DASHIELL HAMMETT

DASHIELL HAMMETT

CRIME STORIES AND
OTHER WRITINGS

Steven Marcus, *editor*

THE LIBRARY OF AMERICA

Contents

CRIME STORIES

Arson Plus

J IM TARR picked up the cigar I rolled across his desk, looked at the band, bit off an end, and reached for a match.

"Fifteen cents straight," he said. "You must want me to break a *couple* of laws for you this time."

I had been doing business with this fat sheriff of Sacramento County for four or five years—ever since I came to the Continental Detective Agency's San Francisco office—and I had never known him to miss an opening for a sour crack; but it didn't mean anything.

"Wrong both times," I told him. "I get two of them for a quarter; and I'm here to do you a favor instead of asking for one. The company that insured Thornburgh's house thinks somebody touched it off."

"That's right enough, according to the fire department. They tell me the lower part of the house was soaked with gasoline, but God knows how they could tell—there wasn't a stick left standing. I've got McClump working on it, but he hasn't found anything to get excited about yet."

"What's the layout? All I know is that there was a fire."

Tarr leaned back in his chair, turned his red face to the ceiling, and bellowed:

"Hey, Mac!"

The pearl push-buttons on his desk are ornaments as far as he is concerned. Deputy sheriffs McHale, McClump and Macklin came to the door together—MacNab apparently wasn't within hearing.

"What's the idea?" the sheriff demanded of McClump. "Are you carrying a bodyguard around with you?"

The two other deputies, thus informed as to who "Mac" referred to this time, went back to their cribbage game.

"We got a city slicker here to catch our firebug for us," Tarr told his deputy. "But we got to tell him what it's all about first."

McClump and I had worked together on an express robbery, several months before. He's a rangy, tow-headed youngster of twenty-five or six, with all the nerve in the world—and most of the laziness.

"Ain't the Lord good to us?"

He had himself draped across a chair by now—always his first objective when he comes into a room.

"Well, here's how she stands: This fellow Thornburgh's house was a couple miles out of town, on the old county road—an old frame house. About midnight, night before last, Jeff Pringle—the nearest neighbor, a half-mile or so to the east—saw a glare in the sky from over that way, and phoned in the alarm; but by the time the fire wagons got there, there wasn't enough of the house left to bother about. Pringle was the first of the neighbors to get to the house, and the roof had already fell in then.

"Nobody saw anything suspicious—no strangers hanging around or nothing. Thornburgh's help just managed to save themselves, and that was all. They don't know much about what happened—too scared, I reckon. But they did see Thornburgh at his window just before the fire got him. A fellow here in town—name of Handerson—saw that part of it too. He was driving home from Wayton, and got to the house just before the roof caved in.

"The fire department people say they found signs of gasoline. The Coonses, Thornburgh's help, say they didn't have no gas on the place. So there you are."

"Thornburgh have any relatives?"

"Yeah. A niece in San Francisco—a Mrs. Evelyn Trowbridge. She was up yesterday, but there wasn't nothing she could do, and she couldn't tell us nothing much, so she went back home."

"Where are the servants now?"

"Here in town. Staying at a hotel on I Street. I told 'em to stick around for a few days."

"Thornburgh own the house?"

"Uh-huh. Bought it from Newning & Weed a couple months ago."

"You got anything to do this morning?"

"Nothing but this."

"Good! Let's get out and dig around."

We found the Coonses in their room at the hotel on I Street. Mr. Coons was a small-boned, plump man with the smooth, meaningless face, and the suavity of the typical male house-servant.

His wife was a tall, stringy woman, perhaps five years older than her husband—say, forty—with a mouth and chin that seemed shaped for gossiping. But he did all the talking, while she nodded her agreement to every second or third word.

"We went to work for Mr. Thornburgh on the fifteenth of June, I think," he said, in reply to my first question. "We came to Sacramento, around the first of the month, and put in applications at the Allis Employment Bureau. A couple of weeks later they sent us out to see Mr. Thornburgh, and he took us on."

"Where were you before you came here?"

"In Seattle, sir, with a Mrs. Comerford; but the climate there didn't agree with my wife—she has bronchial trouble—so we decided to come to California. We most likely would have stayed in Seattle, though, if Mrs. Comerford hadn't given up her house."

"What do you know about Thornburgh?"

"Very little, sir. He wasn't a talkative gentleman. He hadn't any business that I know of. I think he was a retired seafaring man. He never said he was, but he had that manner and look. He never went out or had anybody in to see him, except his niece once, and he didn't write or get any mail. He had a room next to his bedroom fixed up as a sort of workshop. He spent most of his time in there. I always thought he was working on some kind of invention, but he kept the door locked, and wouldn't let us go near it."

"Haven't you any idea at all what it was?"

"No, sir. We never heard any hammering or noises from it, and never smelt anything either. And none of his clothes were ever the least bit soiled, even when they were ready to go out to the laundry. They would have been if he had been working on anything like machinery."

"Was he an old man?"

"He couldn't have been over fifty, sir. He was very erect, and his hair and beard were thick, with no grey hairs."

"Ever have any trouble with him?"

"Oh, no, sir! He was, if I may say it, a very peculiar gentleman in a way; and he didn't care about anything except having his meals fixed right, having his clothes taken care of—he was very particular about them—and not being disturbed. Except early in the morning and at night, we'd hardly see him all day."

"Now about the fire. Tell us the whole thing—everything you remember."

"Well, sir, I and my wife had gone to bed about ten o'clock, our regular time, and had gone to sleep. Our room was on the second floor, in the rear. Some time later—I never did exactly know what time it was—I woke up, coughing. The room was all full of smoke, and my wife was sort of strangling. I jumped up, and dragged her down the back stairs and out the back door, not thinking of anything but getting her out of there.

"When I had her safe in the yard, I thought of Mr. Thornburgh, and tried to get back in the house; but the whole first floor was just flames. I ran around front then, to see if he had got out, but didn't see anything of him. The whole yard was as light as day by then. Then I heard him scream—a horrible scream, sir—I can hear it yet! And I looked up at his window—that was the front second-story room—and saw him there, trying to get out the window. But all the woodwork was burning, and he screamed again and fell back, and right after that the roof over his room fell in.

"There wasn't a ladder or anything that I could have put up to the window for him—there wasn't anything I could have done.

"In the meantime, a gentleman had left his automobile in the road, and come up to where I was standing; but there wasn't anything we could do—the house was burning everywhere and falling in here and there. So we went back to where I had left my wife, and carried her farther away from the fire, and brought her to—she had fainted. And that's all I know about it, sir."

"Hear any noises earlier that night? Or see anybody hanging around?"

"No, sir."

"Have any gasoline around the place?"

"No, sir. Mr. Thornburgh didn't have a car."

"No gasoline for cleaning?"

"No, sir, none at all, unless Mr. Thornburgh had it in his workshop. When his clothes needed cleaning, I took them to town, and all his laundry was taken by the grocer's man, when he brought our provisions."

"Don't know anything that might have some bearing on the fire?"

"No, sir. I was surprised when I heard that somebody had set the house afire. I could hardly believe it. I don't know why anybody should want to do that."

"What do you think of them?" I asked McClump, as we left the hotel.

"They might pad the bills, or even go South with some of the silver, but they don't figure as killers in my mind."

That was my opinion, too; but they were the only persons known to have been there when the fire started except the man who had died. We went around to the Allis Employment Bureau and talked to the manager.

He told us that the Coonses had come into his office on June second, looking for work; and had given Mrs. Edward Comerford, 45 Woodmansee Terrace, Seattle, Washington, as reference. In reply to a letter—he always checked up the references of servants—Mrs. Comerford had written that the Coonses had been in her employ for a number of years, and had been "extremely satisfactory in every respect." On June thirteenth, Thornburgh had telephoned the bureau, asking that a man and his wife be sent out to keep house for him; and Allis had sent two couples that he had listed. Neither had been employed by Thornburgh, though Allis considered them more desirable than the Coonses, who were finally hired by Thornburgh.

All that would certainly seem to indicate that the Coonses hadn't deliberately maneuvered themselves into the place, unless they were the luckiest people in the world—and a detective can't afford to believe in luck or coincidence, unless he has unquestionable proof of it.

At the office of the real estate agents, through whom Thornburgh had bought the house—Newning & Weed—we were told that Thornburgh had come in on the eleventh of June, and had said that he had been told that the house was for sale, had looked it over, and wanted to know the price.

The deal had been closed the next morning, and he had paid for the house with a check for $4,500 on the Seamen's Bank of San Francisco. The house was already furnished.

After luncheon, McClump and I called on Howard Handerson—the man who had seen the fire while driving home from Wayton. He had an office in the Empire Building, with his name and the title "Northern California Agent, Instant-Sheen Cleanser Company," on the door. He was a big, careless-looking man of forty-five or so, with the professionally jovial smile that belongs to the salesman.

He had been in Wayton on business the day of the fire, he said, and had stayed there until rather late, going to dinner and afterward playing pool with a grocer named Hammersmith—one of his customers. He had left Wayton in his machine, at about ten-thirty, and set out for Sacramento. At Tavender he had stopped at the garage for oil and gas and to have one of his tires blown up.

Just as he was about to leave the garage, the garage-man had called his attention to a red glare in the sky, and had told him that it was probably from a fire somewhere along the old county road that paralleled the State road into Sacramento; so Handerson had taken the county road, and had arrived at the burning house just in time to see Thornburgh try to fight his way through the flames that enveloped him.

It was too late to make any attempt to put out the fire, and the man upstairs was beyond saving by then—undoubtedly dead even before the roof collapsed; so Handerson had helped Coons revive his wife, and stayed there watching the fire until it had burned itself out. He had seen no one on that county road while driving to the fire.

"What do you know about Handerson?" I asked McClump, when we were on the street.

"Came here, from somewhere in the East, I think, early in the summer to open that Cleanser agency. Lives at the Garden Hotel. Where do we go next?"

"We get a machine, and take a look at what's left of the Thornburgh house."

An enterprising incendiary couldn't have found a lovelier spot in which to turn himself loose, if he looked the whole county over. Tree-topped hills hid it from the rest of the world, on three sides; while away from the fourth, an uninhabited plain rolled down to the river. The county road that passed the front gate was shunned by automobiles, so McClump said, in favor of the State Highway to the north.

Where the house had been, was now a mound of blackened ruins. We poked around in the ashes for a few minutes—not that we expected to find anything, but because it's the nature of man to poke around in ruins.

A garage in the rear, whose interior gave no evidence of recent occupation, had a badly scorched roof and front, but was otherwise undamaged. A shed behind it, sheltering an ax, a shovel, and various odds and ends of gardening tools, had escaped the fire altogether. The lawn in front of the house, and the garden behind the shed—about an acre in all—had been pretty thoroughly cut and trampled by wagon wheels, and the feet of the firemen and the spectators.

Having ruined our shoe-shines, McClump and I got back in our machine and swung off in a circle around the place, calling at all the houses within a mile radius, and getting little besides jolts for our trouble.

The nearest house was that of Pringle, the man who had turned in the alarm; but he not only knew nothing about the dead man, but said he had never seen him. In fact, only one of the neighbors had ever seen him: a Mrs. Jabine, who lived about a mile to the south.

She had taken care of the key to the house while it was vacant; and a day or two before he bought it, Thornburgh had come to her house, inquiring about the vacant one. She had gone over there with him and showed him through it, and he had told her that he intended buying it, if the price, of which neither of them knew anything, wasn't too high.

He had been alone, except for the chauffeur of the hired car in which he had come from Sacramento, and, save that he had no family, he had told her nothing about himself.

Hearing that he had moved in, she went over to call on him several days later—"just a neighborly visit"—but had been told by Mrs. Coons that he was not at home. Most of the neighbors had talked to the Coonses, and had got the impression that Thornburgh did not care for visitors, so they had let him alone. The Coonses were described as "pleasant enough to talk to when you meet them," but reflecting their employer's desire not to make friends.

McClump summarized what the afternoon had taught us as we pointed our machine toward Tavender: "Any of these folks could have touched off the place, but we got nothing to show that any of 'em even knew Thornburgh, let alone had a bone to pick with him."

Tavender turned out to be a crossroads settlement of a general store and post office, a garage, a church, and six dwellings, about two miles from Thornburgh's place. McClump knew the storekeeper and postmaster, a scrawny little man named Philo, who stuttered moistly.

"I n-n-never s-saw Th-thornburgh," he said, "and I n-n-never had any m-mail for him. C-coons"—it sounded like one of these things butterflies come out of—"used to c-come in once a week t-to order groceries—they d-didn't have a phone. He used to walk in, and I'd s-send the stuff over in my c-c-car. Th-then I'd s-see him once in a while, waiting f-for the stage to S-s-sacramento."

"Who drove the stuff out to Thornburgh's?"

"M-m-my b-boy. Want to t-talk to him?"

The boy was a juvenile edition of the old man, but without the stutter. He had never seen Thornburgh on any of his visits, but his business had taken him only as far as the kitchen. He hadn't noticed anything peculiar about the place.

"Who's the night man at the garage?" I asked him, after we had listened to the little he had to tell.

"Billy Luce. I think you can catch him there now. I saw him go in a few minutes ago."

We crossed the road and found Luce.

"Night before last—the night of the fire down the road—was there a man here talking to you when you first saw it?"

He turned his eyes upward in that vacant stare which people use to aid their memory.

"Yes, I remember now! He was going to town, and I told him that if he took the county road instead of the State Road he'd see the fire on his way in."

"What kind of looking man was he?"

"Middle-aged—a big man, but sort of slouchy. I think he had on a brown suit, baggy and wrinkled."

"Medium complexion?"

"Yes."

"Smile when he talked?"

"Yes, a pleasant sort of fellow."

"Curly brown hair?"

"Have a heart!" Luce laughed. "I didn't put him under a magnifying glass."

From Tavender, we drove over to Wayton. Luce's description had fit Handerson all right; but while we were at it, we thought we might as well check up to make sure that he had been coming from Wayton.

We spent exactly twenty-five minutes in Wayton; ten of them finding Hammersmith, the grocer with whom Handerson had said he dined and played pool; five minutes finding the proprietor of the pool-room; and ten verifying Handerson's story.

"What do you think of it now, Mac?" I asked, as we rolled back toward Sacramento.

Mac's too lazy to express an opinion, or even form one, unless he's driven to it; but that doesn't mean they aren't worth listening to, if you can get them.

"There ain't a hell of a lot to think," he said cheerfully. "Handerson is out of it, if he ever was in it. There's nothing to show that anybody but the Coonses and Thornburgh were there when the fire started—but there may have been a regiment there. Them Coonses ain't too honest looking, maybe, but they ain't killers, or I miss my guess. But the fact remains that they're the only bet we got so far. Maybe we ought to try to get a line on them."

"All right," I agreed. "I'll get a wire off to our Seattle office asking them to interview Mrs. Comerford, and see what she can tell about them as soon as we get back in town. Then I'm going to catch a train for San Francisco, and see Thornburgh's niece in the morning."

Next morning, at the address McClump had given me—a rather elaborate apartment building on California Street—I had to wait three-quarters of an hour for Mrs. Evelyn Trowbridge to dress. If I had been younger, or a social caller, I suppose I'd have felt amply rewarded when she finally came in—a tall, slender woman of less than thirty; in some sort of clinging black affair; with a lot of black hair over a very white face, strikingly set off by a small red mouth and big hazel eyes that looked black until you got close to them.

But I was a busy, middle-aged detective, who was fuming over having his time wasted; and I was a lot more interested in finding the bird who struck the match than I was in feminine beauty. However, I smothered my grouch, apologized for disturbing her at such an early hour, and got down to business.

"I want you to tell me all you know about your uncle—his family, friends, enemies, business connections, everything."

I had scribbled on the back of the card I had sent into her what my business was.

"He hadn't any family," she said; "unless I might be it. He was my mother's brother, and I am the only one of that family now living."

"Where was he born?"

"Here in San Francisco. I don't know the date, but he was about fifty years old, I think—three years older than my mother."

"What was his business?"

"He went to sea when he was a boy, and, so far as I know, always followed it until a few months ago."

"Captain?"

"I don't know. Sometimes I wouldn't see or hear from him for several years, and he never talked about what he was doing; though he would mention some of the places he had visited—Rio de Janeiro, Madagascar, Tobago, Christiania. Then, about three months ago—some time in May—he came here and told me that he was through with wandering; that he was going to take a house in some quiet place where he could work undisturbed on an invention in which he was interested.

"He lived at the Francisco Hotel while he was in San Francisco. After a couple of weeks, he suddenly disappeared. And then, about a month ago, I received a telegram from him, asking me to come to see him at his house near Sacramento. I went up the very next day, and I thought that he was acting very queerly—he seemed very excited over something. He gave me a will that he had just drawn up and some life insurance policies in which I was beneficiary.

"Immediately after that he insisted that I return home, and hinted rather plainly that he did not wish me to either visit him again or write until I heard from him. I thought all that rather peculiar, as he had always seemed fond of me. I never saw him again."

"What was this invention he was working on?"

"I really don't know. I asked him once, but he became so excited—even suspicious—that I changed the subject, and never mentioned it again."

"Are you sure that he really did follow the sea all those years?"

"No, I am not. I just took it for granted; but he may have been doing something altogether different."

"Was he ever married?"

"Not that I know of."

"Know any of his friends or enemies?"

"No, none."

"Remember anybody's name that he ever mentioned?"

"No."

"I don't want you to think this next question insulting, though I admit it is. But it has to be asked. Where were you the night of the fire?"

"At home; I had some friends here to dinner, and they stayed until about midnight. Mr. and Mrs. Walker Kellogg, Mrs. John Dupree, and a Mr. Killmer, who is a lawyer. I can give you their addresses, or you can get them from the phone book, if you want to question them."

From Mrs. Trowbridge's apartment I went to the Francisco Hotel. Thornburgh had been registered there from May tenth to June thirteenth, and hadn't attracted much attention. He had been a tall, broad-shouldered, erect man of about fifty, with rather long brown hair brushed straight back; a short, pointed brown beard, and healthy, ruddy complexion—grave, quiet, punctilious in dress and manner; his hours had been regular and he had had no visitors that any of the hotel employes remembered.

At the Seamen's Bank—upon which Thornburgh's check, in payment of the house, had been drawn—I was told that he had opened an account there on May fifteenth, having been introduced by W. W. Jeffers & Sons, local stock brokers. A balance of a little more than four hundred dollars remained to his credit. The cancelled checks on hand were all to the order of various life insurance companies; and for amounts that, if they represented premiums, testified to rather large policies. I jotted down the names of the life insurance companies, and then went to the offices of W. W. Jeffers & Sons.

Thornburgh had come in, I was told, on the tenth of May with $4,000 worth of Liberty bonds that he wanted sold. During one of his conversations with Jeffers, he had asked the broker to recommend a bank, and Jeffers had given him a letter of introduction to the Seamen's Bank.

That was all Jeffers knew about him. He gave me the numbers of the bonds, but tracing Liberty bonds isn't the easiest thing in the world.

The reply to my Seattle telegram was waiting for me at the Agency when I arrived.

MRS. EDWARD COMERFORD RENTED APARTMENT AT ADDRESS YOU GIVE ON MAY TWENTY-FIVE GAVE IT UP JUNE SIX TRUNKS TO SAN FRANCISCO SAME DAY CHECK NUMBERS GN FOUR FIVE TWO FIVE EIGHT SEVEN AND EIGHT AND NINE

Tracing baggage is no trick at all, if you have the dates and check numbers to start with—as many a bird who is wearing somewhat similar numbers on his chest and back, because he overlooked that detail when making his getaway, can tell you—and twenty-five minutes in a baggage-room at the Ferry and half an hour in the office of a transfer company gave me my answer.

The trunks had been delivered to Mrs. Evelyn Trowbridge's apartment!

I got Jim Tarr on the phone and told him about it.

"Good shooting!" he said, forgetting for once to indulge his wit. "We'll grab the Coonses here and Mrs. Trowbridge there, and that's the end of another mystery."

"Wait a minute!" I cautioned him. "It's not all straightened out yet! There's still a few kinks in the plot."

"It's straight enough for me. I'm satisfied."

"You're the boss, but I think you're being a little hasty. I'm going up and talk with the niece again. Give me a little time before you phone the police here to make the pinch. I'll hold her until they get there."

Evelyn Trowbridge let me in this time, instead of the maid who had opened the door for me in the morning, and she led me to the same room in which we had had our first talk. I let her pick out a seat, and then I selected one that was closer to either door than hers was.

On the way up I had planned a lot of innocent-sounding questions that would get her all snarled up; but after taking a good look at this woman sitting in front of me, leaning comfortably back in her chair, coolly waiting for me to speak my piece, I discarded the trick stuff and came out cold-turkey.

"Ever use the name Mrs. Edward Comerford?"

"Oh, yes." As casual as a nod on the street.

"When?"

"Often. You see, I happen to have been married not so long ago to Mr. Edward Comerford. So it's not really strange that I should have used the name."

"Use it in Seattle recently?"

"I would suggest," she said sweetly, "that if you are leading up to the references I gave Coons and his wife, you might save time by coming right to it?"

"That's fair enough," I said. "Let's do that."

There wasn't a half-tone, a shading, in voice, manner, or expression to indicate that she was talking about anything half so serious or important to her as a possibility of being charged with murder. She might have been talking about the weather, or a book that hadn't interested her particularly.

"During the time that Mr. Comerford and I were married, we lived in Seattle, where he still lives. After the divorce, I left Seattle and resumed my maiden name. And the Coonses *were* in our employ, as you might learn if you care to look it up. You'll find my husband—or former husband—at the Chelsea apartments, I think.

"Last summer, or late spring, I decided to return to Seattle. The truth of it is—I suppose all my personal affairs will be aired anyhow—that I thought perhaps Edward and I might patch up our differences; so I went back and took an apartment on Woodmansee Terrace. As I was known in Seattle as Mrs. Edward Comerford, and as I thought my using his name might influence him a little, perhaps, I used it while I was there.

"Also I telephoned the Coonses to make tentative arrangements in case Edward and I should open our house again; but Coons told me that they were going to California, and so I gladly gave them an excellent recommendation when, some days later, I received a letter of inquiry from an employment bureau in Sacramento. After I had been in Seattle for about two weeks, I changed my mind about the reconciliation— Edward's interest, I learned, was all centered elsewhere; so I returned to San Francisco."

"Very nice! But—"

"If you will permit me to finish," she interrupted. "When I went to see my uncle in response to his telegram, I was surprised to find the Coonses in his house. Knowing my uncle's peculiarities, and finding them now increased, and remembering his extreme secretiveness about his mysterious invention, I cautioned the Coonses not to tell him that they had been in my employ.

"He certainly would have discharged them, and just as certainly would have quarreled with me—he would have thought that I was having him spied upon. Then, when Coons telephoned me after the fire, I knew that to admit that the Coonses had been formerly in my employ, would, in view of the fact that I was my uncle's heir, cast suspicion on all three of us. So we foolishly agreed to say nothing about it and carry on the deception."

That didn't sound all wrong, but it didn't sound all right. I wished Tarr had taken it easier and let us get a better line on these people, before having them thrown in the coop.

"The coincidence of the Coonses stumbling into my uncle's house is, I fancy, too much for your detecting instincts," she went on, as I didn't say anything. "Am I to consider myself under arrest?"

I'm beginning to like this girl; she's a nice, cool piece of work.

"Not yet," I told her. "But I'm afraid it's going to happen pretty soon."

She smiled a little mocking smile at that, and another when the door-bell rang.

It was O'Hara from police headquarters. We turned the apartment upside down and inside out, but didn't find anything of importance except the will she had told me about, dated July eighth, and her uncle's life insurance policies. They were all dated between May fifteenth and June tenth, and added up to a little more than $200,000.

I spent an hour grilling the maid after O'Hara had taken Evelyn Trowbridge away, but she didn't know any more than I did. However, between her, the janitor, the manager of the apartments, and the names Mrs. Trowbridge had given me, I learned that she had really been entertaining friends on the night of the fire—until after eleven o'clock, anyway—and that was late enough.

Half an hour later I was riding the Short Line back to Sacramento. I was getting to be one of the line's best customers, and my anatomy was on bouncing terms with every bump in the road; and the bumps, as "Rubberhead" Davis used to say about the flies and mosquitoes in Alberta in summer, "is freely plentiful."

Between bumps I tried to fit the pieces of this Thornburgh puzzle together. The niece and the Coonses fit in somewhere, but not just where we had them. We had been working on the job sort of lop-sided, but it was the best we could do with it. In the beginning we had turned to the Coonses and Evelyn Trowbridge because there was no other direction to go; and now we had something on them—but a good lawyer could make hash of our case against them.

The Coonses were in the county jail when I got to Sacramento. After some questioning they had admitted their connection with the niece, and had come through with stories that matched hers in every detail.

Tarr, McClump, and I sat around the sheriff's desk and argued.

"Those yarns are pipe-dreams," the sheriff said. "We got all three of 'em cold, and there's nothing else to it. They're as good as convicted of murder!"

McClump grinned derisively at his superior, and then turned to me.

"Go on! You tell him about the holes in his little case. He ain't your boss, and can't take it out on you later for being smarter than he is!"

Tarr glared from one of us to the other.

"Spill it, you wise guys!" he ordered.

"Our dope is," I told him, figuring that McClump's view of it was the same as mine, "that there's nothing to show that even Thornburgh knew he was going to buy that house before the tenth of June, and that the Coonses were in town looking for work on the second. And besides, it was only by luck that they got the jobs. The employment office sent two couples out there ahead of them."

"We'll take a chance on letting the jury figure that out."

"Yes? You'll also take a chance on them figuring out that Thornburgh, who seems to have been a nut all right, might have touched off the place himself! We've got something on these people, Jim, but not enough to go into court with them! How are you going to prove that when the Coonses were planted in Thornburgh's house—if you can even prove they were—they and the Trowbridge woman knew he was going to load up with insurance policies?"

The sheriff spat disgustedly.

"You guys are the limit! You run around in circles, digging up the dope on these people until you get enough to hang 'em, and then you run around hunting for outs! What the hell's the matter with you now?"

I answered him from half-way to the door—the pieces were beginning to fit together under my skull.

"Going to run some more circles! Come on, Mac!"

McClump and I held a conference on the fly, and then I got a machine from the nearest garage and headed for Tavender. We made time going out, and got there before the general store had closed for the night. The stuttering Philo separated himself from the two men with whom he had been talking Hiram Johnson, and followed me to the rear of the store.

"Do you keep an itemized list of the laundry you handle?"

"N-n-no; just the amounts."

"Let's look at Thornburgh's."

He produced a begrimed and rumpled account book and we picked out the weekly items I wanted: $2.60, $3.10, $2.25, and so on.

"Got the last batch of laundry here?"

"Y-yes," he said. "It j-just c-c-came out from the city t-to-day."

I tore open the bundle—some sheets, pillow-cases, table-cloths, towels, napkins; some feminine clothing; some shirts, collars, underwear, sox that were unmistakably Coons's. I thanked Philo while running back to my machine.

Back in Sacramento again, McClump was waiting for me at the garage where I had hired the car.

"Registered at the hotel on June fifteenth, rented the office on the sixteenth. I think he's in the hotel now," he greeted me.

We hurried around the block to the Garden Hotel.

"Mr. Handerson went out a minute or two ago," the night clerk told us. "He seemed to be in a hurry."

"Know where he keeps his car?"

"In the hotel garage around the corner."

We were within two pavements of the garage, when Handerson's automobile shot out and turned up the street.

"Oh, Mr. Handerson!" I cried, trying to keep my voice level and smooth.

He stepped on the gas and streaked away from us.

"Want him?" McClump asked; and, at my nod, stopped a passing roadster by the simple expedient of stepping in front of it.

We climbed aboard, McClump flashed his star at the bewildered driver, and pointed out Handerson's dwindling tail-light. After he had persuaded himself that he wasn't being boarded by a couple of bandits, the commandeered driver did his best, and we picked up Handerson's tail-light after two or three turnings, and closed in on him—though his machine was going at a good clip.

By the time we reached the outskirts of the city, we had crawled up to within safe shooting distance, and I sent a bullet over the fleeing man's head. Thus encouraged, he managed to get a little more speed out of his car; but we were definitely overhauling him now.

Just at the wrong minute Handerson decided to look over his shoulder at us—an unevenness in the road twisted his wheels—his machine swayed—skidded—went over on its side. Almost immediately, from the heart of the tangle, came a flash and a bullet moaned past my ear. Another. And then, while I was still hunting for something to shoot at in the pile of junk we were drawing down upon, McClump's ancient and battered revolver roared in my other ear.

Handerson was dead when we got to him—McClump's bullet had taken him over one eye.

McClump spoke to me over the body.

"I ain't an inquisitive sort of fellow, but I hope you don't mind telling me why I shot this lad."

"Because he was Thornburgh."

He didn't say anything for about five minutes. Then: "I reckon that's right. How'd you guess it?"

We were sitting beside the wreckage now, waiting for the police that we had sent our commandeered chauffeur to phone for.

"He had to be," I said, "when you think it all over. Funny we didn't hit on it before! All that stuff we were told about Thornburgh had a fishy sound. Whiskers and an unknown profession, immaculate and working on a mysterious invention, very secretive and born in San Francisco—where the fire wiped out all the old records—just the sort of fake that could be cooked up easily.

"Then nobody but the Coonses, Evelyn Trowbridge and Handerson ever saw him except between the tenth of May and the middle of June, when he bought the house. The Coonses and the Trowbridge woman were tied up together in this affair somehow, we knew—so that left only Handerson to consider. You had told me he came to Sacramento sometime early this summer—and the dates you got tonight show that he didn't come until after Thornburgh had bought his house. All right! Now compare Handerson with the descriptions we got of Thornburgh.

"Both are about the same size and age, and with the same color hair. The differences are all things that can be manufactured—clothes, a little sunburn, and a month's growth of beard, along with a little acting, would do the trick. Tonight

I went out to Tavender and took a look at the last batch of laundry, and there wasn't any that didn't fit the Coonses—and none of the bills all the way back were large enough for Thornburgh to have been as careful about his clothes as we were told he was."

"It must be great to be a detective!" McClump grinned as the police ambulance came up and began disgorging policemen. "I reckon somebody must have tipped Handerson off that I was asking about him this evening." And then, regretfully: "So we ain't going to hang them folks for murder after all."

"No, but we oughtn't have any trouble convicting them of arson plus conspiracy to defraud, and anything else that the Prosecuting Attorney can think up."

Slippery Fingers

"Y OU are already familiar, of course, with the particulars of my father's—ah—death?"

"The papers are full of it, and have been for three days," I said, "and I've read them; but I'll have to have the whole story first-hand."

"There isn't very much to tell."

This Frederick Grover was a short, slender man of something under thirty years, and dressed like a picture out of *Vanity Fair*. His almost girlish features and voice did nothing to make him more impressive, but I began to forget these things after a few minutes. He wasn't a sap. I knew that downtown, where he was rapidly building up a large and lively business in stocks and bonds without calling for too much help from his father's millions, he was considered a shrewd article; and I wasn't surprised later when Benny Forman, who ought to know, told me that Frederick Grover was the best poker player west of Chicago. He was a cool, well-balanced, quick-thinking little man.

"Father has lived here alone with the servants since mother's death, two years ago," he went on. "I am married, you know, and live in town. Last Saturday evening he dismissed Barton—Barton was his butler-valet, and had been with father for quite a few years—at a little after nine, saying that he did not want to be disturbed during the evening.

"Father was here in the library at the time, looking through some papers. The servants' rooms are in the rear, and none of the servants seem to have heard anything during the night.

"At seven-thirty the following morning—Sunday—Barton found father lying on the floor, just to the right of where you are sitting, dead, stabbed in the throat with the brass paper-knife that was always kept on the table here. The front door was ajar.

"The police found bloody finger-prints on the knife, the table, and the front door; but so far they have not found the man who left the prints, which is why I am employing your agency. The physician who came with the police placed the

22

time of father's death at between eleven o'clock and mid-night.

"Later, on Monday, we learned that father had drawn $10,000 in hundred-dollar bills from the bank Saturday morning. No trace of the money has been found. My finger-prints, as well as the servants', were compared with the ones found by the police, but there was no similarity. I think that is all."

"Do you know of any enemies your father had?"

He shook his head.

"I know of none, though he may have had them. You see, I really didn't know my father very well. He was a very reti-cent man and, until his retirement, about five years ago, he spent most of his time in South America, where most of his mining interests were. He may have had dozens of enemies, though Barton—who probably knew more about him than anyone—seems to know of no one who hated father enough to kill him."

"How about relatives?"

"I was his heir and only child, if that is what you are get-ting at. So far as I know he had no other living relatives."

"I'll talk to the servants," I said.

The maid and the cook could tell me nothing, and I learned very little more from Barton. He had been with Henry Grover since 1912, had been with him in Yunnan, Peru, Mexico, and Central America, but apparently he knew little or nothing of his master's business or acquaintances.

He said that Grover had not seemed excited or worried on the night of the murder, and that nearly every night Grover dismissed him at about the same time, with orders that he not be disturbed; so no importance was to be attached to that part of it. He knew of no one with whom Grover had com-municated during the day, and he had not seen the money Grover had drawn from the bank.

I made a quick inspection of the house and grounds, not expecting to find anything; and I didn't. Half the jobs that come to a private detective are like this one: three or four days—and often as many weeks—have passed since the crime was committed. The police work on the job until they are stumped; then the injured party calls in a private sleuth, dumps him down on a trail that is old and cold and badly trampled, and expects— Oh, well! I picked out this way of making a living, so . . .

I looked through Grover's papers—he had a safe and a desk full of them—but didn't find anything to get excited about. They were mostly columns of figures.

"I'm going to send an accountant out here to go over your father's books," I told Frederick Grover. "Give him everything he asks for, and fix it up with the bank so they'll help him."

I caught a street-car and went back to town, called at Ned Root's office, and headed him out toward Grover's. Ned is a human adding machine with educated eyes, ears, and nose. He can spot a kink in a set of books farther than I can see the covers.

"Keep digging until you find something, Ned, and you can charge Grover whatever you like. Give me something to work on—quick!"

The murder had all the earmarks of one that had grown out of blackmail, though there was—there always is—a chance that it might have been something else. But it didn't look like the work of an enemy or a burglar: either of them would have packed his weapon with him, would not have trusted to finding it on the grounds. Of course, if Frederick Grover, or one of the servants, had killed Henry Grover . . . but the finger-prints said "No."

Just to play safe, I put in a few hours getting a line on Frederick. He had been at a ball on the night of the murder; he had never, so far as I could learn, quarreled with his father; his father was liberal with him, giving him everything he wanted; and Frederick was taking in more money in his brokerage office than he was spending. No motive for a murder appeared on the surface there.

At the city detective bureau I hunted up the police sleuths who had been assigned to the murder; Marty O'Hara and George Dean. It didn't take them long to tell me what they knew about it. Whoever had made the bloody finger-prints was not known to the police here: they had not found the prints in their files. The classifications had been broadcast to every large city in the country, but with no results so far.

A house four blocks from Grover's had been robbed on the night of the murder, and there was a slim chance that the same man *might* have been responsible for both jobs. But the burglary had occurred after one o'clock in the morning, which made the connection look not so good. A burglar who had killed a man, and perhaps picked up $10,000 in the bargain, wouldn't be likely to turn his hand to another job right away.

I looked at the paper-knife with which Grover had been killed, and at the photographs of the bloody prints, but they couldn't help me much just now. There seemed to be nothing to do but get out and dig around until I turned up something somewhere.

Then the door opened, and Joseph Clane was ushered into the room where O'Hara, Dean and I were talking.

Clane was a hard-bitten citizen, for all his prosperous look; fifty or fifty-five, I'd say, with eyes, mouth and jaw that held plenty of humor but none of what is sometimes called the milk of human kindness.

He was a big man, beefy, and all dressed up in a tight-fitting checkered suit, fawn-colored hat, patent-leather shoes with buff uppers, and the rest of the things that go with that sort of combination. He had a harsh voice that was as empty of expression as his hard red face, and he held his body stiffly, as if he was afraid the buttons on his too-tight clothes were about to pop off. Even his arms hung woodenly at his sides, with thick fingers that were lifelessly motionless.

He came right to the point. He had been a friend of the murdered man's, and thought that perhaps what he could tell us would be of value.

He had met Henry Grover—he called him "Henny"—in 1894, in Ontario, where Grover was working a claim: the gold mine that had started the murdered man along the road to wealth. Clane had been employed by Grover as foreman, and the two men had become close friends. A man named Denis Waldeman had a claim adjoining Grover's and a dispute had arisen over their boundaries. The dispute ran on for some time—the men coming to blows once or twice—but finally Grover seems to have triumphed, for Waldeman suddenly left the country.

Clane's idea was that if we could find Waldeman we might find Grover's murderer, for considerable money had been involved in the dispute, and Waldeman was "a mean cuss, for a fact," and not likely to have forgotten his defeat.

Clane and Grover had kept in touch with each other, corresponding or meeting at irregular intervals, but the murdered man had never said or written anything that would throw a light on his death. Clane, too, had given up mining, and now had a small string of race-horses which occupied all his time.

He was in the city for a rest between racing-meets, had arrived two days before the murder, but had been too busy with his own affairs—he had discharged his trainer and was trying to find another—to call upon his friend. Clane was staying at the Marquis hotel, and would be in the city for a week or ten days longer.

"How come you've waited three days before coming to tell us all this?" Dean asked him.

"I wasn't noways sure I had ought to do it. I wasn't never sure in my mind but what maybe Henny done for that fellow Waldeman—he disappeared sudden-like. And I didn't want to do nothing to dirty Henny's name. But finally I decided to do the right thing. And then there's another thing: you found some finger-prints in Henny's house, didn't you? The newspapers said so."

"We did."

"Well, I want you to take mine and match them up. I was out with a girl the night of the murder"—he leered suddenly, boastingly—"all night! And she's a good girl, got a husband and a lot of folks; and it wouldn't be right to drag her into this to prove that I wasn't in Henny's house when he was killed, in case you'd maybe think I killed him. So I thought I better come down here, tell you all about it, and get you to take my finger-prints, and have it all over with."

We went up to the identification bureau and had Clane's prints taken. They were not at all like the murderer's.

After we pumped Clane dry I went out and sent a telegram to our Toronto office, asking them to get a line on the Waldeman angle. Then I hunted up a couple of boys who eat, sleep, and breathe horse racing. They told me that Clane was well known in racing circles as the owner of a small string of near-horses that ran as irregularly as the stewards would permit.

At the Marquis hotel I got hold of the house detective, who is a helpful chap so long as his hand is kept greased. He verified my information about Clane's status in the sporting world, and told me that Clane had stayed at the hotel for several days at a time, off and on, within the past couple years.

He tried to trace Clane's telephone calls for me but—as usual when you want them—the records were jumbled. I arranged to have the girls on the switchboard listen in on any talking he did during the next few days.

Ned Root was waiting for me when I got down to the office the next morning. He had worked on Grover's accounts all night, and had found enough to give me a start. Within the past year—that was as far back as Ned had gone—Grover had drawn out of his bank-accounts nearly fifty thousand dollars that couldn't be accounted for; nearly fifty thousand exclusive of the ten thousand he had drawn the day of the murder. Ned gave me the amounts and the dates:

May 6, 1922,	$15,000
June 10,	5,000
August 1,	5,000
October 10,	10,000
January 3, 1923,	12,500

Forty-seven thousand, five hundred dollars! Somebody was getting fat off him!

The local managers of the telegraph companies raised the usual howl about respecting their patrons' privacy, but I got an order from the Prosecuting Attorney and put a clerk at work on the files of each office.

Then I went back to the Marquis hotel and looked at the old registers. Clane had been there from May 4th to 7th, and from October 8th to 15th last year. That checked off two of the dates upon which Grover had made his withdrawals.

I had to wait until nearly six o'clock for my information from the telegraph companies, but it was worth waiting for. On the third of last January Henry Grover had telegraphed $12,500 to Joseph Clane in San Diego. The clerks hadn't found anything on the other dates I had given them, but I wasn't at all dissatisfied. I had Joseph Clane fixed as the man who had been getting fat off Grover.

I sent Dick Foley—he is the Agency's shadow-ace—and Bob Teal—a youngster who will be a world-beater some day—over to Clane's hotel.

"Plant yourselves in the lobby," I told them. "I'll be over in a few minutes to talk to Clane, and I'll try to bring him down in the lobby where you can get a good look at him. Then I want him shadowed until he shows up at police head-quarters tomorrow. I want to know where he goes and who he talks to. And if he spends much time talking to any one person, or their conversation seems very important, I want one of you boys to trail the other man, to see who he is and what he does. If Clane tries to blow town, grab him and have him thrown in the can, but I don't think he will."

I gave Dick and Bob time enough to get themselves placed, and then went to the hotel. Clane was out, so I waited. He came in a little after eleven and I went up to his room with him. I didn't hem-and-haw, but came out cold-turkey:

"All the signs point to Grover's having been blackmailed. Do you know anything about it?"

"No," he said.

"Grover drew a lot of money out of his banks at different times. You got some of it, I know, and I suppose you got most of it. What about it?"

He didn't pretend to be insulted, or even surprised by my talk. He smiled a little grimly, maybe, but as if he thought it the most natural thing in the world—and it was, at that—for me to suspect him.

"I told you that me and Henny were pretty chummy, didn't I? Well, you ought to know that all us fellows that fool with the bang-tails have our streaks of bad luck. Whenever I'd get up against it I'd hit Henny up for a stake; like at Tijuana last winter where I got into a flock of bad breaks. Henny lent me twelve or fifteen thousand and I got back on my feet again. I've done that often. He ought to have some of my let-ters and wires in his stuff. If you look through his things you'll find them."

I didn't pretend that I believed him.

"Suppose you drop into police headquarters at nine in the morning and we'll go over everything with the city dicks," I told him.

And then, to make my play stronger:

"I wouldn't make it much later than nine—they might be out looking for you."

"Uh-huh," was all the answer I got.

I went back to the Agency and planted myself within reach of a telephone, waiting for word from Dick and Bob. I thought I was sitting pretty. Clane had been blackmailing Grover—I didn't have a single doubt of that—and I didn't think he had been very far away when Grover was killed. That woman alibi of his sounded all wrong!

But the bloody finger-prints were not Clane's—unless the police identification bureau had pulled an awful boner—and the man who had left the prints was the bird I was setting my cap for. Clane had let three days pass between the murder and his appearance at headquarters. The natural explanation for that would be that his partner, the actual murderer, had needed nearly that much time to put himself in the clear.

My present game was simple: I had stirred Clane up with the knowledge that he was still suspected, hoping that he would have to repeat whatever precautions were necessary to protect his accomplice in the first place.

He had taken three days then. I was giving him about nine hours now: time enough to do something, but not too much time, hoping that he would have to hurry things along and that in his haste he would give Dick and Bob a chance to turn up his partner: the owner of the fingers that had smeared blood on the knife, the table, and the door.

At a quarter to one in the morning Dick telephoned that Clane had left the hotel a few minutes behind me, had gone to an apartment house on Polk Street, and was still there.

I went up to Polk Street and joined Dick and Bob. They told me that Clane had gone in apartment number 27, and that the directory in the vestibule showed this apartment was occupied by George Farr. I stuck around with the boys until about two o'clock, when I went home for some sleep.

At seven I was with them again, and was told that our man had not appeared yet. It was a little after eight when he came

out and turned down Geary Street, with the boys trailing
him, while I went into the apartment house for a talk with the
manager. She told me that Farr had been living there for four
or five months, lived alone, and was a photographer by trade,
with a studio on Market Street.

I went up and rang his bell. He was a husky of thirty or
thirty-two with bleary eyes that looked as if they hadn't had
much sleep that night. I didn't waste any time with him.

"I'm from the Continental Detective Agency and I am interested in Joseph Clane. What do you know about him?"

He was wide awake now.

"Nothing."

"Nothing at all?"

"No," sullenly.

"Do you know him?"

"No."

What can you do with a bird like that?

"Farr," I said, "I want you to go down to headquarters
with me."

He moved like a streak and his sullen manner had me a
little off my guard; but I turned my head in time to take the
punch above my ear instead of on the chin. At that, it carried
me off my feet and I wouldn't have bet a nickel that my skull
wasn't dented; but luck was with me and I fell across the
doorway, holding the door open, and managed to scramble
up, stumble through some rooms, and catch one of his feet as
it was going through the bathroom window to join its mate
on the fire-escape. I got a split lip and a kicked shoulder in
the scuffle, but he behaved after a while.

I didn't stop to look at his stuff—that could be done more
regularly later—but put him in a taxicab and took him to the
Hall of Justice. I was afraid that if I waited too long Clane
would take a run-out on me.

Clane's mouth fell open when he saw Farr, but neither of
them said anything.

I was feeling pretty chirp in spite of my bruises.

"Let's get this bird's finger-prints and get it over with," I
said to O'Hara.

Dean was not in.

"And keep an eye on Clane. I think maybe he'll have another story to tell us in a few minutes."

We got in the elevator and took our men up to the identification bureau, where we put Farr's fingers on the pad. Phels—he is the department's expert—took one look at the results and turned to me.

"Well, what of it?"

"What of what?" I asked.

"This isn't the man who killed Henry Grover!"

Clane laughed, Farr laughed, O'Hara laughed, and Phels laughed. I didn't! I stood there and pretended to be thinking, trying to get myself in hand.

"Are you sure you haven't made a mistake?" I blurted, my face a nice, rosy red.

You can tell how badly upset I was by that: it's plain suicide to say a thing like that to a finger-print expert!

Phels didn't answer; just looked me up and down.

Clane laughed again, like a crow cawing, and turned his ugly face to me.

"Do you want to take my prints again, Mr. Slick Private Detective?"

"Yeah," I said, "just that!"

I had to say something.

Clane held his hands out to Phels, who ignored them, speaking to me with heavy sarcasm.

"Better take them yourself this time, so you'll be sure it's been done right."

I was mad clean through—of course it was my own fault—but I was pig-headed enough to go through with anything, particularly anything that would hurt somebody's feelings; so I said:

"That's not a bad idea!"

I walked over and took hold of one of Clane's hands. I'd never taken a finger-print before, but I had seen it done often enough to throw a bluff. I started to ink Clane's fingers and found that I was holding them wrong—my own fingers were in the way.

Then I came back to earth. The balls of Clane's fingers were too smooth—or rather, too slick—without the slight clinging feeling that belongs to flesh. I turned his hand over so fast that I nearly upset him and looked at the fingers. I don't know what I had expected to find but I didn't find anything—not anything that I could name.

"Phels," I called, "look here!"

He forgot his injured feelings and bent to look at Clane's hand.

"I'll be—" he began, and then the two of us were busy for a few minutes taking Clane down and sitting on him, while O'Hara quieted Farr, who had also gone suddenly into action.

When things were peaceful again Phels examined Clane's hands carefully, scratching the fingers with a finger-nail.

He jumped up, leaving me to hold Clane, and paying no attention to my, "What is it?" got a cloth and some liquid, and washed the fingers thoroughly. We took his prints again. They matched the bloody ones taken from Grover's house!

Then we all sat down and had a nice talk.

"I told you about the trouble Henny had with that fellow Waldeman," Clane began, after he and Farr had decided to come clean: there was nothing else they could do. "And how he won out in the argument because Waldeman disappeared. Well, Henny done for him—shot him one night and buried him—and I saw it. Grover was one bad actor in them days, a tough *hombre* to tangle with, so I didn't try to make nothing out of what I knew.

"But after he got older and richer he got soft—a lot of men go like that—and must have begun worrying over it; because when I ran into him in New York accidentally about four years ago it didn't take me long to learn that he was pretty well tamed, and he told me that he hadn't been able to forget the look on Waldeman's face when he drilled him.

"So I took a chance and braced Henny for a couple thousand. I got them easy, and after that, whenever I was flat I either went to him or sent him word, and he always came across. But I was careful not to crowd him too far. I knew what a terror he was in the old days, and I didn't want to push him into busting loose again.

"But that's what I did in the end. I 'phoned him Friday that I needed money and he said he'd call me up and let me know where to meet him the next night. He called up around half past nine Saturday night and told me to come out to the house. So I went out there and he was waiting for me on the porch and took me upstairs and gave me the ten thousand. I told him this was the last time I'd ever bother him—I always told him that—it had a good effect on him.

"Naturally I wanted to get away as soon as I had the money but he must have felt sort of talkative for a change, because he kept me there for half an hour or so, gassing about men we used to know up in the province.

"After awhile I began to get nervous. He was getting a look in his eyes like he used to have when he was young. And then all of a sudden he flared up and tied into me. He had me by the throat and was bending me back across the table when my hand touched that brass knife. It was either me or him—so I let him have it where it would do the most good.

"I beat it then and went back to the hotel. The newspapers were full of it next day, and had a whole lot of stuff about bloody finger-prints. That gave me a jolt! I didn't know nothing about finger-prints, and here I'd left them all over the dump.

"And then I got to worrying over the whole thing, and it seemed like Henny must have my name written down somewheres among his papers, and maybe had saved some of my letters or telegrams—though *they* were wrote in careful enough language. Anyway I figured the police would want to be asking me some questions sooner or later; and there I'd be with fingers that fit the bloody prints, and nothing for what Farr calls a alibi.

"That's when I thought of Farr. I had his address and I knew he had been a finger-print sharp in the East, so I decided to take a chance on him. I went to him and told him the whole story and between us we figured out what to do.

"He said he'd dope my fingers, and I was to come here and tell the story we'd fixed up, and have my finger-prints taken, and then I'd be safe no matter what leaked out about me and Henny. So he smeared up the fingers and told me to be careful not to shake hands with anybody or touch anything, and I came down here and everything went like three of a kind.

"Then that little fat guy"—meaning me—"came around to the hotel last night and as good as told me that he thought I had done for Henny and that I better come down here this morning. I beat it for Farr's right away to see whether I ought to run for it or sit tight, and Farr said, 'Sit tight!' So I stayed there all night and he fixed up my hands this morning. That's my yarn!"

Phels turned to Farr.

"I've seen faked prints before, but never any this good. How'd you do it?"

These scientific birds are funny. Here was Farr looking a nice, long stretch in the face as "accessory after the fact," and yet he brightened up under the admiration in Phel's tone and answered with a voice that was chock-full of pride.

"It's simple! I got hold of a man whose prints I knew weren't in any police gallery—I didn't want any slip up there—and took his prints and put them on a copper plate, using the ordinary photo-engraving process, but etching it pretty deep. Then I coated Clane's fingers with gelatin—just enough to cover all his markings—and pressed them against the plates. That way I got everything, even to the pores, and . . ."

When I left the bureau ten minutes later Farr and Phels were still sitting knee to knee, jabbering away at each other as only a couple of birds who are cuckoo on the same subject can.

Crooked Souls

HARVEY GATEWOOD had issued orders that I was to be admitted as soon as I arrived, so it only took me a little less than fifteen minutes to thread my way past the doorkeepers, office boys, and secretaries who filled up most of the space between the Gatewood Lumber Corporation's front door and the president's private office. His office was large, all mahogany and bronze and green plush, with a mahogany desk as big as a bed in the center of the floor.

Gatewood, leaning across the desk, began to bark at me as soon as the obsequious clerk who had bowed me in bowed himself out.

"My daughter was kidnapped last night! I want the . . . that did it if it takes every cent I got!"

"Tell me about it," I suggested, drawing up the chair that he hadn't thought to offer me.

But he wanted results, it seemed, and not questions, and so I wasted nearly an hour getting information that he could have given me in fifteen minutes.

He's a big bruiser of a man, something over two hundred pounds of hard red flesh, and a czar from the top of his bullet head to the toes of his shoes that would have been at least number twelves if they hadn't been made to measure.

He had made his several millions by sandbagging everybody that stood in his way, and the rage that he's burning up with now doesn't make him any easier to deal with.

His wicked jaw is sticking out like a knob of granite and his eyes are filmed with blood—he's in a lovely frame of mind. For a while it looks as if the Continental Detective Agency is going to lose a client; because I've made up my mind that he's going to tell me all I want to know, or I'm going to chuck up the job. But finally I got the story out of him.

His daughter Audrey had left their house on Clay street at about seven o'clock the preceding evening, telling her maid that she was going for a walk. She had not returned that night—though Gatewood had not known that until after he had read the letter that came this morning.

The letter had been from someone who said that she had been kidnapped. It demanded fifty thousand dollars for her release; and instructed Gatewood to get the money ready in hundred dollar bills, so that there might be no delay when he is told in what manner it is to be paid over to his daughter's captors. As proof that the demand was not a hoax, a lock of the girl's hair, a ring she always wore, and a brief note from her, asking her father to comply with the demands, had been enclosed.

Gatewood had received the letter at his office, and had telephoned to his house immediately. He had been told that the girl's bed had not been slept in the previous night, and that none of the servants had seen her since she started out for her walk. He had then notified the police, turning the letter over to them; and, a few minutes later, he had decided to employ private detectives also.

"Now," he burst out, after I had wormed these things out of him, and he had told me that he knew nothing of his daughter's associates or habits, "go ahead and do something! I'm not paying you to sit around and talk about it!"

"What are you going to do?" I asked.

"Me? I'm going to put those . . . behind the bars if it takes every cent I've got in the world!"

"Sure! But first you can get that fifty thousand ready, so you can give it to them when they ask for it."

He clicked his jaw shut and thrust his face into mine.

"I've never been clubbed into doing anything in my life! And I'm too old to start now!" he said. "I'm going to call these people's bluff!"

"That's going to make it lovely for your daughter. But, aside from what it'll do to her, it's the wrong play. Fifty thousand isn't a whole lot to you, and paying it over will give us two chances that we haven't got now. One when the payment is made—a chance to either nab whoever comes for it or get a line on them. And the other when your daughter is returned. No matter how careful they are it's a cinch that she'll be able to tell us something that will help us grab them."

He shook his head angrily, and I was tired of arguing with him. So I left him, hoping that he'd see the wisdom of the course I had advised before too late.

At the Gatewood residence I found butlers, second men, chauffeurs, cooks, maids, upstairs girls, downstairs girls, and a raft of miscellaneous flunkies—he had enough servants to run a hotel.

What they told me amounted to this: The girl had not received a phone call, note by messenger, or telegram—the time-honored devices for luring a victim out to a murder or abduction—before she left the house. She had told her maid that she would be back within an hour or two; but the maid had not been alarmed when her mistress failed to return all that night.

Audrey was the only child, and since her mother's death she had come and gone to suit herself. She and her father didn't hit it off very well together—their natures were too much alike, I gathered—and he never knew where she was; and there was nothing unusual about her remaining away all night, as she seldom bothered to leave word when she was going to stay overnight with friends.

She was nineteen years old, but looked several years older; about five feet five inches tall, and slender. She had blue eyes, brown hair,—very thick and long,—was pale and very nervous. Her photographs, of which I took a handful, showed that her eyes were large, her nose small and regular, and her chin obstinately pointed.

She was not beautiful, but in the one photograph where a smile had wiped off the sullenness of her mouth, she was at least pretty.

When she left the house she had worn a light tweed skirt and jacket with a London tailor's labels in them, a buff silk shirtwaist with stripes a shade darker, brown wool stockings, low-heeled brown oxfords, and an untrimmed grey felt hat.

I went up to her rooms—she had three on the third floor—and looked through all her stuff. I found nearly a bushel of photographs of men, boys, and girls; and a great stack of letters of varying degrees of intimacy, signed with a wide assortment of names and nicknames. I made notes of all the addresses I found.

Nothing there seemed to have any bearing on her abduction, but there was a chance that one of the names and addresses might be of someone who had served as a decoy. Also, some of her friends might be able to tell us something of value.

I dropped in at the Agency and distributed the names and addresses among the three operatives who were idle, sending them out to see what they could dig up.

Then I reached the police detectives who were working on the case—O'Gar and Thode—by telephone, and went down to the Hall of Justice to meet them. Lusk, a post office inspector, was also there. We turned the job around and around, looking at it from every angle, but not getting very far. We were all agreed, however, that we couldn't take a chance on any publicity, or work in the open, until the girl was safe.

They had had a worse time with Gatewood than I—he had wanted to put the whole thing in the newspapers, with the offer of a reward, photographs and all. Of course, Gatewood was right in claiming that this was the most effective way of catching the kidnappers—but it would have been tough on his daughter if her captors happened to be persons of sufficiently hardened character. And kidnappers as a rule aren't lambs.

I looked at the letter they had sent. It was printed with pencil on ruled paper of the kind that is sold in pads by every stationery dealer in the world. The envelope was just as common, also addressed in pencil, and post-marked "San Francisco, September 20, 9 P.M." That was the night she had been seized.

The letter reads:

"SIR:

WE HAVE YOUR CHARMING DAUGHTER AND PLACE A VALUE OF $50,000 UPON HER. YOU WILL GET THE MONEY READY IN $100 BILLS AT ONCE SO THERE WILL BE NO DELAY WHEN WE TELL YOU HOW IT IS TO BE PAID OVER TO US.

WE BEG TO ASSURE YOU THAT THINGS WILL GO BADLY WITH YOUR DAUGHTER SHOULD YOU NOT DO AS YOU ARE TOLD, OR SHOULD YOU BRING THE POLICE INTO THIS MATTER, OR SHOULD YOU DO ANYTHING FOOLISH.

$50,000 IS ONLY A SMALL FRACTION OF WHAT YOU STOLE WHILE WE WERE LIVING IN MUD AND BLOOD IN

FRANCE FOR YOU, AND WE MEAN TO GET THAT MUCH
OR . . . . !

THREE."

A peculiar note in several ways. They are usually written
with a great pretense of partial illiterateness. Almost always
there's an attempt to lead suspicion astray. Perhaps the ex-
service stuff was there for that purpose . . . or perhaps not.

Then there was a postscript:

"WE KNOW A CHINAMAN WHO WILL BUY HER EVEN
AFTER WE ARE THROUGH WITH HER—IN CASE YOU
WON'T LISTEN TO REASON."

The letter from the girl was written jerkily on the same kind
of paper, apparently with the same pencil.

> "Daddy—
> Please do as they ask! I am so afraid—
> Audrey"

A door at the other end of the room opened, and a head
came through.

"O'Gar! Thode! Gatewood just called up. Get up to his office right away!"

The four of us tumbled out of the Hall of Justice and into
a machine.

Gatewood was pacing his office like a maniac when we
pushed aside enough hirelings to get to him. His face was hot
with blood and his eyes had an insane glare in them.

"She just phoned me!" he cried thickly, when he saw us.

It took a minute or two to get him calm enough to tell us
about it.

"She called me on the phone. Said, 'Oh, daddy! Do something! I can't stand this—they're killing me!' I asked her if
she knew where she was, and she said, 'No, but I can see
Twin Peaks from here. There's three men and a woman,
and—' And then I heard a man curse, and a sound as if he
had struck her, and the phone went dead. I tried to get central to give me the number, but she couldn't! It's a damned
outrage the way the telephone system is run. We pay enough
for service, God knows, and we . . ."

O'Gar scratched his head and turned away from Gatewood.

"In sight of Twin Peaks! There are hundreds of houses that are!"

Gatewood meanwhile had finished denouncing the telephone company and was pounding on his desk with a paper-weight to attract our attention.

"Have you people done anything at all?" he demanded.

I answered him with another question: "Have you got the money ready?"

"No," he said, "I won't be held up by anybody!"

But he said it mechanically, without his usual conviction—the talk with his daughter had shaken him out of some of his stubbornness. He was thinking of her safety a little now instead of altogether of his own fighting spirit.

We went at him hammer and tongs for a few minutes, and after a while he sent a clerk out for the money.

We split up the field then. Thode was to take some men from headquarters and see what he could find in the Twin Peaks end of town; but we weren't very optimistic over the prospects there—the territory was too large.

Lusk and O'Gar were to carefully mark the bills that the clerk brought from the bank, and then stick as close to Gatewood as they could without attracting attention. I was to go out to Gatewood's house and stay there.

The abductors had plainly instructed Gatewood to get the money ready immediately so that they could arrange to get it on short notice—not giving him time to communicate with anyone or make any plans.

Gatewood was to get hold of the newspapers, give them the whole story, with the $10,000 reward he was offering for the abductors' capture, to be published as soon as the girl was safe—so that we would get the help of publicity at the earliest moment possible without jeopardizing the girl.

The police in all the neighboring towns had already been notified—that had been done before the girl's phone message had assured us that she was held in San Francisco.

Nothing happened at the Gatewood residence all that evening. Harvey Gatewood came home early; and after dinner he paced his library floor and drank whiskey until bedtime, demanding every few minutes that we, the detectives in the case, do something besides sit around like a lot of damned mummies. O'Gar, Lusk and Thode were out in the street, keeping an eye on the house and neighborhood.

At midnight Harvey Gatewood went to bed. I declined a bed in favor of the library couch, which I dragged over beside the telephone, an extension of which was in Gatewood's bedroom.

At two-thirty the bell rang. I listened in while Gatewood talked from his bed.

A man's voice, crisp and curt: "Gatewood?"

"Yes."

"Got the dough?"

"Yes."

Gatewood's voice was thick and blurred—I could imagine the boiling that was going on inside him.

"Good!" came the brisk voice. "Put a piece of paper around it, and leave the house with it, right away! Walk down Clay street, keeping on the same side as your house. Don't walk too fast and keep walking. If everything's all right, and there's no elbows tagging along, somebody'll come up to you between your house and the water-front. They'll have a handkerchief up to their face for a second, and then they'll let it fall to the ground.

"When you see that, you'll lay the money on the pavement, turn around and walk back to your house. If the money isn't marked, and you don't try any fancy tricks, you'll get your daughter back in an hour or two. If you try to pull anything—remember what we wrote you about the Chink! Got it straight?"

Gatewood sputtered something that was meant for an affirmative, and the telephone clicked silent.

I didn't waste any of my precious time tracing the call—it would be from a public telephone, I knew—but yelled up the stairs to Gatewood:

"You do as you were told, and don't try any foolishness!"

Then I ran out into the early morning air to find the police detectives and the post office inspector.

They had been joined by two plainclothes men, and had two automobiles waiting. I told them what the situation was, and we laid hurried plans.

O'Gar was to drive in one of the machines down Sacramento street, and Thode, in the other, down Washington street. These streets parallel Clay, one on each side. They were to drive slowly, keeping pace with Gatewood, and stopping at each cross street to see that he passed.

When he failed to cross within a reasonable time they were to turn up to Clay street—and their actions from then on would have to be guided by chance and their own wits.

Lusk was to wander along a block or two ahead of Gatewood, on the opposite side of the street, pretending to be mildly intoxicated, and keeping his eyes and ears open.

I was to shadow Gatewood down the street, with one of the plainclothes men behind me. The other plainclothes man was to turn in a call at headquarters for every available man to be sent to Clay street. They would arrive too late, of course, and as likely as not it would take them some time to find us; but we had no way of knowing what was going to turn up before the night was over.

Our plan was sketchy enough, but it was the best we could do—we were afraid to grab whoever got the money from Gatewood. The girl's talk with her father that afternoon had sounded too much as if her captors were desperate for us to take any chances on going after them rough-shod until she was out of their hands.

We had hardly finished our plans when Gatewood, wearing a heavy overcoat, left his house and turned down the street.

Farther down, Lusk, weaving along, talking to himself, was almost invisible in the shadows. There was no one else in sight. That meant that I had to give Gatewood at least two blocks' lead, so that the man who came for the money wouldn't tumble to me. One of the plainclothes men was half a block behind me, on the other side of the street.

Two blocks down we walked, and then a little chunky man in a derby hat came into sight. He passed Gatewood, passed me, went on.

Three blocks more.

A touring-car, large, black, powerfully engined, and with lowered curtains, came from the rear, passed us, went on. Possibly a scout! I scrawled its license number down on my pad without taking my hand out of my overcoat pocket.

Another three blocks.

A policeman passed, strolling along in ignorance of the game being played under his nose; and then a taxicab with a single male passenger. I wrote down its license number.

Four blocks with no one in sight ahead of me but Gatewood—I couldn't see Lusk any more.

Just ahead of Gatewood a man stepped out of a black door-way—turned around—called up to a window for someone to come down and open the door for him.

We went on.

Coming from nowhere, a woman stood on the sidewalk fifty feet ahead of Gatewood, a handkerchief to her face. It fluttered to the pavement.

Gatewood stopped, standing stiff-legged. I could see his right hand come up, lifting the side of the overcoat in which it was pocketed—and I knew the hand was gripped around a pistol.

For perhaps half a minute he stood like a statue. Then his left hand came out of his pocket, and the bundle of money fell to the sidewalk in front of him, where it made a bright blur in the darkness. Gatewood turned abruptly, and began to retrace his steps homeward.

The woman had recovered her handkerchief. Now she ran to the bundle, picked it up, and scuttled to the black mouth of an alley, a few feet distant—a rather tall woman, bent, and in dark clothes from head to feet.

In the black mouth of the alley she vanished.

I had been compelled to slow up while Gatewood and the woman stood facing each other, and I was more than a block away now. As soon as the woman disappeared I took a chance, and started pounding my rubber soles against the pavement.

The alley was empty when I reached it.

It ran all the way through to the next street, but I knew that the woman couldn't have reached the other end before I got to this one. I carry a lot of weight these days, but I can still step a block or two in good time. Along both sides of the alley were the rears of apartment buildings, each with its back door looking blankly, secretively at me.

The plainclothes man who had been trailing behind me came up, then O'Gar and Thode in their machines, and soon,

Lusk. O'Gar and Thode rode off immediately to wind through the neighboring streets, hunting for the woman. Lusk and the plainclothes man each planted himself on a corner from which two of the streets enclosing the block could be watched.

I went through the alley, hunting vainly for an unlocked door, an open window, a fire-escape that would show recent use—any of the signs that a hurried departure from the alley might leave.

Nothing!

O'Gar came back shortly with some reinforcements from headquarters that he had picked up, and Gatewood.

Gatewood was burning.

"Bungled the damn thing again! I won't pay your agency a nickel, and I'll see that some of these so-called detectives get put back in a uniform and set to walking beats!"

"What'd the woman look like?" I asked him.

"I don't know! I thought you were hanging around to take care of her! She was old and bent, kind of, I guess, but I couldn't see her face for her veil. I don't know! What the hell were you men doing? It's a damned outrage the way . . ."

I finally got him quieted down and took him home, leaving the city men to keep the neighborhood under surveillance. There was fourteen or fifteen of them on the job now, and every shadow held at least one.

The girl would naturally head for home as soon as she was released and I wanted to be there to pump her. There was an excellent chance of catching her abductors before they got very far if she could tell us anything at all about them.

Home, Gatewood went up against the whiskey bottle again, while I kept one ear cocked at the telephone and the other at the front door. O'Gar or Thode phoned every half hour or so to ask if we'd heard from the girl. They had still found nothing.

At nine o'clock they, with Lusk, arrived at the house. The woman in black had turned out to be a man, and had gotten away.

In the rear of one of the apartment buildings that touched the alley—just a foot or so within the back-door—they found a woman's skirt, long coat, hat and veil—all black. Investigating the occupants of the house, they had learned that an apartment had been rented to a young man named Leighton three days before.

Leighton was not at home when they went up to his apartment. His rooms held a lot of cold cigarette butts, and an empty bottle, and nothing else that had not been there when he rented it.

The inference was clear: he had rented the apartment so that he might have access to the building. Wearing woman's clothes over his own, he had gone out of the back door— leaving it unlatched behind him—to meet Gatewood.

Then he had run back into the building, discarded his disguise, and hurried through the building, out the front door, and away before we had our feeble net around the block; perhaps dodging into dark doorways here and there to avoid O'Gar and Thode in their automobiles.

Leighton, it seemed, was a man of about thirty, slender, about five feet eight or nine inches tall, with dark hair and eyes; rather good-looking, and well-dressed, on the two occasions when people living in the building had seen him, in a brown suit and a light brown felt hat.

There was no possibility, according to the opinions of both of the detectives and the post office inspector, that the girl might have been held, even temporarily, in Leighton's apartment.

Ten o'clock came, and no word from the girl.

Gatewood had lost his domineering bull-headedness by now and was breaking up. The suspense was getting him, and the liquor he had put away wasn't helping him. I didn't like him either personally or by reputation, but at that I felt sorry for him this morning.

I talked to the agency over the phone and got the reports of the operatives who had been looking up Audrey's friends. The last person to see her had been an Agnes Dangerfield, who had seen her walking down Market street near Sixth, alone, on the night of her abduction—some time between 8:15 and 8:45. Audrey had been too far away for the Dangerfield girl to speak to her.

For the rest, the boys had learned nothing except that Audrey was a wild, spoiled youngster who hadn't shown any great care in selecting her friends—just the sort of girl who could easily fall into the hands of a mob of highbinders!

Noon struck. No sign of the girl. We told the newspapers to turn loose the story, with the added developments of the past few hours.

Gatewood was broken; he sat with his head in his hands, looking at nothing. Just before I left to follow a hunch I had, he looked up at me, and I'd never have recognized him if I hadn't seen the change take place.

"What do you think is keeping her away?" he asked.

I didn't have the heart to tell him what I was beginning to suspect, now that the money had been paid and she had failed to show up. So I stalled with some vague assurances, and left.

I caught a street-car and dropped off down in the shopping district. I visited the five largest department stores, going to all the women's wear departments from shoes to hats, and trying to learn if a man—perhaps one answering Leighton's description—had been buying clothes that would fit Audrey Gatewood within the past couple days.

Failing to get any results, I turned the rest of the local stores over to one of the boys from the agency, and went across the bay to canvass the Oakland stores.

At the first one I got action. A man who might easily have been Leighton had been in the day before, buying clothes that could easily fit Audrey. He had bought lots of them, everything from lingerie to a cloak, and—my luck was hitting on all its cylinders—had had his purchases delivered to T. Offord, at an address on Fourteenth street.

At the Fourteenth street address, an apartment house, I found Mr. and Mrs. Theodore Offord's names under the vestibule telephone for apartment 202.

I had just found them when the front door opened and a stout, middle-aged woman in a gingham house-dress came out. She looked at me a bit curiously, so I asked:

"Do you know where I can find the manager?"

"I'm the manager," she said.

I handed her a card and stepped indoors with her.

"I'm from the bonding department of the North American Casualty Company"—a repetition of the lie that was printed on the card I had given her—"and a bond for Mr. Offord has been applied for. Is he all right so far as you know?" With the slightly apologetic air of one going through with a necessary but not too important formality.

She frowned.

"A bond? That's funny! He is going away tomorrow."

"Well, I can't say what the bond is for," I said lightly. "We investigators just get the names and addresses. It may be for his present employer, or perhaps the man he is going to work for wherever he's going has applied for it. Or some firms have us look up prospective employees before they hire them, just to be safe."

"Mr. Offord, so far as I know, is a very nice young man," she said, "but he has been here only a week."

"Not staying long, then?"

"No. They came here from Denver, intending to stay, but the low altitude doesn't agree with Mrs. Offord, so they are going back."

"Are you sure they came from Denver?"

"Well," she said, "they told me they did."

"How many of them are there?"

"Only the two of them; they're young people."

"Well, how do they impress you?" I asked, trying to get the impression that I thought her a woman of shrewd judgment over.

"They seem to be a very nice young couple. You'd hardly know they were in their apartment most of the time, they are so quiet. I am sorry they can't stay."

"Do they go out much?"

"I really don't know. They have their keys, and unless I should happen to pass them going in or out I'd never see them."

"Then, as a matter of fact, you couldn't say whether they stayed away all night some nights or not. Could you?"

She eyed me doubtfully—I was stepping way over my pretext now, but I didn't think it mattered—and shook her head.

"No, I couldn't say."

"They have many visitors?"

"I don't know. Mr. Offord is not—"

She broke off as a man came in quietly from the street, brushed past me, and started to mount the steps to the second floor.

"Oh, dear!" she whispered. "I hope he didn't hear me talking about him. That's Mr. Offord."

A slender man in brown, with a light brown hat—Leighton perhaps.

I hadn't seen anything of him except his back, nor he anything except mine. I watched him as he climbed the stairs. If he had heard the manager mention his name he would use the turn at the head of the stairs to sneak a look at me.

He did. I kept my face stolid, but I knew him. He was "Penny" Quayle, a con man who had been active in the East four or five years before. His face was as expressionless as mine. But he knew me.

A door on the second floor shut. I left the manager and started for the stairs.

"I think I'll go up and talk to him," I told her.

Coming silently to the door of apartment 202, I listened. Not a sound. This was no time for hesitation. I pressed the bell-button.

As close together as the tapping of three keys under the fingers of an expert typist, but a thousand times more vicious, came three pistol shots. And waist-high in the door of apartment 202 were three bullet holes.

The three bullets would have been in my fat carcass if I hadn't learned years ago to stand to one side of strange doors when making uninvited calls.

Inside the apartment sounded a man's voice, sharp, commanding.

"Cut it, kid! For God's sake, not that!"

A woman's voice, shrill, bitter, spiteful screaming blasphemies.

Two more bullets came through the door.

"Stop! No! No!" The man's voice had a note of fear in it now.

The woman's voice, cursing hotly. A scuffle. A shot that didn't hit the door.

I hurled my foot against the door, near the knob, and the lock broke away.

On the floor of the room, a man—Quayle—and a woman were tussling. He was bending over her, holding her wrists, trying to keep her down. A smoking automatic pistol was in one of her hands. I got to it in a jump and tore it loose.

"That's enough!" I called to them when I was planted. "Get up and receive company."

Quayle released his antagonist's wrists, whereupon she struck at his eyes with curved, sharp-nailed fingers, tearing his cheek open. He scrambled away from her on hands and knees, and both of them got to their feet.

He sat down on a chair immediately, panting and wiping his bleeding cheek with a handkerchief.

She stood, hands on hips, in the center of the room, glaring at me.

"I suppose," she spat, "you think you've raised hell!"

I laughed—I could afford to.

"If your father is in his right mind," I told her, "he'll do it with a razor strop when he gets you home again. A fine joke you picked out to play on him!"

"If *you'd* been tied to him as long as I have, and had been bullied and held down as much, I guess *you'd* do most anything to get enough money so that you could go away and live your own life."

I didn't say anything to that. Remembering some of the business methods Harvey Gatewood had used—particularly some of his war contracts that the Department of Justice was still investigating—I suppose the worst that could be said about Audrey was that she was her father's own daughter.

"How'd you rap to it?" Quayle asked me, politely.

"Several ways," I said. "First, I'm a little doubtful about grown persons being kidnapped in cities. Maybe it really happens sometimes, but at least nine-tenths of the cases you hear about are fakes. Second, one of Audrey's friends saw her on Market street between 8:15 and 8:45 the night she disappeared; and your letter to Gatewood was post-marked 9 P.M. Pretty fast work. You should have waited a while before mailing it, even if it had to miss the first morning delivery. I suppose she dropped it in the post office on her way over here?"

Quayle nodded.

"Then third," I went on, "there was that phone call of hers. She knew it took anywhere from ten to fifteen minutes to get her father on the wire at the office. If time had been as valuable as it would have been if she had gotten to a phone while imprisoned, she'd have told her story to the first person she got hold of—the phone girl, most likely. So that made it look as if, besides wanting to throw out that Twin Peaks line, she wanted to stir the old man out of his bull-headedness.

"When she failed to show up after the money was paid I figured it was a sure bet that she had kidnapped herself. I knew that if she came back home after faking this thing we'd find it out before we'd talked to her very long—and I figured she knew that too, and would stay away.

"The rest was easy, as I got some good breaks. We knew a man was working with her after we found the woman's clothes you left behind, and I took a chance on there being no one else in it. Then I figured she'd need clothes—she couldn't have taken any from home without tipping her mitt—and there was an even chance that she hadn't laid in a stock beforehand. She's got too many girl friends of the sort that do a lot of shopping to make it safe for her risk showing herself in stores. Maybe, then, the man would buy what she needed for her. And it turned out that he did, and that he was too lazy to carry away his purchases, or perhaps there was too many of them, and so he had them sent out. That's the story."

Quayle nodded again.

"I was damned careless," he said, and then, jerking a contemptuous thumb toward the girl. "But what can you expect? She's had a skin full of hop ever since we started. Took all my time and attention keeping her from running wild and gumming the works. Just now was a sample—I told her you were coming up and she goes crazy and tries to add your corpse to the wreck!"

The Gatewood reunion took place in the office of the captain of inspectors, on the second floor of the Oakland City Hall, and it was a merry little party. For an hour it was a toss-up whether Harvey Gatewood would die of apoplexy, strangle his daughter, or send her off to the state reformatory until she was of age. But Audrey licked him. Besides being a chip off

the old block, she was young enough to be careless of consequences, while her father, for all his bullheadedness, had had
some caution hammered into him.

The card she beat him with was a threat of spilling everything she knew about him to the newspapers, and at least one
of the San Francisco papers had been trying to get his scalp
for years. I don't know what she had on him, and I don't
think he was any too sure himself; but, with his war contracts
even then being investigated by the Department of Justice, he
couldn't afford to take a chance. There was no doubt at all
that she would have done as she threatened.

And so, together, they left for home, sweating hate for each
other at every pore.

We took Quayle upstairs and put him in a cell, but he was
too experienced to let that worry him. He knew that if the
girl was to be spared, he himself couldn't very easily be convicted of anything.

The Tenth Clew

CHAPTER I

"Do you know . . . Emil Bonfils?"

M R. LEOPOLD GANTVOORT is not at home," the servant who opened the door said, "but his son, Mr. Charles, is—if you wish to see him."

"No. I had an appointment with Mr. Leopold Gantvoort for nine or a little after. It's just nine now. No doubt he'll be back soon. I'll wait."

"Very well, sir."

He stepped aside for me to enter the house, took my overcoat and hat, guided me to a room on the second floor—Gantvoort's library—and left me. I picked up a magazine from the stack on the table, pulled an ash tray over beside me, and made myself comfortable.

An hour passed. I stopped reading and began to grow impatient. Another hour passed—and I was fidgeting.

A clock somewhere below had begun to strike eleven when a young man of twenty-five or -six, tall and slender, with remarkably white skin and very dark hair and eyes, came into the room.

"My father hasn't returned yet," he said. "It's too bad that you should have been kept waiting all this time. Isn't there anything I could do for you? I am Charles Gantvoort."

"No, thank you." I got up from my chair, accepting the courteous dismissal. "I'll get in touch with him tomorrow."

"I'm sorry," he murmured, and we moved toward the door together.

As we reached the hall an extension telephone in one corner of the room we were leaving buzzed softly, and I halted in the doorway while Charles Gantvoort went over to answer it.

His back was toward me as he spoke into the instrument.

"Yes. Yes. Yes!"—sharply—"*What?* Yes"—very weakly—"Yes."

He turned slowly around and faced me with a face that was gray and tortured, with wide shocked eyes and gaping mouth—the telephone still in his hand.

"Father," he gasped, "is dead—killed!"

"Where? How?"

"I don't know. That was the police. They want me to come down at once."

He straightened his shoulders with an effort, pulling himself together, put down the telephone, and his face fell into less strained lines.

"You will pardon my—"

"Mr. Gantvoort," I interrupted his apology, "I am connected with the Continental Detective Agency. Your father called up this afternoon and asked that a detective be sent to see him tonight. He said his life had been threatened. He hadn't definitely engaged us, however, so unless you—"

"Certainly! You are employed! If the police haven't already caught the murderer I want you to do everything possible to catch him."

"All right! Let's get down to headquarters."

Neither of us spoke during the ride to the Hall of Justice. Gantvoort bent over the wheel of his car, sending it through the streets at a terrific speed. There were several questions that needed answers, but all his attention was required for his driving if he was to maintain the pace at which he was driving without piling us into something. So I didn't disturb him, but hung on and kept quiet.

Half a dozen police detectives were waiting for us when we reached the detective bureau. O'Gar—a bullet-headed detective-sergeant who dresses like the village constable in a movie, wide-brimmed black hat and all, but who isn't to be put out of the reckoning on that account—was in charge of the investigation. He and I had worked on two or three jobs together before, and hit it off excellently.

He led us into one of the small offices below the assembly room. Spread out on the flat top of a desk there were a dozen or more objects.

"I want you to look these things over carefully," the detective-sergeant told Gantvoort, "and pick out the ones that belonged to your father."

"But where is he?"

"Do this first," O'Gar insisted, "and then you can see him."

I looked at the things on the table while Charles Gantvoort made his selections. An empty jewel case; a memoranda book; three letters in slit envelopes that were addressed to the dead man; some other papers; a bunch of keys; a fountain pen; two white linen handkerchiefs; two pistol cartridges; a gold watch, with a gold knife and a gold pencil attached to it by a gold-and-platinum chain; two black leather wallets, one of them very new and the other worn; some money, both paper and silver; and a small portable typewriter, bent and twisted, and matted with hair and blood. Some of the other things were smeared with blood and some were clean.

Gantvoort picked out the watch and its attachments, the keys, the fountain pen, the memoranda book, the handkerchiefs, the letters and other papers, and the older wallet.

"These were father's," he told us. "I've never seen any of the others before. I don't know, of course, how much money he had with him tonight, so I can't say how much of this is his."

"You're sure none of the rest of this stuff was his?" O'Gar asked.

"I don't think so, but I'm not sure. Whipple could tell you." He turned to me. "He's the man who let you in tonight. He looked after father, and he'd know positively whether any of these other things belonged to him or not."

One of the police detectives went to the telephone to tell Whipple to come down immediately.

I resumed the questioning.

"Is anything that your father usually carried with him missing? Anything of value?"

"Not that I know of. All of the things that he might have been expected to have with him seem to be here."

"At what time tonight did he leave the house?"

"Before seven-thirty. Possibly as early as seven."

"Know where he was going?"

"He didn't tell me, but I supposed he was going to call on Miss Dexter."

The faces of the police detectives brightened, and their eyes grew sharp. I suppose mine did, too. There are many, many murders with never a woman in them anywhere; but seldom a very conspicuous killing.

"Who's this Miss Dexter?" O'Gar took up the inquiry.

"She's well—" Charles Gantvoort hesitated. "Well, father was on very friendly terms with her and her brother. He usually called on them—on her several evenings a week. In fact, I suspected that he intended marrying her."

"Who and what is she?"

"Father became acquainted with them six or seven months ago. I've met them several times, but don't know them very well. Miss Dexter—Creda is her given name—is about twenty-three years old, I should judge, and her brother Madden is four or five years older. He is in New York now, or on his way there, to transact some business for father."

"Did your father tell you he was going to marry her?" O'Gar hammered away at the woman angle.

"No; but it was pretty obvious that he was very much— ah—infatuated. We had some words over it a few days ago— last week. Not a quarrel, you understand, but words. From the way he talked I feared that he meant to marry her."

"What do you mean 'feared'?" O'Gar snapped at that word.

Charles Gantvoort's pale face flushed a little, and he cleared his throat embarrassedly.

"I don't want to put the Dexters in a bad light to you. I don't think—I'm sure they had nothing to do with father's— with this. But I didn't care especially for them—didn't like them. I thought they were—well—fortune hunters, perhaps. Father wasn't fabulously wealthy, but he had considerable means. And, while he wasn't feeble, still he was past fifty-seven, old enough for me to feel that Creda Dexter was interested in his money than in him."

"How about your father's will?"

"The last one of which I have any knowledge—drawn up two or three years ago—left everything to my wife and me jointly. Father's attorney, Mr. Murray Abernathy, could tell you if there was a later will, but I hardly think there was."

"Your father had retired from business, hadn't he?"

"Yes; he turned his import and export business over to me about a year ago. He had quite a few investments scattered around, but he wasn't actively engaged in the management of any concern."

O'Gar tilted his village constable hat back and scratched his bullet head reflectively for a moment. Then he looked at me.

"Anything else you want to ask?"

"Yes. Mr. Gantvoort, do you know, or did you ever hear your father or anyone else speak of an Emil Bonfils?"

"No."

"Did your father ever tell you that he had received a threatening letter? Or that he had been shot at on the street?"

"No."

"Was your father in Paris in 1902?"

"Very likely. He used to go abroad every year up until the time of his retirement from business."

CHAPTER II

"That's Something!"

O'Gar and I took Gantvoort around to the morgue to see his father, then. The dead man wasn't pleasant to look at, even to O'Gar and me, who hadn't known him except by sight. I remembered him as a small wiry man, always smartly tailored, and with a brisk springiness that was far younger than his years.

He lay now with the top of his head beaten into a red and pulpy mess.

We left Gantvoort at the morgue and set out afoot for the Hall of Justice.

"What's this deep stuff you're pulling about Emil Bonfils and Paris in 1902?" the detective-sergeant asked as soon as we were out in the street.

"This: the dead man phoned the Agency this afternoon and said he had received a threatening letter from an Emil Bonfils with whom he had had trouble in Paris in 1902. He also said that Bonfils had shot at him the previous evening, in the street. He wanted somebody to come around and see him about it tonight. And he said that under no circumstances were the police to be let in on it—that he'd rather have

Bonfils get him than have the trouble made public. That's all
he would say over the phone; and that's how I happened to
be on hand when Charles Gantvoort was notified of his father's death."

O'Gar stopped in the middle of the sidewalk and whistled
softly.

"That's something!" he exclaimed. "Wait till we get back
to headquarters—I'll show you something."

Whipple was waiting in the assembly room when we arrived
at headquarters. His face at first glance was as smooth and
mask-like as when he had admitted me to the house on
Russian Hill earlier in the evening. But beneath his perfect
servant's manner he was twitching and trembling.

We took him into the little office where we had questioned
Charles Gantvoort.

Whipple verified all that the dead man's son had told us. He
was positive that neither the typewriter, the jewel case, the two
cartridges, or the newer wallet had belonged to Gantvoort.

We couldn't get him to put his opinion of the Dexters in
words, but that he disapproved of them was easily seen. Miss
Dexter, he said, had called up on the telephone three times
this night at about eight o'clock, at nine, and at nine-thirty.
She had asked for Mr. Leopold Gantvoort each time, but she
had left no message. Whipple was of the opinion that she was
expecting Gantvoort, and he had not arrived.

He knew nothing, he said, of Emil Bonfils or of any threatening letters. Gantvoort had been out the previous night
from eight until midnight. Whipple had not seen him closely
enough when he came home to say whether he seemed excited or not. Gantvoort usually carried about a hundred dollars in his pockets.

"Is there anything that you know of that Gantvoort had on
his person tonight which isn't among these things on the
desk?" O'Gar asked.

"No, sir. Everything seems to be here—watch and chain,
money, memorandum book, wallet, keys, handkerchiefs,
fountain pen—everything that I know of."

"Did Charles Gantvoort go out tonight?"

"No, sir. He and Mrs. Gantvoort were at home all
evening."

"Positive?"

Whipple thought a moment.

"Yes, sir, I'm fairly certain. But I know Mrs. Gantvoort wasn't out. To tell the truth, I didn't see Mr. Charles from about eight o'clock until he came downstairs with this gentleman"—pointing to me—"at eleven. But I'm fairly certain he was home all evening. I think Mrs. Gantvoort said he was."

Then O'Gar put another question—one that puzzled me at the time.

"What kind of collar buttons did Mr. Gantvoort wear?"

"You mean Mr. Leopold?"

"Yes."

"Plain gold ones, made all in one piece. They had a London jeweler's mark on them."

"Would you know them if you saw them?"

"Yes, sir."

We let Whipple go home then.

"Don't you think," I suggested when O'Gar and I were alone with this desk-load of evidence that didn't mean anything at all to me yet, "it's time you were loosening up and telling me what's what?"

"I guess so—listen! A man named Lagerquist, a grocer, was driving through Golden Gate Park tonight, and passed a machine standing on a dark road, with its lights out. He thought there was something funny about the way the man in it was sitting at the wheel, so he told the first patrolman he met about it.

"The patrolman investigated and found Gantvoort sitting at the wheel—dead—with his head smashed in and this dingus"—putting one hand on the bloody typewriter—"on the seat beside him. That was at a quarter of ten. The doc says Gantvoort was killed—his skull crushed—with this typewriter.

"The dead man's pockets, we found, had all been turned inside out; and all this stuff on the desk, except this new wallet, was scattered about in the car—some of it on the floor and some on the seats. This money was there too—nearly a hundred dollars of it. Among the papers was this."

He handed me a sheet of white paper upon which the following had been typewritten:

L. F. G.—

    I want what is mine. 6,000 miles and 21 years are not enough to hide you from the victim of your treachery. I mean to have what you stole.

E. B.

"L. F. G. could be Leopold F. Gantvoort," I said. "And E. B. could be Emil Bonfils. Twenty-one years is the time from 1902 to 1923, and 6,000 miles is, roughly, the distance between Paris and San Francisco."

I laid the letter down and picked up the jewel case. It was a black imitation leather one, lined with white satin, and unmarked in any way.

Then I examined the cartridges. There were two of them, S. W. .45-caliber, and deep crosses had been cut in their soft noses—an old trick that makes the bullet spread out like a saucer when it hits.

"These in the car, too?"

"Yep—and this."

From a vest pocket O'Gar produced a short tuft of blond hair—hairs between an inch and two inches in length. They had been cut off, not pulled out by the roots.

"Any more?"

There seemed to be an endless stream of things.

He picked up the new wallet from the desk—the one that both Whipple and Charles Gantvoort had said did not belong to the dead man—and slid it over to me.

"That was found in the road, three or four feet from the car."

It was of a cheap quality, and had neither manufacturer's name nor owner's initials on it. In it were two ten-dollar bills, three small newspaper clippings, and a typewritten list of six names and addresses, headed by Gantvoort's.

The three clippings were apparently from the Personal columns of three different newspapers—the type wasn't the same—and they read:

GEORGE—

    Everything is fixed. Don't wait too long.

D. D. D.

R. H. T.—
    They do not answer.
                    FLO.

CAPPY.—
    Twelve on the dot and look sharp.
                    BINGO.

The names and addresses on the typewritten list, under Ganvoort's, were:

Quincy Heathcote, 1223 S. Jason Street, Denver; B. D. Thornton, 96 Hughes Circle, Dallas; Luther G. Randall, 615 Columbia Street, Portsmouth; J. H. Boyd Willis, 4544 Harvard Street, Boston; Hannah Hindmarsh, 218 E. 79th Street, Cleveland.

"What else?" I asked when I had studied these.

The detective-sergeant's supply hadn't been exhausted yet.

"The dead man's collar buttons—both front and back— had been taken out, though his collar and tie were still in place. And his left shoe was gone. We hunted high and low all around, but didn't find either shoe or collar buttons."

"Is that all?"

I was prepared for anything now.

"What the hell do you want?" he growled. "Ain't that enough?"

"How about fingerprints?"

"Nothing stirring! All we found belonged to the dead man."

"How about the machine he was found in?"

"A coupé belonging to a Doctor Wallace Girargo. He phoned in at six this evening that it had been stolen from near the corner of McAllister and Polk Streets. We're checking up on him—but I think he's all right."

The things that Whipple and Charles Gantvoort had identified as belonging to the dead man told us nothing. We went over them carefully, but to no advantage. The memoranda book contained many entries, but they all seemed totally foreign to the murder. The letters were quite as irrelevant.

The serial number of the typewriter with which the murder had been committed had been removed, we found—apparently filed out of the frame.

"Well, what do you think?" O'Gar asked when we had given up our examination of our clews and sat back burning tobacco.

"I think we want to find Monsieur Emil Bonfils."

"It wouldn't hurt to do that," he grunted. "I guess our best bet is to get in touch with these five people on the list with Gantvoort's name. Suppose that's a murder list? That this Bonfils is out to get all of them?"

"Maybe. We'll get hold of them anyway. Maybe we'll find that some of them have already been killed. But whether they have been killed or are to be killed or not, it's a cinch they have some connection with this affair. I'll get off a batch of telegrams to the Agency's branches, having the names on the list taken care of. I'll try to have the three clippings traced, too."

O'Gar looked at his watch and yawned.

"It's after four. What say we knock off and get some sleep? I'll leave word for the department's expert to compare the typewriter with that letter signed E. B. and with that list to see if they were written on it. I guess they were, but we'll make sure. I'll have the park searched all around where we found Gantvoort as soon as it gets light enough to see, and maybe the missing shoe and the collar buttons will be found. And I'll have a couple of the boys out calling on all the typewriter shops in the city to see if they can get a line on this one."

I stopped at the nearest telegraph office and got off a wad of messages. Then I went home to dream of nothing even remotely connected with crime or the detecting business.

CHAPTER III

"A sleek kitten that dame!"

At eleven o'clock that same morning, when, brisk and fresh with five hours' sleep under my belt, I arrived at the police detective bureau, I found O'Gar slumped down at his desk, staring dazedly at a black shoe, half a dozen collar buttons, a rusty flat key, and a rumpled newspaper—all lined up before him.

"What's all this? Souvenir of your wedding?"

"Might as well be." His voice was heavy with disgust. "Listen to this: one of the porters of the Seamen's National Bank found a package in the vestibule when he started cleaning up this morning. It was this shoe—Gantvoort's missing one—wrapped in this sheet of a five-day-old *Philadelphia Record*, and with these collar buttons and this old key in it. The heel of the shoe, you'll notice, has been pried off, and is still missing. Whipple identifies it all right, as well as two of the collar buttons, but he never saw the key before. These other four collar buttons are new, and common gold-rolled ones. The key don't look like it had had much use for a long time. What do you make of all that?"

I couldn't make anything out of it.

"How did the porter happen to turn the stuff in?"

"Oh, the whole story was in the morning papers—all about the missing shoe and collar buttons and all."

"What did you learn about the typewriter?" I asked.

"The letter and the list were written with it, right enough; but we haven't been able to find where it came from yet. We checked up the doc who owns the coupe, and he's in the clear. We accounted for all his time last night. Lagerquist, the grocer who found Gantvoort, seems to be all right, too. What did you do?"

"Haven't had any answers to the wires I sent last night. I dropped in at the Agency on my way down this morning, and got four operatives out covering the hotels and looking up all the people named Bonfils they can find—there are two or three families by that name listed in the directory. Also I sent our New York branch a wire to have the steamship records searched to see if an Emil Bonfils had arrived recently; and I put a cable through to our Paris correspondent to see what he could dig up over there."

"I guess we ought to see Gantvoort's lawyer—Abernathy— and that Dexter woman before we do anything else," the detective-sergeant said.

"I guess so," I agreed, "let's tackle the lawyer first. He's the most important one, the way things now stand."

Murray Abernathy, attorney-at-law, was a long, stringy, slow-spoken old gentleman who still clung to starched-bosom shirts. He was too full of what he thought were professional ethics to give us as much help as we had expected; but by letting him talk—letting him ramble along in his own way—we did get a little information from him. What we got amounted to this:

The dead man and Creda Dexter had intended being married the coming Wednesday. His son and her brother were both opposed to the marriage, it seemed, so Gantvoort and the woman had planned to be married secretly in Oakland, and catch a boat for the Orient that same afternoon; figuring that by the time their lengthy honeymoon was over they could return to a son and brother who had become resigned to the marriage.

A new will had been drawn up, leaving half of Gantvoort's estate to his new wife and half to his son and daughter-in-law. But the new will had not been signed yet, and Creda Dexter knew it had not been signed. She knew—and this was one of the few points upon which Abernathy would make a positive statement—that under the old will, still in force, everything went to Charles Gantvoort and his wife.

The Gantvoort estate, we estimated from Abernathy's roundabout statements and allusions, amounted to about a million and a half in cash value. The attorney had never heard of Emil Bonfils, he said, and had never heard of any threats or attempts at murder directed toward the dead man. He knew nothing—or would tell us nothing—that threw any light upon the nature of the thing that the threatening letter had accused the dead man of stealing.

From Abernathy's office we went to Creda Dexter's apartment, in a new and expensively elegant building only a few minutes' walk from the Gantvoort residence.

Creda Dexter was a small woman in her early twenties. The first thing you noticed about her were her eyes. They were large and deep and the color of amber, and their pupils were never at rest. Continuously they changed size, expanded and contracted—slowly at times, suddenly at others—ranging incessantly from the size of pinheads to an extent that threatened to blot out the amber irides.

With the eyes for a guide, you discovered that she was pronouncedly feline throughout. Her every movement was the slow, smooth, sure one of a cat; and the contours of her rather pretty face, the shape of her mouth, her small nose, the set of her eyes, the swelling of her brows, were all cat-like. And the effect was heightened by the way she wore her hair, which was thick and tawny.

"Mr. Gantvoort and I," she told us after the preliminary explanations had been disposed of, "were to have been married the day after tomorrow. His son and daughter-in-law were both opposed to the marriage, as was my brother Madden. They all seemed to think that the difference between our ages was too great. So to avoid any unpleasantness, we had planned to be married quietly and then go abroad for a year or more, feeling sure that they would all have forgotten their grievances by the time we returned.

"That was why Mr. Gantvoort persuaded Madden to go to New York. He had some business there—something to do with the disposal of his interest in a steel mill—so he used it as an excuse to get Madden out of the way until we were off on our wedding trip. Madden lived here with me, and it would have been nearly impossible for me to have made any preparations for the trip without him seeing them."

"Was Mr. Gantvoort here last night?" I asked her.

"No. I expected him—we were going out. He usually walked over—it's only a few blocks. When eight o'clock came and he hadn't arrived, I telephoned his house, and Whipple told me that he had left nearly an hour before. I called up again, twice, after that. Then, this morning, I called up again before I had seen the papers, and I was told that he—"

She broke off with a catch in her voice—the only sign of sorrow she displayed throughout the interview. The impression of her we had received from Charles Gantvoort and Whipple had prepared us for a more or less elaborate display of grief on her part. But she disappointed us. There was nothing crude about her work—she didn't even turn on the tears for us.

"Was Mr. Gantvoort here night before last?"

"Yes. He came over at a little after eight and stayed until nearly twelve. We didn't go out."

"Did he walk over and back?"

"Yes, so far as I know."

"Did he ever say anything to you about his life being threatened?"

"No."

She shook her head decisively.

"Do you know Emil Bonfils?"

"No."

"Ever hear Mr. Gantvoort speak of him?"

"No."

"At what hotel is your brother staying in New York?"

The restless black pupils spread out abruptly, as if they were about to overflow into the white areas of her eyes. That was the first clear indication of fear I had seen. But, outside of those tell-tale pupils, her composure was undisturbed.

"I don't know."

"When did he leave San Francisco?"

"Thursday—four days ago."

O'Gar and I walked six or seven blocks in thoughtful silence after we left Creda Dexter's apartment, and then he spoke.

"A sleek kitten—that dame! Rub her the right way, and she'll purr pretty. Rub her the wrong way—and look out for the claws!"

"What did that flash of her eyes when I asked about her brother tell you?" I asked.

"Something—but I don't know what! It wouldn't hurt to look him up and see if he's really in New York. If he is there today it's a cinch he wasn't here last night—even the mail planes take twenty-six or twenty-eight hours for the trip."

"We'll do that," I agreed. "It looks like this Creda Dexter wasn't any too sure that her brother wasn't in on the killing. And there's nothing to show that Bonfils didn't have help. I can't figure Creda being in on the murder, though. She knew the new will hadn't been signed. There'd be no sense in her working herself out of that three-quarters of a million berries."

We sent a lengthy telegram to the Continental's New York branch, and then dropped in at the Agency to see if any replies had come to the wires I had got off the night before.

They had.

None of the people whose names appeared on the typewritten list with Gantvoort's had been found; not the least trace had been found of any of them. Two of the addresses given were altogether wrong. There were no houses with those numbers on those streets—and there never had been.

CHAPTER IV

"Maybe that ain't so foolish!"

What was left of the afternoon, O'Gar and I spent going over the street between Gantvoort's house on Russian Hill and the building in which the Dexters lived. We questioned everyone we could find—man, woman and child—who lived, worked, or played along any of the three routes the dead man could have taken.

We found nobody who had heard the shots that had been fired by Bonfils on the night before the murder. We found nobody who had seen anything suspicious on the night of the murder. Nobody who remembered having seen him picked up in a coupe.

Then we called at Gantvoort's house and questioned Charles Gantvoort again, his wife, and all the servants—and we learned nothing. So far as they knew, nothing belonging to the dead man was missing—nothing small enough to be concealed in the heel of a shoe.

The shoes he had worn the night he was killed were one of three pairs made in New York for him two months before. He could have removed the heel of the left one, hollowed it out sufficiently to hide a small object in it, and then nailed it on again; though Whipple insisted that he would have noticed the effects of any tampering with the shoe unless it had been done by an expert repairman.

This field exhausted, we returned to the Agency. A telegram had just come from the New York branch, saying that none of the steamship companies' records showed the arrival of an Emil Bonfils from either England, France, or Germany within the past six months.

The operatives who had been searching the city for Bonfils had all come in empty-handed. They had found and investigated eleven persons named Bonfils in San Francisco, Oakland, Berkeley, and Alameda. Their investigations had definitely cleared all eleven. None of these Bonfilses knew an Emil Bonfils. Combing the hotels had yielded nothing.

O'Gar and I went to dinner together—a quiet, grouchy sort of meal during which we didn't speak six words apiece—and then came back to the Agency to find that another wire had come in from New York.

> Madden Dexter arrived McAlpin Hotel this morning with Power of Attorney to sell Gantvoort interest in B. F. and F. Iron Corporation. Denies knowledge of Emil Bonfils or of murder. Expects to finish business and leave for San Francisco tomorrow.

I let the sheet of paper upon which I had decoded the telegram slide out of my fingers, and we sat listlessly facing each other across my desk, looking vacantly each at the other, listening to the clatter of charwomen's buckets in the corridor.

"It's a funny one," O'Gar said softly to himself at last.

I nodded. It was.

"We got nine clews," he spoke again presently, "and none of them have got us a damned thing.

"Number one: the dead man called up you people and told you that he had been threatened and shot at by an Emil Bonfils that he'd had a run-in with in Paris a long time ago.

"Number two: the typewriter he was killed with and that the letter and list were written on. We're still trying to trace it, but with no breaks so far. What the hell kind of a weapon was that, anyway? It looks like this fellow Bonfils got hot and hit Gantvoort with the first thing he put his hand on. But what was the typewriter doing in a stolen car? And why were the numbers filed off it?"

I shook my head to signify that I couldn't guess the answer, and O'Gar went on enumerating our clews.

"Number three: the threatening letter, fitting in with what Gantvoort had said over the phone that afternoon.

"Number four: those two bullets with the crosses in their snoots.

"Number five: the jewel case.

"Number six: that bunch of yellow hair.

"Number seven: the fact that the dead man's shoe and collar buttons were carried away.

"Number eight: the wallet, with two ten-dollar bills, three clippings, and the list in it, found in the road.

"Number nine: finding the shoe next day, wrapped up in a five-day-old Philadelphia paper, and with the missing collar buttons, four more, and a rusty key in it.

"That's the list. If they mean anything at all, they mean that Emil Bonfils whoever he is—was flimflammed out of something by Gantvoort in Paris in 1902, and that Bonfils came to get it back. He picked Gantvoort up last night in a stolen car, bringing his typewriter with him—for God knows what reason! Gantvoort put up an argument, so Bonfils bashed in his noodle with the typewriter, and then went through his pockets, apparently not taking anything. He decided that what he was looking for was in Gantvoort's left shoe, so he took the shoe away with him. And then—but there's no sense to the collar button trick, or the phoney list, or—"

"Yes there is!" I cut in, sitting up, wide awake now. "That's our tenth clew—the one we're going to follow from now on. That list was, except for Gantvoort's name and address, a fake. Our people would have found at least one of the five people whose names were on it if it had been on the level. But they didn't find the least trace of any of them. And two of the addresses were of street numbers that didn't exist!

"That list was faked up, put in the wallet with the clippings and twenty dollars—to make the play stronger—and planted in the road near the car to throw us off-track. And if that's so, then it's a hundred to one that the rest of the things were cooked up too.

"From now on I'm considering all those nine lovely clews as nine bum steers. And I'm going just exactly contrary to them. I'm looking for a man whose name isn't Emil Bonfils, and whose initials aren't either E or B; who isn't French, and who wasn't in Paris in 1902. A man who hasn't light hair, doesn't carry a .45-calibre pistol, and has no interest in Personal advertisements in newspapers. A man who didn't kill Gantvoort to recover anything that could have been hidden in a shoe or on a collar button. That's the sort of a guy I'm hunting for now!"

The detective-sergeant screwed up his little green eyes reflectively and scratched his head.

"Maybe that ain't so foolish!" he said. "You might be right at that. Suppose you are—what then? That Dexter kitten didn't do it—it cost her three-quarters of a million. Her brother didn't do it—he's in New York. And, besides, you don't croak a guy just because you think he's too old to marry your sister. Charles Gantvoort? He and his wife are the only ones who make any money out of the old man dying before the new will was signed. We have only their word for it that Charles was home that night. The servants didn't see him between eight and eleven. You were there, and you didn't see him until eleven. But me and you both believe him when he says he *was* home all that evening. And neither of us think he bumped the old man off—though of course he might. Who then?"

"This Creda Dexter," I suggested, "was marrying Gantvoort for his money, wasn't she? You don't think she was in love with him, do you?"

"No. I figure, from what I saw of her, that she was in love with the million and a half."

"All right," I went on. "Now she isn't exactly homely—not by a long shot. Do you reckon Gantvoort was the only man who ever fell for her?"

"I got you! I got you!" O'Gar exclaimed. "You mean there might have been some young fellow in the running who didn't have any million and a half behind him, and who didn't take kindly to being nosed out by a man who did. Maybe—maybe."

"Well, suppose we bury all this stuff we've been working on and try out that angle."

"Suits me," he said. "Starting in the morning, then, we spend our time hunting for Gantvoort's rival for the paw of this Dexter kitten."

CHAPTER V

"Meet Mr. Smith"

Right or wrong, that's what we did. We stowed all those lovely clews away in a drawer, locked the drawer, and forgot them. Then we set out to find Creda Dexter's masculine acquaintances and sift them for the murderer.

But it wasn't as simple as it sounded.

All our digging into her past failed to bring to light one man who could be considered a suitor. She and her brother had been in San Francisco three years. We traced them back the length of that period, from apartment to apartment. We questioned everyone we could find who even knew her by sight. And nobody could tell us of a single man who had shown an interest in her besides Gantvoort. Nobody, apparently, had ever seen her with any man except Gantvoort or her brother.

All of which, while not getting us ahead, at least convinced us that we were on the right trail. There must have been, we argued, at least one man in her life in those three years besides Gantvoort. She wasn't—unless we were very much mistaken—the sort of woman who would discourage masculine attention; and she was certainly endowed by nature to attract it. And if there was another man, then the very fact that he had been kept so thoroughly under cover strengthened the probability of him having been mixed up in Gantvoort's death.

We were unsuccessful in learning where the Dexters had lived before they came to San Francisco, but we weren't so very interested in their earlier life. Of course it was possible that some old-time lover had come upon the scene again recently; but in that case it should have been easier to find the recent connection than the old one.

There was no doubt, our explorations showed, that Gantvoort's son had been correct in thinking the Dexters were fortune hunters. All their activities pointed to that, although there seemed to be nothing downright criminal in their pasts.

I went up against Creda Dexter again, spending an entire afternoon in her apartment, banging away with question after question, all directed toward her former love affairs. Who had she thrown over for Gantvoort and his million and a half? And the answer was always *nobody*—an answer that I didn't choose to believe.

We had Creda Dexter shadowed night and day—and it carried us ahead not an inch. Perhaps she suspected that she was being watched. Anyway, she seldom left her apartment, and then on only the most innocent of errands. We had her apartment watched whether she was in it or not. Nobody visited it. We tapped her telephone—and all our listening-in netted us nothing. We had her mail covered—and she didn't receive a single letter, not even an advertisement.

Meanwhile, we had learned where the three clippings found in the wallet had come from—from the Personal columns of a New York, a Chicago, and a Portland newspaper. The one in the Portland paper had appeared two days before the murder, the Chicago one four days before, and the New York one five days before. All three of those papers would have been on the San Francisco newsstands the day of the murder—ready to be purchased and cut out by anyone who was looking for material to confuse detectives with.

The Agency's Paris correspondent had found no less than six Emil Bonfilses—all bloomers so far as our job was concerned—and had a line on three more.

But O'Gar and I weren't worrying over Emil Bonfils any more—that angle was dead and buried. We were plugging away at our new task—the finding of Gantvoort's rival.

Thus the days passed, and thus the matter stood when Madden Dexter was due to arrive home from New York.

Our New York branch had kept an eye on him until he left that city, and had advised us of his departure, so I knew what train he was coming on. I wanted to put a few questions to him before his sister saw him. He could tell me what I wanted to know, and he might be willing to if I could get to him before his sister had an opportunity to shut him up.

If I had known him by sight I could have picked him up when he left his train at Oakland, but I didn't know him; and I didn't want to carry Charles Gantvoort or anyone else along with me to pick him out for me.

So I went up to Sacramento that morning, and boarded his train there. I put my card in an envelope and gave it to a messenger boy in the station. Then I followed the boy through the train, while he called out:

"Mr. Dexter! Mr. Dexter!"

In the last car—the observation-club car—a slender, dark-haired man in well-made tweeds turned from watching the station platform through a window and held out his hand to the boy.

I studied him while he nervously tore open the envelope and read my card. His chin trembled slightly just now, emphasizing the weakness of a face that couldn't have been strong at its best. Between twenty-five and thirty, I placed him; with his hair parted in the middle and slicked down; large, too-expressive brown eyes; small well-shaped nose; neat brown mustache; very red, soft lips—that type.

I dropped into the vacant chair beside him when he looked up from the card.

"You are Mr. Dexter?"

"Yes," he said. "I suppose it's about Mr. Gantvoort's death that you want to see me?"

"Uh-huh. I wanted to ask you a few questions, and since I happened to be in Sacramento, I thought that by riding back on the train with you I could ask them without taking up too much of your time."

"If there's anything I can tell you," he assured me, "I'll be only too glad to do it. But I told the New York detectives all I knew, and they didn't seem to find it of much value."

"Well, the situation has changed some since you left New York." I watched his face closely as I spoke. "What we thought of no value then may be just what we want now."

I paused while he moistened his lips and avoided my eyes. He may not know anything, I thought, but he's certainly jumpy. I let him wait a few minutes while I pretended deep thoughtfulness. If I played him right, I was confident I could turn him inside out. He didn't seem to be made of very tough material.

We were sitting with our heads close together, so that the four or five other passengers in the car wouldn't overhear our talk; and that position was in my favor. One of the things that every detective knows is that it's often easy to get information—even a confession—out of a feeble nature simply by putting your face close to his and talking in a loud tone. I couldn't talk loud here, but the closeness of our faces was by itself an advantage.

"Of the men with whom your sister was acquainted," I came out with it at last, "who, outside of Mr. Gantvoort, was the most attentive?"

He swallowed audibly, looked out of the window, fleetingly at me, and then out of the window again.

"Really, I couldn't say."

"All right. Let's get at it this way. Suppose we check off one by one all the men who were interested in her and in whom she was interested."

He continued to stare out of the window.

"Who's first?" I pressed him.

His gaze flickered around to meet mine for a second, with a sort of timid desperation in his eyes.

"I know it sounds foolish, but I, her brother, couldn't give you the name of even one man in whom Creda was interested before she met Gantvoort. She never, so far as I know, had the slightest feeling for any man before she met him. Of course it is possible that there may have been someone that I didn't know anything about, but—"

It did sound foolish, right enough! The Creda Dexter I had talked to—a sleek kitten, as O'Gar had put it—didn't impress me as being at all likely to go very long without having at least one man in tow. This pretty little guy in front of me was lying. There couldn't be any other explanation.

I went at him tooth and nail. But when he reached Oakland early that night he was still sticking to his original statement—that Gantvoort was the only one of his sister's suitors that he knew anything about. And I knew that I had blundered, had underrated Madden Dexter, had played my hand wrong in trying to shake him down too quickly—in driving too directly at the point I was interested in. He was either a lot stronger than I had figured him, or his interest in concealing Gantvoort's murderer was much greater than I had thought it would be.

But I had this much: if Dexter was lying—and there

couldn't be much doubt of that—then Gantvoort *had* had a rival, and Madden Dexter believed or knew that this rival had killed Gantvoort.

When we left the train at Oakland I knew I was licked, that he wasn't going to tell me what I wanted to know—not this night, anyway. But I clung to him, stuck at his side when we boarded the ferry for San Francisco, in spite of the obviousness of his desire to get away from me. There's always a chance of something unexpected happening; so I continued to ply him with questions as our boat left the slip.

Presently a man came toward where we were sitting—a big burly man in a light overcoat, carrying a black bag.

"Hello, Madden!" he greeted my companion, striding over to him with outstretched hand. "Just got in and was trying to remember your phone number," he said, setting down his bag, as they shook hands warmly.

Madden Dexter turned to me.

"I want you to meet Mr. Smith," he told me, and then gave my name to the big man, adding, "he's with the Continental Detective Agency here."

That tag—clearly a warning for Smith's benefit—brought me to my feet, all watchfulness. But the ferry was crowded—a hundred persons were within sight of us, all around us. I relaxed, smiled pleasantly, and shook hands with Smith. Whoever Smith was, and whatever connection he might have with the murder—and if he hadn't any, why should Dexter have been in such a hurry to tip him off to my identity?—he couldn't do anything here. The crowd around us was all to my advantage.

That was my second mistake of the day.

Smith's left hand had gone into his overcoat pocket—or rather, through one of those vertical slits that certain styles of overcoats have so that inside pockets may be reached without unbuttoning the overcoat. His hand had gone through that slit, and his coat had fallen away far enough for me to see a snub-nosed automatic in his hand—shielded from everyone's sight but mine—pointing at my waist-line.

"Shall we go on deck?" Smith asked—and it was an order.

I hesitated. I didn't like to leave all these people who were so blindly standing and sitting around us. But Smith's face wasn't the face of a cautious man. He had the look of one who might easily disregard the presence of a hundred witnesses.

I turned around and walked through the crowd. His right hand lay familiarly on my shoulder as he walked behind me; his left hand held his gun, under the overcoat, against my spine.

The deck was deserted. A heavy fog, wet as rain,—the fog of San Francisco Bay's winter nights,—lay over boat and water, and had driven everyone else inside. It hung about us, thick and impenetrable; I couldn't see so far as the end of the boat, in spite of the lights glowing overhead.

I stopped.

Smith prodded me in the back.

"Farther away, where we can talk," he rumbled in my ear.

I went on until I reached the rail.

The entire back of my head burned with sudden fire . . . tiny points of light glittered in the blackness before me . . . grew larger . . . came rushing toward me. . . .

CHAPTER VI

"Those damned horns!"

Semi-consciousness! I found myself mechanically keeping afloat somehow and trying to get out of my overcoat. The back of my head throbbed devilishly. My eyes burned. I felt heavy and logged, as if I had swallowed gallons of water.

The fog hung low and thick on the water—there was nothing else to be seen anywhere. By the time I had freed myself of the encumbering overcoat my head had cleared somewhat, but with returning consciousness came increased pain.

A light glimmered mistily off to my left, and then vanished. From out of the misty blanket, from every direction, in a dozen different keys, from near and far, fog-horns sounded. I stopped swimming and floated on my back, trying to determine my whereabouts.

After a while I picked out the moaning, evenly spaced blasts of the Alcatraz siren. But they told me nothing. They came to

me out of the fog without direction—seemed to beat down
upon me from straight above.

I was somewhere in San Francisco Bay, and that was all I
knew, though I suspected the current was sweeping me out
toward the Golden Gate.

A little while passed, and I knew that I had left the path of
the Oakland ferries—no boat had passed close to me for some
time. I was glad to be out of that track. In this fog a boat was
a lot more likely to run me down than to pick me up.

The water was chilling me, so I turned over and began
swimming, just vigorously enough to keep my blood circulating while I saved my strength until I had a definite goal to try
for.

A horn began to repeat its roaring note nearer and nearer,
and presently the lights of the boat upon which it was fixed
came into sight. One of the Sausalito ferries, I thought.

It came quite close to me, and I hallooed until I was breathless and my throat was raw. But the boat's siren, crying its
warning, drowned my shouts.

The boat went on and the fog closed in behind it.

The current was stronger now, and my attempts to attract
the attention of the Sausalito ferry had left me weaker. I
floated, letting the water sweep me where it would, resting.

Another light appeared ahead of me suddenly—hung there
for an instant—disappeared.

I began to yell, and worked my arms and legs madly, trying
to drive myself through the water to where it had been.

I never saw it again.

Weariness settled upon me, and a sense of futility. The
water was no longer cold. I was warm with a comfortable,
soothing numbness. My head stopped throbbing; there was
no feeling at all in it now. No lights, now, but the sound of
fog-horns . . . fog-horns . . . fog-horns ahead of me, behind
me, to either side; annoying me, irritating me.

But for the moaning horns I would have ceased all effort.
They had become the only disagreeable detail of my situation—the water was pleasant, fatigue was pleasant. But the
horns tormented me. I cursed them petulantly and decided to
swim until I could no longer hear them, and then, in the
quiet of the friendly fog, go to sleep. . . .

Now and then I would doze, to be goaded into wakefulness by the wailing voice of a siren.

"Those damned horns! Those damned horns!" I complained aloud, again and again.

One of them, I found presently, was bearing down upon me from behind, growing louder and stronger. I turned and waited. Lights, dim and steaming, came into view.

With exaggerated caution to avoid making the least splash, I swam off to one side. When this nuisance was past I could go to sleep. I sniggered softly to myself as the lights drew abreast, feeling a foolish triumph in my cleverness in eluding the boat. Those damned horns. . . .

Life—the hunger for life—all at once surged back into my being.

I screamed at the passing boat, and with every iota of my being struggled toward it. Between strokes I tilted up my head and screamed. . . .

CHAPTER VII

"You have a lot of fun, don't you?"

When I returned to consciousness for the second time that evening, I was lying on my back on a baggage truck, which was moving. Men and women were crowding around, walking beside the truck, staring at me with curious eyes.

I sat up.

"Where are we?" I asked.

A little red-faced man in uniform answered my question.

"Just landing in Sausalito. Lay still. We'll take you over to the hospital."

I looked around.

"How long before this boat goes back to San Francisco?"

"Leaves right away."

I slid off the truck and started back aboard the boat.

"I'm going with it," I said.

Half an hour later, shivering and shaking in my wet clothes, keeping my mouth clamped tight so that my teeth wouldn't sound like a dice-game, I climbed into a taxi at the Ferry Building and went to my flat.

There, I swallowed half a pint of whisky, rubbed myself with a coarse towel until my skin was sore, and, except for an enormous weariness and a worse headache, I felt almost human again.

I reached O'Gar by phone, asked him to come up to my flat right away, and then called up Charles Gantvoort.

"Have you seen Madden Dexter yet?" I asked him.

"No, but I talked to him over the phone. He called me up as soon as he got in. I asked him to meet me in Mr. Abernathy's office in the morning, so we could go over that business he transacted for father."

"Can you call him up now and tell him that you have been called out of town—will have to leave early in the morning—and that you'd like to run over to his apartment and see him tonight?"

"Why yes, if you wish."

"Good! Do that. I'll call for you in a little while and go over to see him with you."

"What is—"

"I'll tell you about it when I see you," I cut him off.

O'Gar arrived as I was finishing dressing.

"So he told you something?" he asked, knowing of my plan to meet Dexter on the train and question him.

"Yes," I said with sour sarcasm, "but I came near forgetting what it was. I grilled him all the way from Sacramento to Oakland, and couldn't get a whisper out of him. On the ferry coming over he introduces me to a man he calls Mr. Smith, and he tells Mr. Smith that I'm a gum-shoe. This, mind you, all happens in the middle of a crowded ferry! Mr. Smith puts a gun in my belly, marches me out on deck, raps me across the back of the head, and dumps me into the bay."

"You have a lot of fun, don't you?" O'Gar grinned, and then wrinkled his forehead. "Looks like Smith would be the man we want then—the buddy who turned the Gantvoort trick. But what the hell did he want to give himself away by chucking you overboard for?"

"Too hard for me," I confessed, while trying to find which of my hats and caps would sit least heavily upon my bruised head. "Dexter knew I was hunting for one of his sister's former lovers, of course. And he must have thought I knew a whole lot more than I do, or he wouldn't have made that raw play—tipping my mitt to Smith right in front of me.

"It may be that after Dexter lost his head and made that break on the ferry, Smith figured that I'd be on to him soon, if not right away; and so he'd take a desperate chance on putting me out of the way. But we'll know all about it in a little while," I said, as we went down to the waiting taxi and set out for Gantvoort's.

"You ain't counting on Smith being in sight, are you?" the detective-sergeant asked.

"No. He'll be holed up somewhere until he sees how things are going. But Madden Dexter will have to be out in the open to protect himself. He has an alibi, so he's in the clear so far as the actual killing is concerned. And with me supposed to be dead, the more he stays in the open, the safer he is. But it's a cinch that he knows what this is all about, though he wasn't necessarily involved in it. As near as I could see, he didn't go out on deck with Smith and me tonight. Anyway he'll be home. And this time he's going to talk—he's going to tell his little story!"

Charles Gantvoort was standing on his front steps when we reached his house. He climbed into our taxi and we headed for the Dexters' apartment. We didn't have time to answer any of the questions that Gantvoort was firing at us with every turning of the wheels.

"He's home and expecting you?" I asked him.

"Yes."

Then we left the taxi and went into the apartment building.

"Mr. Gantvoort to see Mr. Dexter," he told the Philippine boy at the switchboard.

The boy spoke into the phone.

"Go right up," he told us.

At the Dexters' door I stepped past Gantvoort and pressed the button.

Creda Dexter opened the door. Her amber eyes widened and her smile faded as I stepped past her into the apartment.

I walked swiftly down the little hallway and turned into the first room through whose open door a light showed.

And came face to face with Smith!

We were both surprised, but his astonishment was a lot more profound than mine. Neither of us had expected to see the other; but I had known he was still alive, while he had every reason for thinking me at the bottom of the bay.

I took advantage of his greater bewilderment to the extent of two steps toward him before he went into action.

One of his hands swept down.

I threw my right fist at his face—threw it with every ounce of my 180 pounds behind it, re-enforced by the memory of every second I had spent in the water, and every throb of my battered head.

His hand, already darting down for his pistol, came back up too late to fend off my punch.

Something clicked in my hand as it smashed into his face, and my hand went numb.

But he went down—and lay where he fell.

I jumped across his body to a door on the opposite side of the room, pulling my gun loose with my left hand.

"Dexter's somewhere around!" I called over my shoulder to O'Gar, who with Gantvoort and Creda, was coming through the door by which I had entered. "Keep your eyes open!"

I dashed through the four other rooms of the apartment, pulling closet doors open, looking everywhere—and I found nobody.

Then I returned to where Creda Dexter was trying to revive Smith, with the assistance of O'Gar and Gantvoort.

The detective-sergeant looked over his shoulder at me.

"Who do you think this joker is?" he asked.

"My friend Mr. Smith."

"Gantvoort says he's Madden Dexter."

I looked at Charles Gantvoort, who nodded his head.

"This is Madden Dexter," he said.

CHAPTER VIII

"I hope you swing!"

We worked upon Dexter for nearly ten minutes before he opened his eyes.

As soon as he sat up we began to shoot questions and accusations at him, hoping to get a confession out of him before he recovered from his shakiness—but he wasn't that shaky.

All we could get out of him was:

"Take me in if you want to. If I've got anything to say I'll say it to my lawyer, and to nobody else."

Creda Dexter, who had stepped back after her brother came to, and was standing a little way off, watching us, suddenly came forward and caught me by the arm.

"What have you got on him?" she demanded, imperatively.

"I wouldn't want to say," I countered, "but I don't mind telling you this much. We're going to give him a chance in a nice modern court-room to prove that he didn't kill Leopold Gantvoort."

"He was in New York!"

"He was not! He had a friend who went to New York as Madden Dexter and looked after Gantvoort's business under that name. But if this is the real Madden Dexter then the closest he got to New York was when he met his friend on the ferry to get from him the papers connected with the B. F. & F. Iron Corporation transaction; and learned that I had stumbled upon the truth about his alibi—even if I didn't know it myself at the time."

She jerked around to face her brother.

"Is that on the level?" she asked him.

He sneered at her, and went on feeling with the fingers of one hand the spot on his jaw where my fist had landed.

"I'll say all I've got to say to my lawyer," he repeated.

"You will?" she shot back at him. "Well, I'll say what I've got to say right now!"

She flung around to face me again.

"Madden is not my brother at all! My name is Ives. Madden and I met in St. Louis about four years ago, drifted around together for a year or so, and then came to Frisco. He was a con man—still is. He made Mr. Gantvoort's acquaintance six or seven months ago, and was getting him all ribbed up to unload a fake invention on him. He brought him here a couple of times, and introduced me to him as his sister. We usually posed as brother and sister.

"Then, after Mr. Gantvoort had been here a couple times, Madden decided to change his game. He thought Mr. Gantvoort liked me, and that we could get more money out of him by working a fancy sort of badger-game on him. I was to lead the old man on until I had him wrapped around my finger—until we had him tied up so tight he couldn't get away—had something on him—something good and strong. Then we were going to shake him down for plenty of money.

"Everything went along fine for a while. He fell for me— fell hard. And finally he asked me to marry him. We had never figured on that. Blackmail was our game. But when he asked me to marry him I tried to call Madden off. I admit the old man's money had something to do with it—it influenced me—but I had come to like him a little for himself. He was mighty fine in lots of ways—nicer than anybody I had ever known.

"So I told Madden all about it, and suggested that we drop the other plan, and that I marry Gantvoort. I promised to see that Madden was kept supplied with money—I knew I could get whatever I wanted from Mr. Gantvoort. And I was on the level with Madden. I liked Mr. Gantvoort, but Madden had found him and brought him around to me; and so I wasn't going to run out on Madden. I was willing to do all I could for him.

"But Madden wouldn't hear of it. He'd have got more money in the long run by doing as I suggested—but he wanted his little handful right away. And to make him more unreasonable he got one of his jealous streaks. He beat me one night!

"That settled it. I made up my mind to ditch him. I told Mr. Gantvoort that my brother was bitterly opposed to our marrying, and he could see that Madden was carrying a grouch. So he arranged to send Madden East on that steel business, to get him out of the way until we were off on our wedding trip. And we thought Madden was completely deceived—but I should have known that he would see through our scheme. We planned to be gone about a year, and by that time I thought Madden would have forgotten me—or I'd be fixed to handle him if he tried to make any trouble.

"As soon as I heard that Mr. Gantvoort had been killed I had a hunch that Madden had done it. But then it seemed like a certainty that he was in New York the next day, and I thought I had done him an injustice. And I was glad he was out of it. But now—"

She whirled around to her erstwhile confederate.

"Now I hope you swing, you big sap!"

She spun around to me again. No sleek kitten, this, but a furious, spitting cat, with claws and teeth bared.

"What kind of looking fellow was the one who went to New York for him?"

I described the man I had talked to on the train.

"Evan Felter," she said, after a moment of thought. "He used to work with Madden. You'll probably find him hiding in Los Angeles. Put the screws on him and he'll spill all he knows—he's a weak sister! The chances are he didn't know what Madden's game was until it was all over."

"How do you like that?" she spat at Madden Dexter. "How do you like that for a starter? You messed up my little party, did you? Well, I'm going to spend every minute of my time from now until they pop you off helping them pop you!"

And she did, too—with her assistance it was no trick at all to gather up the rest of the evidence we needed to hang him. And I don't believe her enjoyment of her three-quarters of a million dollars is spoiled a bit by any qualms over what she did to Madden. She's a very respectable woman *now*, and glad to be free of the con-man.

Zigzags of Treachery

"ALL I know about Dr. Estep's death," I said, "is the stuff in the papers."

Vance Richmond's lean gray face took on an expression of distaste.

"The newspapers aren't always either thorough or accurate. I'll give you the salient points as I know them; though I suppose you'll want to go over the ground for yourself, and get your information first-hand."

I nodded, and the attorney went on, shaping each word precisely with his thin lips before giving it sound.

"Dr. Estep came to San Francisco in '98 or '99—a young man of twenty-five, just through qualifying for his license. He opened an office here, and, as you probably know, became in time a rather excellent surgeon. He married two or three years after he came here. There were no children. He and his wife seem to have been a bit happier together than the average.

"Of his life before coming to San Francisco, nothing is known. He told his wife briefly that he had been born and raised in Parkersburg, W. Va., but that his home life had been so unpleasant that he was trying to forget it, and that he did not like to talk—or even think—about it. Bear that in mind.

"Two weeks ago—on the third of the month—a woman came to his office, in the afternoon. His office was in his residence on Pine Street. Lucy Coe, who was Dr. Estep's nurse and assistant, showed the woman into his office, and then went back to her own desk in the reception room.

"She didn't hear anything the doctor said to the woman, but through the closed door she heard the woman's voice now and then—a high and anguished voice, apparently pleading. Most of the words were lost upon the nurse, but she heard one coherent sentence. 'Please! Please!' she heard the woman cry. 'Don't turn me away!' The woman was with Dr. Estep for about fifteen minutes, and left sobbing into a handkerchief. Dr. Estep said nothing about the caller either to his nurse or to his wife, who didn't learn of it until after his death.

"The next day, toward evening, while the nurse was putting on her hat and coat preparatory to leaving for home, Dr. Estep came out of his office, with his hat on and a letter in his hand. The nurse saw that his face was pale—'white as my uniform,' she says—and he walked with the care of one who takes pains to keep from staggering.

"She asked him if he was ill. 'Oh, it's nothing!' he told her. 'I'll be all right in a very few minutes.' Then he went on out. The nurse left the house just behind him, and saw him drop the letter he had carried into the mail box on the corner, after which he returned to the house.

"Mrs. Estep, coming downstairs ten minutes later,—it couldn't have been any later than that,—heard, just as she reached the first floor, the sound of a shot from her husband's office. She rushed into it, meeting nobody. Her husband stood by his desk, swaying, with a hole in his right temple and a smoking revolver in his hand. Just as she reached him and put her arms around him, he fell across the desk—dead."

"Anybody else—any of the servants, for instance—able to say that Mrs. Estep didn't go to the office until after the shot?" I asked.

The attorney shook his head sharply.

"No, damn it! That's where the rub comes in!"

His voice, after this one flare of feeling, resumed its level, incisive tone, and he went on with his tale.

"The next day's papers had accounts of Dr. Estep's death, and late that morning the woman who had called upon him the day before his death came to the house. She is Dr. Estep's first wife—which is to say, his legal wife! There seems to be no reason—not the slightest—for doubting it, as much as I'd like to. They were married in Philadelphia in '96. She has a certified copy of the marriage record. I had the matter investigated in Philadelphia, and it's a certain fact that Dr. Estep and this woman—Edna Fife was her maiden name—were really married.

"She says that Estep, after living with her in Philadelphia for two years, deserted her. That would have been in '98, or just before he came to San Francisco. She has sufficient proof of her identity—that she really is the Edna Fife who married him; and my agents in the East found positive proof that Estep had practiced for two years in Philadelphia.

"And here is another point. I told you that Estep had said he was born and raised in Parkersburg. I had inquiries made there, but found nothing to show that he had ever lived there, and found ample to show that he had never lived at the address he had given his wife. There is, then, nothing for us to believe except that his talk of an unhappy early life was a ruse to ward off embarrassing questions."

"Did you do anything toward finding out whether the doctor and his first wife had ever been divorced?" I asked.

"I'm having that taken care of now, but I hardly expect to learn that they had. That would be too crude. To get on with my story: This woman—the first Mrs. Estep—said that she had just recently learned her husband's whereabouts, and had come to see him in an attempt to effect a reconciliation. When she called upon him the afternoon before his death, he asked for a little time to make up his mind what he should do. He promised to give her his decision in two days. My personal opinion, after talking to the woman several times, is that she had learned that he had accumulated some money, and that her interest was more in getting the money than in getting him. But that, of course, is neither here nor there.

"At first the authorities accepted the natural explanation of the doctor's death—suicide. But after the first wife's appearance, the second wife—my client—was arrested and charged with murder.

"The police theory is that after his first wife's visit, Dr. Estep told his second wife the whole story; and that she, brooding over the knowledge that he had deceived her, that she was not his wife at all, finally worked herself up into a rage, went to the office after his nurse had left for the day, and shot him with the revolver that she knew he always kept in his desk.

"I don't know, of course, just what evidence the prosecution has, but from the newspapers I gather that the case against her will be built upon her finger prints on the revolver with which he was killed; an upset inkwell on his desk; splashes of ink on the dress she wore; and an inky print of her hand on a torn newspaper on his desk.

"Unfortunately, but perfectly naturally, one of the first things she did was to take the revolver out of her husband's hand. That accounts for her prints on it. He fell—as I told you—just as she put her arms around him, and, though her memory isn't very clear on this point, the probabilities are that he dragged her with him when he fell across the desk. That accounts for the upset inkwell, the torn paper, and the splashes of ink. But the prosecution will try to persuade the jury that those things all happened before the shooting—that they are proofs of a struggle."

"Not so bad," I gave my opinion.

"Or pretty damned bad—depending on how you look at it. And this is the worst time imaginable for a thing like this to come up! Within the past few months there have been no less than five widely-advertised murders of men by women who were supposed to have been betrayed, or deceived, or one thing or another.

"Not one of those five women was convicted. As a result, we have the press, the public, and even the pulpit, howling for a stricter enforcement of justice. The newspapers are lined up against Mrs. Estep as strongly as their fear of libel suits will permit. The woman's clubs are lined up against her. Everybody is clamoring for an example to be made of her.

"Then, as if all that isn't enough, the Prosecuting Attorney has lost his last two big cases, and he'll be out for blood this time—election day isn't far off."

The calm, even, precise voice was gone now. In its place was a passionate eloquence.

"I don't know what you think," Richmond cried. "You're a detective. This is an old story to you. You're more or less callous, I suppose, and skeptical of innocence in general. But I *know* that Mrs. Estep didn't kill her husband. I don't say it because she's my client! I was Dr. Estep's attorney, and his friend, and if I thought Mrs. Estep guilty, I'd do everything in my power to help convict her. But I know as well as I know anything that she didn't kill him—couldn't have killed him.

"She's innocent. But I know too that if I go into court with no defense beyond what I now have, she'll be convicted! There has been too much leniency shown feminine criminals, public sentiment says. The pendulum will swing the other way—Mrs. Estep, if convicted, will get the limit. I'm putting it up to you! Can you save her?"

"Our best mark is the letter he mailed just before he died," I said, ignoring everything he said that didn't have to do with the facts of the case. "It's good betting that when a man writes and mails a letter and then shoots himself, that the letter isn't altogether unconnected with the suicide. Did you ask the first wife about the letter?"

"I did, and she denies having received one."

"That wasn't right. If the doctor had been driven to suicide by her appearance, then according to all the rules there are, the letter should have been addressed to her. He might have written one to his second wife, but he would hardly have mailed *it*.

"Would she have any reason for lying about it?"

"Yes," the lawyer said slowly, "I think she would. His will leaves everything to the second wife. The first wife, being the only legal wife, will have no difficulty in breaking that will, of course; but if it is shown that the second wife had no knowledge of the first one's existence—that she really believed herself to be Dr. Estep's legal wife—then I think that she will receive at least a portion of the estate. I don't think any court would, under the circumstances, take everything away from her. But if she should be found guilty of murdering Dr. Estep, then no consideration will be shown her, and the first wife will get every penny."

"Did he leave enough to make half of it, say, worth sending an innocent person to the gallows for?"

"He left about half a million, roughly; $250,000 isn't a mean inducement."

"Do you think it would be enough for the first wife—from what you have seen of her?"

"Candidly, I do. She didn't impress me as being a person of many very active scruples."

"Where does this first wife live?" I asked.

"She's staying at the Montgomery Hotel now. Her home is in Louisville, I believe. I don't think you will gain anything by talking to her, however. She has retained Somerset, Somerset, and Quill to represent her—a very reputable firm, by the way—and she'll refer you to them. They will tell you nothing. But if there's anything dishonest about her affairs—such as the concealing of Dr. Estep's letter—I'm confident that Somerset, Somerset and Quill know nothing of it."

"Can I talk to the second Mrs. Estep—your client?"

"Not at present, I'm afraid; though perhaps in a day or two. She is on the verge of collapse just now. She has always been delicate; and the shock of her husband's death, followed by her own arrest and imprisonment, has been too much for her. She's in the city jail, you know, held without bail. I've tried to have her transferred to the prisoner's ward of the City Hospital, even; but the authorities seem to think that her illness is simply a ruse. I'm worried about her. She's really in a critical condition."

His voice was losing its calmness again, so I picked up my hat, said something about starting to work at once, and went out. I don't like eloquence: if it isn't effective enough to pierce your hide, it's tiresome; and if it is effective enough, then it muddles your thoughts.

II

I spent the next couple of hours questioning the Estep servants, to no great advantage. None of them had been near the front of the house at the time of the shooting, and none had seen Mrs. Estep immediately prior to her husband's death.

After a lot of hunting, I located Lucy Coe, the nurse, in an apartment on Vallejo Street. She was a small, brisk, business-like woman of thirty or so. She repeated what Vance Richmond had told me, and could add nothing to it.

That cleaned up the Estep end of the job; and I set out for the Montgomery Hotel, satisfied that my only hope for success—barring miracles, which usually don't happen—lay in finding the letter that I believed Dr. Estep had written to his first wife.

My drag with the Montgomery Hotel management was pretty strong—strong enough to get me anything I wanted that wasn't too far outside the law. So as soon as I got there, I hunted up Stacey, one of the assistant managers.

"This Mrs. Estep who's registered here," I asked, "what do you know about her?"

"Nothing, myself, but if you'll wait a few minutes I'll see what I can learn."

The assistant manager was gone about ten minutes.

"No one seems to know much about her," he told me when he came back. "I've questioned the telephone girls, bell-boys, maids, clerks, and the house detective; but none of them could tell me much.

"She registered from Louisville, on the second of the month. She has never stopped here before, and she seems unfamiliar with the city—asks quite a few questions about how to get around. The mail clerks don't remember handling any mail for her, nor do the girls on the switchboard have any record of phone calls for her.

"She keeps regular hours—usually goes out at ten or later in the morning, and gets in before midnight. She doesn't seem to have any callers or friends."

"Will you have her mail watched—let me know what postmarks and return addresses are on any letters she gets?"

"Certainly."

"And have the girls on the switchboard put their ears up against any talking she does over the wire?"

"Yes."

"Is she in her room now?"

"No, she went out a little while ago."

"Fine! I'd like to go up and take a look at her stuff."

Stacey looked sharply at me, and cleared his throat.

"Is it as—ah—important as all that? I want to give you all the assistance I can, but—"

"It's this important," I assured him, "that another woman's life depends on what I can learn about this one."

"All right!" he said. "I'll tell the clerk to let us know if she comes in before we are through; and we'll go right up."

The woman's room held two valises and a trunk, all unlocked, and containing not the least thing of importance— no letters—nothing. So little, in fact, that I was more than half convinced that she had expected her things to be searched.

Downstairs again, I planted myself in a comfortable chair within sight of the key rack, and waited for a view of this first Mrs. Estep.

She came in at 11:15 that night. A large woman of forty-five or fifty, well dressed, and carrying herself with an air of assurance. Her face was a little too hard as to mouth and chin, but not enough to be ugly. A capable looking woman—a woman who would get what she went after.

III

Eight o'clock was striking as I went into the Montgomery lobby the next morning and picked out a chair, this time, within eye-range of the elevators.

At 10:30 Mrs. Estep left the hotel, with me in her wake. Her denial that a letter from her husband, written immediately before his death, had come to her didn't fit in with the possibilities as I saw them. And a good motto for the detective business is, "When in doubt—shadow 'em."

After eating breakfast at a restaurant on O'Farrell Street, she turned toward the shopping district; and for a long, long time—though I suppose it was a lot shorter than it seemed to me—she led me through the most densely packed portions of the most crowded department stores she could find.

She didn't buy anything, but she did a lot of thorough looking, with me muddling along behind her, trying to act like a little fat guy on an errand for his wife; while stout women bumped me and thin ones prodded me and all sorts got in my way and walked on my feet.

Finally, after I had sweated off a couple of pounds, she left the shopping district, and cut up through Union Square, walking along casually, as if out for a stroll.

Three-quarters way through, she turned abruptly, and retraced her steps, looking sharply at everyone she passed. I was on a bench, reading a stray page from a day-old newspaper, when she went by. She walked on down Post Street to Kearny, stopping every now and then to look—or to pretend to look—in store windows; while I ambled along sometimes beside her, sometimes almost by her side, and sometimes in front.

She was trying to check up the people around her, trying to determine whether she was being followed or not. But here, in the busy part of town, that gave me no cause for worry. On a less crowded street it might have been different, though not necessarily so.

There are four rules for shadowing: Keep behind your subject as much as possible; never try to hide from him; act in a natural manner no matter what happens; and never meet his eye. Obey them, and, except in unusual circumstances, shadowing is the easiest thing that a sleuth has to do.

Assured, after a while, that no one was following her, Mrs. Estep turned back toward Powell Street, and got into a taxi-cab at the St. Francis stand. I picked out a modest touring car from the rank of hire-cars along the Geary Street side of Union Square, and set out after her.

Our route was out Post Street to Laguna, where the taxi presently swung into the curb and stopped. The woman got out, paid the driver, and went up the steps of an apartment building. With idling engine my own car had come to rest against the opposite curb in the block above.

As the taxicab disappeared around a corner, Mrs. Estep came out of the apartment building doorway, went back to the sidewalk, and started down Laguna Street.

"Pass her," I told my chauffeur, and we drew down upon her.

As we came abreast, she went up the front steps of another building, and this time she rang a bell. These steps belonged to a building apparently occupied by four flats, each with its separate door, and the button she had pressed belonged to the right-hand second-story flat.

Under cover of my car's rear curtains, I kept my eye on the doorway while my driver found a convenient place to park in the next block.

I kept my eye on the vestibule until 5:35 P.M., when she came out, walked to the Sutter Street car line, returned to the Montgomery, and went to her room.

I called up the Old Man—the Continental Detective Agency's San Francisco manager—and asked him to detail an operative to learn who and what were the occupants of the Laguna Street flat.

That night Mrs. Estep ate dinner at her hotel, and went to a show afterward, and she displayed no interest in possible shadowers. She went to her room at a little after eleven, and I knocked off for the day.

IV

The following morning I turned the woman over to Dick Foley, and went back to the Agency to wait for Bob Teale, the operative who had investigated the Laguna Street flat. He came in at a little after ten.

"A guy named Jacob Ledwich lives there," Bob said. "He's a crook of some sort, but I don't know just what. He and 'Wop' Healey are friendly, so he must be a crook! 'Porky' Grout says he's an ex-bunco man who is in with a gambling ring now; but 'Porky' would tell you a bishop was a safe-ripper if he thought it would mean five bucks for himself.

"This Ledwich goes out mostly at night, and he seems to be pretty prosperous. Probably a high-class worker of some sort. He's got a Buick—license number 645-221—that he keeps in a garage around the corner from his flat. But he doesn't seem to use the car much."

"What sort of looking fellow is he?"

"A big guy—six feet or better—and he'll weigh a couple hundred easy. He's got a funny mug on him. It's broad and heavy around the cheeks and jaw, but his mouth is a little one that looks like it was made for a smaller man. He's no youngster—middle-aged."

"Suppose you tail him around for a day or two, Bob, and see what he's up to. Try to get a room or apartment in the neighborhood—a place that you can cover his front door from."

V

Vance Richmond's lean face lighted up as soon as I mentioned Ledwich's name to him.

"Yes!" he exclaimed. "He was a friend, or at least an acquaintance, of Dr. Estep's. I met him once—a large man with a peculiarly inadequate mouth. I dropped in to see the doctor one day, and Ledwich was in the office. Dr. Estep introduced us."

"What do you know about him?"

"Nothing."

"Don't you know whether he was intimate with the doctor, or just a casual acquaintance?"

"No. For all I know, he might have been a friend, a patient, or almost anything. The doctor never spoke of him to me, and nothing passed between them while I was there that afternoon. I simply gave the doctor some information he had asked for and left. Why?"

"Dr. Estep's first wife—after going to a lot of trouble to see that she wasn't followed—connected with Ledwich yesterday afternoon. And from what we can learn, he seems to be a crook of some sort."

"What would that indicate?"

"I'm not sure what it means, but I can do a lot of guessing. Ledwich knew both the doctor and the doctor's first wife; then it's not a bad bet that *she* knew where her husband was all the time. If she did, then it's another good bet that she was getting money from him right along. Can you check up his accounts and see whether he was passing out any money that can't be otherwise accounted for?"

The attorney shook his head.

"No, his accounts are in rather bad shape, carelessly kept. He must have had more than a little difficulty with his income tax statements."

"I see. To get back to my guesses: If she knew where he was all the time, and was getting money from him, then why did his first wife finally come to see her husband? Perhaps because—"

"I think I can help you there," Richmond interrupted. "A fortunate investment in lumber nearly doubled Dr. Estep's wealth two or three months ago."

"That's it, then! She learned of it through Ledwich. She demanded, either through Ledwich, or by letter, a rather large share of it—more than the doctor was willing to give. When he refused, she came to see him in person, to demand the money under threat—we'll say—of instant exposure. He thought she was in earnest. Either he couldn't raise the money she demanded, or he was tired of leading a double life. Anyway, he thought it all over, and decided to commit suicide. This is all a guess, or a series of guesses—but it sounds reasonable to me."

"To me, too," the attorney said. "What are you going to do now?"

"I'm still having both of them shadowed—there's no other way of tackling them just now. I'm having the woman looked up in Louisville. But, you understand, I might dig up a whole flock of things on them, and when I got through still be as far as ever from finding the letter Dr. Estep wrote before he died.

"There are plenty of reasons for thinking that the woman destroyed the letter—that would have been her wisest play. But if I can get enough on her, even at that, I can squeeze her into admitting that the letter was written, and that it said something about suicide—if it did. And that will be enough to spring your client. How is she today—any better?"

His thin face lost the animation that had come to it during our discussion of Ledwich, and became bleak.

"She went completely to pieces last night, and was removed to the hospital, where she should have been taken in the first place. To tell you the truth, if she isn't liberated soon, she won't need our help. I've done my utmost to have her released on bail—pulled every wire I know—but there's little likelihood of success in that direction.

"Knowing that she is a prisoner—charged with murdering her husband—is killing her. She isn't young, and she has always been subject to nervous disorders. The bare shock of her husband's death was enough to prostrate her—but now— You've *got* to get her out—and quickly!"

He was striding up and down his office, his voice throbbing with feeling. I left quickly.

VI

From the attorney's office, I returned to the Agency, where I was told that Bob Teale had phoned in the address of a furnished apartment he had rented on Laguna Street. I hopped on a street car, and went up to take a look at it.

But I didn't get that far.

Walking down Laguna Street, after leaving the car, I spied Bob Teale coming toward me. Between Bob and me—also coming toward me—was a big man whom I recognized as Jacob Ledwich: a big man with a big red face around a tiny mouth.

I walked on down the street, passing both Ledwich and Bob, without paying any apparent attention to either. At the next corner I stopped to roll a cigarette, and steal a look at the pair.

And then I came to life!

Ledwich had stopped at a vestibule cigar stand up the street to make a purchase. Bob Teale, knowing his stuff, had passed him and was walking steadily up the street.

He was figuring that Ledwich had either come out for the purpose of buying cigars or cigarettes, and would return to his flat with them; or that after making his purchase the big man would proceed to the car line, where, in either event, Bob would wait.

But as Ledwich had stopped before the cigar stand, a man across the street had stepped suddenly into a doorway, and stood there, back in the shadows. This man, I now remembered, had been on the opposite side of the street from Bob and Ledwich, and walking in the same direction.

He, too, was following Ledwich.

By the time Ledwich had finished his business at the stand, Bob had reached Sutter Street, the nearest car line. Ledwich started up the street in that direction. The man in the doorway stepped out and went after him. I followed that one.

A ferry-bound car came down Sutter Street just as I reached the corner. Ledwich and I got aboard together. The mysterious stranger fumbled with a shoe-string several pavements from the corner until the car was moving again, and then he likewise made a dash for it.

He stood beside me on the rear platform, hiding behind a large man in overalls, past whose shoulder he now and then peeped at Ledwich. Bob had gone to the corner above, and was already seated when Ledwich, this amateur detective,— there was no doubting his amateur status,—and I got on the car.

I sized up the amateur while he strained his neck peeping at Ledwich. He was small, this sleuth, and scrawny and frail. His most noticeable feature was his nose—a limp organ that twitched nervously all the time. His clothes were old and shabby, and he himself was somewhere in his fifties.

After studying him for a few minutes, I decided that he hadn't tumbled to Bob Teale's part in the game. His attention had been too firmly fixed upon Ledwich, and the distance had been too short thus far for him to discover that Bob was also tailing the big man.

So when the seat beside Bob was vacated presently, I chucked my cigarette away, went into the car, and sat down, my back toward the little man with the twitching nose.

"Drop off after a couple of blocks and go back to the apartment. Don't shadow Ledwich any more until I tell you. Just watch his place. There's a bird following him, and I want to see what he's up to," I told Bob in an undertone.

He grunted that he understood, and, after few minutes, left the car.

At Stockton Street, Ledwich got off, the man with the twitching nose behind him, and me in the rear. In that formation we paraded around town all afternoon.

The big man had business in a number of pool rooms, cigar stores, and soft drink parlors—most of which I knew for places where you can get a bet down on any horse that's running in North America, whether at Tanforan, Tijuana, or Timonium.

Just what Ledwich did in these places, I didn't learn. I was bringing up the rear of the procession, and my interest was centered upon the mysterious little stranger. He didn't enter any of the places behind Ledwich, but loitered in their neighborhoods until Ledwich reappeared.

He had a rather strenuous time of it—laboring mightily to keep out of Ledwich's sight, and only succeeding because we were downtown, where you can get away with almost any sort of shadowing. He certainly made a lot of work for himself, dodging here and there.

After a while, Ledwich shook him.

The big man came out of a cigar store with another man. They got into an automobile that was standing beside the curb, and drove away; leaving my man standing on the edge of the sidewalk twitching his nose in chagrin. There was a taxi stand just around the corner, but he either didn't know it or didn't have enough money to pay the fare.

I expected him to return to Laguna Street then, but he didn't. He led me down Kearney Street to Portsmouth Street, where he stretched himself out on the grass, face down, lit a black pipe, and lay looking dejectedly at the Stevenson monument, probably without seeing it.

I sprawled on a comfortable piece of sod some distance away—between a Chinese woman with two perfectly round children and an ancient Portuguese in a gaily checkered suit—and we let the afternoon go by.

When the sun had gone low enough for the ground to become chilly, the little man got up, shook himself, and went back up Kearney Street to a cheap lunch-room, where he ate meagerly. Then he entered a hotel a few doors away, took a key from the row of hooks, and vanished down a dark corridor.

Running through the register, I found that the key he had taken belonged to a room whose occupant was "John Boyd, St. Louis, Mo.," and that he had arrived the day before.

This hotel wasn't of the sort where it is safe to make inquiries, so I went down to the street again, and came to rest on the least conspicuous nearby corner.

Twilight came, and the street and shop lights were turned on. It got dark. The night traffic of Kearney Street went up and down past me: Filipino boys in their too-dapper clothes, bound for the inevitable black-jack game; gaudy women still heavy-eyed from their day's sleep; plain clothes men on their way to headquarters, to report before going off duty; Chinese going to or from Chinatown; sailors in pairs, looking for action of any sort; hungry people making for the Italian and French restaurants; worried people going into the bail bond broker's office on the corner to arrange for the release of friends and relatives whom the police had nabbed; Italians on their homeward journeys from work; odds and ends of furtive-looking citizens on various shady errands.

Midnight came, and no John Boyd, and I called it a day, and went home.

Before going to bed, I talked with Dick Foley over the wire. He said that Mrs. Estep had done nothing of any importance all day, and had received neither mail nor phone calls. I told him to stop shadowing her until I solved John Boyd's game.

I was afraid Boyd might turn his attention to the woman, and I didn't want him to discover that she was being shadowed. I had already instructed Bob Teale to simply watch Ledwich's flat—to see when he came in and went out, and with whom—and now I told Dick to do the same with the woman.

My guess on this Boyd person was that he and the woman were working together—that she had him watching Ledwich for her, so that the big man couldn't double-cross her. But that was only a guess—and I don't gamble too much on my guesses.

VII

The next morning I dressed myself up in an army shirt and shoes, an old faded cap, and a suit that wasn't downright ragged, but was shabby enough not to stand out too noticeably beside John Boyd's old clothes.

It was a little after nine o'clock when Boyd left his hotel and had breakfast at the grease-joint where he had eaten the night before. Then he went up to Laguna Street, picked himself a corner, and waited for Jacob Ledwich.

He did a lot of waiting. He waited all day; because Ledwich didn't show until after dark. But the little man was well-stocked with patience—I'll say that for him. He fidgeted, and stood on one foot and then the other, and even tried sitting on the curb for awhile, but he stuck it out.

I took it easy, myself. The furnished apartment Bob Teale had rented to watch Ledwich's flat from was a ground floor one, across the street, and just a little above the corner where Boyd waited. So we could watch him and the flat with one eye.

Bob and I sat and smoked and talked all day, taking turns watching the fidgeting man on the corner and Ledwich's door.

Night had just definitely settled when Ledwich came out and started up toward the car line. I slid out into the street, and our parade was under way again—Ledwich leading, Boyd following him, and we following *him*.

Half a block of this, and I got an idea!

I'm not what you'd call a brilliant thinker—such results as I get are usually the fruits of patience, industry, and unimaginative plugging, helped out now and then, maybe, by a little luck—but I do have my flashes of intelligence. And this was one of them.

Ledwich was about a block ahead of me; Boyd half that distance. Speeding up, I passed Boyd, and caught up with Ledwich. Then I slackened my pace so as to walk beside him, though with no appearance from the rear of having any interest in him.

"Jake," I said, without turning my head, "there's a guy following you!"

The big man almost spoiled my little scheme by stopping dead still, but he caught himself in time, and, taking his cue from me, kept walking.

"Who the hell are you?" he growled.

"Don't get funny!" I snapped back, still looking and walking ahead. "It ain't my funeral. But I was coming up the street when you came out, and I seen this guy duck behind a pole until you was past, and then follow you up."

That got him.

"You sure?"

"Sure! All you got to do to prove it is turn the next corner and wait."

I was two or three steps ahead of him by this time, I turned the corner, and halted, with my back against the brick building front. Ledwich took up the same position at my side.

"Want any help?" I grinned at him—a reckless sort of grin, unless my acting was poor.

"No."

His little lumpy mouth was set ugly, and his blue eyes were hard as pebbles.

I flicked the tail of my coat aside to show him the butt of my gun.

"Want to borrow the rod?" I asked.

"No."

He was trying to figure me out, and small wonder.

"Don't mind if I stick around to see the fun, do you?" I asked, mockingly.

There wasn't time for him to answer that. Boyd had quickened his steps, and now he came hurrying around the corner, his nose twitching like a tracking dog's.

Ledwich stepped into the middle of the sidewalk, so suddenly that the little man thudded into him with a grunt. For a moment they stared at each other, and there was recognition between them.

Ledwich shot one big hand out and clamped the other by a shoulder.

"What are you snooping around me for, you rat? Didn't I tell you to keep away from 'Frisco?"

"Aw, Jake!" Boyd begged. "I didn't mean no harm. I just thought that—"

Ledwich silenced him with a shake that clicked his mouth shut, and turned to me.

"A friend of mine," he sneered.

His eyes grew suspicious and hard again, and ran up and down me from cap to shoes.

"How'd you know my name?" he demanded.

"A famous man like you?" I asked, in burlesque astonishment.

"Never mind the comedy!" He took a threatening step toward me. "How'd you know my name?"

"None of your damned business," I snapped.

My attitude seemed to reassure him. His face became less suspicious.

"Well," he said slowly, "I owe you something for this trick, and— How are you fixed?"

"I have been dirtier." Dirty is Pacific Coast argot for prosperous.

He looked speculatively from me to Boyd, and back.

"Know 'The Circle'?" he asked me.

I nodded. The underworld calls "Wop" Healey's joint 'The Circle.'

"If you'll meet me there tomorrow night, maybe I can put a piece of change your way."

"Nothing stirring!" I shook my head with emphasis. "I ain't circulating that prominent these days."

A fat chance I'd have of meeting him there! "Wop" Healey and half his customers knew me as a detective. So there was nothing to do but to try to get the impression over that I was a crook who had reasons for wanting to keep away from the more notorious hang-outs for a while. Apparently it got over. He thought a while, and then gave me his Laguna Street number.

"Drop in this time tomorrow and maybe I'll have a proposition to make you—if you've got the guts."

"I'll think it over," I said noncommittally, and turned as if to go down the street.

"Just a minute," he called, and I faced him again. "What's your name?"

"Wisher," I said, "Shine, if you want a front one."

"Shine Wisher," he repeated. "I don't remember ever hearing it before."

It would have surprised me if he had—I had made it up only about fifteen minutes before.

"You needn't yell it," I said sourly, "so that everybody in the burg *will* remember hearing it."

And with that I left him, not at all dissatisfied with myself. By tipping him off to Boyd, I had put him under obligations to me, and had led him to accept me, at least tentatively, as a fellow crook. And by making no apparent effort to gain his good graces, I had strengthened my hand that much more.

I had a date with him for the next day, when I was to be given a chance to earn—illegally, no doubt—"a piece of change."

There was a chance that this proposition he had in view for me had nothing to do with the Estep affair, but then again it might; and whether it did or not, I had my entering wedge at least a little way into Jake Ledwich's business.

I strolled around for about half an hour, and then went back to Bob Teale's apartment.

"Ledwich come back?"

"Yes," Bob said, "with that little guy of yours. They went in about half an hour ago."

"Good! Haven't seen a woman go in?"

"No."

I expected to see the first Mrs. Estep arrive sometime during the evening, but she didn't. Bob and I sat around and talked and watched Ledwich's doorway, and the hours passed.

At one o'clock Ledwich came out alone.

"I'm going to tail him, just for luck," Bob said, and caught up his cap.

Ledwich vanished around a corner, and then Bob passed out of sight behind him.

Five minutes later Bob was with me again.

"He's getting his machine out of the garage."

I jumped for the telephone and put in a rush order for a fast touring car.

Bob, at the window, called out, "Here he is!"

I joined Bob in time to see Ledwich going into his vestibule. His car stood in front of the house. A very few minutes, and Boyd and Ledwich came out together. Boyd was leaning heavily on Ledwich, who was supporting the little man with an arm across his back. We couldn't see their faces in the dark, but the little man was plainly either sick, drunk, or drugged!

Ledwich helped his companion into the touring car. The red tail-light laughed back at us for a few blocks, and then disappeared. The automobile I had ordered arrived twenty minutes later, so we sent it back unused.

At a little after three in the morning, Ledwich, alone and afoot, returned from the direction of his garage. He had been gone exactly two hours.

VIII

Neither Bob nor I went home that night, but slept in the Laguna Street apartment.

Bob went down to the corner grocer's to get what we needed for breakfast in the morning, and he brought a morning paper back with him.

I cooked breakfast while he divided his attention between Ledwich's front door and the newspaper.

"Hey!" he called suddenly, "look here!"

I ran out of the kitchen with a handful of bacon.

"What is it?"

"Listen! 'Park murder mystery!'" he read. "'Early this morning the body of an unidentified man was found near a driveway in Golden Gate Park. His neck had been broken, according to the police, who say that the absence of any considerable bruises on the body, as well as the orderly condition of the clothes and the ground nearby, show that he did not come to his death through falling, or being struck by an automobile. It is believed that he was killed and then carried to the Park in an automobile, to be left there.'"

"Boyd!" I said.

"I bet you!" Bob agreed.

And at the morgue a very little while later, we learned that we were correct. The dead man was John Boyd.

"He was dead when Ledwich brought him out of the house," Bob said.

I nodded.

"He was! He was a little man, and it wouldn't have been much of a stunt for a big bruiser like Ledwich to have dragged him along with one arm the short distance from the door to the curb, pretending to be holding him up, like you do with a drunk. Let's go over to the Hall of Justice and see what the police have got on it—if anything."

At the detective bureau we hunted up O'Gar, the detective-sergeant in charge of the Homicide Detail, and a good man to work with.

"This dead man found in the park," I asked, "know anything about him?"

O'Gar pushed back his village constable's hat—a big black hat with a floppy brim that belongs in vaudeville—scratched his bullet-head, and scowled at me as if he thought I had a joke up my sleeve.

"Not a damned thing except that he's dead!" he said at last.

"How'd you like to know who he was last seen with?"

"It wouldn't hinder me any in finding out who bumped him off, and that's a fact."

"How do you like the sound of this?" I asked. "His name was John Boyd and he was living at a hotel down in the next block. The last person he was seen with was a guy who is tied up with Dr. Estep's first wife. You know—the Dr. Estep whose second wife is the woman you people are trying to prove a murder on. Does that sound interesting?"

"It does," he said. "Where do we go first?"

"This Ledwich—he's the fellow who was last seen with Boyd—is going to be a hard bird to shake down. We better try to crack the woman first—the first Mrs. Estep. There's a chance that Boyd was a pal of hers, and in that case when she finds out that Ledwich rubbed him out, she may open up and spill the works to us.

"On the other hand, if she and Ledwich are stacked up against Boyd together, then we might as well get her safely placed before we tie into him. I don't want to pull him before night, anyway. I got a date with him, and I want to try to rope him first."

Bob Teale made for the door.

"I'm going up and keep my eye on him until you're ready for him," he called over his shoulder.

"Good," I said. "Don't let him get out of town on us. If he tries to blow have him chucked in the can."

In the lobby of the Montgomery Hotel, O'Gar and I talked to Dick Foley first. He told us that the woman was still in her room—had had her breakfast sent up. She had received neither letters, telegrams, or phone calls since we began to watch her.

I got hold of Stacey again.

"We're going up to talk to this Estep woman, and maybe we'll take her away with us. Will you send up a maid to find out whether she's up and dressed yet? We don't want to announce ourselves ahead of time, and we don't want to burst in on her while she's in bed, or only partly dressed."

He kept us waiting about fifteen minutes, and then told us that Mrs. Estep was up and dressed.

We went up to her room, taking the maid with us.

The maid rapped on the door.

"What is it?" an irritable voice demanded.

"The maid; I want to—"

The key turned on the inside, and an angry Mrs. Estep jerked the door open. O'Gar and I advanced, O'Gar flashing his "buzzer."

"From headquarters," he said. "We want to talk to you."

O'Gar's foot was where she couldn't slam the door on us, and we were both walking ahead, so there was nothing for her to do but to retreat into the room, admitting us—which she did with no pretense of graciousness.

We closed the door, and then I threw our big load at her.

"Mrs. Estep, why did Jake Ledwich kill John Boyd?"

The expressions ran over her face like this: Alarm at Ledwich's name, fear at the word "kill," but the name John Boyd brought only bewilderment.

"Why did what?" she stammered meaninglessly, to gain time.

"Exactly," I said. "Why did Jake kill him last night in his flat, and then take him in the park and leave him?"

Another set of expressions: Increased bewilderment until I had almost finished the sentence, and then the sudden understanding of something, followed by the inevitable groping for poise. These things weren't as plain as billboards, you understand, but they were there to be read by anyone who had ever played poker—either with cards or people.

What I got out of them was that Boyd hadn't been working with or for her, and that, though she knew Ledwich had killed somebody at some time, it wasn't Boyd and it wasn't last night. Who, then? And when? Dr. Estep? Hardly! There wasn't a chance in the world that—if he had been murdered—anybody except his wife had done it—his second wife. No possible reading of the evidence could bring any other answer.

Who, then, had Ledwich killed before Boyd? Was he a wholesale murderer?

These things are flitting through my head in flashes and odd scraps while Mrs. Estep is saying:

"This is absurd! The idea of your coming up here and—"

She talked for five minutes straight, the words fairly sizzling from between her hard lips; but the words themselves didn't mean anything. She was talking for time—talking while she tried to hit upon the safest attitude to assume.

And before we could head her off, she had hit upon it—silence!

We got not another word out of her; and that is the only way in the world to beat the grilling game. The average suspect tries to talk himself out of being arrested; and it doesn't matter how shrewd a man is, or how good a liar, if he'll talk to you, and you play your cards right, you can hook him—can make him help you convict him. But if he won't talk you can't do a thing with him.

And that's how it was with this woman. She refused to pay any attention to our questions—she wouldn't speak, nod, grunt, or wave an arm in reply. She gave us a fine assortment of facial expressions, true enough, but we wanted verbal information—and we got none.

We weren't easily licked, however. Three beautiful hours of it we gave her without rest. We stormed, cajoled, threatened, and at times I think we danced; but it was no go. So in the end we took her away with us. We didn't have anything on her, but we couldn't afford to have her running around loose until we nailed Ledwich.

At the Hall of Justice we didn't book her; but simply held her as a material witness, putting her in an office with a matron and one of O'Gar's men, who were to see what they could do with her while we went after Ledwich. We had had her frisked as soon as she reached the Hall, of course; and, as we expected, she hadn't a thing of importance on her.

O'Gar and I went back to the Montgomery and gave her room a thorough overhauling—and found nothing.

"Are you sure you know what you're talking about?" the detective-sergeant asked as we left the hotel. "It's going to be a pretty joke on somebody if you're mistaken."

I let that go by without an answer.

"I'll meet you at 6:30," I said, "and we'll go up against Ledwich."

He grunted an approval, and I set out for Vance Richmond's office.

IX

The attorney sprang up from his desk as soon as his stenographer admitted me. His face was leaner and grayer than ever; its lines had deepened, and there was a hollowness around his eyes.

"You've *got* to do something!" he cried huskily. "I have just come from the hospital. Mrs. Estep is on the point of death! A day more of this—two days at the most—and she will—"

I interrupted him, and swiftly gave him an account of the day's happenings, and what I expected, or hoped, to make out of them. But he received the news without brightening, and shook his head hopelessly.

"But don't you see," he exclaimed when I had finished, "that that won't do? I know you can find proof of her innocence in time. I'm not complaining—you've done all that could be expected, and more! But all that's no good! I've got to have—well—a miracle, perhaps.

"Suppose that you do finally get the truth out of Ledwich and the first Mrs. Estep or it comes out during their trials for Boyd's murder? Or that you even get to the bottom of the matter in three or four days? That will be too late! If I can go to Mrs. Estep and tell her she's free now, she may pull herself together, and come through. But another day of imprisonment—two days, or perhaps even two hours—and she won't need anybody to clear her. Death will have done it! I tell you, she's—"

I left Vance Richmond abruptly again. This lawyer was bound upon getting me worked up; and I like my jobs to be simply jobs—emotions are nuisances during business hours.

x

At a quarter to seven that evening, while O'Gar remained down the street, I rang Jacob Ledwich's bell. As I had stayed with Bob Teale in our apartment the previous night, I was still wearing the clothes in which I had made Ledwich's acquaintance as Shine Wisher.

Ledwich opened the door.

"Hello, Wisher!" he said without enthusiasm, and led me upstairs.

His flat consisted of four rooms, I found, running the full length and half the breadth of the building, with both front and rear exits. It was furnished with the ordinary none-too-spotless appointments of the typical moderately priced furnished flat—alike the world over.

In his front room we sat down and talked and smoked and sized one another up. He seemed a little nervous. I thought he would have been just as well satisfied if I had forgotten to show up.

"About this job you mentioned?" I asked presently.

"Sorry," he said, moistening his little lumpy mouth, "but it's all off." And then he added, obviously as an afterthought, "for the present, at least."

I guessed from that that my job was to have taken care of Boyd—but Boyd had been taken care of for good.

He brought out some whisky after a while, and we talked over it for some time, to no purpose whatever. He was trying not to appear too anxious to get rid of me, and I was cautiously feeling him out.

Piecing together things he let fall here and there, I came to the conclusion that he was a former con man who had fallen into an easier game of late years. That was in line, too, with what "Porky" Grout had told Bob Teale.

I talked about myself with the evasiveness that would have been natural to a crook in my situation; and made one or two carefully planned slips that would lead him to believe that I had been tied up with the "Jimmy the Riveter" hold-up mob, most of whom were doing long hitches at Walla Walla then.

He offered to lend me enough money to tide me over until I could get on my feet again. I told him I didn't need chicken feed so much as a chance to pick up some real jack.

The evening was going along, and we were getting nowhere.

"Jake," I said casually—outwardly casual, that is, "you took a big chance putting that guy out of the way like you did last night."

I meant to stir things up, and I succeeded.

His face went crazy.

A gun came out of his coat.

Firing from my pocket, I shot it out of his hand.

"Now behave!" I ordered.

He sat rubbing his benumbed hand and staring with wide eyes at the smouldering hole in my coat.

Looks like a great stunt—this shooting a gun out of a man's hand, but it's a thing that happens now and then. A man who is a fair shot (and that is exactly what I am—no more, no less), naturally and automatically shoots pretty close to the spot upon which his eyes are focused. When a man goes for his gun in front of you, you shoot at *him*—not at any particular part of him. There isn't time for that—you shoot at *him*. However, you are more than likely to be looking at his gun, and in that case it isn't altogether surprising if your bullet should hit his gun—as mine had done. But it looks impressive.

I beat out the fire around the bullet-hole in my coat, crossed the room to where his revolver had been knocked, and picked it up. I started to eject the bullets from it, but, instead, I snapped it shut again and stuck it in my pocket. Then I returned to my chair, opposite him.

"A man oughtn't to act like that," I kidded him, "he's likely to hurt somebody."

His little mouth curled up at me.

"An elbow, huh?" putting all the contempt he could in his voice; and somehow any synonym for detective seems able to hold a lot of contempt.

I might have tried to talk myself back into the Wisher role. It could have been done, but I doubted that it would be worth it; so I nodded my confession.

His brain was working now, and the passion left his face, while he sat rubbing his right hand, and his little mouth and eyes began to screw themselves up calculatingly.

I kept quiet, waiting to see what the outcome of his thinking would be. I knew he was trying to figure out just what my place in this game was. Since, to his knowledge, I had come into it no later than the previous evening, then the Boyd murder hadn't brought me in. That would leave the Estep affair—unless he was tied up in a lot of other crooked stuff that I didn't know anything about.

"You're not a city dick, are you?" he asked finally; and his voice was on the verge of friendliness now: the voice of one who wants to persuade you of something, or sell you something.

The truth, I thought, wouldn't hurt.

"No," I said, "I'm with the Continental."

He hitched his chair a little closer to the muzzle of my automatic.

"What are you after, then? Where do you come in on it?"

I tried the truth again.

"The second Mrs. Estep. She didn't kill her husband."

"You're trying to dig up enough dope to spring her?"

"Yes."

I waved him back as he tried to hitch his chair still nearer.

"How do you expect to do it?" he asked, his voice going lower and more confidential with each word.

I took still another flier at the truth.

"He wrote a letter before he died."

"Well?"

But I called a halt for the time.

"Just that," I said.

He leaned back in his chair, and his eyes and mouth grew small in thought again.

"What's your interest in the man who died last night?" he asked slowly.

"It's something on you," I said, truthfully again. "It doesn't do the second Mrs. Estep any direct good, maybe; but you and the first wife are stacked up together against her. Anything, therefore, that hurts you two will help her, somehow. I admit I'm wandering around in the dark; but I'm going ahead wherever I see a point of light—and I'll come through to daylight in the end. Nailing you for Boyd's murder is one point of light."

He leaned forward suddenly, his eyes and mouth popping open as far as they would go.

"You'll come out all right," he said very softly, "if you use a little judgment."

"What's that supposed to mean?"

"Do you think," he asked, still very softly, "that you can nail me for Boyd's murder—that you can convict me of murder?"

"I do."

But I wasn't any too sure. In the first place, though we were morally certain of it, neither Bob Teale nor I could swear that the man who had got in the machine with Ledwich was John Boyd.

We knew it was, of course, but the point is that it had been too dark for us to see his face. And, again, in the dark, we had thought him alive; it wasn't until later that we knew he had been dead when he came down the steps.

Little things, those, but a private detective on the witness stand—unless he is absolutely sure of every detail—has an unpleasant and ineffectual time of it.

"I do," I repeated, thinking these things over, "and I'm satisfied to go to the bat with what I've got on you and what I can collect between now and the time you and your accomplice go to trial."

"Accomplice?" he said, not very surprised. "That would be Edna. I suppose you've already grabbed her?"

"Yes."

He laughed.

"You'll have one sweet time getting anything out of her. In the first place, she doesn't know much, and in the second— well, I suppose you've tried, and have found out what a helpful sort she is! So don't try the old gag of pretending that she has talked!"

"I'm not pretending anything."

Silence between us for a few seconds, and then—

"I'm going to make you a proposition," he said. "You can take it or leave it. The note Dr. Estep wrote before he died was to me, and it is positive proof that he committed suicide. Give me a chance to get away—just a chance—a half-hour start—and I'll give you my word of honor to send you the letter."

"I know I can trust you," I said sarcastically.

"I'll trust you, then!" he shot back at me. "I'll turn the note over to you if you'll give me your word that I'm to have half an hour's start."

"For what?" I demanded. "Why shouldn't I take both you and the note?"

"If you can get them! But do I look like the kind of sap who would leave the note where it would be found? Do you think it's here in the room maybe?"

I didn't, but neither did I think that because he had hidden it, it couldn't be found.

"I can't think of any reason why I should bargain with you," I told him. "I've got you cold, and that's enough."

"If I can show you that your only chance of freeing the second Mrs. Estep is through my voluntary assistance, will you bargain with me?"

"Maybe—I'll listen to your persuasion, anyway."

"All right," he said, "I'm going to come clean with you. But most of the things I'm going to tell you can't be proven in court without my help; and if you turn my offer down I'll have plenty of evidence to convince the jury that these things are all false, that I never said them, and that you are trying to frame me."

That part was plausible enough. I've testified before juries all the way from the City of Washington to the State of Washington, and I've never seen one yet that wasn't anxious to believe that a private detective is a double-crossing specialist who goes around with a cold deck in one pocket, a complete forger's outfit in another, and who counts that day lost in which he railroads no innocent to the hoosgow.

XI

"There was once a young doctor in a town a long way from here," Ledwich began. "He got mixed up in a scandal—a pretty rotten one—and escaped the pen only by the skin of his teeth. The state medical board revoked his license.

"In a large city not far away, this young doc, one night when he was drunk,—as he usually was in those days,—told his troubles to a man he had met in a dive. The friend was a resourceful sort; and he offered, for a price, to fix the doc up with a fake diploma, so he could set up in practice in some other state.

"The young doctor took him up, and the friend got the diploma for him. The doc was the man you know as Dr. Estep, and I was the friend. The real Dr. Estep was found dead in the park this morning!"

That was news—if true!

"You see," the big man went on, "when I offered to get the phoney diploma for the young doc—whose real name doesn't matter—I had in mind a forged one. Nowadays they're easy to get—there's a regular business in them,—but twenty-five years ago, while you could manage it, they were hard to get. While I was trying to get one, I ran across a woman I used to work with—Edna Fife. That's the woman you know as the first Mrs. Estep.

"Edna had married a doctor—the real Dr. Humbert Estep. He was a hell of a doctor, though; and after starving with him in Philadelphia for a couple of years, she made him close up his office, and she went back to the bunko game, taking him with her. She was good at it, I'm telling you—a real cleaner—and, keeping him under her thumb all the time, she made him a pretty good worker himself.

"It was shortly after that that I met her, and when she told me all this, I offered to buy her husband's medical diploma and other credentials. I don't know whether he wanted to sell them or not—but he did what she told him, and I got the papers.

"I turned them over to the young doc, who came to San Francisco and opened an office under the name of Humbert Estep. The real Esteps promised not to use that name any more—not much of an inconvenience for them, as they changed names every time they changed addresses.

"I kept in touch with the young doctor, of course, getting my regular rake-off from him. I had him by the neck, and I wasn't foolish enough to pass up any easy money. After a year or so, I learned that he had pulled himself together and was making good. So I jumped on a train and came to San Francisco. He was doing fine; so I camped here, where I could keep my eye on him and watch out for my own interests.

"He got married about then, and, between his practice and his investments, he began to accumulate a roll. But he tightened up on me—damn him! He wouldn't be bled. I got a regular percentage of what he made, and that was all.

"For nearly twenty-five years I got it—but not a nickel over the percentage. He knew I wouldn't kill the goose that laid the golden eggs, so no matter how much I threatened to expose him, he sat tight, and I couldn't budge him. I got my regular cut, and not a nickel more.

"That went along, as I say, for years. I was getting a living out of him, but I wasn't getting any big money. A few months ago I learned that he had cleaned up heavily in a lumber deal so I made up my mind to take him for what he had.

"During all these years I had got to know the Doc pretty well. You do when you're bleeding a man—you get a pretty fair idea of what goes on in his head, and what he's most likely to do if certain things should happen. So I knew the doc pretty well.

"I knew for instance, that he had never told his wife the truth about his past; that he had stalled her with some lie about being born in West Virginia. That was fine—for me! Then I knew that he kept a gun in his desk, and I knew why. It was kept there for the purpose of killing himself if the truth ever came out about his diploma. He figured that if, at the first hint of exposure, he wiped himself out, the authorities, out of respect for the good reputation he had built up, would hush things up.

"And his wife—even if she herself learned the truth—would be spared the shame of a public scandal. I can't see myself dying just to spare some woman's feeling, but the doc was a funny guy in some ways—and he was nutty about his wife.

"That's the way I had him figured out, and that's the way things turned out.

"My plan might sound complicated, but it was simple enough. I got hold of the real Esteps—it took a lot of hunting, but I found them at last. I brought the woman to San Francisco, and told the man to stay away.

"Everything would have gone fine if he had done what I told him; but he was afraid that Edna and I were going to double-cross him, so he came here to keep an eye on us. But I didn't know that until you put the finger on him for me.

"I brought Edna here and, without telling her any more than she had to know, drilled her until she was letter-perfect in her part.

"A couple days before she came I had gone to see the doc, and had demanded a hundred thousand cool smacks. He laughed at me, and I left, pretending to be as hot as hell.

"As soon as Edna arrived, I sent her to call on him. She asked him to perform an illegal operation on her daughter. He, of course, refused. Then she pleaded with him, loud enough for the nurse or whoever else was in the reception-room to hear. And when she raised her voice she was careful to stick to words that could be interpreted the way we wanted them to. She ran off her end to perfection, leaving in tears.

"Then I sprung my other trick! I had a fellow—a fellow who's a whiz at that kind of stuff—make me a plate: an imitation of newspaper printing. It was all worded like the real article, and said that the state authorities were investigating

information that a prominent surgeon in San Francisco was
practising under a license secured by false credentials. This
plate measured four and an eighth by six and three-quarter
inches. If you'll look at the first inside page of the *Evening
Times* any day in the week you'll see a photograph just that
size.

"On the day after Edna's call, I bought a copy of the first
edition of the *Times*—on the street at ten in the morning. I
had this scratcher friend of mine remove the photograph with
acid, and print this fake article in its place.

"That evening I substituted a 'home edition' outer sheet
for the one that had come with the paper we had cooked up,
and made a switch as soon as the doc's newsboy made his delivery. There was nothing to that part of it. The kid just
tossed the paper into the vestibule. It's simply a case of duck
into the doorway, trade papers, and go on, leaving the loaded
one for the doc to read."

I was trying not to look too interested, but my ears were
cocked for every word. At the start, I had been prepared for
a string of lies. But I knew now that he was telling me the
truth! Every syllable was a boast; he was half-drunk with appreciation of his own cleverness—the cleverness with which
he had planned and carried out his program of treachery and
murder.

I knew that he was telling the truth, and I suspected that
he was telling more of it than he had intended. He was fairly
bloated with vanity—the vanity that fills the crook almost invariably after a little success, and makes him ripe for the pen.

His eyes glistened, and his little mouth smiled triumphantly
around the words that continued to roll out of it.

"The doc read the paper, all right—and shot himself. But
first he wrote and mailed a note—to me. I didn't figure on his
wife's being accused of killing him. That was plain luck.

"I figured that the fake piece in the paper would be overlooked in the excitement. Edna would then go forward,
claiming to be his first wife; and his shooting himself after her
first call, with what the nurse had overheard, would make his
death seem a confession that Edna *was* his wife.

"I was sure that she would stand up under any sort of an
investigation. Nobody knew anything about the doc's real

past; except what he had told them, which would be found false.

"Edna had really married a Dr. Humbert Estep in Philadelphia in '96; and the twenty-seven years that had passed since then would do a lot to hide the fact that that Dr. Humbert Estep wasn't this Dr. Humbert Estep.

"All I wanted to do was convince the doc's real wife and her lawyers that she wasn't really his wife at all. And we did that! Everybody took it for granted that Edna was the legal wife.

"The next play would have been for Edna and the real wife to have reached some sort of an agreement about the estate, whereby Edna would have got the bulk—or at least half—of it; and nothing would have been made public.

"If worst came to worst, we were prepared to go to court. We were sitting pretty! But I'd have been satisfied with half the estate. It would have come to a few hundred thousand at the least, and that would have been plenty for me—even deducting the twenty thousand I had promised Edna.

"But when the police grabbed the doc's wife and charged her with his murder, I saw my way into the whole roll. All I had to do was sit tight and wait until they convicted her. Then the court would turn the entire pile over to Edna.

"I had the only evidence that would free the doc's wife: the note he had written me. But I couldn't—even if I had wanted to—have turned it in without exposing my hand. When he read that fake piece in the paper, he tore it out, wrote his message to me across the face of it, and sent it to me. So the note is a dead give-away. However, I didn't have any intention of publishing it, anyhow.

"Up to this point everything had gone like a dream. All I had to do was wait until it was time to cash in on my brains. And that's the time that the real Humbert Estep picked out to mess up the works.

"He shaved his mustache off, put on some old clothes, and came snooping around to see that Edna and I didn't run out on him. As if he could have stopped us! After you put the finger on him for me, I brought him up here.

"I intended salving him along until I could find a place to keep him until all the cards had been played. That's what I was going to hire you for—to take care of him.

"But we got to talking, and wrangling, and I had to knock him down. He didn't get up, and I found that he was dead. His neck was broken. There was nothing to do but take him out to the park and leave him.

"I didn't tell Edna. She didn't have a lot of use for him, as far as I could see, but you can't tell how women will take things. Anyhow, she'll stick, now that it's done. She's on the up and up all the time. And if she should talk, she can't do a lot of damage. She only knows her own part of the lay.

"All this long-winded story is so you'll know just exactly what you're up against. Maybe you think you can dig up the proof of these things I have told you. You can this far. You can prove that Edna wasn't the doc's wife. You can prove that I've been blackmailing him. But you can't prove that the doc's wife didn't *believe* that Edna was his real wife! It's her word against Edna's and mine.

"We'll swear that we had convinced her of it, which will give her a motive. You can't prove that the phoney news article I told you about ever existed. It'll sound like a hop-head's dream to a jury.

"You can't tie last night's murder on me—I've got an alibi that will knock your hat off! I can prove that I left here with a friend of mine who was drunk, and that I took him to his hotel and put him to bed, with the help of a night clerk and a bellboy. And what have you got against that? The word of two private detectives. Who'll believe you?

"You can convict me of conspiracy to defraud, or something—maybe. But, regardless of that, you can't free Mrs. Estep without my help.

"Turn me loose and I'll give you the letter the doc wrote me. It's the goods, right enough! In his own handwriting, written across the face of the fake newspaper story—which ought to fit the torn place in the paper that the police are supposed to be holding—and he wrote that he was going to kill himself, in words almost that plain."

That would turn the trick—there was no doubt of it. And I believed Ledwich's story. The more I thought it over the better I liked it. It fit into the facts everywhere. But I wasn't enthusiastic about giving this big crook his liberty.

"Don't make me laugh!" I said. "I'm going to put you away and free Mrs. Estep—both."

"Go ahead and try it! You're up against it without the letter; and you don't think a man with brains enough to plan a job like this one would be foolish enough to leave the note where it could be found, do you?"

I wasn't especially impressed with the difficulty of convicting this Ledwich and freeing the dead man's widow. His scheme—that cold-blooded zigzag of treachery for everybody he had dealt with, including his latest accomplice, Edna Estep—wasn't as airtight as he thought it. A week in which to run out a few lines in the East, and— But a week was just what I didn't have!

Vance Richmond's words were running through my head: "But another day of imprisonment—two days, or perhaps even two hours—and she won't need anybody to clear her. Death will have done it!"

If I was going to do Mrs. Estep any good, I had to move quick. Law or no law, her life was in my fat hands. This man before me—his eyes bright and hopeful now and his mouth anxiously pursed—was thief, blackmailer, double-crosser, and at least twice a murderer. I hated to let him walk out. But there was the woman dying in a hospital. . . .

XII

Keeping my eye on Ledwich, I went to the telephone, and got Vance Richmond on the wire at his residence.

"How is Mrs. Estep?" I asked.

"Weaker! I talked with the doctor half an hour ago, and he says—"

I cut in on him; I didn't want to listen to the details.

"Get over to the hospital, and be where I can reach you by phone. I may have news for you before the night is over."

"What— Is there a chance? Are you—"

I didn't promise him anything. I hung up the receiver and spoke to Ledwich. "I'll do this much for you. Slip me the note, and I'll give you your gun and put you out the back door. There's a bull on the corner out front, and I can't take you past him."

He was on his feet, beaming.

"Your word on it?" he demanded.

"Yes—get going!"

He went past me to the phone, gave a number (which I made a note of), and then spoke hurriedly into the instrument.

"This is Shuler. Put a boy in a taxi with that envelope I gave you to hold for me, and send him out here right away."

He gave his address, said "Yes" twice and hung up.

There was nothing surprising about his unquestioning acceptance of my word. He couldn't afford to doubt that I'd play fair with him. And, also, all successful bunko men come in time to believe that the world—except for themselves—is populated by a race of human sheep who may be trusted to conduct themselves with true sheep-like docility.

Ten minutes later the door-bell rang. We answered it together, and Ledwich took a large envelope from a messenger boy, while I memorized the number on the boy's cap. Then we went back to the front room.

Ledwich slit the envelope and passed its contents to me: a piece of rough-torn newspaper. Across the face of the fake article he had told me about was written a message in a jerky hand.

> I wouldn't have suspected you, Ledwich, of such profound stupidity. My last thought will be—this bullet that ends my life also ends your years of leisure. You'll have to go to work now.
>
> ESTEP.

The doctor had died game!

I took the envelope from the big man, put the death note in it, and put them in my pocket. Then I went to a front window, flattening a cheek against the glass until I could see O'Gar, dimly outlined in the night, patiently standing where I had left him hours before.

"The city dick is still on the corner," I told Ledwich. "Here's your gat"—holding out the gun I had shot from his fingers a little while back—"take it, and blow through the back door. Remember, that's all I'm offering you—the gun and a fair start. If you play square with me, I'll not do anything to help find you—unless I have to keep myself in the clear."

"Fair enough!"

He grabbed the gun, broke it to see that it was still loaded, and wheeled toward the rear of the flat. At the door he pulled up, hesitated, and faced me again. I kept him covered with my automatic.

"Will you do me a favor I didn't put in the bargain?" he asked.

"What is it?"

"That note of the doc's is in an envelope with my handwriting and maybe my fingerprints on it. Let me put it in a fresh envelope, will you? I don't want to leave any broader trail behind than I have to."

With my left hand—my right being busy with the gun—I fumbled for the envelope and tossed it to him. He took a plain envelope from the table, wiped it carefully with his handkerchief, put the note in it, taking care not to touch it with the balls of his fingers, and passed it back to me; and I put it in my pocket.

I had a hard time to keep from grinning in his face.

That fumbling with the handkerchief told me that the envelope in my pocket was empty, that the death-note was in Ledwich's possession—though I hadn't seen it pass there. He had worked one of his bunko tricks upon me.

"Beat it!" I snapped, to keep from laughing in his face.

He spun on his heel. His feet pounded against the floor. A door slammed in the rear.

I tore into the envelope he had given me. I needed to be sure he had double-crossed me.

The envelope was empty.

Our agreement was wiped out.

I sprang to the front window, threw it wide open, and leaned out. O'Gar saw me immediately—clearer than I could see him. I swung my arm in a wide gesture toward the rear of the house. O'Gar set out for the alley on the run. I dashed back through Ledwich's flat to the kitchen, and stuck my head out of an already open window.

I could see Ledwich against the white-washed fence—throwing the back gate open, plunging through it into the alley.

O'Gar's squat bulk appeared under a light at the end of the alley.

Ledwich's revolver was in his hand. O'Gar's wasn't—not quite.

Ledwich's gun swung up—the hammer clicked.

O'Gar's gun coughed fire.

Ledwich fell with a slow revolving motion over against the white fence, gasped once or twice, and went down in a pile.

I walked slowly down the stairs to join O'Gar; slowly, because it isn't a nice thing to look at a man you've deliberately sent to his death. Not even if it's the surest way of saving an innocent life, and if the man who dies is a Jake Ledwich—altogether treacherous.

"Howcome?" O'Gar asked, when I came into the alley, where he stood looking down at the dead man.

"He got out on me," I said simply.

"He must've."

I stooped and searched the dead man's pockets until I found the suicide note, still crumpled in the handkerchief. O'Gar was examining the dead man's revolver.

"Lookit!" he exclaimed. "Maybe this ain't my lucky day! He snapped at me once, and his gun missed fire. No wonder! Somebody must've been using an ax on it—the firing pin's broke clean off!"

"Is that so?" I asked; just as if I hadn't discovered, when I first picked the revolver up, that the bullet which had knocked it out of Ledwich's hand had made it harmless.

The House in Turk Street

I HAD been told that the man for whom I was hunting lived in a certain Turk Street block, but my informant hadn't been able to give me his house number. Thus it came about that late one rainy afternoon I was canvassing this certain block, ringing each bell, and reciting a myth that went like this:

"I'm from the law office of Wellington and Berkeley. One of our clients—an elderly lady—was thrown from the rear platform of a street car last week and severely injured. Among those who witnessed the accident, was a young man whose name we don't know. But we have been told that he lives in this neighborhood." Then I would describe the man I wanted, and wind up: "Do you know of anyone who looks like that?"

All down one side of the block the answers were:

"No," "No," "No."

I crossed the street and started to work the other side. The first house: "No."

The second: "No."

The third. The fourth.

The fifth—

No one came to the door in answer to my first ring. After a while, I rang again. I had just decided that no one was at home, when the knob turned slowly and a little old woman opened the door. She was a very fragile little old woman, with a piece of grey knitting in one hand, and faded eyes that twinkled pleasantly behind gold-rimmed spectacles. She wore a stiffly starched apron over a black dress and there was white lace at her throat.

"Good evening," she said in a thin friendly voice. "I hope you didn't mind waiting. I always have to peep out to see who's here before I open the door—an old woman's timidity."

She laughed with a little gurgling sound in her throat.

"Sorry to disturb you," I apologized. "But—"

"Won't you come in, please?"

"No; I just want a little information. I won't take much of your time."

"I wish you would come in," she said, and then added with mock severity, "I'm sure my tea is getting cold."

She took my damp hat and coat, and I followed her down a narrow hall to a dim room, where a man got up as we entered. He was old too, and stout, with a thin white beard that fell upon a white vest that was as stiffly starched as the woman's apron.

"Thomas," the little fragile woman told him; "this is Mr.—"

"Tracy," I said, because that was the name I had given the other residents of the block; but I came as near blushing when I said it, as I have in fifteen years. These folks weren't made to be lied to.

Their name, I learned, was Quarre; and they were an affectionate old couple. She called him "Thomas" every time she spoke to him, rolling the name around in her mouth as if she liked the taste of it. He called her "my dear" just as frequently, and twice he got up to adjust a cushion more comfortably to her frail back.

I had to drink a cup of tea with them and eat some little spiced cookies before I could get them to listen to a question. Then Mrs. Quarre made little sympathetic clicking sounds with her tongue and teeth, while I told about the elderly lady who had fallen off a street car. The old man rumbled in his beard that it was "a damn shame," and gave me a fat and oily cigar. I had to assure them that the fictitious elderly lady was being taken care of and was coming along nicely—I was afraid they were going to insist upon being taken to see her.

Finally I got away from the accident itself, and described the man I wanted.

"Thomas," Mrs. Quarre said; "isn't that the young man who lives in the house with the railing—the one who always looks so worried?"

The old man stroked his snowy beard and pondered.

"But, my dear," he rumbled at last; "hasn't he got dark hair?"

She beamed upon her husband and then upon me.

"Thomas is *so* observant," she said with pride. "I had forgotten; but the young man I spoke of does have dark hair, so he couldn't be the one who saw the accident at all."

The old man then suggested that one who lived in the block below might be my man. They discussed this one at some length before they decided that he was too tall and too old. Mrs. Quarre suggested another. They discussed that one, and voted against him. Thomas offered a candidate; he was weighed and discarded. They chattered on:

"But don't you think, Thomas . . . Yes, my dear, but . . . Of course you're right, Thomas, but. . . ."

Two old folks enjoying a chance contact with the world that they had dropped out of.

Darkness settled. The old man turned on a light in a tall lamp that threw a soft yellow circle upon us, and left the rest of the room dim. The room was a large one, and heavy with the thick hangings and bulky horse-hair furniture of a generation ago. I burned the cigar the old man had given me, and slumped comfortably down in my chair, letting them run on, putting in a word or two whenever they turned to me. I didn't expect to get any information here; but I was comfortable, and the cigar was a good one. Time enough to go out into the drizzle when I had finished my smoke.

Something cold touched the nape of my neck.

"Stand up!"

I didn't stand up: I couldn't. I was paralyzed. I sat and blinked at the Quarres.

And looking at them, I knew that something cold *couldn't* be against the back of my neck; a harsh voice *couldn't* have ordered me to stand up. It wasn't possible!

Mrs. Quarre still sat primly upright against the cushions her husband had adjusted to her back; her eyes still twinkled with friendliness behind her glasses; her hands were still motionless in her lap, crossed at the wrists over the piece of knitting. The old man still stroked his white beard, and let cigar smoke drift unhurriedly from his nostrils.

They would go on talking about the young men in the neighborhood who might be the man I wanted. Nothing had happened. I had dozed.

"Get up!"

The cold thing against my neck jabbed deep into the flesh. I stood up.

"Frisk him," the harsh voice came from behind.

The old man carefully laid his cigar down, came to me, and ran his hands over my body. Satisfied that I was unarmed, he emptied my pockets, dropping the contents upon the chair that I had just left.

Mrs. Quarre was pouring herself some more tea.

"Thomas," she said; "you've overlooked that little watch pocket in the trousers."

He found nothing there.

"That's all," he told the man behind me, and returned to his chair and cigar.

"Turn around, you!" the harsh voice ordered.

I turned and faced a tall, gaunt, raw-boned man of about my own age, which is thirty-five. He had an ugly face—hollow-cheeked, bony, and spattered with big pale freckles. His eyes were of a watery blue, and his nose and chin stuck out abruptly.

"Know me?" he asked.

"No."

"You're a liar!"

I didn't argue the point: he was holding a level gun in one big freckled hand.

"You're going to know me pretty well before you're through with me," this big ugly man threatened. "You're going to—"

"Hook!" a voice came from a portièred doorway—the doorway through which the ugly man had no doubt crept up behind me. "Hook, come here!"

The voice was feminine—young, clear, and musical.

"What do you want?" the ugly man called over his shoulder.

"*He's* here."

"All right!" He turned to Thomas Quarre. "Keep this joker safe."

From somewhere among his whiskers, his coat, and his stiff white vest, the old man brought out a big black revolver, which he handled with no signs of either weakness or unfamiliarity.

The ugly man swept up the things that had been taken from my pockets, and carried them through the portières with him.

Mrs. Quarre smiled brightly up at me.

"Do sit down, Mr. Tracy," she said.

I sat.

Through the portières a new voice came from the next room; a drawling baritone voice whose accent was unmistakably British; cultured British.

"What's up, Hook?" this voice was asking.

The harsh voice of the ugly man:

"Plenty's up, I'm telling you! They're onto us! I started out a while ago; and as soon as I got to the street, I seen a man I knowed on the other side. He was pointed out to me in Philly five-six years ago. I don't know his name, but I remembered his mug—he's a Continental Detective Agency man. I came back in right away, and me and Elvira watched him out of the window. He went to every house on the other side of the street, asking questions or something. Then he came over and started to give this side a whirl, and after a while he rings the bell. I tell the old woman and her husband to get him in, stall him along, and see what he says for himself. He's got a song and dance about looking for a guy what seen an old woman bumped by a street car—but that's the bunk! He's gunning for us. There ain't nothing else to it. I went in and stuck him up just now. I meant to wait till you come, but I was scared he'd get nervous and beat it. Here's his stuff if you want to give it the once over."

The British voice:

"You shouldn't have shown yourself to him. The others could have taken care of him."

Hook:

"What's the diff? Chances is he knows us all anyway. But supposing he didn't, what diff does it make?"

The drawling British voice:

"It may make a deal of difference. It was stupid."

Hook, blustering:

"Stupid, huh? You're always bellyaching about other people being stupid. To hell with you, I say! If you don't like my style, to hell with you! Who does all the work? Who's the guy that swings all the jobs? Huh? Where—"

The young feminine voice:

"Now, Hook, for God's sake don't make that speech again. I've listened to it until I know it by heart!"

A rustle of papers, and the British voice:

"I say, Hook, you're correct about his being a detective. Here is an identification card among his things."

The Quarres were listening to the conversation in the next room with as much interest as I, but Thomas Quarre's eyes never left me, and his fat fingers never relaxed about the gun in his lap. His wife sipped tea, with her head cocked on one side in the listening attitude of a bird.

Except for the weapon in the old man's lap, there was not a thing to persuade the eye that melodrama was in the room; the Quarres were in every other detail still the pleasant old couple who had given me tea and expressed sympathy for the elderly lady who had been injured.

The feminine voice from the next room:

"Well, what's to be done? What's our play?"

Hook:

"That's easy to answer. We're going to knock this sleuth off, first thing!"

The feminine voice:

"And put our necks in the noose?"

Hook, scornfully:

"As if they ain't there if we don't! You don't think this guy ain't after us for the L.A. job, do you?"

The British voice:

"You're an ass, Hook, and a quite hopeless one. Suppose this chap is interested in the Los Angeles affair, as is probable; what then? He is a Continental operative. Is it likely that his organization doesn't know where he is? Don't you think they know he was coming up here? And don't they know as much about us—chances are—as he does? There's no use killing him. That would only make matters worse. The thing to do is to tie him up and leave him here. His associates will hardly come looking for him until tomorrow—and that will give us all night to manage our disappearance."

My gratitude went out to the British voice! Somebody was in my favor, at least to the extent of letting me live. I hadn't been feeling very cheerful these last few minutes. Somehow, the fact that I couldn't see these people who were deciding whether I was to live or die, made my plight seem all the more desperate. I felt better now, though far from gay; I had

confidence in the drawling British voice; it was the voice of a
man who habitually carries his point.

Hook, bellowing:

"Let me tell you something, brother: that guy's going to
be knocked off! That's flat! I'm taking no chances. You can
jaw all you want to about it, but I'm looking out for my own
neck and it'll be a lot safer with that guy where he can't talk.
That's flat. He's going to be knocked off!"

The feminine voice, disgustedly:

"Aw, Hook, be reasonable!"

The British voice, still drawling, but dead cold:

"There's no use reasoning with you, Hook, you've the instincts and the intellect of a troglodyte. There is only one sort
of language that you understand; and I'm going to talk that
language to you, my son. If you are tempted to do anything
silly between now and the time of our departure, just say this
to yourself two or three times: 'If he dies, I die. If he dies, I
die.' Say it as if it were out of the Bible—because it's that
true."

There followed a long space of silence, with a tenseness
that made my not particularly sensitive scalp tingle. Beyond
the portière, I knew, two men were matching glances in a
battle of wills, which might any instant become a physical
struggle, and my chances of living were tied up in that battle.

When, at last, a voice cut the silence, I jumped as if a gun
had been fired; though the voice was low and smooth enough.

It was the British voice, confidently victorious, and I
breathed again.

"We'll get the old people away first," the voice was saying.
"You take charge of our guest, Hook. Tie him up neatly. But
remember—no foolishness. Don't waste time questioning
him—he'll lie. Tie him up while I get the bonds, and we'll be
gone in less than half an hour."

The portières parted and Hook came into the room—a
scowling Hook whose freckles had a greenish tinge against
the sallowness of his face. He pointed a revolver at me, and
spoke to the Quarres:

"He wants you."

They got up and went into the next room, and for a while an
indistinguishable buzzing of whispers came from that room.

Hook, meanwhile, had stepped back to the doorway, still menacing me with his revolver; and pulled loose the plush ropes that were around the heavy curtains. Then he came around behind me, and tied me securely to the high-backed chair; my arms to the chair's arms, my legs to the chair's legs, my body to the chair's back and seat; and he wound up by gagging me with the corner of a cushion that was too well-stuffed for my comfort. The ugly man was unnecessarily rough throughout; but I was a lamb. He wanted an excuse for drilling me, and I wanted above all else that he should have no excuse.

As he finished lashing me into place, and stepped back to scowl at me, I heard the street door close softly, and then light footsteps ran back and forth overhead.

Hook looked in the direction of those footsteps, and his little watery blue eyes grew cunning.

"Elvira!" he called softly.

The portières bulged as if someone had touched them, and the musical feminine voice came through.

"What?"

"Come here."

"I'd better not. He wouldn't—"

"Damn him!" Hook flared up. "Come here!"

She came into the room and into the circle of light from the tall lamp; a girl in her early twenties, slender and lithe, and dressed for the street, except that she carried her hat in one hand. A white face beneath a bobbed mass of flame-colored hair. Smoke-grey eyes that were set too far apart for trustworthiness—though not for beauty—laughed at me; and her red mouth laughed at me, exposing the edges of little sharp animal-teeth. She was beautiful; as beautiful as the devil, and twice as dangerous.

She laughed at me—a fat man all trussed up with red plush rope, and with the corner of a green cushion in my mouth—and she turned to the ugly man.

"What do you want?"

He spoke in an undertone, with a furtive glance at the ceiling, above which soft steps still padded back and forth.

"What say we shake him?"

Her smoke-grey eyes lost their merriment and became hard and calculating.

"There's a hundred thousand he's holding—a third of it's mine. You don't think I'm going to take a Mickey Finn on that, do you?"

"Course not! Supposing we get the hundred-grand?"

"How?"

"Leave it to me, kid; leave it to me! If I swing it, will you go with me? You know I'll be good to you."

She smiled contemptuously, I thought—but he seemed to like it.

"You're whooping right you'll be good to me," she said. "But listen, Hook: we couldn't get away with it—not unless you *get him*. I know him! I'm not running away with anything that belongs to him unless he is fixed so that he can't come after it."

Hook moistened his lips and looked around the room at nothing. Apparently he didn't like the thought of tangling with the owner of the British drawl. But his desire for the girl was too strong for his fear of the other man.

"I'll do it!" he blurted. "I'll get him! Do you mean it, kid? If I get him, you'll go with me?"

She held out her hand.

"It's a bet," she said, and he believed her.

His ugly face grew warm and red and utterly happy, and he took a deep breath and straightened his shoulders. In his place, I might have believed her myself—all of us have fallen for that sort of thing at one time or another—but sitting tied up on the side-lines, I knew that he'd have been better off playing with a gallon of nitro than with this baby. She was dangerous! There was a rough time ahead for this Hook!

"This is the lay—" Hook began, and stopped, tongue-tied.

A step had sounded in the next room.

Immediately the British voice came through the portières, and there was an edge of exasperation to the drawl now:

"This is really too much! I can't"—he said *reahly* and *cawnt*—"leave for a moment without having things done all wrong. Now just what got into you, Elvira, that you must go in and exhibit yourself to our detective friend?"

Fear flashed into her smoke-grey eyes, and out again, and she spoke airily:

"Don't be altogether yellow," she said. "Your precious neck can get along all right without so much guarding."

The portières parted, and I twisted my head around as far as I could get it for my first look at this man who was responsible for my still being alive. I saw a short fat man, hatted and coated for the street, and carrying a tan traveling bag in one hand.

Then his face came into the yellow circle of light, and I saw that it was a Chinese face. A short fat Chinese, immaculately clothed in garments that were as British as his accent.

"It isn't a matter of color," he told the girl—and I understood now the full sting of her jibe; "it's simply a matter of ordinary wisdom."

His face was a round yellow mask, and his voice was the same emotionless drawl that I had heard before; but I knew that he was as surely under the girl's sway as the ugly man—or he wouldn't have let her taunt bring him into the room. But I doubted that she'd find this Anglicized oriental as easily handled as Hook.

"There was no particular need," the Chinese was still talking, "for this chap to have seen any of us." He looked at me now for the first time, with little opaque eyes that were like two black seeds. "It's quite possible that he didn't know any of us, even by description. This showing ourselves to him is the most arrant sort of nonsense."

"Aw, hell, Tai!" Hook blustered. "Quit your bellyaching, will you? What's the diff? I'll knock him off, and that takes care of that!"

The Chinese set down his tan bag and shook his head.

"There will be no killing," he drawled, "or there will be quite a bit of killing. You don't mistake my meaning, do you, Hook?"

Hook didn't. His Adam's apple ran up and down with the effort of his swallowing, and behind the cushion that was choking me, I thanked the yellow man again.

Then this red-haired she-devil put her spoon in the dish.

"Hook's always offering to do things that he has no intention of doing," she told the Chinese.

Hook's ugly face blazed red at this reminder of his promise to *get* the Chinese, and he swallowed again, and his eyes looked as if nothing would have suited him better than an opportunity to crawl under something. But the girl had him; her influence was stronger than his cowardice.

He suddenly stepped close to the Chinese, and from his advantage of a full head in height scowled down into the round yellow face that was as expressionless as a clock without hands.

"Tai," the ugly man snarled; "you're done. I'm sick and tired of all this dog you put on—acting like you was a king or something. I've took all the lip I'm going to take from a Chink! I'm going to—"

He faltered, and his words faded away into silence. Tai looked up at him with eyes that were as hard and black and inhuman as two pieces of coal. Hook's lips twitched and he flinched away a little.

I stopped sweating. The yellow man had won again. But I had forgotten the red-haired she-devil.

She laughed now—a mocking laugh that must have been like a knife to the ugly man.

A bellow came from deep in his chest, and he hurled one big fist into the round blank face of the yellow man.

The force of the punch carried Tai all the way across the room, and threw him on his side in one corner.

But he had twisted his body around to face the ugly man even as he went hurtling across the room—a gun was in his hand before he went down—and he was speaking before his legs had settled upon the floor—and his voice was a cultured British drawl.

"Later," he was saying; "we will settle this thing that is between us. Just now you will drop your pistol and stand very still while I get up."

Hook's revolver—only half out of his pocket when the oriental had covered him—thudded to the rug. He stood rigidly still while Tai got to his feet, and Hook's breath came out noisily, and each freckle stood ghastily out against the dirty scared white of his face.

I looked at the girl. There was contempt in the eyes with which she looked at Hook, but no disappointment.

Then I made a discovery: *something had changed in the room near her!*

I shut my eyes and tried to picture that part of the room as it had been before the two men had clashed. Opening my eyes suddenly, I had the answer.

On the table beside the girl had been a book and some magazines. They were gone now. Not two feet from the girl was the tan bag that Tai had brought into the room. Suppose the bag had held the bonds from the Los Angeles job that they had mentioned. It probably had. What then? It probably now held the book and magazines that had been on the table! The girl had stirred up the trouble between the two men to distract their attention while she made a switch. Where would the loot be, then? I didn't know, but I suspected that it was too bulky to be on the girl's slender person.

Just beyond the table was a couch, with a wide red cover that went all the way down to the floor. I looked from the couch to the girl. She was watching me, and her eyes twinkled with a flash of mirth as they met mine coming from the couch. The couch it was!

By now the Chinese had pocketed Hook's revolver, and was talking to him:

"If I hadn't a dislike for murder, and if I didn't think that you will perhaps be of some value to Elvira and me in effecting our departure, I should certainly relieve us of the handicap of your stupidity now. But I'll give you one more chance. I would suggest, however, that you think carefully before you give way to any more of your violent impulses." He turned to the girl. "Have you been putting foolish ideas in our Hook's head?"

She laughed.

"Nobody could put any kind in it."

"Perhaps you're right," he said, and then came over to test the lashings about my arms and body.

Finding them satisfactory, he picked up the tan bag, and held out the gun he had taken from the ugly man a few minutes before.

"Here's your revolver, Hook, now try to be sensible. We may as well go now. The old man and his wife will do as they were told. They are on their way to a city that we needn't mention by name in front of our friend here, to wait for us and their share of the bonds. Needless to say, they will wait a long while—they are out of it now. But between ourselves there must be no more treachery. If we're to get clear, we must help each other."

According to the best dramatic rules, these folks should have made sarcastic speeches to me before they left, but they didn't. They passed me without even a farewell look, and went out of sight into the darkness of the hall.

Suddenly the Chinese was in the room again, running tip-toe—an open knife in one hand, a gun in the other. This was the man I had been thanking for saving my life!

He bent over me.

The knife moved on my right side, and the rope that held that arm slackened its grip. I breathed again, and my heart went back to beating.

"Hook will be back," Tai whispered, and was gone.

On the carpet, three feet in front of me, lay a revolver.

The street door closed, and I was alone in the house for a while.

You may believe that I spent that while struggling with the red plush ropes that bound me. Tai had cut one length, loosening my right arm somewhat and giving my body more play, but I was far from free. And his whispered "Hook will be back" was all the spur I needed to throw my strength against my bonds.

I understood now why the Chinese had insisted so strongly upon my life being spared. I was the weapon with which Hook was to be removed. The Chinese figured that Hook would make some excuse as soon as they reached the street, slip back into the house, knock me off, and rejoin his confederates. If he didn't do it on his own initiative, I suppose the Chinese would suggest it.

So he had put a gun within reach—in case I could get loose—and had loosened my ropes as much as he could, not to have me free before he himself got away.

This thinking was a side-issue. I didn't let it slow up my efforts to get loose. The *why* wasn't important to me just now—the important thing was to have that revolver in my hand when the ugly man came into this room again.

Just as the front door opened, I got my right arm completely free, and plucked the strangling cushion from my mouth. The rest of my body was still held by the ropes—held loosely—but held. There was no time for more.

I threw myself, chair and all, forward, breaking the fall with my free arm. The carpet was thick. I went down on my face, with the heavy chair atop me, all doubled up any which way; but my right arm was free of the tangle, and my right hand grasped the gun.

My left side—the wrong side—was toward the hall door. I twisted and squirmed and wrestled under the bulky piece of furniture that sat on my back.

An inch—two inches—six inches, I twisted. Another inch. Feet were at the hall door. Another inch.

The dim light hit upon a man hurrying into the room—a glint of metal in his hand.

I fired.

He caught both hands to his belly, bent double, and slid out across the carpet.

That was over. But that was far from being all. I wrenched at the plush ropes that held me, while my mind tried to sketch what lay ahead.

The girl had switched the bonds, hiding them under the couch—there was no question of that. She had intended coming back for them before I had time to get free. But Hook had come back first, and she would have to change her plan. What more likely than that she would now tell the Chinese that Hook had made the switch? What then? There was only one answer: Tai would come back for the bonds—both of them would come. Tai knew that I was armed now, but they had said that the bonds represented a hundred thousand dollars. That would be enough to bring them back!

I kicked the last rope loose and scrambled to the couch. The bonds were beneath it: four thick bundles of Liberty Bonds, done up with heavy rubber bands. I tucked them under one arm, and went over to the man who was dying near the door. His gun was under one of his legs. I pulled it out, stepped over him, and went into the dark hall.

Then I stopped to consider.

The girl and the Chinese would split to tackle me. One would come in the front door and the other in the rear. That would be the safest way for them to handle me. My play, obviously, was to wait just inside one of those doors for them. It would be foolish for me to leave the house. That's exactly what they would be expecting at first—and they would be lying in ambush.

Decidedly, my play was to lie low within sight of this front door and wait until one of them came through it—as one of them surely would, when they had tired of waiting for me to come out.

Toward the street door, the hall was lighted with the glow that filtered through the glass from the street lights. The stairway leading to the second-story threw a triangular shadow across part of the hall—a shadow that was black enough for any purpose. I crouched low in this three-cornered slice of night, and waited.

I had two guns: the one the Chinese had given me, and the one I had taken from Hook. I had fired one shot; that would leave me eleven still to use—unless one of the weapons had been used since it was loaded. I broke the gun Tai had given me, and in the dark ran my fingers across the back of the cylinder. My fingers touched *one* shell—under the hammer. Tai had taken no chances; he had given me one bullet—the bullet with which I had dropped Hook.

I put that gun down on the floor, and examined the one I had taken from Hook. It was *empty*. The Chinese had taken no chances at all! He had emptied Hook's gun before returning it to him after their quarrel.

I was in a hole! Alone, unarmed, in a strange house that would presently hold two who were hunting me—and that one of them was a woman didn't soothe me any—she was none the less deadly on that account.

For a moment I was tempted to make a dash for it; the thought of being out in the street again was pleasant; but I put the idea away. That would be foolishness, and plenty of it. Then I remembered the bonds under my arm. They would have to be my weapon; and if they were to serve me, they would have to be concealed.

I slipped out of my triangular shadow and went up the

stairs. Thanks to the street lights, the upstairs rooms were not too dark for me to move around. Around and around I went through the rooms, hunting for a place to hide the Liberty Bonds.

But when suddenly a window rattled, as if from the draught created by the opening of an outside door somewhere, I still had the loot in my hands.

There was nothing to do now but to chuck them out of a window and trust to luck. I grabbed a pillow from a bed, stripped off the white case, and dumped the bonds into it. Then I leaned out of an already open window and looked down into the night, searching for a desirable dumping place: I didn't want the bonds to land on an ash-can or a pile of bottles, or anything that would make a racket.

And, looking out of the window, I found a better hiding-place. The window opened into a narrow court, on the other side of which was a house of the same sort as the one I was in. That house was of the same height as this one, with a flat tin roof that sloped down the other way. The roof wasn't far from me—not too far to chuck the pillow-case. I chucked it. It disappeared over the edge of the roof and crackled softly on the tin.

If I had been a movie actor or something of the sort, I suppose I'd have followed the bonds; I suppose I'd have jumped from the sill, caught the edge of the roof with my fingers, swung a while, and then pulled myself up and away. But dangling in space doesn't appeal to me; I preferred to face the Chinese and the red-head.

Then I did another not at all heroic thing. I turned on all the lights in the room, lighted a cigarette (we all like to pose a little now and then), and sat down on the bed to await my capture. I might have stalked my enemies through the dark house, and possibly have nabbed them; but most likely I would simply have succeeded in getting myself shot. And I don't like to be shot.

The girl found me.

She came creeping up the hall, an automatic in each hand, hesitated for an instant outside the door, and then came in on the jump. And when she saw me sitting peacefully on the side of the bed, her eyes snapped scornfully at me, as if I had done something mean. I suppose she thought I should have given her an opportunity to put lead in me.

"I got him, Tai," she called, and the Chinese joined us.

"What did Hook do with the bonds?" he asked point blank.

I grinned into his round yellow face and led my ace.

"Why don't you ask the girl?"

His face showed nothing, but I imagined that his fat body stiffened a little within its fashionable British clothing. That encouraged me, and I went on with my little lie that was meant to stir things up.

"Haven't you rapped to it," I asked; "that they were fixing up to ditch you?"

"You dirty liar!" the girl screamed, and took a step toward me.

Tai halted her with an imperative gesture. He stared through her with his opaque black eyes, and as he stared the blood slid out of her face. She had this fat yellow man on her string, right enough, but he wasn't exactly a harmless toy.

"So that's how it is?" he said slowly, to no one in particular. "So that's how it is?" Then to me: "Where did they put the bonds?"

The girl went close to him and her words came out tumbling over each other:

"Here's the truth of it, Tai, so help me God! I switched the stuff myself. Hook wasn't in it. I was going to run out on both of you. I stuck them under the couch downstairs, but they're not there now. That's the God's truth!"

He was eager to believe her, and her words had the ring of truth to them. And I knew that—in love with her as he was—he'd more readily forgive her treachery with the bonds than he would forgive her for planning to run off with Hook; so I made haste to stir things up again. The old timer who said *"Divide to conquer,"* or something of the sort, knew what he was talking about.

"Part of that is right enough," I said. "She did stick the bonds under the couch—but Hook was in on it. They fixed it up between them while you were upstairs. He was to pick a fight with you, and during the argument she was to make the switch, and that is exactly what they did."

I had him!

As she wheeled savagely toward me, he stuck the muzzle of an automatic in her side—a smart jab that checked the angry words she was hurling at me.

"I'll take your guns, Elvira," he said, and took them.

There was a purring deadliness in his voice that made her surrender them without a word.

"Where are the bonds now?" he asked me.

I grinned.

"I'm not with you, Tai. I'm against you."

He studied me with his little eyes that were like black seeds for a while, and I studied him; and I hope that his studying was as fruitless as mine.

"I don't like violence," he said slowly, "and I believe you are a sensible person. Let us traffic, my friend."

"You name it," I suggested.

"Gladly! As a basis for our bargaining, we will stipulate that you have hidden the bonds where they cannot be found by anyone else; and that I have you completely in my power, as the shilling shockers used to have it."

"Reasonable enough," I said, "go on."

"The situation, then, is what gamblers call a standoff. Neither of us has the advantage. As a detective, you want us; but we have you. As thieves, we want the bonds; but you have them. I offer you the girl in exchange for the bonds, and that seems to me an equitable offer. It will give me the bonds and a chance to get away. It will give you no small degree of success in your task as a detective. Hook is dead. You will have the girl. All that will remain is to find me and the bonds again—by no means a hopeless task. You will have turned a defeat into more than half of a victory, with an excellent chance to make it a complete one."

"How do I know that you'll give me the girl?"

He shrugged.

"Naturally, there can be no guarantee. But, knowing that she planned to desert me for the swine who lies dead below, you can't imagine that my feelings for her are the most friendly. Too, if I take her with me, she will want a share in the loot."

I turned the lay-out over in my mind, and looked at it from this side and that and the other.

"This is the way it looks to me," I told him at last. "You aren't a killer. I'll come through alive no matter what happens. All right; why should I swap? You and the girl will be easier to find again than the bonds, and they are the most important part of the job anyway. I'll hold on to them, and take my chances on finding you folks again. Yes, I'm playing it safe."

And I meant it, for the time being, at least.

"No, I'm not a killer," he said, very softly; and he smiled the first smile I had seen on his face. It wasn't a pleasant smile: and there was something in it that made you want to shudder. "But I am other things, perhaps, of which you haven't thought. But this talking is to no purpose. Elvira!"

The girl, who had been standing a little to one side, watching us, came obediently forward.

"You will find sheets in one of the bureau drawers," he told her. "Tear one or two of them into strips strong enough to tie up your friend securely."

The girl went to the bureau. I wrinkled my head, trying to find a not too disagreeable answer to the question in my mind. The answer that came first wasn't nice: *torture.*

Then a faint sound brought us all into tense motionlessness.

The room we were in had two doors: one leading into the hall, the other into another bedroom. It was through the hall door that the faint sound had come—the sound of creeping feet.

Swiftly, silently, Tai moved backward to a position from which he could watch the hall door without losing sight of the girl and me—and the gun poised like a live thing in his fat hand was all the warning we needed to make no noise.

The faint sound again, just outside the door.

The gun in Tai's hand seemed to quiver with eagerness.

Through the other door—the door that gave to the next room—popped Mrs. Quarre, an enormous cocked revolver in her thin hand.

"Let go it, you nasty heathen," she screeched.

Tai dropped his pistol before he turned to face her, and he held his hands up high—all of which was very wise.

Thomas Quarre came through the hall door then; he also

held a cocked revolver—the mate of his wife's—though, in front of his bulk, his didn't look so enormously large.

I looked at the old woman again, and found little of the friendly fragile one who had poured tea and chatted about the neighbors. This was a witch if there ever was one—a witch of the blackest, most malignant sort. Her little faded eyes were sharp with ferocity, her withered lips were taut in a wolfish snarl, and her thin body fairly quivered with hate.

"I knew it," she was shrilling. "I told Tom as soon as we got far enough away to think things over. I knew it was a frame-up! I knew this supposed detective was a pal of yours! I knew it was just a scheme to beat Thomas and me out of our shares! Well, I'll show you, you yellow monkey! And the rest of you too! I'll show the whole caboodle of you! Where are them bonds? Where are they?"

The Chinese had recovered his poise, if he had ever lost it.

"Our stout friend can tell you perhaps," he said. "I was about to extract the information from him when you so—ah—dramatically arrived."

"Thomas, for goodness sakes don't stand there dreaming," she snapped at her husband, who to all appearances was still the same mild old man who had given me an excellent cigar. "Tie up this Chinaman! I don't trust him an inch, and I won't feel easy until he's tied up. Tie him up, and then we'll see what's to be done."

I got up from my seat on the side of the bed, and moved cautiously to a spot that I thought would be out of the line of fire if the thing I expected happened.

Tai had dropped the gun that had been in his hand, but he hadn't been searched. The Chinese are a thorough people; if one of them carries a gun at all, he usually carries two or three or more. (I remember picking up one in Oakland during the last tong war, who had five on him—one under each armpit, one on each hip, and one in his waistband.) One gun had been taken from Tai, and if they tried to truss him up without frisking him, there was likely to be fireworks. So I moved off to one side.

Fat Thomas Quarre went phlegmatically up to the Chinese to carry out his wife's orders—and bungled the job perfectly.

He put his bulk between Tai and the old woman's gun.

Tai's hands moved.

An automatic was in each.

Once more Tai ran true to racial form. When a Chinese shoots, he keeps on shooting until his gun is empty.

When I yanked Tai over backward by his fat throat, and slammed him to the floor, his guns were still barking metal; and they clicked empty as I got a knee on one of his arms. I didn't take any chances. I worked on his throat until his eyes and tongue told me that he was out of things for a while.

Then I looked around.

Thomas Quarre was huddled against the bed, plainly dead, with three round holes in his starched white vest—holes that were brown from the closeness of the gun that had put them there.

Across the room, Mrs. Quarre lay on her back. Her clothes had somehow settled in place around her fragile body, and death had given her once more the gentle friendly look she had worn when I first saw her. One thin hand was on her bosom, covering, I found later, the two bullet-holes that were there.

The red-haired girl Elvira was gone.

Presently Tai stirred, and, after taking another gun from his clothes, I helped him sit up. He stroked his bruised throat with one fat hand, and looked coolly around the room.

"So this is how it came out?" he said.

"Uh-huh!"

"Where's Elvira?"

"Got away—for the time being."

He shrugged.

"Well, you can call it a decidedly successful operation. The Quarres and Hook dead; the bonds and I in your hands."

"Not so bad," I admitted, "but will you do me a favor?"

"If I may."

"Tell me what the hell this is all about!"

"All about?" he asked.

"Exactly! From what you people have let me overhear, I gather that you pulled some sort of job in Los Angeles that netted you a hundred-thousand-dollars' worth of Liberty Bonds; but I can't remember any recent job of that size down there."

"Why, that's preposterous!" he said with what, for him, was almost wild-eyed amazement. "Preposterous! Of course you know all about it!"

"I do not! I was trying to find a young fellow named Fisher who left his Tacoma home in anger a week or two ago. His father wants him found on the quiet, so that he can come down and try to talk him into going home again. I was told that I might find Fisher in this block of Turk Street, and that's what brought me here."

He didn't believe me. He never believed me. He went to the gallows thinking me a liar.

When I got out into the street again (and Turk Street was a lovely place when I came free into it after my evening in that house!) I bought a newspaper that told me most of what I wanted to know.

A boy of twenty—a messenger in the employ of a Los Angeles stock and bond house—had disappeared two days before, while on his way to a bank with a wad of Liberty Bonds. That same night this boy and a slender girl with bobbed red hair had registered at a hotel in Fresno as *J. M. Riordan and wife*. The next morning the boy had been found in his room—murdered. The girl was gone. The bonds were gone.

That much the paper told me. During the next few days, digging up a little here and a little there, I succeeded in piecing together most of the story.

The Chinese—whose full name was Tai Choon Tau—had been the brains of the mob. Their game had been a variation of the always-reliable badger game. Tai selected the victims, and he must have been a good judge of humans, for he seems never to have picked a bloomer. He would pick out some youth who was messenger or runner for a banker or broker—one who carried either cash or negotiable securities in large quantities around the city.

The girl Elvira would then *make* this lad, get him all fussed up over her—which shouldn't have been very hard for her—and then lead him gently around to running away with her and whatever he could grab in the way of his employer's bonds or currency.

Wherever they spent the first night of their flight, there Hook would appear—foaming at the mouth and loaded for

bear. The girl would plead and tear her hair and so forth, trying to keep Hook—in his rôle of irate husband—from
butchering the youth. Finally she would succeed, and in the
end the youth would find himself without either girl or the
fruits of his thievery.

Sometimes he had surrendered to the police. Two we
found had committed suicide. The Los Angeles lad had been
built of tougher stuff than the others. He had put up a fight,
and Hook had had to kill him. You can measure the girl's skill
in her end of the game by the fact that not one of the half
dozen youths who had been trimmed had said the least thing
to implicate her; and some of them had gone to great trouble
to keep her out of it.

The house in Turk Street had been the mob's retreat, and,
that it might be always a safe one, they had not worked their
game in San Francisco. Hook and the girl were supposed by
the neighbors to be the Quarres' son and daughter—and Tai
was the Chinese cook. The Quarres' benign and respectable
appearances had also come in handy when the mob had securities to be disposed of.

The Chinese went to the gallows. We threw out the widest
and finest-meshed of drag-nets for the red-haired girl; and we
turned up girls with bobbed red hair by the scores. But the
girl Elvira was not among them.

I promised myself that some day. . . .

The Girl with the Silver Eyes

A BELL jangled me into wakefulness. I rolled to the edge of my bed and reached for the telephone. The neat voice of the Old Man—the Continental Detective Agency's San Francisco manager—came to my ears:

"Sorry to disturb you, but you'll have to go up to the Glenton Apartments on Leavenworth Street. A man named Burke Pangburn, who lives there, phoned me a few minutes ago asking to have someone sent up to see him at once. He seemed rather excited. Will you take care of it? See what he wants."

I said I would and, yawning, stretching and cursing Pangburn—whoever he was—got my fat body out of pajamas and into street clothes.

The man who had disturbed my Sunday morning sleep—I found when I reached the Glenton—was a slim, white-faced person of about twenty-five, with big brown eyes that were red-rimmed just now from either sleeplessness or crying, or both. His long brown hair was rumpled when he opened the door to admit me; and he wore a mauve dressing-robe spotted with big jade parrots over wine-colored silk pajamas.

The room into which he led me resembled an auctioneer's establishment just before the sale—or maybe one of these alley tea-rooms. Fat blue vases, crooked red vases, lanky yellow vases, vases of various shapes and colors; marble statuettes, ebony statuettes, statuettes of any material; lanterns, lamps and candlesticks; draperies, hangings and rugs of all sorts; odds and ends of furniture that were all somehow queerly designed; peculiar pictures hung here and there in unexpected places. A hard room to feel comfortable in.

"My fiancée," he began immediately in a high-pitched voice that was within a notch of hysteria, "has disappeared! Something has happened to her! Foul play of some horrible sort! I want you to find her—to save her from this terrible thing that. . . ."

I followed him this far and then gave it up. A jumble of words came out of his mouth—"spirited away . . . mysterious

something . . . lured into a trap"—but they were too disconnected for me to make anything out of them. So I stopped
trying to understand him, and waited for him to babble himself empty of words.

I have heard ordinarily reasonable men, under stress of excitement, run on even more crazily than this wild-eyed youth;
but his dress—the parroted robe and gay pajamas—and his
surroundings—this deliriously furnished room—gave him too
theatrical a setting; made his words sound utterly unreal.

He himself, when normal, should have been a rather nice-
looking lad: his features were well spaced and, though his
mouth and chin were a little uncertain, his broad forehead
was good. But standing there listening to the occasional
melodramatic phrase that I could pick out of the jumbled
noises he was throwing at me, I thought that instead of parrots on his robe he should have had cuckoos.

Presently he ran out of language and was holding his long,
thin hands out to me in an appealing gesture, saying,

"Will you?" over and over. "Will you? Will you?"

I nodded soothingly, and noticed that tears were on his
thin cheeks.

"Suppose we begin at the beginning," I suggested, sitting
down carefully on a carved bench affair that didn't look any
too strong.

"Yes! Yes!" He was standing legs apart in front of me, running his fingers through his hair. "The beginning. I had a
letter from her every day until—"

"That's not the beginning," I objected. "Who is she? What
is she?"

"She's Jeanne Delano!" he exclaimed in surprise at my ignorance. "And she is my fiancée. And now she is gone, and I
know that—"

The phrases *"victim of foul play," "into a trap"* and so on
began to flow hysterically out again.

Finally I got him quieted down and, sandwiched in between occasional emotional outbursts, got a story out of him
that amounted to this:

This Burke Pangburn was a poet. About two months before, he had received a note from a Jeanne Delano—forwarded
from his publishers—praising his latest book of rhymes. Jeanne

Delano happened to live in San Francisco, too, though she hadn't known that he did. He had answered her note, and had received another. After a little of this they met. If she really was as beautiful as he claimed, then he wasn't to be blamed for falling in love with her. But whether or not she was really beautiful, he thought she was, and he had fallen hard.

This Delano girl had been living in San Francisco for only a little while, and when the poet met her she was living alone in an Ashbury Avenue apartment. He did not know where she came from or anything about her former life. He suspected—from certain indefinite suggestions and peculiarities of conduct which he couldn't put in words—that there was a cloud of some sort hanging over the girl; that neither her past nor her present were free from difficulties. But he hadn't the least idea what those difficulties might be. He hadn't cared. He knew absolutely nothing about her, except that she was beautiful, and he loved her, and she had promised to marry him.

Then, on the third of the month—exactly twenty-one days before this Sunday morning—the girl had suddenly left San Francisco. He had received a note from her, by messenger.

This note, which he showed me after I had insisted point blank on seeing it, read:

Burkelove:

Have just received a wire, and must go East on next train. Tried to get you on the phone, but couldn't. Will write you as soon as I know what my address will be. If anything. (*These two words were erased and could be read only with great difficulty.*) Love me until I'm back with you forever.

Your JEANNE.

Nine days later he had received another letter from her, from Baltimore, Maryland. This one, which I had a still harder time getting a look at, read:

Dearest Poet:

It seems like two years since I have seen you, and I have a fear that it's going to be between one and two months before I see you again.

I can't tell you now, beloved, about what brought me here. There are things that can't be written. But as soon as I'm back with you, I shall tell you the whole wretched story.

If anything should happen—I mean to me—you'll go on loving me forever, won't you, beloved? But that's foolish. Nothing is going to happen. I'm just off the train, and tired from traveling.

Tomorrow I shall write you a long, long letter to make up for this.

My address here is 215 N. Stricker St. Please, Mister, at least one letter a day!

Your own JEANNE.

For nine days he had had a letter from her each day—with two on Monday to make up for the none on Sunday—and then her letters had stopped. And the daily letters he had sent to the address she gave—215 N. Stricker Street—had begun to come back to him, marked "Not known."

He had sent a telegram, and the telegraph company had informed him that its Baltimore office had been unable to find a Jeanne Delano at the North Stricker Street address.

For three days he had waited, expecting hourly to hear from the girl, and no word had come. Then he had bought a ticket for Baltimore.

"But," he wound up, "I was afraid to go. I know she's in some sort of trouble—I can feel that—but I'm a silly poet. I can't deal with mysteries. Either I would find nothing at all or, if by luck I did stumble on the right track, the probabilities are that I would only muddle things; add fresh complications, perhaps endanger her life still further. I can't go blundering at it in that fashion, without knowing whether I am helping or harming her. It's a task for an expert in that sort of thing. So I thought of your agency. You'll be careful, won't you? It may be—I don't know—that she won't want assistance. It may be that you can help her without her knowing anything about it. You are accustomed to that sort of thing; you can do it, can't you?"

II

I turned the job over and over in my mind before answering him. The two great bugaboos of a reputable detective agency are the persons who bring in a crooked plan or a piece of

divorce work all dressed up in the garb of a legitimate operation, and the irresponsible person who is laboring under wild
and fanciful delusions—who wants a dream run out.

This poet—sitting opposite me now twining his long, white
fingers nervously together—was, I thought, sincere; but I
wasn't so sure of his sanity.

"Mr. Pangburn," I said after a while, "I'd like to handle
this thing for you, but I'm not sure that I can. The
Continental is rather strict, and, while I believe this thing is
on the level, still I am only a hired man and have to go by the
rules. Now if you could give us the endorsement of some firm
or person of standing—a reputable lawyer, for instance, or any
legally responsible party—we'd be glad to go ahead with the
work. Otherwise, I am afraid—"

"But I know she's in danger!" he broke out. "I know
that— And I can't be advertising her plight—airing her affairs—to everyone."

"I'm sorry, but I can't touch it unless you can give me
some such endorsement." I stood up. "But you can find
plenty of detective agencies that aren't so particular."

His mouth worked like a small boy's, and he caught his
lower lip between his teeth. For a moment I thought he was
going to burst into tears. But instead he said slowly:

"I dare say you are right. Suppose I refer you to my
brother-in-law, Roy Axford. Will his word be sufficient?"

"Yes."

Roy Axford—R. F. Axford—was a mining man who had a
finger in at least half of the big business enterprises of the
Pacific Coast; and his word on anything was commonly considered good enough for anybody.

"If you can get in touch with him now," I said, "and
arrange for me to see him today, I can get started without
much delay."

Pangburn crossed the room and dug a telephone out from
among a heap of his ornaments. Within a minute or two he
was talking to someone whom he called "Rita."

"Is Roy home? . . . Will he be home this afternoon? . . .
No, you can give him a message for me, though. . . . Tell
him I'm sending a gentleman up to see him this afternoon on
a personal matter—personal with me—and that I'll be very

grateful if he'll do what I want. . . . Yes. . . . You'll find out, Rita. . . . It isn't a thing to talk about over the phone. . . . Yes, thanks!"

He pushed the telephone back into its hiding place and turned to me.

"He'll be at home until two o'clock. Tell him what I told you and if he seems doubtful, have him call me up. You'll have to tell him the whole thing; he doesn't know anything at all about Miss Delano."

"All right. Before I go, I want a description of her."

"She's beautiful!" he exclaimed. "The most beautiful woman in the world!"

That would look nice on a reward circular.

"That isn't exactly what I want," I told him. "How old is she?"

"Twenty-two."

"Height?"

"About five feet eight inches, or possibly nine."

"Slender, medium or plump?"

"She's inclined toward slenderness, but she—"

There was a note of enthusiasm in his voice that made me fear he was about to make a speech, so I cut him off with another question.

"What color hair?"

"Brown—so dark that it's almost black—and it's soft and thick and—"

"Yes, yes. Long or bobbed?"

"Long and thick and—"

"What color eyes?"

"You've seen shadows on polished silver when—"

I wrote down *grey eyes* and hurried on with the interrogation.

"Complexion?"

"Perfect!"

"Uh-huh. But is it light, or dark, or florid, or sallow, or what?"

"Fair."

"Face oval, or square, or long and thin, or what shape?"

"Oval."

"What shaped nose? Large, small, turned-up—"

"Small and regular!" There was a touch of indignation in his voice.

"How did she dress? Fashionably? And did she favor bright or quiet colors?"

"Beaut—" And then as I opened my mouth to head him off he came down to earth with:

"Very quietly—usually dark blues and browns."

"What jewelry did she wear?"

"I've never seen her wear any."

"Any scars, or moles?" The horrified look on his white face urged me on to give him a full shot. "Or warts, or deformities that you know?"

He was speechless, but he managed to shake his head.

"Have you a photograph of her?"

"Yes, I'll show you."

He bounded to his feet, wound his way through the room's excessive furnishings and out through a curtained doorway. Immediately he was back with a large photograph in a carved ivory frame. It was one of these artistic photographs—a thing of shadows and hazy outlines—not much good for identification purposes. She was beautiful—right enough—but that meant nothing; that's the purpose of an artistic photograph.

"This the only one you have?"

"Yes."

"I'll have to borrow it, but I'll get it back to you as soon as I have my copies made."

"No! No!" he protested against having his ladylove's face given to a lot of gumshoes. "That would be terrible!"

I finally got it, but it cost me more words than I like to waste on an incidental.

"I want to borrow a couple of her letters, or something in her writing, too," I said.

"For what?"

"To have photostatic copies made. Handwriting specimens come in handy—give you something to go over hotel registers with. Then, even if going under fictitious names, people now and then write notes and make memorandums."

We had another battle, out of which I came with three envelopes and two meaningless sheets of paper, all bearing the girl's angular writing.

"She have much money?" I asked, when the disputed photograph and handwriting specimens were safely tucked away in my pocket.

"I don't know. It's not the sort of thing that one would pry into. She wasn't poor; that is, she didn't have to practice any petty economies; but I haven't the faintest idea either as to the amount of her income or its source. She had an account at the Golden Gate Trust Company, but naturally I don't know anything about its size."

"Many friends here?"

"That's another thing I don't know. I think she knew a few people here, but I don't know who they were. You see, when we were together we never talked about anything but ourselves. You know what I mean: there was nothing we were interested in but each other. We were simply—"

"Can't you even make a guess at where she came from, who she was?"

"No. Those things didn't matter to me. She was Jeanne Delano, and that was enough for me."

"Did you and she ever have any financial interests in common? I mean, was there ever any transaction in money or other valuables in which both of you were interested?"

What I meant, of course, was had she got into him for a loan, or had she sold him something, or got money out of him in any other way.

He jumped to his feet, and his face went fog-grey. Then he sat down again—slumped down—and blushed scarlet.

"Pardon me," he said thickly. "You didn't know her, and of course you must look at the thing from all angles. No, there was nothing like that. I'm afraid you are going to waste time if you are going to work on the theory that she was an adventuress. There was nothing like that! She was a girl with something terrible hanging over her; something that called her to Baltimore suddenly; something that has taken her away from me. Money? What could money have to do with it? I love her!"

III

R. F. Axford received me in an office-like room in his Russian Hill residence: a big blond man, whose forty-eight or -nine years had not blurred the outlines of an athlete's body. A big, full-blooded man with the manner of one whose self-confidence is complete and not altogether unjustified.

"What's our Burke been up to now?" he asked amusedly when I told him who I was. His voice was a pleasant vibrant bass.

I didn't give him all the details.

"He was engaged to marry a Jeanne Delano, who went East about three weeks ago and then suddenly disappeared. He knows very little about her; thinks something has happened to her; and wants her found."

"Again?" His shrewd blue eyes twinkled. "And to a Jeanne this time! She's the fifth within a year, to my knowledge, and no doubt I missed one or two who were current while I was in Hawaii. But where do I come in?"

"I asked him for responsible endorsement. I think he's all right, but he isn't, in the strictest sense, a responsible person. He referred me to you."

"You're right about his not being, in the strictest sense, a responsible person." The big man screwed up his eyes and mouth in thought for a moment. Then: "Do you think that something has really happened to the girl? Or is Burke imagining things?"

"I don't know. I thought it was a dream at first. But in a couple of her letters there are hints that something was wrong."

"You might go ahead and find her then," Axford said. "I don't suppose any harm will come from letting him have his Jeanne back. It will at least give him something to think about for a while."

"I have your word for it then, Mr. Axford, that there will be no scandal or anything of the sort connected with the affair?"

"Assuredly! Burke is all right, you know. It's simply that he is spoiled. He has been in rather delicate health all his life; and then he has an income that suffices to keep him modestly, with a little over to bring out books of verse and buy doo-daws for his rooms. He takes himself a little too solemnly—is too much the poet—but he's sound at bottom."

"I'll go ahead with it, then," I said, getting up. "By the way, the girl has an account at the Golden Gate Trust

Company, and I'd like to find out as much about it as possible, especially where her money came from. Clement, the cashier, is a model of caution when it comes to giving out information about depositors. If you could put in a word for me it would make my way smoother."

"Be glad to."

He wrote a couple of lines across the back of a card and gave it to me; and, promising to call on him if I needed further assistance, I left.

IV

I telephoned Pangburn that his brother-in-law had given the job his approval. I sent a wire to the agency's Baltimore branch, giving what information I had. Then I went up to Ashbury Avenue, to the apartment house in which the girl had lived.

The manager—an immense Mrs. Clute in rustling black—knew little, if any, more about the girl than Pangburn. The girl had lived there for two and a half months; she had had occasional callers, but Pangburn was the only one that the manager could describe to me. The girl had given up the apartment on the third of the month, saying that she had been called East, and she had asked the manager to hold her mail until she sent her new address. Ten days later Mrs. Clute had received a card from the girl instructing her to forward her mail to 215 N. Stricker Street, Baltimore, Maryland. There had been no mail to forward.

The single thing of importance that I learned at the apartment house was that the girl's two trunks had been taken away by a green transfer truck. Green was the color used by one of the city's largest transfer companies.

I went then to the office of this transfer company, and found a friendly clerk on duty. (A detective, if he is wise, takes pains to make and keep as many friends as possible among transfer company, express company and railroad employees.) I left the office with a memorandum of the transfer company's check numbers and the Ferry baggage-room to which the two trunks had been taken.

At the Ferry Building, with this information, it didn't take me many minutes to learn that the trunks had been checked to Baltimore. I sent another wire to the Baltimore branch, giving the railroad check numbers.

Sunday was well into night by this time, so I knocked off and went home.

V

Half an hour before the Golden Gate Trust Company opened for business the next morning I was inside, talking to Clement, the cashier. All the traditional caution and conservatism of bankers rolled together wouldn't be one-two-three to the amount usually displayed by this plump, white-haired old man. But one look at Axford's card, with *"Please give the bearer all possible assistance"* inked across the back of it, made Clement even eager to help me.

"You have, or have had, an account here in the name of Jeanne Delano," I said. "I'd like to know as much as possible about it: to whom she drew checks, and to what amounts; but especially all you can tell me about where her money came from."

He stabbed one of the pearl buttons on his desk with a pink finger, and a lad with polished yellow hair oozed silently into the room. The cashier scribbled with a pencil on a piece of paper and gave it to the noiseless youth, who disappeared. Presently he was back, laying a handful of papers on the cashier's desk.

Clement looked through the papers and then up at me.

"Miss Delano was introduced here by Mr. Burke Pangburn on the sixth of last month, and opened an account with eight hundred and fifty dollars in cash. She made the following deposits after that: four hundred dollars on the tenth; two hundred and fifty on the twenty-first; three hundred on the twenty-sixth; two hundred on thirtieth; and twenty thousand dollars on the second of this month. All of these deposits except the last were made with cash. The last one was a check—which I have here."

He handed it to me: a Golden Gate Trust Company check.

Pay to the order of Jeanne Delano, twenty thousand dollars.

(Signed) BURKE PANGBURN.

It was dated the second of the month.

"Burke Pangburn!" I exclaimed, a little stupidly. "Was it usual for him to draw checks to that amount?"

"I think not. But we shall see."

He stabbed the pearl button again, ran his pencil across another slip of paper, and the youth with the polished yellow hair made a noiseless entrance, exit, entrance, and exit.

The cashier looked through the fresh batch of papers that had been brought to him.

"On the first of the month, Mr. Pangburn deposited twenty thousand dollars—a check against Mr. Axford's account here."

"Now how about Miss Delano's withdrawals?" I asked.

He picked up the papers that had to do with her account again.

"Her statement and canceled checks for last month haven't been delivered to her yet. Everything is here. A check for eighty-five dollars to the order of H. K. Clute on the fifteenth of last month; one 'to cash' for three hundred dollars on the twentieth, and another of the same kind for one hundred dollars on the twenty-fifth. Both of these checks were apparently cashed here by her. On the third of this month she closed out her account, with a check to her own order for twenty-one thousand, five hundred and fifteen dollars."

"And that check?"

"Was cashed here by her."

I lighted a cigarette, and let these figures drift around in my head. None of them—except those that were fixed to Pangburn's and Axford's signatures—seemed to be of any value to me. The Clute check—the only one the girl had drawn in anyone else's favor—had almost certainly been for rent.

"This is the way of it," I summed up aloud. "On the first of the month, Pangburn deposited Axford's check for twenty thousand dollars. The next day he gave a check to that amount to Miss Delano, which she deposited. On the following day she closed her account, taking between twenty-one and twenty-two thousand dollars in currency."

"Exactly," the cashier said.

VI

Before going up to the Glenton Apartments to find out why Pangburn hadn't come clean with me about the twenty thousand dollars, I dropped in at the agency, to see if any word had come from Baltimore. One of the clerks had just finished decoding a telegram.

It read:

> Baggage arrived Mt. Royal Station on eighth. Taken away same day. Unable to trace. 215 North Stricker Street is Baltimore Orphan Asylum. Girl not known there. Continuing our efforts to find her.

The Old Man came in from luncheon as I was leaving. I went back into his office with him for a couple of minutes. "Did you see Pangburn?" he asked.

"Yes. I'm working on his job now—but I think it's a bust."

"What is it?"

"Pangburn is R. F. Axford's brother-in-law. He met a girl a couple of months ago, and fell for her. She sizes up as a worker. He doesn't know anything about her. The first of the month he got twenty thousand dollars from his brother-in-law and passed it over to the girl. She blew, telling him she had been called to Baltimore, and giving him a phoney address that turns out to be an orphan asylum. She sent her trunks to Baltimore, and sent him some letters from there—but a friend could have taken care of the baggage and could have remailed her letters for her. Of course, she would have needed a ticket to check the trunks on, but in a twenty-thousand-dollar game that would be a small expense. Pangburn held out on me; he didn't tell me a word about the money. Ashamed of being easy pickings, I reckon. I'm going to the bat with him on it now."

The Old Man smiled his mild smile that might mean anything, and I left.

VII

Ten minutes of ringing Pangburn's bell brought no answer. The elevator boy told me he thought Pangburn hadn't been in all night. I put a note in his box and went down to the railroad company's offices, where I arranged to be notified if an unused Baltimore–San Francisco ticket was turned in for redemption.

That done, I went up to the *Chronicle* office and searched the files for weather conditions during the past month, making a memorandum of four dates upon which it had rained steadily day and night. I carried my memorandum to the offices of the three largest taxicab companies.

That was a trick that had worked well for me before. The girl's apartment was some distance from the street car line, and I was counting upon her having gone out—or having had a caller—on one of those rainy dates. In either case, it was very likely that she—or her caller—had left in a taxi in preference to walking through the rain to the car line. The taxicab companies' daily records would show any calls from her address, and the fares' destinations.

The ideal trick, of course, would have been to have the records searched for the full extent of the girl's occupancy of the apartment; but no taxicab company would stand for having that amount of work thrust upon them, unless it was a matter of life and death. It was difficult enough for me to persuade them to turn clerks loose on the four days I had selected.

I called up Pangburn again after I left the last taxicab office, but he was not at home. I called up Axford's residence, thinking that the poet might have spent the night there, but was told that he had not.

Late that afternoon I got my copies of the girl's photograph and handwriting, and put one of each in the mail for Baltimore. Then I went around to the three taxicab companies' offices and got my reports. Two of them had nothing for me. The third's records showed two calls from the girl's apartment.

On one rainy afternoon a taxi had been called, and one passenger had been taken to the Glenton Apartments. That passenger, obviously, was either the girl or Pangburn. At half-past twelve one night another call had come in, and this passenger had been taken to the Marquis Hotel.

The driver who had answered this second call remembered it indistinctly when I questioned him, but he thought that his fare had been a man. I let the matter rest there for the time; the Marquis isn't a large hotel as San Francisco hotels go, but it is too large to make canvassing its guests for the one I wanted practicable.

I spent the evening trying to reach Pangburn, with no success. At eleven o'clock I called up Axford, and asked him if he had any idea where I might find his brother-in-law.

"Haven't seen him for several days," the millionaire said. "He was supposed to come up for dinner last night, but didn't. My wife tried to reach him by phone a couple times today, but couldn't."

VIII

The next morning I called Pangburn's apartment before I got out of bed, and got no answer. Then I telephoned Axford and made an appointment for ten o'clock at his office.

"I don't know what he's up to now," Axford said good-naturedly when I told him that Pangburn had apparently been away from his apartment since Sunday, "and I suppose there's small chance of guessing. Our Burke is nothing if not erratic. How are you progressing with your search for the damsel in distress?"

"Far enough to convince me that she isn't in a whole lot of distress. She got twenty thousand dollars from your brother-in-law the day before she vanished."

"Twenty thousand dollars from Burke? She must be a wonderful girl! But wherever did he get that much money?"

"From you."

Axford's muscular body straightened in his chair.

"From me?"

"Yes—your check."

"He did not."

There was nothing argumentative in his voice; it simply stated a fact.

"You didn't give him a check for twenty thousand dollars on the first of the month?"

"No."

"Then," I suggested, "perhaps we'd better take a run over to the Golden Gate Trust Company."

Ten minutes later we were in Clement's office.

"I'd like to see my cancelled checks," Axford told the cashier.

The youth with the polished yellow hair brought them in presently—a thick wad of them—and Axford ran rapidly through them until he found the one he wanted. He studied that one for a long while, and when he looked up at me he shook his head slowly but with finality.

"I've never seen it before."

Clement mopped his head with a white handkerchief, and tried to pretend that he wasn't burning up with curiosity and fears that his bank had been gypped.

The millionaire turned the check over and looked at the endorsement.

"Deposited by Burke," he said in the voice of one who talks while he thinks of something entirely different, "on the first."

"Could we talk to the teller who took in the twenty-thousand-dollar check that Miss Delano deposited?" I asked Clement.

He pressed one of his desk's pearl buttons with a fumbling pink finger, and in a minute or two a little sallow man with a hairless head came in.

"Do you remember taking a check for twenty thousand from Miss Jeanne Delano a few weeks ago?" I asked him.

"Yes, sir! Yes, sir! Perfectly."

"Just what do you remember about it?"

"Well, sir, Miss Delano came to my window with Mr. Burke Pangburn. It was his check. I thought it was a large check for him to be drawing, but the bookkeepers said he had enough money in his account to cover it. They stood there—Miss Delano and Mr. Pangburn—talking and laughing while I entered the deposit in her book, and then they left, and that was all."

"This check," Axford said slowly, after the teller had gone back to his cage, "is a forgery. But I shall make it good, of course. That ends the matter, Mr. Clement, and there must be no more to-do about it."

"Certainly, Mr. Axford. Certainly."

Clement was all enormously relieved smiles and head-noddings, with this twenty-thousand-dollar load lifted from his bank's shoulders.

Axford and I left the bank then and got into his coupé, in which we had come from his office. But he did not immediately start the engine. He sat for a while staring at the traffic of Montgomery Street with unseeing eyes.

"I want you to find Burke," he said presently, and there was no emotion of any sort in his bass voice. "I want you to find him without risking the least whisper of scandal. If my wife knew of all this— She mustn't know. She thinks her brother is a choice morsel. I want you to find him for me. The girl doesn't matter any more, but I suppose that where you find one you will find the other. I'm not interested in the money, and I don't want you to make any special attempt to recover that; it could hardly be done, I'm afraid, without publicity. I want you to find Burke before he does something else."

"If you want to avoid the wrong kind of publicity," I said, "your best bet is to spread the right kind first. Let's advertise him as missing, fill the papers up with his pictures and so forth. They'll play him up strong. He's your brother-in-law and he's a poet. We can say that he has been ill—you told me that he had been in delicate health all his life—and that we fear he has dropped dead somewhere or is suffering under some mental derangement. There will be no necessity of mentioning the girl or the money, and our explanation may keep people—especially your wife—from guessing the truth when the fact that he is missing leaks out. It's bound to leak out somehow."

He didn't like my idea at first, but I finally won him over.

We went up to Pangburn's apartment then, easily securing admittance on Axford's explanation that we had an engagement with him and would wait there for him. I went through the rooms inch by inch, prying into each hole and hollow and crack; reading everything that was written anywhere, even down to his manuscripts; and I found nothing that threw any light on his disappearance.

I helped myself to his photographs—pocketing five of the dozen or more that were there. Axford did not think that any of the poet's bags or trunks were missing from the pack-room. I did not find his Golden Gate Trust Company deposit book.

I spent the rest of the day loading the newspapers up with what we wished them to have; and they gave my ex-client one grand spread: first-page stuff with photographs and all possible trimmings. Anyone in San Francisco who didn't know that Burke Pangburn—brother-in-law of R. F. Axford and author of *Sandpatches and Other Verse*—was missing, either couldn't read or wouldn't.

IX

This advertising brought results. By the following morning, reports were rolling in from all directions, from dozens of people who had seen the missing poet in dozens of places. A few of these reports looked promising—or at least possible— but the majority were ridiculous on their faces.

I came back to the agency from running out one that had—until run out—looked good, to find a note on my desk asking me to call up Axford.

"Can you come down to my office now?" he asked when I got him on the wire.

There was a lad of twenty-one or -two with Axford when I was ushered into his office: a narrow-chested, dandified lad of the sporting clerk type.

"This is Mr. Fall, one of my employees," Axford told me. "He says he saw Burke Sunday night."

"Where?" I asked Fall.

"Going into a roadhouse near Halfmoon Bay."

"Sure it was him?"

"Absolutely! I've seen him come in here to Mr. Axford's office to know him. It was him all right."

"How'd you come to see him?"

"I was coming up from further down the shore with some friends, and we stopped in at the roadhouse to get something to eat. As we were leaving, a car drove up and Mr. Pangburn and a girl or woman—I didn't notice her particularly—got out and went inside. I didn't think anything of it until I saw in the paper last night that he hadn't been seen since Sunday. So then I thought to myself that—"

"What roadhouse was this?" I cut in, not being interested in his mental processes.

"The White Shack."

"About what time?"

"Somewhere between eleven-thirty and midnight, I guess."

"He see you?"

"No. I was already in our car when he drove up. I don't think he'd know me anyway."

"What did the woman look like?"

"I don't know. I didn't see her face, and I can't remember how she was dressed or even if she was short or tall."

That was all Fall could tell me.

We shooed him out of the office, and I used Axford's telephone to call up "Wop" Healey's dive in North Beach and leave word that when "Porky" Grout came in he was to call up "Jack." That was a standing arrangement by which I got word to Porky whenever I wanted to see him, without giving anybody a chance to tumble to the connection between us.

"Know the White Shack?" I asked Axford, when I was through phoning.

"I know where it is, but I don't know anything about it."

"Well, it's a tough hole. Run by 'Tin-Star' Joplin, an ex-yegg who invested his winnings in the place when Prohibition made the roadhouse game good. He makes more money now than he ever heard of in his piking safe-ripping days. Retailing liquor is a side-line with him; his real profit comes from acting as a relay station for the booze that comes through Halfmoon Bay for points beyond; and the dope is that half the booze put ashore by the Pacific rum fleet is put ashore in Halfmoon Bay.

"The White Shack is a tough hole, and it's no place for your brother-in-law to be hanging around. I can't go down there myself without stirring things up; Joplin and I are old friends. But I've got a man I can put in there for a few nights. Pangburn may be a regular visitor, or he may even be staying there. He wouldn't be the first one Joplin had ever let hide-out there. I'll put this man of mine in the place for a week, anyway, and see what he can find."

"It's all in your hands," Axford said. "Find Burke without scandal—that's all I ask."

X

From Axford's office I went straight to my rooms, left the outer door unlocked, and sat down to wait for Porky Grout. I had waited an hour and a half when he pushed the door open and came in.

" 'Lo! How's tricks?"

He swaggered to a chair, leaned back in it, put his feet on the table and reached for a pack of cigarettes that lay there.

That was Porky Grout. A pasty-faced man in his thirties, neither large nor small, always dressed flashily—even if sometimes dirtily—and trying to hide an enormous cowardice behind a swaggering carriage, a blustering habit of speech, and an exaggerated pretense of self-assurance.

But I had known him for three years; so now I crossed the room and pushed his feet roughly off the table, almost sending him over backward.

"What's the idea?" He came to his feet, crouching and snarling. "Where do you get that stuff? Do you want a smack in the—"

I took a step toward him. He sprang away, across the room.

"Aw, I didn't mean nothin'. I was only kiddin'!"

"Shut up and sit down," I advised him.

I had known this Porky Grout for three years, and had been using him for nearly that long, and I didn't know a single thing that could be said in his favor. He was a coward. He was a liar. He was a thief, and a hophead. He was a traitor to his kind and, if not watched, to his employers. A nice bird to deal with! But detecting is a hard business, and you use whatever tools come to hand. This Porky was an effective tool if handled right, which meant keeping your hand on his throat all the time and checking up every piece of information he brought in.

His cowardice was—for my purpose—his greatest asset. It was notorious throughout the criminal Coast; and though nobody—crook or not—could possibly think him a man to be trusted, nevertheless he was not actually distrusted. Most of his fellows thought him too much the coward to be dangerous; they thought he would be afraid to betray them; afraid of the summary vengeance that crookdom visits upon the squealer. But they didn't take into account Porky's gift for convincing himself that he was a lion-hearted fellow, when no danger was near. So he went freely where he desired and where I sent him, and brought me otherwise unobtainable bits of information upon matters in which I was interested.

For nearly three years I had used him with considerable success, paying him well, and keeping him under my heel. *Informant* was the polite word that designated him in my reports; the underworld has even less lovely names than the common *stool-pigeon* to denote his kind.

"I have a job for you," I told him, now that he was seated again, with his feet on the floor.

His loose mouth twitched up at the left corner, pushing that eye into a knowing squint.

"I thought so."

He always says something like that.

"I want you to go down to Halfmoon Bay and stick around Tin-Star Joplin's joint for a few nights. Here are two photos" —sliding one of Pangburn and one of the girl across the table. "Their names and descriptions are written on the backs. I want to know if either of them shows up down there, what they're doing, and where they're hanging out. It may be that Tin-Star is covering them up."

Porky was looking knowingly from one picture to the other.

"I think I know this guy," he said out of the corner of his mouth that twitches.

That's another thing about Porky. You can't mention a name or give a description that won't bring that same remark, even though you make them up.

"Here's some money." I slid some bills across the table. "If you're down there more than a couple of nights, I'll get some more to you. Keep in touch with me, either over this phone or the under-cover one at the office. And—remember this— lay off the stuff! If I come down there and find you all snowed up, I promise that I'll tip Joplin off to you."

He had finished counting the money by now—there wasn't a whole lot to count—and he threw it contemptuously back on the table.

"Save that for newspapers," he sneered. "How am I goin' to get anywheres if I can't spend no money in the joint?"

"That's plenty for a couple of days' expenses; you'll probably knock back half of it. If you stay longer than a couple of days, I'll get more to you. And you get your pay when the job is done, and not before."

He shook his head and got up.

"I'm tired of pikin' along with you. You can turn your own jobs. I'm through!"

"If you don't get down to Halfmoon Bay tonight, you *are* through," I assured him, letting him get out of the threat whatever he liked.

After a little while, of course, he took the money and left. The dispute over expense money was simply a preliminary that went with every job I sent him out on.

XI

After Porky had cleared out, I leaned back in my chair and burned half a dozen Fatimas over the job. The girl had gone first with the twenty thousand dollars, and then the poet had gone; and both had gone, whether permanently or not, to the White Shack. On its face, the job was an obvious affair. The girl had given Pangburn the *work* to the extent of having him forge a check against his brother-in-law's account; and then, after various moves whose value I couldn't determine at the time, they had gone into hiding together.

There were two loose ends to be taken care of. One of them—the finding of the confederate who had mailed the letters to Pangburn and who had taken care of the girl's baggage—was in the Baltimore branch's hands. The other was: Who had ridden in the taxicab that I had traced from the girl's apartment to the Marquis Hotel?

That might not have any bearing upon the job, or it might. Suppose I could find a connection between the Marquis Hotel and the White Shack. That would make a completed chain of some sort. I searched the back of the telephone directory and found the roadhouse number. Then I went up to the Marquis Hotel.

The girl on duty at the hotel switchboard, when I got there, was one with whom I had done business before.

"Who's been calling Halfmoon Bay numbers?" I asked her.

"My God!" She leaned back in her chair and ran a pink hand gently over the front of her rigidly waved red hair. "I got enough to do without remembering every call that goes through. This ain't a boarding-house. We have more'n one call a week."

"You don't have many Halfmoon Bay calls," I insisted, leaning an elbow on the counter and letting a folded five-spot peep out between the fingers of one hand. "You ought to remember any you've had lately."

"I'll see," she sighed, as if willing to do her best on a hopeless task.

She ran through her tickets.

"Here's one—from room 522, a couple weeks ago."

"What number was called?"

"Halfmoon Bay 51."

That was the roadhouse number. I passed over the five-spot.

"Is 522 a permanent guest?"

"Yes. Mr. Kilcourse. He's been here three or four months."

"What is he?"

"I don't know. A perfect gentleman, if you ask me."

"That's nice. What does he look like?"

"Tall and elegant."

"Be yourself," I pleaded. "What does he look like?"

"He's a young man, but his hair is turning gray. He's dark and handsome. Looks like a movie actor."

"Bull Montana?" I asked, as I moved off toward the desk.

The key to 522 was in its place in the rack. I sat down where I could keep an eye on it. Perhaps an hour later a clerk took it out and gave it to a man who did look somewhat like an actor. He was a man of thirty or so, with dark skin, and dark hair that showed grey around the ears. He stood a good six feet of fashionably dressed slenderness.

Carrying the key, he disappeared into an elevator.

I called up the agency then and asked the Old Man to send Dick Foley over. Ten minutes later Dick arrived. He's a little shrimp of a Canadian—there isn't a hundred and ten pounds of him—who is the smoothest shadow I've ever seen, and I've seen most of them.

"I have a bird in here I want tailed," I told Dick. "His name is Kilcourse and he's in room 522. Stick around outside, and I'll give you the spot on him."

I went back to the lobby and waited some more.

At eight o'clock Kilcourse came down and left the hotel. I went after him for half a block—far enough to turn him over to Dick—and then went home, so that I would be within reach of a telephone if Porky Grout tried to get in touch with me. No call came from him that night.

XII

When I arrived at the agency the next morning, Dick was waiting for me.

"What luck?" I asked.

"Damndest!" The little Canadian talks like a telegram when his peace of mind is disturbed, and just now he was decidedly peevish. "Took me two blocks. Shook me. Only taxi in sight."

"Think he made you?"

"No. Wise head. Playing safe."

"Try him again, then. Better have a car handy, in case he tries the same trick again."

My telephone jingled as Dick was going out. It was Porky Grout, talking over the agency's unlisted line.

"Turn up anything?" I asked.

"Plenty," he bragged.

"Good! Are you in town?"

"Yes."

"I'll meet you in my rooms in twenty minutes," I said.

The pasty-faced informant was fairly bloated with pride in himself when he came through the door I had left unlocked for him. His swagger was almost a cake-walk; and the side of his mouth that twitches was twisted into a knowing leer that would have fit a Solomon.

"I knocked it over for you, kid," he boasted. "Nothin' to it—for me! I went down there and talked to ever'body that knowed anything, seen ever'thing there was to see, and put the X-ray on the whole dump. I made a—"

"Uh-huh," I interrupted. "Congratulations and so forth. But just what did you turn up?"

"Now le'me tell you." He raised a dirty hand in a traffic-cop sort of gesture, and blew a stream of cigarette smoke at the ceiling. "Don't crowd me. I'll give you all the dope."

"Sure," I said. "I know. You're great, and I'm lucky to have you to knock off my jobs for me, and all that! But is Pangburn down there?"

"I'm gettin' around to that. I went down there and—"

"Did you see Pangburn?"

"As I was sayin', I went down there and—"

"Porky," I said, "I don't give a damn what you did! Did you see Pangburn?"

"Yes. I seen him."

"Fine! Now what did you see?"

"He's camping down there with Tin-Star. Him and the broad that you give me a picture of are both there. She's been there a month. I didn't see her, but one of the waiters told me about her. I seen Pangburn myself. They don't show themselves much—stick back in Tin-Star's part of the joint—where he lives—most of the time. Pangburn's been there since Sunday. I went down there and—"

"Learn who the girl is? Or anything about what they're up to?"

"No. I went down there and—"

"All right! *Went down there* again tonight. Call me up as soon as you know positively Pangburn is there—that he hasn't gone out. Don't make any mistakes. I don't want to come down there and scare them up on a false alarm. Use the agency's under-cover line, and just tell whoever answers that you won't be in town until late. That'll mean that Pangburn is there; and it'll let you call up from Joplin's without giving the play away."

"I got to have more dough," he said, as he got up. "It costs—"

"I'll file your application," I promised. "Now beat it, and let me hear from you tonight, the minute you're sure Pangburn is there."

Then I went up to Axford's office.

"I think I have a line on him," I told the millionaire. "I hope to have him where you can talk to him tonight. My man says he was at the White Shack last night, and is probably living there. If he's there tonight, I'll take you down, if you want."

"Why can't we go now?"

"No. The place is too dead in the daytime for my man to hang around without making himself conspicuous, and I don't want to take any chances on either you or me showing ourselves there until we're sure we're coming face to face with Pangburn."

"What do you want me to do then?"

"Have a fast car ready tonight, and be ready to start as soon as I get word to you."

"Righto. I'll be at home after five-thirty. Phone me as soon as you're ready to go, and I'll pick you up."

XIII

At nine-thirty that evening I was sitting beside Axford on the front seat of a powerfully engined foreign car, and we were roaring down a road that led to Halfmoon Bay. Porky's telephone call had come.

Neither of us talked much during that ride, and the imported monster under us made it a rather short ride. Axford sat comfortable and relaxed at the wheel, but I noticed for the first time that he had a rather heavy jaw.

The White Shack is a large building, square-built, of imitation stone. It is set away back from the road, and is approached by two curving driveways, which, together, make a semi-circle whose diameter is the public road. The center of this semi-circle is occupied by sheds under which Joplin's patrons stow their cars, and here and there around the sheds are flower-beds and clumps of shrubbery.

We were still going at a fair clip when we turned into one end of this semi-circular driveway, and—

Axford slammed on his brakes, and the big machine threw us into the windshield as it jolted into an abrupt stop—barely in time to avoid smashing into a cluster of people who had suddenly loomed up before us.

In the glow from our headlights faces stood sharply out; white, horrified faces, furtive faces, faces that were callously curious. Below the faces, white arms and shoulders showed, and bright gowns and jewelry, against the duller background of masculine clothing.

This was the first impression I got, and then, by the time I had removed my face from the windshield, I realized that this cluster of people had a core, a thing about which it centered. I stood up, trying to look over the crowd's heads, but I could see nothing.

Jumping down to the driveway, I pushed through the crowd.

Face down on the white gravel a man sprawled—a thin man in dark clothes—and just above his collar, where the head and neck join, was a hole. I knelt to peer into his face.

Then I pushed through the crowd again, back to where Axford was just getting out of the car, the engine of which was still running.

"Pangburn is dead—shot!"

XIV

Methodically, Axford took off his gloves, folded them and put them in a pocket. Then he nodded his understanding of what I had told him, and walked toward where the crowd stood around the dead poet. I looked after him until he had vanished in the throng. Then I went winding through the outskirts of the crowd, hunting for Porky Grout.

I found him standing on the porch, leaning against a pillar. I passed where he could see me, and went on around to the side of the roadhouse that afforded most shadow.

In the shadows Porky joined me. The night wasn't cool, but his teeth were chattering.

"Who got him?" I demanded.

"I don't know," he whined, and that was the first thing of which I had ever known him to confess complete ignorance. "I was inside, keepin' an eye on the others."

"What others?"

"Tin-Star, and some guy I never seen before, and the broad. I didn't think the kid was going out. He didn't have no hat."

"What *do* you know about it?"

"A little while after I phoned you, the girl and Pangburn came out from Joplin's part of the joint and sat down at a table around on the other side of the porch, where it's fairly dark. They eat for a while and then this other guy comes over and sits down with 'em. I don't know his name, but I think I've saw him around town. He's a tall guy, all rung up in fancy rags."

That would be Kilcourse.

"They talk for a while and then Joplin joins 'em. They sit around the table laughin' and talkin' for maybe a quarter of a hour. Then Pangburn gets up and goes indoors. I got a table that I can watch 'em from, and the place is crowded, and I'm afraid I'll lose my table if I leave it, so I don't follow the kid. He ain't got no hat; I figure he ain't goin' nowhere. But he must of gone through the house and out front, because pretty soon there's a noise that I thought was a auto backfire, and then the sound of a car gettin' away quick. And then some guy squawks that there's a dead man outside. Ever'body runs out here, and it's Pangburn."

"You dead sure that Joplin, Kilcourse and the girl were all at the table when Pangburn was killed?"

"Absolutely," Porky said, "if this dark guy's name is Kilcourse."

"Where are they now?"

"Back in Joplin's hang-out. They went up there as soon as they seen Pangburn had been croaked."

I had no illusions about Porky. I knew he was capable of selling me out and furnishing the poet's murderer with an alibi. But there was this about it: if Joplin, Kilcourse or the girl had fixed him, and had fixed my informant, then it was hopeless for me to try to prove that they weren't on the rear porch when the shot was fired. Joplin had a crowd of hangers-on who would swear to anything he told them without batting an eye. There would be a dozen supposed witnesses to their presence on the rear porch.

Thus the only thing for me to do was to take it for granted that Porky was coming clean with me.

"Have you seen Dick Foley?" I asked, since Dick had been shadowing Kilcourse.

"No."

"Hunt around and see if you can find him. Tell him I've gone up to talk to Joplin, and tell him to come on up. Then you can stick around where I can get hold of you if I want you."

I went in through a French window, crossed an empty dance-floor and went up the stairs that lead to Tin-Star Joplin's living quarters in the rear second story. I knew the way, having been up there before. Joplin and I were old friends.

I was going up now to give him and his friends a shake-down on the off-chance that some good might come of it, though I knew that I had nothing on any of them. I could have tied something on the girl, of course, but not without advertising the fact that the dead poet had forged his brother-in-law's signature to a check. And that was no go.

"Come in," a heavy, familiar voice called when I rapped on Joplin's living-room door.

I pushed the door open and went in.

Tin-Star Joplin was standing in the middle of the floor: a big-bodied ex-yegg with inordinately thick shoulders and an expressionless horse face. Beyond him Kilcourse sat dangling one leg from the corner of a table, alertness hiding behind an amused half-smile on his handsome dark face. On the other side of a room a girl whom I knew for Jeanne Delano sat on the arm of a big leather chair. And the poet hadn't exaggerated when he told me she was beautiful.

"You!" Joplin grunted disgustedly as soon as he recognized me. "What the hell do *you* want?"

"What've you got?"

My mind wasn't on this sort of repartee, however; I was studying the girl. There was something vaguely familiar about her—but I couldn't place her. Perhaps I hadn't seen her before; perhaps much looking at the picture Pangburn had given me was responsible for my feeling of recognition. Pictures will do that.

Meanwhile, Joplin had said:

"Time to waste is one thing I ain't got."

And I had said:

"If you'd saved up all the time different judges have given you, you'd have plenty."

I had seen the girl somewhere before. She was a slender girl in a glistening blue gown that exhibited a generous spread of front, back and arms that were worth showing. She had a mass of dark brown hair above an oval face of the color that pink ought to be. Her eyes were wide-set and of a grey shade that wasn't altogether unlike the shadows on polished silver that the poet had compared them to.

I studied the girl, and she looked back at me with level eyes, and still I couldn't place her. Kilcourse still sat dangling a leg from the table corner.

Joplin grew impatient.

"Will you stop gandering at the girl, and tell me what you want of me?" he growled.

The girl smiled then, a mocking smile that bared the edges of razor-sharp little animal teeth. And with the smile I knew her!

Her hair and skin had fooled me. The last time I had seen her—the only time I had seen her before—her face had been marble-white, and her hair had been short and the color of fire. She and an older woman and three men and I had played hide-and-seek one evening in a house in Turk Street over a matter of the murder of a bank messenger and the theft of a hundred thousand dollars' worth of Liberty Bonds. Through her intriguing three of her accomplices had died that evening, and the fourth—the Chinese—had eventually gone to the gallows at Folsom prison. Her name had been Elvira then, and since her escape from the house that night we had been fruitlessly hunting her from border to border, and beyond.

Recognition must have shown in my eyes in spite of the effort I made to keep them blank, for, swift as a snake, she had left the arm of the chair and was coming forward, her eyes more steel than silver.

I put my gun in sight.

Joplin took a half-step toward me.

"What's the idea?" he barked.

Kilcourse slid off the table, and one of his thin dark hands hovered over his necktie.

"This is the idea," I told them. "I want the girl for a murder a couple months back, and maybe—I'm not sure—for tonight's. Anyway, I'm—"

The snapping of a light-switch behind me, and the room went black.

I moved, not caring where I went so long as I got away from where I had been when the lights went out.

My back touched a wall and I stopped, crouching low.

"Quick, kid!" A hoarse whisper that came from where I thought the door should be.

But both of the room's doors, I thought, were closed, and could hardly be opened without showing gray rectangles. People moved in the blackness, but none got between me and the lighter square of windows.

Something clicked softly in front of me—too thin a click for the cocking of a gun—but it could have been the opening of a spring-knife, and I remembered that Tin-Star Joplin had a fondness for that weapon.

"Let's go! Let's go!" A harsh whisper that cut through the dark like a blow.

Sounds of motion, muffled, indistinguishable . . . one sound not far away. . . .

Abruptly a strong hand clamped one of my shoulders, a hard-muscled body strained against me. I stabbed out with my gun, and heard a grunt.

The hand moved up my shoulder toward my throat.

I snapped up a knee, and heard another grunt.

A burning point ran down my side.

I stabbed again with my gun—pulled it back until the muzzle was clear of the soft obstacle that had stopped it, and squeezed the trigger.

The crash of the shot. Joplin's voice in my ear—a curiously matter-of-fact voice:

"God damn! That got me."

XV

I spun away from him then, toward where I saw the dim yellow of an open door. I had heard no sounds of departure. I had been too busy. But I knew that Joplin had tied into me while the others made their get-away.

Nobody was in sight as I jumped, slid, tumbled down the steps—any number at a time. A waiter got in my path as I plunged toward the dance-floor. I don't know whether his interference was intentional or not. I didn't ask. I slammed the flat of my gun in his face and went on. Once I jumped a leg that came out to trip me; and at the outer door I had to smear another face.

Then I was out in the semi-circular driveway, from one end of which a red tail-light was turning east into the county road.

While I sprinted for Axford's car I noticed that Pangburn's body had been removed. A few people still stood around the spot where he had lain, and they gaped at me now with open mouths.

The car was as Axford had left it, with idling engine. I swung it through a flower-bed and pointed it east on the public road. Five minutes later I picked up the red point of a tail-light again.

The car under me had more power than I would ever need, more than I would have known how to handle. I don't know how fast the one ahead was going, but I closed in as if it had been standing still.

A mile and a half, or perhaps two—

Suddenly a man was in the road ahead—a little beyond the reach of my lights. The lights caught him, and I saw that it was Porky Grout!

Porky Grout standing facing me in the middle of the road, the dull metal of an automatic in each hand.

The guns in his hands seemed to glow dimly red and then go dark in the glare of my headlights—glow and then go dark, like two bulbs in an automatic electric sign.

The windshield fell apart around me.

Porky Grout—the informant whose name was a synonym for cowardice the full length of the Pacific Coast—stood in the center of the road shooting at a metal comet that rushed down upon him. . . .

I didn't see the end.

I confess frankly that I shut my eyes when his set white face showed close over my radiator. The metal monster under me trembled—not very much—and the road ahead was empty except for the fleeing red light. My windshield was gone. The wind tore at my uncovered hair and brought tears to my squinted-up eyes.

Presently I found that I was talking to myself, saying, "That was Porky. That was Porky." It was an amazing fact. It was no surprise that he had double-crossed me. That was to be expected. And for him to have crept up the stairs behind me and turned off the lights wasn't astonishing. But for him to have stood straight up and died—

An orange streak from the car ahead cut off my wonderment. The bullet didn't come near me—it isn't easy to shoot accurately from one moving car into another—but at the pace I was going it wouldn't be long before I was close enough for good shooting.

I turned on the searchlight above the dashboard. It didn't quite reach the car ahead, but it enabled me to see that the girl was driving, while Kilcourse sat screwed around beside her, facing me. The car was a yellow roadster.

I eased up a little. In a duel with Kilcourse here I would have been at a disadvantage, since I would have had to drive as well as shoot. My best play seemed to be to hold my distance until we reached a town, as we inevitably must. It wasn't midnight yet. There would be people on the streets of any town, and policemen. Then I could close in with a better chance of coming off on top.

A few miles of this and my prey tumbled to my plan. The yellow roadster slowed down, wavered, and came to rest with its length across the road. Kilcourse and the girl were out immediately and crouching in the road on the far side of their barricade.

I was tempted to dive pell-mell into them, but it was a weak temptation, and when its short life had passed I put on the brakes and stopped. Then I fiddled with my searchlight until it bore full upon the roadster.

A flash came from somewhere near the roadster's wheels, and the searchlight shook violently, but the glass wasn't touched. It would be their first target, of course, and . . .

Crouching in my car, waiting for the bullet that would smash the lens, I took off my shoes and overcoat.

The third bullet ruined the light.

I switched off the other lights, jumped to the road, and when I stopped running I was squatting down against the near side of the yellow roadster. As easy and safe a trick as can be imagined.

The girl and Kilcourse had been looking into the glare of a powerful light. When that light suddenly died, and the weaker ones around it went, too, they were left in pitch unseeing blackness, which must last for the minute or longer that their eyes would need to readjust themselves to the gray-black of the night. My stockinged feet had made no sound on the macadam road, and now there was only a roadster between us; and I knew it and they didn't.

From near the radiator Kilcourse spoke softly:

"I'm going to try to knock him off from the ditch. Take a shot at him now and then to keep him busy."

"I can't see him," the girl protested.

"Your eyes'll be all right in a second. Take a shot at the car anyway."

I moved toward the radiator as the girl's pistol barked at the empty touring car.

Kilcourse, on hands and knees, was working his way toward the ditch that ran along the south side of the road. I gathered my legs under me, intent upon a spring and a blow with my gun upon the back of his head. I didn't want to kill him, but I wanted to put him out of the way quick. I'd have the girl to take care of, and she was at least as dangerous as he.

As I tensed for the spring, Kilcourse, guided perhaps by some instinct of the hunted, turned his head and saw me—saw a threatening shadow.

Instead of jumping I fired.

I didn't look to see whether I had hit him or not. At that range there was little likelihood of missing. I bent double and slipped back to the rear of the roadster, keeping on my side of it.

Then I waited.

The girl did what I would perhaps have done in her place. She didn't shoot or move toward the place the shot had come from. She thought I had forestalled Kilcourse in using the ditch and that my next play would be to circle around behind her. To offset this, she moved around the rear of the roadster, so that she could ambush me from the side nearest Axford's car.

Thus it was that she came creeping around the corner and poked her delicately chiseled nose plunk into the muzzle of the gun that I held ready for her.

She gave a little scream.

Women aren't always reasonable: they are prone to disregard trifles like guns held upon them. So I grabbed her gun hand, which was fortunate for me. As my hand closed around the weapon, she pulled the trigger, catching a chunk of my forefinger between hammer and frame. I twisted the gun out of her hand; released my finger.

But she wasn't done yet.

With me standing there holding a gun not four inches from her body, she turned and bolted off toward where a clump of trees made a jet-black blot to the north.

When I recovered from my surprise at this amateurish procedure, I stuck both her gun and mine in my pockets, and set out after her, tearing the soles of my feet at every step.

She was trying to get over a wire fence when I caught her.

XVI

"Stop playing, will you?" I said crossly, as I set the fingers of my left hand around her wrist and started to lead her back to the roadster. "This is a serious business. Don't be so childish!"

"You are hurting my arm."

I knew I wasn't hurting her arm, and I knew this girl for the direct cause of four, or perhaps five, deaths; yet I loosened my grip on her wrist until it wasn't much more than a friendly clasp. She went back willingly enough to the roadster, where, still holding her wrist, I switched on the lights.

Kilcourse lay just beneath the headlight's glare, huddled on his face, with one knee drawn up under him.

I put the girl squarely in the line of light.

"Now stand there," I said, "and behave. The first break you make, I'm going to shoot a leg out from under you," and I meant it.

I found Kilcourse's gun, pocketed it, and knelt beside him.

He was dead, with a bullet-hole above his collar-bone.

"Is he—" her mouth trembled.

"Yes."

She looked down at him, and shivered a little.

"Poor Fag," she whispered.

I've gone on record as saying that this girl was beautiful,

and, standing there in the dazzling white of the headlights, she was more than that. She was a thing to start crazy thoughts even in the head of an unimaginative middle-aged thief-catcher. She was—

Anyhow, I suppose that is why I scowled at her and said:

"Yes, poor Fag, and poor Hook, and poor Tai, and poor kind of a Los Angeles bank messenger, and poor Burke," calling the roll, so far as I knew it, of men who had died loving her.

She didn't flare up. Her big grey eyes lifted, and she looked at me with a gaze that I couldn't fathom, and her lovely oval face under the mass of brown hair—which I knew was phoney—was sad.

"I suppose you do think—" she began.

But I had had enough of this; I was uncomfortable along the spine.

"Come on," I said. "We'll leave Kilcourse and the roadster here for the present."

She said nothing, but went with me to Axford's big machine, and sat in silence while I laced my shoes. I found a robe on the back seat and gave it to her.

"Better wrap this around your shoulders. The windshield is gone. It'll be cool."

She followed my suggestion without a word, but when I had edged our vehicle around the rear of the roadster, and had straightened out in the road again, going east, she laid a hand on my arm.

"Aren't we going back to the White Shack?"

"No. Redwood City—the county jail."

A mile perhaps, during which, without looking at her, I knew she was studying my rather lumpy profile. Then her hand was on my forearm again and she was leaning toward me so that her breath was warm against my cheek.

"Will you stop for a minute? There's something—some things I want to tell you."

I brought the car to a halt in a cleared space of hard soil off to one side of the road, and screwed myself a little around in the seat to face her more directly.

"Before you start," I told her, "I want you to understand that we stay here for just so long as you talk about the

Pangburn affair. When you get off on any other line—then we finish our trip to Redwood City."

"Aren't you even interested in the Los Angeles affair?"

"No. That's closed. You and Hook Riordan and Tai Choon Tau and the Quarres were equally responsible for the messenger's death, even if Hook did the actual killing. Hook and the Quarres passed out the night we had our party in Turk Street. Tai was hanged last month. Now I've got you. We had enough evidence to swing the Chinese, and we've even more against you. That is done—finished—completed. If you want to tell me anything about Pangburn's death, I'll listen. Otherwise—"

I reached for the self-starter.

A pressure of her fingers on my arm stopped me.

"I do want to tell you about it," she said earnestly. "I want you to know the truth about it. You'll take me to Redwood City, I know. Don't think that I expect—that I have any foolish hopes. But I'd like you to know the truth about this thing. I don't know why I should care especially what you think, but—"

Her voice dwindled off to nothing.

XVII

Then she began to talk very rapidly—as people talk when they fear interruptions before their stories are told—and she sat leaning slightly forward, so that her beautiful oval face was very close to mine.

"After I ran out of the Turk Street house that night—while you were struggling with Tai—my intention was to get away from San Francisco. I had a couple of thousand dollars, enough to carry me any place. Then I thought that going away would be what you people would expect me to do, and that the safest thing for me to do would be to stay right here. It isn't hard for a woman to change her appearance. I had bobbed red hair, white skin, and wore gay clothes. I simply dyed my hair, bought these transformations to make it look long, put color on my face, and bought some dark clothes. Then I took an apartment on Ashbury Avenue under the name of Jeanne Delano, and I was an altogether different person.

"But, while I knew I was perfectly safe from recognition anywhere, I felt more comfortable staying indoors for a while, and, to pass the time, I read a good deal. That's how I happened to run across Burke's book. Do you read poetry?"

I shook my head. An automobile going toward Halfmoon Bay came into sight just then—the first one we'd seen since we left the White Shack. She waited until it had passed before she went on, still talking rapidly.

"Burke wasn't a genius, of course, but there was something about some of his things that—something that got inside me. I wrote him a little note, telling him how much I had enjoyed these things, and sent it to his publishers. A few days later I had a note from Burke, and I learned that he lived in San Francisco. I hadn't known that.

"We exchanged several notes, and then he asked if he could call, and we met. I don't know whether I was in love with him or not, even at first. I did like him, and, between the ardor of his love for me and the flattery of having a fairly well-known poet for a suitor, I really thought that I loved him. I promised to marry him.

"I hadn't told him anything about myself, though now I know that it wouldn't have made any difference to him. But I was afraid to tell him the truth, and I wouldn't lie to him, so I told him nothing.

"Then Fag Kilcourse saw me one day on the street, and knew me in spite of my new hair, complexion and clothes. Fag hadn't much brains, but he had eyes that could see through anything. I don't blame Fag. He acted according to his code. He came up to my apartment, having followed me home; and I told him that I was going to marry Burke and be a respectable housewife. That was dumb of me. Fag was square. If I had told him that I was ribbing Burke up for a trimming, Fag would have let me alone, would have kept his hands off. But when I told him that I was through with the graft, had 'gone queer,' that made me his meat. You know how crooks are: everyone in the world is either a fellow crook or a prospective victim. So if I was no longer a crook, then Fag considered me fair game.

"He learned about Burke's family connections, and then he put it up to me—twenty thousand dollars, or he'd turn me up. He knew about the Los Angeles job, and he knew how badly I was wanted. I was up against it then. I knew I couldn't hide from Fag or run away from him. I told Burke I had to have twenty thousand dollars. I didn't think he had that much, but I thought he could get it. Three days later he gave me a check for it. I didn't know at the time how he had raised it, but it wouldn't have mattered if I had known. I had to have it.

"But that night he told me where he got the money; that he had forged his brother-in-law's signature. He told me because, after thinking it over, he was afraid that when the forgery was discovered I would be caught with him and considered equally guilty. I'm rotten in spots, but I wasn't rotten enough to let him put himself in the pen for me, without knowing what it was all about. I told him the whole story. He didn't bat an eye. He insisted that the money be paid Kilcourse, so that I would be safe, and began to plan for my further safety.

"Burke was confident that his brother-in-law wouldn't send him over for forgery, but, to be on the safe side, he insisted that I move and change my name again and lay low until we knew how Axford was going to take it. But that night, after he had gone, I made some plans of my own. I did like Burke—I liked him too much to let him be the goat without trying to save him, and I didn't have a great deal of faith in Axford's kindness. This was the second of the month. Barring accidents, Axford wouldn't discover the forgery until he got his cancelled checks early the following month. That gave me practically a month to work in.

"The next day I drew all my money out of the bank, and sent Burke a letter, saying that I had been called to Baltimore, and I laid a clear trail to Baltimore, with baggage and letters and all, which a pal there took care of for me. Then I went down to Joplin's and got him to put me up. I let Fag know I was there, and when he came down I told him I expected to have the money for him in a day or two.

"He came down nearly every day after that, and I stalled him from day to day, and each time it got easier. But my time was getting short. Pretty soon Burke's letters would be coming back from the phoney address I had given him, and I

wanted to be on hand to keep him from doing anything foolish. And I didn't want to get in touch with him until I could
give him the twenty thousand, so he could square the forgery
before Axford learned of it from his cancelled checks.

"Fag was getting easier and easier to handle, but I still didn't
have him where I wanted him. He wasn't willing to give up
the twenty thousand dollars—which I was, of course, holding
all this time—unless I'd promise to stick with him for good.
And I still thought I was in love with Burke, and I didn't
want to tie myself up with Fag, even for a little while.

"Then Burke saw me on the street one Sunday night. I was
careless, and drove into the city in Joplin's roadster—the one
back there. And, as luck would have it, Burke saw me. I told
him the truth, the whole truth. And he told me that he had
just hired a private detective to find me. He was like a child in
some ways: it hadn't occurred to him that the sleuth would
dig up anything about the money. But I knew the forged
check would be found in a day or two at the most. I knew it!

"When I told Burke that he went to pieces. All his faith in
his brother-in-law's forgiveness went. I couldn't leave him the
way he was. He'd have babbled the whole thing to the first
person he met. So I brought him back to Joplin's with me.
My idea was to hold him there for a few days, until we could
see how things were going. If nothing appeared in the papers
about the check, then we could take it for granted that
Axford had hushed the matter up, and Burke could go home
and try to square himself. On the other hand, if the papers
got the whole story, then Burke would have to look for a permanent hiding-place, and so would I.

"Tuesday evening's and Wednesday morning's papers were
full of the news of his disappearance, but nothing was said
about the check. That looked good, but we waited another
day for good measure. Fag Kilcourse was in on the game by
this time, of course, and I had had to pass over the twenty
thousand dollars, but I still had hopes of getting it—or most
of it—back, so I continued to string him along. I had a hard
time keeping him off Burke, though, because he had begun
to think he had some sort of right to me, and jealousy made
him wicked. But I got Tin-Star to throw a scare into him, and
I thought Burke was safe.

"Tonight one of Tin-Star's men came up and told us that a man named Porky Grout, who had been hanging around the place for a couple of nights, had made a couple of cracks that might mean he was interested in us. Grout was pointed out to me, and I took a chance on showing myself in the public part of the place, and sat at a table close to his. He was plain rat—as I guess you know—and in less than five minutes I had him at my table, and half an hour later I knew that he had tipped you off that Burke and I were in the White Shack. He didn't tell me all this right out, but he told me more than enough for me to guess the rest.

"I went up and told the others. Fag was for killing both Grout and Burke right away. But I talked him out of it. That wouldn't help us any, and I had Grout where he would jump in the ocean for me. I thought I had Fag convinced, but— We finally decided that Burke and I would take the roadster and leave, and that when you got here Porky Grout was to pretend he was hopped up, and point out a man and a woman—any who happened to be handy—as the ones he had taken for us. I stopped to get a cloak and gloves, and Burke went on out to the car alone—and Fag shot him. I didn't know he was going to! I wouldn't have let him! Please believe that! I wasn't as much in love with Burke as I had thought, but please believe that after all he had done for me I wouldn't have let them hurt him!

"After that it was a case of stick with the others whether I liked it or not, and I stuck. We ribbed Grout to tell you that all three of us were on the back porch when Burke was killed, and we had any number of others primed with the same story. Then you came up and recognized me. Just my luck that it had to be you—the only detective in San Francisco who knew me!

"You know the rest: how Porky Grout came up behind you and turned off the lights, and Joplin held you while we ran for the car; and then, when you closed in on us, Grout offered to stand you off while we got clear, and now. . . ."

XVIII

Her voice died, and she shivered a little. The robe I had given her had fallen away from her white shoulders. Whether or not it was because she was so close against my shoulder, I shivered, too. And my fingers, fumbling in my pocket for a cigarette, brought it out twisted and mashed.

"That's all there is to the part you promised to listen to," she said softly, her face turned half away. "I wanted you to know. You're a hard man, but somehow I—"

I cleared my throat, and the hand that held the mangled cigarette was suddenly steady.

"Now don't be crude, sister," I said. "Your work has been too smooth so far to be spoiled by rough stuff now."

She laughed—a brief laugh that was bitter and reckless and just a little weary, and she thrust her face still closer to mine, and the grey eyes were soft and placid.

"Little fat detective whose name I don't know"—her voice had a tired huskiness in it, and a tired mockery—"you think I am playing a part, don't you? You think I am playing for liberty. Perhaps I am. I certainly would take it if it were offered me. But— Men have thought me beautiful, and I have played with them. Women are like that. Men have loved me and, doing what I liked with them, I have found men contemptible. And then comes this little fat detective whose name I don't know, and he acts as if I were a hag—an old squaw. Can I help then being piqued into some sort of feeling for him? Women are like that. Am I so homely that any man has a right to look at me without even interest? Am I ugly?"

I shook my head.

"You're quite pretty," I said, struggling to keep my voice as casual as the words.

"You beast!" she spat, and then her smile grew gentle again. "And yet it is because of that attitude that I sit here and turn myself inside out for you. If you were to take me in your arms and hold me close to the chest that I am already leaning against, and if you were to tell me that there is no jail ahead for me just now, I would be glad, of course. But, though for a while you might hold me, you would then be only one of the men with which I am familiar: men who love and are used and are succeeded by other men. But because you do none of these things, because you are a wooden block of a man, I find myself wanting you. Would I tell you this, little fat detective, if I were playing a game?"

I grunted noncommittally, and forcibly restrained my tongue from running out to moisten my dry lips.

"I'm going to this jail tonight if you are the same hard man who has goaded me into whining love into his uncaring ears, but before that, can't I have one whole-hearted assurance that you think me a little more than 'quite pretty'? Or at least a hint that if I were not a prisoner your pulse might beat a little faster when I touch you? I'm going to this jail for a long while—perhaps to the gallows. Can't I take my vanity there not quite in tatters to keep me company? Can't you do some slight thing to keep me from the afterthought of having bleated all this out to a man who was simply bored?"

Her lids had come down half over the silver-grey eyes; her head had tilted back so far that a little pulse showed throbbing in her white throat; her lips were motionless over slightly parted teeth, as the last word had left them. My fingers went deep into the soft white flesh of her shoulders. Her head went further back, her eyes closed, one hand came up to my shoulder.

"You're beautiful as all hell!" I shouted crazily into her face, and flung her against the door.

It seemed an hour that I fumbled with starter and gears before I had the car back in the road and thundering toward the San Mateo County jail. The girl had straightened herself up in the seat again, and sat huddled within the robe I had given her. I squinted straight ahead into the wind that tore at my hair and face, and the absence of the windshield took my thoughts back to Porky Grout.

Porky Grout, whose yellowness was notorious from Seattle to San Diego, standing rigidly in the path of a charging metal monster, with an inadequate pistol in each hand. She had done that to Porky Grout—this woman beside me! She had done that to Porky Grout, and he hadn't even been human! A slimy reptile whose highest thought had been a skinful of dope had gone grimly to death that she might get away— she—this woman whose shoulders I had gripped, whose mouth had been close under mine!

I let the car out another notch, holding the road somehow.

We went through a town: a scurrying of pedestrians for safety, surprised faces staring at us, street lights glistening on the moisture the wind had whipped from my eyes. I passed blindly by the road I wanted, circled back to it, and we were out in the country again.

XIX

At the foot of a long, shallow hill I applied the brakes and we snapped to motionlessness.

I thrust my face close to the girl's.

"Furthermore, you are a liar!" I knew I was shouting foolishly, but I was powerless to lower my voice. "Pangburn never put Axford's name on that check. He never knew anything about it. You got in with him because you knew his brother-in-law was a millionaire. You pumped him, finding out everything he knew about his brother-in-law's account at the Golden Gate Trust. You stole Pangburn's bank book—it wasn't in his room when I searched it—and deposited the forged Axford check to his credit, knowing that under those circumstances the check wouldn't be questioned. The next day you took Pangburn into the bank, saying you were going to make a deposit. You took him in because with him standing beside you the check to which *his* signature had been forged wouldn't be questioned. You knew that, being a gentleman, he'd take pains not to see what you were depositing.

"Then you framed the Baltimore trip. He told the truth to me—the truth so far as he knew it. Then you met him Sunday night—maybe accidentally, maybe not. Anyway, you took him down to Joplin's, giving him some wild yarn that he would swallow and that would persuade him to stay there for a few days. That wasn't hard, since he didn't know anything about either of the twenty-thousand-dollar checks. You and your pal Kilcourse knew that if Pangburn disappeared nobody would ever know that he hadn't forged the Axford check, and nobody would ever suspect that the second check was phoney. You'd have killed him quietly, but when Porky tipped you off that I was on my way down you had to move quick—so you shot him down. That's the truth of it!" I yelled.

All this while she had watched me with wide grey eyes that were calm and tender, but now they clouded a little and a pucker of pain drew her brows together.

I yanked my head away and got the car in motion.

Just before we swept into Redwood City one of her hands came up to my forearm, rested there for a second, patted the arm twice, and withdrew.

I didn't look at her, nor, I think, did she look at me, while she was being booked. She gave her name as Jeanne Delano, and refused to make any statement until she had seen an attorney. It all took a very few minutes.

As she was being led away, she stopped and asked if she might speak privately with me.

We went together to a far corner of the room.

She put her mouth close to my ear so that her breath was warm again on my cheek, as it had been in the car, and whispered the vilest epithet of which the English language is capable.

Then she walked out to her cell.

Women, Politics and Murder

A PLUMP maid with bold green eyes and a loose, full-lipped mouth led me up two flights of steps and into an elaborately furnished boudoir, where a woman in black sat at a window. She was a thin woman of a little more than thirty, this murdered man's widow, and her face was white and haggard.

"You are from the Continental Detective Agency?" she asked before I was two steps inside the room.

"Yes."

"I want you to find my husband's murderer." Her voice was shrill, and her dark eyes had wild lights in them. "The police have done nothing. Four days, and they have done nothing. They say it was a robber, but they haven't found him. They haven't found anything!"

"But, Mrs. Gilmore," I began, not exactly tickled to death with this explosion, "you must—"

"I know! I know!" she broke in. "But they have done nothing, I tell you—nothing. I don't believe they've made the slightest effort. I don't believe they want to find h-him!"

"Him?" I asked, because she had started to say *her*. "You think it was a man?"

She bit her lip and looked away from me, out of the window to where San Francisco Bay, the distance making toys of its boats, was blue under the early afternoon sun.

"I don't know," she said hesitantly; "it might have—"

Her face spun toward me—a twitching face—and it seemed impossible that anyone could talk so fast, hurl words out so rapidly one after the other.

"I'll tell you. You can judge for yourself. Bernard wasn't faithful to me. There was a woman who calls herself Cara Kenbrook. She wasn't the first. But I learned about her last month. We quarreled. Bernard promised to give her up. Maybe he didn't. But if he did, I wouldn't put it past her— A woman like that would do anything—anything. And down in my heart I really believe she did it!"

"And you think the police don't want to arrest her?"

"I didn't mean exactly that. I'm all unstrung, and likely to say anything. Bernard was mixed up in politics, you know; and if the police found, or thought, that politics had anything to do with his death, they might—I don't know just what I mean. I'm a nervous, broken woman, and full of crazy notions." She stretched a thin hand out to me. "Straighten this tangle out for me! Find the person who killed Bernard!"

I nodded with empty assurance, still not any too pleased with my client.

"Do you know this Kenbrook woman?" I asked.

"I've seen her on the street, and that's enough to know what sort of person she is!"

"Did you tell the police about her?"

"No-o." She looked out of the window again, and then, as I waited, she added, defensively:

"The police detectives who came to see me acted as if they thought I might have killed Bernard. I was afraid to tell them that I had cause for jealousy. Maybe I shouldn't have kept quiet about that woman, but I didn't think she had done it until afterward, when the police failed to find the murderer. Then I began to think she had done it; but I couldn't make myself go to the police and tell them that I had withheld information. I knew what they'd think. So I— You can twist it around so it'll look as if I hadn't known about the woman, can't you?"

"Possibly. Now as I understand it, your husband was shot on Pine Street, between Leavenworth and Jones, at about three o'clock Tuesday morning. That right?"

"Yes."

"Where was he going?"

"Coming home, I suppose; but I don't know where he had been. Nobody knows. The police haven't found out, if they have tried. He told me Monday evening that he had a business engagement. He was a building contractor, you know. He went out at about half-past eleven, saying he would probably be gone four or five hours."

"Wasn't that an unusual hour to be keeping a business engagement?"

"Not for Bernard. He often had men come to the house at midnight."

"Can you make any guess at all where he was going that night?"

She shook her head with emphasis.

"No. I knew nothing at all about his business affairs, and even the men in his office don't seem to know where he went that night."

That wasn't unlikely. Most of the B. F. Gilmore Construction Company's work had been on city and state contracts, and it isn't altogether unheard-of for secret conferences to go with that kind of work. Your politician-contractor doesn't always move in the open.

"How about enemies?" I asked.

"I don't know anybody that hated him enough to kill him."

"Where does this Kenbrook woman live, do you know?"

"Yes—in the Garford Apartments on Bush Street."

"Nothing you've forgotten to tell me, is there?" I asked, stressing the *me* a little.

"No, I've told you everything I know—every single thing."

CHAPTER II

Walking over to California Street, I shook down my memory for what I had heard here and there of Bernard Gilmore. I could remember a few things—the opposition papers had been in the habit of exposing him every election year—but none of them got me anywhere. I had known him by sight: a boisterous, red-faced man who had hammered his way up from hod-carrier to the ownership of a half-a-million-dollar business and a pretty place in local politics. "A roughneck with a manicure," somebody had called him; a man with a lot of enemies and more friends; a big, good-natured, hard-hitting rowdy.

Odds and ends of a dozen graft scandals in which he had been mixed up, without anybody ever really getting anything on him, flitted through my head as I rode downtown on the too-small outside seat of a cable-car. Then there had been some talk of a bootlegging syndicate of which he was sup-posed to be the head. . . .

I left the car at Kearny Street and walked over to the Hall of Justice. In the detectives' assembly-room I found O'Gar, the detective-sergeant in charge of the Homicide Detail: a squat man of fifty who goes in for wide-brimmed hats of the movie-sheriff sort, but whose little blue eyes and bullet head aren't handicapped by the trick headgear.

"I want some dope on the Gilmore killing," I told him.

"So do I," he came back. "But if you'll come along I'll tell you what little I know while I'm eating. I ain't had lunch yet."

Safe from eavesdroppers in the clatter of a Sutter Street lunch-room, the detective-sergeant leaned over his clam chowder and told me what he knew about the murder, which wasn't much.

"One of the boys, Kelly, was walking his beat early Tuesday morning, coming down the Jones Street hill from California Street to Pine. It was about three o'clock—no fog or nothing—a clear night. Kelly's within maybe twenty feet of Pine Street when he hears a shot. He whisks around the corner, and there's a man dying on the north sidewalk of Pine Street, halfway between Jones and Leavenworth. Nobody else is in sight. Kelly runs up to the man and finds it's Gilmore. Gilmore dies before he can say a word. The doctors say he was knocked down and then shot; because there's a bruise on his forehead, and the bullet slanted upward in his chest. See what I mean? He was lying on his back when the bullet hit him, with his feet pointing toward the gun it came from. It was a .38."

"Any money on him?"

O'Gar fed himself two spoons of chowder and nodded.

"Six hundred smacks, a coupla diamonds and a watch. Nothing touched."

"What was he doing on Pine Street at that time in the morning?"

"Damned if I know, brother. Chances are he was going home, but we can't find out where he'd been. Don't even know what direction he was walking in when he was knocked over. He was lying across the sidewalk with his feet to the curb; but that don't mean nothing—he could of turned around three or four times after he was hit."

"All apartment buildings in that block, aren't there?"

"Uh-huh. There's an alley or two running off from the south side; but Kelly says he could see the mouths of both

alleys when the shot was fired—before he turned the corner—
and nobody got away through them."

"Reckon somebody who lives in that block did the shooting?" I asked.

O'Gar tilted his bowl, scooped up the last drops of the
chowder, put them in his mouth, and grunted.

"Maybe. But we got nothing to show that Gilmore knew
anybody in that block."

"Many people gather around afterward?"

"A few. There's always people on the street to come running if anything happens. But Kelly says there wasn't anybody
that looked wrong—just the ordinary night crowd. The boys
gave the neighborhood a combing, but didn't turn up anything."

"Any cars around?"

"Kelly says there wasn't, that he didn't see any, and couldn't
of missed seeing it if there'd been one."

"What do you think?" I asked.

He got to his feet, glaring at me.

"I don't think," he said disagreeably; "I'm a police detective."

I knew by that that somebody had been panning him for
not finding the murderer.

"I have a line on a woman," I told him. "Want to come
along and talk to her with me?"

"I want to," he growled, "but I can't. I got to be in court
this afternoon—in half an hour."

CHAPTER III

In the vestibule of the Garford Apartments, I pressed the button tagged Miss Cara Kenbrook several times before the door
clicked open. Then I mounted a flight of stairs and walked
down a hall to her door. It was opened presently by a tall girl
of twenty-three or -four in a black and white crepe dress.

"Miss Cara Kenbrook?"

"Yes."

I gave her a card—one of those that tell the truth about
me.

"I'd like to ask you a few questions; may I come in?"

"Do."

Languidly she stepped aside for me to enter, closed the door behind me, and led me back into a living-room that was littered with newspapers, cigarettes in all stages of consumption from unlighted freshness to cold ash, and miscellaneous articles of feminine clothing. She made room for me on a chair by dumping off a pair of pink silk stockings and a hat, and herself sat on some magazines that occupied another chair.

"I'm interested in Bernard Gilmore's death," I said, watching her face.

It wasn't a beautiful face, although it should have been. Everything was there—perfect features; smooth, white skin; big, almost enormous, brown eyes—but the eyes were dead-dull, and the face was as empty of expression as a china door-knob, and what I said didn't change it.

"Bernard Gilmore," she said without interest. "Oh, yes."

"You and he were pretty close friends, weren't you?" I asked, puzzled by her blankness.

"We had been—yes."

"What do you mean by *had been*?"

She pushed back a lock of her short-cut brown hair with a lazy hand.

"I gave him the air last week," she said casually, as if speaking of something that had happened years ago.

"When was the last time you saw him?"

"Last week—Monday, I think—a week before he was killed."

"Was that the time when you broke off with him?"

"Yes."

"Have a row, or part friends?"

"Not exactly either. I just told him that I was through with him."

"How did he take it?"

"It didn't break his heart. I guess he'd heard the same thing before."

"Where were you the night he was killed?"

"At the Coffee Cup, eating and dancing with friends until about one o'clock. Then I came home and went to bed."

"Why did you split with Gilmore?"

"Couldn't stand his wife."

"Huh?"

"She was a nuisance." This without the faintest glint of either annoyance or humor. "She came here one night and raised a racket; so I told Bernie that if he couldn't keep her away from me he'd have to find another playmate."

"Have you any idea who might have killed him?" I asked.

"Not unless it was his wife—these excitable women are always doing silly things."

"If you had given her husband up, what reason would she have for killing him, do you think?"

"I'm sure I don't know," she replied with complete indifference. "But I'm not the only girl that Bernie ever looked at."

"Think there were others, do you? Know anything, or are you just guessing?"

"I don't know any names," she said, "but I'm not just guessing."

I let that go at that and switched back to Mrs. Gilmore, wondering if this girl could be full of dope.

"What happened the night his wife came here?"

"Nothing but that. She followed Bernie here, rang the bell, rushed past me when I opened the door, and began to cry and call Bernie names. Then she started on me, and I told him that if he didn't take her away I'd hurt her, so he took her home."

Admitting I was licked for the time, I got up and moved to the door. I couldn't do anything with this baby just now. I didn't think she was telling the whole truth, but on the other hand it wasn't reasonable to believe that anybody would lie so woodenly—with so little effort to be plausible.

"I may be back later," I said as she let me out.

"All right."

Her manner didn't even suggest that she hoped I wouldn't.

CHAPTER IV

From this unsatisfactory interview I went to the scene of the killing, only a few blocks away, to get a look at the neighborhood. I found the block just as I had remembered it and as

O'Gar had described it: lined on both sides by apartment buildings, with two blind alleys—one of which was dignified with a name, Touchard Street—running from the south side.

The murder was four days old; I didn't waste any time snooping around the vicinity; but, after strolling the length of the block, boarded a Hyde Street car, transferred at California Street, and went up to see Mrs. Gilmore again. I was curious to know why she hadn't told me about her call on Cara Kenbrook.

The same plump maid who had admitted me earlier in the afternoon opened the door.

"Mrs. Gilmore is not at home," she said. "But I think she'll be back in half an hour or so."

"I'll wait," I decided.

The maid took me into the library, an immense room on the second floor, with barely enough books in it to give it that name. She switched on a light—the windows were too heavily curtained to let in much daylight—crossed to the door, stopped, moved over to straighten some books on a shelf, looked at me with a half-questioning, half-inviting look in her green eyes, started for the door again, and halted.

By that time I knew she wanted to say something, and needed encouragement. I leaned back in my chair and grinned at her, and decided I had made a mistake—the smile into which her slack lips curved held more coquetry than anything else. She came over to me, walking with an exaggerated swing of the hips, and stood close in front of me.

"What's on your mind?" I asked.

"Suppose—suppose a person knew something that nobody else knew; what would it be worth to them?"

"That," I stalled, "would depend on how valuable it was."

"Suppose I knew who killed the boss?" She bent her face close down to mine, and spoke in a husky whisper. "What would that be worth?"

"The newspapers say that one of Gilmore's clubs has offered a thousand-dollar reward. You'd get that."

Her green eyes went greedy, and then suspicious.

"If *you* didn't."

I shrugged. I knew she'd go through with it—whatever it was—now; so I didn't even explain to her that the Continental doesn't touch rewards, and doesn't let its hired men touch them.

"I'll give you my word," I said; "but you'll have to use your own judgment about trusting me."

She licked her lips.

"You're a good fellow, I guess. I wouldn't tell the police, because I know they'd beat me out of the money. But you look like I can trust you." She leered into my face. "I used to have a gentleman friend who was the very image of you, and he was the grandest—"

"Better speak your piece before somebody comes in," I suggested.

She shot a look at the door, cleared her throat, licked her loose mouth again, and dropped on one knee beside my chair.

"I was coming home late Monday night—the night the boss was killed—and was standing in the shadows saying good night to my friend, when the boss came out of the house and walked down the street. And he had hardly got to the corner, when she—Mrs. Gilmore—came out, and went down the street after him. Not trying to catch up with him, you understand; but following him. What do you think of that?"

"What do *you* think of it?"

"*I* think that she finally woke up to the fact that all of her Bernie's dates didn't have anything to do with the building business."

"Do you know that they didn't?"

"Do I know it? I knew that man! He liked 'em—liked 'em all." She smiled into my face, a smile that suggested all evil. "I found *that* out soon after I first came here."

"Do you know when Mrs. Gilmore came back that night—what time?"

"Yes," she said; "at half-past three."

"Sure?"

"Absolutely! After I got undressed I got a blanket and sat at the head of the front stairs. My room's in the rear of the top floor. I wanted to see if they came home together, and if there was a fight. After she came in alone I went back to my room, and it was just twenty-five minutes to four then. I looked at my alarm clock."

"Did you see her when she came in?"

"Just the top of her head and shoulders when she turned toward her room at the landing."

"What's your name?" I asked.

"Lina Best."

"All right, Lina," I told her. "If this is the goods I'll see that you collect on it. Keep your eyes open, and if anything else turns up you can get in touch with me at the Continental office. Now you'd better beat it, so nobody will know we've had our heads together."

Alone in the library, I cocked an eye at the ceiling and considered the information Lina Best had given me. But I soon gave that up—no use trying to guess at things that will work out for themselves in a while. I found a book, and spent the next half-hour reading about a sweet young she-chump and a big strong he-chump and all their troubles.

Then Mrs. Gilmore came in, apparently straight from the street.

I got up and closed the doors behind her, while she watched me with wide eyes.

"Mrs. Gilmore," I said, when I faced her again, "why didn't you tell me that you followed your husband the night he was killed?"

"That's a lie!" she cried; but there was no truth in her voice. "That's a lie!"

"Don't you think you're making a mistake?" I urged. "Don't you think you'd better tell me the whole thing?"

She opened her mouth, but only a dry sobbing sound came out; and she began to sway with a hysterical rocking motion, the fingers of one black-gloved hand plucking at her lower lip, twisting and pulling it.

I stepped to her side and set her down in the chair I had been sitting in, making foolish clucking sounds—meant to soothe her—with my tongue. A disagreeable ten minutes—and gradually she pulled herself together; her eyes lost their glassiness, and she stopped clawing at her mouth.

"I did follow him." It was a hoarse whisper, barely audible.

Then she was out of the chair, kneeling, with arms held up to me, and her voice was a thin scream.

"But I didn't kill him! I didn't! Please believe that I didn't!"

I picked her up and put her back in the chair.

"I didn't say you did. Just tell me what did happen."

"I didn't believe him when he said he had a business engagement," she moaned. "I didn't trust him. He had lied to me before. I followed him to see if he went to that woman's rooms."

"Did he?"

"No. He went into an apartment house on Pine Street, in the block where he was killed. I don't know exactly which house it was—I was too far behind him to make sure. But I saw him go up the steps and into one—near the middle of the block."

"And then what did you do?"

"I waited, hiding in a dark doorway across the street. I knew the woman's apartment was on Bush Street, but I thought she might have moved, or be meeting him here. I waited a long time shivering and trembling. It was chilly and I was frightened—afraid somebody would come into the vestibule where I was. But I made myself stay. I wanted to see if he came out alone, or if that woman came out. I had a right to do it—he had deceived me before.

"It was terrible, horrible—crouching there in the dark—cold and scared. Then—it must have been about half-past two—I couldn't stand it any longer. I decided to telephone the woman's apartment and find out if she were home. I went down to an all-night lunchroom on Ellis Street and called her up."

"Was she home?"

"No! I tried for fifteen minutes, or maybe longer, but nobody answered the phone. So I *knew* she was in that Pine Street building."

"And what did you do then?"

"I went back there, determined to wait until he came out. I walked up Jones Street. When I was between Bush and Pine I heard a shot. I thought it was a noise made by an automobile then, but now I know that it was the shot that killed Bernie.

"When I reached the corner of Pine and Jones, I could see a policeman bending over Bernie on the sidewalk, and I saw people gathering around. I didn't know then that it was

Bernie lying on the sidewalk. In the dark and at that distance I couldn't even see whether it was a man or a woman.

"I was afraid that Bernard would come out to see what was going on, or look out of a window, and discover me; so I didn't go down that way. I was afraid to stay in the neighborhood now, for fear the police would ask me what I was doing loitering in the street at three in the morning—and have it come out that I had been following my husband. So I kept on walking up Jones Street, to California, and then straight home."

"And then what?" I led her on.

"Then I went to bed. I didn't go to sleep—lay there worrying over Bernie; but still not thinking it was he I had seen lying in the street. At nine o'clock that morning two police detectives came and told me Bernie had been killed. They questioned me so sharply that I was afraid to tell them the whole truth. If they had known I had reason for being jealous, and had followed my husband that night, they would have accused me of shooting him. And what could I have done? Everybody would have thought me guilty.

"So I didn't say anything about the woman. I thought they'd find the murderer, and then everything would be all right. I didn't think *she* had done it then, or I would have told you the whole thing the first time you were here. But four days went by without the police finding the murderer, and I began to think they suspected *me!* It was terrible! I couldn't go to them and confess that I had lied to them, and I was sure that the woman had killed him and that the police had failed to suspect her because I hadn't told them about her.

"So I employed you. But I was afraid to tell even you the whole truth. I thought that if I just told you there had been another woman and who she was, you could do the rest without having to know that I had followed Bernie that night. I was afraid *you* would think I had killed him, and would turn me over to the police if I told you everything. And now you *do* believe it! And you'll have me arrested! And they'll hang me! I know it! I know it!"

She began to rock crazily from side to side in her chair.

"Sh-h-h," I soothed her. "You're not arrested yet. Sh-h-h."

I didn't know what to make of her story. The trouble with these nervous, hysterical women is that you can't possibly tell when they're lying and when telling the truth unless you have outside evidence—half of the time they themselves don't know.

"When you heard the shot," I went on when she had quieted down a bit, "you were walking north on Jones, between Bush and Pine? You could see the corner of Pine and Jones?"

"Yes—clearly."

"See anybody?"

"No—not until I reached the corner and looked down Pine Street. Then I saw a policeman bending over Bernie, and two men walking toward them."

"Where were the two men?"

"On Pine Street east of Jones. They didn't have hats on— as if they had come out of a house when they heard the shot."

"Any automobiles in sight either before or after you heard the shot?"

"I didn't see or hear any."

"I have some more questions, Mrs. Gilmore," I said; "but I'm in a hurry now. Please don't go out until you hear from me again."

"I won't," she promised; "but—"

I didn't have any answers for anybody's questions, so I ducked my head and left the library.

Near the street door Lina Best appeared out of a shadow, her eyes bright and inquisitive.

"Stick around," I said without any meaning at all, stepped around her, and went on out into the street.

CHAPTER V

I returned then to the Garford Apartments, walking, because I had a lot things to arrange in my mind before I faced Cara Kenbrook again. And, even though I walked slowly, they weren't all exactly filed in alphabetical order when I got there. She had changed the black and white dress for a plush-like gown of bright green, but her empty doll's face hadn't changed.

"Some more questions," I explained when she opened her door.

She admitted me without word or gesture, and led me back into the room where we had talked before.

"Miss Kenbrook," I asked, standing beside the chair she had offered me, "why did you tell me you were home in bed when Gilmore was killed?"

"Because it's so." Without the flicker of a lash.

"And you wouldn't answer the doorbell?"

I had to twist the facts to make my point. Mrs. Gilmore had phoned, but I couldn't afford to give this girl a chance to shunt the blame for her failure to answer off on central.

She hesitated for a split second.

"No—because I didn't hear it."

One cool article, this baby! I couldn't figure her. I didn't know then, and I don't know now, whether she was the owner of the world's best poker face or was just naturally stupid. But whichever she was, she was thoroughly and completely it!

I stopped trying to guess, and got on with my probing.

"And you wouldn't answer the phone either?"

"It didn't ring—or not enough to awaken me."

I chuckled—an artificial chuckle—because central could have been ringing the wrong number. However . . .

"Miss Kenbrook," I lied, "your phone rang at 2:30 and at 2:40 that morning. And your doorbell rang almost continually from about 2:50 until after 3:00."

"Perhaps," she said; "but I wonder who'd be trying to get me at that hour."

"You didn't hear either?"

"No."

"But you were here?"

"Yes—who was it?" carelessly.

"Get your hat," I bluffed, "and I'll show them to you down at headquarters."

She glanced down at the green gown and walked toward an open bedroom door.

"I suppose I'd better get a cloak, too," she said.

"Yes," I advised her; "and bring your toothbrush."

She turned around then and looked at me, and for a moment it seemed that some sort of expression—surprise maybe—was about to come into her big brown eyes; but none actually came. The eyes stayed dull and empty.

"You mean you're arresting me?"

"Not exactly. But if you stick to your story about being home in bed at 3:00 last Tuesday morning I can promise you you *will* be arrested. If I were you I'd think up another story while we're riding down to the Hall of Justice."

She left the doorway slowly and came back into the room, as far as a chair that stood between us, put her hands on its back, and leaned over it to look at me. For perhaps a minute neither of us spoke—just stood there staring at each other, while I tried to keep my face as expressionless as hers.

"Do you really think," she asked at last, "that I wasn't here when Bernie was killed?"

"I'm a busy man, Miss Kenbrook." I put all the certainty I could fake into my voice. "If you want to stick to your funny story, it's all right with me. But please don't expect me to stand here and argue about it. Get your hat and cloak."

She shrugged, and came around the chair on which she had been leaning.

"I suppose you *do* know something," she said, sitting down. "Well, it's tough on Stan, but women and children first."

My ears twitched at the name *Stan*, but I didn't interrupt her.

"I *was* in the Coffee Cup until one o'clock," she was saying, her voice still flat and emotionless. "And I *did* come home afterward. I'd been drinking *vino* all evening, and it always makes me blue. So after I came home I got to worrying over things. Since Bernie and I split finances haven't been so good. I took stock that night—or morning—and found only four dollars in my purse. The rent was due, and the world looked pretty damned blue.

"Half-lit on Dago wine as I was, I decided to run over and see Stan, tell him all my troubles, and make a touch. Stan is a good egg and he's always willing to go the limit for me. Sober, I wouldn't have gone to see him at three in the morning; but it seemed a perfectly sensible thing to do at the time.

"It's only a few minutes' walk from here to Stan's. I went down Bush Street to Leavenworth, and up Leavenworth to Pine. I was in the middle of that last block when Bernie was shot—I heard it. And when I turned the corner into Pine

Street I saw a copper bending over a man on the pavement right in front of Stan's. I hesitated for a couple of minutes, standing in the shadow of a pole, until three or four men had gathered around the man on the sidewalk. Then I went over.

"It was Bernie. And just as I got there I heard the copper tell one of the men that he had been shot. It was an awful shock to me. You know how things like that will hit you!"

I nodded; though God knows there was nothing in this girl's face, manner, or voice to suggest shock. She might have been talking about the weather.

"Dumfounded, not knowing what to do," she went on, "I didn't even stop. I went on, passing as close to Bernie as I am to you now, and rang Stan's bell. He let me in. He had been half-undressed when I rang. His rooms are in the rear of the building, and he hadn't heard the shot, he said. He didn't know Bernie had been killed until I told him. It sort of knocked the wind out of him. He said Bernie had been there—in Stan's rooms—since midnight, and had just left.

"Stan asked me what I was doing there, and I told him my tale of woe. That was the first time Stan knew that Bernie and I were so thick. I met Bernie through Stan, but Stan didn't know we had got so chummy.

"Stan was worried for fear it would come out that Bernie had been to see him that night, because it would make a lot of trouble for him—some sort of shady deal they had on, I guess. So he didn't go out to see Bernie. That's about all there is to it. I got some money from Stan, and stayed in his rooms until the police had cleared out of the neighborhood; because neither of us wanted to get mixed up in anything. Then I came home. That's straight—on the level."

"Why didn't you get this off your chest before?" I demanded, knowing the answer.

It came.

"I was afraid. Suppose I told about Bernie throwing me down, and said I was close to him—a block or so away—when he was killed, and was half-full of vino? The first thing everybody would have said was that I had shot him! I'd lie about it still if I thought you'd believe me."

"So Bernie was the one who broke off, and not you?"

"Oh, yes," she said lightly.

CHAPTER VI

I lit a Fatima and breathed smoke in silence for a while, and the girl sat placidly watching me.

Here I had two women—neither normal. Mrs. Gilmore was hysterical, abnormally nervous. This girl was dull, subnormal. One was the dead man's wife; the other his mistress; and each with reason for believing she had been thrown down for the other. Liars, both; and both finally confessing that they had been near the scene of the crime at the time of the crime, though neither admitted seeing the other. Both, by their own accounts, had been at that time even further from normal than usual—Mrs. Gilmore filled with jealousy; Cara Kenbrook half-drunk.

What was the answer? Either could have killed Gilmore; but hardly both—unless they had formed some sort of crazy partnership, and in that event—

Suddenly all the facts I had gathered—true and false—clicked together in my head. I had the answer—the one simple, satisfying answer!

I grinned at the girl, and set about filling in the gaps in my solution.

"Who is Stan?" I asked.

"Stanley Tennant—he has something to do with the city."

Stanley Tennant. I knew him by reputation, a—

A key rattled in the hall door.

The hall door opened and closed, and a man's footsteps came toward the open doorway of the room in which we were. A tall, broad-shouldered man in tweeds filled the doorway—a ruddy-faced man of thirty-five or so, whose appearance of athletic blond wholesomeness was marred by close-set eyes of an indistinct blue.

Seeing me, he stopped—a step inside the room.

"Hello, Stan!" the girl said lightly. "This gentleman is from the Continental Detective Agency. I've just emptied myself to him about Bernie. Tried to stall him at first, but it was no good."

The man's vague eyes switched back and forth between the girl and me. Around the pale irises his eyeballs were pink.

He straightened his shoulders and smiled too jovially.

"And what conclusion have you come to?" he inquired.

The girl answered for me.

"I've already had *my* invitation to take a ride."

Tennant bent forward. With an unbroken swing of his arms, he swept a chair up from the floor into my face. Not much force behind it, but quick.

I went back against the wall, fending off the chair with both arms—threw it aside—and looked into the muzzle of a nickeled revolver.

A table drawer stood open—the drawer from which he had grabbed the gun while I was busy with the chair. The revolver, I noticed, was of .38 caliber.

"Now," his voice was thick, like a drunk's, "turn around."

I turned my back to him, felt a hand moving over my body, and my gun was taken away.

"All right," he said, and I faced him again.

He stepped back to the girl's side, still holding the nickel-plated revolver on me. My own gun wasn't in sight—in his pocket perhaps. He was breathing noisily, and his eyeballs had gone from pink to red. His face, too, was red, with veins bulging in the forehead.

"You know me?" he snapped.

"Yes, I know you. You're Stanley Tennant, assistant city engineer, and your record is none too lovely." I chattered away on the theory that conversation is always somehow to the advantage of the man who is looking into the gun. "You're supposed to be the lad who supplied the regiment of well-trained witnesses who turned last year's investigation of graft charges against the engineer's office into a comedy. Yes, Mr. Tennant, I know you. You're the answer to why Gilmore was so lucky in landing city contracts with bids only a few dollars beneath his competitors'. Yes, Mr. Tennant, I know you. You're the bright boy who—"

I had a lot more to tell him, but he cut me off.

"That will do out of you!" he yelled. "Unless you want me to knock a corner off your head with this gun."

Then he addressed the girl, not taking his eyes from me.

"Get up, Cara."

She got out of her chair and stood beside him. His gun was in his right hand, and that side was toward her. He moved around to the other side.

The fingers of his left hand hooked themselves inside of the girl's green gown where it was cut low over the swell of her breasts. His gun never wavered from me. He jerked his left hand, ripping her gown down to the waistline.

"*He* did that, Cara," Tennant said.

She nodded.

His fingers slid inside of the flesh-colored undergarment that was now exposed, and he tore that as he had torn the gown.

"*He* did that."

She nodded again.

His bloodshot eyes darted little measuring glances at her face—swift glances that never kept his eyes from me for the flash of time I would have needed to tie into him.

Then—eyes and gun on me—he smashed his left fist into the girl's blank white face.

One whimper—low and not drawn out—came from her as she went down in a huddle against the wall. Her face—well, there wasn't *much* change in it. She looked dumbly up at Tennant from where she had fallen.

"*He* did that," Tennant was saying.

She nodded, got up from the floor, and returned to her chair.

"Here's our story." The man talked rapidly, his eyes alert on me. "Gilmore was never in my rooms in his life, Cara, and neither were you. The night he was killed you were home shortly after one o'clock, and stayed there. You were sick—probably from the wine you had been drinking—and called a doctor. His name is Howard. I'll see that he's fixed. He got here at 2:30 and stayed until 3:30.

"Today, this gum-shoe, learning that you had been intimate with Gilmore, came here to question you. He knew you hadn't killed Gilmore, but he made certain suggestions to you—you can play them up as strong as you like; maybe say that he's been annoying you for months—and when you turned him down he threatened to frame you.

"You refused to have anything to do with him, and he grabbed you, tearing your clothes, and bruising your face when you resisted. I happened to come along then, having an engagement with you, and heard you scream. Your front door was unlocked, so I rushed in, pulled this fellow away, and disarmed him. Then we held him until the police—whom we will phone for—came. Got that?"

"Yes, Stan."

"Good! Now listen: When the police get here this fellow will spill all he knows, of course, and the chances are that all three of us will be taken in. That's why I want you to know what's what right now. I ought to have enough pull to get you and me out on bail tonight, or, if worst comes to worst, to see that my lawyer gets to me tonight—so I can arrange for the witnesses we'll need. Also I ought to be able to fix it so our little fat friend will be held for a day or two, and not allowed to see anybody until late tomorrow—which will give us a good start on him. I don't know how much he knows, but between your story and the stories of a couple of other smart little ladies I have in mind, I'll fix him up with a rep that will keep any jury in the world from ever believing him about anything."

"How do you like that?" he asked me, triumphantly.

"You big clown," I laughed at him, "I think it's funny!"

But I didn't really think so. In spite of what I thought I knew about Gilmore's murder—in spite of my simple, satisfactory solution—something was crawling up my back, my knees felt jerky, and my hands were wet with sweat. I had had people try to frame me before—no detective stays in the business long without having it happen—but I had never got used to it. There's a peculiar deadliness about the thing—especially if you know how erratic juries can be—that makes your flesh crawl, no matter how safe your judgment tells you you are.

"Phone the police," Tennant told the girl; "and for God's sake keep your story straight!"

As he tried to impress that necessity on the girl his eyes left me.

I was perhaps five feet from him and his level gun.

A jump—not straight at him—off to one side—put me close.

The gun roared under my arm. I was surprised not to feel the bullet. It seemed that he *must* have hit me.

There wasn't a second shot.

I looped my right fist over as I jumped. It landed when I landed. It took him too high—up on the cheekbone—but it rocked him back a couple of steps.

I didn't know what had happened to his gun. It wasn't in his hand any more. I didn't stop to look for it. I was busy, crowding him back—not letting him set himself—staying close to him—driving at him with both hands.

He was a head taller than I, and had longer arms, but he wasn't any heavier or stronger. I suppose he hit me now and then as I hammered him across the room. He must have. But I didn't feel anything.

I worked him into a corner. Jammed him back in a corner with his legs cramped under him—which didn't give him much leverage to hit from. I got my left arm around his body, holding him where I wanted him. And I began to throw my right fist into him.

I liked that. His belly was flabby, and it got softer every time I hit it. I hit it often.

He was chopping at my face, but by digging my nose into his chest and holding it there I kept my beauty from being altogether ruined. Meanwhile I threw my right fist into him.

Then I became aware that Cara Kenbrook was moving around behind me; and I remembered the revolver that had fallen somewhere when I had charged Tennant. I didn't like that; but there was nothing I could do about it—except put more weight in my punches. My own gun, I thought, was in one of his pockets. But neither of us had time to hunt for it now.

Tennant's knees sagged the next time I hit him.

Once more, I said to myself, and then I'll step back, let him have one on the button, and watch him fall.

But I didn't get that far.

Something that I knew was the missing revolver struck me on the top of the head. An ineffectual blow—not clean enough to stun me—but it took the steam out of my punches.

Another.

They weren't hard, these taps, but to hurt a skull with a hunk of metal you don't have to hit it hard.

I tried to twist away from the next bump, and failed. Not only failed, but let Tennant wiggle away from me.

That was the end.

I wheeled on the girl just in time to take another rap on the head, and then one of Tennant's fists took me over the ear.

I went down in one of those falls that get pugs called quitters—my eyes were open, my mind was alive, but my legs and arms wouldn't lift me up from the floor.

Tennant took my own gun out of a pocket, and with it held on me, sat down in a Morris chair, to gasp for the air I had pounded out of him. The girl sat in another chair; and I, finding I could manage it, sat up in the middle of the floor and looked at them.

Tennant spoke, still panting.

"This is fine—all the signs of a struggle we need to make our story good!"

"If they don't believe you were in a fight," I suggested sourly, pressing my aching head with both hands, "you can strip and show them your little tummy."

"And you can show them this!"

He leaned down and split my lip with a punch that spread me on my back.

Anger brought my legs to life. I got up on them. Tennant moved around behind the Morris chair. My black gun was steady in his hand.

"Go easy," he warned me. "My story will work if I have to kill you—maybe work better."

That was sense. I stood still.

"Phone the police, Cara," he ordered.

She went out of the room, closing the door behind her; and all I could hear of her talk was a broken murmur.

CHAPTER VII

Ten minutes later three uniformed policemen arrived. All three knew Tennant, and they treated him with respect. Tennant reeled off the story he and the girl had cooked up, with a few changes to take care of the shot that had been fired from the nickeled gun and our rough-house. She nodded her head vigorously whenever a policeman looked at her. Tennant turned both guns over to the white-haired sergeant in charge.

I didn't argue, didn't deny anything, but told the sergeant:

"I'm working with Detective-Sergeant O'Gar on a job. I want to talk to him over the phone and then I want you to take all three of us down to the detective bureau."

Tennant objected to that, of course; not because he expected to gain anything, but on the off-chance that he might. The white-haired sergeant looked from one of us to the other in puzzlement. Me, with my skinned face and split lip; Tennant, with a red lump under one eye where my first wallop had landed; and the girl, with most of the clothes above the waistline ripped off and a bruised cheek.

"It has a queer look, this thing," the sergeant decided aloud; "and I shouldn't wonder but what the detective bureau was the place for the lot of you."

One of the patrolmen went into the hall with me, and I got O'Gar on the phone at his home. It was nearly ten o'clock by now, and he was preparing for bed.

"Cleaning up the Gilmore murder," I told him. "Meet me at the Hall. Will you get hold of Kelly, the patrolman who found Gilmore, and bring him down there? I want him to look at some people."

"I will that," O'Gar promised, and I hung up.

The "wagon" in which the three policemen had answered Cara Kenbrook's call carried us down to the Hall of Justice, where we all went into the captain of detectives' office. McTighe, a lieutenant, was on duty.

I knew McTighe, and we were on pretty good terms; but I wasn't an influence in local politics, and Tennant was. I don't mean that McTighe would have knowingly helped Tennant frame me; but with me stacked up against the assistant city engineer, I knew who would get the benefit of any doubt there might be.

My head was thumping and roaring just now, with knots all over it where the girl had beaned me. I sat down, kept quiet, and nursed my head while Tennant and Cara Kenbrook, with a lot of details that they had not wasted on the uniformed men, told their tale and showed their injuries.

Tennant was talking—describing the terrible scene that had met his eyes when, drawn by the girl's screams, he had rushed into her apartment—when O'Gar came into the office. He recognized Tennant with a lifted eyebrow, and came over to sit beside me.

"What the hell is all this?" he muttered.

"A lovely mess," I whispered back. "Listen—in that nickel gun on the desk there's an empty shell. Get it for me."

He scratched his head doubtfully, listened to the next few words of Tennant's yarn, glanced at me out of the corner of his eye, and then went over to the desk and picked up the revolver.

McTighe looked at him—a sharp, questioning look.

"Something on the Gilmore killing," the detective-sergeant said, breaking the gun.

The lieutenant started to speak, changed his mind, and O'Gar brought the shell over and handed it to me.

"Thanks," I said, putting it in my pocket. "Now listen to my friend there. It's a good act, if you like it."

Tennant was winding up his history.

". . . Naturally a man who tried a thing like that on an un-protected woman would be yellow; so it wasn't very hard to handle him after I got his gun away from him. I hit him a couple of times, and he quit—begging me to stop, getting down on his knees. Then we called the police."

McTighe looked at me with eyes that were cold and hard. Tennant had made a believer of him, and not only of him—the police-sergeant and his two men were glowering at me. I suspected that even O'Gar—with whom I had been through a dozen storms—would have been half-convinced if the engi-neer hadn't added the neat touches about my kneeling.

"Well, what have *you* got to say?" McTighe challenged me in a tone which suggested that it didn't make much difference what I said.

"I've got nothing to say about this dream," I said shortly. "I'm interested in the Gilmore murder—not in this stuff." I turned to O'Gar. "Is the patrolman here?"

The detective-sergeant went to the door, and called: "Oh, Kelly!"

Kelly came in—a big, straight-standing man, with iron-gray hair and an intelligent fat face.

"You found Gilmore's body?" I asked.

"I did."

I pointed at Cara Kenbrook.

"Ever see her before?"

His gray eyes studied her carefully.

"Not that I remember," he answered.

"Did she come up the street while you were looking at Gilmore, and go into the house he was lying in front of?"

"She did not."

I took out the empty shell O'Gar had got for me, and chucked it down on the desk in front of the patrolman.

"Kelly," I asked, *"why did you kill Gilmore?"*

Kelly's right hand went under his coat-tail at his hip.

I jumped for him.

Somebody grabbed me by the neck. Somebody else piled on my back. McTighe aimed a big fist at my face, but it missed. My legs had been suddenly kicked from under me, and I went down hard with men all over me.

When I was yanked to my feet again, big Kelly stood straight up by the desk, weighing his service revolver in his hand. His clear eyes met mine, and he laid the weapon on the desk. Then he unfastened his shield and put it with the gun.

"It was an accident," he said simply.

By this time the birds who had been manhandling me woke up to the fact that maybe they were missing part of the play—that maybe I wasn't a maniac. Hands dropped off me; and presently everybody was listening to Kelly.

He told his story with unhurried evenness, his eyes never wavering or clouding. A deliberate man, though unlucky.

"I was walkin' my beat that night, an' as I turned the corner of Jones into Pine I saw a man jump back from the steps of a buildin' into the vestibule. A burglar, I thought, an' cat-footed it down there. It was a dark vestibule, an' deep, an' I saw somethin' that looked like a man in it, but I wasn't sure.

" 'Come out o' there!' I called, but there was no answer. I took my gun in my hand an' started up the steps. I saw him move just then, comin' out. An' then my foot slipped. It was worn smooth, the bottom step, an' my foot slipped. I fell forward, the gun went off, an' the bullet hit him. He had come out a ways by then, an' when the bullet hit him he toppled over frontwise, tumblin' down the steps onto the sidewalk.

"When I looked at him I saw it was Gilmore. I knew him to say 'howdy' to, an' he knew me—which is why he must o' ducked out of sight when he saw me comin' around the corner. He didn't want me to see him comin' out of a buildin' where I knew Mr. Tennant lived, I suppose, thinkin' I'd put two an' two together, an' maybe talk.

"I don't say that I did the right thing by lyin', but it didn't hurt anybody. It was an accident; but he was a man with a lot of friends up in high places, an'—accident or no—I stood a good chance of bein' broke, an' maybe sent over for a while. So I told my story the way you people know it. I couldn't say I'd seen anything suspicious without maybe puttin' the blame on some innocent party, an' I didn't want that. I'd made up my mind that if anybody was arrested for the murder, an' things looked bad for them, I'd come out an' say I'd done it. Home, you'll find a confession all written out—written out in case somethin' happened to me—so nobody else'd ever be blamed.

"That's why I had to say I'd never seen the lady here. I did see her—saw her go into the buildin' that night—the buildin' Gilmore had come out of. But I couldn't say so without makin' it look bad for her; so I lied. I could have thought up a better story if I'd had more time, I don't doubt; but I had to think quick. Anyways, I'm glad it's all over."

CHAPTER VIII

Kelly and the other uniformed policeman had left the office, which now held McTighe, O'Gar, Cara Kenbrook, Tennant and me. Tennant had crossed to my side, and was apologizing.

"I hope you'll let me square myself for this evening's work. But you know how it is when somebody you care for is in a jam. I'd have killed you if I had thought it would help Cara—on the level. Why didn't you tell us that you didn't suspect her?"

"But I did suspect the pair of you," I said. "It looked as if Kelly had to be the guilty one; but you people carried on so much that I began to feel doubtful. For a while it was funny— you thinking she had done it, and she thinking you had, though I suppose each had sworn to his or her innocence. But after a time it stopped being funny. You carried it too far."

"How did you rap to Kelly?" O'Gar, at my shoulder, asked.

"Miss Kenbrook was walking north on Leavenworth—and was half-way between Bush and Pine—when the shot was fired. She saw nobody, no cars, until she rounded the corner. Mrs. Gilmore, walking north on Jones, was about the same distance away when *she* heard the shot, and she saw nobody until she reached Pine Street. If Kelly had been telling the truth, she would have seen him on Jones Street. He said he didn't turn the corner until after the shot was fired.

"Either of the women could have killed Gilmore, but hardly both; and I doubted that either could have shot him and got away without running into Kelly or the other. Suppose both of them were telling the truth—what then? Kelly must have been lying! He was the logical suspect any-way—the nearest known person to the murdered man when the shot was fired.

"To back all this up, he had let Miss Kenbrook go into the apartment building at 3:00 in the morning, in front of which a man had just been killed, without questioning her or men-tioning her in his report. That looked as if he *knew* who had done the killing. So I took a chance with the empty shell trick, it being a good bet that he would have thrown his away, and would think that—"

McTighe's heavy voice interrupted my explanation.

"How about this assault charge?" he asked, and had the de-cency to avoid my eye when I turned toward him with the others.

Tennant cleared his throat.

"Er—ah—in view of the way things have turned out, and knowing that Miss Kenbrook doesn't want the disagreeable publicity that would accompany an affair of this sort, why, I'd suggest that we drop the whole thing." He smiled brightly from McTighe to me. "You know nothing has gone on the records yet."

"Make the big heap play his hand out," O'Gar growled in my ear. "Don't let him drop it."

"Of course if Miss Kenbrook doesn't want to press the charge," McTighe was saying, watching me out of the tail of his eye, "I suppose—"

"If everybody understands that the whole thing was a plant," I said, "and if the policemen who heard the story are brought in here now and told by Tennant and Miss Kenbrook that it was all a lie—then I'm willing to let it go at that. Otherwise, I won't stand for a hush-up."

"You're a damned fool!" O'Gar whispered. "Put the screws on them!"

But I shook my head. I didn't see any sense in making a lot of trouble for myself just to make some for somebody else— and suppose Tennant *proved* his story . . .

So the policemen were found, and brought into the office again, and told the truth.

And presently Tennant, the girl, and I were walking together like three old friends through the corridors toward the door, Tennant still asking me to let him make amends for the evening's work.

"You've *got* to let me do something!" he insisted. "It's only right!"

His hand dipped into his coat, and came out with a thick bill-fold.

"Here," he said; "let me—"

We were going, at that happy moment, down the stone vestibule steps that lead to Kearny Street—six or seven steps there are.

"No," I said; "let me—"

He was on the next to the top step, when I reached up and let go.

He settled in a rather limp pile at the bottom.

Leaving his empty-faced lady love to watch over him, I strolled up through Portsmouth Square toward a restaurant where the steaks come thick.

The Golden Horseshoe

I HAVEN'T anything very exciting to offer you this time," Vance Richmond said as we shook hands. "I want you to find a man for me—a man who is not a criminal."

There was an apology in his voice. The last couple of jobs this lean, grey-faced attorney had thrown my way had run to gun-play and other forms of rioting, and I suppose he thought anything less than that would put me to sleep. Was a time when he might have been right—when I was a young sprout of twenty or so, newly attached to the Continental Detective Agency. But the fifteen years that had slid by since then had dulled my appetite for rough stuff. I don't mean that I shuddered whenever I considered the possibility of some bird taking a poke at me; but I didn't call that day a total loss in which nobody tried to puncture my short, fat carcass.

"The man I want found," the lawyer went on, as we sat down, "is an English architect named Norman Ashcraft. He is a man of about thirty-seven, five feet ten inches tall, well built, and fair-skinned, with light hair and blue eyes. Four years ago he was a typical specimen of the clean-cut blond Britisher. He may not be like that now—those four years have been rather hard ones for him, I imagine.

"I want to find him for Mrs. Ashcraft, his wife. I know your Agency's rule against meddling with family affairs, but I can assure you that no matter how things turn out there will be no divorce proceedings in which you will be involved.

"Here is the story. Four years ago the Ashcrafts were living together in England, in Bristol. It seems that Mrs. Ashcraft is of a very jealous disposition, and he was rather high-strung. Furthermore, he had only what money he earned at his profession, while she had inherited quite a bit from her parents. Ashcraft was rather foolishly sensitive about being the husband of a wealthy woman—was inclined to go out of his way to show that he was not dependent upon her money, that he wouldn't be influenced by it. Foolish, of course, but just the sort of attitude a man of his temperament would assume. One

night she accused him of paying too much attention to another woman. They quarreled, and he packed up and left.

"She was repentant within a week—especially repentant
since she had learned that her suspicion had had no foundation outside of her own jealousy—and she tried to find him.
But he was gone. It became manifest that he had left England. She had him searched for in Europe, in Canada, in Australia, and in the United States. She succeeded in tracing him
from Bristol to New York, and then to Detroit, where he had
been arrested and fined for disturbing the peace in a drunken
row of some sort. After that he dropped out of sight until he
bobbed up in Seattle ten months later."

The attorney hunted through the papers on his desk and
found a memorandum.

"On May 23, 1923, he shot and killed a burglar in his room
in a hotel there. The Seattle police seem to have suspected
that there was something funny about the shooting, but had
nothing to hold Ashcraft on. The man he killed was undoubtedly a burglar. Then Ashcraft disappeared again, and
nothing was heard of him until just about a year ago. Mrs.
Ashcraft had advertisements inserted in the personal columns
of papers in the principal American cities.

"One day she received a letter from him, from San
Francisco. It was a very formal letter, and simply requested
her to stop advertising. Although he was through with the
name Norman Ashcraft, he wrote, he disliked seeing it published in every newspaper he read.

"She mailed a letter to him at the General Delivery window
here, and used another advertisement to tell him about it. He
answered it, rather caustically. She wrote him again, asking
him to come home. He refused, though he seemed less bitter
toward her. They exchanged several letters, and she learned
that he had become a drug addict, and what was left of his
pride would not let him return to her until he looked—and
was at least somewhat like—his former self. She persuaded
him to accept enough money from her to straighten himself
out. She sent him this money each month, in care of General
Delivery, here.

"Meanwhile she closed up her affairs in England—she had
no close relatives to hold her there—and came to San Fran-

cisco, to be on hand when her husband was ready to return to her. A year has gone. She still sends him money each month. She still waits for him to come back to her. He has repeatedly refused to see her, and his letters are evasive—filled with accounts of the struggle he is having, making headway against the drug one month, slipping back the next.

"She suspects by now, of course, that he has no intention of ever coming back to her; that he does not intend giving up the drug; that he is simply using her as a source of income. I have urged her to discontinue the monthly allowance for a while. That would at least bring about an interview, I think, and she could learn definitely what to expect. But she will not do that. You see, she blames herself for his present condition. She thinks her foolish flare of jealousy is responsible for his plight, and she is afraid to do anything that might either hurt him or induce him to hurt himself further. Her mind is unchangeably made up in that respect. She wants him back, wants him straightened out; but if he will not come, then she is content to continue the payments for the rest of his life. But she wants to know what she is to expect. She wants to end this devilish uncertainty in which she has been living.

"What we want, then, is for you to find Ashcraft. We want to know whether there is any likelihood of his ever becoming a man again, or whether he is gone beyond redemption. There is your job. Find him, learn whatever you can about him, and then, after we know something, we will decide whether it is wiser to force an interview between them—in hopes that she will be able to influence him—or not."

"I'll try it," I said. "When does Mrs. Ashcraft send him his monthly allowance?"

"On the first of each month."

"Today is the twenty-eighth. That'll give me three days to wind up a job I have on hand. Got a photo of him?"

"Unfortunately, no. In her anger immediately after their row, Mrs. Ashcraft destroyed everything she had that would remind her of him. But I don't think a photograph would be of any great help at the post office. Without consulting me, Mrs. Ashcraft watched for her husband there on several occasions, and did not see him. It is more than likely that he has someone else call for his mail."

I got up and reached for my hat.

"See you around the second of the month," I said, as I left the office.

II

On the afternoon of the first, I went down to the post office and got hold of Lusk, the inspector in charge of the division at the time.

"I've got a line on a scratcher from up north," I told Lusk, "who is supposed to be getting his mail at the window. Will you fix it up so I can get a spot on him?"

Post office inspectors are all tied up with rules and regulations that forbid their giving assistance to private detectives except on certain criminal matters. But a friendly inspector doesn't have to put you through the third degree. You lie to him—so that he will have an alibi in case there's a kick-back—and whether he thinks you're lying or not doesn't matter.

So presently I was downstairs again, loitering within sight of the A to D window, with the clerk at the window instructed to give me the office when Ashcraft's mail was called for. There was no mail for him there at the time. Mrs. Ashcraft's letter would hardly get to the clerks that afternoon, but I was taking no chances. I stayed on the job until the windows closed at eight o'clock, and then went home.

At a few minutes after ten the next morning I got my action. One of the clerks gave me the signal. A small man in a blue suit and a soft gray hat was walking away from the window with an envelope in his hand. A man of perhaps forty years, though he looked older. His face was pasty, his feet dragged, and, although his clothes were fairly new, they needed brushing and pressing.

He came straight to the desk in front of which I stood fiddling with some papers. Out of the tail of my eye I saw that he had not opened the envelope in his hand—was not going to open it. He took a large envelope from his pocket, and I got just enough of a glimpse of its front to see that it was already stamped and addressed. I twisted my neck out of joint trying to read the address, but failed. He kept the addressed side against his body, put the letter he had got from the

window in it, and licked the flap backward, so that there was
no possible way for anybody to see the front of the envelope.
Then he rubbed the flap down carefully and turned toward
the mailing slots. I went after him. There was nothing to do
but to pull the always reliable stumble.

I overtook him, stepped close and faked a fall on the marble floor, bumping into him, grabbing him as if to regain my
balance. It went rotten. In the middle of my stunt my foot
really did slip, and we went down on the floor like a pair of
wrestlers, with him under me. To botch the trick thoroughly,
he fell with the envelope pinned under him.

I scrambled up, yanked him to his feet, mumbled an apology and almost had to push him out of the way to beat him
to the envelope that lay face down on the floor. I had to turn
it over as I handed it to him in order to get the address:

> *Mr. Edward Bohannon,*
> *Golden Horseshoe Cafe,*
> *Tijuana, Baja California, Mexico.*

I had the address, but I had tipped my mitt. There was no
way in God's world for this little man in blue to miss knowing that I had been trying to get that address.

I dusted myself off while he put his envelope through a
slot. He didn't come back past me, but went on down toward
the Mission Street exit. I couldn't let him get away with what
he knew. I didn't want Ashcraft tipped off before I got to
him. I would have to try another trick as ancient as the one
the slippery floor had bungled for me. I set out after the
little man again.

Just as I reached his side he turned his head to see if he was
being followed.

"Hello, Micky!" I hailed him. "How's everything in Chi?"

"You got me wrong." He spoke out of the side of his gray-
lipped mouth, not stopping. "I don't know nothin' about
Chi."

His eyes were pale blue, with needle-point pupils—the eyes
of a heroin or morphine user.

"Quit stalling." I walked along at his side. We had left the
building by this time and were going down Mission Street.
"You fell off the rattler only this morning."

He stopped on the sidewalk and faced me.

"Me? Who do you think I am?"

"You're Micky Parker. The Dutchman gave us the rap that you were headed here. They got him—if you don't already know it."

"You're cuckoo," he sneered. "I don't know what the hell you're talkin' about!"

That was nothing—neither did I. I raised my right hand in my overcoat pocket.

"Now I'll tell one," I growled at him. "And keep your hands away from your clothes or I'll let the guts out of you."

He flinched away from my bulging pocket.

"Hey, listen, brother!" he begged. "You got me wrong—on the level. My name ain't Micky Parker, an' I ain't been in Chi in six years. I been here in Frisco for a solid year, an' that's the truth."

"You got to show me."

"I can do it," he exclaimed, all eagerness. "You come down the drag with me, an' I'll show you. My name's Ryan, an' I been livin' aroun' the corner here on Sixth Street for six or eight months."

"Ryan?" I asked.

"Yes—John Ryan."

I chalked that up against him. Of course there have been Ryans christened John, but not enough of them to account for the number of times that name appears in criminal records. I don't suppose there are three old-time yeggs in the country who haven't used the name at least once; it's the John Smith of yeggdom.

This particular John Ryan led me around to a house on Sixth Street, where the landlady—a rough-hewn woman of fifty, with bare arms that were haired and muscled like the village smithy's—assured me that her tenant had to her positive knowledge been in San Francisco for months, and that she remembered seeing him at least once a day for a couple of weeks back. If I had been really suspicious that this Ryan was my mythical Micky Parker from Chicago, I wouldn't have taken the woman's word for it, but as it was I pretended to be satisfied.

That seemed to be all right then. Mr. Ryan had been led astray, had been convinced that I had mistaken him for another crook, and that I was not interested in the Ashcraft letter. I would be safe—reasonably safe—in letting the situation go as it stood. But loose ends worry me. And you can't always count on people doing and thinking what you want. This bird was a hop-head, and he had given me a phoney-sounding name, so . . .

"What do you do for a living?" I asked him.

"I ain't been doin' nothin' for a coupla months," he pattered, "but I expec' to open a lunch room with a fella nex' week."

"Let's go up to your room," I suggested. "I want to talk to you."

He wasn't enthusiastic, but he took me up. He had two rooms and a kitchen on the third floor. They were dirty, foul-smelling rooms. I dangled a leg from the corner of a table and waved him into a squeaky rocking chair in front of me. His pasty face and dopey eyes were uneasy.

"Where's Ashcraft?" I threw at him.

He jerked, and then looked at the floor.

"I don't know what you're talkin' about," he mumbled.

"You'd better figure it out," I advised him, "or there's a nice cool cell down in the booby-hutch that will be wrapped around you."

"You ain't got nothin' on me."

"What of that? How'd you like to do a thirty or a sixty on a vag charge?"

"Vag, hell!" he snarled, looking up at me. "I got five hundred smacks in my kick. Does that look like you can vag me?"

I grinned down at him.

"You know better than that, Ryan. A pocketful of money'll get you nothing in California. You've got no job. You can't show where your money comes from. You're made to order for the vag law."

I had this bird figured as a dope pedler. If he was—or was anything else off color that might come to light when he was vagged—the chances were that he would be willing to sell Ashcraft out to save himself; especially since, so far as I knew, Ashcraft wasn't on the wrong side of the criminal law.

"If I were you," I went on while he stared at the floor and thought, "I'd be a nice, obliging fellow and do my talking now. You're—"

He twisted sidewise in his chair and one of his hands went behind him.

I kicked him out of his chair.

The table slipped under me or I would have stretched him. As it was, the foot that I aimed at his jaw took him on the chest and carried him over backward, with the rocking-chair piled on top of him. I pulled the chair off and took his gun—a cheap nickel-plated .32. Then I went back to my seat on the corner of the table.

He had only that one flash of fight in him. He got up sniveling.

"I'll tell you. I don't want no trouble, an' it ain't nothin' to me. I didn't know there was nothin' wrong. This Ashcraft told me he was jus' stringin' his wife along. He give me ten bucks a throw to get his letter ever' month an' send it to him in Tijuana. I knowed him here, an' when he went south six months ago—he's got a girl down there—I promised I'd do it for him. I knowed it was money—he said it was his 'alimony'—but I didn't know there was nothin' wrong."

"What sort of a hombre is this Ashcraft? What's his graft?"

"I don't know. He could be a con man—he's got a good front. He's a Englishman, an' mostly goes by the name of Ed Bohannon. He hits the hop. I don't use it myself"—that was a good one—"but you know how it is in a burg like this, a man runs into all kinds of people. I don't know nothin' about what he's up to. I jus' send the money ever' month an' get my ten."

That was all I could get out of him. He couldn't—or wouldn't—tell me where Ashcraft had lived in San Francisco or who he had mobbed up with. However, I had learned that Bohannon was Ashcraft, and not another go-between, and that was something.

Ryan squawked his head off when he found that I was going to vag him anyway. For a moment it looked like I would have to kick him loose from his backbone again.

"You said you'd spring me if I talked," he wailed.

"I did not. But if I had—when a gent flashes a rod on me I figure it cancels any agreement we might have had. Come on."

I couldn't afford to let him run around loose until I got in touch with Ashcraft. He would have been sending a telegram before I was three blocks away, and my quarry would be on his merry way to points north, east, south and west.

It was a good hunch I played in nabbing Ryan. When he was finger-printed at the Hall of Justice he turned out to be one Fred Rooney, alias "Jamocha," a pedler and smuggler who had crushed out of the Federal Prison at Leavenworth, leaving eight years of a tenner still unserved.

"Will you sew him up for a couple of days?" I asked the captain of the city jail. "I've got work to do that will go smoother if he can't get any word out for a while."

"Sure," the captain promised. "The federal people won't take him off our hands for two or three days. I'll keep him air-tight till then."

III

From the jail I went up to Vance Richmond's office and turned my news over to him.

"Ashcraft is getting his mail in Tijuana. He's living down there under the name of Ed Bohannon, and maybe has a woman there. I've just thrown one of his friends—the one who handled the mail and an escaped con—in the cooler."

"Was that necessary?" Richmond asked. "We don't want to work any hardships. We're really trying to help Ashcraft, you know."

"I could have spared this bird," I admitted. "But what for. He was all wrong. If Ashcraft can be brought back to his wife, he's better off with some of his shady friends out of the way. If he can't, what's the difference? Anyway, we've got one line on him safely stowed away where we can find it when we want it."

The attorney shrugged, and reached for the telephone.

He called a number. "Is Mrs. Ashcraft there? . . . This is Mr. Richmond. . . . No, we haven't exactly found him, but I think we know where he is. . . . Yes. . . . In about fifteen minutes."

He put down the telephone and stood up.

"We'll run up to Mrs. Ashcraft's house and see her."

Fifteen minutes later we were getting out of Richmond's car in Jackson Street near Gough. The house was a three-story white stone building, set behind a carefully sodded little lawn with an iron railing around it.

Mrs. Ashcraft received us in a drawing-room on the second floor. A tall woman of less than thirty, slimly beautiful in a gray dress. Clear was the word that best fits her; it described the blue of her eyes, the pink-white of her skin, and the light brown of her hair.

Richmond introduced me to her, and then I told her what I had learned, omitting the part about the woman in Tijuana. Nor did I tell her that the chances were her husband was a crook nowadays.

"Mr. Ashcraft is in Tijuana, I have been told. He left San Francisco about six months ago. His mail is being forwarded to him in care of a cafe there, under the name of Edward Bohannon."

Her eyes lighted up happily, but she didn't throw a fit. She wasn't that sort. She addressed the attorney.

"Shall I go down? Or will you?"

Richmond shook his head.

"Neither. You certainly shouldn't go, and I cannot—not at present. I must be in Eureka by the day after tomorrow, and shall have to spend several days there." He turned to me. "You'll have to go. You can no doubt handle it better than I could. You will know what to do and how to do it. There are no definite instructions I can give you. Your course will have to depend on Mr. Ashcraft's attitude and condition. Mrs. Ashcraft doesn't wish to force herself on him, but neither does she wish to leave anything undone that might help him."

Mrs. Ashcraft held a strong, slender hand out to me.

"You will do whatever you think wisest."

It was partly a question, partly an expression of confidence.

"I will," I promised.

I liked this Mrs. Ashcraft.

IV

Tijuana hadn't changed much in the two years I had been away. Still the same six or seven hundred feet of dusty and dingy street running between two almost solid rows of saloons,—perhaps thirty-five of them to a row,—with dirtier side streets taking care of the dives that couldn't find room on the main street.

The automobile that had brought me down from San Diego dumped me into the center of the town early in the afternoon, and the day's business was just getting under way. That is, there were only two or three drunks wandering around among the dogs and loafing Mexicans in the street, although there was already a bustle of potential drunks moving from one saloon to the next. But this was nothing like the crowd that would be here the following week, when the season's racing started.

In the middle of the next block I saw a big gilded horseshoe. I went down the street and into the saloon behind the sign. It was a fair sample of the local joint. A bar on your left as you came in, running half the length of the building, with three or four slot machines on one end. Across from the bar, against the right-hand wall, a dance floor that ran from the front wall to a raised platform, where a greasy orchestra was now preparing to go to work. Behind the orchestra was a row of low stalls or booths, with open fronts and a table and two benches apiece. Opposite them, in the space between the bar and the rear of the building, a man with a hair-lip was shaking pills out of a keno goose.

It was early in the day, and there were only a few buyers present, so the girls whose business it is to speed the sale of drinks charged down on me in a flock.

"Buy me a drink? Let's have a little drink? Buy a drink, honey?"

I shooed them away—no easy job—and caught a bartender's eye. He was a beefy, red-faced Irishman, with sorrel hair plastered down in two curls that hid what little forehead he had.

"I want to see Ed Bohannon," I told him confidentially.

He turned blank fish-green eyes on me.

"I don't know no Ed Bohannon."

Taking out a piece of paper and a pencil I scribbled, *Jamocha is copped*, and slid the paper over to the bartender.

"If a man who says he's Ed Bohannon asks for that, will you give it to him?"

"I guess so."

"Good," I said. "I'll hang around a while."

I walked down the room and sat at a table in one of the stalls. A lanky girl who had done something to her hair that made it purple was camped beside me before I had settled in my seat.

"Buy me a little drink?" she asked.

The face she made at me was probably meant for a smile. Whatever it was, it beat me. I was afraid she'd do it again, so I surrendered.

"Yes," I said, and ordered a bottle of beer for myself from the waiter who was already hanging over my shoulder.

The beer wasn't bad, for green beer; but at four bits a bottle it wasn't anything to write home about. This Tijuana happens to be in Mexico—by about a mile—but it's an American town, run by Americans, who sell American artificial booze at American prices. If you know your way around the United States you can find lots of places—especially near the Canadian line—where good booze can be bought for less than you are soaked for poison in Tijuana.

The purple-haired woman at my side downed her shot of whiskey, and was opening her mouth to suggest that we have another drink,—hustlers down there don't waste any time at all,—when a voice spoke from behind me.

"Cora, Frank wants you."

Cora scowled, looking over my shoulder.

Then she made that damned face at me again, said "All right, Kewpie. Will you take care of my friend here?" and left me.

Kewpie slid into the seat beside me. She was a little chunky girl of perhaps eighteen—not a day more than that. Just a kid. Her short hair was brown and curly over a round, boyish face with laughing, impudent eyes. Rather a cute little trick.

I bought her a drink and got another bottle of beer.

"What's on your mind?" I asked her.

"Hooch." She grinned at me—a grin that was as boyish as the straight look of her brown eyes. "Gallons of it."

"And besides that?"

I knew this switching of girls on me hadn't been purposeless.

"I hear you're looking for a friend of mine," Kewpie said.

"That might be. What friends have you got?"

"Well, there's Ed Bohannon for one. You know Ed?"

I shook my head.

"No—not yet."

"But you're looking for him?"

"Uh-huh."

"Maybe I could tell you how to find him, if I knew you were all right."

"It doesn't make any difference to me," I said carelessly. "I've a few more minutes to waste, and if he doesn't show up by then it's all one to me."

She cuddled against my shoulder.

"What's the racket? Maybe I could get word to Ed."

I stuck a cigarette in her mouth, one in my own, and lit them.

"Let it go," I bluffed. "This Ed of yours seems to be as exclusive as all hell. Well, it's no skin off *my* face. I'll buy you another drink and then trot along."

She jumped up.

"Wait a minute. I'll see if I can get him. What's your name?"

"Parker will do as well as any other," I said, the name I had used on Ryan popping first into my mind.

"You wait," she called back as she moved toward the back door. "I think I can find him."

"I think so too," I agreed.

Ten minutes went by, and a man came to my table from the front of the establishment. He was a blond Englishman of less than forty, with all the marks of the gentleman gone to pot on him. Not altogether on the rocks yet, but you could see evidence of the downhill slide plainly in the dullness of his blue eyes, in the pouches under his eyes, in the blurred lines around his mouth and the mouth's looseness, and in the grayish tint of his skin. He was still fairly attractive in appearance—enough of his former wholesomeness remained for that.

He sat down facing me across the table.

"You're looking for me?"

There was only a hint of the Britisher in his accent.

"You're Ed Bohannon?"

He nodded.

"Jamocha was picked up a couple of days ago," I told him, "and ought to be riding back to the Kansas big house by now. He got word out for me to give you the rap. He knew I was heading this way."

"How did they come to get him?"

His blue eyes were suspicious on my face.

"Don't know," I said. "Maybe they picked him up on a circular."

He frowned at the table and traced a meaningless design with a finger in a puddle of beer. Then he looked sharply at me again.

"Did he tell you anything else?"

"*He* didn't tell me anything. He got word out to me by somebody's mouthpiece. I didn't see him."

"You're staying down here a while?"

"Yes, for two or three days," I said. "I've got something on the fire."

He stood up and smiled, and held out his hand.

"Thanks for the tip, Parker," he said. "If you'll take a walk with me I'll give you something real to drink."

I didn't have anything against that. He led me out of the Golden Horseshoe and down a side street to an adobe house set out where the town fringed off into the desert. In the front room he waved me to a chair and went into the next room.

"What do you fancy?" he called through the door. "Rye, gin, tequila, Scotch—"

"The last one wins," I interrupted his catalog.

He brought in a bottle of Black and White, a siphon and some glasses, and we settled down to drinking. When that bottle was empty there was another to take its place. We drank and talked, drank and talked, and each of us pretended to be drunker than he really was—though before long we were both as full as a pair of goats.

It was a drinking contest pure and simple. He was trying to drink me into a pulp—a pulp that would easily give up all of its secrets—and I was trying the same game on him. Neither of us made much progress. Neither he nor I was young enough in the world to blab much when we were drunk that wouldn't have come out if we had been sober. Few grown men do, unless they get to boasting, or are very skilfully handled.

All that afternoon we faced each other over the table in the center of the room, drank and entertained each other.

"Y' know," he was saying somewhere along toward dark, "I've been a damn' ass. Got a wife—the nicesh woman in the worl'. Wantsh me t' come back to her, an' all tha' short of thing. Yet I hang around here, lappin' up this shtuff—hittin' the pipe—when I could be shomebody. Arc—architec', y' un'ershtand—good one, too. But I got in rut—got mixsh up with theshe people. C-can't sheem to break 'way. Goin' to, though—no spoofin'. Goin' back to li'l wife, nicesh woman in the worl'. Don't you shay anything t' Kewpie. She'd raishe hell 'f she knew I wash goin' t' shake her. Nishe girl, K-kewpie, but tough. S-shtick a bloomin' knife in me. Good job, too! But I'm goin' back to wife. Breakin' 'way from p-pipe an' ever'thing. Look at me. D' I look like a hop-head? Course not! Curin' m'self, tha's why. I'll show you—take a smoke now—show you I can take it or leave it alone."

Pulling himself dizzily up out of his chair, he wandered into the next room, bawling a song at the top of his voice:

"A dimber mort with a quarter-stone slum,
    A-bubbin' of max with her cove—
A bingo fen in a crack-o'-dawn drum,
    A-waitin' for—"

He came staggering into the room again carrying an elaborate opium layout—all silver and ebony—on a silver tray. He put it on the table and flourished a pipe at me.

"Have a li'l rear on me, Parker."

I told him I'd stick to the Scotch.

"Give y' shot of C. 'f y'd rather have it," he invited me.

I declined the cocaine, so he sprawled himself comfortably on the floor beside the table, rolled and cooked a pill, and our party went on—with him smoking his hop and me punishing the liquor—each of us still talking for the other's benefit, and trying to get the other to talk for our own.

I was holding down a lovely package by the time Kewpie came in, at midnight.

"Looks like you folks are enjoying yourselves," she laughed, leaning down to kiss the Englishman's rumpled hair as she stepped over him.

She perched herself on the table and reached for the Scotch.

"Everything's lovely," I assured her, though probably I didn't say it that clear.

I was fighting a battle with myself just about then. I had an idea that I wanted to dance. Down in Yucatan, four or five months before—hunting for a lad who had done wrong by the bank that employed him—I had seen some natives dance the *naual*. And that naual dance was the one thing in the world I wanted to do just then. (I was carrying a beautiful bun!) But I knew that if I sat still—as I had been sitting all evening—I could keep my cargo in hand, while it wasn't going to take much moving around to knock me over.

I don't remember whether I finally conquered the desire to dance or not. I remember Kewpie sitting on the table, grinning her boy's grin at me, and saying:

"You ought to stay oiled all the time, Shorty; it improves you."

I don't know whether I made any answer to that or not. Shortly afterward, I know, I spread myself beside the Englishman on the floor and went to sleep.

v

The next two days were pretty much like the first one. Ashcraft and I were together twenty-four hours each of the days, and usually the girl was with us, and the only time we weren't drinking was when we were sleeping off what we had been drinking. We spent most of those three days in either the adobe house or the Golden Horseshoe, but we found time to take in most of the other joints in town now and then. I had only a hazy idea of some of the things that went on around me, though I don't think I missed anything entirely. On the second day someone added a first name to the alias I had given the girl—and thereafter I was "Painless" Parker to Tijuana, and still am to some of them. I don't know who christened me, or why.

Ashcraft and I were as thick as thieves, on the surface, but neither of us ever lost his distrust of the other, no matter how drunk we got—and we got plenty drunk. He went up against his mud-pipe regularly. I don't think the girl used the stuff, but she had a pretty capacity for hard liquor. I would go to sleep not knowing whether I was going to wake up or not; but I had nothing on me to give me away, so I figured that I was safe unless I talked myself into a jam. I didn't worry much,—bedtime usually caught me in a state that made worry impossible.

Three days of this, and then, sobering up, I was riding back to San Francisco, making a list of what I knew and guessed about Norman Ashcraft, alias Ed Bohannon.

The list went something like this:

(1) He suspected, if he didn't know, that I had come down to see him on his wife's account: he had been too smooth and had entertained me too well for me to doubt that; (2) he apparently had decided to return to his wife, though there was no guarantee that he would actually do so; (3) he was not incurably addicted to drugs; he merely smoked opium and, regardless of what the Sunday supplements say, an opium smoker is little, if any, worse off than a tobacco smoker; (4) he might pull himself together under his wife's influence, but it was doubtful: physically he hadn't gone to the dogs, but he had had his taste of the gutter and seemed to like it; (5) the girl Kewpie was crazily in love with him, while he liked her, but wasn't turning himself inside out over her.

A good night's sleep on the train between Los Angeles and San Francisco set me down in the Third and Townsend Street station with nearly normal head and stomach and not too many kinks in my nerves. I put away a breakfast that was composed of more food than I had eaten in three days, and went up to Vance Richmond's office.

"Mr. Richmond is still in Eureka," his stenographer told me. "I don't expect him back until the first of the week."

"Can you get him on the phone for me?"

She could, and did.

Without mentioning any names, I told the attorney what I knew and guessed.

"I see," he said. "Suppose you go out to Mrs. A's house and tell her. I will write her tonight, and I probably shall be back in the city by the day after tomorrow. I think we can safely delay action until then."

I caught a street car, transferred at Van Ness Avenue, and went out to Mrs. Ashcraft's house. Nothing happened when I rang the bell. I rang it several times before I noticed that there were two morning newspapers in the vestibule. I looked at the dates—this morning's and yesterday morning's.

An old man in faded overalls was watering the lawn next door.

"Do you know if the people who live here have gone away?" I called to him.

"I don't guess so. The back door's open, I seen this mornin'."

He returned his attention to his hose, and then stopped to scratch his chin.

"They may of gone," he said slowly. "Come to think of it, I ain't seen any of 'em for—I don't remember seein' any of 'em yesterday."

I left the front steps and went around the house, climbed the low fence in back and went up the back steps. The kitchen door stood about a foot open. Nobody was visible in the kitchen, but there was a sound of running water.

I knocked on the door with my knuckles, loudly. There was no answering sound. I pushed the door open and went in. The sound of water came from the sink. I looked in the sink.

Under a thin stream of water running from one of the faucets lay a carving knife with nearly a foot of keen blade. The knife was clean, but the back of the porcelain sink— where water had splashed with only small, scattered drops— was freckled with red-brown spots. I scraped one of them with a finger-nail—dried blood.

Except for the sink, I could see nothing out of order in the kitchen. I opened a pantry door. Everything seemed all right there. Across the room another door led to the front of the house. I opened the door and went into a passageway. Not enough light came from the kitchen to illuminate the passageway. I fumbled in the dusk for the light-button that I knew should be there. I stepped on something soft.

Pulling my foot back, I felt in my pocket for matches, and struck one. In front of me, his head and shoulders on the floor, his hips and legs on the lower steps of a flight of stairs, lay a Filipino boy in his underclothes.

He was dead. One eye was cut, and his throat was gashed straight across, close up under his chin. I could see the killing without even shutting my eyes. At the top of the stairs—the killer's left hand dashing into the Filipino's face—thumb-nail gouging into eye—pushing the brown face back—tightening the brown throat for the knife's edge—the slash—and the shove down the steps.

The light from my second match showed me the button. I clicked on the lights, buttoned my coat, and went up the steps. Dried blood darkened them here and there, and at the second-floor landing the wall paper was stained with a big blot. At the head of the stairs I found another light-button, and pressed it.

I walked down the hall, poked my head into two rooms that seemed in order, and then turned a corner—and pulled up with a jerk, barely in time to miss stumbling over a woman who lay there.

She was huddled on the floor, face down, with knees drawn up under her and both hands clasped to her stomach. She wore a nightgown, and her hair was in a braid down her back.

I put a finger on the back of her neck. Stone-cold.

Kneeling on the floor—to avoid the necessity of turning her over—I looked at her face. She was the maid who had admitted Richmond and me four days ago.

I stood up again and looked around. The maid's head was almost touching a closed door. I stepped around her and pushed the door open. A bedroom, and not the maid's. It was an expensively dainty bedroom in cream and gray, with French prints on the walls. Nothing in the room was disarranged except the bed. The bed clothes were rumpled and tangled, and piled high in the center of the bed—in a pile that was too large. . . .

Leaning over the bed, I began to draw the covers off. The second piece came away stained with blood. I yanked the rest off.

Mrs. Ashcraft was dead there.

Her body was drawn up in a little heap, from which her head hung crookedly, dangling from a neck that had been cut clean through to the bone. Her face was marked with four deep scratches from temple to chin. One sleeve had been torn from the jacket of her blue silk pajamas. Bedding and pajamas were soggy with the blood that the clothing piled over her head kept from drying.

I put the blanket over her again, edged past the dead woman in the hall, and went down the front stairs, switching on more lights, hunting for the telephone. Near the foot of the stairs I found it. I called the police detective bureau first, and then Vance Richmond's office.

"Get word to Mr. Richmond that Mrs. Ashcraft has been murdered," I told his stenographer. "I'm at her house, and he can get in touch with me here any time during the next two or three hours."

Then I went out of the front door and sat on the top step, smoking a cigarette while I waited for the police.

I felt rotten. I've seen dead people in larger quantities than three in my time, and I've seen some that were hacked up pretty badly; but this thing had fallen on me while my nerves were ragged from three days of boozing.

The police automobile swung around the corner and began disgorging men before I had finished my first cigarette. O'Gar, the detective sergeant in charge of the Homicide Detail, was the first man up the steps.

"Hullo," he greeted me. "What have you got hold of this time?"

I was glad to see him. This squat, bullet-headed sergeant is as good a man as the department has, and he and I have always been lucky when we tied up together.

"I found three bodies in there before I quit looking," I told him as I led him indoors. "Maybe a regular detective like you—with a badge and everything—can find more."

"You didn't do bad—for a lad," he said.

My wooziness had passed. I was eager to get to work. These people lying dead around the house were merely counters in a game again—or almost. I remembered the feel of Mrs. Ashcraft's slim hand in mine, but I stuck that memory in the back of my mind. You hear now and then of detectives who have not become callous, who have not lost what you might call the human touch. I always feel sorry for them, and wonder why they don't chuck their jobs and find another line of work that wouldn't be so hard on their emotions. A sleuth who doesn't grow a tough shell is in for a gay life—day in and day out poking his nose into one kind of woe or another.

I showed the Filipino to O'Gar first, and then the two women. We didn't find any more. Detail work occupied all of us—O'Gar, the eight men under him, and me—for the next few hours. The house had to be gone over from roof to cellar. The neighbors had to be grilled. The employment agencies through which the servants had been hired had to be examined. Relatives and friends of the Filipino and the maid had to be traced and questioned. Newsboys, mail carriers, grocers' delivery men, laundrymen, had to be found, questioned and, when necessary, investigated.

When the bulk of the reports were in, O'Gar and I sneaked away from the others—especially away from the newspaper men, who were all over the place by now—and locked ourselves in the library.

"Night before last, huh? Wednesday night?" O'Gar grunted when we were comfortable in a couple of leather chairs, burning tobacco.

I nodded. The report of the doctor who had examined the bodies, the presence of the two newspapers in the vestibule, and the fact that neither neighbor, grocer nor butcher had seen any of them since Wednesday, combined to make Wednesday night—or early Thursday morning—the correct date.

"I'd say the killer cracked the back door," O'Gar went on, staring at the ceiling through smoke, "picked up the carving knife in the kitchen, and went upstairs. Maybe he went straight to Mrs. Ashcraft's room—maybe not. But after a bit he went in there. The torn sleeve and the scratches on her face mean that there was a tussle. The Filipino and the maid heard the noise—heard her scream maybe—and rushed to her room to find out what was the matter. The maid most likely got there just as the killer was coming out—and got hers. I guess the Filipino saw him then and ran. The killer caught him at the head of the back stairs—and finished him. Then he went down to the kitchen, washed his hands, dropped the knife, and blew."

"So far, so good," I agreed; "but I notice you skip lightly over the question of who he was and why he killed."

He pushed his hat back and scratched his bullet head.

"Don't crowd me," he rumbled; "I'll get around to that. There seem to be just three guesses to take your pick from. We know that nobody else lived in the house outside of the three that were killed. So the killer was either a maniac who did the job for the fun of it, a burglar who was discovered and ran wild, or somebody who had a reason for bumping off Mrs. Ashcraft, and then had to kill the two servants when they discovered him.

"Taking the knife from the kitchen would make the burglar guess look like a bum one. And, besides, we're pretty sure nothing was stolen. A good prowler would bring his own weapon with him if he wanted one. But the hell of it is that there are a lot of bum prowlers in the world—half-wits who would be likely to pick up a knife in the kitchen, go to pieces when the house woke up, slash everybody in sight, and then beat it without turning anything over.

"So it could have been a prowler; but my personal guess is that the job was done by somebody who wanted to wipe out Mrs. Ashcraft."

"Not so bad," I applauded. "Now listen to this: Mrs. Ashcraft has a husband in Tijuana, a mild sort of hop-head who is mixed up with a bunch of thugs. She was trying to persuade him to come back to her. He has a girl down there who is young, goofy over him, and a bad actor—one tough youngster. He was planning to run out on the girl and come back home."

"So-o-o?" O'Gar said softly.

"But," I continued, "I was with both him and the girl, in Tijuana, night before last—when this killing was done."

"So-o?"

A knock on the door interrupted our talk. It was a policeman to tell me that I was wanted on the phone. I went down to the first floor, and Vance Richmond's voice came over the wire.

"What is it? Miss Henry delivered your message, but she couldn't give me any details."

I told him the whole thing.

"I'll leave for the city tonight," he said when I had finished. "You go ahead and do whatever you want. You're to have a free hand."

"Right," I replied. "I'll probably be out of town when you get back. You can reach me through the Agency if you want to get in touch with me. I'm going to wire Ashcraft to come up—in your name."

After Richmond had hung up, I called the city jail and asked the captain if John Ryan, alias Fred Rooney, alias Jamocha, was still there.

"No. Federal officers left for Leavenworth with him and two other prisoners yesterday morning."

Up in the library again, I told O'Gar hurriedly:

"I'm catching the evening train south, betting my marbles that the job was made in Tijuana. I'm wiring Ashcraft to come up. I want to get him away from the Mexican town for a day or two, and if he's up here you can keep an eye on him. I'll give you a description of him, and you can pick him up at Vance Richmond's office. He'll probably connect there first thing."

Half an hour of the little time I had left I spent writing and sending three telegrams. The first was to Ashcraft.

> EDWARD BOHANNON,
> GOLDEN HORSESHOE CAFE,
> TIJUANA, MEXICO.
> MRS. ASHCRAFT IS DEAD. CAN YOU COME
> IMMEDIATELY?
>
> VANCE RICHMOND.

The other two were in code. One went to the Continental Detective Agency's Kansas City branch, asking that an operative be sent to Leavenworth to question Jamocha. The other requested the Los Angeles branch to have a man meet me in San Diego the next day.

Then I dashed out to my rooms for a bagful of clean clothes, and went to sleep riding south again.

VI

San Diego was gay and packed when I got off the train early the next afternoon—filled with the crowd that the first Saturday of the racing season across the border had drawn. Movie folk from Los Angeles, farmers from the Imperial Valley, sailors from the Pacific Fleet, gamblers, tourists, grifters, and even regular people, from everywhere. I lunched, registered and left my bag at a hotel, and went up to the U. S. Grant Hotel to pick up the Los Angeles operative I had wired for.

I found him in the lobby—a freckle-faced youngster of twenty-two or so, whose bright gray eyes were busy just now with a racing program, which he held in a hand that had a finger bandaged with adhesive tape. I passed him and stopped at the cigar stand, where I bought a package of cigarettes and straightened out an imaginary dent in my hat. Then I went out to the street again. The bandaged finger and the business with the hat were our introductions. Somebody invented those tricks back before the Civil War, but they still worked smoothly, so their antiquity was no reason for discarding them.

I strolled up Fourth Street, getting away from Broadway— San Diego's main stem—and the operative caught up with me. His name was Gorman, and he turned out to be a pretty good lad. I gave him the lay.

"You're to go down to Tijuana and take a plant on the Golden Horseshoe Café. There's a little chunk of a girl hustling drinks in there—short curly brown hair; brown eyes; round face; rather large red mouth; square shoulders. You can't miss her; she's a nice-looking kid of about eighteen, called Kewpie. She's the target for your eye. Keep away from her. Don't try to rope her. I'll give you an hour's start. Then I'm coming down to talk to her. I want to know what she does right after I leave, and what she does for the next few days. You can get in touch with me at the"—I gave him the name of my hotel and my room number—"each night. Don't give me a tumble anywhere else. I'll most likely be in and out of the Golden Horseshoe often."

We parted, and I went down to the plaza and sat on a bench under the palms for an hour. Then I went up to the corner and fought for a seat on a Tijuana stage.

Fifteen or more miles of dusty riding—packed five in a seat meant for three—a momentary halt at the Immigration Station on the line, and I was climbing out of the stage at the entrance to the race track. The ponies had been running for some time, but the turnstiles were still spinning a steady stream of customers into the track. I turned my back on the gate and went over to the row of jitneys in front of the Monte Carlo—the big wooden casino—got into one, and was driven over to the Old Town.

The Old Town had a deserted look. Nearly everybody was over watching the dogs do their stuff. Gorman's freckled face showed over a drink of mescal when I entered the Golden Horseshoe. I hoped he had a good constitution. He needed one if he was going to do his sleuthing on a distilled cactus diet.

The welcome I got from the Horseshoers was just like a homecoming. Even the bartender with the plastered-down curls gave me a grin.

"Where's Kewpie?" I asked.

"Brother-in-lawing, Ed?" a big Swede girl leered at me. "I'll see if I can find her for you."

Kewpie came through the back door just then.

"Hello, Painless!" She climbed all over me, hugging me, rubbing her face against mine, and the Lord knows what all. "Down for another swell souse?"

"No," I said, leading her back toward the stalls. "Business this time. Where's Ed?"

"Up north. His wife kicked off and he's gone to collect the remains."

"That makes you sorry?"

She showed her big white teeth in a boy's smile of pure happiness.

"You bet! It's tough on me that papa has come into a lot of sugar."

I looked at her out of the corner of my eyes—a glance that was supposed to be wise.

"And you think Ed's going to bring the jack back to you?"

Her eyes snapped darkly at me.

"What's eating you?" she demanded.

I smiled knowingly.

"One of two things is going to happen," I predicted. "Ed's going to ditch you—he was figuring on that, anyway—or he's going to need every brownie he can scrape up to keep his neck from being—"

"You God-damned liar!"

Her right shoulder was to me, touching my left. Her left hand flashed down under her short skirt. I pushed her shoulder forward, twisting her body sharply away from me. The knife her left hand had whipped up from her leg jabbed deep into the underside of the table. A thick-bladed knife, I noticed, balanced for accurate throwing.

She kicked backward, driving one of her sharp heels into my ankle. I slid my left arm around behind her and pinned her elbow to her side just as she freed the knife from the table.

"What th' hell's all 'is?"

I looked up.

Across the table a man stood glaring at me—legs apart, fists on hips. He was a big man, and ugly. A tall, raw-boned man with wide shoulders, out of which a long, skinny yellow neck rose to support a little round head. His eyes were black shoe-buttons stuck close together at the top of a little mashed nose. His mouth looked as if it had been torn in his face, and it was stretched in a snarl now, baring a double row of crooked brown teeth.

"Where d' yuh get 'at stuff?" this lovely person roared at me.

He was too tough to reason with.

"If you're a waiter," I told him, "bring me a bottle of beer and something for the kid. If you're not a waiter—sneak."

He leaned over the table and I gathered my feet in. It looked like I was going to need them to move around on.

"I'll bring yuh a—"

The girl wriggled out of my hands and shut him up.

"Mine's liquor," she said sharply.

He snarled, looked from one of us to the other, showed me his dirty teeth again, and wandered away.

"Who's your friend?"

"You'll do well to lay off him," she advised me, not answering my question.

Then she slid her knife back in its hiding place under her skirt and twisted around to face me.

"Now what's all this about Ed being in trouble?"

"You read about the killing in the papers?"

"Yes."

"You oughtn't need a map, then," I said. "Ed's only out is to put the job on you. But I doubt if he can get away with that. If he can't, he's nailed."

"You're crazy!" she exclaimed. "You weren't too drunk to know that both of us were here with you when the killing was done."

"I'm not crazy enough to think that proves anything," I corrected her. "But I am crazy enough to expect to go back to San Francisco wearing the killer on my wrist."

She laughed at me. I laughed back and stood up.

"See you some more," I said as I strolled toward the door.

I returned to San Diego and sent a wire to Los Angeles, asking for another operative. Then I got something to eat and spent the evening lying across the bed in my hotel room smoking and scheming and waiting for Gorman.

It was late when he arrived, and he smelled of mescal from San Diego to St. Louis and back, but his head seemed level enough.

"Looked like I was going to have to shoot you loose from the place for a moment," he grinned. "Between the twist flashing the pick and the big guy loosening a sap in his pocket, it looked like action was coming."

"You let me alone," I ordered. "Your job is to see what goes on, and that's all. If I get carved, you can mention it in your report, but that's your limit. What did you turn up?"

"After you blew, the girl and the big guy put their noodles together. They seemed kind of agitated—all agog, you might say. He slid out, so I dropped the girl and slid along behind him. He came to town and got a wire off. I couldn't crowd him close enough to see who it was to. Then he went back to the joint. Things were normal when I knocked off."

"Who is the big guy? Did you learn?"

"He's no sweet dream, from what I hear. 'Gooseneck' Flinn is the name on his calling cards. He's bouncer and general utility man for the joint. I saw him in action against a couple of gobs, and he's nobody's meat—as pretty a double throw-out as I've ever seen."

So this Gooseneck party was the Golden Horseshoe's clean-up man, and he hadn't been in sight during my three-day spree? I couldn't possibly have been so drunk that I'd forget his ugliness. And it had been on one of those three days that Mrs. Ashcraft and her servants had been killed.

"I wired your office for another op," I told Gorman. "He's to connect with you. Turn the girl over to him, and you camp on Gooseneck's trail. I think we're going to hang three killings on him, so watch your step. I'll be in to stir things up a little more tomorrow; but remember, no matter what happens, everybody plays his own game. Don't ball things up trying to help me."

"Aye, aye, Cap," and he went off to get some sleep.

The next afternoon I spent at the race track, fooling around with the bangtails while I waited for night. The track was jammed with the usual Sunday crowd. I ran into any number of old acquaintances, some of them on my side of the game, some on the other, and some neutral. One of the second lot was "Trick-hat" Schultz. At our last meeting—a copper was leading him out of a Philadelphia court room toward a fifteen-year bit—he had promised to open me up from my eyebrows to my ankles the next time he saw me. He greeted me this afternoon with an eight-inch smile, bought me a shot of what they sell for gin under the grandstand, and gave me a tip on a horse named Beeswax. I'm not foolish enough to play anybody's tips, so I didn't play this one. Beeswax ran so far ahead of the others that it looked like he and his competitors were in separate races, and he paid twenty-something to one. So Trick-hat had his revenge after all.

After the last race, I got something to eat at the Sunset Inn, and then drifted over to the big casino—the other end of the same building. A thousand or more people of all sorts were jostling one another there, fighting to go up against poker, craps, chuck-a-luck, wheels of fortune, roulette and twenty-one with whatever money the race track had left or given them. I didn't buck any of the games. My playtime was over. I walked around through the crowd looking for my men.

I spotted the first one—a sunburned man who was plainly a farm hand in his Sunday clothes. He was pushing toward the door, and his face held that peculiar emptiness which belongs to the gambler who has gone broke before the end of the game. It's a look of regret that is not so much for the loss of the money as for the necessity of quitting.

I got between the farm hand and the door.

"Clean you?" I asked sympathetically when he reached me.

A sheepish sort of nod.

"How'd you like to pick up five bucks for a few minutes' work?" I tempted him.

He would like it, but what was the work?

"I want you to go over to the Old Town with me and look at a man. Then you get your pay. There are no strings to it."

That didn't exactly satisfy him, but five bucks are five bucks; and he could drop out any time he didn't like the looks of things. He decided to try it.

I put the farm hand over by a door, and went after another—a little, plump man with round, optimistic eyes and a weak mouth. He was willing to earn five dollars in the simple and easy manner I had outlined. The next man I braced was a little too timid to take a chance on a blind game. Then I got a Filipino—glorious in a fawn-colored suit, with a coat split to the neck and pants whose belled bottoms would have held a keg apiece—and a stocky young Greek who was probably either a waiter or a barber.

Four men were enough. My quartet pleased me immensely. They didn't look too intelligent for my purpose, and they didn't look like thugs or sharpers. I put them in a jitney and took them over to the Old Town.

"Now this is it," I coached them when we had arrived. "I'm going into the Golden Horseshoe Café, around the corner. Give me two or three minutes, and then come in and buy yourselves a drink." I gave the farm hand a five-dollar bill. "You pay for the drinks with that—it isn't part of your wages. There's a tall, broad-shouldered man with a long, yellow neck and a small ugly face in there. You can't miss him. I want you all to take a good look at him without letting him get wise. When you're sure you'd know him again anywhere, give me the nod, and come back here and you get your money. Be careful when you give me the nod. I don't want anybody in there to find out that you know me."

It sounded queer to them, but there was the promise of five dollars apiece, and there were the games back in the casino, where five dollars might buy a man into a streak of luck that—write the rest of it yourself. They asked questions, which I refused to answer, but they stuck.

Gooseneck was behind the bar, helping out the bartenders, when I entered the place. They needed help. The joint bulged with customers. The dance floor looked like a mob scene. Thirsts were lined up four deep at the bar. A shotgun wouldn't have sounded above the din: men and women laughing, roaring and cursing; bottles and glasses rattling and banging; and louder and more disagreeable than any of those noises was the noise of the sweating orchestra. Turmoil, uproar, stink—a Tijuana joint on Sunday night.

I couldn't find Gorman's freckled face in the crowd, but I picked out the hatchet-sharp white face of Hooper, another Los Angeles operative, who, I knew then, had been sent down in response to my second telegram. Kewpie was farther down the bar, drinking with a little man whose meek face had the devil-may-care expression of a model husband on a tear. She nodded at me, but didn't leave her client.

Gooseneck gave me a scowl and the bottle of beer I had ordered. Presently my four hired men came in. They did their parts beautifully!

First they peered through the smoke, looking from face to face, and hastily avoiding eyes that met theirs. A little of this, and one of them, the Filipino, saw the man I had described, behind the bar. He jumped a foot in the excitement of his discovery, and then, finding Gooseneck glaring at him, turned his back and fidgeted. The three others spotted Gooseneck now, and sneaked looks at him that were as conspicuously furtive as a set of false whiskers. Gooseneck glowered at them.

The Filipino turned around, looked at me, ducked his head sharply, and bolted for the street. The three who were left shot their drinks down their gullets and tried to catch my eye. I was reading a sign high on the wall behind the bar:

ONLY GENUINE PRE-WAR AMERICAN
AND BRITISH WHISKEYS SERVED HERE

I was trying to count how many lies could be found in those nine words, and had reached four, with promise of more, when one of my confederates, the Greek, cleared his throat with the noise of a gasoline engine's backfire. Gooseneck was edging down the bar, a bungstarter in one hand, his face purple.

I looked at my assistants. Their nods wouldn't have been so terrible had they come one at a time; but they were taking no chances on my looking away again before they could get their reports in. The three heads bobbed together—a signal that nobody within twenty feet could, or did, miss—and they scooted out of the door, away from the long-necked man and his bung-starter.

I emptied my glass of beer, sauntered out of the saloon and around the corner. They were clustered where I had told them to wait.

"We'd know him! We'd know him!" they chorused.

"That's fine," I praised them. "You did great. I think you're all natural-born gumshoes. Here's your pay. Now if I were you boys, I think I'd sort of avoid that place after this; because, in spite of the clever way you covered yourselves up—and you did nobly!—he might possibly suspect something. There's no use taking chances, anyway."

They grabbed their wages and were gone before I had finished my speech. I returned to the Golden Horseshoe—to be on hand in case one of them should decide to sell me out and come back there to spill the deal to Gooseneck.

Kewpie had left her model husband, and met me at the door. She stuck an arm through mine and led me toward the rear of the building. I noticed that Gooseneck was gone from behind the bar. I wondered if he was out gunning for my four ex-employees.

"Business looks good," I chattered as we pushed through the crowd. "You know, I had a tip on Beeswax this afternoon, and wouldn't play the pup." I made two or three more aimless cracks of that sort—just because I knew the girl's mind was full of something else. She paid no attention to anything I said.

But when we had dropped down in front of a vacant table, she asked:

"Who were your friends?"

"What friends?"

"The four jobbies who were at the bar when you were there a few minutes ago."

"Too hard for me, sister." I shook my head. "There were slews of men there. Oh, yes! I know who you mean! Those four gents who seemed kind of smitten with Gooseneck's looks. I wonder what attracted them to him—besides his beauty."

She grabbed my arm with both hands.

"So help me God, Painless," she swore, "if you tie anything on Ed, I'll kill you!"

Her brown eyes were big and damp. She was a hard and wise little baby—had rubbed the world's sharp corners with both shoulders—but she was only a kid, and she was worried sick over this man of hers. However, the business of a sleuth is to catch criminals, not to sympathize with their ladyloves.

I patted her hands.

"I could give you some good advice," I said as I stood up, "but you wouldn't listen to it, so I'll save my breath. It won't do any harm to tell you to keep an eye on Gooseneck, though—he's shifty."

There wasn't any special meaning to that speech, except that it might tangle things up a little more. One way of finding what's at the bottom of either a cup of coffee or a situation is to keep stirring it up until whatever is on the bottom comes to the surface. I had been playing that system thus far on this affair.

Hooper came into my room in the San Diego hotel at a little before two the next morning.

"Gooseneck disappeared, with Gorman tailing him, immediately after your first visit," he said. "After your second visit, the girl went around to a 'dobe house on the edge of town, and she was still there when I knocked off. The place was dark."

Gorman didn't show up.

VII

A bell-hop with a telegram roused me at ten o'clock in the morning. The telegram was from Mexicali:

DROVE HERE LAST NIGHT HOLED UP WITH
FRIENDS SENT TWO WIRES.

GORMAN.

That was good news. The long-necked man had fallen for
my play, had taken my four busted gamblers for four witnesses, had taken their nods for identifications. Gooseneck
was the lad who had done the actual killing, and Gooseneck
was in flight.

I had shed my pajamas and was reaching for my union suit
when the boy came back with another wire. This one was
from O'Gar, through the Agency:

ASHCRAFT DISAPPEARED YESTERDAY

I used the telephone to get Hooper out of bed.

"Get down to Tijuana," I told him. "Stick up the house
where you left the girl last night, unless you run across her at
the Golden Horseshoe. Stay there until she shows. Stay with
her until she connects with a big blond Englishman, and then
switch to him. He's a man of less than forty, tall, with blue
eyes and yellow hair. Don't let him shake you—he's the big
boy in this party just now. I'll be down. If the Englishman
and I stay together and the girl leaves us, take her, but otherwise stick to him."

I dressed, put down some breakfast and caught a stage for
the Mexican town. The boy driving the stage made fair time,
but you would have thought we were standing still to see a
maroon roadster pass us near Palm City. Ashcraft was driving
the roadster.

The roadster was empty, standing in front of the adobe
house, when I saw it again. Up in the next block, Hooper was
doing an imitation of a drunk, talking to two Indians in the
uniforms of the Mexican Army.

I knocked on the door of the adobe house.

Kewpie's voice: "Who is it?"

"Me—Painless. Just heard that Ed is back."

"Oh!" she exclaimed. A pause. "Come in."

I pushed the door open and went in. The Englishman sat
tilted back in a chair, his right elbow on the table, his right

hand in his coat pocket—if there was a gun in that pocket it was pointing at me.

"Hello," he said. "I hear you've been making guesses about me."

"Call 'em anything you like." I pushed a chair over to within a couple of feet of him, and sat down. "But don't let's kid each other. You had Gooseneck knock your wife off so you could get what she had. The mistake you made was in picking a sap like Gooseneck to do the turn—a sap who went on a killing spree and then lost his nerve. Going to read and write just because three or four witnesses put the finger on him! And only going as far as Mexicali! That's a fine place to pick! I suppose he was so scared that the five or six-hour ride over the hills seemed like a trip to the end of the world!"

The man's face told me nothing. He eased himself around in his chair an inch or two, which would have brought the gun in his pocket—if a gun *was* there—in line with my thick middle. The girl was somewhere behind me, fidgeting around. I was afraid of her. She was crazily in love with this man in front of me, and I had seen the blade she wore on one leg. I imagined her fingers itching for it now. The man and his gun didn't worry me much. He was not rattle-brained, and he wasn't likely to bump me off either in panic or for the fun of it.

I kept my chin going.

"You aren't a sap, Ed, and neither am I. I want to take you riding north with bracelets on, but I'm in no hurry. What I mean is, I'm not going to stand up and trade lead with you. This is all in my daily grind. It isn't a matter of life or death with me. If I can't take you today, I'm willing to wait until to-morrow. I'll get you in the end, unless somebody beats me to you—and that won't break my heart. There's a rod between my vest and my belly. If you'll have Kewpie get it out, we'll be all set for the talk I want to make."

He nodded slowly, not taking his eyes from me. The girl came close to my back. One of her hands came over my shoulder, went under my vest, and my old black gun left me. Before she stepped away she laid the point of her knife against the nape of my neck for an instant—a gentle reminder. I managed not to squirm or jump.

"Good," I said when she gave my gun to the Englishman, who pocketed it with his left hand. "Now here's my proposition. You and Kewpie ride across the border with me—so we won't have to fool with extradition papers—and I'll have you locked up. We'll do our fighting in court. I'm not absolutely certain that I can tie the killings on either of you, and if I flop, you'll be free. If I make the grade—as I hope to—you'll swing, of course. But there's always a good chance of beating the courts—especially if you're guilty—and that's the only chance you have that's worth a damn.

"What's the sense of scooting? Spending the rest of your life dodging bulls? Only to be nabbed finally—or bumped off trying to get away? You'll maybe save your neck, but what of the money your wife left? That money is what you are in the game for—it's what you had your wife killed for. Stand trial and you've a chance to collect it. Run—and you kiss it good-by. Are you going to ditch it—throw it away just because your cat's-paw bungled the deal? Or are you going to stick to the finish—win everything or lose everything?"

A lot of these boys who make cracks about not being taken alive have been wooed into peaceful surrender with that kind of talk. But my game just now was to persuade Ed and his girl to bolt. If they let me throw them in the can I might be able to convict one of them, but my chances weren't any too large. It depended on how things turned out later. It depended on whether I could prove that Gooseneck had been in San Francisco on the night of the killings, and I imagined that he would be well supplied with all sorts of proof to the contrary. We had not been able to find a single finger-print of the killer's in Mrs. Ashcraft's house. And if I *could* convince a jury that he was in San Francisco at the time, then I would have to show that he had done the killing. And after that I would have the toughest part of the job still ahead of me—to prove that he had done the killing for one of these two, and not on his own account. I had an idea that when we picked Gooseneck up and put the screws to him he would talk. But that was only an idea.

What I was working for was to make this pair dust out. I didn't care where they went or what they did, so long as they scooted. I'd trust to luck and my own head to get profit out of their scrambling—I was still trying to stir things up.

The Englishman was thinking hard. I knew I had him worried, chiefly through what I had said about Gooseneck Flinn. If I had pulled the moth-eaten stuff—said that Gooseneck had been picked up and had squealed—this Englishman would have put me down as a liar; but the little I had said was bothering him.

He bit his lip and frowned. Then he shook himself and chuckled.

"You're balmy, Painless," he said. "But you—"

I don't know what he was going to say—whether I was going to win or lose.

The front door slammed open, and Gooseneck Flinn came into the room.

His clothes were white with dust. His face was thrust forward to the full length of his long, yellow neck.

His shoe-button eyes focused on me. His hands turned over. That's all you could see. They simply turned over—and there was a heavy revolver in each.

"Your paws on the table, Ed," he snarled.

Ed's gun—if that is what he had in his pocket—was blocked from a shot at the man in the doorway by a corner of the table. He took his hand out of his pocket, empty, and laid both palms down on the table-top.

"Stay where y'r at!" Gooseneck barked at the girl.

She was standing on the other side of the room. The knife with which she had pricked the back of my neck was not in sight.

Gooseneck glared at me for nearly a minute, but when he spoke it was to Ed and Kewpie.

"So this is what y' wired me to come back for, huh? A trap! Me the goat for yur! I'll be y'r goat! I'm goin' to speak my piece, an' then I'm goin' out o' here if I have to smoke my way through the whole damn' Mex army! I killed y'r wife all right— an' her help, too. Killed 'em for the thousand bucks—"

The girl took a step toward him, screaming:

"Shut up, damn you!"

Her mouth was twisting and working like a child's, and there was water in her eyes.

"Shut up, yourself!" Gooseneck roared back at her, and his thumb raised the hammer of the gun that threatened her. "I'm doin' the talkin'. I killed her for—"

Kewpie bent forward. Her left hand went under the hem of her skirt. The hand came up—empty. The flash from Gooseneck's gun lit on a flying steel blade.

The girl spun back across the room—hammered back by the bullets that tore through her chest. Her back hit the wall. She pitched forward to the floor.

Gooseneck stopped shooting and tried to speak. The brown haft of the girl's knife stuck out of his yellow throat. He couldn't get his words past the blade. He dropped one gun and tried to take hold of the protruding haft. Half-way up to it his hand came, and dropped. He went down slowly—to his knees—hands and knees—rolled over on his side—and lay still.

I jumped for the Englishman. The revolver Gooseneck had dropped turned under my foot, spilling me sidewise. My hand brushed the Englishman's coat, but he twisted away from me, and got his guns out.

His eyes were hard and cold and his mouth was shut until you could hardly see the slit of it. He backed slowly across the floor, while I lay still where I had tumbled. He didn't make a speech. A moment of hesitation in the doorway. The door jerked open and shut. He was gone.

I scooped up the gun that had thrown me, sprang to Gooseneck's side, tore the other gun out of his dead hand, and plunged into the street. The maroon roadster was trailing a cloud of dust into the desert behind it. Thirty feet from me stood a dirt-caked black touring car. That would be the one in which Gooseneck had driven back from Mexicali.

I jumped for it, climbed in, brought it to life, and pointed it at the dust-cloud ahead.

VIII

The car under me, I discovered, was surprisingly well engined for its battered looks—its motor was so good that I knew it was a border-runner's car. I nursed it along, not pushing it. There were still four or five hours of daylight left, and while there was any light at all I couldn't miss the cloud of dust from the fleeing roadster.

I didn't know whether we were following a road or not. Sometimes the ground under me looked like one, but mostly it didn't differ much from the rest of the desert. For half an hour or more the dust-cloud ahead and I held our respective positions, and then I found that I was gaining.

The going was roughening. Any road that we might originally have been using had petered out. I opened up a little, though the jars it cost me were vicious. But if I was going to avoid playing Indian among the rocks and cactus, I would have to get within striking distance of my man before he deserted his car and started a game of hide and seek on foot. I'm a city man. I have done my share of work in the open spaces, but I don't like it. My taste in playgrounds runs more to alleys, backyards and cellars than to canyons, mesas and arroyos.

I missed a boulder that would have smashed me up— missed it by a hair—and looked ahead again to see that the maroon roadster was no longer stirring up the grit. It had stopped.

The roadster was empty. I kept on.

From behind the roadster a pistol snapped at me, three times. It would have taken good shooting to plug me at that instant. I was bounding and bouncing around in my seat like a pellet of quicksilver in a nervous man's palm.

He fired again from the shelter of his car, and then dashed for a narrow arroyo—a sharp-edged, ten-foot crack in the earth—off to the left. On the brink, he wheeled to snap another cap at me—and jumped down out of sight.

I twisted the wheel in my hands, jammed on the brakes and slid the black touring car to the spot where I had seen him last. The edge of the arroyo was crumbling under my front wheels. I released the brake. Tumbled out. Shoved.

The car plunged down into the gully after him.

Sprawled on my belly, one of Gooseneck's guns in each hand, I wormed my head over the edge. On all fours, the Englishman was scrambling out of the way of the car. The car was mangled, but still sputtering. One of the man's fists was bunched around a gun—mine.

"Drop it and stand up, Ed!" I yelled.

Snake-quick, he flung himself around in a sitting position on the arroyo bottom, swung his gun up—and I smashed his forearm with my second shot.

He was holding the wounded arm with his left hand when I slid down beside him, picked up the gun he had dropped, and frisked him to see if he had any more.

He grinned at me.

"You know," he drawled, "I fancy your true name isn't Painless Parker at all. You don't act like it."

Twisting a handkerchief into a tourniquet of a sort, I knotted it around his wounded arm, which was bleeding.

"Let's go upstairs and talk," I suggested, and helped him up the steep side of the gully.

We climbed into his roadster.

"Out of gas," he said. "We've got a nice walk ahead of us."

"We'll get a lift. I had a man watching your house, and another one shadowing Gooseneck. They'll be coming out after me, I reckon. Meanwhile, we have time for a nice heart-to-heart talk."

"Go ahead, talk your head off," he invited; "but don't expect me to add much to the conversation. You've got nothing on me." (I'd like to have a dollar, or even a nickel, for every time I've heard that remark!) "You saw Kewpie bump Gooseneck off to keep him from peaching on her."

"So that's your play?" I inquired. "The girl hired Gooseneck to kill your wife—out of jealousy—when she learned that you were planning to shake her and return to your own world?"

"Exactly."

"Not bad, Ed, but there's one rough spot in it."

"Yes?"

"Yes," I repeated. "You are not Ashcraft!"

He jumped, and then laughed.

"Now your enthusiasm is getting the better of your judgment," he kidded me. "Could I have deceived another man's wife? Don't you think her lawyer, Richmond, made me prove my identity?"

"Well, I'll tell you, Ed, I think I'm a smarter baby than either of them. Suppose you had a lot of stuff that belonged to Ashcraft—papers, letters, things in his handwriting? If you were even a fair hand with a pen, you could have fooled his wife. She thought her husband had had four tough years and had become a hop-head. That would account for irregularities in his writing. And I don't imagine you ever got very familiar in your letters—not enough so to risk any missteps. As for the lawyer—his making you identify yourself was only a matter of form. It never occurred to him that you weren't Ashcraft. Identification is easy, anyway. Give me a week and I'll prove that I'm the Sultan of Turkey."

He shook his head sadly.

"That comes from riding around in the sun."

I went on.

"At first your game was to bleed Mrs. Ashcraft for an allowance—to take the cure. But after she closed out her affairs in England and came here, you decided to wipe her out and take everything. You knew she was an orphan and had no close relatives to come butting in. You knew it wasn't likely that there were many people in America who could say you were not Ashcraft. Now if you want to you can do your stalling for just as long as it takes us to send a photograph of you to England—to be shown to the people that knew him there. But you understand that you will do your stalling in the can, so I don't see what it will get you."

"Where do you think Ashcraft would be while I was spending his money?"

There were only two possible guesses. I took the more reasonable one.

"Dead."

I imagined his mouth tightened a little, so I took another shot, and added:

"Up north."

That got to him, though he didn't get excited. But his eyes became thoughtful behind his smile. The United States is all "up north" from Tijuana, but it was even betting that he thought I meant Seattle, where the last record of Ashcraft had come from.

"You may be right, of course," he drawled. "But even at that, I don't see just how you expect to hang me. Can you prove that Kewpie didn't think I was Ashcraft? Can you prove that she knew why Mrs. Ashcraft was sending me money? Can you prove that she knew anything about my game? I rather think not. There are still any number of reasons for her to have been jealous of this other woman.

"I'll do my bit for fraud, Painless, but you're not going to swing me. The only two who could possibly tie anything on me are dead behind us. Maybe one of them told you something. What of it? You know damned well that you won't be allowed to testify to it in court. What someone who is now dead may have told you—unless the person it affects was present—isn't evidence, and you know it."

"You may get away with it," I admitted. "Juries are funny, and I don't mind telling you that I'd be happier if I knew a few things about those murders that I don't know. Do you mind telling me about the ins and outs of your switch with Ashcraft—in Seattle?"

He squinted his blue eyes at me.

"You're a puzzling chap, Painless," he said. "I can't tell whether you know everything, or are just sharp-shooting." He puckered his lips and then shrugged. "I'll tell you. It won't matter greatly. I'm due to go over for this impersonation, so a confession to a little additional larceny won't matter."

IX

"The hotel-sneak used to be my lay," the Englishman said after a pause. "I came to the States after England and the Continent got uncomfortable. I was rather good at it. I had the proper manner—the front. I could do the gentleman without sweating over it, you know. In fact there was a day, not so long ago, when I wasn't 'Liverpool Ed.' But you don't want to hear me brag about the select blood that flows through these veins.

"To get back to our knitting: I had rather a successful tour on my first American voyage. I visited most of the better hotels between New York and Seattle, and profited nicely. Then, one night in a Seattle hotel, I worked the tarrel and put myself into a room on the fourth floor. I had hardly closed the door behind me before another key was rattling in it. The room was night-dark. I risked a flash from my light, picked out a closet door, and got behind it just in time.

"The clothes closet was empty; rather a stroke of luck, since there was nothing in it for the room's occupant to come for. He—it was a man—had switched on the lights by then.

"He began pacing the floor. He paced it for three solid hours—up and down, up and down, up and down—while I stood behind the closet door with my gun in my hand, in case he should pull it open. For three solid hours he paced that damned floor. Then he sat down and I heard a pen scratching on paper. Ten minutes of that and he was back at his pacing; but he kept it up for only a few minutes this time. I heard the latches of a valise click. And a shot!

"I bounded out of my retreat. He was stretched on the floor, with a hole in the side of his head. A bad break for me, and no mistake! I could hear excited voices in the corridor. I stepped over the dead chap, found the letter he had been writing on the writing-desk. It was addressed to Mrs. Norman Ashcraft, at a Wine Street number in Bristol, England. I tore it open. He had written that he was going to kill himself, and it was signed Norman. I felt better. A murder couldn't be made out of it.

"Nevertheless, I was here in this room with a flashlight, skeleton keys, and a gun—to say nothing of a handful of jewelry that I had picked up on the next floor. Somebody was knocking on the door.

" 'Get the police!' I called through the door, playing for time.

"Then I turned to the man who had let me in for all this. I would have pegged him for a fellow Britisher even if I hadn't seen the address on his letter. There are thousands of us on the same order—blond, fairly tall, well set up. I took the only chance there was. His hat and topcoat were on a chair where he had tossed them. I put them on and dropped my hat beside him. Kneeling, I emptied his pockets, and my own, gave him all my stuff, pouched all of his. Then I traded guns with him and opened the door.

"What I had in mind was that the first arrivals might not know him by sight, or not well enough to recognize him immediately. That would give me several seconds to arrange my disappearance in. But when I opened the door I found that my idea wouldn't work out as I had planned. The house detective was there, and a policeman, and I knew I was licked. There would be little chance of sneaking away from them. But I played my hand out. I told them I had come up to my room and found this chap on the floor going through my belongings. I had seized him, and in the struggle had shot him.

"Minutes went by like hours, and nobody denounced me. People were calling me Mr. Ashcraft. My impersonation was succeeding. It had me gasping then, but after I learned more about Ashcraft it wasn't so surprising. He had arrived at the hotel only that afternoon, and no one had seen him except in his hat and coat—the hat and coat I was wearing. We were of the same size and type—typical blond Englishmen.

"Then I got another surprise. When the detective examined the dead man's clothes he found that the maker's labels had been ripped out. When I got a look at his diary, later, I found the explanation of that. He had been tossing mental coins with himself, alternating between a determination to kill himself, and another to change his name and make a new place for himself in the world—putting his old life behind him. It was while he was considering the second plan that he had removed the markers from all of his clothing.

"But I didn't know that while I stood there among those people. All I knew was that miracles were happening. I met the miracles half-way, not turning a hair, accepting everything as a matter of course. I think the police smelled something wrong, but they couldn't put their hands on it. There was the dead man on the floor, with a prowler's outfit in his pockets, a pocketful of stolen jewelry, and the labels gone from his clothes—a burglar's trick. And there I was—a well-to-do Englishman whom the hotel people recognized as the room's rightful occupant.

"I had to talk small just then, but after I went through the dead man's stuff I knew him inside and outside, backward and forward. He had nearly a bushel of papers, and a diary that had everything he had ever done or thought in it. I put in the first night studying those things—memorizing them—and practicing his signature. Among the other things I had taken from his pockets were fifteen hundred dollars' worth of traveler's checks, and I wanted to be able to get them cashed in the morning.

"I stayed in Seattle for three days—as Norman Ashcraft. I had tumbled into something rich and I wasn't going to throw it away. The letter to his wife would keep me from being charged with murder if anything slipped, and I knew I was safer seeing the thing through than running. When the excitement had quieted down I packed up and came down to San Francisco, resuming my own name—Edward Bohannon. But I held onto all of Ashcraft's property, because I had learned from it that his wife had money, and I knew I could get some of it if I played my cards right.

"She saved me the trouble of figuring out a deal for myself. I ran across one of her advertisements in the *Examiner*, answered it, and—here we are."

I looked toward Tijuana. A cloud of yellow dust showed in a notch between two low hills. That would be the machine in which Gorman and Hooper were tracking me. Hooper would have seen me set out after the Englishman, would have waited for Gorman to arrive in the car in which he had followed Gooseneck from Mexicali—Gorman would have had to stay some distance in the rear—and then both of the operatives would have picked up my trail.

I turned to the Englishman.

"But you didn't have Mrs. Ashcraft killed?"

He shook his head.

"You'll never prove it."

"Maybe not," I admitted.

I took a package of cigarettes out of my pocket and put two of them on the seat between us.

"Suppose we play a game. This is just for my own satisfaction. It won't tie anybody to anything—won't prove anything. If you did a certain thing, pick up the cigarette that is nearer me. If you didn't do that thing, pick up the one nearer you. Will you play?"

"No, I won't," he said emphatically. "I don't like your game. But I do want a cigarette."

He reached out his uninjured arm and picked up the cigarette nearer *me*.

"Thanks, Ed," I said. "Now I hate to tell you this, but I'm going to swing you."

"You're balmy, my son."

"You're thinking of the San Francisco job, Ed," I explained. "I'm talking about Seattle. You, a hotel sneak-thief, were discovered in a room with a man who had just died with a bullet in his head. What do you think a jury will make out of that, Ed?"

He laughed at me. And then something went wrong with the laugh. It faded into a sickly grin.

"Of course you did," I said. "When you started to work out your plan to inherit all of Mrs. Ashcraft's wealth by having her killed, the first thing you did was to destroy that suicide letter of her husband's. No matter how carefully you guarded it, there was always a chance that somebody would stumble into it and knock your game on the head. It had served its purpose—you wouldn't need it. It would be foolish to take a chance on it turning up.

"I can't put you up for the murders you engineered in San Francisco; but I can sock you with the one you didn't do in Seattle—so justice won't be cheated. You're going to Seattle, Ed, to hang for Ashcraft's suicide."

And he did.

Nightmare Town

CHAPTER I

A Sensational Arrival

A FORD—whitened by desert travel until it was almost indistinguishable from the dust-clouds that swirled around it—came down Izzard's Main Street. Like the dust, it came swiftly, erratically, zigzagging the breadth of the roadway.

A small woman—a girl of twenty in tan flannel—stepped into the street. The wavering Ford missed her by inches, missing her at all only because her backward jump was bird-quick. She caught her lower lip between white teeth, dark eyes flashed annoyance at the rear of the passing machine, and she essayed the street again.

Near the opposite curb the Ford charged down upon her once more. But turning had taken some of its speed. She escaped it this time by scampering the few feet between her and the sidewalk ahead.

Out of the moving automobile a man stepped. Miraculously he kept his feet, stumbling, sliding, until an arm crooked around an iron awning-post jerked him into an abrupt halt. He was a large man in bleached khaki, tall, broad and thick-armed; his gray eyes were bloodshot; face and clothing were powdered heavily with dust. One of his hands clutched a thick, black stick, the other swept off his hat, and he bowed with exaggerated lowness before the girl's angry gaze.

The bow completed, he tossed his hat carelessly into the street, and grinned grotesquely through the dirt that masked his face—a grin that accented the heaviness of a begrimed and hair-roughened jaw.

"I *beg* y'r par'on," he said. "'F I hadn't been careful I believe I'd a'most hit you. 'S unreli'ble, tha' wagon. Borr'ed it from an engi—eng'neer. Don't ever borrow one from eng'neer. They're unreli'ble."

The girl looked at the place where he stood as if no one stood there, as if, in fact, no one had ever stood there, turned her small back on him, and walked very precisely down the street.

He stared after her with stupid surprise in his eyes until she had vanished through a doorway in the middle of the block. Then he scratched his head, shrugged, and turned to look across the street, where his machine had pushed its nose into the red brick side wall of the Bank of Izzard and now shook and clattered as if in panic at finding itself masterless.

"Look at the son-of-a-gun," he exclaimed.

A hand fastened upon his arm. He turned his head, and then, though he stood a good six feet himself, had to look up to meet the eyes of the giant who held his arm.

"We'll take a little walk," the giant said.

The man in bleached khaki examined the other from the tips of his broad-toed shoes to the creased crown of his black hat, examined him with a whole-hearted admiration that was unmistakable in his red-rimmed eyes. There were nearly seven massive feet of the speaker. Legs like pillars held up a great hogshead of a body, with wide shoulders that sagged a little, as if with their own excessive weight. He was a man of perhaps forty-five, and his face was thick-featured, phlegmatic, with sun-lines around small light eyes—the face of a deliberate man.

"My God, you're big!" the man in khaki exclaimed when he had finished his examination; and then his eyes brightened. "Let's wrestle. Bet you ten bucks against fifteen I can throw you. Come on!"

The giant chuckled deep in his heavy chest, took the man in khaki by the nape of the neck and an arm, and walked down the street with him.

CHAPTER II

Justice and a Slapped Face

Steve Threefall awakened without undue surprise at the unfamiliarity of his surroundings, as one who has awakened in strange places before. Before his eyes were well open he knew the essentials of his position. The feel of the shelf-bunk on which he lay and the sharp smell of disinfectant in his nostrils told him that he was in jail. His head and his mouth told him that he had been drunk; and the three-day growth of beard on his face told him he had been very drunk.

As he sat up and swung his feet down to the floor details came back to him. The two days of steady drinking in Whitetufts on the other side of the Nevada-California line, with Harris, the hotel proprietor, and Whiting, an irrigation engineer. The boisterous arguing over desert travel, with his own Gobi experience matched against the American experiences of the others. The bet that he could drive from Whitetufts to Izzard in daylight with nothing to drink but the especially bitter white liquor they were drinking at the time. The start in the grayness of imminent dawn, in Whiting's Ford, with Whiting and Harris staggering down the street after him, waking the town with their drunken shouts and roared-out mocking advice, until he had reached the desert's edge. Then the drive through the desert, along the road that was hotter than the rest of the desert, with— He chose not to think of the ride. He had made it, though— had won the bet. He couldn't remember the amount of the latter.

"So you've come out of it at last?" a rumbling voice inquired.

The steel-slated door swung open and a man filled the cell's door. Steve grinned up at him. This was the giant who would not wrestle. He was coatless and vestless now, and loomed larger than before. One suspender strap was decorated with a shiny badge that said "Marshal."

"Feel like breakfast?" he asked.

"I could do things to a can of black coffee," Steve admitted.

"All right. But you'll have to gulp it. Judge Denvir is waiting to get a crack at you, and the longer you keep him waiting, the tougher it'll be for you."

The room in which Tobin Denvir, J. P., dealt justice was a large one on the third floor of a wooden building. It was scantily furnished with a table, an ancient desk, a steel engraving of Daniel Webster, a shelf of books sleeping under the dust of weeks, a dozen uncomfortable chairs, and half as many cracked and chipped china cuspidors.

The judge sat between desk and table, with his feet on the latter. They were small feet, and he was a small man. His face was filled with little irritable lines, his lips were thin and tight, and he had the bright, lidless eyes of a bird.

"Well, what's he charged with?" His voice was thin, harshly metallic. He kept his feet on the table.

The marshal drew a deep breath, and recited:

"Driving on the wrong side of the street, exceeding the speed limit, driving while under the influence of liquor, driving without a driver's license, endangering the lives of pedestrians by taking his hands off the wheel, and parking improperly—on the sidewalk up against the bank."

The marshal took another breath, and added, with manifest regret:

"There was a charge of attempted assault, too, but that Vallance girl won't appear, so that'll have to be dropped."

The justice's bright eyes turned upon Steve.

"What's your name?" he growled.

"Steve Threefall."

"Is that your real name?" the marshal asked.

"Of course it is," the justice snapped. "You don't think anybody'd be damn fool enough to give a name like that unless it was his, do you?" Then to Steve: "What have you got to say—guilty or not?"

"I was a little—"

"Are you guilty or not?"

"Oh, I suppose I did—"

"That's enough! You're fined a hundred and fifty dollars and costs. The costs are fifteen dollars and eighty cents, making a total of a hundred and sixty-five dollars and eighty cents. Will you pay it or will you go to jail?"

"I'll pay it if I've got it," Steve said, turning to the marshal. "You took my money. Have I got that much?"

The marshal nodded his massive head.

"You have," he said, "exactly—to the nickel. Funny it should have come out like that—huh?"

"Yes—funny," Steve repeated.

While the justice of the peace was making out a receipt for the fine, the marshal restored Steve's watch, tobacco and matches, pocket-knife, keys, and last of all the black walking-stick. The big man weighed the stick in his hand and examined it closely before he gave it up. It was thick and of ebony, but heavy even for that wood, with a balanced weight that hinted at loaded ferrule and knob. Except for a space the breadth of a man's hand in its middle, the stick was roughened, cut and notched with the marks of hard use—marks that much careful polishing had failed to remove or conceal. The unscarred hand's-breadth was of a softer black than the rest—as soft a black as the knob—as if it had known much contact with a human palm.

"Not a bad weapon in a pinch," the marshal said meaningly as he handed the stick to its owner.

Steve took it with the grasp a man reserves for a favorite and constant companion.

"Not bad," he agreed. "What happened to the flivver?"

"It's in the garage around the corner on Main Street. Pete said it wasn't altogether ruined, and he thinks he can patch it up if you want."

The justice held out the receipt.

"Am I all through here now?" Steve asked.

"I hope so," Judge Denvir said sourly.

"Both of us," Steve echoed, put on his hat, tucked the black stick under his arm, nodded to the big marshal, and left the room.

Steve Threefall went down the wooden stairs toward the street in as cheerful a frame of mind as his body—burnt out inwardly with white liquor and outwardly by a day's scorching desert-riding—would permit. That justice had emptied his pockets of every last cent disturbed him little. That, he knew, was the way of justice everywhere with the stranger, and he had left the greater part of his money with the hotel proprietor in Whitetufts. He had escaped a jail sentence, and he counted himself lucky. He would wire Harris to send him some of his money, wait here until the Ford was repaired, and then drive back to Whitetufts—but not on a whisky ration this time.

"You will not!" a voice cried in his ear.

He jumped, and then laughed at his alcohol-jangled nerves. The words had not been meant for him. Beside him, at a turning of the stairs, was an open window, and opposite it, across a narrow alley, a window in another building was open.

This window belonged to an office in which two men stood facing each other across a flat-topped desk.

One of them was middle-aged and beefy, in a black broadcloth suit out of which a white-vested stomach protruded. His face was purple with rage. The man who faced him was younger—a man of perhaps thirty, with a small dark mustache, finely chiseled features, and satiny brown hair. His slender athlete's body was immaculately clothed in gray suit, gray shirt, gray and silver tie, and on the desk before him lay a Panama hat with gray band. His face was as white as the other's was purple.

The beefy man spoke—a dozen words pitched too low for Steve to catch.

The younger man slapped the speaker viciously across the face with an open hand—a hand that then flashed back to its owner's coat and flicked out a snub-nosed automatic pistol.

"You big lard-can," the younger man cried, his voice sibilant; "you'll lay off or I'll spoil your vest for you!"

He stabbed the protuberant vest with the automatic, and laughed into the scared fat face of the beefy man—laughed with a menacing flash of even teeth and dark slitted eyes. Then he picked up his hat, pocketed the pistol, and vanished from Steve's sight. The fat man sat down.

Steve went on down to the street.

CHAPTER III

Izzard Gains a Citizen

Steve unearthed the garage to which the Ford had been taken, found a greasy mechanic who answered to the name of Pete, and was told that Whiting's automobile would be in condition to move under its own power within two days.

"A beautiful snootful you had yesterday," Pete grinned.

Steve grinned back and went on out. He went down to the telegraph office, next door to the Izzard Hotel, pausing for a moment on the sidewalk to look at a glowing cream-colored Vauxhall-Velox roadster that stood at the curb—as out of place in this grimy factory town as a harlequin opal in a grocer's window.

In the doorway of the telegraph office Steve paused again, abruptly this time.

Behind the counter was a girl in tan flannel—the girl he had nearly run down twice the previous afternoon—the "Vallance girl" who had refrained from adding to justice's account against Steve Threefall. In front of the counter, leaning over it, talking to her with every appearance of intimacy, was one of the two men he had seen from the staircase window half an hour before—the slender dandy in gray who had slapped the other's face and threatened him with an automatic.

The girl looked up, recognized Steve, and stood very erect. He took off his hat, and advanced smiling.

"I'm awfully sorry about yesterday," he said. "I'm a crazy fool when I—"

"Do you wish to send a telegram?" she asked frigidly.

"Yes," Steve said; "I also wish to—"

"There are blanks and pencils on the desk near the window," and she turned her back on him.

Steve felt himself coloring, and since he was one of the men who habitually grin when at a loss, he grinned now, and found himself looking into the dark eyes of the man in gray.

That one smiled back under his little brown mustache, and said:

"Quite a time you had yesterday."

"Quite," Steve agreed, and went to the table the girl had indicated.

He wrote his telegram:

HENRY HARRIS,
  HARRIS HOTEL, WHITETUFTS:
ARRIVED RIGHT SIDE UP, BUT AM IN HOCK. WIRE
ME TWO HUNDRED DOLLARS. WILL BE BACK
SATURDAY.

THREEFALL.

But he did not immediately get up from the desk. He sat there holding the piece of paper in his fingers, studying the man and girl, who were again engaged in confidential conversation over the counter. Steve studied the girl most.

She was quite a small girl, no more than five feet in height, if that; and she had that peculiar rounded slenderness which gives a deceptively fragile appearance. Her face was an oval of skin whose fine whiteness had thus far withstood the grimy winds of Izzard; her nose just missed being upturned, her violet-black eyes just missed being too theatrically large, and her black-brown hair just missed being too bulky for the small head it crowned; but in no respect did she miss being as beautiful as a figure from a Monticelli canvas.

All these things Steve Threefall, twiddling his telegram in sun-brown fingers, considered and as he considered them he came to see the pressing necessity of having his apologies accepted. Explain it as you will—he carefully avoided trying to explain it to himself—the thing was there. One moment there was nothing, in the four continents he knew, of any bothersome importance to Steve Threefall; the next moment he was under an unescapable compulsion to gain the favor of this small person in tan flannel with brown ribbons at wrists and throat.

At this point the man in gray leaned farther over the counter, to whisper something to the girl. She flushed, and her eyes flinched. The pencil in her hand fell to the counter, and she picked it up with small fingers that were suddenly incongruously awkward. She made a smiling reply, and went on with her writing, but the smile seemed forced.

Steve tore up his telegram and composed another:

> I MADE IT, SLEPT IT OFF IN THE COOLER, AND
> AM GOING TO SETTLE HERE A WHILE. THERE ARE
> THINGS ABOUT THE PLACE I LIKE. WIRE MY MONEY
> AND SEND MY CLOTHES TO HOTEL HERE. BUY
> WHITING'S FORD FROM HIM AS CHEAP AS YOU CAN
> FOR ME.

He carried the blank to the counter and laid it down. The girl ran her pencil over it, counting the words.

"Forty-seven," she said, in a tone that involuntarily rebuked the absence of proper telegraphic brevity.

"Long, but it's all right," Steve assured her. "I'm sending it collect.

She regarded him icily.

"I can't accept a collect message unless I know that the sender can pay for it if the addressee refuses it. It's against the rules."

"You'd better make an exception this time," Steve told her solemnly, "because if you don't, you'll have to lend me the money to pay for it."

"I'll have—?"

"You will," he insisted. "You got me into this jam, and it's up to you to help get me out. The Lord knows you've cost me enough as it is—nearly two hundred dollars! The whole thing was your fault."

"*My fault?*"

"It was! Now I'm giving you a chance to square yourself. Hurry it off, please, because I'm hungry and I need a shave. I'll be waiting on the bench outside."

And he spun on his heel and left the office.

CHAPTER IV

A Thin, Sad-Faced Man

One end of the bench in front of the telegraph office was occupied when Steve, paying no attention to the man who sat there, made himself comfortable on the other. He put his black stick between his legs and rolled a cigarette with thoughtful slowness, his mind upon the just completed scene in the office.

Why, he wondered, whenever there was some special reason for gravity, did he always find himself becoming flippant? Why, whenever he found himself face to face with a situation that was important, that meant something to him, did he slip uncontrollably into banter—play the clown? He lit his cigarette and decided scornfully—as he had decided a dozen times before—that it all came from a childish attempt to conceal his self-consciousness; that for all his thirty-three years of life and his eighteen years of rubbing shoulders with the world—its rough corners as well as its polished—he was still a green boy underneath—a big kid.

"A neat package you had yesterday," the man who sat on the other end of the bench remarked.

"Yeah," Steve admitted without turning his head. He supposed he'd be hearing about his crazy arrival as long as he stayed in Izzard.

"I reckon old man Denvir took you to the cleaner's as usual?"

"Uh-huh!" Steve said, turning now for a look at the other.

He saw a very tall and very lean man in rusty brown, slouched down on the small of his back, angular legs thrust out across the sidewalk. A man past forty, whose gaunt melancholy face was marked with lines so deep that they were folds in the skin rather than wrinkles. His eyes were the mournful chestnut eyes of a basset hound, and his nose was as long and sharp as a paper knife. He puffed on a black cigar, getting from it a surprising amount of smoke, which he exhaled upward, his thin nose splitting the smoke into two gray plumes.

"Ever been to our fair young city before?" this melancholy individual asked next. His voice held a monotonous rhythm that was not unpleasant to the ear.

"No, this is my first time."

The thin man nodded ironically.

"You'll like it if you stay," he said. "It's very interesting."

"What's it all about?" Steve asked, finding himself mildly intrigued by his benchmate.

"Soda niter. You scoop it up off the desert, and boil and otherwise cook it, and sell it to fertilizer manufacturers, and nitric acid manufacturers, and any other kind of manufacturers who can manufacture something out of soda niter. The factory in which, for which, and from which you do all this lies yonder, beyond the railroad tracks."

He waved a lazy arm down the street, to where a group of square concrete buildings shut out the desert at the end of the thoroughfare.

"Suppose you don't play with this soda?" Steve asked, more to keep the thin man talking than to satisfy any thirst for local knowledge. "What do you do then?"

The thin man shrugged his sharp shoulders.

"That depends," he said, "on who you are. If you're Dave Brackett"—he wiggled a finger at the red bank across the street—"you gloat over your mortgages, or whatever it is a banker does; if you're Grant Fernie, and too big for a man without being quite big enough for a horse, you pin a badge on your bosom and throw rough-riding strangers into the can until they sober up; or if you're Larry Ormsby, and your old man owns the soda works, then you drive trick cars from across the pond"—nodding at the cream Vauxhall—"and spend your days pursuing beautiful telegraph operators. But I take it that you're broke, and have just wired for money, and are waiting for the more or less doubtful results. Is that it?"

"It is," Steve answered absent-mindedly. So the dandy in gray was named Larry Ormsby and was the factory owner's son.

The thin man drew in his feet and stood upon them.

"In that case it's lunch time, and my name is Roy Kamp, and I'm hungry, and I don't like to eat alone, and I'd be glad to have you face the greasy dangers of a meal at the Finn's with me."

Steve got up and held out his hand.

"I'll be glad to," he said. "The coffee I had for breakfast could stand company. My name's Steve Threefall."

They shook hands, and started up the street together. Coming toward them were two men in earnest conversation; one of them was the beefy man whose face Larry Ormsby had slapped. Steve waited until they had passed, and then questioned Kamp casually:

"And who are those prominent looking folks?"

"The little round one in the checkered college boy suit is Conan Elder, real estate, insurance, and securities. The Wallingford looking personage at his side is W. W. himself—the town's founder, owner, and whatnot—W. W. Ormsby, the Hon. Larry's papa."

The scene in the office, with its slapping of a face and flourish of a pistol, had been a family affair, then; a matter between father and son, with the son in the more forcible rôle. Steve, walking along with scant attention just now for the words Kamp's barytone voice was saying, felt a growing dissatisfaction in the memory of the girl and Larry Ormsby talking over the counter with their heads close together.

The Finn's lunchroom was little more than a corridor squeezed in between a poolroom and a hardware store, of barely sufficient width for a counter and a row of revolving stools. Only one customer was there when the two men entered.

"Hello, Mr. Rymer," said Kamp.

"How are you, Mr. Kamp?" the man at the counter said, and as he turned his head toward them, Steve saw that he was blind. His large blue eyes were filmed over with a gray curtain which gave him the appearance of having dark hollows instead of eyes.

He was a medium-sized man who looked seventy, but there was a suggestion of fewer years in the suppleness of his slender white hands. He had a thick mane of white hair above a face that was crisscrossed with wrinkles, but it was a calm face, the face of a man at peace with his world. He was just finishing his meal, and left shortly, moving to the door with the slow accuracy of the blind man in familiar surroundings.

"Old man Rymer," Kamp told Steve, "lives in a shack behind where the new fire house is going to be, all alone. Supposed to have tons of gold coins under his floor—thus local gossip. Some day we're going to find him all momicked up. But he won't listen to reason. Says nobody would hurt him. Says that in a town as heavy with assorted thugs as this!"

"A tough town, is it?" Steve asked.

"Couldn't help being! It's only three years old—and a desert boom town draws the tough boys."

Kamp left Steve after their meal, saying he probably would run across him later in the evening, and suggesting that there were games of a sort to be found in the next-door poolroom.

"I'll see you there then," Steve said, and went back to the telegraph office.

The girl was alone.

"Anything for me?" he asked her.

She put a green check and a telegram on the counter and returned to her desk.

The telegram read:

COLLECTED BET. PAID WHITING TWO HUNDRED
FOR FORD. SENDING BALANCE SIX HUNDRED FORTY.
SHIPPING CLOTHES. WATCH YOUR STEP.

HARRIS.

"Did you send the wire collect, or do I owe—"

"Collect." She did not look up.

Steve put his elbows on the counter and leaned over; his jaw, still exaggerated by its growth of hair, although he had washed the dirt from it, jutted forward with his determination to maintain a properly serious attitude until he had done this thing that had to be done.

"Now listen, Miss Vallance," he said deliberately. "I was all kinds of a damned fool yesterday, and I'm sorrier than I can say. But, after all, nothing terrible happened, and—"

"Nothing terrible!" she exploded. "Is it nothing to be humiliated by being chased up and down the street like a rabbit by a drunken man with a dirty face in a worse car?"

"I wasn't chasing you. I came back that second time to apologize. But, anyway"—in the uncomfortable face of her uncompromising hostility his determination to be serious went for nothing, and he relapsed into his accustomed defensive mockery—"no matter how scared you were you ought to accept my apology now and let bygones be bygones."

"Scared? Why—"

"I wish you wouldn't repeat words after me," he complained. "This morning you did it, and now you're at it again. Don't you ever think of anything to say on your own account?"

She glared at him, opened her mouth, shut it with a little click. Her angry face bent sharply over the papers on the desk, and she began to add a column of figures.

Steve nodded with pretended approval, and took his check across the street to the bank.

The only man in sight in the bank when Steve came in was a little plump fellow with carefully trimmed salt-and-pepper whiskers hiding nearly all of a jovial round face except the eyes—shrewd, friendly eyes.

This man came to the window in the grille, and said: "Good afternoon. Can I do something for you?"

Steve laid down the telegraph company's check.

"I want to open an account."

The banker picked up the slip of green paper and flicked it with a fat finger.

"You are the gentleman who assaulted my wall with an automobile yesterday?"

Steve grinned. The banker's eyes twinkled, and a smile ruffled his whiskers.

"Are you going to stay in Izzard?"

"For a while."

"Can you give me references?" the banker asked.

"Maybe Judge Denvir or Marshal Fernie will put in a word for me," Steve said. "But if you'll write the Seaman's Bank in San Francisco they'll tell you that so far as they know I'm all right."

The banker stuck a plump hand through the window in the grille.

"I'm very glad to make your acquaintance. My name is David Brackett, and anything I can do to help you get established—call on me."

Outside of the bank ten minutes later, Steve met the huge marshal, who stopped in front of him.

"You still here?" Fernie asked.

"I'm an Izzardite now," Steve said. "For a while, anyhow. I like your hospitality."

"Don't let old man Denvir see you coming out of a bank," Fernie advised him, "or he'll soak you plenty next time."

"There isn't going to be any next time."

"There always is—in Izzard," the marshal said enigmatically as he got his bulk in motion again.

CHAPTER V

A Man Leaves Izzard

That night, shaved and bathed, though still wearing his bleached khaki, Steve, with his black stick beside him, played stud poker with Roy Kamp and four factory workers. They played in the poolroom next door to the Finn's lunchroom. Izzard apparently was a wide-open town. Twelve tables given to craps, poker, red dog, and twenty-one occupied half of the poolroom, and white-hot liquor was to be had at the cost of fifty cents and a raised finger. There was nothing surreptitious about the establishment; obviously its proprietor—a bullet-headed Italian whose customers called him "Gyp"—was in favor with the legal powers of Izzard.

The game in which Steve sat went on smoothly and swiftly, as play does when adepts participate. Though, as most games are, always potentially crooked, it was, in practice, honest. The six men at the table were, without exception, men who knew their way around—men who played quietly and watchfully, winning and losing without excitement or inattention. Not one of the six—except Steve, and perhaps Kamp—would have hesitated to favor himself at the expense of honesty had the opportunity come to him; but where knowledge of trickery is evenly distributed honesty not infrequently prevails.

Larry Ormsby came into the poolroom at a little after eleven and sat at a table some distance from Steve. Faces he had seen in the street during the day were visible through the smoke. At five minutes to twelve the four factory men at Steve's table left for work—they were in the "graveyard" shift—and the game broke up with their departure. Steve, who had kept about even throughout the play, found that he had won something less than ten dollars; Kamp had won fifty some.

Declining invitations to sit in another game, Steve and Kamp left together, going out into the dark and night-cool street, where the air was sweet after the smoke and alcohol of the poolroom. They walked slowly down the dim thoroughfare toward the Izzard Hotel, neither in a hurry to end their first evening together; for each knew by now that the unpainted bench in front of the telegraph office had given him a comrade. Not a thousand words had passed between the two men, but they had as surely become brothers-in-arms as if they had tracked a continent together.

Strolling thus, a dark doorway suddenly vomited men upon them.

Steve rocked back against a building front from a blow on his head, arms were around him, the burning edge of a knife blade ran down his left arm. He chopped his black stick up into a body, freeing himself from encircling grip. He used the moment's respite this gave him to change his grasp on the stick; so that he held it now horizontal, his right hand grasping its middle, its lower half flat against his forearm, its upper half extending to the left.

He put his left side against the wall, and the black stick became a whirling black arm of the night. The knob darted down at a man's head. The man threw an arm up to fend the blow. Spinning back on its axis, the stick reversed—the fer-ruled end darted up under warding arm, hit jawbone with a click, and no sooner struck than slid forward, jabbing deep into throat. The owner of that jaw and throat turned his broad, thick-featured face to the sky; went backward out of the fight, and was lost to sight beneath the curbing.

Kamp, struggling with two men in the middle of the side-walk, broke loose from them, whipped out a gun; but before he could use it his assailants were on him again.

Lower half of stick against forearm once more, Steve whirled in time to take the impact of a blackjack-swinging arm upon it. The stick spun sidewise with thud of knob on temple—spun back with loaded ferrule that missed opposite temple only because the first blow had brought its target down on knees. Steve saw suddenly that Kamp had gone down. He spun his stick and battered a passage to the thin man, kicked a head that bent over the prone, thin form, strad-dled it; and the ebony stick whirled swifter in his hand—spun as quarter staves once spun in Sherwood Forest. Spun to the clicking tune of wood on bone, on metal weapons; to the duller rhythm of wood on flesh. Spun never in full circles, but always in short arcs—one end's recovery from a blow adding velocity to the other's stroke. Where an instant ago knob had swished from left to right, now weighted ferrule struck from right to left—struck under up-thrown arms, over low-thrown arms—put into space a forty-inch sphere, whose radii were whirling black flails.

Behind his stick that had become a living part of him, Steve Threefall knew happiness—that rare happiness which only the expert ever finds—the joy in doing a thing that he can do supremely well. Blows he took—blows that shook him, stag-gered him—but he scarcely noticed them. His whole con-sciousness was in his right arm and the stick it spun. A revolver, tossed from a smashed hand, exploded ten feet over his head, a knife tinkled like a bell on the brick sidewalk, a man screamed as a stricken horse screams.

As abruptly as it had started, the fight stopped. Feet thud-ded away, forms vanished into the more complete darkness of a side street; and Steve was standing alone—alone except for the man stretched out between his feet and the other man who lay still in the gutter.

Kamp crawled from beneath Steve's legs and scrambled briskly to his feet.

"Your work with a bat is what you might call adequate," he drawled.

Steve stared at the thin man. This was the man he had accepted on an evening's acquaintance as a comrade! A man who lay on the street and let his companion do the fighting for both! Hot words formed in Steve's throat.

"You—"

The thin man's face twisted into a queer grimace, as if he were listening to faint, far-off sounds. He caught his hands to his chest, pressing the sides together. Then he turned half around, went down on one knee, went over backward with a leg bent under him.

"Get—word—to—"

The fourth word was blurred beyond recognition. Steve knelt beside Kamp, lifted his head from the bricks, and saw that Kamp's thin body was ripped open from throat to waistline.

"Get—word—to—" the thin man tried desperately to make the last word audible.

A hand gripped Steve's shoulder.

"What the hell's all this?" the roaring voice of Marshal Grant Fernie blotted out Kamp's words.

"Shut up a minute!" Steve snapped, and put his ear again close to Kamp's mouth.

But now the dying man could achieve no articulate sound. He tried with an effort that bulged his eyes; then he shuddered horribly, coughed, the slit in his chest gaped open, and he died.

"What's all this?" the marshal repeated.

"Another reception committee," Steve said bitterly, easing the dead body to the sidewalk, and standing up. "There's one of them in the street; the others beat it around the corner."

He tried to point with his left hand, then let it drop to his side. Looking at it, he saw that his sleeve was black with blood.

The marshal bent to examine Kamp, grunted, "He's dead, all right," and moved over to where the man Steve had knocked into the gutter lay.

"Knocked out," the marshal said, straightening up; "but he'll be coming around in a while. How'd you make out?"

"My arm's slashed, and I've got some sore spots, but I'll live through it."

Fernie took hold of the wounded arm.

"Not bleeding so bad," he decided. "But you better get it patched up. Doc MacPhail's is only a little way up the street. Can you make it, or do you want me to give you a lift?"

"I can make it. How do I find the place?"

"Two blocks up this street, and four to the left. You can't miss it—it's the only house in town with flowers in front of it. I'll get in touch with you when I want you."

CHAPTER VI

The House with Flowers

Steve Threefall found Dr. MacPhail's house without difficulty —a two-story building set back from the street, behind a garden that did its best to make up in floral profusion for Izzard's general barrenness. The fence was hidden under twining virgin's bower, clustered now with white blossoms, and the narrow walk wound through roses, trillium, poppies, tulips, and geraniums that were ghosts in the starlight. The air was heavily sweet with the fragrance of saucerlike moon flowers, whose vines covered the doctor's porch.

Two steps from the latter Steve stopped, and his right hand slid to the middle of his stick. From one end of the porch had come a rustling, faint but not of the wind, and a spot that was black between vines had an instant before been paler, as if framing a peeping face.

"Who is—" Steve began, and went staggering back.

From the vine-blackened porch a figure had flung itself on his chest.

"Mr. Threefall," the figure cried in the voice of the girl of the telegraph office, "there's somebody in the house!"

"You mean a burglar?" he asked stupidly, staring down into the small white face that was upturned just beneath his chin.

"Yes! He's upstairs—in Dr. MacPhail's room!"

"Is the doctor up there?"

"No, no! He and Mrs. MacPhail haven't come home yet."

He patted her soothingly on a velvet-coated shoulder, selecting a far shoulder, so that he had to put his arm completely around her to do the patting.

"We'll fix that," he promised. "You stick here in the shadows, and I'll be back as soon as I have taken care of our friend."

"No, no!" She clung to his shoulder with both hands. "I'll go with you. I couldn't stay here alone; but I won't be afraid with you."

He bent his head to look into her face, and cold metal struck his chin, clicking his teeth together. The cold metal was the muzzle of a big nickel-plated revolver in one of the hands that clung to his shoulder.

"Here, give me that thing," he exclaimed; "and I'll let you come with me."

She gave him the gun and he put it in his pocket.

"Hold on to my coat tails," he ordered; "keep as close to me as you can, and when I say, 'Down,' let go, drop flat on the floor, and stay there."

Thus, the girl whispering guidance to him, they went through the door she had left open, into the house, and mounted to the second floor. From their right, as they stood at the head of the stairs, came cautious rustlings.

Steve put his face down until the girl's hair was on his lips. "How do you get to that room?" he whispered.

"Straight down the hall. It ends there."

They crept down the hall. Steve's outstretched hand touched a door frame.

"Down!" he whispered to the girl.

Her fingers released his coat. He flung the door open, jumped through, slammed it behind him. A head-sized oval was black against the gray of a window. He spun his stick at it. Something caught the stick overhead, glass crashed, showering him with fragments. The oval was no longer visible against the window. He wheeled to the left, flung out an arm toward a sound of motion. His fingers found a neck—a thin neck with skin as dry and brittle as paper.

A kicking foot drove into his shin just below the knee. The paperish neck slid out of his hand. He dug at it with desperate fingers, but his fingers, weakened by the wound in his forearm, failed to hold. He dropped his stick and flashed his right hand to the left's assistance. Too late. The weakened hand had fallen away from the paperish neck, and there was nothing for the right to clutch.

A misshapen blot darkened the center of an open window, vanished with a thud of feet on the roof of the rear porch. Steve sprang to the window in time to see the burglar scramble up from the ground, where he had slid from the porch roof, and make for the low back fence. One of Steve's legs was over the sill when the girl's arms came around his neck.

"No, no!" she pleaded. "Don't leave me! Let him go!"

"All right," he said reluctantly, and then brightened.

He remembered the gun he had taken from the girl, got it out of his pocket as the fleeing shadow in the yard reached the fence; and as the shadow, one hand on the fence top, vaulted high over it, Steve squeezed the trigger. The revolver clicked. Again—another click. Six clicks, and the burglar was gone into the night.

Steve broke the revolver in the dark, and ran his fingers over the back of the cylinder—six empty chambers.

"Turn on the lights," he said brusquely.

CHAPTER VII

Blind Rymer

When the girl had obeyed Steve stepped back into the room, and looked first for his ebony stick. That in his hand, he faced the girl. Her eyes were jet black with excitement and pale lines of strain were around her mouth. As they stood looking into each other's eyes something of bewilderment began to show through her fright. He turned away abruptly and gazed around the room.

The place had been ransacked thoroughly if not expertly. Drawers stood out, their contents strewn on the floor; the bed had been stripped of clothing, and pillows had been dumped out of their cases. Near the door a broken wall light—the obstruction that had checked Steve's stick—hung crookedly. In the center of the floor lay a gold watch and half a length of gold chain. He picked them up and held them out to the girl.

"Dr. MacPhail's?"

She shook her head in denial before she took the watch, and then, examining it closely, she gave a little gasp.

"It's Mr. Rymer's!"

"Rymer?" Steve repeated, and then he remembered. Rymer was the blind man who had been in the Finn's lunchroom, and for whom Kamp had prophesied trouble.

"Yes! Oh, I know something has happened to him!"

She put a hand on Steve's left arm.

"We've got to go see! He lives all alone, and if any harm has—"

She broke off, and looked down at the arm under her hand.

"Your arm! You're hurt!"

"Not as bad as it looks," Steve said. "That's what brought me here. But it has stopped bleeding. Maybe by the time we get back from Rymer's the doctor will be home."

They left the house by the back door, and the girl led him through dark streets and across darker lots. Neither of them spoke during the five minute walk. The girl hurried at a pace that left her little breath for conversation, and Steve was occupied with uncomfortable thinking.

The blind man's cabin was dark when they reached it, but the front door was ajar. Steve knocked his stick against the frame, got no answer, and struck a match. Rymer lay on the floor, sprawled on his back, his arms outflung.

The cabin's one room was topsy turvy. Furniture lay in up-ended confusion, clothing was scattered here and there, and boards had been torn from the floor. The girl knelt beside the unconscious man while Steve hunted for a light. Presently he found an oil lamp that had escaped injury, and got it burning just as Rymer's filmed eyes opened and he sat up. Steve righted an overthrown rocking chair and, with the girl, assisted the blind man to it, where he sat panting.

He had recognized the girl's voice at once, and he smiled bravely in her direction.

"I'm all right, Nova," he said; "not hurt a bit. Some one

knocked at the door, and when I opened it I heard a swishing sound in my ear—and that was all I knew until I came to to find you here."

He frowned with sudden anxiety, got to his feet, and moved across the room. Steve pulled a chair and an upset table from his path, and the blind man dropped on his knees in a corner, fumbling beneath the loosened floor boards. His hands came out empty, and he stood up with a tired droop to his shoulders.

"Gone," he said softly.

Steve remembered the watch then, took it from his pocket, and put it into one of the blind man's hands.

"There was a burglar at our house," the girl explained. "After he had gone we found that on the floor. This is Mr. Threefall."

The blind man groped for Steve's hand, pressed it, then his flexible fingers caressed the watch, his face lighting up happily.

"I'm glad," he said, "to have this back—gladder than I can say. The money wasn't so much—less than three hundred dollars. I'm not the Midas I'm said to be. But this watch was my father's."

He tucked it carefully into his vest, and then, as the girl started to straighten up the room, he remonstrated.

"You'd better run along home, Nova; it's late, and I'm all right. I'll go to bed now, and let the place go as it is until tomorrow."

The girl demurred, but presently she and Steve were walking back to the MacPhails' house, through the black streets; but they did not hurry now. They walked two blocks in silence, Steve looking ahead into dark space with glum thoughtfulness, the girl eying him covertly.

"What is the matter?" she asked abruptly.

Steve smiled pleasantly down at her.

"Nothing. Why?"

"There is," she contradicted him. "You're thinking of something unpleasant, something to do with me."

He shook his head.

"That's wrong, wrong on the face of it—they don't go together."

But she was not to be put off with compliments.

"You're—you're—" She stood still in the dim street, searching for the right word. "You're on your guard—you don't trust me—that's what it is!"

Steve smiled again, but with narrowed eyes. This reading of his mind might have been intuitive, or it might have been something else.

He tried a little of the truth:

"Not distrustful—just wondering. You know you *did* give me an empty gun to go after the burglar with, and you know you *wouldn't* let me chase him."

Her eyes flashed, and she drew herself up to the last inch of her slender five feet.

"So you think," she began indignantly. Then she drooped toward him, her hands fastening upon the lapels of his coat. "Please, please, Mr. Threefall, you've got to believe that I didn't know the revolver was empty. It was Dr. MacPhail's. I took it when I ran out of the house, never dreaming that it wasn't loaded. And as for not letting you chase the burglar— I was afraid to be left alone again. I'm a little coward. I—I— Please believe in me, Mr. Threefall. Be friends with me. I need friends. I—"

Womanhood had dropped from her. She pleaded with the small white face of a child of twelve—a lonely, frightened child. And because his suspicions would not capitulate immediately to her appeal, Steve felt dumbly miserable, with an obscure shame in himself, as if he were lacking in some quality he should have had.

She went on talking, very softly, so that he had to bend his head to catch the words. She talked about herself, as a child would talk.

"It's been terrible! I came here three months ago because there was a vacancy in the telegraph office. I was suddenly alone in the world, with very little money, and telegraphy was all I knew that could be capitalized. It's been terrible here! The town—I can't get accustomed to it. It's so bleak. No children play in the streets. The people are different from those I've known—cruder, more brutal. Even the houses— street after street of them without curtains in the windows, without flowers. No grass in the yards, no trees.

"But I had to stay—there was nowhere else to go. I

thought I could stay until I had saved a little money—enough to take me away. But saving money takes so long. Dr. MacPhail's garden has been like a piece of paradise to me. If it hadn't been for that I don't think I could have—I'd have gone crazy! The doctor and his wife have been nice to me; some people have been nice to me, but most of them are people I can't understand. And not all have been nice. At first it was awful. Men would say things, and women would say things, and when I was afraid of them they thought I was stuck up. Larry—Mr. Ormsby—saved me from that. He made them let me alone, and he persuaded the MacPhails to let me live with them. Mr. Rymer has helped me, too, given me courage; but I lose it again as soon as I'm away from the sight of his face and the sound of his voice.

"I'm scared—scared of everything! Of Larry Ormsby especially! And he's been wonderfully helpful to me. But I can't help it. I'm afraid of him—of the way he looks at me sometimes, of things he says when he has been drinking. It's as if there was something inside of him waiting for something. I shouldn't say this—because I owe him gratitude for— But I'm so afraid! I'm afraid of every person, of every house, of every doorstep even. It's a nightmare!"

Steve found that one of his hands was cupped over the white cheek that was not flat against his chest, and that his other arm was around her shoulders, holding her close.

"New towns are always like this, or worse," he began to tell her. "You should have seen Hopewell, Virginia, when the DuPonts first opened it. It takes time for the undesirables who come with the first rush to be weeded out. And, stuck out here in the desert, Izzard would naturally fare a little worse than the average new town. As for being friends with you—that's why I stayed here instead of going back to Whitetufts. We'll be great friends. We'll—"

He never knew how long he talked, or what he said; though he imagined afterward that he must have made a very long-winded and very stupid speech. But he was not talking for the purpose of saying anything; he was talking to soothe the girl, and to keep her small face between his hand and chest, and her small body close against his for as long a time as possible.

So he talked on and on and on—

CHAPTER VIII

A Pair of Threats

The MacPhails were at home when Nova Vallance and Steve came through the flowered yard again, and they welcomed the girl with evident relief. The doctor was a short man with a round bald head, and a round jovial face, shiny and rosy except where a sandy mustache drooped over his mouth. His wife was perhaps ten years younger than he, a slender blond woman with much of the feline in the set of her blue eyes and the easy grace of her movements.

"The car broke down with us about twenty miles out," the doctor explained in a mellow rambling voice with a hint of a burr lingering around the r's. "I had to perform a major operation on it before we could get going again. When we got home we found you gone, and were just about to rouse the town."

The girl introduced Steve to the MacPhails, and then told them about the burglar, and of what they had found in the blind man's cabin.

Dr. MacPhail shook his round naked head and clicked his tongue on teeth.

"Seems to me Fernie doesn't do all that could be done to tone Izzard down," he said.

Then the girl remembered Steve's wounded arm, and the doctor examined, washed, and bandaged it.

"You won't have to wear the arm in a sling," he said; "if you take a reasonable amount of care of it. It isn't a deep cut, and fortunately it went between the *supinator tongus* and the *great palmar* without injury to either. Get it from our burglar?"

"No. Got it in the street. A man named Kamp and I were walking toward the hotel to-night and were jumped. Kamp was killed. I got this."

An asthmatic clock somewhere up the street was striking three as Steve passed through the MacPhails' front gate and set out for the hotel again. He felt tired and sore in every muscle, and he walked close to the curb.

"If anything else happens to-night," he told himself, "I'm going to run like hell from it. I've had enough for one evening."

At the first cross street he had to pause to let an automobile race by. As it passed him he recognized it—Larry Ormsby's cream Vauxhall. In its wake sped five big trucks, with a speed that testified to readjusted gears. In a roar of engines, a cloud of dust, and a rattling of windows, the caravan vanished toward the desert.

Steve went on toward the hotel, thinking. The factory worked twenty-four hours a day, he knew; but surely no necessity of niter manufacturing would call for such excessive speed in its trucks—if they were factory trucks. He turned into Main Street and faced another surprise. The cream Vauxhall stood near the corner, its owner at the wheel. As Steve came abreast of it Larry Ormsby let its near door swing open, and held out an inviting hand.

Steve stopped and stood by the door.

"Jump in and I'll give you a lift as far as the hotel."

"Thanks."

Steve looked quizzically from the man's handsome, reckless face to the now dimly lighted hotel, less than two blocks away. Then he looked at the man again, and got into the automobile beside him.

"I hear you're a more or less permanent fixture among us," Ormsby said, proffering Steve cigarettes in a lacquered leather case, and shutting off his idling engine.

"For a while."

Steve declined the cigarettes and brought out tobacco and papers from his pocket, adding, "There are things about the place I like."

"I also hear you had a little excitement to-night."

"Some," Steve admitted, wondering whether the other meant the fight in which Kamp had been killed, the burglary at the MacPhails', or both.

"If you keep up the pace you've set," the factory owner's son went on, "it won't take you long to nose me out of my position as Izzard's brightest light."

Tautening nerves tickled the nape of Steve's neck. Larry Ormsby's words and tone seemed idle enough, but underneath them was a suggestion that they were not aimless—that they were leading to some definite place. It was not likely that he had circled around to intercept Steve merely to exchange meaningless chatter with him. Steve, lighting his cigarette, grinned and waited.

"The only thing I ever got from the old man, besides money," Larry Ormsby was saying, "is a deep-rooted proprietary love for my own property. I'm a regular burgher for insisting that my property is mine and must stay mine. I don't know exactly how to feel about a stranger coming in and making himself the outstanding black sheep of the town in two days. A reputation—even for recklessness—is property, you know; and I don't feel that I should give it up—*or any other rights*—without a struggle."

There it was. Steve's mind cleared. He disliked subtleties. But now he knew what the talk was about. He was being warned to keep away from Nova Vallance.

"I knew a fellow once in Onehunga," he drawled, "who thought he owned all of the Pacific south of the Tropic of Capricorn—and had papers to prove it. He'd been that way ever since a Maori bashed in his head with a stone *mere*. Used to accuse us of stealing our drinking water from his ocean."

Larry Ormsby flicked his cigarette into the street and started the engine.

"But the point is"—he was smiling pleasantly—"that a man is moved to protect what he thinks belongs to him. He may be wrong, of course, but that wouldn't affect the—ah—vigor of his protecting efforts."

Steve felt himself growing warm and angry.

"Maybe you're right," he said slowly, with deliberate intent to bring this thing between them to a crisis, "but I've never had enough experience with property to know how I'd feel about being deprived of it. But suppose I had a —well, say— a white vest that I treasured. And suppose a man slapped my face and threatened to spoil the vest. I reckon I'd forget all about protecting the vest in my hurry to tangle with him."

Larry laughed sharply.

Steve caught the wrist that flashed up, and pinned it to Ormsby's side with a hand that much spinning of a heavy stick had muscled with steel.

"Easy," he said into the slitted, dancing eyes; "easy now."

Larry Ormsby's white teeth flashed under his mustache.

"Righto," he smiled. "If you'll turn my wrist loose, I'd

like to shake hands with you—a sort of ante-bellum gesture. I like you, Threefall; you're going to add materially to the pleasures of Izzard."

In his room on the third floor of the Izzard Hotel, Steve Threefall undressed slowly, hampered by a stiff left arm and much thinking. Matter for thought he had in abundance. Larry Ormsby slapping his father's face and threatening him with an automatic; Larry Ormsby and the girl in confidential conversation; Kamp dying in a dark street, his last words lost in the noise of the marshal's arrival; Nova Vallance giving him an empty revolver, and persuading him to let a burglar escape; the watch on the floor and the looting of the blind man's savings; the caravan Larry Ormsby had led toward the desert; the talk in the Vauxhall, with its exchange of threats.

Was there any connection between each of these things and the others? Or were they simply disconnected happenings? If there was a connection—and the whole of that quality in mankind which strives toward simplification of life's phenomena, unification, urged him to belief in a connection—just what was it? Still puzzling, he got into bed; and then out again quickly. An uneasiness that had been vague until now suddenly thrust itself into his consciousness. He went to the door, opened, and closed it. It was a cheaply carpentered door, but it moved easily and silently on well-oiled hinges.

"I reckon I'm getting to be an old woman," he growled to himself; "but I've had all I want to-night."

He blocked the door with the dresser, put his stick where he could reach it quickly, got into bed again, and went to sleep.

CHAPTER IX

"What Next?"

A pounding on the door awakened Steve at nine o'clock the next morning. The pounder was one of Fernie's subordinates, and he told Steve that he was expected to be present at the inquest into Kamp's death within an hour. Steve found that his wounded arm bothered him little; not so much as a bruised area on one shoulder—another souvenir of the fight in the street.

He dressed, ate breakfast in the hotel café, and went up to Ross Amthor's "undertaking parlor," where the inquest was to be held.

The coroner was a tall man with high, narrow shoulders and a sallow, puffy face, who sped proceedings along regardless of the finer points of legal technicality. Steve told his story, the marshal told his, and then produced a prisoner—a thickset Austrian who seemingly neither spoke nor understood English. His throat and lower face were swathed in white bandages.

"Is this the one you knocked down?" the coroner asked.

Steve looked at as much of the Austrian's face as was visible above the bandages.

"I don't know. I can't see enough of him."

"This is the one I picked out of the gutter," Grant Fernie volunteered; "whether you knocked him there or not. I don't suppose you got a good look at him. But this is he all right."

Steve frowned doubtfully.

"I'd know him," he said, "if he turned his face up and I got a good look at him."

"Take off some of his bandages so the witness can see him," the coroner ordered.

Fernie unwound the Austrian's bandages, baring a bruised and swollen jaw.

Steve stared at the man. This fellow may have been one of his assailants, but he most certainly wasn't the one he had knocked into the street. He hesitated. Could he have confused faces in the fight?

"Do you identify him?" the coroner asked impatiently.

Steve shook his head.

"I don't remember ever seeing him."

"Look here, Threefall," the giant marshal scowled down at Steve, "this is the man I hauled out of the gutter—one of the men you said jumped you and Kamp. Now what's the game? What's the idea of forgetting?"

Steve answered slowly, stubbornly:

"I don't know. All I know is that this isn't the first one I hit, the one I knocked out. He was an American—had an American face. He was about this fellow's size, but this isn't he."

The coroner exposed broken yellow teeth in a snarl, the marshal glowered at Steve, the jurors regarded him with frank suspicion. The marshal and the coroner withdrew to a far corner of the room, where they whispered together, casting frequent glances at Steve.

"All right," the coroner told Steve when this conference was over; "that's all."

From the inquest Steve walked slowly back to the hotel, his mind puzzled by this newest addition to Izzard's mysteries. What was the explanation of the certain fact that the man the marshal had produced at the inquest was not the man he had taken from the gutter the previous night? Another thought: the marshal had arrived immediately after the fight of the men who had attacked him and Kamp, had arrived noisily, drowning the dying man's last words. That opportune arrival and the accompanying noise—were they accidental? Steve didn't know; and because he didn't know he strode back to the hotel in frowning meditation.

At the hotel he found that his bag had arrived from Whitetufts. He took it up to his room and changed his clothes. Then he carried his perplexity to the window, where he sat smoking cigarette after cigarette, staring into the alley below, his forehead knotted beneath his tawny hair. Was it possible that so many things should explode around one man in so short a time, in a small city of Izzard's size, without there being a connection between them—and between them and him? And if he was being involved in a vicious maze of crime and intrigue, what was it all about? What had started it? What was the key to it? The girl?

Confused thoughts fell away from him. He sprang to his feet.

Down the other side of the alley a man was walking—a thickset man in soiled blue—a man with bandaged throat and chin. What was visible of his face was the face Steve had seen turned skyward in the fight—the face of the man he had knocked out.

Steve sprang to the door, out of the room, down three flights of stairs, past the desk, and out of the hotel's back door. He gained the alley in time to see a blue trousers-leg disappearing into a doorway in the block below. Thither he went.

The doorway opened into an office building. He searched the corridors, upstairs and down, and did not find the bandaged man. He returned to the ground floor and discovered a sheltered corner near the back door, near the foot of the stairs. The corner was shielded from stairs and from most of the corridor by a wooden closet in which brooms and mops were kept. The man had entered through the rear of the building; he would probably leave that way; Steve waited.

Fifteen minutes passed, bringing no one within sight of his hiding place. Then from the front of the building came a woman's soft laugh, and footsteps moved toward him. He shrank back in his dusky corner. The footsteps passed—a man and a woman laughing and talking together as they walked. They mounted the stairs. Steve peeped out at them, and then drew back suddenly, more in surprise than in fear of detection, for the two who mounted the stairs were completely engrossed in each other.

The man was Elder, the insurance and real estate agent. Steve did not see his face, but the checkered suit on his round figure was unmistakable—"college boy suit," Kamp had called it. Elder's arm was around the woman's waist as they went up the steps, and her cheek leaned against his shoulder as she looked coquettishly into his face. The woman was Dr. MacPhail's feline wife.

"What next?" Steve asked himself, when they had passed from his sight. "Is the whole town wrong? What next, I wonder?"

The answer came immediately—the pounding of crazy footsteps directly over Steve's head—footsteps that might have belonged to a drunken man, or to a man fighting a phantom. Above the noise of heels on wooden floor, a scream rose—a scream that blended horror and pain into a sound that was all the more unearthly because it was unmistakably of human origin.

Steve bolted out of his corner and up the steps three at a time, pivoted into the second floor corridor on the newel, and came face to face with David Brackett, the banker.

Brackett's thick legs were far apart, and he swayed on them. His face was a pallid agony above his beard. Big spots of beard were gone, as if torn out or burned away. From his writhing lips thin wisps of vapor issued.

"They've poisoned me, the damned—"

He came suddenly up on the tips of his toes, his body arched, and he fell stiffly backward, as dead things fall.

Steve dropped on a knee beside him, but he knew nothing could be done—knew Brackett had died while still on his feet. For a moment, as he crouched there over the dead man, something akin to panic swept Steve Threefall's mind clean of reason. Was there never to be an end to this piling of mystery upon mystery, of violence upon violence? He had the sensation of being caught in a monstrous net—a net without beginning or end, and whose meshes were slimy with blood. Nausea—spiritual and physical—gripped him, held him impotent.

Then a shot crashed.

He jerked erect—sprang down the corridor toward the sound; seeking in a frenzy of physical activity escape from the sickness that had filled him.

At the end of the corridor a door was labeled "Ormsby Niter Corporation, W. W. Ormsby, President." There was no need for hesitancy before deciding that the shot had come from behind that label. Even as he dashed toward it, another shot rattled the door and a falling body thudded behind it.

Steve flung the door open—and jumped aside to avoid stepping on the man who lay just inside. Over by a window, Larry Ormsby stood facing the door, a black automatic in his hand. His eyes danced with wild merriment, and his lips curled in a tight-lipped smile.

"Hello, Threefall," he said. "I see you're still keeping close to the storm centers."

Steve looked down at the man on the floor—W. W. Ormsby. Two bullet holes were in the upper left-hand pocket of his vest. The holes, less than an inch apart, had been placed with a precision that left no room for doubting that the man was dead. Steve remembered Larry's threat to his father: "I'll spoil your vest!"

He looked up from killed to killer. Larry Ormsby's eyes were hard and bright; the pistol in his hand was held lightly, with the loose alertness peculiar to professional gunmen.

"This isn't a—ah—personal matter with you, is it?" he asked.

Steve shook his head; and heard the trampling of feet and a confusion of excited voices in the corridor behind him.

"That's nice," the killer was saying; "and I'd suggest that you—"

He broke off as men came into the office. Grant Fernie, the marshal, was one of them.

"Dead?" he asked, with a bare glance at the man on the floor.

"Rather," Larry replied.

"How come?"

Larry Ormsby moistened his lips, not nervously, but thoughtfully. Then he smiled at Steve, and told his story.

"Threefall and I were standing down near the front door talking, when we heard a shot. I thought it had been fired up here, but he said it came from across the street. Anyhow, we came up here to make sure—making a bet on it first; so Threefall owes me a dollar. We came up here, and just as we got to the head of the steps we heard another shot, and Brackett came running out of here with this gun in his hand."

He gave the automatic to the marshal, and went on:

"He took a few steps from the door, yelled, and fell down. Did you see him out there?"

"I did." Fernie said.

"Well, Threefall stopped to look at him while I came on in here to see if my father was all right—and found him dead. That's all there is to it."

CHAPTER X

"*Y' Got To Get Out!*"

Steve went slowly down to the street after the gathering in the dead man's office had broken up, without having either contradicted or corroborated Larry Ormsby's fiction. No one had questioned him. At first he had been too astonished by the killer's boldness to say anything; and when his wits had resumed their functions, he had decided to hold his tongue for a while.

Suppose he had told the truth? Would it have helped justice? Would anything help justice in Izzard? If he had known what lay behind this piling up of crime, he could have decided what to do; but he did not know—did not even know that there was anything behind it. So he had kept silent. The inquest would not be held until the following day—time enough to talk then, after a night's consideration.

He could not grasp more than a fragment of the affair at a time now; disconnected memories made a whirl of meaningless images in his brain. Elder and Mrs. MacPhail going up the stairs—to where? What had become of them? What had become of the man with the bandages on throat and jaw? Had those three any part in the double murder? Had Larry killed the banker as well as his father? By what chance did the marshal appear on the scene immediately after murder had been done?

Steve carried his jumbled thoughts back to the hotel, and lay across his bed for perhaps an hour. Then he got up and went to the Bank of Izzard, drew out the money he had there, put it carefully in his pocket, and returned to his hotel room to lie across the bed again.

Nova Vallance, nebulous in yellow crêpe, was sitting on the lower step of the MacPhails' porch when Steve went up the flowered walk that evening. She welcomed him warmly, concealing none of the impatience with which she had been waiting for him. He sat on the step beside her, twisting around a little for a better view of the dusky oval of her face.

"How is your arm?" she asked.

"Fine!" He opened and shut his left hand briskly. "I suppose you heard all about to-day's excitement?"

"Oh, yes! About Mr. Brackett's shooting Mr. Ormsby, and then dying with one of his heart attacks."

"Huh?" Steve demanded.

"But weren't you there?" she asked in surprise.

"I was, but suppose you tell me just what you heard."

"Oh, I've heard all sorts of things about it! But all I really know is what Dr. MacPhail, who examined both of them, said."

"And what was that?"

"That Mr. Brackett killed Mr. Ormsby—shot him—though nobody seems to know why; and then, before he could get out of the building, his heart failed him and he died."

"And he was supposed to have a bad heart?"

"Yes. Dr. MacPhail told him a year ago that he would have to be careful, that the least excitement might be fatal."

Steve caught her wrist in his hand.

"Think, now," he commanded. "Did you ever hear Dr. MacPhail speak of Brackett's heart trouble until to-day?"

She looked curiously into his face, and a little pucker of bewilderment came between her eyes.

"No," she replied slowly. "I don't think so; but, of course, there was never any reason why he should have mentioned it. Why do you ask?"

"Because," he told her, "Brackett did *not* shoot Ormsby; and any heart attack that killed Brackett was caused by poison—some poison that burned his face and beard."

She gave a little cry of horror.

"You think—" She stopped, glanced furtively over her shoulder at the front door of the house, and leaned close to him to whisper: "Didn't—didn't you say that the man who was killed in the fight last night was named Kamp?"

"Yes."

"Well, the report, or whatever it was that Dr. MacPhail made of his examination, reads Henry Cumberpatch."

"You sure? Sure it's the same man?"

"Yes. The wind blew it off the doctor's desk, and when I handed it back to him, he made some joke"—she colored with a little laugh—"some joke about it nearly being your death certificate instead of your companion's. I glanced down at it then, and saw that it was for a man named Henry Cumberpatch. What does it all mean? What is—"

The front gate clattered open, and a man swayed up the walk. Steve got up, picked up his black stick, and stepped between the girl and the advancing man. The man's face came out of the dark. It was Larry Ormsby; and when he spoke his words had a drunken thickness to match the unsteadiness—not quite a stagger, but nearly so—of his walk.

"Lis'en," he said; "I'm dam' near—"

Steve moved toward him.

"If Miss Vallance will excuse us," he said, "we'll stroll to the gate and talk."

Without waiting for a reply from either of them, Steve linked an arm through one of Ormsby's and urged him down the path. At the gate Larry broke away, pulling his arm loose, and confronting Steve.

"No time for foolishness," he snarled. "Y' got to get out! Get out o' Izzard!"

"Yes?" Steve asked. "And why?"

Larry leaned back against the fence and raised one hand in an impatient gesture.

"Your lives not worth a nickel—neither of you!"

He swayed and coughed. Steve grasped him by a shoulder and peered into his face.

"What's the matter with you?"

Larry coughed again and clapped a hand to his chest, up near the shoulder.

"Bullet—up high—Fernie's. But I got him—the big tramp. Toppled him out a window—down like a kid divin' for pennies." He laughed shrilly, and then became earnest again. "Get th' girl—beat it—now! Now! Now! Ten minutes'll be too late. They're comin'!"

"Who? What? Why?" Steve snapped. "Talk turkey! I don't trust you. I've got to have reasons."

"Reasons, my God!" the wounded man cried. "You'll get your reasons. You think I'm trying to scare you out o' town b'fore th' inquest." He laughed insanely. "Inquest! You fool! There won't be any inquest! There won't be any to-morrow—for Izzard! And you—"

He pulled himself sharply together and caught one of Steve's hands in both of his.

"Listen," he said. "I'll give it to you, but we're wasting time. But if you've got to have it—listen:"

CHAPTER XI

The Naked Soul of Izzard

"Izzard is a plant! The whole damned town is queer. Booze— that's the answer. The man I knocked off this afternoon—the one you thought was my father—originated the scheme. You make soda niter by boiling the nitrate in tanks heated with coils. He got the idea that a niter plant would make a good front for a moonshine factory. And he got the idea that if you had a whole town working together it'd be impossible for the game ever to fall down.

"You can guess how much money there is in this country in the hands of men who'd be glad to invest it in a booze game that was airtight. Not only crooks, I mean, but men who consider themselves honest. Take your guess, whatever it is, and double it, and you still won't be within millions of the right answer. There are men with— But anyway, Ormsby took his scheme East and got his backing—a syndicate that could have raised enough money to build a dozen cities.

"Ormsby, Elder and Brackett were the boys who managed the game. I was here to see that they didn't double-cross the syndicate; and then there's a flock of trusty lieutenants, like Fernie, and MacPhail, and Heman—he's postmaster—and Harker—another doctor, who got his last week—and Leslie, who posed as a minister. There was no trouble to getting the population we wanted. The word went around that the new town was a place where a crook would be safe so long as he did what he was told. The slums of all the cities in America, and half of 'em out of it, emptied themselves here. Every crook that was less than a step ahead of the police, and had car fare here, came and got cover.

"Of course, with every thug in the world blowing in here we had a lot of sleuths coming, too; but they weren't hard to handle, and if worse came to worse, we could let the law take an occasional man; but usually it wasn't hard to take care of the gum-shoes. We have bankers, and ministers, and doctors, and postmasters, and prominent men of all sorts either to tangle the sleuths up with bum leads, or, if necessary to frame them. You'll find a flock of men in the State pen who came here—most of them as narcotic agents or prohibition agents—and got themselves tied up before they knew what it was all about.

"God, there never was a bigger game! It couldn't flop—unless we spoiled it for ourselves. And that's what we've done. It was too big for us! There was too much money in it—it went to our heads! At first we played square with the syndicate. We made booze and shipped it out—shipped it in carload lots, in trucks, did everything but pipe it out, and we made money for the syndicate and for ourselves. Then we got the real idea—the big one! We kept on making the hooch; but we got the big idea going for our own profit. The syndicate wasn't in on that.

"First, we got the insurance racket under way. Elder managed that, with three or four assistants. Between them they became agents of half the insurance companies in the country, and they began to plaster Izzard with policies. Men who had never lived were examined, insured, and then killed—sometimes they were killed on paper, sometimes a real man who had died was substituted, and there were times when a man or two was killed to order. It was soft! We had the insurance agents, the doctors, the coroner, the undertaker, and all the city officials. We had the machinery to swing any deal we wanted! You were with Kamp the night he was killed! That was a good one. He was an insurance company sleuth—the companies were getting suspicious. He came here and was foolish enough to trust his reports to the mail. There aren't many letters from strangers that get through the post office without being read. We read his reports, kept them, and sent phoney ones out in their places. Then we nailed Mr. Kamp, and changed his name on the records to fit a policy in the very company he represented. A rare joke, eh?

"The insurance racket wasn't confined to men—cars, houses, furniture, everything you can insure was plastered. In the last census—by distributing the people we could count on, one in a house, with a list of five or six names—we got a population on the records of at least five times as many as are really here. That gave us room for plenty of policies, plenty of deaths, plenty of property insurance, plenty of everything. It gave us enough political influence in the county and State to strengthen our hands a hundred per cent, make the game safer.

"You'll find street after street of houses with nothing in them out of sight of the front windows. They cost money to put up, but we've made the money right along, and they'll show a wonderful profit when the clean-up comes.

"Then, after the insurance stunt was on its feet, we got the promotion game going. There's a hundred corporations in Izzard that are nothing but addresses on letterheads—but stock certificates and bonds have been sold in them from one end of these United States to the other. And they have bought goods, paid for it, shipped it out to be got rid of— maybe at a loss—and put in larger and larger orders until they've built up a credit with the manufacturers that would make you dizzy to total. Easy! Wasn't Brackett's bank here to give them all the financial references they needed? There was nothing to it; a careful building up of credit until they reached the highest possible point. Then, the goods shipped out to be sold through fences, and—bingo! The town is wiped out by fire. The stocks of goods are presumably burned; the expensive buildings that the out-of-town investors were told about are presumably destroyed; the books and records are burned.

"What a killing! I've had a hell of a time stalling off the syndicate, trying to keep them in the dark about the surprise we're going to give them. They're too suspicious as it is for us to linger much longer. But things are about ripe for the blow-off—the fire that's to start in the factory and wipe out the whole dirty town—and next Saturday was the day we picked. That's the day when Izzard becomes nothing but a pile of ashes—and a pile of collectable insurance policies.

"The rank and file in town won't know anything about the finer points of the game. Those that suspect anything take their money and keep quiet. When the town goes up in smoke there will be hundreds of bodies found in the ruins— all insured—and there will be proof of the death of hundreds of others—likewise insured—whose bodies can't be found.

"There never was a bigger game! But it was too big for us! My fault—some of it—but it would have burst anyway. We always weeded out those who came to town looking too honest or too wise, and we made doubly sure that nobody who was doubtful got into the post office, railroad depot, telegraph office, or telephone exchange. If the railroad company or the telegraph or telephone company sent somebody here to work, and we couldn't make them see things the way we wanted them seen, we managed to make the place disagreeable for them—and they usually flitted elsewhere in a hurry.

"Then the telegraph company sent Nova here and I flopped for her. At first it was just that I liked her looks. We had all sorts of women here—but they were mostly all sorts—and Nova was something different. I've done my share of dirtiness in this world, but I've never been able to get rid of a certain fastidiousness in my taste for women. I— Well, the rest of them—Brackett, Ormsby, Elder and the lot—were all for giving Nova the works. But I talked them out of it. I told them to let her alone and I'd have her on the inside in no time. I really thought I could do it. She liked me, or seemed to, but I couldn't get any further than that. I didn't make any headway. The others got impatient, but I kept putting them off, telling them that everything would be fine, that if necessary I'd marry her, and shut her up that way. They didn't like it. It wasn't easy to keep her from learning what was going on—working in the telegraph office—but we managed it somehow.

"Next Saturday was the day we'd picked for the big fireworks. Ormsby gave me the call yesterday—told me flatly that if I didn't sew Nova up at once they were going to pop her. They didn't know how much she had found out, and they were taking no chances. I told him I'd kill him if he touched her, but I knew I couldn't talk them out of it. To-day the break came. I heard he had given the word that she was to be put out of the way to-night. I went to his office for a showdown. Brackett was there. Ormsby salved me along, denied he had given any order affecting the girl, and poured out drinks for the three of us. The drink looked wrong. I waited to see what was going to happen next. Brackett gulped his down. It was poisoned. He went outside to die, and I nailed Ormsby.

"The game has blown up! It was too rich for us. Everybody is trying to slit everybody else's throat. I couldn't find Elder—but Fernie tried to pot me from a window; and he's Elder's right-hand man. Or he was—he's a stiff now. I think this thing in my chest is the big one—I'm about— But you can get the girl out. You've got to! Elder will go through with the play—try to make the killing for himself. He'll have the town touched off to-night. It's now or never with him. He'll try to—"

A shriek cut through the darkness.

"Steve! *Steve!! Steve!!!*"

CHAPTER XII

Pink Sky

Steve whirled away from the gate, leaping through flower-beds, crossed the porch in a bound, and was in the house. Behind him Larry Ormsby's feet clattered. An empty hallway, an empty room, another. Nobody was in sight on the ground floor. Steve went up the stairs. A strip of golden light lay under a door. He went through the door, not knowing or caring whether it was locked or not. He simply hurled himself shoulder first at it, and was in the room. Leaning back against a table in the center of the room, Dr. MacPhail was struggling with the girl. He was behind her, his arms around her, trying to hold her head still. The girl twisted and squirmed like a cat gone mad. In front of her Mrs. MacPhail poised an uplifted blackjack.

Steve flung his stick at the woman's white arm, flung it instinctively, without skill or aim. The heavy ebony struck arm and shoulder, and she staggered back. Dr. MacPhail, releasing the girl, dived at Steve's legs, got them, and carried him to the floor. Steve's fumbling fingers slid off the doctor's bald head, could get no grip on the back of his thick neck, found an ear, and gouged into the flesh under it.

The doctor grunted and twisted away from the digging fingers. Steve got a knee free—drove it at the doctor's face. Mrs. MacPhail bent over his head, raising the black leather billy she still held. He dashed an arm at her ankles, missed—but the down-crashing blackjack fell obliquely on his shoulder. He twisted away, scrambled to his knees and hands—and sprawled headlong under the impact of the doctor's weight on his back.

He rolled over, got the doctor under him, felt his hot breath on his neck. Steve raised his head and snapped it back—hard. Raised it again, and snapped it down, hammering

MacPhail's face with the back of his skull. The doctor's arms fell away, and Steve lurched upright to find the fight over.

Larry Ormsby stood in the doorway grinning evilly over his pistol at Mrs. MacPhail, who stood sullenly by the table. The blackjack was on the floor at Larry's feet.

Against the other side of the table the girl leaned weakly, one hand on her bruised throat, her eyes dazed and blank with fear. Steve went around to her.

"Get going, Steve! There's no time for playing. You got a car?"

Larry Ormsby's voice was rasping.

"No," Steve said.

Larry cursed bitterly—an explosion of foul blasphemies. Then:

"We'll go in mine—it can outrun anything in the State. But you can't wait here for me to get it. Take Nova over to blind Rymer's shack. I'll pick you up there. He's the only one in town you can trust. Go ahead, damn you!" he yelled.

Steve glanced at the sullen MacPhail woman, and at her husband, now getting up slowly from the floor, his face blood-smeared and battered.

"How about them?"

"Don't worry about them," Larry said. "Take the girl and make Rymer's place. I'll take care of this pair and be over there with the car in fifteen minutes. Get going!"

Steve's eyes narrowed and he studied the man in the doorway. He didn't trust him, but since all Izzard seemed equally dangerous, one place would be as safe as another—and Larry Ormsby might be honest this time.

"All right," he said, and turned to the girl. "Get a heavy coat."

Five minutes later they were hurrying through the same dark streets they had gone through on the previous night. Less than a block from the house, a muffled shot came to their ears, and then another. The girl glanced quickly at Steve but did not speak. He hoped she had not understood what the two shots meant.

They met nobody. Rymer had heard and recognized the girl's footsteps on the sidewalk, and he opened his door before they could knock.

"Come in, Nova," he welcomed her heartily, and then fumbled for Steve's hand. "This is Mr. Threefall, isn't it?"

He led them into the dark cabin, and then lighted the oil lamp on the table. Steve launched at once into a hurried summarizing of what Larry Ormsby had told him. The girl listened with wide eyes and wan face; the blind man's face lost its serenity, and he seemed to grow older and tired as he listened.

"Ormsby said he would come after us with his car," Steve wound up. "If he does, you will go with us, of course, Mr. Rymer. If you'll tell us what you want to take with you we'll get it ready; so that there will be no delay when he comes—if he comes." He turned to the girl. "What do you think, Nova? Will he come? And can we trust him if he does?"

"I—I hope so—he's not all bad, I think."

The blind man went to a wardrobe in the room's other end.

"I've nothing to take," he said, "but I'll get into warmer clothes."

He pulled the wardrobe door open, so that it screened a corner of the room for him to change in. Steve went to a window, and stood there looking between blind and frame, into the dark street where nothing moved. The girl stood close to him, between his arm and side, her fingers twined in his sleeve.

"Will we—? Will we—?"

He drew her closer and answered the whispered question she could not finish.

"We'll make it," he said, "if Larry plays square, or if he doesn't. We'll make it."

A rifle cracked somewhere in the direction of Main Street. A volley of pistol shots. The cream-colored Vauxhall came out of nowhere to settle on the sidewalk, two steps from the door. Larry Ormsby, hatless and with his shirt torn loose to expose a hole under one of his collar-bones, tumbled out of the car, and through the door that Steve threw open for him.

Larry kicked the door shut behind him, and laughed.

"Izzard's frying nicely!" he cried, and clapped his hands together. "Come, come! The desert awaits!"

Steve turned to call the blind man. Rymer stepped out from behind his screening door. In each of Rymer's hands was a heavy revolver. The film was gone from Rymer's eyes.

His eyes, cool and sharp now, held the two men and the girl.

"Put your hands up, all of you," he ordered curtly.

Larry Ormsby laughed insanely.

"Did you ever see a damned fool do his stuff, Rymer?" he asked.

"Put your hands up!"

"Rymer," Larry said, "I'm dying now. To hell with you!"

And without haste he took a black automatic pistol from an inside coat pocket.

The guns in Rymer's hands rocked the cabin with explosion after explosion.

Knocked into a sitting position on the floor by the heavy bullets that literally tore him apart, Larry steadied his back against the wall, and the crisp, sharp reports of his lighter weapon began to punctuate the roars of the erstwhile blind man's guns.

Instinctively jumping aside, pulling the girl with him, at the first shot, Steve now hurled himself upon Rymer's flank. But just as he reached him the shooting stopped. Rymer swayed, the very revolvers in his hands seemed to go limp. He slid out of Steve's clutching hands—his neck scraping one hand with the brittle dryness of paper—and became a lifeless pile on the floor.

Steve kicked the dead man's guns across the floor a way, and then went over to where the girl knelt beside Larry Ormsby. Larry smiled up at Steve with a flash of white teeth.

"I'm gone, Steve," he said. "That Rymer—fooled us all— phoney films on eyes—painted on—spy for rum syndicate."

He writhed, and his smile grew stiff and strained.

"Mind shaking hands, Steve?" he asked a moment later.

Steve found his hand and squeezed it.

"You're a good guy, Larry," was the only thing he could think to say.

The dying man seemed to like that. His smile became real again.

"Luck to you—you can get a hundred and ten out of the Vauxhall," he managed to say.

And then, apparently having forgotten the girl for whom he had given up his life, he flashed another smile at Steve and died.

The front door slammed open—two heads looked in. The heads' owners came in.

Steve bounded upright, swung his stick. A bone cracked like a whip, a man reeled back holding a hand to his temple.

"Behind me—close!" Steve cried to the girl, and felt her hands on his back.

Men filled the doorway. An invisible gun roared and a piece of the ceiling flaked down. Steve spun his stick and charged the door. The light from the lamp behind him glittered and glowed on the whirling wood. The stick whipped backward and forward, from left to right, from right to left. It writhed like a live thing—seemed to fold upon its grasped middle as if spring-hinged with steel. Flashing half-circles merged into a sphere of deadliness. The rhythm of incessant thudding against flesh and clicking on bone became a tune that sang through the grunts of fighting men, the groans and oaths of stricken men. Steve and the girl went through the door.

Between moving arms and legs and bodies the cream of the Vauxhall showed. Men stood upon the automobile, using its height for vantage in the fight. Steve threw himself forward, swinging his stick against shin and thigh, toppling men from the machine. With his left hand he swept the girl around to his side. His body shook and rocked under the weight of blows from men who were packed too closely for any effectiveness except the smothering power of sheer weight.

His stick was suddenly gone from him. One instant he held and spun it; the next, he was holding up a clenched fist that was empty—the ebony had vanished as if in a puff of smoke. He swung the girl up over the car door, hammered her down into the car—jammed her down upon the legs of a man who stood there—heard a bone break; and saw the man go down. Hands gripped him everywhere; hands pounded him. He cried aloud with joy when he saw the girl, huddled on the floor of the car, working with ridiculously small hands at the car's mechanism.

The machine began to move. Holding, with his hands, he lashed both feet out behind. Got them back on the step. Struck over the girl's head with a hand that had neither thought nor time to make a fist—struck stiff-fingered into a broad red face.

The car moved. One of the girl's hands came up to grasp the wheel, holding the car straight along a street she could not see. A man fell on her. Steve pulled him off—tore pieces from him—tore hair and flesh. The car swerved, scraped a building; scraped one side clear of men. The hands that held Steve fell away from him, taking most of his clothing with them. He picked a man off the back of the seat and pushed him down into the street that was flowing past them. Then he fell into the car beside the girl.

Pistols exploded behind them. From a house a little ahead a bitter-voiced rifle emptied itself at them, sieving a mud-guard. Then the desert—white and smooth as a gigantic hospital bed—was around them. Whatever pursuit there had been was left far behind.

Presently the girl slowed down, stopped.

"Are you all right?" Steve asked.

"Yes, but you're—"

"All in one piece," he assured her. "Let me take the wheel."

"No! No!" she protested. "You're bleeding. You're—"

"No! No!" he mocked her. "We'd better keep going until we hit something. We're not far enough from Izzard yet to call ourselves safe."

He was afraid that if she tried to patch him up he would fall apart in her hands. He felt like that.

She started the car, and they went on. A great sleepiness came to him. What a fight! What a fight!

"Look at the sky!" she exclaimed.

He opened his heavy eyes. Ahead of them, above them, the sky was lightening—from blue-black to violet, to mauve, to rose. He turned his head and looked back. Where they had left Izzard, a monstrous bonfire was burning, painting the sky with jeweled radiance.

"Good-by, Izzard," he said drowsily, and settled himself more comfortably in the seat.

He looked again at the glowing pink in the sky ahead.

"My mother has primroses in her garden in Delaware that look like that sometimes," he said dreamily. "You'll like 'em."

His head slid over against her shoulder, and he went to sleep.

The Whosis Kid

IT STARTED in Boston, back in 1917. I ran into Lew Maher on the Tremont street sidewalk of the Touraine Hotel one afternoon, and we stopped to swap a few minutes' gossip in the snow.

I was telling him something or other when he cut in with:

"Sneak a look at this kid coming up the street. The one with the dark cap."

Looking, I saw a gangling youth of eighteen or so; pasty and pimply face, sullen mouth, dull hazel eyes, thick, shapeless nose. He passed the city sleuth and me without attention, and I noticed his ears. They weren't the battered ears of a pug, and they weren't conspicuously deformed, but their rims curved in and out in a peculiar crinkled fashion.

At the corner he went out of sight, turning down Boylston street toward Washington.

"There's a lad that will make a name for hisself if he ain't nabbed or rocked off too soon," Lew predicted. "Better put him on your list. The Whosis Kid. You'll be looking for him some one of these days."

"What's his racket?"

"Stick-up, gunman. He's got the makings of a good one. He can shoot, and he's plain crazy. He ain't hampered by nothing like imagination or fear of consequences. I wish he was. It's these careful, sensible birds that are easiest caught. I'd swear the Kid was in on a coupla jobs that were turned in Brookline last month. But I can't fit him to 'em. I'm going to clamp him some day, though—and that's a promise."

Lew never kept his promise. A prowler killed him in an Audubon Road residence a month later.

A week or two after this conversation I left the Boston branch of the Continental Detective Agency to try army life. When the war was over I returned to the Agency payroll in Chicago, stayed there for a couple of years, and got transferred to San Francisco.

So, all in all, it was nearly eight years later that I found my-self sitting behind the Whosis Kid's crinkled ears at the Dreamland Rink.

Friday night is fight night at the Steiner Street house. This particular one was my first idle evening in several weeks. I had gone up to the rink, fitted myself to a hard wooden chair not too far from the ring, and settled down to watch the boys throw gloves at one another. The show was about a quarter done when I picked out this pair of odd and somehow famil-iar ears two rows ahead of me.

I didn't place them right away. I couldn't see their owner's face. He was watching Kid Cipriani and Bunny Keogh assault each other. I missed most of that fight. But during the brief wait before the next pair of boys went on, the Whosis Kid turned his head to say something to the man beside him. I saw his face and knew him.

He hadn't changed much, and he hadn't improved any. His eyes were duller and his mouth more wickedly sullen than I had remembered them. His face was as pasty as ever, if not so pimply.

He was directly between me and the ring. Now that I knew him, I didn't have to pass up the rest of the card. I could watch the boys over his head without being afraid he would get out on me.

So far as I knew, the Whosis Kid wasn't wanted anywhere—not by the Continental, anyway—and if he had been a pick-pocket, or a con man, or a member of any of the criminal trades in which we are only occasionally interested, I would have let him alone. But stick-ups are always in demand. The Continental's most important clients are insurance companies of one sort or another, and robbery policies make up a good percentage of the insurance business these days.

When the Whosis Kid left in the middle of the main event—along with nearly half of the spectators, not caring what hap-pened to either of the muscle-bound heavies who were putting on a room-mate act in the ring—I went with him.

He was alone. It was the simplest sort of shadowing. The streets were filled with departing fight fans. The Kid walked down to Fillmore street, took on a stack of wheats, bacon and coffee at a lunch room, and caught a No. 22 car.

He—and likewise I—transferred to a No. 5 car at McAllister street, dropped off at Polk, walked north one block, turned back west for a block and a fraction, and went up the front stairs of a dingy light-housekeeping room establishment that occupied the second and third floors over a repair shop on the south side of Golden Gate avenue, between Van Ness and Franklin.

That put a wrinkle in my forehead. If he had left the street car at either Van Ness or Franklin, he would have saved himself a block of walking. He had ridden down to Polk and walked back. For the exercise, maybe.

I loafed across the street for a short while, to see what—if anything—happened to the front windows. None that had been dark before the Kid went in lighted up now. Apparently he didn't have a front room—unless he was a very cautious young man. I knew he hadn't tumbled to my shadowing. There wasn't a chance of that. Conditions had been too favorable to me.

The front of the building giving me no information, I strolled down Van Ness avenue to look at the rear. The building ran through to Redwood street, a narrow back street that split the block in half. Four back windows were lighted, but they told me nothing. There was a back door. It seemed to belong to the repair shop. I doubted that the occupants of the upstairs rooms could use it.

On my way home to my bed and alarm clock, I dropped in at the office, to leave a note for the Old Man:

> Tailing the Whosis Kid, stick-up, 25–27, 135, 5 foot 11 inches, sallow, br. hair, hzl. eyes, thick nose, crooked ears. Origin Boston. Anything on him? Will be vicinity Golden Gate and Van Ness.

CHAPTER II

Eight o'clock the next morning found me a block below the house in which the Kid had gone, waiting for him to appear. A steady, soaking rain was falling, but I didn't mind that. I was closed up inside a black coupé, a type of car whose tamely respectable appearance makes it the ideal one for city work.

This part of Golden Gate avenue is lined with automobile repair shops, second-hand automobile dealers, and the like. There are always dozens of cars standing idle to the block. Although I stayed there all day, I didn't have to worry over my being too noticeable.

That was just as well. For nine solid, end-to-end hours I sat there and listened to the rain on the roof, and waited for the Whosis Kid, with not a glimpse of him, and nothing to eat except Fatimas. I wasn't any too sure he hadn't slipped me. I didn't know that he lived in this place I was watching. He could have gone to his home after I had gone to mine. However, in this detective business pessimistic guesses of that sort are always bothering you, if you let them. I stayed parked, with my eye on the dingy door into which my meat had gone the night before.

At a little after five that evening, Tommy Howd, our pug-nosed office boy, found me and gave me a memorandum from the Old Man:

> Whosis Kid known to Boston branch as robbery-suspect, but have nothing definite on him. Real name believed to be Arthur Cory or Carey. May have been implicated in Tunnicliffe jewelry robbery in Boston last month. Employee killed, $60,000 unset stones taken. No description of two bandits. Boston branch thinks this angle worth running out. They authorize surveillance.

After I had read this memorandum, I gave it back to the boy,—there's no wisdom in carrying around a pocketful of stuff relating to your job,—and asked him:

"Will you call up the Old Man and ask him to send somebody up to relieve me while I get a bite of food? I haven't chewed since breakfast."

"Swell chance!" Tommy said. "Everybody's busy. Hasn't been an op in all day. I don't see why you fellas don't carry a hunk or two of chocolate in your pockets to—"

"You've been reading about Arctic explorers," I accused him. "If a man's starving he'll eat anything, but when he's just ordinarily hungry he doesn't want to clutter up his stomach with a lot of candy. Scout around and see if you can pick me up a couple of sandwiches and a bottle of milk."

He scowled at me, and then his fourteen-year-old face grew cunning.

"I tell you what," he suggested. "You tell me what this fella looks like, and which building he's in, and I'll watch while you go get a decent meal. Huh? Steak, and French fried potatoes, and pie, and coffee."

Tommy has dreams of being left on the job in some such circumstance, of having everything break for him while he's there, and of rounding up regiments of desperadoes all by himself. I don't think he'd muff a good chance at that, and I'd be willing to give him a whack at it. But the Old Man would scalp me if he knew I turned a child loose among a lot of thugs.

So I shook my head.

"This guy wears four guns and carries an ax, Tommy. He'd eat you up."

"Aw, applesauce! You ops are all the time trying to make out nobody else could do your work. These crooks can't be such tough mugs—or they wouldn't let you catch 'em!"

There was some truth in that, so I put Tommy out of the coupé into the rain.

"One tongue sandwich, one ham, one bottle of milk. And make it sudden."

But I wasn't there when he came back with the food. He had barely gone out of sight when the Whosis Kid, his overcoat collar turned up against the rain that was driving down in close-packed earnest just now, came out of the rooming-house doorway.

He turned south on Van Ness.

When the coupé got me to the corner he was not in sight. He couldn't have reached McAllister street. Unless he had gone into a building, Redwood street—the narrow one that split the block—was my best bet. I drove up Golden Gate avenue another block, turned south, and reached the corner of Franklin and Redwood just in time to see my man ducking into the back door of an apartment building that fronted on McAllister street.

I drove on slowly, thinking.

The building in which the Kid had spent the night and this building into which he had just gone had their rears on the same back street, on opposite sides, a little more than half a block apart. If the Kid's room was in the rear of his building, and he had a pair of strong glasses, he could keep a pretty sharp eye on all the windows—and probably much of the interiors—of the rooms on that side of the McAllister street building.

Last night he had ridden a block out of his way. Having seen him sneak into the back door just now, my guess was that he had not wished to leave the street car where he could be seen from this building. Either of his more convenient points of departure from the car would have been in sight of this building. This would add up to the fact that the Kid was watching someone in this building, and did not want them to be watching him.

He had now gone calling through the back door. That wasn't difficult to explain. The front door was locked, but the back door—as in most large buildings—probably was open all day. Unless the Kid ran into a janitor or someone of the sort, he could get in with no trouble. The Kid's call was furtive, whether his host was at home or not.

I didn't know what it was all about, but that didn't bother me especially. My immediate problem was to get to the best place from which to pick up the Kid when he came out.

If he left by the back door, the next block of Redwood street—between Franklin and Gough—was the place for me and my coupé. But he hadn't promised me he would leave that way. It was more likely that he would use the front door. He would attract less attention walking boldly out the front of the building than sneaking out the back. My best bet was the corner of McAllister and Van Ness. From there I could watch the front door as well as one end of Redwood street.

I slid the coupé down to that corner and waited.

Half an hour passed. Three quarters.

The Whosis Kid came down the front steps and walked toward me, buttoning his overcoat and turning up the collar as he walked, his head bent against the slant of the rain.

A curtained black Cadillac touring car came from behind me, a car I thought had been parked down near the City Hall when I took my plant here.

It curved around my coupé, slid with chainless recklessness in to the curb, skidded out again, picking up speed somehow on the wet paving.

A curtain whipped loose in the rain.

Out of the opening came pale fire-streaks. The bitter voice of a small-caliber pistol. Seven times.

The Whosis Kid's wet hat floated off his head—a slow balloon-like rising.

There was nothing slow about the Kid's moving.

Plunging, in a twisting swirl of coat-skirts, he flung into a shop vestibule.

The Cadillac reached the next corner, made a dizzy sliding turn, and was gone up Franklin street. I pointed the coupé at it.

Passing the vestibule into which the Kid had plunged, I got a one-eyed view of him, on his knees, still trying to get a dark gun untangled from his overcoat. Excited faces were in the doorway behind him. There was no excitement in the street. People are too accustomed to automobile noises nowadays to pay much attention to the racket of anything less than a six-inch gun.

By the time I reached Franklin street, the Cadillac had gained another block on me. It was spinning to the left, up Eddy street.

I paralleled it on Turk street, and saw it again when I reached the two open blocks of Jefferson Square. Its speed was decreasing. Five or six blocks further, and it crossed ahead of me—on Steiner street—close enough for me to read the license plate. Its pace was moderate now. Confident that they had made a clean getaway, its occupants didn't want to get in trouble through speeding. I slid into their wake, three blocks behind.

Not having been in sight during the early blocks of the flight, I wasn't afraid that they would suspect my interest in them now.

Out on Haight street near the park panhandle, the Cadillac stopped to discharge a passenger. A small man—short and slender—with cream-white face around dark eyes and a tiny black mustache. There was something foreign in the cut of his dark coat and the shape of his gray hat. He carried a walking-stick.

The Cadillac went on out Haight street without giving me a look at the other occupants. Tossing a mental nickel, I stuck to the man afoot. The chances always are against you being able to trace a suspicious car by its license number, but there is a slim chance.

My man went into a drug store on the corner and used the telephone. I don't know what else he did in there, if anything. Presently a taxicab arrived. He got in and was driven to the Marquis Hotel. A clerk gave him the key to room 761. I dropped him when he stepped into an elevator.

CHAPTER III

At the Marquis I am among friends.

I found Duran, the house copper, on the mezzanine floor, and asked him:

"Who is 761?"

Duran is a white-haired old-timer who looks, talks, and acts like the president of an exceptionally strong bank. He used to be captain of detectives in one of the larger Middle Western cities. Once he tried too hard to get a confession out of a safe-ripper, and killed him. The newspapers didn't like Duran. They used that accident to howl him out of his job.

"761?" he repeated in his grandfatherly manner. "That is Mr. Maurois, I believe. Are you especially interested in him?"

"I have hopes," I admitted. "What do you know about him?"

"Not a great deal. He has been here perhaps two weeks. We shall go down and see what we can learn."

We went to the desk, the switchboard, the captain of bell-hops, and upstairs to question a couple of chambermaids. The occupant of 761 had arrived two weeks ago, had registered as *Edouard Maurois, Dijon, France*, had frequent telephone calls, no mail, no visitors, kept irregular hours and tipped freely. Whatever business he was in or had was not known to the hotel people.

"What is the occasion of your interest in him, if I may ask?" Duran inquired after we had accumulated these facts. He talks like that.

"I don't exactly know yet," I replied truthfully. "He just connected with a bird who is wrong, but this Maurois may be all right himself. I'll give you a rap the minute I get anything solid on him."

I couldn't afford to tell Duran I had seen his guest snapping caps at a gunman under the eyes of the City Hall in daylight. The Marquis Hotel goes in for respectability. They would have shoved the Frenchman out in the streets. It wouldn't help me to have him scared up.

"Please do," Duran said. "You owe us something for our help, you know, so please don't withhold any information that might save us unpleasant notoriety."

"I won't," I promised. "Now will you do me another favor? I haven't had my teeth in anything except my mouth since seven-thirty this morning. Will you keep an eye on the elevators, and let me know if Maurois goes out? I'll be in the grill, near the door."

"Certainly."

On my way to the grillroom I stopped at the telephone booths and called up the office. I gave the night office man the Cadillac's license number.

"Look it up on the list and see whom it belongs to."

The answer was: "H. J. Paterson, San Pablo, issued for a Buick roadster."

That about wound up that angle. We could look up Paterson, but it was safe betting it wouldn't get us anything. License plates, once they get started in crooked ways, are about as easy to trace as Liberty Bonds.

All day I had been building up hunger. I took it into the grillroom and turned it loose. Between bites I turned the day's events over in my mind. I didn't think hard enough to spoil my appetite. There wasn't that much to think about.

The Whosis Kid lived in a joint from which some of the McAllister street apartments could be watched. He visited the apartment building furtively. Leaving, he was shot at, from a car that must have been waiting somewhere in the vicinity. Had the Frenchman's companion in the Cadillac—or his companions, if more than one—been the occupant of the apartment the Kid had visited? Had they expected him to visit it? Had they tricked him into visiting it, planning to shoot him down as he was leaving? Or were they watching the front while the Kid watched the rear? If so, had either known that the other was watching? And who lived there?

I couldn't answer any of these riddles. All I knew was that the Frenchman and his companions didn't seem to like the Whosis Kid.

Even the sort of meal I put away doesn't take forever to eat. When I finished it, I went out to the lobby again.

Passing the switchboard, one of the girls—the one whose red hair looks as if it had been poured into its waves and hardened—gave me a nod.

I stopped to see what she wanted.

"Your friend just had a call," she told me.

"You get it?"

"Yes. A man is waiting for him at Kearny and Broadway. Told him to hurry."

"How long ago?"

"None. They're just through talking."

"Any names?"

"No."

"Thanks."

I went on to where Duran was stalling with an eye on the elevators.

"Shown yet?" I asked.

"No."

"Good. The red-head on the switchboard just told me he had a phone call to meet a man at Kearny and Broadway. I think I'll beat him to it."

Around the corner from the hotel, I climbed into my coupé and drove down to the Frenchman's corner.

The Cadillac he had used that afternoon was already there, with a new license plate. I passed it and took a look at its one occupant—a thick-set man of forty-something with a cap pulled low over his eyes. All I could see of his features was a wide mouth slanting over a heavy chin.

I put the coupé in a vacant space down the street a way. I didn't have to wait long for the Frenchman. He came around the corner afoot and got into the Cadillac. The man with the big chin drove. They went slowly up Broadway. I followed.

CHAPTER IV

We didn't go far, and when we came to rest again, the Cadillac was placed conveniently for its occupants to watch the Venetian Café, one of the gaudiest of the Italian restaurants that fill this part of town.

Two hours went by.

I had an idea that the Whosis Kid was eating at the Venetian. When he left, the fireworks would break out, continuing the celebration from where it had broken off that afternoon on McAllister street. I hoped the Kid's gun wouldn't get caught in his coat this time. But don't think I meant to give him a helping hand in his two-against-one fight.

This party had the shape of a war between gunmen. It would be a private one as far as I was concerned. My hope was that by hovering on the fringes until somebody won, I could pick up a little profit for the Continental, in the form of a wanted crook or two among the survivors.

My guess at the Frenchman's quarry was wrong. It wasn't the Whosis Kid. It was a man and a woman. I didn't see their faces. The light was behind them. They didn't waste any time between the Venetian's door and their taxicab.

The man was big—tall, wide, and thick. The woman looked small at his side. I couldn't go by that. Anything weighing less than a ton would have seemed tiny beside him.

As the taxicab pulled away from the café, the Cadillac went after it. I ran in the Cadillac's wake.

It was a short chase.

The taxicab turned into a dark block on the edge of Chinatown. The Cadillac jumped to its side, bearing it over to the curb.

A noise of brakes, shouting voices, broken glass. A woman's scream. Figures moving in the scant space between touring car and taxicab. Both cars rocking. Grunts. Thuds. Oaths.

A man's voice: "Hey! You can't do that! Nix! Nix!"

It was a stupid voice.

I had slowed down until the coupé was barely moving toward this tussle ahead. Peering through the rain and darkness,

I tried to pick out a detail or so as I approached, but I could see little.

I was within twenty feet when the curbward door of the taxicab banged open. A woman bounced out. She landed on her knees on the sidewalk, jumped to her feet, and darted up the street.

Putting the coupé closer to the curb, I let the door swing open. My side windows were spattered with rain. I wanted to get a look at the woman when she passed. If she should take the open door for an invitation, I didn't mind talking to her.

She accepted the invitation, hurrying as directly to the car as if she had expected me to be waiting for her. Her face was a small oval above a fur collar.

"Help me!" she gasped. "Take me from here—quickly."

There was a suggestion of foreignness too slight to be called an accent.

"How about—?"

I shut my mouth. The thing she was jabbing me in the body with was a snub-nosed automatic.

"Sure! Get in," I urged her.

She bent her head to enter. I looped an arm over her neck, throwing her down across my lap. She squirmed and twisted—a small-boned, hard-fleshed body with strength in it.

I wrenched the gun out of her hand and pushed her back on the seat beside me.

Her fingers dug into my arms.

"Quick! Quick! Ah, please, quickly! Take me—"

"What about your friend?" I asked.

"Not him! He is of the others! Please, quickly!"

A man filled the open coupé door—the big-chinned man who had driven the Cadillac.

His hand seized the fur at the woman's throat.

She tried to scream—made the gurgling sound of a man with a slit throat. I smacked his chin with the gun I had taken from her.

He tried to fall into the coupé. I pushed him out.

Before his head had hit the sidewalk, I had the door closed, and was twisting the coupé around in the street.

We rode away. Two shots sounded just as we turned the first corner. I don't know whether they were fired at us or

not. I turned other corners. The Cadillac did not appear
again.

So far, so good. I had started with the Whosis Kid, dropped
him to take Maurois, and now let him go to see who this
woman was. I didn't know what this confusion was all about,
but I seemed to be learning *who* it was all about.

"Where to?" I asked presently.

"To home," she said, and gave me an address.

I pointed the coupé at it with no reluctance at all. It was
the McAllister street apartments the Whosis Kid had visited
earlier in the evening.

We didn't waste any time getting there. My companion
might know it or might not, but I knew that all the other
players in this game knew that address. I wanted to get there
before the Frenchman and Big Chin.

Neither of us said anything during the ride. She crouched
close to me, shivering. I was looking ahead, planning how I
was to land an invitation into her apartment. I was sorry I
hadn't held on to her gun. I had let it fall when I pushed Big
Chin out of the car. It would have been an excuse for a later
call if she didn't invite me in.

I needn't have worried. She didn't invite me. She insisted
that I go in with her. She was scared stiff.

"You will not leave me?" she pleaded as we drove up
McAllister street. "I am in complete terror. You cannot go
from me! If you will not come in, I will stay with you."

I was willing enough to go in, but I didn't want to leave
the coupé where it would advertise me.

"We'll ride around the corner and park the car," I told her,
"and then I'll go in with you."

I drove around the block, with an eye in each direction for
the Cadillac. Neither eye found it. I left the coupé on Franklin
street and we returned to the McAllister street building.

She had me almost running through the rain that had
lightened now to a drizzle.

The hand with which she tried to fit a key to the front door
was a shaky, inaccurate hand. I took the key and opened the
door. We rode to the third floor in an automatic elevator, seeing no one. I unlocked the door to which she led me, near
the rear of the building.

Holding my arm with one hand, she reached inside and snapped on the lights in the passageway.

I didn't know what she was waiting for, until she cried: "Frana! Frana! Ah, Frana!"

The muffled yapping of a small dog replied. The dog did not appear.

She grabbed me with both arms, trying to crawl up my damp coat-front.

"They are here!" she cried in the thin dry voice of utter terror. "They are here!"

CHAPTER V

"Is anybody supposed to be here?" I asked, putting her around to one side, where she wouldn't be between me and the two doors across the passageway.

"No! Just my little dog Frana, but—"

I slid my gun half out of my pocket and back again, to make sure it wouldn't catch if I needed it, and used my other hand to get rid of the woman's arms.

"You stay here. I'll see if you've got company."

Moving to the nearest door, I heard a seven-year-old voice—Lew Maher's—saying: *"He can shoot and he's plain crazy. He ain't hampered by nothing like imagination or fear of consequences."*

With my left hand I turned the first door's knob. With my left foot I kicked it open.

Nothing happened.

I put a hand around the frame, found the button, switched on the lights.

A sitting-room, all orderly.

Through an open door on the far side of the room came the muffled yapping of Frana. It was louder now and more excited. I moved to the doorway. What I could see of the next room, in the light from this, seemed peaceful and unoccupied enough. I went into it and switched on the lights.

The dog's voice came through a closed door. I crossed to it, pulled it open. A dark fluffy dog jumped snapping at my leg. I grabbed it where its fur was thickest and lifted it squirming and snarling. The light hit it. It was purple—purple as a grape! Dyed purple!

Carrying this yapping, yelping artificial hound a little away from my body with my left hand, I moved on to the next room—a bedroom. It was vacant. Its closet hid nobody. I found the kitchen and bathroom. Empty. No one was in the apartment. The purple pup had been imprisoned by the Whosis Kid earlier in the day.

Passing through the second room on my way back to the woman with her dog and my report, I saw a slitted envelope lying face-down on a table. I turned it over. The stationery of a fashionable store, it was addressed to Mrs. Inés Almad, here.

The party seemed to be getting international. Maurois was French; the Whosis Kid was Boston American; the dog had a Bohemian name (at least I remember nabbing a Czech forger a few months before whose first name was Frana); and Inés, I imagine, was either Spanish or Portuguese. I didn't know what Almad was, but she was undoubtedly foreign, and not, I thought, French.

I returned to her. She hadn't moved an inch.

"Everything seems to be all right," I told her. "The dog got himself caught in a closet."

"There is no one here?"

"No one."

She took the dog in both hands, kissing its fluffy stained head, crooning affectionate words to it in a language that made no sense to me.

"Do your friends—the people you had your row with tonight—know where you live?" I asked.

I knew they did. I wanted to see what she knew.

She dropped the dog as if she had forgotten it, and her brows puckered.

"I do not know that," she said slowly. "Yet it may be. If they do—"

She shuddered, spun on her heel, and pushed the hall door violently shut.

"They may have been here this afternoon," she went on. "Frana has made himself prisoner in closets before, but I fear everything. I am coward-like. But there is none here now?"

"No one," I assured her again.

We went into the sitting-room. I got my first good look at her when she shed her hat and dark cape.

She was a trifle under medium height, a dark-skinned woman of thirty in a vivid orange gown. She was dark as an Indian, with bare brown shoulders round and sloping, tiny feet and hands, her fingers heavy with rings. Her nose was thin and curved, her mouth full-lipped and red, her eyes—long and thickly lashed—were of an extraordinary narrowness. They were dark eyes, but nothing of their color could be seen through the thin slits that separated the lids. Two dark gleams through veiling lashes. Her black hair was disarranged just now in fluffy silk puffs. A rope of pearls hung down on her dark chest. Earrings of black iron—in a peculiar club-like design—swung beside her cheeks.

Altogether, she was an odd trick. But I wouldn't want to be quoted as saying that she wasn't beautiful—in a wild way.

She was shaking and shivering as she got rid of her hat and cloak. White teeth held her lower lip as she crossed the room to turn on an electric heater. I took advantage of this opportunity to shift my gun from my overcoat pocket to my pants. Then I took off the coat.

Leaving the room for a second, she returned with a brown-filled quart bottle and two tumblers on a bronze tray, which she put on a little table near the heater.

The first tumbler she filled to within half an inch of its rim. I stopped her when she had the other nearly half full.

"That'll do fine for me," I said.

It was brandy, and not at all hard to get down. She shot her tumblerful into her throat as if she needed it, shook her bare shoulders, and sighed in a satisfied way.

"You will think, certainly, I am lunatic," she smiled at me. "Flinging myself on you, a stranger in the street, demanding of you time and troubles."

"No," I lied seriously. "I think you're pretty level-headed for a woman who, no doubt, isn't used to this sort of stuff."

She was pulling a little upholstered bench closer to the electric heater, within reach of the table that held the brandy. She sat down now, with an inviting nod at the bench's empty half.

The purple dog jumped into her lap. She pushed it out. It started to return. She kicked it sharply in the side with the pointed toe of her slipper. It yelped and crawled under a chair across the room.

I avoided the window by going the long way around the room. The window was curtained, but not thickly enough to hide all of the room from the Whosis Kid—if he happened to be sitting at his window just now with a pair of field-glasses to his eyes.

"But I am not level-headed, really," the woman was saying as I dropped beside her. "I am coward-like, terribly. And even becoming accustomed— It is my husband, or he who was my husband. I should tell you. Your gallantry deserves the explanation, and I do not wish you should think a thing that is not so."

I tried to look trusting and credulous. I expected to disbelieve everything she said.

"He is most crazily jealous," she went on in her low-pitched, soft voice, with a peculiar way of saying words that just missed being marked enough to be called a foreign accent. "He is an old man, and incredibly wicked. These men he has sent to me! A woman there was once—tonight's men are not first. I don't know what—what they mean. To kill me, perhaps—to maim, to disfigure—I do not know."

"And the man in the taxi with you was one of them?" I asked. "I was driving down the street behind you when you were attacked, and I could see there was a man with you. He was one of them?"

"Yes! I did not know it, but it must have been that he was. He does not defend me. A pretense, that is all."

"Ever try sicking the cops on this hubby of yours?"

"It is what?"

"Ever notify the police?"

"Yes, but"—she shrugged her brown shoulders—"I would as well have kept quiet, or better. In Buffalo it was, and they—they bound my husband to keep the peace, I think you call it. A thousand dollars! Poof! What is that to him in his jealousy? And I—I cannot stand the things the newspapers say—the jesting of them. I must leave Buffalo. Yes, once I do try sicking the cops on him. But not more."

"Buffalo?" I explored a little. "I lived there for a while—on Crescent avenue."

"Oh, yes. That is out by the Delaware Park."

That was right enough. But her knowing something about Buffalo didn't prove anything about the rest of her story.

CHAPTER VI

She poured more brandy. By speaking quick I held my drink down to a size suitable for a man who has work to do. Hers was as large as before. We drank, and she offered me cigarettes in a lacquered box—slender cigarettes, hand-rolled in black paper.

I didn't stay with mine long. It tasted, smelt and scorched like gun-powder.

"You don't like my cigarettes?"

"I'm an old-fashioned man," I apologized, rubbing its fire out in a bronze dish, fishing in my pocket for my own deck. "Tobacco's as far as I've got. What's in these fireworks?"

She laughed. She had a pleasant laugh, with a sort of coo in it.

"I am so very sorry. So many people do not like them. I have a Hindu incense mixed with the tobacco."

I didn't say anything to that. It was what you would expect of a woman who would dye her dog purple.

The dog moved under its chair just then, scratching the floor with its nails.

The brown woman was in my arms, in my lap, her arms wrapped around my neck. Close-up, opened by terror, her eyes weren't dark at all. They were gray-green. The blackness was in the shadow from her heavy lashes.

"It's only the dog," I assured her, sliding her back on her own part of the bench. "It's only the dog wriggling around under the chair."

"Ah!" she blew her breath out with enormous relief.

Then we had to have another shot of brandy.

"You see, I am most awfully the coward," she said when the third dose of liquor was in her. "But, ah, I have had so much trouble. It is a wonder that I am not insane."

I could have told her she wasn't far enough from it to do much bragging, but I nodded with what was meant for sympathy.

She lit another cigarette to replace the one she had dropped in her excitement. Her eyes became normal black slits again.

"I do not think it is nice"—there was a suggestion of a dimple in her brown cheek when she smiled like that—"that I throw myself into the arms of a man even whose name I do not know, or anything of him."

"That's easy to fix. My name is Young," I lied; "and I can let you have a case of Scotch at a price that will astonish you. I think maybe I could stand it if you call me Jerry. Most of the ladies I let sit in my lap do."

"Jerry Young," she repeated, as if to herself. "That is a nice name. And you are the bootlegger?"

"Not *the*," I corrected her, "just *a*. This is San Francisco."

The going got tough after that.

Everything else about this brown woman was all wrong, but her fright was real. She was scared stiff. And she didn't intend being left alone this night. She meant to keep me there—to massage any more chins that stuck themselves at her. Her idea—she being that sort—was that I would be most surely held with affection. So she must turn herself loose on me. She wasn't hampered by any pruderies or puritanisms at all.

I also have an idea. Mine is that when the last gong rings I'm going to be leading this baby and some of her playmates to the city prison. That is an excellent reason—among a dozen others I could think of—why I shouldn't get mushy with her.

I was willing enough to camp there with her until something happened. That apartment looked like the scene of the next action. But I had to cover up my own game. I couldn't let her know she was only a minor figure in it. I had to pretend there was nothing behind my willingness to stay but a desire to protect her. Another man might have got by with a chivalrous, knight-errant, protector-of-womanhood-without-personal-interest attitude. But I don't look, and can't easily act, like that kind of person. I had to hold her off without letting her guess that my interest wasn't personal. It was no cinch. She was too damned direct, and she had too much brandy in her.

I didn't kid myself that my beauty and personality were responsible for any of her warmth. I was a thick-armed male with big fists. She was in a jam. She spelled my name P-r-o-t-e-c-t-i-o-n. I was something to be put between her and trouble.

Another complication: I am neither young enough nor old enough to get feverish over every woman who doesn't make me think being blind isn't so bad. I'm at that middle point around forty where a man puts other feminine qualities—amiability, for one—above beauty on his list. This brown woman annoyed me. She was too sure of herself. Her work was rough. She was trying to handle me as if I were a farmer boy. But in spite of all this, I'm constructed mostly of human ingredients. This woman got more than a stand-off when faces and bodies were dealt. I didn't like her. I hoped to throw her in the can before I was through. But I'd be a liar if I didn't admit that she had me stirred up inside—between her cuddling against me, giving me the come-on, and the brandy I had drunk.

The going was tough—no fooling.

A couple of times I was tempted to bolt. Once I looked at my watch—2:06. She put a ring-heavy brown hand on the timepiece and pushed it down to my pocket.

"Please, Jerry!" the earnestness in her voice was real. "You cannot go. You cannot leave me here. I will not have it so. I will go also, through the streets following. You cannot leave me to be murdered here!"

I settled down again.

A few minutes later a bell rang sharply.

She went to pieces immediately. She piled over on me, strangling me with her bare arms. I pried them loose enough to let me talk.

"What bell is that?"

"The street door. Do not heed it."

I patted her shoulder.

"Be a good girl and answer it. Let's see who it is."

Her arms tightened.

"No! No! No! They have come!"

The bell rang again.

"Answer it," I insisted.

Her face was flat against my coat, her nose digging into my chest.

"No! No!"

"All right," I said. "I'll answer it myself."

I untangled myself from her, got up and went into the passageway. She followed me. I tried again to persuade her to do the talking. She would not, although she didn't object to my talking. I would have liked it better if whoever was downstairs didn't learn that the woman wasn't alone. But she was too stubborn in her refusal for me to do anything with her.

"Well?" I said into the speaking-tube.

"Who the hell are you?" a harsh, deep-chested voice asked. "What do you want?"

"I want to talk to Inés."

"Speak your piece to me," I suggested, "and I'll tell her about it."

The woman, holding one of my arms, had an ear close to the tube.

"Billie, it is," she whispered. "Tell him that he goes away."

"You're to go away," I passed the message on.

"Yeah?" the voice grew harsher and deeper. "Will you open the door, or will I bust it in?"

There wasn't a bit of playfulness in the question. Without consulting the woman, I put a finger on the button that unlocks the street door.

"Welcome," I said into the tube.

"He's coming up," I explained to the woman. "Shall I stand behind the door and tap him on the skull when he comes in? Or do you want to talk to him first?"

"Do not strike him!" she exclaimed. "It is Billie."

That suited me. I hadn't intended putting the slug to him—not until I knew who and what he was, anyway. I had wanted to see what she would say.

CHAPTER VII

Billie wasn't long getting up to us. I opened the door when he rang, the woman standing beside me. He didn't wait for an invitation. He was through the doorway before I had the door half opened. He glared at me. There was plenty of him!

A big, red-faced, red-haired bale of a man—big in any direction you measured him—and none of him was fat. The skin was off his nose, one cheek was clawed, the other swollen. His hatless head was a tangled mass of red hair. One pocket had been ripped out of his coat, and a button dangled on the end of a six-inch ribbon of torn cloth.

This was the big heaver who had been in the taxicab with the woman.

"Who's this mutt?" he demanded, moving his big paws toward me.

I knew the woman was a goof. It wouldn't have surprised me if she had tried to feed me to the battered giant. But she didn't. She put a hand on one of his and soothed him.

"Do not be nasty, Billie. He is a friend. Without him I would not this night have escaped."

He scowled. Then his face straightened out and he caught her hand in both of his.

"So you got away it's all right," he said huskily. "I'd a done better if we'd been outside. There wasn't no room in that taxi for me to turn around. And one of them guys crowned me."

That was funny. This big clown was apologizing for getting mangled up protecting a woman who had scooted, leaving him to get out as well as he could.

The woman led him into the sitting-room, I tagging along behind. They sat on the bench. I picked out a chair that wasn't in line with the window the Whosis Kid ought to be watching.

"What did happen, Billie?" She touched his grooved cheek and skinned nose with her fingertips. "You are hurt."

He grinned with a sort of shamefaced delight. I saw that what I had taken for a swelling in one cheek was only a big hunk of chewing tobacco.

"I don't know all that happened," he said. "One of 'em crowned me, and I didn't wake up till a coupla hours afterwards. The taxi driver didn't give me no help in the fight, but he was a right guy and knowed where his money would come from. He didn't holler or nothing. He took me around to a doc that wouldn't squawk, and the doc straightened me out, and then I come up here."

"Did you see each one of those men?" she asked.

"Sure! I seen 'em, and felt 'em, and maybe tasted 'em."

"They were how many?"

"Just two of 'em. A little fella with a trick tickler, and a husky with a big chin on him."

"There was no other? There was not a younger man, tall and thin?"

That could be the Whosis Kid. She thought he and the Frenchman were working together?

Billie shook his shaggy, banged-up head.

"Nope. They was only two of 'em."

She frowned and chewed her lip.

Billie looked sidewise at me—a look that said "Beat it."

The woman caught the glance. She twisted around on the bench to put a hand on his head.

"Poor Billie," she cooed; "his head most cruelly hurt saving me, and now, when he should be at his home giving it rest, I keep him here talking. You go, Billie, and when it is morning and your poor head is better, you will telephone to me?"

His red face got dark. He glowered at me.

Laughing, she slapped him lightly on the cheek that bulged around his cud of tobacco.

"Do not become jealous of Jerry. Jerry is enamored of one yellow and white lady somewhere, and to her he is most faithful. Not even the smallest liking has he for dark women." She smiled a challenge at me. "Is it not so, Jerry?"

"No," I denied. "And, besides, all women are dark."

Billie shifted his chew to the scratched cheek and bunched his shoulders.

"What the hell kind of a crack is that to be making?" he rumbled.

"That means nothing it should not, Billie," she laughed at him. "It is only an epigram."

"Yeah?" Billie was sour and truculent. I was beginning to think he didn't like me. "Well, tell your little fat friend to keep his smart wheezes to himself. I don't like 'em."

That was plain enough. Billie wanted an argument. The woman, who held him securely enough to have steered him off, simply laughed again. There was no profit in trying to find the reason behind any of her actions. She was a nut.

Maybe she thought that since we weren't sociable enough for her to keep both on hand, she'd let us tangle, and hold on to the one who rubbed the other out of the picture.

Anyway, a row was coming. Ordinarily I am inclined to peace. The day is past when I'll fight for the fun of it. But I've been in too many rumpuses to mind them much. Usually nothing very bad happens to you, even if you lose. I wasn't going to back down just because this big stiff was meatier than I. I've always been lucky against the large sizes. He had been banged up earlier in the evening. That would cut down his steam some. I wanted to hang around this apartment a little longer, if it could be managed. If Billie wanted to tussle— and it looked as if he did—he could.

It was easy to meet him half-way: anything I said would be used against me.

I grinned at his red face, and suggested to the woman, solemnly:

"I think if you'd dip him in blueing he'd come out the same color as the other pup."

As silly as that was, it served. Billie reared up on his feet and curled his paws into fists.

"Me and you'll take a walk," he decided; "out where there's space enough."

I got up, pushed my chair back with a foot, and quoted "Red" Burns to him: "If you're close enough, there's room enough."

He wasn't a man you had to talk to much. We went around and around.

It was fists at first. He started it by throwing his right at my head. I went in under it and gave him all I had in a right and left to the belly. He swallowed his chew of tobacco. But he didn't bend. Few big men are as strong as they look. Billie was.

He didn't know anything at all. His idea of a fight was to stand up and throw fists at your head—right, left, right, left. His fists were as large as wastebaskets. They wheezed through the air. But always at the head—the easiest part to get out of the way.

There was room enough for me to go in and out. I did that. I hammered his belly. I thumped his heart. I mauled his belly again. Every time I hit him he grew an inch, gained a pound and picked up another horsepower. I don't fool when I hit, but nothing I did to this human mountain—not even making him swallow his hunk of tobacco—had any visible effect on him.

I've always had a reasonable amount of pride in my ability to sock. It was disappointing to have this big heaver take the best I could give him without a grunt. But I wasn't discouraged. He couldn't stand it forever. I settled down to make a steady job of it.

Twice he clipped me. Once on the shoulder. A big fist spun me half around. He didn't know what to do next. He came in on the wrong side. I made him miss, and got clear. The other time he caught me on the forehead. A chair kept me from going down. The smack hurt me. It must have hurt him more. A skull is tougher than a knuckle. I got out of his way when he closed in, and let him have something to remember on the back of his neck.

The woman's dusky face showed over Billie's shoulder as he straightened up. Her eyes were shiny behind their heavy lashes, and her mouth was open to let white teeth gleam through.

Billie got tired of the boxing after that, and turned the set-to into a wrestling match, with trimmings. I would rather have kept on with the fists. But I couldn't help myself. It was his party. He grabbed one of my wrists, yanked, and we thudded chest to chest.

He didn't know any more about this than he had about that. He didn't have to. He was big enough and strong enough to play with me.

I was underneath when we tumbled down on the floor and began rolling around. I did my best. It wasn't anything. Three times I put a scissors on him. His body was too big for my short legs to clamp around. He chucked me off as if he were amusing the baby. There was no use at all in trying to do things to his legs. No hold known to man could have held them. His arms were almost as strong. I quit trying.

Nothing I knew was any good against this monster. He was out of my range. I was satisfied to spend all that was left of my strength trying to keep him from crippling me—and waiting for a chance to out-smart him.

He threw me around a lot. Then my chance came.

I was flat on my back, with everything but one or two of my most centrally located intestines squeezed out. Kneeling astride me, he brought his big hands up to my throat and fastened them there.

That's how much he didn't know!

You can't choke a man that way—not if his hands are loose and he knows a hand is stronger than a finger.

I laughed in his purple face and brought my own hands up. Each of them picked one of his little fingers out of my flesh. It wasn't a dream at that. I was all in, and he wasn't. But no man's little finger is stronger than another's hand. I twisted them back. They broke together.

He yelped. I grabbed the next—the ring fingers.

One of them snapped. The other was ready to pop when he let go.

Jerking up, I butted him in the face. I twisted from between his knees. We came on our feet together.

The doorbell rang.

CHAPTER VIII

Fight interest went out of the woman's face. Fear came in. Her fingers picked at her mouth.

"Ask who's there," I told her.

"Who—who is there?"

Her voice was flat and dry.

"Mrs. Keil," came from the corridor, the words sharp with indignation. "You will have to stop this noise immediately! The tenants are complaining—and no wonder! A pretty hour to be entertaining company and carrying on so!"

"The landlady," the dark woman whispered. Aloud: "I am sorry, Mrs. Keil. There will not be more noises."

Something like a sniff came through the door, and the sound of dimming footsteps.

Inés Almad frowned reproachfully at Billie.

"You should not have done this," she blamed him.

He looked humble, and at the floor, and at me. Looking at me, the purple began to flow back into his face.

"I'm sorry," he mumbled. "I told this fella we ought to take a walk. We'll do it now, and there won't be no more noise here."

"Billie!" her voice was sharp. She was reading the law to him. "You will go out and have attention for your hurts. If you have not won these fights, because of that am I to be left here alone to be murdered?"

The big man shuffled his feet, avoided her gaze and looked utterly miserable. But he shook his head stubbornly.

"I can't do it, Inés," he said. "Me and this guy has got to finish it. He busted my fingers, and I got to bust his jaw."

"Billie!"

She stamped one small foot and looked imperiously at him. He looked as if he'd like to roll over on his back and hold his paws in the air. But he stood his ground.

"I got to," he repeated. "There ain't no way out of it."

Anger left her face. She smiled very tenderly at him.

"Dear old Billie," she murmured, and crossed the room to a secretary in a corner.

When she turned, an automatic pistol was in her hand. Its one eye looked at Billie.

"Now, *lechón*," she purred, "go out!"

The red man wasn't a quick thinker. It took a full minute for him to realize that this woman he loved was driving him away with a gun. The big dummy might have known that his three broken fingers had disqualified him. It took another minute for him to get his legs in motion. He went toward the door in slow bewilderment, still only half believing this thing was really happening.

The woman followed him step by step. I went ahead to open the door.

I turned the knob. The door came in, pushing me back against the opposite wall.

In the doorway stood Edouard Maurois and the man I had swatted on the chin. Each had a gun.

I looked at Inés Almad, wondering what turn her craziness would take in the face of this situation. She wasn't so crazy as I had thought. Her scream and the thud of her gun on the floor sounded together.

"Ah!" the Frenchman was saying. "The gentlemen were leaving? May we detain them?"

The man with the big chin—it was larger than ever now with the marks of my tap—was less polite.

"Back up, you birds!" he ordered, stooping for the gun the woman had dropped.

I still was holding the doorknob. I rattled it a little as I took my hand away—enough to cover up the click of the lock as I pushed the button that left it unlatched. If I needed help, and it came, I wanted as few locks as possible between me and it.

Then—Billie, the woman and I walking backward—we all paraded into the sitting-room. Maurois and his companion both wore souvenirs of the row in the taxicab. One of the Frenchman's eyes was bruised and closed—a beautiful shiner. His clothes were rumpled and dirty. He wore them jauntily in spite of that, and he still had his walking stick, crooked under the arm that didn't hold his gun.

Big Chin held us with his own gun and the woman's while Maurois ran his hand over Billie's and my clothes, to see if we were armed. He found my gun and pocketed it. Billie had no weapons.

"Can I trouble you to step back against the wall?" Maurois asked when he was through.

We stepped back as if it was no trouble at all. I found my shoulder against one of the window curtains. I pressed it against the frame, and turned far enough to drag the curtain clear of a foot or more of pane.

If the Whosis Kid was watching, he should have had a clear view of the Frenchman—the man who had shot at him earlier in the evening. I was putting it up to the Kid. The corridor door was unlocked. If the Kid could get into the building— no great trick—he had a clear path. I didn't know where he fit in, but I wanted him to join us, and I hoped he wouldn't disappoint me. If everybody got together here, maybe whatever was going on would come out where I could see it and understand it.

Meanwhile, I kept as much of myself as possible out of the window. The Kid might decide to throw lead from across the alley.

Maurois was facing Inés. Big Chin's guns were on Billie and me.

"I do not *comprends* ze *anglais* ver' good," the Frenchman was mocking the woman. "So it is when you say you meet wit' me, I t'ink you say in New Orleans. I do not know you say San Francisc'. I am ver' sorry to make ze mistake. I am mos' sorry zat I keep you wait. But now I am here. You have ze share for me?"

"I have not." She held her hands out in an empty gesture. "The Kid took those—everything from me."

"What?" Maurois dropped his taunting smile and his vaudeville accent. His one open eye flashed angrily. "How could he, unless—?"

"He suspected us, Edouard." Her mouth trembled with earnestness. Her eyes pleaded for belief. She was lying. "He had me followed. The day after I am there he comes. He takes all. I am afraid to wait for you. I fear your unbelief. You would not—"

"*C'est incroyable!*" Maurois was very excited over it. "I was on the first train south after our—our theatricals. Could the Kid have been on that train without my knowing it? *Non!* And how else could he have reached you before I? You are playing with me, *ma petite* Inés. That you did join the Kid, I do not doubt. But not in New Orleans. You did not go there. You came here to San Francisco."

"Edouard!" she protested, fingering his sleeve with one brown hand, the other holding her throat as if she were having trouble getting the words out. "You cannot think that thing! Do not those weeks in Boston say it is not possible? For one like the Kid—or like any other—am I to betray you? You know me not more than to think I am like that?"

She was an actress. She was appealing, and pathetic, and anything else you like—including dangerous.

The Frenchman took his sleeve away from her and stepped back a step. White lines ringed his mouth below his tiny mustache, and his jaw muscles bulged. His one good eye was worried. She had got to him, though not quite enough to upset him altogether. But the game was young yet.

"I do not know what to think," he said slowly. "If I have

been wrong—I must find the Kid first. Then I will learn the truth."

"You don't have to look no further, brother. I'm right among you!"

The Whosis Kid stood in the passageway door. A black revolver was in each of his hands. Their hammers were up.

CHAPTER IX

It was a pretty tableau.

There is the Whosis Kid in the door—a lean lad in his twenties, all the more wicked-looking because his face is weak and slack-jawed and dull-eyed. The cocked guns in his hands are pointing at everybody or at nobody, depending on how you look at them.

There is the brown woman, her cheeks pinched in her two fists, her eyes open until their green-grayishness shows. The fright I had seen in her face before was nothing to the fright that is there now.

There is the Frenchman—whirled doorward at the Kid's first word—his gun on the Kid, his cane still under his arm, his face a tense white blot.

There is Big Chin, his body twisted half around, his face over one shoulder to look at the door, with one of his guns following his face around.

There is Billie—a big, battered statue of a man who hasn't said a word since Inés Almad started to gun him out of the apartment.

And, last, here I am—not feeling so comfortable as I would home in bed, but not actually hysterical either. I wasn't altogether dissatisfied with the shape things were taking. Something was going to happen in these rooms. But I wasn't friendly enough to any present to care especially what happened to whom. For myself, I counted on coming through all in one piece. Few men *get* killed. Most of those who meet sudden ends *get themselves* killed. I've had twenty years of experience at dodging that. I can count on being one of the survivors of whatever blow-up there is. And I hope to take most of the other survivors for a ride.

But right now the situation belonged to the men with guns—the Whosis Kid, Maurois and Big Chin.

The Kid spoke first. He had a whining voice that came disagreeably through his thick nose.

"This don't look nothing like Chi to me, but, anyways, we're all here."

"Chicago!" Maurois exclaimed. "You did not go to Chicago!"

The Kid sneered at him.

"Did you? Did she? What would I be going there for? You think me and her run out on you, don't you? Well, we would of if she hadn't put the two X's to me the same as she done to you, and the same as the three of us done to the boob."

"That may be," the Frenchman replied; "but you do not expect me to believe that you and Inés are not friends? Didn't I see you leaving here this afternoon?"

"You seen me, all right," the Kid agreed; "but if my rod hadn't of got snagged in my flogger you wouldn't have seen nothing else. But I ain't got nothing against you now. I thought you and her had ditched me, just as you think me and her done you. I know different now, from what I heard while I was getting in here. She twisted the pair of us, Frenchy, just like we twisted the boob. Ain't you got it yet?"

Maurois shook his head slowly.

What put an edge to this conversation was that both men were talking over their guns.

"Listen," the Kid asked impatiently. "We was to meet up in Chi for a three-way split, wasn't we?"

The Frenchman nodded.

"But she tells me," the Kid went on, "she'll connect with me in St. Louis, counting you out; and she ribs you up to meet her in New Orleans, ducking me. And then she gyps the pair of us by running out here to Frisco with the stuff.

"We're a couple of suckers, Frenchy, and there ain't no use of us getting hot at each other. There's enough of it for a fat two-way cut. What I say is let's forget what's done, and me and you make it fifty-fifty. Understand, I ain't begging you. I'm making a proposition. If you don't like it, to hell with you! You know me. You never seen the day I wouldn't shoot it out with you or anybody else. Take your pick!"

The Frenchman didn't say anything for a while. He was converted, but he didn't want to weaken his hand by coming in too soon. I don't know whether he believed the Kid's words or not, but he believed the Kid's guns. You can get a bullet out of a cocked revolver a lot quicker than out of a hammerless automatic. The Kid had the bulge there. And the Kid had him licked because the Kid had the look of one who doesn't give a damn what happens next.

Finally Maurois looked a question at Big Chin. Big Chin moistened his lips, but said nothing.

Maurois looked at the Kid again, and nodded his head.

"You are right," he said. "We will do that."

"Good!" The Kid did not move from his door. "Now who are these plugs?"

"These two"—Maurois nodded at Billie and me—"are friends of our Inés. This"—indicating Big Chin—"is a confrere of mine."

"You mean he's in with you? That's all right with me." The Kid spoke crisply. "But, you understand, his cut comes out of yours. I get half, and no trimming."

The Frenchman frowned, but he nodded in agreement.

"Half is yours, if we find it."

"Don't get no headache over that," the Kid advised him. "It's here and we'll get it."

He put one of his guns away and came into the room, the other gun hanging loosely at his side. When he walked across the room to face the woman, he managed it so that Big Chin and Maurois were never behind him.

"Where's the stuff?" he demanded.

Inés Almad wet her red mouth with her tongue and let her mouth droop a little and looked softly at the Kid, and made her play.

"One of us is as bad as are the others, Kid. We all—each of us tried to get for ourselves everything. You and Edouard have put aside what is past. Am I more wrong than you? I have them, true, but I have not them here. Until tomorrow will you wait? I will get them. We will divide them among us three, as it was to have been. Shall we not do that?"

"Not any!" The Kid's voice had finality in it.

"Is that just?" she pleaded, letting her chin quiver a bit. "Is there a treachery of which I am guilty that also you and Edouard are not? Do you—?"

"That ain't the idea at all," the Kid told her. "Me and Frenchy are in a fix where we got to work together to get anywhere. So we're together. With you it's different. We don't need you. We can take the stuff away from you. You're out! Where's the stuff?"

"Not here! Am I foolish sufficient to leave them here where so easily you could find them? You *do* need my help to find them. Without me you cannot—"

"You're silly! I might flop for that if I didn't know you. But I know you're too damned greedy to let 'em get far away from you. And you're yellower than you're greedy. If you're smacked a couple of times, you'll kick in. And don't think I got any objections to smacking you over!"

She cowered back from his upraised hand.

The Frenchman spoke quickly.

"We should search the rooms first, Kid. If we don't find them there, then we can decide what to do next."

The Whosis Kid laughed sneeringly at Maurois.

"All right. But, get this, I'm not going out of here without that stuff—not if I have to take this rat apart. My way's quicker, but we'll hunt first if you want to. Your con-what-ever-you-call-him can keep these plugs tucked in while me and you upset the joint."

They went to work. The Kid put away his gun and brought out a long-bladed spring-knife. The Frenchman unscrewed the lower two-thirds of his cane, baring a foot and a half of sword-blade.

No cursory search, theirs. They took the room we were in first. They gutted it thoroughly, carved it to the bone. Furniture and pictures were taken apart. Upholstering gave up its stuffing. Floor coverings were cut. Suspicious lengths of wallpaper were scraped loose. They worked slowly. Neither would let the other get behind him. The Kid would not turn his back on Big Chin.

The sitting-room wrecked, they went into the next room, leaving the woman, Billie and me standing among the litter. Big Chin and his two guns watched over us.

As soon as the Frenchman and the Kid were out of sight, the woman tried her stuff out on our guardian. She had a lot of confidence in her power with men, I'll say that for her.

For a while she worked her eyes on Big Chin, and then, very softly:

"Can I—?"

"You can't!" Big Chin was loud and gruff. "Shut up!"

The Whosis Kid appeared at the door.

"If nobody don't say nothing maybe nobody won't get hurt," he snarled, and went back to his work.

The woman valued herself too highly to be easily discouraged. She didn't put anything in words again, but she looked things at Big Chin—things that had him sweating and blushing. He was a simple man. I didn't think she'd get anywhere. If there had been no one present but the two of them, she might have put Big Chin over the jumps; but he wouldn't be likely to let her get to him with a couple of birds standing there watching the show.

Once a sharp yelp told us that the purple Frana—who had fled rearward when Maurois and Big Chin arrived—had got in trouble with the searchers. There was only that one yelp, and it stopped with a suddenness that suggested trouble for the dog.

The two men spent nearly an hour in the other rooms. They didn't find anything. Their hands, when they joined us again, held nothing but the cutlery.

CHAPTER X

"I said to you it was not here," Inés told them triumphantly. "Now will you—?"

"You can't tell me nothing I'll believe." The Kid snapped his knife shut and dropped it in his pocket. "I still think it's here."

He caught her wrist, and held his other hand, palm up, under her nose.

"You can put 'em in my hand, or I'll take 'em."

"They are not here! I swear it!"

His mouth lifted at the corner in a savage grimace.

"Liar!"

He twisted her arm roughly, forcing her to her knees. His free hand went to the shoulder-strap of her orange gown.

"I'll damn soon find out," he promised.

Billie came to life.

"Hey!" he protested, his chest heaving in and out. "You can't do that!"

"Wait, Kid!" Maurois—putting his sword-cane together again—called. "Let us see if there is not another way."

The Whosis Kid let go of the woman and took three slow steps back from her. His eyes were dead circles without any color you could name—the dull eyes of the man whose nerves quit functioning in the face of excitement. His bony hands pushed his coat aside a little and rested where his vest bulged over the sharp corners of his hip-bones.

"Let's me and you get this right, Frenchy," he said in his whining voice. "Are you with me or her?"

"You, most certainly, but—"

"All right. Then *be* with me! Don't be trying to gum every play I make. I'm going to frisk this dolly, and don't think I ain't. What are you going to do about it?"

The Frenchman pursed his mouth until his little black mustache snuggled against the tip of his nose. He puckered his eyebrows and looked thoughtfully out of his one good eye. But he wasn't going to do anything at all about it, and he knew he wasn't. Finally he shrugged.

"You are right," he surrendered. "She should be searched."

The Kid grunted contemptuous disgust at him and went toward the woman again.

She sprang away from him, to me. Her arms clamped around my neck in the habit they seemed to have.

"Jerry!" she screamed in my face. "You will not allow him! Jerry, please not!"

I didn't say anything.

I didn't think it was exactly genteel of the Kid to frisk her, but there were several reasons why I didn't try to stop him. First, I didn't want to do anything to delay the unearthing of this "stuff" there had been so much talk about. Second, I'm no Galahad. This woman had picked her playmates, and was largely responsible for this angle of their game. If they played rough, she'd have to make the best of it. And, a good strong third, Big Chin was prodding me in the side with a gun-muzzle to remind me that I couldn't do anything if I wanted to—except get myself slaughtered.

The Kid dragged Inés away. I let her go.

He pulled her over to what was left of the bench by the electric heater, and called the Frenchman there with a jerk of his head.

"You hold her while I go through her," he said.

She filled her lungs with air. Before she could turn it loose in a shriek, the Kid's long fingers had fit themselves to her throat.

"One chirp out of you and I'll tie a knot in your neck," he threatened.

She let the air wheeze out of her nose.

Billie shuffled his feet. I turned my head to look at him. He was puffing through his mouth. Sweat polished his forehead under his matted red hair. I hoped he wasn't going to turn his wolf loose until the "stuff" came to the surface. If he would wait a while I might join him.

He wouldn't wait. He went into action when—Maurois holding her—the Kid started to undress the woman.

He took a step toward them. Big Chin tried to wave him back with a gun. Billie didn't even see it. His eyes were red on the three by the bench.

"Hey, you can't do that!" he rumbled. "You can't do that!"

"No?" The Kid looked up from his work. "Watch me."

"Billie!" the woman urged the big man on in his foolishness.

Billie charged.

Big Chin let him go, playing safe by swinging both guns on me. The Whosis Kid slid out of the plunging giant's path. Maurois hurled the girl straight at Billie—and got his gun out.

Billie and Inés thumped together in a swaying tangle.

The Kid spun behind the big man. One of the Kid's hands came out of his pocket with the spring-knife. The knife clicked open as Billie regained his balance.

The Kid jumped close.

He knew knives. None of your clumsy downward strokes with the blade sticking out the bottom of his fist.

Thumb and crooked forefinger guided blade. He struck upward. Under Billie's shoulder. Once. Deep.

Billie pitched forward, smashing the woman to the floor under him. He rolled off her and was dead on his back among the furniture-stuffing. Dead, he seemed larger than ever, seemed to fill the room.

The Whosis Kid wiped his knife clean on a piece of carpet, snapped it shut, and dropped it back in his pocket. He did this with his left hand. His right was close to his hip. He did not look at the knife. His eyes were on Maurois.

But if he expected the Frenchman to squawk, he was disappointed. Maurois' little mustache twitched, and his face was white and strained, but:

"We'd better hurry with what we have to do, and get out of here," he suggested.

The woman sat up beside the dead man, whimpering. Her face was ashy under her dark skin. She was licked. A shaking hand fumbled beneath her clothes. It brought out a little flat silk bag.

Maurois—nearer than the Kid—took it. It was sewed too securely for his fingers to open. He held it while the Kid ripped it with his knife. The Frenchman poured part of the contents out in one cupped hand.

Diamonds. Pearls. A few colored stones among them.

CHAPTER XI

Big Chin blew his breath out in a faint whistle. His eyes were bright on the sparkling stones. So were the eyes of Maurois, the woman, and the Kid.

Big Chin's inattention was a temptation. I could reach his jaw. I could knock him over. The strength Billie had mauled out of me had nearly all come back by now. I could knock Big Chin over and have at least one of his guns by the time the Kid and Maurois got set. It was time for me to do something. I had let these comedians run the show long enough. The stuff had come to light. If I let the party break up there was no telling when, if ever, I could round up these folks again.

But I put the temptation away and made myself wait a bit longer. No use going off half-cocked. With a gun in my hand, facing the Kid and Maurois, I still would have less than an even break. That's not enough. The idea in this detective business is to catch crooks, not to put on heroics.

Maurois was pouring the stones back in the bag when I looked at him again. He started to put the bag in his pocket. The Whosis Kid stopped him with a hand on his arm.

"I'll pack 'em."

Maurois' eyebrows went up.

"There's two of you and one of me," the Kid explained. "I trust you, and all the like of that, but just the same I'm carrying my own share."

"But—"

The doorbell interrupted Maurois' protest.

The Kid spun to the girl.

"You do the talking—and no wise breaks!"

She got up from the floor and went to the passageway.

"Who is there?" she called.

The landlady's voice, stern and wrathful:

"Another sound, Mrs. Almad, and I shall call the police. This is disgraceful!"

I wondered what she would have thought if she had opened the unlocked door and taken a look at her apartment—furniture whittled and gutted; a dead man—the noise of whose dying had brought her up here this second time—lying in the middle of the litter.

I wondered—I took a chance.

"Aw, go jump down the sewer!" I told her.

A gasp, and we heard no more from her. I hoped she was speeding her injured feelings to the telephone. I might need the police she had mentioned.

The Kid's gun was out. For a while it was a toss-up. I would lie down beside Billie, or I wouldn't. If I could have been knifed quietly, I would have gone. But nobody was behind me. The Kid knew I wouldn't stand still and quiet while he carved me. He didn't want any more racket than necessary, now that the jewels were on hand.

"Keep your clam shut or I'll shut it for you!" was the worst I got out of it.

The Kid turned to the Frenchman again. The Frenchman had used the time spent in this side-play to pocket the gems.

"Either we divvy here and now, or I carry the stuff," the Kid announced. "There's two of you to see I don't take a Micky Finn on you."

"But, Kid, we cannot stay here! Is not the landlady even now calling the police? We will go elsewhere to divide. Why cannot you trust me when you are with me?"

Two steps put the Kid between the door and both Maurois and Big Chin. One of the Kid's hands held the gun he had flashed on me. The other was conveniently placed to his other gun.

"Nothing stirring!" he said through his nose. "My cut of them stones don't go out of here in nobody else's kick. If you want to split 'em here, good enough. If you don't, I'll do the carrying. That's flat!"

"But the police!"

"You worry about them. I'm taking one thing at a time, and it's the stones right now."

A vein came out blue in the Frenchman's forehead. His small body was rigid. He was trying to collect enough courage to swap shots with the Kid. He knew, and the Kid knew, that one of them was going to have all the stuff when the curtain came down. They had started off by double-crossing each other. They weren't likely to change their habits. One would have the stones in the end. The other would have nothing—except maybe a burial.

Big Chin didn't count. He was too simple a thug to last long in his present company. If he had known anything, he would have used one of his guns on each of them right now. Instead, he continued to cover me, trying to watch them out of the tail of his eye.

The woman stood near the door, where she had gone to talk to the landlady. She was staring at the Frenchman and the Kid. I wasted precious minutes that seemed to run into hours trying to catch her eye. I finally got it.

I looked at the light-switch, only a foot from her. I looked at her. I looked at the switch again. At her. At the switch.

She got me. Her hand crept sidewise along the wall.

I looked at the two principal players in this button-button game.

The Kid's eyes were dead—and deadly—circles. Maurois' one open eye was watery. He couldn't make the grade. He put a hand in his pocket and brought out the silk bag.

The woman's brown finger topped the light-button. God knows she was nothing to gamble on, but I had no choice. I had to be in motion when the lights went. Big Chin would pump metal. I had to trust Inés not to balk. If she did, my name was Denis.

Her nail whitened.

I went for Maurois.

Darkness—streaked with orange and blue—filled with noise.

My arms had Maurois. We crashed down on dead Billie. I twisted around, kicking the Frenchman's face. Loosened one arm. Caught one of his. His other hand gouged at my face. That told me the bag was in the one I held. Clawing fingers tore my mouth. I put my teeth in them and kept them there. One of my knees was on his face. I put my weight on it. My teeth still held his hand. Both of my hands were free to get the bag.

Not nice, this work, but effective.

The room was the inside of a black drum on which a giant was beating the long roll. Four guns worked together in a prolonged throbbing roar.

Maurois' fingernails dug into my thumb. I had to open my mouth—let his hand escape. One of my hands found the bag. He wouldn't let go. I screwed his thumb. He cried out. I had the bag.

I tried to leave him then. He grabbed my legs. I kicked at him—missed. He shuddered twice—and stopped moving. A flying bullet had hit him, I took it. Rolling over to the floor, snuggling close to him, I ran a hand over him. A hard bulge came under my hand. I put my hand in his pocket and took back my gun.

On hands and knees—one fist around my gun, the other clutching the silk sack of jewels—I turned to where the door to the next room should have been. A foot wrong, I corrected my course. As I went through the door, the racket in the room behind me stopped.

CHAPTER XII

Huddled close to the wall inside the door, I stowed the silk bag away, and regretted that I hadn't stayed plastered to the floor behind the Frenchman. This room was dark. It hadn't been dark when the woman switched off the sitting-room lights. Every room in the apartment had been lighted then. All were dark now. Not knowing who had darkened them, I didn't like it.

No sounds came from the room I had quit.

The rustle of gently falling rain came from an open window that I couldn't see, off to one side.

Another sound came from behind me. The muffled tattoo of teeth on teeth.

That cheered me. Inés the scary, of course. She had left the sitting-room in the dark and put out the rest of the lights. Maybe nobody else was behind me.

Breathing quietly through wide-open mouth, I waited. I couldn't hunt for the woman in the dark without making noises. Maurois and the Kid had strewn furniture and parts of furniture everywhere. I wished I knew if she was holding a gun. I didn't want to have her spraying me.

Not knowing, I waited where I was.

Her teeth clicked on for minutes.

Something moved in the sitting-room. A gun thundered.

"Inés!" I hissed toward the chattering teeth.

No answer. Furniture scraped in the sitting-room. Two guns went off together. A groaning broke out.

"I've got the stuff," I whispered under cover of the groaning.

That brought an answer.

"Jerry! Ah, come here to me!"

The groans went on, but fainter, in the other room. I crawled toward the woman's voice. I went on hands and knees, bumping as carefully as possible against things. I couldn't see anything. Midway, I put a hand down on a soggy bundle of fur—the late purple Frana. I went on.

Inés touched my shoulder with an eager hand.

"Give them to me," were her first words.

I grinned at her in the dark, patted her hand, found her head, and put my mouth to her ear.

"Let's get back in the bedroom," I breathed, paying no attention to her request for the loot. "The Kid will be coming." I didn't doubt that he had bested Big Chin. "We can handle him better in the bedroom."

I wanted to receive him in a room with only one door.

She led me—both of us on hands and knees—to the bedroom. I did what thinking seemed necessary as we crawled. The Kid couldn't know yet how the Frenchman and I had come out. If he guessed, he would guess that the Frenchman had survived. He would be likely to put me in the chump class with Billie, and think the Frenchman could handle me. The chances were that he had got Big Chin, and knew it by now. It was black as black in the sitting-room, but he must know by now that he was the only living thing there.

He blocked the only exit from the apartment. He would think, then, that Inés and Maurois were still alive in it, with the spoils. What would he do about it? There was no pretense of partnership now. That had gone with the lights. The Kid was after the stones. The Kid was after them alone.

I'm no wizard at guessing the other guy's next move. But my idea was that the Kid would be on his way after us, soon. He knew—he must know—that the police were coming; but I had him doped as crazy enough to disregard the police until they appeared. He'd figure that there would be only a couple of them—prepared for nothing more violent than a drinking-party. He could handle them—or he would think he could. Meanwhile, he would come after the stones.

The woman and I reached the bedroom, the room farthest back in the apartment, a room with only one door. I heard her fumbling with the door, trying to close it. I couldn't see, but I got my foot in the way.

"Leave it open," I whispered.

I didn't want to shut the Kid out. I wanted to take him in.

On my belly, I crawled back to the door, felt for my watch, and propped it on the sill, in the angle between door and frame. I wriggled back from it until I was six or eight feet away, looking diagonally across the open doorway at the watch's luminous dial.

The phosphorescent numbers could not be seen from the other side of the door. They faced me. Anybody who came through the door—unless he jumped—must, if only for a split-second, put some part of himself between me and the watch.

On my belly, my gun cocked, its butt steady on the floor, I waited for the faint light to be blotted out.

I waited a time. Pessimism: perhaps he wasn't coming; perhaps I would have to go after him; perhaps he would run out, and I would lose him after all my trouble.

Inés, beside me, breathed quaveringly in my ear, and shivered.

"Don't touch me," I growled at her as she tried to cuddle against me.

She was shaking my arm.

Glass broke in the next room.

Silence.

The luminous patches on the watch burnt my eyes. I couldn't afford to blink. A foot could pass the dial while I was blinking. I couldn't afford to blink, but I had to blink. I blinked. I couldn't tell whether something had passed the watch or not. I had to blink again. Tried to hold my eyes stiffly opened. Failed. I almost shot at the third blink. I could have sworn something had gone between me and the watch.

The Kid, whatever he was up to, made no sound.

The dark woman began to sob beside me. Throat noises that could guide bullets.

I lumped her with my eyes and cursed the lot—not aloud, but from the heart.

My eyes smarted. Moisture filmed them. I blinked it away, losing sight of the watch for precious instants. The butt of my gun was slimy with my hand's sweat. I was thoroughly uncomfortable, inside and out.

Gunpowder burned at my face.

A screaming maniac of a woman was crawling all over me.

My bullet hit nothing lower than the ceiling.

I flung, maybe kicked, the woman off, and snaked backward. She moaned somewhere to one side. I couldn't see the Kid—couldn't hear him. The watch was visible again, farther away. A rustling.

The watch vanished.

I fired at it.

Two points of light near the floor gave out fire and thunder.

My gun-barrel as close to the floor as I could hold it, I fired between those points. Twice.

Twin flames struck at me again.

My right hand went numb. My left took the gun. I sped two more bullets on their way. That left one in my gun.

I don't know what I did with it. My head filled up with funny notions. There wasn't any room. There wasn't any darkness. There wasn't anything. . . .

I opened my eyes in dim light. I was on my back. Beside me the dark woman knelt, shivering and sniffling. Her hands were busy—in my clothes.

One of them came out of my vest with the jewel-bag.

Coming to life, I grabbed her arm. She squealed as if I were a stirring corpse. I got the bag again.

"Give them back, Jerry," she wailed, trying frantically to pull my fingers loose. "They are my things. Give them!"

Sitting up, I looked around.

Beside me lay a shattered bedside lamp, whose fall—caused by carelessness with my feet, or one of the Kid's bullets—had KO'd me. Across the room, face down, arms spread in a crucified posture, the Whosis Kid sprawled. He was dead.

From the front of the apartment—almost indistinguishable from the throbbing in my head—came the pounding of heavy blows. The police were kicking down the unlocked door.

The woman went quiet. I whipped my head around. The knife stung my cheek—put a slit in the lapel of my coat. I took it away from her.

There was no sense to this. The police were already here. I humored her, pretending a sudden coming to full consciousness.

"Oh, it's you!" I said. "Here they are."

I handed her the silk bag of jewels just as the first policeman came into the room.

CHAPTER XIII

I didn't see Inés again before she was taken back East to be hit with a life-sentence in the Massachusetts big house. Neither of the policemen who crashed into her apartment that night knew me. The woman and I were separated before I ran into anyone who did know me, which gave me an opportunity to arrange that she would not be tipped off to my identity. The most difficult part of the performance was to keep myself out of the newspapers, since I had to tell the coroner's jury about the deaths of Billie, Big Chin, Maurois and the Whosis Kid. But I managed it. So far as I know, the dark woman still thinks I am Jerry Young, the bootlegger.

The Old Man talked to her before she left San Francisco. Fitting together what he got from her and what the Boston branch got, the history runs like this:

A Boston jeweler named Tunnicliffe had a trusted employee named Binder. Binder fell in with a dark woman named Inés Almad. The dark woman, in turn, had a couple of shifty friends—a Frenchman named Maurois, and a native of Boston whose name was either Carey or Cory, but who was better known as the Whosis Kid. Out of that sort of combination almost anything was more than likely to come.

What came was a scheme. The faithful Binder—part of whose duties it was to open the shop in the morning and close it at night—was to pick out the richest of the unset stones bought for the holiday trade, carry them off with him one evening, and turn them over to Inés. She was to turn them into money.

To cover up Binder's theft, the Whosis Kid and the Frenchman were to rob the jeweler's shop immediately after the door was opened the following morning. Binder and the porter—who would not notice the absence of the most valuable pieces from the stock—would be the only ones in the shop. The robbers would take whatever they could get. In addition to their pickings, they were to be paid two hundred and fifty dollars apiece, and in case either was caught later, Binder could be counted on not to identify them.

That was the scheme as Binder knew it. There were angles he didn't suspect.

Between Inés, Maurois and the Kid there was another agreement. She was to leave for Chicago with the stones as soon as Binder gave them to her, and wait there for Maurois and the Kid. She and the Frenchman would have been satisfied to run off and let Binder hold the sack. The Whosis Kid

insisted that the hold-up go through as planned, and that the
foolish Binder be killed. Binder knew too much about them,
the Kid said, and he would squawk his head off as soon as he
learned he had been double-crossed.

The Kid had his way, and he had shot Binder.

Then had come the sweet mess of quadruple and sextuple
crossing that had led all three into calamity: the woman's private agreements with the Kid and Maurois—to meet one in
St. Louis and the other in New Orleans—and her flight alone
with the loot to San Francisco.

Billie was an innocent bystander—or almost. A lumber-
handler Inés had run into somewhere, and picked up as a sort
of cushion against the rough spots along the rocky road she
traveled.

The Scorched Face

"WE EXPECTED them home yesterday," Alfred Banbrock wound up his story. "When they had not come by this morning, my wife telephoned Mrs. Walden. Mrs. Walden said they had not been down there—had not been expected, in fact."

"On the face of it, then," I suggested, "it seems that your daughters went away of their own accord, and are staying away on their own accord?"

Banbrock nodded gravely. Tired muscles sagged in his fleshy face.

"It would seem so," he agreed. "That is why I came to your agency for help instead of going to the police."

"Have they ever disappeared before?"

"No. If you read the papers and magazines, you've no doubt seen hints that the younger generation is given to irregularity. My daughters came and went pretty much as they pleased. But, though I can't say I ever knew what they were up to, we always knew where they were in a general way."

"Can you think of any reason for their going like this?"

He shook his weary head.

"Any recent quarrels?" I probed.

"N—" He changed it to: "Yes—although I didn't attach any importance to it, and wouldn't have recalled it if you hadn't jogged my memory. It was Thursday evening—the evening before they went away."

"And it was about—?"

"Money, of course. We never disagreed over anything else. I gave each of my daughters an adequate allowance—perhaps a very liberal one. Nor did I keep them strictly within it. There were few months in which they didn't exceed it. Thursday evening they asked for an amount of money even more than usual in excess of what two girls should need. I wouldn't give it to them, though I finally did give them a somewhat smaller amount. We didn't exactly quarrel—not in the strict sense of the word—but there was a certain lack of friendliness between us."

"And it was after this disagreement that they said they were going down to Mrs. Walden's, in Monterey, for the week-end?"

"Possibly. I'm not sure of that point. I don't think I heard of it until the next morning, but they may have told my wife before that. I shall ask her if you wish."

"And you know of no other possible reason for their running away?"

"None. I can't think that our dispute over money—by no means an unusual one—had anything to do with it."

"What does their mother think?"

"Their mother is dead," Banbrock corrected me. "My wife is their stepmother. She is only two years older than Myra, my older daughter. She is as much at sea as I."

"Did your daughters and their stepmother get along all right together?"

"Yes! Yes! Excellently! If there was a division in the family, I usually found them standing together against me."

"Your daughters left Friday afternoon?"

"At noon, or a few minutes after. They were going to drive down."

"The car, of course, is still missing?"

"Naturally."

"What was it?"

"A Locomobile, with a special cabriolet body. Black."

"You can give me the license and engine numbers?"

"I think so."

He turned in his chair to the big roll-top desk that hid a quarter of one office wall, fumbled with papers in a compartment, and read the numbers over his shoulder to me. I put them on the back of an envelope.

"I'm going to have this car put on the police department list of stolen machines," I told him. "It can be done without mentioning your daughters. The police bulletin might find the car for us. That would help us find your daughters."

"Very well," he agreed, "if it can be done without disagreeable publicity. As I told you at first, I don't want any more advertising than is absolutely necessary—unless it becomes likely that harm has come to the girls."

I nodded understanding, and got up.

"I want to go out and talk to your wife," I said. "Is she home now?"

"Yes, I think so. I'll phone her and tell her you are coming."

II

In a big limestone fortress on top a hill in Sea Cliff, looking down on ocean and bay, I had my talk with Mrs. Banbrock. She was a tall dark girl of not more than twenty-two years, inclined to plumpness.

She couldn't tell me anything her husband hadn't at least mentioned, but she could give me finer details.

I got descriptions of the two girls:

Myra—20 years old; 5 feet 8 inches; 150 pounds; athletic; brisk, almost masculine manner and carriage; bobbed brown hair; brown eyes; medium complexion; square face, with large chin and short nose; scar over left ear, concealed by hair; fond of horses and all outdoor sports. When she left the house she wore a blue and green wool dress, small blue hat, short black seal coat, and black slippers.

Ruth—18 years; 5 feet 4 inches; 105 pounds; brown eyes; brown bobbed hair; medium complexion; small oval face; quiet, timid, inclined to lean on her more forceful sister. When last seen she had worn a tobacco-brown coat trimmed with brown fur over a grey silk dress, and a wide brown hat.

I got two photographs of each girl, and an additional snapshot of Myra standing in front of the cabriolet. I got a list of the things they had taken with them—such things as would naturally be taken on a week-end visit. What I valued most of what I got was a list of their friends, relatives, and other acquaintances, so far as Mrs. Banbrock knew them.

"Did they mention Mrs. Walden's invitation before their quarrel with Mr. Banbrock?" I asked, when I had my lists stowed away.

"I don't think so," Mrs. Banbrock said thoughtfully. "I didn't connect the two things at all. They didn't really quarrel with their father, you know. It wasn't harsh enough to be called a quarrel."

"Did you see them when they left?"

"Assuredly! They left at about half-past twelve Friday afternoon. They kissed me as usual when they went, and there was certainly nothing in their manner to suggest anything out of the ordinary."

"You've no idea at all where they might have gone?"

"None."

"Can't even make a guess?"

"I can't. Among the names and addresses I have given you are some of friends and relatives of the girls in other cities. They may have gone to one of those. Do you think we should—?"

"I'll take care of that," I promised. "Could you pick out one or two of them as the most likely places for the girls to have gone?"

She wouldn't try it.

"No," she said positively, "I could not."

From this interview I went back to the Agency, and put the Agency machinery in motion; arranging to have operatives from some of the Continental's other branches call on the out-of-town names on my list; having the missing Locomobile put on the police department list; turning one photograph of each girl over to a photographer to be copied.

That done, I set out to talk to the persons on the list Mrs. Banbrock had given me. My first call was on a Constance Delee, in an apartment building on Post Street. I saw a maid. The maid said Miss Delee was out of town. She wouldn't tell me where her mistress was, or when she would be back.

From there I went up on Van Ness Avenue and found a Wayne Ferris in an automobile salesroom: a sleek-haired young man whose very nice manners and clothes completely hid anything else—brains for instance—he might have had. He was very willing to help me, and he knew nothing. It took him a long time to tell me so. A nice boy.

Another blank: "Mrs. Scott is in Honolulu."

In a real estate office on Montgomery Street I found my next one—another sleek, stylish, smooth-haired young man with nice manners and nice clothes. His name was Raymond Elwood. I would have thought him a no more distant relative of Ferris than cousin if I hadn't known that the world—

especially the dancing, teaing world—was full of their sort. I learned nothing from him.

Then I drew some more blanks: "Out of town," "Shopping," "I don't know where you can find him."

I found one more of the Banbrock girls' friends before I called it a day. Her name was Mrs. Stewart Correll. She lived in Presidio Terrace, not far from the Banbrocks. She was a small woman, or girl, of about Mrs. Banbrock's age. A little fluffy blonde person with wide eyes of that particular blue which always looks honest and candid no matter what is going on behind it.

"I haven't seen either Ruth or Myra for two weeks or more," she said in answer to my question.

"At that time—the last time you saw them—did either say anything about going away?"

"No."

Her eyes were wide and frank. A little muscle twitched in her upper lip.

"And you've no idea where they might have gone?"

"No."

Her fingers were rolling her lace handkerchief into a little ball.

"Have you heard from them since you last saw them?"

"No."

She moistened her mouth before she said it.

"Will you give me the names and addresses of all the people you know who were also known by the Banbrock girls?"

"Why—? Is there—?"

"There's a chance that some of them may have seen them more recently than you," I explained. "Or may even have seen them since Friday."

Without enthusiasm, she gave me a dozen names. All were already on my list. Twice she hesitated as if about to speak a name she did not want to speak. Her eyes stayed on mine, wide and honest. Her fingers, no longer balling the handkerchief, picked at the cloth of her skirt.

I didn't pretend to believe her. But my feet weren't solidly enough on the ground for me to put her on the grill. I gave her a promise before I left, one that she could get a threat out of if she liked.

"Thanks, very much," I said. "I know it's hard to remember things exactly. If I run across anything that will help your memory, I'll be back to let you know about it."

"Wha—? Yes, do!" she said.

Walking away from the house, I turned my head to look back just before I passed out of sight. A curtain swung into place at a second-floor window. The street lights weren't bright enough for me to be sure the curtain had swung in front of a blonde head.

My watch told me it was nine-thirty: too late to line up any more of the girls' friends. I went home, wrote my report for the day, and turned in, thinking more about Mrs. Correll than about the girls.

She seemed worth an investigation.

III

Some telegraphic reports were in when I got to the office the next morning. None was of any value. Investigation of the names and addresses in other cities had revealed nothing. An investigation in Monterey had established reasonably—which is about as well as anything is ever established in the detecting business—that the girls had not been there recently; that the Locomobile had not been there.

The early editions of the afternoon papers were on the street when I went out to get some breakfast before taking up the grind where I had dropped it the previous night. I bought a paper to prop behind my grapefruit.

It spoiled my breakfast for me.

BANKER'S WIFE SUICIDE

Mrs. Stewart Correll, wife of the vice-president of the Golden Gate Trust Company, was found dead early this morning by the maid in her bedroom, in her home in Presidio Terrace. A bottle believed to have contained poison was on the floor beside the bed.

The dead woman's husband could give no reason for his wife's suicide. He said she had not seemed depressed or . . .

I gave my eggs and toast a quick play, put my coffee down in a lump, and got going.

At the Correll residence I had to do a lot of talking before I could get to Correll. He was a tall, slim man of less than thirty-five, with a sallow, nervous face and blue eyes that fidgeted.

"I'm sorry to disturb you at a time like this," I apologized when I had finally insisted my way into his presence. "I won't take up more of your time than necessary. I am an operative of the Continental Detective Agency. I have been trying to find Ruth and Myra Banbrock, who disappeared several days ago. You know them, I think."

"Yes," he said without interest. "I know them."

"You knew they had disappeared?"

"No." His eyes switched from a chair to a rug. "Why should I?"

"Have you seen either of them recently?" I asked, ignoring his question.

"Last week—Wednesday, I think. They were just leaving— standing at the door talking to my wife—when I came home from the bank."

"Didn't your wife say anything to you about their vanishing?"

"No. Really, I can't tell you anything about the Misses Banbrock. If you'll excuse me—"

"Just a moment longer," I said. "I wouldn't have bothered you if it hadn't been necessary. I was here last night, to question Mrs. Correll. She seemed nervous. My impression was that some of her answers to my questions were—uh—evasive. I want—"

He was up out of his chair. His face was red in front of mine.

"You!" he cried. "I can thank you for—"

"Now, Mr. Correll," I tried to quiet him, "there's no use—"

But he had himself all worked up.

"You drove my wife to her death," he accused me. "You killed her with your damned prying—with your bulldozing threats; with your—"

That was silly. I felt sorry for this young man whose wife had killed herself. Apart from that, I had work to do. I tightened the screws.

"We won't argue, Correll," I told him. "The point is that I came here to see if your wife could tell me anything about the

Banbrocks. She told me less than the truth. Later, she committed suicide. I want to know why. Come through for me, and I'll do what I can to keep the papers and the public from linking her death with the girls' disappearance."

"Linking her death with their disappearance?" he exclaimed. "That's absurd!"

"Maybe—but the connection is there!" I hammered away at him. I felt sorry for him, but I had work to do. "It's there. If you'll give it to me, maybe it won't have to be advertised. I'm going to get it, though. You give it to me—or I'll go after it out in the open."

For a moment I thought he was going to take a poke at me. I wouldn't have blamed him. His body stiffened—then sagged, and he dropped back into his chair. His eyes fidgeted away from mine.

"There's nothing I can tell," he mumbled. "When her maid went to her room to call her this morning, she was dead. There was no message, no reason, nothing."

"Did you see her last night?"

"No. I was not home for dinner. I came in late and went straight to my own room, not wanting to disturb her. I hadn't seen her since I left the house that morning."

"Did she seem disturbed or worried then?"

"No."

"Why do you think she did it?"

"My God, man, I don't know! I've thought and thought, but I don't know!"

"Health?"

"She seemed well. She was never ill, never complained."

"Any recent quarrels?"

"We never quarreled—never in the year and a half we have been married!"

"Financial trouble?"

He shook his head without speaking or looking up from the floor.

"Any other worry?"

He shook his head again.

"Did the maid notice anything peculiar in her behavior last night?"

"Nothing."

"Have you looked through her things—for papers, letters?"

"Yes—and found nothing." He raised his head to look at me. "The only thing"—he spoke very slowly—"there was a little pile of ashes in the grate in her room, as if she had burned papers, or letters."

Correl held nothing more for me—nothing I could get out of him, anyway.

The girl at the front gate in Alfred Banbrock's Shoreman's Building suite told me he was *in conference*. I sent my name in. He came out of conference to take me into his private office. His tired face was full of questions.

I didn't keep him waiting for the answers. He was a grown man. I didn't edge around the bad news.

"Things have taken a bad break," I said as soon as we were locked in together. "I think we'll have to go to the police and newspapers for help. A Mrs. Correll, a friend of your daughters, lied to me when I questioned her yesterday. Last night she committed suicide."

"Irma Correll? Suicide?"

"You knew her?"

"Yes! Intimately! She was—that is, she was a close friend of my wife and daughters. She killed herself?"

"Yes. Poison. Last night. Where does she fit in with your daughters' disappearance?"

"Where?" he repeated. "I don't know. Must she fit in?"

"I think she must. She told me she hadn't seen your daughters for a couple of weeks. Her husband told me just now that they were talking to her when he came home from the bank last Wednesday afternoon. She seemed nervous when I questioned her. She killed herself shortly afterward. There's hardly a doubt that she fits in somewhere."

"And that means—?"

"That means," I finished for him, "that your daughters may be perfectly safe, but that we can't afford to gamble on that possibility."

"You think harm has come to them?"

"I don't think anything," I evaded, "except that with a death tied up closely with their going, we can't afford to play around."

Banbrock got his attorney on the phone—a pink-faced, white-haired old boy named Norwall, who had the reputation of knowing more about corporations than all the Morgans, but who hadn't the least idea as to what police procedure was all about—and told him to meet us at the Hall of Justice.

We spent an hour and a half there, getting the police turned loose on the affair, and giving the newspapers what we wanted them to have. That was plenty of dope on the girls, plenty of photographs and so forth; but nothing about the connection between them and Mrs. Correll. Of course we let the police in on that angle.

IV

After Banbrock and his attorney had gone away together, I went back to the detectives' assembly room to chew over the job with Pat Reddy, the police sleuth assigned to it.

Pat was the youngest member of the detective bureau—a big blond Irishman who went in for the spectacular in his lazy way.

A couple of years ago he was a new copper, pounding his feet in harness on a hillside beat. One night he tagged an automobile that was parked in front of a fireplug. The owner came out just then and gave him an argument. She was Althea Wallach, only and spoiled daughter of the owner of the Wallach Coffee Company—a slim, reckless youngster with hot eyes. She must have told Pat plenty. He took her over to the station and dumped her in a cell.

Old Wallach, so the story goes, showed up the next morning with a full head of steam and half the lawyers in San Francisco. But Pat made his charge stick, and the girl was fined. Old Wallach did everything but take a punch at Pat in the corridor afterward. Pat grinned his sleepy grin at the coffee importer, and drawled:

"You better lay off me—or I'll stop drinking your coffee."

That crack got into most of the newspapers in the country, and even into a Broadway show.

But Pat didn't stop with the snappy come-back. Three days later he and Althea Wallach went over to Alameda and got themselves married. I was in on that part. I happened to be on the ferry they took, and they dragged me along to see the deed done.

Old Wallach immediately disowned his daughter, but that didn't seem to worry anybody else. Pat went on pounding his beat, but, now that he was conspicuous, it wasn't long before his qualities were noticed. He was boosted into the detective bureau. Old Wallach relented before he died, and left Althea both of his millions.

Pat took the afternoon off to go to the funeral, and went back to work that night, catching a wagonload of gunmen. He kept on working. I don't know what his wife did with her money, but Pat didn't even improve the quality of his cigars— though he should have. He lived now in the Wallach mansion, true enough, and now and then on rainy mornings he would be driven down to the Hall in a Hispano-Suiza brougham; but there was no difference in him beyond that.

That was the big blond Irishman who sat across a desk from me in the assembly room and fumigated me with something shaped like a cigar.

He took the cigar-like thing out of his mouth presently, and spoke through the fumes.

"This Correll woman you think's tied up with the Banbrocks—she was stuck-up a couple of months back and nicked for eight hundred dollars. Know that?"

I hadn't known it.

"Lose anything besides cash?" I asked.

"No."

"You believe it?"

He grinned.

"That's the point," he said. "We didn't catch the bird who did it. With women who lose things that way—especially money—it's always a question whether it's a hold-up or a hold-out."

He teased some more poison-gas out of the cigar-thing, and added:

"The hold-up might have been on the level, though. What are you figuring on doing now?"

"Let's go up to the Agency and see if anything new has turned up. Then I'd like to talk to Mrs. Banbrock again. Maybe she can tell us something about the Correll woman."

At the office I found that reports had come in on the rest of the out-of-town names and addresses. Apparently none of these people knew anything about the girls' whereabouts. Reddy and I went on up to Sea Cliff to the Banbrock home.

Banbrock had telephoned the news of Mrs. Correll's death to his wife, and she had read the papers. She told us she could think of no reason for the suicide. She could imagine no possible connection between the suicide and her stepdaughters' vanishing.

"Mrs. Correll seemed as nearly contented and happy as usual the last time I saw her, two or three weeks ago," Mrs. Banbrock said. "Of course she was by nature inclined to be dissatisfied with things, but not to the extent of doing a thing like this."

"Do you know of any trouble between her and her husband?"

"No. So far as I know, they were happy, though—"

She broke off. Hesitancy, embarrassment showed in her dark eyes.

"Though?" I repeated.

"If I don't tell you now, you'll think I am hiding something," she said, flushing, and laughing a little laugh that held more nervousness than amusement. "It hasn't any bearing, but I was always just a little jealous of Irma. She and my husband were—well, everyone thought they would marry. That was a little before he and I married. I never let it show, and I dare say it was a foolish idea, but I always had a suspicion that Irma married Stewart more in pique than for any other reason, and that she was still fond of Alfred—Mr. Banbrock."

"Was there anything definite to make you think that?"

"No, nothing—really! I never thoroughly believed it. It was just a sort of vague feeling. Cattiness, no doubt, more than anything else."

It was getting along toward evening when Pat and I left the Banbrock house. Before we knocked off for the day, I called up the Old Man—the Continental's San Francisco branch manager, and therefore my boss—and asked him to sic an operative on Irma Correll's past.

I took a look at the morning papers—thanks to their custom of appearing almost as soon as the sun is out of sight—

before I went to bed. They had given our job a good spread. All the facts except those having to do with the Correll angle were there, plus photographs, and the usual assortment of guesses and similar garbage.

The following morning I went after the friends of the missing girls to whom I had not yet talked. I found some of them, and got nothing of value from them. Late in the morning I telephoned the office to see if anything new had turned up.

It had.

"We've just had a call from the sheriff's office at Martinez," the Old Man told me. "An Italian grapegrower near Knob Valley picked up a charred photograph a couple of days ago, and recognized it as Ruth Banbrock when he saw her picture in this morning's paper. Will you get up there? A deputy sheriff and the Italian are waiting for you in the Knob Valley marshal's office."

"I'm on my way," I said.

At the ferry building I used the four minutes before my boat left trying to get Pat Reddy on the phone, with no success.

Knob Valley is a town of less than a thousand people, a dreary, dirty town in Contra Costa county. A San Francisco–Sacramento local set me down there while the afternoon was still young.

I knew the marshal slightly—Tom Orth. I found two men in the office with him. Orth introduced us. Abner Paget, a gawky man of forty-something, with a slack chin, scrawny face, and pale intelligent eyes, was the deputy sheriff. Gio Cereghino, the Italian grapegrower, was a small, nut-brown man with strong yellow teeth that showed in an everlasting smile under his black mustache, and soft brown eyes.

Paget showed me the photograph. A scorched piece of paper the size of a half-dollar, apparently all that had not been burned of the original picture. It was Ruth Banbrock's face. There was little room for doubting that. She had a peculiarly excited—almost drunken—look, and her eyes were larger than in the other pictures of her I had seen. But it was her face.

"He says he found it day 'fore yesterday," Paget explained dryly, nodding at the Italian. "The wind blew it against his foot when he was walkin' up a piece of road near his place. He picked it up an' stuck it in his pocket, he says, for no special reason, I guess, except maybe that guineas like pictures."

He paused to regard the Italian meditatively. The Italian nodded his head in vigorous affirmation.

"Anyways," the deputy sheriff went on, "he was in town this mornin', an' seen the pictures in the papers from 'Frisco. So he come in here an' told Tom about it. Tom an' me decided the best thing was to phone your agency—since the papers said you was workin' on it."

I looked at the Italian.

Paget, reading my mind, explained:

"Cereghino lives over in the hills. Got a grape-ranch there. Been around here five or six years, an' ain't killed nobody that I know of."

"Remember the place where you found the picture?" I asked the Italian.

His grin broadened under his mustache, and his head went up and down.

"For sure, I remember that place."

"Let's go there," I suggested to Paget.

"Right. Comin' along, Tom?"

The marshal said he couldn't. He had something to do in town. Cereghino, Paget and I went out and got into a dusty Ford that the deputy sheriff drove.

We rode for nearly an hour, along a county road that bent up the slope of Mount Diablo. After a while, at a word from the Italian, we left the county road for a dustier and ruttier one.

A mile of this one.

"This place," Cereghino said.

Paget stopped the Ford. We got out in a clearing. The trees and bushes that had crowded the road retreated here for twenty feet or so on either side, leaving a little dusty circle in the woods.

"About this place," the Italian was saying. "I think by this stump. But between that bend ahead and that one behind, I know for sure."

v

Paget was a countryman. I am not. I waited for him to move.

He looked around the clearing, slowly, standing still between the Italian and me. His pale eyes lighted presently. He went around the Ford to the far side of the clearing. Cereghino and I followed.

Near the fringe of brush at the edge of the clearing, the scrawny deputy stopped to grunt at the ground. The wheel-marks of an automobile were there. A car had turned around here.

Paget went on into the woods. The Italian kept close to his heels. I brought up the rear. Paget was following some sort of track. I couldn't see it, either because he and the Italian blotted it out ahead of me, or because I'm a shine Indian.

We went back quite a way.

Paget stopped. The Italian stopped.

Paget said, "Uh-huh," as if he had found an expected thing.

The Italian said something with the name of God in it.

I trampled a bush, coming beside them to see what they saw.

I saw it.

At the base of a tree, on her side, her knees drawn up close to her body, a girl was dead.

She wasn't nice to see. Birds had been at her.

A tobacco-brown coat was half on, half off her shoulders. I knew she was Ruth Banbrock before I turned her over to look at the side of her face the ground had saved from the birds.

Cereghino stood watching me while I examined the girl. His face was mournful in a calm way. The deputy sheriff paid little attention to the body. He was off in the brush, moving around, looking at the ground.

He came back as I finished my examination.

"Shot," I told him, "once in the right temple. Before that, I think, there was a fight. There are marks on the arm that was under her body. There's nothing on her—no jewelry, money—nothing."

"That goes," Paget said. "Two women got out of the car back in the clearin', an' came here. Could've been three women—if the others carried this one. Can't make out how many went back. One of 'em was larger than this one. There was a scuffle here. Find the gun?"

"No," I said.

"Neither did I. It went away in the car, then. There's what's left of a fire over there." He ducked his head to the left. "Paper an' rags burnt. Not enough left to do us any good. I reckon the photo Cereghino found blew away from the fire. Late Friday, I'd put it, or maybe Saturday mornin'. . . . No nearer than that."

I took the deputy sheriff's word for it. He seemed to know his stuff.

"Come here. I'll show you somethin'," he said, and led me over to a little black pile of ashes.

He hadn't anything to show me. He wanted to talk to me away from the Italian's ears.

"I think the guinea's all right," he said, "but I reckon I'd best hold him a while to make sure. This is some way from his place, an' he stuttered a little bit too much tellin' me how he happened to be passin' here. Course, that don't mean nothin' much. All these guineas peddle *vino*, an' I guess that's what brought him out this way. I'll hold him a day or two, anyways."

"Good," I agreed. "This is your country, and you know the people. Can you visit around and see what you can pick up? Whether anybody saw anything? Saw a Locomobile cabriolet? Or anything else? You can get more than I could."

"I'll do that," he promised.

"All right. Then I'll go back to San Francisco now. I suppose you'll want to camp here with the body?"

"Yeah. You drive the Ford back to Knob Valley, an' tell Tom what's what. He'll come or send out. I'll keep the guinea here with me."

Waiting for the next west-bound train out of Knob Valley, I got the office on the telephone. The Old Man was out. I told my story to one of the office men and asked him to get the news to the Old Man as soon as he could.

Everybody was in the office when I got back to San Francisco. Alfred Banbrock, his face a pink-grey that was deader than solid grey could have been. His pink and white old lawyer. Pat Reddy, sprawled on his spine with his feet on another chair. The Old Man, with his gentle eyes behind gold spectacles and his mild smile, hiding the fact that fifty years of sleuthing had left him without any feelings at all on any subject. (Whitey Clayton used to say the Old Man could spit icicles in August.)

Nobody said anything when I came in. I said my say as briefly as possible.

"Then the other woman—the woman who killed Ruth was—?"

Banbrock didn't finish his question. Nobody answered it.

"We don't know what happened," I said after a while. "Your daughter and someone we don't know may have gone there. Your daughter may have been dead before she was taken there. She may have—"

"But Myra!" Banbrock was pulling at his collar with a finger inside. "Where is Myra?"

I couldn't answer that, nor could any of the others.

"You are going up to Knob Valley now?" I asked him.

"Yes, at once. You will come with me?"

I wasn't sorry I could not.

"No. There are things to be done here. I'll give you a note to the marshal. I want you to look carefully at the piece of your daughter's photograph the Italian found—to see if you remember it."

Banbrock and the lawyer left.

VI

Reddy lit one of his awful cigars.

"We found the car," the Old Man said.

"Where?"

"In Sacramento. It was left in a garage there either late Friday night or early Saturday. Foley has gone up to investigate it. And Reddy has uncovered a new angle."

Pat nodded through his smoke.

"A hock-shop dealer came in this morning," Pat said, "and told us that Myra Banbrock and another girl came to his joint last week and hocked a lot of stuff. They gave him phoney names, but he swears one of them was Myra. He recognized her picture as soon as he saw it in the paper. Her companion wasn't Ruth. It was a little blonde."

"Mrs. Correll?"

"Uh-huh. The shark can't swear to that, but I think that's the answer. Some of the jewelry was Myra's, some Ruth's, and some we don't know. I mean we can't prove it belonged to Mrs. Correll—though we will."

"When did all this happen?"

"They soaked the stuff Monday before they went away."

"Have you seen Correll?"

"Uh-huh," Pat said. "I did a lot of talking to him, but the answers weren't worth much. He says he don't know whether any of her jewelry is gone or not, and doesn't care. It was hers, he says, and she could do anything she wanted with it. He was kind of disagreeable. I got along a little better with one of the maids. She says some of Mrs. Correll's pretties disappeared last week. Mrs. Correll said she had lent them to a friend. I'm going to show the stuff the hock-shop has to the maid tomorrow, to see if she can identify it. She didn't know anything else—except that Mrs. Correll was out of the picture for a while on Friday—the day the Banbrock girls went away."

"What do you mean, out of the picture?" I asked.

"She went out late in the morning and didn't show up until somewhere around three the next morning. She and Correll had a row over it, but she wouldn't tell him where she had been."

I liked that. It could mean something.

"And," Pat went on, "Correll has just remembered that his wife had an uncle who went crazy in Pittsburgh in 1902, and that she had a morbid fear of going crazy herself, and that she had often said she would kill herself if she thought she was going crazy. Wasn't it nice of him to remember those things at last? To account for her death?"

"It was," I agreed, "but it doesn't get us anywhere. It doesn't even prove that he knows anything. Now my guess is—"

"To hell with your guess," Pat said, getting up and pushing his hat in place. "Your guesses all sound like a lot of static to me. I'm going home, eat my dinner, read my Bible, and go to bed."

I suppose he did. Anyway, he left us.

We all might as well have spent the next three days in bed for all the profit that came out of our running around. No place we visited, nobody we questioned, added to our knowledge. We were in a blind alley.

We learned that the Locomobile was left in Sacramento by Myra Banbrock, and not by anyone else, but we didn't learn where she went afterward. We learned that some of the jewelry in the pawnshop was Mrs. Correll's. The Locomobile was brought back from Sacramento. Mrs. Correll was buried. Ruth Banbrock was buried. The newspapers found other mysteries. Reddy and I dug and dug, and all we brought up was dirt.

The following Monday brought me close to the end of my rope. There seemed nothing more to do but sit back and hope that the circulars with which we had plastered North America would bring results. Reddy had already been called off and put to running out fresher trails. I hung on because Banbrock wanted me to keep at it so long as there was the shadow of anything to keep at. But by Monday I had worked myself out.

Before going to Banbrock's office to tell him I was licked, I dropped in at the Hall of Justice to hold a wake over the job with Pat Reddy. He was crouched over his desk, writing a report on some other job.

"Hello!" he greeted me, pushing his report away and smearing it with ashes from his cigar. "How do the Banbrock doings?"

"They don't," I admitted. "It doesn't seem possible, with the stack-up what it is, that we should have come to a dead stop! It's there for us, if we can find it. The need of money before both the Banbrock and the Correll calamities: Mrs. Correll's suicide after I had questioned her about the girls; her burning things before she died and the burning of things immediately before or after Ruth Banbrock's death."

"Maybe the trouble is," Pat suggested, "that you're not such a good sleuth."

"Maybe."

We smoked in silence for a minute or two after that insult.

"You understand," Pat said presently, "there doesn't have to be any connection between the Banbrock death and disappearance and the Correll death."

"Maybe not. But there has to be a connection between the Banbrock death and the Banbrock disappearance. There was a connection—in a pawnshop—between the Banbrock and Correll actions before these things. If there is that connection, then—"

I broke off, all full of ideas.

"What's the matter?" Pat asked. "Swallow your gum?"

"Listen!" I let myself get almost enthusiastic. "We've got what happened to three women hooked up together. If we could tie up some more in the same string—I want the names and addresses of all the women and girls in San Francisco who have committed suicide, been murdered, or have disappeared within the past year."

"You think this is a wholesale deal?"

"I think the more we can tie up together, the more lines we'll have to run out. And they can't all lead nowhere. Let's get our list, Pat!"

We spent all the afternoon and most of the night getting it. Its size would have embarrassed the Chamber of Commerce. It looked like a hunk of the telephone book. Things happen in a city in a year. The section devoted to strayed wives and daughters was the largest; suicides next; and even the smallest division—murders—wasn't any too short.

We could check off most of the names against what the police department had already learned of them and their motives, weeding out those positively accounted for in a manner nowise connected with our present interest. The remainder we split into two classes; those of unlikely connection, and those of more possible connection. Even then, the second list was longer than I had expected, or hoped.

There were six suicides in it, three murders, and twenty-one disappearances.

Reddy had other work to do. I put the list in my pocket and went calling.

VII

For four days I ground at the list. I hunted, found, questioned, and investigated friends and relatives of the women and girls on my list. My questions all hit in the same direction. Had she been acquainted with Myra Banbrock? Ruth? Mrs. Correll? Had she been in need of money before her death or disappearance? Had she destroyed anything before her death or disappearance? Had she known any of the other women on my list?

Three times I drew yeses.

Sylvia Varney, a girl of twenty, who had killed herself on November 5th, had drawn six hundred dollars from the bank the week before her death. No one in her family could say what she had done with the money. A friend of Sylvia Varney's—Ada Youngman, a married woman of twenty-five or -six—had disappeared on December 2nd, and was still gone. The Varney girl had been at Mrs. Youngman's home an hour before she—the Varney girl—killed herself.

Mrs. Dorothy Sawdon, a young widow, had shot herself on the night of January 13th. No trace was found of either the money her husband had left her or the funds of a club whose treasurer she was. A bulky letter her maid remembered having given her that afternoon was never found.

These three women's connection with the Banbrock-Correll affair was sketchy enough. None of them had done anything that isn't done by nine out of ten women who kill themselves or run away. But the troubles of all three had come to a head within the past few months—and all three were women of about the same financial and social position as Mrs. Correll and the Banbrocks.

Finishing my list with no fresh leads, I came back to these three.

I had the names and addresses of sixty-two friends of the Banbrock girls. I set about getting the same sort of catalogue on the three women I was trying to bring into the game. I didn't have to do all the digging myself. Fortunately, there were two or three operatives in the office with nothing else to do just then.

We got something.

Mrs. Sawdon had known Raymond Elwood. Sylvia Varney had known Raymond Elwood. There was nothing to show Mrs. Youngman had known him, but it was likely she had. She and the Varney girl had been thick.

I had already interviewed this Raymond Elwood in connection with the Banbrock girls, but had paid no especial attention to him. I had considered him just one of the sleek-headed, high-polished young men of whom there was quite a few listed.

I went back at him, all interest now. The results were promising.

He had, as I have said, a real estate office on Montgomery Street. We were unable to find a single client he had ever served, or any signs of one's existence. He had an apartment out in the Sunset District, where he lived alone. His local record seemed to go back no farther than ten months, though we couldn't find its definite starting point. Apparently he had no relatives in San Francisco. He belonged to a couple of fashionable clubs. He was vaguely supposed to be "well connected in the East." He spent money.

I couldn't shadow Elwood, having too recently interviewed him. Dick Foley did. Elwood was seldom in his office during the first three days Dick tailed him. He was seldom in the financial district. He visited his clubs, he danced and tea'd and so forth, and each of those three days he visited a house on Telegraph Hill.

The first afternoon Dick had him, Elwood went to the Telegraph Hill house with a tall fair girl from Burlingame. The second day—in the evening—with a plump young woman who came out of a house out on Broadway. The third evening with a very young girl who seemed to live in the same building as he.

Usually Elwood and his companion spent from three to four hours in the house on Telegraph Hill. Other people—all apparently well-to-do—went in and out of the house while it was under Dick's eye.

I climbed Telegraph Hill to give the house the up-and-down. It was a large house—a big frame house painted egg-yellow. It hung dizzily on a shoulder of the hill, a shoulder that was sharp where rock had been quarried away. The house seemed about to go ski-ing down on the roofs far below.

It had no immediate neighbors. The approach was screened by bushes and trees.

I gave that section of the hill a good strong play, calling at all the houses within shooting distance of the yellow one. Nobody knew anything about it, or about its occupants. The folks on the Hill aren't a curious lot—perhaps because most of them have something to hide on their own account.

My climbing uphill and downhill got me nothing until I succeeded in learning who owned the yellow house. The owner was an estate whose affairs were in the hands of the West Coast Trust Company.

I took my investigations to the trust company, with some satisfaction. The house had been leased eight months ago by Raymond Elwood, acting for a client named T. F. Maxwell.

We couldn't find Maxwell. We couldn't find anybody who knew Maxwell. We couldn't find any evidence that Maxwell was anything but a name.

One of the operatives went up to the yellow house on the hill, and rang the bell for half an hour with no result. We didn't try that again, not wanting to stir things up at this stage.

I made another trip up the hill, house-hunting. I couldn't find a place as near the yellow house as I would have liked, but I succeeded in renting a three-room flat from which the approach to it could be watched.

Dick and I camped in the flat—with Pat Reddy, when he wasn't off on other duties—and watched machines turn into the screened path that led to the egg-tinted house. Afternoon and night there were machines. Most of them carried women. We saw no one we could place as a resident of the house. Elwood came daily, once alone, the other time with women whose faces we couldn't see from our window.

We shadowed some of the visitors away. They were without exception reasonably well off financially, and some were socially prominent. We didn't go up against any of them with talk. Even a carefully planned pretext is as likely as not to tip your mitt when you're up against a blind game.

Three days of this—and our break came.

It was early evening, just dark. Pat Reddy had phoned that he had been up on a job for two days and a night, and was going to sleep the clock around. Dick and I were sitting at the window of our flat, watching automobiles turn toward the yellow house, writing down their license numbers as they passed through the blue-white patch of light an arc-lamp put in the road just beyond our window.

A woman came climbing the hill, afoot. She was a tall woman, strongly built. A dark veil, not thick enough to advertise the fact that she wore it to hide her features, nevertheless did hide them. Her way was up the hill, past our flat, on the other side of the roadway.

A night-wind from the Pacific was creaking a grocer's sign down below, swaying the arc-light above. The wind caught the woman as she passed out of our building's sheltered area. Coat and skirts tangled. She put her back to the wind, a hand to her hat. Her veil whipped out straight from her face.

Her face was a face from a photograph—Myra Banbrock's face.

Dick made her with me.

"Our Baby!" he cried, bouncing to his feet.

"Wait," I said. "She's going into the joint on the edge of the hill. Let her go. We'll go after her when she's inside. That's our excuse for frisking the joint."

I went into the next room, where our telephone was, and called Pat Reddy's number.

"She didn't go in," Dick called from the window. "She went past the path."

"After her!" I ordered. "There's no sense to that! What's the matter with her?" I felt sort of indignant about it. "She's got to go in! Tail her. I'll find you after I get Pat."

Dick went.

Pat's wife answered the telephone. I told her who I was.

"Will you shake Pat out of the covers and send him up here? He knows where I am. Tell him I want him in a hurry."

"I will," she promised. "I'll have him there in ten minutes—wherever it is."

Outdoors, I went up the road, hunting for Dick and Myra Banbrock. Neither was in sight. Passing the bushes that masked the yellow house, I went on, circling down a stony path to the left. No sign of either.

I turned back in time to see Dick going into our flat. I followed.

"She's in," he said when I joined him. "She went up the road, cut across through some bushes, came back to the edge of the cliff, and slid feet-first through a cellar window."

That was nice. The crazier the people you are sleuthing act, as a rule, the nearer you are to an ending of your troubles.

Reddy arrived within a minute or two of the time his wife had promised. He came in buttoning his clothes.

"What the hell did you tell Althea?" he growled at me. "She gave me an overcoat to put over my pajamas, dumped the rest of my clothes in the car, and I had to get in them on the way over."

"I'll cry with you after awhile," I dismissed his troubles. "Myra Banbrock just went into the joint through a cellar window. Elwood has been there an hour. Let's knock it off."

Pat is deliberate.

"We ought to have papers, even at that," he stalled.

"Sure," I agreed, "but you can get them fixed up afterward. That's what you're here for. Contra Costa county wants her—maybe to try her for murder. That's all the excuse we need to get into the joint. We go there for her. If we happen to run into anything else—well and good."

Pat finished buttoning his vest.

"Oh, all right!" he said sourly. "Have it your way. But if you get me smashed for searching a house without authority, you'll have to give me a job with your law-breaking agency."

"I will." I turned to Foley. "You'll have to stay outside, Dick. Keep your eye on the getaway. Don't bother anybody else, but if the Banbrock girl gets out, stay behind her."

"I expected it," Dick howled. "Any time there's any fun I can count on being stuck off somewhere on a street corner!"

VIII

Pat Reddy and I went straight up the bush-hidden path to the yellow house's front door, and rang the bell.

A big black man in a red fez, red silk jacket over red-striped silk shirt, red zouave pants and red slippers, opened the door. He filled the opening, framed in the black of the hall behind him.

"Is Mr. Maxwell home?" I asked.

The black man shook his head and said words in a language I don't know.

"Mr. Elwood, then?"

Another shaking of the head. More strange language.

"Let's see whoever is home then," I insisted.

Out of the jumble of words that meant nothing to me, I picked three in garbled English, which I thought were "master," "not," and "home."

The door began to close. I put a foot against it.

Pat flashed his buzzer.

Though the black man had poor English, he had knowledge of police badges.

One of his feet stamped on the floor behind him. A gong boomed deafeningly in the rear of the house.

The black man bent his weight to the door.

My weight on the foot that blocked the door, I leaned sidewise, swaying to the negro.

Slamming from the hip, I put my fist in the middle of him.

Reddy hit the door and we went into the hall.

"'Fore God, Fat Shorty," the black man gasped in good black Virginian, "you done hurt me!"

Reddy and I went by him, down the hall whose bounds were lost in darkness.

The bottom of a flight of steps stopped my feet.

A gun went off upstairs. It seemed to point at us. We didn't get the bullets.

A babel of voices—women screaming, men shouting—came and went upstairs; came and went as if a door was being opened and shut.

"Up, my boy!" Reddy yelped in my ear.

We went up the stairs. We didn't find the man who had shot at us.

At the head of the stairs, a door was locked. Reddy's bulk forced it.

We came into a bluish light. A large room, all purple and gold. Confusion of overturned furniture and rumpled rugs. A gray slipper lay near a far door. A green silk gown was in the center of the floor. No person was there.

I raced Pat to the curtained door beyond the slipper. The door was not locked. Reddy yanked it wide.

A room with three girls and a man crouching in a corner, fear in their faces. Neither of them was Myra Banbrock, or Raymond Elwood, or anyone we knew.

Our glances went away from them after the first quick look. The open door across the room grabbed our attention.

The door gave to a small room.

The room was chaos.

A small room, packed and tangled with bodies. Live bodies, seething, writhing. The room was a funnel into which men and women had been poured. They boiled noisily toward the one small window that was the funnel's outlet. Men and women, youths and girls, screaming, struggling, squirming, fighting. Some had no clothes.

"We'll get through and block the window!" Pat yelled in my ear.

"Like hell—" I began, but he was gone ahead into the confusion.

I went after him.

I didn't mean to block the window. I meant to save Pat from his foolishness. No five men could have fought through that boiling turmoil of maniacs. No ten men could have turned them from the window.

Pat—big as he is—was down when I got to him. A half dressed girl—a child—was driving at his face with sharp highheels. Hands, feet, were tearing him apart.

I cleared him with a play of gun-barrel on shins and wrists—dragged him back.

"Myra's not there!" I yelled into his ear as I helped him up. "Elwood's not there!"

I wasn't sure, but I hadn't seen them, and I doubted that they would be in this mess. These savages, boiling again to the window, with no attention for us, whoever they were, weren't insiders. They were the mob, and the principals shouldn't be among them.

"We'll try the other rooms," I yelled again. "We don't want these."

Pat rubbed the back of his hand across his torn face and laughed.

"It's a cinch I don't want 'em any more," he said.

We went back to the head of the stairs the way we had come. We saw no one. The man and girls who had been in the next room were gone.

At the head of the stairs we paused. There was no noise behind us except the now fainter babel of the lunatics fighting for their exit.

A door shut sharply downstairs.

A body came out of nowhere, hit my back, flattened me to the landing.

The feel of silk was on my cheek. A brawny hand was fumbling at my throat.

I bent my wrist until my gun, upside down, lay against my cheek. Praying for my ear, I squeezed.

My cheek took fire. My head was a roaring thing, about to burst.

The silk slid away.

Pat hauled me upright.

We started down the stairs.

Swish!

A thing came past my face, stirring my bared hair.

A thousand pieces of glass, china, plaster, exploded upward at my feet.

I tilted head and gun together.

A negro's red-silk arms were still spread over the balustrade above.

I sent him two bullets. Pat sent him two.

The negro teetered over the rail.

He came down on us, arms outflung—a dead man's swan-dive.

We scurried down the stairs from under him.

He shook the house when he landed, but we weren't watching him then.

The smooth sleek head of Raymond Elwood took our attention.

In the light from above, it showed for a furtive split-second around the newel-post at the foot of the stairs. Showed and vanished.

Pat Reddy, closer to the rail than I, went over it in a one-hand vault down into the blackness below.

I made the foot of the stairs in two jumps, jerked myself around with a hand on the newel, and plunged into the suddenly noisy dark of the hall.

A wall I couldn't see hit me. Caroming off the opposite wall, I spun into a room whose curtained grayness was the light of day after the hall.

IX

Pat Reddy stood with one hand on a chair-back, holding his belly with the other. His face was mouse-colored under its blood. His eyes were glass agonies. He had the look of a man who had been kicked.

The grin he tried failed. He nodded toward the rear of the house. I went back.

In a little passageway I found Raymond Elwood.

He was sobbing and pulling frantically at a locked door. His face was the hard white of utter terror.

I measured the distance between us.

He turned as I jumped.

I put everything I had in the downswing of my gun-barrel—

A ton of meat and bone crashed into my back.

I went over against the wall, breathless, giddy, sick.

Red-silk arms that ended in brown hands locked around me.

I wondered if there was a whole regiment of these gaudy negroes—or if I was colliding with the same one over and over.

This one didn't let me do much thinking.

He was big. He was strong. He didn't mean any good.

My gun-arm was flat at my side, straight down. I tried a shot at one of the negro's feet. Missed. Tried again. He moved his feet. I wriggled around, half facing him.

Elwood piled on my other side.

The negro bent me backward, folding my spine on itself like an accordion.

I fought to hold my knees stiff. Too much weight was hanging on me. My knees sagged. My body curved back.

Pat Reddy, swaying in the doorway, shone over the negro's shoulder like the Angel Gabriel.

Gray pain was in Pat's face, but his eyes were clear. His right hand held a gun. His left was getting a blackjack out of his hip pocket.

He swung the sap down on the negro's shaven skull.

The black man wheeled away from me, shaking his head.

Pat hit him once more before the negro closed with him—
hit him full in the face, but couldn't beat him off.

Twisting my freed gun-hand up, I drilled Elwood neatly
through the chest, and let him slide down me to the floor.

The negro had Pat against the wall, bothering him a lot.
His broad red back was a target.

But I had used five of the six bullets in my gun. I had more
in my pocket, but reloading takes time.

I stepped out of Elwood's feeble hands, and went to work
with the flat of my gun on the negro. There was a roll of fat
where his skull and neck fit together. The third time I hit it,
he flopped, taking Pat with him.

I rolled him off. The blond police detective—not very
blond now—got up.

At the other end of the passageway, an open door showed
an empty kitchen.

Pat and I went to the door that Elwood had been playing with. It was a solid piece of carpentering, and neatly
fastened.

Yoking ourselves together, we began to beat the door with
our combined three hundred and seventy or eighty pounds.

It shook, but held. We hit it again. Wood we couldn't see
tore.

Again.

The door popped away from us. We went through—down
a flight of steps—rolling, snowballing down—until a cement
floor stopped us.

Pat came back to life first.

"You're a hell of an acrobat," he said. "Get off my neck!"

I stood up. He stood up. We seemed to be dividing the
evening between falling on the floor and getting up from the
floor.

A light-switch was at my shoulder. I turned it on.

If I looked anything like Pat, we were a fine pair of nightmares. He was all raw meat and dirt, with not enough clothes
left to hide much of either.

I didn't like his looks, so I looked around the basement in
which we stood. To the rear was a furnace, coal-bins and a

woodpile. To the front was a hallway and rooms, after the manner of the upstairs.

The first door we tried was locked, but not strongly. We smashed through it into a photographer's dark-room.

The second door was unlocked, and put us in a chemical laboratory: retorts, tubes, burners and a small still. There was a little round iron stove in the middle of the room. No one was there.

We went out into the hallway and to the third door, not so cheerfully. This cellar looked like a bloomer. We were wasting our time here, when we should have stayed upstairs. I tried the door.

It was firm beyond trembling.

We smacked it with our weight, together, experimentally. It didn't shake.

"Wait."

Pat went to the woodpile in the rear and came back with an axe.

He swung the axe against the door, flaking out a hunk of wood. Silvery points of light sparkled in the hole. The other side of the door was an iron or steel plate.

Pat put the axe down and leaned on the helve.

"You write the next prescription," he said.

I didn't have anything to suggest, except:

"I'll camp here. You beat it upstairs, and see if any of your coppers have shown up. This is a God-forsaken hole, but somebody may have sent in an alarm. See if you can find another way into this room—a window, maybe—or man-power enough to get us in through this door."

Pat turned toward the steps.

A sound stopped him—the clicking of bolts on the other side of the iron-lined door.

A jump put Pat on one side of the frame. A step put me on the other.

Slowly the door moved in. Too slowly.

I kicked it open.

Pat and I went into the room on top of my kick.

His shoulder hit the woman. I managed to catch her before she fell.

Pat took her gun. I steadied her back on her feet.

Her face was a pale blank square.

She was Myra Banbrock, but she now had none of the mas-
culinity that had been in her photographs and description.

Steadying her with one arm—which also served to block
her arms—I looked around the room.

A small cube of a room whose walls were brown-painted
metal. On the floor lay a queer little dead man.

A little man in tight-fitting black velvet and silk. Black velvet blouse and breeches, black silk stockings and skull cap,
black patent leather pumps. His face was small and old and
bony, but smooth as stone, without line or wrinkle.

A hole was in his blouse, where it fit high under his chin.
The hole bled very slowly. The floor around him showed it
had been bleeding faster a little while ago.

Beyond him, a safe was open. Papers were on the floor in
front of it, as if the safe had been tilted to spill them out.

The girl moved against my arm.

"You killed him?" I asked.

"Yes," too faint to have been heard a yard away.

"Why?"

She shook her short brown hair out of her eyes with a tired
jerk of her head.

"Does it make any difference?" she asked. "I did kill him."

"It might make a difference," I told her, taking my arm
away, and going over to shut the door. People talk more
freely in a room with a closed door. "I happen to be in your
father's employ. Mr. Reddy is a police detective. Of course,
neither of us can smash any laws, but if you'll tell us what's
what, maybe we can help you."

"My father's employ?" she questioned.

"Yes. When you and your sister disappeared, he engaged
me to find you. We found your sister, and—"

Life came into her face and eyes and voice.

"I didn't kill Ruth!" she cried. "The papers lied! I didn't
kill her! I didn't know she had the revolver. I didn't know it!
We were going away to hide from—from everything. We
stopped in the woods to burn the—those things. That's the
first time I knew she had the revolver. We had talked about
suicide at first, but I had persuaded her—thought I had persuaded her—not to. I tried to take the revolver away from

her, but I couldn't. She shot herself while I was trying to get it away. I tried to stop her. I didn't kill her!"

This was getting somewhere.

"And then?" I encouraged her.

"And then I went to Sacramento and left the car there, and came back to San Francisco. Ruth told me she had written Raymond Elwood a letter. She told me that before I persuaded her not to kill herself—the first time. I tried to get the letter from Raymond. She had written him she was going to kill herself. I tried to get the letter, but Raymond said he had given it to Hador.

"So I came here this evening to get it. I had just found it when there was a lot of noise upstairs. Then Hador came in and found me. He bolted the door. And—and I shot him with the revolver that was in the safe. I—I shot him when he turned around, before he could say anything. It had to be that way, or I couldn't."

"You mean you shot him without being threatened or attacked by him?" Pat asked.

"Yes. I was afraid of him, afraid to let him speak. I hated him! I couldn't help it. It had to be that way. If he had talked I couldn't have shot him. He—he wouldn't have let me!"

"Who was this Hador?" I asked.

She looked away from Pat and me, at the walls, at the ceiling, at the queer little dead man on the floor.

X

"He was a———" She cleared her throat, and started again, staring down at her feet. "Raymond Elwood brought us here the first time. We thought it was funny. But Hador was a devil. He told you things and you believed them. You couldn't help it. He told you *everything* and you believed it. Perhaps we were drugged. There was always a warm bluish wine. It must have been drugged. We couldn't have done those things if it hadn't. Nobody would— He called himself a priest—a priest of Alzoa. He taught a freeing of the spirit from the flesh by—"

Her voice broke huskily. She shuddered.

"It was horrible!" she went on presently in the silence Pat and I had left for her. "But you believed him. That is the whole thing. You can't understand it unless you understand that. The things he taught could not be so. But he said they were, and you *believed* they were. Or maybe—I don't know—maybe you pretended you believed them, because you were crazy and drugs were in your blood. We came back again and again, for weeks, months, before the disgust that had to come drove us away.

"We stopped coming, Ruth and I—and Irma. And then we found out what he was. He demanded money, more money than we had been paying while we believed—or pretended belief—in his cult. We couldn't give him the money he demanded. I told him we wouldn't. He sent us photographs—of us—taken during the—the times here. They were—*pictures—you—couldn't—explain*. And they were true! We knew them true! What could we do? He said he would send copies to our father, every friend, everyone we knew—unless we paid.

"What could we do—except pay? We got the money somehow. We gave him money—more—more—more. And then we had no more—could get no more. We didn't know what to do! There was nothing to do, except— Ruth and Irma wanted to kill themselves. I thought of that, too. But I persuaded Ruth not to. I said we'd go away. I'd take her away—keep her safe. And then—then—this!"

She stopped talking, went on staring at her feet.

I looked again at the little dead man on the floor, weird in his black cap and clothes. No more blood came from his throat.

It wasn't hard to put the pieces together. This dead Hador, self-ordained priest of something or other, staging orgies under the alias of religious ceremonies. Elwood, his confederate, bringing women of family and wealth to him. A room lighted for photography, with a concealed camera. Contributions from his converts so long as they were faithful to the cult. Blackmail—with the help of the photographs—afterward.

I looked from Hador to Pat Reddy. He was scowling at the dead man. No sound came from outside the room.

"You have the letter your sister wrote Elwood?" I asked the girl.

Her hand flashed to her bosom, and crinkled paper there. "Yes."

"It says plainly she meant to kill herself?"

"Yes."

"That ought to square her with Contra Costa county," I said to Pat.

He nodded his battered head.

"It ought to," he agreed. "It's not likely that they could prove murder on her even without that letter. With it, they'll not take her into court. That's a safe bet. Another is that she won't have any trouble over this shooting. She'll come out of court free, and thanked in the bargain."

Myra Banbrock flinched away from Pat as if he had hit her in the face.

I was her father's hired man just now. I saw her side of the affair.

I lit a cigarette and studied what I could see of Pat's face through blood and grime. Pat is a right guy.

"Listen, Pat," I wheedled him, though with a voice that was as if I were not trying to wheedle him at all. "Miss Banbrock can go into court and come out free and thanked, as you say. But to do it, she's got to use everything she knows. She's got to have all the evidence there is. She's got to have all those photographs Hador took—or all we can find of them.

"Some of those pictures have sent women to suicide, Pat—at least two that we know. If Miss Banbrock goes into court, we've got to make the photographs of God knows how many other women public property. We've got to advertise things that will put Miss Banbrock—and you can't say how many other women and girls—in a position that at least two women have killed themselves to escape."

Pat scowled at me and rubbed his dirty chin with a dirtier thumb.

I took a deep breath and made my play.

"Pat, you and I came here to question Raymond Elwood, having traced him here. Maybe we suspected him of being tied up with the mob that knocked over the St. Louis bank last month. Maybe we suspected him of handling the stuff that was taken from the mail cars in that stick-up near Denver week before last. Anyway, we were after him, knowing that he had a lot of money that came from nowhere, and a real estate office that did no real estate business.

"We came here to question him in connection with one of these jobs I've mentioned. We were jumped by a couple of the shines upstairs when they found we were sleuths. The rest of it grew out of that. This religious cult business was just something we ran into, and didn't interest us especially. So far as we knew, all these folks jumped us just through friendship for the man we were trying to question. Hador was one of them, and, tussling with you, you shot him with his own gun, which, of course, is the one Miss Banbrock found in the safe."

Reddy didn't seem to like my suggestion at all. The eyes with which he regarded me were decidedly sour.

"You're goofy," he accused me. "What'll that get anybody? That won't keep Miss Banbrock out of it. She's here, isn't she, and the rest of it will come out like thread off a spool."

"But Miss Banbrock *wasn't* here," I explained. "Maybe the upstairs is full of coppers by now. Maybe not. Anyway, you're going to take Miss Banbrock out of here and turn her over to Dick Foley, who will take her home. She's got nothing to do with this party. Tomorrow she, and her father's lawyer, and I, will all go up to Martinez and make a deal with the prosecuting attorney of Contra Costa county. We'll show him how Ruth killed herself. If somebody happens to connect the Elwood who I hope is dead upstairs with the Elwood who knew the girls and Mrs. Correll, what of it? If we keep out of court—as we'll do by convincing the Contra Costa people they can't possibly convict her of her sister's murder—we'll keep out of the newspapers—and out of trouble."

Pat hung fire, thumb still to chin.

"Remember," I urged him, "it's not only Miss Banbrock we're doing this for. It's a couple of dead ones, and a flock of live ones, who certainly got mixed up with Hador of their own accords, but who don't stop being human beings on that account."

Pat shook his head stubbornly.

"I'm sorry," I told the girl with faked hopelessness. "I've done all I can, but it's a lot to ask of Reddy. I don't know that I blame him for being afraid to take a chance on—"

Pat is Irish.

"Don't be so damned quick to fly off," he snapped at me, cutting short my hypocrisy. "But why do I have to be the one that shot this Hador? Why not you?"

I had him!

"Because," I explained, "you're a bull and I'm not. There'll be less chance of a slip-up if he was shot by a bona fide, star-wearing, flat-footed officer of the peace. I killed most of those birds upstairs. You ought to do something to show you were here."

That was only part of the truth. My idea was that if Pat took the credit, he couldn't very well ease himself out afterward, no matter what happened. Pat's a right guy, and I'd trust him anywhere—but you can trust a man just as easily if you have him sewed up.

Pat grumbled and shook his head, but:

"I'm ruining myself, I don't doubt," he growled, "but I'll do it, this once."

"Attaboy!" I went over to pick up the girl's hat from the corner in which it lay. "I'll wait here until you come back from turning her over to Dick." I gave the girl her hat and orders together. "You go to your home with the man Reddy turns you over to. Stay there until I come, which will be as soon as I can make it. Don't tell anybody anything, except that I told you to keep quiet. That includes your father. Tell him I told you not to tell him even where you saw me. Got it?"

"Yes, and I—"

Gratitude is nice to think about afterward, but it takes time when there's work to be done.

"Get going, Pat!"

They went.

XI

As soon as I was alone with the dead man I stepped over him and knelt in front of the safe, pushing letters and papers away, hunting for photographs. None was in sight. One compartment of the safe was locked.

I frisked the corpse. No key. The locked compartment wasn't very strong, but neither am I the best safe-burglar in the West. It took me a while to get into it.

What I wanted was there. A thick sheaf of negatives. A stack of prints—half a hundred of them.

I started to run through them, hunting for the Banbrock girls' pictures. I wanted to have them pocketed before Pat came back. I didn't know how much farther he would let me go.

Luck was against me—and the time I had wasted getting into the compartment. He was back before I had got past the sixth print in the stack. Those six had been—pretty bad.

"Well, that's done," Pat growled at me as he came into the room. "Dick's got her. Elwood is dead, and so is the only one of the negroes I saw upstairs. Everybody else seems to have beat it. No bulls have shown—so I put in a call for a wagonful."

I stood up, holding the sheaf of negatives in one hand, the prints in the other.

"What's all that?" he asked.

I went after him again.

"Photographs. You've just done me a big favor, Pat, and I'm not hoggish enough to ask another. But I'm going to put something in front of you, Pat. I'll give you the lay, and you can name it.

"These"—I waved the pictures at him—"are Hador's meal-tickets—the photos he was either collecting on or planning to collect on. They're photographs of people, Pat, mostly women and girls, and some of them are pretty rotten.

"If tomorrow's papers say that a flock of photos were found in this house after the fireworks, there's going to be a fat suicide-list in the next day's papers, and a fatter list of disappearances. If the papers say nothing about the photos, the lists may be a little smaller, but not much. Some of the people whose pictures are here know they are here. They will expect the police to come hunting for them. We know this much about the photographs—two women have killed themselves to get away from them. This is an armful of stuff that can dynamite a lot of people, Pat, and a lot of families—no matter which of those two ways the papers read.

"But, suppose, Pat, the papers say that just before you shot Hador he succeeded in burning a lot of pictures and papers, burning them beyond recognition. Isn't it likely, then, that there won't be any suicides? That some of the disappearances of recent months may clear themselves up? There she is, Pat—you name it."

Looking back, it seems to me I had come a lot nearer being eloquent than ever before in my life.

But Pat didn't applaud.

He cursed me. He cursed me thoroughly, bitterly, and with an amount of feeling that told me I had won another point in my little game. He called me more things than I ever listened to before from a man who was built of meat and bone, and who therefore could be smacked.

When he was through, we carried the papers and photographs and a small book of addresses we found in the safe into the next room, and fed them to the little round iron stove there. The last of them was ash before we heard the police overhead.

"That's absolutely all!" Pat declared when we got up from our work. "Don't ever ask me to do anything else for you if you live to be a thousand."

"That's absolutely all," I echoed.

I like Pat. He is a right guy. The sixth photograph in the stack had been of his wife—the coffee importer's reckless, hot-eyed daughter.

Dead Yellow Women

SHE WAS sitting straight and stiff in one of the Old Man's chairs when he called me into his office—a tall girl of perhaps twenty-four, broad-shouldered, deep-bosomed, in mannish grey clothes. That she was Oriental showed only in the black shine of her bobbed hair, in the pale yellow of her unpowdered skin, and in the fold of her upper lids at the outer eye-corners, half hidden by the dark rims of her spectacles. But there was no slant to her eyes, her nose was almost aquiline, and she had more chin than Mongolians usually have. She was modern Chinese-American from the flat heels of her tan shoes to the crown of her untrimmed felt hat.

I knew her before the Old Man introduced me. The San Francisco papers had been full of her affairs for a couple of days. They had printed photographs and diagrams, interviews, editorials, and more or less expert opinions from various sources. They had gone back to 1912 to remember the stubborn fight of the local Chinese—mostly from Fokien and Kwangtung, where democratic ideas and hatred of Manchus go together—to have her father kept out of the United States, to which he had scooted when the Manchu rule flopped. The papers had recalled the excitement in Chinatown when Shan Fang was allowed to land—insulting placards had been hung in the streets, an unpleasant reception had been planned.

But Shan Fang had fooled the Cantonese. Chinatown had never seen him. He had taken his daughter and his gold—presumably the accumulated profits of a life-time of provincial misrule—down to San Mateo County, where he had built what the papers described as a palace on the edge of the Pacific. There he had lived and died in a manner suitable to a *Ta Jen* and a millionaire.

So much for the father. For the daughter—this young woman who was coolly studying me as I sat down across the table from her: she had been ten-year-old Ai Ho, a very Chinese little girl, when her father had brought her to California. All that was Oriental of her now were the features I have mentioned and the money her father had left her. Her

name, translated into English, had become Water Lily, and
then, by another step, Lillian. It was as Lillian Shan that she
had attended an eastern university, acquired several degrees,
won a tennis championship of some sort in 1919, and published a book on the nature and significance of fetishes, whatever all that is or are.

Since her father's death, in 1921, she had lived with her four
Chinese servants in the house on the shore, where she had
written her first book and was now at work on another. A
couple of weeks ago, she had found herself stumped, so she
said—had run into a blind alley. There was, she said, a certain
old cabalistic manuscript in the Arsenal Library in Paris that
she believed would solve her troubles for her. So she had
packed some clothes and, accompanied by her maid, a
Chinese woman named Wang Ma, had taken a train for New
York, leaving the three other servants to take care of the
house during her absence. The decision to go to France for a
look at the manuscript had been formed one morning—she
was on the train before dark.

On the train between Chicago and New York, the key to
the problem that had puzzled her suddenly popped into her
head. Without pausing even for a night's rest in New York,
she had turned around and headed back for San Francisco. At
the ferry here she had tried to telephone her chauffeur to
bring a car for her. No answer. A taxicab had carried her and
her maid to her house. She rang the door-bell to no effect.

When her key was in the lock the door had been suddenly
opened by a young Chinese man—a stranger to her. He had
refused her admittance until she told him who she was. He
mumbled an unintelligible explanation as she and the maid
went into the hall.

Both of them were neatly bundled up in some curtains.

Two hours later Lillian Shan got herself loose—in a linen
closet on the second floor. Switching on the light, she started
to untie the maid. She stopped. Wang Ma was dead. The rope
around her neck had been drawn too tight.

Lillian Shan went out into the empty house and telephoned
the sheriff's office in Redwood City.

Two deputy sheriffs had come to the house, had listened to
her story, had poked around, and had found another Chinese

body—another strangled woman—buried in the cellar. Apparently she had been dead a week or a week and a half; the dampness of the ground made more positive dating impossible. Lillian Shan identified her as another of her servants—Wan Lan, the cook.

The other servants—Hoo Lun and Yin Hung—had vanished. Of the several hundred thousand dollars' worth of furnishings old Shan Fang had put into the house during his life, not a nickel's worth had been removed. There were no signs of a struggle. Everything was in order. The closest neighboring house was nearly half a mile away. The neighbors had seen nothing, knew nothing.

That's the story the newspapers had hung headlines over, and that's the story this girl, sitting very erect in her chair, speaking with businesslike briskness, shaping each word as exactly as if it were printed in black type, told the Old Man and me.

"I am not at all satisfied with the effort the San Mateo County authorities have made to apprehend the murderer or murderers," she wound up. "I wish to engage your agency."

The Old Man tapped the table with the point of his inevitable long yellow pencil and nodded at me.

"Have you any idea of your own on the murders, Miss Shan?" I asked.

"I have not."

"What do you know about the servants—the missing ones as well as the dead?"

"I really know little or nothing about them." She didn't seem very interested. "Wang Ma was the most recent of them to come to the house, and she has been with me for nearly seven years. My father employed them, and I suppose he knew something about them."

"Don't you know where they came from? Whether they have relatives? Whether they have friends? What they did when they weren't working?"

"No," she said. "I did not pry into their lives."

"The two who disappeared—what do they look like?"

"Hoo Lun is an old man, quite white-haired and thin and stooped. He did the housework. Yin Hung, who was my chauffeur and gardener, is younger, about thirty years old, I think. He is quite short, even for a Cantonese, but sturdy. His nose has been broken at some time and not set properly. It is very flat, with a pronounced bend in the bridge."

"Do you think this pair, or either of them, could have killed the women?"

"I do not think they did."

"The young Chinese—the stranger who let you in the house—what did he look like?"

"He was quite slender, and not more than twenty or twenty-one years old, with large gold fillings in his front teeth. I think he was quite dark."

"Will you tell me exactly why you are dissatisfied with what the sheriff is doing, Miss Shan?"

"In the first place, I am not sure they are competent. The ones I saw certainly did not impress me with their brilliance."

"And in the second place?"

"Really," she asked coldly, "is it necessary to go into all my mental processes?"

"It is."

She looked at the Old Man, who smiled at her with his polite, meaningless smile—a mask through which you can read nothing.

For a moment she hung fire. Then: "I don't think they are looking in very likely places. They seem to spend the greater part of their time in the vicinity of the house. It is absurd to think the murderers are going to return."

I turned that over in my mind.

"Miss Shan," I asked, "don't you think they suspect you?"

Her dark eyes burned through her glasses at me and, if possible, she made herself more rigidly straight in her chair.

"Preposterous!"

"That isn't the point," I insisted. "Do they?"

"I am not able to penetrate the police mind," she came back. "Do *you*?"

"I don't know anything about this job but what I've read and what you've just told me. I need more foundation than that to suspect anybody. But I can understand why the sheriff's office would be a little doubtful. You left in a hurry. They've got your word for why you went and why you came back, and your word is all. The woman found in the cellar could have been killed just before you left as well as just after. Wang Ma, who could have told things, is dead. The other servants are missing. Nothing was stolen. That's plenty to make the sheriff think about you!"

"Do you suspect me?" she asked again.

"No," I said truthfully. "But that proves nothing."

She spoke to the Old Man, with a chin-tilting motion, as if she were talking over my head.

"Do you wish to undertake this work for me?"

"We shall be very glad to do what we can," he said, and then to me, after they had talked terms and while she was writing a check, "you handle it. Use what men you need."

"I want to go out to the house first and look the place over," I said.

Lillian Shan was putting away her check-book.

"Very well. I am returning home now. I will drive you down."

It was a restful ride. Neither the girl nor I wasted energy on conversation. My client and I didn't seem to like each other very much. She drove well.

II

The Shan house was a big brownstone affair, set among sodded lawns. The place was hedged shoulder-high on three sides. The fourth boundary was the ocean, where it came in to make a notch in the shore-line between two small rocky points.

The house was full of hangings, rugs, pictures, and so on—a mixture of things American, European and Asiatic. I didn't spend much time inside. After a look at the linen-closet, at the still open cellar grave, and at the pale, thick-featured Danish woman who was taking care of the house until Lillian Shan could get a new corps of servants, I went outdoors again. I poked around the lawns for a few minutes, stuck my head in the garage, where two cars, besides the one in which we had come from town, stood, and then went off to waste the rest of the afternoon talking to the girl's neighbors. None of them knew anything. Since we were on opposite sides of the game, I didn't hunt up the sheriff's men.

By twilight I was back in the city, going into the apartment building in which I lived during my first year in San Francisco. I found the lad I wanted in his cubby-hole room, getting his small body into a cerise silk shirt that was something to look at. Cipriano was the bright-faced Filipino boy who looked after the building's front door in the daytime. At night, like all the Filipinos in San Francisco, he could be found down on Kearny Street, just below Chinatown, except when he was in a Chinese gambling-house passing his money over to the yellow brothers.

I had once, half-joking, promised to give the lad a fling at gum-shoeing if the opportunity ever came. I thought I could use him now.

"Come in, sir!"

He was dragging a chair out of a corner for me, bowing and smiling. Whatever else the Spaniards do for the people they rule, they make them polite.

"What's doing in Chinatown these days?" I asked as he went on with his dressing.

He gave me a white-toothed smile.

"I take eleven bucks out of bean-game last night."

"And you're getting ready to take it back tonight?"

"Not all of 'em, sir! Five bucks I spend for this shirt."

"That's the stuff," I applauded his wisdom in investing part of his fan-tan profits. "What else is doing down there?"

"Nothing unusual, sir. You want to find something?"

"Yeah. Hear any talk about the killings down the country last week? The two Chinese women?"

"No, sir. Chinaboy don't talk much about things like that. Not like us Americans. I read about those things in newspapers, but I have not heard."

"Many strangers in Chinatown nowadays?"

"All the time there's strangers, sir. But I guess maybe some new Chinaboys are there. Maybe not, though."

"How would you like to do a little work for me?"

"Yes, sir! Yes, sir! Yes, sir!" He said it oftener than that, but that will give you the idea. While he was saying it he was down on his knees, dragging a valise from under the bed. Out of the valise he took a pair of brass knuckles and a shiny revolver.

"Here! I want some information. I don't want you to knock anybody off for me."

"I don't knock 'em," he assured me, stuffing his weapons in his hip pockets. "Just carry these—maybe I need 'em."

I let it go at that. If he wanted to make himself bow-legged carrying a ton of iron it was all right with me.

"Here's what I want. Two of the servants ducked out of the house down there." I described Yin Hung and Hoo Lun. "I want to find them. I want to find what anybody in Chinatown knows about the killings. I want to find who the dead women's friends and relatives are, where they came from, and the same thing for the two men. I want to know about those strange Chinese—where they hang out, where they sleep, what they're up to.

"Now, don't try to get all this in a night. You'll be doing fine if you get any of it in a week. Here's twenty dollars. Five of it is your night's pay. You can use the other to carry you around. Don't be foolish and poke your nose into a lot of grief. Take it easy and see what you can turn up for me. I'll drop in tomorrow."

From the Filipino's room I went to the office. Everybody except Fiske, the night man, was gone, but Fiske thought the Old Man would drop in for a few minutes later in the night.

I smoked, pretended to listen to Fiske's report on all the jokes that were at the Orpheum that week, and grouched over my job. I was too well known to get anything on the quiet in Chinatown. I wasn't sure Cipriano was going to be much help. I needed somebody who was in right down there.

This line of thinking brought me around to "Dummy" Uhl. Uhl was a dummerer who had lost his store. Five years before, he had been sitting on the world. Any day on which his sad face, his package of pins, and his *I am deaf and dumb* sign didn't take twenty dollars out of the office buildings along his route was a rotten day. His big card was his ability to play the statue when skeptical people yelled or made sudden noises behind him. When the Dummy was right, a gun going off beside his ear wouldn't make him twitch an eye-lid. But too much heroin broke his nerves until a whisper was enough to make him jump. He put away his pins and his sign—another man whose social life had ruined him.

Since then Dummy had become an errand boy for whoever would stake him to the price of his necessary nose-candy. He slept somewhere in Chinatown, and he didn't care especially how he played the game. I had used him to get me some information on a window-smashing six months before. I decided to try him again.

I called "Loop" Pigatti's place—a dive down on Pacific Street, where Chinatown fringes into the Latin Quarter. Loop is a tough citizen, who runs a tough hole, and who minds his own business, which is making his dive show a profit. Everybody looks alike to Loop. Whether you're a yegg, stool-pigeon, detective, or settlement worker, you get an even break out of Loop and nothing else. But you can be sure that, unless it's something that might hurt his business, anything you tell Loop will get no further. And anything he tells you is more than likely to be right.

He answered the phone himself.

"Can you get hold of Dummy Uhl for me?" I asked after I had told him who I was.

"Maybe."

"Thanks. I'd like to see him tonight."

"You got nothin' on him?"

"No, Loop, and I don't expect to. I want him to get something for me."

"All right. Where d'you want him?"

"Send him up to my joint. I'll wait there for him."

"If he'll come," Loop promised and hung up.

I left word with Fiske to have the Old Man call me up when he came in, and then I went up to my rooms to wait for my informant.

He came in a little after ten—a short, stocky, pasty-faced man of forty or so, with mouse-colored hair streaked with yellow-white.

"Loop says y'got sumpin' f'r me."

"Yes," I said, waving him to a chair, and closing the door. "I'm buying news."

He fumbled with his hat, started to spit on the floor, changed his mind, licked his lips, and looked up at me.

"What kind o' news? I don't know nothin'."

I was puzzled. The Dummy's yellowish eyes should have showed the pin-point pupils of the heroin addict. They didn't. The pupils were normal. That didn't mean he was off the stuff—he had put cocaine into them to distend them to normal. The puzzle was—why? He wasn't usually particular enough about his appearance to go to that trouble.

"Did you hear about the Chinese killings down the shore last week?" I asked him.

"No."

"Well," I said, paying no attention to the denial, "I'm hunting for the pair of yellow men who ducked out—Hoo Lun and Yin Hung. Know anything about them?"

"No."

"It's worth a couple of hundred dollars to you to find either of them for me. It's worth another couple hundred to find out about the killings for me. It's worth another to find the slim Chinese youngster with gold teeth who opened the door for the Shan girl and her maid."

"I don't know nothin' about them things," he said.

But he said it automatically while his mind was busy counting up the hundreds I had dangled before him. I suppose his dope-addled brains made the total somewhere in the thousands. He jumped up.

"I'll see what I c'n do. S'pose you slip me a hundred now, on account."

I didn't see that.

"You get it when you deliver."

We had to argue that point, but finally he went off grumbling and growling to get me my news.

I went back to the office. The Old Man hadn't come in yet. It was nearly midnight when he arrived.

"I'm using Dummy Uhl again," I told him, "and I've put a Filipino boy down there too. I've got another scheme, but I don't know anybody to handle it. I think if we offered the missing chauffeur and house-man jobs in some out-of-the-way place up the country, perhaps they'd fall for it. Do you know anybody who could pull it for us?"

"Exactly what have you in mind?"

"It must be somebody who has a house out in the country,

the farther the better, the more secluded the better. They would phone one of the Chinese employment offices that they needed three servants—cook, house-man, and chauffeur. We throw in the cook for good measure, to cover the game. It's got to be air-tight on the other end, and, if we're going to catch our fish, we have to give 'em time to investigate. So whoever does it must have some servants, and must put up a bluff—I mean in his own neighborhood—that they are leaving, and the servants must be in on it. And we've got to wait a couple of days, so our friends here will have time to investigate. I think we'd better use Fong Yick's employment agency, on Washington Street.

"Whoever does it could phone Fong Yick tomorrow morning, and say he'd be in Thursday morning to look the applicants over. This is Monday—that'll be long enough. Our helper gets at the employment office at ten Thursday morning. Miss Shan and I arrive in a taxicab ten minutes later, when he'll be in the middle of questioning the applicants. I'll slide out of the taxi into Fong Yick's, grab anybody that looks like one of our missing servants. Miss Shan will come in a minute or two behind me and check me up—so there won't be any false-arrest mixups."

The Old Man nodded approval.

"Very well," he said. "I think I can arrange it. I will let you know tomorrow."

I went home to bed. Thus ended the first day.

III

At nine the next morning, Tuesday, I was talking to Cipriano in the lobby of the apartment building that employs him. His eyes were black drops of ink in white saucers. He thought he had got something.

"Yes, sir! Strange Chinaboys are in town, some of them. They sleep in a house on Waverly Place—on the western side, four houses from the house of Jair Quon, where I sometimes play dice. And there is more—I talk to a white man who knows they are hatchet-men from Portland and Eureka and Sacramento. They are Hip Sing men—a tong war starts—pretty soon, maybe."

"Do these birds look like gunmen to you?"

Cipriano scratched his head.

"No, sir, maybe not. But a fellow can shoot sometimes if he don't look like it. This man tells me they are Hip Sing men."

"Who was this white man?"

"I don't know the name, but he lives there. A short man—snow-bird."

"Grey hair, yellowish eyes?"

"Yes, sir."

That, as likely as not, would be Dummy Uhl. One of my men was stringing the other. The tong stuff hadn't sounded right to me anyhow. Once in a while they mix things, but usually they are blamed for somebody else's crimes. Most wholesale killings in Chinatown are the result of family or clan feuds—such as the ones the "Four Brothers" used to stage.

"This house where you think the strangers are living—know anything about it?"

"No, sir. But maybe you could go through there to the house of Chang Li Ching on other street—Spofford Alley."

"So? And who is this Chang Li Ching?"

"I don't know, sir. But he is there. Nobody sees him, but all Chinaboys say he is great man."

"So? And his house is in Spofford Alley?"

"Yes, sir, a house with red door and red steps. You find it easy, but better not fool with Chang Li Ching."

I didn't know whether that was advice or just a general remark.

"A big gun, huh?" I probed.

But my Filipino didn't really know anything about this Chang Li Ching. He was basing his opinion of the Chinese's greatness on the attitude of his fellow countrymen when they mentioned him.

"Learn anything about the two Chinese men?" I asked after I had fixed this point.

"No, sir, but I will—you bet!"

I praised him for what he had done, told him to try it again that night, and went back to my rooms to wait for Dummy Uhl, who had promised to come there at ten-thirty. It was not quite ten when I got there, so I used some of my spare time to call up the office. The Old Man said Dick Foley—our shadow ace—was idle, so I borrowed him. Then I fixed my gun and sat down to wait for my stool-pigeon.

He rang the bell at eleven o'clock. He came in frowning tremendously.

"I don't know what t' hell to make of it, kid," he spoke importantly over the cigarette he was rolling. "There's sumpin' makin' down there, an' that's a fact. Things ain't been anyways quiet since the Japs began buyin' stores in the Chink streets, an' maybe that's got sumpin' to do with it. But there ain't no strange Chinks in town—not a damn one! I got a hunch your men have gone down to L. A., but I expec' t' know f'r certain tonight. I got a Chink ribbed up t' get the dope; 'f I was you, I'd put a watch on the boats at San Pedro. Maybe those fellas'll swap papers wit' a coupla Chink sailors that'd like t' stay here."

"And there are no strangers in town?"

"Not any."

"Dummy," I said bitterly, "you're a liar, and you're a boob, and I've been playing you for a sucker. You were in on that killing, and so were your friends, and I'm going to throw you in the can, and your friends on top of you!"

I put my gun in sight, close to his scared-grey face.

"Keep yourself still while I do my phoning!"

Reaching for the telephone with my free hand, I kept one eye on the Dummy.

It wasn't enough. My gun was too close to him.

He yanked it out of my hand. I jumped for him.

The gun turned in his fingers. I grabbed it—too late. It went off, its muzzle less than a foot from where I'm thickest. Fire stung my body.

Clutching the gun with both hands I folded down to the floor. Dummy went away from there, leaving the door open behind him.

One hand on my burning belly, I crossed to the window and waved an arm at Dick Foley, stalling on a corner down the street. Then I went to the bathroom and looked to my wound. A blank cartridge does hurt if you catch it close up!

My vest and shirt and union suit were ruined, and I had a nasty scorch on my body. I greased it, taped a cushion over it, changed my clothes, loaded the gun again, and went down to the office to wait for word from Dick. The first trick in the game looked like mine. Heroin or no heroin, Dummy Uhl would not have jumped me if my guess—based on the trouble he was taking to make his eyes look right and the lie he had sprung on me about there being no strangers in Chinatown—hadn't hit close to the mark.

Dick wasn't long in joining me.

"Good pickings!" he said when he came in. The little Canadian talks like a thrifty man's telegram. "Beat it for phone. Called Hotel Irvington. Booth—couldn't get anything but number. Ought to be enough. Then Chinatown. Dived in cellar west side Waverly Place. Couldn't stick close enough to spot place. Afraid to take chance hanging around. How do you like it?"

"I like it all right. Let's look up 'The Whistler's' record."

A file clerk got it for us—a bulky envelope the size of a brief case, crammed with memoranda, clippings and letters. The gentleman's biography, as we had it, ran like this:

Neil Conyers, alias The Whistler, was born in Philadelphia—out on Whiskey Hill—in 1883. In '94, at the age of eleven, he was picked up by the Washington police. He had gone there to join Coxey's Army. They sent him home. In '98 he was arrested in his home town for stabbing another lad in a row over an election-night bonfire. This time he was released in his parents' custody. In 1901 the Philadelphia police grabbed him again, charging him with being the head of the first organized automobile-stealing ring. He was released without trial, for lack of evidence. But the district attorney lost his job in the resultant scandal. In 1908 Conyers appeared on the Pacific Coast—at Seattle, Portland, San Francisco, and Los Angeles—in company with a con-man known as "Duster" Hughes. Hughes was shot and killed the following year by a man whom he'd swindled in a fake airplane manufacturing deal. Conyers was arrested on the same deal. Two juries disagreed and he was turned loose. In 1910 the Post Office Department's famous raid on get-rich-quick promoters caught him. Again there wasn't enough evidence against him to put him away. In 1915 the law scored on him for the first time. He went to San Quentin for buncoing some visitors to the Panama-Pacific International Exposition. He stayed there for three years. In 1919 he and a Jap named Hasegawa nicked the Japanese colony of Seattle for $20,000, Conyers posing as an American who had held a commission in the Japanese army during that late war. He had a counterfeit medal of the Order of the Rising Sun which the emperor was supposed to have pinned on him. When the game fell through, Hasegawa's family made good the $20,000—Conyers got out of it with a good profit and not even any disagreeable publicity. The thing had been hushed. He returned to San Francisco after that, bought the Hotel Irvington, and had been living there now for five years without anybody being able to add another word to his criminal record. He was up to something, but nobody could learn what. There wasn't a chance in the world of getting a detective into his hotel as a guest. Apparently the joint was always without vacant rooms. It was as exclusive as the Pacific-Union Club.

This, then, was the proprietor of the hotel Dummy Uhl had got on the phone before diving into his hole in Chinatown.

I had never seen Conyers. Neither had Dick. There were a couple of photographs in his envelope. One was the profile and full-face photograph of the local police, taken when he had been picked up on the charge that led him to San Quentin. The other was a group picture: all rung up in evening clothes, with the phoney Japanese medal on his chest, he stood among half a dozen of the Seattle Japs he had trimmed—a flashlight picture taken while he was leading them to the slaughter.

These pictures showed him to be a big bird, fleshy, pompous-looking, with a heavy, square chin and shrewd eyes.

"Think you could pick him up?" I asked Dick.

"Sure."

"Suppose you go up there and see if you can get a room or apartment somewhere in the neighborhood—one you can watch the hotel from. Maybe you'll get a chance to tail him around now and then."

I put the pictures in my pocket, in case they'd come in handy, dumped the rest of the stuff back in its envelope, and went into the Old Man's office.

"I arranged that employment office stratagem," he said. "A Frank Paul, who has a ranch out beyond Martinez, will be in

Fong Yick's establishment at ten Thursday morning, carrying out his part."

"That's fine! I'm going calling in Chinatown now. If you don't hear from me for a couple of days, will you ask the street-cleaners to watch what they're sweeping up?"

He said he would.

IV

San Francisco's Chinatown jumps out of the shopping district at California Street and runs north to the Latin Quarter—a strip two blocks wide by six long. Before the fire nearly twenty-five thousand Chinese lived in those dozen blocks. I don't suppose the population is a third of that now.

Grant Avenue, the main street and spine of this strip, is for most of its length a street of gaudy shops catering to the tourist trade and flashy chop-suey houses, where the racket of American jazz orchestras drowns the occasional squeak of a Chinese flute. Farther out, there isn't so much paint and gilt, and you can catch the proper Chinese smell of spices and vinegar and dried things. If you leave the main thoroughfares and show places and start poking around in alleys and dark corners, and nothing happens to you, the chances are you'll find some interesting things—though you won't like some of them.

However, I wasn't poking around as I turned off Grant Avenue at Clay Street, and went up to Spofford Alley, hunting for the house with red steps and red door, which Cipriano had said was Chang Li Ching's. I did pause for a few seconds to look up Waverly Place when I passed it. The Filipino had told me the strange Chinese were living there, and that he thought their house might lead through to Chang Li Ching's; and Dick Foley had shadowed Dummy Uhl there.

But I couldn't guess which was the important house. Four doors from Jair Quon's gambling house, Cipriano had said, but I didn't know where Jair Quon's was. Waverly Place was a picture of peace and quiet just now. A fat Chinese was stacking crates of green vegetables in front of a grocery. Half a dozen small yellow boys were playing at marbles in the middle of the street. On the other side, a blond young man in tweeds was climbing the six steps from a cellar to the street, a painted Chinese woman's face showing for an instant before she closed the door behind him. Up the street a truck was unloading rolls of paper in front of one of the Chinese newspaper plants. A shabby guide was bringing four sightseers out of the Temple of the Queen of Heaven—a joss house over the Sue Hing headquarters.

I went on up to Spofford Alley and found my house with no difficulty at all. It was a shabby building with steps and door the color of dried blood, its windows solidly shuttered with thick, tight-nailed planking. What made it stand out from its neighbors was that its ground floor wasn't a shop or place of business. Purely residential buildings are rare in Chinatown: almost always the street floor is given to business, with the living quarters in cellar or upper stories.

I went up the three steps and tapped the red door with my knuckles.

Nothing happened.

I hit it again, harder. Still nothing. I tried it again, and this time was rewarded by the sounds of scraping and clicking inside.

At least two minutes of this scraping and clicking, and the door swung open—a bare four inches.

One slanting eye and a slice of wrinkled brown face looked out of the crack at me, above the heavy chain that held the door.

"Whata wan'?"

"I want to see Chang Li Ching."

"No savvy. Maybe closs stleet."

"Bunk! You fix your little door and run back and tell Chang Li Ching I want to see him."

"No can do! No savvy Chang."

"You tell him I'm here," I said, turning my back on the door. I sat down on the top step, and added, without looking around, "I'll wait."

While I got my cigarettes out there was silence behind me. Then the door closed softly and the scraping and clicking broke out behind it. I smoked a cigarette and another and let time go by, trying to look like I had all the patience there was.

I hoped this yellow man wasn't going to make a chump of me by letting me sit there until I got tired of it.

Chinese passed up and down the alley, scuffling along in American shoes that can never be made to fit them. Some of them looked curiously at me, some gave me no attention at all. An hour went to waste, and a few minutes, and then the familiar scraping and clicking disturbed the door.

The chain rattled as the door swung open. I wouldn't turn my head.

"Go 'way! No catch 'em Chang!"

I said nothing. If he wasn't going to let me in he would have let me sit there without further attention.

A pause.

"Whata wan'?"

"I want to see Chang Li Ching," I said without looking around.

Another pause, ended by the banging of the chain against the door-frame.

"All light."

I chucked my cigarette into the street, got up and stepped into the house. In the dimness I could make out a few pieces of cheap and battered furniture. I had to wait while the Chinese put four arm-thick bars across the door and pad-locked them there. Then he nodded at me and scuffled across the floor, a small, bent man with hairless yellow head and a neck like a piece of rope.

Out of this room, he led me into another, darker still, into a hallway, and down a flight of rickety steps. The odors of musty clothing and damp earth were strong. We walked through the dark across a dirt floor for a while, turned to the left, and cement was under my feet. We turned twice more in the dark, and then climbed a flight of unplaned wooden steps into a hall that was fairly light with the glow from shaded electric lights.

In this hall my guide unlocked a door, and we crossed a room where cones of incense burned, and where, in the light of an oil lamp, little red tables with cups of tea stood in front of wooden panels, marked with Chinese characters in gold paint, which hung on the walls. A door on the opposite side of this room let us into pitch blackness, where I had to hold the tail of my guide's loose made-to-order blue coat.

So far he hadn't once looked back at me since our tour began, and neither of us had said anything. This running upstairs and downstairs, turning to the right and turning to the left, seemed harmless enough. If he got any fun out of confusing me, he was welcome. I was confused enough now, so far as the directions were concerned. I hadn't the least idea where I might be. But that didn't disturb me so much. If I was going to be cut down, a knowledge of my geographical position wouldn't make it any more pleasant. If I was going to come out all right, one place was still as good as another.

We did a lot more of the winding around, we did some stair-climbing and some stair-descending, and the rest of the foolishness. I figured I'd been indoors nearly half an hour by now, and I had seen nobody but my guide.

Then I saw something else.

We were going down a long, narrow hall that had brown-painted doors close together on either side. All these doors were closed—secretive-looking in the dim light. Abreast of one of them, a glint of dull metal caught my eye—a dark ring in the door's center.

I went to the floor.

Going down as if I'd been knocked, I missed the flash. But I heard the roar, smelled the powder.

My guide spun around, twisting out of one slipper. In each of his hands was an automatic as big as a coal scuttle. Even while trying to get my own gun out I wondered how so puny a man could have concealed so much machinery on him.

The big guns in the little man's hands flamed at me. Chinese-fashion, he was emptying them—crash! crash! crash!

I thought he was missing me until I had my finger tight on my trigger. Then I woke up in time to hold my fire.

He wasn't shooting at me. He was pouring metal into the door behind me—the door from which I had been shot at.

I rolled away from it, across the hall.

The scrawny little man stepped closer and finished his bombardment. His slugs shredded the wood as if it had been paper. His guns clicked empty.

The door swung open, pushed by the wreck of a man who was trying to hold himself up by clinging to the sliding panel in the door's center.

Dummy Uhl—all the middle of him gone—slid down to the floor and made more of a puddle than a pile there.

The hall filled with yellow men, black guns sticking out like briars in a blackberry patch.

I got up. My guide dropped his guns to his side and sang out a guttural solo. Chinese began to disappear through various doors, except four who began gathering up what twenty bullets had left of Dummy Uhl.

The stringy old boy tucked his empty guns away and came down the hall to me, one hand held out toward my gun.

"You give 'em," he said politely.

I gave 'em. He could have had my pants.

My gun stowed away in his shirt-bosom, he looked casually at what the four Chinese were carrying away, and then at me.

"No like 'em fella, huh?" he asked.

"Not so much," I admitted.

"All light. I take you."

Our two-man parade got under way again. The ring-around-the-rosy game went on for another flight of stairs and some right and left turns, and then my guide stopped before a door and scratched it with his finger-nails.

V

The door was opened by another Chinese. But this one was none of your Cantonese runts. He was a big meat-eating wrestler—bull-throated, mountain-shouldered, gorilla-armed, leather-skinned. The god that made him had plenty of material, and gave it time to harden.

Holding back the curtain that covered the door, he stepped to one side. I went in, and found his twin standing on the other side of the door.

The room was large and cubical, its doors and windows—if any—hidden behind velvet hangings of green and blue and silver. In a big black chair, elaborately carved, behind an inlaid black table, sat an old Chinese man. His face was round and plump and shrewd, with a straggle of thin white whiskers on his chin. A dark, close-fitting cap was on his head; a purple robe, tight around his neck, showed its sable lining at the bottom, where it had fallen back in a fold over his blue satin trousers.

He did not get up from his chair, but smiled mildly over his whiskers and bent his head almost to the tea things on the table.

"It was only the inability to believe that one of your excellency's heaven-born splendor would waste his costly time on so mean a clod that kept the least of your slaves from running down to prostrate himself at your noble feet as soon as he heard the Father of Detectives was at his unworthy door."

That came out smoothly in English that was a lot clearer than my own. I kept my face straight, waiting.

"If the Terror of Evildoers will honor one of my deplorable chairs by resting his divine body on it, I can assure him the chair shall be burned afterward, so no lesser being may use it. Or will the Prince of Thief-catchers permit me to send a servant to his palace for a chair worthy of him?"

I went slowly to a chair, trying to arrange words in my mind. This old joker was spoofing me with an exaggeration—a burlesque—of the well-known Chinese politeness. I'm not hard to get along with: I'll play anybody's game up to a certain point.

"It's only because I'm weak-kneed with awe of the mighty Chang Li Ching that I dare to sit down," I explained, letting myself down on the chair, and turning my head to notice that the giants who had stood beside the door were gone.

I had a hunch they had gone no farther than the other side of the velvet hangings that hid the door.

"If it were not that the King of Finders-out"—he was at it again—"knows everything, I should marvel that he had heard my lowly name."

"Heard it? Who hasn't?" I kidded back. "Isn't the word *change*, in English, derived from Chang? Change, meaning alter, is what happens to the wisest man's opinions after he has heard the wisdom of Chang Li Ching!" I tried to get away from this vaudeville stuff, which was a strain on my head. "Thanks for having your man save my life back there in the passage."

He spreads his hands out over the table.

"It was only because I feared the Emperor of Hawkshaws would find the odor of such low blood distasteful to his elegant nostrils that the foul one who disturbed your excellency was struck down quickly. If I have erred, and you would have chosen that he be cut to pieces inch by inch, I can only offer to torture one of my sons in his place."

"Let the boy live," I said carelessly, and turned to business. "I wouldn't have bothered you except that I am so ignorant that only the help of your great wisdom could ever bring me up to normal."

"Does one ask the way of a blind man?" the old duffer asked, cocking his head to one side. "Can a star, however willing, help the moon? If it pleases the Grandfather of Bloodhounds to flatter Chang Li Ching into thinking he can add to the great one's knowledge, who is Chang to thwart his master by refusing to make himself ridiculous?"

I took that to mean he was willing to listen to my questions.

"What I'd like to know is, who killed Lillian Shan's servants, Wang Ma and Wan Lan?"

He played with a thin strand of his white beard, twisting it in a pale, small finger.

"Does the stag-hunter look at the hare?" he wanted to know. "And when so mighty a hunter pretends to concern himself with the death of servants, can Chang think anything except that it pleases the great one to conceal his real object? Yet it may be, because the dead were servants and not girdle-wearers, that the Lord of Snares thought the lowly Chang Li Ching, insignificant one of the Hundred Names, might have knowledge of them. Do not rats know the way of rats?"

He kept this stuff up for some minutes, while I sat and listened and studied his round, shrewd yellow mask of a face, and hoped that something clear would come of it all. Nothing did.

"My ignorance is even greater than I had arrogantly supposed," he brought his speech to an end. "This simple question you put is beyond the power of my muddled mind. I do not know who killed Wang Ma and Wan Lan."

I grinned at him, and put another question:

"Where can I find Hoo Lun and Yin Hung?"

"Again I must grovel in my ignorance," he murmured, "only consoling myself with the thought that the Master of Mysteries knows the answers to his questions, and is pleased to conceal his infallibly accomplished purpose from Chang."

And that was as far as I got.

There were more crazy compliments, more bowing and scraping, more assurances of eternal reverence and love, and then I was following my rope-necked guide through winding, dark halls, across dim rooms, and up and down rickety stairs again.

At the street door—after he had taken down the bars—he slid my gun out of his shirt and handed it to me. I squelched the impulse to look at it then and there to see if anything had been done to it. Instead I stuck it in my pocket and stepped through the door.

"Thanks for the killing upstairs," I said.

The Chinese grunted, bowed, and closed the door.

I went up to Stockton Street, and turned toward the office, walking along slowly, punishing my brains.

First, there was Dummy Uhl's death to think over. Had it been arranged before-hand: to punish him for bungling that morning and, at the same time, to impress me? And how? And why? Or was it supposed to put me under obligations to the Chinese? And, if so, why? Or was it just one of those complicated tricks the Chinese like? I put the subject away and pointed my thoughts at the little plump yellow man in the purple robe.

I liked him. He had humor, brains, nerve, everything. To jam him in a cell would be a trick you'd want to write home about. He was my idea of a man worth working against.

But I didn't kid myself into thinking I had anything on him. Dummy Uhl had given me a connection between The Whistler's Hotel Irvington and Chang Li Ching. Dummy Uhl had gone into action when I accused him of being mixed up in the Shan killings. That much I had—and that was all, except that Chang had said nothing to show he wasn't interested in the Shan troubles.

In this light, the chances were that Dummy's death had not been a planned performance. It was more likely that he had seen me coming, had tried to wipe me out, and had been knocked off by my guide because he was interfering with the audience Chang had granted me. Dummy couldn't have had a very valuable life in the Chinese's eye—or in anybody else's.

I wasn't at all dissatisfied with the day's work so far. I hadn't done anything brilliant, but I had got a look at my destination, or thought I had. If I was butting my head against a stone wall, I at least knew where the wall was and had seen the man who owned it.

In the office, a message from Dick Foley was waiting for me. He had rented a front apartment up the street from the Irvington and had put in a couple of hours trailing The Whistler.

The Whistler had spent half an hour in "Big Fat" Thomson's place on Market Street, talking to the proprietor and some of the sure-thing gamblers who congregate there. Then he had taxi-cabbed out to an apartment house on O'Farrell Street—the Glenway—where he had rung one of the bells. Getting no answer, he had let himself into the building with a key. An hour later he had come out and returned to his hotel. Dick hadn't been able to determine which bell he had rung, or which apartment he had visited.

I got Lillian Shan on the telephone.

"Will you be in this evening?" I asked. "I've something I want to go into with you, and I can't give it to you over the wire."

"I will be at home until seven-thirty."

"All right, I'll be down."

It was seven-fifteen when the car I had hired put me down at her front door. She opened the door for me. The Danish woman who was filling in until new servants were employed stayed there only in the daytime, returning to her own home—a mile back from the shore—at night.

The evening gown Lillian Shan wore was severe enough, but it suggested that if she would throw away her glasses and do something for herself, she might not be so unfeminine looking after all. She took me upstairs, to the library, where a clean-cut lad of twenty-something in evening clothes got up from a chair as we came in—a well-set-up boy with fair hair and skin.

His name, I learned when we were introduced, was Garthorne. The girl seemed willing enough to hold our conference in his presence. I wasn't. After I had done everything but insist point-blank on seeing her alone, she excused her-self—calling him Jack—and took me out into another room.

By then I was a bit impatient.

"Who's that?" I demanded.

She put her eyebrows up for me.

"Mr. John Garthorne," she said.

"How well do you know him?"

"May I ask why you are so interested?"

"You may. Mr. John Garthorne is all wrong, I think."

"Wrong?"

I had another idea.

"Where does he live?"

She gave me an O'Farrell Street number.

"The Glenway Apartments?"

"I think so." She was looking at me without any affectation at all. "Will you please explain?"

"One more question and I will. Do you know a Chinese named Chang Li Ching?"

"No."

"All right. I'll tell you about Garthorne. So far I've run into two angles on this trouble of yours. One of them has to do with this Chang Li Ching in Chinatown, and one with an ex-convict named Conyers. This John Garthorne was in Chinatown today. I saw him coming out of a cellar that prob-ably connects with Chang Li Ching's house. The ex-convict Conyers visited the building where Garthorne lives, early this afternoon."

Her mouth popped open and then shut.

"That is absurd!" she snapped. "I have known Mr. Gar-thorne for some time, and——"

"Exactly how long?"

"A long—several months."

"Where'd you meet him?"

"Through a girl I knew at college."

"What does he do for a living?"

She stood stiff and silent.

"Listen, Miss Shan," I said. "Garthorne may be all right, but I've got to look him up. If he's in the clear there'll be no harm done. I want to know what you know about him."

I got it, little by little. He was, or she thought he was, the youngest son of a prominent Richmond, Virginia, family, in disgrace just now because of some sort of boyish prank. He had come to San Francisco four months ago, to wait until his father's anger cooled. Meanwhile his mother kept him in money, leaving him without the necessity of toiling during his exile. He had brought a letter of introduction from one of Lillian Shan's schoolmates. Lillian Shan had, I gathered, a lot of liking for him.

"You're going out with him tonight?" I asked when I had got this.

"Yes."

"In his car or yours?"

She frowned, but she answered my question.

"In his. We are going to drive down to Half Moon for dinner."

"I'll need a key, then, because I am coming back here after you have gone."

"You're what?"

"I'm coming back here. I'll ask you not to say anything about my more or less unworthy suspicions to him, but my honest opinion is that he's drawing you away for the evening. So if the engine breaks down on the way back, just pretend you see nothing unusual in it."

That worried her, but she wouldn't admit I might be right. I got the key, though, and then I told her of my employment agency scheme that needed her assistance, and she promised to be at the office at half past nine Thursday morning.

I didn't see Garthorne again before I left the house.

VI

In my hired car again, I had the driver take me to the nearest village, where I bought a plug of chewing tobacco, a flashlight, and a box of cartridges at the general store. My gun is a .38 Special, but I had to take the shorter, weaker cartridges, because the storekeeper didn't keep the specials in stock.

My purchases in my pocket, we started back toward the Shan house again. Two bends in the road this side of it, I stopped the car, paid the chauffeur, and sent him on his way, finishing the trip afoot.

The house was dark all around.

Letting myself in as quietly as possible, and going easy with the flashlight, I gave the interior a combing from cellar to roof. I was the only occupant. In the kitchen, I looted the ice-box for a bite or two, which I washed down with milk. I could have used some coffee, but coffee is too fragrant.

The luncheon done, I made myself comfortable on a chair in the passageway between the kitchen and the rest of the house. On one side of the passageway, steps led down to the basement. On the other, steps led upstairs. With every door in the house except the outer ones open, the passageway was the center of things so far as hearing noises was concerned.

An hour went by—quietly except for the passing of cars on the road a hundred yards away and the washing of the Pacific down in the little cove. I chewed on my plug of tobacco—a substitute for cigarettes—and tried to count up the hours of my life I'd spent like this, sitting or standing around waiting for something to happen.

The telephone rang.

I let it ring. It might be Lillian Shan needing help, but I couldn't take a chance. It was too likely to be some egg trying to find out if anybody was in the house.

Another half hour went by with a breeze springing up from the ocean, rustling trees outside.

A noise came that was neither wind nor surf nor passing car. Something clicked somewhere.

It was at a window, but I didn't know which. I got rid of my chew, got gun and flashlight out.

It sounded again, harshly.

Somebody was giving a window a strong play—too strong. The catch rattled, and something clicked against the pane. It was a stall. Whoever he was, he could have smashed the glass with less noise than he was making.

I stood up, but I didn't leave the passageway. The window noise was a fake to draw the attention of anyone who might be in the house. I turned my back on it, trying to see into the kitchen.

The kitchen was too black to see anything.

I saw nothing there. I heard nothing there.

Damp air blew on me from the kitchen.

That was something to worry about. I had company, and he was slicker than I. He could open doors or windows under my nose. That wasn't so good.

Weight on rubber heels, I backed away from my chair until the frame of the cellar door touched my shoulder. I wasn't sure I was going to like this party. I like an even break or better, and this didn't look like one.

So when a thin line of light danced out of the kitchen to hit the chair in the passageway, I was three steps cellar-ward, my back flat against the stair-wall.

The light fixed itself on the chair for a couple of seconds, and then began to dart around the passageway, through it into the room beyond. I could see nothing but the light.

Fresh sounds came to me—the purr of automobile engines close to the house on the road side, the soft padding of feet on the back porch, on the kitchen linoleum, quite a few feet. An odor came to me—an unmistakable odor—the smell of unwashed Chinese.

Then I lost track of these things. I had plenty to occupy me close up.

The proprietor of the flashlight was at the head of the cellar steps. I had ruined my eyes watching the light: I couldn't see him.

The first thin ray he sent downstairs missed me by an inch—which gave me time to make a map there in the dark. If he was of medium size, holding the light in his left hand, a gun in his right, and exposing as little of himself as possible—his noodle should have been a foot and a half above the beginning of the light-beam, the same distance behind it, six inches to the left—my left.

The light swung sideways and hit one of my legs.

I swung the barrel of my gun at the point I had marked X in the night.

His gun-fire cooked my cheek. One of his arms tried to take me with him. I twisted away and let him dive alone into the cellar, showing me a flash of gold teeth as he went past.

The house was full of "Ah yahs" and pattering feet.

I had to move—or I'd be pushed.

Downstairs might be a trap. I went up to the passageway again.

The passageway was solid and alive with stinking bodies. Hands and teeth began to take my clothes away from me. I knew damned well I had declared myself in on something!

I was one of a struggling, tearing, grunting and groaning mob of invisibles. An eddy of them swept me toward the kitchen. Hitting, kicking, butting, I went along.

A high-pitched voice was screaming Chinese orders.

My shoulder scraped the door-frame as I was carried into the kitchen, fighting as best I could against enemies I couldn't see, afraid to use the gun I still gripped.

I was only one part of the mad scramble. The flash of my gun might have made me the center of it. These lunatics were fighting panic now: I didn't want to show them something tangible to tear apart.

I went along with them, cracking everything that got in my way, and being cracked back. A bucket got between my feet.

I crashed down, upsetting my neighbors, rolled over a body, felt a foot on my face, squirmed from under it, and came to rest in a corner, still tangled up with the galvanized bucket.

Thank God for that bucket!

I wanted these people to go away. I didn't care who or what they were. If they'd depart in peace I'd forgive their sins.

I put my gun inside the bucket and squeezed the trigger. I got the worst of the racket, but there was enough to go around. It sounded like a crump going off.

I cut loose in the bucket again, and had another idea. Two fingers of my left hand in my mouth, I whistled as shrill as I could while I emptied the gun.

It was a sweet racket!

When my gun had run out of bullets and my lungs out of air, I was alone. I was glad to be alone. I knew why men go off and live in caves by themselves. And I didn't blame them!

Sitting there alone in the dark, I reloaded my gun.

On hands and knees I found my way to the open kitchen door, and peeped out into the blackness that told me nothing. The surf made guzzling sounds in the cove. From the other side of the house came the noise of cars. I hoped it was my friends going away.

I shut the door, locked it, and turned on the kitchen light.

The place wasn't as badly upset as I had expected. Some pans and dishes were down and a chair had been broken, and the place smelled of unwashed bodies. But that was all—except a blue cotton sleeve in the middle of the floor, a straw sandal near the passageway door, and a handful of short black hairs, a bit blood-smeared, beside the sandal.

In the cellar I did not find the man I had sent down there. An open door showed how he had left me. His flashlight was there, and my own, and some of his blood.

Upstairs again, I went through the front of the house. The front door was open. Rugs had been rumpled. A blue vase was broken on the floor. A table was pushed out of place, and a couple of chairs had been upset. I found an old and greasy brown felt hat that had neither sweat-band nor hat-band. I found a grimy photograph of President Coolidge—apparently cut from a Chinese newspaper—and six wheat-straw cigarette papers.

I found nothing upstairs to show that any of my guests had gone up there.

It was half past two in the morning when I heard a car drive up to the front door. I peeped out of Lillian Shan's bedroom window, on the second floor. She was saying good-night to Jack Garthorne.

I went back to the library to wait for her.

"Nothing happened?" were her first words, and they sounded more like a prayer than anything else.

"It did," I told her, "and I suppose you had your breakdown."

For a moment I thought she was going to lie to me, but she nodded, and dropped into a chair, not as erect as usual.

"I had a lot of company," I said, "but I can't say I found out much about them. The fact is, I bit off more than I could chew, and had to be satisfied with chasing them out."

"You didn't call the sheriff's office?" There was something strange about the tone in which she put the question.

"No—I don't want Garthorne arrested yet."

That shook the dejection out of her. She was up, tall and straight in front of me, and cold.

"I'd rather not go into that again," she said.

That was all right with me, but:

"You didn't say anything to him, I hope."

"Say anything to him?" She seemed amazed. "Do you think I would insult him by repeating your guesses—your absurd guesses?"

"That's fine," I applauded her silence if not her opinion of my theories. "Now, I'm going to stay here tonight. There isn't a chance in a hundred of anything happening, but I'll play it safe."

She didn't seem very enthusiastic about that, but she finally went off to bed.

Nothing happened between then and sun-up, of course. I left the house as soon as daylight came and gave the grounds the once over. Footprints were all over the place, from water's edge to driveway. Along the driveway some of the sod was cut where machines had been turned carelessly.

Borrowing one of the cars from the garage, I was back in San Francisco before the morning was far gone.

In the office, I asked the Old Man to put an operative behind Jack Garthorne; to have the old hat, flashlight, sandal and the rest of my souvenirs put under the microscope and searched for finger prints, foot prints, tooth-prints or what have you; and to have our Richmond branch look up the Garthornes. Then I went up to see my Filipino assistant.

He was gloomy.

"What's the matter?" I asked. "Somebody knock you over?"

"Oh, no, sir!" he protested. "But maybe I am not so good a detective. I try to follow one fella, and he turns a corner and he is gone."

"Who was he, and what was he up to?"

"I do not know, sir. There is four automobiles with men getting out of them into that cellar of which I tell you the strange Chinese live. After they are gone in, one man comes out. He wears his hat down over bandage on his upper face, and he walks away rapidly. I try to follow him, but he turns that corner, and where is he?"

"What time did all this happen?"

"Twelve o'clock, maybe."

"Could it have been later than that, or earlier?"

"Yes, sir."

My visitors, no doubt, and the man Cipriano had tried to shadow could have been the one I swatted. The Filipino hadn't thought to get the license numbers of the automobiles. He didn't know whether they had been driven by white men or Chinese, or even what make cars they were.

"You've done fine," I assured him. "Try it again tonight. Take it easy, and you'll get there."

From him I went to a telephone and called the Hall of Justice. Dummy Uhl's death had not been reported, I learned.

Twenty minutes later I was skinning my knuckles on Chang Li Ching's front door.

VII

The little old Chinese with the rope neck didn't open for me this time. Instead, a young Chinese with a smallpox-pitted face and a wide grin.

"You wanna see Chang Li Ching," he said before I could speak, and stepped back for me to enter.

I went in and waited while he replaced all the bars and locks. We went to Chang by a shorter route than before, but it was still far from direct. For a while I amused myself trying to map the route in my head as he went along, but it was too complicated, so I gave it up.

The velvet-hung room was empty when my guide showed me in, bowed, grinned, and left me. I sat down in a chair near the table and waited.

Chang Li Ching didn't put on the theatricals for me by materializing silently, or anything of the sort. I heard his soft slippers on the floor before he parted the hangings and came in. He was alone, his white whiskers ruffled in a smile that was grandfatherly.

"The Scatterer of Hordes honors my poor residence again," he greeted me, and went on at great length with the same sort of nonsense that I'd had to listen to on my first visit.

The Scatterer of Hordes part was cool enough—if it was a reference to last night's doings.

"Not knowing who he was until too late, I beaned one of your servants last night," I said when he had run out of flowers for the time. "I know there's nothing I can do to square myself for such a terrible act, but I hope you'll let me cut my throat and bleed to death in one of your garbage cans as a sort of apology."

A little sighing noise that could have been a smothered chuckle disturbed the old man's lips, and the purple cap twitched on his round head.

"The Disperser of Marauders knows all things," he murmured blandly, "even to the value of noise in driving away demons. If he says the man he struck was Chang Li Ching's servant, who is Chang to deny it?"

I tried him with my other barrel.

"I don't know much—not even why the police haven't yet heard of the death of the man who was killed here yesterday."

One of his hands made little curls in his white beard.

"I had not heard of the death," he said.

I could guess what was coming, but I wanted to take a look at it.

"You might ask the man who brought me here yesterday," I suggested.

Chang Li Ching picked up a little padded stick from the table and struck a tasseled gong that hung at his shoulder. Across the room the hangings parted to admit the pock-marked Chinese who had brought me in.

"Did death honor our hovel yesterday?" Chang asked in English.

"No, *Ta Jen*," the pock-marked one said.

"It was the nobleman who guided me here yesterday," I explained, "not this son of an emperor."

Chang imitated surprise.

"Who welcomed the King of Spies yesterday?" he asked the man at the door.

"I bring 'em, *Ta Jen*."

I grinned at the pock-marked man, he grinned back, and Chang smiled benevolently.

"An excellent jest," he said.

It was.

The pock-marked man bowed and started to duck back through the hangings. Loose shoes rattled on the boards behind him. He spun around. One of the big wrestlers I had seen the previous day loomed above him. The wrestler's eyes were bright with excitement, and grunted Chinese syllables poured out of his mouth. The pock-marked one talked back. Chang Li Ching silenced them with a sharp command. All this was in Chinese—out of my reach.

"Will the Grand Duke of Manhunters permit his servant to depart for a moment to attend to his distressing domestic affairs?"

"Sure."

Chang bowed with his hands together, and spoke to the wrestler.

"You will remain here to see that the great one is not disturbed and that any wishes he expresses are gratified."

The wrestler bowed and stood aside for Chang to pass through the door with the pock-marked man. The hangings swung over the door behind them.

I didn't waste any language on the man at the door, but got a cigarette going and waited for Chang to come back. The cigarette was half gone when a shot sounded in the building, not far away.

The giant at the door scowled.

Another shot sounded, and running feet thumped in the hall. The pock-marked man's face came through the hangings. He poured grunts at the wrestler. The wrestler scowled at me and protested. The other insisted.

The wrestler scowled at me again, rumbled, "You wait," and was gone with the other.

I finished my cigarette to the tune of muffled struggle-sounds that seemed to come from the floor below. There were two more shots, far apart. Feet ran past the door of the room I was in. Perhaps ten minutes had gone since I had been left alone.

I found I wasn't alone.

Across the room from the door, the hangings that covered the wall were disturbed. The blue, green and silver velvet bulged out an inch and settled back in place.

The disturbance happened the second time perhaps ten feet farther along the wall. No movement for a while, and then a tremor in the far corner.

Somebody was creeping along between hangings and wall.

I let them creep, still slumping in my chair with idle hands. If the bulge meant trouble, action on my part would only bring it that much quicker.

I traced the disturbance down the length of that wall and halfway across the other, to where I knew the door was. Then I lost it for some time. I had just decided that the creeper had gone through the door when the curtains opened and the creeper stepped out.

She wasn't four and a half feet high—a living ornament from somebody's shelf. Her face was a tiny oval of painted beauty, its perfection emphasized by the lacquer-black hair that was flat and glossy around her temples. Gold earrings swung beside her smooth cheeks, a jade butterfly was in her hair. A lavender jacket, glittering with white stones, covered her from under her chin to her knees. Lavender stockings showed under her short lavender trousers, and her bound-small feet were in slippers of the same color, shaped like kittens, with yellow stones for eyes and aigrettes for whiskers.

The point of all this our-young-ladies'-fashion stuff is that she was impossibly dainty. But there she was—neither a carving nor a painting, but a living small woman with fear in her black eyes and nervous, tiny fingers worrying the silk at her bosom.

Twice as she came toward me—hurrying with the awkward, quick step of the foot-bound Chinese woman—her head twisted around for a look at the hangings over the door.

I was on my feet by now, going to meet her.

Her English wasn't much. Most of what she babbled at me I missed, though I thought "yung hel-lup" might have been meant for "You help?"

I nodded, catching her under the elbows as she stumbled against me.

She gave me some more language that didn't make the situation any clearer—unless "sul-lay-vee gull" meant slave-girl and "tak-ka wah" meant take away.

"You want me to get you out of here?" I asked.

Her head, close under my chin, went up and down, and her red flower of a mouth shaped a smile that made all the other smiles I could remember look like leers.

She did some more talking. I got nothing out of it. Taking one of her elbows out of my hand, she pushed up her sleeve, baring a forearm that an artist had spent a life-time carving out of ivory. On it were five finger-shaped bruises ending in cuts where the nails had punctured the flesh.

She let the sleeve fall over it again, and gave me more words. They didn't mean anything to me, but they tinkled prettily.

"All right," I said, sliding my gun out. "If you want to go, we'll go."

Both her hands went to the gun, pushing it down, and she talked excitedly into my face, winding up with a flicking of one hand across her collar—a pantomime of a throat being cut.

I shook my head from side to side and urged her toward the door.

She balked, fright large in her eyes.

One of her hands went to my watch-pocket. I let her take the watch out.

She put the tiny tip of one pointed finger over the twelve and then circled the dial three times. I thought I got that. Thirty-six hours from noon would be midnight of the following night—Thursday.

"Yes," I said.

She shot a look at the door and led me to the table where the tea things were. With a finger dipped in cold tea she began to draw on the table's inlaid top. Two parallel lines I took for a street. Another pair crossed them. The third pair crossed the second and paralleled the first.

"Waverly Place?" I guessed.

Her face bobbed up and down, delightedly.

On what I took for the east side of Waverly Place she drew a square—perhaps a house. In the square she set what could have been a rose. I frowned at that. She erased the rose and in its place put a crooked circle, adding dots. I thought I had it. The rose had been a cabbage. This thing was a potato. The square represented the grocery store I had noticed on Waverly Place. I nodded.

Her finger crossed the street and put a square on the other side, and her face turned up to mine, begging me to understand her.

"The house across the street from the grocer's," I said slowly, and then, as she tapped my watch-pocket, I added, "at midnight tomorrow."

I don't know how much of it she caught, but she nodded her little head until her earrings were swinging like crazy pendulums.

With a quick diving motion, she caught my right hand, kissed it, and with a tottering, hoppy run vanished behind the velvet curtains.

I used my handkerchief to wipe the map off the table and was smoking in my chair when Chang Li Ching returned some twenty minutes later.

I left shortly after that, as soon as we had traded a few dizzy compliments. The pock-marked man ushered me out.

At the office there was nothing new for me. Foley hadn't been able to shadow The Whistler the night before.

I went home for the sleep I had not got last night.

VIII

At ten minutes after ten the next morning Lillian Shan and I arrived at the front door of Fong Yick's employment agency on Washington Street.

"Give me just two minutes," I told her as I climbed out. "Then come in."

"Better keep your steam up," I suggested to the driver. "We might have to slide away in a hurry."

In Fong Yick's, a lanky, grey-haired man whom I thought was the Old Man's Frank Paul was talking around a chewed cigar to half a dozen Chinese. Across the battered counter a fat Chinese was watching them boredly through immense steel-rimmed spectacles.

I looked at the half-dozen. The third from me had a crooked nose—a short, squat man.

I pushed aside the others and reached for him.

I don't know what the stuff he tried on me was—jiu jitsu,

maybe, or its Chinese equivalent. Anyhow, he crouched and moved his stiffly open hands trickily.

I took hold of him here and there, and presently had him by the nape of his neck, with one of his arms bent up behind him.

Another Chinese piled on my back. The lean, grey-haired man did something to his face, and the Chinese went over in a corner and stayed there.

That was the situation when Lillian Shan came in.

I shook the flat-nosed boy at her.

"Yin Hung!" she exclaimed.

"Hoo Lun isn't one of the others?" I asked, pointing to the spectators.

She shook her head emphatically, and began jabbering Chinese at my prisoner. He jabbered back, meeting her gaze.

"What are you going to do with him?" she asked me in a voice that wasn't quite right.

"Turn him over to the police to hold for the San Mateo sheriff. Can you get anything out of him?"

"No."

I began to push him toward the door. The steel-spectacled Chinese blocked the way, one hand behind him.

"No can do," he said.

I slammed Yin Hung into him. He went back against the wall.

"Get out!" I yelled at the girl.

The grey-haired man stopped two Chinese who dashed for the door, sent them the other way—back hard against the wall.

We left the place.

There was no excitement in the street. We climbed into the taxicab and drove the block and a half to the Hall of Justice, where I yanked my prisoner out. The rancher Paul said he wouldn't go in, that he had enjoyed the party, but now had some of his own business to look after. He went on up Kearney Street afoot.

Half-out of the taxicab, Lillian Shan changed her mind.

"Unless it's necessary," she said, "I'd rather not go in either. I'll wait here for you."

"Righto," and I pushed my captive across the sidewalk and up the steps.

Inside, an interesting situation developed.

The San Francisco police weren't especially interested in Yin Hung, though willing enough, of course, to hold him for the sheriff of San Mateo County.

Yin Hung pretended he didn't know any English, and I was curious to know what sort of story he had to tell, so I hunted around in the detectives' assembly room until I found Bill Thode of the Chinatown detail, who talks the language some.

He and Yin Hung jabbered at each other for some time.

Then Bill looked at me, laughed, bit off the end of a cigar, and leaned back in his chair.

"According to the way he tells it," Bill said, "that Wan Lan woman and Lillian Shan had a row. The next day Wan Lan's not anywheres around. The Shan girl and Wang Ma, her maid, say Wan Lan has left, but Hoo Lun tells this fellow he saw Wang Ma burning some of Wan Lan's clothes.

"So Hoo Lun and this fellow think something's wrong, and the next day they're damned sure of it, because this fellow misses a spade from his garden tools. He finds it again that night, and it's still wet with damp dirt, and he says no dirt was dug up anywheres around the place—not outside of the house anyways. So him and Hoo Lun put their heads together, didn't like the result, and decided they'd better dust out before they went wherever Wan Lan had gone. That's the message."

"Where is Hoo Lun now?"

"He says he don't know."

"So Lillian Shan and Wang Ma were still in the house when this pair left?" I asked. "They hadn't started for the East yet?"

"So he says."

"Has he got any idea why Wan Lan was killed?"

"Not that I've been able to get out of him."

"Thanks, Bill! You'll notify the sheriff that you're holding him?"

"Sure."

Of course Lillian Shan and the taxicab were gone when I came out of the Hall of Justice door.

I went back into the lobby and used one of the booths to phone the office. Still no report from Dick Foley—nothing of any value—and none from the operative who was trying to shadow Jack Garthorne. A wire had come from the Richmond branch. It was to the effect that the Garthornes were a wealthy and well-known local family, that young Jack was usually in trouble, that he had slugged a Prohibition agent during a cafe raid a few months ago, that his father had taken him out of his will and chased him from the house, but that his mother was believed to be sending him money.

That fit in with what the girl had told me.

A street car carried me to the garage where I had stuck the roadster I had borrowed from the girl's garage the previous morning. I drove around to Cipriano's apartment building. He had no news of any importance for me. He had spent the night hanging around Chinatown, but had picked up nothing.

I was a little inclined toward grouchiness as I turned the roadster west, driving out through Golden Gate Park to the Ocean Boulevard. The job wasn't getting along as snappily as I wanted it to.

I let the roadster slide down the boulevard at a good clip, and the salt air blew some of my kinks away.

A bony-faced man with pinkish mustache opened the door when I rang Lillian Shan's bell. I knew him—Tucker, a deputy sheriff.

"Hullo," he said. "What d'you want?"

"I'm hunting for her too."

"Keep on hunting," he grinned. "Don't let me stop you."

"Not here, huh?"

"Nope. The Swede woman that works for her says she was in and out half an hour before I got here, and I've been here about ten minutes now."

"Got a warrant for her?" I asked.

"You bet you! Her chauffeur squawked."

"Yes, I heard him," I said. "I'm the bright boy who gathered him in."

I spent five or ten minutes more talking to Tucker and then climbed in the roadster again.

"Will you give the agency a ring when you nab her?" I asked as I closed the door.

"You bet you."

I pointed the roadster at San Francisco again.

Just outside of Daly City a taxicab passed me, going south. Jack Garthorne's face looked through the window.

I snapped on the brakes and waved my arm. The taxicab turned and came back to me. Garthorne opened the door, but did not get out.

I got down into the road and went over to him.

"There's a deputy sheriff waiting in Miss Shan's house, if that's where you're headed."

His blue eyes jumped wide, and then narrowed as he looked suspiciously at me.

"Let's go over to the side of the road and have a little talk," I invited.

He got out of the taxicab and we crossed to a couple of comfortable-looking boulders on the other side.

"Where is Lil—Miss Shan?" he asked.

"Ask The Whistler," I suggested.

This blond kid wasn't so good. It took him a long time to get his gun out. I let him go through with it.

"What do you mean?" he demanded.

I hadn't meant anything. I had just wanted to see how the remark would hit him. I kept quiet.

"Has The Whistler got her?"

"I don't think so," I admitted, though I hated to do it. "But the point is that she has had to go in hiding to keep from being hanged for the murders The Whistler framed."

"Hanged?"

"Uh-huh. The deputy waiting in her house has a warrant for her—for murder."

He put away his gun and made gurgling noises in his throat.

"I'll go there! I'll tell everything I know!"

He started for his taxicab.

"Wait!" I called. "Maybe you'd better tell me what you know first. I'm working for her, you know."

He spun around and came back.

"Yes, that's right. You'll know what to do."

"Now what do you really know, if anything?" I asked when he was standing in front of me.

"I know the whole thing!" he cried. "About the deaths and the booze and——"

"Easy! Easy! There's no use wasting all that knowledge on the chauffeur."

He quieted down, and I began to pump him. I spent nearly an hour getting all of it.

IX

The history of his young life, as he told it to me, began with his departure from home after falling into disgrace through slugging the Prohi. He had come to San Francisco to wait until his father cooled off. Meanwhile his mother kept him in funds, but she didn't send him all the money a young fellow in a wild city could use.

That was the situation when he ran into The Whistler, who suggested that a chap with Garthorne's front could pick up some easy money in the rum-running game if he did what he was told to do. Garthorne was willing enough. He didn't like Prohibition—it had caused most of his troubles. Rum-running sounded romantic to him—shots in the dark, signal lights off the starboard bow, and so on.

The Whistler, it seemed, had boats and booze and waiting customers, but his landing arrangements were out of whack. He had his eye on a little cove down the shore line that was an ideal spot to land hooch. It was neither too close nor too far from San Francisco. It was sheltered on either side by rocky points, and screened from the road by a large house and high hedges. Given the use of that house, his troubles would be over. He could land his hooch in the cove, run it into the house, repack it innocently there, put it through the front door into his automobiles, and shoot it to the thirsty city.

The house, he told Garthorne, belonged to a Chinese girl named Lillian Shan, who would neither sell nor rent it. Garthorne was to make her acquaintance—The Whistler was already supplied with a letter of introduction written by a former classmate of the girl's, a classmate who had fallen a lot since university days—and try to work himself in with her to a degree of intimacy that would permit him to make her an offer for the use of the house. That is, he was to find out if she was the sort of person who could be approached with a more or less frank offer of a share in the profits of The Whistler's game.

Garthorne had gone through with his part, or the first of it, and had become fairly intimate with the girl, when she suddenly left for the East, sending him a note saying she would be gone several months. That was fine for the rum-runners. Garthorne, calling at the house, the next day, had learned that Wang Ma had gone with her mistress, and that the three other servants had been left in charge of the house.

That was all Garthorne knew firsthand. He had not taken part in the landing of the booze, though he would have liked to. But The Whistler had ordered him to stay away, so that he could continue his original part when the girl returned.

The Whistler told Garthorne he had bought the help of the three Chinese servants, but that the woman, Wan Lan, had been killed by the two men in a fight over their shares of the money. Booze had been run through the house once during Lillian Shan's absence. Her unexpected return gummed things. The house still held some of the booze. They had to grab her and Wang Ma and stick them in a closet until they got the stuff away. The strangling of Wang Ma had been accidental—a rope tied too tight.

The worst complication, however, was that another cargo was scheduled to land in the cove the following Tuesday night, and there was no way of getting word out to the boat that the place was closed. The Whistler sent for our hero and ordered him to get the girl out of the way and keep her out of the way until at least two o'clock Wednesday morning.

Garthorne had invited her to drive down to Half Moon with him for dinner that night. She had accepted. He had faked engine trouble, and had kept her away from the house until two-thirty, and The Whistler had told him later that everything had gone through without a hitch.

After this I had to guess at what Garthorne was driving at—he stuttered and stammered and let his ideas rattle looser than ever. I think it added up to this: he hadn't thought much about the ethics of his play with the girl. She had no attraction for him—too severe and serious to seem really feminine. And he had not pretended—hadn't carried on what could possibly be called a flirtation with her. Then he suddenly woke up to the fact that she wasn't as indifferent as he. That had been a shock to him—one he couldn't stand. He had seen things straight for the first time. He had thought of it before as simply a wit-matching game. Affection made it different—even though the affection was all on one side.

"I told The Whistler I was through this afternoon," he finished.

"How did he like it?"

"Not a lot. In fact, I had to hit him."

"So? And what were you planning to do next?"

"I was going to see Miss Shan, tell her the truth, and then—then I thought I'd better lay low."

"I think you'd better. The Whistler might not like being hit."

"I won't hide now! I'll go give myself up and tell the truth."

"Forget it!" I advised him. "That's no good. You don't know enough to help her."

That wasn't exactly the truth, because he did know that the chauffeur and Hoo Lun had still been in the house the day after her departure for the East. But I didn't want him to get out of the game yet.

"If I were you," I went on, "I'd pick out a quiet hiding place and stay there until I can get word to you. Know a good place?"

"Yes," slowly. "I have a—a friend who will hide me—down near—near the Latin Quarter."

"Near the Latin Quarter?" That could be Chinatown. I did some sharp shooting. "Waverly Place?"

He jumped.

"How did you know?"

"I'm a detective. I know everything. Ever hear of Chang Li Ching?"

"No."

I tried to keep from laughing into his puzzled face.

The first time I had seen this cut-up he was leaving a house in Waverly Place, with a Chinese woman's face showing dimly in the doorway behind him. The house had been across the street from a grocery. The Chinese girl with whom I had talked at Chang's had given me a slave-girl yarn and an invitation to that same house. Big-hearted Jack here had fallen for the same game, but he didn't know that the girl had anything to do with Chang Li Ching, didn't know that Chang existed, didn't know Chang and The Whistler were playmates. Now Jack is in trouble, and he's going to the girl to hide!

I didn't dislike this angle of the game. He was walking into a trap, but that was nothing to me—or, rather, I hoped it was going to help me.

"What's your friend's name?" I asked.

He hesitated.

"What is the name of the tiny woman whose door is across the street from the grocery?" I made myself plain.

"Hsiu Hsiu."

"All right," I encouraged him in his foolishness. "You go there. That's an excellent hiding place. Now if I want to get a Chinese boy to you with a message, how will he find you?"

"There's a flight of steps to the left as you go in. He'll have to skip the second and third steps, because they are fitted with some sort of alarm. So is the handrail. On the second floor you turn to the left again. The hall is dark. The second door to the right—on the right-hand side of the hall—lets you into a room. On the other side of the room is a closet, with a door hidden behind old clothes. There are usually people in the room the door opens into, so he'll have to wait for a chance to get through it. This room has a little balcony outside, that you can get to from either of the windows. The balcony's sides are solid, so if you crouch low you can't be seen from the street or from other houses. At the other end of the balcony there are two loose floor boards. You slide down under them into a little room between walls. The trap-door there will let you down into another just like it where I'll probably be. There's another way out of the bottom room, down a flight of steps, but I've never been that way."

A fine mess! It sounded like a child's game. But even with all this frosting on the cake our young chump hadn't tumbled. He took it seriously.

"So that's how it's done!" I said. "You'd better get there as soon as you can, and stay there until my messenger gets to you. You'll know him by the cast in one of his eyes, and maybe I'd better give him a password. Haphazard—that'll be the word. The street door—is it locked?"

"No. I've never found it locked. There are forty or fifty Chinamen—or perhaps a hundred—living in that building, so I don't suppose the door is ever locked."

"Good. Beat it now."

X

At 10:15 that night I was pushing open the door opposite the grocery in Waverly Place—an hour and three-quarters early for my date with Hsiu Hsiu. At 9:55 Dick Foley had phoned that The Whistler had gone into the red-painted door on Spofford Alley.

I found the interior dark, and closed the door softly, concentrating on the childish directions Garthorne had given me. That I knew they were silly didn't help me, since I didn't know any other route.

The stairs gave me some trouble, but I got over the second and third without touching the handrail, and went on up. I found the second door in the hall, the closet in the room behind it, and the door in the closet. Light came through the cracks around it. Listening, I heard nothing.

I pushed the door open—the room was empty. A smoking oil lamp stunk there. The nearest window made no sound as I raised it. That was inartistic—a squeak would have impressed Garthorne with his danger.

I crouched low on the balcony, in accordance with instructions, and found the loose floorboards that opened up a black hole. Feet first, I went down in, slanting at an angle that made descent easy. It seemed to be a sort of slot cut diagonally through the wall. It was stuffy, and I don't like narrow holes. I went down swiftly, coming into a small room, long and narrow, as if placed inside a thick wall.

No light was there. My flashlight showed a room perhaps eighteen feet long by four wide, furnished with table, couch and two chairs. I looked under the one rug on the floor. The trapdoor was there—a crude affair that didn't pretend it was part of the floor.

Flat on my belly, I put an ear to the trapdoor. No sound. I raised it a couple of inches. Darkness and a faint murmuring of voices. I pushed the trapdoor wide, let it down easily on the floor and stuck head and shoulders into the opening, discovering then that it was a double arrangement. Another door was below, fitting no doubt in the ceiling of the room below.

Cautiously I let myself down on it. It gave under my foot. I could have pulled myself up again, but since I had disturbed it I chose to keep going.

I put both feet on it. It swung down. I dropped into light. The door snapped up over my head. I grabbed Hsiu Hsiu and clapped a hand over her tiny mouth in time to keep her quiet.

"Hello," I said to the startled Garthorne; "this is my boy's evening off, so I came myself."

"Hello," he gasped.

This room, I saw, was a duplicate of the one from which I had dropped, another cupboard between walls, though this one had an unpainted wooden door at one end.

I handed Hsiu Hsiu to Garthorne.

"Keep her quiet," I ordered, "while——"

The clicking of the door's latch silenced me. I jumped to the wall on the hinged side of the door just as it swung open—the opener hidden from me by the door.

The door opened wide, but not much wider than Jack Garthorne's blue eyes, nor than his mouth. I let the door go back against the wall and stepped out behind my balanced gun.

The queen of something stood there!

She was a tall woman, straight-bodied and proud. A butterfly-shaped headdress decked with the loot of a dozen jewelry stores exaggerated her height. Her gown was amethyst fili-greed with gold above, a living rainbow below. The clothes were nothing!

She was—maybe I can make it clear this way. Hsiu Hsiu was as perfect a bit of feminine beauty as could be imagined. She was perfect! Then comes this queen of something—and Hsiu Hsiu's beauty went away. She was a candle in the sun. She was still pretty—prettier than the woman in the doorway, if it came to that—but you didn't pay any attention to her.

Hsiu Hsiu was a pretty girl: this royal woman in the doorway was—I don't know the words.

"My God!" Garthorne was whispering harshly. "I never knew it!"

"What are you doing here?" I challenged the woman.

She didn't hear me. She was looking at Hsiu Hsiu as a tigress might look at an alley cat. Hsiu Hsiu was looking at her as an alley cat might look at a tigress. Sweat was on Garthorne's face and his mouth was the mouth of a sick man.

"What are you doing here?" I repeated, stepping closer to Lillian Shan.

"I am here where I belong," she said slowly, not taking her eyes from the slave-girl. "I have come back to my people."

That was a lot of bunk. I turned to the goggling Garthorne.

"Take Hsiu Hsiu to the upper room, and keep her quiet, if you have to strangle her. I want to talk to Miss Shan."

Still dazed, he pushed the table under the trapdoor, climbed up on it, hoisted himself through the ceiling, and reached down. Hsiu Hsiu kicked and scratched, but I heaved her up to him. Then I closed the door through which Lillian Shan had come, and faced her.

"How did you get here?" I demanded.

"I went home after I left you, knowing what Yin Hung would say, because he had told me in the employment office, and when I got home— When I got home I decided to come here where I belong."

"Nonsense!" I corrected her. "When you got home you found a message there from Chang Li Ching, asking you—ordering you to come here."

She looked at me, saying nothing.

"What did Chang want?"

"He thought perhaps he could help me," she said, "and so I stayed here."

More nonsense.

"Chang told you Garthorne was in danger—had split with The Whistler."

"The Whistler?"

"You made a bargain with Chang," I accused her, paying no attention to her question. The chances were she didn't know The Whistler by that name.

She shook her head, jiggling the ornaments on her head-dress.

"There was no bargain," she said, holding my gaze too steadily.

I didn't believe her. I said so.

"You gave Chang your house—or the use of it—in exchange for his promise that"—the boob were the first words I thought of, but I changed them—"Garthorne would be saved from The Whistler, and that you would be saved from the law."

She drew herself up.

"I did," she said calmly.

I caught myself weakening. This woman who looked like the queen of something wasn't easy to handle the way I wanted to handle her. I made myself remember that I knew her when she was homely as hell in mannish clothes.

"You ought to be spanked!" I growled at her. "Haven't you had enough trouble without mixing yourself now with a flock of highbinders? Did you see The Whistler?"

"There was a man up there," she said. "I don't know his name."

I hunted through my pocket and found the picture of him taken when he was sent to San Quentin.

"That is he," she told me when I showed it to her.

"A fine partner you picked," I raged. "What do you think his word on anything is worth?"

"I did not take his word for anything. I took Chang Li Ching's word."

"That's just as bad. They're mates. What was your bargain?"

She balked again, straight, stiff-necked and level-eyed. Because she was getting away from me with this Manchu princess stuff I got peevish.

"Don't be a chump all your life!" I pleaded. "You think you made a deal. They took you in! What do you think they're using your house for?"

She tried to look me down. I tried another angle of attack.

"Here, you don't mind who you make bargains with. Make one with me. I'm still one prison sentence ahead of The Whistler, so if his word is any good at all, mine ought to be highly valuable. You tell me what the deal was. If it's half-way decent, I'll promise you to crawl out of here and forget it. If you don't tell me, I'm going to empty a gun out of the first window I can find. And you'd be surprised how many cops a shot will draw in this part of town, and how fast it'll draw them."

The threat took some of the color out of her face.

"If I tell, you will promise to do nothing?"

"You missed part of it," I reminded her. "If I think the deal is half-way on the level I'll keep quiet."

She bit her lips and let her fingers twist together, and then it came.

"Chang Li Ching is one of the leaders of the anti-Japanese movement in China. Since the death of Sun Wen—or Sun Yat-Sen, as he is called in the south of China and here—the Japanese have increased their hold on the Chinese government until it is greater than it ever was. It is Sun Wen's work that Chang Li Ching and his friends are carrying on.

"With their own government against them, their immediate necessity is to arm enough patriots to resist Japanese aggression when the time comes. That is what my house is used for. Rifles and ammunition are loaded into boats there and sent out to ships lying far offshore. This man you call The Whistler is the owner of the ships that carry the arms to China."

"And the death of the servants?" I asked.

"Wan Lan was a spy for the Chinese government—for the Japanese. Wang Ma's death was an accident, I think, though she, too, was suspected of being a spy. To a patriot, the death of traitors is a necessary thing, you can understand that? Your people are like that too when your country is in danger."

"Garthorne told me a rum-running story," I said. "How about it?"

"He believed it," she said, smiling softly at the trapdoor through which he had gone. "They told him that, because they did not know him well enough to trust him. That is why they would not let him help in the loading."

One of her hands came out to rest on my arm.

"You will go away and keep silent?" she pleaded. "These things are against the law of your country, but would you not break another country's laws to save your own country's life? Have not four hundred million people the right to fight an alien race that would exploit them? Since the day of Taou-kwang my country has been the plaything of more aggressive nations. Is any price too great for patriotic Chinese to pay to end that period of dishonor? You will not put yourself in the way of my people's liberty?"

"I hope they win," I said, "but you've been tricked. The only guns that have gone through your house have gone through in pockets! It would take a year to get a shipload through there. Maybe Chang is running guns to China. It's likely. But they don't go through your place.

"The night I was there coolies went through—coming in, not going out. They came from the beach, and they left in machines. Maybe The Whistler is running the guns over for Chang and bringing coolies back. He can get anything from a thousand dollars up for each one he lands. That's about the how of it. He runs the guns over for Chang, and brings his own stuff—coolies and no doubt some opium—back, getting his big profit on the return trip. There wouldn't be enough money in the guns to interest him.

"The guns would be loaded at a pier, all regular, mas-querading as something else. Your house is used for the re-turn. Chang may or may not be tied up with the coolie and opium game, but it's a cinch he'll let The Whistler do what-ever he likes if only The Whistler will run his guns across. So, you see, you have been gypped!"

"But——"

"But nothing! You're helping Chang by taking part in the coolie traffic. And, my guess is, your servants were killed, not because they were spies, but because they wouldn't sell you out."

She was white-faced and unsteady on her feet. I didn't let her recover.

"Do you think Chang trusts The Whistler? Did they seem friendly?"

I knew he couldn't trust him, but I wanted something specific.

"No-o-o," she said slowly. "There was some talk about a missing boat."

That was good.

"They still together?"

"Yes."

"How do I get there?"

"Down these steps, across the cellar—straight across—and up two flights of steps on the other side. They were in a room to the right of the second-floor landing."

Thank God I had a direct set of instructions for once!

I jumped up on the table and rapped on the ceiling.

"Come on down, Garthorne, and bring your chaperon."

"Don't either of you budge out of here until I'm back," I told the boob and Lillian Shan when we were all together again. "I'm going to take Hsiu Hsiu with me. Come on, sister, I want you to talk to any bad men I meet. We go to see Chang Li Ching, you understand?" I made faces. "One yell out of you, and—" I put my fingers around her collar and pressed them lightly.

She giggled, which spoiled the effect a little.

"To Chang," I ordered, and, holding her by one shoulder, urged her toward the door.

We went down into the dark cellar, across it, found the other stairs, and started to climb them. Our progress was slow. The girl's bound feet weren't made for fast walking.

A dim light burned on the first floor, where we had to turn to go up to the second floor. We had just made the turn when footsteps sounded behind us.

I lifted the girl up two steps, out of the light, and crouched beside her, holding her still. Four Chinese in wrinkled street clothes came down the first-floor hall, passed our stairs without a glance, and started on.

Hsiu Hsiu opened her red flower of a mouth and let out a squeal that could have been heard over in Oakland.

I cursed, turned her loose, and started up the steps. The four Chinese came after me. On the landing ahead one of Chang's big wrestlers appeared—a foot of thin steel in his paw. I looked back.

Hsiu Hsiu sat on the bottom step, her head over her shoulder, experimenting with different sorts of yells and screams, enjoyment all over her laughing doll's face. One of the climbing yellow men was loosening an automatic.

My legs pushed me on up toward the man-eater at the head of the steps.

When he crouched close above me I let him have it.

My bullet cut the gullet out of him.

I patted his face with my gun as he tumbled down past me.

A hand caught one of my ankles.

Clinging to the railing, I drove my other foot back. Something stopped my foot. Nothing stopped me.

A bullet flaked some of the ceiling down as I made the head of the stairs and jumped for the door to the right.

Pulling it open, I plunged in.

The other of the big man-eaters caught me—caught my plunging hundred and eighty-some pounds as a boy would catch a rubber ball.

Across the room, Chang Li Ching ran plump fingers through his thin whiskers and smiled at me. Beside him, a man I knew for The Whistler started up from his chair, his beefy face twitching.

"The Prince of Hunters is welcome," Chang said, and added something in Chinese to the man-eater who held me.

The man-eater set me down on my feet, and turned to shut the door on my pursuers.

The Whistler sat down again, his red-veined eyes shifty on me, his bloated face empty of enjoyment.

I tucked my gun inside my clothes before I started across the room toward Chang. And crossing the room, I noticed something.

Behind The Whistler's chair the velvet hangings bulged just the least bit, not enough to have been noticed by anyone who hadn't seen them bulge before. So Chang didn't trust his confederate at all!

"I have something I want you to see," I told the old Chinese when I was standing in front of him, or, rather, in front of the table that was in front of him.

"That eye is privileged indeed which may gaze on anything brought by the Father of Avengers."

"I have heard," I said, as I put my hand in my pocket, "that all that starts for China doesn't get there."

The Whistler jumped up from his chair again, his mouth a snarl, his face a dirty pink. Chang Li Ching looked at him, and he sat down again.

I brought out the photograph of The Whistler standing in a group of Japs, the medal of the Order of the Rising Sun on his chest. Hoping Chang had not heard of the swindle and would not know the medal for a counterfeit, I dropped the photograph on the table.

The Whistler craned his neck, but could not see the picture.

Chang Li Ching looked at it for a long moment over his clasped hands, his old eyes shrewd and kindly, his face gentle. No muscle in his face moved. Nothing changed in his eyes.

The nails of his right hand slowly cut a red gash across the back of the clasped left hand.

"It is true," he said softly, "that one acquires wisdom in the company of the wise."

He unclasped his hands, picked up the photograph, and held it out to the beefy man. The Whistler seized it. His face drained grey, his eyes bulged out.

"Why, that's—" he began, and stopped, let the photograph drop to his lap, and slumped down in an attitude of defeat.

That puzzled me. I had expected to argue with him, to convince Chang that the medal was not the fake it was.

"You may have what you wish in payment for this," Chang Li Ching was saying to me.

"I want Lillian Shan and Garthorne cleared, and I want your fat friend here, and I want anybody else who was in on the killings."

Chang's eyes closed for a moment—the first sign of weariness I had seen on his round face.

"You may have them," he said.

"The bargain you made with Miss Shan is all off, of course," I pointed out. "I may need a little evidence to make sure I can hang this baby," nodding at The Whistler.

Chang smiled dreamily.

"That, I am regretful, is not possible."

"Why—?" I began, and stopped.

There was no bulge in the velvet curtain behind The Whistler now, I saw. One of the chair legs glistened in the light. A red pool spread on the floor under him. I didn't have to see his back to know he was beyond hanging.

"That's different," I said, kicking a chair over to the table. "Now we'll talk business."

I sat down and we went into conference.

XI

Two days later everything was cleared up to the satisfaction of police, press and public. The Whistler had been found in a dark street, hours dead from a cut in his back, killed in a bootlegging war, I heard. Hoo Lun was found. The gold-toothed Chinese who had opened the door for Lillian Shan was found. Five others were found. These seven, with Yin Hung, the chauffeur, eventually drew a life sentence apiece. They were The Whistler's men, and Chang sacrificed them without batting an eye. They had as little proof of Chang's complicity as I had, so they couldn't hit back, even if they knew that Chang had given me most of my evidence against them.

Nobody but the girl, Chang and I knew anything about Garthorne's part, so he was out, with liberty to spend most of his time at the girl's house.

I had no proof that I could tie on Chang, couldn't get any. Regardless of his patriotism, I'd have given my right eye to put the old boy away. That would have been something to write home about. But there hadn't been a chance of nailing him, so I had had to be content with making a bargain whereby he turned everything over to me except himself and his friends.

I don't know what happened to Hsiu Hsiu, the squealing slave-girl. She deserved to come through all right. I might have gone back to Chang's to ask about her, but I stayed away. Chang had learned that the medal in the photo was a trick one. I had a note from him:

> Greetings and Great Love to the Unveiler of
>   Secrets:
>   One whose patriotic fervor and inherent stupid-
> ity combined to blind him, so that he broke a

valuable tool, trusts that the fortunes of worldly traffic will not again ever place his feeble wits in opposition to the irresistible will and dazzling intellect of the Emperor of Untanglers.

You can take that any way you like. But I know the man who wrote it, and I don't mind admitting that I've stopped eating in Chinese restaurants, and that if I never have to visit Chinatown again it'll be soon enough.

The Gutting of Couffignal

W EDGE-SHAPED Couffignal is not a large island, and not far from the mainland, to which it is linked by a wooden bridge. Its western shore is a high, straight cliff that jumps abruptly up out of San Pablo Bay. From the top of this cliff the island slopes eastward, down to a smooth pebble beach that runs into the water again, where there are piers and a clubhouse and moored pleasure boats.

Couffignal's main street, paralleling the beach, has the usual bank, hotel, moving-picture theater, and stores. But it differs from most main streets of its size in that it is more carefully arranged and preserved. There are trees and hedges and strips of lawn on it, and no glaring signs. The buildings seem to belong beside one another, as if they had been de-signed by the same architect, and in the stores you will find goods of a quality to match the best city stores.

The intersecting streets—running between rows of neat cottages near the foot of the slope—become winding hedged roads as they climb toward the cliff. The higher these roads get, the farther apart and larger are the houses they lead to. The occupants of these higher houses are the owners and rulers of the island. Most of them are well-fed old gentlemen who, the profits they took from the world with both hands in their younger days now stowed away at safe percentages, have bought into the island colony so they may spend what is left of their lives nursing their livers and improving their golf among their kind. They admit to the island only as many storekeepers, working-people, and similar riffraff as are needed to keep them comfortably served.

That is Couffignal.

It was some time after midnight. I was sitting in a second-story room in Couffignal's largest house, surrounded by wedding presents whose value would add up to something between fifty and a hundred thousand dollars.

Of all the work that comes to a private detective (except di-vorce work, which the Continental Detective Agency doesn't handle) I like weddings as little as any. Usually I manage to avoid them, but this time I hadn't been able to. Dick Foley, who had been slated for the job, had been handed a black eye by an unfriendly pickpocket the day before. That let Dick out and me in. I had come up to Couffignal—a two-hour ride from San Francisco by ferry and auto stage—that morning, and would return the next.

This had been neither better nor worse than the usual wedding detail. The ceremony had been performed in a little stone church down the hill. Then the house had begun to fill with reception guests. They had kept it filled to overflowing until some time after the bride and groom had sneaked off to their eastern train.

The world had been well represented. There had been an admiral and an earl or two from England; an ex-president of a South American country; a Danish baron; a tall young Russian princess surrounded by lesser titles, including a fat, bald, jovial and black-bearded Russian general who had talked to me for a solid hour about prize fights, in which he had a lot of interest, but not so much knowledge as was possible; an ambassador from one of the Central European countries; a justice of the Supreme Court; and a mob of people whose prominence and near-prominence didn't carry labels.

In theory, a detective guarding wedding presents is supposed to make himself indistinguishable from the other guests. In practice, it never works out that way. He has to spend most of his time within sight of the booty, so he's easily spotted. Besides that, eight or ten people I recognized among the guests were clients or former clients of the Agency, and so knew me. However, being known doesn't make so much difference as you might think, and everything had gone off smoothly.

A couple of the groom's friends, warmed by wine and the necessity of maintaining their reputations as cut-ups, had tried to smuggle some of the gifts out of the room where they were displayed and hide them in the piano. But I had been expecting that familiar trick, and blocked it before it had gone far enough to embarrass anybody.

Shortly after dark a wind smelling of rain began to pile storm clouds up over the bay. Those guests who lived at a distance, especially those who had water to cross, hurried off for their homes. Those who lived on the island stayed until the first raindrops began to patter down. Then they left.

The Hendrixson house quieted down. Musicians and extra servants left. The weary house servants began to disappear in the direction of their bedrooms. I found some sandwiches, a couple of books and a comfortable armchair, and took them up to the room where the presents were now hidden under grey-white sheeting.

Keith Hendrixson, the bride's grandfather—she was an orphan—put his head in at the door.

"Have you everything you need for your comfort?" he asked.

"Yes, thanks."

He said good night and went off to bed—a tall old man, slim as a boy.

The wind and the rain were hard at it when I went downstairs to give the lower windows and doors the up-and-down. Everything on the first floor was tight and secure, everything in the cellar. I went upstairs again.

Pulling my chair over by a floor lamp, I put sandwiches, books, ash-tray, gun and flashlight on a small table beside it. Then I switched off the other lights, set fire to a Fatima, sat down, wriggled my spine comfortably into the chair's padding, picked up one of the books, and prepared to make a night of it.

The book was called *The Lord of the Sea*, and had to do with a strong, tough and violent fellow named Hogarth, whose modest plan was to hold the world in one hand. There were plots and counterplots, kidnappings, murders, prison-breakings, forgeries and burglaries, diamonds large as hats and floating forts larger than Couffignal. It sounds dizzy here, but in the book it was as real as a dime.

Hogarth was still going strong when the lights went out.

II

In the dark, I got rid of the glowing end of my cigarette by grinding it in one of the sandwiches. Putting the book down, I picked up gun and flashlight, and moved away from the chair.

Listening for noises was no good. The storm was making hundreds of them. What I needed to know was why the lights had gone off. All the other lights in the house had been turned off some time ago. So the darkness of the hall told me nothing.

I waited. My job was to watch the presents. Nobody had touched them yet. There was nothing to get excited about.

Minutes went by, perhaps ten of them.

The floor swayed under my feet. The windows rattled with a violence beyond the strength of the storm. The dull boom of a heavy explosion blotted out the sounds of wind and falling water. The blast was not close at hand, but not far enough away to be off the island.

Crossing to the window, peering through the wet glass, I could see nothing. I should have seen a few misty lights far down the hill. Not being able to see them settled one point. The lights had gone out all over Couffignal, not only in the Hendrixson house.

That was better. The storm could have put the lighting system out of whack, could have been responsible for the explosion—maybe.

Staring through the black window, I had an impression of great excitement down the hill, of movement in the night. But all was too far away for me to have seen or heard even had there been lights, and all too vague to say what was moving. The impression was strong but worthless. It didn't lead anywhere. I told myself I was getting feeble-minded, and turned away from the window.

Another blast spun me back to it. This explosion sounded nearer than the first, maybe because it was stronger. Peering through the glass again, I still saw nothing. And still had the impression of things that were big moving down there.

Bare feet pattered in the hall. A voice was anxiously calling my name. Turning from the window again, I pocketed my gun and snapped on the flashlight. Keith Hendrixson, in pajamas and bathrobe, looking thinner and older than anybody could be, came into the room.

"Is it—"

"I don't think it's an earthquake," I said, since that is the first calamity your Californian thinks of. "The lights went off a little while ago. There have been a couple of explosions down the hill since the—"

I stopped. Three shots, close together, had sounded. Rifle-shots, but of the sort that only the heaviest of rifles could make. Then, sharp and small in the storm, came the report of a far-away pistol.

"What is it?" Hendrixson demanded.

"Shooting."

More feet were pattering in the halls, some bare, some shod. Excited voices whispered questions and exclamations. The butler, a solemn, solid block of a man, partly dressed, and carrying a lighted five-pronged candlestick, came in.

"Very good, Brophy," Hendrixson said as the butler put the candlestick on the table beside my sandwiches. "Will you try to learn what is the matter?"

"I have tried, sir. The telephone seems to be out of order, sir. Shall I send Oliver down to the village?"

"No-o. I don't suppose it's that serious. Do you think it is anything serious?" he asked me.

I said I didn't think so, but I was paying more attention to the outside than to him. I had heard a thin screaming that could have come from a distant woman, and a volley of small-arms shots. The racket of the storm muffled these shots, but when the heavier firing we had heard before broke out again, it was clear enough.

To have opened the window would have been to let in gallons of water without helping us to hear much clearer. I stood with an ear tilted to the pane, trying to arrive at some idea of what was happening outside.

Another sound took my attention from the window—the ringing of the doorbell. It rang loudly and persistently.

Hendrixson looked at me. I nodded.

"See who it is, Brophy," he said.

The butler went solemnly away, and came back even more solemnly.

"Princess Zhukovski," he announced.

She came running into the room—the tall Russian girl I had seen at the reception. Her eyes were wide and dark with excitement. Her face was very white and wet. Water ran in streams down her blue waterproof cape, the hood of which covered her dark hair.

"Oh, Mr. Hendrixson!" She had caught one of his hands in both of hers. Her voice, with nothing foreign in its accents, was the voice of one who is excited over a delightful surprise. "The bank is being robbed, and the—what do you call him?—marshal of police has been killed!"

"What's that?" the old man exclaimed, jumping awkwardly, because water from her cape had dripped down on one of his bare feet. "Weegan killed? And the bank robbed?"

"Yes! Isn't it terrible?" She said it as if she were saying wonderful. "When the first explosion woke us, the general sent Ignati down to find out what was the matter, and he got down there just in time to see the bank blown up. Listen!"

We listened, and heard a wild outbreak of mixed gun-fire.

"That will be the general arriving!" she said. "He'll enjoy himself most wonderfully. As soon as Ignati returned with the news, the general armed every male in the household from Aleksandr Sergyeevich to Ivan the cook, and led them out happier than he's been since he took his division to East Prussia in 1914."

"And the duchess?" Hendrixson asked.

"He left her at home with me, of course, and I furtively crept out and away from her while she was trying for the first time in her life to put water in a samovar. This is not the night for one to stay at home!"

"H-m-m," Hendrixson said, his mind obviously not on her words. "And the bank!"

He looked at me. I said nothing. The racket of another volley came to us.

"Could you do anything down there?" he asked.

"Maybe, but—" I nodded at the presents under their covers.

"Oh, those!" the old man said. "I'm as much interested in the bank as in them; and, besides, we will be here."

"All right!" I was willing enough to carry my curiosity down the hill. "I'll go down. You'd better have the butler stay in here, and plant the chauffeur inside the front door. Better give them guns if you have any. Is there a raincoat I can borrow? I brought only a light overcoat with me."

Brophy found a yellow slicker that fit me. I put it on, stowed gun and flashlight conveniently under it, and found my hat while Brophy was getting and loading an automatic pistol for himself and a rifle for Oliver, the mulatto chauffeur.

Hendrixson and the princess followed me downstairs. At the door I found she wasn't exactly following me—she was going with me.

"But, Sonya!" the old man protested.

"I'm not going to be foolish, though I'd like to," she promised him. "But I'm going back to my Irinia Androvana, who will perhaps have the samovar watered by now."

"That's a sensible girl!" Hendrixson said, and let us out into the rain and the wind.

It wasn't weather to talk in. In silence we turned downhill between two rows of hedging, with the storm driving at our backs. At the first break in the hedge I stopped, nodding toward the black blot a house made.

"That is your—"

Her laugh cut me short. She caught my arm and began to urge me down the road again.

"I only told Mr. Hendrixson that so he would not worry," she explained. "You do not think I am not going down to see the sights."

III

She was tall. I am short and thick. I had to look up to see her face—to see as much of it as the rain-grey night would let me see.

"You'll be soaked to the hide, running around in this rain," I objected.

"What of that? I am dressed for it."

She raised a foot to show me a heavy waterproof boot and a woolen-stockinged leg.

"There's no telling what we'll run into down there, and I've got work to do," I insisted. "I can't be looking out for you."

"I can look out for myself."

She pushed her cape aside to show me a square automatic pistol in one hand.

"You'll be in my way."

"I will not," she retorted. "You'll probably find I can help you. I'm as strong as you, and quicker, and I can shoot."

The reports of scattered shooting had punctuated our argument, but now the sound of heavier firing silenced the dozen objections to her company that I could still think of. After all, I could slip away from her in the dark if she became too much of a nuisance.

"Have it your own way," I growled, "but don't expect anything from me."

"You're so kind," she murmured as we got under way again, hurrying now, with the wind at our backs speeding us along.

Occasionally dark figures moved on the road ahead of us, but too far away to be recognizable. Presently a man passed us, running uphill—a tall man whose nightshirt hung out of his trousers, down below his coat, identifying him as a resident.

"They've finished the bank and are at Medcraft's!" he yelled as he went by.

"Medcraft is the jeweler," the girl informed me.

The sloping under our feet grew less sharp. The houses—dark but with faces vaguely visible here and there at windows—came closer together. Below, the flash of a gun could be seen now and then—orange streaks in the rain.

Our road put us into the lower end of the main street just as a staccato rat-ta-tat broke out.

I pushed the girl into the nearest doorway, and jumped in after her.

Bullets ripped through walls with the sound of hail tapping on leaves.

That was the thing I had taken for an exceptionally heavy rifle—a machine gun.

The girl had fallen back in a corner, all tangled up with something. I helped her up. The something was a boy of seventeen or so, with one leg and a crutch.

"It's the boy who delivers papers," Princess Zhukovski said, "and you've hurt him with your clumsiness."

The boy shook his head, grinning as he got up.

"No'm, I ain't hurt none, but you kind of scared me, jumping on me like that."

She had to stop and explain that she hadn't jumped on him, that she had been pushed into him by me, and that she was sorry and so was I.

"What's happening?" I asked the newsboy when I could get a word in.

"Everything," he boasted, as if some of the credit were his. "There must be a hundred of them, and they've blowed the bank wide open, and now some of 'em is in Medcraft's, and I guess they'll blow that up, too. And they killed Tom Weegan. They got a machine gun on a car in the middle of the street. That's it shooting now."

"Where's everybody—all the merry villagers?"

"Most of 'em are up behind the Hall. They can't do nothing, though, because the machine gun won't let 'em get near enough to see what they're shooting at, and that smart Bill Vincent told me to clear out, 'cause I've only got one leg, as if I couldn't shoot as good as the next one, if I only had something to shoot with!"

"That wasn't right of them," I sympathized. "But you can do something for me. You can stick here and keep your eye on this end of the street, so I'll know if they leave in this direction."

"You're not just saying that so I'll stay here out of the way, are you?"

"No," I lied. "I need somebody to watch. I was going to leave the princess here, but you'll do better."

"Yes," she backed me up, catching the idea. "This gentleman is a detective, and if you do what he asks you'll be helping more than if you were up with the others."

The machine gun was still firing, but not in our direction now.

"I'm going across the street," I told the girl. "If you—"

"Aren't you going to join the others?"

"No. If I can get around behind the bandits while they're busy with the others, maybe I can turn a trick.

"Watch sharp now!" I ordered the boy, and the princess and I made a dash for the opposite sidewalk.

We reached it without drawing lead, sidled along a building for a few yards, and turned into an alley. From the alley's other end came the smell and wash and the dull blackness of the bay.

While we moved down this alley I composed a scheme by which I hoped to get rid of my companion, sending her off on a safe wild-goose chase. But I didn't get a chance to try it out.

The big figure of a man loomed ahead of us.

Stepping in front of the girl, I went on toward him. Under my slicker I held my gun on the middle of him.

He stood still. He was larger than he had looked at first. A big, slope-shouldered, barrel-bodied husky. His hands were empty. I spotted the flashlight on his face for a split second. A flat-cheeked, thick-featured face, with high cheek-bones and a lot of ruggedness in it.

"Ignati!" the girl exclaimed over my shoulder.

He began to talk what I suppose was Russian to the girl. She laughed and replied. He shook his big head stubbornly, insisting on something. She stamped her foot and spoke sharply. He shook his head again and addressed me.

"General Pleshskev, he tell me bring Princess Sonya to home."

His English was almost as hard to understand as his Russian. His tone puzzled me. It was as if he was explaining some absolutely necessary thing that he didn't want to be blamed for, but that nevertheless he was going to do.

While the girl was speaking to him again, I guessed the answer. This big Ignati had been sent out by the general to bring the girl home, and he was going to obey his orders if he had to carry her. He was trying to avoid trouble with me by explaining the situation.

"Take her," I said, stepping aside.

The girl scowled at me, laughed.

"Very well, Ignati," she said in English, "I shall go home," and she turned on her heel and went back up the alley, the big man close behind her.

Glad to be alone, I wasted no time in moving in the opposite direction until the pebbles of the beach were under my feet. The pebbles ground harshly under my heels. I moved back to more silent ground and began to work my way as swiftly as I could up the shore toward the center of action.

The machine gun barked on. Smaller guns snapped. Three concussions, close together—bombs, hand grenades, my ears and my memory told me.

The stormy sky glared pink over a roof ahead of me and to the left. The boom of the blast beat my ear-drums. Fragments I couldn't see fell around me. That, I thought, would be the jeweler's safe blowing apart.

I crept on up the shore line. The machine gun went silent. Lighter guns snapped, snapped, snapped. Another grenade went off. A man's voice shrieked pure terror.

Risking the crunch of pebbles, I turned down to the water's edge again. I had seen no dark shape on the water that could have been a boat. There had been boats moored along this beach in the afternoon. With my feet in the water of the bay I still saw no boat. The storm could have scattered them, but I didn't think it had. The island's western height shielded this shore. The wind was strong here, but not violent.

My feet sometimes on the edge of the pebbles, sometimes in the water, I went on up the shore line. Now I saw a boat. A gently bobbing black shape ahead. No light was on it. Nothing I could see moved on it. It was the only boat on that shore. That made it important.

Foot by foot, I approached.

A shadow moved between me and the dark rear of a building. I froze. The shadow, man-size, moved again, in the direction from which I was coming.

Waiting, I didn't know how nearly invisible, or how plain, I might be against my background. I couldn't risk giving myself away by trying to improve my position.

Twenty feet from me the shadow suddenly stopped.

I was seen. My gun was on the shadow.

"Come on," I called softly. "Keep coming. Let's see who you are."

The shadow hesitated, left the shelter of the building, drew nearer. I couldn't risk the flashlight. I made out dimly a handsome face, boyishly reckless, one cheek dark-stained.

"Oh, how d'you do?" the face's owner said in a musical baritone voice. "You were at the reception this afternoon."

"Yes."

"Have you seen Princess Zhukovski? You know her?"

"She went home with Ignati ten minutes or so ago."

"Excellent!" He wiped his stained cheek with a stained handkerchief, and turned to look at the boat. "That's Hendrixson's boat," he whispered. "They've got it and they've cast the others off."

"That would mean they are going to leave by water."

"Yes," he agreed, "unless— Shall we have a try at it?"

"You mean jump it?"

"Why not?" he asked. "There can't be very many aboard. God knows there are enough of them ashore. You're armed. I've a pistol."

"We'll size it up first," I decided, "so we'll know what we're jumping."

"That is wisdom," he said, and led the way back to the shelter of the buildings.

Hugging the rear walls of the buildings, we stole toward the boat.

The boat grew clearer in the night. A craft perhaps forty-five feet long, its stern to the shore, rising and falling beside a small pier. Across the stern something protruded. Something I couldn't quite make out. Leather soles scuffled now and then on the wooden deck. Presently a dark head and shoulders showed over the puzzling thing in the stern.

The Russian lad's eyes were better than mine.

"Masked," he breathed in my ear. "Something like a stocking over his head and face."

The masked man was motionless where he stood. We were motionless where we stood.

"Could you hit him from here?" the lad asked.

"Maybe, but night and rain aren't a good combination for sharpshooting. Our best bet is to sneak as close as we can, and start shooting when he spots us."

"That is wisdom," he agreed.

Discovery came with our first step forward. The man in the boat grunted. The lad at my side jumped forward. I recognized the thing in the boat's stern just in time to throw out a leg and trip the young Russian. He tumbled down, all sprawled out on the pebbles. I dropped behind him.

The machine gun in the boat's stern poured metal over our heads.

IV

"No good rushing that!" I said. "Roll out of it!"

I set the example by revolving toward the back of the building we had just left.

The man at the gun sprinkled the beach, but sprinkled it at random, his eyes no doubt spoiled for night-seeing by the flash of his gun.

Around the corner of the building, we sat up.

"You saved my life by tripping me," the lad said coolly.

"Yes. I wonder if they've moved the machine gun from the street, or if—"

The answer to that came immediately. The machine gun in the street mingled its vicious voice with the drumming of the one in the boat.

"A pair of them!" I complained. "Know anything about the layout?"

"I don't think there are more than ten or twelve of them," he said, "although it is not easy to count in the dark. The few I have seen are completely masked—like the man in the boat. They seem to have disconnected the telephone and light lines first and then to have destroyed the bridge. We attacked them while they were looting the bank, but in front they had a machine gun mounted in an automobile, and we were not equipped to combat on equal terms."

"Where are the islanders now?"

"Scattered, and most of them in hiding, I fancy, unless General Pleshskev has succeeded in rallying them again."

I frowned and beat my brains together. You can't fight machine guns and hand grenades with peaceful villagers and retired capitalists. No matter how well led and armed they are, you can't do anything with them. For that matter, how could anybody do much against a game of that toughness?

"Suppose you stick here and keep your eye on the boat," I suggested. "I'll scout around and see what's doing further up, and if I can get a few good men together, I'll try to jump the boat again, probably from the other side. But we can't count on that. The get-away will be by boat. We can count on that, and try to block it. If you lie down you can watch the boat around the corner of the building without making much of a target of yourself. I wouldn't do anything to attract attention until the break for the boat comes. Then you can do all the shooting you want."

"Excellent!" he said. "You'll probably find most of the islanders up behind the church. You can get to it by going straight up the hill until you come to an iron fence, and then follow that to the right."

"Right."

I moved off in the direction he had indicated.

At the main street I stopped to look around before venturing across. Everything was quiet there. The only man I could see was spread out face-down on the sidewalk near me.

On hands and knees I crawled to his side. He was dead. I didn't stop to examine him further, but sprang up and streaked for the other side of the street.

Nothing tried to stop me. In a doorway, flat against a wall, I peeped out. The wind had stopped. The rain was no longer a driving deluge, but a steady down-pouring of small drops. Couffignal's main street, to my senses, was a deserted street.

I wondered if the retreat to the boat had already started. On the sidewalk, walking swiftly toward the bank, I heard the answer to that guess.

High up on the slope, almost up to the edge of the cliff, by the sound, a machine gun began to hurl out its stream of bullets.

Mixed with the racket of the machine gun were the sounds of smaller arms, and a grenade or two.

At the first crossing, I left the main street and began to run up the hill. Men were running toward me. Two of them passed, paying no attention to my shouted, "What's up now?"

The third man stopped because I grabbed him—a fat man whose breath bubbled, and whose face was fish-belly white.

"They've moved the car with the machine gun on it up behind us," he gasped when I had shouted my question into his ear again.

"What are you doing without a gun?" I asked.

"I—I dropped it."

"Where's General Pleshskev?"

"Back there somewhere. He's trying to capture the car, but he'll never do it. It's suicide! Why don't help come?"

Other men had passed us, running downhill, as we talked. I let the white-faced man go, and stopped four men who weren't running so fast as the others.

"What's happening now?" I questioned them.

"They's going through the houses up the hill," a sharp-featured man with a small mustache and a rifle said.

"Has anybody got word off the island yet?" I asked.

"Can't," another informed me. "They blew up the bridge first thing."

"Can't anybody swim?"

"Not in that wind. Young Catlan tried it and was lucky to get out again with a couple of broken ribs."

"The wind's gone down," I pointed out.

The sharp-featured man gave his rifle to one of the others and took off his coat.

"I'll try it," he promised.

"Good! Wake up the whole country, and get word through to the San Francisco police boat and to the Mare Island Navy Yard. They'll lend a hand if you tell 'em the bandits have machine guns. Tell 'em the bandits have an armed boat waiting to leave in. It's Hendrixson's."

The volunteer swimmer left.

"A boat?" two of the men asked together.

"Yes. With a machine gun on it. If we're going to do anything, it'll have to be now, while we're between them and their get-away. Get every man and every gun you can find down there. Tackle the boat from the roofs if you can. When the bandits' car comes down there, pour it into it. You'll do better from the buildings than from the street."

The three men went on downhill. I went uphill, toward the crackling of firearms ahead. The machine gun was working irregularly. It would pour out its rat-tat-tat for a second or so, and then stop for a couple of seconds. The answering fire was thin, ragged.

I met more men, learned from them that the general, with less than a dozen men, was still fighting the car. I repeated the advice I had given the other men. My informants went down to join them. I went on up.

A hundred yards farther along, what was left of the general's dozen broke out of the night, around and past me, flying downhill, with bullets hailing after them.

The road was no place for mortal man. I stumbled over two bodies, scratched myself in a dozen places getting over a hedge. On soft, wet sod I continued my uphill journey.

The machine gun on the hill stopped its clattering. The one in the boat was still at work.

The one ahead opened again, firing too high for anything near at hand to be its target. It was helping its fellow below, spraying the main street.

Before I could get closer it had stopped. I heard the car's motor racing. The car moved toward me.

Rolling into the hedge, I lay there, straining my eyes through the spaces between the stems. I had six bullets in a gun that hadn't yet been fired on this night that had seen tons of powder burned.

When I saw wheels on the lighter face of the road, I emptied my gun, holding it low.

The car went on.

I sprang out of my hiding-place.

The car was suddenly gone from the empty road.

There was a grinding sound. A crash. The noise of metal folding on itself. The tinkle of glass.

I raced toward those sounds.

V

Out of a black pile where an engine sputtered, a black figure leaped—to dash off across the soggy lawn. I cut after it, hoping that the others in the wreck were down for keeps.

I was less than fifteen feet behind the fleeing man when he cleared a hedge. I'm no sprinter, but neither was he. The wet grass made slippery going.

He stumbled while I was vaulting the hedge. When we straightened out again I was not more than ten feet behind him.

Once I clicked my gun at him, forgetting I had emptied it. Six cartridges were wrapped in a piece of paper in my vest pocket, but this was no time for loading.

I was tempted to chuck the empty gun at his head. But that was too chancy.

A building loomed ahead. My fugitive bore off to the right, to clear the corner.

To the left a heavy shotgun went off.

The running man disappeared around the house-corner.

"Sweet God!" General Pleshskev's mellow voice complained. "That with a shotgun I should miss all of a man at the distance!"

"Go round the other way!" I yelled, plunging around the corner after my quarry.

His feet thudded ahead. I could not see him. The general puffed around from the other side of the house.

"You have him?"

"No."

In front of us was a stone-faced bank, on top of which ran a path. On either side of us was a high and solid hedge.

"But, my friend," the general protested. "How could he have—?"

A pale triangle showed on the path above—a triangle that could have been a bit of shirt showing above the opening of a vest.

"Stay here and talk!" I whispered to the general, and crept forward.

"It must be that he has gone the other way," the general carried out my instructions, rambling on as if I were standing beside him, "because if he had come my way I should have seen him, and if he had raised himself over either of the hedges or the embankment, one of us would surely have seen him against . . ."

He talked on and on while I gained the shelter of the bank on which the path sat, while I found places for my toes in the rough stone facing.

The man on the road, trying to make himself small with his back in a bush, was looking at the talking general. He saw me when I had my feet on the path.

He jumped, and one hand went up.

I jumped, with both hands out.

A stone, turning under my foot, threw me sidewise, twisting my ankle, but saving my head from the bullet he sent at it.

My outflung left arm caught his legs as I spilled down. He came over on top of me. I kicked him once, caught his gun-arm, and had just decided to bite it when the general puffed up over the edge of the path and prodded the man off me with the muzzle of the shotgun.

When it came my turn to stand up, I found it not so good. My twisted ankle didn't like to support its share of my hun-dred-and-eighty-some pounds. Putting most of my weight on the other leg, I turned my flashlight on the prisoner.

"Hello, Flippo!" I exclaimed.

"Hello!" he said without joy in the recognition.

He was a roly-poly Italian youth of twenty-three or -four. I had helped send him to San Quentin four years ago for his part in a payroll stick-up. He had been out on parole for sev-eral months now.

"The prison board isn't going to like this," I told him.

"You got me wrong," he pleaded. "I ain't been doing a thing. I was up here to see some friends. And when this thing busted loose I had to hide, because I got a record, and if I'm picked up I'll be railroaded for it. And now you got me, and you think I'm in on it!"

"You're a mind reader," I assured him, and asked the gen-eral: "Where can we pack this bird away for a while, under lock and key?"

"In my house there is a lumber-room with a strong door and not a window."

"That'll do it. March, Flippo!"

General Pleshskev collared the youth, while I limped along behind them, examining Flippo's gun, which was loaded ex-cept for the one shot he had fired at me, and reloading my own.

We had caught our prisoner on the Russian's grounds, so we didn't have far to go.

The general knocked on the door and called out something in his language Bolts clicked and grated, and the door was swung open by a heavily mustached Russian servant. Behind him the princess and a stalwart older woman stood.

We went in while the general was telling his household about the capture, and took the captive up to the lumber-room. I frisked him for his pocket-knife and matches—he had nothing else that could help him get out—locked him in and braced the door solidly with a length of board. Then we went downstairs again.

"You are injured!" the princess, seeing me limp across the floor, cried.

"Only a twisted ankle," I said. "But it does bother me some. Is there any adhesive tape around?"

"Yes," and she spoke to the mustached servant, who went out of the room and presently returned, carrying rolls of gauze and tape and a basin of steaming water.

"If you'll sit down," the princess said, taking these things from the servant.

But I shook my head and reached for the adhesive tape.

"I want cold water, because I've got to go out in the wet again. If you'll show me the bathroom, I can fix myself up in no time."

We had to argue about that, but I finally got to the bathroom, where I ran cold water on my foot and ankle, and strapped it with adhesive tape, as tight as I could without stopping the circulation altogether. Getting my wet shoe on again was a job, but when I was through I had two firm legs under me, even if one of them did hurt some.

When I rejoined the others I noticed that the sound of firing no longer came up the hill, and that the patter of rain was lighter, and a grey streak of coming daylight showed under a drawn blind.

I was buttoning my slicker when the knocker rang on the front door. Russian words came through, and the young Russian I had met on the beach came in.

"Aleksandr, you're—" the stalwart older woman screamed when she saw the blood on his cheek, and fainted.

He paid no attention to her at all, as if he was used to having her faint.

"They've gone in the boat," he told me while the girl and two men servants gathered up the woman and laid her on an ottoman.

"How many?" I asked.

"I counted ten, and I don't think I missed more than one or two, if any."

"The men I sent down there couldn't stop them?"

He shrugged.

"What would you? It takes a strong stomach to face a machine gun. Your men had been cleared out of the buildings almost before they arrived."

The woman who had fainted had revived by now and was pouring anxious questions in Russian at the lad. The princess was getting into her blue cape. The woman stopped questioning the lad and asked her something.

"It's all over," the princess said. "I am going to view the ruins."

That suggestion appealed to everybody. Five minutes later all of us, including the servants, were on our way downhill. Behind us, around us, in front of us, were other people going downhill, hurrying along in the drizzle that was very gentle now, their faces tired and excited in the bleak morning light.

Halfway down, a woman ran out of a cross-path and began to tell me something. I recognized her as one of Hendrixson's maids.

I caught some of her words.

"Presents gone. . . . Mr. Brophy murdered. . . . Oliver. . . ."

VI

"I'll be down later," I told the others, and set out after the maid.

She was running back to the Hendrixson house. I couldn't run, couldn't even walk fast. She and Hendrixson and more of his servants were standing on the front porch when I arrived.

"They killed Oliver and Brophy," the old man said.

"How?"

"We were in the back of the house, the rear second story, watching the flashes of the shooting down in the village. Oliver was down here, just inside the front door, and Brophy in the room with the presents. We heard a shot in there, and immediately a man appeared in the doorway of our room, threatening us with two pistols, making us stay there for perhaps ten minutes. Then he shut and locked the door and went away. We broke the door down—and found Brophy and Oliver dead."

"Let's look at them."

The chauffeur was just inside the front door. He lay on his back, with his brown throat cut straight across the front, almost back to the vertebrae. His rifle was under him. I pulled it out and examined it. It had not been fired.

Upstairs, the butler Brophy was huddled against a leg of one of the tables on which the presents had been spread. His gun was gone. I turned him over, straightened him out, and found a bullet-hole in his chest. Around the hole his coat was charred in a large area.

Most of the presents were still here. But the most valuable pieces were gone. The others were in disorder, lying around any which way, their covers pulled off.

"What did the one you saw look like?" I asked.

"I didn't see him very well," Hendrixson said. "There was no light in our room. He was simply a dark figure against the candle burning in the hall. A large man in a black rubber raincoat, with some sort of black mask that covered his whole head and face, with small eyeholes."

"No hat?"

"No, just the mask over his entire face and head."

As we went downstairs again I gave Hendrixson a brief account of what I had seen and heard and done since I had left him. There wasn't enough of it to make a long tale.

"Do you think you can get information about the others from the one you caught?" he asked, as I prepared to go out.

"No. But I expect to bag them just the same."

Couffignal's main street was jammed with people when I limped into it again. A detachment of Marines from Mare Island was there, and men from a San Francisco police boat. Excited citizens in all degrees of partial nakedness boiled around them. A hundred voices were talking at once, recounting their personal adventures and braveries and losses and what they had seen. Such words as machine gun, bomb, bandit, car, shot, dynamite, and killed sounded again and again, in every variety of voice and tone.

The bank had been completely wrecked by the charge that had blown the vault. The jewelry store was another ruin. A grocer's across the street was serving as a field hospital. Two doctors were toiling there, patching up damaged villagers.

I recognized a familiar face under a uniform cap—Sergeant Roche of the harbor police—and pushed through the crowd to him.

"Just get here?" he asked as we shook hands. "Or were you in on it?"

"In on it."

"What do you know?"

"Everything."

"Who ever heard of a private detective that didn't," he joshed as I led him out of the mob.

"Did you people run into an empty boat out in the bay?" I asked when we were away from audiences.

"Empty boats have been floating around the bay all night," he said.

I hadn't thought of that.

"Where's your boat now?" I asked him.

"Out trying to pick up the bandits. I stayed with a couple of men to lend a hand here."

"You're in luck," I told him. "Now sneak a look across the street. See the stout old boy with the black whiskers? Standing in front of the druggist's."

General Pleshskev stood there, with the woman who had fainted, the young Russian whose bloody cheek had made her faint, and a pale, plump man of forty-something who had been with them at the reception. A little to one side stood big Ignati, the two men-servants I had seen at the house, and another who was obviously one of them. They were chatting together and watching the excited antics of a red-faced property-owner who was telling a curt lieutenant of Marines that it was his own personal private automobile that the bandits had stolen to mount their machine gun on, and what he thought should be done about it.

"Yes," said Roche, "I see your fellow with the whiskers."

"Well, he's your meat. The woman and two men with him are also your meat. And those four Russians standing to the left are some more of it. There's another missing, but I'll take care of that one. Pass the word to the lieutenant, and you can round up those babies without giving them a chance to fight back. They think they're safe as angels."

"Sure, are you?" the sergeant asked.

"Don't be silly!" I growled, as if I had never made a mistake in my life.

I had been standing on my one good prop. When I put my weight on the other to turn away from the sergeant, it stung me all the way to the hip. I pushed my back teeth together and began to work painfully through the crowd to the other side of the street.

The princess didn't seem to be among those present. My idea was that, next to the general, she was the most important member of the push. If she was at their house, and not yet suspicious, I figured I could get close enough to yank her in without a riot.

Walking was hell. My temperature rose. Sweat rolled out on me.

"Mister, they didn't none of 'em come down that way."

The one-legged newsboy was standing at my elbow. I greeted him as if he were my pay-check.

"Come on with me," I said, taking his arm. "You did fine down there, and now I want you to do something else for me."

Half a block from the main street I led him up on the porch of a small yellow cottage. The front door stood open, left that way when the occupants ran down to welcome police and Marines, no doubt. Just inside the door, beside a hall rack, was a wicker porch chair. I committed unlawful entry to the extent of dragging that chair out on the porch.

"Sit down, son," I urged the boy.

He sat, looking up at me with puzzled freckled face. I took a firm grip on his crutch and pulled it out of his hand.

"Here's five bucks for rental," I said, "and if I lose it I'll buy you one of ivory and gold."

And I put the crutch under my arm and began to propel myself up the hill.

It was my first experience with a crutch. I didn't break any records. But it was a lot better than tottering along on an unassisted bum ankle.

The hill was longer and steeper than some mountains I've seen, but the gravel walk to the Russians' house was finally under my feet.

I was still some dozen feet from the porch when Princess Zhukovski opened the door.

VII

"Oh!" she exclaimed, and then, recovering from her surprise, "your ankle is worse!"

She ran down the steps to help me climb them. As she came I noticed that something heavy was sagging and swinging in the right-hand pocket of her grey flannel jacket.

With one hand under my elbow, the other arm across my back, she helped me up the steps and across the porch. That assured me she didn't think I had tumbled to the game. If she had, she wouldn't have trusted herself within reach of my hands. Why, I wondered, had she come back to the house after starting downhill with the others?

While I was wondering we went into the house, where she planted me in a large and soft leather chair.

"You must certainly be starving after your strenuous night," she said. "I will see if——"

"No, sit down." I nodded at a chair facing mine. "I want to talk to you."

She sat down, clasping her slender white hands in her lap. In neither face nor pose was there any sign of nervousness, not even of curiosity. And that was overdoing it.

"Where have you cached the plunder?" I asked.

The whiteness of her face was nothing to go by. It had been white as marble since I had first seen her. The darkness of her eyes was as natural. Nothing happened to her other features. Her voice was smoothly cool.

"I am sorry," she said. "The question doesn't convey anything to me."

"Here's the point," I explained. "I'm charging you with complicity in the gutting of Couffignal, and in the murders that went with it. And I'm asking you where the loot has been hidden."

Slowly she stood up, raised her chin, and looked at least a mile down at me.

"How dare you? How dare you speak so to me, a Zhukovski!"

"I don't care if you're one of the Smith Brothers!" Leaning forward, I had pushed my twisted ankle against a leg of the chair, and the resulting agony didn't improve my disposition. "For the purpose of this talk you are a thief and a murderer."

Her strong slender body became the body of a lean crouching animal. Her white face became the face of an enraged animal. One hand—claw now—swept to the heavy pocket of her jacket.

Then, before I could have batted an eye—though my life seemed to depend on my not batting it—the wild animal had vanished. Out of it—and now I know where the writers of the old fairy stories got their ideas—rose the princess again, cool and straight and tall.

She sat down, crossed her ankles, put an elbow on an arm of her chair, propped her chin on the back of that hand, and looked curiously into my face.

"However," she murmured, "did you chance to arrive at so strange and fanciful a theory?"

"It wasn't chance, and it's neither strange nor fanciful," I said. "Maybe it'll save time and trouble if I show you part of the score against you. Then you'll know how you stand and won't waste your brains pleading innocence."

"I should be grateful," she smiled, "very!"

I tucked my crutch in between one knee and the arm of my chair, so my hands would be free to check off my points on my fingers.

"First—whoever planned the job knew the island—not fairly well, but every inch of it. There's no need to argue about that. Second—the car on which the machine gun was mounted was local property, stolen from the owner here. So was the boat in which the bandits were supposed to have escaped. Bandits from the outside would have needed a car or a boat to bring their machine guns, explosives, and grenades here and there doesn't seem to be any reason why they shouldn't have used that car or boat instead of stealing a fresh one. Third—there wasn't the least hint of the professional bandit touch on this job. If you ask me, it was a military job from beginning to end. And the worst safe-burglar in the world could have got into both the bank vault and the jeweler's safe without wrecking the buildings. Fourth—bandits from the outside wouldn't have destroyed the bridge. They might have blocked it, but they wouldn't have destroyed it. They'd have saved it in case they had to make their get-away in that direction. Fifth—bandits figuring on a get-away by boat would have cut the job short, wouldn't have spread it over the whole night. Enough racket was made here to wake up California all the way from Sacramento to Los Angeles. What you people did was to send one man out in the boat, shooting, and he didn't go far. As soon as he was at a safe distance, he went overboard, and swam back to the island. Big Ignati could have done it without turning a hair."

That exhausted my right hand. I switched over, counting on my left.

"Sixth—I met one of your party, the lad, down on the beach, and he was coming from the boat. He suggested that we jump it. We were shot at, but the man behind the gun was playing with us. He could have wiped us out in a second if he had been in earnest, but he shot over our heads. Seventh—that same lad is the only man on the island, so far as I know, who saw the departing bandits. Eighth—all of your people that I ran into were especially nice to me, the general even spending an hour talking to me at the reception this afternoon. That's a distinctive amateur crook trait. Ninth—after the machine gun car had been wrecked I chased its occupant. I lost him around this house. The Italian boy I picked up wasn't him. He couldn't have climbed up on the path without my seeing him. But he could have run around to the general's side of the house and vanished indoors there. The general liked him, and would have helped him. I know that, because the general performed a downright miracle by missing him at some six feet with a shotgun. Tenth—you called at Hendrixson's house for no other purpose than to get me away from there."

That finished the left hand. I went back to the right.

"Eleventh—Hendrixson's two servants were killed by someone they knew and trusted. Both were killed at close quarters and without firing a shot. I'd say you got Oliver to let you into the house, and were talking to him when one of your men cut his throat from behind. Then you went upstairs and probably shot the unsuspecting Brophy yourself. He wouldn't have been on his guard against you. Twelfth—but that ought to be enough, and I'm getting a sore throat from listing them."

She took her chin off her hand, took a fat white cigarette out of a thin black case, and held it in her mouth while I put a match to the end of it. She took a long pull at it—a draw that accounted for a third of its length—and blew the smoke down at her knees.

"That would be enough," she said when all these things had been done, "if it were not that you yourself know it was impossible for us to have been so engaged. Did you not see us—did not everyone see us—time and time again?"

"That's easy!" I argued. "With a couple of machine guns, a trunkful of grenades, knowing the island from top to bottom, in the darkness and in a storm, against bewildered civilians—it was duck soup. There are nine of you that I know of, including two women. Any five of you could have carried on the work, once it was started, while the others took turns appearing here and there, establishing alibis. And that is what you did. You took turns slipping out to alibi yourselves. Everywhere I went I ran into one of you. And the general! That whiskered old joker running around leading the simple citizens to battle! I'll bet he led 'em plenty! They're lucky there are any of 'em alive this morning!"

She finished her cigarette with another inhalation, dropped the stub on the rug, ground out the light with one foot, sighed wearily, put her hands on her hips, and asked:

"And now what?"

"Now I want to know where you have stowed the plunder."

The readiness of her answer surprised me.

"Under the garage, in a cellar we dug secretly there some months ago."

I didn't believe that, of course, but it turned out to be the truth.

I didn't have anything else to say. When I fumbled with my borrowed crutch, preparing to get up, she raised a hand and spoke gently:

"Wait a moment, please. I have something to suggest."

Half standing, I leaned toward her, stretching out one hand until it was close to her side.

"I want the gun," I said.

She nodded, and sat still while I plucked it from her pocket, put it in one of my own, and sat down again.

VIII

"You said a little while ago that you didn't care who I was," she began immediately. "But I want you to know. There are so many of us Russians who once were somebodies and who now are nobodies that I won't bore you with the repetition of a tale the world has grown tired of hearing. But you must remember that this weary tale is real to us who are its subjects. However, we fled from Russia with what we could carry of our property, which fortunately was enough to keep us in bearable comfort for a few years.

"In London we opened a Russian restaurant, but London was suddenly full of Russian restaurants, and ours became, instead of a means of livelihood, a source of loss. We tried teaching music and languages, and so on. In short, we hit on all the means of earning our living that other Russian exiles hit upon, and so always found ourselves in overcrowded, and thus unprofitable, fields. But what else did we know—could we do?

"I promised not to bore you. Well, always our capital shrank, and always the day approached on which we should be shabby and hungry, the day when we should become familiar to readers of your Sunday papers—charwomen who had been princesses, dukes who now were butlers. There was no place for us in the world. Outcasts easily become outlaws. Why not? Could it be said that we owed the world any fealty? Had not the world sat idly by and seen us despoiled of place and property and country?

"We planned it before we had heard of Couffignal. We could find a small settlement of the wealthy, sufficiently isolated, and, after establishing ourselves there, we would plunder it. Couffignal, when we found it, seemed to be the ideal place. We leased this house for six months, having just enough capital remaining to do that and to live properly here while our plans matured. Here we spent four months establishing ourselves, collecting our arms and our explosives, mapping our offensive, waiting for a favorable night. Last night seemed to be that night, and we had provided, we thought, against every eventuality. But we had not, of course, provided against your presence and your genius. They were simply others of the unforeseen misfortunes to which we seem eternally condemned."

She stopped, and fell to studying me with mournful large eyes that made me feel like fidgeting.

"It's no good calling me a genius," I objected. "The truth is you people botched your job from beginning to end. Your general would get a big laugh out of a man without military training who tried to lead an army. But here are you people with absolutely no criminal experience trying to swing a trick that needed the highest sort of criminal skill. Look at how you all played around with me! Amateur stuff! A professional crook with any intelligence would have either let me alone or knocked me off. No wonder you flopped! As for the rest of it—your troubles—I can't do anything about them."

"Why?" very softly. "Why can't you?"

"Why should I?" I made it blunt.

"No one else knows what you know." She bent forward to put a white hand on my knee. "There is wealth in that cellar beneath the garage. You may have whatever you ask."

I shook my head.

"You aren't a fool!" she protested. "You know——"

"Let me straighten this out for you," I interrupted. "We'll disregard whatever honesty I happen to have, sense of loyalty to employers, and so on. You might doubt them, so we'll throw them out. Now I'm a detective because I happen to like the work. It pays me a fair salary, but I could find other jobs that would pay more. Even a hundred dollars more a month would be twelve hundred a year. Say twenty-five or thirty thousand dollars in the years between now and my sixtieth birthday.

"Now I pass up that twenty-five or thirty thousand of honest gain because I like being a detective, like the work. And liking work makes you want to do it as well as you can. Otherwise there'd be no sense to it. That's the fix I am in. I don't know anything else, don't enjoy anything else, don't want to know or enjoy anything else. You can't weigh that against any sum of money. Money is good stuff. I haven't anything against it. But in the past eighteen years I've been getting my fun out of chasing crooks and tackling puzzles, my satisfaction out of catching crooks and solving riddles. It's the only kind of sport I know anything about, and I can't imagine a pleasanter future than twenty-some years more of it. I'm not going to blow that up!"

She shook her head slowly, lowering it, so that now her dark eyes looked up at me under the thin arcs of her brows.

"You speak only of money," she said. "I said you may have whatever you ask."

That was out. I don't know where these women get their ideas.

"You're still all twisted up," I said brusquely, standing now and adjusting my borrowed crutch. "You think I'm a man and you're a woman. That's wrong. I'm a manhunter and you're something that has been running in front of me. There's nothing human about it. You might just as well expect a hound to play tiddly-winks with the fox he's caught. We're wasting time anyway. I've been thinking the police or Marines might come up here and save me a walk. You've been waiting for your mob to come back and grab me. I could have told you they were being arrested when I left them."

That shook her. She had stood up. Now she fell back a step, putting a hand behind her for steadiness, on her chair. An exclamation I didn't understand popped out of her mouth. Russian, I thought, but the next moment I knew it had been Italian.

"Put your hands up."

It was Flippo's husky voice. Flippo stood in the doorway, holding an automatic.

IX

I raised my hands as high as I could without dropping my supporting crutch, meanwhile cursing myself for having been too careless, or too vain, to keep a gun in my hand while I talked to the girl.

So this was why she had come back to the house. If she freed the Italian, she had thought, we would have no reason for suspecting that he hadn't been in on the robbery, and so we would look for the bandits among his friends. A prisoner, of course, he might have persuaded us of his innocence. She had given him the gun so he could either shoot his way clear, or, what would help her as much, get himself killed trying.

While I was arranging these thoughts in my head, Flippo had come up behind me. His empty hand passed over my body, taking away my own gun, his, and the one I had taken from the girl.

"A bargain, Flippo," I said when he had moved away from me, a little to one side, where he made one corner of a triangle whose other corners were the girl and I. "You're out on parole, with some years still to be served. I picked you up with a gun on you. That's plenty to send you back to the big house. I know you weren't in on this job. My idea is that you were up here on a smaller one of your own, but I can't prove that and don't want to. Walk out of here, alone and neutral, and I'll forget I saw you."

Little thoughtful lines grooved the boy's round, dark face.

The princess took a step toward him.

"You heard the offer I just now made him?" she asked. "Well, I make that offer to you, if you will kill him."

The thoughtful lines in the boy's face deepened.

"There's your choice, Flippo," I summed up for him. "All I can give you is freedom from San Quentin. The princess can give you a fat cut of the profits in a busted caper, with a good chance to get yourself hanged."

The girl, remembering her advantage over me, went at him hot and heavy in Italian, a language in which I know only four words. Two of them are profane and the other two obscene. I said all four.

The boy was weakening. If he had been ten years older, he'd have taken my offer and thanked me for it. But he was young and she—now that I thought of it—was beautiful. The answer wasn't hard to guess.

"But not to bump him off," he said to her, in English, for my benefit. "We'll lock him up in there where I was at."

I suspected Flippo hadn't any great prejudice against murder. It was just that he thought this one unnecessary, unless he was kidding me to make the killing easier.

The girl wasn't satisfied with his suggestion. She poured more hot Italian at him. Her game looked sure-fire, but it had a flaw. She couldn't persuade him that his chances of getting any of the loot away were good. She had to depend on her charms to swing him. And that meant she had to hold his eye.

He wasn't far from me.

She came close to him. She was singing, chanting, crooning Italian syllables into his round face.

She had him.

He shrugged. His whole face said yes. He turned—

I knocked him on the noodle with my borrowed crutch.

The crutch splintered apart. Flippo's knees bent. He stretched up to his full height. He fell on his face on the floor. He lay there, dead-still, except for a thin worm of blood that crawled out of his hair to the rug.

A step, a tumble, a foot or so of hand-and-knee scrambling put me within reach of Flippo's gun.

The girl, jumping out of my path, was half-way to the door when I sat up with the gun in my hand.

"Stop!" I ordered.

"I shan't," she said, but she did, for the time at least. "I am going out."

"You are going out when I take you."

She laughed, a pleasant laugh, low and confident.

"I'm going out before that," she insisted good-naturedly.

I shook my head.

"How do you purpose stopping me?" she asked.

"I don't think I'll have to," I told her. "You've got too much sense to try to run while I'm holding a gun on you."

She laughed again, an amused ripple.

"I've got too much sense to stay," she corrected me. "Your crutch is broken, and you're lame. You can't catch me by running after me, then. You pretend you'll shoot me, but I don't believe you. You'd shoot me if I attacked you, of course, but I shan't do that. I shall simply walk out, and you know you won't shoot me for that. You'll wish you could, but you won't. You'll see."

Her face turned over her shoulder, her dark eyes twinkling at me, she took a step toward the door.

"Better not count on that!" I threatened.

For answer to that she gave me a cooing laugh. And took another step.

"Stop, you idiot!" I bawled at her.

Her face laughed over her shoulder at me. She walked without haste to the door, her short skirt of grey flannel shaping itself to the calf of each grey wool-stockinged leg as its mate stepped forward.

Sweat greased the gun in my hand.

When her right foot was on the doorsill, a little chuckling sound came from her throat.

"Adieu!" she said softly.

And I put a bullet in the calf of her left leg.

She sat down—plump! Utter surprise stretched her white face. It was too soon for pain.

I had never shot a woman before. I felt queer about it.

"You ought to have known I'd do it!" My voice sounded harsh and savage and like a stranger's in my ears. "Didn't I steal a crutch from a cripple?"

The Assistant Murderer

The Man in Gray

GOLD on the door, edged with black, said *Alexander Rush, Private Detective*. Inside, an ugly man sat tilted back in a chair, his feet on a yellow desk.

The office was in no way lovely. Its furnishings were few and old with the shabby age of second-handom. A shredding square of dun carpet covered the floor. On one buff wall hung a framed certificate that licensed Alexander Rush to pursue the calling of private detective in the city of Baltimore in accordance with certain red-numbered regulations. A map of the city hung on another wall. Beneath the map a frail bookcase, small as it was, gaped emptily around its contents: a yellowish railway guide, a smaller hotel directory, and street and telephone directories for Baltimore, Washington and Philadelphia. An insecure oaken clothes-tree held up a black derby and a black overcoat beside a white sink in one corner. The four chairs in the room were unrelated to one another in everything except age. The desk's scarred top held, in addition to the proprietor's feet, a telephone, a black-clotted inkwell, a disarray of papers having generally to do with criminals who had escaped from one prison or another, and a grayed ashtray that held as much ash and as many black cigar stumps as a tray of its size could expect to hold.

An ugly office—the proprietor was uglier.

His head was squatly pear-shaped. Excessively heavy, wide, blunt at the jaw, it narrowed as it rose to the close-cropped, erect grizzled hair that sprouted above a low, slanting forehead. His complexion was of a rich darkish red, his skin tough in texture and rounded over thick cushions of fat. These fundamental inelegancies were by no means all his ugliness. Things had been done to his features.

One way you looked at his nose, you said it was crooked. Another way, you said it could not be crooked; it had no shape at all. Whatever your opinion of its form, you could not deny its color. Veins had been broken to pencil its already florid surface with brilliant red stars and curls and puzzling scrawls that looked as if they must have some secret meanings. His lips were thick, tough-skinned. Between them showed the brassy glint of two solid rows of gold teeth, the lower row lapping the upper, so undershot was the bulging jaw. His eyes—small, deep-set and pale blue of iris—were bloodshot to a degree that made you think he had a heavy cold. His ears accounted for some of his earlier years: they were the thickened, twisted cauliflower ears of the pugilist.

A man of forty-something, ugly, sitting tilted back in his chair, feet on desk.

The gilt-labeled door opened and another man came into the office. Perhaps ten years younger than the man at the desk, he was, roughly speaking, everything that one was not. Fairly tall, slender, fair-skinned, brown-eyed, he would have been as little likely to catch your eye in a gambling house as in an art gallery. His clothes—suit and hat were gray—were fresh and properly pressed, and even fashionable in that inconspicuous manner which is one sort of taste. His face was likewise unobtrusive, which was surprising when you considered how narrowly it missed handsomeness through the least meagerness of mouth—a mark of the too cautious man.

Two steps into the office he hesitated, brown eyes glancing from shabby furnishings to ill-visaged proprietor. So much ugliness seemed to disconcert the man in gray. An apologetic smile began on his lips, as if he were about to murmur, "I beg your pardon, I'm in the wrong office."

But when he finally spoke it was otherwise. He took another step forward, asking uncertainly:

"You are Mr. Rush?"

"Yeah." The detective's voice was hoarse with a choking harshness that seemed to corroborate the heavy-cold testimony of his eyes. He put his feet down on the floor and jerked a fat, red hand at a chair. "Sit down, sir."

The man in gray sat down, tentatively upright on the chair's front edge.

"Now what can I do for you?" Alec Rush croaked amiably.

"I want—I wish—I would like—" and further than that the man in gray said nothing.

"Maybe you'd better just tell me what's wrong," the detective suggested. "Then I'll know what you want of me," and he smiled.

There was kindliness in Alec Rush's smile, and it was not easily resisted. True, his smile was a horrible grimace out of a nightmare, but that was its charm. When your gentle-countenanced man smiles there is small gain: his smile expresses little more than his reposed face. But when Alec Rush distorted his ogre's mask so that jovial friendliness peeped incongruously from his savage red eyes, from his brutal metal-studded mouth—then that was a heartening, a winning thing.

"Yes, I daresay that would be better." The man in gray sat back in his chair, more comfortably, less transiently. "Yesterday on Fayette Street, I met a—a young woman I know. I hadn't—we hadn't met for several months. That isn't really pertinent, however. But after we separated—we had talked for a few minutes—I saw a man. That is, he came out of a doorway and went down the street in the same direction she had taken, and I got the idea he was following her. She turned into Liberty Street and he did likewise. Countless people walk along that same route, and the idea that he was following her seemed fantastic, so much so that I dismissed it and went on about my business.

"But I couldn't get the notion out of my head. It seemed to me there had been something peculiarly intent in his carriage, and no matter how much I told myself the notion was absurd, it persisted in worrying me. So last night, having nothing especial to do, I drove out to the neighborhood of—of the young woman's house. And I saw the same man again. He was standing on a corner two blocks from her house. It was the same man—I'm certain of it. I tried to watch him, but while I was finding a place for my car he disappeared and I did not see him again. Those are the circumstances. Now will you look into it, learn if he is actually following her, and why?"

"Sure," the detective agreed hoarsely, "but didn't you say anything to the lady or to any of her family?"

The man in gray fidgeted in his chair and looked at the stringy dun carpet.

"No, I didn't. I didn't want to disturb her, frighten her, and still don't. After all, it may be no more than a meaningless coincidence, and—and—well—I don't— That's impossible! What I had in mind was for you to find out what is wrong, if anything, and remedy it without my appearing in the matter at all."

"Maybe, but, mind you, I'm not saying I will. I'd want to know more first."

"More? You mean more——"

"More about you and her."

"But there is nothing about us!" the man in gray protested. "It is exactly as I have told you. I might add that the young woman is—is married, and that until yesterday I had not seen her since her marriage."

"Then your interest in her is—?" The detective let the husky interrogation hang incompleted in the air.

"Of friendship—past friendship."

"Yeah. Now who is this young woman?"

The man in gray fidgeted again.

"See here, Rush," he said, coloring, "I'm perfectly willing to tell you, and shall, of course, but I don't want to tell you unless you are going to handle this thing for me. I mean I don't want to be bringing her name into it if—if you aren't. Will you?"

Alec Rush scratched his grizzled head with a stubby forefinger.

"I don't know," he growled. "That's what I'm trying to find out. I can't take hold of a job that might be anything. I've got to know that you're on the up-and-up."

II

Two Names

Puzzlement disturbed the clarity of the younger man's brown eyes. "But I didn't think you'd be——" He broke off and looked away from the ugly man.

"Of course you didn't." A chuckle rasped in the detective's burly throat, the chuckle of a man touched in a once sore spot that is no longer tender. He raised a big hand to arrest his prospective client in the act of rising from his chair. "What you did, on a guess, was to go to one of the big agencies and tell 'em your story. They wouldn't touch it unless you cleared up the fishy points. Then you ran across my name, remembered I was chucked out of the department a couple of years ago. 'There's my man,' you said to yourself, 'a baby who won't be so choicy!' "

The man in gray protested with head and gesture and voice that this was not so. But his eyes were sheepish.

Alec Rush laughed harshly again and said, "No matter. I ain't sensitive about it. I can talk about politics, and being made the goat, and all that, but the records show the Board of Police Commissioners gave me the air for a list of crimes that would stretch from here to Canton Hollow. All right, sir! I'll take your job. It sounds phony, but maybe it ain't. It'll cost you fifteen a day and expenses."

"I can see that it sounds peculiar," the younger man assured the detective, "but you'll find that it's quite all right. You'll want a retainer, of course."

"Yes, say fifty."

The man in gray took five new ten-dollar bills from a pigskin billfold and put them on the desk. With a thick pen Alec Rush began to make muddy ink-marks on a receipt blank.

"Your name?" he asked.

"I would rather not. I'm not to appear in it, you know. My name would not be of importance, would it?"

Alec Rush put down his pen and frowned at his client.

"Now! Now!" he grumbled good-naturedly. "How am I going to do business with a man like you?"

The man in gray was sorry, even apologetic, but he was stubborn in his reticence. He would not give his name. Alec Rush growled and complained, but pocketed the five ten-dollar bills.

"It's in your favor, maybe," the detective admitted as he surrendered, "though it ain't to your credit. But if you were off-color I guess you'd have sense enough to fake a name. Now this young woman—who is she?"

"Mrs. Hubert Landow."

"Well, well, we've got a name at last! And where does Mrs. Landow live?"

"On Charles-Street Avenue," the man in gray said, and gave a number.

"Her description?"

"She is twenty-two or -three years old, rather tall, slender in an athletic way, with auburn hair, blue eyes and very white skin."

"And her husband? You know him?"

"I have seen him. He is about my age—thirty—but larger than I, a tall, broad-shouldered man of the clean-cut blond type."

"And your mystery man? What does he look like?"

"He's quite young, not more than twenty-two at the most, and not very large—medium size, perhaps, or a little under. He's very dark, with high cheek-bones and a large nose. High, straight shoulders, too, but not broad. He walks with small, almost mincing, steps."

"Clothes?"

"He was wearing a brown suit and a tan cap when I saw him on Fayette Street yesterday afternoon. I suppose he wore the same last night, but I'm not positive."

"I suppose you'll drop in here for my reports," the detective wound up, "since I won't know where to send them to you?"

"Yes." The man in gray stood up and held out his hand. "I'm very grateful to you for undertaking this, Mr. Rush."

Alec Rush said that was all right. They shook hands, and the man in gray went out.

The ugly man waited until his client had had time to turn off into the corridor that led to the elevators. Then the detective said, "Now, Mr. Man!" got up from his chair, took his hat from the clothes-tree in the corner, locked his office door behind him, and ran down the back stairs.

He ran with the deceptive heavy agility of a bear. There was something bear-like, too, in the looseness with which his blue suit hung on his stout body, and in the set of his heavy shoulders—sloping, limber-jointed shoulders whose droop concealed much of their bulk.

He gained the ground floor in time to see the gray back of his client issuing into the street. In his wake Alec Rush sauntered. Two blocks, a turn to the left, another block and a turn to the right. The man in gray went into the office of a trust company that occupied the ground floor of a large office building.

The rest was the mere turning of a hand. Half a dollar to a porter: the man in gray was Ralph Millar, assistant cashier.

Darkness was settling in Charles-Street Avenue when Alec Rush, in a modest black coupé, drove past the address Ralph Millar had given him. The house was large in the dusk, spaced from its fellows as from the paving by moderate expanses of fenced lawn.

Alec Rush drove on, turned to the left at the first crossing, again to the left at the next, and at the next. For half an hour he guided his car along a many-angled turning and returning route until, when finally he stopped beside the curb at some distance from, but within sight of, the Landow house, he had driven through every piece of thoroughfare in the vicinity of that house.

He had not seen Millar's dark, high-shouldered young man.

Lights burned brightly in Charles-Street Avenue, and the night traffic began to purr southward into the city. Alec Rush's heavy body slumped against the wheel of his coupé while he filled its interior with pungent fog from a black cigar, and held patient, bloodshot eyes on what he could see of the Landow residence.

Three-quarters of an hour passed, and there was motion in the house. A limousine left the garage in the rear for the front door. A man and a woman, faintly distinguishable at that distance, left the house for the limousine. The limousine moved out into the cityward current. The third car behind it was Alec Rush's modest coupé.

III
The Man in the Doorway

Except for a perilous moment at North Avenue, when the interfering cross-stream of traffic threatened to separate him from his quarry, Alec Rush followed the limousine without difficulty. In front of a Howard Street theatre it discharged its freight: a youngish man and a young woman, both tall, evening-clad, and assuringly in agreement with the descriptions the detective had got from his client.

The Landows went into the already dark theatre while Alec Rush was buying his ticket. In the light of the first intermission he discovered them again. Leaving his seat for the rear of the auditorium, he found an angle from which he could study them for the remaining five minutes of illumination.

Hubert Landow's head was rather small for his stature, and the blond hair with which it was covered threatened each moment to escape from its imposed smoothness into crisp curls. His face, healthily ruddy, was handsome in a muscular, very masculine way, not indicative of any great mental nimbleness. His wife had that beauty which needs no cataloguing. However, her hair was auburn, her eyes blue, her skin white, and she looked a year or two older than the maximum twenty-three Millar had allowed her.

While the intermission lasted Hubert Landow talked to his wife eagerly, and his bright eyes were the eyes of a lover. Alec Rush could not see Mrs. Landow's eyes. He saw her replying now and again to her husband's words. Her profile showed no answering eagerness. She did not show she was bored.

Midway the last act, Alec Rush left the theatre to maneuver his coupé into a handy position from which to cover the Landows' departure. But their limousine did not pick them up when they left the theatre. They turned down Howard Street afoot, going to a rather garish second-class restaurant, where an abbreviated orchestra succeeded by main strength in concealing its smallness from the ear.

His coupé conveniently parked, Alec Rush found a table from which he could watch his subjects without being himself noticeable. Husband still wooed wife with incessant, eager talking. Wife was listless, polite, unkindled. Neither more than touched the food before them. They danced once, the woman's face as little touched by immediate interest as when she listened to her husband's words. A beautiful face, but empty.

The minute hand of Alec Rush's nickel-plated watch had scarcely begun its last climb of the day from where VI is inferred to XII when the Landows left the restaurant. The limousine—against its side a young Norfolk-jacketed Negro smoking—was two doors away. It bore them back to their house. The detective, having seen them into the house, having seen the limousine into the garage, drove his coupé again around and around through the neighboring thoroughfares. And saw nothing of Millar's dark young man.

Then Alec Rush went home and to bed.

At eight o'clock the next morning ugly man and modest coupé were stationary in Charles-Street Avenue again. Male Charles-Street Avenue went with the sun on its left toward its offices. As the morning aged and the shadows grew shorter and thicker, so, generally, did the individuals who composed this morning procession. Eight-o'clock was frequently young and slender and brisk, Eight-thirty less so, Nine still less, and rear-guard Ten-o'clock was preponderantly neither young nor slender, and more often sluggish than brisk.

Into this rear guard, though physically he belonged to no later period than eight-thirty, a blue roadster carried Hubert Landow. His broad shoulders were blue-coated, his blond hair gray-capped, and he was alone in the roadster. With a glance around to make sure Millar's dark young man was not in sight, Alec Rush turned his coupé in the blue car's wake.

They rode swiftly into the city, down into its financial center, where Hubert Landow deserted his roadster before a Redwood Street stock-broker's office. The morning had become noon before Landow was in the street again, turning his roadster northward.

When shadowed and shadower came to rest again they were in Mount Royal Avenue. Landow got out of his car and strode briskly into a large apartment building. A block distant, Alec Rush lighted a black cigar and sat still in his coupé. Half an hour passed. Alec Rush turned his head and sank his gold teeth deep into his cigar.

Scarcely twenty feet behind the coupé, in the doorway of a garage, a dark young man with high cheek-bones, high, straight shoulders, loitered. His nose was large. His suit was brown, as were the eyes with which he seemed to pay no especial attention to anything through the thin blue drift of smoke from the tip of a drooping cigarette.

Alec Rush took his cigar from his mouth to examine it, took a knife from his pocket to trim the bitten end, restored cigar to mouth and knife to pocket, and thereafter was as indifferent to all Mount Royal Avenue as the dark youth behind him. The one drowsed in his doorway. The other dozed in his car. And the afternoon crawled past one o'clock, past one-thirty.

Hubert Landow came out of the apartment building, vanished swiftly in his blue roadster. His going stirred neither of the motionless men, scarcely their eyes. Not until another fifteen minutes had gone did either of them move.

Then the dark youth left his doorway. He moved without haste, up the street, with short, almost mincing, steps. The back of Alec Rush's black-derbied head was to the youth when he passed the coupé, which may have been chance, for none could have said that the ugly man had so much as glanced at the other since his first sight of him. The dark young man let his eyes rest on the detective's back without interest as he passed. He went on up the street toward the apartment building Landow had visited, up its steps and out of sight into it.

When the dark young man had disappeared, Alec Rush threw away his cigar, stretched, yawned, and awakened the coupé's engine. Four blocks and two turnings from Mount Royal Avenue, he got out of the automobile, leaving it locked and empty in front of a gray stone church. He walked back to Mount Royal Avenue, to halt on a corner two blocks above his earlier position.

He had another half-hour of waiting before the dark young man appeared. Alec Rush was buying a cigar in a glass-fronted cigar store when the other passed. The young man boarded a street car at North Avenue and found a seat. The detective boarded the same car at the next corner and stood on the rear platform. Warned by an indicative forward hitching of the young man's shoulders and head, Alec Rush was the first passenger off the car at Madison Avenue, and the first aboard a southbound car there. And again, he was off first at Franklin Street.

The dark youth went straight to a rooming-house in this street, while the detective came to rest beside the window of a corner drug store specializing in theatrical make-up. There he loafed until half-past three. When the dark young man came into the street again it was to walk—Alec Rush behind him—to Eutaw Street, board a car, and ride to Camden Station.

There, in the waiting-room, the dark young man met a young woman who frowned and asked:

"Where in the hell have you been at?"

IV

The Man in the Picture

Passing them, the detective heard the petulant greeting, but the young man's reply was pitched too low for him to catch, nor did he hear anything else the young woman said. They talked for perhaps ten minutes, standing together in a deserted end of the waiting-room, so that Alec Rush could not have approached them without making himself conspicuous.

The young woman seemed to be impatient, urgent. The young man seemed to explain, to reassure. Now and then he gestured with the ugly, deft hands of a skilled mechanic. His companion became more agreeable. She was short, square, as if carved economically from a cube. Consistently, her nose also was short and her chin square. She had, on the whole, now that her earlier displeasure was passing, a merry face, a pert, pugnacious, rich-blooded face that advertised inexhaustible vitality. That advertisement was in every feature, from the live ends of her cut brown hair to the earth-gripping pose of her feet on the cement flooring. Her clothes were dark, quiet, expensive, but none too gracefully worn, hanging just the least bit bunchily here and there on her sturdy body.

Nodding vigorously several times, the young man at length tapped his cap-visor with two careless fingers and went out into the street. Alec Rush let him depart unshadowed. But when, walking slowly out to the iron train-shed gates, along them to the baggage window, thence to the street door, the young woman passed out of the station, the ugly man was behind her. He was still behind her when she joined the four o'clock shopping crowd at Lexington Street.

The young woman shopped with the whole-hearted air of one with nothing else on her mind. In the second department store she visited, Alec Rush left her looking at a display of laces while he moved as swiftly and directly as intervening shoppers would permit toward a tall, thick-shouldered, gray-haired woman in black, who seemed to be waiting for someone near the foot of a flight of stairs.

"Hello, Alec!" she said when he touched her arm, and her humorous eyes actually looked with pleasure at his uncouth face. "What are you doing in my territory?"

"Got a booster for you," he mumbled. "The chunky girl in blue at the lace counter. Make her?"

The store detective looked and nodded.

"Yes. Thanks, Alec. You're sure she's boosting, of course?"

"Now, Minnie!" he complained, his rasping voice throttled down to a metallic growl. "Would I be giving you a bum rumble? She went south with a couple of silk pieces, and it's more than likely she's got herself some lace by now."

"Um-hmm," said Minnie. "Well, when she sticks her foot on the sidewalk, I'll be with her."

Alec Rush put his hand on the store detective's arm again.

"I want a line on her," he said. "What do you say we tail her around and see what she's up to before we knock her over?"

"If it doesn't take all day," the woman agreed. And when the chunky girl in blue presently left the lace counter and the store, the detectives followed, into another store, ranging too far behind her to see any thieving she might have done, content to keep her under surveillance. From this last store their prey went down to where Pratt Street was dingiest, into a dingy three-story house of furnished flats.

Two blocks away a policeman was turning a corner.

"Take a plant on the joint while I get the copper," Alec Rush ordered.

When he returned with the policeman the store detective was waiting in the vestibule.

"Second floor," she said.

Behind her the house's street door stood open to show a dark hallway and the foot of a tattered-carpeted flight of steps. Into this dismal hallway appeared a slovenly thin woman in rumpled gray cotton, saying whiningly as she came forward, "What do you want? I keep a respectable house, I'll have you understand, and I——"

"Chunky, dark-eyed girl living here," Alec Rush croaked. "Second floor. Take us up."

The woman's scrawny face sprang into startled lines, faded eyes wide, as if mistaking the harshness of the detective's voice for the harshness of great emotion.

"Why—why—" she stammered, and then remembered the first principle of shady rooming-house management—never to stand in the way of the police. "I'll take you up," she agreed, and, hitching her wrinkled skirt in one hand, led the way up the stairs.

Her sharp fingers tapped on a door near the head of the stairs.

"Who's that?" a casually curt feminine voice asked.

"Landlady."

The chunky girl in blue, without her hat now, opened the door. Alec Rush moved a big foot forward to hold it open, while the landlady said, "This is her," the policeman said, "You'll have to come along," and Minnie said, "Dearie, we want to come in and talk to you."

"My God!" exclaimed the girl. "There'd be just as much sense to it if you'd all jumped out at me and yelled 'Boo!'"

"This ain't any way," Alec Rush rasped, moving forward, grinning his hideous friendly grin. "Let's go in where we can talk it over."

Merely by moving his loose-jointed bulk a step this way, a half-step that, turning his ugly face on this one and that one, he herded the little group as he wished, sending the landlady discontentedly away, marshaling the others into the girl's rooms.

"Remember, I got no idea what this is all about," said the girl when they were in her living-room, a narrow room where blue fought with red without ever compromising on purple. "I'm easy to get along with, and if you think this is a nice place to talk about whatever you want to talk about, go ahead! But if you're counting on me talking, too, you'd better smart me up."

"Boosting, dearie," Minnie said, leaning forward to pat the girl's arm. "I'm at Goodbody's."

"You think I've been shoplifting? Is that the idea?"

"Yeah. Exactly. Uh-huh. That's what." Alec Rush left her no doubt on the point.

The girl narrowed her eyes, puckered her red mouth, squinted sidewise at the ugly man.

"It's all right with me," she announced, "so long as Goodbody's hanging the rap on me—somebody I can sue for a million when it flops. I've got nothing to say. Take me for my ride."

"You'll get your ride, sister," the ugly man rasped good-naturedly. "Nobody's going to beat you out of it. But do you mind if I look around your place a little first?"

"Got anything with a judge's name on it that says you can?"

"No."

"Then you don't get a peep!"

Alec Rush chuckled, thrust his hands into his trouser pockets, and began to wander through the rooms, of which there were three. Presently he came out of the bedroom carrying a photograph in a silver frame.

"Who's this?" he asked the girl.

"Try and find out!"

"I am trying," he lied.

"You big bum!" said she. "You couldn't find water in the ocean!"

Alec Rush laughed with coarse heartiness. He could afford to. The photograph in his hand was of Hubert Landow.

v

The Overpaid Assassin

Twilight was around the gray stone church when the owner of the deserted coupé returned to it. The chunky girl—Polly Vanness was the name she had given—had been booked and lodged in a cell in the Southwestern Police Station. Quantities of stolen goods had been found in her flat. Her harvest of that afternoon was still on her person when Minnie and a police matron searched her. She had refused to talk. The detective had said nothing to her about his knowledge of the photograph's subject, or of her meeting in the railroad station with the dark young man. Nothing found in her rooms threw any light on either of these things.

Having eaten his evening meal before coming back to his car, Alec Rush now drove out to Charles-Street Avenue.

Lights glowed normally in the Landow house when he passed it. A little beyond it he turned his coupé so that it pointed toward the city, and brought it to rest in a tree-darkened curbside spot within sight of the house.

The night went along and no one left or entered the Landow house.

Finger nails clicked on the coupé's glass door.

A man stood there. Nothing could be said of him in the darkness except that he was not large, and that to have escaped the detective's notice until now he must have stealthily stalked the car from the rear.

Alec Rush put out a hand and the door swung open.

"Got a match?" the man asked.

The detective hesitated, said, "Yeah," and held out a box.

A match scraped and flared into a dark young face: large nose, high cheekbones: the young man Alec Rush had shadowed that afternoon.

But recognition, when it was voiced, was voiced by the dark young man.

"I thought it was you," he said simply as he applied the flaming match to his cigarette. "Maybe you don't know me, but I knew you when you were on the force."

The ex-detective-sergeant gave no meaning at all to a husky "Yeah."

"I thought it was you in the heap on Mount Royal this afternoon, but I couldn't make sure," the young man continued, entering the coupé, sitting beside the detective, closing the door. "Scuttle Zeipp's me. I ain't as well known as Napoleon, so if you've never heard of me there's no hard feelings."

"Yeah."

"That's the stuff! When you once think up a good answer, stick to it." Scuttle Zeipp's face was a sudden bronze mask in the glow of his cigarette. "The same answer'll do for my next question. You're interested in these here Landows? Yeah," he added in hoarse mimicry of the detective's voice.

Another inhalation lighted his face, and his words came smokily out as the glow faded.

"You ought to want to know what I'm doing hanging around 'em. I ain't tight. I'll tell you. I've been slipped half a grand to bump off the girl—twice. How do you like that?"

"I hear you," said Alec Rush. "But anybody can talk that knows the words."

"Talk? Sure it's talk," Zeipp admitted cheerfully. "But so's it talk when the judge says 'hanged by the neck until dead and may God have mercy on your soul!' Lots of things are talk, but that don't always keep 'em from being real."

"Yeah?"

"Yeah, brother, yeah! Now listen to this: it's one for the cuff. A certain party comes to me a couple of days ago with a knock-down from a party that knows me. See? This certain party asks me what I want to bump off a broad. I thought a grand would be right, and said so. Too stiff. We come to-gether on five hundred. I got two-fifty down and get the rest when the Landow twist is cold. Not so bad for a soft trick—a slug through the side of a car—huh?"

"Well, what are you waiting for?" the detective asked. "You want to make it a fancy caper—kill her on her birthday or a legal holiday?"

Scuttle Zeipp smacked his lips and poked the detective's chest with a finger in the dark.

"Not any, brother! I'm thinking way ahead of you! Listen to this: I pocket my two-fifty advance and come up here to give the ground a good casing, not wanting to lam into any-thing I didn't know was here. While I'm poking around, I run into another party that's poking around. This second party gives me a tumble, I talk smart, and bingo! First thing you know she's propositioning me. What do you guess? She wants to know what I want to bump off a broad! Is it the same one *she* wants stopped? I hope to tell you it is!

"I ain't so silly! I get my hands on another two hundred and fifty berries, with that much more coming when I put over the fast one. Now do you think I'm going to do any-thing to that Landow baby? You're dumb if you do. She's my meal ticket. If she lives till I pop her, she'll be older than ei-ther you or the bay. I've got five hundred out of her so far. What's the matter with sticking around and waiting for more customers that don't like her? If two of 'em want to buy her out of the world, why not more? The answer is, 'Yeah!' And on top of that, here you are snooping around her. Now there it is, brother, for you to look at and taste and smell."

Silence held for several minutes, in the darkness of the coupé's interior, and then the detective's harsh voice put a skeptical question:

"And who are these certain parties that want her out of the way?"

"Be yourself!" Scuttle Zeipp admonished him. "I'm laying down on 'em, right enough, but I ain't feeding 'em to you."

"What are you giving me all this for then?"

"What for? Because you're in on the lay somewhere. Crossing each other, neither of us can make a thin dimmer. If we don't hook up we'll just ruin the racket for each other. I've already made half a grand off this Landow. That's mine, but there's more to be picked up by a couple of men that know what they're doing. All right. I'm offering to throw in with you on a two-way cut of whatever else we can get. But my parties are out! I don't mind throwing them down, but I ain't rat enough to put the finger on them for you."

Alec Rush grunted and croaked another dubious inquiry.

"How come you trust me so much, Scuttle?"

The hired killer laughed knowingly.

"Why not? You're a right guy. You can see a profit when it's showed to you. They didn't chuck you off the force for forgetting to hang up your stocking. Besides, suppose you want to double-cross me, what can you do? You can't prove anything. I told you I didn't mean the woman any harm. I ain't even packing a gun. But all that's the bunk. You're a wise head. You know what's what. Me and you, Alec, we can get plenty!"

Silence again, until the detective spoke slowly, thoughtfully.

"The first thing would be to get a line on the reasons your parties want the girl put out. Got anything on that?"

"Not a whisper."

"Both of 'em women, I take it."

Scuttle Zeipp hesitated.

"Yes," he admitted. "But don't be asking me anything about 'em. In the first place, I don't know anything, and in the second, I wouldn't tip their mitts if I did."

"Yeah," the detective croaked, as if he quite understood his companion's perverted idea of loyalty. "Now if they're women, the chances are the racket hangs on a man. What do you think of Landow? He's a pretty lad."

Scuttle Zeipp leaned over to put his finger against the detective's chest again.

"You've got it, Alec! That could be it, damned if it couldn't!"

"Yeah," Alec Rush agreed, fumbling with the levers of his car. "We'll get away from here and stay away until I look into him."

At Franklin Street, half a block from the rooming-house into which he had shadowed the young man that afternoon, the detective stopped his coupé.

"You want to drop out here?" he asked.

Scuttle Zeipp looked sidewise, speculatively, into the elder man's ugly face.

"It'll do," the young man said, "but you're a damned good guesser, just the same." He stopped with a hand on the door. "It's a go, is it, Alec? Fifty-fifty?"

"I wouldn't say so," Alec Rush grinned at him with hideous good-nature. "You're not a bad lad, Scuttle, and if there's any gravy you'll get yours, but don't count on me mobbing up with you."

Zeipp's eyes jerked to slits, his lips snarled back from yellow teeth that were set edge to edge.

"You sell me out, you damned gorilla, and I'll—" He laughed the threat out of being, his dark face young and careless again. "Have it your own way, Alec. I didn't make no mistake when I throwed in with you. What you say goes."

"Yeah," the ugly man agreed. "Lay off that joint out there until I tell you. Maybe you'd better drop in to see me tomorrow. The phone book'll tell you where my office is. So long, kid."

"So long, Alec."

VI

Cathedral Street

In the morning Alec Rush set about investigating Hubert Landow. First he went to the City Hall, where he examined the gray books in which marriage licenses are indexed. Hubert Britman Landow and Sara Falsoner had been married six months before, he learned.

The bride's maiden name thickened the red in the detective's bloodshot eyes. Air hissed sharply from his flattened nostrils. "Yeah! Yeah!" he said to himself, so raspingly that a lawyer's skinny clerk, fiddling with other records at his elbow, looked frightenedly at him and edged a little away.

From the City Hall, Alec Rush carried the bride's name to two newspaper offices, where, after studying the files, he bought an armful of six-months-old papers. He took the papers to his office, spread them on his desk, and attacked them with a pair of shears. When the last one had been cut and thrown aside, there remained on his desk a thick sheaf of clippings.

Arranging his clippings in chronological order, Alec Rush lighted a black cigar, put his elbows on the desk, his ugly head between his palms, and began to read a story with which newspaper-reading Baltimore had been familiar half a year before.

Purged of irrelevancies and earlier digressions, the story was essentially this:

Jerome Falsoner, aged forty-five, was a bachelor who lived alone in a flat in Cathedral Street, on an income more than sufficient for his comfort. He was a tall man, but of delicate physique, the result, it may have been, of excessive indulgence in pleasure on a constitution none too strong in the beginning. He was well known, at least by sight, to all night-living Baltimoreans, and to those who frequented race-track, gambling-house, and the furtive cockpits that now and then materialize for a few brief hours in the forty miles of country that lie between Baltimore and Washington.

One Fanny Kidd, coming as was her custom at ten o'clock one morning to "do" Jerome Falsoner's rooms, found him lying on his back in his living-room, staring with dead eyes at a spot on the ceiling, a bright spot that was reflected sunlight—reflected from the metal hilt of his paper-knife, which protruded from his chest.

Police investigation established four facts:

First, Jerome Falsoner had been dead for fourteen hours when Fanny Kidd found him, which placed his murder at about eight o'clock the previous evening.

Second, the last persons known to have seen him alive were a woman named Madeline Boudin, with whom he had been intimate, and three of her friends. They had seen him, alive, at some time between seven-thirty and eight o'clock, or less than half an hour before his death. They had been driving down to a cottage on the Severn River, and Madeline Boudin had told the others she wanted to see Falsoner before she went. The others had remained in their car while she rang the bell. Jerome Falsoner opened the street door and she went in. Ten minutes later she came out and rejoined her friends. Jerome Falsoner came to the door with her, waving a hand at one of the men in the car—a Frederick Stoner, who knew Falsoner slightly, and who was connected with the district attorney's office. Two women, talking on the steps of a house across the street, had also seen Falsoner, and had seen Madeline Boudin and her friends drive away.

Third, Jerome Falsoner's heir and only near relative was his niece, Sara Falsoner, who, by some vagary of chance, was marrying Hubert Landow at the very hour that Fanny Kidd was finding her employer's dead body. Niece and uncle had seldom seen one another. The niece—for police suspicion settled on her for a short space—was definitely proved to have been at home, in her apartment in Carey Street, from six o'clock the evening of the murder until eight-thirty the next morning. Her husband, her fiancé then, had been there with her from six until eleven that evening. Prior to her marriage, the girl had been employed as stenographer by the same trust company that employed Ralph Millar.

Fourth, Jerome Falsoner, who had not the most even of dispositions, had quarreled with an Icelander named Einer Jokumsson in a gambling-house two days before he was murdered. Jokumsson had threatened him. Jokumsson—a short, heavily built man, dark-haired, dark-eyed—had vanished from his hotel, leaving his bags there, the day the body was found, and had not been seen since.

The last of these clippings carefully read, Alec Rush rocked back in his chair and made a thoughtful monster's face at the ceiling. Presently he leaned forward again to look into the telephone directory, and to call the number of Ralph Millar's trust company. But when he got his number he changed his mind.

"Never mind," he said into the instrument, and, called a number that was Goodbody's. Minnie, when she came to the telephone, told him that Polly Vanness had been identified as one Polly Bangs, arrested in Milwaukee two years ago for shoplifting, and given a two-year sentence. Minnie also said that Polly Bangs had been released on bail early that morning.

Alec Rush pushed back the telephone and looked through his clippings again until he found the address of Madeline Boudin, the woman who had visited Falsoner so soon before his death. It was a Madison Avenue number. Thither his coupé carried the detective.

No, Miss Boudin did not live there. Yes, she had lived there, but had moved four months ago. Perhaps Mrs. Blender, on the third floor, would know where she lived now. Mrs. Blender did not know. She knew Miss Boudin had moved to an apartment-house in Garrison Avenue, but did not think she was living there now. At the Garrison Avenue house: Miss Boudin had moved away a month and a half ago—somewhere in Mount Royal Avenue, perhaps. The number was not known.

The coupé carried its ugly owner to Mount Royal Avenue, to the apartment building he had seen first Hubert Landow and then Scuttle Zeipp visit the previous day. At the manager's office he made inquiries about a Walter Boyden, who was thought to live there. Walter Boyden was not known to the manager. There was a Miss Boudin in 604, but her name was B-o-u-d-i-n, and she lived alone.

Alec Rush left the building and got in his car again. He screwed up his savage red eyes, nodded his head in a satisfied way, and with one finger described a small circle in the air. Then he returned to his office.

Calling the trust company's number again, he gave Ralph Millar's name, and presently was speaking to the assistant cashier.

"This is Rush. Can you come up to the office right away?"

"What's that? Certainly. But how—how—? Yes, I'll be up in a minute."

None of the surprise that had been in Millar's telephoned voice was apparent when he reached the detective's office. He asked no questions concerning the detective's knowledge of his identity. In brown today, he was as neatly inconspicuous as he had been yesterday in gray.

504 THE ASSISTANT MURDERER

"Come in," the ugly man welcomed him. "Sit down. I've got to have some more facts, Mr. Millar."

Millar's thin mouth tightened and his brows drew together with obstinate reticence.

"I thought we settled that point, Rush. I told you——"

Alec Rush frowned at his client with jovial, though frightful exasperation.

"I know what you told me," he interrupted. "But that was then and this is now. The thing's coming unwound on me, and I can see just enough to get myself tangled up if I don't watch Harvey. I found your mysterious man, talked to him. He was following Mrs. Landow, right enough. According to the way he tells it, he's been hired to kill her."

Millar leaped from his chair to lean over the yellow desk, his face close to the detective's.

"My God, Rush, what are you saying? To kill her?"

"Now, now! Take it easy. He's not going to kill her. I don't think he ever meant to. But he claims he was hired to do it."

"You've arrested him? You've found the man who hired him?"

The detective squinted up his bloodshot eyes and studied the younger man's passionate face.

"As a matter of fact," he croaked calmly when he had finished his examination, "I haven't done either of those things. She's in no danger just now. Maybe the lad was stringing me, maybe he wasn't, but either way he wouldn't have spilled it to me if he meant to do anything. And when it comes right down to it, Mr. Millar, do you want him arrested?"

"Yes! That is—" Millar stepped back from the desk, sagged limply down on the chair again, and put shaking hands over his face. "My God, Rush, I don't know!" he gasped.

VII
Millar Talks

"Exactly," said Alec Rush. "Now here it is. Mrs. Landow was Jerome Falsoner's niece and heir. She worked for your trust company. She married Landow the morning her uncle was found dead. Yesterday Landow visited the building where

Madeline Boudin lives. She was the last person known to have
been in Falsoner's rooms before he was killed. But her alibi
seems to be as air-tight as the Landows'. The man who claims
he was hired to kill Mrs. Landow also visited Madeline
Boudin's building yesterday. I saw him go in. I saw him meet
another woman. A shoplifter, the second one. In her rooms I
found a photograph of Hubert Landow. Your dark man
claims he was hired twice to kill Mrs. Landow—by two
women, neither knowing the other had hired him. He won't
tell me who they are, but he doesn't have to."

The hoarse voice stopped and Alec Rush waited for Millar
to speak. But Millar was for the time without a voice. His eyes
were wide and despairingly empty. Alec Rush raised one big
hand, folded it into a fist that was almost perfectly spherical,
and thumped his desk softly.

"There it is, Mr. Millar," he rasped. "A pretty tangle. If
you'll tell me what you know, we'll get it straightened out,
never fear. If you don't—I'm out!"

Now Millar found words, however jumbled.

"You couldn't, Rush! You can't desert me—us—her! It's
not— You're not——"

But Alec Rush shook his ugly pear-shaped head with slow
emphasis.

"There's murder in this and the Lord knows what all. I've
got no liking for a blindfolded game. How do I know what
you're up to? You can tell me what you know—everything—
or you can find yourself another detective. That's flat."

Ralph Millar's fingers picked at each other, his teeth pulled
at his lips, his harassed eyes pleaded with the detective.

"You can't, Rush," he begged. "She's still in danger. Even
if you are right about that man not attacking her, she's not
safe. The women who hired him can hire another. You've got
to protect her, Rush."

"Yeah? Then you've got to talk."

"I've got to—? Yes, I'll talk, Rush. I'll tell you anything you
ask. But there's really nothing—or almost nothing—I know
beyond what you've already learned."

"She worked for your trust company?"

"Yes, in my department."

"Left there to be married?"

"Yes. That is— No, Rush, the truth is she was discharged. It was an outrage, but——"

"When was this?"

"It was the day before the—before she was married."

"Tell me about it."

"She had— I'll have to explain her situation to you first, Rush. She is an orphan. Her father, Ben Falsoner, had been wild in his youth—and perhaps not only in his youth—as I believe all the Falsoners have been. However, he had quarreled with his father—old Howard Falsoner—and the old man had cut him out of the will. But not altogether out. The old man hoped Ben would mend his ways, and he didn't mean to leave him with nothing in that event. Unfortunately he trusted it to his other son, Jerome.

"Old Howard Falsoner left a will whereby the income from his estate was to go to Jerome during Jerome's life. Jerome was to provide for his brother Ben as he saw fit. That is, he had an absolutely free hand. He could divide the income equally with his brother, or he could give him a pittance, or he could give him nothing, as Ben's conduct deserved. On Jerome's death the estate was to be divided equally among the old man's grandchildren.

"In theory, that was a fairly sensible arrangement, but not in practice—not in Jerome Falsoner's hands. You didn't know him? Well, he was the last man you'd ever trust with a thing of that sort. He exercised his power to the utmost. Ben Falsoner never got a cent from him. Three years ago Ben died, and so the girl, his only daughter, stepped into his position in relation to her grandfather's money. Her mother was already dead. Jerome Falsoner never paid her a cent.

"That was her situation when she came to the trust company two years ago. It wasn't a happy one. She had at least a touch of the Falsoner recklessness and extravagance. There she was: heiress to some two million dollars—for Jerome had never married and she was the only grandchild—but without any present income at all, except her salary, which was by no means a large one.

"She got in debt. I suppose she tried to economize at times, but there was always that two million dollars ahead to make scrimping doubly distasteful. Finally, the trust company officials heard of her indebtedness. A collector or two came to the office, in fact. Since she was employed in my department, I had the disagreeable duty of warning her. She promised to pay her debts and contract no more, and I suppose she did try, but she wasn't very successful. Our officials are old-fashioned, ultra-conservative. I did everything I could to save her, but it was no good. They simply would not have an employee who was heels over head in debt."

Millar paused a moment, looked miserably at the floor, and went on:

"I had the disagreeable task of telling her her services were no longer needed. I tried to— It was awfully unpleasant. That was the day before she married Landow. It—" he paused and, as if he could think of nothing else to say, repeated, "Yes, it was the day before she married Landow," and fell to staring miserably at the floor again.

Alec Rush, who had sat as still through the recital of this history as a carven monster on an old church, now leaned over his desk and put a husky question:

"And who is this Hubert Landow? What is he?"

Ralph Millar shook his downcast head.

"I don't know him. I've seen him. I know nothing of him."

"Mrs. Landow ever speak of him? I mean when she was in the trust company?"

"It's likely, but I don't remember."

"So you didn't know what to make of it when you heard she'd married him?"

The younger man looked up with frightened brown eyes.

"What are you getting at, Rush? You don't think— Yes, as you say, I was surprised. What are you getting at?"

"The marriage license," the detective said, ignoring his client's repeated question, "was issued to Landow four days before the wedding-day, four days before Jerome Falsoner's body was found."

Millar chewed a finger nail and shook his head hopelessly.

"I don't know what you're getting at," he mumbled around the finger. "The whole thing is bewildering."

"Isn't it a fact, Mr. Millar," the detective's voice filled the office with hoarse insistence, "that you were on more friendly terms with Sara Falsoner than with anyone else in the trust company?"

The younger man raised his head and looked Alec Rush in the eye—held his gaze with brown eyes that were doggedly level.

"Your fact is," he said quietly, "that I asked Sara Falsoner to marry me the day she left."

"Yeah. And she——?"

"And she—I suppose it was my fault. I was clumsy, crude, whatever you like. God knows what she thought—that I was asking her to marry me out of pity, that I was trying to force her into marriage by discharging her when I knew she was over her head in debt! She might have thought anything. Anyhow, it was—it was disagreeable."

"You mean she not only refused you, but was—well—disagreeable about it?"

"I do mean that."

Alec Rush sat back in his chair and brought fresh grotesqueries into his face by twisting his thick mouth crookedly up at one corner. His red eyes were evilly reflective on the ceiling.

"The only thing for it," he decided, "is to go to Landow and give him what we've got."

"But are you sure he——?" Millar objected indefinitely.

"Unless he's one whale of an actor, he's a lot in love with his wife," the detective said with certainty. "That's enough to justify taking the story to him."

Millar was not convinced.

"You're sure it would be wisest?"

"Yeah. We've got to go to one of three people with the tale—him, her, or the police. I think he's the best bet, but take your choice."

The younger man nodded reluctantly.

"All right. But you don't have to bring me into it, do you?" with quick alarm. "You can handle it so I won't be involved. You understand what I mean? She's his wife, and it would be——"

"Sure," Alec Rush promised, "I'll keep you covered up."

VIII
Sara Talks

Hubert Landow, twisting the detective's card in his fingers, received Alec Rush in a somewhat luxuriously furnished room in the second story of the Charles-Street Avenue house. He was standing—tall, blond, boyishly handsome—in the middle of the floor, facing the door, when the detective—fat, grizzled, battered and ugly—was shown in.

"You wish to see me? Here, sit down."

Hubert Landow's manner was neither restrained nor hearty. It was precisely the manner that might be expected of a young man receiving an unexpected call from so savage-visaged a detective.

"Yeah," said Alec Rush as they sat in facing chairs. "I've got something to tell you. It won't take much time, but it's kind of wild. It might be a surprise to you, and it might not. But it's on the level. I don't want you to think I'm kidding you."

Hubert Landow bent forward, his face all interest.

"I won't," he promised. "Go on."

"A couple of days ago I got a line on a man who might be tied up in a job I'm interested in. He's a crook. Trailing him around, I discovered he was interested in your affairs, and your wife's. He's shadowed you and he's shadowed her. He was loafing down the street from a Mount Royal Avenue apartment that you went in yesterday, and he went in there later himself."

"But what the devil is he up to?" Landow exclaimed. "You think he's——"

"Wait," the ugly man advised. "Wait until you've heard it all, and then you can tell me what you make of it. He came out of there and went to Camden Station, where he met a young woman. They talked a bit, and later in the afternoon she was picked up in a department store—shoplifting. Her name is Polly Bangs, and she's done a hitch in Wisconsin for the same racket. Your photograph was on her dresser."

"My photograph?"

Alec Rush nodded placidly up into the face of the young man who was now standing.

"Yours. You know this Polly Bangs? A chunky, square-built girl of twenty-six or so, with brown hair and eyes—saucy looking?"

Hubert Landow's face was a puzzled blank.

"No! What the devil could she be doing with my picture?" he demanded. "Are you sure it was mine?"

"Not dead sure, maybe, but sure enough to need proof that it wasn't. Maybe she's somebody you've forgotten, or maybe she ran across the picture somewhere and kept it because she liked it."

"Nonsense!" The blond man squirmed at this tribute to his face, and blushed a vivid red beside which Alec Rush's complexion was almost colorless. "There must be some sensible reason. She has been arrested, you say?"

"Yeah, but she's out on bail now. But let me get along with my story. Last night this thug I've told you about and I had a talk. He claims he has been hired to kill your wife."

Hubert Landow, who had returned to his chair, now jerked in it so that its joints creaked strainingly. His face, crimson a second ago, drained paper-white. Another sound than the chair's creaking was faint in the room: the least of muffled gasps. The blond young man did not seem to hear it, but Alec Rush's bloodshot eyes flicked sidewise for an instant to focus fleetingly on a closed door across the room.

Landow was out of his chair again, leaning down to the detective, his fingers digging into the ugly man's loose muscular shoulders.

"This is horrible!" he was crying. "We've got to—"

The door at which the detective had looked a moment ago opened. A beautiful tall girl came through—Sara Landow. Her hair rumpled, was an auburn cloud around her white face. Her eyes were dead things. She walked slowly toward the men, her body inclined a little forward, as if against a strong wind.

"It's no use, Hubert." Her voice was dead as her eyes. "We may as well face it. It's Madeline Boudin. She has found out that I killed my uncle."

"Hush, darling, hush!" Landow caught his wife in his arms and tried to soothe her with a caressing hand on her shoulder. "You don't know what you're saying."

"Oh, but I do." She shrugged herself listlessly out of his arms and sat in the chair Alec Rush had just vacated. "It's Madeline Boudin, you know it is. She knows I killed Uncle Jerome."

Landow whirled to the detective, both hands going out to grip the ugly man's arm.

"You won't listen to what she's saying, Rush?" he pleaded. "She hasn't been well. She doesn't know what she's saying."

Sara Landow laughed with weary bitterness.

"Haven't been well?" she said. "No, I haven't been well, not since I killed him. How could I be well after that? You are a detective." Her eyes lifted their emptiness to Alec Rush. "Arrest me. I killed Jerome Falsoner."

Alec Rush, standing arms akimbo, legs apart, scowled at her, saying nothing.

"You can't, Rush!" Landow was tugging at the detective's arm again. "You can't, man. It's ridiculous! You—"

"Where does this Madeline Boudin fit in?" Alec Rush's harsh voice demanded. "I know she was chummy with Jerome, but why should she want your wife killed?"

Landow hesitated, shifting his feet, and when he replied it was reluctantly.

"She was Jerome's mistress, had a child by him. My wife, when she learned of it, insisted on making her a settlement out of the estate. It was in connection with that that I went to see her yesterday."

"Yeah. Now to get back to Jerome: you and your wife were supposed to be in her apartment at the time he was killed, if I remember right?"

Sara Landow sighed with spiritless impatience.

"Must there be all this discussion?" she asked in a small, tired voice. "I killed him. No one else killed him. No one else was there when I killed him. I stabbed him with the paper-knife when he attacked me, and he said, 'Don't! Don't!' and began to cry, down on his knees, and I ran out."

Alec Rush looked from the girl to the man. Landow's face was wet with perspiration, his hands were white fists, and something quivered in his chest. When he spoke his voice was as hoarse as the detective's, if not so loud.

"Sara, will you wait here until I come back? I'm going out for a little while, possibly an hour. You'll wait here and not do anything until I return?"

"Yes," the girl said, neither curiosity nor interest in her voice. "But it's no use, Hubert. I should have told you in the beginning. It's no use."

"Just wait for me, Sara," he pleaded, and then bent his head to the detective's deformed ear. "Stay with her, Rush, for God's sake!" he whispered, and went swiftly out of the room.

The front door banged shut. An automobile purred away from the house. Alec Rush spoke to the girl.

"Where's the phone?"

"In the next room," she said, without looking up from the handkerchief her fingers were measuring.

The detective crossed to the door through which she had entered the room, found that it opened into a library, where a telephone stood in a corner. On the other side of the room a clock indicated three-thirty-five. The detective went to the telephone and called Ralph Millar's office, asked for Millar, and told him:

"This is Rush. I'm at the Landow's. Come up right away."

"But I can't, Rush. Can't you understand my—"

"Can't hell!" croaked Alec Rush. "Get here quick!"

IX

The Shadow

The young woman with dead eyes, still playing with the hem of her handkerchief, did not look up when the ugly man returned to the room. Neither of them spoke. Alec Rush, standing with his back to a window, twice took out his watch to glare savagely at it.

The faint tingling of the doorbell came from below. The detective went across to the hall door and down the front stairs, moving with heavy swiftness. Ralph Millar, his face a field in which fear and embarrassment fought, stood in the vestibule, stammering something unintelligible to the maid who had opened the door. Alec Rush put the girl brusquely aside, brought Millar in, guided him upstairs.

"She says she killed Jerome," he muttered into his client's ear as they mounted.

Ralph Millar's face went dreadfully white, but there was no surprise in it.

"You knew she killed him?" Alec Rush growled.

Millar tried twice to speak and made no sound. They were on the second-floor landing before the words came.

"I saw her on the street that night, going toward his flat!"

Alec Rush snorted viciously and turned the younger man toward the room where Sara Landow sat.

"Landow's out," he whispered hurriedly. "I'm going out. Stay with her. She's shot to hell—likely to do anything if she's left alone. If Landow gets back before I do, tell him to wait for me."

Before Millar could voice the confusion in his face they were across the sill and into the room. Sara Landow raised her head. Her body was lifted from the chair as if by an invisible power. She came up tall and erect on her feet. Millar stood just inside the door. They looked eye into eye, posed each as if in the grip of a force pushing them together, another holding them apart.

Alec Rush hurried clumsily and silently down to the street.

In Mount Royal Avenue, Alec Rush saw the blue roadster at once. It was standing empty before the apartment building in which Madeline Boudin lived. The detective drove past it and turned his coupé in to the curb three blocks below. He had barely come to rest there when Landow ran out of the apartment building, jumped into his car, and drove off. He drove to a Charles Street hotel. Behind him went the detective.

In the hotel, Landow walked straight to the writing room. For half an hour he sat there, bending over a desk, covering sheet after sheet of paper with rapidly written words, while the detective sat behind a newspaper in a secluded angle of the lobby, watching the writing-room exit. Landow came out of the room stuffing a thick envelope in his pocket, left the hotel, got into his machine, and drove to the office of a messenger service company in St. Paul Street.

He remained in this office for five minutes. When he came out he ignored his roadster at the curb, walking instead to

Calvert Street, where he boarded a northbound street-car. Alec Rush's coupé rolled along behind the car. At Union Station, Landow left the street-car and went to the ticket window. He had just asked for a one-way ticket to Philadelphia when Alec Rush tapped him on the shoulder.

Hubert Landow turned slowly, the money for his ticket still in his hand. Recognition brought no expression to his handsome face.

"Yes," he said coolly, "what is it?"

Alec Rush nodded his ugly head at the ticket-window, at the money in Landow's hand.

"This is nothing for you to be doing," he growled.

"Here you are," the ticket-seller said through his grille. Neither of the men in front paid any attention to him. A large woman in pink, red and violet, jostling Landow, stepped on his foot and pushed past him to the window. Landow stepped back, the detective following.

"You shouldn't have left Sara alone," said Landow. "She's—"

"She's not alone. I got somebody to stay with her."

"Not—?"

"Not the police, if that's what you're thinking."

Landow began to pace slowly down the long concourse, the detective keeping step with him. The blond man stopped and looked sharply into the other's face.

"Is it that fellow Millar who's with her?" he demanded.

"Yeah."

"Is he the man you're working for, Rush?"

"Yeah."

Landow resumed his walking. When they had reached the northern extremity of the concourse, he spoke again.

"What does he want, this Millar?"

Alec Rush shrugged his thick, limber shoulders and said nothing.

"Well, what do you want?" the young man asked with some heat, facing the detective squarely now.

"I don't want you going out of town."

Landow pondered that, scowling.

"Suppose I insist on going," he asked, "how will you stop me?"

"Accomplice after the fact in Jerome's murder would be a charge I could hold you on."

Silence again, until broken by Landow.

"Look here, Rush. You're working for Millar. He's out at my house. I've just sent a letter out to Sara by messenger. Give them time to read it, and then phone Millar there. Ask him if he wants me held or not."

Alec Rush shook his head decidedly.

"No good," he rasped. "Millar's too rattle-brained for me to take his word for anything like that over the phone. We'll go back there and have a talk all around."

Now it was Landow who balked.

"No," he snapped. "I won't!" He looked with cool calculation at the detective's ugly face. "Can I buy you, Rush?"

"No, Landow. Don't let my looks and my record kid you."

"I thought not." Landow looked at the roof and at his feet, and he blew his breath out sharply. "We can't talk here. Let's find a quiet place."

"The heap's outside," Alec Rush said, "and we can sit in that."

X

Bangs

Seated in Alec Rush's coupé, Hubert Landow lighted a cigarette, the detective one of his black cigars.

"That Polly Bangs you were talking about, Rush," the blond man said without preamble, "is my wife. My name is Henry Bangs. You won't find my fingerprints anywhere. When Polly was picked up in Milwaukee a couple of years ago and sent over, I came east and fell in with Madeline Boudin. We made a good team. She had brains in chunks, and if I've got somebody to do my thinking for me, I'm a pretty good worker myself."

He smiled at the detective, pointing at his own face with his cigarette. While Alec Rush watched, a tide of crimson surged into the blond man's face until it was rosy as a blushing schoolgirl's. He laughed again and the blush began to fade.

"That's my best trick," he went on. "Easy if you have the gift and keep in practice: fill your lungs, try to force the air out while keeping it shut off at the larynx. It's a gold mine for a grifter! You'd be surprised how people will trust me after I've turned on a blush or two for 'em. So Madeline and I were in the money. She had brains, nerve and a good front. I have everything but brains. We turned a couple of tricks—one con and one blackmail—and then she ran into Jerome Falsoner. We were going to give him the squeeze at first. But when Madeline found out that Sara was his heiress, that she was in debt, and that she and her uncle were on the outs, we ditched that racket and cooked a juicier one. Madeline found somebody to introduce me to Sara. I made myself agreeable, playing the boob—the shy but worshipful young man.

"Madeline had brains, as I've said. She used 'em all this time. I hung around Sara, sending her candy, books, flowers, taking her to shows and dinner. The books and shows were part of Madeline's work. Two of the books mentioned the fact that a husband can't be made to testify against his wife in court, nor wife against husband. One of the plays touched the same thing. That was planting the seeds. We planted another with my blushing and mumbling—persuaded Sara, or rather let her discover for herself, that I was the clumsiest liar in the world.

"The planting done, we began to push the game along. Madeline kept on good terms with Jerome. Sara was getting deeper in debt. We helped her in still deeper. We had a burglar clean out her apartment one night—Ruby Sweeger, maybe you know him. He's in stir now for another caper. He got what money she had and most of the things she could have hocked in a pinch. Then we stirred up some of the people she owed, sent them anonymous letters warning them not to count too much on her being Jerome's heir. Foolish letters, but they did the trick. A couple of her creditors sent collectors to the trust company.

"Jerome got his income from the estate quarterly. Madeline knew the dates, and Sara knew them. The day before the next one, Madeline got busy on Sara's creditors again. I don't know what she told them this time, but it was enough. They descended on the trust company in a flock, with the result that the next day Sara was given two weeks' pay and discharged. When she came out I met her—by chance—yes, I'd been watching for her since morning. I took her for a drive and got her back to her apartment at six o'clock. There we found more frantic creditors waiting to pounce on her. I chased them out, played the big-hearted boy, making embarrassed offers of all sorts of help. She refused them, of course, and I could see decision coming into her face. She knew this was the day on which Jerome got his quarterly check. She determined to go see him, to demand that he pay her debts at least. She didn't tell me where she was going, but I could see it plain enough, since I was looking for it.

"I left her and waited across the street from her apartment, in Franklin Square, until I saw her come out. Then I found a telephone, called up Madeline, and told her Sara was on her way to her uncle's flat."

Landow's cigarette scorched his fingers. He dropped it, crushed it under his foot, lighted another.

"This is a long-winded story, Rush," he apologized, "but it'll soon be over now."

"Keep talking, son," said Alec Rush.

"There were some people in Madeline's place when I phoned her—people trying to persuade her to go down the country on a party. She agreed now. They would give her an even better alibi than the one she had cooked up. She told them she had to see Jerome before she left, and they drove her over to his place and waited in their car while she went in with him.

"She had a pint bottle of cognac with her, all doped and ready. She poured out a drink of it for Jerome, telling him of the new bootlegger she had found who had a dozen or more cases of this cognac to sell at a reasonable price. The cognac was good enough and the price low enough to make Jerome think she had dropped in to let him in on something good. He gave her an order to pass on to the bootlegger. Making sure his steel paper-knife was in full view on the table, Madeline rejoined her friends, taking Jerome as far as the door so they would see he was still alive, and drove off.

"Now I don't know what Madeline had put in that cognac. If she told me, I've forgotten. It was a powerful drug—not a poison, you understand, but an excitant. You'll see what I mean when you hear the rest. Sara must have reached her uncle's flat ten or fifteen minutes after Madeline's departure. Her uncle's face, she says, was red, inflamed, when he opened the door for her. But he was a frail man, while she was strong, and she wasn't afraid of the devil himself, for that matter. She went in and demanded that he settle her debts, even if he didn't choose to make her an allowance out of his income.

"They were both Falsoners, and the argument must have grown hot. Also the drug was working on Jerome, and he had no will with which to fight it. He attacked her. The paper-knife was on the table, as Madeline had seen. He was a maniac. Sara was not one of your corner-huddling, screaming girls. She grabbed the paper-knife and let him have it. When he fell, she turned and ran.

"Having followed her as soon as I'd finished telephoning to Madeline, I was standing on Jerome's front steps when she dashed out. I stopped her and she told me she'd killed her uncle. I made her wait there while I went in, to see if he was really dead. Then I took her home, explaining my presence at Jerome's door by saying, in my boobish, awkward way, that I had been afraid she might do something reckless and had thought it best to keep an eye on her.

"Back in her apartment, she was all for giving herself up to the police. I pointed out the danger in that, arguing that, in debt, admittedly going to her uncle for money, being his heiress, she would most certainly be convicted of having murdered him so she would get the money. Her story of his attack, I persuaded her, would be laughed at as a flimsy yarn. Dazed, she wasn't hard to convince. The next step was easy. The police would investigate her, even if they didn't especially suspect her. I was, so far as we knew, the only person whose testimony could convict her. I was loyal enough, but wasn't I the clumsiest liar in the world? Didn't the mildest lie make me blush like an auctioneer's flag? The way around that difficulty lay in what two of the books I had given her, and one of the plays we had seen, had shown: if I was her husband I couldn't be made to testify against her. We were married the next morning, on a license I had been carrying for nearly a week.

"Well, there we were. I was married to her. She had a couple of millions coming when her uncle's affairs were straightened out. She couldn't possibly, it seemed, escape arrest and conviction. Even if no one had seen her entering or leaving her uncle's flat, everything still pointed to her guilt, and the foolish course I had persuaded her to follow would simply ruin her chance of pleading self-defense. If they hanged her, the two million would come to me. If she got a long term in prison, I'd have the handling of the money at least."

Landow dropped and crushed his second cigarette and stared for a moment straight ahead into distance.

"Do you believe in God, or Providence, or Fate, or any of that, Rush?" he asked. "Well, some believe in one thing and some in another, but listen. Sara was never arrested, never even really suspected. It seems there was some sort of Finn or Swede who had had a run-in with Jerome and threatened him. I suppose he couldn't account for his whereabouts the night of the killing, so he went into hiding when he heard of Jerome's murder. The police suspicion settled on him. They looked Sara up, of course, but not very thoroughly. No one seems to have seen her in the street, and the people in her apartment house, having seen her come in at six o'clock with me, and not having seen her—or not remembering if they did—go out or in again, told the police she had been in all evening. The police were too much interested in the missing Finn, or whatever he was, to look any further into Sara's affairs.

"So there we were again. I was married into the money, but I wasn't fixed so I could hand Madeline her cut. Madeline said we'd let things run along as they were until the estate was settled up, and then we could tip Sara off to the police. But by the time the money was settled up there was another hitch. This one was my doing. I—I—well, I wanted to go on just as we were. Conscience had nothing to do with it, you understand? It was simply that—well—that living on with Sara was the only thing I wanted. I wasn't even sorry for what I'd done, because if it hadn't been for that I would never have had her.

"I don't know whether I can make this clear to you, Rush, but even now I don't regret any of it. If it could have been different—but it couldn't. It had to be this way or none. And I've had those six months. I can see that I've been a chump. Sara was never for me. I got her by a crime and a trick, and while I held on to a silly hope that some day she'd—she'd look at me as I did at her, I knew in my heart all the time it was no use. There had been a man—your Millar. She's free now that it's out about my being married to Polly, and I hope she—I hope— Well, Madeline began to howl for action. I told Sara that Madeline had had a child by Jerome, and Sara agreed to settle some money on her. But that didn't satisfy Madeline. It wasn't sentiment with her. I mean, it wasn't any feeling for me, it was just the money. She wanted every cent she could get, and she couldn't get enough to satisfy her in a settlement of the kind Sara wanted to make.

"With Polly, it was that too, but maybe a little more. She's fond of me, I think. I don't know how she traced me here after she got out of the Wisconsin big house, but I can see how she figured things. I was married to a wealthy woman. If the woman died—shot by a bandit in a hold-up attempt—then I'd have money, and Polly would have both me and money. I haven't seen her, wouldn't know she was in Baltimore if you hadn't told me, but that's the way it would work out in her mind. The killing idea would have occurred just as easily to Madeline. I had told her I wouldn't stand for pushing the game through on Sara. Madeline knew that if she went ahead on her own hook and hung the Falsoner murder on Sara I'd blow up the whole racket. But if Sara died, then I'd have the money and Madeline would draw her cut. So that was it.

"I didn't know that until you told me, Rush. I don't give a damn for your opinion of me, but it's God's truth that I didn't know that either Polly or Madeline was trying to have Sara killed. Well, that's about all. Were you shadowing me when I went to the hotel?"

"Yeah."

"I thought so. That letter I wrote and sent home told just about what I've told you, spilled the whole story. I was going to run for it, leaving Sara in the clear. She's clear, all right, but now I'll have to face it. But I don't want to see her again, Rush."

"I wouldn't think you would," the detective agreed. "Not after making a killer of her."

"But I didn't," Landow protested. "She isn't. I forgot to tell you that, but I put it in the letter. Jerome Falsoner was not dead, not even dying, when I went past her into the flat. The knife was too high in his chest. I killed him, driving the knife into the same wound again, but downward. That's what I went in for, to make sure he was finished!"

Alec Rush screwed up his savage bloodshot eyes, looked long into the confessed murderer's face.

"That's a lie," he croaked at last, "but a decent one. Are you sure you want to stick to it? The truth will be enough to clear the girl, and maybe won't swing you."

"What difference does it make?" the younger man asked. "I'm a gone baby anyhow. And I might as well put Sara in the clear with herself as well as with the law. I'm caught to rights and another rap won't hurt. I told you Madeline had brains. I was afraid of them. She'd have had something up her sleeve to spring on us—to ruin Sara with. She could out-smart me without trying. I couldn't take any chances."

He laughed into Alec Rush's ugly face and, with a somewhat theatrical gesture, jerked one cuff an inch or two out of his coat-sleeve. The cuff was still damp with a maroon stain.

"I killed Madeline an hour ago," said Henry Bangs, alias Hubert Landow.

Creeping Siamese

STANDING beside the cashier's desk in the front office of the Continental Detective Agency's San Francisco branch, I was watching Porter check up my expense account when the man came in. He was a tall man, raw-boned, hard-faced. Grey clothes bagged loosely from his wide shoulders. In the late afternoon sunlight that came through partially drawn blinds, his skin showed the color of new tan shoes.

He opened the door briskly, and then hesitated, standing in the doorway, holding the door open, turning the knob back and forth with one bony hand. There was no indecision in his face. It was ugly and grim, and its expression was the expression of a man who is remembering something disagreeable.

Tommy Howd, our freckled and snub-nosed office boy, got up from his desk and went to the rail that divided the office.

"Do you—?" Tommy began, and jumped back.

The man had let go the doorknob. He crossed his long arms over his chest, each hand gripping a shoulder. His mouth stretched wide in a yawn that had nothing to do with relaxation. His mouth clicked shut. His lips snarled back from clenched yellow teeth.

"Hell!" he grunted, full of disgust, and pitched down on the floor.

I heaved myself over the rail, stepped across his body, and went out into the corridor.

Four doors away, Agnes Braden, a plump woman of thirty-something who runs a public stenographic establishment, was going into her office.

"Miss Braden!" I called, and she turned, waiting for me to come up. "Did you see the man who just came in our office?"

"Yes." Curiosity put lights in her green eyes. "A tall man who came up in the elevator with me. Why?"

"Was he alone?"

"Yes. That is, he and I were the only ones who got off at this floor. Why?"

"Did you see anybody close to him?"

"No, though I didn't notice him in the elevator. Why?"

"Did he act funny?"

"Not that I noticed. Why?"

"Thanks. I'll drop in and tell you about it later."

I made a circuit of the corridors on our floor, finding nothing.

The raw-boned man was still on the floor when I returned to the office, but he had been turned over on his back. He was as dead as I had thought. The Old Man, who had been examining him, straightened up as I came in. Porter was at the telephone, trying to get the police. Tommy Howd's eyes were blue half-dollars in a white face.

"Nothing in the corridors," I told the Old Man. "He came up in the elevator with Agnes Braden. She says he was alone, and she saw nobody close to him."

"Quite so." The Old Man's voice and smile were as pleasantly polite as if the corpse at his feet had been a part of the pattern in the carpet. Fifty years of sleuthing have left him with no more emotion than a pawnbroker. "He seems to have been stabbed in the left breast, a rather large wound that was staunched with this piece of silk"—one of his feet poked at a rumpled ball of red cloth on the floor—"which seems to be a sarong."

Today is never Tuesday to the Old Man: it *seems* to be Tuesday.

"On his person," he went on, "I have found some nine hundred dollars in bills of various denominations, and some silver; a gold watch and a pocket knife of English manufacture; a Japanese silver coin, 50 *sen*; tobacco, pipe and matches; a Southern Pacific timetable; two handkerchiefs without laundry marks; a pencil and several sheets of blank paper; four two-cent stamps; and a key labeled *Hotel Montgomery, Room 540*.

"His clothes seem to be new. No doubt we shall learn something from them when we make a more thorough examination, which I do not care to make until the police come. Meanwhile, you had better go to the Montgomery and see what you can learn there."

In the Hotel Montgomery's lobby the first man I ran into was the one I wanted: Pederson, the house copper, a blond-mustached ex-bartender who doesn't know any more about gum-shoeing than I do about saxaphones, but who does know people and how to handle them, which is what his job calls for.

"Hullo!" he greeted me. "What's the score?"

"Six to one, Seattle, end of the fourth. Who's in 540, Pete?"

"They're not playing in Seattle, you chump! Portland! A man that hasn't got enough civic spirit to know where his team—"

"Stop it, Pete! I've got no time to be fooling with your childish pastimes. A man just dropped dead in our joint with one of your room-keys in his pocket—540."

Civic spirit went blooey in Pederson's face.

"540?" He stared at the ceiling. "That would be that fellow Rounds. Dropped dead, you say?"

"Dead. Tumbled down in the middle of the floor with a knife-cut in him. Who is this Rounds?"

"I couldn't tell you much off-hand. A big bony man with leathery skin. I wouldn't have noticed him excepting he was such a sour looking body."

"That's the bird. Let's look him up."

At the desk we learned that the man had arrived the day before, registering as H. R. Rounds, New York, and telling the clerk he expects to leave within three days. There was no record of mail or telephone calls for him. Nobody knew when he had gone out, since he had not left his key at the desk. Neither elevator boys nor bell-hops could tell us anything.

His room didn't add much to our knowledge. His baggage consisted of one pigskin bag, battered and scarred, and covered with the marks of labels that had been scraped off. It was locked, but traveling bags locks don't amount to much. This one held us up about five minutes.

Rounds' clothes—some in the bag, some in the closet—were neither many nor expensive, but they were all new. The washable stuff was without laundry marks. Everything was of popular makes, widely advertised brands that could be bought in any city in the country. There wasn't a piece of paper with anything written on it. There wasn't an identifying tag. There wasn't anything in the room to tell where Rounds had come from or why.

Pederson was peevish about it.

"I guess if he hadn't got killed he'd of beat us out of a week's bill! These guys that don't carry anything to identify 'em, and that don't leave their keys at the desk when they go out, ain't to be trusted too much!"

We had just finished our search when a bell-hop brought Detective Sergeant O'Gar, of the police department Homicide Detail, into the room.

"Been down to the Agency?" I asked him.

"Yeah, just came from there."

"What's new?"

O'Gar pushed back his wide-brimmed black village-constable's hat and scratched his bullet head.

"Not a heap. The doc says he was opened with a blade at least six inches long by a couple wide, and that he couldn't of lived two hours after he got the blade—most likely not more'n one. We didn't find any news on him. What've you got here?"

"His name is Rounds. He registered here yesterday from New York. His stuff is new, and there's nothing on any of it to tell us anything except that he didn't want to leave a trail. No letters, no memoranda, nothing. No blood, no signs of a row, in the room."

O'Gar turned to Pederson.

"Any brown men been around the hotel? Hindus or the like?"

"Not that I saw," the house copper said. "I'll find out for you."

"Then the red silk was a sarong?" I asked.

"And an expensive one," the detective sergeant said. "I saw a lot of 'em the four years I was soldiering on the islands, but I never saw as good a one as that."

"Who wears them?"

"Men and women in the Philippines, Borneo, Java, Sumatra, Malay Peninsula, parts of India."

"Is it your idea that whoever did the carving advertised himself by running around in the streets in a red petticoat?"

"Don't try to be funny!" he growled at me. "They're often enough twisted or folded up into sashes or girdles. And how do I know he was knifed in the street? For that matter, how do I know he wasn't cut down in your joint?"

"We always bury our victims without saying anything about 'em. Let's go down and give Pete a hand in the search for your brown men."

That angle was empty. Any brown men who had snooped around the hotel had been too good at it to be caught.

I telephoned the Old Man, telling him what I had learned—which didn't cost me much breath—and O'Gar and I spent the rest of the evening sharp-shooting around without ever getting on the target once. We questioned taxicab drivers, questioned the three Roundses listed in the telephone book, and our ignorance was as complete when we were through as when we started.

The morning papers, on the streets at a little after eight o'clock that evening, had the story as we knew it.

At eleven o'clock O'Gar and I called it a night, separating in the direction of our respective beds.

We didn't stay apart long.

II

I opened my eyes sitting on the side of my bed in the dim light of a moon that was just coming up, with the ringing telephone in my hand.

O'Gar's voice: "1856 Broadway! On the hump!"

"1856 Broadway," I repeated, and he hung up.

I finished waking up while I phoned for a taxicab, and then wrestled my clothes on. My watch told me it was 12:55 A.M. as I went downstairs. I hadn't been fifteen minutes in bed.

1856 Broadway was a three-story house set behind a pocket-size lawn in a row of like houses behind like lawns. The others were dark. 1856 shed light from every window, and from the open front door. A policeman stood in the vestibule.

"Hello, Mac! O'Gar here?"

"Just went in."

I walked into a brown and buff reception hall, and saw the detective sergeant going up the wide stairs.

"What's up?" I asked as I joined him.

"Don't know."

On the second floor we turned to the left, going into a library or sitting room that stretched across the front of the house.

A man in pajamas and bathrobe sat on a davenport there, with one bared leg stretched out on a chair in front of him. I recognized him when he nodded to me: Austin Richter, owner of a Market Street moving picture theater. He was a round-faced man of forty-five or so, partly bald, for whom the Agency had done some work a year or so before in connection with a ticket-seller who had departed without turning in the day's receipts.

In front of Richter a thin white-haired man with doctor written all over him stood looking at Richter's leg, which was wrapped in a bandage just below the knee. Beside the doctor, a tall woman in a fur-trimmed dressing-gown stood, a roll of gauze and a pair of scissors in her hands. A husky police corporal was writing in a notebook at a long narrow table, a thick hickory walking stick laying on the bright blue table cover at his elbow.

All of them looked around at us as we came into the room. The corporal got up and came over to us.

"I knew you were handling the Rounds job, sergeant, so I thought I'd best get word to you as soon as I heard they was brown men mixed up in this."

"Good work, Flynn," O'Gar said. "What happened here?"

"Burglary, or maybe only attempted burglary. They was four of them—crashed the kitchen door."

Richter was sitting up very straight, and his blue eyes were suddenly excited, as were the brown eyes of the woman.

"I beg your pardon," he said, "but is there—you mentioned brown men in connection with another affair—is there another?"

O'Gar looked at me.

"You haven't seen the morning papers?" I asked the theatre owner.

"No."

"Well, a man came into the Continental office late this afternoon, with a stab in his chest, and died there. Pressed against the wound, as if to stop the bleeding, was a sarong, which is where we got the brown men idea."

"His name?"

"Rounds, H. R. Rounds."

The name brought no recognition into Richter's eyes.

"A tall man, thin, with dark skin?" he asked. "In a grey suit?"

"All of that."

Richter twisted around to look at the woman.

"Molloy!" he exclaimed.

"Molloy!" she exclaimed.

"So you know him?"

Their faces came back toward me.

"Yes. He was here this afternoon. He left—"

Richter stopped, to turn to the woman again, questioningly.

"Yes, Austin," she said, putting gauze and scissors on the table, and sitting down beside him on the davenport. "Tell them."

He patted her hand and looked up at me again with the expression of a man who has seen a nice spot on which to lay down a heavy load.

"Sit down. It isn't a long story, but sit down."

We found ourselves chairs.

"Molloy—Sam Molloy—that is his name, or the name I have always known him by. He came here this afternoon. He'd either called up the theater or gone there, and they had told him I was home. I hadn't seen him for three years. We could see—both my wife and I—that there was something the matter with him when he came in.

"When I asked him, he said he'd been stabbed, by a Siamese, on his way here. He didn't seem to think the wound amounted to much, or pretended he didn't. He wouldn't let us fix it for him, or look at it. He said he'd go to a doctor after he left, after he'd got rid of the thing. That was what he had come to me for. He wanted me to hide it, to take care of it until he came for it again.

"He didn't talk much. He was in a hurry, and suffering. I didn't ask him any questions. I couldn't refuse him anything. I couldn't question him even though he as good as told us that it was illegal as well as dangerous. He saved our lives once—more than my wife's life—down in Mexico, where we first knew him. That was in 1916. We were caught down there during the Villa troubles. Molloy was running guns over the border, and he had enough influence with the bandits to have us released when it looked as if we were done for.

"So this time, when he wanted me to do something for him, I couldn't ask him about it. I said, 'Yes,' and he gave me the package. It wasn't a large package: about the size of— well—a loaf of bread, perhaps, but quite heavy for its size. It was wrapped in brown paper. We unwrapped it after he had gone, that is, we took the paper off. But the inner wrapping was of canvas, tied with silk cord, and sealed, so we didn't open that. We put it upstairs in the pack room, under a pile of old magazines.

"Then, at about a quarter to twelve tonight—I had only been in bed a few minutes, and hadn't gone to sleep yet—I heard a noise in here. I don't own a gun, and there's nothing you could properly call a weapon in the house, but that walking stick"—indicating the hickory stick on the table—"was in a closet in our bedroom. So I got that and came in here to see what the noise was.

"Right outside the bedroom door I ran into a man. I could see him better than he could see me, because this door was open and he showed against the window. He was between me and it, and the moonlight showed him fairly clear. I hit him with the stick, but didn't knock him down. He turned and ran in here. Foolishly, not thinking that he might not be alone, I ran after him. Another man shot me in the leg just as I came through the door.

"I fell, of course. While I was getting up, two of them came in with my wife between them. There were four of them. They were medium-sized men, brown-skinned, but not so dark. I took it for granted that they were Siamese, because Molloy had spoken of Siamese. They turned on the lights here, and one of them, who seemed to be the leader, asked me:

" 'Where is it?'

"His accent was pretty bad, but you could understand his words good enough. Of course I knew they were after what Molloy had left, but I pretended I didn't. They told me, or rather the leader did, that he knew it had been left here, but they called Molloy by another name—Dawson. I said I didn't know any Dawson, and nothing had been left here, and I tried to get them to tell me what they expected to find. They wouldn't though—they just called it '*it.*'

"They talked among themselves, but of course I couldn't make out a word of what they were saying, and then three of them went out, leaving one here to guard us. He had a Luger pistol. We could hear the others moving around the house. The search must have lasted an hour. Then the one I took for the leader came in, and said something to our guard. Both of them looked quite elated.

" 'It is not wise if you will leave this room for many minutes,' the leader said to me, and they left us—both of them—closing the door behind them.

"I knew they were going, but I couldn't walk on this leg. From what the doctor says, I'll be lucky if I walk on it inside of a couple of months. I didn't want my wife to go out, and perhaps run into one of them before they'd got away, but she insisted on going. She found they'd gone, and she phoned the police, and then ran up to the pack room and found Molloy's package was gone."

"And this Molloy didn't give you any hint at all as to what was in the package?" O'Gar asked when Richter had finished.

"Not a word, except that it was something the Siamese were after."

"Did he know the Siamese who stabbed him?" I asked.

"I think so," Richter said slowly, "though I am not sure he said he did."

"Do you remember his words?"

"Not exactly, I'm afraid."

"I think I remember them," Mrs. Richter said. "My husband, Mr. Richter, asked him, 'What's the matter, Molloy? Are you hurt, or sick?'

"Molloy gave a little laugh, putting a hand on his chest, and said, 'Nothing much. I run into a Siamese who was looking for me on my way here, and got careless and let him scratch me. But I kept my little bundle!' And he laughed again, and patted the package."

"Did he say anything else about the Siamese?"

"Not directly," she replied, "though he did tell us to watch out for any Asiatics we saw around the neighborhood. He said he wouldn't leave the package if he thought it would make trouble for us, but that there was always a chance that something would go wrong, and we'd better be careful. And he told my husband"—nodding at Richter—"that the Siamese had been dogging him for months, but now that he had a safe place for the package he was going to 'take them for a walk and forget to bring them back.' That was the way he put it."

"How much do you know about Molloy?"

"Not a great deal, I'm afraid," Richter took up the answering again. "He liked to talk about the places he had been and the things he had seen, but you couldn't get a word out of him about his own affairs. We met him first in Mexico, as I have told you, in 1916. After he saved us down there and got us away, we didn't see him again for nearly four years. He rang the bell one night, and came in for an hour or two. He was on his way to China, he said, and had a lot of business to attend to before he left the next day.

"Some months later I had a letter from him, from the Queen's Hotel in Kandy, asking me to send him a list of the importers and exporters in San Francisco. He wrote me a letter thanking me for the list, and I didn't hear from him again until he came to San Francisco for a week, about a year later. That was in 1921, I think.

"He was here for another week about a year after that, telling us that he had been in Brazil, but, as usual, not saying what he had been doing there. Some months later I had a letter from him, from Chicago, saying he would be here the following week. However, he didn't come. Instead, some time later, he wrote from Vladivostok, saying he hadn't been able to make it. Today was the first we'd heard of him since then."

"Where's his home? His people?"

"He always says he has neither. I've an idea he was born in England, though I don't know that he ever said so, or what made me think so."

"Got any more questions?" I asked O'Gar.

"No. Let's give the place the eye, and see if the Siamese left any leads behind 'em."

The eye we gave the house was thorough. We didn't split the territory between us, but went over everything together—everything from roof to cellar—every nook, drawer, corner.

The cellar did most for us: it was there, in the cold furnace, that we found the handful of black buttons and the fire-darkened garter clasps. But the upper floors hadn't been altogether worthless: in one room we had found the crumpled sales slip of an Oakland store, marked *1 table cover*; and in another room we had found no garters.

"Of course it's none of my business," I told Richter when O'Gar and I joined the others again, "but I think maybe if you plead self-defense you might get away with it."

He tried to jump up from the davenport, but his shot leg failed him.

The woman got up slowly.

"And maybe that would leave an out for you," O'Gar told her. "Why don't you try to persuade him?"

"Or maybe it would be better if you plead the self-defense," I suggested to her. "You could say that Richter ran to your help when your husband grabbed you, that your husband shot him and was turning his gun on you when you stabbed him. That would sound smooth enough."

"My husband?"

"Uh-huh, Mrs. Rounds-Molloy-Dawson. Your late husband, anyway."

Richter got his mouth far enough closed to get words out of it.

"What is the meaning of this damned nonsense?" he demanded.

"Them's harsh words to come from a fellow like you," O'Gar growled at him. "If this is nonsense, what do you make of that yarn you told us about creeping Siamese and mysterious bundles, and God knows what all?"

"Don't be too hard on him," I told O'Gar. "Being around movies all the time has poisoned his idea of what sounds plausible. If it hadn't, he'd have known better than to see a Siamese in the moonlight at 11:45, when the moon was just coming up at somewhere around 12:45, when you phoned me."

Richter stood up on his one good leg.

The husky police corporal stepped close to him.

"Hadn't I better frisk him, sergeant?"

O'Gar shook his bullet head.

"Waste of time. He's got nothing on him. They cleaned the

place of weapons. The chances are the lady dropped them in the bay when she rode over to Oakland to get a table cover to take the place of the sarong her husband carried away with him."

That shook the pair of them. Richter pretended he hadn't gulped, and the woman had a fight of it before she could make her eyes stay still on mine.

O'Gar struck while the iron was hot by bringing the buttons and garters clasps we had salvaged out of his pocket, and letting them trickle from one hand to another. That used up the last bit of the facts we had.

I threw a lie at them.

"Never me to knock the press, but you don't want to put too much confidence in what the papers say. For instance, a fellow might say a few pregnant words before he died, and the papers might say he didn't. A thing like that would confuse things."

The woman reared up her head and looked at O'Gar.

"May I speak to Austin alone?" she asked. "I don't mean out of your sight."

The detective sergeant scratched his head and looked at me. This letting your victims go into conference is always a ticklish business: they may decide to come clean, and then again, they may frame up a new out. On the other hand, if you don't let them, the chances are they get stubborn on you, and you can't get anything out of them. One way was as risky as another. I grinned at O'Gar and refused to make a suggestion. He could decide for himself, and, if he was wrong, I'd have him to dump the blame on. He scowled at me, and then nodded to the woman.

"You can go over into that corner and whisper together for a couple of minutes," he said, "but no foolishness."

She gave Richter the hickory stick, took his other arm, helped him hobble to a far corner, pulled a chair over there for him. He sat with his back to us. She stood behind him, leaning over his shoulder, so that both their faces were hidden from us.

O'Gar came closer to me.

"What do you think?" he muttered.

"I think they'll come through."

"That shot of yours about being Molloy's wife hit center. I missed that one. How'd you make it?"

"When she was telling us what Molloy had said about the Siamese she took pains both times she said 'my husband' to show that she meant Richter."

"So? Well—"

The whispering in the far corner had been getting louder, so that the s's had become sharp hisses. Now a clear emphatic sentence came from Richter's mouth.

"I'll be damned if I will!"

Both of them looked furtively over their shoulders, and they lowered their voices again, but not for long. The woman was apparently trying to persuade him to do something. He kept shaking his head. He put a hand on her arm. She pushed it away, and kept on whispering.

He said aloud, deliberately:

"Go ahead, if you want to be a fool. It's your neck. I didn't put the knife in him."

She jumped away from him, her eyes black blazes in a white face. O'Gar and I moved softly toward them.

"You rat!" she spat at Richter, and spun to face us.

"I killed him!" she cried. "This thing in the chair tried to and—"

Richter swung the hickory stick.

I jumped for it—missed—crashed into the back of his chair. Hickory stick, Richter, chair, and I sprawled together on the floor. The corporal helped me up. He and I picked Richter up and put him on the davenport again.

The woman's story poured out of her angry mouth:

"His name wasn't Molloy. It was Lange, Sam Lange. I married him in Providence in 1913 and went to China with him—to Canton, where he had a position with a steamship line. We didn't stay there long, because he got into some trouble through being mixed up in the revolution that year. After that we drifted around, mostly around Asia.

"We met this thing"—she pointed at the now sullenly quiet Richter—"in Singapore, in 1919, I think—right after the World War was over. His name is Holley, and Scotland Yard can tell you something about him. He had a proposition. He knew of a gem-bed in upper Burma, one of many that were hidden from the British when they took the country. He knew the natives who were working it, knew where they were hiding their gems.

"My husband went in with him, with two other men that were killed. They looted the natives' cache, and got away with a whole sackful of sapphires, topazes and even a few rubies. The two other men were killed by the natives and my husband was badly wounded.

"We didn't think he could live. We were hiding in a hut near the Yunnan border. Holley persuaded me to take the gems and run away with them. It looked as if Sam was done for, and if we stayed there long we'd be caught. I can't say that I was crazy about Sam anyway; he wasn't the kind you would be, after living with him for a while.

"So Holley and I took it and lit out. We had to use a lot of the stones to buy our way through Yunnan and Kwangsi and Kwangtung, but we made it. We got to San Francisco with enough to buy this house and the movie theater, and we've been here since. We've been honest since we came here, but I don't suppose that means anything. We had enough money to keep us comfortable.

"Today Sam showed up. We hadn't heard of him since we left him on his back in Burma. He said he'd been caught and jailed for three years. Then he'd got away, and had spent the other three hunting for us. He was that kind. He didn't want me back, but he did want money. He wanted everything we had. Holley lost his nerve. Instead of bargaining with Sam, he lost his head and tried to shoot him.

"Sam took his gun away from him and shot him in the leg. In the scuffle Sam had dropped a knife—a kris, I think. I picked it up, but he grabbed me just as I got it. I don't know how it happened. All I saw was Sam staggering back, holding his chest with both hands—and the kris shining red in my hand.

"Sam had dropped his gun. Holley got it and was all for shooting Sam, but I wouldn't let him. It happened in this room. I don't remember whether I gave Sam the sarong we used for a cover on the table or not. Anyway, he tried to stop the blood with it. He went away then, while I kept Holley from shooting him.

"I knew Sam wouldn't go to the police, but I didn't know

what he'd do. And I knew he was hurt bad. If he dropped dead somewhere, the chances are he'd be traced here. I watched from a window as he went down the street, and nobody seemed to pay any attention to him, but he looked so conspicuously wounded to me that I thought everybody would be sure to remember him if it got into the papers that he had been found dead somewhere.

"Holley was even more scared than I. We couldn't run away, because he had a shot leg. So we made up that Siamese story, and I went over to Oakland, and bought the table cover to take the place of the sarong. We had some guns and even a few oriental knives and swords here. I wrapped them up in paper, breaking the swords, and dropped them off the ferry when I went to Oakland.

"When the morning papers came out we read what had happened, and then we went ahead with what we had planned. We burned the suit Holley had worn when he was shot, and his garters—because the pants had a bullet-hole in them, and the bullet had cut one garter. We fixed a hole in his pajama-leg, unbandaged his leg,—I had fixed it as well as I could,—and washed away the clotted blood until it began to bleed again. Then I gave the alarm."

She raised both hands in a gesture of finality and made a clucking sound with her tongue.

"And there you are," she said.

"You got anything to say?" I asked Holley, who was staring at his bandaged leg.

"To my lawyer," he said without looking up.

O'Gar spoke to the corporal.

"The wagon, Flynn."

Ten minutes later we were in the street, helping Holley and the woman into a police car.

Around the corner on the other side of the street came three brown-skinned men, apparently Malay sailors. The one in the middle seemed to be drunk, and the other two were supporting him. One of them had a package that could have held a bottle under his arm.

O'Gar looked from them to me and laughed.

"We wouldn't be doing a thing to those babies right now if we had fallen for that yarn, would we?" he whispered.

"Shut up, you, you big heap!" I growled back, nodding at Holley, who was in the car by now. "If that bird sees them he'll identify 'em as his Siamese, and God knows what a jury would make of it!"

We made the puzzled driver twist the car six blocks out of his way to be sure we'd miss the brown men. It was worth it, because nothing interfered with the twenty years apiece that Holley and Mrs. Lange drew.

The Big Knock-Over

I FOUND Paddy the Mex in Jean Larrouy's dive.

Paddy—an amiable con man who looked like the King of Spain—showed me his big white teeth in a smile, pushed a chair out for me with one foot, and told the girl who shared his table:

"Nellie, meet the biggest-hearted dick in San Francisco. This little fat guy will do anything for anybody, if only he can send 'em over for life in the end." He turned to me, waving his cigar at the girl: "Nellie Wade, and you can't get anything on her. She don't have to work—her old man's a bootlegger."

She was a slim girl in blue—white skin, long green eyes, short chestnut hair. Her sullen face livened into beauty when she put a hand across the table to me, and we both laughed at Paddy.

"Five years?" she asked.

"Six," I corrected.

"Damn!" said Paddy, grinning and hailing a waiter. "Some day I'm going to fool a sleuth."

So far he had fooled all of them—he had never slept in a hoosegow.

I looked at the girl again. Six years before, this Angel Grace Cardigan had buncoed half a dozen Philadelphia boys out of plenty. Dan Morey and I had nailed her, but none of her victims would go to the bat against her, so she had been turned loose. She was a kid of nineteen then, but already a smooth grifter.

In the middle of the floor one of Larrouy's girls began to sing *Tell Me What You Want and I'll Tell You What You Get.* Paddy the Mex tipped a gin-bottle over the glasses of gin-gerale the waiter had brought. We drank and I gave Paddy a piece of paper with a name and address penciled on it.

"Itchy Maker asked me to slip you that," I explained. "I saw him in the Folsom big house yesterday. It's his mother, he says, and he wants you to look her up and see if she wants anything. What he means, I suppose, is that you're to give her his cut from the last trick you and he turned."

"You hurt my feelings," Paddy said, pocketing the paper and bringing out the gin again.

I downed the second gin-gingerale and gathered in my feet, preparing to rise and trot along home. At that moment four of Larrouy's clients came in from the street. Recognition of one of them kept me in my chair. He was tall and slender and all dolled up in what the well-dressed man should wear. Sharp-eyed, sharp-faced, with lips thin as knife-edges under a small pointed mustache—Bluepoint Vance. I wondered what he was doing three thousand miles away from his New York hunting-grounds.

While I wondered I put the back of my head to him, pretending interest in the singer, who was now giving the customers *I Want to Be a Bum.* Beyond her, back in a corner, I spotted another familiar face that belonged in another city— Happy Jim Hacker, round and rosy Detroit gunman, twice sentenced to death and twice pardoned.

When I faced front again, Bluepoint Vance and his three companions had come to rest two tables away. His back was to us. I sized up his playmates.

Facing Vance sat a wide-shouldered young giant with red hair, blue eyes and a ruddy face that was good-looking in a tough, savage way. On his left was a shifty-eyed dark girl in a floppy hat. She was talking to Vance. The red-haired giant's attention was all taken by the fourth member of the party, on his right. She deserved it.

She was neither tall nor short, thin nor plump. She wore a black Russian tunic affair, green-trimmed and hung with silver dinguses. A black fur coat was spread over the chair behind her. She was probably twenty. Her eyes were blue, her mouth red, her teeth white, the hair-ends showing under her black-green-and-silver turban were brown, and she had a nose. Without getting steamed up over the details, she was nice. I said so. Paddy the Mex agreed with a "That's what," and Angel Grace suggested that I go over and tell Red O'Leary I thought her nice.

"Red O'Leary the big bird?" I asked, sliding down in my seat so I could stretch a foot under the table between Paddy and Angel Grace. "Who's his nice girl friend?"

"Nancy Regan, and the other one's Sylvia Yount."

"And the slicker with his back to us?" I probed.

Paddy's foot, hunting the girl's under the table, bumped mine.

"Don't kick me, Paddy," I pleaded. "I'll be good. Anyway, I'm not going to stay here to be bruised. I'm going home."

I swapped so-longs with them and moved toward the street, keeping my back to Bluepoint Vance.

At the door I had to step aside to let two men come in. Both knew me, but neither gave me a tumble—Sheeny Holmes (not the old-timer who staged the Moose Jaw looting back in the buggy-riding days) and Denny Burke, Baltimore's King of Frog Island. A good pair—neither of them would think of taking a life unless assured of profit and political protection.

Outside, I turned down toward Kearny Street, strolling along, thinking that Larrouy's joint had been full of crooks this one night, and that there seemed to be more than a sprinkling of prominent visitors in our midst. A shadow in a doorway interrupted my brain-work.

The shadow said, "Ps-s-s-s! Ps-s-s-s!"

Stopping, I examined the shadow until I saw it was Beno, a hophead newsie who had given me a tip now and then in the past—some good, some phoney.

"I'm sleepy," I growled as I joined Beno and his arm-load of newspapers in the doorway, "and I've heard the story about the Mormon who stuttered, so if that's what's on your mind, say so, and I'll keep going."

"I don't know nothin' about no Mormons," he protested, "but I know somethin' else."

"Well?"

"'S all right for you to say 'Well,' but what I want to know is, what am I gonna get out of it?"

"Flop in the nice doorway and go shut-eye," I advised him, moving toward the street again. "You'll be all right when you wake up."

"Hey! Listen, I got somethin' for you. Hones' to Gawd!"

"Well?"

"Listen!" He came close, whispering. "There's a caper rigged for the Seaman's National. I don't know what's the racket, but it's real. Hones' to Gawd! I ain't stringin' you. I can't give you no monickers. You know I would if I knowed 'em. Hones' to Gawd! Gimme ten bucks. It's worth that to you, ain't it? This is straight dope—hones' to Gawd!"

"Yeah, straight from the nose-candy!"

"No! Hones' to Gawd! I—"

"What *is* the caper, then?"

"I don't know. All I got was that the Seaman's is gonna be nicked, Hones' to—"

"Where'd you get it?"

Beno shook his head. I put a silver dollar in his hand.

"Get another shot and think up the rest of it," I told him, "and if it's amusing enough I'll give you the other nine bucks."

I walked on down to the corner, screwing up my forehead over Beno's tale. By itself, it sounded like what it probably was—a yarn designed to get a dollar out of a trusting gumshoe. But it wasn't altogether by itself. Larrouy's—just one drum in a city that had a number—had been heavy with grifters who were threats against life and property. It was worth a look-see, especially since the insurance company covering the Seaman's National Bank was a Continental Detective Agency client.

Around the corner, twenty feet or so along Kearny Street, I stopped.

From the street I had just quit came two bangs—the reports of a heavy pistol. I went back the way I had come. As I rounded the corner I saw men gathering in a group up the street. A young Armenian—a dapper boy of nineteen or twenty—passed me, going the other way, sauntering along, hands in pockets, softly whistling *Broken-hearted Sue.*

I joined the group—now becoming a crowd—around Beno. Beno was dead, blood from two holes in his chest staining the crumpled newspapers under him.

I went up to Larrouy's and looked in. Red O'Leary, Bluepoint Vance, Nancy Regan, Sylvia Yount, Paddy the Mex, Angel Grace, Denny Burke, Sheeny Holmes, Happy Jim Hacker—not one of them was there.

Returning to Beno's vicinity, I loitered with my back to a wall while the police arrived, asked questions, learned nothing, found no witnesses, and departed, taking what was left of the newsie with them.

I went home and to bed.

In the morning I spent on hour in the Agency file-room, digging through the gallery and records. We didn't have anything on Red O'Leary, Denny Burke, Nancy Regan, Sylvia Yount, and only some guesses on Paddy the Mex. Nor were there any open jobs definitely chalked against Angel Grace, Bluepoint Vance, Sheeny Holmes and Happy Jim Hacker, but their photos were there. At ten o'clock—bank opening time—I set out for the Seaman's National, carrying these photos and Beno's tip.

The Continental Detective Agency's San Francisco office is located in a Market Street office building. The Seaman's National Bank occupies the ground floor of a tall gray building in Montgomery Street, San Francisco's financial center. Ordinarily, since I don't like even seven blocks of unnecessary walking, I would have taken a street car. But there was some sort of traffic jam on Market Street, so I set out afoot, turning off along Grant Avenue.

A few blocks of walking, and I began to see that something was wrong with the part of town I was heading for. Noises for one thing—roaring, rattling, explosive noises. At Sutter Street a man passed me, holding his face with both hands and groaning as he tried to push a dislocated jaw back in place. His cheek was scraped red.

I went down Sutter Street. Traffic was in a tangle that reached to Montgomery Street. Excited, bare-headed men were running around. The explosive noises were clearer. An automobile full of policemen went down past me, going as fast as traffic would let it. An ambulance came up the street, clanging its gong, taking to the sidewalks where the traffic tangle was worst.

I crossed Kearny Street on the trot. Down the other side of the street two patrolmen were running. One had his gun out. The explosive noises were a drumming chorus ahead.

Rounding into Montgomery Street, I found few sightseers ahead of me. The middle of the street was filled with trucks, touring cars, taxis—deserted there. Up in the next block—between Bush and Pine Streets—hell was on a holiday.

The holiday spirit was gayest in the middle of the block, where the Seaman's National Bank and the Golden Gate Trust Company faced each other across the street.

For the next six hours I was busier than a flea on a fat woman.

III

Late that afternoon I took a recess from bloodhounding and went up to the office for a pow-wow with the Old Man. He was leaning back in his chair, staring out the window, tapping on his desk with the customary long yellow pencil.

A tall, plump man in his seventies, this boss of mine, with a white-mustached, baby-pink grandfatherly face, mild blue eyes behind rimless spectacles, and no more warmth in him than a hangman's rope. Fifty years of crook-hunting for the Continental had emptied him of everything except brains and a soft-spoken, gently smiling shell of politeness that was the same whether things went good or bad—and meant as little at one time as another. We who worked under him were proud of his cold-bloodedness. We used to boast that he could spit icicles in July, and we called him Pontius Pilate among ourselves, because he smiled politely when he sent us out to be crucified on suicidal jobs.

He turned from the window as I came in, nodded me to a chair, and smoothed his mustache with the pencil. On his desk the afternoon papers screamed the news of the Seaman's National Bank and Golden Gate Trust Company double-looting in five colors.

"What is the situation?" he asked, as one would ask about the weather.

"The situation is a pip," I told him. "There were a hundred and fifty crooks in the push if there was one. I saw a hundred myself—or think I did—and there were slews of them that I didn't see—planted where they could jump out and bite when fresh teeth were needed. They bit, too. They bushwacked the police and made a merry wreck out of 'em—going and coming. They hit the two banks at ten sharp—took over the whole block—chased away the reasonable people—dropped the others. The actual looting was duck soup to a mob of that size. Twenty or thirty of 'em to each of the banks while the others held the street. Nothing to it but wrap up the spoils and take 'em home.

"There's a highly indignant business men's meeting down there now—wild-eyed stockbrokers up on their hind legs yelling for the chief of police's heart's blood. The police didn't do any miracles, that's a cinch, but no police department is equipped to handle a trick of that size—no matter how well they think they are. The whole thing lasted less than twenty minutes. There were, say, a hundred and fifty thugs in on it, loaded for bear, every play mapped to the inch. How are you going to get enough coppers down there, size up the racket, plan your battle, and put it over in that little time? It's easy enough to say the police should look ahead—should have a dose for every emergency—but these same birds who are yelling, 'Rotten,' down there now would be the first to squawk, 'Robbery,' if their taxes were boosted a couple of cents to buy more policemen and equipment.

"But the police fell down—there's no question about that—and there will be a lot of beefy necks feel the ax. The armored cars were no good, the grenading was about fifty-fifty, since the bandits knew how to play that game, too. But the real disgrace of the party was the police machine-guns. The bankers and brokers are saying they were fixed. Whether they were deliberately tampered with, or were only carelessly taken care of, is anybody's guess, but only one of the damned things would shoot, and it not very well.

"The getaway was north on Montgomery to Columbus. Along Columbus the parade melted, a few cars at a time, into side streets. The police ran into an ambush between Washington and Jackson, and by the time they had shot their way through it the bandit cars had scattered all over the city. A lot of 'em have been picked up since then—empty.

"All the returns aren't in yet, but right now the score stands something like this: The haul will run God only knows how far into the millions—easily the richest pickings ever got with civilian guns. Sixteen coppers were knocked off, and three times that many wounded. Twelve innocent spectators, bank clerks, and the like, were killed and about as many banged around. There are two bandits and five shot-ups who might be either thugs or spectators that got too close. The bandits lost seven dead that we know of and thirty-one prisoners, most of them bleeding somewhere.

"One of the dead was Fat Boy Clarke. Remember him? He shot his way out of a Des Moines courtroom three or four years ago. Well, in his pocket we found a piece of paper, a map of Montgomery Street between Pine and Bush, the block of the looting. On the back of the map were typed instructions, telling him exactly what to do and when to do it. An X on the map showed him where he was to park the car in which he arrived with his seven men, and there was a circle where he was to stand with them, keeping an eye on things in general and on the windows and roofs of the buildings across the street in particular. Figures 1, 2, 3, 4, 5, 6, 7, 8 on the map marked doorways, steps, a deep window, and so on, that were to be used for shelter if shots had to be traded with those windows and roofs. Clarke was to pay no attention to the Bush Street end of the block, but if the police charged the Pine Street end he was to move his men up there, distributing them among points marked a, b, c, d, e, f, g, and h. (His body was found on the spot marked a.) Every five minutes during the looting he was to send a man to an automobile standing in the street at a point marked on the map with a star, to see if there were any new instructions. He was to tell his men that if he were shot down one of them must report to the car, and a new leader would be given them. When the signal for the getaway was given, he was to send one of his men to the car in which he had come. If it was still in commission, this man was to drive it, not passing the car ahead of him. If it was out of whack, the man was to report to the star-marked car for instructions how to get a new one. I suppose they counted on finding enough parked cars to take care of this end. While Clarke waited for his car he and his men were to throw as much lead as possible at every target in their district, and none of them was to board the car until it came abreast of them. Then they were to drive out Montgomery to Columbus to—blank.

"Get that?" I asked. "Here are a hundred and fifty gunmen, split into groups under group-leaders, with maps and schedules showing what each man is to do, showing the fire-plug he's to kneel behind, the brick he's to stand on, where he's to spit—everything but the name and address of the policeman he's to shoot! It's just as well Beno couldn't give me the details—I'd have written it off as a hop-head's dream!"

"Very interesting," the Old Man said, smiling blandly.

"The Fat Boy's was the only timetable we found," I went on with my history. "I saw a few friends among the killed and caught, and the police are still identifying others. Some are local talent, but most of 'em seem to be imported stock. Detroit, Chi, New York, St. Louis, Denver, Portland, L.A., Philly, Baltimore—all seem to have sent delegates. As soon as the police get through identifying them I'll make out a list.

"Of those who weren't caught, Bluepoint Vance seems to be the main squeeze. He was in the car that directed operations. I don't know who else was there with him. The Shivering Kid was in on the festivities, and I think Alphabet Shorty McCoy, though I didn't get a good look at him. Sergeant Bender told me he spotted Toots Salda and Darby M'Laughlin in the push, and Morgan saw the Did-and-Dat Kid. That's a good cross-section of the layout—gunmen, swindlers, hijackers from all over Rand-McNally.

"The Hall of Justice has been a slaughter-house all afternoon. The police haven't killed any of their guests—none that I know of—but they're sure-God making believers out of them. Newspaper writers who like to sob over what they call the third degree should be down there now. After being knocked around a bit, some of the guests have talked. But the hell of it is they don't know a whole lot. They know some names—Denny Burke, Toby the Lugs, Old Pete Best, Fat Boy Clarke and Paddy the Mex were named—and that helps some, but all the smacking power in the police force arm can't bring out anything else.

"The racket seems to have been organized like this: Denny Burke, for instance, is known as a shifty worker in Baltimore. Well, Denny talks to eight or ten likely boys, one at a time. 'How'd you like to pick up a piece of change out on the Coast?' he asks them. 'Doing what?' the candidate wants to know. 'Doing what you're told,' the King of Frog Island says. 'You know me. I'm telling you this is the fattest picking ever rigged, a kick in the pants to go through—air-tight. Everybody in on it will come home lousy with cush—and they'll all come home if they don't dog it. That's all I'm spilling. If you don't like it—forget it.'

"And these birds did know Denny, and if he said the job was good that was enough for them. So they put in with him. He told them nothing. He saw that they had guns, gave 'em each a ticket to San Francisco and twenty bucks, and told them where to meet him here. Last night he collected them and told them they went to work this morning. By that time they had moved around the town enough to see that it was bubbling over with visiting talent, including such moguls as Toots Salda, Bluepoint Vance and the Shivering Kid. So this morning they went forth eagerly with the King of Frog Island at their head to do their stuff.

"The other talkers tell varieties of the same tale. The police found room in their crowded jail to stick in a few stool-pigeons. Since few of the bandits knew very many of the others, the stools had an easy time of it, but the only thing they could add to what we've got is that the prisoners are looking for a wholesale delivery tonight. They seem to think their mob will crash the prison and turn 'em loose. That's probably a lot of chewing-gum, but anyway this time the police will be ready.

"That's the situation as it stands now. The police are sweeping the streets, picking up everybody who needs a shave or can't show a certificate of attendance signed by his parson, with special attention to outward bound trains, boats and automobiles. I sent Jack Counihan and Dick Foley down North Beach way to play the joints and see if they can pick up anything."

"Do you think Bluepoint Vance was the actual directing intelligence in this robbery?" the Old Man asked.

"I hope so—we know him."

The Old Man turned his chair so his mild eyes could stare out the window again, and he tapped his desk reflectively with the pencil.

"I'm afraid not," he said in a gently apologetic tone. "Vance is a shrewd, resourceful and determined criminal, but his weakness is one common to his type. His abilities are all for present action and not for planning ahead. He has executed some large operations, but I've always thought I saw in them some other mind at work behind him."

I couldn't quarrel with that. If the Old Man said something was so, then it probably was, because he was one of these cautious babies who'll look out of the window at a cloudburst and say, "It seems to be raining," on the off-chance that somebody's pouring water off the roof.

"And who is this arch-gonnif?" I asked.

"You'll probably know that before I do," he said, smiling benignantly.

IV

I went back to the Hall and helped boil more prisoners in oil until around eight o'clock, when my appetite reminded me I hadn't eaten since breakfast. I attended to that, and then turned down toward Larrouy's, ambling along leisurely, so the exercise wouldn't interfere with my digestion. I spent three-quarters of an hour in Larrouy's, and didn't see anybody who interested me especially. A few gents I knew were present, but they weren't anxious to associate with me—it's not always healthy in criminal circles to be seen wagging your chin with a sleuth right after a job has been turned.

Not getting anything there, I moved up the street to Wop Healy's—another hole. My reception was the same here—I was given a table and let alone. Healy's orchestra was giving *Don't You Cheat*, all they had, while those customers who felt athletic were romping it out on the dance-floor. One of the dancers was Jack Counihan, his arms full of a big olive-skinned girl with a pleasant, thick-featured, stupid face.

Jack was a tall, slender lad of twenty-three or four who had drifted into the Continental's employ a few months before. It was the first job he'd ever had, and he wouldn't have had it if his father hadn't insisted that if sonny wanted to keep his fingers in the family till he'd have to get over the notion that squeezing through a college graduation was enough work for one lifetime. So Jack came to the Agency. He thought gum-shoeing would be fun. In spite of the fact that he'd rather catch the wrong man than wear the wrong necktie, he was a promising young thief-catcher. A likable youngster, well-muscled for all his slimness, smooth-haired, with a gentleman's face and a gentleman's manner, nervy, quick with head and hands, full of the don't-give-a-damn gaiety that belonged to his youthfulness. He was jingle-brained, of course, and needed holding, but I would rather work with him than with a lot of old-timers I knew.

Half an hour passed with nothing to interest me.

Then a boy came into Healy's from the street—a small kid, gaudily dressed, very pressed in the pants-legs, very shiny in the shoes, with an impudent sallow face of pronounced cast. This was the boy I had seen sauntering down Broadway a moment after Beno had been rubbed out.

Leaning back in my chair so that a woman's wide-hatted head was between us, I watched the young Armenian wind between tables to one in a far corner, where three men sat. He spoke to them—off-hand—perhaps a dozen words—and moved away to another table where a snub-nosed, black-haired man sat alone. The boy dropped into the chair facing snub-nose, spoke a few words, sneered at snub-nose's questions, and ordered a drink. When his glass was empty he crossed the room to speak to a lean, buzzard-faced man, and then went out of Healy's.

I followed him out, passing the table where Jack sat with the girl, catching his eye. Outside, I saw the young Armenian half a block away. Jack Counihan caught up with me, passed me. With a Fatima in my mouth I called to him:

"Got a match, brother?"

While I lighted my cigarette with a match from the box he gave me I spoke behind my hands:

"The goose in the glad rags—tail him. I'll string behind you. I don't know him, but if he blipped Beno off for talking to me last night, he knows me. On his heels!"

Jack pocketed his matches and went after the boy. I gave Jack a lead and then followed him. And then an interesting thing happened.

The street was fairly well filled with people, mostly men, some walking, some loafing on corners and in front of soft-drink parlors. As the young Armenian reached the corner of an alley where there was a light, two men came up and spoke to him, moving a little apart so that he was between them. The boy would have kept walking apparently paying no attention to them, but one checked him by stretching an arm out in front of him. The other man took his right hand out of his pocket and flourished it in the boy's face so that the nickel-plated knuckles on it twinkled in the light. The boy ducked swiftly under threatening hand and outstretched arm, and went on across the alley, walking, and not even looking over his shoulder at the two men who were now closing on his back.

Just before they reached him another reached them—a broad-backed, long-armed, ape-built man I had not seen before. His gorilla's paws went out together. Each caught a man. By the napes of their necks he yanked them away from the boy's back, shook them till their hats fell off, smacked their skulls together with a crack that was like a broom-handle breaking, and dragged their rag-limp bodies out of sight up the alley. While this was happening the boy walked jauntily down the street, without a backward glance.

When the skull-cracker came out of the alley I saw his face in the light—a dark-skinned, heavily-lined face, broad and flat, with jaw-muscles bulging like abscesses under his ears. He spit, hitched his pants, and swaggered down the street after the boy.

The boy went into Larrouy's. The skull-cracker followed him in. The boy came out, and in his rear—perhaps twenty feet behind—the skull-cracker rolled. Jack had tailed them into Larrouy's while I had held up the outside.

"Still carrying messages?" I asked.

"Yes. He spoke to five men in there. He's got plenty of body-guard, hasn't he?"

"Yeah," I agreed. "And you be damned careful you don't get between them. If they split, I'll shadow the skull-cracker, you keep the goose."

We separated and moved after our game. They took us to all the hangouts in San Francisco, to cabarets, grease-joints, pool-rooms, saloons, flop-houses, hook-shops, gambling-joints and what have you. Everywhere the kid found men to speak his dozen words to, and between calls, he found them on street-corners.

I would have liked to get behind some of these birds, but I
didn't want to leave Jack alone with the boy and his bodyguard—they seemed to mean too much. And I couldn't stick
Jack on one of the others, because it wasn't safe for me to
hang too close to the Armenian boy. So we played the game
as we had started it, shadowing our pair from hole to hole,
while night got on toward morning.

It was a few minutes past midnight when they came out of
a small hotel up on Kearny Street, and for the first time since
we had seen them they walked together, side by side, up to
Green Street, where they turned east along the side of
Telegraph Hill. Half a block of this, and they climbed the
front steps of a ramshackle furnished-room house and disappeared inside. I joined Jack Counihan on the corner where he
had stopped.

"The greetings have all been delivered," I guessed, "or he
wouldn't have called in his bodyguard. If there's nothing stirring within the next half hour I'm going to beat it. You'll
have to take a plant on the joint till morning."

Twenty minutes later the skull-cracker came out of the
house and walked down the street.

"I'll take him," I said. "You stick to the other baby."

The skull-cracker took ten or twelve steps from the house
and stopped. He looked back at the house, raising his face to
look at the upper stories. Then Jack and I could hear what
had stopped him. Up in the house a man was screaming. It
wasn't much of a scream in volume. Even now, when it had
increased in strength, it barely reached our ears. But in it—in
that one wailing voice—everything that fears death seemed to
cry out its fear. I heard Jack's teeth click. I've got horny skin
all over what's left of my soul, but just the same my forehead
twitched. The scream was so damned weak for what it said.

The skull-cracker moved. Five gliding strides carried him
back to the house. He didn't touch one of the six or seven
front steps. He went from pavement to vestibule in a spring
no monkey could have beaten for swiftness, ease or silence.
One minute, two minutes, three minutes, and the screaming
stopped. Three more minutes and the skull-cracker was leaving the house again. He paused on the sidewalk to spit and
hitch his pants. Then he swaggered off down the street.

"He's your meat, Jack," I said. "I'm going to call on the boy. He won't recognize me now."

V

The street-door of the rooming-house was not only unlocked but wide open. I went through it into a hallway, where a dim light burning upstairs outlined a flight of steps. I climbed them and turned toward the front of the house. The scream had come from the front—either this floor or the third. There was a fair likelihood of the skull-cracker having left the room-door unlocked, just as he had not paused to close the street-door.

I had no luck on the second floor, but the third knob I cautiously tried on the third floor turned in my hand and let its door edge back from the frame. In front of this crack I waited a moment, listening to nothing but a throbbing snore somewhere far down the hallway. I put a palm against the door and eased it open another foot. No sound. The room was black as an honest politician's prospects. I slid my hand across the frame, across a few inches of wall-paper, found a light button, pressed it. Two globes in the center of the room threw their weak yellow light on the shabby room and on the young Armenian who lay dead across the bed.

I went into the room, closed the door and stepped over to the bed. The boy's eyes were wide and bulging. One of his temples was bruised. His throat gaped with a red slit that ran actually from ear to ear. Around the slit, in the few spots not washed red, his thin neck showed dark bruises. The skull-cracker had dropped the boy with a poke in the temple and had choked him until he thought him dead. But the kid had revived enough to scream—not enough to keep from screaming. The skull-cracker had returned to finish the job with a knife. Three streaks on the bed-clothes showed where the knife had been cleaned.

The lining of the boy's pockets stuck out. The skull-cracker had turned them out. I went through his clothes, but with no better luck than I expected—the killer had taken everything. The room gave me nothing—a few clothes, but not a thing out of which information could be squeezed.

My prying done, I stood in the center of the floor scratching my chin and considering. In the hall a floor-board creaked. Three backward steps on my rubber heels put me in the musty closet, dragging the door all but half an inch shut behind me.

Knuckles rattled on the room door as I slid my gun off my hip. The knuckles rattled again and a feminine voice said, "Kid, oh, Kid!" Neither knuckles nor voice was loud. The lock clicked as the knob was turned. The door opened and framed the shifty-eyed girl who had been called Sylvia Yount by Angel Grace.

Her eyes lost their shiftiness for surprise when they settled on the boy.

"Holy hell!" she gasped, and was gone.

I was half out of the closet when I heard her tip-toeing back. In my hole again, I waited, my eye to the crack. She came in swiftly, closed the door silently, and went to lean over the dead boy. Her hands moved over him, exploring the pockets whose linings I had put back in place.

"Damn such luck!" she said aloud when the unprofitable frisking was over, and went out of the house.

I gave her time to reach the sidewalk. She was headed toward Kearny Street when I left the house. I shadowed her down Kearny to Broadway, up Broadway to Larrouy's. Larrouy's was busy, especially near the door, with customers going and coming. I was within five feet of the girl when she stopped a waiter and asked, in a whisper that was excited enough to carry, "Is Red here?"

The waiter shook his head.

"Ain't been in tonight."

The girl went out of the dive, hurrying along on clicking heels to a hotel in Stockton Street.

While I looked through the glass front, she went to the desk and spoke to the clerk. He shook his head. She spoke again and he gave her paper and envelope, on which she scribbled with the pen beside the register. Before I had to leave for a safer position from which to cover her exit, I saw which pigeon-hole the note went into.

From the hotel the girl went by street-car to Market and Powell Streets, and then walked up Powell to O'Farrell, where a fat-faced young man in gray overcoat and gray hat left the curb to link arms with her and lead her to a taxi stand up O'Farrell Street. I let them go, making a note of the taxi number—the fat-faced man looked more like a customer than a pal.

It was a little shy of two in the morning when I turned back into Market Street and went up to the office. Fiske, who holds down the Agency at night, said Jack Counihan had not reported, nothing else had come in. I told him to rouse me an operative, and in ten or fifteen minutes he succeeded in getting Mickey Linehan out of bed and on the wire.

"Listen, Mickey," I said, "I've got the nicest corner picked out for you to stand on the rest of the night. So pin on your diapers and toddle down there, will you?"

In between his grumbling and cursing I gave him the name and number of the Stockton Street hotel, described Red O'Leary, and told him which pigeon-hole the note had been put in.

"It mightn't be Red's home, but the chance is worth covering," I wound up. "If you pick him up, try not to lose him before I can get somebody down there to take him off your hands."

I hung up during the outburst of profanity this insult brought.

The Hall of Justice was busy when I reached it, though nobody had tried to shake the upstairs prison loose yet. Fresh lots of suspicious characters were being brought in every few minutes. Policemen in and out of uniform were everywhere. The detective bureau was a bee-hive.

Trading information with the police detectives, I told them about the Armenian boy. We were making up a party to visit the remains when the captain's door opened and Lieutenant Duff came into the assembly room.

"*Allez! Oop!*" he said, pointing a thick finger at O'Gar, Tully, Reeder, Hunt and me. "There's a thing worth looking at in Fillmore."

We followed him out to an automobile.

VI

A gray frame house in Fillmore Street was our destination. A lot of people stood in the street looking at the house. A police-wagon stood in front of it, and police uniforms were indoors and out.

A red-mustached corporal saluted Duff and led us into the house, explaining as we went, "'Twas the neighbors give us the rumble, complaining of the fighting, and when we got here, faith, there weren't no fight left in nobody."

All the house held was fourteen dead men.

Eleven of them had been poisoned—over-doses of knock-out drops in their booze, the doctors said. The other three had been shot, at intervals along the hall. From the looks of the remains, they had drunk a toast—a loaded one—and those who hadn't drunk, whether because of temperance or suspicious natures, had been gunned as they tried to get away.

The identity of the bodies gave us an idea of what their toast had been. They were all thieves—they had drunk their poison to the day's looting.

We didn't know all the dead men then, but all of us knew some of them, and the records told us who the others were later. The completed list read like *Who's Who in Crookdom*.

There was the Dis-and-Dat Kid, who had crushed out of Leavenworth only two months before; Sheeny Holmes; Snohomish Whitey, supposed to have died a hero in France in 1919; L.A. Slim, from Denver, sockless and underwearless as usual, with a thousand-dollar bill sewed in each shoulder of his coat; Spider Girrucci wearing a steel-mesh vest under his shirt and a scar from crown to chin where his brother had carved him years ago; Old Pete Best, once a congressman; Nigger Vojan, who once won $175,000 in a Chicago crap-game—*Abacadbra* tattooed on him in three places; Alphabet Shorty McCoy; Tom Brooks, Alphabet Shorty's brother-in-law, who invented the Richmond *razzle-dazzle*, and bought three hotels with the profits; Red Cudahy, who stuck up a Union Pacific train in 1924; Denny Burke; Bull McGonickle, still pale from fifteen years in Joliet; Toby the Lugs, Bull's running-mate, who used to brag about picking President Wilson's pocket in a Washington vaudeville theater; and Paddy the Mex.

Duff looked them over and whistled.

"A few more tricks like this," he said, "and we'll all be out of jobs. There won't be any grifters left to protect the tax-payers from."

"I'm glad you like it," I told him. "Me—I'd hate like hell to be a San Francisco copper the next few days."

"Why especially?"

"Look at this—one grand piece of double-crossing. This village of ours is full of mean lads who are waiting right now for these stiffs to bring 'em their cut of the stick-up. What do you think's going to happen when the word gets out that there's not going to be any gravy for the mob? There are going to be a hundred and more stranded thugs busy raising getaway dough. There'll be three burglaries to a block and a stick-up to every corner until the carfare's raised. God bless you, my son, you're going to sweat for your wages!"

Duff shrugged his thick shoulders and stepped over bodies to get to the telephone. When he was through I called the Agency.

"Jack Counihan called a couple of minutes ago," Fiske told me, and gave me an Army Street address. "He says he put his man in there, with company."

I phoned for a taxi, and then told Duff, "I'm going to run out for a while. I'll give you a ring here if there's anything to the angle, or if there isn't. You'll wait?"

"If you're not too long."

I got rid of my taxicab two blocks from the address Fiske had given me, and walked down Army Street to find Jack Counihan planted on a dark corner.

"I got a bad break," was what he welcomed me with. "While I was phoning from the lunch-room up the street some of my people ran out on me."

"Yeah? What's the dope?"

"Well, after that apey chap left the Green Street house he trolleyed to a house in Fillmore Street, and——"

"What number?"

The number Jack gave was that of the death-house I had just left.

"In the next ten or fifteen minutes just about that many other chaps went into the same house. Most of them came afoot, singly or in pairs. Then two cars came up together, with nine men in them—I counted them. They went into the house, leaving their machines in front. A taxi came past a little later, and I stopped it, in case my chap should motor away.

"Nothing happened for at least half an hour after the nine chaps went in. Then everybody in the house seemed to become demonstrative—there was a quantity of yelling and shooting. It lasted long enough to awaken the whole neighborhood. When it stopped, ten men—I counted them—ran out of the house, got into the two cars, and drove away. My man was one of them.

"My faithful taxi and I cried *Yoicks* after them, and they brought us here, going into that house down the street in front of which one of their motors still stands. After half an hour or so I thought I'd better report, so, leaving my taxi around the corner—where it's still running up expenses—I went up to yon all-night caravansary and phoned Fiske. And when I came back, one of the cars was gone—and I, woe is me!—don't know who went with it. Am I rotten?"

"Sure! You should have taken their cars along to the phone with you. Watch the one that's left while I collect a strong-arm squad."

I went up to the lunch-room and phoned Duff, telling him where I was, and:

"If you bring your gang along maybe there'll be profit in it. A couple of carloads of folks who were in Fillmore Street and didn't stay there came here, and part of 'em may still be here, if you make it sudden."

Duff brought his four detectives and a dozen uniformed men with him. We hit the house front and back. No time was wasted ringing the bell. We simply tore down the doors and went in. Everything inside was black until flashlights lit it up. There was no resistance. Ordinarily the six men we found in there would have damned near ruined us in spite of our outnumbering them. But they were too dead for that.

We looked at one another sort of open-mouthed.

"This is getting monotonous," Duff complained, biting off a hunk of tobacco. "Everybody's work is pretty much the same thing over and over, but I'm tired of walking into roomfuls of butchered crooks."

The catalog here had fewer names than the other, but they were bigger names. The Shivering Kid was here—nobody would collect all the reward money piled up on him now; Darby M'Laughlin, his horn-rimmed glasses crooked on his nose, ten thousand dollars' worth of diamonds on fingers and tie; Happy Jim Hacker; Donkey Marr, the last of the bow-legged Marrs, killers all, father and five sons; Toots Salda, the strongest man in crookdom, who had once picked up and run away with two Savannah coppers to whom he was hand-cuffed; and Rumdum Smith, who killed Lefty Read in Chi in 1916—a rosary wrapped around his left wrist.

No gentlemanly poisoning here—these boys had been mowed down with a 30-30 rifle fitted with a clumsy but ef-fective home-made silencer. The rifle lay on the kitchen table. A door connected the kitchen with the dining-room. Directly opposite that door, double doors—wide open—opened into the room in which the dead thieves lay. They were all close to the front wall, lying as if they had been lined up against the wall to be knocked off.

The gray-papered wall was spattered with blood, punctured with holes where a couple of bullets had gone all the way through. Jack Counihan's young eyes picked out a stain on the paper that wasn't accidental. It was close to the floor, be-side the Shivering Kid, and the Kid's right hand was stained with blood. He had written on the wall before he died—with fingers dipped in his own and Toots Salda's blood. The letters in the words showed breaks and gaps where his fingers had run dry, and the letters were crooked and straggly, because he must have written them in the dark.

By filling in the gaps, allowing for the kinks, and guessing where there weren't any indications to guide us, we got two words: *Big Flora*.

"They don't mean anything to me," Duff said, "but it's a name and most of the names we have belong to dead men now, so it's time we were adding to our list."

"What do you make of it?" asked bullet-headed O'Gar, detective-sergeant in the Homicide Detail, looking at the bodies. "Their pals got the drop on them, lined them against the wall, and the sharpshooter in the kitchen shot 'em down—bing-bing-bing-bing-bing-bing?"

"It reads that way," the rest of us agreed.

"Ten of 'em came here from Fillmore Street," I said. "Six stayed here. Four went to another house—where part of 'em are now cutting down the other part. All that's necessary is to trail the corpses from house to house until there's only one man left—and he's bound to play it through by croaking himself, leaving the loot to be recovered in the original packages. I hope you folks don't have to stay up all night to find the remains of that last thug. Come on, Jack, let's go home for some sleep."

VII

It was exactly 5 a.m. when I separated the sheets and crawled into my bed. I was asleep before the last draw of smoke from my good-night Fatima was out of my lungs. The telephone woke me at 5:15.

Fiske was talking: "Mickey Linehan just phoned that your Red O'Leary came home to roost half an hour ago."

"Have him booked," I said, and was asleep again by 5:17.

With the help of the alarm clock I rolled out of bed at nine, breakfasted, and went down to the detective bureau to see how the police had made out with the red-head. Not so good.

"He's got us stopped," the captain told me. "He's got alibis for the time of the looting and for last night's doings. And we can't even vag the son-of-a-gun. He's got means of support. He's salesman for Humperdickel's Universal Encyclopædiac Dictionary of Useful and Valuable Knowledge, or something like it. He started peddling these pamphlets the day before the knock-over, and at the time it was happening he was ringing doorbells and asking folks to buy his durned books. Anyway, he's got three witnesses that say so. Last night he was in a hotel from eleven to four-thirty this morning, playing cards, and he's got witnesses. We didn't find a durned thing on him or in his room."

I borrowed the captain's phone to call Jack Counihan's house.

"Could you identify any of the men you saw in the cars last night?" I asked when he had been stirred out of bed.

"No. It was dark and they moved too fast. I could barely make sure of my chap."

"Can't, huh?" the captain said. "Well, I can hold him twenty-four hours without laying charges, and I'll do that, but I'll have to spring him then unless you can dig up something."

"Suppose you turn him loose now," I suggested after thinking through my cigarette for a few minutes. "He's got himself all alibied up, so there's no reason why he should hide out on us. We'll let him alone all day—give him time to make sure he isn't being tailed—and then we'll get behind him tonight and stay behind him. Any dope on Big Flora?"

"No. That kid that was killed in Green Street was Bernie Bernheimer, alias the Motsa Kid. I guess he was a dip—he ran with dips—but he wasn't very—"

The buzz of the phone interrupted him. He said, "Hello, yes," and "Just a minute," into the instrument, and slid it across the desk to me.

A feminine voice: "This is Grace Cardigan. I called your Agency and they told me where to get you. I've got to see you. Can you meet me now?"

"Where are you?"

"In the telephone station on Powell Street."

"I'll be there in fifteen minutes," I said.

Calling the Agency, I got hold of Dick Foley and asked him to meet me at Ellis and Market right away. Then I gave the captain back his phone, said "See you later," and went uptown to keep my dates.

Dick Foley was on his corner when I got there. He was a swarthy little Canadian who stood nearly five feet in his high-heeled shoes, weighed a hundred pounds minus, talked like a Scotchman's telegram, and could have shadowed a drop of salt water from the Golden Gate to Hongkong without ever losing sight of it.

"You know Angel Grace Cardigan?" I asked him.

He saved a word by shaking his head, no.

"I'm going to meet her in the telephone station. When I'm through, stay behind her. She's smart, and she'll be looking for you, so it won't be duck soup, but do what you can."

Dick's mouth went down at the corners and one of his rare long-winded streaks hit him.

"Harder they look, easier they are," he said.

He trailed along behind me while I went up to the station. Angel Grace was standing in the doorway. Her face was more

sullen than I had ever seen it, and therefore less beautiful—
except her green eyes, which held too much fire for sullenness. A rolled newspaper was in one of her hands. She neither
spoke, smiled nor nodded.

"We'll go to Charley's, where we can talk," I said, guiding
her down past Dick Foley.

Not a murmur did I get out of her until we were seated
cross-table in the restaurant booth, and the waiter had gone
off with our orders. Then she spread the newspaper out on
the table with shaking hands.

"Is this on the level?" she demanded.

I looked at the story her shaking finger tapped—an account
of the Fillmore and Army Street findings, but a cagey account. A glance showed that no names had been given, that
the police had censored the story quite a bit. While I pretended to read I wondered whether it would be to my advantage to tell the girl the story was a fake. But I couldn't see
any clear profit in that, so I saved my soul a lie.

"Practically straight," I admitted.

"You were there?"

She had pushed the paper aside to the floor and was leaning over the table.

"With the police."

"Was—?" Her voice broke huskily. Her white fingers wadded
the tablecloth in two little bunches half-way between us. She
cleared her throat. "Who was—?" was as far as she got this time.

A pause. I waited. Her eyes went down, but not before I
had seen water dulling the fire in them. During the pause the
waiter came in, put our food down, went away.

"You know what I want to ask," she said presently, her
voice low, choked. "Was he? Was he? For God's sake tell me!"

I weighed them—truth against lie, lie against truth. Once
more truth triumphed.

"Paddy the Mex was shot—killed—in the Fillmore Street
house," I said.

The pupils of her eyes shrank to pinpoints—spread again
until they almost covered the green irises. She made no
sound. Her face was empty. She picked up a fork and lifted a
forkful of salad to her mouth—another. Reaching across the
table, I took the fork out of her hand.

"You're only spilling it on your clothes," I growled. "You can't eat without opening your mouth to put the food in."

She put her hands across the table, reaching for mine, trembling, holding my hand with fingers that twitched so that the nails scratched me.

"You're not lying to me?" she half sobbed, half chattered. "You're on the square! You were white to me that time in Philly! Paddy always said you were one white dick! You're not tricking me?"

"Straight up," I assured her. "Paddy meant a lot to you?"

She nodded dully, pulling herself together, sinking back in a sort of stupor.

"The way's open to even up for him," I suggested.

"You mean—?"

"Talk."

She stared at me blankly for a long while, as if she was trying to get some meaning out of what I had said. I read the answer in her eyes before she put it in words.

"I wish to God I could! But I'm Paper-box-John Cardigan's daughter. It isn't in me to turn anybody up. You're on the wrong side. I can't go over. I wish I could. But there's too much Cardigan in me. I'll be hoping every minute that you nail them, and nail them dead right, but—"

"Your sentiments are noble, or words to that effect," I sneered at her. "Who do you think you are—Joan of Arc? Would your brother Frank be in stir now if his partner, Johnny the Plumber, hadn't put the finger on him for the Great Falls bulls? Come to life, dearie! You're a thief among thieves, and those who don't double-cross get crossed. Who rubbed your Paddy the Mex out? Pals! But you mustn't slap back at 'em because it wouldn't be clubby. My God!"

My speech only thickened the sullenness in her face.

"I'm going to slap back," she said, "but I can't, can't split. I can't, I tell you. If you were a gun, I'd— Anyway, what help I get will be on my side of the game. Let it go at that, won't you? I know how you feel about it, but— Will you tell me who besides—who else was—was found in those houses?"

"Oh, sure!" I snarled. "I'll tell you everything. I'll let you pump me dry. But you mustn't give me any hints, because it might not be in keeping with the ethics of your highly honorable profession!"

Being a woman, she ignored all this, repeating, "Who else?"

"Nothing stirring. But I will do this—I'll tell you a couple who weren't there—Big Flora and Red O'Leary."

Her dopiness was gone. She studied my face with green eyes that were dark and savage.

"Was Bluepoint Vance?" she demanded.

"What do you guess?" I replied.

She studied my face for a moment longer and then stood up.

"Thanks for what you've told me," she said, "and for meeting me like this. I do hope you win."

She went out to be shadowed by Dick Foley. I ate my lunch.

VIII

At four o'clock that afternoon Jack Counihan and I brought our hired automobile to rest within sight of the front door of the Stockton Street hotel.

"He cleared himself with the police, so there's no reason why he should have moved, maybe," I told Jack, "and I'd rather not monkey with the hotel people, not knowing them. If he doesn't show by late we'll have to go up against them then."

We settled down to cigarettes, guesses on who'd be the next heavyweight champion and when, the possibilities of Prohibition being either abolished or practiced, where to get good gin and what to do with it, the injustice of the new Agency ruling that for purposes of expense accounts Oakland was not to be considered out of town, and similar exciting topics, which carried us from four o'clock to ten minutes past nine.

At 9:10 Red O'Leary came out of the hotel.

"God is good," said Jack as he jumped out of the machine to do the footwork while I stirred the motor.

The fire-topped giant didn't take us far. Larrouy's front door gobbled him. By the time I had parked the car and gone into the dive, both O'Leary and Jack had found seats. Jack's table was on the edge of the dance-floor. O'Leary's was on the other side of the establishment, against the wall, near a corner. A fat blond couple were leaving the table back in that corner when I came in, so I persuaded the waiter who was guiding me to a table to make it that one.

O'Leary's face was three-quarters turned away from me. He was watching the front door, watching it with an earnestness that turned suddenly to happiness when a girl appeared there. She was the girl Angel Grace had called Nancy Regan. I have already said she was nice. Well, she was. And the cocky little blue hat that hid all her hair didn't handicap her niceness any tonight.

The red-head scrambled to his feet and pushed a waiter and a couple of customers out of his way as he went to meet her. As reward for his eagerness he got some profanity that he didn't seem to hear and a blue-eyed, white-toothed smile that was—well—nice. He brought her back to his table and put her in a chair facing me, while he sat very much facing her.

His voice was a baritone rumble out of which my snooping ears could pick no words. He seemed to be telling her a lot, and she listened as if she liked it.

"But, Reddy, dear, you shouldn't," she said once. Her voice—I know other words, but we'll stick to this one—was nice. Outside of the music in it, it had quality. Whoever this gunman's moll was, she either had had a good start in life or had learned her stuff well. Now and then, when the orchestra came up for air, I would catch a few words, but they didn't tell me anything except that neither she nor her rowdy playmate had anything against the other.

The joint had been nearly empty when she came in. By ten o'clock it was fairly crowded, and ten o'clock is early for Larrouy's customers. I began to pay less attention to Red's girl—even if she was nice—and more to my other neighbors. It struck me that there weren't many women in sight. Checking up on that, I found damned few women in proportion to the men. Men—rat-faced men, hatchet-faced men, square-jawed men, slack-chinned men, pale men, ruddy men, dark men, bull-necked men, scrawny men, funny-looking men, tough-looking men, ordinary men—sitting two to a table, four to a table, more coming in—and damned few women.

These men talked to one another, as if they weren't much interested in what they were saying. They looked casually around the joint, with eyes that were blankest when they came to O'Leary. And always those casual—bored—glances did rest on O'Leary for a second or two.

I returned my attention to O'Leary and Nancy Regan. He was sitting a little more erect in his chair than he had been, but it was an easy, supple erectness, and though his shoulders had hunched a bit, there was no stiffness in them. She said something to him. He laughed, turning his face toward the center of the room, so that he seemed to be laughing not only at what she had said, but also at these men who sat around him, waiting. It was a hearty laugh, young and careless.

The girl looked surprised for a moment, as if something in the laugh puzzled her, then she went on with whatever she was telling him. She didn't know she was sitting on dynamite, I decided. O'Leary knew. Every inch of him, every gesture, said, "I'm big, strong, young, tough and red-headed. When you boys want to do your stuff I'll be here."

Time slid by. Few couples danced. Jean Larrouy went around with dark worry in his round face. His joint was full of customers, but he would rather have had it empty.

By eleven o'clock I stood up and beckoned to Jack Counihan. He came over, we shook hands, exchanged *How's everythings* and *Getting muches*, and he sat at my table.

"What is happening?" he asked under cover of the orchestra's din. "I can't see anything, but there is something in the air. Or am I being hysterical?"

"You will be presently. The wolves are gathering, and Red O'Leary's the lamb. You could pick a tenderer one if you had a free hand, maybe. But these bimbos once helped pluck a bank, and when pay-day came there wasn't anything in their envelopes, not even any envelopes. The word got out that maybe Red knew how-come. Hence this. They're waiting now—maybe for somebody—maybe till they get enough hooch in them."

"And we sit here because it's the nearest table to the target for all these fellows' bullets when the blooming lid blows off?" Jack inquired. "Let's move over to Red's table. It's still nearer, and I rather like the appearance of the girl with him."

"Don't be impatient, you'll have your fun," I promised him. "There's no sense in having this O'Leary killed. If they bargain with him in a gentlemanly way, we'll lay off. But if they start heaving things at him, you and I are going to pry him and his girl friend loose."

"Well spoken, my hearty!" He grinned, whitening around the mouth. "Are there any details, or do we just simply and unostentatiously pry 'em loose?"

"See the door behind me, to the right? When the pop-off comes, I'm going back there and open it up. You hold the line midway between. When I yelp, you give Red whatever help he needs to get back there."

"Aye, aye!" He looked around the room at the assembled plug-uglies, moistened his lips, and looked at the hand holding his cigarette, a quivering hand. "I hope you won't think I'm in a funk," he said. "But I'm not an antique murderer like you. I get a reaction out of this prospective slaughtering."

"Reaction, my eye," I said. "You're scared stiff. But no nonsense, mind! If you try to make a vaudeville act out of it I'll ruin whatever these guerrillas leave of you. You do what you're told, and nothing else. If you get any bright ideas, save 'em to tell me about afterward."

"Oh, my conduct will be most exemplary!" he assured me.

IX

It was nearly midnight when what the wolves waited for came. The last pretense of indifference went out of faces that had been gradually taking on tenseness. Chairs and feet scraped as men pushed themselves back a little from their tables. Muscles flexed bodies into readiness for action. Tongues licked lips and eyes looked eagerly at the front door.

Bluepoint Vance was coming into the room. He came alone, nodding to acquaintances on this side and that, carrying his tall body gracefully, easily, in its well-cut clothing. His sharp-featured face was smilingly self-confident. He came without haste and without delay to Red O'Leary's table. I couldn't see Red's face, but muscles thickened the back of his neck. The girl smiled cordially at Vance and gave him her hand. It was naturally done. She didn't know anything.

Vance turned his smile from Nancy Regan to the red-haired giant—a smile that was a trifle cat-to-mousey.

"How's everything, Red?" he asked.

"Everything suits me," bluntly.

The orchestra had stopped playing. Larrouy, standing by the street door, was mopping his forehead with a handkerchief. At the table to my right, a barrel-chested, broken-nosed bruiser in a widely striped suit was breathing heavily between his gold teeth, his watery gray eyes bulging at O'Leary, Vance and Nancy. He was in no way conspicuous—there were too many others holding the same pose.

Bluepoint Vance turned his head, called to a waiter: "Bring me a chair."

The chair was brought and put at the unoccupied side of the table, facing the wall. Vance sat down, slumping back in the chair, leaning indolently toward Red, his left arm hooked over the chair-back, his right hand holding a cigarette.

"Well, Red," he said when he was thus installed, "have you got any news for me?"

His voice was suave, but loud enough for those at nearby tables to hear.

"Not a word." O'Leary's voice made no pretense of friendliness, nor of caution.

"What, no spinach?" Vance's thin-lipped smile spread, and his dark eyes had a mirthful but not pleasant glitter. "Nobody gave you anything to give me?"

"No," said O'Leary, emphatically.

"My goodness!" said Vance, the smile in his eyes and mouth deepening, and getting still less pleasant. "That's ingratitude! Will you help me collect, Red?"

"No."

I was disgusted with this red-head—half-minded to let him go under when the storm broke. Why couldn't he have stalled his way out—fixed up a fancy tale that Bluepoint would have had to half-way accept? But no—this O'Leary boy was so damned childishly proud of his toughness that he had to make a show of it when he should have been using his bean. If it had been only his own carcass that was due for a beating, it would have been all right. But it wasn't all right that Jack and I should have to suffer. This big chump was too valuable to lose. We'd have to get ourselves all battered up saving him from the rewards of his own pig-headedness. There was no justice in it.

"I've got a lot of money coming to me, Red." Vance spoke lazily, tauntingly. "And I need that money." He drew on his cigarette, casually blew the smoke into the red-head's face, and drawled, "Why, do you know the laundry charges twenty-six cents just for doing a pair of pajamas? I need money."

"Sleep in your underclothes," said O'Leary.

Vance laughed. Nancy Regan smiled, but in a bewildered way. She didn't seem to know what it was all about, but she couldn't help knowing that it was about something.

O'Leary leaned forward and spoke deliberately, loud enough for any to hear:

"Bluepoint, I've got nothing to give you—now or ever. And that goes for anybody else that's interested. If you or them think I owe you something—try and get it. To hell with you, Bluepoint Vance! If you don't like it—you've got friends here. Call 'em on!"

What a prime young idiot! Nothing would suit him but an ambulance—and I must be dragged along with him.

Vance grinned evilly, his eyes glittering into O'Leary's face.

"You'd like that, Red?"

O'Leary hunched his big shoulders and let them drop.

"I don't mind a fight," he said. "But I'd like to get Nancy out of it." He turned to her. "Better run along, honey, I'm going to be busy."

She started to say something, but Vance was talking to her. His words were lightly spoken, and he made no objection to her going. The substance of what he told her was that she was going to be lonely without Red. But he went intimately into the details of that loneliness.

Red O'Leary's right hand rested on the table. It went up to Vance's mouth. The hand was a fist when it got there. A wallop of that sort is awkward to deliver. The body can't give it much. It has to depend on the arm muscles, and not on the best of those. Yet Bluepoint Vance was driven out of his chair and across to the next table.

Larrouy's chairs went empty. The shindig was on.

"On your toes," I growled at Jack Counihan, and, doing my best to look like the nervous little fat man I was, I ran toward the back door, passing men who were moving not yet swiftly toward O'Leary. I must have looked the part of a scared trouble-dodger, because nobody stopped me, and I reached the door before the pack had closed on Red. The door was closed, but not locked. I wheeled with my back to it, black-jack in right hand, gun in left. Men were in front of me, but their backs were to me.

O'Leary was towering in front of his table, his tough red face full of bring-on-your-hell, his big body balanced on the balls of his feet. Between us, Jack Counihan stood, his face turned to me, his mouth twitching in a nervous grin, his eyes dancing with delight. Bluepoint Vance was on his feet again. Blood trickled from his thin lips, down his chin. His eyes were cool. They looked at Red O'Leary with the businesslike look of a logger sizing up the tree he's going to bring down. Vance's mob watched Vance.

"Red!" I bawled into the silence. "This way, Red!"

Faces spun to me—every face in the joint—millions of them.

"Come on, Red!" Jack Counihan yelped, taking a step forward, his gun out.

Bluepoint Vance's hand flashed to the V of his coat. Jack's gun snapped at him. Bluepoint had thrown himself down before the boy's trigger was yanked. The bullet went wide, but Vance's draw was gummed.

Red scooped the girl up with his left arm. A big automatic blossomed in his right fist. I didn't pay much attention to him after that. I was busy.

Larrouy's home was pregnant with weapons—guns, knives, saps, knucks, club-swung chairs and bottles, miscellaneous implements of destruction. Men brought their weapons over to mingle with me. The game was to nudge me away from my door. O'Leary would have liked it. But I was no fire-haired young rowdy. I was pushing forty, and I was twenty pounds overweight. I had the liking for ease that goes with that age and weight. Little ease I got.

A squint-eyed Portuguese slashed at my neck with a knife that spoiled my necktie. I caught him over the ear with the side of my gun before he could get away, saw the ear tear loose. A grinning kid of twenty went down for my legs—football stuff. I felt his teeth in the knee I pumped up, and felt them break. A pock-marked mulatto pushed a gun-barrel over the shoulder of the man in front of him. My blackjack crunched the arm of the man in front. He winced sidewise as the mulatto pulled the trigger—and had the side of his face blown away.

I fired twice—once when a gun was leveled within a foot of my middle, once when I discovered a man standing on a table not far off taking careful aim at my head. For the rest I trusted to my arms and legs, and saved bullets. The night was young and I had only a dozen pills—six in the gun, six in my pocket.

It was a swell bag of nails. Swing right, swing left, kick, swing right, swing left, kick. Don't hesitate, don't look for targets. God will see that there's always a mug there for your gun or blackjack to sock, a belly for your foot.

A bottle came through and found my forehead. My hat saved me some, but the crack didn't do me any good. I swayed and broke a nose where I should have smashed a skull. The room seemed stuffy, poorly ventilated. Somebody ought to tell Larrouy about it. How do you like that lead-and-leather pat on the temple, blondy? This rat on my left is getting too close. I'll draw him in by bending to the right to poke the mulatto, and then I'll lean back into him and let him have it. Not bad! But I can't keep this up all night. Where are Red and Jack? Standing off watching me?

Somebody socked me in the shoulder with something—a piano from the feel of it. A bleary-eyed Greek put his face where I couldn't miss it. Another thrown bottle took my hat and part of my scalp. Red O'Leary and Jack Counihan smashed through, dragging the girl between them.

X

While Jack put the girl through the door, Red and I cleared a little space in front of us. He was good at that. When he chucked them back they went back. I didn't dog it on him, but I did let him get all the exercise he wanted.

"All right!" Jack called.

Red and I went through the door, slammed it shut. It wouldn't hold even if locked. O'Leary sent three slugs through it to give the boys something to think about, and our retreat got under way.

We were in a narrow passageway lighted by a fairly bright light. At the other end was a closed door. Halfway down, to the right, steps led up.

"Straight ahead?" asked Jack, who was in front.

O'Leary said, "Yes." and I said, "No. Vance will have that blocked by now if the bulls haven't. Upstairs—the roof."

We reached the stairs. The door behind us burst open. The light went out. The door at the other end of the passage slammed open. No light came through either door. Vance would want light. Larrouy must have pulled the switch, trying to keep his dump from being torn to toothpicks.

Tumult boiled in the dark passage as we climbed the stairs by the touch system. Whoever had come through the back door was mixing it with those who had followed us—mixing it with blows, curses and an occasional shot. More power to them! We climbed, Jack leading, the girl next, then me, and last of all, O'Leary.

Jack was gallantly reading road-signs to the girl: "Careful of the landing, half a turn to the left now, put your right hand on the wall and—"

"Shut up!" I growled at him. "It's better to have her falling down than to have everybody in the drum fall on us."

We reached the second floor. It was black as black. There were three stories to the building.

"I've mislaid the blooming stairs," Jack complained.

We poked around in the dark, hunting for the flight that should lead up toward our roof. We didn't find it. The riot downstairs was quieting. Vance's voice was telling his push that they were mixing it with each other, asking where we had gone. Nobody seemed to know. We didn't know, either.

"Come on," I grumbled, leading the way down the dark hall toward the back of the building. "We've got to go somewhere."

There was still noise downstairs, but no more fighting. Men were talking about getting lights. I stumbled into a door at the end of the hall, pushed it open. A room with two windows through which came a pale glow from the street lights. It seemed brilliant after the hall. My little flock followed me in and we closed the door.

Red O'Leary was across the room, his noodle to an open window.

"Back street," he whispered. "No way down unless we drop."

"Anybody in sight?" I asked.

"Don't see any."

I looked around the room—bed, couple of chairs, chest of drawers, and a table.

"The table will go through the window," I said. "We'll chuck it as far as we can and hope the racket will lead 'em out there before they decide to look up here."

Red and the girl were assuring each other that each was still all in one piece. He broke away from her to help me with the table. We balanced it, swung it, let it go. It did nicely, crashing into the wall of the building opposite, dropping down into a backyard to clang and clatter on a pile of tin, or a collection of garbage cans, or something beautifully noisy. You couldn't have heard it more than a block and a half away.

We got away from the window as men bubbled out of Larrouy's back door.

The girl, unable to find any wounds on O'Leary, had turned to Jack Counihan. He had a cut cheek. She was monkeying with it and a handkerchief.

"When you finish that," Jack was telling her, "I'm going out and get one on the other side."

"I'll never finish if you keep talking—you jiggle your cheek."

"That's a swell idea," he exclaimed. "San Francisco is the second largest city in California. Sacramento is the State capital. Do you like geography? Shall I tell you about Java? I've never been there, but I drink their coffee. If—"

"Silly!" she said, laughing. "If you don't hold still I'll stop now."

"Not so good," he said. "I'll be still."

She wasn't doing anything except wiping blood off his cheek, blood that had better been let dry there. When she finished this perfectly useless surgery, she took her hand away slowly, surveying the hardly noticeable results with pride. As her hand came on a level with his mouth, Jack jerked his head forward to kiss the tip of one passing finger.

"Silly!" she said again, snatching her hand away.

"Lay off that," said Red O'Leary, "or I'll knock you off."

"Pull in your neck," said Jack Counihan.

"Reddy!" the girl cried, too late.

The O'Leary right looped out. Jack took the punch on the button, and went to sleep on the floor. The big red-head spun on the balls of his feet to loom over me.

"Got anything to say?" he asked.

I grinned down at Jack, up at Red.

"I'm ashamed of him," I said. "Letting himself be stopped by a paluka who leads with his right."

"You want to try it?"

"Reddy! Reddy!" the girl pleaded, but nobody was listening to her.

"If you'll lead with your right," I said.

"I will," he promised, and did.

I grandstanded, slipping my head out of the way, laying a forefinger on his chin.

"That could have been a knuckle," I said.

"Yes? This one is."

I managed to get under his left, taking the forearm across the back of my neck. But that about played out the acrobatics. It looked as if I would have to see what I could do to him, if any. The girl grabbed his arm and hung on.

"Reddy, darling, haven't you had enough fighting for one night? Can't you be sensible, even if you are Irish?"

I was tempted to paste the big chaw while his playmate had him tied up.

He laughed down at her, ducked his head to kiss her mouth, and grinned at me.

"There's always some other time," he said good-naturedly.

XI

"We'd better get out of here if we can," I said. "You've made too much rumpus for it to be safe."

"Don't get it up in your neck, little man," he told me. "Hold on to my coat-tails and I'll pull you out."

The big tramp. If it hadn't been for Jack and me he wouldn't have had any coat-tail by now.

We moved to the door, listened there, heard nothing.

"The stairs to the third floor must be up front," I whispered. "We'll try for them now."

We opened the door carefully. Enough light went past us into the hall to show a promise of emptiness. We crept down the hall, Red and I each holding one of the girl's hands. I hoped Jack would come out all right, but he had put himself to sleep, and I had troubles of my own.

I hadn't known that Larrouy's was large enough to have two miles of hallway. It did. It was an even mile in the darkness to the head of the stairs we had come up. We didn't pause there to listen to the voices below. At the end of the next mile O'Leary's foot found the bottom step of the flight leading up.

Just then a yell broke out at the head of the other flight.

"All up—they're up here!"

A white light beamed up on the yeller, and a brogue addressed him from below: "Come on down, ye windbag."

"The police," Nancy Regan whispered, and we hustled up our new-found steps to the third floor.

More darkness, just like that we'd left. We stood still at the top of the stairs. We didn't seem to have any company.

"The roof," I said. "We'll risk matches."

Back in a corner our feeble match-light found us a ladder nailed to the wall, leading to a trap in the ceiling. As little later as possible we were on Larrouy's roof, the trap closed behind us.

"All silk so far," said O'Leary, "and if Vance's rats and the bulls will play a couple of seconds longer—bingavast."

I led the way across the roofs. We dropped ten feet to the next building, climbed a bit to the next, and found on the other side of it a fire-escape that ran down to a narrow court with an opening into the back street.

"This ought to do it," I said, and went down.

The girl came behind me, and then Red. The court into which we dropped was empty—a narrow cement passage between buildings. The bottom of the fire-escape creaked as it hinged down under my weight, but the noise didn't stir anything. It was dark in the court, but not black.

"When we hit the street, we split," O'Leary told me, without a word of gratitude for my help—the help he didn't seem to know he had needed. "You roll your hoop, we'll roll ours."

"Uh-huh," I agreed, chasing my brains around in my skull. "I'll scout the alley first."

Carefully I picked my way down to the end of the court and risked the top of my hatless head to peep into the back street. It was quiet, but up at the corner, a quarter of a block above, two loafers seemed to be loafing attentively. They weren't coppers. I stepped out into the back street and beckoned them down. They couldn't recognize me at that distance, in that light, and there was no reason why they shouldn't think me one of Vance's crew, if they belonged to him.

As they came toward me I stepped back into the court and hissed for Red. He wasn't a boy you had to call twice to a row. He got to me just as they arrived. I took one. He took the other.

Because I wanted a disturbance, I had to work like a mule to get it. These bimbos were a couple of lollipops for fair. There wouldn't have been an ounce of fight in a ton of them. The one I had didn't know what to make of my roughing him around. He had a gun, but he managed to drop it first thing, and in the wrestling it got kicked out of reach. He hung on while I sweated ink jockeying him around into position. The darkness helped, but even at that it was no cinch to pretend he was putting up a battle while I worked him around behind O'Leary, who wasn't having any trouble at all with his man.

Finally I made it. I was behind O'Leary, who had his man pinned against the wall with one hand, preparing to sock him again with the other. I clamped my left hand on my playmate's wrist, twisted him to his knees, got my gun out, and shot O'Leary in the back, just below the right shoulder.

Red swayed, jamming his man into the wall. I beaned mine with the gun-butt.

"Did he get you, Red?" I asked, steadying him with an arm, knocking his prisoner across the noodle.

"Yeah."

"Nancy," I called.

She ran to us.

"Take his other side," I told her. "Keep on your feet, Red, and we'll make the sneak O.K."

The bullet was too freshly in him to slow him up yet, though his right arm was out of commission. We ran down the back street to the corner. We had pursuers before we made it. Curious faces looked at us in the street. A policeman a block away began to move our way. The girl helping O'Leary on one side, me on the other, we ran half a block away from the copper, to where I had left the automobile Jack and I had used. The street was active by the time I got the machinery grinding and the girl had Red stowed safely in the back seat. The copper sent a yell and a high bullet after us. We left the neighborhood.

I didn't have any special destination yet, so, after the necessary first burst of speed, I slowed up a little, went around lots of corners, and brought the bus to rest in a dark street beyond Van Ness Avenue.

Red was drooping in one corner of the back, the girl holding him up, when I screwed around in my seat to look at them.

"Where to?" I asked.

"A hospital, a doctor, something!" the girl cried. "He's dying!"

I didn't believe that. If he was, it was his own fault. If he had had enough gratitude to take me along with him as a friend I wouldn't have had to shoot him so I could go along as nurse.

"Where to, Red?" I asked him, prodding his knee with a finger.

He spoke thickly, giving me the address of the Stockton Street hotel.

"That's no good," I objected. "Everybody in town knows you bunk there, and if you go back, it's lights out for yours. Where to?"

"Hotel," he repeated.

I got up, knelt on the seat, and leaned back to work on him. He was weak. He couldn't have much resistance left.

Bulldozing a man who might after all be dying wasn't gentle-manly, but I had invested a lot of trouble in this egg, trying to get him to lead me to his friends, and I wasn't going to quit in the stretch. For a while it looked as if he wasn't weak enough yet, as if I'd have to shoot him again. But the girl sided with me, and between us we finally convinced him that his only safe bet was to go somewhere where he could hide while he got the right kind of care. We didn't actually convince him—we wore him out and he gave in because he was too weak to argue longer. He gave me an address out by Holly Park.

Hoping for the best, I pointed the machine thither.

XII

The house was a small one in a row of small houses. We took the big boy out of the car and between us to the door. He could just about make it with our help. The street was dark. No light showed from the house. I rang the bell.

Nothing happened. I rang again, and then once more.

"Who is it?" a harsh voice demanded from the inside.

"Red's been hurt," I said.

Silence for a while. Then the door opened half a foot. Through the opening a light came from the interior, enough light to show the flat face and bulging jaw-muscles of the skull-cracker who had been the Motsa Kid's guardian and executioner.

"What the hell?" he asked.

"Red was jumped. They got him," I explained, pushing the limp giant forward.

We didn't crash the gate that way. The skull-cracker held the door as it was.

"You'll wait," he said, and shut the door in our faces. His voice sounded from within, "Flora." That was all right—Red had brought us to the right place.

When he opened the door again he opened it all the way, and Nancy Regan and I took our burden into the hall. Beside the skull-cracker stood a woman in a low-cut black silk gown—Big Flora, I supposed.

She stood at least five feet ten in her high-heeled slippers. They were small slippers, and I noticed that her ringless hands were small. The rest of her wasn't. She was broad-shouldered, deep-bosomed, thick-armed, with a pink throat which, for all its smoothness, was muscled like a wrestler's. She was about my age—close to forty—with very curly and very yellow bobbed hair, very pink skin, and a handsome, brutal face. Her deep-set eyes were gray, her thick lips were well-shaped, her nose was just broad enough and curved enough to give her a look of strength, and she had chin enough to support it. From forehead to throat her pink skin was underlaid with smooth, thick, strong muscles.

This Big Flora was no toy. She had the look and the poise of a woman who could have managed the looting and the double-crossing afterward. Unless her face and body lied, she had all the strength of physique, mind and will that would be needed, and some to spare. She was made of stronger stuff than either the ape-built bruiser at her side or the red-haired giant I was holding.

"Well?" she asked, when the door had been closed behind us. Her voice was deep but not masculine—a voice that went well with her looks.

"Vance ganged him in Larrouy's. He took one in the back," I said.

"Who are you?"

"Get him to bed," I stalled. "We've got all night to talk."

She turned, snapping her fingers. A shabby little old man darted out of a door toward the rear. His brown eyes were very scary.

"Get to hell upstairs," she ordered. "Fix the bed, get hot water and towels."

The little old man scrambled up the stairs like a rheumatic rabbit.

The skull-cracker took the girl's side of Red, and he and I carried the giant up to a room where the little man was scurrying around with basins and cloth. Flora and Nancy Regan followed us. We spread the wounded man face-down on the bed and stripped him. Blood still ran from the bullet-hole. He was unconscious.

Nancy Regan went to pieces.

"He's dying! He's dying! Get a doctor! Oh, Reddy, dearest—"

"Shut up!" said Big Flora. "The damned fool ought to croak—going to Larrouy's tonight!" She caught the little man by the shoulder and threw him at the door. "Zonite and more water," she called after him. "Give me your knife, Pogy."

The ape-built man took from his pocket a spring-knife with a long blade that had been sharpened until it was narrow and thin. This is the knife, I thought, that cut the Motsa Kid's throat.

With it, Big Flora cut the bullet out of Red O'Leary's back.

The ape-built Pogy kept Nancy Regan over in a corner of the room while the operating was done. The little scared man knelt beside the bed, handing the woman what she asked for, mopping up Red's blood as it ran from the wound.

I stood beside Flora, smoking cigarettes from the pack she had given me. When she raised her head, I would transfer the cigarette from my mouth to hers. She would fill her lungs with a draw that ate half the cigarette and nod. I would take the cigarette from her mouth. She would blow out the smoke and bend to her work again. I would light another cigarette from what was left of that one, and be ready for her next smoke.

Her bare arms were blood to the elbows. Her face was damp with sweat. It was a gory mess, and it took time. But when she straightened up for the last smoke, the bullet was out of Red, the bleeding had stopped, and he was bandaged.

"Thank God that's over," I said, lighting one of my own cigarettes. "Those pills you smoke are terrible."

The little scared man was cleaning up. Nancy Regan had fainted in a chair across the room, and nobody was paying any attention to her.

"Keep your eye on this gent, Pogy," Big Flora told the skull-cracker, nodding at me, "while I wash up."

I went over to the girl, rubbed her hands, put some water on her face, and got her awake.

"The bullet's out. Red's sleeping. He'll be picking fights again within a week," I told her.

She jumped up and ran over to the bed.

Flora came in. She had washed and had changed her blood-stained black gown for a green kimono affair, which gaped here and there to show a lot of orchid-colored underthings.

"Talk," she commanded, standing in front of me. "Who, what and why?"

"I'm Percy Maguire," I said, as if this name, which I had just thought up, explained everything.

"That's the who," she said, as if my phoney alias explained nothing. "Now what's the what and why?"

The ape-built Pogy, standing on one side, looked me up and down. I'm short and lumpy. My face doesn't scare children, but it's a more or less truthful witness to a life that hasn't been overburdened with refinement and gentility. The evening's entertainment had decorated me with bruises and scratches, and had done things to what was left of my clothes.

"Percy," he echoed, showing wide-spaced yellow teeth in a grin. "My Gawd, brother, your folks must have been color-blind!"

"That's the what and why," I insisted to the woman, paying no attention to the wheeze from the zoo. "I'm Percy Maguire, and I want my hundred and fifty thousand dollars."

The muscles in her brows came down over her eyes.

"You've got a hundred and fifty thousand dollars, have you?"

I nodded up into her handsome brutal face.

"Yeah," I said. "That's what I came for."

"Oh, you haven't got them? You want them?"

"Listen, sister, I want my dough." I had to get tough if this play was to go over. "This swapping *Oh-have-yous* and *Yes-I-haves* don't get me anything but a thirst. We were in the big knock-over, see? And after that, when we find the pay-off's a bust, I said to the kid I was training with, 'Never mind, Kid, we'll get our whack. Just follow Percy.' And then Bluepoint comes to me and asks me to throw in with him, and I said, 'Sure!' and me and the kid throw in with him until we all come across Red in the dump tonight. Then I told the kid, 'These coffee-and-doughnut guns are going to rub Red out, and that won't get us anything. We'll take him away from 'em and make him steer us to where Big Flora's sitting on the jack. We ought to be good for a hundred and fifty grand apiece, now that there's damned few in on it. After we get that, if we want to bump Red off, all right. But business before pleasure, and a hundred and fifty thou is business.' So we did. We opened an out for the big boy when he didn't have any. The kid got mushy with the broad along the road and got knocked for a loop. That was all-right with me. If she was worth a hundred and fifty grand to him—fair enough. I came on with Red. I pulled the big tramp out after he stopped the slug. By rights I ought to collect the kid's dib, too—making three hundred thou for me—but give me the hundred and fifty I started out for and we'll call it even-steven."

I thought this hocus ought to stick. Of course I wasn't counting on her ever giving me any money, but if the rank and file of the mob hadn't known these people, why should these people know everybody in the mob?

Flora spoke to Pogy:

"Get that damned heap away from the front door."

I felt better when he went out. She wouldn't have sent him out to move the car if she had meant to do anything to me right away.

"Got any food in the joint?" I asked, making myself at home.

She went to the head of the steps and yelled down, "Get something for us to eat."

Red was still unconscious. Nancy Regan sat beside him, holding one of his hands. Her face was drained white. Big Flora came into the room again, looked at the invalid, put a hand on his forehead, felt his pulse.

"Come on downstairs," she said.

"I—I'd rather stay here, if I may," Nancy Regan said. Voice and eyes showed utter terror of Flora.

The big woman, saying nothing, went downstairs. I followed her to the kitchen, where the little man was working on ham and eggs at the range. The window and back door, I saw, were reinforced with heavy planking and braced with timbers nailed to the floor. The clock over the sink said 2.50 a.m.

Flora brought out a quart of liquor and poured drinks for herself and me. We sat at the table and while we waited for our food she cursed Red O'Leary and Nancy Regan, because he had got himself disabled keeping a date with her at a time when Flora needed his strength most. She cursed them individually, as a pair, and was making it a racial matter by cursing all the Irish when the little man gave us our ham and eggs.

We had finished the solids and were stirring hooch in our second cups of coffee when Pogy came back. He had news.

"There's a couple of mugs hanging around the corner that I don't much like."

"Bulls or——?" Flora asked.

"Or," he said.

Flora began to curse Red and Nancy again. But she had pretty well played that line out already. She turned to me.

"What the hell did you bring them here for?" she demanded. "Leaving a mile-wide trail behind you! Why didn't you let the lousy bum die where he got his dose?"

"I brought him here for my hundred and fifty grand. Slip it to me and I'll be on my way. You don't owe me anything else. I don't owe you anything. Give me my rhino instead of lip and I'll pull my freight."

"Like hell you will," said Pogy.

The woman looked at me under lowered brows and drank her coffee.

XIII

Fifteen minutes later the shabby little old man came running into the kitchen, saying he had heard feet on the roof. His faded brown eyes were dull as an ox's with fright, and his withered lips writhed under his straggly yellow-white mustache.

Flora profanely called him a this-and-that kind of old one-thing-and-another and chased him upstairs again. She got up from the table and pulled the green kimono tight around her big body.

"You're here," she told me, "and you'll put in with us. There's no other way. Got a rod?"

I admitted I had a gun but shook my head at the rest of it.

"This is not my wake—yet," I said. "It'll take one hundred and fifty thousand berries, spot cash, paid in the hand, to buy Percy in on it."

I wanted to know if the loot was on the premises.

Nancy Regan's tearful voice came from the stairs:

"No, no, darling! Please, please, go back to bed! You'll kill yourself, Reddy, dear!"

Red O'Leary strode into the kitchen. He was naked except for a pair of gray pants and his bandage. His eyes were feverish and happy. His dry lips were stretched in a grin. He had a gun in his left hand. His right arm hung useless. Behind him trotted Nancy. She stopped pleading and shrank behind him when she saw Big Flora.

"Ring the gong, and let's go," the half-naked red-head laughed. "Vance is in our street."

Flora went over to him, put her fingers on his wrist, held them there a couple of seconds, and nodded:

"You crazy son-of-a-gun," she said in a tone that was more like maternal pride than anything else. "You're good for a fight right now. And a damned good thing, too, because you're going to get it."

Red laughed—a triumphant laugh that boasted of his toughness—then his eyes turned to me. Laughter went out of them and a puzzled look drew them narrow.

"Hello," he said. "I dreamed about you, but I can't remember what it was. It was— Wait. I'll get it in a minute. It was— By God! I dreamed it was you that plugged me!"

Flora smiled at me, the first time I had seen her smile, and she spoke quickly:

"Take him, Pogy!"

I twisted obliquely out of my chair.

Pogy's fist took me in the temple. Staggering across the room, struggling to keep my feet, I thought of the bruise on the dead Motsa Kid's temple.

Pogy was on me when the wall bumped me upright.

I put a fist—spat!—in his flat nose. Blood squirted, but his hairy paws gripped me. I tucked my chin in, ground the top of my head into his face. The scent Big Flora used came strong to me. Her silk clothes brushed against me. With both hands full of my hair she pulled my head back, stretching my neck for Pogy. He took hold of it with his paws. I quit. He didn't throttle me any more than was necessary, but it was bad enough.

Flora frisked me for gun and blackjack.

".38 special," she named the caliber of the gun. "I dug a .38

special bullet out of you, Red." The words came faintly to me through the roaring in my ears.

The little old man's voice was chattering in the kitchen. I couldn't make out anything he said. Pogy's hands went away from me. I put my own hands to my throat. It was hell not to have any pressure at all there. The blackness went slowly away from my eyes, leaving a lot of little purple clouds that floated around and around. Presently I could sit up on the floor. I knew by that I had been lying down on it.

The purple clouds shrank until I could see past them enough to know there were only three of us in the room now. Cringing in a chair, back in a corner, was Nancy Regan. On another chair, beside the door, a black pistol in his hand, sat the scared little old man. His eyes were desperately frightened. Gun and hand shook at me. I tried to ask him to either stop shaking or move his gun away from me, but I couldn't get any words out yet.

Upstairs, guns boomed, their reports exaggerated by the smallness of the house.

The little man winced.

"Let me get out," he whispered with unexpected abruptness, "and I will give you everything. I will! Everything—if you will let me get out of this house!"

This feeble ray of light where there hadn't been a dot gave me back the use of my vocal apparatus.

"Talk turkey," I managed to say.

"I will give you those upstairs—that she-devil. I will give you the money. I will give you all—if you will let me go out. I am old. I am sick. I cannot live in prison. What have I to do with robberies? Nothing. Is it my fault that she-devil—? You have seen it here. I am a slave—I who am near the end of my life. Abuse, cursings, beatings—and those are not enough. Now I must go to prison because that she-devil is a she-devil. I am an old man who cannot live in prisons. You let me go out. You do me that kindness. I will give you that she-devil—those other devils—the money they stole. That I will do!"

Thus this panic-stricken little old man, squirming and fidgeting on his chair.

"How can I get you out?" I asked, getting up from the floor, my eye on his gun. If I could get to him while we talked. . . .

"How not? You are a friend of the police—that I know. The police are here now—waiting for daylight before they come into this house. I myself with my old eyes saw them take that Bluepoint Vance. You can take me out past your friends, the police. You do what I ask, and I will give you those devils and their moneys."

"Sounds good" I said, taking a careless step toward him. "But can I just stroll out of here when I want to?"

"No! No!" he said, paying no attention to the second step I took toward him. "But first I will give you those three devils. I will give them to you alive but without power. And their money. That I will do, and then you will take me out—and this girl here." He nodded suddenly at Nancy, whose white face, still nice in spite of its terror, was mostly wide eyes just now. "She, too, has nothing to do with those devils' crimes. She must go with me."

I wondered what this old rabbit thought he could do. I frowned exceedingly thoughtful while I took still another step toward him.

"Make no mistake," he whispered earnestly. "When that she-devil comes back into this room you will die—she will kill you certainly."

Three more steps and I would be close enough to take hold of him and his gun.

Footsteps were in the hall. Too late for a jump.

"Yes?" he hissed desperately.

I nodded a split-second before Big Flora came through the door.

XIV

She was dressed for action in a pair of blue pants that were probably Pogy's, beaded moccasins, a silk waist. A ribbon held her curly yellow hair back from her face. She had a gun in one hand, one in each hip pocket.

The one in her hand swung up.

"You're done," she told me, quite matter-of-fact.

My newly acquired confederate whined, "Wait, wait, Flora! Not here like this, please! Let me take him into the cellar."

She scowled at him, shrugging her silken shoulders.

"Make it quick," she said. "It'll be light in another half-hour."

I felt too much like crying to laugh at them. Was I supposed to think this woman would let the rabbit change her plans? I suppose I must have put some value on the old gink's help, or I wouldn't have been so disappointed when this little comedy told me it was a frame-up. But any hole they worked me into couldn't be any worse than the one I was in.

So I went ahead of the old man into the hall, opened the door he indicated, switched on the basement light, and went down the rough steps.

Close behind me he was whispering, "I'll first show you the moneys, and then I will give to you those devils. And you will not forget your promise? I and that girl shall go out through the police?"

"Oh, yes," I assured the old joker.

He came up beside me, sticking a gun-butt in my hand.

"Hide it," he hissed, and, when I had pocketed that one, gave me another, producing them with his free hand from under his coat.

Then he actually showed me the loot. It was still in the boxes and bags in which it had been carried from the banks. He insisted on opening some of them to show me the money—green bundles belted with the bank's yellow wrappers. The boxes and bags were stacked in a small brick cell that was fitted with a padlocked door, to which he had the key.

He closed the door when we were through looking, but he did not lock it, and he led me back part of the way we had come.

"That, as you see, is the money," he said. "Now for those. You will stand here, hiding behind these boxes."

A partition divided the cellar in half. It was pierced by a doorway that had no door. The place the old man told me to hide was close beside this doorway, between the partition and four packing-cases. Hiding there, I would be to the right of, and a little behind, anyone who came downstairs and walked through the cellar toward the cell that held the money. That is, I would be in that position when they went to go through the doorway in the partition.

The old man was fumbling beneath one of the boxes. He brought out an eighteen-inch length of lead pipe stuffed in a similar length of black garden hose. He gave this to me as he explained everything.

"They will come down here one at a time. When they are about to go through this door, you will know what to do with this. And then you will have them, and I will have your promise. Is it not so?"

"Oh, yes," I said, all up in the air.

He went upstairs. I crouched behind the boxes, examining the guns he had given me—and I'm damned if I could find anything wrong with them. They were loaded and they seemed to be in working order. That finishing touch completely balled me up. I didn't know whether I was in a cellar or a balloon.

When Red O'Leary, still naked except for pants and bandage, came into the cellar, I had to shake my head violently to clear it in time to bat him across the back of the noodle as his first bare foot stepped through the doorway. He sprawled down on his face.

The old man scurried down the steps, full of grins.

"Hurry! Hurry!" he panted, helping me drag the redhead back into the money cell. Then he produced two pieces of cord and tied the giant hand and foot.

"Hurry!" he panted again as he left me to run upstairs, while I went back to my hiding-place and hefted the lead-pipe, wondering if Flora had shot me and I was now enjoying the rewards of my virtue—in a heaven where I could enjoy myself forever and ever socking folks who had been rough with me down below.

The ape-built skull-cracker came down, reached the door. I cracked his skull. The little man came scurrying. We dragged Pogy to the cell, tied him up.

"Hurry!" panted the old gink, dancing up and down in his excitement. "That she-devil next—and strike hard!"

He scrambled upstairs and I could hear his feet pattering overhead.

I got rid of some of my bewilderment, making room for a little intelligence in my skull. This foolishness we were up to wasn't so. It couldn't be happening. Nothing ever worked out just that way. You didn't stand in corners and knock down people one after the other like a machine, while a scrawny little bozo up at the other end fed them to you. It was too damned silly! I had enough!

I passed up my hiding place, put down the pipe and found another spot to crouch in, under some shelves, near the steps. I hunkered down there with a gun in each fist. This game I was playing in was—it had to be—gummy around the edges. I wasn't going to stay put any longer.

Flora came down the steps. Two steps behind her the little man trotted.

Flora had a gun in each hand. Her gray eyes were everywhere. Her head was down like an animal's coming to a fight. Her nostrils quivered. Her body, coming down neither slowly nor swiftly, was balanced like a dancer's. If I live to a million I'll never forget the picture this handsome brutal woman made coming down those unplaned cellar stairs. She was a beautiful fight-bred animal going to a fight.

She saw me as I straightened.

"Drop 'em!" I said, but I knew she wouldn't.

The little man flicked a limp brown blackjack out of his sleeve and knocked her behind the ear just as she swung her left gun on me.

I jumped over and caught her before she hit the cement.

"Now, you see!" the old man said gleefully. "You have the money and you have them. And now you will get me and that girl out."

"First we'll stow this with the others," I said.

After he had helped me do that I told him to lock the cell door. He did, and I took the key with one hand, his neck with the other. He squirmed like a snake while I ran my other hand over his clothes, removing the blackjack and a gun, and finding a money-belt around his waist.

"Take it off," I ordered. "You don't carry anything out with you."

His fingers worked with the buckle, dragged the belt from under his clothes, let it fall on the floor. It was padded fat.

Still holding his neck, I took him upstairs, where the girl still sat frozen on the kitchen chair. It took a stiff hooker of whisky and a lot of words to thaw her into understanding that she was going out with the old man and that she wasn't to say a word to anybody, especially not to the police.

"Where's Reddy?" she asked when color had come back into her face—which had even at the worst never lost its niceness—and thoughts to her head.

I told her he was all right, and promised her he would be in a hospital before the morning was over. She didn't ask anything else. I shooed her upstairs for her hat and coat, went with the old man while he got his hat, and then put the pair of them in the front ground-floor room.

"Stay here till I come for you," I said, and I locked the door and pocketed the key when I went out.

xv

The front door and the front window on the ground floor had been planked and braced like the rear ones. I didn't like to risk opening them, even though it was fairly light by now. So I went upstairs, fashioned a flag of truce out of a pillow-slip and a bed-slat, hung it out a window, waited until a heavy voice said, "All right, speak your piece," and then I showed myself and told the police I'd let them in.

It took five minutes' work with a hatchet to pry the front door loose. The chief of police, the captain of detectives, and half the force were waiting on the front steps and pavement when I got the door open. I took them to the cellar and turned Big Flora, Pogy and Red O'Leary over to them, with the money. Flora and Pogy were awake, but not talking.

While the dignitaries were crowded around the spoils I went upstairs. The house was full of police sleuths. I swapped greetings with them as I went through to the room where I had left Nancy Regan and the old gink. Lieutenant Duff was trying the locked door, while O'Gar and Hunt stood behind him.

I grinned at Duff and gave him the key.

He opened the door, looked at the old man and the girl—mostly at her—and then at me. They were standing in the center of the room. The old man's faded eyes were miserably worried, the girl's blue ones darkly anxious. Anxiety didn't ruin her looks a bit.

"If that's yours I don't blame you for locking it up," O'Gar muttered in my ear.

"You can run along now," I told the two in the room. "Get all the sleep you need before you report for duty again."

They nodded and went out of the house.

"That's how your Agency evens up?" Duff said. "The she-employees make up in looks for the ugliness of the he's."

Dick Foley came into the hall.

"How's your end?" I asked.

"Finis. The Angel led me to Vance. He led here. I led the bulls here. They got him—got her."

Two shots crashed in the street.

We went to the door and saw excitement in a police car down the street. We went down there. Bluepoint Vance, handcuffs on his wrists, was writhing half on the seat, half on the floor.

"We were holding him here in the car, Houston and me," a hard-mouthed plain-clothes man explained to Duff. "He made a break, grabbed Houston's gat with both hands. I had to drill him—twice. The cap'll raise hell! He specially wanted him kept here to put up against the others. But God knows I wouldn't of shot him if it hadn't been him or Houston!"

Duff called the plain-clothesman a damned clumsy mick as they lifted Vance up on the seat. Bluepoint's tortured eyes focused on me.

"I—know—you?" he asked painfully. "Continental—New—York?"

"Yes," I said.

"Couldn't—place—you—Larrouy's—with—Red."

He stopped to cough blood.

"Got—Red?"

"Yeah," I told him. "Got Red, Flora, Pogy and the cush."

"But—not—Papa—dop—oul—os."

"Papa does what?" I asked impatiently, a shiver along my spine.

He pulled himself up on the seat.

"Papadopoulos," he repeated, with an agonizing summoning of the little strength left in him. "I tried—shoot him—saw him—walk 'way—with girl—bull—too damn quick—wish . . ."

His words ran out. He shuddered. Death wasn't a sixteenth of an inch behind his eyes. A white-coated intern tried to get past me into the car. I pushed him out of the way and leaned in, taking Vance by the shoulders. The back of my neck was ice. My stomach was empty.

"Listen, Bluepoint," I yelled in his face. "Papadopoulos? Little old man? Brains of the push?"

"Yes," Vance said, and the last live blood in him came out with the word.

I let him drop back on the seat and walked away.

Of course! How had I missed it? The little old scoundrel—if he hadn't, for all his scariness, been the works, how could he have so neatly turned the others over to me one at a time? They had been absolutely cornered. It was be killed fighting, or surrender and be hanged. They had no other way out. The police had Vance, who could and would tell them that the little buzzard was the headman—there wasn't even a chance for him beating the courts with his age, his weakness and his mask of being driven around by the others.

And there I had been—with no choice but to accept his offer. Otherwise lights out for me. I had been putty in his hands, his accomplices had been putty. He had slipped the cross over on them as they had helped him slip it over on the others—and I had sent him safely away.

Now I could turn the city upside down for him—my promise had been only to get him out of the house—but . . .

What a life!

$106,000 Blood Money

I'M Tom-Tom Carey," he said, drawling the words.
I nodded at the chair beside my desk and weighed him
in while he moved to it. Tall, wide-shouldered, thick-chested,
thin-bellied, he would add up to say a hundred and ninety
pounds. His swarthy face was hard as a fist, but there was
nothing ill-humored in it. It was the face of a man of forty-
something who lived life raw and thrived on it. His blue
clothes were good and he wore them well.

In the chair, he twisted brown paper around a charge of
Bull Durham and finished introducing himself:

"I'm Paddy the Mex's brother."

I thought maybe he was telling the truth. Paddy had been
like this fellow in coloring and manner.

"That would make your real name Carrera," I suggested.

"Yes," he was lighting his cigarette. "Alfredo Estanislao
Cristobal Carrera, if you want all the details."

I asked him how to spell Estanislao, wrote the name down
on a slip of paper, adding *alias Tom-Tom Carey*, rang for
Tommy Howd, and told him to have the file clerk see if we
had anything on it.

"While your people are opening graves I'll tell you why I'm
here," the swarthy man drawled through smoke when
Tommy had gone away with the paper.

"Tough—Paddy being knocked off like that," I said.

"He was too damned trusting to live long," his brother explained. "This is the kind of hombre he was—the last time I
saw him was four years ago, here in San Francisco. I'd come
in from an expedition down to—never mind where. Anyway I
was flat. Instead of pearls all I'd got out of the trip was a
bullet-crease over my hip. Paddy was dirty with fifteen thousand or so he'd just nicked somebody for. The afternoon I
saw him he had a date that he was leery of toting so much
money to. So he gives me the fifteen thousand to hold for
him till that night."

Tom-Tom Carey blew out smoke and smiled softly past me
at a memory.

"That's the kind of hombre he was," he went on. "He'd trust even his own brother. I went to Sacramento that afternoon and caught a train East. A girl in Pittsburgh helped me spend the fifteen thousand. Her name was Laurel. She liked rye whisky with milk for a chaser. I used to drink it with her till I was all curdled inside, and I've never had any appetite for *schmierkäse* since. So there's a hundred thousand dollars reward on this Papadopoulos, is there?"

"And six. The insurance companies put up a hundred thousand, the bankers' association five, and the city a thousand."

Tom-Tom Carey chucked the remains of his cigarette in the cuspidor and began to assemble another one.

"Suppose I hand him to you?" he asked. "How many ways will the money have to go?"

"None of it will stop here," I assured him. "The Continental Detective Agency doesn't touch reward money—and won't let its hired men. If any of the police are in on the pinch they'll want a share."

"But if they aren't, it's all mine?"

"If you turn him in without help, or without any help except ours."

"I'll do that." The words were casual. "So much for the arrest. Now for the conviction part. If you get him, are you sure you can nail him to the cross?"

"I ought to be, but he'll have to go up against a jury—and that means anything can happen."

The muscular brown hand holding the brown cigarette made a careless gesture.

"Then maybe I'd better get a confession out of him before I drag him in," he said off-hand.

"It would be safer that way," I agreed. "You ought to let that holster down an inch or two. It brings the gun-butt too high. The bulge shows when you sit down."

"Uh-huh. You mean the one on the left shoulder. I took it away from a fellow after I lost mine. Strap's too short. I'll get another one this afternoon."

Tommy came in with a folder labeled, *Carey, Tom-Tom, 1361-C*. It held some newspaper clippings, the oldest dated ten years back, the youngest eight months. I read them through, passing each one to the swarthy man as I finished it. Tom-

Tom Carey was written down in them as soldier of fortune, gun-runner, seal poacher, smuggler and pirate. But it was all alleged, supposed and suspected. He had been captured variously but never convicted of anything.

"They don't treat me right," he complained placidly when we were through reading. "For instance, stealing that Chinese gunboat wasn't my fault. I was forced to do it—I was the one that was double-crossed. After they'd got the stuff aboard they wouldn't pay for it. I couldn't unload it. I couldn't do anything but take gunboat and all. The insurance companies must want this Papadopoulos plenty to hang a hundred thousand on him."

"Cheap enough if it lands him," I said. "Maybe he's not all the newspapers picture him as, but he's more than a handful. He gathered a whole damned army of strong-arm men here, took over a block in the center of the financial district, looted the two biggest banks in the city, fought off the whole police department, made his getaway, ditched the army, used some of his lieutenants to bump off some more of them,—that's where your brother Paddy got his,—then, with the help of Pogy Reeve, Big Flora Brace and Red O'Leary, wiped out the rest of his lieutenants. And remember, these lieutenants weren't schoolboys—they were slick grifters like Bluepoint Vance and the Shivering Kid and Darby M'Laughlin—birds who knew their what's what."

"Uh-huh." Carey was unimpressed. "But it was a bust just the same. You got all the loot back, and he just managed to get away himself."

"A bad break for him," I explained. "Red O'Leary broke out with a complication of love and vanity. You can't chalk that against Papadopoulos. Don't get the idea he's half-smart. He's dangerous, and I don't blame the insurance companies for thinking they'll sleep better if they're sure he's not out where he can frame some more tricks against their policy-holding banks."

"Don't know much about this Papadopoulos, do you?"

"No." I told the truth. "And nobody does. The hundred thousand offer made rats out of half the crooks in the country. They're as hot after him as we—not only because of the reward but because of his wholesale double-crossing. And they know just as little about him as we do—that he's had his fingers in a dozen or more jobs, that he was the brains behind Bluepoint Vance's bond tricks, and that his enemies have a habit of dying young. But nobody knows where he came from, or where he lives when he's home. Don't think I'm touting him as a Napoleon or a Sunday-supplement master mind—but he's a shifty, tricky old boy. As you say, I don't know much about him—but there are lots of people I don't know much about."

Tom-Tom Carey nodded to show he understood the last part and began making his third cigarette.

"I was in Nogales when Angel Grace Cardigan got word to me that Paddy had been done in," he said. "That was nearly a month ago. She seemed to think I'd romp up here pronto—but it was no skin off my face. I let it sleep. But last week I read in a newspaper about all this reward money being posted on the hombre she blamed for Paddy's rub-out. That made it different—a hundred thousand dollars different. So I shipped up here, talked to her, and then came in to make sure there'll be nothing between me and the blood money when I put the loop on this Papadoodle."

"Angel Grace sent you to me?" I inquired.

"Uh-huh—only she don't know it. She dragged you into the story—said you were a friend of Paddy's, a good guy for a sleuth, and hungry as hell for this Papadoodle. So I thought you'd be the gent for me to see."

"When did you leave Nogales?"

"Tuesday—last week."

"That," I said, prodding my memory, "was the day after Newhall was killed across the border."

The swarthy man nodded. Nothing changed in his face.

"How far from Nogales was that?" I asked.

"He was gunned down near Oquitoa—that's somewhere around sixty miles southwest of Nogales. You interested?"

"No—except I was wondering about your leaving the place where he was killed the day after he was killed, and coming up where he had lived. Did you know him?"

"He was pointed out to me in Nogales as a San Francisco millionaire going with a party to look at some mining property in Mexico. I was figuring on maybe selling him something later, but the Mexican patriots got him before I did."

"And so you came north?"

"Uh-huh. The hubbub kind of spoiled things for me. I had a nice little business in—call it supplies—to and fro across the line. This Newhall killing turned the spotlight on that part of the country. So I thought I'd come up and collect that hundred thousand and give things a chance to settle down there. Honest, brother, I haven't killed a millionaire in weeks, if that's what's worrying you."

"That's good. Now, as I get it, you're counting on landing Papadopoulos. Angel Grace sent for you, thinking you'd run him down just to even up for Paddy's killing, but it's the money you want, so you figure on playing with me as well as the Angel. That right?"

"Check."

"You know what'll happen if she learns you're stringing along with me?"

"Uh-huh. She'll chuck a convulsion—kind of balmy on the subject of keeping clear of the police, isn't she?"

"She is—somebody told her something about honor among thieves once and she's never got over it. Her brother's doing a hitch up north now—Johnny the Plumber sold him out. Her man Paddy was mowed down by his pals. Did either of those things wake her up? Not a chance. She'd rather have Papadopoulos go free than join forces with us."

"That's all right," Tom-Tom Carey assured me. "She thinks I'm the loyal brother—Paddy couldn't have told her much about me—and I'll handle her. You having her shadowed?"

I said: "Yes—ever since she was turned loose. She was picked up the same day Flora and Pogy and Red were grabbed, but we hadn't anything on her except that she had been Paddy's lady-love, so I had her sprung. How much dope did you get out of her?"

"Descriptions of Papadoodle and Nancy Regan, and that's all. She don't know any more about them than I do. Where does this Regan girl fit in?"

"Hardly any, except that she might lead us to Papadopoulos. She was Red's girl. It was keeping a date with her that he upset the game. When Papadopoulos wriggled out he took the girl with him. I don't know why. She wasn't in on the stick-ups."

Tom-Tom Carey finished making and lighting his fifth cigarette and stood up.

"Are we teamed?" he asked as he picked up his hat.

"If you turn in Papadopoulos I'll see that you get every nickel you're entitled to," I replied. "And I'll give you a clear field—I won't handicap you with too much of an attempt to keep my eyes on your actions."

He said that was fair enough, told me he was stopping at a hotel in Ellis Street, and went away.

II

Calling the late Taylor Newhall's office on the phone, I was told that if I wanted any information about his affairs I should try his country residence, some miles south of San Francisco. I tried it. A ministerial voice that said it belonged to the butler told me that Newhall's attorney, Franklin Ellert, was the person I should see. I went over to Ellert's office.

He was a nervous, irritable old man with a lisp and eyes that stuck out with blood pressure.

"Is there any reason," I asked point-blank, "for supposing that Newhall's murder was anything more than a Mexican bandit outburst? Is it likely that he was killed purposely, and not resisting capture?"

Lawyers don't like to be questioned. This one sputtered and made faces at me and let his eyes stick out still further and, of course, didn't give me an answer.

"How? How?" he snapped disagreeably. "Exthplain your meaning, thir!"

He glared at me and then at the desk, pushing papers around with excited hands, as if he were hunting for a police whistle. I told my story—told him about Tom-Tom Carey.

Ellert sputtered some more, demanded, "What the devil do you mean?" and made a complete jumble of the papers on his desk.

"I don't mean anything," I growled back. "I'm just telling you what was said."

"Yeth! Yeth! I know!" He stopped glaring at me and his voice was less peevish. "But there ith abtholutely no reathon for thuthpecting anything of the thort. None at all, thir, none at all!"

"Maybe you're right." I turned to the door. "But I'll poke into it a little anyway."

"Wait! Wait!" He scrambled out of his chair and ran around the desk to me. "I think you are mithtaken, but if you are going to invethtigate it I would like to know what you dithcover. Perhapth you'd better charge me with your regular fee for whatever ith done, and keep me informed of your progreth. Thatithfactory?"

I said it was, came back to his desk and began to question him. There was, as the lawyer had said, nothing in Newhall's affairs to stir us up. The dead man was several times a million-aire, with most of his money in mines. He had inherited nearly half his money. There was no shady practice, no claim-jumping, no trickery in his past, no enemies. He was a widower with one daughter. She had everything she wanted while he lived, and she and her father had been very fond of one another. He had gone to Mexico with a party of mining men from New York who expected to sell him some property there. They had been attacked by bandits, had driven them off, but Newhall and a geologist named Parker had been killed during the fight.

Back in the office, I wrote a telegram to our Los Angeles branch, asking that an operative be sent to Nogales to pry into Newhall's killing and Tom-Tom Carey's affairs. The clerk to whom I gave it to be coded and sent told me the Old Man wanted to see me. I went into his office and was introduced to a short, rolly-polly man named Hook.

"Mr. Hook," the Old Man said, "is the proprietor of a restaurant in Sausalito. Last Monday he employed a waitress named Nelly Riley. She told him she had come from Los Angeles. Her description, as Mr. Hook gives it, is quite simi-lar to the description you and Counihan have given of Nancy Regan. Isn't it?" he asked the fat man.

"Absolutely. It's exactly what I read in the papers. She's five feet five inches tall, about, and medium in size, and she's got blue eyes and brown hair, and she's around twenty-one or two, and she's got looks, and the thing that counts most is she's high-hat as the devil—she don't think nothin's good enough for her. Why, when I tried to be a little sociable she told me to keep my 'dirty paws' to myself. And then I found out she didn't know hardly nothing about Los Angeles, though she claimed to have lived there two or three years. I bet you she's the girl, all right," and he went on talking about how much reward money he ought to get.

"Are you going back there now?" I asked him.

"Pretty soon. I got to stop and see about some dishes. Then I'm going back."

"This girl will be working?"

"Yes."

"Then we'll send a man over with you—one who knows Nancy Regan."

I called Jack Counihan in from the operatives' room and introduced him to Hook. They arranged to meet in half an hour at the ferry and Hook waddled out.

"This Nelly Riley won't be Nancy Regan," I said. "But we can't afford to pass up even a hundred to one chance."

I told Jack and the Old Man about Tom-Tom Carey and my visit to Ellert's office. The Old Man listened with his usual polite attentiveness. Young Counihan—only four months in the man-hunting business—listened with wide eyes.

"You'd better run along now and meet Hook," I said when I had finished, leaving the Old Man's office with Jack. "And if she should be Nancy Regan—grab her and hang on." We were out of the Old Man's hearing, so I added, "And for God's sake don't let your youthful gallantry lead you to a poke in the jaw this time. Pretend you're grown up."

The boy blushed, said, "Go to hell!" adjusted his necktie, and set off to meet Hook.

I had some reports to write. After I had finished them I put my feet on my desk, made cavities in a package of Fatimas, and thought about Tom-Tom Carey until six o'clock. Then I went down to the States for my abalone chowder and minute steak and home to change clothes before going out Sea Cliff way to sit in a poker game.

The telephone interrupted my dressing. Jack Counihan was on the other end.

"I'm in Sausalito. The girl wasn't Nancy, but I've got hold of something else. I'm not sure how to handle it. Can you come over?"

"Is it important enough to cut a poker game for?"

"Yes, it's—I think it's big." He was excited. "I wish you would come over. I really think it's a lead."

"Where are you?"

"At the ferry there. Not the Golden Gate, the other."

"All right. I'll catch the first boat."

III

An hour later I walked off the boat in Sausalito. Jack Counihan pushed through the crowd and began talking:

"Coming down here on my way back——"

"Hold it till we get out of the mob," I advised him. "It must be tremendous—the eastern point of your collar is bent."

He mechanically repaired this defect in his otherwise immaculate costuming while we walked to the street, but he was too intent on whatever was on his mind to smile.

"Up this way," he said, guiding me around a corner. "Hook's lunch-room is on the corner. You can take a look at the girl if you like. She's of the same size and complexion as Nancy Regan, but that is all. She's a tough little job who probably was fired for dropping her chewing gum in the soup the last place she worked."

"All right. That let's her out. Now what's on your mind?"

"After I saw her I started back to the ferry. A boat came in while I was still a couple of blocks away. Two men who must have come in on it came up the street. They were Greeks, rather young, tough, though ordinarily I shouldn't have paid much attention to them. But, since Papadopoulos is a Greek, we have been interested in them, of course, so I looked at these chaps. They were arguing about something as they walked, not talking loud, but scowling at one another. As they passed me the chap on the gutter side said to the other, 'I tell him it's been twenty-nine days.'

"Twenty-nine days. I counted back and it's just twenty-nine days since we started hunting for Papadopoulos. He is a Greek and these chaps were Greeks. When I had finished counting I turned around and began to follow them. They took me all the way through the town and up a hill on the fringe. They went to a little cottage—it couldn't have more than three rooms—set back in a clearing in the woods by itself. There was a 'For Sale' sign on it, and no curtains in the windows, no sign of occupancy—but on the ground behind the back door there was a wet place, as if a bucket or pan of water had been thrown out.

"I stayed in the bushes until it got a little darker. Then I went closer. I could hear people inside, but I couldn't see anything through the windows. They're boarded up. After a while the two chaps I had followed came out, saying something in a language I couldn't understand to whoever was in the cottage. The cottage door stayed open until the two men had gone out of sight down the path—so I couldn't have followed them without being seen by whoever was at the door.

"Then the door was closed and I could hear people moving around inside—or perhaps only one person—and could smell cooking, and some smoke came out of the chimney. I waited and waited and nothing more happened and I thought I had better get in touch with you."

"Sounds interesting," I agreed.

We were passing under a street light. Jack stopped me with a hand on my arm and fished something out of his overcoat pocket.

"Look!" He held it out to me. A charred piece of blue cloth. It could have been the remains of a woman's hat that had been three-quarters burned. I looked at it under the street light and then used my flashlight to examine it more closely.

"I picked it up behind the cottage while I was nosing around," Jack said, "and—"

"And Nancy Regan wore a hat of that shade the night she and Papadopoulos vanished," I finished for him. "On to the cottage."

We left the street lights behind, climbed the hill, dipped down into a little valley, turned into a winding sandy path, left that to cut across sod between trees to a dirt road, trod half a mile of that, and then Jack led the way along a narrow path that wound through a black tangle of bushes and small trees. I hoped he knew where he was going.

"Almost there," he whispered to me.

A man jumped out of the bushes and took me by the neck.

My hands were in my overcoat pockets—one holding the flashlight, the other my gun.

I pushed the muzzle of the pocketed gun toward the man—pulled the trigger.

The shot ruined seventy-five dollars' worth of overcoat for me. But it took the man away from my neck.

That was lucky. Another man was on my back.

I tried to twist away from him—didn't altogether make it—felt the edge of a knife along my spine.

That wasn't so lucky—but it was better than getting the point.

I butted back at his face—missed—kept twisting and squirming while I brought my hands out of my pockets and clawed at him.

The blade of his knife came flat against my cheek. I caught the hand that held it and let myself go—down backward—him under.

He said: "Uh!"

I rolled over, got hands and knees on the ground, was grazed by a fist, scrambled up.

Fingers dragged at my ankle.

My behavior was ungentlemanly. I kicked the fingers away—found the man's body—kicked it twice—hard.

Jack's voice whispered my name. I couldn't see him in the blackness, nor could I see the man I had shot.

"All right here," I told Jack. "How did you come out?"

"Top-hole. Is that all of it?"

"Don't know, but I'm going to risk a peek at what I've got."

Tilting my flashlight down at the man under my foot, I snapped it on. A thin blond man, his face blood-smeared, his pink-rimmed eyes jerking as he tried to play 'possum in the glare.

"Come out of it!" I ordered.

A heavy gun went off back in the bush—another, lighter one. The bullets ripped through the foliage.

I switched off the light, bent to the man on the ground, knocked him on the top of the head with my gun.

"Crouch down low," I whispered to Jack.

The smaller gun snapped again, twice. It was ahead, to the left.

I put my mouth to Jack's ear.

"We're going to that damned cottage whether anybody likes it or no. Keep low and don't do any shooting unless you can see what you're shooting at. Go ahead."

Bending as close to the ground as I could, I followed Jack up the path. The position stretched the slash in my back—a scalding pain from between my shoulders almost to my waist. I could feel blood trickling down over my hips—or thought I could.

The going was too dark for stealthiness. Things crackled under our feet, rustled against our shoulders. Our friends in the bush used their guns. Luckily, the sound of twigs breaking and leaves rustling in pitch blackness isn't the best of targets. Bullets zipped here and there, but we didn't stop any of them. Neither did we shoot back.

We halted where the end of the bush left the night a weaker gray.

"That's it," Jack said about a square shape ahead.

"On the jump," I grunted and lit out for the dark cottage.

Jack's long slim legs kept him easily at my side as we raced across the clearing.

A man-shape oozed from behind the blot of the building and his gun began to blink at us. The shots came so close together that they sounded like one long stuttering bang.

Pulling the youngster with me, I flopped, flat to the ground except where a ragged-edged empty tin-can held my face up.

From the other side of the building another gun coughed. From a tree-stem to the right, a third.

Jack and I began to burn powder back at them.

A bullet kicked my mouth full of dirt and pebbles. I spit mud and cautioned Jack:

"You're shooting too high. Hold it low and pull easy."

A hump showed in the house's dark profile. I sent a bullet at it.

A man's voice yelled: "Ow—ooh!" and then, lower but very bitter, "Oh, damn you—damn you!"

For a warm couple of seconds bullets spattered all around

us. Then there was not a sound to spoil the night's quiet-
ness.

When the silence had lasted five minutes, I got myself up
on hands and knees and began to move forward, Jack following. The ground wasn't made for that sort of work. Ten feet
of it was enough. We stood up and walked the rest of the way
to the building.

"Wait," I whispered, and leaving Jack at one corner of the
building, I circled it, seeing nobody, hearing nothing but the
sounds I made.

We tried the front door. It was locked but rickety.

Bumping it open with my shoulder, I went indoors—flashlight and gun in my fists.

The shack was empty.

Nobody—no furnishings—no traces of either in the two
bare rooms—nothing but bare wooden walls, bare floor, bare
ceiling, with a stove-pipe connected to nothing sticking
through it.

Jack and I stood in the middle of the floor, looked at the
emptiness, and cursed the dump from back door to front for
being empty. We hadn't quite finished when feet sounded
outside, a white light beamed on the open doorway, and a
cracked voice said:

"Hey! You can come out one at a time—kind of easy like!"

"Who says so?" I asked, snapping off the flashlight, moving
over close to a side wall.

"A whole goldurned flock of deputy sheriffs," the voice answered.

"Couldn't you push one of 'em in and let us get a look at
him?" I asked. "I've been choked and carved and shot at tonight until I haven't got much faith left in anybody's word."

A lanky, knock-kneed man with a thin leathery face appeared in the doorway. He showed me a buzzer, I fished out
my credentials, and the other deputies came in. There were
three of them in all.

"We were driving down the road bound for a little job near
the point when we heard the shooting," the lanky one explained. "What's up?"

I told him.

"This shack's been empty a long while," he said when I had

finished. "Anybody could have camped in it easy enough. Think it was that Papadopoulos, huh? We'll kind of look around for him and his friends—especial since there's that nice reward money."

We searched the woods and found nobody. The man I had knocked down and the man I had shot were both gone.

Jack and I rode back to Sausalito with the deputies. I hunted up a doctor there and had my back bandaged. He said the cut was long but shallow. Then we returned to San Francisco and separated in the direction of our homes.

And thus ended the day's doings.

IV

Here is something that happened next morning. I didn't see it. I heard about it a little before noon and read about it in the papers that afternoon. I didn't know then that I had any personal interest in it, but later I did—so I'll put it in here where it happened.

At ten o'clock that morning, into busy Market Street, staggered a man who was naked from the top of his battered head to the soles of his blood-stained feet. From his bare chest and sides and back, little ribbons of flesh hung down, dripping blood. His left arm was broken in two places. The left side of his bald head was smashed in. An hour later he died in the emergency hospital—without having said a word to anyone, with the same vacant, distant look in his eyes.

The police easily ran back the trail of blood drops. They ended with a red smear in an alley beside a small hotel just off Market Street. In the hotel, the police found the room from which the man had jumped, fallen, or been thrown. The bed was soggy with blood. On it were torn and twisted sheets that had been knotted and used rope-wise. There was also a towel that had been used as a gag.

The evidence read that the naked man had been gagged, trussed up and worked on with a knife. The doctors said the ribbons of flesh had been cut loose, not torn or clawed. After the knife-user had gone away, the naked man had worked free of his bonds, and, probably crazed by pain, had either jumped or fallen out of the window. The fall had crushed his skull and broken his arm, but he had managed to walk a block and a half in that condition.

The hotel management said the man had been there two days. He was registered as H. F. Barrows, City. He had a black gladstone bag in which, besides clothes, shaving implements and so on, the police found a box of .38 cartridges, a black handkerchief with eye-holes cut in it, four skeleton keys, a small jimmy, and a quantity of morphine, with a needle and the rest of the kit. Elsewhere in the room they found the rest of his clothes, a .38 revolver and two quarts of liquor. They didn't find a cent.

The supposition was that Barrows had been a burglar, and that he had been tied up, tortured and robbed, probably by pals, between eight and nine that morning. Nobody knew anything about him. Nobody had seen his visitor or visitors. The room next to his on the left was unoccupied. The occupant of the room on the other side had left for his work in a furniture factory before seven o'clock.

While this was happening I was at the office, sitting forward in my chair to spare my back, reading reports, all of which told how operatives attached to various Continental Detective Agency branches had continued to fail to turn up any indications of the past, present, or future whereabouts of Papadopoulos and Nancy Regan. There was nothing novel about these reports—I had been reading similar ones for three weeks.

The Old Man and I went out to luncheon together, and I told him about the previous night's adventures in Sausalito while we ate. His grandfatherly face was as attentive as always, and his smile as politely interested, but when I was half through my story he turned his mild blue eyes from my face to his salad and he stared at his salad until I had finished talking. Then, still not looking up, he said he was sorry I had been cut. I thanked him and we ate a while.

Finally he looked at me. The mildness and courtesy he habitually wore over his cold-bloodedness were in face and eyes and voice as he said:

"This first indication that Papadopoulos is still alive came immediately after Tom-Tom Carey's arrival."

It was my turn to shift my eyes.

I looked at the roll I was breaking while I said: "Yes."

That afternoon a phone call came in from a woman out in the Mission who had seen some highly mysterious happenings and was sure they had something to do with the well-advertised bank robberies. So I went out to see her and spent most of the afternoon learning that half of her happenings were imaginary and the other half were the efforts of a jealous wife to get the low-down on her husband.

It was nearly six o'clock when I returned to the Agency. A few minutes later Dick Foley called me on the phone. His teeth were chattering until I could hardly get the words.

"C-c-canyoug-g-get-t-townt-t-tooth-ar-r-rbr-r-spittle?"

"What?" I asked, and he said the same thing again, or worse. But by this time I had guessed that he was asking me if I could get down to the Harbor Hospital.

I told him I could in ten minutes, and with the help of a taxi I did.

V

The little Canadian operative met me at the hospital door. His clothes and hair were dripping wet, but he had had a shot of whisky and his teeth had stopped chattering.

"Damned fool jumped in bay!" he barked as if it were my fault.

"Angel Grace?"

"Who else was I shadowing? Got on Oakland ferry. Moved off by self by rail. Thought she was going to throw something over. Kept eye on her. Bingo! She jumps." Dick sneezed. "I was goofy enough to jump after her. Held her up. Were fished out. In there," nodding his wet head toward the interior of the hospital.

"What happened before she took the ferry?"

"Nothing. Been in joint all day. Straight out to ferry."

"How about yesterday?"

"Apartment all day. Out at night with man. Roadhouse. Home at four. Bad break. Couldn't tail him off."

"What did he look like?"

The man Dick described was Tom-Tom Carey.

"Good," I said. "You'd better beat it home for a hot bath and some dry rags."

I went in to see the near-suicide.

She was lying on her back on a cot, staring at the ceiling. Her face was pale, but it always was, and her green eyes were no more sullen than usual. Except that her short hair was dark with dampness she didn't look as if anything out of the ordinary had happened.

"You think of the funniest things to do," I said when I was beside the bed.

She jumped and her face jerked around to me, startled. Then she recognized me and smiled—a smile that brought into her face the attractiveness that habitual sullenness kept out.

"You have to keep in practice—sneaking up on people?" she asked. "Who told you I was here?"

"Everybody knows it. Your pictures are all over the front pages of the newspapers, with your life history and what you said to the Prince of Wales."

She stopped smiling and looked steadily at me.

"I got it!" she exclaimed after a few seconds. "That runt who came in after me was one of your ops—tailing me. Wasn't he?"

"I didn't know anybody had to go in after you," I answered. "I thought you came ashore after you had finished your swim. Didn't you want to land?"

She wouldn't smile. Her eyes began to look at something horrible.

"Oh! Why didn't they let me alone?" she wailed, shuddering. "It's a rotten thing, living."

I sat down on a small chair beside the white bed and patted the lump her shoulder made in the sheets.

"What was it?" I was surprised at the fatherly tone I achieved. "What did you want to die for, Angel?"

Words that wanted to be said were shiny in her eyes, tugged at muscles in her face, shaped her lips—but that was all. The words she said came out listlessly, but with a reluctant sort of finality. They were:

"No. You're law. I'm thief. I'm staying on my side of the fence. Nobody can say—"

"All right! All right!" I surrendered. "But for God's sake don't make me listen to another of those ethical arguments. Is there anything I can do for you?"

"Thanks, no."

"There's nothing you want to tell me?"

She shook her head.

"You're all right now?"

"Yes. I was being shadowed, wasn't I? Or you wouldn't have known about it so soon."

"I'm a detective—I know everything. Be a good girl."

From the hospital I went up to the Hall of Justice, to the police detective bureau. Lieutenant Duff was holding down the captain's desk. I told him about the Angel's dive.

"Got any idea what she was up to?" he wanted to know when I had finished.

"She's too far off center to figure. I want her vagged."

"Yeah? I thought you wanted her loose so you could catch her."

"That's about played out now. I'd like to try throwing her in the can for thirty days. Big Flora is in waiting trial. The Angel knows Flora was one of the troupe that rubbed out her Paddy. Maybe Flora don't know the Angel. Let's see what will come of mixing the two babies for a month."

"Can do," Duff agreed. "This Angel's got no visible means of support, and it's a cinch she's got no business running around jumping in people's bays. I'll put the word through."

From the Hall of Justice I went up to the Ellis Street hotel at which Tom-Tom Carey had told me he was registered. He was out. I left word that I would be back in an hour, and used that hour to eat. When I returned to the hotel the tall swarthy man was sitting in the lobby. He took me up to his room and set out gin, orange juice and cigars.

"Seen Angel Grace?" I asked.

"Yes, last night. We did the dumps."

"Seen her today?"

"No."

"She jumped in the bay this afternoon."

"The hell she did." He seemed moderately surprised. "And then?"

"She was fished out. She's O.K."

The shadow in his eyes could have been some slight disappointment.

"She's a funny sort of kid," he remarked. "I wouldn't say Paddy didn't show good taste when he picked her, but she's a queer one!"

"How's the Papadopoulos hunt progressing?"

"It is. But you oughtn't have split on your word. You half-way promised you wouldn't have me shadowed."

"I'm not the big boss," I apologized. "Sometimes what I want don't fit in with what the headman wants. This shouldn't bother you much—you can shake him, can't you?"

"Uh-huh. That's what I've been doing. But it's a damned nuisance jumping in and out of taxis and back doors."

We talked and drank a few minutes longer, and then I left Carey's room and hotel, and went to a drug-store telephone booth, where I called Dick Foley's home, and gave Dick the swarthy man's description and address.

"I don't want you to tail Carey, Dick. I want you to find out who is trying to tail him—and that shadower is the bird you're to stick to. The morning will be time enough to start—get yourself dried out."

And that was the end of that day.

VI

I woke to a disagreeable rainy morning. Maybe it was the weather, maybe I'd been too frisky the day before, anyway the slit in my back was like a foot-long boil. I phoned Dr. Canova, who lived on the floor below me, and had him look at the cut before he left for his downtown office. He rebandaged it and told me to take life easy for a couple of days. It felt better after he had fooled with it, but I phoned the Agency and told the Old Man that unless something exciting broke I was going to stay on sick-call all day.

I spent the day propped up in front of the gas-log, reading, and smoking cigarettes that wouldn't burn right on account of the weather. That night I used the phone to organize a poker game, in which I got very little action one way or the other. In the end I was fifteen dollars ahead, which was just about five dollars less than enough to pay for the booze my guests had drunk on me.

My back was better the following day, and so was the day. I went down to the Agency. There was a memorandum on my desk saying Duff had phoned that Angel Grace Cardigan had been vagged—thirty days in the city prison. There was a familiar pile of reports from various branches on their operatives' inability to pick up anything on Papadopoulos and Nancy Regan. I was running through these when Dick Foley came in.

"Made him," he reported. "Thirty or thirty-two. Five, six. Hundred, thirty. Sandy hair, complexion. Blue eye. Thin face, some skin off. Rat. Lives dump in Seventh Street."

"What did he do?"

"Tailed Carey one block. Carey shook him. Hunted for Carey till two in morning. Didn't find him. Went home. Take him again?"

"Go up to his flophouse and find out who he is."

The little Canadian was gone half an hour.

"Sam Arlie," he said when he returned. "Been there six months. Supposed to be barber—when he's working—if ever."

"I've got two guesses about this Arlie," I told Dick. "The first is that he's the gink who carved me in Sausalito the other night. The second is that something's going to happen to him."

It was against Dick's rules to waste words, so he said nothing.

I called Tom-Tom Carey's hotel and got the swarthy man on the wire.

"Come over," I invited him. "I've got some news for you."

"As soon as I'm dressed and breakfasted," he promised.

"When Carey leaves here you're to go along behind him," I told Dick after I had hung up. "If Arlie connects with him now, maybe there'll be something doing. Try to see it."

Then I phoned the detective bureau and made a date with Sergeant Hunt to visit Angel Grace Cardigan's apartment. After that I busied myself with paper work until Tommy came in to announce the swarthy man from Nogales.

"The jobbie who's tailing you," I informed him when he had sat down and begun work on a cigarette, "is a barber named Arlie," and I told him where Arlie lived.

"Yes. A slim-faced, sandy lad?"

I gave him the description Dick had given me.

"That's the hombre," Tom-Tom Carey said. "Know anything else about him?"

"No."

"You had Angel Grace vagged."

It was neither an accusation nor a question, so I didn't answer it.

"It's just as well," the tall man went on. "I'd have had to send her away. She was bound to gum things with her foolishness when I got ready to swing the loop."

"That'll be soon?"

"That all depends on how it happens." He stood up, yawned and shook his wide shoulders. "But nobody would starve to death if they decided not to eat any more till I'd got him. I oughtn't have accused you of having me shadowed."

"It didn't spoil my day."

Tom-Tom Carey said, "So long," and sauntered out.

I rode down to the Hall of Justice, picked up Hunt, and we went to the Bush Street apartment house in which Angel Grace Cardigan had lived. The manager—a highly scented fat woman with a hard mouth and soft eyes—already knew her tenant was in the cooler. She willingly took us up to the girl's rooms.

The Angel wasn't a good housekeeper. Things were clean enough, but upset. The kitchen sink was full of dirty dishes. The folding bed was worse than loosely made up. Clothes and odds and ends of feminine equipment hung over everything from bathroom to kitchen.

We got rid of the landlady and raked the place over thoroughly. We came away knowing all there was to know about the girl's wardrobe, and a lot about her personal habits. But we didn't find anything pointing Papadopoulosward.

No report came in on the Carey-Arlie combination that afternoon or evening, though I expected to hear from Dick every minute.

At three o'clock in the morning my bedside phone took my ear out of the pillows. The voice that came over the wire was the Canadian op's.

"Exit Arlie," he said.

"R.I.P.?"

"Yep."

"How?"

"Lead."

"Our lad's?"

"Yep."

"Keep till morning?"

"Yep."

"See you at the office," and I went back to sleep.

VII

When I arrived at the Agency at nine o'clock, one of the clerks had just finished decoding a night letter from the Los Angeles operative who had been sent over to Nogales. It was a long telegram, and meaty.

It said that Tom-Tom Carey was well known along the border. For some six months he had been engaged in over-the-line traffic—guns going south, booze, and probably dope and immigrants, coming north. Just before leaving there the previous week he had made inquiries concerning one Hank Barrows. This Hank Barrows' description fit the H. F. Barrows who had been cut into ribbons, who had fallen out the hotel window and died.

The Los Angeles operative hadn't been able to get much of a line on Barrows, except that he hailed from San Francisco, had been on the border only a few days, and had apparently returned to San Francisco. The operative had turned up nothing new on the Newhall killing—the signs still read that he had been killed resisting capture by Mexican patriots.

Dick Foley came into my office while I was reading the news. When I had finished he gave me his contribution to the history of Tom-Tom Carey.

"Tailed him out of here. To hotel. Arlie on corner. Eight o'clock, Carey out. Garage. Hire car without driver. Back hotel. Checked out. Two bags. Out through park. Arlie after him in flivver. My boat after Arlie. Down boulevard. Off cross-road. Dark. Lonely. Arlie steps on gas. Closes in. Bang! Carey stops. Two guns going. Exit Arlie. Carey back to city.

Hotel Marquis. Registers George F. Danby, San Diego. Room 622."

"Did Tom-Tom frisk Arlie after he dropped him?"

"No. Didn't touch him."

"So? Take Mickey Linehan with you. Don't let Carey get out of your sight. I'll get somebody up to relieve you and Mickey late tonight, if I can, but he's got to be shadowed twenty-four hours a day until—" I didn't know what came after that so I stopped talking.

I took Dick's story into the Old Man's office and told it to him, winding up:

"Arlie shot first, according to Foley, so Carey gets a self-defense on it, but we're getting action at last and I don't want to do anything to slow it up. So I'd like to keep what we know about this shooting quiet for a couple of days. It won't increase our friendship any with the county sheriff if he finds out what we're doing, but I think it's worth it."

"If you wish," the Old Man agreed, reaching for his ringing phone.

He spoke into the instrument and passed it on to me. Detective-sergeant Hunt was talking:

"Flora Brace and Grace Cardigan crushed out just before daylight. The chances are they—"

I wasn't in a humor for details.

"A clean sneak?" I asked.

"Not a lead on 'em so far, but—"

"I'll get the details when I see you. Thanks," and I hung up.

"Angel Grace and Big Flora have escaped from the city prison," I passed the news on to the Old Man.

He smiled courteously, as if at something that didn't especially concern him.

"You were congratulating yourself on getting action," he murmured.

I turned my scowl to a grin, mumbled, "Well, maybe," went back to my office and telephoned Franklin Ellert. The lisping attorney said he would be glad to see me, so I went over to his office.

"And now, what progreth have you made?" he asked eagerly when I was seated beside his desk.

"Some. A man named Barrows was also in Nogales when Newhall was killed, and also came to San Francisco right after. Carey followed Barrows up here. Did you read about the man found walking the streets naked, all cut up?"

"Yeth."

"That was Barrows. Then another man comes into the game—a barber named Arlie. He was spying on Carey. Last night, in a lonely road south of here, Arlie shot at Carey. Carey killed him."

The old lawyer's eyes came out another inch.

"What road?" he gasped.

"You want the exact location?"

"Yeth!"

I pulled his phone over, called the Agency, had Dick's report read to me, gave the attorney the information he wanted.

It had an effect on him. He hopped out of his chair. Sweat was shiny along the ridges wrinkles made in his face.

"Mith Newhall ith down there alone! That plath ith only half a mile from her houth!"

I frowned and beat my brains together, but I couldn't make anything out of it.

"Suppose I put a man down there to look after her?" I suggested.

"Exthellent!" His worried face cleared until there weren't more than fifty or sixty wrinkles in it. "The would prefer to thtay there during her firth grief over her fatherth death. You will thend a capable man?"

"The Rock of Gibraltar is a leaf in the breeze beside him. Give me a note for him to take down. Andrew MacElroy is his name."

While the lawyer scribbled the note I used his phone again to call the Agency, to tell the operator to get hold of Andy and tell him I wanted him. I ate lunch before I returned to the Agency. Andy was waiting when I got there.

Andy MacElroy was a big boulder of a man—not very tall, but thick and hard of head and body. A glum, grim man with no more imagination than an adding machine. I'm not even sure he could read. But I was sure that when Andy was told to do something, he did it and nothing else. He didn't know enough not to.

I gave him the lawyer's note to Miss Newhall, told him where to go and what to do, and Miss Newhall's troubles were off my mind.

Three times that afternoon I heard from Dick Foley and Mickey Linehan. Tom-Tom Carey wasn't doing anything very exciting, though he had bought two boxes of .44 cartridges in a Market Street sporting goods establishment.

The afternoon papers carried photographs of Big Flora Brace and Angel Grace Cardigan, with a story of their escape. The story was as far from the probable facts as newspaper stories generally are. On another page was an account of the discovery of the dead barber in the lonely road. He had been shot in the head and in the chest, four times in all. The county officials' opinion was that he had been killed resisting a stick-up, and that the bandits had fled without robbing him.

At five o'clock Tommy Howd came to my door.

"That guy Carey wants to see you again," the freckle-faced boy said.

"Shoot him in."

The swarthy man sauntered in, said "Howdy," sat down, and made a brown cigarette.

"Got anything special on for tonight?" he asked when he was smoking.

"Nothing I can't put aside for something better. Giving a party?"

"Uh-huh. I had thought of it. A kind of surprise party for Papadoodle. Want to go along?"

It was my turn to say, "Uh-huh."

"I'll pick you up at eleven—Van Ness and Geary," he drawled. "But this has got to be a kind of tight party—just you and me—and him."

"No. There's one more who'll have to be in on it. I'll bring him along."

"I don't like that." Tom-Tom Carey shook his head slowly, frowning amiably over his cigarette. "You sleuths oughtn't out-number me. It ought to be one and one."

"You won't be out-numbered," I explained. "This jobbie I'm bringing won't be on my side more than yours. And it'll pay you to keep as sharp an eye on him as I do—and to see he don't get behind either of us if we can help it."

"Then what do you want to lug him along for?"

"Wheels within wheels," I grinned.

The swarthy man frowned again, less amiably now.

"The hundred and six thousand reward money—I'm not figuring on sharing that with anybody."

"Right enough," I agreed. "Nobody I bring along will declare themselves in on it."

"I'll take your word for it." He stood up. "And we've got to watch this hombre, huh?"

"If we want everything to go all right."

"Suppose he gets in the way—cuts up on us. Can we put it to him, or do we just say, 'Naughty! Naughty!'?"

"He'll have to take his own chances."

"Fair enough." His hard face was good-natured again as he moved toward the door. "Eleven o'clock at Van Ness and Geary."

VIII

I went back into the operatives' room, where Jack Counihan was slumped down in a chair reading a magazine.

"I hope you've thought up something for me to do," he greeted me. "I'm getting bed-sores from sitting around."

"Patience, son, patience—that's what you've got to learn if you're ever going to be a detective. Why when I was a child of your age, just starting in with the Agency, I was lucky—"

"Don't start that," he begged. Then his good-looking young face got earnest. "I don't see why you keep me cooped up here. I'm the only one besides you who really got a good look at Nancy Regan. I should think you would have me out hunting for her."

"I told the Old Man the same thing," I sympathized. "But he is afraid to risk something happening to you. He says in all his fifty years of gum-shoeing he's never seen such a handsome op, besides being a fashion plate and a social butterfly and the heir to millions. His idea is we ought to keep you as a sort of show piece, and not let you—"

"Go to hell!" Jack said, all red in the face.

"But I persuaded him to let me take the cotton packing off you tonight," I continued. "So meet me at Van Ness and Geary before eleven o'clock."

"Action?" He was all eagerness.

"Maybe."

"What are we going to do?"

"Bring your little pop-gun along." An idea came into my head and I worded it. "You'd better be all dressed up—evening duds."

"Dinner coat?"

"No—the limit—everything but the high hat. Now for your behavior: you're not supposed to be an op. I'm not sure just what you're supposed to be, but it doesn't make any difference. Tom-Tom Carey will be along. You act as if you were neither my friend nor his—as if you didn't trust either of us. We'll be cagey with you. If anything is asked that you don't know the answer to—you fall back on hostility. But don't crowd Carey too far. Got it?"

"I—I think so." He spoke slowly, screwing up his forehead. "I'm to act as if I was going along on the same business as you, but that outside of that we weren't friends. As if I wasn't willing to trust you. That it?"

"Very much. Watch yourself. You'll be swimming in nitro-glycerine all the way."

"What is up? Be a good chap and give me some idea."

I grinned up at him. He was a lot taller than I.

"I could," I admitted, "but I'm afraid it would scare you off. So I'd better tell you nothing. Be happy while you can. Eat a good dinner. Lots of condemned folks seem to eat hearty breakfasts of ham and eggs just before they parade out to the rope. Maybe you wouldn't want 'em for dinner, but—"

At five minutes to eleven that night Tom-Tom Carey brought a black touring car to the corner where Jack and I stood waiting in a fog that was like a damp fur coat.

"Climb in," he ordered as we came to the curb.

I opened the front door and motioned Jack in. He rang up the curtain on his little act, looking coldly at me and opening the rear door.

"I'm going to sit back here," he said bluntly.

"Not a bad idea," and I climbed in beside him.

Carey twisted around in his seat and he and Jack stared at each other for a while. I said nothing, did not introduce them. When the swarthy man had finished sizing the youngster up, he looked from the boy's collar and tie—all of his evening clothes not hidden by his overcoat—to me, grinned, and drawled:

"Your friend's a waiter, huh?"

I laughed, because the indignation that darkened the boy's face and popped his mouth open was natural, not part of his acting. I pushed my foot against his. He closed his mouth, said nothing, looked at Tom-Tom Carey and me as if we were specimens of some lower form of animal life.

I grinned back at Carey and asked, "Are we waiting for anything?"

He said we weren't, left off staring at Jack, and put the machine in motion. He drove us out through the park, down the boulevard. Traffic going our way and the other loomed out of and faded into the fog-thick night. Presently we left the city behind, and ran out of the fog into clear moonlight. I didn't look at any of the machines running behind us, but I knew that in one of them Dick Foley and Mickey Linehan should be riding.

Tom-Tom Carey swung our car off the boulevard, into a road that was smooth and well made, but not much traveled.

"Wasn't a man killed down along here somewhere last night?" I asked.

Carey nodded his head without turning it, and, when we had gone another quarter-mile, said: "Right here."

We rode a little slower now, and Carey turned off his lights. In the road that was half moon-silver, half shadow-gray, the machine barely crept along for perhaps a mile. We stopped in the shade of tall shrubs that darkened a spot of the road.

"All ashore that's going ashore," Tom-Tom Carey said, and got out of the car.

Jack and I followed him. Carey took off his overcoat and threw it into the machine.

"The place is just around the bend, back from the road," he told us. "Damn this moon! I was counting on fog."

I said nothing, nor did Jack. The boy's face was white and excited.

"We'll bee-line it," Carey said, leading the way across the road to a high wire fence.

He went over the fence first, then Jack, then—the sound of someone coming along the road from ahead stopped me. Signalling silence to the two men on the other side of the fence, I made myself small beside a bush. The coming steps were light, quick, feminine.

A girl came into the moonlight just ahead. She was a girl of twenty-something, neither tall nor short, thin nor plump. She was short-skirted, bare-haired, sweatered. Terror was in her white face, in the carriage of her hurrying figure—but something else was there too—more beauty than a middle-aged sleuth was used to seeing.

When she saw Carey's automobile bulking in the shadow, she stopped abruptly, with a gasp that was almost a cry.

I walked forward, saying:

"Hello, Nancy Regan."

This time the gasp was a cry.

"Oh! Oh!" Then, unless the moonlight was playing tricks, she recognized me and terror began to go away from her. She put both hands out to me, with relief in the gesture.

"Well?" A bearish grumble came from the big boulder of a man who had appeared out of the darkness behind her. "What's all this?"

"Hello, Andy," I greeted the boulder.

"Hullo," MacElroy echoed and stood still.

Andy always did what he was told to do. He had been told to take care of Miss Newhall. I looked at the girl and then at him again.

"Is this Miss Newhall?" I asked.

"Yeah," he rumbled. "I came down like you said, but she told me she didn't want me—wouldn't let me in the house. But you hadn't said anything about coming back. So I just camped outside, moseying around, keeping my eyes on things. And when I seen her shinnying out a window a little while ago, I just went on along behind her to take care of her, like you said I was to do."

Tom-Tom Carey and Jack Counihan came back into the road, crossed it to us. The swarthy man had an automatic in one hand. The girl's eyes were glued on mine. She paid no attention to the others.

"What is it all about?" I asked her.

"I don't know," she babbled, her hands holding on to mine, her face close to mine. "Yes, I'm Ann Newhall. I didn't know. I thought it was fun. And then when I found out it wasn't I couldn't get out of it."

Tom-Tom Carey grunted and stirred impatiently. Jack Counihan was staring down the road. Andy MacElroy stood stolid in the road, waiting to be told what to do next. The girl never once looked from me to any of these others.

"How did you get in with them?" I demanded. "Talk fast."

IX

I had told the girl to talk fast. She did. For twenty minutes she stood there and turned out words in a chattering stream that had no breaks except where I cut in to keep her from straying from the path I wanted her to follow. It was jumbled, almost incoherent in spots, and not always plausible, but the notion stayed with me throughout that she was trying to tell the truth—most of the time.

And not for a fraction of a second did she turn her gaze from my eyes. It was as if she was afraid to look anywhere else.

This millionaire's daughter had, two months before, been one of a party of four young people returning late at night from some sort of social affair down the coast. Somebody suggested that they stop at a roadhouse along their way—a particularly tough joint. Its toughness was its attraction, of course—toughness was more or less of a novelty to them. They got a first-hand view of it that night, for, nobody knew just how, they found themselves taking part in a row before they had been ten minutes in the dump.

The girl's escort had shamed her by showing an unreasonable amount of cowardice. He had let Red O'Leary turn him over his knee and spank him—and had done nothing about it afterward. The other youth in the party had been not much braver. The girl, insulted by this meekness, had walked across to the red-haired giant who had wrecked her escort, and she had spoken to him loud enough for everybody to hear:

"Will you please take me home?"

Red O'Leary was glad to do it. She left him a block or two from her city house. She told him her name was Nancy Regan. He probably doubted it, but he never asked her any questions, pried into her affairs. In spite of the difference in their worlds, a genuine companionship had grown up between them. She liked him. He was so gloriously a roughneck that she saw him as a romantic figure. He was in love with her, knew she was miles above him, and so she had no trouble making him behave so far as she was concerned.

They met often. He took her to all the rowdy holes in the bay district, introduced her to yeggs, gunmen, swindlers, told her wild tales of criminal adventuring. She knew he was a crook, knew he was tied up in the Seamen's National and Golden Gate Trust jobs when they broke. But she saw it all as a sort of theatrical spectacle. She didn't see it as it was.

She woke up the night they were in Larrouy's and were jumped by the crooks that Red had helped Papadopoulos and the others double-cross. But it was too late then for her to wriggle clear. She was blown along with Red to Papadopoulos' hangout after I had shot the big lad. She saw then what her romantic figures really were—what she had mixed herself with.

When Papadopoulos escaped, taking her with him, she was wide awake, cured, through forever with her dangerous trifling with outlaws. So she thought. She thought Papadopoulos was the little, scary old man he seemed to be—Flora's slave, a harmless old duffer too near the grave to have any evil in him. He had been whining and terrified. He begged her not to forsake him, pleaded with her while tears ran down his withered cheeks, begging her to hide him from Flora. She took him to her country house and let him fool around in the garden, safe from prying eyes. She had no idea that he had known who she was all along, had guided her into suggesting this arrangement.

Even when the newspapers said he had been the commander-in-chief of the thug army, when the hundred and six thousand dollar reward was offered for his arrest, she believed in his innocence. He convinced her that Flora and Red had simply put the blame for the whole thing on him so they could get off with lighter sentences. He was such a frightened old gink—who wouldn't have believed him?

Then her father's death in Mexico had come and grief had occupied her mind to the exclusion of most other things until this day, when Big Flora and another girl—probably Angel Grace Cardigan—had come to the house. She had been deathly afraid of Big Flora when she had seen her before. She was more afraid now. And she soon learned that Papadopoulos was not Flora's slave but her master. She saw the old buzzard as he really was. But that wasn't the end of her awakening.

Angel Grace had suddenly tried to kill Papadopoulos. Flora had overpowered her. Grace, defiant, had told them she was Paddy's girl. Then she had screamed at Ann Newhall:

"And you, you damned fool, don't you know they killed your father? Don't you know—?"

Big Flora's fingers, around Angel Grace's throat, stopped her words. Flora tied up the Angel and turned to the Newhall girl.

"You're in it," she said brusquely. "You're in it up to your neck. You'll play along with us, or else— Here's how it stands, dearie. The old man and I are both due to step off if we're caught. And you'll do the dance with us. I'll see to that. Do what you're told, and we'll all come through all right. Get funny, and I'll beat holy hell out of you."

The girl didn't remember much after that. She had a dim recollection of going to the door and telling Andy she didn't want his services. She did this mechanically, not even needing to be prompted by the big blonde woman who stood close behind her. Later, in the same fearful daze, she had gone out her bedroom window, down the vine-covered side of the porch, and away from the house, running along the road, not going anywhere, just escaping.

That was what I learned from the girl. She didn't tell me all of it. She told me very little of it in those words. But that is the story I got by combining her words, her manner of telling them, her facial expressions, with what I already knew, and what I could guess.

And not once while she talked had her eyes turned from mine. Not once had she shown that she knew there were other men standing in the road with us. She stared into my face with a desperate fixity, as if she was afraid not to, and her hands held mine as if she might sink through the ground if she let go.

"How about your servants?" I asked.

"There aren't any there now."

"Papadopoulos persuaded you to get rid of them?"

"Yes—several days ago."

"Then Papadopoulos, Flora and Angel Grace are alone in the house now?"

"Yes."

"They know you ducked?"

"I don't know. I don't think they do. I had been in my room some time. I don't think they suspected I'd dare do anything but what they told me."

It annoyed me to find I was staring into the girl's eyes as fixedly as she into mine, and that when I wanted to take my gaze away it wasn't easily done. I jerked my eyes away from her, took my hands away.

"The rest of it you can tell me later," I growled, and turned to give Andy MacElroy his orders. "You stay here with Miss Newhall until we get back from the house. Make yourselves comfortable in the car."

The girl put a hand on my arm.

"Am I—? Are you—?"

"We're going to turn you over to the police, yes," I assured her.

"No! No!"

"Don't be childish," I begged. "You can't run around with a mob of cutthroats, get yourself tied up in a flock of crimes, and then when you're tripped say, 'Excuse it, please,' and go free. If you tell the whole story in court—including the parts you haven't told me—the chances are you'll get off. But there's no way in God's world for you to escape arrest. Come on," I told Jack and Tom-Tom Carey. "We've got to shake it up if we want to find our folks at home."

Looking back as I climbed the fence, I saw that Andy had put the girl in the car and was getting in himself.

"Just a moment," I called to Jack and Carey, who were already starting across the field.

"Thought of something else to kill time," the swarthy man complained.

I went back across the road to the car and spoke quickly and softly to Andy:

"Dick Foley and Mickey Linehan should be hanging around the neighborhood. As soon as we're out of sight, hunt 'em up. Turn Miss Newhall over to Dick. Tell him to take her with him and beat it for a phone—rouse the sheriff. Tell Dick he's to turn the girl over to the sheriff, to hold for the San Francisco police. Tell him he's not to give her up to anybody else—not even to me. Got it?"

"Got it."

"All right. After you've told him that and have given him the girl, then you bring Mickey Linehan to the Newhall house as fast as you can make it. We'll likely need all the help we can get as soon as we can get it."

"Got you," Andy said.

X

"What are you up to?" Tom-Tom Carey asked suspiciously when I rejoined Jack and him.

"Detective business."

"I ought to have come down and turned the trick all by myself," he grumbled. "You haven't done a damned thing but waste time since we started."

"I'm not the one that's wasting it now."

He snorted and set out across the field again, Jack and I following him. At the end of the field there was another fence to be climbed. Then we came over a little wooded ridge and the Newhall house lay before us—a large white house, glistening in the moonlight, with yellow rectangulars where blinds were down over the windows of lighted rooms. The lighted rooms were on the ground floor. The upper floor was dark. Everything was quiet.

"Damn the moonlight!" Tom-Tom Carey repeated, bringing another automatic out of his clothes, so that he now had one in each hand.

Jack started to take his gun out, looked at me, saw I was letting mine rest, let his slide back in his pocket.

Tom-Tom Carey's face was a dark stone mask—slits for eyes, slit for mouth—the grim mask of a manhunter, a man-killer. He was breathing softly, his big chest moving gently. Beside him, Jack Counihan looked like an excited school-boy. His face was ghastly, his eyes all stretched out of shape, and he was breathing like a tire-pump. But his grin was genuine, for all the nervousness in it.

"We'll cross to the house on this side," I whispered. "Then one of us can take the front, one the back, and the other can wait till he sees where he's needed most. Right?"

"Right," the swarthy one agreed.

"Wait!" Jack exclaimed. "The girl came down the vines from an upper window. What's the matter with my going up that way? I'm lighter than either of you. If they haven't missed her, the window would still be open. Give me ten minutes to find the window, get through it, and get myself placed. Then when you attack I'll be there behind them. How's that?" he demanded applause.

"And what if they grab you as soon as you light?" I objected.

"Suppose they do. I can make enough racket for you to hear. You can gallop to the attack while they're busy with me. That'll be just as good."

"Blue hell!" Tom-Tom Carey barked. "What good's all that? The other way's best. One of us at the front door, one at the back, kick 'em in and go in shooting."

"If this new one works, it'll be better," I gave my opinion. "If you want to jump in the furnace, Jack, I won't stop you. I won't cheat you out of your heroics."

"No!" the swarthy man snarled. "Nothing doing!"

"Yes," I contradicted him. "We'll try it. Better take twenty minutes, Jack. That won't give you any time to waste."

He looked at his watch and I at mine, and he turned toward the house.

Tom-Tom Carey, scowling darkly, stood in his way. I cursed and got between the swarthy man and the boy. Jack went around my back and hurried away across the too-bright space between us and the house.

"Keep your feet on the ground," I told Carey. "There are a lot of things to this game you don't know anything about."

"Too damned many!" he snarled, but he let the boy go.

There was no open second-story window on our side of the building. Jack rounded the rear of the house and went out of sight.

A faint rustling sounded behind us. Carey and I spun together. His guns went up. I stretched out an arm across them, pushing them down.

"Don't have a hemorrhage," I cautioned him. "This is just another of the things you don't know about."

The rustling had stopped.

"All right," I called softly.

Mickey Linehan and Andy MacElroy came out of the tree-shadows.

Tom-Tom Carey stuck his face so close to mine that I'd have been scratched if he had forgotten to shave that day.

"You double-crossing—"

"Behave! Behave! A man of your age!" I admonished him. "None of these boys want any of your blood money."

"I don't like this gang stuff," he snarled. "We—"

"We're going to need all the help we can get," I interrupted, looking at my watch. I told the two operatives: "We're going to close in on the house now. Four of us ought to be able to wrap it up snug. You know Papadopoulos, Big Flora and Angel Grace by description. They're in there. Don't take any chances with them—Flora and Papadopoulos are dynamite. Jack Counihan is trying to ease inside now. You two look after the back of the joint. Carey and I will take the front. We'll make the play. You see that nobody leaks out on us. Forward march!"

The swarthy man and I headed for the front porch—a wide porch, grown over with vines on the side, yellowly illuminated now by the light that came through four curtained French windows.

We hadn't taken our first steps across the porch when one of these tall windows moved—opened.

The first thing I saw was Jack Counihan's back.

He was pushing the casement open with a hand and foot, not turning his head.

Beyond the boy—facing him across the brightly lighted room—stood a man and a woman. The man was old, small, scrawny, wrinkled, pitifully frightened—Papadopoulos. I saw he had shaved off his straggly white mustache. The woman was tall, full-bodied, pink-fleshed and yellow-haired—a she-athlete of forty with clear gray eyes set deep in a handsome brutal face—Big Flora Brace. They stood very still, side by side, watching the muzzle of Jack Counihan's gun.

While I stood in front of the window looking at this scene, Tom-Tom Carey, his two guns up, stepped past me, going through the tall window to the boy's side. I did not follow him into the room.

Papadopoulos' scary brown eyes darted to the swarthy man's face. Flora's gray ones moved there deliberately, and then looked past him to me.

"Hold it, everybody!" I ordered, and moved away from the window, to the side of the porch where the vines were thinnest.

Leaning out between the vines, so my face was clear in the moonlight, I looked down the side of the building. A shadow in the shadow of the garage could have been a man. I put an arm out in the moonlight and beckoned. The shadow came toward me—Mickey Linehan. Andy MacElroy's head peeped around the back of the house. I beckoned again and he followed Mickey.

I returned to the open window.

Papadopoulos and Flora—a rabbit and a lioness—stood looking at the guns of Carey and Jack. They looked again at me when I appeared, and a smile began to curve the woman's full lips.

Mickey and Andy came up and stood beside me. The woman's smile died grimly.

"Carey," I said, "you and Jack stay as is. Mickey, Andy, go in and take hold of our gifts from God."

When the two operatives stepped through the window—things happened.

Papadopoulos screamed.

Big Flora lunged against him, knocking him at the back door.

"Go! Go!" she roared.

Stumbling, staggering, he scrambled across the room.

Flora had a pair of guns—sprung suddenly into her hands. Her big body seemed to fill the room, as if by will-power she had become a giantess. She charged—straight at the guns Jack and Carey held—blotting the back door and the fleeing man from their fire.

A blur to one side was Andy MacElroy moving.

I had a hand on Jack's gun-arm.

"Don't shoot," I muttered in his ear.

Flora's guns thundered together. But she was tumbling. Andy had crashed into her. Had thrown himself at her legs as a man would throw a boulder.

When Flora tumbled, Tom-Tom Carey stopped waiting.

His first bullet was sent so close past her that it clipped her curled yellow hair. But it went past—caught Papadopoulos just as he went through the door. The bullet took him low in the back—smeared him out on the floor.

Carey fired again—again—again—into the prone body.

"It's no use," I growled. "You can't make him any deader."

He chuckled and lowered his guns.

"Four into a hundred and six." All his ill-humor, his grimness was gone. "That's twenty-six thousand, five hundred dollars each of those slugs was worth to me."

Andy and Mickey had wrestled Flora into submission and were hauling her up off the floor.

I looked from them back to the swarthy man, muttering, "It's not all over yet."

"No?" He seemed surprised. "What next?"

"Stay awake and let your conscience guide you," I replied, and turned to the Counihan youngster. "Come along Jack."

I led the way out through the window and across the porch, where I leaned against the railing. Jack followed and stood in front of me, his gun still in his hand, his face white and tired from nervous tension. Looking over his shoulder, I could see the room we had just quit. Andy and Mickey had Flora sitting between them on a sofa. Carey stood a little to one side, looking curiously at Jack and me. We were in the middle of the band of light that came through the open window. We could see inside—except that Jack's back was that way—and could be seen from there, but our talk couldn't be overheard unless we made it loud.

All that was as I wanted it.

"Now tell me about it," I ordered Jack.

XI

"Well, I found the open window," the boy began.

"I know all that part," I cut in. "You came in and told your friends—Papadopoulos and Flora—about the girl's escape, and that Carey and I were coming. You advised them to make out you had captured them single-handed. That would draw Carey and me in. With you unsuspected behind us, it would be easy for the three of you to grab the two of us. After that you could stroll down the road and tell Andy I had sent you for the girl. That was a good scheme—except that you didn't know I had Dick and Mickey up my sleeve, didn't know I wouldn't let you get behind me. But all that isn't what I want to know. I want to know why you sold us out—and what you think you're going to do now."

"Are you crazy?" His young face was bewildered, his young eyes horrified. "Or is this some—?"

"Sure, I'm crazy," I confessed. "Wasn't I crazy enough to let you lead me into that trap in Sausalito? But I wasn't too crazy to figure it out afterward. I wasn't too crazy to see that Ann Newhall was afraid to look at you. I'm not crazy enough to think you could have captured Papadopoulos and Flora unless they wanted you to. I'm crazy—but in moderation."

Jack laughed—a reckless young laugh, but too shrill. His eyes didn't laugh with mouth and voice. While he was laughing his eyes looked from me to the gun in his hand and back to me.

"Talk, Jack," I pleaded huskily, putting a hand on his shoulder. "For God's sake why did you do it?"

The boy shut his eyes, gulped, and his shoulders twitched. When his eyes opened they were hard and glittering and full of merry hell.

"The worst part of it," he said harshly, moving his shoulder from under my hand, "is that I wasn't a very good crook, was I? I didn't succeed in deluding you."

I said nothing.

"I suppose you've earned your right to the story," he went on after a little pause. His voice was consciously monotonous, as if he was deliberately keeping out of it every tone or accent that might seem to express emotion. He was too young to talk naturally. "I met Ann Newhall three weeks ago, in my own home. She had gone to school with my sisters, though I had never met her before. We knew each other at once, of course—I knew she was Nancy Regan, she knew I was a Continental operative.

"So we went off by ourselves and talked things over. Then she took me to see Papadopoulos. I liked the old boy and he liked me. He showed me how we together could accumulate unheard-of piles of wealth. So there you are. The prospect of all that money completely devastated my morals. I told him about Carey as soon as I had heard from you, and I led you into that trap, as you say. He thought it would be better if you stopped bothering us before you found the connection between Newhall and Papadopoulos.

"After that failure, he wanted me to try again, but I refused to have a hand in any more fiascos. There's nothing sillier than a murder that doesn't come off. Ann Newhall is quite innocent of everything except folly. I don't think she has the slightest suspicion that I have had any part in the dirty work beyond refraining from having everybody arrested. That, my dear Sherlock, about concludes the confession."

I had listened to the boy's story with a great show of sympathetic attentiveness. Now I scowled at him and spoke accusingly, but still not without friendliness.

"Stop spoofing! The money Papadopoulos showed you didn't buy you. You met the girl and were too soft to turn her in. But your vanity—your pride in looking at yourself as a pretty cold proposition—wouldn't let you admit it even to yourself. You had to have a hard-boiled front. So you were meat to Papadopoulos' grinder. He gave you a part you could play to yourself—a super-gentleman-crook, a master-mind, a desperate suave villain, and all that kind of romantic garbage. That's the way you went, my son. You went as far as possible beyond what was needed to save the girl from the hoosegow—just to show the world, but chiefly yourself, that you were not acting through sentimentality, but according to your own reckless desires. There you are. Look at yourself."

Whatever he saw in himself—what I had seen or something else—his face slowly reddened, and he wouldn't look at me. He looked past me at the distant road.

I looked into the lighted room beyond him. Tom-Tom Carey had advanced to the center of the floor, where he stood watching us. I jerked a corner of my mouth at him—a warning.

"Well," the boy began again, but he didn't know what to say after that. He shuffled his feet and kept his eyes from my face.

I stood up straight and got rid of the last trace of my hypocritical sympathy.

"Give me your gun, you lousy rat!" I snarled at him.

He jumped back as if I had hit him. Craziness writhed in his face. He jerked his gun chest-high.

Tom-Tom Carey saw the gun go up. The swarthy man fired twice. Jack Counihan was dead at my feet.

Mickey Linehan fired once. Carey was down on the floor, bleeding from the temple.

I stepped over Jack's body, went into the room, knelt beside the swarthy man. He squirmed, tried to say something, died before he could get it out. I waited until my face was straight before I stood up.

Big Flora was studying me with narrowed gray eyes. I stared back at her.

"I don't get it all yet," she said slowly, "but if you—"

"Where's Angel Grace?" I interrupted.

"Tied to the kitchen table," she informed me, and went on with her thinking aloud. "You've dealt a hand that—"

"Yeah," I said sourly, "I'm another Papadopoulos."

Her big body suddenly quivered. Pain clouded her handsome brutal face. Two tears came out of her lower eye-lids.

I'm damned if she hadn't loved the old scoundrel!

XII

It was after eight in the morning when I got back to the city. I ate breakfast and then went up to the Agency, where I found the Old Man going through his morning mail.

"It's all over," I told him. "Papadopoulos knew Nancy Regan was Taylor Newhall's heiress. When he needed a hiding-place after the bank jobs flopped, he got her to take him down to the Newhall country place. He had two holds on her. She pitied him as a misused old duffer, and she was—even if innocently—an accomplice after the fact in the stick-ups.

"Pretty soon Papa Newhall had to go to Mexico on business. Papadopoulos saw a chance to make something. If Newhall was knocked off, the girl would have millions—and the old thief knew he could take them away from her. He sent Barrows down to the border to buy the murder from some Mexican bandits. Barrows put it over, but talked too much. He told a girl in Nogales that he had to go back 'to 'Frisco to collect plenty from an old Greek,' and then he'd return and buy her the world. The girl passed the news on to Tom-Tom Carey. Carey put a lot of twos together and got at least a dozen for an answer. He followed Barrows up here.

"Angel Grace was with him the morning he called on Barrows here—to find out if his 'old Greek' really was Papadopoulos, and where he could be found. Barrows was too full of morphine to listen to reason. He was so dope-deadened that even after the dark man began to reason with a knife-blade he had to whittle Barrows all up before he began to feel hurt. The carving sickened Angel Grace. She left, after vainly trying to stop Carey. And when she read in the afternoon papers what a finished job he had made of it, she tried to commit suicide, to stop the images from crawling around in her head.

"Carey got all the information Barrows had, but Barrows didn't know where Papadopoulos was hiding. Papadopoulos learned of Carey's arrival—you know how he learned. He sent Arlie to stop Carey. Carey wouldn't give the barber a chance—until the swarthy man began to suspect Papadopoulos might be at the Newhall place. He drove down there, letting Arlie follow. As soon as Arlie discovered his destination, Arlie closed in, hell-bent on stopping Carey at any cost. That was what Carey wanted. He gunned Arlie, came back to town, got hold of me, and took me down to help wind things up.

"Meanwhile, Angel Grace, in the cooler, had made friends with Big Flora. She knew Flora but Flora didn't know her. Papadopoulos had arranged a crush-out for Flora. It's always easier for two to escape than one. Flora took the Angel along, took her to Papadopoulos. The Angel went for him, but Flora knocked her for a loop.

"Flora, Angel Grace and Ann Newhall, alias Nancy Regan, are in the county jail," I wound up. "Papadopoulos, Tom-Tom Carey and Jack Counihan are dead."

I stopped talking and lighted a cigarette, taking my time, watching cigarette and match carefully throughout the operation. The Old Man picked up a letter, put it down without reading it, picked up another.

"They were killed in course of making the arrests?" His mild voice held nothing but its usual unfathomable politeness.

"Yes. Carey killed Papadopoulos. A little later he shot Jack. Mickey—not knowing—not knowing anything except that the dark man was shooting at Jack and me—we were standing apart talking—shot and killed Carey." The words twisted around my tongue, wouldn't come out straight. "Neither Mickey nor Andy know that Jack— Nobody but you and I know exactly what the thing—exactly what Jack was doing. Flora Brace and Ann Newhall did know, but if we say he was acting on orders all the time, nobody can deny it."

The Old Man nodded his grandfatherly face and smiled, but for the first time in the years I had known him I knew what he was thinking. He was thinking that if Jack had come through alive we would have had the nasty choice between letting him go free or giving the Agency a black-eye by advertising the fact that one of our operatives was a crook.

I threw away my cigarette and stood up. The Old Man stood also, and held out a hand to me.

"Thank you," he said.

I took his hand, and I understood him, but I didn't have anything I wanted to confess—even by silence.

"It happened that way," I said deliberately. "I played the cards so we would get the benefit of the breaks—but it just happened that way."

He nodded, smiling benignantly.

"I'm going to take a couple of weeks off," I said from the door.

I felt tired, washed out.

The Main Death

THE CAPTAIN told me Hacken and Begg were handling the job. I caught them leaving the detectives' assembly room. Begg was a freckled heavyweight, as friendly as a Saint Bernard puppy, but less intelligent. Lanky detective-sergeant Hacken, not so playful, carried the team's brains behind his worried hatchet face.

"In a hurry?" I inquired.

"Always in a hurry when we're quitting for the day," Begg said, his freckles climbing up his face to make room for his grin.

"What do you want?" Hacken asked.

"I want the low-down on the Main doings—if any."

"You going to work on it?"

"Yes," I said, "for Main's boss—Gungen."

"Then you can tell us something. Why'd he have the twenty thou in cash?"

"Tell you in the morning," I promised. "I haven't seen Gungen yet. Got a date with him tonight."

While we talked we had gone into the assembly room, with its school-room arrangement of desks and benches. Half a dozen police detectives were scattered among them, doing reports. We three sat around Hacken's desk and the lanky detective-sergeant talked:

"Main got home from Los Angeles at eight, Sunday night, with twenty thousand in his wallet. He'd gone down there to sell something for Gungen. You find out why he had that much in cash. He told his wife he had driven up from L.A. with a friend—no name. She went to bed around ten-thirty, leaving him reading. He had the money—two hundred hundred-dollar bills—in a brown wallet.

"So far, so good. He's in the living-room reading. She's in the bedroom sleeping. Just the two of them in the apartment. A racket wakes her. She jumps out of bed, runs into the living-room. There's Main wrestling with a couple of men. One's tall and husky. The other's little—kind of girlish built. Both have got black handkerchiefs over their mugs and caps pulled down.

636

"When Mrs. Main shows, the little one breaks away from Main and sticks her up. Puts a gun in Mrs. Main's face and tells her to behave. Main and the other guy are still scuffling. Main has got his gun in his hand, but the thug has him by the wrist, trying to twist it. He makes it pretty soon—Main drops the rod. The thug flashes his own, holding Main off while he bends down to pick up the one that fell.

"When the man stoops, Main piles on him. He manages to knock the fellow's gun out of his hand, but by that time the fellow had got the one on the floor—the one Main had dropped. They're heaped up there for a couple of seconds. Mrs. Main can't see what's happening. Then bang! Main's falling away, his vest burning where the shot had set fire to it, a bullet in his heart, his gun smoking in the masked guy's fist. Mrs. Main passes out.

"When she comes to there's nobody in the apartment but herself and her dead husband. His wallet's gone, and so is his gun. She was unconscious for about half an hour. We know that, because other people heard the shot and could give us the time—even if they didn't know where it came from.

"The Main's apartment is on the sixth floor. It's an eight-story building. Next door to it, on the corner of Eighteenth Avenue, is a two-story building—grocery downstairs, grocer's flat upstairs. Behind these buildings runs a narrow back street —an alley. All right.

"Kinney—the patrolman on that beat—was walking down Eighteenth Avenue. He heard the shot. It was clear to him, because the Mains' apartment is on that side of the building—the side overlooking the grocer's—but Kinney couldn't place it right away. He wasted time scouting around up the street. By the time he got down as far as the alley in his hunting, the birds had flown. Kinney found signs of 'em though— they had dropped a gun in the alley—the gun they'd taken from Main and shot him with. But Kinney didn't see 'em— didn't see anybody who might have been them.

"Now, from a hall window of the apartment house's third floor to the roof of the grocer's building is easy going. Anybody but a cripple could make it—in or out—and the window's never locked. From the grocer's roof to the back street is almost as easy. There's a cast iron pipe, a deep window, a door with heavy hinges sticking out—a regular ladder up and down that back wall. Begg and I did it without working up a sweat. The pair could have gone in that way. We know they left that way. On the grocer's roof we found Main's wallet—empty, of course—and a handkerchief. The wallet had metal corners. The handkerchief had caught on one of 'em, and went with it when the crooks tossed it away."

"Main's handkerchief?"

"A woman's—with an E in one corner."

"Mrs. Main's?"

"Her name is Agnes," Hacken said. "We showed her the wallet, the gun, and the handkerchief. She identified the first two as her husband's, but the handkerchief was a new one on her. However, she could give us the name of the perfume on it—*Dèsir du Cœur*. And—with it for a guide—she said the smaller of the masked pair could have been a woman. She had already described him as kind of girlish built."

"Any fingerprints, or the like?" I asked.

"No. Phels went over the apartment, the window, the roof, the wallet and the gun. Not a smear."

"Mrs. Main identify 'em?"

"She says she'd know the little one. Maybe she would."

"Got anything on the who?"

"Not yet," the lanky detective-sergeant said as we moved toward the door.

In the street I left the police sleuths and set out for Bruno Gungen's home in Westwood Park.

The dealer in rare and antique jewelry was a little bit of a man and a fancy one. His dinner jacket was corset-tight around his waist, padded high and sharp at the shoulders. Hair, mustache and spade-shaped goatee were dyed black and greased until they were as shiny as his pointed pink fingernails. I wouldn't bet a cent that the color in his fifty-year-old cheeks wasn't rouge.

He came out of the depths of a leather library chair to give me a soft, warm hand that was no larger than a child's, bowing and smiling at me with his head tilted to one side.

Then he introduced me to his wife, who bowed without getting up from her seat at the table. Apparently she was a

little more than a third of his age. She couldn't have been a
day over nineteen, and she looked more like sixteen. She was
as small as he, with a dimpled olive-skinned face, round brown
eyes, a plump painted mouth and the general air of an expensive doll in a toy-store window.

Bruno Gungen explained to her at some length that I was
connected with the Continental Detective Agency, and that
he had employed me to help the police find Jeffrey Main's
murderers and recover the stolen twenty thousand dollars.

She murmured, "Oh, yes!" in a tone that said she was not
the least bit interested, and stood up, saying, "Then I'll leave
you to—"

"No, no, my dear!" Her husband was waving his pink fingers at her. "I would have no secrets from you."

His ridiculous little face jerked around to me, cocked itself
sidewise, and he asked, with a little giggle:

"Is not that so? That between husband and wife there
should be no secrets?"

I pretended I agreed with him.

"You, I know, my dear," he addressed his wife, who had sat
down again, "are as much interested in this as I, for did we
not have an equal affection for dear Jeffrey? Is it not so?"

She repeated, "Oh, yes!" with the same lack of interest.

Her husband turned to me and said, "Now?" encouragingly.

"I've seen the police," I told him. "Is there anything you
can add to their story? Anything new? Anything you didn't
tell them?"

He whisked his face around toward his wife.

"Is there, Enid, dear?"

"I know of nothing," she replied.

He giggled and made a delighted face at me.

"That is it," he said. "We know of nothing."

"He came back to San Francisco eight o'clock Sunday
night—three hours before he was killed and robbed—with
twenty thousand dollars in hundred-dollar bills. What was he
doing with it?"

"It was the proceeds of a sale to a customer," Bruno
Gungen explained. "Mr. Nathaniel Ogilvie, of Los Angeles."

"But why cash?"

The little man's painted face screwed itself up into a shrewd leer.

"A bit of hanky-panky," he confessed complacently, "a trick of the trade, as one says. You know the genus collector? Ah, there is a study for you! Observe. I obtain a golden tiara of early Grecian workmanship, or let me be correct—purporting to be of early Grecian workmanship, purporting also to have been found in Southern Russia, near Odessa. Whether there is any truth in either of these suppositions I do not know, but certainly the tiara is a thing of beauty."

He giggled.

"Now I have a client, a Mr. Nathaniel Ogilvie, of Los Angeles, who has an appetite for curios of the sort—a very devil of a *cacoethes carpendi*. The value of these items, you will comprehend, is exactly what one can get for them—no more, little less. This tiara—now ten thousand dollars is the least I could have expected for it, if sold as one sells an ordinary article of the sort. But can one call a golden cap made long ago for some forgotten Scythian king an ordinary article of any sort? No! No! So, swaddled in cotton, intricately packed, Jeffrey carries this tiara to Los Angeles to show our Mr. Ogilvie.

"In what manner the tiara came into our hands Jeffrey will not say. But he will hint at devious intrigues, smuggling, a little of violence and lawlessness here and there, the necessity for secrecy. For your true collector, there is the bait! Nothing is anything to him except as it is difficultly come by. Jeffrey will not lie. No! *Mon Dieu*, that would be dishonest, despicable! But he will suggest much, and he will refuse, oh, so emphatically! to take a check for the tiara. No check, my dear sir! Nothing which may be traced! Cash moneys!

"Hanky-panky, as you see. But where is the harm? Mr. Ogilvie is certainly going to buy the tiara, and our little deceit simply heightens his pleasure in his purchase. He will enjoy its possession so much the more. Besides, who is to say that this tiara is not authentic? If it is, then these things Jeffrey suggests are indubitably true. Mr. Ogilvie does buy it, for twenty thousand dollars, and that is why poor Jeffrey had in his possession so much cash money."

He flourished a pink hand at me, nodded his dyed head vigorously, and finished with:

"*Voilà!* That is it!"

"Did you hear from Main after he got back?" I asked.

The dealer smiled as if my question tickled him, turning his head so that the smile was directed at his wife.

"Did we, Enid, darling?" he passed on the question.

She pouted and shrugged her shoulders indifferently.

"The first we knew he had returned," Gungen interpreted these gestures to me, "was Monday morning, when we heard of his death. Is it not so, my dove?"

His dove murmured, "Yes," and left her chair, saying, "You'll excuse me? I have a letter to write."

"Certainly, my dear," Gungen told her as he and I stood up.

She passed close to him on her way to the door. His small nose twitched over his dyed mustache and he rolled his eyes in a caricature of ecstasy.

"What a delightful scent, my precious!" he exclaimed. "What a heavenly odor! What a song to the nostrils! Has it a name, my love?"

"Yes," she said, pausing in the doorway, not looking back.

"And it is?"

"*Dèsir du Cœur,*" she replied over her shoulder as she left us.

Bruno Gungen looked at me and giggled.

I sat down again and asked him what he knew about Jeffrey Main.

"Everything, no less," he assured me. "For a dozen years, since he was a boy of eighteen he has been my right eye, my right hand."

"Well, what sort of man was he?"

Bruno Gungen showed me his pink palms side by side.

"What sort is any man?" he asked over them.

That didn't mean anything to me, so I kept quiet, waiting.

"I shall tell you," the little man began presently. "Jeffrey had the eye and the taste for this traffic of mine. No man living save myself alone has a judgment in these matters which I would prefer to Jeffrey's. And, honest, mind you! Let nothing I say mislead you on that point. Never a lock have I to which Jeffrey had not also the key, and might have it forever, if he had lived so long.

"But there is a but. In his private life, rascal is a word that only does him justice. He drank, he gambled, he loved, he spent—dear God, how he spent! He was, in this drinking and gaming and loving and spending, a most promiscuous fellow, beyond doubt. With moderation he had nothing to do. Of the moneys he got by inheritance, of the fifty thousand dollars or more his wife had when they were married, there is no remainder. Fortunately, he was well insured—else his wife would have been left penniless. Oh, he was a true Heliogabalus, that fellow!"

Bruno Gungen went down to the front door with me when I left. I said, "Good night," and walked down the gravel path to where I had left my car. The night was clear, dark, moonless. High hedges were black walls on both sides of the Gungen place. To the left there was a barely noticeable hole in the blackness—a dark-gray hole—oval—the size of a face.

I got into my car, stirred up the engine and drove away. Into the first cross-street I turned, parked the machine, and started back toward Gungen's afoot. I was curious about that face-size oval.

When I reached the corner, I saw a woman coming toward me from the direction of Gungen's. I was in the shadow of a wall. Cautiously, I backed away from the corner until I came to a gate with brick buttresses sticking out. I made myself flat between them.

The woman crossed the street, went on up the driveway, toward the car-line. I couldn't make out anything about her, except that she was a woman. Maybe she was coming from Gungen's grounds, maybe not. Maybe it was her face I had seen against the hedge, maybe not. It was a heads or tails proposition. I guessed yes and tailed her up the drive.

Her destination was a drugstore on the car line. Her business there was with the telephone. She spent ten minutes at it. I didn't go into the store to try for an earful, but stayed on the other side of the street, contenting myself with a good look at her.

She was a girl of about twenty-five, medium in height, chunky in build, with pale gray eyes that had little pouches under them, a thick nose and a prominent lower lip. She had no hat over her brown hair. Her body was wrapped in a long blue cape.

From the drug store I shadowed her back to the Gungen house. She went in the back door. A servant, probably, but not the maid who had opened the door for me earlier in the evening.

I returned to my car, drove back to town, to the office.

"Is Dick Foley working on anything?" I asked Fiske, who sits on the Continental Detective Agency's affairs at night.

"No. Did you ever hear the story about the fellow who had his neck operated on?"

With the slightest encouragement, Fiske is good for a dozen stories without a stop, so I said:

"Yes. Get hold of Dick and tell him I've got a shadow job out Westwood Park way for him to start on in the morning."

I gave Fiske—to be passed on to Dick—Gungen's address and a description of the girl who had done the phoning from the drugstore. Then I assured the night man that I had also heard the story about the pickaninny named Opium, and likewise the one about what the old man said to his wife on their golden wedding anniversary. Before he could try me with another, I escaped to my own office, where I composed and coded a telegram to our Los Angeles branch, asking that Main's recent visit to that city be dug into.

The next morning Hacken and Begg dropped in to see me and I gave them Gungen's version of why the twenty thousand had been in cash. The police detectives told me a stool-pigeon had brought them word that Bunky Dahl—a local guerrilla who did a moderate business in hijacking—had been flashing a roll since about the time of Main's death.

"We haven't picked him up yet," Hacken said. "Haven't been able to place him, but we've got a line on his girl. Course, he might have got his dough somewhere else."

At ten o'clock that morning I had to go over to Oakland to testify against a couple of flimflammers who had sold bushels of stock in a sleight-of-hand rubber manufacturing business. When I got back to the Agency, at six that evening, I found a wire from Los Angeles on my desk.

Jeffrey Main, the wire told me, had finished his business with Ogilvie Saturday afternoon, had checked out of his hotel immediately, and had left on the Owl that evening, which would have put him in San Francisco early Sunday morning. The hundred-dollar bills with which Ogilvie had paid for the tiara had been new ones, consecutively numbered, and Ogilvie's bank had given the Los Angeles operative the numbers.

Before I quit for the day, I phoned Hacken, gave him these numbers, as well as the other dope in the telegram.

"Haven't found Dahl yet," he told me.

Dick Foley's report came in the next morning. The girl had left the Gungen house at 9:15 the previous night, had gone to the corner of Miramar Avenue and Southwood Drive, where a man was waiting for her in a Buick coupe. Dick described him: Age about 30; height about five feet ten; slender, weight about 140; medium complexion; brown hair and eyes; long, thin face with pointed chin; brown hat, suit and shoes and gray overcoat.

The girl got into the car with him and they drove out to the beach, along the Great Highway for a little while, and then back to Miramar and Southwood, where the girl got out. She seemed to be going back to the house, so Dick let her go and tailed the man in the Buick down to the Futurity Apartments in Mason Street.

The man stayed in there for half an hour or so and then came out with another man and two women. This second man was of about the same age as the first, about five feet eight inches tall, would weigh about a hundred and seventy pounds, had brown hair and eyes, a dark complexion, a flat, broad face with high cheek bones, and wore a blue suit, gray hat, tan overcoat, black shoes, and a pear-shaped pearl tie-pin.

One of the women was about twenty-two years old, small, slender and blonde. The other was probably three or four years older, red-haired, medium in height and build, with a turned-up nose.

The quartet had got in the car and gone to the Algerian Café, where they had stayed until a little after one in the morning. Then they had returned to the Futurity Apartments. At half-past three the two men had left, driving the Buick to a garage in Post Street, and then walking to the Mars Hotel.

When I had finished reading this I called Mickey Linehan in from the operatives' room, gave him the report and instructions:

"Find out who these folks are."

Mickey went out. My phone rang.

Bruno Gungen: "Good morning. May you have something to tell me today?"

"Maybe," I said. "You're downtown?"

"Yes, in my shop. I shall be here until four."

"Right. I'll be in to see you this afternoon."

At noon Mickey Linehan returned. "The first bloke," he reported, "the one Dick saw with the girl, is named Benjamin Weel. He owns the Buick and lives in the Mars—room 410. He's a salesman, though it's not known what of. The other man is a friend of his who has been staying with him for a couple of days. I couldn't get anything on him. He's not registered. The two women in the Futurity are a couple of hustlers. They live in apartment 303. The larger one goes by the name of Mrs. Effie Roberts. The little blonde is Violet Evarts."

"Wait," I told Mickey, and went back into the file room, to the index-card drawers.

I ran through the W's—*Weel, Benjamin, alias Coughing Ben, 36,312 W.*

The contents of folder No. 36,312W told me that Coughing Ben Weel had been arrested in Amador County in 1916 on a highgrading charge and had been sent to San Quentin for three years. In 1922 he had been picked up again in Los Angeles and charged with trying to blackmail a movie actress, but the case had fallen through. His description fit the one Dick had given of the man in the Buick. His photograph—a copy of the one taken by the Los Angeles police in '22—showed a sharp-featured young man with a chin like a wedge.

I took the photo back to my office and showed it to Mickey.

"This is Weel five years ago. Follow him around a while."

When the operative had gone I called the police detective bureau. Neither Hacken nor Begg was in. I got hold of Lewis, in the identification department.

"What does Bunky Dahl look like?" I asked him.

"Wait a minute," Lewis said, and then: "32, 67½, 174, medium, brown, brown, broad flat face with prominent cheek-bones, gold bridge work in lower left jaw, brown mole under right ear, deformed little toe on right foot."

"Have you a picture of him to spare?"

"Sure."

"Thanks, I'll send a boy down for it."

I told Tommy Howd to go down and get it, and then went out for some food. After luncheon I went up to Gungen's establishment in Post Street. The little dealer was gaudier than ever this afternoon in a black coat that was even more padded in the shoulders and tighter in the waist than his dinner coat had been the other night, striped gray pants, a vest that leaned toward magenta, and a billowy satin tie wonderfully embroidered with gold thread.

We went back through his store, up a narrow flight of stairs to a small cube of an office on the mezzanine floor.

"And now you have to tell me?" he asked when we were seated, with the door closed.

"I've got more to ask than tell. First, who is the girl with the thick nose, the thick lower lip, and the pouches under grey eyes, who lives in your house?"

"That is one Rose Rubury." His little painted face was wrinkled in a satisfied smile. "She is my dear wife's maid."

"She goes riding with an ex-convict."

"She does?" He stroked his dyed goatee with a pink hand, highly pleased. "Well, she is my dear wife's maid, that she is."

"Main didn't drive up from Los Angeles with a friend, as he told his wife. He came up on the train Saturday night—so he was in town twelve hours before he showed up at home."

Bruno Gungen giggled, cocking his delighted face to one side.

"Ah!" he tittered. "We progress! We progress! Is it not so?"

"Maybe. Do you remember if this Rose Rubury was in the house on Sunday night—say from eleven to twelve?"

"I do remember. She was. I know it certainly. My dear wife was not feeling well that night. My darling had gone out early that Sunday morning, saying she was going to drive out into the country with some friends—what friends I do not know.

But she came home at eight o'clock that night complaining of a distressing headache. I was quite frightened by her appearance, so that I went often to see how she was, and thus it happens that I know her maid was in the house all of that night, until one o'clock, at least."

"Did the police show you the handkerchief they found with Main's wallet?"

"Yes." He squirmed on the edge of his chair, his face like the face of a kid looking at a Christmas tree.

"You're sure it's your wife's?"

His giggle interfered with his speech, so he said, "Yes," by shaking his head up and down until the goatee seemed to be a black whiskbroom brushing his tie.

"She could have left it at the Mains' some time when she was visiting Mrs. Main," I suggested.

"That is not possible," he corrected me eagerly. "My darling and Mrs. Main are not acquainted."

"But your wife and Main were acquainted?"

He giggled and brushed his tie with his whisker again.

"How well acquainted?"

He shrugged his padded shoulders up to his ears.

"I know not," he said merrily. "I employ a detective."

"Yeah?" I scowled at him. "You employ this one to find out who killed and robbed Main—and for nothing else. If you think you're employing him to dig up your family secrets, you're as wrong as Prohibition."

"But why? But why?" He was flustered. "Have I not the right to know? There will be no trouble over it, no scandal, no divorce suing, of that be assured. Even Jeffrey is dead, so it is what one calls ancient history. While he lived I knew nothing, was blind. After he died I saw certain things. For my own satisfaction—that is all, I beg you to believe—I should like to know with certainty."

"You won't get it out of me," I said bluntly. "I don't know anything about it except what you've told me, and you can't hire me to go further into it. Besides, if you're not going to do anything about it, why don't you keep your hands off—let it sleep?"

"No, no, my friend." He had recovered his bright-eyed cheerfulness. "I am not an old man, but I am fifty-two. My dear wife is eighteen, and a truly lovely person." He giggled. "This thing happened. May it not happen again? And would it not be the part of husbandly wisdom to have—shall I say— a hold on her? A rein? A check? Or if it never happen again, still might not one's dear wife be the more docile for certain information which her husband possesses?"

"It's your business." I stood up, laughing. "But I don't want any part of it."

"Ah, do not let us quarrel!" He jumped up and took one of my hands in his. "If you will not, you will not. But there remains the criminal aspect of the situation—the aspect that has engaged you thus far. You will not forsake that? You will fulfil your engagement there? Surely?"

"Suppose—just suppose—it should turn out that your wife had a hand in Main's death. What then?"

"That"—he shrugged, holding his hands out, palms up— "would be a matter for the law."

"Good enough. I'll stick—if you understand that you're entitled to no information except what touches your 'criminal aspect.' "

"Excellent! And if it so happens you cannot separate my darling from that—"

I nodded. He grabbed my hand again, patting it. I took it away from him and returned to the Agency.

A memorandum on my desk asked me to phone detective-sergeant Hacken. I did.

"Bunky Dahl wasn't in on the Main job," the hatchet-faced man told me. "He and a pal named Coughing Ben Weel were putting on a party in a roadhouse near Vallejo that night. They were there from around ten until they were thrown out after two in the morning for starting a row. It's on the up-and-up. The guy that gave it to me is right—and I got a check-up on it from two others."

I thanked Hacken and phoned Gungen's residence, asking for Mrs. Gungen, asking her if she would see me if I came out there.

"Oh, yes," she said. It seemed to be her favorite expression, though the way she said it didn't express anything.

Putting the photos of Dahl and Weel in my pocket, I got a taxi and set out for Westwood Park. Using Fatima-smoke on my brains while I rode, I concocted a wonderful series of lies to be told my client's wife—a series that I thought would get me the information I wanted.

A hundred and fifty yards or so up the drive from the house I saw Dick Foley's car standing.

A thin, pasty-faced maid opened the Gungens' door and took me into a sitting room on the second floor, where Mrs. Gungen put down a copy of *The Sun Also Rises* and waved a cigarette at a nearby chair. She was very much the expensive doll this afternoon in a Persian orange dress, sitting with one foot tucked under her in a brocaded chair.

Looking at her while I lighted a cigarette, remembering my first interview with her and her husband, and my second one with him, I decided to chuck the tale-of-woe I had spent my ride building.

"You've a maid—Rose Rubury," I began. "I don't want her to hear what's said."

She said, "Very well," without the least sign of surprise, added, "Excuse me a moment," and left her chair and the room.

Presently she was back, sitting down with both feet tucked under her now.

"She will be away for at least half an hour."

"That will be long enough. This Rose is friendly with an ex-convict named Weel."

The doll face frowned, and the plump painted lips pressed themselves together. I waited, giving her time to say something. She didn't say it. I took Weel's and Dahl's pictures out and held them out to her.

"The thin-faced one is your Rose's friend. The other's a pal of his—also a crook."

She took the photographs with a tiny hand that was as steady as mine, and looked at them carefully. Her mouth became smaller and tighter, her brown eyes darker. Then, slowly, her face cleared, she murmured, "Oh, yes," and returned the pictures to me.

"When I told your husband about it"—I spoke deliberately—"he said, 'She's my wife's maid,' and laughed."

Enid Gungen said nothing.

"Well?" I asked. "What did he mean by that?"

"How should I know?" she sighed.

"You know your handkerchief was found with Main's empty wallet." I dropped this in a by-the-way tone, pretending to be chiefly occupied putting cigarette ash in a jasper tray that was carved in the form of a lidless coffin.

"Oh, yes," she said wearily, "I've been told that."

"How do you think it happened?"

"I can't imagine."

"I can," I said, "but I'd rather know positively. Mrs. Gungen, it would save a lot of time if we could talk plain language."

"Why not?" she asked listlessly. "You are in my husband's confidence, have his permission to question me. If it happens to be humiliating to me—well, after all, I am only his wife. And it is hardly likely that any new indignities either of you can devise will be worse than those to which I have already submitted."

I grunted at this theatrical speech and went ahead.

"Mrs. Gungen, I'm only interested in learning who robbed and killed Main. Anything that points in that direction is valuable to me, but only in so far as it points in that direction. Do you understand what I mean?"

"Certainly," she said. "I understand you are in my husband's employ."

That got us nowhere. I tried again:

"What impression do you suppose I got the other evening, when I was here?"

"I can't imagine."

"Please try."

"Doubtless"—she smiled faintly—"you got the impression that my husband thought I had been Jeffrey's mistress."

"Well?"

"Are you"—her dimples showed; she seemed amused—"asking me if I really was his mistress?"

"No—though of course I'd like to know."

"Naturally you would," she said pleasantly.

"What impression did you get that evening?" I asked.

"I?" She wrinkled her forehead. "Oh, that my husband had hired you to prove that I had been Jeffrey's mistress." She repeated the word mistress as if she liked the shape of it in her mouth.

"You were wrong."

"Knowing my husband, I find that hard to believe."

"Knowing myself, I'm sure of it," I insisted. "There's no uncertainty about it between your husband and me, Mrs. Gungen. It is understood that my job is to find who stole and killed—nothing else."

"Really?" It was a polite ending of an argument of which she had grown tired.

"You're tying my hands," I complained, standing up, pretending I wasn't watching her carefully. "I can't do anything now but grab this Rose Rubury and the two men and see what I can squeeze out of them. You said the girl would be back in half an hour?"

She looked at me steadily with her round brown eyes.

"She should be back in a few minutes. You're going to question her?"

"But not here," I informed her. "I'll take her down to the Hall of Justice and have the men picked up. Can I use your phone?"

"Certainly. It's in the next room." She crossed to open the door for me.

I called Davenport 20 and asked for the detective bureau.

Mrs. Gungen, standing in the sitting room, said, so softly I could barely hear it:

"Wait."

Holding the phone, I turned to look through the door at her. She was pinching her red mouth between thumb and finger, frowning. I didn't put down the phone until she took the hand from her mouth and held it out toward me. Then I went back into the sitting-room.

I was on top. I kept my mouth shut. It was up to her to make the plunge. She studied my face for a minute or more before she began:

"I won't pretend I trust you." She spoke hesitantly, half as if to herself, "You're working for my husband, and even the money would not interest him so much as whatever I had done. It's a choice of evils—certain on the one hand, more than probable on the other."

She stopped talking and rubbed her hands together. Her round eyes were becoming indecisive. If she wasn't helped along she was going to balk.

"There's only the two of us," I urged her. "You can deny everything afterward. It's my word against yours. If you don't tell me—I know now I can get it from the others. Your calling me from the phone lets me know that. You think I'll tell your husband everything. Well, if I have to fry it out of the others, he'll probably read it all in the papers. Your one chance is to trust me. It's not as slim a chance as you think. Anyway, it's up to you."

A half-minute of silence.

"Suppose," she whispered, "I should pay you to——"

"What for? If I'm going to tell your husband, I could take your money and still tell him, couldn't I?"

Her red mouth curved, her dimples appeared and her eyes brightened.

"That is reassuring," she said. "I shall tell you. Jeffrey came back from Los Angeles early so we could have the day together in a little apartment we kept. In the afternoon two men came in—with a key. They had revolvers. They robbed Jeffrey of the money. That was what they had come for. They seemed to know all about it and about us. They called us by name, and taunted us with threats of the story they would tell if we had them arrested.

"We couldn't do anything after they had gone. It was a ridiculously hopeless plight they had put us in. There wasn't anything we could do—since we couldn't possibly replace the money. Jeffrey couldn't even pretend he had lost it or had been robbed of it while he was alone. His secret early return to San Francisco would have been sure to throw suspicion on him. Jeffrey lost his head. He wanted me to run away with him. Then he wanted to go to my husband and tell him the truth. I wouldn't permit either course—they were equally foolish.

"We left the apartment, separating, a little after seven. We weren't, the truth is, on the best of terms by then. He wasn't—now that we were in trouble—as—— No, I shouldn't say that."

She stopped and stood looking at me with a placid doll's face that seemed to have got rid of all its troubles by simply passing them to me.

"The pictures I showed you are the two men?" I asked.

"Yes."

"This maid of yours knew about you and Main? Knew about the apartment? Knew about his trip to Los Angeles and his plan to return early with the cash?"

"I can't say she did. But she certainly could have learned most of it by spying and eavesdropping and looking through my— I had a note from Jeffrey telling me about the Los Angeles trip, making the appointment for Sunday morning. Perhaps she could have seen it. I'm careless."

"I'm going now," I said. "Sit tight till you hear from me. And don't scare up the maid."

"Remember, I've told you nothing," she reminded me as she followed me to the sitting-room door.

From the Gungen house I went direct to the Mars Hotel. Mickey Linehan was sitting behind a newspaper in a corner of the lobby.

"They in?" I asked him.

"Yep."

"Let's go up and see them."

Mickey rattled his knuckles on door number 410. A metallic voice asked: "Who's there?"

"Package," Mickey replied in what was meant for a boy's voice.

A slender man with a pointed chin opened the door. I gave him a card. He didn't invite us into the room, but he didn't try to keep us out when we walked in.

"You're Weel?" I addressed him while Mickey closed the door behind us, and then, not waiting for him to say yes, I turned to the broad-faced man sitting on the bed. "And you're Dahl?"

Weel spoke to Dahl, in a casual, metallic voice:

"A couple of gum-shoes."

The man on the bed looked at us and grinned.

I was in a hurry.

"I want the dough you took from Main," I announced.

They sneered together, as if they had been practicing.

I brought out my gun.

Weel laughed harshly.

"Get your hat, Bunky," he chuckled. "We're being taken into custody."

"You've got the wrong idea," I explained. "This isn't a pinch. It's a stick-up. Up go the hands!"

Dahl's hands went up quick. Weel hesitated until Mickey prodded him in the ribs with the nose of a .38-special.

"Frisk 'em," I ordered Mickey.

He went through Weel's clothes, taking a gun, some papers, some loose money, and a money-belt that was fat. Then he did the same for Dahl.

"Count it," I told him.

Mickey emptied the belts, spit on his fingers and went to work.

"Nineteen thousand, one hundred and twenty-six dollars and sixty-two cents," he reported when he was through.

With the hand that didn't hold my gun, I felt in my pocket for the slip on which I had written the numbers of the hundred-dollar bills Main had got from Ogilvie. I held the slip out to Mickey.

"See if the hundreds check against this."

He took the slip, looked, said, "They do."

"Good—pouch the money and the guns and see if you can turn up any more in the room."

Coughing Ben Weel had got his breath by now.

"Look here!" he protested. "You can't pull this, fellow! Where do you think you are? You can't get away with this!"

"I can try," I assured him. "I suppose you're going to yell, *Police!* Like hell you are! The only squawk you've got coming is at your own dumbness in thinking because your squeeze on the woman was tight enough to keep her from having you copped, you didn't have to worry about anything. I'm playing the same game you played with her and Main—only mine's better, because you can't get tough afterward without facing stir. Now shut up!"

"No more jack," Mickey said. "Nothing but four postage stamps."

"Take 'em along," I told him. "That's practically eight cents. Now we'll go."

"Hey, leave us a couple of bucks," Weel begged.

"Didn't I tell you to shut up?" I snarled at him, backing to the door, which Mickey was opening.

The hall was empty. Mickey stood in it, holding his gun on Weel and Dahl while I backed out of the room and switched the key from the inside to the outside. Then I slammed the door, twisted the key, pocketed it, and we went downstairs and out of the hotel.

Mickey's car was around the corner. In it, we transferred our spoils—except the guns—from his pockets to mine. Then he got out and went back to the Agency. I turned the car toward the building in which Jeffrey Main had been killed.

Mrs. Main was a tall girl of less than twenty-five, with curled brown hair, heavily-lashed gray-blue eyes, and a warm, full-featured face. Her ample body was dressed in black from throat to feet.

She read my card, nodded at my explanation that Gungen had employed me to look into her husband's death, and took me into a gray and white living room.

"This is the room?" I asked.

"Yes." She had a pleasant, slightly husky voice.

I crossed to the window and looked down on the grocer's roof, and on the half of the back street that was visible. I was still in a hurry.

"Mrs. Main," I said as I turned, trying to soften the abruptness of my words by keeping my voice low, "after your husband was dead, you threw the gun out the window. Then you stuck the handkerchief to the corner of the wallet and threw that. Being lighter than the gun, it didn't go all the way to the alley, but fell on the roof. Why did you put the handkerchief——?"

Without a sound she fainted.

I caught her before she reached the floor, carried her to a sofa, found Cologne and smelling salts, applied them.

"Do you know whose handkerchief it was?" I asked when she was awake and sitting up.

She shook her head from left to right.

"Then why did you take that trouble?"

"It was in his pocket. I didn't know what else to do with it. I thought the police would ask about it. I didn't want anything to start them asking questions."

"Why did you tell the robbery story?"

No answer.

"The insurance?" I suggested.

She jerked up her head, cried defiantly:

"Yes! He had gone through his own money and mine. And then he had to—to do a thing like that. He——"

I interrupted her complaint:

"He left a note, I hope—something that will be evidence." Evidence that she hadn't killed him, I meant.

"Yes." She fumbled in the bosom of her black dress.

"Good," I said, standing. "The first thing in the morning, take that note down to your lawyer and tell him the whole story."

I mumbled something sympathetic and made my escape.

Night was coming down when I rang the Gungens' bell for the second time that day. The pasty-faced maid who opened the door told me Mr. Gungen was at home. She led me upstairs.

Rose Rubury was coming down the stairs. She stopped on the landing to let us pass. I halted in front of her while my guide went on toward the library.

"You're done, Rose," I told the girl on the landing. "I'll give you ten minutes to clear out. No word to anybody. If you don't like that—you'll get a chance to see if you like the inside of the can."

"Well—the idea!"

"The racket's flopped." I put a hand into a pocket and showed her one wad of the money I had got at the Mars Hotel. "I've just come from visiting Coughing Ben and Bunky."

That impressed her. She turned and scurried up the stairs.

Bruno Gungen came to the library door, searching for me. He looked curiously from the girl—now running up the steps to the third story—to me. A question was twisting the little man's lips, but I headed it off with a statement:

"It's done."

"Bravo!" he exclaimed as we went into the library. "You hear that, my darling? It is done!"

His darling, sitting by the table, where she had sat the other night, smiled with no expression in her doll's face, and murmured, "Oh, yes," with no expression in her words.

I went to the table and emptied my pockets of money.

"Nineteen thousand, one hundred and twenty-six dollars and seventy cents, including the stamps," I announced. "The other eight hundred and seventy-three dollars and thirty cents is gone."

"Ah!" Bruno Gungen stroked his spade-shaped black beard with a trembling pink hand and pried into my face with hard bright eyes. "And where did you find it? By all means sit down and tell us the tale. We are famished with eagerness for it, eh, my love?"

His love yawned, "Oh, yes!"

"There isn't much story," I said. "To recover the money I had to make a bargain, promising silence. Main was robbed Sunday afternoon. But it happens that we couldn't convict the robbers if we had them. The only person who could identify them—won't."

"But who killed Jeffrey?" The little man was pawing my chest with both pink hands. "Who killed him that night?"

"Suicide. Despair at being robbed under circumstances he couldn't explain."

"Preposterous!" My client didn't like the suicide.

"Mrs. Main was awakened by the shot. Suicide would have canceled his insurance—would have left her penniless. She threw the gun and wallet out the window, hid the note he left, and framed the robber story."

"But the handkerchief!" Gungen screamed. He was all worked up.

"That doesn't mean anything," I assured him solemnly, "except that Main—you said he was promiscuous—had probably been fooling with your wife's maid, and that she—like a lot of maids—helped herself to your wife's belongings."

He puffed up his rouged cheeks, and stamped his feet, fairly dancing. His indignation was as funny as the statement that caused it.

"We shall see!" He spun on his heel and ran out of the room, repeating over and over, "We shall see!"

Enid Gungen held a hand out to me. Her doll face was all curves and dimples.

"I thank you," she whispered.

"I don't know what for," I growled, not taking the hand. "I've got it jumbled so anything like proof is out of the question. But he can't help knowing—didn't I practically tell him?"

"Oh, that!" She put it behind her with a toss of her small head. "I'm quite able to look out for myself so long as he has no definite proof."

I believed her.

Bruno Gungen came fluttering back into the library, frothing at the mouth, tearing his dyed goatee, raging that Rose Rubury was not to be found in the house.

The next morning Dick Foley told me the maid had joined Weel and Dahl and had left for Portland with them.

This King Business

THE train from Belgrade set me down in Stefania, capital of Muravia, in early afternoon—a rotten afternoon. Cold wind blew cold rain in my face and down my neck as I left the square granite barn of a railroad station to climb into a taxi-cab.

English meant nothing to the chauffeur, nor French. Good German might have failed. Mine wasn't good. It was a hodge-podge of grunts and gargles. This chauffeur was the first person who had ever pretended to understand it. I suspected him of guessing, and I expected to be taken to some distant sub-urban point. Maybe he was a good guesser. Anyhow, he took me to the Hotel of the Republic.

The hotel was a new six-story affair, very proud of its elevators, American plumbing, private baths, and other modern tricks. After I had washed and changed clothes I went down to the café for luncheon. Then, supplied with minute instructions in English, French, and sign-language by a highly uniformed head porter, I turned up my raincoat collar and crossed the muddy plaza to call on Roy Scanlan, United States *chargé d'affaires* in this youngest and smallest of the Balkan States.

He was a pudgy man of thirty, with smooth hair already far along the gray route, a nervous, flabby face, plump white hands that twitched, and very nice clothes. He shook hands with me, patted me into a chair, barely glanced at my letter of introduction, and stared at my necktie while saying:

"So you're a private detective from San Francisco?"

"Yes."

"And?"

"Lionel Grantham."

"Surely not!"

"Yes."

659

"But he's—" The diplomat realized he was looking into my eyes, hurriedly switched his gaze to my hair, and forgot what he had started to say.

"But he's what?" I prodded him.

"Oh!"—with a vague upward motion of head and eyebrows—"not that sort."

"How long has he been here?" I asked.

"Two months. Possibly three or three and a half or more."

"You know him well?"

"Oh, no! By sight, of course, and to talk to. He and I are the only Americans here, so we're fairly well acquainted."

"Know what he's doing here?"

"No, I don't. He just happened to stop here in his travels, I imagine, unless, of course, he's here for some special reason. No doubt there's a girl in it—she is General Radnjak's daughter—though I don't think so."

"How does he spend his time?"

"I really haven't any idea. He lives at the Hotel of the Republic, is quite a favorite among our foreign colony, rides a bit, lives the usual life of a young man of family and wealth."

"Mixed up with anybody who isn't all he ought to be?"

"Not that I know of, except that I've seen him with Mahmoud and Einarson. They are certainly scoundrels, though they may not be."

"Who are they?"

"Nubar Mahmoud is private secretary to Doctor Semich, the President. Colonel Einarson is an Icelander, just now virtually the head of the army. I know nothing about either of them."

"Except that they are scoundrels?"

The *chargé d'affaires* wrinkled his round white forehead in pain and gave me a reproachful glance.

"Not at all," he said. "Now, may I ask, of what is Grantham suspected?"

"Nothing."

"Then?"

"Seven months ago, on his twenty-first birthday, this Lionel Grantham got hold of the money his father had left him—a nice wad. Till then the boy had had a tough time of it. His mother had, and has, highly developed middle-class notions of refinement. His father had been a genuine aristocrat in the old manner—a hard-souled, soft-spoken individual who got what he wanted by simply taking it; with a liking for old wine and young women, and plenty of both, and for cards and dice and running horses—and fights, whether he was in them or watching them.

"While he lived the boy had a he-raising. Mrs. Grantham thought her husband's tastes low, but he was a man who had things his own way. Besides, the Grantham blood was the best in America. She was a woman to be impressed by that. Eleven years ago—when Lionel was a kid of ten—the old man died. Mrs. Grantham swapped the family roulette wheel for a box of dominoes and began to convert the kid into a patent leather Galahad.

"I've never seen him, but I'm told the job wasn't a success. However, she kept him bundled up for eleven years, not even letting him escape to college. So it went until the day when he was legally of age and in possession of his share of his father's estate. That morning he kisses Mamma and tells her casually that he's off for a little run around the world—alone. Mamma does and says all that might be expected of her, but it's no good. The Grantham blood is up. Lionel promises to drop her a post-card now and then, and departs.

"He seems to have behaved fairly well during his wandering. I suppose just being free gave him all the excitement he needed. But a few weeks ago the trust company that handles his affairs got instructions from him to turn some railroad bonds into cash and ship the money to him in care of a Belgrade bank. The amount was large—over the three million mark—so the trust company told Mrs. Grantham about it. She chucked a fit. She had been getting letters from him— from Paris, without a word said about Belgrade.

"Mamma was all for dashing over to Europe at once. Her brother, Senator Walbourn, talked her out of it. He did some cabling, and learned that Lionel was neither in Paris nor in Belgrade, unless he was hiding. Mrs. Grantham packed her trunks and made reservations. The Senator headed her off again, convincing her that the lad would resent her interference, telling her the best thing was to investigate on the quiet. He brought the job to the Agency. I went to Paris, learned that a friend of Lionel's there was relaying his mail, and that Lionel was here in Stefania. On the way down I stopped off in Belgrade and learned that the money was being sent here to him—most of it already has been. So here I am."

Scanlan smiled happily.

"There's nothing I can do," he said. "Grantham is of age, and it's his money."

"Right," I agreed, "and I'm in the same fix. All I can do is poke around, find out what he's up to, try to save his dough if he's being gypped. Can't you give me even a guess at the answer? Three million dollars—what could he put it into?"

"I don't know." The *chargé d'affaires* fidgeted uncomfortably. "There's no business here that amounts to anything. It's purely an agricultural country, split up among small landowners—ten, fifteen, twenty acre farms. There's his association with Einarson and Mahmoud, though. They'd certainly rob him if they got the chance. I'm positive they're robbing him. But I don't think they would. Perhaps he isn't acquainted with them. It's probably a woman."

"Well, whom should I see? I'm handicapped by not knowing the country, not knowing the language. To whom can I take my story and get help?"

"I don't know," he said gloomily. Then his face brightened. "Go to Vasilije Djudakovich. He is Minister of Police. He is the man for you! He can help you, and you may trust him. He has a digestion instead of a brain. He'll not understand a thing you tell him. Yes, Djudakovich is your man!"

"Thanks," I said, and staggered out into the muddy street.

CHAPTER II

ROMAINE

I FOUND the Minister of Police's offices in the Administration Building, a gloomy concrete pile next to the Executive Residence at the head of the plaza. In French that was even worse than my German, a thin, white-whiskered clerk, who looked like a consumptive Santa Claus, told me His Excellency was not in. Looking solemn, lowering my voice to a whisper, I repeated that I had come from the United States *chargé d'affaires*. This hocus-pocus seemed to impress Saint

Nicholas. He nodded understandingly and shuffled out of the room. Presently he was back, bowing at the door, asking me to follow him.

I tailed him along a dim corridor to a wide door marked "15." He opened it, bowed me through it, wheezed, "*Asseyez-vous, s'il vous plait,*" closed the door and left me. I was in an office, a large, square one. Everything in it was large. The four windows were double-size. The chairs were young benches, except the leather one at the desk, which could have been the rear half of a touring car. A couple of men could have slept on the desk. Twenty could have eaten at the table.

A door opposite the one through which I had come opened, and a girl came in, closing the door behind her, shutting out a throbbing purr, as of some heavy machine, that had sounded through.

"I'm Romaine Frankl," she said in English, "His Excellency's secretary. Will you tell me what you wish?"

She might have been any age from twenty to thirty, something less than five feet in height, slim without boniness, with curly hair as near black as brown can get, black-lashed eyes whose gray irises had black rims, a small, delicate-featured face, and a voice that seemed too soft and faint to carry as well as it did. She wore a red woolen dress that had no shape except that which her body gave it, and when she moved—to walk or raise a hand—it was as if it cost her no energy—as if someone else were moving her.

"I'd like to see him," I said while I was accumulating this data.

"Later, certainly," she promised, "but it's impossible now." She turned, with her peculiar effortless grace, back to the door, opening it so that the throbbing purr sounded in the room again. "Hear?" she said. "He's taking his nap."

She shut the door against His Excellency's snoring and floated across the room to climb up in the immense leather chair at the desk.

"Do sit down," she said, wriggling a tiny forefinger at a chair beside the desk. "It will save time if you will tell me your business, because, unless you speak our tongue, I'll have to interpret your message to His Excellency."

I told her about Lionel Grantham and my interest in him, in practically the same words I had used on Scanlan, winding up:

"You see, there's nothing I can do except try to learn what the boy's up to and give him a hand if he needs it. I can't go to him—he's too much Grantham, I'm afraid, to take kindly to what he'd think was nursemaid stuff. Mr. Scanlan advised me to come to the Minister of Police."

"You were fortunate." She looked as if she wanted to make a joke about my country's representative but weren't sure how I'd take it. "Your *chargé d'affaires* is not always easy to understand."

"Once you get the hang of it, it's not hard," I said. "You just throw out all his statements that have *no's* or *not's* or *nothing's* or *don't's* in them."

"That's it! That's it, exactly!" She leaned toward me, laughing. "I've always known there was some key to it, but nobody's been able to find it before. You've solved our national problem."

"For reward, then, I should be given all the information you have about Grantham."

"You should, but I'll have to speak to His Excellency first. He'll wake presently."

"You can tell me unofficially what you think of Grantham. You know him?"

"Yes. He's charming. A nice boy, delightfully naïf, inexperienced, but really charming."

"Who are his friends here?"

She shook her head and said:

"No more of that until His Excellency wakes. You're from San Francisco? I remember the funny little street cars, and the fog, and the salad right after the soup, and Coffee Dan's."

"You've been there?"

"Twice. I was in the United States for a year and a half, in vaudeville, bringing rabbits out of hats."

We were still talking about that half an hour later when the door opened and the Minister of Police came in.

The over-size furniture immediately shrank to normal, the girl became a midget, and I felt like somebody's little boy.

This Vasilije Djudakovich stood nearly seven feet tall, and that was nothing to his girth. Maybe he wouldn't weigh more than five hundred pounds, but, looking at him, it was hard to think except in terms of tons. He was a blond-haired, blond-bearded mountain of meat in a black frock coat. He wore a necktie, so I suppose he had a collar, but it was hidden all the way around by the red rolls of his neck. His white vest was the size and shape of a hoop-skirt, and in spite of that it strained at the buttons. His eyes were almost invisible between the cushions of flesh around them, and were shaded into a colorless darkness, like water in a deep well. His mouth was a fat red oval among the yellow hairs of his whiskers and mustache. He came into the room slowly, ponderously, and I was surprised that the floor didn't creak nor the room tremble.

Romaine Frankl was watching me attentively as she slid out of the big leather chair and introduced me to the Minister. He gave me a fat, sleepy smile and a hand that had the general appearance of a naked baby, and let himself down slowly into the chair the girl had quit. Planted there, he lowered his head until it rested on the pillows of his several chins, and then he seemed to go to sleep.

I drew up another chair for the girl. She took another sharp look at me—she seemed to be hunting for something in my face—and began to talk to him in what I suppose was the native lingo. She talked rapidly for about twenty minutes, while he gave no sign that he was listening or that he was even awake.

When she was through, he said: "*Da.*" He spoke dreamily, but there was a volume to the syllable that could have come from no place smaller than his gigantic belly.

The girl turned to me, smiling.

"His Excellency will be glad to give you every possible assistance. Officially, of course, he does not care to interfere in the affairs of a visitor from another country, but he realizes the importance of keeping Mr. Grantham from being victimized while here. If you will return tomorrow afternoon, at, say, three o'clock . . ."

I promised to do that, thanked her, shook hands with the mountain again, and went out into the rain.

CHAPTER III

SHADOWING

BACK at the hotel, I had no trouble learning that Lionel Grantham occupied a suite on the sixth floor and was in it at that time. I had his photograph in my pocket and his description in my head. I spent what was left of the afternoon and the early evening waiting for a look at him. At a little after seven I got it.

He stepped out of the elevator, a tall, flat-backed boy with a supple body that tapered from broad shoulders to narrow hips, carried erectly on long, muscular legs—the sort of frame that tailors like. His pink, regular-featured, really handsome face wore an expression of aloof superiority that was too marked to be anything else than a cover for youthful self-consciousness.

Lighting a cigarette, he passed into the street. The rain had stopped, though clouds overhead promised more shortly. He turned down the street afoot. So did I.

We went to a much gilded restaurant two blocks from the hotel, where a gypsy orchestra played on a little balcony stuck insecurely high on one wall. All the waiters and half the diners seemed to know the boy. He bowed and smiled to this side and that as he walked down to a table near the far end, where two men were waiting for him.

One of them was tall and thick-bodied, with bushy dark hair and a flowing dark mustache. His florid, short-nosed face wore the expression of a man who doesn't mind a fight now and then. This one was dressed in a green and gold military uniform, with high boots of the shiniest black leather. His companion was in evening clothes, a plump, swarthy man of medium height, with oily black hair and a suave, oval face.

While young Grantham joined this pair I found a table some distance from them for myself. I ordered dinner and looked around at my neighbors. There was a sprinkling of uniforms in the room, some dress coats and evening gowns, but most of the diners were in ordinary daytime clothes. I saw a couple of faces that were probably British, a Greek or two, a few Turks. The food was good and so was my appetite. I was smoking a cigarette over a tiny cup of syrupy coffee when Grantham and the big florid officer got up and went away.

I couldn't have got my bill and paid it in time to follow them, without raising a disturbance, so I let them go. Then I settled for my meal and waited until the dark, plump man they had left behind called for his check. I was in the street a minute or more ahead of him, standing, looking up toward the dimly electric-lighted plaza with what was meant for the expression of a tourist who didn't quite know where to go next.

He passed me, going up the muddy street with the soft, careful-where-you-put-your-foot tread of a cat.

A soldier—a bony man in sheepskin coat and cap, with a gray mustache bristling over gray, sneering lips—stepped out of a dark doorway and stopped the swarthy man with whining words.

The swarthy man lifted hands and shoulders in a gesture that held both anger and surprise.

The soldier whined again, but the sneer on his gray mouth became more pronounced. The plump man's voice was low, sharp, angry, but he moved a hand from pocket to soldier, and the brown of Muravian paper money showed in the hand. The soldier pocketed the money, raised a hand in a salute, and went across the street.

When the swarthy man had stopped staring after the soldier, I moved toward the corner around which sheepskin coat and cap had vanished. My soldier was a block and a half down the street, striding along with bowed head. He was in a hurry. I got plenty of exercise keeping up with him. Presently the city began to thin out. The thinner it got, the less I liked this expedition. Shadowing is at its best in daytime, downtown in a familiar large city. This was shadowing at its worst.

He led me out of the city along a cement road bordered by few houses. I stayed as far back as I could, so he was a faint, blurred shadow ahead. He turned a sharp bend in the road. I hustled toward the bend, intending to drop back again as soon as I had rounded it. Speeding, I nearly gummed the works.

The soldier suddenly appeared around the curve, coming toward me.

A little behind me, a small pile of lumber on the roadside was the only cover within a hundred feet. I stretched my short legs thither.

Irregularly piled boards made a shallow cavity in one end of the pile, almost large enough to hold me. On my knees in the mud, I huddled into that cavity.

The soldier came into sight through a chink between boards. Bright metal gleamed in one of his hands. A knife, I thought. But when he halted in front of my shelter I saw it was a revolver of the old-style nickel-plated sort.

He stood still, looking at my shelter, looking up the road and down the road. He grunted, came toward me. Slivers stung my cheek as I rubbed myself flatter against the timber-ends. My gun was with my blackjack—in my gladstone bag, in my room in my hotel. A fine place to have them now! The soldier's gun was bright in his hand.

Rain began to patter on boards and ground. The soldier turned up the collar of his coat as he came. Nobody ever did anything I liked more. A man stalking another wouldn't have done that. He didn't know I was there. He was hunting a hiding place for himself. The game was even. If he found me, he had the gun, but I had seen him first.

His sheepskin coat rasped against the wood as he went by me, bending low as he passed my corner for the back of the pile, so close to me that the same raindrops seemed to be hitting both of us. I undid my fists after that. I couldn't see him, but I could hear him breathing, scratching himself, even humming.

A couple of weeks went by.

The mud I was kneeling in soaked through my pants-legs, wetting my knees and shins. The rough wood filed skin off my face every time I breathed. My mouth was as dry as my knees were wet, because I was breathing through it for silence.

An automobile came around the bend, headed for the city. I heard the soldier grunt softly, heard the click of his gun as he cocked it. The car came abreast, went on. The soldier blew out his breath and started scratching himself and humming again.

Another couple of weeks passed.

Men's voices came through the rain, barely audible, louder, quite clear. Four soldiers in sheepskin coats and hats walked down the road the way we had come, their voices presently shrinking into silence as they disappeared around the curve.

In the distance an automobile horn barked two ugly notes. The soldier grunted—a grunt that said clearly: "Here it is." His feet slopped in the mud, and the lumber pile creaked under his weight. I couldn't see what he was up to.

White light danced around the bend in the road, and an automobile came into view—a high-powered car going cityward with a speed that paid no attention to the wet slipperiness of the road. Rain and night and speed blurred its two occupants, who were in the front seat.

Over my head a heavy revolver roared. The soldier was working. The speeding car swayed crazily along the wet cement, its brakes screaming.

When the sixth shot told me the nickel-plated gun was probably empty, I jumped out of my hollow.

The soldier was leaning over the lumber pile, his gun still pointing at the skidding car while he peered through the rain.

He turned as I saw him, swung the gun around to me, snarled an order I couldn't understand. I was betting the gun was empty. I raised both hands high over my head, made an astonished face, and kicked him in the belly.

He folded over on me, wrapping himself around my leg. We both went down. I was underneath, but his head was against my thigh. His cap fell off. I caught his hair with both hands and yanked myself into a sitting position. His teeth went into my leg. I called him disagreeable things and put my thumbs in the hollows under his ears. It didn't take much pressure to teach him that he oughtn't to bite people. When he lifted his face to howl, I put my right fist in it, pulling him into the punch with my left hand in his hair. It was a nice solid sock.

I pushed him off my leg, got up, took a handful of his coat collar, and dragged him out into the road.

CHAPTER IV

INTRODUCTIONS

WHITE light poured over us. Squinting into it, I saw the automobile standing down the road, its spotlight turned on me and my sparring partner. A big man in green and gold came into the light—the florid officer who had been one of Grantham's companions in the restaurant. An automatic was in one of his hands.

He strode over to us, stiff-legged in his high boots, ignored the soldier on the ground, and examined me carefully with sharp little dark eyes.

"British?" he asked.

"American."

He bit a corner of his mustache and said meaninglessly:

"Yes, that is better."

His English was guttural, with a German accent.

Lionel Grantham came from the car to us. His face wasn't as pink as it had been.

"What is it?" he asked the officer, but he looked at me.

"I don't know," I said. "I took a stroll after dinner and got mixed up on my directions. Finding myself out here, I decided I was headed the wrong way. When I turned around to go back I saw this fellow duck behind the lumber pile. He had a gun in his hand. I took him for a stick-up, so I played Indian on him. Just as I got to him he jumped up and began spraying you people. I reached him in time to spoil his aim. Friend of yours?"

"You're an American," the boy said. "I'm Lionel Grantham. This is Colonel Einarson. We're very grateful to you." He screwed up his forehead and looked at Einarson. "What do you think of it?"

The officer shrugged his shoulders, growled, "One of my children—we'll see," and kicked the ribs of the man on the ground.

The kick brought the soldier to life. He sat up, rolled over on hands and knees, and began a broken, long-winded entreaty, plucking at the Colonel's tunic with dirty hands.

"Ach!" Einarson knocked the hands down with a tap of pistol barrel across knuckles, looked with disgust at the muddy marks on his tunic, and growled an order.

The soldier jumped to his feet, stood at attention, got another order, did an about-face, and marched to the automobile. Colonel Einarson strode stiff-legged behind him, holding his automatic to the man's back. Grantham put a hand on my arm.

"Come along," he said. "We'll thank you properly and get better acquainted after we've taken care of this fellow."

Colonel Einarson got into the driver's seat, with the soldier beside him. Grantham waited while I found the soldier's revolver. Then we got into the rear seat. The officer looked doubtfully at me out of his eye-corners, but said nothing. He drove the car back the way it had come. He liked speed, and we hadn't far to go. By the time we were settled in our seats the car was whisking us through a gateway in a high stone wall, with a sentry on each side presenting arms. We did a sliding half-circle into a branching driveway and jerked to a standstill in front of a square whitewashed building.

Einarson prodded the soldier out ahead of him. Grantham and I got out. To the left a row of long, low buildings showed pale gray in the rain—barracks. The door of the square, white building was opened by a bearded orderly in green. We went in. Einarson pushed his prisoner across the small reception hall and through the open door of a bedroom. Grantham and I followed them in. The orderly stopped in the doorway, traded some words with Einarson, and went away, closing the door.

The room we were in looked like a cell, except that there were no bars over the one small window. It was a narrow room, with bare, whitewashed walls and ceiling. The wooden floor, scrubbed with lye until it was almost as white as the walls, was bare. For furniture there was a black iron cot, three folding chairs of wood and canvas, and an unpainted chest of drawers, with comb, brush, and a few papers on top. That was all.

"Be seated, gentlemen," Einarson said, indicating the camp chairs. "We'll get at this thing now."

The boy and I sat down. The officer laid his pistol on the top of the chest of drawers, rested one elbow beside the pistol, took a corner of his mustache in one big red hand, and addressed the soldier. His voice was kindly, paternal. The soldier, standing rigidly upright in the middle of the floor, replied, whining, his eyes focused on the officer's with a blank, in-turned look.

They talked for five minutes or more. Impatience grew in the Colonel's voice and manner. The soldier kept his blank abjectness. Einarson ground his teeth together and looked angrily at the boy and me.

"This pig!" he exclaimed, and began to bellow at the soldier.

Sweat sprang out on the soldier's gray face, and he cringed out of his military stiffness. Einarson stopped bellowing at him and yelled two words at the door. It opened and the bearded orderly came in with a short, thick, leather whip. At a nod from Einarson, he put the whip beside the automatic on the top of the chest of drawers and went out.

The soldier whimpered. Einarson spoke curtly to him. The soldier shuddered, began to unfasten his coat with shaking fingers, pleading all the while with whining, stuttering words. He took off his coat, his green blouse, his gray undershirt, letting them fall on the floor, and stood there, his hairy, not exactly clean body naked from the waist up. He worked his fingers together and cried.

Einarson grunted a word. The soldier stiffened at attention, hands at sides, facing us, his left side to Einarson.

Slowly Colonel Einarson removed his own belt, unbuttoned his tunic, took it off, folded it carefully, and laid it on the cot. Beneath it he wore a white cotton shirt. He rolled the sleeves up above his elbows and picked up the whip.

"This pig!" he said again.

Lionel Grantham stirred uneasily on his chair. His face was white, his eyes dark.

CHAPTER V

A FLOGGING

LEANING his left elbow on the chest of drawers again, playing with his mustache-end with his left hand, standing indolently cross-legged, Einarson began to flog the soldier. His right arm raised the whip, brought the lash whistling down to the soldier's back, raised it again, brought it down again. It was especially nasty because he was not hurrying himself, not exerting himself. He meant to flog the man until he got what he wanted, and he was saving his strength so that he could keep it up as long as necessary.

With the first blow the terror went out of the soldier's eyes. They dulled sullenly and his lips stopped twitching. He stood woodenly under the beating, staring over Grantham's head. The officer's face had also become expressionless. Anger was gone. He showed no pleasure in his work, not even that of relieving his feelings. His air was the air of a stoker shoveling coal, of a carpenter sawing a board, of a stenographer typing a letter. Here was a job to be done in a workmanlike manner, without haste or excitement or wasted effort, without either enthusiasm or repulsion. It was nasty, but it taught me respect for this Colonel Einarson.

Lionel Grantham sat on the edge of his folding chair, staring at the soldier with white-ringed eyes. I offered the boy a cigarette, making an unnecessary complicated operation out of lighting it and my own—to break up his score-keeping. He had been counting the strokes, and that wasn't good for him.

The whip curved up, swished down, cracked on the naked back—up, down, up, down. Einarson's florid face took on the damp glow of moderate exercise. The soldier's gray face was a lump of putty. He was facing Grantham and me. We couldn't see the marks of the whip.

Grantham said something to himself in a whisper. Then he gasped:

"I can't stand this!"

Einarson didn't look around from his work.

"Don't stop it now," I muttered. "We've gone this far."

The boy got up unsteadily and went to the window, opened it and stood looking out into the rainy night. Einarson paid no attention to him. He was putting more weight into the whipping now, standing with his feet far apart, leaning forward a little, his left hand on his hip, his right carrying the whip up and down with increasing swiftness.

The soldier swayed and a sob shook his hairy chest. The

whip cut—cut—cut. I looked at my watch. Einarson had been at it for forty minutes, and looked good for the rest of the night.

The soldier moaned and turned toward the officer. Einarson did not break the rhythm of his stroke. The lash cut the man's shoulder. I caught a glimpse of his back—raw meat. Einarson spoke sharply. The soldier jerked himself to attention again, his left side to the officer. The whip went on with its work—up, down, up, down, up, down.

The soldier flung himself on hands and knees at Einarson's feet and began to pour out sob-broken words. Einarson looked down at him, listening carefully, holding the lash of the whip in his left hand, the butt still in his right. When the man had finished, Einarson asked questions, got answers, nodded, and the soldier stood up. Einarson put a friendly hand on the man's shoulder, turned him around, looked at his mangled red back, and said something in a sympathetic tone. Then he called the orderly in and gave him some orders. The soldier, moaning as he bent, picked up his discarded clothes and followed the orderly out of the bedroom.

Einarson tossed the whip up on top of the chest of drawers and crossed to the bed to pick up his tunic. A leather pocketbook slid from an inside pocket to the floor. When he recovered it, a soiled newspaper clipping slipped out and floated across to my feet. I picked it up and gave it back to him—a photograph of a man, the Shah of Persia, according to the French caption under it.

"That pig!" he said—meaning the soldier, not the Shah—as he put on his tunic and buttoned it. "He has a son, also until last week of my troops. This son drinks too much of wine. I reprimand him. He is insolent. What kind of army is it without discipline? Pigs! I knock this pig down, and he produces a knife. Ach! What kind of army is it where a soldier may attack his officers with knives? After I—personally, you comprehend—have finished with this swine, I have him court-martialed and sentenced to twenty years in the prison. This elder pig, his father, does not like that. So he will shoot me to-night. Ach! What kind of army is that?"

Lionel Grantham came away from his window. His young face was haggard. His young eyes were ashamed of the haggardness of his face.

Colonel Einarson made me a stiff bow and a formal speech of thanks for spoiling the soldier's aim—which I hadn't—and saving his life. Then the conversation turned to my presence in Muravia. I told them briefly that I had held a captain's commission in the military intelligence department during the war. That much was the truth, and that was all the truth I gave them. After the war—so my fairy tale went—I had decided to stay in Europe, had taken my discharge there and had drifted around, doing odd jobs at one place and another. I was vague, trying to give them the impression that those odd jobs had not always, or usually, been ladylike. I gave them more definite—though still highly imaginary—details of my recent employment with a French syndicate, admitting that I had come to this corner of the world because I thought it better not to be seen in Western Europe for a year or so.

"Nothing I could be jailed for," I said, "but things could be made uncomfortable for me. So I roamed over into *Mitteleuropa*, learned that I might find a connection in Belgrade, got there to find it a false alarm, and came on down here. I may pick up something here. I've got a date with the Minister of Police to-morrow. I think I can show him where he can use me."

"The gross Djudakovich!" Einarson said with frank contempt. "You find him to your liking?"

"No work, no eat," I said.

"Einarson," Grantham began quickly, hesitated, then said: "Couldn't we—don't you think——" and didn't finish.

The Colonel frowned at him, saw I had noticed the frown, cleared his throat, and addressed me in a gruffly hearty tone:

"Perhaps it would be well if you did not too speedily engage yourself to this fat minister. It may be—there is a possibility that we know of another field where your talents might find employment more to your taste—and profit."

I let the matter stand there, saying neither yes nor no.

CHAPTER VI

CARDS ON THE TABLE

WE returned to the city in the officer's car. He and Grantham
sat in the rear. I sat beside the soldier who drove. The boy and
I got out at our hotel. Einarson said good night and was driven
away as if he were in a hurry.

"It's early," Grantham said as we went indoors. "Come up
to my room."

I stopped at my own room to wash off the mud I'd gathered around the lumber stack and to change my clothes, and
then went up with him. He had three rooms on the top floor,
overlooking the plaza.

He set out a bottle of whisky, a syphon, lemons, cigars and
cigarettes, and we drank, smoked, and talked. Fifteen or
twenty minutes of the talk came from no deeper than the
mouth on either side—comments on the night's excitement,
our opinions of Stefania, and so on. Each of us had something to say to the other. Each was weighing the other in before he said it.

I decided to put mine over first.

"Colonel Einarson was spoofing us to-night," I said.

"Spoofing?" The boy sat up straight, blinking.

"His soldier shot for money, not revenge."

"You mean——?" His mouth stayed open.

"I mean the little dark man you ate with gave the soldier
money."

"Mahmoud! Why, that's—— You are sure?"

"I saw it."

He looked at his feet, yanking his gaze away from mine as if
he didn't want me to see that he thought I was lying.

"The soldier may have lied to Einarson," he said presently,
still trying to keep me from knowing he thought me the liar.
"I can understand some of the language, as spoken by the
educated Muravians, but not the country dialect the soldier
talked, so I don't know what he said, but he may have lied,
you know."

"Not a chance," I said. "I'd bet my pants he told the
truth."

He continued to stare at his outstretched feet, fighting to hold his face cool and calm. Part of what he was thinking slipped out in words:

"Of course, I owe you a tremendous debt for saving us from——"

"You don't. You owe that to the soldier's bad aim. I didn't jump him till his gun was empty."

"But——" His young eyes were wide before mine, and if I had pulled a machine gun out of my cuff he wouldn't have been surprised. He suspected me of everything on the blotter. I cursed myself for overplaying my hand. There was nothing to do now but spread the cards.

"Listen, Grantham. Most of what I told you and Einarson about myself is the bunk. Your uncle, Senator Walbourn, sent me down here. You were supposed to be in Paris. A lot of your dough was being shipped to Belgrade. The Senator was leery of the racket, didn't know whether you were playing a game or somebody was putting over a fast one. I went to Belgrade, traced you here, and came here, to run into what I ran into. I've traced the money to you, have talked to you. That's all I was hired to do. My job's done—unless there's anything I can do for you now."

"Not a thing," he said very calmly. "Thanks, just the same." He stood up, yawning. "Perhaps I'll see you again before you leave for the United States."

"Yeah." It was easy for me to make my voice match his in indifference: I hadn't a cargo of rage to hide. "Good night."

I went down to my room, got into bed, and, not having anything to think about, went to sleep.

CHAPTER VII
LIONEL'S PLANS

I SLEPT till late the next morning and then had breakfast in my room. I was in the middle of it when knuckles tapped my door. A stocky man in a wrinkled gray uniform, set off with a short, thick sword, came in, saluted, gave me a square white envelope, looked hungrily at the American cigarettes on my table, smiled and took one when I offered them, saluted again, and went out.

The square envelope had my name written on it in a small,

very plain and round, but not childish, handwriting. Inside
was a note from the same pen:

> The Minister of Police regrets that departmental
> affairs prevent his receiving you this afternoon.

It was signed "Romaine Frankl," and had a postscript:

> If it's convenient for you to call on me after
> nine this evening, perhaps I can save you some
> time.
>
> R. F.

Below this an address was written.

I put the note in my pocket and called: "Come in," to another set of knocking knuckles.

Lionel Grantham entered. His face was pale and set.

"Good morning," I said, making it cheerfully casual, as if I
attached no importance to last night's rumpus. "Had breakfast yet? Sit down, and——"

"Oh, yes, thanks. I've eaten." His handsome red face was
reddening. "About last night—I was——"

"Forget it! Nobody likes to have his business pried into."

"That's good of you," he said, twisting his hat in his hands.
He cleared his throat. "You said you'd—ah—do—ah—help
me if I wished."

"Yeah. I will. Sit down."

He sat down, coughed, ran his tongue over his lips.

"You haven't said anything to anyone about last night's affair with the soldier?"

"No," I said.

"Will you not say anything about it?"

"Why?"

He looked at the remains of my breakfast and didn't answer. I lit a cigarette to go with my coffee and waited. He
stirred uneasily in his chair and, without looking up, asked:

"You know Mahmoud was killed last night?"

"The man in the restaurant with you and Einarson?"

"Yes. He was shot down in front of his house a little after
midnight."

"Einarson?"

The boy jumped.

"No!" he cried. "Why do you say that?"

"Einarson knew Mahmoud had paid the soldier to wipe him out, so he plugged Mahmoud, or had him plugged. Did you tell him what I told you last night?"

"No." He blushed. "It's embarrassing to have one's family sending guardians after one."

I made a guess:

"He told you to offer me the job he spoke of last night, and to caution me against talking about the soldier. Didn't he?"

"Y-e-s."

"Well, go ahead and offer."

"But he doesn't know you're——"

"What are you going to do, then?" I asked. "If you don't make me the offer, you'll have to tell him why."

"Oh, Lord, what a mess!" he said wearily, putting elbows on knees, face between palms, looking at me with the harried eyes of a boy finding life too complicated.

He was ripe for talk. I grinned at him, finished my coffee, and waited.

"You know I'm not going to be led home by an ear," he said with a sudden burst of rather childish defiance.

"You know I'm not going to try to take you," I soothed him.

We had some more silence after that. I smoked while he held his head and worried. After a while he squirmed in his chair, sat stiffly upright, and his face turned perfectly crimson from hair to collar.

"I'm going to ask for your help," he said, pretending he didn't know he was blushing. "I'm going to tell you the whole foolish thing. If you laugh, I'll—— You won't laugh, will you?"

"If it's funny I probably will, but that needn't keep me from helping you."

"Yes, do laugh! It's silly! You ought to laugh!" He took a deep breath. "Did you ever—did you ever think you'd like to be a——" he stopped, looked at me with a desperate sort of shyness, pulled himself together, and almost shouted the last word—"king?"

"Maybe. I've thought of a lot of things I'd like to be, and that might be one of 'em."

"I met Mahmoud at an embassy ball in Constantinople," he dashed into the story, dropping his words quickly as if glad to get rid of them. "He was President Semich's secretary. We got quite friendly, though I wasn't especially fond of him. He persuaded me to come here with him, and introduced me to Colonel Einarson. Then they—there's really no doubt that the country is wretchedly governed. I wouldn't have gone into it if that hadn't been so.

"A revolution was being prepared. The man who was to lead it had just died. It was handicapped, too, by a lack of money. Believe this—it wasn't all vanity that made me go into it. I believed—I still believe—that it would have been—will be—for the good of the country. The offer they made me was that if I would finance the revolution I could be—could be king.

"Now wait! The Lord knows it's bad enough, but don't think it sillier than it is. The money I have would go a long way in this small, impoverished country. Then, with an American ruler, it would be easier—it ought to be—for the country to borrow in America or England. Then there's the political angle. Muravia is surrounded by four countries, any one of which is strong enough to annex it if it wants. Even Albania, now that it is a protégé of Italy's. Muravia has stayed independent so far only because of the jealousy among its stronger neighbors and because it hasn't a seaport. But with the balance shifting—with Greece, Italy, and Albania allied against Jugoslavia for control of the Balkans—it's only a matter of time before something will happen here, as it now stands.

"But with an American ruler—and if loans in America and England were arranged, so we had their capital invested here—there would be a change in the situation. Muravia would be in a stronger position, would have at least some slight claim on the friendship of stronger powers. That would be enough to make the neighbors cautious.

"Albania, shortly after the war, thought of the same thing, and offered its crown to one of the wealthy American Bonapartes. He didn't want it. He was an older man and had already made his career. I did want my chance when it came. There were"—some of the embarrassment that had left him during his talking returned—"there were kings back in the Grantham lines. We trace our descent from James the Fourth, of Scotland. I wanted—it was nice to think of carrying the line back to a crown.

"We weren't planning a violent revolution. Einarson holds the army. We simply had to use the army to force the Deputies—those who were not already with us—to change the form of government and elect me king. My descent would make it easier than if the candidate were one who hadn't royal blood in him. It would give me a certain standing in spite—in spite of my being young, and—and the people really want a king, especially the peasants. They don't think they're really entitled to call themselves a nation without one. A president means nothing to them—he's simply an ordinary man like themselves. So, you see, I—— It was—— Go ahead, laugh! You've heard enough to know how silly it is!" His voice was high-pitched, screechy. "Laugh! Why don't you laugh?"

"What for?" I asked. "It's crazy, God knows, but not silly. Your judgment was gummy, but your nerve's all right. You've been talking as if this were all dead and buried. Has it flopped?"

"No, it hasn't," he said slowly, frowning, "but I keep thinking it has. Mahmoud's death shouldn't change the situation, yet I've a feeling it's all over."

"Much of your money sunk?"

"I don't mind that. But—well—suppose the American newspapers get hold of the story, and they probably will. You know how ridiculous they could make it. And then the others who'll know about it—my mother and uncle and the trust company. I won't pretend I'm not ashamed to face them. And then——" His face got red and shiny. "And then Valeska—Miss Radnjak—her father was to have led the revolution. He did lead it—until he was murdered. She is—I never could be good enough for her." He said this in a peculiarly idiotic tone of awe. "But I've hoped that perhaps by carrying on her father's work, and if I had something besides mere money to offer her—if I had done something—made a place for myself—perhaps she'd—you know."

I said: "Uh-huh."

"What shall I do?" he asked earnestly. "I can't run away.

I've got to see it through for her, and to keep my own self-respect. But I've got the feeling that it's all over. You offered to help me. Help me. Tell me what I ought to do!"

"You'll do what I tell you—if I promise to bring you through with a clean face?" I asked, just as if steering millionaire descendants of Scotch kings through Balkan plots were an old story to me, merely part of the day's work.

"Yes!"

"What's the next thing on the revolutionary program?"

"There's a meeting to-night. I'm to bring you."

"What time?"

"Midnight."

"I'll meet you here at eleven-thirty. How much am I supposed to know?"

"I was to tell you about the plot, and to offer you whatever inducements were necessary to bring you in. There was no definite arrangement as to how much or how little I was to tell you."

CHAPTER VIII
AN ENLIGHTENING INTERVIEW

AT NINE-THIRTY that night a cab set me down in front of the address the Minister of Police's secretary had given in her note. It was a small two-story house in a badly paved street on the city's eastern edge. A middle-aged woman in very clean, stiffly starched, ill-fitting clothes opened the door for me. Before I could speak, Romaine Frankl, in a sleeveless pink satin gown, floated into sight behind the woman, smiling, holding out a small hand to me.

"I didn't know you'd come," she said.

"Why?" I asked, with a great show of surprise at the notion that any man would ignore an invitation from her, while the servant closed the door and took my coat and hat.

We were standing in a dull-rose-papered room, finished and carpeted with oriental richness. There was one discordant note in the room—an immense leather chair.

"We'll go upstairs," the girl said, and addressed the servant with words that meant nothing to me, except the name

Marya. "Or would you"—she turned to me and English again—"prefer beer to wine?"

I said I wouldn't, and we went upstairs, the girl climbing ahead of me with her effortless appearance of being carried. She took me into a black, white, and gray room that was very daintily furnished with as few pieces as possible, its otherwise perfect feminine atmosphere spoiled by the presence of another of the big padded chairs.

The girl sat on a gray divan, pushing away a stack of French and Austrian magazines to make a place for me beside her. Through an open door I could see the painted foot of a Spanish bed, a short stretch of purple counterpane, and half of a purple-curtained window.

"His Excellency was very sorry," the girl began, and stopped.

I was looking—not staring—at the big leather chair. I knew she had stopped because I was looking at it, so I wouldn't take my eyes away.

"Vasilije," she said, more distinctly than was really necessary, "was very sorry he had to postpone this afternoon's appointment. The assassination of the President's secretary—you heard of it?—made us put everything else aside for the moment."

"Oh, yes, that fellow Mahmoud—" slowly shifting my eyes from the leather chair to her. "Found out who killed him?"

Her black-ringed, black-centered eyes seemed to study me from a distance while she shook her head, jiggling the nearly black curls.

"Probably Einarson," I said.

"You haven't been idle." Her lower lids lifted when she smiled, giving her eyes a twinkling effect.

The servant Marya came in with wine and fruit, put them on a small table beside the divan, and went away. The girl poured wine and offered me cigarettes in a silver box. I passed them up for one of my own. She smoked a king-size Egyptian cigarette—big as a cigar. It accentuated the smallness of her face and hand—which is probably why she favored that size.

"What sort of revolution is this they've sold my boy?" I asked.

"It was a very nice one until it died."

"How come it died?"

"It—do you know anything about our history?"

"No."

"Well, Muravia came into existence as a result of the fear and jealousy of four countries. The nine or ten thousand square miles that make this country aren't very valuable land. There's little here that any of those four countries especially wanted, but no three of them would agree to let the fourth have it. The only way to settle the thing was to make a separate country out of it. That was done in 1923.

"Doctor Semich was elected the first president, for a ten-year term. He is not a statesman, not a politician, and never will be. But since he was the only Muravian who had ever been heard of outside his own town, it was thought that his election would give the new country some prestige. Besides, it was a fitting honor for Muravia's only great man. He was not meant to be anything but a figure-head. The real governing was to be done by General Danilo Radnjak, who was elected vice-president, which, here, is more than equivalent to Prime Minister. General Radnjak was a capable man. The army worshiped him, the peasants trusted him, and our *bourgeoisie* knew him to be honest, conservative, intelligent, and as good a business administrator as a military one.

"Doctor Semich is a very mild, elderly scholar with no knowledge whatever of worldly affairs. You can understand him from this—he is easily the greatest of living bacteriologists, but he'll tell you, if you are on intimate terms with him, that he doesn't believe in the value of bacteriology at all. 'Mankind must learn to live with bacteria as with friends,' he'll say. 'Our bodies must adapt themselves to diseases, so there will be little difference between having tuberculosis, for example, or not having it. That way lies victory. This making war on bacteria is a futile business. Futile but interesting. So we do it. Our poking around in laboratories is perfectly useless—but it amuses us.'

"Now when this delightful old dreamer was honored by his countrymen with the presidency, he took it in the worst possible way. He determined to show his appreciation by locking up his laboratory and applying himself heart and soul to running the government. Nobody expected or wanted that. Radnjak was to have been the government. For a while he did control the situation, and everything went well enough.

"But Mahmoud had designs of his own. He was Doctor Semich's secretary, and he was trusted. He began calling the President's attentions to various trespasses of Radnjak's on the presidential powers. Radnjak, in an attempt to keep Mahmoud from control, made a terrible mistake. He went to Doctor Semich and told him frankly and honestly that no one expected him, the President, to give all his time to executive business, and that it had been the intention of his countrymen to give him the honor of being the first president rather than the duties.

"Radnjak had played into Mahmoud's hands—the secretary became the actual government. Doctor Semich was now thoroughly convinced that Radnjak was trying to steal his authority, and from that day on Radnjak's hands were tied. Doctor Semich insisted on handling every governmental detail himself, which meant that Mahmoud handled it, because the President knows as little about statesmanship to-day as he did when he took office. Complaints—no matter who made them—did no good. Doctor Semich considered every dissatisfied citizen a fellow-conspirator of Radnjak's. The more Mahmoud was criticized in the Chamber of Deputies, the more faith Doctor Semich had in him. Last year the situation became intolerable, and the revolution began to form.

"Radnjak headed it, of course, and at least ninety percent of the influential men in Muravia were in it. The attitude of people as a whole, it is difficult to judge. They are mostly peasants, small land-owners, who ask only to be let alone. But there's no doubt they'd rather have a king than a president, so the form was to be changed to please them. The army, which worshiped Radnjak, was in it. The revolution matured slowly. General Radnjak was a cautious, careful man, and, as this is not a wealthy country, there was not much money available.

"Two months before the date set for the outbreak, Radnjak

was assassinated. And the revolution went to pieces, split up into half a dozen factions. There was no other man strong enough to hold them together. Some of these groups still meet and conspire, but they are without general influence, without real purpose. And this is the revolution that has been sold Lionel Grantham. We'll have more information in a day or two, but what we've learned so far is that Mahmoud, who spent a month's vacation in Constantinople, brought Grantham back here with him and joined forces with Einarson to swindle the boy.

"Mahmoud was very much out of the revolution, of course, since it was aimed at him. But Einarson had been in it with his superior, Radnjak. Since Radnjak's death Einarson has succeeded in transferring to himself much of the allegiance that the soldiers gave the dead general. They do not love the Icelander as they did Radnjak, but Einarson is spectacular, theatrical—has all the qualities that simple men like to see in their leaders. So Einarson had the army and could get enough of the late revolution's machinery in his hands to impress Grantham. For money he'd do it. So he and Mahmoud put on a show for your boy. They used Valeska Radnjak, the general's daughter, too. She, I think, was also a dupe. I've heard that the boy and she are planning to be king and queen. How much did he invest in this little farce?"

"Maybe as much as three million American dollars."

Romaine Frankl whistled softly and poured more wine.

CHAPTER IX

CONJECTURES

"HOW did the Minister of Police stand, when the revolution was alive?" I asked.

"Vasilije," she told me, sipping wine between phrases, "is a peculiar man, an original. He is interested in nothing except his comfort. Comfort to him means enormous amounts of food and drink and at least sixteen hours of sleep each day, and not having to move around much during his eight waking hours. Outside of that he cares for nothing. To guard his comfort he has made the police department a model one. They've got to do their work smoothly and neatly. If they don't, crimes will go unpunished, people will complain, and those complaints might disturb His Excellency. He might even have to shorten his afternoon nap to attend a conference or meeting. That wouldn't do. So he insists on an organization that will keep crime down to a minimum, and catch the perpetrators of that minimum. And he gets it."

"Catch Radnjak's assassin?"

"Killed resisting arrest ten minutes after the murder."

"One of Mahmoud's men?"

The girl emptied her glass, frowning at me, her lifted lower lids putting a twinkle in the frown.

"You're not so bad," she said slowly, "but now it's my turn to ask: Why did you say Einarson killed Mahmoud?"

"Einarson knew Mahmoud had tried to have him and Grantham shot earlier in the evening."

"Really?"

"I saw a soldier take money from Mahmoud, ambush Einarson and Grantham, and miss 'em with six shots."

She clicked a fingernail against her teeth.

"That's not like Mahmoud," she objected, "to be seen paying for his murders."

"Probably not," I agreed. "But suppose his hired man decided he wanted more pay, or maybe he'd only been paid part of his wages. What better way to collect than to pop out and ask for it in the street a few minutes before he was scheduled to turn the trick?"

She nodded, and spoke as if thinking aloud:

"Then they've got all they expect to get from Grantham, and each was trying to hog it by removing the other."

"Where you go wrong," I told her, "is in thinking that the revolution is dead."

"But Mahmoud wouldn't, for three million dollars, conspire to remove himself from power."

"Right! Mahmoud thought he was putting on a show for the boy. When he learned it wasn't a show—learned Einarson was in earnest—he tried to have him knocked off."

"Perhaps." She shrugged her smooth bare shoulders. "But now you're guessing."

"Yes? Einarson carries a picture of the Shah of Persia. It's worn, as if he handled it a lot. The Shah of Persia is a Russian soldier who went in there after the war, worked himself up until he had the army in his hands, became dictator, then Shah. Correct me if I'm wrong. Einarson is an Icelandic soldier who came in here after the war and has worked himself up until he's got the army in his hands. If he carries the Shah's picture and looks at it often enough to have it shabby from handling, does it mean he hopes to follow his example? Or doesn't it?"

Romaine Frankl got up and roamed around the room, moving a chair two inches here, adjusting an ornament there, shaking out the folds of a window-curtain, pretending a picture wasn't quite straight on the wall, moving from place to place with the appearance of being carried—a graceful small girl in pink satin.

She stopped in front of a mirror, moved a little to one side so she could see my reflection in it, and fluffed her curls while saying:

"Very well, Einarson wants a revolution. What will your boy do?"

"What I tell him."

"What will you tell him?"

"Whatever pays best. I want to take him home with all his money."

She left the mirror and came over to me, rumpled my hair, kissed my mouth, and sat on my knees, holding my face between small warm hands.

"Give me a revolution, nice man!" Her eyes were black with excitement, her voice throaty, her mouth laughing, her body trembling. "I detest Einarson. Use him and break him for me. But give me a revolution!"

I laughed, kissed her, and turned her around on my lap so her head would fit against my shoulder.

"We'll see," I promised. "I'm to meet the folks at midnight. Maybe I'll know then."

"You'll come back after the meeting?"

"Try to keep me away!"

CHAPTER X

EINARSON IN CONTROL

I GOT back to the hotel at eleven-thirty, loaded my hips with gun and blackjack, and went upstairs to Grantham's suite. He was alone, but said he expected Einarson. He seemed glad to see me.

"Tell me, did Mahmoud go to any of the meetings?" I asked.

"No. His part in the revolution was hidden even from most of those in it. There were reasons why he couldn't appear."

"There were. The chief one was that everybody knew he didn't want any revolts, didn't want anything but money."

Grantham chewed his lower lip and said: "Oh, Lord, what a mess!"

Colonel Einarson arrived, in a dinner coat, but very much the soldier, the man of action. His hand-clasp was stronger than it needed to be. His little dark eyes were hard and bright.

"You are ready, gentlemen?" he addressed the boy and me as if we were a multitude. "Excellent! We shall go now. There will be difficulties to-night. Mahmoud is dead. There will be those of our friends who will ask: 'Why now revolt?' Ach!" He yanked a corner of his flowing dark mustache. "I will answer that. Good souls, our confrères, but given to timidity. There is no timidity under capable leadership. You shall see!" And he yanked his mustache again. This military gent seemed to be feeling Napoleonic this evening. But I didn't write him off as a musical-comedy revolutionist—I remembered what he had done to the soldier.

We left the hotel, got into a machine, rode seven blocks, and went into a small hotel on a side street. The porter bowed to the belt when he opened the door for Einarson. Grantham and I followed the officer up a flight of stairs, down a dim hall. A fat, greasy man in his fifties came bowing and clucking to meet us. Einarson introduced him to me— the proprietor of the hotel. He took us into a low-ceilinged room where thirty or forty men got up from chairs and looked at us through tobacco smoke.

Einarson made a short, very formal speech which I couldn't understand, introducing me to the gang. I ducked my head at them and found a seat beside Grantham. Einarson sat on his other side. Everybody else sat down again, in no especial order.

Colonel Einarson smoothed his mustache and began to talk to this one and that, shouting over the clamor of other voices when necessary. In an undertone, Lionel Grantham pointed out the more important conspirators to me—a dozen or more members of the Chamber of Deputies, a banker, a brother of the Minister of Finance (supposed to represent that official), half a dozen officers (all in civilian clothes tonight), three professors from the university, the president of a labor union, a newspaper publisher and his editor, the secretary of a students' club, a politician from out in the country, and a handful of small business men.

The banker, a white-bearded fat man of sixty, stood up and began a speech, staring intently at Einarson. He spoke deliberately, softly, but with a faintly defiant air. The Colonel didn't let him get far.

"Ach!" Einarson barked and reared up on his feet. None of the words he said meant anything to me, but they took the pinkness out of the banker's cheeks and brought uneasiness into the eyes around us.

"They want to call it off," Grantham whispered in my ear. "They won't go through with it now. I know they won't."

The meeting became rough. A lot of people were yelping at once, but nobody talked down Einarson's bellow. Everybody was standing up, either very red or very white in the face. Fists, fingers, and heads were shaking. The Minister of Finance's brother—a slender, elegantly dressed man with a long, intelligent face—took off his nose glasses so savagely that they broke in half, screamed words at Einarson, spun on his heel, and walked to the door.

He pulled it open and stopped.

The hall was full of green uniforms. Soldiers leaned against the wall, sat on their heels, stood in little groups. They hadn't guns—only bayonets in scabbards at their sides. The Minister of Finance's brother stood very still at the door, looking at the soldiers.

A brown-whiskered, dark-skinned, big man, in coarse clothes and heavy boots, glared with red-rimmed eyes from the soldiers to Einarson, and took two heavy steps toward the Colonel. This was the country politician. Einarson blew out his lips and stepped forward to meet him. Those who were between them got out of the way.

Einarson roared and the countryman roared. Einarson made the most noise, but the countryman wouldn't stop on that account.

Colonel Einarson said: "Ach!" and spat in the country-man's face.

The countryman staggered back a step and one of his paws went under his brown coat. I stepped around Einarson and shoved the muzzle of my gun in the countryman's ribs.

Einarson laughed, called two soldiers into the room. They took the countryman by the arms and led him out. Somebody closed the door. Everybody sat down. Einarson made another speech. Nobody interrupted him. The white-whiskered banker made another speech. The Minister of Finance's brother rose to say half a dozen polite words, staring near-sightedly at Einarson, holding half of his broken glasses in each slender hand. Grantham, at a word from Einarson, got up and talked. Everybody listened very respectfully.

Einarson spoke again. Everybody got excited. Everybody talked at once. It went on for a long time. Grantham explained to me that the revolution would start early Thursday morning—it was now early Wednesday morning—and that the details were now being arranged for the last time. I doubted that anybody was going to know anything about the details, with all this hub-bub going on. They kept it up until half-past three. The last couple of hours I spent dozing in a chair, tilted back against the wall in a corner.

Grantham and I walked back to our hotel after the meet-ing. He told me we were to gather in the plaza at four o'clock the next morning. It would be daylight by six, and by then the government buildings, the President, most of the officials and Deputies who were not on our side, would be in our hands. A meeting of the Chamber of Deputies would be held under the eyes of Einarson's troops, and everything would be done as swiftly and regularly as possible.

I was to accompany Grantham as a sort of bodyguard, which meant, I imagined, that both of us were to be kept out of the way as much as possible. That was all right with me.

I left Grantham at the fifth floor, went to my room, ran cold water over my face and hands, and then left the hotel again. There was no chance of getting a cab at this hour, so I set out afoot for Romaine Frankl's house.

I had a little excitement on the way.

A wind was blowing in my face as I walked. I stopped and put my back to it to light a cigarette. A shadow down the street slid over into a building's shadow. I was being tailed, and not very skillfully. I finished lighting my cigarette and went on my way until I came to a sufficiently dark side street. Turning into it, I stopped in a street-level dark doorway.

A man came puffing around the corner. My first crack at him went wrong—the blackjack took him too far forward, on the cheek. The second one got him fairly behind the ear. I left him sleeping there and went on to Romaine Frankl's house.

CHAPTER XI

A ROMANTIC INTERLUDE

THE servant Marya, in a woolly gray bathrobe, opened the door and sent me up to the black, white, and gray room, where the Minister's secretary, still in the pink gown, was propped up among cushions on the divan. A tray full of cigarette butts showed how she'd been spending her time.

"Well?" she asked as I moved her over to make a seat for myself beside her.

"Thursday morning at four we revolute."

"I knew you'd do it," she said, patting my hand.

"It did itself, though there were a few minutes when I could have stopped it by simply knocking our Colonel behind the ear and letting the rest of them tear him apart. That reminds me—somebody's hired man tried to follow me here tonight."

"What sort of a man?"

"Short, beefy, forty—just about my size and age."

"But he didn't succeed?"

"I slapped him flat and left him sleeping there."

She laughed and pulled my ear.

"That was Gopchek, our very best detective. He'll be furious."

"Well, don't sic any more of 'em on me. You can tell him I'm sorry I had to hit him twice, but it was his own fault. He shouldn't have jerked his head back the first time."

She laughed, then frowned, finally settling on an expression that held half of each.

"Tell me about the meeting," she commanded.

I told her what I knew. When I had finished she pulled my head down to kiss me, and held it down to whisper:

"You do trust me, don't you, dear?"

"Yeah. Just as much as you trust me."

"That's far from being enough," she said, pushing my face away with a hand flat against my nose.

Marya came in with a tray of food. We pulled the table around in front of the divan and ate.

"I don't quite understand you," Romaine said over a stalk of asparagus. "If you don't trust me why do you tell me things? As far as I know, you haven't done much lying to me. Why should you tell me the truth if you've no faith in me?"

"My susceptible nature," I explained. "I'm so overwhelmed by your beauty and charm and one thing and another that I can't refuse you anything."

"Don't!" she exclaimed, suddenly serious. "I've capitalized that beauty and charm in half the countries in the world. Don't say things like that to me ever again. It hurts, be-cause—because——" She pushed her plate back, started to reach for a cigarette, stopped her hand in midair, and looked at me with disagreeable eyes. "I love you," she said.

I took the hand that was hanging in the air, kissed the palm of it, and asked:

"You love me more than anyone else in the world?"

She pulled the hand away from me.

"Are you a bookkeeper?" she demanded. "Must you have amounts, weights, and measurements for everything?"

I grinned at her and tried to go on with my meal. I had been hungry. Now, though I had eaten only a couple of mouthfuls, my appetite was gone. I tried to pretend I still had the hunger I had lost, but it was no go. The food didn't want to be swallowed. I gave up the attempt and lighted a cigarette.

She used her left hand to fan away the smoke between us.

"You don't trust me," she insisted. "Then why do you put yourself in my hands?"

"Why not? You can make a flop of the revolution. That's nothing to me. It's not my party, and its failure needn't mean that I can't get the boy out of the country with his money."

"You don't mind a prison, an execution, perhaps?"

"I'll take my chances," I said. But what I was thinking was: if, after twenty years of scheming and slickering in big-time cities, I let myself get trapped in this hill village, I'd deserve all I got.

"And you've no feeling at all for me?"

"Don't be foolish." I waved my cigarette at my uneaten meal. "I haven't had anything to eat since eight o'clock last night."

She laughed, put a hand over my mouth, and said:

"I understand. You love me, but not enough to let me interfere with your plans. I don't like that. It's effeminate."

"You going to turn out for the revolution?" I asked.

"I'm not going to run through the streets throwing bombs, if that's what you mean."

"And Djudakovich?"

"He sleeps till eleven in the morning. If you start at four, you'll have seven hours before he's up." She said all this perfectly seriously. "Get it done in that time. Or he might decide to stop it."

"Yeah? I had a notion he wanted it."

"Vasilije wants nothing but peace and comfort."

"But listen, sweetheart," I protested. "If your Vasilije is any good at all, he can't help finding out about it ahead of time. Einarson and his army are the revolution. These bankers and deputies and the like that he's carrying with him to give the party a responsible look are a lot of movie conspirators. Look at 'em! They hold their meetings at midnight, and all that kind of foolishness. Now that they're actually signed up to something, they won't be able to keep from spreading the news. All day they'll be going around trembling and whispering together in odd corners."

"They've been doing that for months," she said. "Nobody pays any attention to them. And I promise you Vasilije shan't hear anything new. I won't tell him, and he never listens to anything any one else says."

"All right." I wasn't sure it was all right, but it might be. "Now this row is going through—if the army follows Einarson?"

"Yes, and the army will follow him."

"Then, after it's over, our real job begins?"

She rubbed a flake of cigarette ash into the table cloth with a small pointed finger, and said nothing.

"Einarson's got to be dumped," I continued.

"We'll have to kill him," she said thoughtfully. "You'd better do it yourself."

CHAPTER XII

THE NIGHT BEFORE

I SAW Einarson and Grantham that evening, and spent several hours with them. The boy was fidgety, nervous, without confidence in the revolution's success, though he tried to pretend he was taking things as a matter of course. Einarson was full of words. He gave us every detail of the next day's plans. I was more interested in him than in what he was saying. He could put the revolution over, I thought, and I was willing to leave it to him. So while he talked I studied him, combing him over for weak spots.

I took him physically first—a tall, thick-bodied man in his prime, not as quick as he might have been, but strong and tough. He had an amply jawed, short-nosed, florid face that a fist wouldn't bother much. He wasn't fat, but he ate and drank too much to be hard-boiled, and your florid man can seldom stand much poking around the belt. So much for the gent's body.

Mentally, he wasn't a heavyweight. His revolution was crude stuff. It would get over chiefly because there wasn't much opposition. He had plenty of will-power, I imagined, but I didn't put a big number on that. People who haven't much brains have to develop will-power to get anywhere. I didn't know whether he had guts or not, but before an audience I guessed he'd make a grand showing, and most of this act would be before an audience. Off in a dark corner I had an idea he would go watery. He believed in himself—absolutely. That's ninety percent of leadership, so there was no flaw in him there. He didn't trust me. He had taken me in because as things turned out it was easier to do so than to shut the door against me.

He kept on talking about his plans. There was nothing to talk about. He was going to bring his soldiers in town in the early morning and take over the government. That was all the plan that was needed. The rest of it was the lettuce around the dish, but this lettuce part was the only part we could discuss. It was dull.

At eleven o'clock Einarson stopped talking and left us, making this sort of speech:

"Until four o'clock, gentlemen, when Muravia's history begins." He put a hand on my shoulder and commanded me: "Guard His Majesty!"

I said, "Uh-huh," and immediately sent His Majesty to bed. He wasn't going to sleep, but he was too young to confess it, so he went off willingly enough. I got a taxi and went out to Romaine's.

She was like a child the night before a picnic. She kissed me and she kissed the servant Marya. She sat on my knees, beside me, on the floor, on all the chairs, changing her location every half-minute. She laughed and talked incessantly, about the revolution, about me, about herself, about anything at all. She nearly strangled herself trying to talk while swallowing wine. She lit her big cigarettes and forgot to smoke them, or forgot to stop smoking them until they scorched her lips. She sang lines from songs in half a dozen languages. She made puns and jokes and goofy rhymes.

I left at three o'clock. She went down to the door with me, pulled my head down to kiss my eyes and mouth.

"If anything goes wrong," she said, "come to the prison. We'll hold that until——"

"If it goes wrong enough I'll be brought there," I promised.

She wouldn't joke now.

"I'm going there now," she said. "I'm afraid Einarson's got my house on his list."

"Good idea," I said. "If you hit a bad spot get word to me."

I walked back to the hotel through the dark streets—the lights were turned off at midnight—without seeing a single other person, not even one of the gray-uniformed policemen. By the time I reached home rain was falling steadily.

In my room, I changed into heavier clothes and shoes, dug an extra gun—an automatic—out of my bag and hung it in a shoulder holster. Then I filled my pocket with enough ammunition to make me bow-legged, picked up hat and rain-coat, and went upstairs to Lionel Grantham's suite.

"It's ten to four," I told him. "We might as well go down to the plaza. Better put a gun in your pocket."

He hadn't slept. His handsome young face was as cool and pink and composed as it had been the first time I saw him, though his eyes were brighter now.

He got into an overcoat, and we went downstairs.

CHAPTER XIII

PROGRESS GOES "BETUNE"

RAIN drove into our faces as we went toward the center of the dark plaza. Other figures moved around us, though none came near. We halted at the foot of an iron statue of some-body on a horse.

A pale young man of extraordinary thinness came up and began to talk rapidly, gesturing with both hands, sniffing every now and then, as if he had a cold in his head. I couldn't understand a word he said.

The rumble of other voices began to compete with the pat-ter of rain. The fat, white-whiskered face of the banker who had been at the meeting appeared suddenly out of the darkness and went back into it just as suddenly, as if he didn't want to be recognized. Men I hadn't seen before gathered around us, saluting Grantham with a sheepish sort of respect. A little man in a too big cape ran up and began to tell us something in a cracked, jerky voice. A thin, stooped man with glasses freckled by raindrops translated the little man's story into English for us:

"He says the artillery has betrayed us, and guns are being mounted in the government buildings to sweep the plaza at daybreak." There was an odd sort of hopefulness in his voice, and he added: "In that event we can, naturally, do nothing."

"We can die," Lionel Grantham said gently.

There wasn't the least bit of sense to that crack. Nobody was here to die. They were all here because it was so unlikely that anybody would have to die, except perhaps a few of Einarson's soldiers. That's the sensible view of the boy's speech. But it's God's own truth that even I—a middle-aged detective who had forgotten what it was like to believe in fairies—felt suddenly warm inside my wet clothes. And if anybody had said to me: "This boy is a real king," I wouldn't have argued the point.

An abrupt hush came in the murmuring around us, leaving only the rustle of rain, and the tramp, tramp, tramp of orderly marching up the street—Einarson's men. Everybody commenced to talk at once, happily, expectantly, cheered by the approach of those whose part it was to do the heavy work.

An officer in a glistening slicker pushed through the crowd—a small, dapper boy with too large a sword. He saluted Grantham elaborately, and said in English, of which he seemed proud:

"Colonel Einarson's respects, Mister, and this progress goes betune."

I wondered what the last word meant.

Grantham smiled and said: "Convey my thanks to Colonel Einarson."

The banker appeared again, bold enough now to join us. Others who had been at the meeting appeared. We made an inner group around the statue, with the mob around us—

more easily seen now in the gray of early morning. I didn't
see the countryman into whose face Einarson had spat.

The rain soaked us. We shifted our feet, shivered, and
talked. Daylight came slowly, showing more and more who
stood around us wet and curious-eyed. On the edge of the
crowd men burst into cheers. The rest of them took it up.
They forgot their wet misery, laughed and danced, hugged
and kissed one another. A bearded man in a leather coat came
to us, bowed to Grantham, and explained that Einarson's
own regiment could be seen occupying the Administration
Building and the Executive Residence.

Day came fully. The mob around us opened to make way
for an automobile that was surrounded by a squad of cavalrymen. It stopped in front of us. Colonel Einarson, holding a
bare sword in his hand, stepped out of the car, saluted, and
held the door open for Grantham and me. He followed us in,
smelling of victory like a chorus girl of Coty. The cavalrymen
closed around the car again, and we were driven to the
Administration Building, through a crowd that yelled and ran
red-faced and happy after us. It was all quite theatrical.

CHAPTER XIV

CORONATION

"THE city is ours," said Einarson, leaning forward in his
seat, his sword's point on the car floor, his hands on its
hilt. "The President, the Deputies, nearly every official of
importance, is taken. Not a single shot fired, not a window
broken!"

He was proud of his revolution, and I didn't blame him. I
wasn't sure that he might not have brains, after all. He had
had sense enough to park his civilian adherents in the plaza
until his soldiers had done their work.

We got out at the Administration Building, walking up the
steps between rows of infantrymen at present-arms, rain
sparkling on their fixed bayonets. More green-uniformed soldiers presented arms along the corridors. We went into an
elaborately furnished dining-room, where fifteen or twenty
officers stood up to receive us. There were lots of speeches
made. Everybody was triumphant. All through breakfast there

was much talking. I didn't understand any of it. I attended to my eating.

After the meal we went to the Deputies' Chamber, a large, oval room with curved rows of benches and desks facing a raised platform. Besides three desks on the platform, some twenty chairs had been put there, facing the curved seats. Our breakfast party occupied these chairs. I noticed that Grantham and I were the only civilians on the platform. None of our fellow conspirators were there, except those who were in Einarson's army. I wasn't so fond of that.

Grantham sat in the first row of chairs, between Einarson and me. We looked down on the Deputies. There were perhaps a hundred of them distributed among the curved benches, split sharply in two groups. Half of them, on the right side of the room, were revolutionists. They stood up and hurrahed at us. The other half, on the left, were prisoners. Most of them seemed to have dressed hurriedly. They looked at us with uneasy eyes.

Around the room, shoulder to shoulder against the wall except on the platform and where the doors were, stood Einarson's soldiers.

An old man came in between two soldiers—a mild-eyed old gentleman, bald, stooped, with a wrinkled, clean-shaven, scholarly face.

"Doctor Semich," Grantham whispered.

The President's guards took him to the center one of the three desks on the platform. He paid no attention to us who were sitting on the platform, and he did not sit down.

A red-haired Deputy—one of the revolutionary party—got up and talked. His fellows cheered when he had finished. The President spoke—three words in a very dry, very calm voice, and left the platform to walk back the way he had come, the two soldiers accompanying him.

"Refused to resign," Grantham informed me.

The red-haired Deputy came up on the platform and took the center desk. The legislative machinery began to grind. Men talked briefly, apparently to the point—revolutionists. None of the prisoner Deputies rose. A vote was taken. A few of the in-wrongs didn't vote. Most of them seemed to vote with the ins.

"They've revoked the constitution," Grantham whispered.

The Deputies were hurrahing again—those who were there voluntarily. Einarson leaned over and mumbled to Grantham and me:

"That is as far as we may safely go to-day. It leaves all in our hands."

"Time to listen to a suggestion?" I asked.

"Yes."

"Will you excuse us a moment?" I said to Grantham, and got up and walked to one of the rear corners of the platform.

Einarson followed me, frowning suspiciously.

"Why not give Grantham his crown now?" I asked when we were standing in the corner, my right shoulder touching his left, half facing each other, half facing the corner, our backs to the officers who sat on the platform, the nearest less than ten feet away. "Push it through. You can do it. There'll be a howl, of course. To-morrow, as a concession to that howl, you'll make him abdicate. You'll get credit for that. You'll be fifty percent stronger with the people. Then you will be in a position to make it look as if the revolution was his party, and that you were the patriot who kept this newcomer from grabbing the throne. Meanwhile you'll be dictator, and whatever else you want to be when the time comes. See what I mean? Let him bear the brunt. You catch yours on the rebound."

He liked the idea, but he didn't like it to come from me. His little dark eyes pried into mine.

"Why should you suggest this?" he asked.

"What do you care? I promise you he'll abdicate within twenty-four hours."

He smiled under his mustache and raised his head. I knew a major in the A.E.F. who always raised his head like that when he was going to issue an unpleasant order. I spoke quickly:

"My raincoat—do you see it's folded over my left arm?"

He said nothing, but his eyelids crept together.

"You can't see my left hand," I went on.

His eyes were slits, but he said nothing.

"There's an automatic in it," I wound up.

"Well?" he asked contemptuously.

"Nothing—only—get funny, and I'll let your guts out."

"Ach!"—he didn't take me seriously—"and after that?"

"I don't know. Think it over carefully, Einarson. I've deliberately put myself in a position where I've got to go ahead if you don't give in. I can kill you before you do anything. I'm going to do it if you don't give Grantham his crown now. Understand? I've got to. Maybe—most likely—your boys would get me afterward, but you'd be dead. If I back down now, you'll certainly have me shot. So I can't back down. If neither of us backs down, we'll both take the leap. *I've* gone too far to weaken now. *You'll* have to give in. Think it over. I can't possibly be bluffing."

He thought it over. Some of the color washed out of his face, and a little rippling movement appeared in the flesh of his chin. I crowded him along by moving the raincoat enough to show him the muzzle of the gun that actually was there in my left hand. I had the big heaver—he hadn't nerve enough to take a chance on dying in his hour of victory. A little earlier, a little later, I might have had to gun him. Now I had him.

He strode across the platform to the desk at which the red-head sat, drove the red-head away with a snarl and a gesture, leaned over the desk, and bellowed down into the chamber. I stood a little to one side of him, a little behind, so no one could get between us.

No Deputy made a sound for a long minute after the Colonel's bellow had stopped. Then one of the anti-revolutionists jumped to his feet and yelped bitterly. Einarson pointed a long brown finger at him. Two soldiers left their places by the wall, took the Deputy roughly by neck and arms, and dragged him out. Another Deputy stood up, talked, and was removed. After the fifth drag-out everything was peaceful.

Einarson put a question and got a unanimous answer.

He turned to me, his gaze darting from my face to my raincoat and back, and said: "That is done."

"We'll have the coronation now," I commanded. "Any kind of ceremony, so it's short."

I missed most of the ceremony. I was busy keeping my hold on the florid officer, but finally Lionel Grantham was officially installed as Lionel the First, King of Muravia. Einarson and I congratulated him, or whatever it was, together. Then I took the officer aside.

"We're going to take a walk," I said. "No foolishness. Take me out a side door."

I had him now, almost without needing the gun. He would have to deal quietly with Grantham and me—kill us without any publicity—if he were to avoid being laughed at—this man who had let himself be stuck up and robbed of a throne in the middle of his army.

We went roundabout from the Administration Building to the Hotel of the Republic without meeting any one who knew us. The population was all in the plaza. We found the hotel deserted. I made him run the elevator to my floor, and herded him down the corridor to my room.

I tried the door, found it unlocked, let go the knob, and told him to go in. He pushed the door open and stopped.

Romaine Frankl was sitting crosslegged in the middle of my bed, sewing a button on one of my union suits.

CHAPTER XV

BARGAIN HUNTER

I PRODDED Einarson into the room and closed the door. Romaine looked at him and at the automatic that was now uncovered in my hand. With burlesque disappointment she said:

"Oh, you haven't killed him yet!"

Colonel Einarson stiffened. He had an audience now—one that saw his humiliation. He was likely to do something. I'd have to handle him with gloves, or—maybe the other way was better. I kicked him on the ankle and snarled:

"Get over in the corner and sit down!"

He spun around to me. I jabbed the muzzle of the pistol in his face, grinding his lip between it and his teeth. When his head jerked back I slammed him in the belly with my other fist. He grabbed for air with a wide mouth. I pushed him over to a chair in one corner of the room.

Romaine laughed and shook a finger at me, saying:

"You're a rowdy!"

"What else can I do?" I protested, chiefly for my prisoner's benefit. "When somebody's watching him he gets notions that he's a hero. I stuck him up and made him crown the boy king. But this bird has still got the army, which is the government. I can't let go of him, or both Lionel the Once and I will gather lead. It hurts me more than it does him to have to knock him around, but I can't help myself. I've got to keep him sensible."

"You're doing wrong by him," she replied. "You've got no right to mistreat him. The only polite thing for you to do is to cut his throat in a gentlemanly manner."

"Ach!" Einarson's lungs were working again.

"Shut up," I yelled at him, "or I'll knock you double-jointed."

He glared at me, and I asked the girl: "What'll we do with him? I'd be glad to cut his throat, but the trouble is, his army might avenge him, and I'm not a fellow who likes to have anybody's army avenging on him."

"We'll give him to Vasilije," she said, swinging her feet over the side of the bed and standing up. "He'll know what to do."

"Where is he?"

"Upstairs in Grantham's suite, finishing his morning nap, I suppose."

Then she said lightly, casually, as if she hadn't been thinking seriously about it: "So you had the boy crowned?"

"I did. You want it for your Vasilije? Good! We want five million American dollars for our abdication. Grantham put in three to finance the doings, and he deserves a profit. He's been regularly elected by the Deputies. He's got no real backing here, but he can get support from the neighbors. Don't overlook that. There are a couple of countries not a million miles away that would gladly send in an army to support a legitimate king in exchange for whatever concessions they liked. But Lionel the First isn't unreasonable. He thinks it would be better for you to have a native ruler. All he asks is a decent provision from the government. Five million is low enough, and he'll abdicate tomorrow. Tell that to your Vasilije."

She went around me to avoid passing between my gun and its target, stood on tiptoe to kiss my ear, and said:

"You and your king are a couple of brigands. I'll be back in a few minutes."

She went out.

"Ten millions," Colonel Einarson said.

"I can't trust you now," I said. "You'd pay us off in front of a firing squad."

"You can trust this pig Djudakovich?"

"He's got no reason to hate us."

"He will when he's told of you and his Romaine."

I laughed.

"Besides, how can he be king? Ach! What is his promise to pay if he cannot become in a position to pay? Suppose even I am dead. What will he do with my army? Ach! You have seen the pig! What kind of king is he?"

"I don't know," I said truthfully. "I'm told he was a good Minister of Police because inefficiency would spoil his comfort. Maybe he'd be a good dictator or king for the same reason. I've seen him once. He's a bloated mountain, but there's nothing ridiculous about him. He weighs a ton, and moves without shaking the floor. I'd be afraid to try on him what I did to you."

This insult brought the soldier up on his feet, very tall and straight. His eyes burned at me while his mouth hardened in a thin line. He was going to make trouble for me before I was rid of him. I scowled at him and wondered what I should do next.

The door opened and Vasilije Djudakovich came in, followed by the girl. I grinned at the fat Minister. He nodded without smiling. His little dark eyes moved coldly from me to Einarson.

The girl said:

"The government will give Lionel the First a draft for four million dollars, American, on either a Vienna or Athens bank, in exchange for his abdication." She dropped her official tone and added: "That's every nickel I could get out of him."

"You and your Vasilije are a couple of rotten bargain hunters," I complained. "But we'll take it. We've got to have a special train to Saloniki—one that will put us across the border before the abdication goes into effect."

"That will be arranged," she promised.

"Good! Now to do all this your Vasilije has got to take the army away from Einarson. Can he do it?"

"Ach!" Colonel Einarson reared up his head, swelled his thick chest. "That is precisely what he has got to do!"

The fat man grumbled sleepily through his yellow beard. Romaine came over and put a hand on my arm.

"Vasilije wants a private talk with Einarson. Leave it to him. We'll go upstairs."

I agreed and offered Djudakovich my automatic. He paid no attention to the gun or to me. He was looking with a clammy sort of patience at the officer. I went out with the girl and closed the door. At the foot of the stairs I took her by the shoulders and turned her around.

"Can I trust your Vasilije?" I asked.

"Oh my dear, he could handle half a dozen Einarsons."

"I don't mean that. He won't try to gyp me?"

She frowned at me, asking: "Why should you start worrying about that now?"

"He doesn't seem to be exactly all broken out with friendliness."

She laughed, and twisted her face around to bite at one of my hands on her shoulders.

"He's got ideals," she explained. "He despises you and your king for a pair of adventurers who are making a profit out of his country's troubles. That's why he's so sniffy. But he'll keep his word."

Maybe he would, I thought, but he hadn't given me his word—the girl had.

"I'm going over to see His Majesty," I said. "I won't be long—then I'll join you up in his suite. What was the idea of the sewing act? I had no buttons off."

"You did," she contradicted me, rummaging in my pocket for cigarettes. "I pulled one off when one of our men told me you and Einarson were headed this way. I thought it would look domestic."

CHAPTER XVI
LIONEL REX

I FOUND my king in a wine and gold drawing-room in the Executive Residence, surrounded by Muravia's socially and politically ambitious. Uniforms were still in the majority, but a sprinkling of civilians had finally got to him, along with their wives and daughters. He was too occupied to see me for a few minutes, so I stood around, looking the folks over. Particularly one—a tall girl in black, who stood apart from the others, at a window.

I noticed her first because she was beautiful in face and body, and then I studied her more closely because of the expression in the brown eyes with which she watched the new king. If ever anybody looked proud of anybody else, this girl did of Grantham. The way she stood there, alone, by the window, and looked at him—he would have had to be at least a combination of Apollo, Socrates, and Alexander to deserve half of it. Valeska Radnjak, I supposed.

I looked at the boy. His face was proud and flushed, and every two seconds turned toward the girl at the window while he listened to the jabbering of the worshipful group around him. I knew he wasn't any Apollo-Socrates-Alexander, but he managed to look the part. He had found a spot in the world that he liked. I was half sorry he couldn't hang on to it, but my regrets didn't keep me from deciding that I had wasted enough time.

I pushed through the crowd toward him. He recognized me with the eyes of a park sleeper being awakened from sweet dreams by a night-stick on his shoe-soles. He excused himself to the others and took me down a corridor to a room with stained glass windows and richly carved office furniture.

"This was Doctor Semich's office," he told me. "I shall——" He broke off and looked away from me.

"You'll be in Greece by to-morrow," I said bluntly.

He frowned at his feet, a stubborn frown.

"You ought to know you can't hold on," I argued. "You may think everything is going smoothly. If you do, you're deaf, dumb, and blind. I put you in with the muzzle of a gun against Einarson's liver. I've kept you in this long by kidnaping him. I've made a deal with Djudakovich—the only strong man I've seen here. It's up to him to handle Einarson. I can't hold him any longer. Djudakovich will make a good dictator, and a good king later, if he wants it. He promises you four million dollars and a special train and safe-conduct to Saloniki. You go out with your head up. You've been a king.

You've taken a country out of bad hands and put it into good—this fat guy is real. And you've made yourself a million profit."

Grantham looked at me and said:

"No. You go. I shall see it through. These people have trusted me, and I shall——"

"My God, that's old Doc Semich's line! These people haven't trusted you—not a bit of it. I'm the people who trusted you. I made you king, understand? I made you king so you could go home with your chin up—not so you could stay here and make an ass of yourself! I bought help with promises. One of them was that you'd get out within twenty-four hours. You've got to keep the promises I made in your name. The people trusted you, huh? You were crammed down their throats, my son! And I did the cramming! Now I'm going to uncram you. If it happens to be tough on your romance—if your Valeska won't take any price less than this lousy country's throne—that's——"

"That's enough." His voice came from some point at least fifty feet above me. "You shall have your abdication. I don't want the money. You will send word to me when the train is ready."

"Write the get-out now," I ordered.

He went over to the desk, found a sheet of paper, and with a steady hand wrote that in leaving Muravia he renounced his throne and all rights to it. He signed the paper *Lionel Rex* and gave it to me. I pocketed it and began sympathetically:

"I can understand your feelings, and I'm sorry that—"

He put his back to me and walked out of the room. I returned to the hotel.

At the fifth floor I left the elevator and walked softly to the door of my room. No sound came through. I tried the door, found it unlocked, and went in. Emptiness. Even my clothes and bags were gone. I went up to Grantham's suite.

Djudakovich, Romaine, Einarson, and half the police force were there.

CHAPTER XVII
MOB LAW

COLONEL EINARSON sat very erect in an armchair in the middle of the room. Dark hair and mustache bristled. His chin was out, muscles bulged everywhere in his florid face, his eyes were hot—he was in one of his finest scrapping moods. That came of giving him an audience.

I scowled at Djudakovich, who stood on wide-spread giant's legs with his back to a window. Why hadn't the fat fool known enough to keep Einarson off in a lonely corner, where he could be handled? Djudakovich looked sleepily at my scowl.

Romaine floated around and past the policemen who stood or sat everywhere in the room, and came to where I stood, inside the door.

"Are your arrangements all made?" she asked.

"Got the abdication in my pocket."

"Give it to me."

"Not yet," I said. "First I've got to know that your Vasilije is as big as he looks. Einarson doesn't look squelched to me. Your fat boy ought to have known he'd blossom out in front of an audience."

"There's no telling what Vasilije is up to," she said lightly, "except that it will be adequate."

I wasn't as sure of that as she was. Djudakovich rumbled a question at her, and she gave him a quick answer. He rumbled some more—at the policemen. They began to go away from us, singly, in pairs, in groups. When the last one had gone the fat man pushed words out between his yellow whiskers at Einarson. Einarson stood up, chest out, shoulders back, grinning confidently under his flowing dark mustache.

"What now?" I asked the girl.

"Come along and you'll see," she said. Her breath came and went quickly, and the gray of her eyes was almost as dark as the black.

The four of us went downstairs and out the hotel's front door. The rain had stopped. In the plaza was gathered most of Stefania's population, thickest in front of the Administration Building and Executive Residence. Over their heads we could see the sheepskin caps of Einarson's regiment, still around those buildings as he had left them.

We—or at least Einarson—were recognized and cheered as we crossed the plaza. Einarson and Djudakovich went side by side in front, the soldier marching, the fat giant waddling. Romaine and I went close behind them. We headed straight for the Administration Building.

"What is he up to?" I asked irritably.

She patted my arm, smiled excitedly, and said:

"Wait and see."

There didn't seem to be anything else to do—except worry while I waited.

We arrived at the foot of the Administration Building's stone steps. Bayonets had an uncomfortably cold gleam in the early evening light as Einarson's troops presented arms. We climbed the steps. On the broad top step Einarson and Djudakovich turned to face soldiers and citizens below. The girl and I moved around behind the pair. Her teeth were chattering, her fingers were digging into my arm, but her lips and eyes were smiling recklessly.

The soldiers who were around the Executive Residence came to join those already before us, pushing back the citizens to make room. Another detachment came up. Einarson raised his hand, bawled a dozen words, growled at Djudakovich, and stepped back, giving the blond giant the center of the stage.

Djudakovich spoke, a drowsy, effortless roar that could have been heard as far as the hotel. As he spoke, he took a paper out of his pocket and held it before him. There was nothing theatrical in his voice or manner. He might have been talking about anything not too important. But—looking at his audience, you'd have known it was important.

The soldiers had broken ranks to crowd nearer, faces were reddening, a bayoneted gun was shaken aloft here and there. Behind them the citizens were looking at one another with frightened faces, jostling each other, some trying to get nearer, some trying to get away.

Djudakovich talked on. The turmoil grew. A soldier pushed

through his fellows and started up the steps, others at his heels. Angry voices raised cries.

Einarson cut in on the fat man's speech, stepping to the edge of the top step, bawling down at the upturned faces, with the voice of a man accustomed to being obeyed.

The soldiers on the steps tumbled down. Einarson bawled again. The broken ranks were slowly straightened, flourished guns were grounded. Einarson stood silent a moment, glowering at his troops, and then began an address. I couldn't understand his words any more than I had the fat man's, but there was no question about his impressiveness. And there was no doubt that the anger was going out of the faces below.

I looked at Romaine. She shivered and was no longer smiling. I looked at Djudakovich. He was as still and as emotionless as the mountain he resembled.

I wished I knew what it was all about, so I'd know whether it was wisest to shoot Einarson and duck through the apparently empty building behind us or not. I could guess that the paper in Djudakovich's hand had been evidence of some sort against the Colonel, evidence that would have stirred the soldiers to the point of attacking him if they hadn't been too accustomed to obeying him.

While I was wishing and guessing, Einarson finished his address, stepped to one side, clicked his heels together, pointed a finger at Djudakovich, barked an order.

Down below, soldiers' faces were indecisive, shifty-eyed, but four of them stepped briskly out at their colonel's order and came up the steps. "So," I thought, "my fat candidate has lost! Well, he can have the firing squad. The back door for mine." My hand had been holding the gun in my coat pocket for a long time. I kept it there while I took a slow step back, drawing the girl with me.

"Move when I tell you," I muttered.

"Wait!" she gasped. "Look!"

The fat giant, sleepy-eyed as ever, put out an enormous paw and caught the wrist of Einarson's pointing hand. Pulled Einarson down. Let go the wrist and caught the Colonel's shoulder. Lifted him off his feet with that one hand that held his shoulder. Shook him at the soldiers below. Shook Einarson at them with one hand. Shook his piece of paper—whatever it was—at them with the other. And I'm damned if one seemed any more strain on his monstrous arms than the other!

While he shook them—man and paper—he roared sleepily, and when he had finished roaring he flung his two handfuls down to the wild-eyed ranks. Flung them with a gesture that said, *"Here is the man and here is the evidence against him. Do what you like."*

And the soldiers who had cringed back into ranks at Einarson's command when he stood tall and domineering above them, did what could have been expected when he was tossed down to them.

They tore him apart—actually—piece by piece. They dropped their guns and fought to get at him. Those farther away climbed over those nearer, smothering them, trampling them. They surged back and forth in front of the steps, an insane pack of men turned wolves, savagely struggling to destroy a man who must have died before he had been down half a minute.

I put the girl's hand off my arm and went to face Djudakovich.

"Muravia's yours," I said. "I don't want anything but our draft and train. Here's the abdication."

Romaine swiftly translated my words and then Djuda-kovich's:

"The train is ready now. The draft will be delivered there. Do you wish to go over for Grantham?"

"No. Send him down. How do I find the train?"

"I'll take you," she said. "We'll go through the building and out a side door."

One of Djudakovich's detectives sat at the wheel of a car in front of the hotel. Romaine and I got in it. Across the plaza tumult was still boiling. Neither of us said anything while the car whisked us through darkening streets. She sat as far from me as the width of the rear seat would let her.

Presently she asked very softly:

"And now you despise me?"

"No." I reached for her. "But I hate mobs, lynchings—they sicken me. No matter how wrong the man is, if a mob's against him, I'm for him. The only thing I ever pray to God for is a chance some day to squat down behind a machine gun with a lynching party in front of me. I had no use for Einarson, but I wouldn't have given him that! Well, what's done is done. What was the document?"

"A letter from Mahmoud. He had left it with a friend to be given to Vasilije if anything ever happened to him. He knew Einarson, it seems, and prepared his revenge. The letter confessed his—Mahmoud's—part in the assassination of General Radnjak, and said that Einarson was also implicated. The army worshiped Radnjak, and Einarson wanted the army."

"Your Vasilije could have used that to chase Einarson out—without feeding him to the wolves," I complained.

She shook her head and said:

"Vasilije was right. Bad as it was, that was the way to do it. It's over and settled forever, with Vasilije in power. An Einarson alive, an army not knowing he had killed their idol—too risky. Up to the end Einarson thought he had power enough to hold his troops, no matter what they knew. He——"

"All right—it's done. And I'm glad to be through with this king business. Kiss me."

She did, and whispered:

"When Vasilije dies—and he can't live long, the way he eats—I'm coming to San Francisco."

"You're a cold-blooded hussy," I said.

Lionel Grantham, ex-king of Muravia, was only five minutes behind us in reaching our train. He wasn't alone. Valeska Radnjak, looking as much like the queen of something as if she had been, was with him. She didn't seem to be all broken up over the loss of her throne.

The boy was pleasant and polite enough to me during our rattling trip to Saloniki, but obviously not very comfortable in my company. His bride-to-be didn't know anybody but the boy existed, unless she happened to find some one else directly in front of her. So I didn't wait for their wedding, but left Saloniki on a boat that pulled out a couple of hours after we arrived.

I left the draft with them, of course. They decided to take out Lionel's three millions and return the fourth to Muravia. And I went back to San Francisco to quarrel with my boss over what he thought were unnecessary five- and ten-dollar items in my expense account.

Fly Paper

I T WAS a wandering daughter job.

The Hambletons had been for several generations a wealthy and decently prominent New York family. There was nothing in the Hambleton history to account for Sue, the youngest member of the clan. She grew out of childhood with a kink that made her dislike the polished side of life, like the rough. By the time she was twenty-one, in 1926, she definitely preferred Tenth Avenue to Fifth, grifters to bankers, and Hymie the Riveter to the Honorable Cecil Windown, who had asked her to marry him.

The Hambletons tried to make Sue behave, but it was too late for that. She was legally of age. When she finally told them to go to hell and walked out on them there wasn't much they could do about it. Her father, Major Waldo Hambleton, had given up all the hopes he ever had of salvaging her, but he didn't want her to run into any grief that could be avoided. So he came into the Continental Detective Agency's New York office and asked to have an eye kept on her.

Hymie the Riveter was a Philadelphia racketeer who had moved north to the big city, carrying a Thompson submachine-gun wrapped in blue-checkered oil cloth, after a disagreement with his partners. New York wasn't so good a field as Philadelphia for machine-gun work. The Thompson lay idle for a year or so while Hymie made expenses with an automatic, preying on small-time crap games in Harlem.

Three or four months after Sue went to live with Hymie he made what looked like a promising connection with the first of the crew that came into New York from Chicago to organize the city on the western scale. But the boys from Chi didn't want Hymie; they wanted the Thompson. When he showed it to them, as the big item in his application for employment, they shot holes in the top of Hymie's head and went away with the gun.

Sue Hambleton buried Hymie, had a couple of lonely weeks in which she hocked a ring to eat, and then got a job as hostess in a speakeasy run by a Greek named Vassos.

One of Vassos' customers was Babe McCloor, two hundred and fifty pounds of hard Scotch-Irish-Indian bone and muscle, a black-haired, blue-eyed, swarthy giant who was resting up after doing a fifteen-year hitch in Leavenworth for ruining most of the smaller post offices between New Orleans and Omaha. Babe was keeping himself in drinking money while he rested by playing with pedestrians in dark streets.

Babe liked Sue. Vassos liked Sue. Sue liked Babe. Vassos didn't like that. Jealousy spoiled the Greek's judgment. He kept the speakeasy door locked one night when Babe wanted to come in. Babe came in, bringing pieces of the door with him. Vassos got his gun out, but couldn't shake Sue off his arm. He stopped trying when Babe hit him with the part of the door that had the brass knob on it. Babe and Sue went away from Vassos' together.

Up to that time the New York office had managed to keep in touch with Sue. She hadn't been kept under constant surveillance. Her father hadn't wanted that. It was simply a matter of sending a man around every week or so to see that she was still alive, to pick up whatever information he could from her friends and neighbors, without, of course, letting her know she was being tabbed. All that had been easy enough, but when she and Babe went away after wrecking the gin mill, they dropped completely out of sight.

After turning the city upside-down, the New York office sent a journal on the job to the other Continental branches throughout the country, giving the information above and enclosing photographs and descriptions of Sue and her new playmate. That was late in 1927.

We had enough copies of the photographs to go around, and for the next month or so whoever had a little idle time on his hands spent it looking through San Francisco and Oakland for the missing pair. We didn't find them. Operatives in other cities, doing the same thing, had the same luck.

Then, nearly a year later, a telegram came to us from the New York office. Decoded, it read:

> Major Hambleton today received telegram from daughter in San Francisco *quote* Please wire me thousand dollars care apartment two hundred

six number six hundred one Eddis Street *stop* I will come home if you will let me *stop* Please tell me if I can come but please please wire money anyway *unquote* Hambleton authorizes payment of money to her immediately *stop* Detail competent operative to call on her with money and to arrange for her return home *stop* If possible have man and woman operative accompany her here *stop* Hambleton wiring her *stop* Report immediately by wire.

II

The Old Man gave me the telegram and a check, saying:

"You know the situation. You'll know how to handle it."

I pretended I agreed with him, went down to the bank, swapped the check for a bundle of bills of several sizes, caught a street car, and went up to 601 Eddis Street, a fairly large apartment building on the corner of Larkin.

The name on Apartment 206's vestibule mail box was J. M. Wales.

I pushed 206's button. When the locked door buzzed off I went into the building, past the elevator to the stairs, and up a flight. 206 was just around the corner from the stairs.

The apartment door was opened by a tall, slim man of thirty-something in neat dark clothes. He had narrow dark eyes set in a long pale face. There was some gray in the dark hair brushed flat to his scalp.

"Miss Hambleton," I said.

"Uh—what about her?" His voice was smooth, but not too smooth to be agreeable.

"I'd like to see her."

His upper eyelids came down a little and the brows over them came a little closer together. He asked, "Is it—?" and stopped, watching me steadily.

I didn't say anything. Presently he finished his question:

"Something to do with a telegram?"

"Yeah."

His long face brightened immediately. He asked:

"You're from her father?"

"Yeah."

He stepped back and swung the door wide open, saying:

"Come in. Major Hambleton's wire came to her only a few minutes ago. He said someone would call."

We went through a small passageway into a sunny living-room that was cheaply furnished, but neat and clean enough.

"Sit down," the man said, pointing at a brown rocking chair.

I sat down. He sat on the burlap-covered sofa facing me. I looked around the room. I didn't see anything to show that a woman was living there.

He rubbed the long bridge of his nose with a longer fore-finger and asked slowly:

"You brought the money?"

I said I'd feel more like talking with her there.

He looked at the finger with which he had been rubbing his nose, and then up at me, saying softly:

"But I'm her friend."

I said, "Yeah?" to that.

"Yes," he repeated. He frowned slightly, drawing back the corners of his thin-lipped mouth. "I've only asked whether you've brought the money."

I didn't say anything.

"The point is," he said quite reasonably, "that if you brought the money she doesn't expect you to hand it over to anybody except her. If you didn't bring it she doesn't want to see you. I don't think her mind can be changed about that. That's why I asked if you had brought it."

"I brought it."

He looked doubtfully at me. I showed him the money I had got from the bank. He jumped up briskly from the sofa.

"I'll have her here in a minute or two," he said over his shoulder as his long legs moved him toward the door. At the door he stopped to ask: "Do you know her? Or shall I have her bring means of identifying herself?"

"That would be best," I told him.

He went out, leaving the corridor door open.

III

In five minutes he was back with a slender blonde girl of twenty-three in pale green silk. The looseness of her small mouth and the puffiness around her blue eyes weren't yet pronounced enough to spoil her prettiness.

I stood up.

"This is Miss Hambleton," he said.

She gave me a swift glance and then lowered her eyes again, nervously playing with the strap of a handbag she held.

"You can identify yourself?" I asked.

"Sure," the man said. "Show them to him, Sue."

She opened the bag, brought out some papers and things, and held them up for me to take.

"Sit down, sit down," the man said as I took them.

They sat on the sofa. I sat in the rocking chair again and examined the things she had given me. There were two letters addressed to Sue Hambleton here, her father's telegram welcoming her home, a couple of receipted department store bills, an automobile driver's license, and a savings account pass book that showed a balance of less than ten dollars.

By the time I had finished my examination the girl's embarrassment was gone. She looked levelly at me, as did the man beside her. I felt in my pocket, found my copy of the photograph New York had sent us at the beginning of the hunt, and looked from it to her.

"Your mouth could have shrunk, maybe," I said, "but how could your nose have got that much longer?"

"If you don't like my nose," she said, "how'd you like to go to hell?" Her face had turned red.

"That's not the point. It's a swell nose, but it's not Sue's." I held the photograph out to her. "See for yourself."

She glared at the photograph and then at the man.

"What a smart guy you are," she told him.

He was watching me with dark eyes that had a brittle shine to them between narrow-drawn eyelids. He kept on watching me while he spoke to her out the side of his mouth, crisply:

"Pipe down."

She piped down. He sat and watched me. I sat and watched him. A clock ticked seconds away behind me. His eyes began shifting their focus from one of my eyes to the other. The girl sighed.

He said in a low voice: "Well?"

I said: "You're in a hole."

"What can you make out of it?" he asked casually.

"Conspiracy to defraud."

The girl jumped up and hit one of his shoulders angrily with the back of a hand, crying:

"What a smart guy you are, to get me in a jam like this. It was going to be duck soup—yeh! Eggs in the coffee—yeh! Now look at you. You haven't even got guts enough to tell this guy to go chase himself." She spun around to face me, pushing her red face down at me—I was still sitting in the rocker—snarling: "Well, what are you waiting for? Waiting to be kissed good-by? We don't owe you anything, do we? We didn't get any of your lousy money, did we? Outside, then. Take the air. Dangle."

"Stop it, sister," I growled. "You'll bust something."

The man said:

"For God's sake stop that bawling, Peggy, and give somebody else a chance." He addressed me: "Well, what do you want?"

"How'd you get into this?" I asked.

He spoke quickly, eagerly:

"A fellow named Kenny gave me that stuff and told me about this Sue Hambleton, and her old man having plenty. I thought I'd give it a whirl. I figured the old man would either wire the dough right off the reel or wouldn't send it at all. I didn't figure on this send-a-man stuff. Then when his wire came, saying he was sending a man to see her, I ought to have dropped it.

"But hell! Here was a man coming with a grand in cash. That was too good to let go of without a try. It looked like there still might be a chance of copping, so I got Peggy to do Sue for me. If the man was coming today, it was a cinch he belonged out here on the Coast, and it was an even bet he wouldn't know Sue, would only have a description of her. From what Kenny had told me about her, I knew Peggy would come pretty close to fitting her description. I still don't see how you got that photograph. Television? I only wired the old man yesterday. I mailed a couple of letters to Sue, here, yesterday, so we'd have them with the other identification stuff to get the money from the telegraph company on."

"Kenny gave you the old man's address?"

"Sure he did."

"Did he give you Sue's?"

"No."

"How'd Kenny get hold of the stuff?"

"He didn't say."

"Where's Kenny now?"

"I don't know. He was on his way east, with something else on the fire, and couldn't fool with this. That's why he passed it on to me."

"Big-hearted Kenny," I said. "You know Sue Hambleton?"

"No," emphatically. "I'd never even heard of her till Kenny told me."

"I don't like this Kenny," I said, "though without him your story's got some good points. Could you tell it leaving him out?"

He shook his head slowly from side to side, saying:

"It wouldn't be the way it happened."

"That's too bad. Conspiracies to defraud don't mean as much to me as finding Sue. I might have made a deal with you."

He shook his head again, but his eyes were thoughtful, and his lower lip moved up to overlap the upper a little.

The girl had stepped back so she could see both of us as we talked, turning her face, which showed she didn't like us, from one to the other as we spoke our pieces. Now she fastened her gaze on the man, and her eyes were growing angry again.

I got up on my feet, telling him:

"Suit yourself. But if you want to play it that way I'll have to take you both in."

He smiled with indrawn lips and stood up.

The girl thrust herself in between us, facing him.

"This is a swell time to be dummying up," she spit at him. "Pop off, you lightweight, or I will. You're crazy if you think I'm going to take the fall with you."

"Shut up," he said in his throat.

"Shut me up," she cried.

He tried to, with both hands. I reached over her shoulders and caught one of his wrists, knocked the other hand up.

She slid out from between us and ran around behind me, screaming:

"Joe does know her. He got the things from her. She's at the St. Martin on O'Farrell Street—her and Babe McCloor."

While I listened to this I had to pull my head aside to let Joe's right hook miss me, had got his left arm twisted behind him, had turned my hip to catch his knee, and had got the palm of my left hand under his chin. I was ready to give his chin the Japanese tilt when he stopped wrestling and grunted:

"Let me tell it."

"Hop to it," I consented, taking my hands away from him and stepping back.

He rubbed the wrist I had wrenched, scowling past me at the girl. He called her four unlovely names, the mildest of which was "a dumb twist," and told her:

"He was bluffing about throwing us in the can. You don't think old man Hambleton's hunting for newspaper space, do you?" That wasn't a bad guess.

He sat on the sofa again, still rubbing his wrist. The girl stayed on the other side of the room, laughing at him through her teeth.

I said: "All right, roll it out, one of you."

"You've got it all," he muttered. "I glaumed that stuff last week when I was visiting Babe, knowing the story and hating to see a promising layout like that go to waste."

"What's Babe doing now?" I asked.

"I don't know."

"Is he still puffing them?"

"I don't know."

"Like hell you don't."

"I don't," he insisted. "If you know Babe you know you can't get anything out of him about what he's doing."

"How long have he and Sue been here?"

"About six months that I know of."

"Who's he mobbed up with?"

"I don't know. Any time Babe works with a mob he picks them up on the road and leaves them on the road."

"How's he fixed?"

"I don't know. There's always enough grub and liquor in the joint."

Half an hour of this convinced me that I wasn't going to get much information about my people here.

I went to the phone in the passageway and called the Agency. The boy on the switchboard told me MacMan was in the operatives' room. I asked to have him sent up to me, and went back to the living-room. Joe and Peggy took their heads apart when I came in.

MacMan arrived in less than ten minutes. I let him in and told him:

"This fellow says his name's Joe Wales, and the girl's supposed to be Peggy Carroll who lives upstairs in 421. We've got them cold for conspiracy to defraud, but I've made a deal with them. I'm going out to look at it now. Stay here with them, in this room. Nobody goes in or out, and nobody but you gets to the phone. There's a fire-escape in front of the window. The window's locked now. I'd keep it that way. If the deal turns out O.K. we'll let them go, but if they cut up on you while I'm gone there's no reason why you can't knock them around as much as you want."

MacMan nodded his hard round head and pulled a chair out between them and the door. I picked up my hat.

Joe Wales called:

"Hey, you're not going to uncover me to Babe, are you? That's got to be part of the deal."

"Not unless I have to."

"I'd just as leave stand the rap," he said. "I'd be safer in jail."

"I'll give you the best break I can," I promised, "but you'll have to take what's dealt you."

IV

Walking over to the St. Martin—only half a dozen blocks from Wales's place—I decided to go up against McCloor and the girl as a Continental op who suspected Babe of being in on a branch bank stick-up in Alameda the previous week. He hadn't been in on it—if the bank people had described half-correctly the men who had robbed them—so it wasn't likely my supposed suspicions would frighten him much. Clearing himself, he might give me some information I could use. The chief thing I wanted, of course, was a look at the girl, so I could report to her father that I had seen her. There was no reason for supposing that she and Babe knew her father was trying to keep an eye on her. Babe had a record. It was natural enough for sleuths to drop in now and then and try to hang something on him.

The St. Martin was a small three-story apartment house of red brick between two taller hotels. The vestibule register showed, *R. K. McCloor, 313*, as Wales and Peggy had told me.

I pushed the bell button. Nothing happened. Nothing happened any of the four times I pushed it. I pushed the button labeled *Manager*.

The door clicked open. I went indoors. A beefy woman in a pink-striped cotton dress that needed pressing stood in an apartment doorway just inside the street door.

"Some people named McCloor live here?" I asked.

"Three-thirteen," she said.

"Been living here long?"

She pursed her fat mouth, looked intently at me, hesitated, but finally said: "Since last June."

"What do you know about them?"

She balked at that, raising her chin and her eyebrows.

I gave her my card. That was safe enough; it fit in with the pretext I intended using upstairs.

Her face, when she raised it from reading the card, was oily with curiosity.

"Come in here," she said in a husky whisper, backing through the doorway.

I followed her into her apartment. We sat on a Chesterfield and she whispered:

"What is it?"

"Maybe nothing." I kept my voice low, playing up to her theatricals. "He's done time for safe-burglary. I'm trying to get a line on him now, on the off chance that he might have been tied up in a recent job. I don't know that he was. He may be going straight for all I know." I took his photograph—front and profile, taken at Leavenworth—out of my pocket. "This him?"

She seized it eagerly, nodded, said, "Yes, that's him, all right," turned it over to read the description on the back, and repeated, "Yes, that's him, all right."

"His wife is here with him?" I asked.

She nodded vigorously.

"I don't know her," I said. "What sort of looking girl is she?"

She described a girl who could have been Sue Hambleton. I couldn't show Sue's picture, that would have uncovered me if she and Babe heard about it.

I asked the woman what she knew about the McCloors. What she knew wasn't a great deal; paid their rent on time, kept irregular hours, had occasional drinking parties, quarreled a lot.

"Think they're in now?" I asked. "I got no answer on the bell."

"I don't know," she whispered. "I haven't seen either of them since night before last, when they had a fight."

"Much of a fight?"

"Not much worse than usual."

"Could you find out if they're in?" I asked.

She looked at me out of the ends of her eyes.

"I'm not going to make any trouble for you," I assured her. "But if they've blown I'd like to know it, and I reckon you would too."

"All right, I'll find out." She got up, patting a pocket in which keys jingled. "You wait here."

"I'll go as far as the third floor with you," I said, "and wait out of sight there."

"All right," she said reluctantly.

On the third floor, I remained by the elevator. She disappeared around a corner of the dim corridor, and presently a muffled electric bell rang. It rang three times. I heard her keys jingle and one of them grate in a lock. The lock clicked. I heard the doorknob rattle as she turned it.

Then a long moment of silence was ended by a scream that filled the corridor from wall to wall.

I jumped for the corner, swung around it, saw an open door ahead, went through it, and slammed the door shut behind me.

The scream had stopped.

I was in a small dark vestibule with three doors besides the one I had come through. One door was shut. One opened into a bathroom. I went to the other.

The fat manager stood just inside it, her round back to me. I pushed past her and saw what she was looking at.

Sue Hambleton, in pale yellow pajamas trimmed with black lace, was lying across a bed. She lay on her back. Her arms were stretched out over her head. One leg was bent under her, one stretched out so that its bare foot rested on the floor. That bare foot was whiter than a live foot could be. Her face was white as her foot, except for a mottled swollen area from the right eyebrow to the right cheek-bone and dark bruises on her throat.

"Phone the police," I told the woman, and began poking into corners, closets and drawers.

It was late afternoon when I returned to the Agency. I asked the file clerk to see if we had anything on Joe Wales and Peggy Carroll, and then went into the Old Man's office.

He put down some reports he had been reading, gave me a nodded invitation to sit down, and asked:

"You've seen her?"

"Yeah. She's dead."

The Old Man said, "Indeed," as if I had said it was raining, and smiled with polite attentiveness while I told him about it—from the time I had rung Wales's bell until I had joined the fat manager in the dead girl's apartment.

"She had been knocked around some, was bruised on the face and neck," I wound up. "But that didn't kill her."

"You think she was murdered?" he asked, still smiling gently.

"I don't know. Doc Jordan says he thinks it could have been arsenic. He's hunting for it in her now. We found a funny thing in the joint. Some thick sheets of dark gray paper were stuck in a book—*The Count of Monte Cristo*—wrapped in a month-old newspaper and wedged into a dark corner between the stove and the kitchen wall."

"Ah, arsenical fly paper," the Old Man murmured. "The Maybrick-Seddons trick. Mashed in water, four to six grains of arsenic can be soaked out of a sheet—enough to kill two people."

I nodded, saying:

"I worked on one in Louisville in 1916. The mulatto janitor saw McCloor leaving at half-past nine yesterday morning. She was probably dead before that. Nobody's seen him since.

Earlier in the morning the people in the next apartment had heard them talking, her groaning. But they had too many fights for the neighbors to pay much attention to that. The landlady told me they had a fight the night before that. The police are hunting for him."

"Did you tell the police who she was?"

"No. What do we do on that angle? We can't tell them about Wales without telling them all."

"I dare say the whole thing will have to come out," he said thoughtfully. "I'll wire New York."

I went out of his office. The file clerk gave me a couple of newspaper clippings. The first told me that, fifteen months ago, Joseph Wales, alias Holy Joe, had been arrested on the complaint of a farmer named Toomey that he had been taken for twenty-five hundred dollars on a phoney "Business Opportunity" by Wales and three other men. The second clipping said the case had been dropped when Toomey failed to appear against Wales in court—bought off in the customary manner by the return of part or all of his money. That was all our files held on Wales, and they had nothing on Peggy Carroll.

V

MacMan opened the door for me when I returned to Wales's apartment.

"Anything doing?" I asked him.

"Nothing—except they've been bellyaching a lot."

Wales came forward, asking eagerly:

"Satisfied now?"

The girl stood by the window, looking at me with anxious eyes.

I didn't say anything.

"Did you find her?" Wales asked, frowning. "She was where I told you?"

"Yeah," I said.

"Well, then." Part of his frown went away. "That lets Peggy and me out, doesn't—" He broke off, ran his tongue over his lower lip, put a hand to his chin, asked sharply: "You didn't give them the tip-off on me, did you?"

I shook my head, no.

He took his hand from his chin and asked irritably:

"What's the matter with you, then? What are you looking like that for?"

Behind him the girl spoke bitterly.

"I knew damned well it would be like this," she said. "I knew damned well we weren't going to get out of it. Oh, what a smart guy you are!"

"Take Peggy into the kitchen, and shut both doors," I told MacMan. "Holy Joe and I are going to have a real heart-to-heart talk."

The girl went out willingly, but when MacMan was closing the door she put her head in again to tell Wales:

"I hope he busts you in the nose if you try to hold out on him."

MacMan shut the door.

"Your playmate seems to think you know something," I said.

Wales scowled at the door and grumbled: "She's more help to me than a broken leg." He turned his face to me, trying to make it look frank and friendly. "What do you want? I came clean with you before. What's the matter now?"

"What do you guess?"

He pulled his lips in between his teeth.

"What do you want to make me guess for?" he demanded. "I'm willing to play ball with you. But what can I do if you won't tell me what you want? I can't see inside your head."

"You'd get a kick out of it if you could."

He shook his head wearily and walked back to the sofa, sitting down bent forward, his hands together between his knees.

"All right," he sighed. "Take your time about asking me. I'll wait for you."

I went over and stood in front of him. I took his chin between my left thumb and fingers, raising his head and bending my own down until our noses were almost touching. I said:

"Where you stumbled, Joe, was in sending the telegram right after the murder."

"He's dead?" It popped out before his eyes had even had time to grow round and wide.

The question threw me off balance. I had to wrestle with my forehead to keep it from wrinkling, and I put too much calmness in my voice when I asked:

"Is who dead?"

"Who? How do I know? Who do you mean?"

"Who did you think I meant?" I insisted.

"How do I know? Oh, all right! Old man Hambleton, Sue's father."

"That's right," I said, and took my hand away from his chin.

"And he was murdered, you say?" He hadn't moved his face an inch from the position into which I had lifted it. "How?"

"Arsenic—fly paper."

"Arsenic fly paper." He looked thoughtful. "That's a funny one."

"Yeah, very funny. Where'd you go about buying some if you wanted it?"

"Buying it? I don't know. I haven't seen any since I was a kid. Nobody uses fly paper here in San Francisco anyway. There aren't enough flies."

"Somebody used some here," I said, "on Sue."

"Sue?" He jumped so that the sofa squeaked under him.

"Yeah. Murdered yesterday morning—arsenical fly paper."

"Both of them?" he asked incredulously.

"Both of who?"

"Her and her father."

"Yeah."

He put his chin far down on his chest and rubbed the back of one hand with the palm of the other.

"Then I am in a hole," he said slowly.

"That's what," I cheerfully agreed. "Want to try talking yourself out of it?"

"Let me think."

I let him think, listening to the tick of the clock while he thought. Thinking brought drops of sweat out on his gray-white face. Presently he sat up straight, wiping his face with a fancily colored handkerchief.

"I'll talk," he said. "I've got to talk now. Sue was getting ready to ditch Babe. She and I were going away. She— Here, I'll show you."

He put his hand in his pocket and held out a folded sheet of thick notepaper to me. I took it and read:

> Dear Joe:—
>   I can't stand this much longer—we've simply got to go soon. Babe beat me again tonight. Please, if you really love me, let's make it soon.
>   Sue

The handwriting was a nervous woman's, tall, angular, and piled up.

"That's why I made the play for Hambleton's grand," he said. "I've been shatting on my uppers for a couple of months, and when that letter came yesterday I just had to raise dough somehow to get her away. She wouldn't have stood for tapping her father though, so I tried to swing it without her knowing."

"When did you see her last?"

"Day before yesterday, the day she mailed that letter. Only I saw her in the afternoon—she was here—and she wrote it that night."

"Babe suspect what you were up to?"

"We didn't think he did. I don't know. He was jealous as hell all the time, whether he had any reason to be or not."

"How much reason did he have?"

Wales looked me straight in the eye and said:

"Sue was a good kid."

I said: "Well, she's been murdered."

He didn't say anything.

Day was darkening into evening. I went to the door and pressed the light button. I didn't lose sight of Holy Joe Wales while I was doing it.

As I took my finger away from the button, something clicked at the window. The click was loud and sharp.

I looked at the window.

A man crouched there on the fire-escape, looking in through glass and lace curtain. He was a thick-featured dark man whose size identified him as Babe McCloor. The muzzle of a big black automatic was touching the glass in front of him. He had tapped the glass with it to catch our attention.

He had our attention.

There wasn't anything for me to do just then. I stood there and looked at him. I couldn't tell whether he was looking at me or at Wales. I could see him clearly enough, but the lace curtain spoiled my view of details like that. I imagined he wasn't neglecting either of us, and I didn't imagine the lace curtain hid much from him. He was closer to the curtain than we, and I had turned on the room's lights.

Wales, sitting dead still on the sofa, was looking at McCloor. Wales's face wore a peculiar, stiffly sullen expression. His eyes were sullen. He wasn't breathing.

McCloor flicked the nose of his pistol against the pane, and a triangular piece of glass fell out, tinkling apart on the floor. It didn't, I was afraid, make enough noise to alarm MacMan in the kitchen. There were two closed doors between here and there.

Wales looked at the broken pane and closed his eyes. He closed them slowly, little by little, exactly as if he were falling asleep. He kept his stiffly sullen blank face turned straight to the window.

McCloor shot him three times.

The bullets knocked Wales down on the sofa, back against the wall. Wales's eyes popped open, bulging. His lips crawled back over his teeth, leaving them naked to the gums. His tongue came out. Then his head fell down and he didn't move any more.

When McCloor jumped away from the window I jumped to it. While I was pushing the curtain aside, unlocking the window and raising it, I heard his feet land on the cement paving below.

MacMan flung the door open and came in, the girl at his heels.

"Take care of this," I ordered as I scrambled over the sill. "McCloor shot him."

VI

Wales's apartment was on the second floor. The fire-escape ended there with a counter-weighted iron ladder that a man's weight would swing down into a cement-paved court.

I went down as Babe McCloor had gone, swinging down on the ladder till within dropping distance of the court, and then letting go.

There was only one street exit to the court. I took it.

A startled looking, smallish man was standing in the middle of the sidewalk close to the court, gaping at me as I dashed out.

I caught his arm, shook it.

"A big guy running." Maybe I yelled. "Where?"

He tried to say something, couldn't, and waved his arm at billboards standing across the front of a vacant lot on the other side of the street.

I forgot to say, "Thank you," in my hurry to get over there.

I got behind the billboards by crawling under them instead of going to either end, where there were openings. The lot was large enough and weedy enough to give cover to any-body who wanted to lie down and bushwhack a pursuer— even anybody as large as Babe McCloor.

While I considered that, I heard a dog barking at one cor-ner of the lot. He could have been barking at a man who had run by. I ran to that corner of the lot. The dog was in a board-fenced backyard, at the corner of a narrow alley that ran from the lot to a street.

I chinned myself on the board fence, saw a wire-haired ter-rier alone in the yard, and ran down the alley while he was charging my part of the fence.

I put my gun back into my pocket before I left the alley for the street.

A small touring car was parked at the curb in front of a cigar store some fifteen feet from the alley. A policeman was talking to a slim dark-faced man in the cigar store doorway.

"The big fellow that come out of the alley a minute ago," I said. "Which way did he go?"

The policeman looked dumb. The slim man nodded his head down the street, said, "Down that way," and went on with his conversation.

I said, "Thanks," and went on down to the corner. There was a taxi phone there and two idle taxis. A block and a half below, a street car was going away.

"Did the big fellow who came down here a minute ago take a taxi or the street car?" I asked the two taxi chauffeurs who were leaning against one of the taxis.

The rattier looking one said:

"He didn't take a taxi."

I said:

"I'll take one. Catch that street car for me."

The street car was three blocks away before we got going. The street wasn't clear enough for me to see who got on and off it. We caught it when it stopped at Market Street.

"Follow along," I told the driver as I jumped out.

On the rear platform of the street car I looked through the glass. There were only eight or ten people aboard.

"There was a great big fellow got on at Hyde Street," I said to the conductor. "Where'd he get off?"

The conductor looked at the silver dollar I was turning over in my fingers and remembered that the big man got off at Taylor Street. That won the silver dollar.

I dropped off as the street car turned into Market Street. The taxi, close behind, slowed down, and its door swung open.

"Sixth and Mission," I said as I hopped in.

McCloor could have gone in any direction from Taylor Street. I had to guess. The best guess seemed to be that he would make for the other side of Market Street.

It was fairly dark by now. We had to go down to Fifth Street to get off Market, then over to Mission, and back up to Sixth. We got to Sixth Street without seeing McCloor. I couldn't see him on Sixth Street—either way from the crossing.

"On up to Ninth," I ordered, and while we rode told the driver what kind of man I was looking for.

We arrived at Ninth Street. No McCloor. I cursed and pushed my brains around.

The big man was a yegg. San Francisco was on fire for him. The yegg instinct would be to use a rattler to get away from trouble. The freight yards were in this end of town. Maybe he would be shifty enough to lie low instead of trying to powder. In that case, he probably hadn't crossed Market Street at all. If he stuck, there would still be a chance of picking him up tomorrow. If he was high-tailing, it was catch him now or not at all.

"Down to Harrison," I told the driver.

We went down to Harrison Street, and down Harrison to Third, up Bryant to Eighth, down Brannan to Third again, and over to Townsend—and we didn't see Babe McCloor.

"That's tough, that is," the driver sympathized as we stopped across the street from the Southern Pacific passenger station.

"I'm going over and look around in the station," I said. "Keep your eyes open while I'm gone."

When I told the copper in the station my trouble he introduced me to a couple of plain-clothes men who had been planted there to watch for McCloor. That had been done after Sue Hambleton's body was found. The shooting of Holy Joe Wales was news to them.

I went outside again and found my taxi in front of the door, its horn working over-time, but too asthmatically to be heard indoors. The ratty driver was excited.

"A guy like you said come up out of King Street just now and swung on a No. 16 car as it pulled away," he said.

"Going which way?"

"That-away," pointing southeast.

"Catch him," I said, jumping in.

The street car was out of sight around a bend in Third Street two blocks below. When we rounded the bend, the street car was slowing up, four blocks ahead. It hadn't slowed up very much when a man leaned far out and stepped off. He was a tall man, but didn't look tall on account of his shoulder spread. He didn't check his momentum, but used it to carry him across the sidewalk and out of sight.

We stopped where the man had left the car.

I gave the driver too much money and told him:

"Go back to Townsend Street and tell the copper in the station that I've chased Babe McCloor into the S. P. yards."

VII

I thought I was moving silently down between two strings of box cars, but I had gone less than twenty feet when a light flashed in my face and a sharp voice ordered:

"Stand still, you."

I stood still. Men came from between cars. One of them spoke my name, adding: "What are you doing here? Lost?" It was Harry Pebble, a police detective.

I stopped holding my breath and said:

"Hello, Harry. Looking for Babe?"

"Yes. We've been going over the rattlers."

"He's here. I just tailed him in from the street."

Pebble swore and snapped the light off.

"Watch, Harry," I advised. "Don't play with him. He's packing plenty of gun and he's cut down one boy tonight."

"I'll play with him," Pebble promised, and told one of the men with him to go over and warn those on the other side of the yard that McCloor was in, and then to ring for reinforcements.

"We'll just sit on the edge and hold him in till they come," he said.

That seemed a sensible way to play it. We spread out and waited. Once Pebble and I turned back a lanky bum who tried to slip into the yard between us, and one of the men below us picked up a shivering kid who was trying to slip out. Otherwise nothing happened until Lieutenant Duff arrived with a couple of carloads of coppers.

Most of our force went into a cordon around the yard. The rest of us went through the yard in small groups, working it over car by car. We picked up a few hoboes that Pebble and his men had missed earlier, but we didn't find McCloor.

We didn't find any trace of him until somebody stumbled over a railroad bull huddled in the shadow of a gondola. It took a couple of minutes to bring him to, and he couldn't talk then. His jaw was broken. But when we asked if McCloor had slugged him, he nodded, and when we asked in which direction McCloor had been headed, he moved a feeble hand to the east.

We went over and searched the Santa Fe yards.

We didn't find McCloor.

VIII

I rode up to the Hall of Justice with Duff. MacMan was in the captain of detectives' office with three or four police sleuths.

"Wales die?" I asked.

"Yep."

"Say anything before he went?"

"He was gone before you were through the window."

"You held on to the girl?"

"She's here."

"She say anything?"

"We were waiting for you before we tapped her," detective-sergeant O'Gar said, "not knowing the angle on her."

"Let's have her in. I haven't had any dinner yet. How about the autopsy on Sue Hambleton?"

"Chronic arsenic poisoning."

"Chronic? That means it was fed to her little by little, and not in a lump?"

"Uh-huh. From what he found in her kidney, intestines, liver, stomach and blood, Jordan figures there was less than a grain of it in her. That wouldn't be enough to knock her off. But he says he found arsenic in the tips of her hair, and she'd have to be given some at least a month ago for it to have worked out that far."

"Any chance that it wasn't arsenic that killed her?"

"Not unless Jordan's a bum doctor."

A policewoman came in with Peggy Carroll.

The blonde girl was tired. Her eyelids, mouth corners and body drooped, and when I pushed a chair out toward her she sagged down in it.

O'Gar ducked his grizzled bullet head at me.

"Now, Peggy," I said, "tell us where you fit into this mess."

"I don't fit into it." She didn't look up. Her voice was tired. "Joe dragged me into it. He told you."

"You his girl?"

"If you want to call it that," she admitted.

"You jealous?"

"What," she asked, looking up at me, her face puzzled, "has that got to do with it?"

"Sue Hambleton was getting ready to go away with him when she was murdered."

The girl sat up straight in the chair and said deliberately:

"I swear to God I didn't know she was murdered."

"But you did know she was dead," I said positively.

"I didn't," she replied just as positively.

I nudged O'Gar with my elbow. He pushed his undershot jaw at her and barked:

"What are you trying to give us? You knew she was dead. How could you kill her without knowing it?"

While she looked at him I waved the others in. They crowded close around her and took up the chorus of the sergeant's song. She was barked, roared, and snarled at plenty in the next few minutes.

The instant she stopped trying to talk back to them I cut in again.

"Wait," I said, very earnestly. "Maybe she didn't kill her."

"The hell she didn't," O'Gar stormed, holding the center of the stage so the others could move away from the girl without their retreat seeming too artificial. "Do you mean to tell me this baby—"

"I didn't say she didn't," I remonstrated. "I said maybe she didn't."

"Then who did?"

I passed the question to the girl: "Who did?"

"Babe," she said immediately.

O'Gar snorted to make her think he didn't believe her.

I asked, as if I were honestly perplexed:

"How do you know that if you didn't know she was dead?"

"It stands to reason he did," she said. "Anybody can see that. He found out she was going away with Joe, so he killed her and then came to Joe's and killed him. That's just exactly what Babe would do when he found it out."

"Yeah? How long have *you* known they were going away together?"

"Since they decided to. Joe told me a month or two ago."

"And you didn't mind?"

"You've got this all wrong," she said. "Of course I didn't mind. I was being cut in on it. You know her father had the bees. That's what Joe was after. She didn't mean anything to him but an in to the old man's pockets. And I was to get my dib. And you needn't think I was crazy enough about Joe or anybody else to step off in the air for them. Babe got next and fixed the pair of them. That's a cinch."

"Yeah? How do you figure Babe would kill her?"

"That guy? You don't think he'd—"

"I mean, how would he go about killing her?"

"Oh!" She shrugged. "With his hands, likely as not."

"Once he'd made up his mind to do it, he'd do it quick and violent?" I suggested.

"That would be Babe," she agreed.

"But you can't see him slow-poisoning her—spreading it out over a month?"

Worry came into the girl's blue eyes. She put her lower lip between her teeth, then said slowly:

"No, I can't see him doing it that way. Not Babe."

"Who can you see doing it that way?"

She opened her eyes wide, asking:

"You mean Joe?"

I didn't say anything.

"Joe might have," she said persuasively. "God only knows what he'd want to do it for, why he'd want to get rid of the kind of meal ticket she was going to be. But you couldn't always guess what he was getting at. He pulled plenty of dumb ones. He was too slick without being smart. If he was going to kill her, though, that would be about the way he'd go about it."

"Were he and Babe friendly?"

"No."

"Did he go to Babe's much?"

"Not at all that I know about. He was too leary of Babe to take a chance on being caught there. That's why I moved upstairs, so Sue could come over to our place to see him."

"Then how could Joe have hidden the fly paper he poisoned her with in her apartment?"

"Fly paper!" Her bewilderment seemed honest enough.

"Show it to her," I told O'Gar.

He got a sheet from the desk and held it close to the girl's face.

She stared at it for a moment and then jumped up and grabbed my arm with both hands.

"I didn't know what it was," she said excitedly. "Joe had some a couple of months ago. He was looking at it when I came in. I asked him what it was for, and he smiled that wisenheimer smile of his and said, 'You make angels out of it,' and wrapped it up again and put it in his pocket. I didn't pay much attention to him: he was always fooling with some kind of tricks that were supposed to make him wealthy, but never did."

"Ever see it again?"

"No."

"Did you know Sue very well?"

"I didn't know her at all. I never even saw her. I used to keep out of the way so I wouldn't gum Joe's play with her."

"But you know Babe?"

"Yes, I've been on a couple of parties where he was. That's all I know him."

"Who killed Sue?"

"Joe," she said. "Didn't he have that paper you say she was killed with?"

"Why did he kill her?"

"I don't know. He pulled some awful dumb tricks sometimes."

"You didn't kill her?"

"No, no, no!"

I jerked the corner of my mouth at O'Gar.

"You're a liar," he bawled, shaking the fly paper in her face. "You killed her." The rest of the team closed in, throwing accusations at her. They kept it up until she was groggy and the policewoman beginning to look worried.

Then I said angrily:

"All right. Throw her in a cell and let her think it over." To her: "You know what you told Joe this afternoon: this is no time to dummy up. Do a lot of thinking tonight."

"Honest to God I didn't kill her," she said.

I turned my back to her. The policewoman took her away.

"Ho-hum," O'Gar yawned. "We gave her a pretty good ride at that, for a short one."

"Not bad," I agreed. "If anybody else looked likely, I'd say she didn't kill Sue. But if she's telling the truth, then Holy Joe did it. And why should he poison the goose that was going to lay nice yellow eggs for him? And how and why did he cache the poison in their apartment? Babe had the motive, but damned if he looks like a slow-poisoner to me. You can't tell, though; he and Holy Joe could even have been working together on it."

"Could," Duff said. "But it takes a lot of imagination to get that one down. Anyway you twist it, Peggy's our best bet so far. Go up against her again, hard, in the morning?"

"Yeah," I said. "And we've got to find Babe."

The others had had dinner. MacMan and I went out and got ours. When we returned to the detective bureau an hour later it was practically deserted of the regular operatives.

"All gone to Pier 42 on a tip that McCloor's there," Steve Ward told us.

"How long ago?"

"Ten minutes."

MacMan and I got a taxi and set out for Pier 42. We didn't get to Pier 42.

On First Street, half a block from the Embarcadero, the taxi suddenly shrieked and slid to a halt.

"What—?" I began, and saw a man standing in front of the machine. He was a big man with a big gun. "Babe," I grunted, and put my hand on MacMan's arm to keep him from getting his gun out.

"Take me to—" McCloor was saying to the frightened driver when he saw us. He came around to my side and pulled the door open, holding the gun on us.

He had no hat. His hair was wet, plastered to his head. Little streams of water trickled down from it. His clothes were dripping wet.

He looked surprised at us and ordered:

"Get out."

As we got out he growled at the driver:

"What the hell you got your flag up for if you had fares?"

The driver wasn't there. He had hopped out the other side and was scooting away down the street. McCloor cursed him and poked his gun at me, growling:

"Go on, beat it."

Apparently he hadn't recognized me. The light here wasn't good, and I had a hat on now. He had seen me for only a few seconds in Wales's room.

I stepped aside. MacMan moved to the other side.

McCloor took a backward step to keep us from getting him between us and started an angry word.

MacMan threw himself on McCloor's gun arm.

I socked McCloor's jaw with my fist. I might just as well have hit somebody else for all it seemed to bother him.

He swept me out of his way and pasted MacMan in the mouth. MacMan fell back till the taxi stopped him, spit out a tooth, and came back for more.

I was trying to climb up McCloor's left side.

MacMan came in on his right, failed to dodge a chop of the gun, caught it square on the top of the noodle, and went down hard. He stayed down.

I kicked McCloor's ankle, but couldn't get his foot from under him. I rammed my right fist into the small of his back and got a left-handful of his wet hair, swinging on it. He shook his head, dragging me off my feet.

He punched me in the side and I could feel my ribs and guts flattening together like leaves in a book.

I swung my fist against the back of his neck. That bothered him. He made a rumbling noise down in his chest, crunched my shoulder in his left hand, and chopped at me with the gun in his right.

I kicked him somewhere and punched his neck again.

Down the street, at the Embarcadero, a police whistle was blowing. Men were running up First Street toward us.

McCloor snorted like a locomotive and threw me away from him. I didn't want to go. I tried to hang on. He threw me away from him and ran up the street.

I scrambled up and ran after him, dragging my gun out.

At the first corner he stopped to squirt metal at me—three shots. I squirted one at him. None of the four connected.

He disappeared around the corner. I swung wide around it, to make him miss if he were flattened to the wall waiting for me. He wasn't. He was a hundred feet ahead, going into a space between two warehouses. I went in after him, and out after him at the other end, making better time with my hundred and ninety pounds than he was making with his two-fifty.

He crossed a street, turning up, away from the waterfront. There was a light on the corner. When I came into its glare he wheeled and leveled his gun at me. I didn't hear it click, but I knew it had when he threw it at me. The gun went past with a couple of feet to spare and raised hell against a door behind me.

McCloor turned and ran up the street. I ran up the street after him.

I put a bullet past him to let the others know where we were. At the next corner he started to turn to the left, changed his mind, and went straight on.

I sprinted, cutting the distance between us to forty or fifty feet, and yelped:

"Stop or I'll drop you."

He jumped sidewise into a narrow alley.

I passed it on the jump, saw he wasn't waiting for me, and went in. Enough light came in from the street to let us see each other and our surroundings. The alley was blind—walled on each side and at the other end by tall concrete buildings with steel-shuttered windows and doors.

McCloor faced me, less than twenty feet away. His jaw stuck out. His arms curved down free of his sides. His shoulders were bunched.

"Put them up," I ordered, holding my gun level.

"Get out of my way, little man," he grumbled, taking a stiff-legged step toward me. "I'll eat you up."

"Keep coming," I said, "and I'll put you down."

"Try it." He took another step, crouching a little. "I can still get to you *with* slugs in me."

"Not where I'll put them." I was wordy, trying to talk him into waiting till the others came up. I didn't want to have to kill him. We could have done that from the taxi. "I'm no Annie Oakley, but if I can't pop your kneecaps with two shots at this distance, you're welcome to me. And if you think smashed kneecaps are a lot of fun, give it a whirl."

"Hell with that," he said and charged.

I shot his right knee.

He lurched toward me.

I shot his left knee.

He tumbled down.

"You would have it," I complained.

He twisted around, and with his arms pushed himself into a sitting position facing me.

"I didn't think you had sense enough to do it," he said through his teeth.

IX

I talked to McCloor in the hospital. He lay on his back in bed with a couple of pillows slanting his head up. The skin was pale and tight around his mouth and eyes, but there was nothing else to show he was in pain.

"You sure devastated me, bo," he said when I came in.

"Sorry," I said, "but—"

"I ain't beefing. I asked for it."

"Why'd you kill Holy Joe?" I asked, off-hand, as I pulled a chair up beside the bed.

"Uh-uh—you're tooting the wrong ringer."

I laughed and told him I was the man in the room with Joe when it happened.

McCloor grinned and said:

"I thought I'd seen you somewheres before. So that's where it was. I didn't pay no attention to your mug, just so your hands didn't move."

"Why'd you kill him?"

He pursed his lips, screwed up his eyes at me, thought something over, and said:

"He killed a broad I knew."

"He killed Sue Hambleton?" I asked.

He studied my face a while before he replied: "Yep."

"How do you figure that out?"

"Hell," he said, "I don't have to. Sue told me. Give me a butt."

I gave him a cigarette, held a lighter under it, and objected:

"That doesn't exactly fit in with other things I know. Just what happened and what did she say? You might start back with the night you gave her the goog."

He looked thoughtful, letting smoke sneak slowly out of his nose, then said:

"I hadn't ought to hit her in the eye, that's a fact. But, see, she had been out all afternoon and wouldn't tell me where she'd been, and we had a row over it. What's this—Thursday morning? That was Monday, then. After the row I went out and spent the night in a dump over on Army Street. I got home about seven the next morning. Sue was sick as hell, but she wouldn't let me get a croaker for her. That was kind of funny, because she was scared stiff."

McCloor scratched his head meditatively and suddenly drew in a great lungful of smoke, practically eating up the rest of the cigarette. He let the smoke leak out of mouth and nose together, looking dully through the cloud at me. Then he said bruskly:

"Well, she went under. But before she went she told me she'd been poisoned by Holy Joe."

"She say how he'd given it to her?"

McCloor shook his head.

"I'd been asking her what was the matter, and not getting anything out of her. Then she starts whining that she's poisoned. 'I'm poisoned, Babe,' she whines. 'Arsenic. That damned Holy Joe,' she says. Then she won't say anything else, and it's not a hell of a while after that that she kicks off."

"Yeah? Then what'd you do?"

"I went gunning for Holy Joe. I knew him but didn't know where he jungled up, and didn't find out till yesterday. You was there when I came. You know about that. I had picked up a boiler and parked it over on Turk Street, for the getaway. When I got back to it, there was a copper standing close to it. I figured he might have spotted it as a hot one and was waiting to see who came for it, so I let it alone, and caught a street car instead, and cut for the yards. Down there I ran into a whole flock of hammer and saws and had to go overboard in China Basin, swimming up to a pier, being ranked again by a watchman there, swimming off to another, and finally getting through the line only to run into another bad break. I wouldn't of flagged that taxi if the *For Hire* flag hadn't been up."

"You knew Sue was planning to take a run-out on you with Joe?"

"I don't know it yet," he said. "I knew damned well she was cheating on me, but I didn't know who with."

"What would you have done if you had known that?" I asked.

"Me?" He grinned wolfishly. "Just what I did."

"Killed the pair of them," I said.

He rubbed his lower lip with a thumb and asked calmly:

"You think I killed Sue?"

"You did."

"Serves me right," he said. "I must be getting simple in my old age. What the hell am I doing barbering with a lousy dick? That never got nobody nothing but grief. Well, you might just as well take it on the heel and toe now, my lad. I'm through spitting."

And he was. I couldn't get another word out of him.

X

The Old Man sat listening to me, tapping his desk lightly with the point of a long yellow pencil, staring past me with mild blue, rimless-spectacled, eyes. When I had brought my story up to date, he asked pleasantly:

"How is MacMan?"

"He lost two teeth, but his skull wasn't cracked. He'll be out in a couple of days."

The Old Man nodded and asked:

"What remains to be done?"

"Nothing. We can put Peggy Carroll on the mat again, but it's not likely we'll squeeze much more out of her. Outside of that, the returns are pretty well all in."

"And what do you make of it?"

I squirmed in my chair and said: "Suicide."

The Old Man smiled at me, politely but skeptically.

"I don't like it either," I grumbled. "And I'm not ready to write it in a report yet. But that's the only total that what we've got will add up to. That fly paper was hidden behind the kitchen stove. Nobody would be crazy enough to try to hide something from a woman in her own kitchen like that. But the woman might hide it there.

"According to Peggy, Holy Joe had the fly paper. If Sue hid it, she got it from him. For what? They were planning to go away together, and were only waiting till Joe, who was on the nut, raised enough dough. Maybe they were afraid of Babe, and had the poison there to slip him if he tumbled to their plan before they went. Maybe they meant to slip it to him before they went anyway.

"When I started talking to Holy Joe about murder, he thought Babe was the one who had been bumped off. He was surprised, maybe, but as if he was surprised that it had happened so soon. He was more surprised when he heard that Sue had died too, but even then he wasn't so surprised as when he saw McCloor alive at the window.

"She died cursing Holy Joe, and she knew she was poisoned, and she wouldn't let McCloor get a doctor. Can't that mean that she had turned against Joe, and had taken the poison herself instead of feeding it to Babe? The poison was hidden from Babe. But even if he found it, I can't figure him as a poisoner. He's too rough. Unless he caught her trying to poison him and made her swallow the stuff. But that doesn't account for the month-old arsenic in her hair."

"Does your suicide hypothesis take care of that?" the Old Man asked.

"It could," I said. "Don't be kicking holes in my theory. It's got enough as it stands. But, if she committed suicide this time, there's no reason why she couldn't have tried it once before—say after a quarrel with Joe a month ago—and failed to bring it off. That would have put the arsenic in her. There's no real proof that she took any between a month ago and day before yesterday."

"No real proof," the Old Man protested mildly, "except the autopsy's finding—chronic poisoning."

I was never one to let experts' guesses stand in my way. I said:

"They base that on the small amount of arsenic they found in her remains—less than a fatal dose. And the amount they find in your stomach after you're dead depends on how much you vomit before you die."

The Old Man smiled benevolently at me and asked:

"But you're not, you say, ready to write this theory into a report? Meanwhile what do you purpose doing?"

"If there's nothing else on tap, I'm going home, fumigate my brains with Fatimas, and try to get this thing straightened out in my head. I think I'll get a copy of *The Count of Monte Cristo* and run through it. I haven't read it since I was a kid.

It looks like the book was wrapped up with the fly paper to make a bundle large enough to wedge tightly between the wall and stove, so it wouldn't fall down. But there might be something in the book. I'll see anyway."

"I did that last night," the Old Man murmured.

I asked: "And?"

He took a book from his desk drawer, opened it where a slip of paper marked a place, and held it out to me, one pink finger marking a paragraph.

"Suppose you were to take a millegramme of this poison the first day, two millegrammes the second day, and so on. Well, at the end of ten days you would have taken a centi-gramme: at the end of twenty days, increasing another mille-gramme, you would have taken three hundred centigrammes; that is to say, a dose you would support without inconve-nience, and which would be very dangerous for any other person who had not taken the same precautions as yourself. Well, then, at the end of the month, when drinking water from the same carafe, you would kill the person who had drunk this water, without your perceiving otherwise than from slight inconvenience that there was any poisonous sub-stance mingled with the water."

"That does it," I said. "That does it. They were afraid to go away without killing Babe, too certain he'd come after them. She tried to make herself immune from arsenic poisoning by getting her body accustomed to it, taking steadily increasing doses, so when she slipped the big shot in Babe's food she could eat it with him without danger. She'd be taken sick, but wouldn't die, and the police couldn't hang his death on her because she too had eaten the poisoned food.

"That clicks. After the row Monday night, when she wrote Joe the note urging him to make the getaway soon, she tried to hurry up her immunity, and increased her preparatory doses too quickly, took too large a shot. That's why she cursed Joe at the end: it was his plan."

"Possibly she overdosed herself in an attempt to speed it along," the Old Man agreed, "but not necessarily. There are people who can cultivate an ability to take large doses of ar-senic without trouble, but it seems to be a sort of natural gift with them, a matter of some constitutional peculiarity.

Ordinarily, any one who tried it would do what Sue Hambleton did—slowly poison themselves until the cumulative effect was strong enough to cause death."

Babe McCloor was hanged, for killing Holy Joe Wales, six months later.

The Farewell Murder

I was the only one who left the train at Farewell.

A man came through the rain from the passenger shed. He was a small man. His face was dark and flat. He wore a gray waterproof cap and a gray coat cut in military style.

He didn't look at me. He looked at the valise and gladstone bag in my hands. He came forward quickly, walking with short, choppy steps.

He didn't say anything when he took the bags from me. I asked:

"Kavalov's?"

He had already turned his back to me and was carrying my bags towards a tan Stutz coach that stood in the roadway beside the gravel station platform. In answer to my question he bowed twice at the Stutz without looking around or checking his jerky half-trot.

I followed him to the car.

Three minutes of riding carried us through the village. We took a road that climbed westward into the hills. The road looked like a seal's back in the rain.

The flat-faced man was in a hurry. We purred over the road at a speed that soon carried us past the last of the cottages sprinkled up the hillside.

Presently we left the shiny black road for a paler one curving south to run along a hill's wooded crest. Now and then this road, for a hundred feet or more at a stretch, was turned into a tunnel by tall trees' heavily leafed boughs interlocking overhead.

Rain accumulated in fat drops on the boughs and came down to thump the Stutz's roof. The dulness of rainy early evening became almost the blackness of night inside these tunnels.

The flat-faced man switched on the lights, and increased our speed.

He sat rigidly erect at the wheel. I sat behind him. Above his military collar, among the hairs that were clipped short on the nape of his neck, globules of moisture made tiny shining points. The moisture could have been rain. It could have been sweat.

We were in the middle of one of the tunnels.

The flat-faced man's head jerked to the left, and he screamed:

"A-a-a-a-a-a!"

It was a long, quivering, high-pitched bleat, thin with terror.

I jumped up, bending forward to see what was the matter with him.

The car swerved and plunged ahead, throwing me back on the seat again.

Through the side window I caught a one-eyed glimpse of something dark lying in the road.

I twisted around to try the back window, less rain-bleared.

I saw a black man lying on his back in the road, near the left edge. His body was arched, as if its weight rested on his heels and the back of his head. A knife handle that couldn't have been less than six inches long stood straight up in the air from the left side of his chest.

By the time I had seen this much we had taken a curve and were out of the tunnel.

"Stop," I called to the flat-faced man.

He pretended he didn't hear me. The Stutz was a tan streak under us. I put a hand on the driver's shoulder.

His shoulder squirmed under my hand, and he screamed "A-a-a-a-a!" again as if the dead black man had him.

I reached past him and shut off the engine.

He took his hands from the wheel and clawed up at me. Noises came from his mouth, but they didn't make any words that I knew.

I got a hand on the wheel. I got my other forearm under his chin. I leaned over the back of his seat so that the weight of my upper body was on his head, mashing it down against the wheel.

Between this and that and the help of God, the Stutz hadn't left the road when it stopped moving.

I got up off the flat-faced man's head and asked:

"What the hell's the matter with you?"

He looked at me with white eyes, shivered, and didn't say anything.

"Turn it around," I said. "We'll go back there."

He shook his head from side to side, desperately, and made some more of the mouth-noises that might have been words if I could have understood them.

"You know who that was?" I asked.

He shook his head.

"You do," I growled.

He shook his head.

By then I was beginning to suspect that no matter what I said to this fellow I'd get only head-shakes out of him.

I said:

"Get away from the wheel, then. I'm going to drive back there."

He opened the door and scrambled out.

"Come back here," I called.

He backed away, shaking his head.

I cursed him, slid in behind the wheel, said, "All right, wait here for me," and slammed the door.

He retreated backwards slowly, watching me with scared, whitish eyes while I backed and turned the coach.

I had to drive back farther than I had expected, something like a mile.

I didn't find the black man.

The tunnel was empty.

If I had known the exact spot in which he had been lying, I might have been able to find something to show how he had been removed. But I hadn't had time to pick out a landmark, and now any one of four or five places looked like the spot.

With the help of the coach's lamps I went over the left side of the road from one end of the tunnel to the other.

I didn't find any blood. I didn't find any footprints. I didn't find anything to show that anybody had been lying in the road. I didn't find anything.

It was too dark by now for me to try searching the woods.

I returned to where I had left the flat-faced man.

He was gone.

It looked, I thought, as if Mr. Kavalov might be right in thinking he needed a detective.

II

Half a mile beyond the place where the flat-faced man had de-serted me, I stopped the Stutz in front of a grilled steel gate that blocked the road. The gate was padlocked on the inside. From either side of it tall hedging ran off into the woods. The upper part of a brown-roofed small house was visible over the hedge-top to the left.

I worked the Stutz's horn.

The racket brought a gawky boy of fifteen or sixteen to the other side of the gate. He had on bleached whipcord pants and a wildly striped sweater. He didn't come out to the mid-dle of the road, but stood at one side, with one arm out of sight as if holding something that was hidden from me by the hedge.

"This Kavalov's?" I asked.

"Yes, sir," he said uneasily.

I waited for him to unlock the gate. He didn't unlock it. He stood there looking uneasily at the car and at me.

"Please, mister," I said, "can I come in?"

"What—who are you?"

"I'm the guy that Kavalov sent for. If I'm not going to be let in, tell me, so I can catch the six-fifty back to San Francisco."

The boy chewed his lip, said, "Wait till I see if I can find the key," and went out of sight behind the hedge.

He was gone long enough to have had a talk with somebody.

When he came back he unlocked the gate, swung it open, and said:

"It's all right, sir. They're expecting you."

When I had driven through the gate I could see lights on a hilltop a mile or so ahead and to the left.

"Is that the house?" I asked.

"Yes, sir. They're expecting you."

Close to where the boy had stood while talking to me through the gate, a double-barrel shotgun was propped up against the hedge.

I thanked the boy and drove on. The road wound gently uphill through farm land. Tall, slim trees had been planted at regular intervals on both sides of the road.

The road brought me at last to the front of a building that looked like a cross between a fort and a factory in the dusk. It was built of concrete. Take a flock of squat cones of various sizes, round off the points bluntly, mash them together with the largest one somewhere near the center, the others grouped around it in not too strict accordance with their sizes, adjust the whole collection to agree with the slopes of a hilltop, and you would have a model of the Kavalov house. The windows were steel-sashed. There weren't very many of them. No two were in line either vertically or horizontally. Some were lighted.

As I got out of the car, the narrow front door of this house opened.

A short, red-faced woman of fifty or so, with faded blonde hair wound around and around her head, came out. She wore a high-necked, tight-sleeved, gray woolen dress. When she smiled her mouth seemed wide as her hips.

She said:

"You're the gentleman from the city?"

"Yeah. I lost your chauffeur somewhere back on the road."

"Lord bless you," she said amiably, "that's all right."

A thin man with thin dark hair plastered down above a thin, worried face came past her to take my bags when I had lifted them out of the car. He carried them indoors.

The woman stood aside for me to enter, saying:

"Now I suppose you'll want to wash up a little bit before you go in to dinner, and they won't mind waiting for you the few minutes you'll take if you hurry."

I said, "Yeah, thanks," waited for her to get ahead of me again, and followed her up a curving flight of stairs that climbed along the inside of one of the cones that made up the building.

She took me to a second-story bedroom where the thin man was unpacking my bags.

"Martin will get you anything you need," she assured me from the doorway, "and when you're ready, just come on downstairs."

I said I would, and she went away. The thin man had finished unpacking by the time I had got out of coat, vest, collar and shirt. I told him there wasn't anything else I needed, washed up in the adjoining bathroom, put on a fresh shirt and collar, my vest and coat, and went downstairs.

The wide hall was empty. Voices came through an open doorway to the left.

One voice was a nasal whine. It complained:

"I will not have it. I will not put up with it. I am not a child, and I will not have it."

This voice's t's were a little too thick for t's, but not thick enough to be d's.

Another voice was a lively, but slightly harsh, barytone. It said cheerfully:

"What's the good of saying we won't put up with it, when we are putting up with it?"

The third voice was feminine, a soft voice, but flat and spiritless. It said:

"But perhaps he did kill him."

The whining voice said: "I do not care. I will not have it."

The barytone voice said, cheerfully as before: "Oh, won't you?"

A doorknob turned farther down the hall. I didn't want to be caught standing there listening. I advanced to the open doorway.

III

I was in the doorway of a low-ceilinged oval room furnished and decorated in gray, white and silver. Two men and a woman were there.

The older man—he was somewhere in his fifties—got up from a deep gray chair and bowed ceremoniously at me. He was a plump man of medium height, completely bald, dark-skinned and pale-eyed. He wore a wax-pointed gray mustache and a straggly gray imperial.

"Mr. Kavalov?" I asked.

"Yes, sir." His was the whining voice.

I told him who I was. He shook my hand and then introduced me to the others.

The woman was his daughter. She was probably thirty. She had her father's narrow, full-lipped mouth, but her eyes were dark, her nose was short and straight, and her skin was almost colorless. Her face had Asia in it. It was pretty, passive, unintelligent.

The man with the barytone voice was her husband. His name was Ringgo. He was six or seven years older than his wife, neither tall nor heavy, but well setup. His left arm was in splints and a sling. The knuckles of his right hand were darkly bruised. He had a lean, bony, quick-witted face, bright dark eyes with plenty of lines around them, and a good-natured hard mouth.

He gave me his bruised hand, wriggled his bandaged arm at me, grinned, and said:

"I'm sorry you missed this, but the future injuries are yours."

"How did it happen?" I asked.

Kavalov raised a plump hand.

"Time enough it is to go into that when we have eaten," he said. "Let us have our dinner first."

We went into a small green and brown dining-room where a small square table was set. I sat facing Ringgo across a silver basket of orchids that stood between tall silver candlesticks in the center of the table. Mrs. Ringgo sat to my right, Kavalov to my left. When Kavalov sat down I saw the shape of an automatic pistol in his hip pocket.

Two men servants waited on us. There was a lot of food and all of it was well turned out. We ate caviar, some sort of consommé, sand dabs, potatoes and cucumber jelly, roast lamb, corn and string beans, asparagus, wild duck and hominy cakes, artichoke-and-tomato salad, and orange ice. We drank white wine, claret, Burgundy, coffee and *crème de menthe*.

Kavalov ate and drank enormously. None of us skimped.

Kavalov was the first to disregard his own order that nothing be said about his troubles until after we had eaten. When he had finished his soup he put down his spoon and said:

"I am not a child. I will not be frightened."

He blinked pale, worried eyes defiantly at me, his lips pouting between mustache and imperial.

Ringgo grinned pleasantly at him. Mrs. Ringgo's face was as serene and inattentive as if nothing had been said.

"What is there to be frightened of?" I asked.

"Nothing," Kavalov said. "Nothing excepting a lot of idiotic and very pointless trickery and play-acting."

"You can call it anything you want to call it," a voice grumbled over my shoulder, "but I seen what I seen."

The voice belonged to one of the men who was waiting on the table, a sallow, youngish man with a narrow, slack-lipped face. He spoke with a subdued sort of stubbornness, and without looking up from the dish he was putting before me.

Since nobody else paid any attention to the servant's clearly audible remark, I turned my face to Kavalov again. He was trimming the edge of a sand dab with the side of his fork.

"What kind of trickery and play-acting?" I asked.

Kavalov put down his fork and rested his wrists on the edge of the table. He rubbed his lips together and leaned over his plate towards me.

"Supposing"—he wrinkled his forehead so that his bald scalp twitched forward—"you have done injury to a man ten years ago." He turned his wrists quickly, laying his hands palms-up on the white cloth. "You have done this injury in the ordinary business manner—you understand?—for profit. There is not anything personal concerned. You do not hardly know him. And then supposing he came to you after all those ten years and said to you: 'I have come to watch you die.'" He turned his hands over, palms down. "Well, what would you think?"

"I wouldn't," I replied, "think I ought to hurry up my dying on his account."

The earnestness went out of his face, leaving it blank. He blinked at me for a moment and then began eating his fish. When he had chewed and swallowed the last piece of sand dab he looked up at me again. He shook his head slowly, drawing down the corners of his mouth.

"That was not a good answer," he said. He shrugged, and spread his fingers. "However, you will have to deal with this Captain Cat-and-mouse. It is for that I engaged you."

I nodded.

Ringgo smiled and patted his bandaged arm, saying:

"I wish you more luck with him than I had."

Mrs. Ringgo put out a hand and let the pointed fingertips touch her husband's wrist for a moment.

I asked Kavalov:

"This injury I was to suppose I had done: how serious was it?"

He pursed his lips, made little wavy motions with the fingers of his right hand, and said:

"Oh—ah—ruin."

"We can take it for granted, then, that your captain's really up to something?"

"Good God!" said Ringgo, dropping his fork. "I wouldn't like to think he'd broken my arm just in fun."

Behind me the sallow servant spoke to his mate:

"He wants to know if we think the captain's really up to something."

"I heard him," the other said gloomily. "A lot of help he's going to be to us."

Kavalov tapped his plate with a fork and made angry faces at the servants.

"Shut up," he said. "Where is the roast?" He pointed the fork at Mrs. Ringgo. "Her glass is empty." He looked at the fork. "See what care they take of my silver," he complained, holding it out to me. "It has not been cleaned decently in a month."

He put the fork down. He pushed back his plate to make room for his forearms on the table. He leaned over them, hunching his shoulders. He sighed. He frowned. He stared at me with pleading pale eyes.

"Listen," he whined. "Am I a fool? Would I send to San Francisco for a detective if I did not need a detective? Would I pay you what you are charging me, when I could get plenty good enough detectives for half of that, if I did not require the best detective I could secure? Would I require so expensive a one if I did not know this captain for a completely dangerous fellow?"

I didn't say anything. I sat still and looked attentive.

"Listen," he whined. "This is not April-foolery. This captain means to murder me. He came here to murder me. He will certainly murder me if somebody does not stop him from it."

"Just what has he done so far?" I asked.

"That is not it." Kavalov shook his bald head impatiently. "I do not ask you to undo anything that he has done. I ask you to keep him from killing me. What has he done so far? Well, he has terrorized my people most completely. He has broken Dolph's arm. He has done these things so far, if you must know."

"How long has this been going on? How long has he been here?"

"A week and two days."

"Did your chauffeur tell you about the black man we saw in the road?"

Kavalov pushed his lips together and nodded slowly.

"He wasn't there when I went back," I said.

He blew out his lips with a little puff and cried excitedly:

"I do not care anything about your black men and your roads. I care about not being murdered."

"Have you said anything to the sheriff's office?" I asked, trying to pretend I wasn't getting peevish.

"That I have done. But to what good? Has he threatened me? Well, he has told me he has come to watch me die. From him, the way he said it, that is a threat. But to your sheriff it is not a threat. He has terrorized my people. Have I proof that he has done that? The sheriff says I have not. What absurdity! Do I need proof? Don't I know? Must he leave fingerprints on the fright he causes? So it comes to this: the sheriff will keep an eye on him. 'An eye,' he said, mind you. Here I have twenty people, servants and farm hands, with forty eyes. And he comes and goes as he likes. An eye!"

"How about Ringgo's arm?" I asked.

Kavalov shook his head impatiently and began to cut up his lamb.

Ringgo said:

"There's nothing we can do about that. I hit him first." He looked at his bruised knuckles. "I didn't think he was that tough. Maybe I'm not as good as I used to be. Anyway, a dozen people saw me punch his jaw before he touched me. We performed at high noon in front of the post office."

"Who is this captain?"

"It's not him," the sallow servant said. "It's that black devil."

Ringgo said:

"Sherry's his name, Hugh Sherry. He was a captain in the British army when we knew him before—quarter-masters department in Cairo. That was in 1917, all of twelve years ago. The commodore"—he nodded his head at his father-in-law— "was speculating in military supplies. Sherry should have been a line officer. He had no head for desk work. He wasn't timid enough. Somebody decided the commodore wouldn't have made so much money if Sherry hadn't been so careless. They knew Sherry hadn't made any money for himself. They cashiered Sherry at the same time they asked the commodore please to go away."

Kavalov looked up from his plate to explain:

"Business is like that in wartime. They wouldn't let me go away if I had done anything they could keep me there for."

"And now, twelve years after you had him kicked out of the army in disgrace," I said, "he comes here, threatens to kill you, so you believe, and sets out to spread panic among your people. Is that it?"

"That is not it," Kavalov whined. "That is not it at all. I did not have him kicked out of any armies. I am a man of business. I take my profits where I find them. If somebody lets me take a profit that angers his employers, what is their anger to me? Second, I do not believe he means to kill me. I know that."

"I'm trying to get it straight in my mind."

"There is nothing to get straight. A man is going to murder me. I ask you not to let him do it. Is not that simple enough?"

"Simple enough," I agreed, and stopped trying to talk to him.

Kavalov and Ringgo were smoking cigars, Mrs. Ringgo and I cigarettes over *crème de menthe* when the red-faced blonde woman in gray wool came in.

She came in hurriedly. Her eyes were wide open and dark. She said:

"Anthony says there's a fire in the upper field."

Kavalov crunched his cigar between his teeth and looked pointedly at me.

I stood up, asking:

"How do I get there?"

"I'll show you the way," Ringgo said, leaving his chair.

"Dolph," his wife protested, "your arm."

He smiled gently at her and said:

"I'm not going to interfere. I'm only going along to see how an expert handles these things."

IV

I ran up to my room for hat, coat, flashlight and gun.

The Ringgos were standing at the front door when I started downstairs again.

He had put on a dark raincoat, buttoned tight over his injured arm, its left sleeve hanging empty. His right arm was around his wife. Both of her bare arms were around his neck. She was bent far back, he far forward over her. Their mouths were together.

Retreating a little, I made more noise with my feet when I came into sight again. They were standing apart at the door, waiting for me. Ringgo was breathing heavily, as if he had been running. He opened the door.

Mrs. Ringgo addressed me:

"Please don't let my foolish husband be too reckless."

I said I wouldn't, and asked him:

"Worth while taking any of the servants or farm hands along?"

He shook his head.

"Those that aren't hiding would be as useless as those that are," he said. "They've all had it taken out of them."

He and I went out, leaving Mrs. Ringgo looking after us from the doorway. The rain had stopped for the time, but a black muddle overhead promised more presently.

Ringgo led me around the side of the house, along a narrow path that went downhill through shrubbery, past a group of small buildings in a shallow valley, and diagonally up another, lower, hill.

The path was soggy. At the top of the hill we left the path, going through a wire gate and across a stubby field that was both gummy and slimy under our feet. We moved along swiftly. The gumminess of the ground, the sultriness of the night air, and our coats, made the going warm work.

When we had crossed this field we could see the fire, a spot of flickering orange beyond intervening trees. We climbed a low wire fence and wound through the trees.

A violent rustling broke out among the leaves overhead, starting at the left, ending with a solid thud against a tree trunk just to our right. Then something *plopped* on the soft ground under the tree.

Off to the left a voice laughed, a savage, hooting laugh.

The laughing voice couldn't have been far away. I went after it.

The fire was too small and too far away to be of much use to me: blackness was nearly perfect among the trees.

I stumbled over roots, bumped into trees, and found nothing. The flashlight would have helped the laugher more than me, so I kept it idle in my hand.

When I got tired of playing peekaboo with myself, I cut through the woods to the field on the other side, and went down to the fire.

The fire had been built in one end of the field, a dozen feet or less from the nearest tree. It had been built of dead twigs and broken branches that the rain had missed, and had nearly burnt itself out by the time I reached it.

Two small forked branches were stuck in the ground on opposite sides of the fire. Their forks held the ends of a length of green sapling. Spitted on the sapling, hanging over the fire, was an eighteen-inch-long carcass, headless, tailless, footless, skinless, and split down the front.

On the ground a few feet away lay an airedale puppy's head, pelt, feet, tail, insides, and a lot of blood.

There were some dry sticks, broken in convenient lengths, beside the fire. I put them on as Ringgo came out of the woods to join me. He carried a stone the size of a grapefruit in his hand.

"Get a look at him?" he asked.

"No. He laughed and went."

He held out the stone to me, saying:

"This is what was chucked at us."

Drawn on the smooth gray stone, in red, were round blank eyes, a triangular nose, and a grinning, toothy mouth—a crude skull.

I scratched one of the red eyes with a fingernail, and said:

"Crayon."

Ringgo was staring at the carcass sizzling over the fire and at the trimmings on the ground.

"What do you make of that?" I asked.

He swallowed and said:

"Mickey was a damned good little dog."

"Yours?"

He nodded.

I went around with my flashlight on the ground. I found some footprints, such as they were.

"Anything?" Ringgo asked.

"Yeah." I showed him one of the prints. "Made with rags tied around his shoes. They're no good."

We turned to the fire again.

"This is another show," I said. "Whoever killed and cleaned the pup knew his stuff; knew it too well to think he could cook him decently like that. The outside will be burnt before the inside's even warm, and the way he's put on the spit he'd fall off if you tried to turn him."

Ringgo's scowl lightened a bit.

"That's a little better," he said. "Having him killed is rotten enough, but I'd hate to think of anybody eating Mickey, or even meaning to."

"They didn't," I assured him. "They were putting on a show. This the sort of thing that's been happening?"

"Yes."

"What's the sense of it?"

He glumly quoted Kavalov:

"Captain Cat-and-mouse."

I gave him a cigarette, took one myself, and lighted them with a stick from the fire.

He raised his face to the sky, said, "Raining again; let's go back to the house," but remained by the fire, staring at the cooking carcass. The stink of scorched meat hung thick around us.

"You don't take this very seriously yet, do you?" he asked presently, in a low, matter-of-fact voice.

"It's a funny layout."

"He's cracked," he said in the same low voice. "Try to see this. Honor meant something to him. That's why we had to trick him instead of bribing him, back in Cairo. Less than ten years of dishonor can crack a man like that. He'd go off and hide and brood. It would be either shoot himself when the blow fell—or that. I was like you at first." He kicked at the fire. "This is silly. But I can't laugh at it now, except when I'm around Miriam and the commodore. When he first showed up I didn't have the slightest idea that I couldn't handle him. I had handled him all right in Cairo. When I discovered I couldn't handle him I lost my head a little. I went down and picked a row with him. Well, that was no good either. It's the silliness of this that makes it bad. In Cairo he was the kind of man who combs his hair before he shaves, so his mirror will show an orderly picture. Can you understand some of this?"

"I'll have to talk to him first," I said. "He's staying in the village?"

"He has a cottage on the hill above. It's the first one on the left after you turn into the main road." Ringgo dropped his cigarette into the fire and looked thoughtfully at me, biting his lower lip. "I don't know how you and the commodore are going to get along. You can't make jokes with him. He doesn't understand them, and he'll distrust you on that account."

"I'll try to be careful," I promised. "No good offering this Sherry money?"

"Hell, no," he said softly. "He's too cracked for that."

We took down the dog's carcass, kicked the fire apart, and trod it out in the mud before we returned to the house.

V

The country was fresh and bright under clear sunlight the next morning. A warm breeze was drying the ground and chasing raw-cotton clouds across the sky.

At ten o'clock I set out afoot for Captain Sherry's. I didn't have any trouble finding his house, a pinkish stuccoed bungalow with a terra cotta roof, reached from the road by a cobbled walk.

A white-clothed table with two places set stood on the tiled veranda that stretched across the front of the bungalow.

Before I could knock, the door was opened by a slim black man, not much more than a boy, in a white jacket. His features were thinner than most American negroes', aquiline, pleasantly intelligent.

"You're going to catch colds lying around in wet roads," I said, "if you don't get run over."

His mouth-ends ran towards his ears in a grin that showed me a lot of strong yellow teeth.

"Yes, sir," he said, buzzing his s's, rolling the r, bowing. "The *capitaine* have waited breakfast that you be with him. You do sit down, sir. I will call him."

"Not dog meat?"

His mouth-ends ran back and up again and he shook his head vigorously.

"No, sir." He held up his black hands and counted the fingers. "There is orange and kippers and kidneys grilled and eggs and marmalade and toast and tea or coffee. There is not dog meat."

"Fine," I said, and sat down in one of the wicker armchairs on the veranda.

I had time to light a cigarette before Captain Sherry came out.

He was a gaunt tall man of forty. Sandy hair, parted in the middle, was brushed flat to his small head, above a sunburned face. His eyes were gray, with lower lids as straight as ruler-edges. His mouth was another hard straight line under a close-clipped sandy mustache. Grooves like gashes ran from his nostrils past his mouth-corners. Other grooves, just as deep, ran down his cheeks to the sharp ridge of his jaw. He wore a gaily striped flannel bathrobe over sand-colored pajamas.

"Good morning," he said pleasantly, and gave me a semi-salute. He didn't offer to shake hands. "Don't get up. It will be some minutes before Marcus has breakfast ready. I slept late. I had a most abominable dream." His voice was a deliberately languid drawl. "I dreamed that Theodore Kavalov's throat had been cut from here to here." He put bony fingers under his ears. "It was an atrociously gory business. He bled and screamed horribly, the swine."

I grinned up at him, asking:

"And you didn't like that?"

"Oh, getting his throat cut was all to the good, but he bled and screamed so filthily." He raised his nose and sniffed. "That's honeysuckle somewhere, isn't it?"

"Smells like it. Was it throat-cutting that you had in mind when you threatened him?"

"When I threatened him," he drawled. "My dear fellow, I did nothing of the sort. I was in Udja, a stinking Moroccan town close to the Algerian frontier, and one morning a voice spoke to me from an orange tree. It said: 'Go to Farewell, in California, in the States, and there you will see Theodore Kavalov die.' I thought that a capital idea. I thanked the voice, told Marcus to pack, and came here. As soon as I arrived I told Kavalov about it, thinking perhaps he would die then and I wouldn't be hung up here waiting. He didn't, though, and too late I regretted not having asked the voice for a definite date. I should hate having to waste months here."

"That's why you've been trying to hurry it up?" I asked.

"I beg your pardon?"

"*Schrecklichkeit*," I said, "rocky skulls, dog barbecues, vanishing corpses."

"I've been fifteen years in Africa," he said. "I've too much faith in voices that come from orange trees where no one is to try to give them a hand. You needn't fancy I've had anything to do with whatever has happened."

"Marcus?"

Sherry stroked his freshly shaven cheeks and replied:

"That's possible. He has an incorrigible bent for the ruder sort of African horse-play. I'll gladly cane him for any misbehavior of which you've reasonably definite proof."

"Let me catch him at it," I said, "and I'll do my own caning."

Sherry leaned forward and spoke in a cautious undertone:

"Be sure he suspects nothing till you've a firm grip on him. He's remarkably effective with either of his knives."

"I'll try to remember that. The voice didn't say anything about Ringgo?"

"There was no need. When the body dies, the hand is dead."

Black Marcus came out carrying food. We moved to the table and I started on my second breakfast.

Sherry wondered whether the voice that had spoken to him from the orange tree had also spoken to Kavalov. He had asked Kavalov, he said, but hadn't received a very satisfactory answer. He believed that voices which announced deaths to people's enemies usually also warned the one who was to die. "That is," he said, "the conventional way of doing it, I believe."

"I don't know," I said. "I'll try to find out for you. Maybe I ought to ask him what he dreamed last night, too."

"Did he look nightmarish this morning?"

"I don't know. I left before he was up."

Sherry's eyes became hot gray points.

"Do you mean," he asked, "that you've no idea what shape he's in this morning, whether he's alive or not, whether my dream was a true one or not?"

"Yeah."

The hard line of his mouth loosened into a slow delighted smile.

"By Jove," he said, "That's capital! I thought—you gave me the impression of knowing positively that there was nothing to my dream, that it was only a meaningless dream."

He clapped his hands sharply.

Black Marcus popped out of the door.

"Pack," Sherry ordered. "The bald one is finished. We're off."

Marcus bowed and backed grinning into the house.

"Hadn't you better wait to make sure?" I asked.

"But I am sure," he drawled, "as sure as when the voice spoke from the orange tree. There is nothing to wait for now: I have seen him die."

"In a dream."

"Was it a dream?" he asked carelessly.

When I left, ten or fifteen minutes later, Marcus was making noises indoors that sounded as if he actually was packing.

Sherry shook hands with me, saying:

"Awfully glad to have had you for breakfast. Perhaps we'll meet again if your work ever brings you to northern Africa. Remember me to Miriam and Dolph. I can't sincerely send condolences."

Out of sight of the bungalow, I left the road for a path along the hillside above, and explored the country for a higher spot from which Sherry's place could be spied on. I found a pip, a vacant ramshackle house on a jutting ridge off to the northeast. The whole of the bungalow's front, part of one side, and a good stretch of the cobbled walk, including its juncture with the road, could be seen from the vacant house's front porch. It was a rather long shot for naked eyes, but with field glasses it would be just about perfect, even to a screen of over-grown bushes in front.

When I got back to the Kavalov house Ringgo was propped up on gay cushions in a reed chair under a tree, with a book in his hand.

"What do you think of him?" he asked. "Is he cracked?"

"Not very. He wanted to be remembered to you and Mrs. Ringgo. How's the arm this morning?"

"Rotten. I must have let it get too damp last night. It gave me hell all night."

"Did you see Captain Cat-and-mouse?" Kavalov's whining voice came from behind me. "And did you find any satisfaction in that?"

I turned around. He was coming down the walk from the house. His face was more gray than brown this morning, but what I could see of his throat, above the v of a wing collar, was uncut enough.

"He was packing when I left," I said. "Going back to Africa."

VI

That day was Thursday. Nothing else happened that day.

Friday morning I was awakened by the noise of my bedroom door being opened violently.

Martin, the thin-faced valet, came dashing into my room and began shaking me by the shoulder, though I was sitting up by the time he reached my bedside.

His thin face was lemon-yellow and ugly with fear.

"It's happened," he babbled. "Oh, my God, it's happened!"

"What's happened?"

"It's happened. It's happened."

I pushed him aside and got out of bed. He turned suddenly and ran into my bathroom. I could hear him vomiting as I pushed my feet into slippers.

Kavalov's bedroom was three doors below mine, on the same side of the building.

The house was full of noises, excited voices, doors opening and shutting, though I couldn't see anybody.

I ran down to Kavalov's door. It was open.

Kavalov was in there, lying on a low Spanish bed. The bedclothes were thrown down across the foot.

Kavalov was lying on his back. His throat had been cut, a curving cut that paralleled the line of his jaw between points an inch under his ear lobes.

Where his blood had soaked into the blue pillow case and blue sheet it was purple as grape-juice. It was thick and sticky, already clotting.

Ringgo came in wearing a bathrobe like a cape.

"It's happened," I growled, using the valet's words.

Ringgo looked dully, miserably, at the bed and began cursing in a choked, muffled, voice.

The red-faced blonde woman—Louella Qually, the housekeeper—came in, screamed, pushed past us, and ran to the bed, still screaming. I caught her arm when she reached for the covers.

"Let things alone," I said.

"Cover him up. Cover him up, the poor man!" she cried.

I took her away from the bed. Four or five servants were in the room by now. I gave the housekeeper to a couple of them, telling them to take her out and quiet her down. She went away laughing and crying.

Ringgo was still staring at the bed.

"Where's Mrs. Ringgo?" I asked.

He didn't hear me. I tapped his good arm and repeated the question.

"She's in her room. She—she didn't have to see it to know what had happened."

"Hadn't you better look after her?"

He nodded, turned slowly, and went out.

The valet, still lemon-yellow, came in.

"I want everybody on the place, servants, farm hands, everybody downstairs in the front room," I told him. "Get them all there right away, and they're to stay there till the sheriff comes."

"Yes, sir," he said and went downstairs, the others following him.

I closed Kavalov's door and went across to the library, where I phoned the sheriff's office in the county seat. I talked to a deputy named Hilden. When I had told him my story he said the sheriff would be at the house within half an hour.

I went to my room and dressed. By the time I had finished, the valet came up to tell me that everybody was assembled in the front room—everybody except the Ringgos and Mrs. Ringgo's maid.

I was examining Kavalov's bedroom when the sheriff arrived. He was a white-haired man with mild blue eyes and a mild voice that came out indistinctly under a white mustache. He had brought three deputies, a doctor and a coroner with him.

"Ringgo and the valet can tell you more than I can," I said when we had shaken hands all around. "I'll be back as soon as I can make it. I'm going to Sherry's. Ringgo will tell you where he fits in."

In the garage I selected a muddy Chevrolet and drove to the bungalow. Its doors and windows were tight, and my knocking brought no answer.

I went back along the cobbled walk to the car, and rode down into Farewell. There I had no trouble learning that Sherry and Marcus had taken the two-ten train for Los Angeles the afternoon before, with three trunks and half a dozen bags that the village expressman had checked for them.

After sending a telegram to the Agency's Los Angeles branch, I hunted up the man from whom Sherry had rented the bungalow.

He could tell me nothing about his tenants except that he was disappointed in their not staying even a full two weeks. Sherry had returned the keys with a brief note saying he had been called away unexpectedly.

I pocketed the note. Handwriting specimens are always convenient to have. Then I borrowed the keys to the bungalow and went back to it.

I didn't find anything of value there, except a lot of fingerprints that might possibly come in handy later. There was nothing there to tell me where my men had gone.

I returned to Kavalov's.

The sheriff had finished running the staff through the mill.

"Can't get a thing out of them," he said. "Nobody heard anything and nobody saw anything, from bedtime last night, till the valet opened the door to call him at eight o'clock this morning, and saw him dead like that. You know any more than that?"

"No. They tell you about Sherry?"

"Oh, yes. That's our meat, I guess, huh?"

"Yeah. He's supposed to have cleared out yesterday afternoon, with his black man, for Los Angeles. We ought to be able to find the work in that. What does the doctor say?"

"Says he was killed between three and four this morning, with a heavyish knife—one clean slash from left to right, like a left-handed man would do it."

"Maybe one clean cut," I agreed, "but not exactly a slash. Slower than that. A slash, if it curved, ought to curve up, away from the slasher, in the middle, and down towards him at the ends—just the opposite of what this does."

"Oh, all right. Is this Sherry a southpaw?"

"I don't know." I wondered if Marcus was. "Find the knife?"

"Nary hide nor hair of it. And what's more, we didn't find anything else, inside or out. Funny a fellow as scared as Kavalov was, from all accounts, didn't keep himself locked up tighter. His windows were open. Anybody could of got in them with a ladder. His door wasn't locked."

"There could be half a dozen reasons for that. He—"

One of the deputies, a big-shouldered blond man, came to the door and said:

"We found the knife."

The sheriff and I followed the deputy out of the house, around to the side on which Kavalov's room was situated. The knife's blade was buried in the ground, among some shrubs that bordered a path leading down to the farm hands' quarters.

The knife's wooden handle—painted red—slanted a little toward the house. A little blood was smeared on the blade, but the soft earth had cleaned off most. There was no blood on the painted handle, and nothing like a fingerprint.

There were no footprints in the soft ground near the knife. Apparently it had been tossed into the shrubbery.

"I guess that's all there is here for us," the sheriff said. "There's nothing much to show that anybody here had anything to do with it, or didn't. Now we'll look after this here Captain Sherry."

I went down to the village with him. At the post office we learned that Sherry had left a forwarding address: General Delivery, St. Louis, Mo. The postmaster said Sherry had received no mail during his stay in Farewell.

We went to the telegraph office, and were told that Sherry had neither received nor sent any telegrams. I sent one to the Agency's St. Louis branch.

The rest of our poking around in the village brought us nothing—except we learned that most of the idlers in Farewell had seen Sherry and Marcus board the southbound two-ten train.

Before we returned to the Kavalov house a telegram came from the Los Angeles branch for me:

> Sherry's trunks and bags in baggage room here
> not yet called for are keeping them under sur-
> veillance.

When we got back to the house I met Ringgo in the hall, and asked him:

"Is Sherry left-handed?"

He thought, and then shook his head.

"I can't remember," he said. "He might be. I'll ask Miriam. Perhaps she'll know—women remember things like that."

When he came downstairs again he was nodding:

"He's very nearly ambidextrous, but uses his left hand more than his right. Why?"

"The doctor thinks it was done with a left hand. How is Mrs. Ringgo now?"

"I think the worst of the shock is over, thanks."

VII

Sherry's baggage remained uncalled for in the Los Angeles passenger station all day Saturday. Late that afternoon the sheriff made public the news that Sherry and the black were wanted for murder, and that night the sheriff and I took a train south.

Sunday morning, with a couple of men from the Los Angeles police department, we opened the baggage. We didn't find anything except legitimate clothing and personal belongings that told us nothing.

That trip paid no dividends.

I returned to San Francisco and had bales of circulars printed and distributed.

Two weeks went by, two weeks in which the circulars brought us nothing but the usual lot of false alarms.

Then the Spokane police picked up Sherry and Marcus in a Stevens Street rooming house.

Some unknown person had phoned the police that one Fred Williams living there had a mysterious black visitor nearly every day, and that their actions were very suspicious. The Spokane police had copies of our circular. They hardly needed the H.S. monograms on Fred Williams' cuff links and handkerchiefs to assure them that he was our man.

After a couple of hours of being grilled, Sherry admitted his identity, but denied having murdered Kavalov.

Two of the sheriff's men went north and brought the prisoners down to the county seat.

Sherry had shaved off his mustache. There was nothing in his face or voice to show that he was the least bit worried.

"I knew there was nothing more to wait for after my dream," he drawled, "so I went away. Then, when I heard the dream had come true, I knew you johnnies would be hot after me—as if one can help his dreams—and I—ah—sought seclusion."

He solemnly repeated his orange-tree-voice story to the sheriff and district attorney. The newspapers liked it.

He refused to map his route for us, to tell us how he had spent his time.

"No, no," he said. "Sorry, but I shouldn't do it. It may be I shall have to do it again some time, and it wouldn't do to reveal my methods."

He wouldn't tell us where he had spent the night of the murder. We were fairly certain that he had left the train before it reached Los Angeles, though the train crew had been able to tell us nothing.

"Sorry," he drawled. "But if you chaps don't know where I was, how do you know that I was where the murder was?"

We had even less luck with Marcus. His formula was:

"Not understand the English very good. Ask the *capitaine*. I don't know."

The district attorney spent a lot of time walking his office floor, biting his finger nails, and telling us fiercely that the case was going to fall apart if we couldn't prove that either Sherry or Marcus was within reach of the Kavalov house at, or shortly before or after, the time of the murder.

The sheriff was the only one of us who hadn't a sneaky feeling that Sherry's sleeves were loaded with assorted aces. The sheriff saw him already hanged.

Sherry got a lawyer, a slick looking pale man with hornrim glasses and a thin twitching mouth. His name was Schaeffer. He went around smiling to himself and at us.

When the district attorney had only thumb nails left and was starting to work on them, I borrowed a car from Ringgo and started following the railroad south, trying to learn where Sherry had left the train. We had mugged the pair, of course, so I carried their photographs with me.

I displayed those damned photographs at every railroad stop between Farewell and Los Angeles, at every village within twenty miles of the tracks on either side, and at most of the houses in between. And it got me nothing.

There was no evidence that Sherry and Marcus hadn't gone through to Los Angeles.

Their train would have put them there at ten-thirty that night. There was no train out of Los Angeles that would have carried them back to Farewell in time to kill Kavalov. There were two possibilities: an airplane could have carried them back in plenty of time; and an automobile might have been able to do it, though that didn't look reasonable.

I tried the airplane angle first, and couldn't find a flyer who had had a passenger that night. With the help of the Los Angeles police and some operatives from the Continental's Los Angeles branch, I had everybody who owned a plane—public or private—interviewed. All the answers were no.

We tried the less promising automobile angle. The larger taxicab and hire-car companies said, "No." Four privately owned cars had been reported stolen between ten and twelve o'clock that night. Two of them had been found in the city the next morning: they couldn't have made the trip to Farewell and back. One of the others had been picked up in San Diego the next day. That let that one out. The other was still loose, a Packard sedan. We got a printer working on post card descriptions of it.

To reach all the small-fry taxi and hire-car owners was quite a job, and then there were the private car owners who might have hired out for one night. We went into the newspapers to cover these fields.

We didn't get any automobile information, but this new line of inquiry—trying to find traces of our men here a few hours before the murder—brought results of another kind.

At San Pedro (Los Angeles's seaport, twenty-five miles away) a negro had been arrested at one o'clock on the morning of the murder. The negro spoke English poorly, but had papers to prove that he was Pierre Tisano, a French sailor. He had been arrested on a drunk and disorderly charge.

The San Pedro police said that the photograph and description of the man we knew as Marcus fit the drunken sailor exactly.

That wasn't all the San Pedro police said.

Tisano had been arrested at one o'clock. At a little after two o'clock, a white man who gave his name as Henry Somerton had appeared and had tried to bail the negro out. The desk sergeant had told Somerton that nothing could be done till morning, and that, anyway, it would be better to let Tisano sleep off his jag before removing him. Somerton had readily agreed to that, had remained talking to the desk sergeant for more than half an hour, and had left at about three. At ten o'clock that morning he had reappeared to pay the black man's fine. They had gone away together.

The San Pedro police said that Sherry's photograph—without the mustache—and description were Henry Somerton's.

Henry Somerton's signature on the register of the hotel to which he had gone between his two visits to the police matched the handwriting in Sherry's note to the bungalow's owner.

It was pretty clear that Sherry and Marcus had been in San Pedro—a nine-hour train ride from Farewell—at the time that Kavalov was murdered.

Pretty clear isn't quite clear enough in a murder job: I carried the San Pedro desk sergeant north with me for a look at the two men.

"Them's them, all righty," he said.

VIII

The district attorney ate up the rest of his thumb nails.

The sheriff had the bewildered look of a child who had held a balloon in his hand, had heard a pop, and couldn't understand where the balloon had gone.

I pretended I was perfectly satisfied.

"Now we're back where we started," the district attorney wailed disagreeably, as if it was everybody's fault but his, "and with all those weeks wasted."

The sheriff didn't look at the district attorney, and didn't say anything.

I said:

"Oh, I wouldn't say that. We've made some progress."

"What?"

"We know that Sherry and the dinge have alibis."

The district attorney seemed to think I was trying to kid him. I didn't pay any attention to the faces he made at me, and asked:

"What are you going to do with them?"

"What can I do with them but turn them loose? This shoots the case to hell."

"It doesn't cost the county much to feed them," I suggested. "Why not hang on to them as long as you can, while we think it over? Something new may turn up, and you can always drop the case if nothing does. You don't think they're innocent, do you?"

He gave me a look that was heavy and sour with pity for my stupidity.

"They're guilty as hell, but what good's that to me if I can't get a conviction? And what's the good of saying I'll hold them? Damn it, man, you know as well as I do that all they've got to do now is ask for their release and any judge will hand it to them."

"Yeah," I agreed. "I'll bet you the best hat in San Francisco that they don't ask for it."

"What do you mean?"

"They want to stand trial," I said, "or they'd have sprung that alibi before we dug it up. I've an idea that they tipped off the Spokane police themselves. And I'll bet you that hat that you get no *habeas corpus* motions out of Schaeffer."

The district attorney peered suspiciously into my eyes.

"Do you know something that you're holding back?" he demanded.

"No, but you'll see I'm right."

I was right. Schaeffer went around smiling to himself and making no attempt to get his clients out of the county prison.

Three days later something new turned up.

A man named Archibald Weeks, who had a small chicken farm some ten miles south of the Kavalov place, came to see the district attorney. Weeks said he had seen Sherry on his—Weeks's—place early on the morning of the murder.

Weeks had been leaving for Iowa that morning to visit his parents. He had got up early to see that everything was in order before driving twenty miles to catch an early morning train.

At somewhere between half-past five and six o'clock he had gone to the shed where he kept his car, to see if it held enough gasoline for the trip.

A man ran out of the shed, vaulted the fence, and dashed away down the road. Weeks chased him for a short distance, but the other was too speedy for him. The man was too well-dressed for a hobo: Weeks supposed he had been trying to steal the car.

Since Weeks's trip east was a necessary one, and during his absence his wife would have only their two sons—one seventeen, one fifteen—there with her, he had thought it wisest not to frighten her by saying anything about the man he had surprised in the shed.

He had returned from Iowa the day before his appearance in the district attorney's office, and after hearing the details of the Kavalov murder, and seeing Sherry's picture in the papers, had recognized him as the man he had chased.

We showed him Sherry in person. He said Sherry was the man. Sherry said nothing.

With Weeks's evidence to refute the San Pedro police's, the district attorney let the case against Sherry come to trial. Marcus was held as a material witness, but there was nothing to weaken his San Pedro alibi, so he was not tried.

Weeks told his story straight and simply on the witness stand, and then, under cross-examination, blew up with a loud bang. He went to pieces completely.

He wasn't, he admitted in answer to Schaeffer's questions, quite as sure that Sherry was the man as he had been before. The man had certainly, the little he had seen of him, looked something like Sherry, but perhaps he had been a little hasty in saying positively that it was Sherry. He wasn't, now that he had had time to think it over, really sure that he had actually got a good look at the man's face in the dim morning light. Finally, all that Weeks would swear to was that he had seen a man who had seemed to look a little bit like Sherry.

It was funny as hell.

The district attorney, having no nails left, nibbled his finger-bones.

The jury said, "Not guilty."

Sherry was freed, forever in the clear so far as the Kavalov murder was concerned, no matter what might come to light later.

Marcus was released.

The district attorney wouldn't say good-bye to me when I left for San Francisco.

IX

Four days after Sherry's acquittal, Mrs. Ringgo was shown into my office.

She was in black. Her pretty, unintelligent, Oriental face was not placid. Worry was in it.

"Please, you won't tell Dolph I have come here?" were the first words she spoke.

"Of course not, if you say not," I promised and pulled a chair over for her.

She sat down and looked big-eyed at me, fidgeting with her gloves in her lap.

"He's so reckless," she said.

I nodded sympathetically, wondering what she was up to.

"And I'm so afraid," she added, twisting her gloves. Her chin trembled. Her lips formed words jerkily: "They've come back to the bungalow."

"Yeah?" I sat up straight. I knew who *they* were.

"They can't," she cried, "have come back for any reason except that they mean to murder Dolph as they did father. And he won't listen to me. He's so sure of himself. He laughs and calls me a foolish child, and tells me he can take care of himself. But he can't. Not, at least, with a broken arm. And they'll kill him as they killed father. I know it. I know it."

"Sherry hates your husband as much as he hated your father?"

"Yes. That's it. He does. Dolph was working for father, but Dolph's part in the—the business that led up to Hugh's trouble was more—more active than father's. Will you—will you keep them from killing Dolph? Will you?"

"Surely."

"And you mustn't let Dolph know," she insisted, "and if he does find out you're watching them, you mustn't tell him I got you to. He'd be angry with me. I asked him to send for you, but he—" She broke off, looking embarrassed: I supposed her husband had mentioned my lack of success in keeping Kavalov alive. "But he wouldn't."

"How long have they been back?"

"Since the day before yesterday."

"Any demonstrations?"

"You mean things like happened before? I don't know. Dolph would hide them from me."

"I'll be down tomorrow," I promised. "If you'll take my advice you'll tell your husband that you've employed me, but I won't tell him if you don't."

"And you won't let them harm Dolph?"

I promised to do my best, took some money away from her, gave her a receipt, and bowed her out.

Shortly after dark that evening I reached Farewell.

X

The bungalow's windows were lighted when I passed it on my way uphill. I was tempted to get out of my coupé and do some snooping, but was afraid that I couldn't out-Indian Marcus on his own grounds, and so went on.

When I turned into the dirt road leading to the vacant house I had spotted on my first trip to Farewell, I switched off the coupé's lights and crept along by the light of a very white moon overhead.

Close to the vacant house I got the coupé off the path and at least partly hidden by bushes.

Then I went up on the rickety porch, located the bungalow, and began to adjust my field glasses to it.

I had them partly adjusted when the bungalow's front door opened, letting out a slice of yellow light and two people.

One of the people was a woman.

Another least turn of the set-screw and her face came clear in my eyes—Mrs. Ringgo.

She raised her coat collar around her face and hurried away down the cobbled walk. Sherry stood on the veranda looking after her.

When she reached the road she began running uphill, towards her house.

Sherry went indoors and shut the door.

I took the glasses away from my eyes and looked around for a place where I could sit. The only spot I could find where sitting wouldn't interfere with my view of the bungalow was the porch-rail. I made myself as comfortable as possible there, with a shoulder against the corner post, and prepared for an evening of watchful waiting.

Two hours and a half later a man turned into the cobbled walk from the road. He walked swiftly to the bungalow, with a cautious sort of swiftness, and he looked from side to side as he walked.

I suppose he knocked on the door.

The door opened, throwing a yellow glow on his face, Dolph Ringgo's face.

He went indoors. The door shut.

My watch-tower's fault was that the bungalow could only be reached from it roundabout by the path and road. There was no way of cutting cross-country.

I put away the field glasses, left the porch, and set out for the bungalow. I wasn't sure that I could find another good spot for the coupé, so I left it where it was and walked.

I was afraid to take a chance on the cobbled walk.

Twenty feet above it, I left the road and moved as silently as I could over sod and among trees, bushes and flowers. I knew the sort of folks I was playing with: I carried my gun in my hand.

All of the bungalow's windows on my side showed lights, but all the windows were closed and their blinds drawn. I didn't like the way the light that came through the blinds helped the moon illuminate the surrounding ground. That had been swell when I was up on the ridge getting cock-eyed squinting through glasses. It was sour now that I was trying to get close enough to do some profitable listening.

I stopped in the closest dark spot I could find—fifteen feet from the building—to think the situation over.

Crouching there, I heard something.

It wasn't in the right place. It wasn't what I wanted to hear. It was the sound of somebody coming down the walk towards the house.

I wasn't sure that I couldn't be seen from the path. I turned my head to make sure. And by turning my head I gave myself away.

Mrs. Ringgo jumped, stopped dead still in the path, and then cried:

"Is Dolph in there? Is he? Is he?"

I was trying to tell her that he was by nodding, but she made so much noise with her *Is he's* that I had to say "Yeah" out loud to make her hear.

I don't know whether the noise we made hurried things up indoors or not, but guns had started going off inside the bungalow.

You don't stop to count shots in circumstances like those, and anyway these were too blurred together for accurate score-keeping, but my impression was that at least fifty of them had been fired by the time I was bruising my shoulder on the front door.

Luckily, it was a California door. It went in the second time I hit it.

Inside was a reception hall opening through a wide arched doorway into a living-room. The air was hazy and the stink of burnt powder was sharp.

Sherry was on the polished floor by the arch, wriggling sidewise on one elbow and one knee, trying to reach a Luger that lay on an amber rug some four feet away. His upper teeth were sunk deep into his lower lip, and he was coughing little stomach coughs as he wriggled.

At the other end of the room, Ringgo was upright on his knees, steadily working the trigger of a black revolver in his good hand. The pistol was empty. It went snap, snap, snap, snap foolishly, but he kept on working the trigger. His broken arm was still in the splints, but had fallen out of the sling and was hanging down. His face was puffy and florid with blood. His eyes were wide and dull. The white bone handle of a knife stuck out of his back, just over one hip, its blade all the way in. He was clicking the empty pistol at Marcus.

The black boy was on his feet, feet far apart under bent knees. His left hand was spread wide over his chest, and the black fingers were shiny with blood. In his right hand he held a white bone-handled knife—its blade a foot long—held it, knife-fighter fashion, as you'd hold a sword. He was moving toward Ringgo, not directly, but from side to side, obliquely, closing in with shuffling steps, crouching, his hand turning the knife restlessly, but holding the point always towards Ringgo. Marcus's eyes were bulging and red-veined. His mouth was a wide grinning crescent. His tongue, far out, ran slowly around and around the outside of his lips. Saliva trickled down his chin.

He didn't see us. He didn't hear us. All of his world just then was the man on his knees, the man in whose back a knife—brother of the one in the black hand—was wedged.

Ringgo didn't see us. I don't suppose he even saw the black. He knelt there and persistently worked the trigger of his empty gun.

I jumped over Sherry and swung the barrel of my gun at the base of Marcus's skull. It hit. Marcus dropped.

Ringgo stopped working the gun and looked surprised at me.

"That's the idea; you've got to put bullets in them or they're no good," I told him, pulled the knife out of Marcus's hand, and went back to pick up the Luger that Sherry had stopped trying to get.

Mrs. Ringgo ran past me to her husband.

Sherry was lying on his back now. His eyes were closed.

He looked dead, and he had enough bullet holes in him to make death a good guess.

Hoping he wasn't dead, I knelt beside him—going around him so I could kneel facing Ringgo—and lifted his head up a little from the floor.

Sherry stirred then, but I couldn't tell whether he stirred because he was still alive or because he had just died.

"Sherry," I said sharply. "Sherry."

He didn't move. His eyelids didn't even twitch.

I raised the fingers of the hand that was holding up his head, making his head move just a trifle.

"Did Ringgo kill Kavalov?" I asked the dead or dying man.

Even if I hadn't known Ringgo was looking at me I could have felt his eyes on me.

"Did he, Sherry?" I barked into the still face.

The dead or dying man didn't move.

I cautiously moved my fingers again so that his dead or dying head nodded, twice.

Then I made his head jerk back, and let it gently down on the floor again.

"Well," I said, standing up and facing Ringgo, "I've got you at last."

XI

I've never been able to decide whether I would actually have gone on the witness stand and sworn that Sherry was alive when he nodded, and nodded voluntarily, if it had been necessary for me to do so to convict Ringgo.

I don't like perjury, but I knew Ringgo was guilty, and there I had him.

Fortunately, I didn't have to decide.

Ringgo believed Sherry had nodded, and then, when Marcus gave the show away, there was nothing much for Ringgo to do but try his luck with a plea of guilty.

We didn't have much trouble getting the story out of Marcus. Ringgo had killed his beloved *capitaine*. The black boy was easily persuaded that the law would give him his best revenge.

After Marcus had talked, Ringgo was willing to talk.

He stayed in the hospital until the day before his trial opened. The knife Marcus had planted in his back had permanently paralyzed one of his legs, though aside from that he recovered from the stabbing.

Marcus had three of Ringgo's bullets in him. The doctors fished two of them out, but were afraid to touch the third. It didn't seem to worry him. By the time he was shipped north to begin an indeterminate sentence in San Quentin for his part in the Kavalov murder he was apparently as sound as ever.

Ringgo was never completely convinced that I had ever suspected him before the last minute when I had come charging into the bungalow.

"Of course I had, right along," I defended my skill as a sleuth. That was while he was still in the hospital. "I didn't believe Sherry was cracked. He was one hard, sane-looking scoundrel. And I didn't believe he was the sort of man who'd be worried much over any disgrace that came his way. I was willing enough to believe that he was out for Kavalov's scalp, but only if there was some profit in it. That's why I went to sleep and let the old man's throat get cut. I figured Sherry was scaring him up—nothing more—to get him in shape for a big-money shakedown. Well, when I found out I had been wrong there I began to look around.

"So far as I knew, your wife was Kavalov's heir. From what I had seen, I imagined your wife was enough in love with you to be completely in your hands. All right, you, as the husband of his heir, seemed the one to profit most directly by Kavalov's death. You were the one who'd have control of his fortune when he died. Sherry could only profit by the murder if he was working with you."

"But didn't his breaking my arm puzzle you?"

"Sure. I could understand a phoney injury, but that seemed carrying it a little too far. But you made a mistake there that helped me. You were too careful to imitate a left-hand cut on Kavalov's throat; did it by standing by his head, facing his body when you cut him, instead of by his body, facing his head, and the curve of the slash gave you away. Throwing the knife out the window wasn't so good, either. How'd he happen to break your arm? An accident?"

"You can call it that. We had that supposed fight arranged to fit in with the rest of the play, and I thought it would be fun to really sock him. So I did. And he was tougher than I thought, tough enough to even up by snapping my arm. I suppose that's why he killed Mickey too. That wasn't on the schedule. On the level, did you suspect us of being in cahoots?"

I nodded.

"Sherry had worked the game up for you, had done everything possible to draw suspicion on himself, and then, the day before the murder, had run off to build himself an alibi. There couldn't be any other answer to it: he had to be working with you. There it was, but I couldn't prove it. I couldn't prove it till you were trapped by the thing that made the whole game possible—your wife's love for you sent her to hire me to protect you. Isn't that one of the things they call ironies of life?"

Ringgo smiled ruefully and said:

"They should call it that. You know what Sherry was trying on me, don't you?"

"I can guess. That's why he insisted on standing trial."

"Exactly. The scheme was for him to dig out and keep going, with his alibi ready in case he was picked up, but staying uncaught as long as possible. The more time they wasted hunting him, the less likely they were to look elsewhere, and the colder the trail would be when they found he wasn't their man. He tricked me there. He had himself picked up, and his lawyer hired that Weeks fellow to egg the district attorney into not dropping the case. Sherry wanted to be tried and acquitted, so he'd be in the clear. Then he had me by the neck. He was legally cleared forever. I wasn't. He had me. He was supposed to get a hundred thousand dollars for his part. Kavalov had left Miriam something more than three million dollars. Sherry demanded one-half of it. Otherwise, he said, he'd go to the district attorney and make a complete confession. They couldn't do anything to him. He'd been acquitted. They'd hang me. That was sweet."

"You'd have been wise at that to have given it to him," I said.

"Maybe. Anyway I suppose I would have given it to him if Miriam hadn't upset things. There'd have been nothing else to do. But after she came back from hiring you she went to see Sherry, thinking she could talk him into going away. And he lets something drop that made her suspect I had a hand in her father's death, though she doesn't even now actually believe that I cut his throat.

"She said you were coming down the next day. There was nothing for me to do but go down to Sherry's for a showdown that night, and have the whole thing settled before you came poking around. Well, that's what I did, though I didn't tell Miriam I was going. The showdown wasn't going along very well, too much tension, and when Sherry heard you outside he thought I had brought friends, and—fireworks."

"What ever got you into a game like that in the first place?" I asked. "You were sitting pretty enough as Kavalov's son-in-law, weren't you?"

"Yes, but it was tiresome being cooped up in that hole with him. He was young enough to live a long time. And he wasn't always easy to get along with. I'd no guarantee that he wouldn't get up on his ear and kick me out, or change his will, or anything of the sort.

"Then I ran across Sherry in San Francisco, and we got to talking it over, and this plan came out of it. Sherry had brains. On the deal back in Cairo that you know about, both he and I made plenty that Kavalov didn't know about. Well, I was a chump. But don't think I'm sorry that I killed Kavalov. I'm sorry I got caught. I'd done his dirty work since he picked me up as a kid of twenty, and all I'd got out of it was damned little except the hopes that since I'd married his daughter I'd probably get his money when he died—if he didn't do something else with it."

They hanged him.

Woman in the Dark

H ER right ankle turned under her and she fell. The wind blowing downhill from the south, whipping the trees beside the road, made a whisper of her exclamation and snatched her scarf away into the darkness. She sat up slowly, palms on the gravel pushing her up, and twisted her body sidewise to release the leg bent beneath her.

Her right slipper lay in the road close to her feet. When she put it on she found its heel was missing. She peered around, then began to hunt for the heel, hunting on hands and knees uphill into the wind, wincing a little when her right knee touched the road. Presently she gave it up and tried to break the heel off her left slipper, but could not. She replaced the slipper and rose with her back to the wind, leaning back against the wind's violence and the road's steep sloping. Her gown clung to her back, flew fluttering out before her. Hair lashed her cheeks. Walking high on the ball of her right foot to make up for the missing heel, she hobbled on down the hill.

At the bottom of the hill there was a wooden bridge, and, a hundred yards beyond, a sign that could not be read in the darkness marked a fork in the road. She halted there, not looking at the sign but around her, shivering now, though the wind had less force than it had had on the hill. Foliage to her left moved to show and hide yellow light. She took the left-hand fork.

In a little while she came to a gap in the bushes beside the road and sufficient light to show a path running off the road through the gap. The light came from the thinly curtained window of a house at the other end of the path.

She went up the path to the door and knocked. When there was no answer she knocked again.

A hoarse unemotional masculine voice said: "Come in."

She put her hand on the latch; hesitated. No sound came from within the house. Outside the wind was noisy everywhere. She knocked once more, gently.

The voice said exactly as before: "Come in."

She opened the door. The wind blew it in sharply, her hold on the latch dragging her with it so that she had to cling to the door with both hands to keep from falling. The wind went past her into the room, to balloon curtains and scatter the sheets of a newspaper that had been on a table. She forced the door shut and, still leaning against it, said: "I am sorry." She took pains with her words to make them clear notwithstanding her accent.

The man cleaning a pipe at the hearth said: "It's all right." His copperish eyes were as impersonal as his hoarse voice. "I'll be through in a minute." He did not rise from his chair. The edge of the knife in his hand rasped inside the brier bowl of his pipe.

She left the door and came forward, limping, examining him with perplexed eyes under brows drawn a little together. She was a tall woman and carried herself proudly, for all she was lame and the wind had tousled her hair and the gravel of the road had cut and dirtied her hands and bare arms and the red crêpe of her gown.

She said, still taking pains with her words: "I must go to the railroad. I have hurt my ankle on the road. Eh?"

He looked up from his work then. His sallow, heavily featured face, under coarse hair nearly the color of his eyes, was definitely neither hostile nor friendly. He looked at the woman's face, at her torn skirt. He did not turn his head to call: "Hey, Evelyn."

A girl—slim maturing body in tan sport clothes, slender sunburned face with dark bright eyes and dark short hair—came into the room through a doorway behind him.

The man did not look around at her. He nodded at the woman in red and said: "This—"

The woman interrupted him: "My name is Luise Fischer."

The man said: "She's got a bum leg."

Evelyn's dark prying eyes shifted their focus from the woman to the man—she could not see his face—and to the woman again. She smiled, speaking hurriedly: "I'm just leaving. I can drop you at Mile Valley on my way home."

The woman seemed about to smile. Under her curious gaze Evelyn suddenly blushed and her face became defiant while it reddened. The girl was pretty. Facing her the woman had become beautiful; her eyes were long, heavily lashed, set well apart under a smooth broad brow, her mouth was not small but sensitively carved and mobile, and in the light from the open fire the surfaces of her face were as clearly defined as sculptured planes.

The man blew through his pipe, forcing out a small cloud of black powder. "No use hurrying," he said. "There's no train till six." He looked up at the clock on the mantelpiece. It said ten thirty-three. "Why don't you help her with her leg?"

The woman said: "No, it is not necessary. I—" She put her weight on her injured leg and flinched, steadying herself with a hand on the back of a chair.

The girl hurried to her, stammering contritely: "I—I didn't think. Forgive me." She put an arm around the woman and helped her into the chair.

The man stood up to put his pipe on the mantelpiece beside the clock. He was of medium height, but his sturdiness made him look shorter. His neck, rising from the V of a gray sweater, was short, powerfully muscled. Below the sweater he wore loose gray trousers and heavy brown shoes. He clicked his knife shut and put it in his pocket before turning to look at Luise Fischer.

Evelyn was on her knees in front of the woman, pulling off her right stocking, making sympathetic clucking noises, chattering nervously: "You've cut your knee too. Tch-tch-tch! And look how your ankle's swelling. You shouldn't've tried to walk all that distance in these slippers." Her body hid the woman's bare leg from the man. "Now sit still and I'll fix it up in a minute." She pulled the torn red skirt down over the bare leg.

The woman's smile was polite. She said carefully: "You are very kind."

The girl ran out of the room.

The man had a paper package of cigarettes in his hand. He shook it until three cigarettes protruded half an inch and held them out to her. "Smoke?"

"Thank you." She took a cigarette, put it between her lips, and looked at his hand when he held a match to it. His hand was thick-boned, muscular, but not a laborer's. She looked through her lashes at his face while he was lighting his cigarette. He was younger than he had seemed at first glance—perhaps no older than thirty-two or three—and his features, in the flare of his match, seemed less stolid than disciplined.

"Bang it up much?" His tone was merely conversational.

"I hope I have not." She drew up her skirt to look first at her ankle, then at her knee. The ankle was perceptibly though not greatly swollen; the knee was cut once deeply, twice less seriously. She touched the edges of the cuts gently with a forefinger. "I do not like pain," she said very earnestly.

Evelyn came in with a basin of steaming water, cloths, a roll of bandage, salve. Her dark eyes widened at the man and woman, but were hidden by lowered lids by the time their faces had turned toward her. "I'll fix it now. I'll have it all fixed in a minute." She knelt in front of the woman again, nervous hand sloshing water on the floor, body between Luise Fischer's leg and the man.

He went to the door and looked out, holding the door half a foot open against the wind.

The woman asked the girl bathing her ankle: "There is not a train before it is morning?" She pursed her lips thoughtfully.

"No."

The man shut the door and said: "It'll be raining in an hour." He put more wood on the fire, then stood—legs apart, hands in pockets, cigarette dangling from one side of his mouth—watching Evelyn attend to the woman's leg. His face was placid.

The girl dried the ankle and began to wind a bandage around it, working with increasing speed, breathing more rapidly now. Once more the woman seemed about to smile at the girl, but instead she said, "You are very kind."

The girl murmured, "It's nothing."

Three sharp knocks sounded on the door.

Luise Fischer started, dropped her cigarette, looked swiftly around the room with frightened eyes. The girl did not raise her head from her work. The man, with nothing in his face or manner to show he had noticed the woman's fright, turned his face toward the door and called in his hoarse matter-of-fact voice: "All right. Come in."

The door opened and a spotted great Dane came in, followed by two tall men in dinner clothes. The dog walked straight to Luise Fischer and nuzzled her hand. She was looking at the two men who had just entered. There was no timidity, no warmth in her gaze.

One of the men pulled off his cap—it was a gray tweed matching his topcoat—and came to her smiling. "So this is where you landed?" His smile vanished as he saw her leg and the bandages. "What happened?" He was perhaps forty years old, well groomed, graceful of carriage, with smooth dark hair, intelligent dark eyes—solicitous at the moment—and a close-clipped dark mustache. He pushed the dog aside and took the woman's hand.

"It is not serious, I think." She did not smile. Her voice was cool. "I stumbled in the road and twisted my ankle. These people have been very—"

He turned to the man in the gray sweater, holding out his hand, saying briskly: "Thanks ever so much for taking care of *Fräulein* Fischer. You're Brazil, aren't you?"

The man in the sweater nodded. "And you'd be Kane Robson."

"Right." Robson jerked his head at the man who still stood just inside the door. "Mr. Conroy."

Brazil nodded. Conroy said, "How do you do," and advanced toward Luise Fischer. He was an inch or two taller than Robson—who was nearly six feet himself—and some ten years younger, blond, broad-shouldered, and lean, with a beautifully shaped small head and remarkably symmetrical features. A dark overcoat hung over one of his arms and he carried a black hat in his hand. He smiled down at the woman and said: "Your idea of a lark's immense."

She addressed Robson: "Why have you come here?"

He smiled amiably, raised his shoulders a little. "You said you weren't feeling well and were going to lie down. When Helen went up to your room to see how you were, you weren't there. We were afraid you had gone out and something had happened to you." He looked at her leg, moved his shoulders again. "Well, we were right."

Nothing in her face responded to his smile. "I am going to the city," she told him. "Now you know."

"All right, if you want to"—he was good-natured—"but you can't go like that." He nodded at her torn evening dress. "We'll take you back home, where you can change your clothes and pack a bag and—" He turned to Brazil. "When's the next train?"

Brazil said: "Six." The dog was sniffing at his legs.

"You see," Robson said blandly, speaking to the woman again. "There's plenty of time."

She looked down at her clothes and seemed to find them satisfactory. "I go like this," she replied.

"Now look here, Luise," Robson began again, quite reasonably. "You've got hours before train time—time enough to get some rest and a nap and to—"

She said simply: "I have gone."

Robson grimaced impatiently, half humorously, and turned his palms out in a gesture of helplessness. "But what are you going to do?" he asked in a tone that matched the gesture. "You're not going to expect Brazil to put you up till train time and then drive you to the station?"

She looked at Brazil with level eyes and asked calmly: "Is it too much?"

Brazil shook his head carelessly. "Uh-uh."

Robson and Conroy turned together to look at Brazil. There was considerable interest in their eyes, but no visible hostility. He bore the inspection placidly.

Luise Fischer said coolly, with an air of finality: "So."

Conroy looked questioningly at Robson, who sighed wearily and asked: "Your mind's made up on this, Luise?"

"Yes."

Robson shrugged again, said: "You always know what you want." Face and voice were grave. He started to turn away toward the door, then stopped to ask: "Have you got enough money?" One of his hands went to the inner breast pocket of his dinner jacket.

"I want nothing," she told him.

"Right. If you want anything later let me know. Come on, Dick."

He went to the door, opened it, twisted his head around to direct a brisk "Thanks, good night" at Brazil, and went out.

Conroy touched Luise Fischer's forearm lightly with three fingers, said "Good luck" to her, bowed to Evelyn and Brazil, and followed Robson out.

The dog raised his head to watch the two men go out. The girl Evelyn stared at the door with despairing eyes and worked her hands together. Luise Fischer told Brazil: "You will be wise to lock your door."

He stared at her for a long moment, brooding, and while no actual change seemed to take place in his expression all his facial muscles stiffened. "No," he said finally, "I won't lock it."

The woman's eyebrows went up a little, but she said nothing. The girl spoke, addressing Brazil for the first time since Luise Fischer's arrival. Her voice was peculiarly emphatic. "They were drunk."

"They've been drinking," he conceded. He looked thoughtfully at her, apparently only then noticing her perturbation. "You look like a drink would do *you* some good."

She became confused. Her eyes evaded his. "Do—do you want one?"

"I think so." He looked inquiringly at Luise Fischer, who nodded and said: "Thank you."

The girl went out of the room. The woman leaned forward a little to look intently up at Brazil. Her voice was calm enough, but the deliberate slowness with which she spoke made her words impressive: "Do not make the mistake of thinking Mr. Robson is not dangerous."

He seemed to weigh this speech almost sleepily; then, regarding her with a slight curiosity, he asked: "I've made an enemy?"

Her nod was sure.

He accepted that with a faint grin, offering her his cigarettes again, asking: "Have you?"

She stared through him as if studying some distant thing and replied slowly: "Yes, but I have lost a worse friend."

Evelyn came in carrying a tray that held glasses, mineral water, and a bottle of whisky. Her dark eyes, glancing from man to woman, were inquisitive, somewhat furtive. She went to the table and began to mix drinks.

Brazil finished lighting his cigarette and asked: "Leaving him for good?"

For the moment during which she stared haughtily at him it seemed that the woman did not intend to answer his question; but suddenly her face was distorted by an expression of utter hatred and she spit out a venomous "*Ja!*"

He set his glass on the mantelpiece and went to the door. He went through the motions of looking out into the night; yet he opened the door a bare couple of inches and shut it immediately, and his manner was so far from nervous that he seemed preoccupied with something else.

He turned to the mantelpiece, picked up his glass, and drank. Then, his eyes focused contemplatively on the lowered glass, he was about to speak when a telephone bell rang behind a door facing the fireplace. He opened the door, and as soon as he had passed out of sight his hoarse unemotional voice could be heard. "Hello? . . . Yes. . . . Yes, Nora. . . . Just a moment." He reëntered the room saying to the girl: "Nora wants to talk to you." He shut the bedroom door behind her.

Luise said: "You cannot have lived here long if you did not know Kane Robson before tonight."

"A month or so; but of course he was in Europe till he came back last week"—he paused—"with you." He picked up his glass. "Matter of fact, he is my landlord."

"Then you—" She broke off as the bedroom door opened. Evelyn stood in the doorway, hands to breast, and cried: "Father's coming—somebody phoned him I was here." She hurried across the room to pick up hat and coat from a chair.

Brazil said: "Wait. You'll meet him on the road if you go now. You'll have to wait till he gets here, then duck out back and beat him home while he's jawing at me. I'll stick your car down at the foot of the back road." He drained his glass and started for the bedroom door.

"But you won't"—her lip quivered—"won't fight with him? Promise me you won't."

"I won't." He went into the bedroom, returning almost immediately with a soft brown hat on his head and one of his arms in a raincoat. "It'll only take me five minutes." He went out the front door.

Luise Fischer said: "Your father does not approve?"

The girl shook her head miserably. Then suddenly she turned to the woman, holding her hands out in an appealing gesture, lips—almost colorless—moving jerkily as her words tumbled out: "You'll be here. Don't let them fight. They mustn't."

The woman took the girl's hands and put them together between her own, saying: "I will do what I can, I promise you."

"He mustn't get in trouble again," the girl moaned. "He mustn't!"

The door opened and Brazil came in.

"That's done," he said cheerfully, and took off his raincoat, dropping it on a chair, putting his damp hat on it. "I left it at the end of the fence." He picked up the woman's empty glass and his own and went to the table. "Better slide out to the kitchen in case he pops in suddenly." He began to pour whisky into the glasses.

The girl wet her lips with her tongue, said, "Yes, I guess so," indistinctly, smiled timidly, pleadingly, at Luise Fischer, hesitated, and touched his sleeve with her fingers. "You— you'll behave?"

"Sure." He did not stop preparing their drinks.

"I'll call you up tomorrow." She smiled at Luise Fischer and moved reluctantly toward the door.

Brazil gave the woman her glass, pulled a chair around to face her more directly, and sat down.

"Your little friend," the woman said, "she loves you very much."

He seemed doubtful. "Oh, she's just a kid," he said.

"But her father," she suggested, "he is not nice—eh?"

"He's cracked," he replied carelessly, then became thoughtful. "Suppose Robson phoned him?"

"Would he know?"

He smiled a little. "In a place like this everybody knows all about everybody."

"Then about me," she began, "you—"

She was interrupted by a pounding on the door that shook it on its hinges and filled the room with thunder. The dog came up stiff-legged on its feet.

Brazil gave the woman a brief grim smile and called: "All right. Come in." His hoarse voice was unemotional.

The door was violently opened by a medium-sized man in a glistening black rubber coat that hung to his ankles. Dark eyes set too close together burned under the down-turned brim of a gray hat. A pale bony nose jutted out above ragged short-cut grizzled mustache and beard. One fist gripped a heavy applewood walking stick.

"Where is my daughter?" this man demanded. His voice was deep, powerful, resounding.

Brazil's face was a phlegmatic mask. "Hello, Grant," he said.

The man in the doorway took another step forward. "Where is my daughter?"

The dog growled and showed its teeth. Luise Fischer said: "Franz!" The dog looked at her and moved its tail sidewise an inch or two and back.

Brazil said: "Evelyn's not here."

Grant glared at him. "Where is she?"

Brazil was placid. "I don't know."

"That's a lie!" Grant's eyes darted their burning gaze around the room. The knuckles of his hand holding the stick were white. "Evelyn!" he called.

Luise Fischer, smiling as if entertained by the bearded man's rage, said: "It is so, Mr. Grant. There is nobody else here."

He glanced briefly at her, with loathing in his mad eyes. "Bah! The strumpet's word confirms the convict's!" He strode to the bedroom door and disappeared inside.

Brazil grinned. "See? He's cracked. He always talks like that—like a guy in a bum book."

She smiled at him and said: "Be patient."

"I'm being," he said dryly.

Grant came out of the bedroom and stamped across to the rear door, opening it and disappearing through it.

Brazil emptied his glass and put it on the floor beside his chair. "There'll be more fireworks when he comes back."

When the bearded man returned to the room he stalked in silence to the front door, pulled it open, and holding the latch with one hand, banging the ferrule of his walking stick on the floor with the other, roared at Brazil: "For the last time, I'm telling you not to have anything to do with my daughter! I shan't tell you again." He went out, slamming the door.

Brazil exhaled heavily and shook his head. "Cracked," he sighed. "Absolutely cracked."

Luise Fischer said: "He called me a strumpet. Do people here—"

He was not listening to her. He had left his chair and was picking up his hat and coat. "I want to slip down and see if she got away all right. If she gets home first she'll be O.K. Nora—that's her stepmother—will take care of her. But if she doesn't— I won't be long." He went out the back way.

Luise Fischer kicked off her remaining slipper and stood up, experimenting with her weight on her injured leg. Three tentative steps proved her leg stiff but serviceable. She saw then that her hands and arms were still dirty from the road and, exploring, presently found a bathroom opening off the bedroom. She hummed a tune to herself while she washed and, in the bedroom again, while she combed her hair and brushed her clothes—but broke off impatiently when she failed to find powder or lipstick. She was studying her reflection in a tall looking-glass when she heard the outer door opening.

Her face brightened. "I am here," she called, and went into the other room.

Robson and Conroy were standing inside the door.

"So you are, my dear," Robson said, smiling at her start of surprise. He was paler than before and his eyes were glassier, but he seemed otherwise unchanged. Conroy, however, was somewhat disheveled; his face was flushed and he was obviously rather drunk.

The woman had recovered composure. "What do you want?" she demanded bluntly.

Robson looked around. "Where's Brazil?"

"What do you want?" she repeated.

He looked past her at the open bedroom door, grinned, and crossed to it. When he turned from the empty room she sneered at him. Conroy had gone to the fireplace, where the great Dane was lying, and was standing with his back to the fire watching them.

Robson said: "Well, it's like this, Luise: you're going back home with me."

She said: "No."

He wagged his head up and down, grinning. "I haven't got my money's worth out of you yet." He took a step toward her.

She retreated to the table, caught up the whisky bottle by its neck. "Do not touch me!" Her voice, like her face, was cold with fury.

The dog rose growling.

Robson's dark eyes jerked sidewise to focus on the dog, then on Conroy—and one eyelid twitched—then on the woman again.

Conroy—with neither tenseness nor furtiveness to alarm woman or dog—put his right hand into his overcoat pocket, brought out a black pistol, put its muzzle close behind one of the dog's ears, and shot the dog through the head. The dog tried to leap, fell on its side, and its legs stirred feebly. Conroy, smiling foolishly, returned the pistol to his pocket.

Luise Fischer spun around at the sound of the shot. Screaming at Conroy, she raised the bottle to hurl it. But Robson caught her wrist with one hand, wrenched the bottle away with the other. He was grinning, saying, "No, no, my sweet," in a bantering voice.

He put the bottle on the table again, but kept his grip on her wrist.

The dog's legs stopped moving.

Robson said: "All right. Now are you ready to go?"

She made no attempt to free her wrist. She drew herself up straight and said very seriously: "My friend, you do not know me yet if you think I am going with you."

Robson chuckled. "You don't know me if you think you're not," he told her.

The front door opened and Brazil came in. His sallow face was phlegmatic, though there was a shade of annoyance in his eyes. He shut the door carefully behind him, then addressed his guests. His voice was that of one who complains without anger. "What the hell is this?" he asked. "Visitors' day? Am I supposed to be running a road house?"

Robson said: "We are going now. *Fräulein* Fischer's going with us."

Brazil was looking at the dead dog, annoyance deepening in his copperish eyes. "That's all right if she wants to," he said indifferently.

The woman said: "I am not going."

Brazil was still looking at the dog. "That's all right too," he muttered, and with more interest: "But who did this?" He walked over to the dog and prodded its head with his foot. "Blood all over the floor," he grumbled.

Then, without raising his head, without the slightest shifting of balance or stiffening of his body, he drove his right fist up into Conroy's handsome drunken face.

Conroy fell away from the fist rigidly, with unbent knees, turning a little as he fell. His head and one shoulder struck the stone fireplace, and he tumbled forward, rolling completely over, face upward, on the floor.

Brazil whirled to face Robson.

Robson had dropped the woman's wrist and was trying to get a pistol out of his overcoat pocket. But she had flung herself on his arm, hugging it to her body, hanging with her full weight on it, and he could not free it, though he tore her hair with his other hand.

Brazil went around behind Robson, struck his chin up with a fist so he could slide his forearm under it across the taller man's throat. When he had tightened the forearm there and had his other hand wrapped around Robson's wrist, he said: "All right. I've got him."

Luise Fischer released the man's arm and fell back on her haunches. Except for the triumph in it, her face was as businesslike as Brazil's.

Brazil pulled Robson's arm up sharply behind his back. The pistol came up with it, and when the pistol was horizontal Robson pulled the trigger. The bullet went between his back and Brazil's chest, to splinter the corner of a bookcase in the far end of the room.

Brazil said: "Try that again, baby, and I'll break your arm. Drop it!"

Robson hesitated, let the pistol clatter down on the floor. Luise Fischer scrambled forward on hands and knees to pick it up. She sat on a corner of the table holding the pistol in her hand.

Brazil pushed Robson away from him and crossed the room, to kneel beside the man on the floor, feeling his pulse, running hands over his body, rising with Conroy's pistol, which he thrust into a hip pocket.

Conroy moved one leg, his eyelids fluttered sleepily, and he groaned.

Brazil jerked a thumb at him and addressed Robson curtly: "Take him and get out."

Robson went over to Conroy, stooped to lift his head and shoulders a little, shaking him and saying irritably: "Come on, Dick, wake up. We're going."

Conroy mumbled, "I'm a' ri'," and tried to lie down again.

"Get up, get up," Robson snarled, and slapped his cheeks.

Conroy shook his head and mumbled: "Do' wan'a."

Robson slapped the blond face again. "Come on, get up, you louse."

Conroy groaned and mumbled something unintelligible.

Brazil said impatiently: "Get him out anyway. The rain'll bring him around."

Robson started to speak, changed his mind, picked up his hat from the floor, put it on, and bent over the blond man again. He pulled him up into something approaching a sitting position, drew one limp arm over his shoulder, got a hand around Conroy's back and under his armpit, and rose, slowly lifting the other on unsteady legs beside him.

Brazil held the front door open. Half dragging, half carrying Conroy, Robson went out.

Brazil shut the door, leaned his back against it, and shook his head in mock resignation.

Luise Fischer put Robson's pistol down on the table and stood up. "I am sorry," she said gravely. "I did not mean to bring to you all this—"

He interrupted her carelessly: "That's all right." There was some bitterness in his grin, though his tone remained careless. "I go on like this all the time. God! I need a drink."

She turned swiftly to the table and began to fill glasses.

He looked her up and down reflectively, sipped, and asked: "You walked out just like that?"

She looked down at her clothes and nodded yes.

He seemed amused. "What are you going to do?"

"When I go to the city? I shall sell these things"—she moved her hands to indicate her rings—"and then—I do not know."

"You mean you haven't any money at all?" he demanded.

"That is it," she replied coolly.

"Not even enough for your ticket?"

She shook her head no, raised her eyebrows a little, and her calmness was almost insolence. "Surely that is a small amount you can afford to lend me."

"Sure," he said, and laughed. "But you're a pip."

She did not seem to understand him.

He drank again, then leaned forward. "Listen, you're going to look funny riding the train like that." He flicked two fingers at her gown. "Suppose I drive you in and I've got some friends that'll put you up till you get hold of some clothes you can go out in?"

She studied his face carefully before replying: "If it is not too much trouble for you."

"That's settled, then," he said. "Want to catch a nap first?"

He emptied his glass and went to the front door, where he made a pretense of looking out at the night.

As he turned from the door he caught her expression, though she hastily put the frown off her face. His smile, voice were mockingly apologetic: "I can't help it. They had me away for a while—in prison, I mean—and it did that to me. I've got to keep making sure I'm not locked in." His smile became more twisted. "There's a name for it—claustrophobia—but that doesn't make it any better."

"I am sorry," she said. "Was it—very long ago?"

"Plenty long ago when I went in," he said dryly, "but only a few weeks ago that I got out. That's what I came up here for—to try to get myself straightened out, see how I stood, what I wanted to do."

"And?" she asked softly.

"And what? Have I found out where I stand, what I want to do? I don't know." He was standing in front of her, hands in pockets, lowering down at her. "I suppose I've just been waiting for something to turn up, something I could take as a sign which way I was to go. Well, what turned up was you. That's good enough. I'll go along with you."

He took his hands from his pockets, leaned down, lifted her to her feet, and kissed her savagely.

For a moment she was motionless. Then she squirmed out of his arms and struck at his face with curved fingers. She was white with anger.

He caught her hand, pushed it down carelessly, and growled: "Stop it. If you don't want to play you don't want to play, that's all."

"That is exactly all," she said furiously.

"Fair enough." There was no change in his face, none in his voice.

Presently she said: "That man—your little friend's father— called me a strumpet. Do people here talk very much about me?"

He made a deprecatory mouth. "You know how it is. The Robsons have been the big landowners, the local gentry, for generations, and anything they do is big news. Everybody knows everything they do and so—"

"And what do they say about me?"

He grinned. "The worst, of course. What do you expect? They know him."

"And what do you think?"

"About you?"

She nodded. Her eyes were intent on his.

"I can't very well go round panning people," he said, "only I wonder why you ever took up with him. You must've seen him for the rat he is."

"I did not altogether," she said simply. "And I was stranded in a little Swiss village."

"Actress?"

She nodded. "A singer."

The telephone bell rang.

He went unhurriedly into the bedroom. His unemotional voice came out: "Hello? . . . Yes, Evelyn. . . . Yes." There was a long pause. "Yes; all right, and thanks."

He returned to the other room as unhurriedly as he had left, but at the sight of him Luise Fischer half rose from the table. His face was pasty, yellow, glistening with sweat on forehead and temples, and the cigarette between fingers of his right hand was mashed and broken.

"That was Evelyn. Her father's justice of the peace. Conroy's got a fractured skull—dying. Robson just phoned he's going down to swear out a warrant. That damned fireplace. I can't live in a cell again!"

PART TWO — THE POLICE CLOSE IN

Luise came to him with her hands out. "But you are not to blame. They can't—"

"You don't get it," his monotonous voice went on. He turned away from her toward the front door, walking mechanically. "This is what they sent me up for the other time. It was a drunken free-for-all in a road house, with bottles and everything, and a guy died. I couldn't say they were wrong in tying it on me." He opened the door, made his automatic pretense of looking out, shut the door, and moved back toward her.

"It was manslaughter that time. They'll make it murder if this guy dies. See? I'm on record as a killer." He put a hand up to his chin. "It's air-tight."

"No, no." She stood close to him and took one of his hands. "It was an accident that his head struck the fireplace. I can tell them that. I can tell them what brought it all about. They cannot—"

He laughed with bitter amusement, and quoted Grant: "'The strumpet's word confirms the convict's.'"

She winced.

"That's what they'll do to me," he said, less monotonously now. "If he dies I haven't got a chance. If he doesn't they'll hold me without bail till they see how it's coming out—assault with intent to kill or murder. What good'll your word be? Robson's mistress leaving him with me! Tell the truth and it'll only make it worse. They've got me"—his voice rose—"and I can't live in a cell again!" His eyes jerked around toward the door. Then he raised his head with a rasping noise in his throat that might have been a laugh. "Let's get out of here. I'll go screwy indoors tonight."

"Yes," she said eagerly, putting a hand on his shoulder, watching his face with eyes half frightened, half pitying. "We will go."

"You'll need a coat." He went into the bedroom.

She found her slippers, put on the right one, and held the left one out to him when he returned. "Will you break off the heel?"

He draped the rough brown overcoat he carried over her shoulders, took the slipper from her, and wrenched off the heel with a turn of his wrist. He was at the front door by the time she had her foot in the slipper.

She glanced swiftly once around the room and followed him out. . . .

She opened her eyes and saw daylight had come. Rain no longer dabbled the coupé's windows and windshield and the automatic wiper was still. Without moving she looked at Brazil. He was sitting low and lax on the seat beside her, one hand on the steering wheel, the other holding a cigarette on his knee. His sallow face was placid and there was no weariness in it. His eyes were steady on the road ahead.

"Have I slept long?" she asked.

He smiled at her. "An hour this time. Feel better?" He raised the hand holding the cigarette to switch off the headlights.

"Yes." She sat up a little, yawning. "Will we be much longer?"

"An hour or so." He put a hand in his pocket and offered her cigarettes.

She took one and leaned forward to use the electric lighter in the dashboard. "What will you do?" she asked when the cigarette was burning.

"Hide out till I see what's what."

She glanced sidewise at his placid face, said: "You too feel better."

He grinned somewhat shamefacedly. "I lost my head back there, all right."

She patted the back of his hand once gently, and they rode in silence for a while. Then she asked: "We are going to those friends of whom you spoke?"

"Yes."

A dark coupé with two uniformed policemen in it came toward them, went past. The woman looked sharply at Brazil. His face was expressionless.

She touched his hand again, approvingly.

"I'm all right outdoors," he explained. "It's walls that get me."

She screwed her head around to look back. The policemen's car had passed out of sight.

Brazil said: "They didn't mean anything." He lowered the window on his side and dropped his cigarette out. Air blew in fresh and damp. "Want to stop for coffee?"

"Had we better?"

An automobile overtook them, crowded them to the edge of the road in passing, and quickly shot ahead. It was a black sedan traveling at the rate of sixty-five or more miles an hour. There were four men in it, one of whom looked back at Brazil's car.

Brazil said: "Maybe it'd be safer to get under cover as soon as we can; but if you're hungry—"

"No; I too think we should hurry."

The black sedan disappeared around a bend in the road.

"If the police should find you, would"—she hesitated—"would you fight?"

"I don't know," he said gloomily. "That's what's the matter with me. I never know ahead of time what I'd do." He lost some of his gloominess. "There's no use worrying. I'll be all right."

They rode through a crossroads settlement of a dozen houses, bumped over railroad tracks, and turned into a long straight stretch of road paralleling the tracks. Halfway down the level stretch, the sedan that had passed them was stationary on the edge of the road. A policeman stood beside it—between it and his motorcycle—and stolidly wrote on a leaf of a small book while the man at the sedan's wheel talked and gestured excitedly.

Luise Fischer blew breath out and said: "Well, they were not police."

Brazil grinned.

Neither of them spoke again until they were riding down a suburban street. Then she said: "They—your friends—will not dislike our coming to them like this?"

"No," he replied carelessly; "they've been through things themselves."

The houses along the suburban street became cheaper and meaner, and presently they were in a shabby city street where grimy buildings with cards saying "Flats to Let" in their windows stood among equally grimy factories and warehouses. The street into which Brazil after a little while steered the car was only slightly less dingy and the rental signs were almost as many.

He stopped the car in front of a four-story red brick building with broken brownstone steps. "This is it," he said, opening the door.

She sat looking at the building's unlovely face until he came around and opened the door on her side. Her face was inscrutable. Three dirty children stopped playing with the skeleton of an umbrella to stare at her as she went with him up the broken steps.

The street door opened when he turned the knob, letting them into a stuffy hallway where a dim light illuminated stained wall paper of a once vivid design, ragged carpet, and a worn brass-bound staircase.

"Next floor," he said, and went up the stairs behind her.

Facing the head of the stairs was a door shiny with new paint of a brown peculiarly unlike any known wood. Brazil went to this door and pushed the bell button four times—long, short, long, short. The bell rang noisily just inside the door.

After a moment of silence vague rustling noises came through the door, followed by a cautious masculine voice: "Who's there?"

Brazil put his head close to the door and kept his voice low: "Brazil."

The fastenings of the door rattled and it was opened by a small wiry blond man of about forty in crumpled green cotton pyjamas. His feet were bare. His hollow-cheeked and sharp-featured face wore a cordial smile and his voice was cordial. "Come in, kid," he said. "Come in." His small pale eyes appraised Luise Fischer from head to foot while he was stepping back to make way for them.

Brazil put a hand on the woman's arm and urged her forward saying: "Miss Fischer, this is Mr. Link."

Link said, "Pleased to meet you," and shut the door behind them.

Luise Fischer bowed.

Link slapped Brazil on the shoulder. "I'm glad to see you, kid. We were wondering what had happened to you. Come on in."

He led them into a living room that needed airing. There were articles of clothing lying around, sheets of newspaper here and there, a few not quite empty glasses and coffeecups, and a great many cigarette stubs. Link took a vest off a chair, threw it across the back of another, and said: "Take off your things and set down, Miss Fischer."

A very blonde full-bodied woman in her late twenties said, "My God, look who's here!" from the doorway and ran to Brazil with wide arms, hugging him violently, kissing him on the mouth. She had on a pink wrapper over a pink silk nightgown and green mules decorated with yellow feathers.

Brazil said, "Hello, Fan," and put his arms around her. Then, turning to Luise Fischer, who had taken off her coat: "Fan, this is Miss Fischer. Mrs. Link."

Fan went to Luise Fischer with her hand out. "Glad to know you," she said, shaking hands warmly. "You look tired, both of you. Sit down and I'll get you some breakfast, and maybe Donny'll get you a drink after he covers up his nakedness."

Luise Fischer said, "You are very kind," and sat down.

Link said, "Sure, sure," and went out.

Fan asked: "Been up all night?"

"Yes," Brazil said. "Driving most of it." He sat down on the sofa.

She looked sharply at him. "Anything the matter you'd just as lief tell me about?"

He nodded. "That's what we came for."

Link, in bath robe and slippers now, came in with a bottle of whisky and some glasses.

Brazil said: "The thing is, I slapped a guy down last night and he didn't get up."

"Hurt bad?"

Brazil made a wry mouth. "Maybe dying."

Link whistled, said: "When you slap 'em, boy, they stay slapped."

"He cracked his head on the fireplace," Brazil explained. He scowled at Link.

Fan said: "Well, there's no sense of worrying about it now. The thing to do is get something in your stomachs and get some rest. Come on, Donny, pry yourself loose from some of that booze." She beamed on Luise Fischer. "You just sit still and I'll have some breakfast in no time at all." She hurried out of the room.

Link, pouring whisky, asked: "Anybody see it?"

Brazil nodded. "Uh-huh—the wrong people." He sighed wearily. "I want to hide out a while, Donny, till I see how it's coming out."

"This dump's yours," Link said. He carried glasses of whisky to Luise Fischer and Brazil. He looked at the woman whenever she was not looking at him.

Brazil emptied his glass with a gulp.

Luise Fischer sipped and coughed.

"Want a chaser?" Link asked.

"No, I thank you," she said. "This is very good. I caught a little cold from the rain." She held the glass in her hand, but did not drink again.

Brazil said: "I left my car out front. I ought to bury it."

"I'll take care of that, kid," Link promised.

"And I'll want somebody to see what's happening up Mile Valley way."

Link wagged his head up and down. "Harry Klaus is the mouthpiece for you. I'll phone him."

"And we both want some clothes."

Luise Fischer spoke: "First I must sell these rings."

Link's pale eyes glistened. He moistened his lips and said: "I know the—"

"That can wait a day," Brazil said. "They're not hot, Donny. You don't have to fence them."

Donny seemed disappointed.

The woman said: "But I have no money for clothes until—"

Brazil said: "We've got enough for that."

Donny, watching the woman, addressed Brazil: "And you know I can always dig up some for you, kid."

"Thanks. We'll see." Brazil held out his empty glass, and when it had been filled said: "Hide the car, Donny."

"Sure." The blond man went to the telephone in an alcove and called a number.

Brazil emptied his glass. "Tired?" he asked.

She rose, went over to him, took the whisky glass out of his hand and put it on the table with her own, which was still almost full.

He chuckled, asked: "Had enough trouble with drunks last night?"

"Yes," she replied, not smiling, and returned to her chair.

Donny was speaking into the telephone: "Hello, Duke? . . . Listen; this is Donny. There's a ride standing outside my joint." He described Brazil's coupé. "Will you stash it for me? . . . Yes. . . . Better switch the plates too. . . . Yes, right away, will you? . . . Right." He hung up the receiver, turned back to the others saying:

"Voily!"

"Donny!" Fan called from elsewhere in the flat.

"Coming!" He went out.

Brazil leaned toward Luise Fischer and spoke in a low voice: "Don't give him the rings."

She stared at him in surprise. "But why?"

"He'll gyp you to hell and gone."

"You mean he will cheat me?"

He nodded, grinning.

"But you say he is your friend. You are trusting him now."

"He's O.K. on a deal like this," he assured her. "He'd never turn anybody up. But dough's different. Anyhow, even if he didn't trim you, anybody he sold them to would think they were stolen and wouldn't give half of what they're worth."

"Then he is a—" She hesitated.

"A crook. We were cellmates a while."

She frowned and said: "I do not like this."

Fan came to the door, smiling, saying: "Breakfast is served."

In the passageway Brazil turned and took a tentative step toward the front door, but checked himself when he caught

Luise Fischer's eye, and, grinning a bit sheepishly, followed her and the blonde woman into the dining room.

Fan would not sit down with them. "I can't eat this early," she told Luise Fischer. "I'll get you a hot bath ready and fix your bed, because I know you're all in and'll be ready to fall over as soon as you're done."

She went out, paying no attention to Luise Fischer's polite remonstrances.

Donny stuck a fork into a small sausage and said: "Now, about them rings. I can—"

"That can wait," Brazil said. "We've got enough to go on a while."

"Maybe; but it's just as well to have a get-away stake ready in case you need it all of a sudden." Donny put the sausage into his mouth. "And you can't have too big a one."

He chewed vigorously. "Now, for instance, you take the case of Shuffling Ben Devlin. You remember Ben? He was in the carpenter shop. Remember? The big guy with the gam?"

"I remember," Brazil replied without enthusiasm.

Donny stabbed another sausage. "Well, Ben was in a place called Finehaven once and—"

"He was in a place called the pen when we knew him," Brazil said.

"Sure; that's what I'm telling you. It was all on account of Ben thought—"

Fan came in. "Everything's ready whenever you are," she told Luise Fischer.

Luise Fischer put down her coffee cup and rose. "It is a lovely breakfast," she said, "but I am too tired to eat much."

As she left the room Donny was beginning again: "It was all on account of—"

Fan took her to a room in the rear of the flat where there was a wide wooden bed with smooth white covers turned down. A white nightgown and a red wrapper lay on the bed. On the floor there was a pair of slippers. The blonde woman halted at the door and gestured with one pink hand. "If there's anything else you need, just sing out. The bathroom's just across the hall and I turned the water on."

"Thank you," Luise Fischer said; "you are very kind. I am imposing on you most—"

Fan patted her shoulder. "No friend of Brazil's can ever impose on me, darling. Now you get your bath and a good sleep, and if there's anything you want, yell." She went out and shut the door.

Luise Fischer, standing just inside the door, looked slowly, carefully around the cheaply furnished room, and then, going to the side of the bed, began to take off her clothes. When she had finished she put on the red wrapper and the slippers and, carrying the nightgown over her arm, crossed the hallway to the bathroom. The bathroom was warm with steam. She ran cold water into the tub while she took the bandages off her knee and ankle.

After she had bathed she found fresh bandages in the cabinet over the basin, and rewrapped her knee but not her ankle. Then she put on nightgown, wrapper, and slippers, and returned to the bedroom. Brazil was there, standing with his back to her, looking out a window.

He did not turn around. Smoke from his cigarette drifted back past his head.

She shut the door slowly, leaning against it, the faintest of contemptuous smiles curving her mobile lips.

He did not move.

She went slowly to the bed and sat on the side farthest from him. She did not look at him but at a picture of a horse on the wall. Her face was proud and cold. She said: "I am what I am, but I pay my debts." This time the deliberate calmness of her voice was insolence. "I brought this trouble to you. Well, now if you can find any use for me—" She shrugged.

He turned from the window without haste. His copperish eyes, his face were expressionless. He said: "O.K." He rubbed the fire of his cigarette out in an ash tray on the dressing table and came around the bed to her.

She stood up straight and tall awaiting him.

He stood close to her for a moment, looking at her with eyes that weighed her beauty as impersonally as if she had been inanimate. Then he pushed her head back rudely and kissed her.

She made neither sound nor movement of her own, submitting completely to his caress, and when he released her and stepped back her face was as unaffected, as masklike, as his.

He shook his head slowly. "No, you're no good at your job." And suddenly his eyes were burning and he had her in his arms and she was clinging to him and laughing softly in her throat while he kissed her mouth and cheeks and eyes and forehead.

Donny opened the door and came in. He leered knowingly at them as they stepped apart, and said: "I just phoned Klaus. He'll be over as soon's he's had breakfast."

"O.K.," Brazil said.

Donny, still leering, withdrew, shutting the door.

"Who is this Klaus?" Luise Fischer asked.

"Lawyer," Brazil replied absent-mindedly. He was scowling thoughtfully at the floor. "I guess he's our best bet, though I've heard things about him that—" He broke off impatiently. "When you're in a jam you have to take your chances." His scowl deepened. "And the best you can expect is the worst of it."

She took his hand and said earnestly: "Let us go away from here. I do not like these people. I do not trust them."

His face cleared and he put an arm around her again, but abruptly turned his attention to the door when a bell rang beyond it.

There was a pause; then Donny's guarded voice could be heard asking: "Who is it?"

The answer could not be heard.

Donny's voice, raised a little: "Who?"

Nothing was heard for a short while after that. The silence was broken by the creaking of a floor board just outside the bedroom door. The door was opened by Donny. His pinched face was a caricature of alertness. "Bulls," he whispered. "Take the window." He was swollen with importance.

Brazil's face jerked around to Luise Fischer.

"Go!" she cried, pushing him toward the window. "I will be all right."

"Sure," Donny said; "me and Fan'll take care of her. Beat it, kid, and slip us the word when you can. Got enough dough?"

"Uh-huh." Brazil was kissing Luise Fischer.

"Go, go!" she gasped.

His sallow face was phlegmatic. He was laconic. "Be seeing you," he said, and pushed up the window. His foot was over the sill by the time the window was completely raised. His other foot followed the first immediately, and, turning on his chest, he lowered himself, grinning cheerfully at Luise Fischer for an instant before he dropped out of sight.

She ran to the window and looked down. He was rising from among weeds in the unkempt back yard. His head turned swiftly from right to left. Moving with a swiftness that seemed mere unhesitancy, he went to the left-hand fence, up it, and over into the next dooryard.

Donny took her arm and pulled her from the window. "Stay away from there. You'll tip his mitt. He's all right, though Christ help the copper he runs into—if they're close."

Something heavy was pounding on the flat's front door. A heavy authoritative voice came through: "Open up!"

Donny sneered in the general direction of the front door. "I guess I better let 'em in or they'll be making toothpicks of my front gate." He seemed to be enjoying the situation.

She stared at him with blank eyes.

He looked at her, looked at the floor and at her again, and said defensively: "Look—I love the guy. I love him!"

The pounding on the front door became louder.

"I guess I better," Donny said, and went out.

Through the open window came the sound of a shot. She ran to the window and, hands on sill, leaned far out.

Fifty feet to the left, on the top of a long fence that divided the long row of back yards from the alley behind, Brazil was poised, crouching. As Luise Fischer looked, another shot sounded and Brazil fell down out of sight into the alley behind the fence. She caught her breath with a sob.

The pounding on the flat's front door suddenly stopped. She drew her head in through the window. She took her hands from the sill. Her face was an automaton's. She pulled the window down without seeming conscious of what she was doing, and was standing in the center of the room looking critically at her finger nails when a tired-faced huge man in wrinkled clothes appeared in the doorway.

He asked: "Where's he at?"

She looked up at him from her finger nails as she had looked at her finger nails. "Who?"

He sighed wearily. "Brazil." He went to a closet door, opened it. "You the Fischer woman?" He shut the door and moved toward the window, looking around the room, not at her, with little apparent interest.

"I am Luise Fischer," she said to his back.

He raised the window and leaned out. "How's it, Tom?" he called to someone below. Whatever answer he received was inaudible in the room.

Luise Fischer put attentiveness off her face as he turned to her. "I ain't had breakfast yet," he said.

Donny's voice came through the doorway from another part of the flat: "I tell you I don't know where he's gone to. He just dropped the dame here and high-tailed. He didn't tell me nothing. He—"

A metallic voice said "I bet you!" disagreeably. There was the sound of a blow.

Donny's voice: "If I did know I wouldn't tell you, you big crum! Now sock me again."

The metallic voice: "If that's what you want." There was the sound of another blow.

Fan's voice, shrill with anger, screamed, "Stop that, you—" and ceased abruptly.

The huge man went to the bedroom door and called toward the front of the flat: "Never mind, Ray." He addressed Luise Fischer: "Get some clothes on."

"Why?" she asked coolly.

"They want you back in Mile Valley."

"For what?" She did not seem to think it was true.

"I don't know," he grumbled impatiently. "This ain't my job. We're just picking you up for them. Something about some rings that belonged to a guy's mother and disappeared from the house the same time you did."

She held up her hands and stared at the rings. "But they didn't. He bought them for me in Paris and—"

The huge man scowled wearily. "Well, don't argue with me about it. It's none of my business. Where was this fellow Brazil meaning to go when he left here?"

"I do not know." She took a step forward, holding out her hand in an appealing gesture. "Is he—"

"Nobody ever does," he complained, ignoring the question he had interrupted. "Get your clothes on." He held a hand out to her. "Better let me take care of the junk."

She hesitated, then slipped the rings from her fingers and dropped them into his hand.

"Shake it up," he said. "I ain't had breakfast yet." He went out and shut the door.

She dressed hurriedly in the clothes she had taken off a short while before, though she did not again put on the one stocking she had worn down from Brazil's house. When she had finished, she went quietly, with a backward glance at the closed door, to the window, and began slowly, cautiously to raise the sash.

The tired-faced huge man opened the door. "Good thing I was peeping through the keyhole," he said patiently. "Now come on."

Fan came into the room behind him. Her face was very pink; her voice was shrill. "What're you picking on her for?" she demanded. "She didn't do anything. Why don't you—"

"Stop it, stop it," the huge man begged. His weariness seemed to have become almost unbearable. "I'm only a copper told to bring her in on a larceny charge. I got nothing to do with it, don't know anything about it."

"It is all right, Mrs. Link," Luise Fischer said with dignity. "It will be all right."

"But you can't go like that," Fan protested, and turned to the huge man. "You got to let her put on some decent clothes."

He sighed and nodded. "Anything, if you'll only hurry it up and stop arguing with me."

Fan hurried out.

Luise Fischer addressed the huge man: "He too is charged with larceny?"

He sighed. "Maybe one thing, maybe another," he said spiritlessly.

She said: "He has done nothing."

"Well, I haven't neither," he complained.

Fan came in with some clothes, a blue suit and hat, dark slippers, stockings, and a white blouse.

"Just keep the door open," the huge man said. He went out of the room and stood leaning against an opposite wall, where he could see the windows in the bedroom.

Luise Fischer changed her clothes, with Fan's assistance, in a corner of the room where they were hidden from him.

"Did they catch him?" Fan whispered.

"I do not know."

"I don't think they did."

"I hope they did not."

Fan was kneeling in front of Luise Fischer, putting on her stockings. "Don't let them make you talk till you've seen Harry Klaus," she whispered rapidly. "You tell them he's your lawyer and you got to see him first. We'll send him down and he'll get you out all right." She looked up abruptly. "You didn't cop them, did you?"

"Steal the rings?" Luise Fischer asked in surprise.

"I didn't think so," the blonde woman said. "So you won't have to—"

The huge man's weary voice came to them: "Come on—cut out the barbering and get into the duds."

Fan said: "Go take a run at yourself."

Luise Fischer carried her borrowed hat to the looking-glass and put it on; then, smoothing down the suit, looked at her reflection. The clothes did not fit her so badly as might have been expected.

Fan said: "You look swell."

The man outside the door said: "Come on."

Luise Fischer turned to Fan. "Good-by and I—"

The blonde woman put her arms around her. "There's nothing to say and you'll be back here in a couple of hours. Harry'll show those saps they can't put anything like this over on you."

The huge man said: "Come on."

Luise Fischer joined him and they went toward the front of the flat.

As they passed the living-room door Donny, rising from the sofa, called cheerfully: "Don't let them worry you, baby. We'll—"

A tall man in brown put a hand over Donny's face and pushed him back on the sofa.

Luise Fischer and the huge man went out. A police-department automobile was standing in front of the house where Brazil had left his coupé. A dozen or more adults and children were standing around it, solemnly watching the door through which she came.

A uniformed policeman pushed some of them aside to make passageway for her and her companion and got into the car behind them. "Let her go, Tom," he called to the chauffeur, and they drove off.

The huge man shut his eyes and groaned softly. "God, I'm *schwach!*"

They rode seven blocks and halted in front of a square red brick building on a corner. The huge man helped her out of the automobile and took her between two large frosted globes into the building and into a room where a bald fat man in uniform sat behind a high desk.

The huge man said: "It's that Luise Fischer for Mile Valley." He took a hand from a pocket and tossed her rings on the desk. "That's the stuff, I guess."

The bald man said: "Nice picking. Get the guy?"

"Hospital, I guess."

Luise Fischer turned to him: "Was he—was he badly hurt?"

The huge man grumbled: "I don't know about it. Can't I guess?"

The bald man called: "Luke!"

A thin white-mustached policeman came in.

The fat man said: "Put her in the royal suite."

Luise Fischer said: "I wish to see my lawyer."

The three men looked unblinkingly at her.

"His name is Harry Klaus," she said. "I wish to see him."

Luke said: "Come back this way."

She followed him down a bare corridor to the far end, where he opened a door and stood aside for her to go through. The room into which the door opened was a small one furnished with cot, table, two chairs, and some magazines. The window was large, fitted with a heavy wire grating.

In the center of the room she turned to say again: "I wish to see my lawyer."

The white-mustached man shut the door and she could hear him locking it.

Two hours later he returned with a bowl of soup, some cold meat and a slice of bread on a plate, and a cup of coffee.

She had been lying on the cot, staring at the ceiling. She rose and faced him imperiously. "I wish to see—"

"Don't start that again," he said irritably. "We got nothing to do with you. Tell it to them Mile Valley fellows when they come for you."

He put the food on the table and left the room. She ate everything he had brought her.

It was late afternoon when the door opened again. "There you are," the white-mustached man said, and stood aside to let his companions enter. There were two of them, men of medium height, in dull clothes, one thick-chested and florid, the other less heavy, older.

The thick-chested florid one looked Luise Fischer up and down and grinned admiringly at her. The other said: "We want you to come back to the Valley with us, Miss Fischer."

She rose from her chair and began to put on her hat and coat.

"That's it," the older of the two said approvingly. "Don't give us no trouble and we won't give you none."

She looked curiously at him.

They went to the street and got into a dusty blue sedan. The thick-chested man drove. Luise Fischer sat behind him, beside the older man. They retraced the route she and Brazil had taken that morning.

Once, before they left the city, she had said: "I wish to see my lawyer. His name is Harry Klaus."

The man beside her was chewing gum. He made noises with his lips, then told her politely enough:

"We can't stop now."

The man at the wheel spoke before she could reply. He did not turn his head. "How come Brazil socked him?"

Luise said quickly: "It was not his fault. He was—"

The older man, addressing the man at the wheel, interrupted her: "Let it alone, Pete. Let the D.A. do his own work."

Pete said: "Oke."

The woman turned to the man beside her. "Was—was Brazil hurt?"

He studied her face for a long moment, then nodded slightly. "Stopped a slug, I hear."

Her eyes widened. "He was shot?"

He nodded again.

She put both hands on his forearm. "How badly?"

He shook his head. "I don't know."

Her fingers dug into his arm. "Did they arrest him?"

"I can't tell you, miss. Maybe the District Attorney wouldn't like me to." He smacked his lips over his gum-chewing.

"But please!" she insisted. "I must know."

He shook his head again. "We ain't worrying you with a lot of questions. Don't be worrying us."

PART THREE — CONCLUSION

It was nearly nine o'clock by the dial in the dashboard, and quite dark, when Luise Fischer and her captors passed a large square building whose illuminated sign said "Mile Valley Lumber Co." and turned into what was definitely a town street, though its irregularly spaced houses were not many. Ten minutes later the sedan came to rest at the curb in front of a gray public building. The driver got out. The other man held the door open for Luise. They took her into a ground-floor room in the gray building.

Three men were in the room. A sad-faced man of sixty-some years, with ragged white hair and mustache, was tilted back in a chair with his feet on a battered yellowish desk. He wore a hat but no coat. A pasty-faced young blond man, straddling a chair in front of the filing cabinet on the other side of the room, was saying, "So the traveling salesman asked the farmer if he could put him up for the night and—" but broke off when Luise Fischer and her companions came in.

The third man stood with his back to the window. He was a slim man of medium height, not far past thirty, thin-lipped, pale, flashily dressed in brown and red. His collar was very tight. He advanced swiftly toward Luise Fischer, showing white teeth in a smile. "I'm Harry Klaus. They wouldn't let me see you down there, so I came on up to wait for you." He spoke rapidly and with assurance. "Don't worry. I've got everything fixed."

The story-teller hesitated, changed his position. The two men who had brought Luise Fischer up from the city looked at the lawyer with obvious disapproval.

Klaus smiled again with complete assurance. "You know she's not going to tell you anything at all till we've talked it over, don't you? Well, what the hell, then?"

The man at the desk said: "All right, all right." He looked at the two men standing behind the woman. "If Tuft's office is empty let 'em use that."

"Thanks." Harry Klaus picked up a brown briefcase from a chair, took Luise Fischer's elbow in his hand, and turned her to follow the thick-chested florid man.

He led them down the corridor a few feet to an office that was similar to the one they had just left. He did not go in with them. He said, "Come on back when you're finished," and, when they had gone in, slammed the door.

Klaus jerked his head at the door. "A lot of whittlers," he said cheerfully. "We'll stand them on their heads." He tossed his briefcase on the desk. "Sit down."

"Brazil?" she asked. "He is—"

His shrug lifted his shoulders almost to his ears. "I don't know. Can't get anything out of these people."

"Then—?"

"Then he got away," he said.

"Do you think he did?"

He shrugged his shoulders again. "We can always hope."

"But one of those policemen told me he had been shot and—"

"That don't have to mean anything but that they hope they hit him." He put his hands on her shoulders and pushed her down in a chair. "There's no use of worrying about Brazil till we know whether we've got anything to worry about." He drew another chair up close to hers and sat in it. "Let's worry about you now. I want the works—no song and dance—just what happened, the way it happened."

She drew her brows together in a puzzled frown. "But you told me everything—"

"I told you everything was all fixed, and it is." He patted her knee. "I've got the bail all fixed so you can walk out of here as soon as they get through asking you questions. But we've got to decide what kind of answers you're going to give them." He looked sharply at her from under his hat brim. "You want to help Brazil, don't you?"

"Yes."

"That's the stuff." He patted her knee again and his hand remained on it. "Now give me everything from the beginning."

"You mean from when I first met Kane Robson?"

He nodded.

She crossed her knees, dislodging his hand. Staring at the opposite wall as if not seeing it, she said earnestly: "Neither of us did anything wrong. It is not right that we should suffer."

"Don't worry." His tone was light, confident. "I'll get the pair of you out of it." He proffered her cigarettes in a shiny case.

She took a cigarette, leaned forward to hold its end in the flame from his lighter, and, still leaning forward, asked: "I will not have to stay here tonight?"

He patted her cheek. "I don't think so. It oughtn't to take them more than an hour to grill you." He dropped his hand to her knee. "And the sooner we get through here the sooner you'll be through with them."

She took a deep breath and sat back in her chair. "There is not a lot to say," she began, pronouncing her words carefully so they were clear in spite of her accent. "I met him in a little place in Switzerland. I was without any money at all, any friends. He liked me and he was rich." She made a little gesture with the cigarette in her hand. "So I said yes."

Klaus nodded sympathetically and his fingers moved on her knee.

"He bought me clothes, that jewelry, in Paris. They were not his mother's and he gave them to me."

The lawyer nodded again and his fingers moved again on her knee.

"He brought me over here then and"—she put the burning end of her cigarette on the back of his hand—"I stayed at his—"

Klaus had snatched his hand from her knee to his mouth, was sucking the back of his hand. "What's the matter with you?" he demanded indignantly, the words muffled by the hand to his mouth. He lowered the hand and looked at the burn. "If there's something you don't like, you can say so, can't you?"

She did not smile. "I no speak Inglis good," she said, burlesquing a heavy accent. "I stayed at his house for two weeks—not quite two weeks—until—"

"If it wasn't for Brazil you could take your troubles to another lawyer!" He pouted over his burnt hand.

"Until last night," she continued, "when I could stand him no longer. We quarreled and I left. I left just as I was, in evening clothes, with . . ."

She was finishing her story when the telephone bell rang. The attorney went to the desk and spoke into the telephone: "Hello? . . . Yes. . . . Just a couple of minutes more. . . . That's right. Thanks." He turned. "They're getting impatient."

She rose from her chair saying: "I have finished. Then the police came and he escaped through the window and they arrested me about those rings."

"Did you do any talking after they arrested you?"

She shook her head. "They would not let me. Nobody would listen to me. Nobody cared."

A young man in blue clothes that needed pressing came up to Luise Fischer and Klaus as they left the courthouse. He took off his hat and tucked it under an arm. "Mith Fither, I'm from the Mile Valley Potht. Can you—"

Klaus, smiling, said: "There's nothing now. Look me up at the hotel in the morning and I'll give you a statement." He handed the reporter a card. He cleared his throat. "We're hunting food now. Maybe you'll tell us where to find it—and join us."

The young man's face flushed. He looked at the card in his hand and then up at the lawyer. "Thank you, Mithter Klauth, I'll be glad to. The Tavern'th jutht around the corner. It'th the only plathe that'th any good that'th open now."

He turned to indicate the south. "My name'th George Dunne."

Klaus shook his hand and said, "Glad to know you," Luise Fischer nodded and smiled, and they went down the street.

"How's Conroy?" Klaus asked.

"He hathn't come to yet," the young man replied. "They don't know yet how bad it ith."

"Where is he?"

"Thtill at Robthon'th. They're afraid to move him."

They turned the corner. Klaus asked: "Any news of Brazil?"

The reporter craned his neck to look past Luise Fischer at the lawyer. "I thought you'd know."

"Know what?"

"What—whatever there wath to know. Thith ith it."

He led them into a white-tiled restaurant. By the time they were seated at a table the dozen or more people at counter and tables were staring at Luise Fischer and there was a good deal of whispering among them.

Luise Fischer, sitting in the chair Dunne had pulled out for her, taking one of the menus from the rack on the table, seemed neither disturbed by nor conscious of anyone's interest in her. She said: "I am very hungry."

A plump bald-headed man with a pointed white beard, sitting three tables away, caught Dunne's eye as the young man went around to his chair, and beckoned with a jerk of his head.

Dunne said, "Pardon me—it'th my both," and went over to the bearded man's table.

Klaus said: "He's a nice boy."

Luise Fischer said: "We must telephone the Links. They have surely heard from Brazil."

Klaus pulled the ends of his mouth down, shook his head. "You can't trust these county-seat telephone exchanges."

"But—"

"Have to wait till tomorrow. It's late anyhow." He looked at his watch and yawned. "Play this kid. Maybe he knows something."

Dunne came back to them. His face was flushed and he seemed embarrassed.

"Anything new?" Klaus asked.

The young man shook his head violently. "Oh, no!" he said with emphasis.

A waiter came to their table. Luise Fischer ordered soup, a steak, potatoes, asparagus, a salad, cheese, and coffee. Klaus ordered scrambled eggs and coffee. Dunne pie and milk.

When the waiter stepped back from the table Dunne's eyes opened wide. He stared past Klaus. Luise Fischer turned her head to follow the reporter's gaze. Kane Robson was coming into the restaurant. Two men were with him. One of them—a fat pale youngish man—smiled and raised his hat.

Luise Fischer addressed Klaus in a low voice: "It's Robson."

The lawyer did not turn his head. He said, "That's all right," and held his cigarette case out to her.

She took a cigarette without removing her gaze from Robson. When he saw her he raised his hat and bowed and smiled ironically. Then he said something to his companions and, leaving them, came toward her. His face was pale; his dark eyes glittered.

She was smoking by the time he reached her table. He said, "Hello, darling," and sat in the empty chair facing her across the table. He turned his head to the reporter for an instant to say a careless "Hello, Dunne."

Luise Fischer said: "This is Mr. Klaus. Mr. Robson."

Robson did not look at the lawyer. He addressed the woman: "Get your bail fixed up all right?"

"As you see."

He smiled mockingly. "I meant to leave word that I'd put it up if you couldn't get it anywhere else, but I forgot."

There was a moment of silence. Then she said: "I shall send for my clothes in the morning. Will you have Ito pack them?"

"*Your* clothes?" He laughed. "You didn't have a stitch besides what you had on when I picked you up. Let your new man buy you new clothes."

Young Dunne blushed and looked at the tablecloth in embarrassment. Klaus's face was, except for the brightness of his eyes, expressionless.

Luise Fischer said softly: "Your friends will miss you if you stay away too long."

"Let them. I want to talk to you, Luise." He addressed Dunne impatiently: "Why don't you two go play in a corner somewhere?"

The reporter jumped up from his chair stammering: "Th-thertainly, Mr. Robthon."

Klaus looked questioningly at Luise Fischer. Her nod was barely perceptible. He rose and left the table with Dunne.

Robson said: "Come back with me and I'll call off all this foolishness about the rings."

She looked curiously at him. "You want me back knowing I despise you?"

He nodded, grinning. "I can get fun out of even that."

She narrowed her eyes, studying his face. Then she asked: "How is Dick?"

His face and voice were gay with malice. "He's dying fast enough."

She seemed surprised. "You hate him?"

"I don't hate him—I don't love him. You and he were too fond of each other. I won't have my male and female parasites mixing like that."

She smiled contemptuously. "So. Then suppose I go back with you. What?"

"I explain to these people that it was all a mistake about the rings, that you really thought I had given them to you. That's all." He was watching her closely. "There's no bargaining about your boy friend Brazil. He takes what he gets."

Her face showed nothing of what she might be thinking. She leaned across the table a little toward him and spoke carefully: "If you were as dangerous as you think you are, I would be afraid to go back with you—I would rather go to prison. But I am not afraid of you. You should know by this time that you will never hurt me very much, that I can take very good care of myself."

"Maybe you've got something to learn," he said quickly; then, recovering his consciously matter-of-fact tone: "Well, what's the answer?"

"I am not a fool," she said. "I have no money, no friends who can help me. You have both and I am not afraid of you. I try to do what is best for myself. First I try to get out of this trouble without you. If I cannot then I come back to you."

"If I'll have you."

She shrugged her shoulders. "Yes, certainly that."

✳

Luise Fischer and Harry Klaus reached the Links' flat late the next morning.

Fan opened the door for them. She put her arms around Luise Fischer. "See, I told you Harry would get you out all right." She turned her face quickly toward the lawyer and demanded: "You didn't let them hold her all night?"

"No," he said; "but we missed the last train and had to stay at the hotel."

They went into the living room.

Evelyn Grant rose from the sofa. She came to Luise Fischer saying: "It's my fault. It's all my fault!" Her eyes were red and swollen. She began to cry again. "He had told me about Donny—Mr. Link—and I thought he'd come here and I tried to phone him and papa caught me and told the police. And I only wanted to help him and—"

From the doorway Donny snarled: "Shut up. Stop it. Pipe down." He addressed Klaus petulantly: "She's been doing this for an hour. She's got me screwy."

Fan said: "Lay off the kid. She feels bad."

Donny said: "She ought to." He smiled at Luise Fischer. "Hello, baby. Everything O.K.?"

She said: "How do you do? I think it is."

He looked at her hands. "Where's the rings?"

"We had to leave them up there."

"I told you!" His voice was bitter. "I told you you'd ought to let me sold them." He turned to Klaus. "Can you beat that?"

The lawyer did not say anything.

Fan had taken Evelyn to the sofa and was soothing her.

Luise Fischer asked: "Have you heard from—"

"Brazil?" Donny said before she could finish her question. He nodded. "Yep. He's O.K." He glanced over his shoulder at the girl on the sofa, then spoke rapidly in a low voice. "He's at the Hilltop Sanatorium outside of town—supposed to have D.T.s. You know he got plugged in the side. He's O.K., though—Doc Barry'll keep him under cover and fix him up good as new. He—"

Luise Fischer's eyes were growing large. She put a hand to her throat. "But he—Dr. Ralph Barry?" she demanded.

Donny wagged his head up and down. "Yep. He's a good guy. He'll—"

"But he is a friend of Kane Robson's!" she cried. "I met him there at Robson's house." She turned to Klaus. "He was with him in the restaurant last night—the fat one."

The men stared at her.

She caught Klaus's arm and shook him. "That is why he was there last night—to see Kane—to ask him what he should do."

Fan and Evelyn had risen from the sofa and were listening.

Donny began: "Aw, maybe it's O.K. Doc's a good guy. I don't think he—"

"Cut it out!" Klaus growled. "This is serious—serious as hell." He scowled thoughtfully at Luise Fischer. "No chance of a mistake on this?"

"No."

Evelyn thrust herself between the two men to confront Luise Fischer. She was crying again, but was angry now.

"Why did you have to get him into all this? Why did you have to come to him with your troubles? It's your fault that they'll put him in prison and he'll go crazy in prison! If it hadn't been for you none of this would have happened. You—"

Donny touched Evelyn's shoulder. "I think I'll take a sock at you," he said.

She cringed away from him.

Klaus said: "For God's sake let's stop this fiddledeedee and decide what we'd better do." He scowled at Luise Fischer again. "Didn't Robson say anything to you about it last night?"

She shook her head.

Donny said: "Well, listen. We got to get him out of there. It don't—"

"That's easy," Klaus said with heavy sarcasm. "If he's in wrong there"—he shrugged—"it's happened already. We've got to find out. Can you get to see him?"

Donny nodded. "Sure."

"Then go. Wise him up—find out what the layout is."

Donny and Luise Fischer left the house by the back door, went through the yard to the alley behind, and down the alley for two blocks. They saw nobody following them.

"I guess we're in the clear," Donny said, and led the way down a cross street.

On the next corner there was a garage and repair shop. A small dark man was tinkering with an engine.

"Hello, Tony," Donny said. "Lend me a boat."

The dark man looked curiously at Luise Fischer while saying: "Surest thing you know. Take the one in the corner."

They got into a black sedan and drove away.

"It ain't far," Donny said. Then: "I'd like to pull him out of there."

Luise Fischer was silent.

After half an hour Donny turned the machine into a road at the end of which a white building was visible. "That's her," he said.

Leaving the sedan in front of the building, they walked under a black-and-gold sign that said Hilltop Sanatorium into an office.

"We want to see Mr. Lee," Donny told the nurse at the desk. "He's expecting us."

She moistened her lips nervously and said: "It's two hundred and three, right near the head of the stairs."

They went up a dark flight of stairs to the second floor. "This is it," Donny said, halting. He opened the door without knocking and waved Luise Fischer inside.

Besides Brazil, lying in bed, his sallowness more pronounced than usual, there were two men in the room. One of them was the huge tired-faced man who had arrested Luise Fischer. He said: "I oughtn't let you people see him."

Brazil half rose in bed and stretched a hand out toward Luise Fischer.

She went around the huge man to the bed and took Brazil's hand. "Oh, I'm sorry—sorry!" she murmured.

He grinned without pleasure. "Hard luck, all right. And I'm scared stiff of those damned bars."

She leaned over and kissed him.

The huge man said: "Come on, now. You got to get out. I'm liable to catch hell for this."

Donny took a step toward the bed. "Listen, Brazil. Is there—"

The huge man put out a hand and wearily pushed Donny back. "Go 'way. There's nothing for you to hang around here for." He put a hand on Luise Fischer's shoulder. "Go ahead, please, will you? Say good-by to him now—and maybe you can see him afterwards."

She kissed Brazil again and stood up.

He said: "Look after her, will you, Donny?"

"Sure," Donny promised. "And don't let them worry you. I'll send Harry over to see you and—"

The huge man groaned. "Is this going to keep up all day?"

He took Luise Fischer's arm and put her and Donny out.

They went in silence down to the sedan, and neither spoke until they were entering the city again. Then Luise Fischer said: "Will you kindly lend me ten dollars?"

"Sure." Donny took one hand from the wheel, felt in his pants pocket, and gave her two five-dollar bills.

Then she said: "I wish to go to the railroad station."

He frowned. "What for?"

"I want to go to the railroad station," she repeated.

When they reached the station she got out of the sedan.

"Thank you very much," she said. "Do not wait. I will come over later."

Luise Fischer went into the railroad station and to the news stand, where she bought a package of cigarettes. Then she went to a telephone booth, asked for long distance, and called a Mile Valley number.

"Hello, Ito? . . . Is Mr. Robson there? This is *Fräulein* Fischer. . . . Yes." There was a pause. "Hello, Kane. . . . Well, you have won. You might have saved yourself the delay if you had told me last night what you knew. . . . Yes. . . . Yes, I am."

She put the receiver on its prong and stared at it for a long moment. Then she left the booth, went to the ticket window, and said:

"A ticket to Mile Valley—one way—please."

The room was wide and high-ceilinged. Its furniture was Jacobean. Kane Robson was sprawled comfortably in a deep chair. At his elbow was a small table on which were a crystal-and-silver coffee service, a crystal-and-silver decanter—half full—some glasses, cigarettes, and an ash tray. His eyes glittered in the light from the fireplace.

Ten feet away, partly facing him, partly the fireplace, Luise Fischer sat, more erectly, in a smaller chair. She was in a pale negligee and had pale slippers on her feet.

Somewhere in the house a clock struck midnight. Robson heard it out attentively before he went on speaking: "And you are making a great mistake, my dear, in being too sure of yourself."

She yawned. "I slept very little last night," she said. "I am too sleepy to be frightened."

He rose grinning at her. "I didn't get any either. Shall we take a look at the invalid before we turn in?"

A nurse—a scrawny middle-aged woman in white—came into the room, panting. "Mr. Conroy's recovering consciousness, I do believe," she said.

Robson's mouth tightened and his eyes, after a momentary flickering, became steady. "Phone Dr. Blake," he said. "He'll want to know right away." He turned to Luise Fischer. "I'll run up and stay with him till she is through phoning."

Luise Fischer rose. "I'll go with you."

He pursed his lips. "I don't know. Maybe the excitement of too many people—the surprise of seeing you back here again—might not be good for him."

The nurse had left the room.

Ignoring Luise Fischer's laughter, he said: "No; you had better stay here, my dear."

She said: "I will not."

He shrugged. "Very well, but—" He went upstairs without finishing the sentence.

Luise Fischer went up behind him, but not with his speed. She arrived at the sick-room doorway, however, in time to catch the look of utter fear in Conroy's eyes, before they closed, as his bandaged head fell back on the pillow.

Robson, standing just inside the door, said softly: "Ah, he's passed out again." His eyes were unwary.

Her eyes were probing.

They stood there and stared at each other until the Japanese butler came to the door and said: "A Mr. Brazil to see *Fräulein* Fischer."

Into Robson's face little by little came the expression of one considering a private joke. He said: "Show Mr. Brazil into the living room. *Fräulein* Fischer will be down immediately. Phone the deputy sheriff."

Robson smiled at the woman. "Well?"

She said nothing.

"A choice?" he asked.

The nurse came in. "Dr. Blake is out, but I left word."

Luise Fischer said: "I do not think Mr. Conroy should be left alone, Miss George." . . .

Brazil was standing in the center of the living room, balancing himself on legs spread far apart. He held his left arm tight to his side, straight down. He had on a dark overcoat that was buttoned high against his throat. His face was a ghastly yellow mask in which his eyes burned redly. He said through his teeth: "They told me you'd come back. I had to see it." He spit on the floor. "Strumpet!"

She stamped a foot. "Do not be a fool. I—" She broke off as the nurse passed the doorway. She said sharply: "Miss George, what are you doing?"

The nurse said: "Mr. Robson said he thought I might be able to reach Dr. Blake on the phone at Mrs. Webber's."

Luise Fischer turned, paused to kick off her slippers, and ran up the steps on stockinged feet. The door to Conroy's room was shut. She flung it open.

Robson was leaning over the sick man. His hands were on the sick man's bandaged head, holding it almost face down in the pillow.

His thumbs were pressing the back of the skull. All his weight seemed on his thumbs. His face was insane. His lips were wet.

Luise Fischer screamed, "Brazil!" and flung herself at Robson and clawed at his legs.

Brazil came into the room, lurching blindly, his left arm tight to his side. He swung his right fist, missed Robson's head by a foot, was struck twice in the face by Robson, did not seem to know it, and swung his right fist into Robson's belly. The woman's grip on Robson's ankles kept him from recovering his balance. He went down heavily.

The nurse was busy with her patient, who was trying to sit up in bed. Tears ran down his face. He was sobbing: "He stumbled over a piece of wood while he was helping me to the car, and he hit me on the head with it."

Luise Fischer had Brazil sitting upon the floor with his back to the wall, wiping his face with her handkerchief.

He opened one eye and murmured: "The guy was screwy, wasn't he?"

She put an arm around him and laughed with a cooing sound in her throat. "All men are."

Robson had not moved.

There was a commotion and three men came in.

The tallest one looked at Robson and then at Brazil and chuckled.

"There's our lad that don't like hospitals," he said. "It's a good thing he didn't escape from a gymnasium or he might've hurt somebody."

Luise Fischer took off her rings and put them on the floor beside Robson's left foot.

Two Sharp Knives

O N MY way home from the regular Wednesday night poker game at Ben Kamsley's I stopped at the railroad station to see the 2:11 come in—what we called putting the town to bed—and as soon as this fellow stepped down from the smoking-car I recognized him. There was no mistaking his face, the pale eyes with lower lids that were as straight as if they had been drawn with a ruler, the noticeably flat-tipped bony nose, the deep cleft in his chin, the slightly hollow gray-ish cheeks. He was tall and thin and very neatly dressed in a dark suit, long dark overcoat, derby hat, and carried a black Gladstone bag. He looked a few years older than the forty he was supposed to be. He went past me towards the street steps.

When I turned around to follow him I saw Wally Shane coming out of the waiting-room. I caught Wally's eye and nodded at the man carrying the black bag. Wally examined him carefully as he went by. I could not see whether the man noticed the examination. By the time I came up to Wally the man was going down the steps to the street.

Wally rubbed his lips together and his blue eyes were bright and hard. "Look," he said out of the side of his mouth, "that's a ringer for the guy we got—"

"That's the guy," I said, and we went down the steps behind him.

Our man started towards one of the taxicabs at the curb, then saw the lights of the Deerwood Hotel two blocks away, shook his head at the taxi driver, and went up the street afoot.

"What do we do?" Wally asked. "See what he's—?"

"It's nothing to us. We take him. Get my car. It's at the corner of the alley."

I gave Wally the few minutes he needed to get the car and then closed in. "Hello, Furman," I said when I was just be-hind the tall man.

His face jerked around to me. "How do you—" He halted. "I don't believe I—" He looked up and down the street. We had the block to ourselves.

"You're Lester Furman, aren't you?" I asked.

He said "Yes" quickly.

"Philadelphia?"

He peered at me in the light that was none too strong where we stood. "Yes."

"I'm Scott Anderson," I said, "Chief of Police here. I—"

His bag thudded down on the pavement. "What's happened to her?" he asked hoarsely.

"Happened to who?"

Wally arrived in my car then, abruptly, skidding into the curb. Furman, his face stretched by fright, leaped back away from me. I went after him, grabbing him with my good hand, jamming him back against the front wall of Henderson's warehouse. He fought with me there until Wally got out of the car. Then he saw Wally's uniform and immediately stopped fighting.

"I'm sorry," he said weakly. "I thought—for a second I thought maybe you weren't the police. You're not in uniform and— It was silly of me. I'm sorry."

"It's all right," I told him. "Let's get going before we have a mob around us." Two cars had stopped just a little beyond mine and I could see a bellboy and a hatless man coming towards us from the direction of the hotel.

Furman picked up his bag and went willingly into my car ahead of me. We sat in the rear, Wally drove.

We rode a block in silence, then Furman asked, "You're taking me to police headquarters?"

"Yes."

"What for?"

"Philadelphia."

"I—" he cleared his throat, "—I don't think I understand you."

"You understand that you're wanted in Philadelphia, don't you, for murder?"

He said indignantly, "That's ridiculous. Murder! That's—" He put a hand on my arm, his face close to mine, and instead of indignation in his voice there now was a desperate sort of earnestness. "Who told you that?"

"I didn't make it up. Well, here we are. Come on, I'll show you."

We took him into my office. George Propper, who had been dozing in a chair in the front office, followed us in. I found the Trans-American Detective Agency circular and handed it to Furman. In the usual form it offered fifteen hundred dollars for the arrest and conviction of Lester Furman, alias Lloyd Fields, alias J. D. Carpenter, for the murder of Paul Frank Dunlap in Philadelphia on the 26th of the previous month.

Furman's hands holding the circular were steady and he read it carefully. His face was pale, but no muscles moved in it until he opened his mouth to speak. He tried to speak calmly. "It's a lie." He did not look up from the circular.

"You're Lester Furman, aren't you?" I asked.

He nodded, still not looking up.

"That's your description, isn't it?"

He nodded.

"That's your photograph, isn't it?"

He nodded, and then, staring at his photograph on the circular, he began to tremble—his lips, his hands, his legs.

I pushed a chair up behind him and said, "Sit down," and he dropped down on it and shut his eyes, pressing the lids together. I took the circular from his limp hands.

George Propper, leaning against a side of the doorway, turned his loose grin from me to Wally and said, "So that's that and so you lucky stiffs split a grand and a half reward money. Lucky Wally! If it ain't vacations in New York at the city's expense it's reward money."

Furman jumped up from the chair and screamed, "It's a lie. It's a frame-up. You can't prove anything. There's nothing to prove. I never killed anybody. I won't be framed. I won't be—"

I pushed him down on the chair again. "Take it easy," I told him. "You're wasting your breath on us. Save it for the Philadelphia police. We're just holding you for them. If anything's wrong it's there, not here."

"But it's not the police. It's the Trans-American De—"

"We turn you over to the police."

He started to say something, broke off, sighed, made a little hopeless gesture with his hands, and tried to smile. "Then there's nothing I can do now?"

"There's nothing any of us can do till morning," I said. "We'll have to search you, then we won't bother you any more till they come for you."

In the black Gladstone bag we found a couple of changes of clothes, some toilet articles, and a loaded .38 automatic. In his pockets we found a hundred and sixty-some dollars, a book of checks on a Philadelphia bank, business cards and a few letters that seemed to show he was in the real estate business, and the sort of odds and ends that you usually find in men's pockets.

While Wally was putting these things in the vault I told George Propper to lock Furman up.

George rattled keys in his pocket and said, "Come along, darling. We ain't had anybody in our little hoosegow for three days. You'll have it all to yourself, just like a suite in the Ritz."

Furman said, "Good night and thank you," to me and followed George out.

When George came back he leaned against the door frame again and asked, "How about you big-hearted boys cutting me in on a little of that blood money?"

Wally said, "Sure. I'll forget that two and a half you been owing me three months."

I said, "Make him as comfortable as you can, George. If he wants anything sent in, O.K."

"He's valuable, huh? If it was some bum that didn't mean a nickel to you. . . . Maybe I ought to take a pillow off my bed for him." He spit at the cuspidor and missed. "He's just like the rest of 'em to me."

I thought, "Any day now I'm going to forget that your uncle is county chairman and throw you back in the gutter." I said, "Do all the talking you want, but do what I tell you."

It was about four o'clock when I got home—my farm was a little outside the town—and maybe half an hour after that before I went to sleep. The telephone woke me up at five minutes past six.

Wally's voice: "You better come down, Scott. The fellow Furman's hung himself."

"What?"

"By his belt—from a window bar—deader'n hell."

"All right. I'm on my way. Phone Ben Kamsley I'll pick him up on my way in."

"No doctor's going to do this man any good, Scott."

"It won't hurt to have him looked at," I insisted. "You'd better phone Douglassville too." Douglassville was the county seat.

"O.K."

Wally phoned me back while I was dressing to tell me that Ben Kamsley had been called out on an emergency case and was somewhere on the other side of town, but that his wife would get in touch with him and tell him to stop at headquarters on his way home.

When, riding into town, I was within fifty or sixty feet of the Red Top Diner, Heck Jones ran out with a revolver in his hand and began to shoot at two men in a black roadster that had just passed me.

I leaned out and yelled, "What's it?" at him while I was turning my car.

"Holdup," he bawled angrily. "Wait for me." He let loose another shot that couldn't have missed my front tire by more than an inch and galloped up to me, his apron flapping around his fat legs. I opened the door for him, he squeezed his bulk in beside me, and we set off after the roadster.

"What gets me," he said when he had stopped panting, "is they done it like a joke. They come in, they don't want nothing but ham and eggs and coffee and then they get kind of kidding together under their breath and then they put the guns on me like a joke."

"How much did they take?"

"Sixty or thereabouts, but that ain't what gripes me so much. It's them doing it like a joke."

"Never mind," I said. "We'll get 'em."

We very nearly didn't, though. They led us a merry chase. We lost them a couple of times and finally picked them up more by luck than anything else, a couple of miles over the state line.

We didn't have any trouble taking them, once we had caught up to them, but they knew they had crossed the state line and they insisted on regular extradition or nothing, so we had to carry them on to Badington and stick them in the jail there until the necessary papers could be sent through. It was ten o'clock before I got a chance to phone my office.

Hammill answered the phone and told me Ted Carroll, our district attorney, was there, so I talked to Ted—though not as much as he talked to me.

"Listen, Scott," he asked excitedly, "what is all this?"

"All what?"

"This fiddle-de-dee, this hanky-panky."

"I don't know what you mean," I said. "Wasn't it suicide?"

"Sure it was suicide, but I wired the Trans-American and they phoned me just a few minutes ago and said they'd never sent out any circulars on Furman, didn't know about any murder he was wanted for. All they knew about him was he used to be a client of theirs."

I couldn't think of anything to say except that I would be back in Deerwood by noon. And I was.

Ted was at my desk with the telephone receiver clamped to his ear, saying, "Yes. . . . Yes. . . . Yes," when I went into the office. He put down the receiver and asked, "What happened to you?"

"A couple of boys knocked over the Red Top Diner and I had to chase 'em almost to Badington."

He smiled with one side of his mouth. "The town getting out of your hands?" He and I were on opposite sides of the fence politically and we took our politics seriously in Candle County.

I smiled back at him. "Looks like it—with one felony in six months."

"And this." He jerked a thumb towards the rear of the building, where the cells were.

"What about this? Let's talk about this."

"It's plenty wrong," he said. "I just finished talking to the Philly police. There wasn't any Paul Frank Dunlap murdered there that they know about; they've got no unexplained murder on the 26th of last month." He looked at me as if it were my fault. "What'd you get out of Furman before you let him hang himself?"

"That he was innocent."

"Didn't you grill him? Didn't you find out what he was doing in town? Didn't you—"

"What for?" I asked. "He admitted his name was Furman, the description fit him, the photograph was him, the Trans-American's supposed to be on the level. Philadelphia wanted him: I didn't. Sure, if I'd known he was going to hang himself— You said he'd been a client of the Trans-American. They tell you what the job was?"

"His wife left him a couple of years ago and he had them hunting for her for five or six months, but they never found her. They're sending a man up tonight to look it over." He stood up. "I'm going to get some lunch." At the door he turned his head over his shoulder to say, "There'll probably be trouble over this."

I knew that; there usually is when somebody dies in a cell.

George Propper came in grinning happily. "So what's become of that fifteen hundred fish?"

"What happened last night?" I asked.

"Nothing. He hung hisself."

"Did you find him?"

He shook his head. "Wally took a look in there to see how things was before he went off duty and found him."

"You were asleep, I suppose."

"Well, I was catching a nap, I guess," he mumbled; "but everybody does that sometimes—even Wally sometimes when he comes in off his beat between rounds—and I always wake up when the phone rings or anything. And suppose I had been awake. You can't hear a guy hanging hisself."

"Did Kamsley say how long he'd been dead?"

"He done it about five o'clock, he said he guessed. You want to look at the remains? They're over at Fritz's undertaking parlor."

I said, "Not now. You'd better go home and get some more sleep, so your insomnia won't keep you awake tonight."

He said, "I feel almost as bad about you and Wally losing all that dough as you do," and went out; went out chuckling.

Ted Carroll came back from lunch with the notion that perhaps there was some connection between Furman and the two men who had robbed Heck Jones. That didn't seem to make much sense, but I promised to look into it. Naturally, we never did find any such connection.

That evening a fellow named Rising, assistant manager of

the Trans-American Detective Agency's Philadelphia branch, arrived. He brought the dead man's lawyer, a scrawny, asthmatic man named Wheelock, with him. After they had identified the body we went back to my office for a conference.

It didn't take me long to tell them all I knew, with the one additional fact I had picked up during the afternoon, which was that the police in most towns in our corner of the state had received copies of the reward circular.

Rising examined the circular and called it an excellent forgery: paper, style, type were all almost exactly those ordinarily used by his agency.

They told me the dead man was a well-known, respectable and prosperous citizen of Philadelphia. In 1928 he had married a twenty-two-year-old girl named Ethel Brian, the daughter of a respectable, if not prosperous, Philadelphia family. They had a child born in 1930, but it lived only a few months. In 1931 Furman's wife had disappeared and neither he nor her family had heard of her since, though he had spent a good deal of money trying to find her. Rising showed me a photograph of her, a small-featured, pretty blonde with a weak mouth and large, somewhat staring, eyes.

"I'd like to have a copy made," I said.

"You can keep that. It's one of them that we had made. Her description's on the back."

"Thanks. And he didn't divorce her?"

Rising shook his head with emphasis. "No, sir. He was a lot in love with her and he seemed to think the kid's dying had made her a little screwy and she didn't know what she was doing." He looked at the lawyer. "That right?"

Wheelock made a couple of asthmatic sounds and said, "That is my belief."

"You said he had money. About how much, and who gets it?"

The scrawny lawyer wheezed some more, said, "I should say his estate will amount to perhaps a half a million dollars, left in its entirety to his wife."

That gave me something to think about, but the thinking didn't help me out then.

They couldn't tell me why he had come to Deerwood. He seemed to have told nobody where he was going, had simply told his servants and his employees that he was leaving town for a day or two. Neither Rising nor Wheelock knew of any enemies he had. That was the crop.

And that was still the crop at the inquest the next day. Everything showed that somebody had framed Furman into our jail and that the frame-up had driven him to suicide. Nothing showed anything else. And there had to be something else, a lot else.

Some of the else began to show up immediately after the inquest. Ben Kamsley was waiting for me when I left the undertaking parlor, where the inquest had been held. "Let's get out of the crowd," he said. "I want to tell you something."

"Come on over to the office."

We went over there. He shut the door, which usually stayed open, and sat on a corner of my desk. His voice was low: "Two of those bruises showed."

"What bruises?"

He looked curiously at me for a second, then put a hand on the top of his head. "Furman—up under the hair—there were two bruises."

I tried to keep from shouting. "Why didn't you tell me?"

"I am telling you. You weren't here that morning. This is the first time I've seen you since."

I cursed the two hoodlums who had kept me away by sticking up the Red Top Diner and demanded, "Then why didn't you spill it when you were testifying at the inquest?"

He frowned. "I'm a friend of yours. Do I want to put you in a spot where people can say you drove this chap to suicide by third-degreeing him too rough?"

"You're nuts," I said. "How bad was his head?"

"That didn't kill him, if that's what you mean. There's nothing the matter with his skull. Just a couple of bruises nobody would notice unless they parted the hair."

"It killed him just the same," I growled. "You and your *friendship* that—"

The telephone rang. It was Fritz. "Listen, Scott," he said, "there's a couple ladies here that want a look at that fellow. Is it all right?"

"Who are they?"

"I don't know 'em—strangers."

"What do they want to see him for?"

"I don't know. Wait a minute."

A woman's voice came over the wire: "Can't I please see him?" It was a very pleasant, earnest voice.

"Why do you want to see him?" I asked.

"Well, I"—there was a long pause—"I am"—a shorter pause, and when she finished the sentence her voice was not much more than a whisper—"his wife."

"Oh, certainly," I said. "I'll be right over."

I hurried out.

Leaving the building, I ran into Wally Shane. He was in civilian clothes, since he was off duty. "Hey, Scott!" He took my arm and dragged me back into the vestibule, out of sight of the street. "A couple of dames came into Fritz's just as I was leaving. One of 'em's Hotcha Randall, a baby with a record as long as your arm. You know she's one of that mob you had me in New York working on last summer."

"She know you?"

He grinned. "Sure. But not by my right name, and she thinks I'm a Detroit rum-runner."

"I mean did she know you just now?"

"I don't think she saw me. Anyways, she didn't give me a tumble."

"You don't know the other one?"

"No. She's a blonde, kind of pretty."

"O.K.," I said. "Stick around a while, but out of sight. Maybe I'll be bringing them back with me." I crossed the street to the undertaking parlor.

Ethel Furman was prettier than her photograph had indicated. The woman with her was five or six years older, quite a bit larger, handsome in a big, somewhat coarse way. Both of them were attractively dressed in styles that hadn't reached Deerwood yet.

The big woman was introduced to me as Mrs. Crowder. I said, "I thought your name was Randall."

She laughed. "What do you care, Chief? I'm not hurting your town."

I said, "Don't call me Chief. To you big-city slickers I'm the Town Whittler. We go back through here."

Ethel Furman didn't make any fuss over her husband when

she saw him. She simply looked gravely at his face for about three minutes, then turned away and said, "Thank you," to me.

"I'll have to ask you some questions," I said, "so if you'll come across the street . . ."

She nodded. "And I'd like to ask you some." She looked at her companion. "If Mrs. Crowder will—"

"Call her Hotcha," I said. "We're all among friends. Sure, she'll come along, too."

The Randall woman said, "Aren't you the cut-up?" and took my arm.

In my office I gave them chairs and said, "Before I ask you anything I want to tell you something. Furman didn't commit suicide. He was murdered."

Ethel Furman opened her eyes wide. "Murdered?"

Hotcha Randall said as if she had had the words on the tip of her tongue right along, "We've got alibis. We were in New York. We can prove it."

"You're likely to get a chance to, too," I told her. "How'd you people happen to come down here?"

Ethel Furman repeated, "Murdered?" in a dazed tone.

The Randall woman said, "Who's got a better right to come down here? She was still his wife, wasn't she? She's entitled to some of his estate, isn't she? She's got a right to look out for her own interests, hasn't she?"

That reminded me of something. I picked up the telephone and told Hammill to have somebody get hold of the lawyer Wheelock—he had stayed over for the inquest, of course—before he left town and tell him I wanted to see him. "And is Wally around?"

"He's not here. He said you told him to keep out of sight. I'll find him, though."

"Right. Tell him I want him to go to New York tonight. Send Mason home to get some sleep: he'll have to take over Wally's night trick."

Hammill said, "Oke," and I turned back to my guests.

Ethel Furman had come out of her daze. She leaned forward and asked, "Mr. Anderson, do you think I had—had anything to do with Lester's—with his death?"

"I don't know. I know he was killed. I know he left you something like half a million."

The Randall woman whistled softly. She came over and put a diamond-ringed hand on my shoulder. "Dollars?"

When I nodded, the delight went out of her face, leaving it serious. "All right, Chief," she said, "now don't be a clown. The kid didn't have a thing to do with whatever you think happened. We read about him committing suicide in yesterday morning's paper, and about there being something funny about it, and I persuaded her she ought to come down and—"

Ethel Furman interrupted her friend: "Mr. Anderson, I wouldn't have done anything to hurt Lester. I left him because I wanted to leave him, but I wouldn't have done anything to him for money or anything else. Why, if I'd wanted money from him all I'd've had to do would've been to ask him. Why, he used to put ads in papers telling me if I wanted anything to let him know, but I never did. You can—his lawyer—anybody who knew anything about it can tell you that."

The Randall woman took up the story: "That's the truth, Chief. For years I've been telling her she was a chump not to tap him, but she never would. I had a hard enough time getting her to come for her share now he's dead and got nobody else to leave it to."

Ethel Furman said, "I wouldn't've hurt him."

"Why'd you leave him?"

She moved her shoulders. "I don't know how to say it. The way we lived wasn't the way I wanted to live. I wanted—I don't know what. Anyway, after the baby died I couldn't stand it any more and cleared out, but I didn't want anything from him and I wouldn't've hurt him. He was always good to me. I was—I was the one that was wrong."

The telephone rang. Hammill's voice: "I found both of 'em. Wally's home. I told him. The old guy Wheelock is on his way over."

I dug out the phony reward circular and showed it to Ethel Furman. "This is what got him into the can. Did you ever see that picture before?"

She started to say "No"; then a frightened look came into her face. "Why, that's—it can't be. It's—it's a snapshot I had—have. It's an enlargement of it."

"Who else has one?"

Her face became more frightened, but she said, "Nobody that I know of. I don't think anybody else could have one."

"You've still got yours?"

"Yes. I don't remember whether I've seen it recently—it's with some old papers and things—but I must have it."

I said, "Well, Mrs. Furman, it's stuff like that that's got to be checked up, and neither of us can dodge it. Now there are two ways we can play it. I can hold you here on suspicion till I've had time to check things up, or I can send one of my men back to New York with you for the check-up. I'm willing to do that if you'll speed things up by helping him all you can and if you'll promise me you won't try any tricks."

"I promise," she said. "I'm as anxious as you are to—"

"All right. How'd you come down?"

"I drove," the Randall woman said. "That's my car, the big green one across the street."

"Fine. Then he can ride back with you, but remember, no funny business."

The telephone rang again while they were assuring me there would be no funny business. Hammill: "Wheelock's here."

"Send him in."

The lawyer's asthma nearly strangled him when he saw Ethel Furman. Before he could get himself straightened out I asked, "This is really Mrs. Furman?"

He wagged his head up and down, still wheezing.

"Fine," I said. "Wait for me. I'll be back in a little while." I herded the two women out and across the street to the green car. "Straight up to the end of the street and then two blocks left," I told the Randall woman, who was at the wheel.

"Where are we going?" she asked.

"To see Shane, the man who's going to New York with you."

Mrs. Dober, Wally's landlady, opened the door for us.

"Wally in?" I asked.

"Yes, indeedy, Mr. Anderson. Go right on up." She was staring with wide-eyed curiosity at my companions while talking to me.

We went up a flight of stairs and I knocked on his door.

"Who is it?" he called.

"Scott."

"Come on in."

I pushed the door open and stepped aside to let the women in.

Ethel Furman gasped, "Harry!" and stepped back, treading on my foot.

Wally had a hand behind him, but my gun was already out in my hand. "I guess you win," he said.

I said I guessed I did and we all went back to headquarters.

"I'm a sap," he complained when he and I were alone in my office. "I knew it was all up as soon as I saw those two dames going into Fritz's. Then, when I was ducking out of sight and ran into you, I was afraid you'd take me over with you, so I had to tell you one of 'em knew me, figuring you'd want to keep me under cover for a little while anyhow—long enough for me to get out of town. And then I didn't have sense enough to do it.

"I drop in home to pick up a couple of things before I scram and that call of Hammill's catches me and I fall for it plenty. I figure I'm getting a break. I figure you're not on yet and are going to send me back to New York as the Detroit rum-runner again to see what dope I can get out of these folks and I'll be sitting pretty. Well, you fooled me, brother, or didn't— Listen, Scott, you didn't just stumble into that accidentally, did you?"

"No. Furman had to be murdered by a copper. A copper was most likely to know reward circulars well enough to make a good job of forging one. Who printed that for you?"

"Go on with your story," he said. "I'm not dragging anybody in with me. It was only a poor mug of a printer that needed dough."

"O.K. Only a copper would be sure enough of the routine to know how things would be handled. Only a copper—one of my coppers—would be able to walk into his cell, bang him across the head and string him up on the— Those bruises showed, you know."

"They did? I wrapped the blackjack in a towel, figuring it would knock him out without leaving a mark anybody'd find under the hair. I seem to've slipped up a lot."

"So that narrows it down to my coppers," I went on,

"and—well—you told me you knew the Randall woman, and there it was, only I figured you were working with them. What got you into this?"

He made a sour mouth. "What gets most saps in jams? A yen for easy dough. I'm in New York, see, working on that Dutton job for you, palling around with bootleggers and racketeers, passing for one of them; and I get to figuring that here my work takes as much brains as theirs, and is as tough and dangerous as theirs, but they're taking in big money and I'm working for coffee and doughnuts. That kind of stuff gets you; anyway, it got me.

"Then I run into this Ethel and she goes for me like a house afire. I like her, too, so that's dandy; but one night she tells me about this husband of hers and how much dough he's got and how nuts he is about her and how he's still trying to find her, and I get to thinking. I think she's nuts enough about me to marry me. I still think she'd marry me if she didn't know I killed him. Divorcing him's no good, because the chances are she wouldn't take any money from him and, anyway, it would only be part. So I got to thinking about suppose he died and left her the roll.

"That was more like it. I ran down to Philly a couple of afternoons and looked him up and everything looked fine. He didn't even have anybody else close enough to leave more than a little of his dough to. So I did it. Not right away; I took my time working out the details, meanwhile writing to her through a fellow in Detroit.

"And then I did it. I sent those circulars out—to a lot of places—not wanting to point too much at this one. And when I was ready I phoned him, telling him if he'd come to the Deerwood Hotel that night, sometime between then and the next night, he'd hear from Ethel. And, like I thought, he'd've fallen for any trap that was baited with her. You picking him up at the station was a break. If you hadn't, I'd've had to discover he was registered at the hotel that night. Anyway, I'd've killed him and pretty soon I'd've started drinking or something and you'd've fired me and I'd've gone off and married Ethel and her half-million under my Detroit name." He made the sour mouth again. "Only I guess I'm not as sharp as I thought I was."

"Maybe you are," I said, "but that doesn't always help. Old man Kamsley, Ben's father, used to have a saying, 'To a sharp knife comes a tough steak.' I'm sorry you did it, Wally. I always liked you."

He smiled wearily. "I know you did," he said. "I was counting on that."

OTHER WRITINGS

The Thin Man:
An Early Typescript

T HE TRAIN went north among the mountains. The dark man crossed the tracks to the ticket-window and said: "Can you tell me how to get to Mr. Wynant's place? Mr. Walter Irving Wynant's."

The man within stopped writing on a printed form. His eyes became brightly inquisitive behind tight rimless spectacles. His voice was eager. "Are you a newspaper reporter?"

"Why?" The dark man's eyes were very blue. They looked idly at the other. "Does it make any difference?"

"Then you ain't," the ticket-agent said. He was disappointed. He looked at a clock on a wall. "Hell, I ought to've known that. You wouldn't've had time to get here." He picked up the pencil he had put down.

"Know where his place is?"

"Sure. Up there on the hill." The ticket-agent waved his pencil vaguely westward. "All the taxi-drivers know it, but if it's Wynant you want to see you're out of luck."

"Why?"

The ticket-agent's mien brightened. He put his forearms on the counter, hunching his shoulders, and said: "Because the fact is he went and murdered everybody on the place and jumped in the river not more than an hour ago."

The dark man exclaimed, "No!" softly.

The ticket-agent smacked his lips. "Uh-huh—killed all three of them—the whole shooting match—chopped them up in pieces with an ax and then tied a weight around his own neck and jumped in the river."

The dark man asked solemnly: "What'd he do that for?"

A telephone-bell began to ring behind the ticket-agent. "You don't know him or you wouldn't have to ask," he replied as he reached for the telephone. "Crazy as they make them and always was. The only wonder is he didn't do it long before this." He said, "Hello," into the telephone.

The dark man went through the waiting-room and downstairs to the street. The half a dozen automobiles parked near the station were apparently private cars. A large red and white sign in the next block said *Taxi*. The dark man walked under the sign into a small grimy office where a bald fat man was reading a newspaper.

"Can I get a taxi?" the dark man asked.

"All out now, brother, but I'm expecting one of them back any minute. In a hurry?"

"A little bit."

The bald man brought his chair down on all its legs and lowered his newspaper. "Where do you want to go?"

"Wynant's."

The bald man dropped his newspaper and stood up, saying heartily: "Well, I'll run you up there myself." He covered his baldness with a sweat-stained brown hat.

They left the office and—after the fat man had paused at the real-estate-office next door to yell, "Take care of my phone if it rings, Toby"—got into a dark sedan, took the left turn at the first crossing, and rode uphill towards the west.

When they had ridden some three hundred yards the fat man said in a tone whose casualness was belied by the shine of his eyes: "That must be a hell of a mess up there and no fooling."

The dark man was lighting a cigarette. "What happened?" he asked.

The fat man looked sharply sidewise at him. "Didn't you hear?"

"Only what the ticket-agent told me just now"—the dark man leaned forward to return the lighter to its hole in the dashboard—"that Wynant had killed three people with an ax and then drowned himself."

The fat man laughed scornfully. "Christ, you can't beat Lew," he said. "If you sprained your ankle he could get a broken back out of it. Wynant didn't kill but two of them—the Hopkins woman got away because it was her that phoned—and he choked them to death and then shot himself. I bet you if you'd go back there right now Lew'd tell you there was a cool half a dozen of them killed and likely as not with dynamite."

The dark man took his cigarette from his mouth. "Then he wasn't right about Wynant being crazy?"

"Yes," the fat man said reluctantly, "but nobody could go wrong on that."

"No?"

"Nope. Holy hell! didn't he used to come down to town in his pajamas last summer? And then when people didn't like it and got Ray to say something to him about it didn't he get mad and stop coming in at all? Don't he make as much fuss about people trespassing on his place as if he had a gold mine there? Didn't I see him with my own eyes heave a rock at a car that had gone past him raising dust once?"

The dark man smiled meagerly. "I don't know any of the answers," he said. "I didn't know him."

Beside a painted warning against trespass they left their graveled road for an uneven narrow crooked one of dark earth running more steeply uphill to the right. Protruding undergrowth brushed the sedan's sides and now and then an overhanging tree-branch its top. Their speed made their ride rougher than it need have been.

"This is his place," the fat man said. He sat stiffly at the wheel fighting the road's unevenness. His eyes were shiny, expectant.

The house they presently came to was a rambling structure of grey native stone and wood needing grey paint under low Dutch roofs. Five cars stood in the clearing in front of the house. The man who sat at the wheel of one of them, and the two men standing beside it, stopped talking and watched the sedan draw up.

"Here we are," the fat man said and got out. His manner had suddenly become important. He put importance in the nod he gave the three men.

The dark man, leaving the other side of the sedan, went towards the house. The fat man hurried to walk beside him.

A man came out of the house before they reached it. He was a middle-aged giant in baggy worn clothes. His hair was grey, his eyes small, and he chewed gum. He said, "Howdy, Fern," to the fat man and, looking steadily at the dark man, stood in the path confronting them squarely.

Fern said, "Hello, Nick," and then told the dark man: "This is Sheriff Petersen." He narrowed one eye shrewdly and addressed the Sheriff again: "He came up to see Wynant."

Sheriff Nick Petersen stopped chewing. "What's the name?" he asked.

The dark man said: "John Guild."

The Sheriff said: "So. Now what were you wanting to see Wynant about?"

The man who had said his name was John Guild smiled. "Does it make any difference now he's dead?"

The Sheriff asked, "What?" with considerable force.

"Now that he's dead," Guild repeated patiently. He put a fresh cigarette between his lips.

"How do you know he's dead?" The Sheriff emphasized "you."

Guild looked with curious blue eyes at the giant. "They told me in the village," he said carelessly. He moved his cigarette an inch to indicate the fat man. "He told me."

The Sheriff frowned skeptically, but when he spoke it was to utter a vague "Oh." He chewed his gum. "Well, what was it you were wanting to see him about?"

Guild said: "Look here: is he dead or isn't he?"

"Not that I know of."

"Fine," Guild said, his eyes lighting up. "Where is he?"

"I'd like to know," the Sheriff replied gloomily. "Now what is it you want with him?"

"I'm from his bank. I want to see him on business." Guild's eyes became drowsy. "It's confidential business."

"So?" Sheriff Petersen's frown seemed to hold more discomfort than annoyance. "Well, none of his business is confidential from me any more. I got a right to know anything and everything that anybody knows about him."

Guild's eyes narrowed a little. He blew smoke out.

"I have," the Sheriff insisted in a tone of complaint. "Listen, Guild, you haven't got any right to hide any of his business from me. He's a murderer and I'm responsible for law and order in this county."

Guild pursed his lips. "Who'd he kill?"

"This here Columbia Forrest," Petersen said, jerking a thumb at the house, "shot her stone dead and lit out for God only knows where."

"Didn't kill anybody else?"

"My God," the Sheriff asked peevishly, "ain't that enough?"

"Enough for me, but down in the village they've got it all very plural." Guild stared thoughtfully at the Sheriff. "Got away clean?"

"So far," Petersen grumbled, "but we're phoning descriptions of him and his car around." He sighed, moved his big shoulders uncomfortably. "Well, come on now, let's have it. What's your business with him?" but when Guild would have replied the giant said: "Wait a minute. We might as well go in and get hold of Boyer and Ray and get it over with at one crack."

Leaving the fat man, Guild and the Sheriff went indoors, into a pleasantly furnished tan room in the front of the house, where they were soon joined by two more men. One of these was nearly tall as the Sheriff, a raw-boned blond man in his early thirties, hard of jaw and mouth, somber of eye. One was younger, shorter, with boyishly rosy cheeks, quick dark eyes, and smoothed dark hair. When the Sheriff introduced them to Guild he said the taller one was Ray Callaghan, a Deputy Sheriff, the other District Attorney Bruce Boyer. He told them John Guild was a fellow who wanted to see Wynant.

The youthful District Attorney, standing close to Guild, smiled ingratiatingly and asked: "What business are you in, Mr. Guild?"

"I came up to see Wynant about his bank-account," the dark man replied slowly.

"What bank?"

"Seaman's National of San Francisco."

"I see. Now what did you want to see him about? I mean, what was there about his account that you had to come up here to see him about?"

"Call it an over-draft," Guild said with deliberate evasiveness.

The District Attorney's eyes became anxious.

Guild made a small gesture with the brown hand holding his cigarette. "Look here, Boyer," he said, "if you want me to go all the way with you you ought to go all the way with me."

Boyer looked at Petersen. The Sheriff met his gaze with noncommittal eyes. Boyer turned back to Guild. "We're not hiding anything from you," he said earnestly. "We've nothing to hide."

Guild nodded. "Swell. What happened here?"

"Wynant caught the Forrest girl getting ready to leave him and he shot her and jumped in his car and drove away," he said quickly. "That's all there is to it."

"Who's the Forrest girl?"

"His secretary."

Guild pursed his lips, asked: "Only that?"

The raw-boned Deputy Sheriff said, "None of that, now!" in a strained croaking voice. His pale eyes were bloodshot and glaring.

The Sheriff growled, "Take it easy there, Ray," avoiding his Deputy's eyes.

The District Attorney glanced impatiently at the Deputy Sheriff. Guild stared gravely, attentively at him.

The Deputy Sheriff's face flushed a little and he shifted his feet. He spoke to the dark man again, in the same croaking voice: "She's dead and you might just as well talk decently about her."

Guild moved his shoulders a little. "I didn't know her," he said coldly. "I'm trying to find out what happened." He stared for a moment longer at the raw-boned man and then shifted his gaze to Boyer. "What was she leaving him for?"

"To get married. She told him when he caught her packing after she came back from town and—and they had a fight and when she wouldn't change her mind he shot her."

Guild's blue eyes moved sidewise to focus on the raw-boned Deputy Sheriff's face. "She was living with Wynant, wasn't she?" he asked bluntly.

"You son of a bitch!" the Deputy Sheriff cried hoarsely and struck with his right fist at Guild's face.

Guild avoided the fist by stepping back with no appearance of haste. He had begun to step back before the fist started towards his face. His eyes gravely watched the fist go past his face.

Big Petersen lurched against his Deputy, wrapping his arms around him. "Cut it out, Ray," he grumbled. "Why don't you behave yourself? This is no time to be losing your head."

The Deputy Sheriff did not struggle against him.

"What's the matter with him?" Guild asked the District Attorney. There was no resentment in his manner. "In love with her or something?"

Boyer nodded furtively, then frowned and shook his head in a warning gesture.

"That's all right," Guild said. "Where'd you get your information about what happened?"

"From the Hopkinses. They look after the place for Wynant. They were in the kitchen and heard the whole fight. They ran upstairs when they heard the shots and he stood them off with the gun and told them he'd come back and kill them if they told anybody before he'd an hour's start, but they phoned Ray as soon as he'd gone."

Guild tossed the stub of his cigarette into the fireplace and lit a fresh one. Then he took a card from a brown case brought from an inner pocket and gave the card to Boyer.

John Guild

Associated Detective Bureaus, Inc.

Frost Building, San Francisco

"Last week Wynant deposited a ten-thousand-dollar New York check in his account at the Seaman's National Bank," Guild said. "Yesterday the bank learned the check had been raised from one thousand to ten. The bank's nicked for six thousand on the deal."

"But in the case of an altered check," Boyer said, "I understand——"

"I know," Guild agreed, "the bank's not responsible—theoretically—but there are usually loopholes and it's—— Well, we're working for the insurance company that covers the Seaman's and it's good business to go after him and recover as much as we can."

"I'm glad that's the way you feel about it," the District Attorney said with enthusiasm. "I'm mighty glad you're going to work with us." He held out his hand.

"Thanks," Guild said as he took the hand. "Let's look at the Hopkinses and the body."

CHAPTER TWO

Columbia Forrest had been a long-limbed smoothly slender young woman. Her body, even as it lay dead in a blue sport suit, seemed supple. Her short hair was a faintly reddish brown. Her features were small and regular, appealing in their lack of strength. There were three bullet-holes in her left temple. Two of them touched. The third was down beside the eye.

Guild put the tip of his dark forefinger lightly on the edge of the lower hole. "A thirty-two," he said. "He made sure: any of the three would have done it." He turned his back on the corpse. "Let's see the Hopkinses."

"They're in the dining-room, I think," the District Attorney said. He hesitated, cleared his throat. His young face was worried. He touched Guild's elbow with the back of one hand and said: "Go easy with Ray, will you? He was a little bit—or a lot, I guess—in love with her and it's tough on him."

"The Deputy?"

"Yes, Ray Callaghan."

"That's all right if he doesn't get in the way," Guild said carelessly. "What sort of person is this Sheriff?"

"Oh, Petersen's all right."

Guild seemed to consider this statement critically. Then he said: "But he's not what you'd call a feverish manhunter?"

"Well, no, that's not—you know—a sheriff has other things to do most of the time, but even if he'd just as lief have somebody else do the work he won't interfere." Boyer moistened his lips and leaned close to the dark man. His face was boyishly alight. "I wish you'd—I'm glad you're going to work with me on this, Guild," he said in a low earnest voice. "I—this is my first murder and I'd like to—well—show them"—he blushed—"that I'm not as young as some of them said."

"Fair enough. Let's see the Hopkinses—in here."

The District Attorney studied Guild's dark face uneasily for a moment, started to say something, changed his mind, and left the room.

A man and a woman came with him when he returned. The man was probably fifty years old, of medium stature, with thin greying hair above a round phlegmatic face. He wore tan trousers held up by new blue suspenders and a faded blue shirt open at the neck. The woman was of about the same age, rather short, plump, and dressed neatly in grey. She wore gold-rimmed spectacles. Her eyes were round and pale and bright.

The District Attorney shut the door and said: "This is Mr. and Mrs. Hopkins, Mr. Guild." He addressed them: "Mr. Guild is working with me. Please give him all the assistance you can."

The Hopkinses nodded in unison.

Guild asked: "How'd this happen?" He indicated with a small backward jerk of his head the dead young woman.

Hopkins said, "I always knew he'd do something like that sometime," while his wife was saying: "It was right in this room and they were talking so loud you could hear it all over the place."

Guild shook his cigarette at them. "One at a time." He spoke to the man: "How'd you know he was going to do it?"

The woman replied quickly: "Oh, he was crazy-jealous of her all the time—if she got out of his sight for a minute—and when she came back from the city and told him she was going to leave to get married he——"

Again Guild used his cigarette to interrupt her. "What do you think? Is he really crazy?"

"He was then, sir," she said. "Why, when we ran in here when we heard the shooting and he told us to keep our mouths shut he was—his eyes—you never saw anything like them in your life—nor his voice either and he was shaking and jerking like he was going to fall apart."

"I don't mean that," Guild explained. "I mean, is he crazy?" Before the woman could reply he put another question to her: "How long have you been with him?"

"Going on about ten months, ain't it, Willie?" she asked her husband.

"Yes," he agreed, "since last fall."

"That's right," she told Guild. "It was last November."

"Then you ought to know whether he's crazy. Is he?"

"Well, I'll tell you," she said slowly, wrinkling her forehead. "He was certainly the most peculiar person you ever heard tell of, but I guess geniuses are like that and I wouldn't want to say he was out and out crazy except about her." She looked at her husband.

He said tolerantly: "Sure, all geniuses are like that. It's—it's eccentric."

"So you think he was a genius," Guild said. "Did you read the things he wrote?"

"No, sir," Mrs. Hopkins said, squirming, "though I did try sometimes, but it was too—I couldn't make heads or tails of it—much—but I ain't an educated woman and——"

"Who was she going to marry?" Guild asked.

Mrs. Hopkins shook her head vigorously. "I don't know. I didn't catch the name if she said it. It was him that was talking so loud."

"What'd she go to town for?"

Mrs. Hopkins shook her head again. "I don't know that either. She used to go in every couple of weeks and he always got mad about it."

"She drive in?"

"Mostly she did, but she didn't yesterday, but she drove out in that new blue car out there."

Guild looked questioningly at the District Attorney, who said: "We're trying to trace it now. It's apparently a new one, but we ought to know whose it is soon."

Guild nodded and returned his attention to the Hopkinses. "She went to San Francisco by train yesterday and came back in this new car at what time today?"

"Yes, sir. At about three o'clock, I guess it was, and she started packing." She pointed at the traveling bags and clothing scattered around the room. "And he came in and the fuss started. I could hear them downstairs and I went to the window and beckoned at Willie—Mr. Hopkins, that is—and we stood at the foot of the stairs, there by the dining-room-door and listened to them."

Guild turned aside to mash his cigarette in a bronze tray on a table. "She usually stay over-night when she went to the city?"

"Mostly always."

"You must have some idea of what she went to the city for," Guild insisted.

"No, I haven't," the woman said earnestly. "We never did know, did we, Willie? Jealous like he was, I guess if she was going in to see some fellow she wouldn't be likely to tell anybody that might tell him, though the Lord knows I can keep my mouth shut as tight as anybody. I've seen the——"

Guild stopped lighting a fresh cigarette to ask: "How about her mail? You must've seen that sometimes."

"No, Mr. Gould, we never did, and that's a funny thing, because all the time we've been here I never saw any mail for her except magazines and never knew her to write any."

Guild frowned. "How long had she been here?"

"She was here when we came. I don't know how long she'd been here, but it must've been a long time."

Boyer said: "Three years. She came here in March three years ago."

"How about her relatives, friends?"

The Hopkinses shook their heads. Boyer shook his head. "His?"

Mrs. Hopkins shook her head again. "He didn't have any. That's what he would always say, that he didn't have a relative or a friend in the world."

"Who's his lawyer?"

Mrs. Hopkins looked blank. "If he's got one I don't know it, Mr. Gould. Maybe you could find something like that in his letters and things."

"That'll do," Guild said abruptly around the cigarette in his mouth, and opened the door for the Hopkinses. They left the room.

He shut the door behind them and with his back against it looked around the room, at the blanketed dead figure on the bed, at the clothing scattered here and there, at the three traveling bags, and finally at the bloodstained center of the light blue rug.

Boyer watched him expectantly.

Staring at the bloodstain, Guild asked: "You've notified the police in San Francisco?"

"Oh, yes, we've sent his description and the description and license-number of his car all over—from Los Angeles to Seattle and as far east as Salt Lake."

"What is the number?" Guild took a pencil and an envelope from his pockets.

Boyer told him, adding: "It's a Buick coupe, last year's."

"What does he look like?"

"I've never seen him, but he's very tall—well over six feet—and thin. Won't weigh more than a hundred and thirty, they say. You know he's tubercular: that's how he happened to come up here. He's about forty-five years old, sunburned, but sallow, with brown eyes and very dark brown hair and whiskers. He's got whiskers—maybe five or six inches long—thick and shaggy, and his eyebrows are thick and shaggy. There's a lot of pictures of him in his room. You can help yourself to them. He had on a baggy grey tweed suit and a soft grey hat and heavy brown shoes. His shoulders are high and straight and he walks on the balls of his feet with long steps. He doesn't smoke or drink and he has a habit of talking to himself."

Guild put away his pencil and envelope. "Had your finger-print people go over the place yet?"

"No, I——"

"It might help in case he's picked up somewhere and we're doubtful. I suppose we can get specimens of his handwriting. Anyway we'll be able to get them from the bank. We'll try to——"

Someone knocked on the door.

"Come in," Boyer called.

The door opened to admit a man's head. He said: "They want you on the phone."

The District Attorney followed the man downstairs. During his absence Guild smoked and looked somberly around the room.

The District Attorney came back saying: "The car belongs to a Charles Fremont, on Guerrero Street, in San Francisco."

"What number." Guild brought out his pencil and envelope again. Boyer told him the number and he wrote it down. "I think I'll trot back right now and see him."

The District Attorney looked at his watch. "I wonder if I couldn't manage to get away to go with you," he said.

Guild pursed his lips. "I don't think you ought to. One of us ought to be here looking through his stuff, gathering up the loose ends. I haven't seen anybody else we ought to trust with it."

Though Boyer seemed disappointed he said, "Righto," readily enough. "You'll keep in touch with me?"

"Sure. Let me have that card I gave you and I'll put my home address and phone-number on it." Guild's eyes became drowsy. "What do you say I drive Fremont's car in?"

The District Attorney wrinkled his forehead. "I don't know," he said slowly. "It might— Oh, sure, if you want. You'll phone me as soon as you've seen him—let me know what's what?"

"Um-hmm."

CHAPTER THREE

A red-haired girl in white opened the door.

Guild said: "I want to see Mr. Charles Fremont."

"Yes, sir," the girl said amiably in a resonant throaty voice. "Come in."

She took him into a comfortably furnished living-room to the right of the entrance. "Sit down. I'll call my brother." She went through another doorway and her voice could be heard singing: "Charley, a gentleman to see you."

Upstairs a hard masculine voice replied: "Be right down."

The red-haired girl came back to the room where Guild was. "He'll be down in a minute," she said.

Guild thanked her.

"Do sit down," she said, sitting on an end of the sofa. Her legs were remarkably beautiful.

He sat in a large chair facing her across the room, but got up again immediately to offer her cigarettes and to hold his lighter to hers. "What I wanted to see your brother about," he said as he sat down again, "was to ask if he knows a Miss Columbia Forrest."

The girl laughed. "He probably does," she said. "She's— They're going to be married tomorrow."

Guild said: "Well, that's——" He stopped when he heard footsteps running down stairs from the second floor.

A man came into the room. He was a man of perhaps thirty-five years, a little above medium height, trimly built, rather gaily dressed in grey with lavender shirt, tie, and protruding pocket-handkerchief. His face was lean and good-looking in a shrewd tight-lipped fashion.

"This is my brother," the girl said.

Guild stood up. "I'm trying to get some information about Miss Columbia Forrest," he said and gave Charles Fremont one of his cards.

The curiosity that had come into Fremont's face with Guild's words became frowning amazement when he had read Guild's card. "What——?"

Guild was saying: "There's been some trouble up at Hell Bend."

Fremont's eyes widened in his paling face. "Wynant has——?"

Guild nodded. "He shot Miss Forrest this afternoon."

The Fremonts stared at each other's blank horrified faces. She said through the fingers of one hand, trembling so she stuttered: "I t-t-told you, Charlie!"

Charles Fremont turned savagely on Guild. "How bad is she hurt? Tell me!"

The dark man said: "She's dead."

Fremont sobbed and sat down with his face in his hands. His sister knelt beside him with her arms around him. Guild stood watching them.

Presently Fremont raised his head. "Wynant?" he asked.

"Gone."

Fremont let his breath out in a low groan. He sat up straight, patting one of his sister's hands, freeing himself from her arms. "I'm going up there now," he told her, rising.

Guild had finished lighting a cigarette. He said: "That's all right, but you'll do most good by telling me some things before you go."

"Anything I can," Fremont promised readily.

"You were to be married tomorrow?"

"Yes. She was down here last night and stayed with us and I persuaded her. We were going to leave here tomorrow morning and drive up to Portland—where we wouldn't have to wait three days for the license—and then go up to Banff. I've just wired the hotel there for reservations. So she took the car—the new one we were going in—to go up to Hell Bend and get her things. I asked her not to—we both tried to persuade her—because we knew Wynant would make trouble, but—but we never thought he would do anything like this."

"You know him pretty well?"

"No, I've only seen him once—about three weeks ago—when he came to see me."

"What'd he come to see you for?"

"To quarrel with me about her—to tell me to stay away from her."

Guild seemed about to smile. "What'd you say to that?"

Fremont drew his thin lips back tight against his teeth. "Do I look like I'd tell him anything except to go to hell?" he demanded.

The dark man nodded. "All right. What do you know about him?"

"Nothing."

Guild frowned. "You must know something. She'd've talked about him."

Anger went out of Fremont's lean face, leaving it gloomy. "I didn't like her to," he said, "so she didn't."

"Why?"

"Jesus!" Fremont exclaimed. "She was living up there. I was nuts about her. I knew he was. What the hell?" He bit his lip. "Do you think that was something I liked to talk about?"

Guild stared thoughtfully at the other man for a moment and then addressed the girl: "What'd she tell you?"

"Not anything. She didn't like to talk about him any more than Charley liked to have her."

Guild drew his brows together. "What'd she stay with him for then?"

Fremont said painfully: "She was going to leave. That's why he killed her."

The dark man put his hands in his pockets and walked down the room to the front windows and back, squinting a little in the smoke rising from his cigarette. "You don't know where he's likely to go? who he's likely to connect with? how we're likely to find him?"

Fremont shook his head. "Don't you think I'd tell you if I knew?" he asked bitterly.

Guild did not reply to that. He asked: "Where are her people?"

"I don't know. I think she's got a father still alive in Texas somewhere. I know she's an only child and her mother's dead."

"How long have you known her?"

"Four—nearly five months."

"Where'd you meet her?"

"In a speakeasy on Powell Street, a couple of blocks beyond the Fairmont. She was in a party with some people I know— Helen Robier—I think she lives at the Cathedral—and a fellow named MacWilliams."

Guild walked to the windows again and back. "I don't like this," he said aloud, but apparently not to the Fremonts. "It doesn't make sense. It's— Look here." He halted in front of them and took some photographs from his pocket. "Are these good pictures of her?" He spread three out fanwise. "I've only seen her dead."

The Fremonts looked and nodded together. "The middle one especially," the girl said. "You have one of those, Charley."

Guild put the dead girl's photographs away and displayed two of a bearded man. "Are they good of him?"

The girl said, "I've never seen him," but her brother nodded and said: "They look like him."

Guild seemed dissatisfied with the answers he had been given. He put the photographs in his pocket again. "Then it's not that," he said, "but there's something funny somewhere."

He scowled at the floor, looked up quickly. "You people aren't putting up some kind of game on me, are you?"

Charles Fremont said: "Don't be a sap."

"All right, but there's something wrong somewhere."

The girl spoke: "What? Maybe if you'd tell us what you think is wrong——"

Guild shook his head. "If I knew what was wrong I could find out for myself what made it wrong. Never mind, I'll get it. I want the names and addresses of all the friends she had, the people she knew that you know of."

"I've told you Helen Robier lives—I'm pretty sure—at the Cathedral," Fremont said. "MacWilliams works in the Russ Building, for a stockbroker, I think. That's all I know about him and I don't believe Columbia knows—" he swallowed "—knew him very well. They're the only ones I know."

"I don't believe they're all you know," Guild said.

"Please, Mr. Guild," the girl said, coming around to his side, "don't be unfair to Charley. He's trying to help you— we're both trying—but——" She stamped her foot and cried angrily, tearfully: "Can't you have some consideration for him now?"

Guild said: "Oh, all right." He reached for his hat. "I drove your car down," he told Fremont. "It's out front now."

"Thank you, Guild."

Something struck one of the front windows, knocking a triangle of glass from its lower left-hand corner in on the floor. Charles Fremont, facing the window, yelled inarticulately and threw himself down on the floor. A pistol was fired through the gap in the pane. The bullet went over Fremont's head and made a small hole in the green plastered wall there.

Guild was moving towards the street-door by the time the bullet-hole appeared in the wall. A black pistol came into his right hand. Outside, that block of Guerrero Street was deserted. Guild went swiftly, though with many backward glances, to the nearest corner. From there he began to retrace his steps slowly, stopping to peer into shadowy doorways and the dark basement-entrances under the high front steps.

Charles Fremont came out to join him. Windows were being raised along the street and people were looking out.

"Get inside," Guild said curtly to Fremont. "You're the one he's gunning for. Get inside and phone the police."

"Elsa's doing that now. He's shaved his whiskers off, Guild."

"That'd be the first thing he did. Go back in the house."

Fremont said, "No," and went with Guild as he searched the block. They were still at it when the police arrived. They did not find Wynant. Around a corner two blocks from the Fremonts' house they found a year-old Buick coupe bearing the license-numbers Boyer had given Guild—Wynant's car.

CHAPTER FOUR

After dinner, which Guild ate alone at Solari's in Maiden Lane, he went to an apartment in Hyde Street. He was admitted by a young woman whose pale tired face lighted up as she said: "Hello, John. We've been wondering what had become of you."

"Been away. Is Chris home?"

"I'd let you in anyhow," she said as she pushed the door farther open.

They went back to a square bookish room where a thick-set man with rumpled sandy hair was half buried in an immense shabby chair. He put his book down, reached for the tall glass of beer at his elbow, and said jovially: "Enter the sleuth. Get some more beer, Kay. I've been wanting to see you, John. What do you say you do some detective-story reviews for my page—you know—The Detective Looks at Detective Fiction?"

"You asked me that before," Guild said. "Nuts."

"It's a good idea, though," the thick-set man said cheerfully. "And I've got another one. I was going to save it till I got around to writing a detective story, but you might be able to use it in your work sometime, so I'll give it to you free."

Guild took the glass of beer Kay held out to him, said, "Thanks," to her and then to the man: "Do I have to listen to it?"

"Yes. You see, this fellow's suspected of a murder that requires quite a bit of courage. All the evidence points right at him—that kind of thing. But he's a great lover of Sam Johnson—got his books all over the place—so you know he didn't do it, because only timid men—the kind that say, 'Yes, sir,' to their wives and, 'Yes, Ma'am,' to policemen—love Johnson. You see, he's only loved for his boorishness and the boldness of his rudeness and bad manners and that's the kind of thing that appeals to——"

"So I look for a fellow named Sam Johnson and he's guilty?" the dark man said.

Kay said: "Chris has one of his nights."

Chris said: "Sneer at me and be damned to you, but there's a piece of psychology that might come in handy some day. Remember it. It's a law. Love of Doctor Johnson is the mark of the pathologically meek."

Guild made a face. "God knows I'm earning me beer," he said and drank. "If you've got to talk, talk about Walter Irving Wynant. That'll do me some good maybe."

"Why?" Chris asked. "How?"

"I'm hunting for him. He slaughtered his secretary this afternoon and lit out for parts unknown."

Kay exclaimed: "Not really!"

Chris said: "The hell he did!"

Guild nodded and drank more beer. "He only paused long enough to take a shot at the fellow his secretary was supposed to marry tomorrow."

Chris and Kay looked at each other with delighted eyes.

Chris lay back in his chair. "Can you beat that? But, you know, I'm not nearly as surprised as I ought to be. The last time I saw him I thought there was something wrong there, though he always was a bit on the goofy side. Remember I said something to you about it, Kay? And it's a cinch this magazine stuff he's been doing lately is woozy. Even parts of his last book— No, I'm being smart-alecky now. I'll stick to what I wrote about his book when it came out: in spite of occasional flaws his 'departmentalization' comes nearer supplying an answer to Pontius Pilate's question than anything ever offered by anybody else."

"What kind of writing does he do?" Guild asked.

"This sort of thing." Chris rose grunting, went to one of his bookcases, picked out a bulky black volume entitled, in large gold letters, *Knowledge and Belief*, opened it at random, and read: "Science is concerned with percepts. A percept is a defined, that is a limited, difference. The scientific datum that white occurs means that white is the difference between a certain perceptual field and the rest of the perceiver. If you look at an unbroken expanse of white you perceive white because your perception of it is limited to your visual field: the surrounding, contrasting, extra-visual area of non-white gives you your percept of white. These are not scientific definitions. They cannot be. Science cannot define, cannot limit, itself. Definitions of science must be philosophical definitions. Science cannot know what it cannot know. Science cannot know there is anything it does not know. Science deals with percepts and not with non-percepts. Thus, Einstein's theory of relativity—that the phenomena of nature will be the same, that is not different, to two observers who move with any uniform velocity whatever relative to one another—is a philosophical, and not a scientific, hypothesis.

"Philosophy, like science, cannot define, cannot limit, itself. Definitions of philosophy must be made from a viewpoint that will bear somewhat the same relation to philosophy that the philosophical viewpoint bears to science. These definitions may be——"

"That'll be enough of that," Guild said.

Chris shut the book with a bang. "That's the kind of stuff he writes," he said cheerfully and went back to his chair and beer.

"What do you know about him?" Guild asked. "I mean outside his writing. Don't start that again. I want to know if he was only crazy with jealousy or has blown his top altogether—and how to catch up with him either way."

"I haven't seen him for six or seven months or maybe longer," Chris said. "He always was a little cracked and unsociable as hell. Maybe just erratic, maybe worse than that."

"What do you know about him?"

"What everybody knows," Chris said depreciatively. "Born somewhere in Devonshire. Went to Oxford. Went native in India and came out with a book on economics—a pretty good book, but visionary. Married an actress named Hana Drix—or something like that—in Paris and lived with her there for three or four years and came out of it with his second book. I think they had a couple of children. After she divorced him he went to Africa and later, I believe, to South America. Anyway he did a lot of traveling and then settled down in Berlin long enough to write his *Speculative Anthropology* and to do some lecturing. I don't know where he was during the War. He popped up over here a couple of years later with a two-volume piece of metaphysics called *Conscious Drifting*. He's been in America ever since—the last five or six years up in the mountains here doing that *Knowledge and Belief*."

"How about relatives, friends?"

Chris shook his tousled head. "Maybe his publishers would know—Dale & Dale."

"And as a critic you think——"

"I'm no critic," Chris said. "I'm a reviewer."

"Well, as whatever you are, you think his stuff is sane?"

Chris moved his thick shoulders in a lazy shrug. "Parts of his books I know are damned fine. Other parts—maybe they're over my head. Even that's possible. But the magazine stuff he's been doing lately—since *Knowledge and Belief*—I know is tripe and worse. The paper sent a kid up to get an interview out of him a couple of weeks ago—when everybody was making the fuss over that Russian anthropologist—and he came back with something awful. We wouldn't have run it if it hadn't been for the weight Wynant's name carries and the kid's oaths that he had written it exactly as it was given to him. I'd say it was likely enough his mind's cracked up."

"Thanks," Guild said, and reached for his hat, but both the others began questioning him then, so they sat there and talked and smoked and drank beer until midnight was past.

In his hotel-room Guild had his coat off when the telephone-bell rang. He went to the telephone. "Hello. . . . Yes. . . . Yes." He waited. "Yes? . . . Yes, Boyer. . . . He showed up at Fremont's and took a shot at him. . . . No, no harm done except that he made a clean sneak. . . . Yes, but we found his car. . . . Where? . . . Yes, I know where it is. . . . What time? . . . . Yes, I see. . . . Tomorrow? What time? . . . Fine. Suppose you pick me up here at my hotel. . . . Right."

He left the telephone, started to unbutton his vest, stopped, looked at the watch on his wrist, put his coat on again, picked up his hat, and went out.

At California Street he boarded an eastbound cable-car and rode over the top of the hill and down it to Chinatown, leaving the car at Grant Avenue. Rain nearly fine as mist was beginning to blow down from the north. Guild went out beyond the curb to avoid a noisy drunken group coming out of a Chinese restaurant, walked a block, and halted across the street from another restaurant. This was a red brick building that tried to seem oriental by means of much gilding and colored lighting, obviously pasted-on corbelled cornices and three-armed brackets marking its stories—some carrying posts above in the shape of half-pillars—and a tent-shaped terra cotta roof surmounted by a mast bearing nine aluminumed rings. There was a huge electric sign—*Manchu.*

He stood looking at this gaudy building until he had lit a cigarette. Then he went over to it. The girl in the cloak-room would not take his hat. "We close at one," she said.

He looked at the people getting into an elevator, at her again. "They're coming in."

"That's upstairs. Have you a card?"

He smiled. "Of course I have. I left it in my other suit."

She looked severely blank.

He said, "Oh, all right, sister," gave her a silver dollar, took his hat-check, and squeezed himself into the crowded elevator.

At the fourth floor he left the elevator with the others and went into a large shabby oblong room where, running out from a small stage, an oblong dance-floor was a peninsula among tables waited on by Chinese in dinner clothes. There were forty or fifty people in the place. Some of them were dancing to music furnished by a piano, a violin, and a French horn.

Guild was given a small table near a shuttered window. He ordered a sandwich and coffee.

The dance ended and a woman with a middle-aged harpy's face and a beautiful satin-skinned body sang a modified version of *Christopher Colombo.* There was another dance after that. Then Elsa Fremont came out to the center of the dance-floor and sang *Hollywood Papa*. Her low-cut green gown set off the red of her hair and brought out the greenness of her narrowly lanceolate eyes. Guild smoked, sipped coffee, and watched her. When she was through he applauded with the others.

She came straight to his table, smiling, and said: "What are you doing here?" She sat down facing him.

He sat down again. "I didn't know you worked here."

"No?" Her smile was merry, her eyes skeptical.

"No," he said, "but maybe I should have known it. A man named Lane, who lives near Wynant in Hell Bend, saw him coming in this place early this evening."

"That would be downstairs," the girl said. "We don't open up here till midnight."

"Lane didn't know about the murder till he got home late tonight. Then he phoned the District Attorney and told him he'd seen Wynant and the D.A. phoned me. I thought I'd drop in just on the off-chance that I might pick up something."

Frowning a little, she asked: "Well?"

"Well, I found you here."

"But I wasn't downstairs earlier this evening," she said. "What time was it?"

"Half an hour before he took his shot at your brother."

"You see"—triumphantly—"you know I was home then talking to you."

"I know that one," Guild said.

CHAPTER FIVE

At ten o'clock next morning Guild went into the Seaman's National Bank, to a desk marked *Mr. Coler, Assistant Cashier*. The sunburned blond man who sat there greeted Guild eagerly.

Guild sat down and said: "Saw the papers this morning, I suppose."

"Yes. Thank the Lord for insurance."

"We ought to get him in time to get some of it back,"

Guild said. "I'd like to get a look at his account and whatever canceled checks are on hand."

"Surely." Coler got up from his desk and went away. When he came back he was carrying a thin pack of checks in one hand, a sheet of typed paper in the other. Sitting down, he looked at the sheet and said: "This is what happened: on the second of the month Wynant deposited that ten-thousand-dollar check on——"

"Bring it in himself?"

"No. He always mailed his deposits. It was a Modern Publishing Company check on the Madison Trust Company of New York. He had a balance of eleven hundred sixty-two dollars and fifty-five cents: the check brought it up to eleven thousand and so on. On the fifth a check"—he took one from the thin pack—"for nine thousand dollars to the order of Laura Porter came through the clearing house." He looked at the check. "Dated the third, the day after he deposited his check." He turned the check over. "It was deposited in the Golden Gate Trust Company." He passed it across the desk to Guild. "Well, that left him with a balance of twenty-one hundred sixty-two dollars and fifty-five cents. Yesterday we received a wire telling us the New York check had been raised from one thousand to ten."

"Do you let your customers draw against out-of-town checks like that before they've had time to go through?"

Coler raised his eyebrows. "Old accounts of the standing of Mr. Wynant—yes."

"He's got a swell standing now," Guild said. "What other checks are there in there?"

Coler looked through them. His eyes brightened. He said: "There are two more Laura Porter ones—a thousand and a seven hundred and fifty. The rest seem to be simply salaries and household expenses." He passed them to Guild.

Guild examined the checks slowly one by one. Then he said: "See if you can find out how long this has been going on and how much of it."

Coler willingly rose and went away. He was gone half an hour. When he returned he said: "As near as I can learn, she's been getting checks for several months at least and has been getting about all he deposited, with not much more than enough left over to cover his ordinary expenses."

Guild said, "Thanks," softly through cigarette-smoke.

From the Seaman's National Bank, Guild went to the Golden Gate Trust Company in Montgomery Street. A girl stopped typewriting to carry his card into the cashier's office and presently ushered him into the office. There he shook hands with a round white-haired man who said: "Glad to see you, Mr. Guild. Which of us criminals are you looking for now?"

"I don't know whether I'm looking for any this time. You've got a depositor named Laura Porter. I'd like to get her address."

The cashier's smile set. "Now, now, I'm always willing to do all I can to help you chaps, but——"

Guild said: "She may have had something to do with gypping the Seaman's National out of eight thou."

Curiosity took some of the stiffness from the cashier's smile.

Guild said: "I don't know that she had a finger in it, but it's because I think she might that I'm here. All I want's her address—now—and I won't want anything else unless I'm sure."

The cashier rubbed his lips together, frowned, cleared his throat, finally said: "Well, if I give it to you you'll understand it's——"

"Strictly confidential," Guild said, "just like the information that the Seaman's been nicked."

Five minutes later he was leaving the Golden Gate Trust Company carrying, in a pocket, a slip of paper on which was written *Laura Porter, 1157 Leavenworth.*

He caught a cable car and rode up California Street. When his car passed the Cathedral Apartments he stood up suddenly and he left the car at the next corner, walking back to the apartment-building.

At the desk he said: "Miss Helen Robier."

The man on the other side of the counter shook his head. "We've nobody by that name—unless she's visiting someone."

"Can you tell me if she lived here—say—five months ago?"

"I'll try." He went back and spoke to another man. The other man came over to Guild. "Yes," he said, "Miss Robier did live here, but she's dead."

"Dead?"

"She was killed in an automobile accident the Fourth of July."

Guild pursed his lips. "Have you a MacWilliams here?"

"No."

"Ever have one?"

"I don't think so. I'll look it up." When he came back he was positive. "No."

Outside the Cathedral, Guild looked at his watch. It was a quarter to twelve. He walked over to his hotel. Boyer rose from a chair in the lobby and came to meet him, saying: "Good morning. How are you? Anything new?"

Guild shrugged. "Some things that might mean something. Let's do our talking over a lunch-table." He turned beside the District Attorney and guided him into the hotel grill.

When they were seated and had given their orders he told Boyer about his conversation with the Fremonts, the shot that had interrupted them, and their search for Wynant that had resulted in their finding his car; about his conversation with Chris—"Christopher Maxim," he said, "book-critic on the *Dispatch*"; about his visit to the Manchu and his meeting Elsa Fremont there; and about his visits that morning to the two banks and the apartment-house. He spoke rapidly, wasting few words, missing no salient point.

"Do you suppose Wynant went to that Chinese restaurant, knowing the girl worked there, to find out where she and her brother lived?" Boyer asked when Guild had finished.

"Not if he'd been at Fremont's house raising hell a couple of weeks ago."

Boyer's face flushed. "That's right. Well, do you——?"

"Let me know what's doing on your end," Guild said, "and maybe we can do our supposing together. Wait till this waiter gets out of the way."

When their food had been put in front of them and they were alone again the District Attorney said: "I told you about Lane seeing Wynant going in this Chinese place."

Guild said, "Yes. How about the finger-prints?" and put some food in his mouth.

"I had the place gone over and we took the prints of everybody we knew had been there, but the matching-up hadn't been done when I left early this morning."

"Didn't forget to take the dead girl's?"

"Oh, no. And you were in there: you can send us yours."

"All right, though I made a point of not touching anything. Any reports from the general alarm?"

"None."

"Anyway, we know he came to San Francisco. How about the circulars?"

"They're being printed now—photo, description, handwriting specimens. We'll get out a new batch when we've got his finger-prints: I wanted to get something out quick."

"Fine. I asked the police here to get us some of his prints off the car. What else happened on your end?"

"That's about all."

"Didn't get anything out of his papers?"

"Nothing. Outside of what seemed to be notes for his work there wasn't a handful of papers. You can look at them yourself when you come up."

Guild, eating, nodded as if he were thoroughly satisfied. "We'll go up for a look at Miss Porter first thing this afternoon," he said, "and maybe something'll come of that."

"Do you suppose she was blackmailing him?"

"People have blackmailed people," Guild admitted.

"I'm just talking at random," the District Attorney said a bit sheepishly, "letting whatever pops into my mind come out."

"Keep it up," Guild said encouragingly.

"Do you suppose she could be a daughter he had by that actress wife in Paris?"

"We can try to find out what happened to her and the children. Maybe Columbia Forrest was his daughter."

"But you know what the situation was up there," Boyer protested. "That would be incest."

"It's happened before," Guild said gravely. "That's why they've got a name for it."

∗

Guild pushed the button beside Laura Porter's name in the vestibule of a small brown stone apartment-building at 1157 Leavenworth Street. Boyer, breathing heavily, stood beside him. There was no response. There was no response the second and third times he pushed the button, but when he touched the one labeled *Manager* the door-lock buzzed.

They opened the door and went into a dim lobby. A door straight ahead of them opened and a woman said: "Yes? What is it?" She was small and sharp-featured, grey-haired, hook-nosed, bright-eyed.

Guild advanced towards her saying: "We wanted to see Miss Laura Porter—three ten—but she doesn't answer the bell."

"I don't think she's in," the grey-haired woman said. "She's not in much. Can I take a message?"

"When do you expect her back?"

"I don't know, I'm sure."

"Do you know when she went out?"

"No, sir. Sometimes I see my people when they come in and go out and sometimes I don't. I don't watch them and Miss Porter I see less than any."

"Oh, she's not here most of the time?"

"I don't know, mister. So long as they pay their rent and don't make too much noise I don't bother them."

"Them? Does she live with somebody?"

"No. I meant them—all my people here."

Guild turned to the District Attorney. "Here. One of your cards."

Boyer fumbled for his cards, got one of them out, and handed it to Guild, who gave it to the woman.

"We want a little information about her," the dark man said in a low confidential voice while she was squinting at the card in the dim light. "She's all right as far as we know, but——"

The woman's eyes, when she raised them, were wide and inquisitive. "What is it?" she asked.

Guild leaned down towards her impressively. "How long has she been here?" he asked in a stage whisper.

"Almost six months," she replied. "It is six months."

"Does she have many visitors?"

"I don't know. I don't remember ever seeing any, but I don't pay much attention and when I see people coming in here I don't know what apartment they're going to."

Guild straightened, put his left hand out, and pressed an electric-light-button, illuminating the lobby. He put his right hand to his inner coat-pocket and brought out pictures of Wynant and his dead secretary. He gave them to the woman. "Ever see either of these?"

She looked at the man's picture and shook her head. "No," she said, "and that ain't a man I'd ever forget if I'd once seen him." She looked at Columbia Forrest's picture. "That!" she cried. "That *is* Miss Porter!"

CHAPTER SIX

Boyer looked round-eyed at Guild.

The dark man, after a little pause, spoke to the woman. "That's Columbia Forrest," he said, "the girl who was killed up in Hell Bend yesterday."

The woman's eyes became round as the District Attorney's. "Well!" she exclaimed, looking at the photograph again, "I never would've thought she was a thief. Why, she was such a pleasant mild-looking little thing——"

"A thief?" Boyer asked incredulously.

"Why, yes." She raised puzzled eyes from the photograph. "At least that's what the paper says, about her going——"

"What paper?"

"The afternoon paper." Her face became bright, eager. "Didn't you see it?"

"No. Have you——?"

"Yes. I'll show you." She turned quickly and went through the doorway open behind her.

Guild, pursing his lips a little, raising his eyebrows, looked at Boyer.

The District Attorney whispered loudly: "She wasn't blackmailing him? She was stealing from him?"

Guild shook his head. "We don't know anything yet," he said.

The woman hurried back to them carrying a newspaper. She turned the newspaper around and thrust it into Guild's hand, leaning over it, tapping the paper with a forefinger. "There it is." Her voice was metallic with excitement. "That's it. You read that."

Boyer went around behind the dark man to his other side, where he stood close to him, almost hanging on his arm, craning for a better view of the paper.

They read:

MURDERED SECRETARY KNOWN TO N.Y. POLICE

NEW YORK, Sept. 8 (A.P.).—Columbia Forrest, in connection with whose murder at Hell Bend, Calif., yesterday the police are now searching for Walter Irving Wynant, famous scientist, philosopher and author, was convicted of shoplifting in New York City three years ago, according to former police magistrate Erle Gardner.

Ex-magistrate Gardner stated that the girl pleaded guilty to a charge brought against her by two department stores and was given a six-month sentence by him, but that the sentence was suspended due to the intervention of Walter Irving Wynant, who offered to reimburse the stores and to give her employment as his secretary. The girl had formerly been a typist in the employ of a Wall St. brokerage house.

Boyer began to speak, but Guild forestalled him by addressing the woman crisply: "That's interesting. Thanks a lot. Now we'd like a look at her rooms."

The woman, chattering with the utmost animation, took them upstairs and unlocked the door of apartment 310. She went into the apartment ahead of them, but the dark man, holding the corridor-door open, said pointedly: "We'll see you again before we leave." She went away reluctantly and Guild shut the door.

"Now we're getting somewhere," Boyer said.

"Maybe we are," Guild agreed.

Words ran swiftly from the District Attorney's mouth. "Do

you suppose she handled the details of his banking and forged those Laura Porter checks and juggled his books to cover them? The chances are he didn't spend much and thought he had a fat balance. Then when she had his account drained she raised the last check, drew against it, and was running away?"

"Maybe, but——" Guild stared thoughtfully at the District Attorney's feet.

"But what?"

Guild raised his eyes. "Why didn't she run away while she was away instead of driving back there in another man's car to tell him she was going away with another man?"

Boyer had a ready answer. "Thieves are funny and women are funny and when you get a woman thief there's no telling what she'll do or why. She could've had a quarrel with him and wanted to rub it in that she was going. She could have forgotten something up there. She might've had some idea of throwing suspicion away from the bank-account-juggling for awhile. She could've had any number of reasons, they need not've been sensible ones. She could've——"

Guild smiled politely. "Let's see what the place'll tell us."

On a table in the living-room they found a flat brass key that unlocked the corridor-door. Nothing else they found anywhere except in the bathroom seemed to interest them. In the bathroom, on a table, they found an obviously new razor holding a blade freshly spotted with rust, an open tube of shaving-cream from which very little had been squeezed, a new shaving-brush that had been used and not rinsed, and a pair of scissors. Hanging over the edge of the tub beside the table was a face-towel on which smears of lather had dried.

Guild blew cigarette-smoke at these things and said: "Looks like our thin man came here to get rid of his whiskers."

Boyer, frowning in perplexity, asked: "But how would he know?"

"Maybe he got it out of her before he killed her and let himself in with the key on the table—hers." Guild pointed his cigarette at the scissors. "They make it look like him and not—well—Fremont for instance. He'd need them for the whiskers and the things are new, as if he'd bought them on his way here." He bent over to examine the table, the inside of the tub, the floor. "Though I don't see any hairs."

"What does it mean, then—his coming here?" the District Attorney asked anxiously.

The dark man smiled a little. "Something or other, maybe," he said. He straightened from his examination of the floor. "He could've been careful not to drop any of his whiskers when he hacked them off, though God knows why he'd try." He looked thoughtfully at the shaving-tools on the table. "We ought to do some more talking to her boy friend."

Downstairs they found the manager waiting in the lobby for them. She stood in front of them using a bright smile to invite speech.

Guild said: "Thanks a lot. How far ahead is her rent paid?"

"Up to the fifteenth of the month it's paid."

"Then it won't cost you anything to let nobody in there till then. Don't and if you go in don't touch anything. There'll be some policemen up. Sure you didn't see a man in there early last night?"

"Yes, sir, I'm sure I didn't see anybody go in there or come out of there, though the Lord knows they could if they had a key without me——"

"How many keys did she have?"

"I only gave her one, but she could've had them made, all she wanted to, and likely enough did if she was—— What'd she do, mister?"

"I don't know. She get much mail?"

"Well, not so very much and most of that looked like ads and things."

"Remember where any of it was from?"

The woman's face colored. "That I don't. I don't look at my people's mail like that. I was always one to mind my own business as long as they paid their rent and don't make so much noise that other people——"

"That's right," Guild said. "Thanks a lot." He gave her one of his cards. "I'll probably be back, but if anything happens—anything that looks like it might have anything to do with her—will you call me up? If I'm not there leave the message."

"Yes, sir, I certainly will," she promised. "Is there——?"

"Thanks a lot," Guild said once more and he and the District Attorney went out.

They were sitting in the District Attorney's automobile when Boyer asked: "What do you suppose Wynant left the key there for, if it was hers and he used it?"

"Why not? He only went there to shave and maybe frisk the place. He wouldn't take a chance on going there again and leaving it there was easier than throwing it away."

Boyer nodded dubiously and put the automobile in motion. Guild directed him to the vicinity of the Golden Gate Trust Company, where they parked the automobile. After a few minutes' wait they were shown into the white-haired cashier's office.

He rose from his chair as they entered. Neither his smile nor his bantering "You are shadowing me" concealed his uneasy curiosity.

Guild said: "Mr. Bliss, this is Mr. Boyer, District Attorney of Whitfield County."

Boyer and Bliss shook hands. The cashier motioned his visitors into chairs.

Guild said: "Our Laura Porter is the Columbia Forrest that was murdered up at Hell Bend yesterday."

Bliss's face reddened. There was something akin to indignation in the voice with which he said: "That's preposterous, Guild."

The dark man's smile was small with malice. "You mean as soon as anybody becomes one of your depositors they're sure of a long and happy life?"

The cashier smiled then. "No, but——" He stopped smiling. "Did she have any part in the Seaman's National swindle?"

"She did," Guild replied and added, still with smiling malice, "unless you're sure none of your clients could possibly touch anybody else's nickels."

The cashier, paying no attention to the latter part of Guild's speech, squirmed in his chair and looked uneasily at the door.

The dark man said: "We'd like to get a transcript of her account and I want to send a handwriting man down for a look at her checks, but we're in a hurry now. We'd like to know when she opened her account, what references she gave, and how much she's got in it."

Bliss pressed one of the buttons on his desk, but before anyone came into the room he rose with a muttered "Excuse me" and went out.

Guild smiled after him. "He'll be ten pounds lighter before he learns whether he's been gypped or not and twenty if he finds he has."

When the cashier returned he shut the door, leaned back against it, and spoke as if he had rehearsed his words. "Miss Porter's account shows a balance of thirty-eight dollars and fifty cents. She drew out twelve thousand dollars in cash yesterday morning."

"Herself?"

"Yes."

Guild addressed Boyer: "We'll show the teller her photo on the way out just to be doubly sure." He turned to the cashier again: "And about the date she opened it and the references she gave?"

The white-haired man consulted a card in his hand. "She opened her account on November the eighth, last year," he said. "The references she gave were Francis X. Kearny, proprietor of the Manchu Restaurant on Grant Avenue, and Walter Irving Wynant."

CHAPTER SEVEN

"The Manchu's only five or six blocks from here," Guild told Boyer as they left the Golden Gate Trust Company. "We might as well stop in now and see what we can get out of Francis Xavier Kearny."

"Do you know him?"

"Uh-uh, except by rep. He's in solid with the police here and is supposed to be plenty tough."

The District Attorney nodded. He chewed his lips in frowning silence until they reached his automobile. Then he said: "What we've learned today seems to tie him, her, the Fremonts, and Wynant all up together."

"Yes," Guild agreed, "it seems to."

"Or do you suppose she could have given Wynant's name because she knew, being his secretary, she could catch the bank's letter of inquiry and answer it without his knowing anything about it?"

"That sounds reasonable enough," the dark man said, "but there's Wynant's visit to the Manchu yesterday."

The District Attorney's frown deepened. "What do you suppose Wynant was up to—if he was in it with them?"

"I don't know. I know somebody's got the twelve thousand she drew out yesterday. I know I want six of it for the Seaman's National. Turn left at the next corner."

They went into the Manchu Restaurant together. A smiling Chinese waiter told them Mr. Kearny was not in, was not expected until nine o'clock that night. They could not learn where he might be found before nine o'clock. They left the restaurant and got into Boyer's automobile again.

"Guerrero Street," Guild said, "though we ought to stop first at a booth where I can phone the police about the Leavenworth Street place and the office to pick up cancelled checks from both banks, so we'll know if any of them are forgeries." He cupped his hands around the cigarette he was lighting. "This'll do. Pull in here."

The District Attorney turned the automobile in at the Mark Hopkins.

Guild, saying, "I'll hurry," jumped out and went indoors. When he came out ten minutes later his face was thoughtful. "The police didn't find any finger-prints on Wynant's car," he said. "I wonder why."

"He could've taken the trouble to——"

"Uh-huh," the dark man agreed, "but I'm wondering why he did. Well, on to Guerrero Street. If Fremont's not back from Hell Bend we'll see what we can shake the girl down for. She ought to know where Kearny hangs out in the daytime."

A Filipino maid opened the Fremonts' door.

"Is Mr. Charles Fremont in?" Guild asked.

"No, sir."

"Miss Fremont?"

"I'll see if she's up yet."

The maid took them into the living-room and went up-stairs.

Guild pointed at the broken window-pane. "That's where the shot was taken at him." He pointed at the hole in the green wall. "That's where it hit." He took a misshapen bullet from his vest-pocket and showed it to Boyer. "It."

Boyer's face had become animated. He moved close to Guild and began to talk in a low excited voice. "Do you sup-pose they could all have been in some game together and Wynant discovered that his secretary was double-crossing him besides getting ready to go off with——"

Guild jerked his head at the hall-door. "Sh-h-h."

Light footsteps ran down the stairs and Elsa Fremont in a brightly figured blue *haori* coat over light green silk pajamas entered the room. "Good morning," she said, holding a hand out to Guild. "It is for me anyway." She used her other hand to partly cover a yawn. "We didn't close the jernt till nearly eight this morning."

Guild introduced the District Attorney to her, then asked: "Your brother go up to Hell Bend?"

"Yes. He was leaving when I got home." She dropped down on the sofa with a foot drawn up under her. Her feet were stockingless in blue embroidered slippers. "Do sit down."

The District Attorney sat in a chair facing her. The dark man went over to the sofa to sit beside her. "We've just come from the Manchu," he said.

Her lanceolate eyes became a little narrower. "Have a nice lunch?" she asked.

Guild smiled and said: "We didn't go there for that."

She said: "Oh." Her eyes were clear and unwary now.

Guild said: "We went to see Frank Kearny."

"Did you?"

"See him? No."

"There's not much chance of finding him there during the day," she said carelessly, "but he's there every night."

"So we were told." Guild took cigarettes from his pocket and held them out to her. "Where do you think we could find him now?"

The girl shook her red head as she took a cigarette. "You can search me. He used to live in Sea Cliff, but I don't know where he moved to." She leaned forward as Guild held his lighter to her cigarette. "Won't whatever you want to see him about wait till night?" she asked when her cigarette was burning.

Guild offered his cigarettes to the District Attorney, who shook his head and murmured: "No, thanks."

The dark man put a cigarette between his lips and set fire to it before he answered the girl's question. Then he said: "We wanted to find out what he knows about Columbia Forrest."

Elsa Fremont said evenly: "I don't think Frank knew her at all."

"Yes, he did, at least as Laura Porter."

Her surprise seemed genuine. She leaned towards Guild. "Say that again."

"Columbia Forrest," Guild said in a deliberately monotonous voice, "had an apartment on Leavenworth Street where she was known as Laura Porter and Frank Kearny knew her."

The girl, frowning, said earnestly: "If you didn't seem to know what you're talking about I wouldn't believe it."

"But you do believe it?"

She hesitated, finally said: "Well, knowing Frank, I'll say it's possible."

"You didn't know about the Leavenworth Street place?"

She shook her head, meeting his gaze with candid eyes. "I didn't."

"Did you know she'd ever gone as Laura Porter?"

"No."

"Ever hear of Laura Porter?"

"No."

Guild drew smoke in and breathed it out. "I think I believe you," he said in a casual tone. "But your brother must have known about it."

She frowned at the cigarette in her hand, at the foot she was not sitting on, and then at Guild's dark face. "You don't have to believe me," she said slowly, "but I honestly don't think he did."

Guild smiled politely. "I can believe you and still think you're wrong," he said.

"I wish," she said naively, "you'd believe me and think I'm right."

Guild moved his cigarette in a vague gesture. "What does your brother do, Miss Fremont?" he asked. "For a living, I mean?"

"He's managing a couple of fighters now," she said, "only one of them isn't. The other's Sammy Deep."

Guild nodded. "The Chinese bantam."

"Yes. Charley thinks he's got a champ in him."

"He's a good boy. Who's the other?"

"A stumble-bum named Terry Moore. If you go to fights much you're sure to've seen him knocked out."

Boyer spoke for the first time since he had declined a cigarette. "Miss Fremont, where were you born?"

"Right here in San Francisco, up on Pacific Avenue."

Boyer seemed disappointed. He asked: "And your brother?"

"Here in San Francisco too."

Disappointment deepened in the District Attorney's young face and there was little hopefulness in his voice asking: "Was your mother also an actress, an entertainer?"

The girl shook her head with emphasis. "She was a school-teacher. Why?"

Boyer's explanation was given more directly to Guild. "I was thinking of Wynant's marriage in Paris."

The dark man nodded. "Fremont's too old. He's only ten or twelve years younger than Wynant." He smiled guilelessly. "Want another idea to play with? Fremont and the dead girl have the same initials—C.F."

Elsa Fremont laughed. "More than that," she said, "they had the same birthdays—May twenty-seventh—though of course Charley is older."

Guild smiled carelessly at this information while the District Attorney's eyes took on a troubled stare.

The dark man looked at his watch. "Did your brother say how long he was going to stay in Hell Bend?" he asked.

"No."

Guild spoke to Boyer. "Why don't you call up and see if he's there. If he is, ask him to wait for us. If he's left, we'll wait here for him."

The District Attorney rose from his chair, but before he could speak the girl was asking anxiously: "Is there anything special you want to see Charley about? Anything I could tell you?"

"You said you didn't know," Guild said. "It's the Laura Porter angle we want to find out about."

"Oh." Some of her anxiety went away.

"Your brother knows Frank Kearny, doesn't he?" Guild asked.

"Oh, yes. That's how I happened to go to work there."

"Is there a phone here we can use?"

"Certainly." She jumped up and, saying, "Back here," opened a door into an adjoining room. When the District Attorney had passed through she shut the door behind him and returned to her place on the sofa beside Guild. "Have you learned anything else?" she asked, "anything besides about her being known as Laura Porter and having the apartment?"

"Some odds and ends," he said, "but it's too early to say what they'll add up to when they're sorted. I didn't ask you whether Kearny and Wynant know each other, did I?"

She shook her head from side to side. "If they do I don't know it. I don't. I'm telling you the truth, Mr. Guild."

"All right, but Wynant was seen going into the Manchu."

"I know, but——" She finished the sentence with a jerk of her shoulders. She moved closer to Guild on the sofa. "You don't think Charley has done anything he oughtn't've done, do you?"

Guild's face was placid. "I won't lie to you," he said. "I think everybody connected with the job has done things they oughtn't've done."

She made an impatient grimace. "I believe you're just trying to make things confusing, to make work for yourself," she said, "so you'll be looking like you're doing something even if you can't find Wynant. Why don't you find him?" Her voice was rising. "That's all you've got to do. Why don't you find him instead of trying to make trouble for everybody else? He's the only one that did anything. He killed her and tried to kill Charley and he's the one you want—not Charley, not me, not Frank. Wynant's the one you want."

Guild laughed indulgently. "You make it sound simple as hell," he told her. "I wish you were right."

Her indignation faded. She put a hand on his hand. Her eyes held a frightened gleam. "There isn't anything else, is there?" she asked, "something we don't know about?"

Guild put his other hand over to pat the back of hers. "There is," he assured her pleasantly. "There's a lot none of us knows and what we do know don't make sense."

"Then——"

The District Attorney opened the door and stood in the doorway. He was pale and he was sweating. "Fremont isn't up there," he said blankly. "He didn't go up there."

Elsa Fremont said, "Jesus Christ!" under her breath.

CHAPTER EIGHT

Night was settling between the mountains when Guild and Boyer arrived at Hell Bend. The District Attorney drove into the village, saying: "We'll go to Ray's. We can come back to Wynant's later if you want to."

"All right," Guild said, "unless Fremont might be there."

"He won't if he came up to see the body. She's at Schumach's funeral parlor."

"Inquest tomorrow?"

"Yes, unless there's some reason for putting it off."

"There's none that I know of," Guild said. He looked side-wise at Boyer. "You'll see that as little as possible comes out at the inquest?"

"Oh, yes!"

They were in Hell Bend now, running between irregularly spaced cottages towards lights that glittered up along the railroad, but before they reached the railroad they turned off to the right and stopped before a small square house where softer lights burned behind yellow blinds.

Callaghan, the raw-boned blond Deputy Sheriff, opened the door for them. He said, "Hello, Bruce," to the District Attorney and nodded politely if without warmth at Guild.

They went indoors, into an inexpensively furnished room where three men sat at a table playing stud poker and a huge

German sheep dog lay attentive in a corner. Boyer spoke to the three men and introduced Guild while the Deputy Sheriff sat down at the table and picked up his cards.

One of the men—thin, bent, old, white-haired, white-mustached—was Callaghan's father. Another—stocky, broad-browed over wide-spaced clear eyes, sunburned almost dark as Guild—was Ross Lane. The third—small, pale, painfully neat—was Schumach, the undertaker.

Boyer turned from the introductions to Callaghan. "You're sure Fremont didn't show up?"

The Deputy Sheriff replied without looking up from his cards. "He didn't show up at Wynant's place. King's been there all day. And he didn't show up at Ben's to—to see her. Where else'd he go if he came up here?" He pushed a chip out on the table. "I'll crack it." He had two kings in his hand.

Schumach pushed a chip out and said: "No, sir, he didn't show up to look at the *corpus delicti.*"

Lane dropped his cards face-down on the table. The elder Callaghan put in a chip and picked up the rest of the deck.

His son said, "Three cards," and then to Boyer: "You can phone King if you want." He moved his head to indicate the telephone by the door.

Boyer looked questioningly at Guild, who said: "Might as well."

Guild addressed a question to Lane while the other three men at the table were making their bets and Boyer was using the telephone. "You're the man who saw Wynant going into the Manchu?"

"Yes." Lane's voice was a quiet bass.

"Was anybody with him?"

Lane said, "No," with certainty, then hesitated thoughtfully and added: "unless they went in ahead of him. I don't think so, but it's possible. He was just going in when I saw him and it could've happened that he'd stopped to shut his car-door or take his key out or something and whoever was with him had gone on ahead."

"Did you see enough of him to make sure it was him?"

"I couldn't go wrong on that, even if I did see only his back. My place being next to his, I guess I've seen a lot more of him than most people around here and then, tall and skinny, with those high shoulders and that funny walk, you couldn't miss him. Besides, his car was there."

"Had he cut his whiskers off, or was he still wearing them?"

Lane opened his eyes wide and laughed. "By God, I don't know," he said. "I heard he shaved them, but I never thought of that. You've got me there. His back was to me and I wouldn't've seen them unless they happened to be sticking out sideways or I got a slanting look at him. I don't remember seeing them, yet I might've and thought nothing of it. If I'd seen his face without them it's a cinch I'd've noticed, but—— You've got me there, brother."

"Know him pretty well?"

Lane picked up the cards the younger Callaghan dealt him and smiled. "Well, I don't guess anybody could say they know him pretty well." He spread his cards apart to look at them.

"Did you know the Forrest girl pretty well?"

The Deputy Sheriff's face began to redden. He said somewhat sharply to the undertaker: "Can you do it?"

The undertaker rapped the table with his knuckles to say he could not.

Lane had a pair of sixes and a pair of fours. He said, "I'll do it," pushed out a chip and replied to the dark man's question: "I don't know just what you mean by that. I knew her. She used to come over sometimes and watch me work the dogs when I had them over in the field near their place."

Boyer had finished telephoning and had come to stand beside Guild. He explained: "Ross raises and trains police dogs."

The elder Callaghan said: "I hope she didn't have you going around talking to yourself like she had Ray." His voice was a nasal whine.

His son slammed his cards down on the table. His face was red and swollen. In a loud accusing tone he began: "I guess I ought to go around chasing after——"

"Ray! Ray!" A stringy white-haired woman in faded blue had come a step in from the next room. Her voice was chiding. "You oughtn't to——"

"Well, make him stop jawing about her, then," the Deputy Sheriff said. "She was as good as anybody else and a lot better than most I know." He glowered at the table in front of him.

In the uncomfortable silence that followed, Boyer said: "Good evening, Mrs. Callaghan. How are you?"

"Just fine," she said. "How's Lucy?"

"She's always well, thanks. This is Mr. Guild, Mrs. Callaghan."

Guild bowed murmuring something polite. The woman ducked her head at him and took a backward step. "If you can't play cards without rowing I wish you'd stop," she told her son and husband as she withdrew.

Boyer addressed Guild: "King, the Deputy stationed at Wynant's place, says he hasn't seen anything of Fremont all day."

Guild looked at his watch. "He's had eleven hours to make it in," he said. He smiled pleasantly. "Or eleven hours start if he headed in another direction."

The undertaker leaned over the table. "You think——?"

"I don't know," Guild said. "I don't know anything. That's the hell of it. We don't know anything."

"There's nothing to know," the Deputy Sheriff said querulously, "except that Wynant was jealous and killed her and ran away and you haven't been able to find him."

Guild, staring bleakly at the younger Callaghan, said nothing.

Boyer cleared his throat. "Well, Ray," he began, "Mr. Guild and I have found quite a bit of confusing evidence in the——"

The elder Callaghan prodded his son with a gnarled forefinger. "Did you tell them about that Smoot boy?"

The Deputy Sheriff pulled irritably away from his father's finger. "That don't amount to nothing," he said, "and, besides, what chance've I got to tell anything with all the talking you've been doing?"

"What was it?" Boyer asked eagerly.

"It don't amount to nothing. Just that this kid—maybe you know him, Pete Smoot's boy—had a telegram for Wynant and took it up to his house. He got there at five minutes after two. He wrote down the time because nobody answered the door and he had to poke the telegram under the door."

"This was yesterday afternoon?" Guild asked.

"Yes," the Deputy Sheriff said gruffly. "Well, the kid says the blue car, the one she drove out from the city in, was there then and Wynant's wasn't."

"He knew Wynant's car?" Guild asked.

Pointedly ignoring Guild, the Deputy Sheriff said: "He says there wasn't any other car there, either in the shed or outside. He'd've seen it if there was. So he put the telegram under the door, got on his bike, and rode back to the telegraph office. Coming back along the road he says he saw the Hopkinses cutting across the field. They'd been down at Hooper's buying Hopkins a suit. The kid says they didn't see him and they were too far from the road for him to holler at them about the telegram." The Deputy Sheriff's face began to redden again. "So if that's right, and I guess it is, they'd've got back to the house, I reckon, around twenty past two—not before that, anyway." He picked up the cards and began to shuffle them, though he had dealt the last hand. "You see, that—well—it don't mean anything or help us any."

Guild had finished lighting a cigarette. He asked Callaghan, before Boyer could speak: "What do you figure? She was alone in the house and didn't answer the kid's knock because she was hurrying to get her packing done before Wynant came home? Or because she was already dead?"

Boyer began in a tone of complete amazement: "But the Hopkinses said——"

Guild said: "Wait. Let Callaghan answer."

Callaghan said in a voice hoarse with anger: "Let Callaghan answer if he wants to, but he don't happen to want to, and what do you think of that?" He glared at Guild. "I got nothing to do with you." He glared at Boyer. "You got nothing to do with me. I'm a deputy sheriff and Petersen's my boss. Go to him for anything you want. Understand that?"

Guild's dark face was impassive. His voice was even. "You're not the first deputy sheriff that ever tried to make a name for himself by holding back information." He started to put his cigarette in his mouth, lowered it, and said: "You got the Hopkinses' call. You were first on the scene, weren't you? What'd you find there that you've kept to yourself?"

Callaghan stood up. Lane and the undertaker rose hastily from their places at the table.

Boyer said: "Now, wait, gentlemen, there's no use of our quarreling."

Guild, smiling, addressed the Deputy Sheriff blandly: "You're not in such a pretty spot, Callaghan. You had a yen for the girl. You were likely to be just as jealous as Wynant when you heard she was going off with Fremont. You've got a childish sort of hot temper. Where were you around two o'clock yesterday afternoon?"

Callaghan, snarling unintelligible curses, lunged at Guild.

Lane and the undertaker sprang between the two men, struggling with the Deputy Sheriff. Lane turned his head to give the growling dog in the corner a quieting command. The elder Callaghan did not get up, but leaned over the table whining remonstrances at his son's back. Mrs. Callaghan came in and began to scold her son.

Boyer said nervously to Guild: "I think we'd better go."

Guild shrugged. "Whatever you say, though I would like to know where he spent the early part of yesterday afternoon." He glanced calmly around the room and followed Boyer to the front door.

Outside, the District Attorney exclaimed: "Good God! You don't think Ray killed her!"

"Why not?" Guild snapped the remainder of his cigarette to the middle of the roadbed in a long red arc. "I don't know. Somebody did and I'll tell you a secret. I'm damned if I think Wynant did."

CHAPTER NINE

Hopkins and a tall younger man with a reddish mustache came out of Wynant's house when Boyer stopped his automobile in front of it.

The District Attorney got down on the ground saying: "Good evening, gentlemen." Indicating the red-mustached man, he said to Guild: "This is Deputy Sheriff King, Mr. Guild. Mr. Guild," he explained, "is working with me."

The Deputy Sheriff nodded, looking the dark man up and down. "Yes," he said, "I been hearing about him. Howdy, Mr. Guild."

Guild's nod included Hopkins and King.

"No sign of Fremont yet?" Boyer asked.

"No."

Guild spoke: "Is Mrs. Hopkins still up?"

"Yes, sir," her husband said, "she's doing some sewing."

The four men went indoors.

Mrs. Hopkins, sitting in a rocking chair hemming an un-bleached linen handkerchief, started to rise, but sank back in her chair with a "How do you do" when Boyer said: "Don't get up. We'll find chairs."

Guild did not sit down. Standing by the door, he lit a ciga-rette while the others were finding seats. Then he addressed the Hopkinses: "You told us it was around three o'clock yes-terday afternoon that Columbia Forrest got back from the city."

"Oh, no, sir!" The woman dropped her sewing on her knees. "Or at least we never meant to say anything like that. We meant to say it was around three o'clock when we heard them—him—quarreling. You can ask Mr. Callaghan what time it was when I called him up and——"

"I'm asking you," Guild said in a pleasant tone. "Was she here when you got back from the village—from buying the suit—at two-twenty?"

The woman peered nervously through her spectacles at him. "Well, yes, sir, she was, if that's what time it was. I thought it was later, Mr. Gould, but if you say that's what time it was I guess you know, but she'd only just got home."

"How do you know that?"

"She said so. She called downstairs to know if it was us coming in and she said she'd just that minute got home."

"Was there a telegram under the door when you came in?"

The Hopkinses looked at each other in surprise and shook their heads. "No, there was not," the man said.

"Was he here?"

"Mr. Wynant?"

"Yes. Was he here when you got home?"

"Yes. I—I think he was?"

"Do you know?"

"Well, it—" she looked appealingly at her husband—"he was here when we heard them fighting not much after that, so he must've been——"

"Or did he come in after you got back?"

"Not—we didn't see him come in."

"Hear him?"

She shook her head certainly. "No, sir."

"Was his car here when you got back?"

The woman started to say Yes, stopped midway, and looked questioningly at her husband. His round face was uncomfortably confused. "We—we didn't notice," she stammered.

"Would you have heard him if he'd driven up while you were here?"

"I don't know, Mr. Gould. I think—I don't know. If I was in the kitchen with the water running and Willie—Mr. Hopkins that is—don't hear any too good anyway. Maybe we——"

Guild turned his back to her and addressed the District Attorney. "There's no sense to their story. If I were you I'd throw them in the can and charge them with the murder."

Boyer gaped. Hopkins's face went yellow. His wife leaned over her sewing and began to cry. King stared at the dark man as at some curio seen for the first time.

The District Attorney was the first to speak. "But—but why?"

"You don't believe them, do you?" Guild asked in an amused tone.

"I don't know. I——"

"If it was up to me I'd do it," Guild said good-naturedly, "but if you want to wait till we locate Wynant, all right. I want to get some more specimens of Wynant's and the girl's handwriting." He turned back to the Hopkinses and asked casually: "Who was Laura Porter?"

The name seemed to mean nothing to them. Hopkins shook his head dumbly. His wife did not stop crying.

"I didn't think you knew," Guild said. "Let's go up and get those scratch samples, Boyer."

The District Attorney's face, as he went upstairs with Guild, was a theater where anxiety played. He stared at the dark man with troubled pleading eyes. "I—I wish you'd tell me why you think Wynant didn't do it," he said in a wheedling voice, "and why you think Ray and the Hopkinses are mixed up in it." He made a despairing gesture with his hands. "What do you really think, Guild? Do you really suspect these people or are you——?" His face flushed under the dark man's steady unreadable gaze and he lowered his eyes.

"I suspect everybody," Guild said in a voice that was devoid of feeling. "Where were you between two and three o'clock yesterday afternoon?"

Boyer jumped and a look of fear came into his young face. Then he laughed sheepishly and said: "Well, I suppose you're right. I want you to understand, Guild, that I keep asking you things not because I think you're off on the wrong track, but because I think you know so much more about this kind of thing than I do."

Guild was in San Francisco by two o'clock in the morning. He went straight to the Manchu.

Elsa Fremont was singing when he stepped out of the elevator. She was wearing a taffeta gown—snug of bodice, billowy of skirt—whereon great red roses were printed against a chalky blue background, with two rhinestone buckles holding a puffy sash in place. The song she sang had a recurring line, *Boom, chisel, chisel!*

When she had finished her second encore she started towards Guild's table, but two men and a woman at an intervening table stopped her, and it was ten minutes or more before she joined him. Her eyes were dark, her face and voice nervous. "Did you find Charley?"

Guild, on his feet, said: "No. He didn't go up to Hell Bend."

She sat down twisting her wrist-scarf, nibbling her lip, frowning.

The dark man sat down asking: "Did you think he'd gone there?"

She jerked her head up indignantly. "I told you I did. Don't you ever believe anything that anybody tells you?"

"Sometimes I do and am wrong," Guild said. He tapped a

cigarette on the table. "Wherever he's gone, he's got a new car and an all-day start."

She put her hands on the table suddenly, palms up in a suppliant gesture. "But why should he want to go anywhere else?"

Guild was looking at her hands. "I don't know, but he did." He bent his head further over her hands as if studying their lines. "Is Frank Kearny here now and can I talk to him?"

She uttered a brief throaty laugh. "Yes." Letting her hands lie as they were on the table, she turned her head and caught a passing waiter's attention. "Lee, ask Frank to come here." She looked at the dark man again, somewhat curiously. "I told him you wanted to see him. Was that all right?"

He was still studying her palms. "Oh, yes, sure," he said good-naturedly. "That would give him time to think."

She laughed again and took her hands off the table.

A man came to the table. He was a full six feet tall, but the width of his shoulders made him seem less than that. His face was broad and flat, his eyes small, his lips wide and thick, and when he smiled he displayed crooked teeth set apart. His age could have been anything between thirty-five and forty-five.

"Frank, this is Mr. Guild," Elsa Fremont said.

Kearny threw his right hand out with practiced heartiness. "Glad to know you, Guild."

They shook hands and Kearny sat down with them. The orchestra was playing *Love Is Like That* for dancers.

"Do you know Laura Porter?" Guild asked Kearny.

The proprietor shook his ugly head. "Never heard of her. Elsa asked me."

"Did you know Columbia Forrest?"

"No. All I know is she's the girl that got clipped up there in Whitfield County and I only know that from the papers and from Elsa."

"Know Wynant?"

"No, and if somebody saw him coming in here all I got to say is that if lots of people I don't know didn't come in here I couldn't stay in business."

"That's all right," Guild said pleasantly, "but here's the thing: when Columbia Forrest opened a bank-account seven months ago under the name of Laura Porter you were one of the references she gave the bank."

Kearny's grin was undisturbed. "That might be, right enough," he said, "but that still don't mean I know her." He put out a long arm and stopped a waiter. "Tell Sing to give you that bottle and bring ginger ale set-ups." He turned his attention to Guild again. "Look it, Guild. I'm running a joint. Suppose some guy from the Hall or the Municipal Building that can do me good or bad, or some guy that spends with me, comes to me and says he's got a friend—or a broad—that's hunting a job or wants to open some kind of account or get a bond, and can they use my name? Well, what the hell! It happens all the time."

Guild nodded. "Sure. Well, who asked you to OK Laura Porter?"

"Seven months ago?" Kearny scoffed. "A swell chance I got of remembering! Maybe I didn't even hear her name then."

"Maybe you did. Try to remember."

"No good," Kearny insisted. "I tried when Elsa first told me about you wanting to see me."

Guild said: "The other name she gave was Wynant's. Does that help?"

"No. I don't know him, don't know anybody that knows him."

"Charley Fremont knows him."

Kearny moved his wide shoulders carelessly. "I didn't know that," he said.

The waiter came, gave the proprietor a dark quart bottle, put glasses of cracked ice on the table, and began to open bottles of ginger ale.

Elsa Fremont said: "I told you I didn't think Frank knew anything about any of them."

"You did," the dark man said, "and now he's told me." He made his face solemnly thoughtful. "I'm glad he didn't contradict you."

Elsa stared at him while Kearny put whisky and the waiter ginger ale into the glasses.

The proprietor, patting the stopper into the bottle again, asked: "Is it your idea this fellow Wynant's still hanging around San Francisco?"

Elsa said in a low hoarse voice: "I'm scared! He tried to shoot Charley before. Where"—she put a hand on the dark man's wrist—"where is Charley?"

Before Guild could reply Kearny was saying to her: "It might help if you'd do some singing now and then for all that dough you're getting." He watched her walk out on the dance-floor and said to Guild: "The kid's worried. Think anything happened to Charley? Or did he have reasons to scram?"

"You people should ask me things," Guild said and drank.

The proprietor picked up his glass. "People can waste a lot of time," he said reflectively, "once they get the idea that people that don't know anything do." He tilted his glass abruptly, emptying most of its contents into his throat, set the glass down, and wiped his mouth with the back of his hand. "You sent a friend of mine over a couple of months ago—Deep Ying."

"I remember," Guild said. "He was the fattest of the three *boo how doy* who tried to spread their tong war out to include sticking up a Japanese bank."

"There was likely a tong angle to it, guns stashed there or something."

The dark man said, "Maybe," indifferently and drank again.

Kearny said: "His brother's here now."

Some of Guild's indifference went away. "Was he in on the job too?"

The proprietor laughed. "No," he said, "but you never can tell how close brothers are and I thought you'd like to know."

The dark man seemed to weigh this statement carefully. Then he said: "In that case maybe you ought to point him out to me."

"Sure." Kearny stood up grinning, raised a hand, and sat down.

Elsa Fremont was singing *Kitty From Kansas City*.

A plump Chinese with a round smooth merry face came between tables to their table. He was perhaps forty years old, of less than medium stature, and though his grey suit was of good quality it did not fit him. He halted beside Kearny and said: "How you do, Frank."

The proprietor said: "Mr. Guild, I want you to meet a friend of mine, Deep Kee."

"I'm your friend, you bet you." The Chinese, smiling broadly, ducked his head vigorously at both men.

Guild said: "Kearny tells me you're Deep Ying's brother."

"You bet you." Deep Kee's eyes twinkled merrily. "I hear about you, Mr. Guild. Number one detective. You catch 'em my brother. You play trick on 'em. You bet you."

Guild nodded and said solemnly: "No play trick on 'em, no catch 'em. You bet you."

The Chinese laughed heartily.

Kearny said: "Sit down and have a drink."

Deep Kee sat down beaming on Guild, who was lighting a cigarette, while the proprietor brought his bottle from beneath the table.

A woman at the next table, behind Guild, was saying oratorically: "I can always tell when I'm getting swacked because the skin gets tight across my forehead, but it don't ever do me any good because by that time I'm too swacked to care whether I'm getting swacked or not."

Elsa Fremont was finishing her song.

Guild asked Deep Kee: "You know Wynant?"

"Please, no."

"A thin man, tall, used to have whiskers before he cut them off," Guild went on. "Killed a woman up at Hell Bend."

The Chinese, smiling, shook his head from side to side.

"Ever been in Hell Bend?"

The smiling Chinese head continued to move from side to side.

Kearny said humorously: "He's a high-class murderer, Guild. He wouldn't take a job in the country."

Deep Kee laughed delightedly.

Elsa Fremont came to the table and sat down. She seemed tired and drank thirstily from her glass.

The Chinese, smiling, bowing, leaving his drink barely tasted, went away. Kearny, looking after him, told Guild: "That's a good guy to have liking you."

"Tong gunman?"

"I don't know. I know him pretty well, but I don't know that. You know how they are."

"I don't know," Guild said.

A quarrel had started in the other end of the room. Two men were standing cursing each other over a table. Kearny screwed himself around in his chair to stare at them for a moment. Then, grumbling, "Where do these bums think they are?" he got up and went over to them.

Elsa Fremont stared moodily at her glass. Guild watched Kearny go to the table where the two men were cursing, quiet them, and sit down with them.

The woman who had talked about the skin tightening on her forehead was now saying in the same tone: "Character actress—that's the old stall. She's just exactly the same kind of character actress I was. She's doing bits—when she can get them."

Elsa Fremont, still staring at her glass, whispered: "I'm scared."

"Of what?" Guild asked as if moderately interested.

"Of Wynant, of what he might——" She raised her eyes, dark and harried. "Has he done anything to Charley, Mr. Guild?"

"I don't know."

She put a tight fist on the table and cried angrily: "Why don't you do something? Why don't you find Wynant? Why don't you find Charley? Haven't you got any blood, any heart, any guts? Can't you do anything but sit there like a——" She broke off with a sob. Anger went out of her face and the fingers that had been clenched opened in appeal. "I—I'm sorry. I didn't mean—— But, oh, Mr. Guild, I'm so——" She put her head down and bit her lower lip.

Guild, impassive, said: "That's all right."

A man rose drunkenly from a nearby table and came up behind Elsa's chair. He put a fat hand on her shoulder and said: "There, there, darling." He said to Guild: "You cannot annoy this little girl in this way. You cannot. You ought to be ashamed of yourself, a man of your complexion." He leaned forward sharply, peering into Guild's face. "By Jesus, I believe you're a mulatto. I really do."

Elsa, squirming from under the fat drunken hand, flung a "Let me alone" up at the man. Guild said nothing. The fat man looked uncertainly from one to the other of them until a hardly less drunken man, mumbling unintelligible apologies, came and led him away.

Elsa looked humbly at the dark man. "I'm going to tell Frank I'm going," she said in a small tired voice. "Will you take me home?"

"Sure."

They rose and moved towards the door. Kearny was standing by the elevator.

"I don't feel like working tonight, Frank," the girl told him. "I'm going to knock off."

"Oke," he said. "Give yourself a hot drink and some aspirin." He held his hand out to Guild. "Glad I met you. Drop in any time. Anything I can ever do for you, let me know. You going to take the kid home? Swell! Be good."

CHAPTER TEN

Elsa Fremont was a dusky figure beside Guild in a taxicab riding west up Nob Hill. Her eyes glittered in a splash of light from a street-lamp. She drew breath in and asked: "You think Charley's run away, don't you?"

"It's likely," Guild said, "but maybe he'll be home when we get there."

"I hope so," she said earnestly. "I do hope so, but—I'm afraid."

He looked obliquely at her. "You've said that before. Mean you're afraid something's happened to him or will happen to you?"

She shivered. "I don't know. I'm just afraid." She put a hand in his, asking plaintively: "Aren't you ever going to catch Wynant?"

"Your hand's cold," he said.

She pulled her hand away. Her voice was not loud: intensity made it shrill. "Aren't you ever human?" she demanded. "Are you always like this? Or is it a pose?" She drew herself far back in a corner of the taxicab. "Are you a damned corpse?"

"I don't know," the dark man said. He seemed mildly puzzled. "I don't know what you mean."

She did not speak again, but sulked in her corner until they reached her house. Guild sat at ease and smoked until the taxicab stopped. Then he got out saying: "I'll stop long enough to see if he's home."

The girl crossed the sidewalk and unlocked the door while he was paying the chauffeur. She had gone indoors leaving the door open when he mounted the front steps. He followed her in. She had turned on ground-floor lights and was calling upstairs: "Charley!" There was no answer.

She uttered an impatient exclamation and ran upstairs. When she came down again she moved wearily. "He's not in," she said. "He hasn't come."

Guild nodded without apparent disappointment. "I'll give you a ring when I wake up," he said, stepping back towards the street-door, "or if I get any news of him."

She said quickly: "Don't go yet, please, unless you have to. I don't—I wish you'd stay a little while."

He said, "Sure," and they went into the living-room.

When she had taken off her coat she left him for a few minutes, going into the kitchen, returning with Scotch whisky, ice, lemons, glasses, and a siphon of water. They sat on the sofa with drinks in their hands.

Presently, looking inquisitively at him, she said: "I really meant what I said in the cab. Aren't you actually human? Isn't there any way anybody can get to you, get to the real inside you? I think you're the most—" she frowned, selecting words "—most untouchable, unreal, person I've ever known. Trying to—to really come in contact with you is just like trying to hold a handful of smoke."

Guild, who had listened attentively, now nodded. "I think I know what you're trying to say. It's an advantage when I'm working."

"I didn't ask you that," she protested, moving the glass in her hand impatiently. "I asked you if that's the way you really are or if you just do it."

He smiled and shook his head noncommittally.

"That isn't a smile," she said. "It's painted on." She leaned to him swiftly and kissed him, holding her mouth to his mouth for an appreciable time. When she took her mouth from his her narrow green eyes examined his face carefully. She made a moue. "You're not even a corpse—you're a ghost."

Guild said pleasantly, "I'm working," and drank from his glass.

Her face flushed. "Do you think I'm trying to make you?" she asked hotly.

He laughed at her. "I'd like it if you were, but I didn't mean it that way."

"You wouldn't like it," she said. "You'd be scared."

"Uh-uh," he explained blandly. "I'm working. It'd make you easier for me to handle."

Nothing in her face responded to his bantering. She said, with patient earnestness: "If you'd only listen to me and believe me when I tell you I don't know any more what it's all about than you do, if that much. You're just wasting your time when you ought to be finding Wynant. I don't know anything. Charley doesn't. We'd both tell you if we did. We've both already told you all we know. Why can't you believe me when I tell you that?"

"Sorry," Guild said lightly. "It don't make sense." He looked at his watch. "It's after five. I'd better run along."

She put a hand out to detain him, but instead of speaking she stared thoughtfully at her dangling wrist-scarf and worked her lips together.

Guild lit another cigarette and waited with no appearance of impatience.

Presently she shrugged her bare shoulders and said: "It doesn't make any difference." She turned her head to look uneasily behind her. "But will you—will you do something for me before you go? Go through the house and see that everything is all right. I'm—I'm nervous, upset."

"Sure," he said readily, and then, suggestively: "If you've got anything to tell me, the sooner the better for both of us."

"No, no, there's nothing," she said. "I've told you everything."

"All right. Have you got a flashlight?"

She nodded and brought him one from the next room.

When Guild returned to the living-room Elsa Fremont was standing where he had left her. She looked at his face and anxiety went out of her eyes. "It was silly of me," she said, "but I do thank you."

He put the flashlight on the table and felt for his cigarettes. "Why'd you ask me to look?"

She smiled in embarrassment and murmured: "It was a silly notion."

"Why'd you bring me home with you?" he asked.

She stared at him with eyes in which fear was awakening. "Wh-what do you mean? Is there——?"

He nodded.

"What is it?" she cried. "What did you find?"

He said: "I found something wrong down in the cellar."

Her hand went to her mouth.

"Your brother," he said.

She screamed: "What?"

"Dead."

The hand over her mouth muffled her voice: "K-killed?"

He nodded. "Suicide, from the looks of it. The gun could be the one the girl was killed with. The——" He broke off and caught her arm as she tried to run past him towards the door. "Wait. There's plenty of time for you to look at him. I want to talk to you."

She stood motionless staring at him with open blank eyes.

He said: "And I want you to talk to me."

She did not show she had heard him.

He said: "Your brother did kill Columbia Forrest, didn't he?"

Her eyes held their blank stare. Her lips barely moved. "You fool, you fool," she muttered in a tired flat voice.

He was still holding her arm. He ran the tip of his tongue over his lips and asked in a low persuasive tone: "How do you know he didn't?"

She began to tremble. "He couldn't've," she cried. Life had come back to her voice and face now. "He couldn't've."

"Why?"

She jerked her arm out of his hand and thrust her face up towards his. "He couldn't've, you idiot. He wasn't there. You can find out where he was easily enough. You'd've found out long before this if you'd had any brains. He was at a meeting of the Boxing Commission that afternoon, seeing about a permit or something for Sammy. They'll tell you that. They'll have a record of it."

The dark man did not seem surprised. His blue eyes were meditative under brows drawn a little together. "He didn't kill her, but he committed suicide," he said slowly and with an air of listening to himself say it. "That don't make sense too."

From the Memoirs of a Private Detective

I

WISHING to get some information from members of the W.C.T.U. in an Oregon city, I introduced myself as the secretary of the Butte Civic Purity League. One of them read me a long discourse on the erotic effects of cigarettes upon young girls. Subsequent experiments proved this trip worthless.

2

A man whom I was shadowing went out into the country for a walk one Sunday afternoon and lost his bearings completely. I had to direct him back to the city.

3

House burglary is probably the poorest paid trade in the world; I have never known anyone to make a living at it. But for that matter few criminals of any class are self-supporting unless they toil at something legitimate between times. Most of them, however, live on their women.

4

I know an operative who while looking for pickpockets at the Havre de Grace race track had his wallet stolen. He later became an official in an Eastern detective agency.

5

Three times I have been mistaken for a Prohibition agent, but never had any trouble clearing myself.

6

Taking a prisoner from a ranch near Gilt Edge, Mont., to Lewistown one night, my machine broke down and we had to sit there until daylight. The prisoner, who stoutly affirmed his innocence, was clothed only in overalls and shirt. After shivering all night on the front seat his morale was low, and I had no difficulty in getting a complete confession from him while walking to the nearest ranch early the following morning.

7

Of all the men embezzling from their employers with whom I have had contact, I can't remember a dozen who smoked, drank, or had any of the vices in which bonding companies are so interested.

8

I was once falsely accused of perjury and had to perjure my-self to escape arrest.

9

A detective agency official in San Francisco once substi-tuted "truthful" for "voracious" in one of my reports on the grounds that the client might not understand the latter. A few days later in another report "simulate" became "quicken" for the same reason.

10

Of all the nationalities haled into the criminal courts, the Greek is the most difficult to convict. He simply denies every-thing, no matter how conclusive the proof may be; and noth-ing so impresses a jury as a bare statement of fact, regardless of the fact's inherent improbability or obvious absurdity in the face of overwhelming contrary evidence.

11

I know a man who will forge the impressions of any set of fingers in the world for $50.

12

I have never known a man capable of turning out first-rate work in a trade, a profession or an art, who was a professional criminal.

13

I know a detective who once attempted to disguise himself thoroughly. The first policeman he met took him into custody.

14

I know a deputy sheriff in Montana who, approaching the cabin of a homesteader for whose arrest he had a warrant, was confronted by the homesteader with a rifle in his hands. The deputy sheriff drew his revolver and tried to shoot over the homesteader's head to frighten him. The range was long and a strong wind was blowing. The bullet knocked the rifle from the homesteader's hands. As time went by the deputy sheriff came to accept as the truth the reputation for expertness that this incident gave him, and he not only let his friends enter him in a shooting contest, but wagered everything he owned upon his skill. When the contest was held he missed the target completely with all six shots.

15

Once in Seattle the wife of a fugitive swindler offered to sell me a photograph of her husband for $15. I knew where I could get one free, so I didn't buy it.

16

I was once engaged to discharge a woman's housekeeper.

17

The slang in use among criminals is for the most part a conscious, artificial growth, designed more to confuse outsiders than for any other purpose, but sometimes it is singularly expressive; for instance, *two-time loser*—one who has been convicted twice; and the older *gone to read and write*—found it advisable to go away for a while.

18

Pocket-picking is the easiest to master of all the criminal trades. Anyone who is not crippled can become an adept in a day.

19

In 1917, in Washington, D.C., I met a young woman who did not remark that my work must be very interesting.

20

Even where the criminal makes no attempt to efface the prints of his fingers, but leaves them all over the scene of the crime, the chances are about one in ten of finding a print that is sufficiently clear to be of any value.

21

The chief of police of a Southern city once gave me a description of a man, complete even to a mole on his neck, but neglected to mention that he had only one arm.

22

I know a forger who left his wife because she had learned to smoke cigarettes while he was serving a term in prison.

23

Second only to "Dr. Jekyll and Mr. Hyde" is "Raffles" in the affections of the daily press. The phrase "gentleman crook" is used on the slightest provocation. A composite portrait of the gentry upon whom the newspapers have bestowed this title would show a laudanum-drinker, with a large rhinestone horseshoe aglow in the soiled bosom of his shirt below a bow tie, leering at his victim, and saying: "Now don't get scared, lady, I ain't gonna crack you on the bean. I ain't a rough-neck!"

24

The cleverest and most uniformly successful detective I have ever known is extremely myopic.

25

Going from the larger cities out into the remote rural communities, one finds a steadily decreasing percentage of crimes that have to do with money and a proportionate increase in the frequency of sex as a criminal motive.

26

While trying to peer into the upper story of a roadhouse in northern California one night—and the man I was looking for was in Seattle at the time—part of the porch roof crumbled under me and I fell, spraining an ankle. The proprietor of the roadhouse gave me water to bathe it in.

27

The chief difference between the exceptionally knotty problem confronting the detective of fiction and that facing the real detective is that in the former there is usually a paucity of clues, and in the latter altogether too many.

28

I know a man who once stole a Ferris-wheel.

29

That the law-breaker is invariably soon or late apprehended is probably the least challenged of extant myths. And yet the files of every detective bureau bulge with the records of unsolved mysteries and uncaught criminals.

"Suggestions to Detective Story Writers"

A FELLOW who takes detective stories seriously, I am annoyed by the stupid recurrence of these same blunders
in book after book. It would be silly to insist that nobody
who has not been a detective should write detective stories,
but it is certainly not unreasonable to ask any one who is going to write a book of any sort to make some effort at least to
learn something about his subject. Most writers do. Only detective story writers seem to be free from a sense of obligation
in this direction, and, curiously, the more established and prolific detective story writers seem to be the worst offenders.
Nearly all writers of Western tales at least get an occasional
glimpse of their chosen territory from a car-window while en
route to Hollywood; writers of sea stories have been seen on
the waterfront; surely detective story writers could afford to
speak to policemen now and then.

Meanwhile, a couple of months' labor in this arena has
convinced me that the following suggestions might be of
value to somebody:

(1) There was an automatic revolver, the Webley-Fosbery,
made in England some years ago. The ordinary automatic pistol, however, is not a revolver. A pistol, to be a revolver, must
have something on it that revolves.

(2) The Colt's .45 automatic pistol has no chambers. The
cartridges are put in a magazine.

(3) A silencer may be attached to a revolver, but the effect
will be altogether negligible. I have never seen a silencer used
on an automatic pistol, but am told it would cause the pistol
to jam. A silencer may be used on a single-shot target pistol
or on a rifle, but both would still make quite a bit of noise.
"Silencer" is a rather optimistic name for this device which
has generally fallen into disuse.

(4) When a bullet from a Colt's .45, or any firearm of approximately the same size and power, hits you, even if not in
a fatal spot, it usually knocks you over. It is quite upsetting at
any reasonable range.

(5) A shot or stab wound is simply felt as a blow or push at first. It is some little time before any burning or other painful sensation begins.

(6) When you are knocked unconscious you do not feel the blow that does it.

(7) A wound made after the death of the wounded is usually recognizable as such.

(8) Finger-prints of any value to the police are seldom found on anybody's skin.

(9) The pupils of many drug-addicts' eyes are apparently normal.

(10) It is impossible to see anything by the flash of an ordinary gun, though it is easy to imagine you have seen things.

(11) Not nearly so much can be seen by moonlight as you imagine. This is especially true of colors.

(12) All Federal snoopers are not members of the Secret Service. That branch is chiefly occupied with pursuing counterfeiters and guarding Presidents and prominent visitors to our shores.

(13) A sheriff is a county officer who usually has no official connection with city, town or State police.

(14) Federal prisoners convicted in Washington, D.C., are usually sent to the Atlanta prison and not to Leavenworth.

(15) The California State prison at San Quentin is used for convicts serving first terms. Two-time losers are usually sent to Folsom.

(16) Ventriloquists do not actually "throw" their voices and such doubtful illusions as they manage depend on their gestures. Nothing at all could be done by a ventriloquist standing behind his audience.

(17) Even detectives who drop their final g's should not be made to say "anythin' "—an oddity that calls for vocal acrobatics.

(18) "Youse" is the plural of "you."

(19) A trained detective shadowing a subject does not ordinarily leap from doorway to doorway and does not hide behind trees and poles. He knows no harm is done if the subject sees him now and then.

—

A few weeks ago, having no books on hand that I cared to talk much about, I listed in this column nineteen suggestions to detective story writers. Those suggestions having been received with extreme enthusiasm—to the extent at least of one publisher offering me a hundred dollars for a slightly more complete list—I, not needing that particular hundred dollars at the moment, herewith present a few more suggestions at the mere usual space rate:

(20) The current practice in most places in the United States is to make the coroner's inquest an empty formality in which nothing much is brought out except that somebody has died.

(21) Fingerprints are fragile affairs. Wrapping a pistol or other small object up in a handkerchief is much more likely to obliterate than to preserve any prints it may have.

(22) When an automatic pistol is fired the empty cartridge-shell flies out the right-hand side. The empty cartridge-case remains in a revolver until ejected by hand.

(23) A lawyer cannot impeach his own witness.

(24) The length of time a corpse has been a corpse can be approximated by an experienced physician, but only approximated, and the longer it has been a corpse, the less accurate the approximation is likely to be.

Chronology

1894   Samuel Dashiell Hammett born May 27 on "Hopewell and Aim," tobacco farm of paternal grandfather Samuel Hammett in St. Mary's County, Maryland, second of three children of Richard Thomas Hammett and Annie Bond Dashiell. (Hammett family has been in America since the 17th century, Dashiell family since the 18th. Mother, who suffers from chronic tuberculosis, is of French Huguenot ancestry but converted to Catholicism on marrying Hammett. Father works on family tobacco farm and pursues career in local politics with little success.) Baptized a Catholic at St. Nicholas Church.

1895–97   Family, including older sister, Aronia, and younger brother, Richard, moves briefly to Philadelphia.

1898–1907 Family settles in Baltimore, where father works as clerk and later as salesman, bus conductor, factory foreman, and security guard. Hammett attends Public School 72.

1908–14   Attends Baltimore Polytechnic Institute in 1908. Leaves school after less than a year to work as newsboy, office boy and freight clerk for B&O Railroad, and clerk for Poe and Davies stockbrokerage. Family struggles financially. Paternal grandfather dies in 1911.

1915–17   Works as detective for Baltimore office of Pinkerton detective agency, located in the Continental Building. Learns job from older employee James Wright (later described by Hammett as model for his character the Continental Op).

1918   Leaves Pinkerton to enlist in army. Undergoes basic training at Camp Mead, Maryland; in July is assigned to a motor ambulance company. In October, complains of flu-like symptoms and is hospitalized with high fever; diagnosed with bronchopneumonia and released after 20 days.

1919   Hospitalized again in February; is diagnosed with tuberculosis and given discharge from army with small disability pension. Moves back with family. Despite frail condition, returns to work at Pinkerton; after six months is again hospitalized. Bureau of War Risk Insurance reviews his case and grants him a higher pension.

1920   Leaves home permanently in May; travels to Spokane, Washington, where he resumes work for Pinkerton. Serves as Pinkerton operative in Idaho and Montana, becoming involved as strikebreaker in Anaconda miners' strike. Health deteriorates; admitted in November to Cushman Hospital in Tacoma.

1921   Falls in love with nurse Josephine ("Jose") Dolan. After four months, is transferred to treatment center at Camp Kearny, near San Diego, California. Mother dies in April; Hammett does not return to Baltimore for funeral. Learns from Jose that she is pregnant; by letter, they agree to marry. Released from Camp Kearny in May, but physical condition remains fragile (will continue to suffer cyclical recurrence of lung problems). Moves to San Francisco in June. Marries Jose on July 7 at Saint Mary's Cathedral. Settles with Jose in apartment on Eddy Street and resumes work for Pinkerton. Daughter Mary Jane born October 15.

1922–23   Serious relapse makes it impossible for Hammett to work; reluctantly asks his family for financial help. With subsidy from Veterans Bureau, studies stenography and writing at Munson's Business College; decides to seek work in advertising. In October 1922 first published short story, "The Parthian Shot," appears in *The Smart Set*; publishes four more pieces in the magazine over the next year, including autobiographical "From the Memoirs of a Private Detective," based on his Pinkerton experience. Publishes "The Road Home," his first contribution to *Black Mask*, under pseudonym Peter Collinson in December 1922. In *Black Mask* story "Arson Plus" (October 1923) introduces anonymous operative later known as the Continental Op (the Op will be the protagonist of 28 stories and two novels).

1924–25   Wife and daughter go to live with her family in Montana for six months. Regularly publishes stories in *Black Mask*, including "The Tenth Clew," "The House in Turk Street," "The Whosis Kid," "The Scorched Face," and "Dead Yellow Women." Starts and then abandons a novel, "The Secret Emperor."

1926   Takes full-time job as advertising manager for jeweler Albert Samuels. Daughter Josephine Rebecca born May 24. Hammett, who has been drinking heavily for years, suffers lung hemorrhage and collapses at work in July. Diagnosed with hepatitis and is unable to continue working. Lives apart from family. Receives literary encouragement from Joseph T. Shaw, who assumes editorship of *Black Mask* in November.

1927   Begins reviewing crime fiction for *Saturday Review of Literature* in January (continues to publish there for next three years). After hiatus of a year, resumes writing fiction; continues series of Continental Op stories for *Black Mask* with "The Big Knock-Over" (February), "$106,000 Blood Money" (May), and "The Main Death" (June). Jose moves with children to San Anselmo in spring (family will live together only sporadically over next two years). Begins novel *Red Harvest* (originally titled "Poisonville"); first episode is serialized as "The Cleansing of Poisonville" in the November issue of *Black Mask*.

1928   Submits completed manuscript of novel to Alfred A. Knopf in February; Blanche Knopf offers publication but suggests revisions, including toning down of violence; Hammett agrees to some changes, and then makes extensive revisions in collaboration with Knopf editor Harry Block. Receives offer of scriptwriting work from William Fox Studios and goes to Hollywood in June, but no deal materializes. Completes second novel *The Dain Curse* in June (serialized in *Black Mask*, Nov. 1928–Feb. 1929). By end of year, completes his next novel, *The Maltese Falcon*.

1929   *Red Harvest* is published in February; Paramount buys movie rights. Knopf accepts *The Dain Curse* but requests extensive changes, which Hammett makes reluctantly. Hammett's health improves, and he moves into new, more expensive apartment with writer and actress Nell Martin, with whom he maintains longtime relationship. Manuscript of *The Maltese Falcon* is accepted by Knopf with requests for only minor revisions. *The Dain Curse* is published in July to favorable reviews and sells better than *Red Harvest*. *The Maltese Falcon* is serialized in *Black Mask* (Sept. 1929–Jan. 1930). Hammett and Martin travel to New York in the fall for extended stay; he works on new novel, *The Glass Key*.

1930   *The Maltese Falcon* is published in February; it receives excellent reviews from influential critics, including Will Cuppy and Franklin P. Adams, and is reprinted seven times in the course of the year. Paramount releases film *Roadhouse Nights*, loosely derived from *Red Harvest*. Hammett completes *The Glass Key* (serialized in *Black Mask*, March–June). Takes job as regular reviewer of crime fiction for the *New York Evening Post*. Warner Brothers acquires movie rights to *The Maltese Falcon* in June. At urging of David O. Selznick, Hammett is offered writing contract with Paramount, which he fulfills with hastily written seven-page story outline. Works on several other projects, and leaves Paramount at end of year. Meets Lillian Hellman, then married to writer Arthur Kober, at Hollywood party in November; they become lovers (relationship continues for the rest of their lives although they are frequently separated and often have other partners).

1931   Remains in Hollywood through the spring. Sees other writers socially, including Arthur Kober and Lillian Hellman, Dorothy Parker, and S. J. Perelman and his wife, Laura; drinks heavily and has many affairs. Writes treatment of an original Sam Spade story for Darryl Zanuck at Warner Brothers, but after receiving $10,000 for the story, it is rejected. *City Streets*, film based on Hammett's initial Paramount story, released in April. *The Glass Key* is published by Knopf in April, receiving strong reviews and selling well. Hammett moves to New York. Forms friendly relationship with William Faulkner. Completes first 65 pages of an early version of *The Thin Man*, then puts it aside. A film version of *The Maltese Falcon*, starring Ricardo Cortez and Bebe Daniels, is released by Warner Brothers in May.

1932   Found guilty in absentia on June 30 of battery and attempted rape in civil suit brought against him by actress Elise De Vianne, who is awarded $2,500 in damages.

Works on a second version of *The Thin Man*. Unable to pay his bill at Hotel Pierre, leaves surreptitiously and goes to live at Sutton Club Hotel on East 56th Street, which is managed by Nathanael West.

1933   Publishes novella "Woman in the Dark" as a three-part serial in *Liberty*. Finishes *The Thin Man* in May (condensed version appears in December *Redbook*). Travels with Hellman to Florida Keys for extended stay in fishing camp, where he helps her with her play *The Children's Hour*. Rents house in Huntington, Long Island, in summer.

1934   *The Thin Man* is published by Knopf in January. MGM movie version of the novel, starring William Powell and Myrna Loy, is released in June (five other movies featuring the novel's protagonists, Nick and Nora Charles, will be released between 1934 and 1947). *Secret Agent X-9*, King Features comic strip with script credited to Hammett and art by Alex Raymond, first appears in January (Hammett's byline is dropped after fifteen months). Publishes three stories in *Collier's*, January–March. Spends spring in Florida Keys with Hellman. Signs contract with MGM in October for a second movie in *Thin Man* series; stays at the Beverly Wilshire Hotel and socializes with friends, including Herbert Asbury, Nunnally Johnson, Joel Sayre, Arthur Kober, and Edward G. Robinson. Drinks heavily.

1935   Submits draft of story to MGM in January. Meets Gertrude Stein, who admires his work greatly, at dinner party in April. In June signs three-year contract with MGM, paying him minimum of $1,000 per week as writer and executive (Hammett frequently fails to meet terms of contract and is periodically taken off salary). Runs up heavy debts and is sued over the next several years by various creditors. Has brief affair with Laura Perelman during summer. In the fall divides time between Los Angeles and New York. Universal releases movie *Mister Dynamite*, starring Edmund Lowe, based on a Hammett story originally written in 1931; Paramount releases film version of *The Glass Key* starring George Raft and Edward Arnold.

1936   Meets Raymond Chandler at *Black Mask* dinner in January. Begins long-term affair with Pru Whitfield, wife of

Black Mask writer Raoul Whitfield. Becomes increasingly involved with Communist Party, which he joins as a secret member. Stays with Hellman on Tavern Island near Norwalk, Connecticut, during spring. Moves to Princeton, New Jersey, in October. *Satan Met a Lady*, a second film version of *The Maltese Falcon* starring Warren William and Bette Davis, released by Warner Brothers. *After the Thin Man*, based on Hammett's story, opens in December. Released from contract with Knopf after he fails to deliver promised novel.

1937   Returns to Hollywood in April to work on third *Thin Man* movie, under new agreement that pays him only for completed work. Publicly supports the Anti-Nazi League and the Western Writers Congress, and donates money to Abraham Lincoln Brigade fighting in Spain in support of Loyalist government. Becomes active in movement to gain recognition from studios for Screen Writers Guild. Begins 14-month period of abstinence from drinking. Jose Hammett files for mail-order divorce in Sonora, Mexico, court (after Hammett's death, divorce is ruled illegal and Jose is recognized as entitled to widow's benefits).

1938   Completes treatment for *Another Thin Man*. Along with other writers including Hellman, Langston Hughes, Dorothy Parker, and Malcolm Cowley, signs statement in defense of Moscow purge trials in April. Becomes ill after resuming drinking and is flown back to New York to enter Lenox Hill Hospital; moves into Plaza Hotel after his release in June. Signs contract with Bennett Cerf of Modern Library for new novel. Tells friends that he is at work on novel tentatively titled "My Brother Felix." Stays with Hellman on Tavern Island during summer and early fall, where he gives her detailed assistance on revisions of her play *The Little Foxes*. Speaks at anti-Nazi rallies sponsored by Communist Party in New York in November. MGM rejects his scenario for a *Thin Man* sequel.

1939   MGM cancels Hammett's contract in July. Modern Library announces new Hammett novel, "There Was a Young Man," for publication in the fall, but he does not deliver a manuscript. Hammett becomes member of editorial board of Equality Publishers, press sponsored by the Communist Party whose declared aim is "to defend democracy and combat anti-Semitism and Fascism" (press publishes monthly magazine *Equality* but ceases publication after signing of Nazi-Soviet pact in late August). Becomes a regular guest at Hardscrabble Farm, 130-acre property purchased by Hellman in Pleasantville, New York. *Another Thin Man* opens in November.

1940   Helps publisher Ralph Ingersoll in assembling staff for his newspaper *PM*; after public protests over Communist influence on the paper, Ingersoll repudiates Hammett in memo to stockholders. Serves as national chairman of Committee on Election Rights—1940, organization seeking to get Communist candidates on local ballots, and supports presidential campaign of Communist Party general secretary Earl Browder.

1941   In accordance with Communist policy shift following Nazi-Soviet pact, publicly opposes lend-lease policy of aid to Britain and American entry into war. (Becomes a supporter of the war effort following the shift in the Communist Party line after the German attack on the Soviet Union in June.) Elected president of League of American Writers. Receives $500 a week for nominal authorship of NBC radio serial *The Adventures of the Thin Man*, for which he does no writing. John Huston films highly successful adaptation of *The Maltese Falcon*, starring Humphrey Bogart and Mary Astor.

1942   Works on screen adaptation of Hellman's play *Watch on the Rhine*, with Hellman making extensive revisions (Hammett receives primary screen credit when film opens in September 1943). Returns advance on unwritten novel to Random House in March. Knopf issues all five novels as *The Complete Dashiell Hammett*. A second film version of *The Glass Key*, starring Brian Donlevy and Alan Ladd, opens. After previous rejections on health grounds, Hammett is accepted into the army as a private; he is inducted in September and undergoes Signal Corps Training at Fort Monmouth, New Jersey, where his tasks include composing lessons for trainees and giving orientation lectures.

1943   To avoid further dental problems, has all his teeth pulled at army hospital in March. Promoted to corporal in May.

Sent in June to Camp Shenango in Transfer, Pennsylvania, a facility used by the army to isolate soldiers with subversive political views. After he has been there a week, camp is dispersed following protest by Eleanor Roosevelt, and Hammett is sent to Fort Lawton near Tacoma, Washington, and then to Fort Randall, Alaska. Assigned to provide orientation for troops in the Aleutian Islands, arrives in September on small volcanic island of Adak. Starts a camp newspaper, *The Adakian*, under orders of Brigadier General Harry Thompson.

1944   First issue of *The Adakian* published in January (Hammett continues as editor for 15 months, contributing 13 signed articles). Establishes editorial staff that includes future journalists Bernard Kalb and Eliot Asinof and that is racially integrated, despite the overall segregation of the armed forces. Promoted to sergeant in August. *The Battle of the Aleutians*, pamphlet co-written by Hammett, published for distribution to troops. Sent on tour of the Aleutians to give educational lectures to servicemen.

1945   Joins training unit at Fort Richardson, near Anchorage. Promoted to master sergeant in June, and discharged in September. Moves to New York, living in apartment on East 66th Street. Lives on royalties from three radio serials based on his characters.

1946   Divides time between New York apartment and Hardscrabble Farm. Elected president of Communist-sponsored Civil Rights Congress of New York in June (position is nominal), and named a trustee of CRC bail fund. Begins teaching courses in mystery writing at Jefferson School of Social Sciences, devoted to "Marxism as the philosophy and social science of the working class" (continues teaching there until 1956).

1947   Moves to apartment in Greenwich Village. Hires full-time housekeeper, Rose Evans, who assumes close management of Hammett's affairs. Resumes contact with his brother Richard. Daughter Mary Jane stays with Hammett for an extended period; both drink heavily.

1948   Hammett's father, whom he had recently visited for the first time in nearly two decades, dies in Maryland in

March. Warner Brothers brings lawsuit against radio series *The Adventures of Sam Spade* on grounds that Warners owns all broadcast rights to *The Maltese Falcon*; Hammett files complaint seeking to affirm his right to use of the name Sam Spade. Health breaks after long period of heavy drinking and he is admitted to Lenox Hill Hospital; quits drinking permanently when warned that his life is in immediate danger if he continues.

1949   Lives mostly at Hardscrabble Farm. Loses suit against Warners regarding *Adventures of Sam Spade*; studio files plagiarism complaint against Hammett. Elected to board of trustees of Jefferson School of Social Sciences in August. Civil Rights Congress posts bail in November for eleven Communist leaders appealing convictions under the Smith Act of 1940 for conspiring to advocate the violent overthrow of the U.S. government.

1950   Goes to Hollywood to work on screenplay of William Wyler's *Detective Story*, but is unable to write. Lives with Jose during six-month stay, and enjoys company of daughter Josephine. Works with Hellman on her play *The Autumn Garden*.

1951   Visits Josephine and her daughter Ann in Los Angeles; returns with them for stay at Hardscrabble Farm. When four of the Communists convicted for Smith Act violations fail to surrender to authorities, subpoenas are issued for the trustees of the Civil Rights Congress bail fund. Hammett appears before U.S. District Court Judge Sylvester Ryan on July 9 and repeatedly invokes the Fifth Amendment when questioned about the CRC, the bail fund, and the whereabouts of the fugitives. At the conclusion of his testimony, Ryan finds him guilty of contempt of court and sentences him to six months in prison. Serves his sentence at the Federal House of Detention in New York until September, when he is moved to the federal prison in Ashland, Kentucky. Released on December 9 with time off for good behavior. Health is further damaged by imprisonment. Warner Brothers suit decided in Hammett's favor in December (studio's appeal is rejected in 1954).

1952   Finds himself impoverished due to cancellation of radio shows based on his work and liens on his income by

Internal Revenue Service for back taxes owed since 1943; all his books are out of print. Takes up residence at Katonah, New York, on estate of friend Dr. Samuel Rosen, living rent-free in gatekeeper's cottage. Writes 12,500 words of a novel which he abandons (it is published as "Tulip" in *The Big Knockover*, a collection of Hammett's stories published in 1966).

1953   Subpoenaed by Senator Joseph McCarthy to testify before his subcommittee of the Committee on Government Operations, where he is questioned about purchase of his books for libraries by U.S. State Department, and whether he ever donated royalties from such sales to the Communist Party. When asked by McCarthy whether he thinks it reasonable for the government to purchase and distribute books by Communists when it is fighting Communism, Hammett replies: "If I were fighting Communism, I don't think I would do it by giving people any books at all."

1955   Called to testify in February before New York State Joint Legislative Committee about his involvement with Civil Rights Congress; during questioning says, "Communism to me is not a dirty word. When you are working for the advance of mankind it never occurs to you whether a guy is a Communist." Suffers heart attack while visiting Lillian Hellman on Martha's Vineyard in August.

1956   Questioned by F.B.I. in March about his ability to pay tax judgment of over $140,000; Hammett asserts that he has no income or savings. In an interview given to the *Washington Daily News* the same month, states: "I stopped writing because I was repeating myself. It is the beginning of the end when you discover you have style." Fails to appear in court to answer federal suit for back taxes.

1957–61 Ordered to pay $104,795 in back taxes for the years 1950–54 in February 1957. Health continues to deteriorate severely; moves into Lillian Hellman's New York apartment in spring of 1958. Granted small pension by Veterans Administration in May 1959 on grounds of severe respiratory illness. Goes out in public for last time in February 1960 to see opening of Hellman's play *Toys in the Attic*.

Dies of lung cancer on January 10, 1961, at Lenox Hill Hospital. Funeral is held at Frank E. Campbell funeral home in New York. Buried at Arlington National Cemetery on January 13.

Note on the Texts

This volume presents, in the order of their first publication, a selection of 24 crime stories by Dashiell Hammett, followed by "The Thin Man: An Early Typescript" (an unfinished novel in ten chapters), and two short pieces about detective work and detective fiction.

All of the stories included in this volume appeared initially in magazines, principally in the pulp *Black Mask* (titled *The Black Mask* until early in 1927), where Hammett also first published *Red Harvest* (1929), *The Dain Curse* (1929), *The Maltese Falcon* (1930), and *The Glass Key* (1931). For a brief period, Hammett considered revising his stories and collecting them in book form. In a letter of June 16, 1929, to Harry Block, his editor at Alfred A. Knopf, he suggested two possible volumes, *The Continental Op* (a collection of stories featuring his character of the same name) and *The Big Knock-Over* (to include "The Big Knock-Over" and the related story "$106,000 Blood Money"). "I'd want to rewrite the stories," he told Block, "and there are possibly fifty or sixty thousand words out of the quarter-million that I'd throw out as not worth bothering about. In the remainder there are some good stories, and altogether I think they'd give a more complete and true picture of the detective at work than has been given anywhere else." Within a month, however, Hammett had reconsidered; "I don't think I want to do anything with them," he wrote Block again on July 14, 1929.

Hammett continued to decline Knopf proposals over subsequent years to publish story collections, but he did allow his stories to appear in print elsewhere: in magazine anthologies, in newspaper syndication (through King Features), and in paperback collections, the first series of which was published by Lawrence E. Spivak in New York beginning in 1943, edited by Ellery Queen (a pseudonym used jointly by Frederick Dannay and Manfred B. Lee). Two stories included in this volume, "The Golden Horseshoe" and "Dead Yellow Women," appeared in a British hardcover collection, *The Dashiell Hammett Omnibus* (London: Cassell, 1950), along with Hammett's novels.

Numerous textual changes, large and small (including alterations to titles, substantial verbal revision, and the omission of sentences and paragraphs), are introduced in these later reprintings. In almost all cases, Hammett is known not to have been or is not likely to have been responsible for these changes. As William F. Nolan comments in *Hammett: A Life at the Edge* (1983), "Aside from the money he received from these collections of his early fiction, Hammett had nothing to do with them. He did not revise the works as they went into book form." He did suggest, in a letter to Lillian Hellman written from the Aleutian Islands on July 26, 1944, that the story "Two Sharp Knives" be retitled "To a Sharp Knife" when it appeared in book form; the latter was Hammett's original title, the former "thought up by *Collier's*" where the story was first published.

The texts of all of Hammett's stories in this volume have been taken from their initial magazine appearances. A copy of the issue of *Mystery Stories* in which "This King Business" was first published has been located and kindly provided by Terry Zobeck, a private collector. Two stories—"Arson Plus" and "Slippery Fingers"—were originally printed under the pseudonym Peter Collinson.

The following list gives details about the first serial and first book versions of each of the stories included in this volume; when the first book version is a collection of the work of various authors, the first appearance in a Hammett collection is also noted:

Arson Plus
The Black Mask 6.13 (October 1, 1923): 25–36.
Woman in the Dark. New York: Lawrence E. Spivak, 1951.

Slippery Fingers
The Black Mask 6.14 (October 15, 1923): 96–103.
Woman in the Dark. New York: Lawrence E. Spivak, 1951.

Crooked Souls
The Black Mask 6.14 (October 15, 1923): 35–44.
The Big Knockover. New York: Random House, 1966. [As "The Gatewood Caper"]

The Tenth Clew
The Black Mask 6.19 (January 1, 1924): 3–23.
The Return of the Continental Op. New York: Lawrence E. Spivak, 1945. [As "The Tenth Clue"]

Zigzags of Treachery
The Black Mask 6.23 (March 1, 1924): 80–102.
The Continental Op. New York: Lawrence E. Spivak, 1945.

The House in Turk Street
The Black Mask 7.2 (April 15, 1924): 9–22.
Hammett Homicides. New York: Lawrence E. Spivak, 1946.

The Girl with the Silver Eyes
The Black Mask 7.4 (June 1924): 45–70.
Hammett Homicides. New York: Lawrence E. Spivak, 1946.

Women, Politics and Murder
The Black Mask 7.7 (September 1924): 67–83.
The Continental Op. New York: Lawrence E. Spivak, 1945. [As "Death on Pine Street"]

The Golden Horseshoe
The Black Mask 7.9 (November 1924): 37–62.
Dead Yellow Women. New York: Lawrence E. Spivak, 1947.

Nightmare Town
Argosy All-Story Weekly 165.4 (December 27, 1924): 502–26.
Nightmare Town. New York: Lawrence E. Spivak, 1948.

The Whosis Kid
The Black Mask 8.1 (March 1925): 7–32.
The Return of the Continental Op. New York: Lawrence E. Spivak, 1945.

The Scorched Face
The Black Mask 8.3 (May 1925): 9–31.
Nightmare Town. New York: Lawrence E. Spivak, 1948.

Dead Yellow Women
The Black Mask 8.9 (November 1925): 9–39.
Dead Yellow Women. New York: Lawrence E. Spivak, 1947.

The Gutting of Couffignal
The Black Mask 8.10 (December 1925): 30–48.
The Return of the Continental Op. New York: Lawrence E. Spivak, 1945.

The Assistant Murderer
The Black Mask 8.12 (February 1926): 57–79.
The Adventures of Sam Spade and Other Stories. New York: Lawrence E. Spivak, 1944.

Creeping Siamese
The Black Mask 9.1 (March 1926): 38–47.
The Creeping Siamese. New York: Lawrence E. Spivak, 1950.

The Big Knock-Over
Black Mask 9.12 (February 1927): 7–38.
$106,000 Blood Money. New York: Lawrence E. Spivak, 1943.

$106,000 Blood Money
Black Mask 10.3 (May 1927): 9–34.
$106,000 Blood Money. New York: Lawrence E. Spivak, 1943.

The Main Death
Black Mask 10.4 (June 1927): 44–57.
Hammett Homicides. New York: Lawrence E. Spivak, 1946.

This King Business
Mystery Stories 13:1 (January 1928): 5–39.
The Creeping Siamese. New York: Lawrence E. Spivak, 1950.

Fly Paper
Black Mask 12.6 (August 1929): 7–26.
Best Stories from Ellery Queen's Mystery Magazine. New York:
     Detective Book Club, 1944.
The Continental Op. New York: Lawrence E. Spivak, 1945.

The Farewell Murder
Black Mask 12.12 (February 1930): 9–30.
The Best American Mystery Stories of the Year. New York:
     John Day, 1932.
The Continental Op. New York: Lawrence E. Spivak, 1945.

Woman in the Dark
Liberty 10.14 (April 8, 1933): 5–11; 10.15 (April 15, 1933): 12–18;
     10.16 (April 22, 1933): 44–49.
Woman in the Dark. New York: Lawrence E. Spivak, 1951.

Two Sharp Knives
Collier's 93.2 (January 13, 1934): 12–13.
The Avon Annual. New York: Avon, 1945. [As "To a Sharp Knife"]
Hammett Homicides. New York: Lawrence E. Spivak, 1946.

"The Thin Man: An Early Typescript" has been reprinted from
Hammett's original typescript, in the Guymon Collection, Mary
Norton Clapp Library, Occidental College Library, Los Angeles. A
handwritten note accompanying the typescript, signed by Hammett
and dated Hardscrabble Farm, Pleasantville, N.Y., January 14, 1942,
explains the unfinished novel's relation to *The Thin Man* (1934):

> In 1930 I started writing a book entitled "The Thin
> Man." By the time I had written these 65 pages my pub-
> lisher and I agreed that it might be wise to postpone the
> publication of "The Glass Key"—scheduled for that
> fall—until the following spring. This meant that "The
> Thin Man" could not be published until the fall of 1931.
> So—having plenty of time—I put these 65 pages aside

and went to Hollywood for a year. One thing and/or
another intervening after that, I didn't return to work
on the story until a couple of more years had passed—
and then I found it easier, or at least generally more satisfactory, to keep only the basic idea of the plot and
otherwise to start anew. Some of the incidents in this
original version I later used in "After The Thin Man," a
motion picture sequel, but—except for that and for the
use of the characters' names Guild and Wynant—this
unfinished manuscript has a clear claim to virginity.

The unfinished "Thin Man" remained unpublished during Hammett's lifetime, and no other manuscript version is known to be extant; it first appeared in print in its entirety in *City Magazine* 9.17
(November 4, 1975): 1–12 (insert).

"From the Memoirs of a Private Detective" is reprinted here from
The Smart Set (March 1923, pages 87–90), where it was first published; Hammett did not make further revisions to this work.

" 'Suggestions to Detective Story Writers' " has been assembled-
from two installments of "The Crime Wave," a book-review column
Hammett contributed to the *New York Evening Post* between April
and October of 1930; its first section (from 914.1 to 915.39 in this volume) reprints all but the title, list of books reviewed, and opening
paragraph of the review of June 7, 1930, and its second (from 916.1
onward in this volume) reprints the penultimate section of the review of July 5, 1930. The title has been supplied for this volume.
Hammett did not revise "The Crime Wave" columns after their initial appearances.

This volume presents the texts of the original printings and the
typescript chosen for inclusion here, but it does not attempt to reproduce features of their design and layout. The texts are printed
without change, except for the correction of typographical errors.
Spelling, punctuation, and capitalization often are expressive features
and they are not altered, even when inconsistent or irregular. The
following is a list of typographical errors corrected, cited by page and
line number: 4.23, The; 8.25, "It; 11.3, complection; 15.8, talk,; 15.13,
womai; 19.2, $2.60;; 28.19, came old; 28.34, Tiajuana; 36.17, "No,";
50.19, mit; 50.34, wreck!; 54.9, back; 54.36, going."; 67.14, busines;
72.38, with out; 78.12, him him; 84.21, unpleasand; 85.8, minutes.";
88.12, *it*."; 91.1, same; 91.10, Estop; 91.17, that; 96.20, direcion; 102.12,
in you; 104.1, police;; 104.21, Homocide; 105.21, Stacy; 108.9, Mrs.
Ledwich; 114.20, Francico; 114.28, layed; 114.33, wan't; 115.19, Francico; 115.21, afrad; 121.2, clear.; 123.17, "No, "No; 126.7, trousers.;
131.6, wet; 131.14, way; 140.31, it complete; 141.37, heathen"; 174.35,

that."; 178.36, lense; 183.3, "I; 183.35, 'gone; 194.27, "O'Gar; 204.19,
"'It; 223.18, *Tiajuana*; 227.14, CHAPTER III; 233.7, architect'; 237.20,
he hair; 238.34, mind; 240.34, wrie; 241.37, gablers; 259.24, chapter
ix; 262.29, no,; 263.1, Ed.; 290.18, *mele*; 316.24, paralled; 318.4, eves;
353.1, night; 364.32, 'And; 377.17, tead; 392.17, once.'; 401.38, gun off;
417.21, run; 440.26, this; 458.35, trick."; 473.4, surprnse; 484.1, it
color; 484.9, cold His; 484.19–20, in conspicuous; 502.40, Goodbody's; 504.26, wouldn't spilled; 506.10, Falsoner's; 514.1, street;
514.9, "What; 516.32, crediors; 525.9, there?; 525.34, Peninsular;
526.18, i; 530.2, we; 530.9, our our; 530.32, sick?"; 532.16, self-defense.;
533.5, him.; 533.31, can over; 578.28, upstairs"; 579.1, up!'; 594.39,
bcause; 600.33, "I ... days."; 609.21, troup; 614.24, "I; 629.22, five- ;
637.20, come; 678.36, midinght; 697.17–18, amunition; 709.36, "THE;
719.19, levely; 746.36, doing?; 756.29, wouldn't,'; 757.3, husbands;
757.6, it?'; 776.32, Week's; 786.4, Then; 795.18, said.; 804.29, now. If;
829.17, repeated,; 837.24, get's; 839.14–15, became; 858.1, they way;
869.34–35, occassional; 875.11, depositer; 877.22, up.; 883.4, where;
883.19, County.; 887.7, murmurred; 895.5, Wyanant; 904.25, earnestly.
I; 910.17, or.

Notes

In the notes below, the reference numbers denote page and line of this volume (the line count includes chapter headings). No note is made for material included in standard desk-reference books such as Webster's *Collegiate, Biographical,* and *Geographical* dictionaries. For further information and references to other studies, see Diane Johnson, *Dashiell Hammett: A Life* (New York: Random House, 1983); Richard Layman, *Dashiell Hammett: A Descriptive Bibliography* (Pittsburgh: University of Pittsburgh Press, 1979); Richard Layman, *Shadow Man: The Life of Dashiell Hammett* (New York: Harcourt Brace Jovanovich, 1981); Richard Layman and Julie M. Rivett, eds., *Selected Letters of Dashiell Hammett, 1921–1960* (New York: Counterpoint, 2001); Joan Mellen, *Hellman and Hammett: The Legendary Passion of Lillian Hellman and Dashiell Hammett* (New York: HarperCollins, 1996); and William F. Nolan, *Hammett: A Life at the Edge* (New York: Congdon & Weed, 1983).

18.35   Hiram Johnson] Johnson (1866–1945) was governor of California (1911–17) and Theodore Roosevelt's presidential running mate on the Progressive ticket in 1912. He later served four terms as senator.

82.4   badger-game] Confidence game in which the victim is lured into a compromising sexual situation and then subjected to blackmail or extortion.

98.2   Stevenson monument] The monument to Robert Louis Stevenson in Portsmouth Square, San Francisco.

164.25   piking] Cheating; conning.

168.30   Bull Montana] Italian-born wrestler and movie actor whose films included *When the Clouds Roll By* (1919), *The Lost World* (1925), and *Son of the Sheik* (1926).

222.8   scratcher] Forger.

229.24   keno goose] Container from which, in the game of keno, numbered balls are released.

234.10–11   carrying a beautiful bun] Drunk.

249.3   bungstarter] Wooden mallet used for opening a cask.

252.10–11   read and write] See page 912.1–2 in this volume.

290.18   *mere*] Short warclub, usually made of jade.

336.23   *lechón*]   Pig.

348.12   kick]   Bag for holding loot.

373.7   soaked]   Pawned.

395.31   Ta Jen]   Great man; a term of respect and also an official rank in the Chinese bureaucracy.

402.14   settlement worker]   Provider of social services or charitable assistance through a settlement house.

405.14–15   clan feuds . . . the "Four Brothers" used to stage]   The Four Brothers was a Chinese clan amalgamated from four lineages (Lau, Quan, Cheung, and Chew) and embroiled in an extended gang war in New York, 1909–10, in which at least 12 people were killed.

407.22   Coxey's Army]   Group of unemployed workers, led by Jacob Coxey (1854–1951), who traveled to Washington, D.C., in 1894 to demonstrate in favor of paper money and the funding of public works projects.

442.19   highbinders]   Chinese extortion gangs in San Francisco preying on gamblers and prostitutes.

444.3–4   Taoukwang]   Daoguang (1782–1850), Chinese emperor who, following the Chinese defeat in the first Opium War (1839–42), opened five treaty ports to British merchants and ceded Hong Kong to Great Britain.

452.26   *The Lord of the Sea*]   Novel (1901) by M. P. Shiel.

472.10   push]   Gang.

498.10   knock-down]   Introduction.

547.2   cush]   Money; profit.

574.33   bingavast]   Get away.

579.3   Zonite]   Brand name of a liquid antiseptic douche.

582.16   rhino]   Money.

593.7   *schmierkäse*]   Cream cheese.

640.14   *cacoethes carpendi*]   Mania for enjoyment, consumption, selection.

645.27   highgrading]   Stealing ore, or dealing in stolen ore.

649.8   *The Sun Also Rises*]   Novel (1926) by Ernest Hemingway.

663.5–6   *"Asseyez-vous, s'il vous plaît,"*]   "Please be seated."

722.26   puffing]   Blowing safes with explosives.

726.29   *The Count of Monte Cristo*]   Novel (1844) by Alexandre Dumas.

726.33   Maybrick-Seddons trick] Florence Maybrick was convicted in
1889 of poisoning her husband, James Maybrick, with arsenic extracted from
fly paper; her death sentence was commuted and she was released after 15
years' imprisonment. Frederick Seddon was hanged in 1912 for the murder, by
means of repeated exposure to arsenic-coated flypaper, of Eliza Barrow the
previous year; Seddon's wife, Maggie, was acquitted.

730.11   shatting on my uppers]   Broke.

733.32–33   to powder]   To run away.

765.27   *Schrecklichkeit*]   Terror.

817.13   *schwach*]   Weak; faint.

869.36   Pontius Pilate's question]   "What is truth?"; cf. John 18:38.

886.15   *haori*]   Knee-length Japanese coat.

901.22   *boo how doy*]   Enforcer for Chinese tongs; often translated as
"hatchet man."

912.24   Raffles]   Gentleman burglar depicted in stories by E. W. Hornung
collected in *The Amateur Cracksman* (1895) and other volumes.

Library of Congress Cataloging-in-Publication Data

Hammett, Dashiell, 1894–1961
　[Selections. 2001]
　Crime stories and other writings/Dashiell Hammett.
　　p. cm.—(The Library of America ; 125)

Includes bibliographical references (p.).
ISBN 1–931082–00–6 (alk. paper)
　1. Detective and mystery stories, American. I. Title. II. Series.

PS3515.A4347 A6 2001
813'.52—dc21   00–054594

THE LIBRARY OF AMERICA SERIES

The Library of America fosters appreciation and pride in America's literary heritage by publishing, and keeping permanently in print, authoritative editions of America's best and most significant writing. An independent nonprofit organization, it was founded in 1979 with seed funding from the National Endowment for the Humanities and the Ford Foundation.

To subscribe to the series or to order individual copies, please visit www.loa.org or call (800) 964–5778.

This book is set in 10 point Linotron Galliard,
a face designed for photocomposition by Matthew Carter
and based on the sixteenth-century face Granjon. The paper
is acid-free lightweight opaque and meets the requirements
for permanence of the American National Standards Institute.
The binding material is Brillianta, a woven rayon cloth made
by Van Heek–Scholco Textielfabrieken, Holland. Composition
by The Clarinda Company. Printing and binding
by Edwards Brothers Malloy, Ann Arbor.
Designed by Bruce Campbell.

DASHIELL HAMMETT

DASHIELL HAMMETT

COMPLETE NOVELS
Red Harvest
The Dain Curse
The Maltese Falcon
The Glass Key
The Thin Man

Steven Marcus, *editor*

THE LIBRARY OF AMERICA

Eighth Printing
The Library of America—110

Contents

RED HARVEST

To
Joseph Thompson Shaw

TABLE OF CONTENTS

A Woman in Green and a Man in Gray

I FIRST heard Personville called Poisonville by a red-haired mucker named Hickey Dewey in the Big Ship in Butte. He also called his shirt a shoit. I didn't think anything of what he had done to the city's name. Later I heard men who could manage their r's give it the same pronunciation. I still didn't see anything in it but the meaningless sort of humor that used to make richardsnary the thieves' word for dictionary. A few years later I went to Personville and learned better.

Using one of the phones in the station, I called the *Herald*, asked for Donald Willsson, and told him I had arrived.

"Will you come out to my house at ten this evening?" He had a pleasantly crisp voice. "It's 2101 Mountain Boulevard. Take a Broadway car, get off at Laurel Avenue, and walk two blocks west."

I promised to do that. Then I rode up to the Great Western Hotel, dumped my bags, and went out to look at the city.

The city wasn't pretty. Most of its builders had gone in for gaudiness. Maybe they had been successful at first. Since then the smelters whose brick stacks stuck up tall against a gloomy mountain to the south had yellow-smoked everything into uniform dinginess. The result was an ugly city of forty thousand people, set in an ugly notch between two ugly mountains that had been all dirtied up by mining. Spread over this was a grimy sky that looked as if it had come out of the smelters' stacks.

The first policeman I saw needed a shave. The second had a couple of buttons off his shabby uniform. The third stood in the center of the city's main intersection—Broadway and Union Street—directing traffic, with a cigar in one corner of his mouth. After that I stopped checking them up.

At nine-thirty I caught a Broadway car and followed the directions Donald Willsson had given me. They brought me to a house set in a hedged grass-plot on a corner.

The maid who opened the door told me Mr. Willsson was

not home. While I was explaining that I had an appointment with him a slender blonde woman of something less than thirty in green crêpe came to the door. When she smiled her blue eyes didn't lose their stoniness. I repeated my explanation to her.

"My husband isn't in now." A barely noticeable accent slurred her s's. "But if he's expecting you he'll probably be home shortly."

She took me upstairs to a room on the Laurel Avenue side of the house, a brown and red room with a lot of books in it. We sat in leather chairs, half facing each other, half facing a burning coal grate, and she set about learning my business with her husband.

"Do you live in Personville?" she asked first.

"No. San Francisco."

"But this isn't your first visit?"

"Yes."

"Really? How do you like our city?"

"I haven't seen enough of it to know." That was a lie. I had. "I got in only this afternoon."

Her shiny eyes stopped prying while she said:

"You'll find it a dreary place." She returned to her digging with: "I suppose all mining towns are like this. Are you engaged in mining?"

"Not just now."

She looked at the clock on the mantel and said:

"It's inconsiderate of Donald to bring you out here and then keep you waiting, at this time of night, long after business hours."

I said that was all right.

"Though perhaps it isn't a business matter," she suggested.

I didn't say anything.

She laughed—a short laugh with something sharp in it.

"I'm really not ordinarily so much of a busybody as you probably think," she said gaily. "But you're so excessively secretive that I can't help being curious. You aren't a bootlegger, are you? Donald changes them so often."

I let her get whatever she could out of a grin.

A telephone bell rang downstairs. Mrs. Willsson stretched her green-slippered feet out toward the burning coal and pretended she hadn't heard the bell. I didn't know why she thought that necessary.

She began: "I'm afraid I'll ha—" and stopped to look at the maid in the doorway.

The maid said Mrs. Willsson was wanted at the phone. She excused herself and followed the maid out. She didn't go downstairs, but spoke over an extension within earshot.

I heard: "Mrs. Willsson speaking. . . . Yes. . . . I beg your pardon? . . . Who? . . . Can't you speak a little louder? . . . *What?* . . . Yes. . . . Yes. . . . Who is this? . . . Hello! Hello!"

The telephone hook rattled. Her steps sounded down the hallway—rapid steps.

I set fire to a cigarette and stared at it until I heard her going down the steps. Then I went to a window, lifted an edge of the blind, and looked out at Laurel Avenue, and at the square white garage that stood in the rear of the house on that side.

Presently a slender woman in dark coat and hat came into sight hurrying from house to garage. It was Mrs. Willsson. She drove away in a Buick coupé. I went back to my chair and waited.

Three-quarters of an hour went by. At five minutes after eleven, automobile brakes screeched outside. Two minutes later Mrs. Willsson came into the room. She had taken off hat and coat. Her face was white, her eyes almost black.

"I'm awfully sorry," she said, her tight-lipped mouth moving jerkily, "but you've had all this waiting for nothing. My husband won't be home tonight."

I said I would get in touch with him at the *Herald* in the morning.

I went away wondering why the green toe of her left slipper was dark and damp with something that could have been blood.

I walked over to Broadway and caught a street car. Three blocks north of my hotel I got off to see what the crowd was doing around a side entrance of the City Hall.

Thirty or forty men and a sprinkling of women stood on the sidewalk looking at a door marked *Police Department.*

There were men from mines and smelters still in their working clothes, gaudy boys from pool rooms and dance halls, sleek men with slick pale faces, men with the dull look of respectable husbands, a few just as respectable and dull women, and some ladies of the night.

On the edge of this congregation I stopped beside a square-set man in rumpled gray clothes. His face was grayish too, even the thick lips, though he wasn't much older than thirty. His face was broad, thick-featured and intelligent. For color he depended on a red windsor tie that blossomed over his gray flannel shirt.

"What's the rumpus?" I asked him.

He looked at me carefully before he replied, as if he wanted to be sure that the information was going into safe hands. His eyes were gray as his clothes, but not so soft.

"Don Willsson's gone to sit on the right hand of God, if God don't mind looking at bullet holes."

"Who shot him?" I asked.

The gray man scratched the back of his neck and said:

"Somebody with a gun."

I wanted information, not wit. I would have tried my luck with some other member of the crowd if the red tie hadn't interested me. I said:

"I'm a stranger in town. Hang the Punch and Judy on me. That's what strangers are for."

"Donald Willsson, Esquire, publisher of the *Morning* and *Evening Heralds*, was found in Hurricane Street a little while ago, shot very dead by parties unknown," he recited in a rapid singsong. "Does that keep your feelings from being hurt?"

"Thanks." I put out a finger and touched a loose end of his tie. "Mean anything? Or just wearing it?"

"I'm Bill Quint."

"The hell you are!" I exclaimed, trying to place the name. "By God, I'm glad to meet you!"

I dug out my card case and ran through the collection of credentials I had picked up here and there by one means or another. The red card was the one I wanted. It identified me as Henry F. Neill, A.B. seaman, member in good standing of the Industrial Workers of the World. There wasn't a word of truth in it.

I passed this card to Bill Quint. He read it carefully, front and back, returned it to my hand, and looked me over from hat to shoes, not trustfully.

"He's not going to die any more," he said. "Which way you going?"

"Any."

We walked down the street together, turned a corner, aimlessly as far as I knew.

"What brought you in here, if you're a sailor?" he asked casually.

"Where'd you get that idea?"

"There's the card."

"I got another that proves I'm a timber beast," I said. "If you want me to be a miner I'll get one for that tomorrow."

"You won't. I run 'em here."

"Suppose you got a wire from Chi?" I asked.

"Hell with Chi! I run 'em here." He nodded at a restaurant door and asked: "Drink?"

"Only when I can get it."

We went through the restaurant, up a flight of steps, and into a narrow second-story room with a long bar and a row of tables. Bill Quint nodded and said, "Hullo!" to some of the boys and girls at tables and bar, and steered me into one of the green-curtained booths that lined the wall opposite the bar.

We spent the next two hours drinking whiskey and talking.

The gray man didn't think I had any right to the card I had showed him, nor to the other one I had mentioned. He didn't think I was a good wobbly. As chief muckademuck of the I.W.W. in Personville, he considered it his duty to get the low-down on me, and to not let himself be pumped about radical affairs while he was doing it.

That was all right with me. I was interested in Personville affairs. He didn't mind discussing them between casual pokings into my business with the red cards.

What I got out of him amounted to this:

For forty years old Elihu Willsson—father of the man who had been killed this night—had owned Personville, heart, soul, skin and guts. He was president and majority stockholder of the Personville Mining Corporation, ditto of the First National Bank, owner of the *Morning Herald* and *Evening*

Herald, the city's only newspapers, and at least part owner of nearly every other enterprise of any importance. Along with these pieces of property he owned a United States senator, a couple of representatives, the governor, the mayor, and most of the state legislature. Elihu Willsson was Personville, and he was almost the whole state.

Back in the war days the I.W.W.—in full bloom then throughout the West—had lined up the Personville Mining Corporation's help. The help hadn't been exactly pampered. They used their new strength to demand the things they wanted. Old Elihu gave them what he had to give them, and bided his time.

In 1921 it came. Business was rotten. Old Elihu didn't care whether he shut down for a while or not. He tore up the agreements he had made with his men and began kicking them back into their pre-war circumstances.

Of course the help yelled for help. Bill Quint was sent out from I.W.W. headquarters in Chicago to give them some action. He was against a strike, an open walk-out. He advised the old sabotage racket, staying on the job and gumming things up from the inside. But that wasn't active enough for the Personville crew. They wanted to put themselves on the map, make labor history.

They struck.

The strike lasted eight months. Both sides bled plenty. The wobblies had to do their own bleeding. Old Elihu hired gunmen, strike-breakers, national guardsmen and even parts of the regular army, to do his. When the last skull had been cracked, the last rib kicked in, organized labor in Personville was a used firecracker.

But, said Bill Quint, old Elihu didn't know his Italian history. He won the strike, but he lost his hold on the city and the state. To beat the miners he had to let his hired thugs run wild. When the fight was over he couldn't get rid of them. He had given his city to them and he wasn't strong enough to take it away from them. Personville looked good to them and they took it over. They had won his strike for him and they took the city for their spoils. He couldn't openly break with them. They had too much on him. He was responsible for all they had done during the strike.

Bill Quint and I were both fairly mellow by the time we had got this far. He emptied his glass again, pushed his hair out of his eyes and brought his history up to date:

"The strongest of 'em now is probably Pete the Finn. This stuff we're drinking's his. Then there's Lew Yard. He's got a loan shop down on Parker Street, does a lot of bail bond business, handles most of the burg's hot stuff, so they tell me, and is pretty thick with Noonan, the chief of police. This kid Max Thaler—Whisper—has got a lot of friends too. A little slick dark guy with something wrong with his throat. Can't talk. Gambler. Those three, with Noonan, just about help Elihu run his city—help him more than he wants. But he's got to play with 'em or else—"

"This fellow who was knocked off tonight—Elihu's son— where did he stand?" I asked.

"Where papa put him, and he's where papa put him now."

"You mean the old man had him—?"

"Maybe, but that's not my guess. This Don just came home and began running the papers for the old man. It wasn't like the old devil, even if he was getting close to the grave, to let anybody cop anything from him without hitting back. But he had to be cagey with these guys. He brought the boy and his French wife home from Paris and used him for his monkey—a damned nice fatherly trick. Don starts a reform campaign in the papers. Clear the burg of vice and corruption—which means clear it of Pete and Lew and Whisper, if it goes far enough. Get it? The old man's using the boy to shake 'em loose. I guess they got tired of being shook."

"There seems to be a few things wrong with that guess," I said.

"There's more than a few things wrong with everything in this lousy burg. Had enough of this paint?"

I said I had. We went down to the street. Bill Quint told me he was living in the Miners' Hotel in Forest Street. His way home ran past my hotel, so we walked down together. In front of my hotel a beefy fellow with the look of a plain clothes man stood on the curb and talked to the occupant of a Stutz touring car.

"That's Whisper in the car," Bill Quint told me.

I looked past the beefy man and saw Thaler's profile. It was young, dark and small, with pretty features as regular as if they had been cut by a die.

"He's cute," I said.

"Uh-huh," the gray man agreed, "and so's dynamite."

CHAPTER II

The Czar of Poisonville

THE *Morning Herald* gave two pages to Donald Willsson and his death. His picture showed a pleasant intelligent face with curly hair, smiling eyes and mouth, a cleft chin and a striped necktie.

The story of his death was simple. At ten-forty the previous night he had been shot four times in stomach, chest and back, dying immediately. The shooting had taken place in the eleven-hundred block of Hurricane Street. Residents of that block who looked out after hearing the shots saw the dead man lying on the sidewalk. A man and a woman were bending over him. The street was too dark for anyone to see anybody or anything clearly. The man and woman had disappeared before anybody else reached the street. Nobody knew what they looked like. Nobody had seen them go away.

Six shots had been fired at Willsson from a .32 calibre pistol. Two of them had missed him, going into the front wall of a house. Tracing the course of these two bullets, the police had learned that the shooting had been done from a narrow alley across the street. That was all anybody knew.

Editorially the *Morning Herald* gave a summary of the dead man's short career as a civic reformer and expressed a belief that he had been killed by some of the people who didn't want Personville cleaned up. The *Herald* said the chief of police could best show his own lack of complicity by speedily catching and convicting the murderer or murderers. The editorial was blunt and bitter.

I finished it with my second cup of coffee, jumped a Broadway car, dropped off at Laurel Avenue, and turned down toward the dead man's house.

I was half a block from it when something changed my mind and my destination.

A smallish young man in three shades of brown crossed the street ahead of me. His dark profile was pretty. He was Max Thaler, alias Whisper. I reached the corner of Mountain Boulevard in time to catch the flash of his brown-covered rear leg vanishing into the late Donald Willsson's doorway.

I went back to Broadway, found a drug store with a phone booth in it, searched the directory for Elihu Willsson's residence number, called it, told somebody who claimed to be the old man's secretary that I had been brought from San Francisco by Donald Willsson, that I knew something about his death, and that I wanted to see his father.

When I made it emphatic enough I got an invitation to call.

The czar of Poisonville was propped up in bed when his secretary—a noiseless slim sharp-eyed man of forty—brought me into the bedroom.

The old man's head was small and almost perfectly round under its close-cut crop of white hair. His ears were too small and plastered too flat to the sides of his head to spoil the spherical effect. His nose also was small, carrying down the curve of his bony forehead. Mouth and chin were straight lines chopping the sphere off. Below them a short thick neck ran down into white pajamas between square meaty shoulders. One of his arms was outside the covers, a short compact arm that ended in a thick-fingered blunt hand. His eyes were round, blue, small and watery. They looked as if they were hiding behind the watery film and under the bushy white brows only until the time came to jump out and grab something. He wasn't the sort of man whose pocket you'd try to pick unless you had a lot of confidence in your fingers.

He ordered me into a bedside chair with a two-inch jerk of his round head, chased the secretary away with another, and asked:

"What's this about my son?"

His voice was harsh. His chest had too much and his mouth too little to do with his words for them to be very clear.

"I'm a Continental Detective Agency operative, San Francisco branch," I told him. "A couple of days ago we got a check from your son and a letter asking that a man be sent here to do some work for him. I'm the man. He told me to come out to his house last night. I did, but he didn't show up. When I got downtown I learned he had been killed."

Elihu Willsson peered suspiciously at me and asked:

"Well, what of it?"

"While I was waiting your daughter-in-law got a phone message, went out, came back with what looked like blood on her shoe, and told me her husband wouldn't be home. He was shot at ten-forty. She went out at ten-twenty, came back at eleven-five."

The old man sat straight up in bed and called young Mrs. Willsson a flock of things. When he ran out of words of that sort he still had some breath left. He used it to shout at me:

"Is she in jail?"

I said I didn't think so.

He didn't like her not being in jail. He was nasty about it. He bawled a lot of things I didn't like, winding up with:

"What the hell are you waiting for?"

He was too old and too sick to be smacked. I laughed and said:

"For evidence."

"Evidence? What do you need? You've—"

"Don't be a chump," I interrupted his bawling. "Why should she kill him?"

"Because she's a French hussy! Because she—"

The secretary's frightened face appeared at the door.

"Get out of here!" the old man roared at it, and the face went.

"She jealous?" I asked before he could go on with his shouting. "And if you don't yell maybe I'll be able to hear you anyway. My deafness is a lot better since I've been eating yeast."

He put a fist on top of each hump his thighs made in the covers and pushed his square chin at me.

"Old as I am and sick as I am," he said very deliberately, "I've a great mind to get up and kick your behind."

I paid no attention to that, repeating:

"Was she jealous?"

"She was," he said, not yelling now, "and domineering, and spoiled, and suspicious, and greedy, and mean, and unscrupulous, and deceitful, and selfish, and damned bad—altogether damned bad!"

"Any reason for her jealousy?"

"I hope so," he said bitterly. "I'd hate to think a son of mine would be faithful to her. Though likely enough he was. He'd do things like that."

"But you don't know any reason why she should have killed him?"

"Don't know any reason?" He was bellowing again. "Haven't I been telling you that—"

"Yeah. But none of that means anything. It's kind of childish."

The old man flung the covers back from his legs and started to get out of bed. Then he thought better of it, raised his red face and roared:

"Stanley!"

The door opened to let the secretary glide in.

"Throw this bastard out!" his master ordered, waving a fist at me.

The secretary turned to me. I shook my head and suggested:

"Better get help."

He frowned. We were about the same age. He was weedy, nearly a head taller than I, but fifty pounds lighter. Some of my hundred and ninety pounds were fat, but not all of them. The secretary fidgeted, smiled apologetically, and went away.

"What I was about to say," I told the old man: "I intended talking to your son's wife this morning. But I saw Max Thaler go into the house, so I postponed my visit."

Elihu Willsson carefully pulled the covers up over his legs again, leaned his head back on the pillows, screwed his eyes up at the ceiling, and said:

"Hm-m-m, so that's the way it is, is it?"

"Mean anything?"

"She killed him," he said certainly. "That's what it means."

Feet made noises in the hall, huskier feet than the secretary's. When they were just outside the door I began a sentence:

"You were using your son to run a—"

"Get out of here!" the old man yelled at those in the doorway. "And keep that door closed." He glowered at me and demanded: "What was I using my son for?"

"To put the knife in Thaler, Yard and the Finn."

"You're a liar."

"I didn't invent the story. It's all over Personville."

"It's a lie. I gave him the papers. He did what he wanted with them."

"You ought to explain that to your playmates. They'd believe you."

"What they believe be damned! What I'm telling you is so."

"What of it? Your son won't come back to life just because he was killed by mistake—if he was."

"That woman killed him."

"Maybe."

"Damn you and your maybes! She did."

"Maybe. But the other angle has got to be looked into too—the political end. You can tell me—"

"I can tell you that that French hussy killed him, and I can tell you that any other damned numbskull notions you've got are way off the lode."

"But they've got to be looked into," I insisted. "And you know the inside of Personville politics better than anyone else I'm likely to find. He was your son. The least you can do is—"

"The least I can do," he bellowed, "is tell you to get to hell back to Frisco, you and your numbskull—"

I got up and said unpleasantly:

"I'm at the Great Western Hotel. Don't bother me unless you want to talk sense for a change."

I went out of the bedroom and down the stairs. The secretary hovered around the bottom step, smiling apologetically.

"A fine old rowdy," I growled.

"A remarkably vital personality," he murmured.

At the office of the *Herald*, I hunted up the murdered man's secretary. She was a small girl of nineteen or twenty with wide chestnut eyes, light brown hair and a pale pretty face. Her name was Lewis.

She said she hadn't known anything about my being called to Personville by her employer.

"But then," she explained, "Mr. Willsson always liked to keep everything to himself as long as he could. It was— I don't think he trusted anybody here, completely."

"Not you?"

She flushed and said:

"No. But of course he had been here such a short while and didn't know any of us very well."

"There must have been more to it than that."

"Well," she bit her lip and made a row of forefinger prints down the polished edge of the dead man's desk, "his father wasn't—wasn't in sympathy with what he was doing. Since his father really owned the papers, I suppose it was natural for Mr. Donald to think some of the employes might be more loyal to Mr. Elihu than to him."

"The old man wasn't in favor of the reform campaign? Why did he stand for it, if the papers were his?"

She bent her head to study the finger prints she had made. Her voice was low.

"It's not easy to understand unless you know— The last time Mr. Elihu was taken sick he sent for Donald—Mr. Donald. Mr. Donald had lived in Europe most of his life, you know. Dr. Pride told Mr. Elihu that he'd have to give up the management of his affairs, so he cabled his son to come home. But when Mr. Donald got here Mr. Elihu couldn't make up his mind to let go of everything. But he wanted Mr. Donald to stay here, so he gave him the newspapers—that is, made him publisher. Mr. Donald liked that. He had been interested in journalism in Paris. When he found out how terrible everything was here—in civic affairs and so on—he started that reform campaign. He didn't know—he had been away since he was a boy—he didn't know—"

"He didn't know his father was in it as deep as anybody else," I helped her along.

She squirmed a little over her examination of the finger prints, didn't contradict me, and went on:

"Mr. Elihu and he had a quarrel. Mr. Elihu told him to stop stirring things up, but he wouldn't stop. Maybe he would have stopped if he had known—all there was to know. But I don't suppose it would ever have occurred to him that his father was really seriously implicated. And his father wouldn't tell him. I suppose it would be hard for a father to tell a son a thing like that. He threatened to take the papers away from Mr. Donald. I don't know whether he intended to or not. But he was taken sick again, and everything went along as it did."

"Donald Willsson didn't confide in you?" I asked.

"No." It was almost a whisper.

"Then you learned all this where?"

"I'm trying—trying to help you learn who murdered him," she said earnestly. "You've no right to—"

"You'll help me most just now by telling me where you learned all this," I insisted.

She stared at the desk, chewing her lower lip. I waited. Presently she said:

"My father is Mr. Willsson's secretary."

"Thanks."

"But you mustn't think that we—"

"It's nothing to me," I assured her. "What was Willsson doing in Hurricane Street last night when he had a date with me at his house?"

She said she didn't know. I asked her if she had heard him tell me, over the phone, to come to his house at ten o'clock. She said she had.

"What did he do after that? Try to remember every least thing that was said and done from then until you left at the end of the day."

She leaned back in her chair, shut her eyes and wrinkled her forehead.

"You called up—if it was you he told to come to his house—at about two o'clock. After that Mr. Donald dictated some letters, one to a paper mill, one to Senator Keefer about some changes in post office regulations, and— Oh, yes! He went out for about twenty minutes, a little before three. And before he went he wrote out a check."

"Who for?"

"I don't know, but I saw him writing it."

"Where's his check book? Carry it with him?"

"It's here." She jumped up, went around to the front of his desk, and tried the top drawer. "Locked."

I joined her, straightened out a wire clip, and with that and a blade of my knife fiddled the drawer open.

The girl took out a thin, flat First National Bank check book. The last used stub was marked $5,000. Nothing else. No name. No explanation.

"He went out with this check," I said, "and was gone twenty minutes? Long enough to get to the bank and back?"

"It wouldn't have taken him more than five minutes to get there."

"Didn't anything else happen before he wrote out the check? Think. Any messages? Letters? Phone calls?"

"Let's see." She shut her eyes again. "He was dictating some mail and— Oh, how stupid of me! He did have a phone call. He said: 'Yes, I can be there at ten, but I shall have to hurry away.' Then again he said: 'Very well, at ten.' That was all he said except, 'Yes, yes,' several times."

"Talking to a man or a woman?"

"I didn't know."

"Think. There'd be a difference in his voice."

She thought and said:

"Then it was a woman."

"Which of you—you or he—left first in the evening?"

"I did. He— I told you my father is Mr. Elihu's secretary. He and Mr. Donald had an engagement for the early part of the evening—something about the paper's finances. Father came in a little after five. They were going to dinner together, I think."

That was all the Lewis girl could give me. She knew nothing that would explain Willsson's presence in the eleven-hundred block of Hurricane Street, she said. She admitted knowing nothing about Mrs. Willsson.

We frisked the dead man's desk, and dug up nothing in any way informative. I went up against the girls at the switch-board, and learned nothing. I put in an hour's work on messengers, city editors, and the like, and my pumping brought up nothing. The dead man, as his secretary said, had been a good hand at keeping his affairs to himself.

CHAPTER III

Dinah Brand

AT THE First National Bank I got hold of an assistant cashier named Albury, a nice-looking blond youngster of twenty-five or so.

"I certified the check for Willsson," he said after I had explained what I was up to. "It was drawn to the order of Dinah Brand—$5,000."

"Know who she is?"

"Oh, yes! I know her."

"Mind telling me what you know about her?"

"Not at all. I'd be glad to, but I'm already eight minutes overdue at a meeting with—"

"Can you have dinner with me this evening and give it to me then?"

"That'll be fine," he said.

"Seven o'clock at the Great Western?"

"Righto."

"I'll run along and let you get to your meeting, but tell me, has she an account here?"

"Yes, and she deposited the check this morning. The police have it."

"Yeah? And where does she live?"

"1232 Hurricane Street."

I said: "Well, well!" and, "See you tonight," and went away.

My next stop was in the office of the chief of police, in the City Hall.

Noonan, the chief, was a fat man with twinkling greenish eyes set in a round jovial face. When I told him what I was doing in his city he seemed glad of it. He gave me a handshake, a cigar and a chair.

"Now," he said when we were settled, "tell me who turned the trick."

"The secret's safe with me."

"You and me both," he said cheerfully through smoke. "But what do you guess?"

"I'm no good at guessing, especially when I haven't got the facts."

" 'Twon't take long to give you all the facts there is," he said. "Willsson got a five-grand check in Dinah Brand's name certified yesterday just before bank closing. Last night he was killed by slugs from a .32 less than a block from her house. People that heard the shooting saw a man and a woman bending over the remains. Bright and early this morning the said Dinah Brand deposits the said check in the said bank. Well?"

"Who is this Dinah Brand?"

The chief dumped the ash off his cigar in the center of his desk, flourished the cigar in his fat hand, and said:

"A soiled dove, as the fellow says, a de luxe hustler, a big-league gold-digger."

"Gone up against her yet?"

"No. There's a couple of slants to be taken care of first. We're keeping an eye on her and waiting. This I've told you is under the hat."

"Yeah. Now listen to this," and I told him what I had seen and heard while waiting in Donald Willsson's house the previous night.

When I had finished the chief bunched his fat mouth, whistled softly, and exclaimed:

"Man, that's an interesting thing you've been telling me! So it was blood on her slipper? And she said her husband wouldn't be home?"

"That's what I took it for," I said to the first question, and, "Yeah," to the second.

"Have you done any talking to her since then?" he asked.

"No. I was up that way this morning, but a young fellow named Thaler went into the house ahead of me, so I put off my visit."

"Grease us twice!" His greenish eyes glittered happily. "Are you telling me the Whisper was there?"

"Yeah."

He threw his cigar on the floor, stood up, planted his fat hands on the desk top, and leaned over them toward me, oozing delight from every pore.

"Man, you've done something," he purred. "Dinah Brand

is this Whisper's woman. Let's me and you just go out and kind of talk to the widow."

We climbed out of the chief's car in front of Mrs. Willsson's residence. The chief stopped for a second with one foot on the bottom step to look at the black crêpe hanging over the bell. Then he said, "Well, what's got to be done has got to be done," and we went up the steps.

Mrs. Willsson wasn't anxious to see us, but people usually see the chief of police if he insists. This one did. We were taken upstairs to where Donald Willsson's widow sat in the library. She was in black. Her blue eyes had frost in them.

Noonan and I took turns mumbling condolences and then he began:

"We just wanted to ask you a couple of questions. For instance, like where'd you go last night?"

She looked disagreeably at me, then back to the chief, frowned, and spoke haughtily:

"May I ask why I am being questioned in this manner?"

I wondered how many times I had heard that question, word for word and tone for tone, while the chief, disregarding it, went on amiably:

"And then there was something about one of your shoes being stained. The right one, or maybe the left. Anyways it was one or the other."

A muscle began twitching in her upper lip.

"Was that all?" the chief asked me. Before I could answer he made a clucking noise with his tongue and turned his genial face to the woman again. "I almost forgot. There was a matter of how you knew your husband wouldn't be home."

She got up, unsteadily, holding the back of her chair with one white hand.

"I'm sure you'll excuse—"

" 'S all right." The chief made a big-hearted gesture with one beefy paw. "We don't want to bother you. Just where you went, and about the shoe, and how you knew he wasn't coming back. And, come to think of it, there's another——What Thaler wanted here this morning."

Mrs. Willsson sat down again, very rigidly. The chief looked at her. A smile that tried to be tender made funny lines and humps in his fat face. After a little while her shoulders began to relax, her chin went lower, a curve came in her back.

I put a chair facing her and sat on it.

"You'll have to tell us, Mrs. Willsson," I said, making it as sympathetic as I could. "These things have got to be explained."

"Do you think I have anything to hide?" she asked defiantly, sitting up straight and stiff again, turning each word out very precisely, except that the s's were a bit slurred. "I did go out. The stain was blood. I knew my husband was dead. Thaler came to see me about my husband's death. Are your questions answered now?"

"We knew all that," I said. "We're asking you to explain them."

She stood up again, said angrily:

"I dislike your manner. I refuse to submit to—"

Noonan said:

"That's perfectly all right, Mrs. Willsson, only we'll have to ask you to go down to the Hall with us."

She turned her back to him, took a deep breath and threw words at me:

"While we were waiting here for Donald I had a telephone call. It was a man who wouldn't give his name. He said Donald had gone to the home of a woman named Dinah Brand with a check for five thousand dollars. He gave me her address. Then I drove out there and waited down the street in the car until Donald came out.

"While I was waiting there I saw Max Thaler, whom I knew by sight. He went to the woman's house, but didn't go in. He went away. Then Donald came out and walked down the street. He didn't see me. I didn't want him to. I intended to drive home—get here before he came. I had just started the engine when I heard the shots, and I saw Donald fall. I got out of the car and ran over to him. He was dead. I was frantic. Then Thaler came. He said if I were found there they would say I had killed him. He made me run back to the car and drive home."

Tears were in her eyes. Through the water her eyes studied my face, apparently trying to learn how I took the story. I didn't say anything. She asked:

"Is that what you wanted?"

"Practically," Noonan said. He had walked around to one side. "What did Thaler say this afternoon?"

"He urged me to keep quiet." Her voice had become small and flat. "He said either or both of us would be suspected if anyone learned we were there, because Donald had been killed coming from the woman's house after giving her money."

"Where did the shots come from?" the chief asked.

"I don't know. I didn't see anything—except—when I looked up—Donald falling."

"Did Thaler fire them?"

"No," she said quickly. Then her mouth and eyes spread. She put a hand to her breast. "I don't know. I didn't think so, and he said he didn't. I don't know where he was. I don't know why I never thought he might have."

"What do you think now?" Noonan asked.

"He—he may have."

The chief winked at me, an athletic wink in which all his facial muscles took part, and cast a little farther back:

"And you don't know who called you up?"

"He wouldn't tell me his name."

"Didn't recognize his voice?"

"No."

"What kind of voice was it?"

"He talked in an undertone, as if afraid of being overheard. I had difficulty understanding him."

"He whispered?" The chief's mouth hung open as the last sound left it. His greenish eyes sparkled greedily between their pads of fat.

"Yes, a hoarse whisper."

The chief shut his mouth with a click, opened it again to say persuasively:

"You've heard Thaler talk. . . ."

The woman started and stared big-eyed from the chief to me.

"It was he," she cried. "It was he."

Robert Albury, the young assistant cashier of the First National Bank, was sitting in the lobby when I returned to the Great Western Hotel. We went up to my room, had some ice-water brought, used its ice to put chill in Scotch, lemon juice, and grenadine, and then went down to the dining room.

"Now tell me about the lady," I said when we were working on the soup.

"Have you seen her yet?" he asked.

"Not yet."

"But you've heard something about her?"

"Only that she's an expert in her line."

"She is," he agreed. "I suppose you'll see her. You'll be disappointed at first. Then, without being able to say how or when it happened, you'll find you've forgotten your disappointment, and the first thing you know you'll be telling her your life's history, and all your troubles and hopes." He laughed with boyish shyness. "And then you're caught, absolutely caught."

"Thanks for the warning. How'd you come by the information?"

He grinned shamefacedly across his suspended soup spoon and confessed:

"I bought it."

"Then I suppose it cost you plenty. I hear she likes *dinero*."

"She's money-mad, all right, but somehow you don't mind it. She's so thoroughly mercenary, so frankly greedy, that there's nothing disagreeable about it. You'll understand what I mean when you know her."

"Maybe. Mind telling me how you happened to part with her?"

"No, I don't mind. I spent it all, that's how."

"Cold-blooded like that?"

His face flushed a little. He nodded.

"You seem to have taken it well," I said.

"There was nothing else to do." The flush in his pleasant young face deepened and he spoke hesitantly. "It happens I owe her something for it. She— I'm going to tell you this. I want you to see this side of her. I had a little money. After that was gone— You must remember I was young and head over heels. After my money was gone there was the bank's. I had— You don't care whether I had actually done anything or was simply thinking about it. Anyway, she found it out. I never could hide anything from her. And that was the end."

"She broke off with you?"

"Yes, thank God! If it hadn't been for her you might be looking for me now—for embezzlement. I owe her that!" He wrinkled his forehead earnestly. "You won't say anything about this—you know what I mean. But I wanted you to know she has her good side too. You'll hear enough about the other."

"Maybe she has. Or maybe it was just that she didn't think she'd get enough to pay for the risk of being caught in a jam."

He turned this over in his mind and then shook his head.

"That may have had something to do with it, but not all."

"I gathered she was strictly pay-as-you-enter."

"How about Dan Rolff?" he asked.

"Who's he?"

"He's supposed to be her brother, or half-brother, or something of the sort. He isn't. He's a down-and-outer—t.b. He lives with her. She keeps him. She's not in love with him or anything. She simply found him somewhere and took him in."

"Any more?"

"There was that radical chap she used to run around with. It's not likely she got much money out of him."

"What radical chap?"

"He came here back during the strike—Quint is his name."

"So he was on her list?"

"That's supposed to be the reason he stayed here after the strike was over."

"So he's still on her list?"

"No. She told me she was afraid of him. He had threatened to kill her."

"She seems to have had everybody on her string at one time or another," I said.

"Everybody she wanted," he said, and he said it seriously.

"Donald Willsson was the latest?" I asked.

"I don't know," he said. "I had never heard anything about them, had never seen anything. The chief of police had us try to find any checks he may have issued to her before yesterday, but we found nothing. Nobody could remember ever having seen any."

"Who was her last customer, so far as you know?"

"Lately I've seen her around town quite often with a chap named Thaler—he runs a couple of gambling houses here. They call him Whisper. You've probably heard of him."

At eight-thirty I left young Albury and set out for the Miner's Hotel in Forest Street. Half a block from the hotel I met Bill Quint.

"Hello!" I hailed him. "I was on my way down to see you."

He stopped in front of me, looked me up and down, growled:

"So you're a gum-shoe."

"That's the bunk," I complained. "I come all the way down here to rope you, and you're smarted up."

"What do you want to know now?" he asked.

"About Donald Willsson. You knew him, didn't you?"

"I knew him."

"Very well?"

"No."

"What did you think of him?"

He pursed his gray lips, by forcing breath between them made a noise like a rag tearing, and said:

"A lousy liberal."

"You know Dinah Brand?" I asked.

"I know her." His neck was shorter and thicker than it had been.

"Think she killed Willsson?"

"Sure. It's a kick in the pants."

"Then you didn't?"

"Hell, yes," he said, "the pair of us together. Got any more questions?"

"Yeah, but I'll save my breath. You'd only lie to me."

I walked back to Broadway, found a taxi, and told the driver to take me to 1232 Hurricane Street.

CHAPTER IV

Hurricane Street

M Y DESTINATION was a gray frame cottage. When I rang
the bell the door was opened by a thin man with a
tired face that had no color in it except a red spot the size of
a half-dollar high on each cheek. This, I thought, is the
lunger Dan Rolff.

"I'd like to see Miss Brand," I told him.

"What name shall I tell her?" His voice was a sick man's
and an educated man's.

"It wouldn't mean anything to her. I want to see her about
Willsson's death."

He looked at me with level tired dark eyes and said:
"Yes?"

"I'm from the San Francisco office of the Continental
Detective Agency. We're interested in the murder."

"That's nice of you," he said ironically. "Come in."

I went in, into a ground-floor room where a young woman
sat at a table that had a lot of papers on it. Some of the papers were financial service bulletins, stock and bond market
forecasts. One was a racing chart.

The room was disorderly, cluttered up. There were too
many pieces of furniture in it, and none of them seemed to be
in its proper place.

"Dinah," the lunger introduced me, "this gentleman has
come from San Francisco on behalf of the Continental Detective Agency to inquire into Mr. Donald Willsson's demise."

The young woman got up, kicked a couple of newspapers
out of her way, and came to me with one hand out.

She was an inch or two taller than I, which made her about
five feet eight. She had a broad-shouldered, full-breasted,
round-hipped body and big muscular legs. The hand she gave
me was soft, warm, strong. Her face was the face of a girl of
twenty-five already showing signs of wear. Little lines crossed
the corners of her big ripe mouth. Fainter lines were beginning to make nets around her thick-lashed eyes. They were
large eyes, blue and a bit blood-shot.

Her coarse hair—brown—needed trimming and was parted crookedly. One side of her upper lip had been rouged higher than the other. Her dress was of a particularly unbecoming wine color, and it gaped here and there down one side, where she had neglected to snap the fasteners or they had popped open. There was a run down the front of her left stocking.

This was the Dinah Brand who took her pick of Poison-ville's men, according to what I had been told.

"His father sent for you, of course," she said while she moved a pair of lizard-skin slippers and a cup and saucer off a chair to make room for me.

Her voice was soft, lazy.

I told her the truth:

"Donald Willsson sent for me. I was waiting to see him while he was being killed."

"Don't go away, Dan," she called to Rolff.

He came back into the room. She returned to her place at the table. He sat on the opposite side, leaning his thin face on a thin hand, looking at me without interest.

She drew her brows together, making two creases between them, and asked:

"You mean he knew someone meant to kill him?"

"I don't know. He didn't say what he wanted. Maybe just help in the reform campaign."

"But do you—?"

I made a complaint:

"It's no fun being a sleuth when somebody steals your stuff, does all the questioning."

"I like to find out what's going on," she said, a little laugh gurgling down in her throat.

"I'm that way too. For instance, I'd like to know why you made him have the check certified."

Very casually, Dan Rolff shifted in his chair, leaning back, lowering his thin hands out of sight below the table's edge.

"So you found out about that?" Dinah Brand asked. She crossed left leg over right and looked down. Her eyes fo-cussed on the run in her stocking. "Honest to God, I'm going to stop wearing them!" she complained. "I'm going barefooted. I paid five bucks for these socks yesterday. Now look at the damned things. Every day—runs, runs, runs!"

"It's no secret," I said. "I mean the check, not the runs. Noonan's got it."

She looked at Rolff, who stopped watching me long enough to nod once.

"If you talked my language," she drawled, looking narrow-eyed at me, "I might be able to give you some help."

"Maybe if I knew what it was."

"Money," she explained, "the more the better. I like it."

I became proverbial:

"Money saved is money earned. I can save you money and grief."

"That doesn't mean anything to me," she said, "though it sounds like it's meant to."

"The police haven't asked you anything about the check?"

She shook her head, no.

I said:

"Noonan's figuring on hanging the rap on you as well as on Whisper."

"Don't scare me," she lisped. "I'm only a child."

"Noonan knows that Thaler knew about the check. He knows that Thaler came here while Willsson was here, but didn't get in. He knows that Thaler was hanging around the neighborhood when Willsson was shot. He knows that Thaler and a woman were seen bending over the dead man."

The girl picked up a pencil from the table and thoughtfully scratched her cheek with it. The pencil made little curly black lines over the rouge.

Rolff's eyes had lost their weariness. They were bright, feverish, fixed on mine. He leaned forward, but kept his hands out of sight below the table.

"Those things," he said, "concern Thaler, not Miss Brand."

"Thaler and Miss Brand aren't strangers," I said. "Willsson brought a five-thousand dollar check here, and was killed leaving. That way, Miss Brand might have had trouble cashing it—if Willsson hadn't been thoughtful enough to get it certified."

"My God!" the girl protested, "if I'd been going to kill him I'd have done it in here where nobody could have seen it, or waited until he got out of sight of the house. What kind of a dumb onion do you take me for?"

"I'm not sure you killed him," I said. "I'm just sure that the fat chief means to hang it on you."

"What are you trying to do?" she asked.

"Learn who killed him. Not who could have or might have, but who did."

"I could give you some help," she said, "but there'd have to be something in it for me."

"Safety," I reminded her, but she shook her head.

"I mean it would have to get me something in a financial way. It'd be worth something to you, and you ought to pay something, even if not a fortune."

"Can't be done." I grinned at her. "Forget the bank roll and go in for charity. Pretend I'm Bill Quint."

Dan Rolff started up from his chair, lips white as the rest of his face. He sat down again when the girl laughed—a lazy, good-natured laugh.

"He thinks I didn't make any profit out of Bill, Dan." She leaned over and put a hand on my knee. "Suppose you knew far enough ahead that a company's employes were going to strike, and when, and then far enough ahead when they were going to call the strike off. Could you take that info and some capital to the stock market and do yourself some good playing with the company's stock? You bet you could!" she wound up triumphantly. "So don't go around thinking that Bill didn't pay his way."

"You've been spoiled," I said.

"What in the name of God's the use of being so tight?" she demanded. "It's not like it had to come out of your pocket. You've got an expense account, haven't you?"

I didn't say anything. She frowned at me, at the run in her stocking, and at Rolff. Then she said to him:

"Maybe he'd loosen up if he had a drink."

The thin man got up and went out of the room.

She pouted at me, prodded my shin with her toe, and said:

"It's not so much the money. It's the principle of the thing. If a girl's got something that's worth something to somebody, she's a boob if she doesn't collect."

I grinned.

"Why don't you be a good guy?" she begged.

Dan Rolff came in with a siphon, a bottle of gin, some

lemons, and a bowl of cracked ice. We had a drink apiece. The lunger went away. The girl and I wrangled over the money question while we had more drinks. I kept trying to keep the conversation on Thaler and Willsson. She kept switching it to the money she deserved. It went on that way until the gin bottle was empty. My watch said one-fifteen.

She chewed a piece of lemon peel and said for the thirtieth or fortieth time:

"It won't come out of your pocket. What do you care?"

"It's not the money," I said, "it's the principle of the thing."

She made a face at me and put her glass where she thought the table was. She was eight inches wrong. I don't remember if the glass broke when it hit the floor, or what happened to it. I do remember that I was encouraged by her missing the table.

"Another thing," I opened up a new argumentative line, "I'm not sure I really need whatever you can tell me. If I have to get along without it, I think I can."

"It'll be nice if you can, but don't forget I'm the last person who saw him alive, except whoever killed him."

"Wrong," I said. "His wife saw him come out, walk away, and fall."

"His wife!"

"Yeah. She was sitting in a coupé down the street."

"How did she know he was here?"

"She says Thaler phoned her that her husband had come here with the check."

"You're trying to kid me," the girl said. "Max couldn't have known it."

"I'm telling you what Mrs. Willsson told Noonan and me."

The girl spit what was left of the lemon peel out on the floor, further disarranged her hair by running her fingers through it, wiped her mouth with the back of her hand, and slapped the table.

"All right, Mr. Knowitall," she said, "I'm going to play with you. You can think it's not going to cost you anything, but I'll get mine before we're through. You think I won't?" she challenged me, peering at me as if I were a block away.

This was no time to revive the money argument, so I said:
"I hope you do." I think I said it three or four times, quite
earnestly.

"I will. Now listen to me. You're drunk, and I'm drunk,
and I'm just exactly drunk enough to tell you anything you
want to know. That's the kind of girl I am. If I like a person
I'll tell them anything they want to know. Just ask me. Go
ahead, ask me."

I did:

"What did Willsson give you five thousand dollars for?"

"For fun." She leaned back to laugh. Then: "Listen. He
was hunting for scandal. I had some of it, some affidavits and
things that I thought might be good for a piece of change
some day. I'm a girl that likes to pick up a little jack when she
can. So I had put these things away. When Donald began
going after scalps I let him know that I had these things, and
that they were for sale. I gave him enough of a peep at them
to let him know they were good. And they were good. Then
we talked how much. He wasn't as tight as you—nobody ever
was—but he was a little bit close. So the bargain hung fire, till
yesterday.

"Then I gave him the rush, phoned him and told him I had
another customer for the stuff and that if he wanted it he'd
have to show up that night with either five thousand smacks
in cash or a certified check. That was hooey, but he hadn't
been around much, so he fell for it."

"Why ten o'clock?" I asked.

"Why not? That's as good a time as any other. The main
thing on a deal like that is to give them a definite time. Now
you want to know why it had to be cash or a certified check?
All right, I'll tell you. I'll tell you anything you want to know.
That's the kind of girl I am. Always was."

She went on that way for five minutes, telling me in detail
just which and what sort of a girl she was, and always had
been, and why. I yes-yes'd her until I got a chance to cut in
with:

"All right, now why did it have to be a certified check?"

She shut one eye, waggled a forefinger at me, and said:

"So he couldn't stop payment. Because he couldn't have
used the stuff I sold him. It was good, all right. It was too

good. It would have put his old man in jail with the rest of them. It would have nailed Papa Elihu tighter than anyone else."

I laughed with her while I tried to keep my head above the gin I had guzzled.

"Who else would it nail?" I asked.

"The whole damned lot of them." She waved a hand. "Max, Lew Yard, Pete, Noonan, and Elihu Willsson—the whole damned lot of them."

"Did Max Thaler know what you were doing?"

"Of course not—nobody but Donald Willsson."

"Sure of that?"

"Sure I'm sure. You don't think I was going around bragging about it ahead of time, do you?"

"Who do you think knows about it now?"

"I don't care," she said. "It was only a joke on him. He couldn't have used the stuff."

"Do you think the birds whose secrets you sold will see anything funny in it? Noonan's trying to hang the killing on you and Thaler. That means he found the stuff in Donald Willsson's pocket. They all thought old Elihu was using his son to break them, didn't they?"

"Yes, sir," she said, "and I'm one who thinks the same thing."

"You're probably wrong, but that doesn't matter. If Noonan found the things you sold Donald Willsson in his pocket, and learned you had sold them to him, why shouldn't he add that up to mean that you and your friend Thaler had gone over to old Elihu's side?"

"He can see that old Elihu would be hurt as much as anybody else."

"What was this junk you sold him?"

"They built a new City Hall three years ago," she said, "and none of them lost any money on it. If Noonan got the papers he'll pretty soon find out that they tied as much on old Elihu, or more, than on anybody else."

"That doesn't make any difference. He'll take it for granted that the old man had found an out for himself. Take my word for it, sister, Noonan and his friends think you and Thaler and Elihu are double-crossing them."

"I don't give a damn what they think," she said obstinately. "It was only a joke. That's all I meant it for. That's all it was."

"That's good," I growled. "You can go to the gallows with a clear conscience. Have you seen Thaler since the murder?"

"No, but Max didn't kill him, if that's what you think, even if he was around."

"Why?"

"Lots of reasons. First place, Max wouldn't have done it himself. He'd have had somebody else do it, and he'd have been way off with an alibi nobody could shake. Second place, Max carries a .38, and anybody he sent to do the job would have had that much gun or more. What kind of a gunman would use a .32?"

"Then who did it?"

"I've told you all I know," she said. "I've told you too much."

I stood up and said:

"No, you've told me just exactly enough."

"You mean you think you know who killed him?"

"Yeah, though there's a couple of things I'll have to cover before I make the pinch."

"Who? Who?" She stood up, suddenly almost sober, tugging at my lapels. "Tell me who did it."

"Not now."

"Be a good guy."

"Not now."

She let go my lapels, put her hands behind her, and laughed in my face.

"All right. Keep it to yourself—and try to figure out which part of what I told you is the truth."

I said:

"Thanks for the part that is, anyhow, and for the gin. And if Max Thaler means anything to you, you ought to pass him the word that Noonan's trying to rib him."

CHAPTER V

Old Elihu Talks Sense

IT WAS close to two-thirty in the morning when I reached the hotel. With my key the night clerk gave me a memorandum that asked me to call Poplar 605. I knew the number. It was Elihu Willsson's.

"When did this come?" I asked the clerk.

"A little after one."

That sounded urgent. I went back to a booth and put in the call. The old man's secretary answered, asking me to come out at once. I promised to hurry, asked the clerk to get me a taxi, and went up to my room for a shot of Scotch.

I would rather have been cold sober, but I wasn't. If the night held more work for me I didn't want to go to it with alcohol dying in me. The snifter revived me a lot. I poured more of the King George into a flask, pocketed it, and went down to the taxi.

Elihu Willsson's house was lighted from top to bottom. The secretary opened the front door before I could get my finger on the button. His thin body was shivering in pale blue pajamas and dark blue bath robe. His thin face was full of excitement.

"Hurry!" he said. "Mr. Willsson is waiting. And, please, will you try to persuade him to let us have the body removed?"

I promised and followed him up to the old man's bedroom.

Old Elihu was in bed as before, but now a black automatic pistol lay on the covers close to one of his pink hands.

As soon as I appeared he took his head off the pillows, sat upright and barked at me:

"Have you got as much guts as you've got gall?"

His face was an unhealthy dark red. The film was gone from his eyes. They were hard and hot.

I let his question wait while I looked at the corpse on the floor between door and bed.

A short thick-set man in brown lay on his back with dead eyes staring at the ceiling from under the visor of a gray cap. A piece of his jaw had been knocked off. His chin was tilted to show where another bullet had gone through tie and collar to make a hole in his neck. One arm was bent under him. The other hand held a blackjack as big as a milk bottle. There was a lot of blood.

I looked up from this mess to the old man. His grin was vicious and idiotic.

"You're a great talker," he said. "I know that. A two-fisted, you-be-damned man with your words. But have you got anything else? Have you got the guts to match your gall? Or is it just the language you've got?"

There was no use in trying to get along with the old boy. I scowled and reminded him:

"Didn't I tell you not to bother me unless you wanted to talk sense for a change?"

"You did, my lad." There was a foolish sort of triumph in his voice. "And I'll talk you your sense. I want a man to clean this pig-sty of a Poisonville for me, to smoke out the rats, little and big. It's a man's job. Are you a man?"

"What's the use of getting poetic about it?" I growled. "If you've got a fairly honest piece of work to be done in my line, and you want to pay a decent price, maybe I'll take it on. But a lot of foolishness about smoking rats and pig-pens doesn't mean anything to me."

"All right. I want Personville emptied of its crooks and grafters. Is that plain enough language for you?"

"You didn't want it this morning," I said. "Why do you want it now?"

The explanation was profane and lengthy and given to me in a loud and blustering voice. The substance of it was that he had built Personville brick by brick with his own hands and he was going to keep it or wipe it off the side of the hill. Nobody could threaten him in his own city, no matter who they were. He had let them alone, but when they started telling him, Elihu Willsson, what he had to do and what he couldn't do, he would show them who was who. He brought the speech to an end by pointing at the corpse and boasting:

"That'll show them there's still a sting in the old man."

I wished I were sober. His clowning puzzled me. I couldn't put my finger on the something behind it.

"Your playmates sent him?" I asked, nodding at the dead man.

"I only talked to him with this," he said, patting the automatic on the bed, "but I reckon they did."

"How did it happen?"

"It happened simple enough. I heard the door opening, and I switched on the light, and there he was, and I shot him, and there he is."

"What time?"

"It was about one o'clock."

"And you've let him lie there all this time?"

"That I have." The old man laughed savagely and began blustering again: "Does the sight of a dead man turn your stomach? Or is it his spirit you're afraid of?"

I laughed at him. Now I had it. The old boy was scared stiff. Fright was the something behind his clowning. That was why he blustered, and why he wouldn't let them take the body away. He wanted it there to look at, to keep panic away, visible proof of his ability to defend himself. I knew where I stood.

"You really want the town cleaned up?" I asked.

"I said I did and I do."

"I'd have to have a free hand—no favors to anybody—run the job as I pleased. And I'd have to have a ten-thousand dollar retainer."

"Ten thousand dollars! Why in hell should I give that much to a man I don't know from Adam? A man who's done nothing I know of but talk?"

"Be serious. When I say *me*, I mean the Continental. You know them."

"I do. And they know me. And they ought to know I'm good for—"

"That's not the idea. These people you want taken to the cleaners were friends of yours yesterday. Maybe they will be friends again next week. I don't care about that. But I'm not playing politics for you. I'm not hiring out to help you kick them back in line—with the job being called off then. If you want the job done you'll plank down enough money to pay for a complete job. Any that's left over will be returned to you. But you're going to get a complete job or nothing. That's the way it'll have to be. Take it or leave it."

"I'll damned well leave it," he bawled.

He let me get half-way down the stairs before he called me back.

"I'm an old man," he grumbled. "If I was ten years younger—" He glared at me and worked his lips together. "I'll give you your damned check."

"And authority to go through with it in my own way?"

"Yes."

"We'll get it done now. Where's your secretary?"

Willsson pushed a button on his bedside table and the silent secretary appeared from wherever he had been hiding. I told him:

"Mr. Willsson wants to issue a ten-thousand dollar check to the Continental Detective Agency, and he wants to write the Agency—San Francisco branch—a letter authorizing the Agency to use the ten thousand dollars investigating crime and political corruption in Personville. The letter is to state clearly that the Agency is to conduct the investigation as it sees fit."

The secretary looked questioningly at the old man, who frowned and ducked his round white head.

"But first," I told the secretary as he glided toward the door, "you'd better phone the police that we've got a dead burglar here. Then call Mr. Willsson's doctor."

The old man declared he didn't want any damned doctors.

"You're going to have a nice shot in the arm so you can sleep," I promised him, stepping over the corpse to take the black gun from the bed. "I'm going to stay here tonight and we'll spend most of tomorrow sifting Poisonville affairs."

The old man was tired. His voice, when he profanely and somewhat long-windedly told me what he thought of my impudence in deciding what was best for him, barely shook the windows.

I took off the dead man's cap for a better look at his face. It didn't mean anything to me. I put the cap back in place.

When I straightened up the old man asked, moderately:

"Are you getting anywhere in your hunt for Donald's murderer?"

"I think so. Another day ought to see it finished."

"Who?" he asked.

The secretary came in with the letter and the check. I gave them to the old man instead of an answer to his question. He put a shaky signature on each, and I had them folded in my pocket when the police arrived.

The first copper into the room was the chief himself, fat Noonan. He nodded amiably at Willsson, shook hands with me, and looked with twinkling greenish eyes at the dead man.

"Well, well," he said. "It's a good job he did, whoever did it. Yakima Shorty. And will you look at the sap he's toting?" He kicked the blackjack out of the dead man's hand. "Big enough to sink a battleship. You drop him?" he asked me.

"Mr. Willsson."

"Well, that certainly is fine," he congratulated the old man. "You saved a lot of people a lot of troubles, including me. Pack him out, boys," he said to the four men behind him.

The two in uniform picked Yakima Shorty up by legs and arm-pits and went away with him, while one of the others gathered up the blackjack and a flashlight that had been under the body.

"If everybody did that to their prowlers, it would certainly be fine," the chief babbled on. He brought three cigars out of a pocket, threw one over on the bed, stuck one at me, and put the other in his mouth. "I was just wondering where I could get hold of you," he told me as we lighted up. "I got a little job ahead that I thought you'd like to be in on. That's how I happened to be on tap when the rumble came." He put his mouth close to my ear and whispered: "Going to pick up Whisper. Want to go along?"

"Yeah."

"I thought you would. Hello, Doc!"

He shook hands with a man who had just come in, a little plump man with a tired oval face and gray eyes that still had sleep in them.

The doctor went to the bed, where one of Noonan's men was asking Willsson about the shooting. I followed the secretary into the hall and asked him:

"Any men in the house besides you?"

"Yes, the chauffeur, the Chinese cook."

"Let the chauffeur stay in the old man's room tonight. I'm going out with Noonan. I'll get back as soon as I can. I don't think there'll be any more excitement here, but no matter what happens don't leave the old man alone. And don't leave him alone with Noonan or any of Noonan's crew."

The secretary's mouth and eyes popped wide.

"What time did you leave Donald Willsson last night?" I asked.

"You mean night before last, the night he was killed?"

"Yeah."

"At precisely half-past nine."

"You were with him from five o'clock till then?"

"From a quarter after five. We went over some statements and that sort of thing in his office until nearly eight o'clock. Then we went to Bayard's and finished our business over our dinners. He left at half-past nine, saying he had an engagement."

"What else did he say about this engagement?"

"Nothing else."

"Didn't give you any hint of where he was going, who he was going to meet?"

"He merely said he had an engagement."

"And you didn't know anything about it?"

"No. Why? Did you think I did?"

"I thought he might have said something." I switched back to tonight's doings: "What visitors did Willsson have today, not counting the one he shot?"

"You'll have to pardon me," the secretary said, smiling apologetically, "I can't tell you that without Mr. Willsson's permission. I'm sorry."

"Weren't some of the local powers here? Say Lew Yard, or—"

The secretary shook his head, repeating:

"I'm sorry."

"We won't fight over it," I said, giving it up and starting back toward the bedroom door.

The doctor came out, buttoning his overcoat.

"He will sleep now," he said hurriedly. "Someone should

stay with him. I shall be in in the morning." He ran down-stairs.

I went into the bedroom. The chief and the man who had questioned Willsson were standing by the bed. The chief grinned as if he were glad to see me. The other man scowled. Willsson was lying on his back, staring at the ceiling.

"That's about all there is here," Noonan said. "What say we mosey along?"

I agreed and said, "Good-night," to the old man. He said, "Good-night," without looking at me. The secretary came in with the chauffeur, a tall sunburned young husky.

The chief, the other sleuth—a police lieutenant named McGraw—and I went downstairs and got into the chief's car. McGraw sat beside the driver. The chief and I sat in back.

"We'll make the pinch along about daylight," Noonan ex-plained as we rode. "Whisper's got a joint over on King Street. He generally leaves there along about daylight. We could crash the place, but that'd mean gun-play, and it's just as well to take it easy. We'll pick him up when he leaves."

I wondered if he meant pick him up or pick him off. I asked:

"Got enough on him to make the rap stick?"

"Enough?" He laughed good-naturedly. "If what the Willsson dame give us ain't enough to stretch him I'm a pick-pocket."

I thought of a couple of wisecrack answers to that. I kept them to myself.

CHAPTER VI

Whisper's Joint

O UR RIDE ended under a line of trees in a dark street not far from the center of town. We got out of the car and walked down to the corner.

A burly man in a gray overcoat, with a gray hat pulled down over his eyes, came to meet us.

"Whisper's hep," the burly man told the chief. "He phoned Donohoe that he's going to stay in his joint. If you think you can pull him out, try it, he says."

Noonan chuckled, scratched an ear, and asked pleasantly:

"How many would you say was in there with him?"

"Fifty, anyhow."

"Aw, now! There wouldn't be that many, not at this time of morning."

"The hell there wouldn't," the burly man snarled. "They been drifting in since midnight."

"Is that so? A leak somewheres. Maybe you oughtn't to have let them in."

"Maybe I oughtn't." The burly man was angry. "But I did what you told me. You said let anybody go in or out that wanted to, but when Whisper showed to—"

"To pinch him," the chief said.

"Well, yes," the burly man agreed, looking savagely at me.

More men joined us and we held a talk-fest. Everybody was in a bad humor except the chief. He seemed to enjoy it all. I didn't know why.

Whisper's joint was a three-story brick building in the middle of the block, between two two-story buildings. The ground floor of his joint was occupied by a cigar store that served as entrance and cover for the gambling establishment upstairs. Inside, if the burly man's information was to be depended on, Whisper had collected half a hundred friends, loaded for a fight. Outside, Noonan's force was spread around the building, in the street in front, in the alley in back, and on the adjoining roofs.

"Well, boys," the chief said amiably after everybody had

had his say, "I don't reckon Whisper wants trouble any more than we do, or he'd have tried to shoot his way out before this, if he's got that many with him, though I don't mind saying I don't think has—not that many."

The burly man said: "The hell he ain't."

"So if he don't want trouble," Noonan went on, "maybe talking might do some good. You run over, Nick, and see if you can't argue him into being peaceable."

The burly man said: "The hell I will."

"Phone him, then," the chief suggested.

The burly man growled: "That's more like it," and went away.

When he came back he looked completely satisfied.

"He says," he reported, " 'Go to hell.' "

"Get the rest of the boys down here," Noonan said cheerfully. "We'll knock it over as soon as it gets light."

The burly Nick and I went around with the chief while he made sure his men were properly placed. I didn't think much of them—a shabby, shifty-eyed crew without enthusiasm for the job ahead of them.

The sky became a faded gray. The chief, Nick, and I stopped in a plumber's doorway diagonally across the street from our target.

Whisper's joint was dark, the upper windows blank, blinds down over cigar store windows and door.

"I hate to start this without giving Whisper a chance," Noonan said. "He's not a bad kid. But there's no use me trying to talk to him. He never did like me much."

He looked at me. I said nothing.

"You wouldn't want to make a stab at it?" he asked.

"Yeah, I'll try it."

"That's fine of you. I'll certainly appreciate it if you will. You just see if you can talk him into coming along without any fuss. You know what to say—for his own good and all that, like it is."

"Yeah," I said and walked across to the cigar store, taking pains to let my hands be seen swinging empty at my sides.

Day was still a little way off. The street was the color of smoke. My feet made a lot of noise on the pavement.

I stopped in front of the door and knocked the glass with a

knuckle, not heavily. The green blind down inside the door made a mirror of the glass. In it I saw two men moving up the other side of the street.

No sound came from inside. I knocked harder, then slid my hand down to rattle the knob.

Advice came from indoors:

"Get away from there while you're able."

It was a muffled voice, but not a whisper, so probably not Whisper's.

"I want to talk to Thaler," I said.

"Go talk to the lard-can that sent you."

"I'm not talking for Noonan. Is Thaler where he can hear me?"

A pause. Then the muffled voice said: "Yes."

"I'm the Continental op who tipped Dinah Brand off that Noonan was framing you," I said. "I want five minutes' talk with you. I've got nothing to do with Noonan except to queer his racket. I'm alone. I'll drop my rod in the street if you say so. Let me in."

I waited. It depended on whether the girl had got to him with the story of my interview with her. I waited what seemed a long time.

The muffled voice said:

"When we open, come in quick. And no stunts."

"All set."

The latch clicked. I plunged in with the door.

Across the street a dozen guns emptied themselves. Glass shot from door and windows tinkled around us.

Somebody tripped me. Fear gave me three brains and half a dozen eyes. I was in a tough spot. Noonan had slipped me a pretty dose. These birds couldn't help thinking I was playing his game.

I tumbled down, twisting around to face the door. My gun was in my hand by the time I hit the floor.

Across the street, burly Nick had stepped out of a doorway to pump slugs at us with both hands.

I steadied my gun-arm on the floor. Nick's body showed over the front sight. I squeezed the gun. Nick stopped shooting. He crossed his guns on his chest and went down in a pile on the sidewalk.

Hands on my ankles dragged me back. The floor scraped pieces off my chin. The door slammed shut. Some comedian said:

"Uh-huh, people don't like you."

I sat up and shouted through the racket:

"I wasn't in on this."

The shooting dwindled, stopped. Door and window blinds were dotted with gray holes. A husky whisper said in the darkness:

"Tod, you and Slats keep an eye on things down here. The rest of us might as well go upstairs."

We went through a room behind the store, into a passageway, up a flight of carpeted steps, and into a second-story room that held a green table banked for crap-shooting. It was a small room, had no windows, and the lights were on.

There were five of us. Thaler sat down and lit a cigarette, a small dark young man with a face that was pretty in a chorusman way until you took another look at the thin hard mouth. An angular blond kid of no more than twenty in tweeds sprawled on his back on a couch and blew cigarette smoke at the ceiling. Another boy, as blond and as young, but not so angular, was busy straightening his scarlet tie, smoothing his yellow hair. A thin-faced man of thirty with little or no chin under a wide loose mouth wandered up and down the room looking bored and humming *Rosy Cheeks*.

I sat in a chair two or three feet from Thaler's.

"How long is Noonan going to keep this up?" he asked. There was no emotion in his hoarse whispering voice, only a shade of annoyance.

"He's after you this trip," I said. "I think he's going through with it."

The gambler smiled a thin, contemptuous smile.

"He ought to know what a swell chance he's got of hanging a one-legged rap like that on me."

"He's not figuring on proving anything in court," I said.

"No?"

"You're to be knocked off resisting arrest, or trying to make a getaway. He won't need much of a case after that."

"He's getting tough in his old age." The thin lips curved in another smile. He didn't seem to think much of the fat chief's deadliness. "Any time he rubs me out I deserve rubbing. What's he got against you?"

"He's guessed I'm going to make a nuisance of myself."

"Too bad. Dinah told me you were a pretty good guy, except kind of Scotch with the roll."

"I had a nice visit. Will you tell me what you know about Donald Willsson's killing?"

"His wife plugged him."

"You saw her?"

"I saw her the next second—with the gat in her hand."

"That's no good to either of us," I said. "I don't know how far you've got it cooked. Rigged right, you could make it stick in court, maybe, but you'll not get a chance to make your play there. If Noonan takes you at all he'll take you stiff. Give me the straight of it. I only need that to pop the job."

He dropped his cigarette on the floor, mashed it under his foot, and asked:

"You that hot?"

"Give me your slant on it and I'm ready to make the pinch—if I can get out of here."

He lit another cigarette and asked:

"Mrs. Willsson said it was me that phoned her?"

"Yeah—after Noonan had persuaded her. She believes it now—maybe."

"You dropped Big Nick," he said. "I'll take a chance on you. A man phoned me that night. I don't know him, don't know who he was. He said Willsson had gone to Dinah's with a check for five grand. What the hell did I care? But, see, it was funny somebody I didn't know cracked it to me. So I went around. Dan stalled me away from the door. That was all right. But still it was funny as hell that guy phoned me.

"I went up the street and took a plant in a vestibule. I saw Mrs. Willsson's heap standing in the street, but I didn't know then that it was hers or that she was in it. He came out pretty soon and walked down the street. I didn't see the shots. I heard them. Then this woman jumps out of the heap and runs over to him. I knew she hadn't done the shooting. I ought to have beat it. But it was all funny as hell, so when I saw the woman was Willsson's wife I went over to them, trying to find out what it was all about. That was a break, see?

So I had to make an out for myself, in case something slipped. I strung the woman. That's the whole damned works—on the level."

"Thanks," I said. "That's what I came for. Now the trick is to get out of here without being mowed down."

"No trick at all," Thaler assured me. "We go any time we want to."

"I want to now. If I were you, I'd go too. You've got Noonan pegged as a false-alarm, but why take a chance? Make the sneak and keep under cover till noon, and his frame-up will be a wash-out."

Thaler put his hand in his pants pocket and brought out a fat roll of paper money. He counted off a hundred or two, some fifties, twenties, tens, and held them out to the chinless man, saying:

"Buy us a get-away, Jerry, and you don't have to give anybody any more dough than he's used to."

Jerry took the money, picked up a hat from the table, and strolled out. Half an hour later he returned and gave some of the bills back to Thaler, saying casually:

"We wait in the kitchen till we get the office."

We went down to the kitchen. It was dark there. More men joined us.

Presently something hit the door.

Jerry opened the door and we went down three steps into the back yard. It was almost full daylight. There were ten of us in the party.

"This all?" I asked Thaler.

He nodded.

"Nick said there were fifty of you."

"Fifty of us to stand off that crummy force!" he sneered.

A uniformed copper held the back gate open, muttering nervously:

"Hurry it up, boys, please."

I was willing to hurry, but nobody else paid any attention to him.

We crossed an alley, were beckoned through another gate by a big man in brown, passed through a house, out into the next street, and climbed into a black automobile that stood at the curb.

One of the blond boys drove. He knew what speed was.

I said I wanted to be dropped off somewhere in the neighborhood of the Great Western Hotel. The driver looked at Whisper, who nodded. Five minutes later I got out in front of my hotel.

"See you later," the gambler whispered, and the car slid away.

The last I saw of it was its police department license plate vanishing around a corner.

CHAPTER VII

That's Why I Sewed You Up

IT WAS half-past five. I walked around a few blocks until I came to an unlighted electric sign that said *Hotel Crawford*, climbed a flight of steps to the second-floor office, registered, left a call for ten o'clock, was shown into a shabby room, moved some of the Scotch from my flask to my stomach, and took old Elihu's ten-thousand dollar check and my gun to bed with me.

At ten I dressed, went up to the First National Bank, found young Albury, and asked him to certify Willsson's check for me. He kept me waiting a while. I suppose he phoned the old man's residence to find out if the check was on the up-and-up. Finally he brought it back to me, properly scribbled on.

I sponged an envelope, put the old man's letter and check in it, addressed it to the Agency in San Francisco, stuck a stamp on it, and went out and dropped it in the mail-box on the corner.

Then I returned to the bank and said to the boy:

"Now tell me why you killed him."

He smiled and asked:

"Cock Robin or President Lincoln?"

"You're not going to admit off-hand that you killed Donald Willsson?"

"I don't want to be disagreeable," he said, still smiling, "but I'd rather not."

"That's going to make it bad," I complained. "We can't stand here and argue very long without being interrupted. Who's the stout party with cheaters coming this way?"

The boy's face pinkened. He said:

"Mr. Dritton, the cashier."

"Introduce me."

The boy looked uncomfortable, but he called the cashier's name. Dritton—a large man with a smooth pink face, a fringe of white hair around an otherwise bald pink head, and rimless nose glasses—came over to us.

The assistant cashier mumbled the introductions. I shook Dritton's hand without losing sight of the boy.

"I was just saying," I addressed Dritton, "that we ought to have a more private place to talk in. He probably won't confess till I've worked on him a while, and I don't want everybody in the bank to hear me yelling at him."

"Confess?" The cashier's tongue showed between his lips.

"Sure." I kept my face, voice and manner bland, mimicking Noonan. "Didn't you know that Albury is the fellow who killed Donald Willsson?"

A polite smile at what he thought an asinine joke started behind the cashier's glasses, and changed to puzzlement when he looked at his assistant. The boy was rouge-red and the grin he was forcing his mouth to wear was a terrible thing.

Dritton cleared his throat and said heartily:

"It's a splendid morning. We've been having splendid weather."

"But isn't there a private room where we can talk?" I insisted.

Dritton jumped nervously and questioned the boy:

"What—what is this?"

Young Albury said something nobody could have understood.

I said: "If there isn't I'll have to take him down to the City Hall."

Dritton caught his glasses as they slid down his nose, jammed them back in place and said:

"Come back here."

We followed him down the length of the lobby, through a gate, and into an office whose door was labeled *President*— old Elihu's office. Nobody was in it.

I motioned Albury into one chair and picked another for myself. The cashier fidgeted with his back against the desk, facing both of us.

"Now, sir, will you explain this," he said.

"We'll get around to that," I told him and turned to the boy. "You're an ex-boy-friend of Dinah's who was given the air. You're the only one who knew her intimately who could have known about the certified check in time to phone Mrs.

Willsson and Thaler. Willsson was shot with a .32. Banks like that caliber. Maybe the gun you used wasn't a bank gun, but I think it was. Maybe you didn't put it back. Then there'll be one missing. Anyway I'm going to have a gun expert put his microscopes and micrometers on the bullets that killed Willsson and bullets fired from all the bank guns."

The boy looked calmly at me and said nothing. He had himself under control again. That wouldn't do. I had to be nasty. I said:

"You were cuckoo over the girl. You confessed to me that it was only because she wouldn't stand for it that you didn't—"

"Don't—please don't," he gasped. His face was red again.

I made myself sneer at him until his eyes went down. Then I said:

"You talked too much, son. You were too damned anxious to make your life an open book for me. That's a way you amateur criminals have. You've always got to overdo the frank and open business."

He was watching his hands. I let him have the other barrel:

"You know you killed him. You know if you used a bank gun, and if you put it back. If you did you're nailed now, without an out. The gun-sharks will take care of that. If you didn't, I'm going to nail you anyhow. All right. I don't have to tell you whether you've got a chance or not. You know.

"Noonan is framing Whisper Thaler for the job. He can't convict him, but the frame-up is tight enough that if Thaler's killed resisting arrest, the chief will be in the clear. That's what he means to do—kill Thaler. Thaler stood off the police all night in his King Street joint. He's still standing them off—unless they've got to him. The first copper that gets to him—exit Thaler.

"If you figure you've got a chance to beat your rap, and you want to let another man be killed on your account, that's your business. But if you know you haven't got a chance—and you haven't if the gun can be found—for God's sake give Thaler one by clearing him."

"I'd like," Albury's voice was an old man's. He looked up from his hands, saw Dritton, said, "I'd like," again and stopped.

"Where is the gun?" I asked.

"In Harper's cage," the boy said.

I scowled at the cashier and asked him:

"Will you get it?"

He went out as if he were glad to go.

"I didn't mean to kill him," the youngster said. "I don't think I meant to."

I nodded encouragingly, trying to look solemnly sympathetic.

"I don't think I meant to kill him," he repeated, "though I took the gun with me. You were right about my being cuckoo over Dinah—then. It was worse some days than others. The day Willsson brought the check in was one of the bad ones. All I could think about was that I had lost her because I had no more money, and he was taking five thousand dollars to her. It was the check. Can you understand that? I had known that she and Thaler were—you know. If I had learned that Willsson and she were too, without seeing the check, I wouldn't have done anything. I'm sure of it. It was seeing the check—and knowing I'd lost her because my money was gone.

"I watched her house that night and saw him go in. I was afraid of what I might do, because it was one of the bad days, and I had the gun in my pocket. Honestly I didn't want to do anything. I was afraid. I couldn't think of anything but the check, and why I had lost her. I knew Willsson's wife was jealous. Everybody knew that. I thought if I called her up and told her— I don't know exactly what I thought, but I went to a store around the corner and phoned her. Then I phoned Thaler. I wanted them there. If I could have thought of anyone else who had anything to do with either Dinah or Willsson I'd have called them too.

"Then I went back and watched Dinah's house again. Mrs. Willsson came, and then Thaler, and both of them stayed there, watching the house. I was glad of that. With them there I wasn't so afraid of what I might do. After a while Willsson came out and walked down the street. I looked up at Mrs. Willsson's car and at the doorway where I knew Thaler was. Neither of them did anything, and Willsson was walking away. I knew then why I had wanted them there. I had hoped they would do something—and I wouldn't have to. But they didn't, and he was walking away. If one of them had gone over and said something to him, or even followed him, I wouldn't have done anything.

"But they didn't. I remember taking the gun out of my pocket. Everything was blurred in front of my eyes, like I was crying. Maybe I was. I don't remember shooting—I mean I don't remember deliberately aiming and pulling the trigger—but I can remember the sound the shots made, and that I knew the noise was coming from the gun in my hand. I don't remember how Willsson looked, if he fell before I turned and ran up the alley, or not. When I got home I cleaned and re-loaded the pistol, and put it back in the paying teller's cage the next morning."

On the way down to the City Hall with the boy and the gun I apologized for the village cut-up stuff I had put in the early part of the shake-down, explaining:

"I had to get under your skin, and that was the best way I knew. The way you'd talked about the girl showed me you were too good an actor to be broken down by straight hammering."

He winced, and said slowly:

"That wasn't acting, altogether. When I was in danger, facing the gallows, she didn't—didn't seem so important to me. I couldn't—I can't now—quite understand—fully—why I did what I did. Do you know what I mean? That somehow makes the whole thing—and me—cheap. I mean, the whole thing from the beginning."

I couldn't find anything to say except something meaningless, like:

"Things happen that way."

In the chief's office we found one of the men who had been on the storming party the night before—a red-faced official named Biddle. He goggled at me with curious gray eyes, but asked no questions about the King Street doings.

Biddle called in a young lawyer named Dart from the prosecuting attorney's office. Albury was repeating his story to Biddle, Dart and a stenographer, when the chief of police, looking as if he had just crawled out of bed, arrived.

"Well, it certainly is fine to see you," Noonan said, pumping my hand up and down while patting my back. "By God! you had a narrow one last night—the rats! I was dead sure they'd got you till we kicked in the doors and found the joint empty. Tell me how those son-of-a-guns got out of there."

"A couple of your men let them out the back door, took them through the house in back, and sent them away in a department car. They took me along so I couldn't tip you off."

"A couple of my men did that?" he asked, with no appearance of surprise. "Well, well! What kind of looking men were they?"

I described them.

"Shore and Riordan," he said. "I might of known it. Now what's all this?" nodding his fat face at Albury.

I told him briefly while the boy went on dictating his statement.

The chief chuckled and said:

"Well, well, I did Whisper an injustice. I'll have to hunt him up and square myself. So you landed the boy? That certainly is fine. Congratulations and thanks." He shook my hand again. "You'll not be leaving our city now, will you?"

"Not just yet."

"That's fine," he assured me.

I went out for breakfast-and-lunch. Then I treated myself to a shave and hair-cut, sent a telegram to the Agency asking to have Dick Foley and Mickey Linehan shipped to Personville, stopped in my room for a change of clothes, and set out for my client's house.

Old Elihu was wrapped in blankets in an armchair at a sunny window. He gave me a stubby hand and thanked me for catching his son's murderer.

I made some more or less appropriate reply. I didn't ask him how he had got the news.

"The check I gave you last night," he said, "is only fair pay for the work you have done."

"Your son's check more than covered that."

"Then call mine a bonus."

"The Continental's got rules against taking bonuses or rewards," I said.

His face began to redden.

"Well, damn it—"

"You haven't forgotten that your check was to cover the cost of investigating crime and corruption in Personville, have you?" I asked.

"That was nonsense," he snorted. "We were excited last night. That's called off."

"Not with me."

He threw a lot of profanity around. Then:

"It's my money and I won't have it wasted on a lot of damn-foolery. If you won't take it for what you've done, give it back to me."

"Stop yelling at me," I said. "I'll give you nothing except a good job of city-cleaning. That's what you bargained for, and that's what you're going to get. You know now that your son was killed by young Albury, and not by your playmates. They know now that Thaler wasn't helping you double-cross them. With your son dead, you've been able to promise them that the newspapers won't dig up any more dirt. All's lovely and peaceful again.

"I told you I expected something like that. That's why I sewed you up. And you are sewed up. The check has been certified, so you can't stop payment. The letter of authority may not be as good as a contract, but you'll have to go into court to prove that it isn't. If you want that much of that kind of publicity, go ahead. I'll see that you get plenty.

"Your fat chief of police tried to assassinate me last night. I don't like that. I'm just mean enough to want to ruin him for it. Now I'm going to have my fun. I've got ten thousand dollars of your money to play with. I'm going to use it opening Poisonville up from Adam's apple to ankles. I'll see that you get my reports as regularly as possible. I hope you enjoy them."

And I went out of the house with his curses sizzling around my head.

CHAPTER VIII

A Tip on Kid Cooper

I SPENT most of the afternoon writing my three days' reports on the Donald Willsson operation. Then I sat around, burned Fatimas, and thought about the Elihu Willsson operation until dinner time.

I went down to the hotel dining room and had just decided in favor of pounded rump steak with mushrooms when I heard myself being paged.

The boy took me to one of the lobby booths. Dinah Brand's lazy voice came out of the receiver:

"Max wants to see you. Can you drop in tonight?"

"Your place?"

"Yes."

I promised to drop in and returned to the dining room and my meal. When I had finished eating I went up to my room, fifth floor front. I unlocked the door and went in, snapping on the light.

A bullet kissed a hole in the door-frame close to my noodle.

More bullets made more holes in door, door-frame and wall, but by that time I had carried my noodle into a safe corner, one out of line with the window.

Across the street, I knew, was a four-story office building with a roof a little above the level of my window. The roof would be dark. My light was on. There was no percentage in trying to peep out under those conditions.

I looked around for something to chuck at the light globe, found a Gideon Bible, and chucked it. The bulb popped apart, giving me darkness.

The shooting had stopped.

I crept to the window, kneeling with an eye to one of its lower corners. The roof across the street was dark and too high for me to see beyond its rim. Ten minutes of this one-eyed spying got me nothing except a kink in my neck.

I went to the phone and asked the girl to send the house copper up.

He was a portly, white-mustached man with the round un-developed forehead of a child. He wore a too-small hat on the back of his head to show the forehead. His name was Keever. He got too excited over the shooting.

The hotel manager came in, a plump man with carefully controlled face, voice and manner. He didn't get excited at all. He took the this-is-unheard-of-but-not-really-serious-of-course attitude of a street fakir whose mechanical dingus flops during a demonstration.

We risked light, getting a new globe, and added up the bullet-holes. There were ten of them.

Policemen came, went, and returned to report no luck in picking up whatever trail there might have been. Noonan called up. He talked to the sergeant in charge of the police detail, and then to me.

"I just this minute heard about the shooting," he said. "Now who do you reckon would be after you like that?"

"I couldn't guess," I lied.

"None of them touched you?"

"No."

"Well, that certainly is fine," he said heartily. "And we'll nail that baby, whoever he was, you can bet your life on that. Would you like me to leave a couple of the boys with you, just to see nothing else happens?"

"No, thanks."

"You can have them if you want them," he insisted.

"No, thanks."

He made me promise to call on him the first chance I got, told me the Personville police department was at my disposal, gave me to understand that if anything happened to me his whole life would be ruined, and I finally got rid of him.

The police went away. I had my stuff moved into another room, one into which bullets couldn't be so easily funneled. Then I changed my clothes and set out for Hurricane Street, to keep my date with the whispering gambler.

Dinah Brand opened the door for me. Her big ripe mouth was rouged evenly this evening, but her brown hair still needed trimming, was parted haphazardly, and there were spots down the front of her orange silk dress.

"So you're still alive," she said. "I suppose nothing can be done about it. Come on in."

We went into her cluttered-up living room. Dan Rolff and Max Thaler were playing pinochle there. Rolff nodded to me. Thaler got up to shake hands.

His hoarse whispering voice said:

"I hear you've declared war on Poisonville."

"Don't blame me. I've got a client who wants the place ventilated."

"Wanted, not wants," he corrected me as we sat down. "Why don't you chuck it?"

I made a speech:

"No. I don't like the way Poisonville has treated me. I've got my chance now, and I'm going to even up. I take it you're back in the club again, all brothers together, let bygones be bygones. You want to be let alone. There was a time when I wanted to be let alone. If I had been, maybe now I'd be riding back to San Francisco. But I wasn't. Especially I wasn't let alone by that fat Noonan. He's had two tries at my scalp in two days. That's plenty. Now it's my turn to run him ragged, and that's exactly what I'm going to do. Poisonville is ripe for the harvest. It's a job I like, and I'm going to it."

"While you last," the gambler said.

"Yeah," I agreed. "I was reading in the paper this morning about a fellow choking to death eating a chocolate eclair in bed."

"That may be good," said Dinah Brand, her big body sprawled in an arm-chair, "but it wasn't in this morning's paper."

She lit a cigarette and threw the match out of sight under the Chesterfield. The lunger had gathered up the cards and was shuffling them over and over, purposelessly.

Thaler frowned at me and said:

"Willsson's willing for you to keep the ten grand. Let it go at that."

"I've got a mean disposition. Attempted assassinations make me mad."

"That won't get you anything but a box. I'm for you. You kept Noonan from framing me. That's why I'm telling you, forget it and go back to Frisco."

"I'm for you," I said. "That's why I'm telling you, split with them. They crossed you up once. It'll happen again. Anyway, they're slated for the chutes. Get out while the getting's good."

"I'm sitting too pretty," he said. "And I'm able to take care of myself."

"Maybe. But you know the racket's too good to last. You've had the cream of the pickings. Now it's get-away day."

He shook his little dark head and told me:

"I think you're pretty good, but I'm damned if I think you're good enough to crack this camp. It's too tight. If I thought you could swing it, I'd be with you. You know how I stand with Noonan. But you'll never make it. Chuck it."

"No. I'm in it to the last nickel of Elihu's ten thousand."

"I told you he was too damned pig-headed to listen to reason," Dinah Brand said, yawning. "Isn't there anything to drink in the dump, Dan?"

The lunger got up from the table and went out of the room.

Thaler shrugged, said:

"Have it your way. You're supposed to know what you're doing. Going to the fights tomorrow night?"

I said I thought I would. Dan Rolff came in with gin and trimmings. We had a couple of drinks apiece. We talked about the fights. Nothing more was said about me versus Poisonville. The gambler apparently had washed his hands of me, but he didn't seem to hold my stubbornness against me. He even gave me what seemed to be a straight tip on the fights—telling me any bet on the main event would be good if its maker remembered that Kid Cooper would probably knock Ike Bush out in the sixth round. He seemed to know what he was talking about, and it didn't seem to be news to the others.

I left a little after eleven, returning to the hotel without anything happening.

CHAPTER IX

A Black Knife

I WOKE next morning with an idea in my skull. Personville had only some forty thousand inhabitants. It shouldn't be hard to spread news. Ten o'clock found me out spreading it.

I did my spreading in pool rooms, cigar stores, speakeasies, soft drink joints, and on street corners—wherever I found a man or two loafing. My spreading technique was something like this:

"Got a match? . . . Thanks. . . . Going to the fights tonight? . . . I hear Ike Bush takes a dive in the sixth. . . . It ought to be straight: I got it from Whisper. . . . Yeah, they all are."

People like inside stuff, and anything that had Thaler's name to it was very inside in Personville. The news spread nicely. Half the men I gave it to worked almost as hard as I did spreading it, just to show they knew what was what.

When I started out, seven to four was being offered that Ike Bush would win, and two to three that he would win by a knock-out. By two o'clock none of the joints taking bets were offering anything better than even money, and by half-past three Kid Cooper was a two-to-one favorite.

I made my last stop a lunch counter, where I tossed the news out to a waiter and a couple of customers while eating a hot beef sandwich.

When I went out I found a man waiting by the door for me. He had bowed legs and a long sharp jaw, like a hog's. He nodded and walked down the street beside me, chewing a toothpick and squinting sidewise into my face. At the corner he said:

"I know for a fact that ain't so."

"What?" I asked.

"About Ike Bush flopping. I know for a fact that ain't so."

"Then it oughtn't bother you any. But the wise money's going two to one on Cooper, and he's not that good unless Bush lets him be."

The hog jaw spit out the mangled toothpick and snapped yellow teeth at me.

"He told me his own self that Cooper was a set-up for him, last night, and he wouldn't do nothing like that—not to me."

"Friend of yours?"

"Not exactly, but he knows I— Hey, listen! Did Whisper give you that, on the level?"

"On the level."

He cursed bitterly. "And I put my last thirty-five bucks in the world on that rat on his say-so. Me, that could send him over for—" He broke off and looked down the street.

"Could send him over for what?" I asked.

"Plenty," he said. "Nothing."

I had a suggestion:

"If you've got something on him, maybe we ought to talk it over. I wouldn't mind seeing Bush win, myself. If what you've got is any good, what's the matter with putting it up to him?"

He looked at me, at the sidewalk, fumbled in his vest pocket for another toothpick, put it in his mouth, and mumbled:

"Who are you?"

I gave him a name, something like Hunter or Hunt or Huntington, and asked him his. He said his name was MacSwain, Bob MacSwain, and I could ask anybody in town if it wasn't right.

I said I believed him and asked:

"What do you say? Will we put the squeeze to Bush?"

Little hard lights came into his eyes and died.

"No," he gulped. "I ain't that kind of fellow. I never—"

"You never did anything but let people gyp you. You don't have to go up against him, MacSwain. Give me the dope, and I'll make the play—if it's any good."

He thought that over, licking his lips, letting the toothpick fall down to stick on his coat front.

"You wouldn't let on about me having any part in it?" he asked. "I belong here, and I wouldn't stand a chance if it got out. And you won't turn him up? You'll just use it to make him fight?"

"Right."

He took my hand excitedly and demanded:

"Honest to God?"

"Honest to God."

"His real monicker is Al Kennedy. He was in on the Keystone Trust knock-over in Philly two years ago, when Scissors Haggerty's mob croaked two messengers. Al didn't do the killing, but he was in on the caper. He used to scrap around Philly. The rest of them got copped, but he made the sneak. That's why he's sticking out here in the bushes. That's why he won't never let them put his mug in the papers or on any cards. That's why he's a pork-and-beaner when he's as good as the best. See? This Ike Bush is Al Kennedy that the Philly bulls want for the Keystone trick. See? He was in on the—"

"I see. I see," I stopped the merry-go-round. "The next thing is to get to see him. How do we do that?"

"He flops at the Maxwell, on Union Street. I guess maybe he'd be there now, resting up for the mill."

"Resting for what? He doesn't know he's going to fight. We'll give it a try, though."

"We! We! Where do you get that *we* at? You said—you swore you'd keep me covered."

"Yeah," I said, "I remember that now. What does he look like?"

"A black-headed kid, kind of slim, with one tin ear and eyebrows that run straight across. I don't know if you can make him like it."

"Leave that to me. Where'll I find you afterwards?"

"I'll be hanging around Murry's. Mind you don't tip my mitt. You promised."

The Maxwell was one of a dozen hotels along Union Street with narrow front doors between stores, and shabby stairs leading up to second-story offices. The Maxwell's office was simply a wide place in the hall, with a key- and mail-rack behind a wooden counter that needed paint just as badly. A brass bell and a dirty day-book register were on the counter. Nobody was there.

I had to run back eight pages before I found *Ike Bush, Salt Lake City, 214*, written in the book. The pigeon-hole that had that number was empty. I climbed more steps and knocked on a door that had it. Nothing came of that. I tried it two or three times more and then turned back to the stairs.

Somebody was coming up. I stood at the top, waiting for a look at him. There was just light enough to see by.

He was a slim muscular lad in army shirt, blue suit, gray cap. Black eyebrows made a straight line above his eyes.

I said: "Hello."

He nodded without stopping or saying anything.

"Win tonight?" I asked.

"Hope so," he said shortly, passing me.

I let him take four steps toward his room before I told him: "So do I. I'd hate to have to ship you back to Philly, Al."

He took another step, turned around very slowly, rested a shoulder against the wall, let his eyes get sleepy, and grunted: "Huh?"

"If you were smacked down in the sixth or any other round by a palooka like Kid Cooper, it'd make me peevish," I said. "Don't do it, Al. You don't want to go back to Philly."

The youngster put his chin down in his neck and came back to me. When he was within arm's reach, he stopped, letting his left side turn a bit to the front. His hands were hanging loose. Mine were in my overcoat pockets.

He said, "Huh?" again.

I said:

"Try to remember that—if Ike Bush doesn't turn in a win tonight, Al Kennedy will be riding east in the morning."

He lifted his left shoulder an inch. I moved the gun around in my pocket, enough. He grumbled:

"Where do you get that stuff about me not winning?"

"Just something I heard. I didn't think there was anything in it, except maybe a ducat back to Philly."

"I oughta bust your jaw, you fat crook."

"Now's the time to do it," I advised him. "If you win tonight you're not likely to see me again. If you lose, you'll see me, but your hands won't be loose."

I found MacSwain in Murry's, a Broadway pool room.

"Did you get to him?" he asked.

"Yeah. It's all fixed—if he doesn't blow town, or say something to his backers, or just pay no attention to me, or—"

MacSwain developed a lot of nervousness.

"You better damn sight be careful," he warned me. "They might try to put you out the way. He— I got to see a fellow down the street," and he deserted me.

Poisonville's prize fighting was done in a big wooden ex-casino in what had once been an amusement park on the edge of town. When I got there at eight-thirty, most of the population seemed to be on hand, packed tight in close rows of folding chairs on the main floor, packed tighter on benches in two dinky balconies.

Smoke. Stink. Heat. Noise.

My seat was in the third row, ringside. Moving down to it, I discovered Dan Rolff in an aisle seat not far away, with Dinah Brand beside him. She had had her hair trimmed at last, and marcelled, and looked like a lot of money in a big gray fur coat.

"Get down on Cooper?" she asked after we had swapped hellos.

"No. You playing him heavy?"

"Not as heavy as I'd like. We held off, thinking the odds would get better, but they went to hell."

"Everybody in town seems to know Bush is going to dive," I said. "I saw a hundred put on Cooper at four to one a few minutes ago." I leaned past Rolff and put my mouth close to where the gray fur collar hid the girl's ear, whispering: "The dive is off. Better copper your bets while there's time."

Her big bloodshot eyes went wide and dark with anxiety, greed, curiosity, suspicion.

"You mean it?" she asked huskily.

"Yeah."

She chewed her reddened lips, frowned, asked:

"Where'd you get it?"

I wouldn't say. She chewed her mouth some more and asked:

"Is Max on?"

"I haven't seen him. Is he here?"

"I suppose so," she said absent-mindedly, a distant look in her eyes. Her lips moved as if she were counting to herself.

I said: "Take it or leave it, but it's a gut."

She leaned forward to look sharply into my eyes, clicked

her teeth together, opened her bag, and dragged out a roll of bills the size of a coffee can. Part of the roll she pushed at Rolff.

"Here, Dan, get it down on Bush. You've got an hour anyway to look over the odds."

Rolff took the money and went off on his errand. I took his seat. She put a hand on my forearm and said:

"Christ help you if you've made me drop that dough."

I pretended the idea was ridiculous.

The preliminary bouts got going, four-round affairs between assorted hams. I kept looking for Thaler, but couldn't see him. The girl squirmed beside me, paying little attention to the fighting, dividing her time between asking me where I had got my information and threatening me with hell-fire and damnation if it turned out to be a bust.

The semi-final was on when Rolff came back and gave the girl a handful of tickets. She was straining her eyes over them when I left for my own seat. Without looking up she called to me:

"Wait outside for us when it's over."

Kid Cooper climbed into the ring while I was squeezing through to my seat. He was a ruddy straw-haired solid-built boy with a dented face and too much meat around the top of his lavender trunks. Ike Bush, alias Al Kennedy, came through the ropes in the opposite corner. His body looked better—slim, nicely ridged, snaky—but his face was pale, worried.

They were introduced, went to the center of the ring for the usual instructions, returned to their corners, shed bath robes, stretched on the ropes, the gong rang, and the scrap was on.

Cooper was a clumsy bum. He had a pair of wide swings that might have hurt when they landed, but anybody with two feet could have kept away from them. Bush had class—nimble legs, a smooth fast left hand, and a right that got away quick. It would have been murder to put Cooper in the ring with the slim boy if he had been trying. But he wasn't. That is, he wasn't trying to win. He was trying not to, and had his hands full doing it.

Cooper waddled flat-footed around the ring, throwing his wide swings at everything from the lights to the corner posts.

His system was simply to turn them loose and let them take their chances. Bush moved in and out, putting a glove on the ruddy boy whenever he wanted to, but not putting anything in the glove.

The customers were booing before the first round was over. The second round was just as sour. I didn't feel so good. Bush didn't seem to have been much influenced by our little conversation. Out of the corner of my eye I could see Dinah Brand trying to catch my attention. She looked hot. I took care not to have my attention caught.

The room-mate act in the ring was continued in the third round to the tune of yelled Throw-em-outs, Why-don't-you-kiss-hims and Make-em-fights from the seats. The pugs' waltz brought them around to the corner nearest me just as the booing broke off for a moment.

I made a megaphone of my hands and bawled:

"Back to Philly, Al."

Bush's back was to me. He wrestled Cooper around, shoving him into the ropes, so he—Bush—faced my way.

From somewhere far back in another part of the house another yelling voice came:

"Back to Philly, Al."

MacSwain, I supposed.

A drunk off to one side lifted his puffy face and bawled the same thing, laughing as if it were a swell joke. Others took up the cry for no reason at all except that it seemed to disturb Bush.

His eyes jerked from side to side under the black bar of his eyebrows.

One of Cooper's wild mitts clouted the slim boy on the side of the jaw.

Ike Bush piled down at the referee's feet.

The referee counted five in two seconds, but the gong cut him off.

I looked over at Dinah Brand and laughed. There wasn't anything else to do. She looked at me and didn't laugh. Her face was sick as Dan Rolff's, but angrier.

Bush's handlers dragged him into his corner and rubbed him up, not working very hard at it. He opened his eyes and watched his feet. The gong was tapped.

Kid Cooper paddled out hitching up his trunks. Bush waited until the bum was in the center of the ring, and then came to him, fast.

Bush's left glove went down, out—practically out of sight in Cooper's belly. Cooper said, "Ugh," and backed away, folding up.

Bush straightened him with a right-hand poke in the mouth, and sank the left again. Cooper said, "Ugh," again and had trouble with his knees.

Bush cuffed him once on each side of the head, cocked his right, carefully pushed Cooper's face into position with a long left, and threw his right hand straight from under his jaw to Cooper's.

Everybody in the house felt the punch.

Cooper hit the floor, bounced, and settled there. It took the referee half a minute to count ten seconds. It would have been just the same if he had taken half an hour. Kid Cooper was out.

When the referee had finally stalled through the count, he raised Bush's hand. Neither of them looked happy.

A high twinkle of light caught my eye. A short silvery streak slanted down from one of the small balconies.

A woman screamed.

The silvery streak ended its flashing slant in the ring, with a sound that was partly a thud, partly a snap.

Ike Bush took his arm out of the referee's hand and pitched down on top of Kid Cooper. A black knife-handle stuck out of the nape of Bush's neck.

CHAPTER X

Crime Wanted—Male or Female

HALF AN HOUR later, when I left the building, Dinah
Brand was sitting at the wheel of a pale blue little Marmon, talking to Max Thaler, who stood in the road.

The girl's square chin was tilted up. Her big red mouth was
brutal around the words it shaped, and the lines crossing its
ends were deep, hard.

The gambler looked as unpleasant as she. His pretty face
was yellow and tough as oak. When he talked his lips were
paper-thin.

It seemed to be a nice family party. I wouldn't have joined
it if the girl hadn't seen me and called:

"My God, I thought you were never coming."

I went over to the car. Thaler looked across the hood at me
with no friendliness at all.

"Last night I advised you to go back to Frisco." His whisper was harsher than anybody's shout could have been. "Now
I'm telling you."

"Thanks just the same," I said as I got in beside the
girl.

While she was stirring the engine up he said to her:

"This isn't the first time you've sold me out. It's the last."

She put the car in motion, turned her head back over her
shoulder, and sang to him:

"To hell, my love, with you!"

We rode into town rapidly.

"Is Bush dead?" she asked as she twisted the car into
Broadway.

"Decidedly. When they turned him over the point of the
knife was sticking out in front."

"He ought to have known better than to double-cross
them. Let's get something to eat. I'm almost eleven hundred
ahead on the night's doings, so if the boy friend doesn't like
it, it's just too bad. How'd you come out?"

"Didn't bet. So your Max doesn't like it?"

"Didn't bet?" she cried. "What kind of an ass are you?

Whoever heard of anybody not betting when they had a thing like that sewed up?"

"I wasn't sure it was sewed up. So Max didn't like the way things turned out?"

"You guessed it. He dropped plenty. And then he gets sore with me because I had sense enough to switch over and get in on the win." She stopped the car violently in front of a Chinese restaurant. "The hell with him, the little tin-horn runt!"

Her eyes were shiny because they were wet. She jabbed a handkerchief into them as we got out of the car.

"My God, I'm hungry," she said, dragging me across the sidewalk. "Will you buy me a ton of *chow mein?*"

She didn't eat a ton of it, but she did pretty well, putting away a piled-up dish of her own and half of mine. Then we got back into the Marmon and rode out to her house.

Dan Rolff was in the dining room. A water glass and a brown bottle with no label stood on the table in front of him. He sat straight up in his chair, staring at the bottle. The room smelled of laudanum.

Dinah Brand slid her fur coat off, letting it fall half on a chair and half on the floor, and snapped her fingers at the lunger, saying impatiently:

"Did you collect?"

Without looking up from the bottle, he took a pad of paper money out of his inside coat pocket and dropped it on the table. The girl grabbed it, counted the bills twice, smacked her lips, and stuffed the money in her bag.

She went out to the kitchen and began chopping ice. I sat down and lit a cigarette. Rolff stared at his bottle. He and I never seemed to have much to say to one another. Presently the girl brought in some gin, lemon juice, seltzer and ice.

We drank and she told Rolff:

"Max is sore as hell. He heard you'd been running around putting last-minute money on Bush, and the little monkey thinks I double-crossed him. What did I have to do with it? All I did was what any sensible person would have done—get in on the win. I didn't have any more to do with it than a baby, did I?" she asked me.

"No."

"Of course not. What's the matter with Max is he's afraid the others will think he was in on it too, that Dan was putting his dough down as well as mine. Well, that's his hard luck. He can go climb trees for all I care, the lousy little runt. Another drink would go good."

She poured another for herself and for me. Rolff hadn't touched his first one. He said, still staring at the brown bottle:

"You can hardly expect him to be hilarious about it."

The girl scowled and said disagreeably:

"I can expect anything I want. And he's got no right to talk to me that way. He doesn't own me. Maybe he thinks he does, but I'll show him different." She emptied her glass, banged it on the table, and twisted around in her chair to face me. "Is that on the level about your having ten thousand dollars of Elihu Willsson's money to use cleaning up the city?"

"Yeah."

Her bloodshot eyes glistened hungrily.

"And if I help you will I get some of the ten—?"

"You can't do that, Dinah." Rolff's voice was thick, but gently firm, as if he were talking to a child. "That would be utterly filthy."

The girl turned her face slowly toward him. Her mouth took on the look it had worn while talking to Thaler.

"I am going to do it," she said. "That makes me utterly filthy, does it?"

He didn't say anything, didn't look up from the bottle. Her face got red, hard, cruel. Her voice was soft, cooing:

"It's just too bad that a gentleman of your purity, even if he is a bit consumptive, has to associate with a filthy bum like me."

"That can be remedied," he said slowly, getting up. He was laudanumed to the scalp.

Dinah Brand jumped out of her chair and ran around the table to him. He looked at her with blank dopey eyes. She put her face close to his and demanded:

"So I'm too utterly filthy for you now, am I?"

He said evenly:

"I said to betray your friends to this chap would be utterly filthy, and it would."

She caught one of his thin wrists and twisted it until he was on his knees. Her other hand, open, beat his hollow-cheeked face, half a dozen times on each side, rocking his head from side to side. He could have put his free arm up to protect his face, but didn't.

She let go his wrist, turned her back on him, and reached for gin and seltzer. She was smiling. I didn't like the smile.

He got up, blinking. His wrist was red where she had held it, his face bruised. He steadied himself upright and looked at me with dull eyes.

With no change in the blankness of his face and eyes, he put a hand under his coat, brought out a black automatic pistol, and fired at me.

But he was too shaky for either speed or accuracy. I had time to toss a glass at him. The glass hit his shoulder. His bullet went somewhere overhead.

I jumped before he got the next one out—jumped at him—was close enough to knock the gun down. The second slug went into the floor.

I socked his jaw. He fell away from me and lay where he fell.

I turned around.

Dinah Brand was getting ready to bat me over the head with the seltzer bottle, a heavy glass siphon that would have made pulp of my skull.

"Don't," I yelped.

"You didn't have to bust him like that," she snarled.

"Well, it's done. You'd better get him straightened out."

She put down the siphon and I helped her carry him up to his bedroom. When he began moving his eyes, I left her to finish the work and went down to the dining room again. She joined me there fifteen minutes later.

"He's all right," she said. "But you could have handled him without that."

"Yeah, but I did that for him. Know why he took the shot at me?"

"So I'd have nobody to sell Max out to?"

"No. Because I'd seen you maul him around."

"That doesn't make sense to me," she said. "I was the one who did it."

"He's in love with you, and this isn't the first time you've done it. He acted like he had learned there was no use matching muscle with you. But you can't expect him to enjoy having another man see you slap his face."

"I used to think I knew men," she complained, "but, by God! I don't. They're lunatics, all of them."

"So I poked him to give him back some of his self-respect. You know, treated him as I would a man instead of a down-and-outer who could be slapped around by girls."

"Anything you say," she sighed. "I give it up. We ought to have a drink."

We had the drink, and I said:

"You were saying you'd work with me if there was a cut of the Willsson money in it for you. There is."

"How much?"

"Whatever you earn. Whatever what you do is worth."

"That's uncertain."

"So's your help, so far as I know."

"Is it? I can give you the stuff, brother, loads of it, and don't think I can't. I'm a girl who knows her Poisonville." She looked down at her gray-stockinged knees, waved one leg at me, and exclaimed indignantly: "Look at that. Another run. Did you ever see anything to beat it? Honest to God! I'm going barefoot."

"Your legs are too big," I told her. "They put too much strain on the material."

"That'll do out of you. What's your idea of how to go about purifying our village?"

"If I haven't been lied to, Thaler, Pete the Finn, Lew Yard and Noonan are the men who've made Poisonville the sweet-smelling mess it is. Old Elihu comes in for his share of the blame, too, but it's not all his fault, maybe. Besides, he's my client, even if he doesn't want to be, so I'd like to go easy on him.

"The closest I've got to an idea is to dig up any and all the dirty work I can that might implicate the others, and run it out. Maybe I'll advertise—*Crime Wanted—Male or Female*. If they're as crooked as I think they are I shouldn't have a lot of trouble finding a job or two that I can hang on them."

"Is that what you were up to when you uncooked the fight?"

"That was only an experiment—just to see what would happen."

"So that's the way you scientific detectives work. My God! for a fat, middle-aged, hard-boiled, pig-headed guy, you've got the vaguest way of doing things I ever heard of."

"Plans are all right sometimes," I said. "And sometimes just stirring things up is all right—if you're tough enough to survive, and keep your eyes open so you'll see what you want when it comes to the top."

"That ought to be good for another drink," she said.

CHAPTER XI

The Swell Spoon

W̲E HAD another drink.

She put her glass down, licked her lips, and said:

"If stirring things up is your system, I've got a swell spoon for you. Did you ever hear of Noonan's brother Tim, the one who committed suicide out at Mock Lake a couple of years ago?"

"No."

"You wouldn't have heard much good. Anyway, he didn't commit suicide. Max killed him."

"Yeah?"

"For God's sake wake up. This I'm giving you is real. Noonan was like a father to Tim. Take the proof to him and he'll be after Max like nobody's business. That's what you want, isn't it?"

"We've got proof?"

"Two people got to Tim before he died, and he told them Max had done it. They're both still in town, though one won't live a lot longer. How's that?"

She looked as if she were telling the truth, though with women, especially blue-eyed women, that doesn't always mean anything.

"Let's listen to the rest of it," I said. "I like details and things."

"You'll get them. You ever been out to Mock Lake? Well, it's our summer resort, thirty miles up the canyon road. It's a dump, but it's cool in summer, so it gets a good play. This was summer a year ago, the last week-end in August. I was out there with a fellow named Holly. He's back in England now, but you don't care anything about that, because he's got nothing to do with it. He was a funny sort of old woman—used to wear white silk socks turned inside out so the loose threads wouldn't hurt his feet. I got a letter from him last week. It's around here somewhere, but that doesn't make any difference.

"We were up there, and Max was up there with a girl he

used to play around with—Myrtle Jennison. She's in the hospital now—City—dying of Bright's disease or something. She was a classy looking kid then, a slender blonde. I always liked her, except that a few drinks made her too noisy. Tim Noonan was crazy about her, but she couldn't see anybody but Max that summer.

"Tim wouldn't let her alone. He was a big good-looking Irishman, but a sap and a cheap crook who only got by because his brother was chief of police. Wherever Myrtle went, he'd pop up sooner or later. She didn't like to say anything to Max about it, not wanting Max to do anything to put him in wrong with Tim's brother, the chief.

"So of course Tim showed up at Mock Lake this Saturday. Myrtle and Max were just by themselves. Holly and I were with a bunch, but I saw Myrtle to talk to and she told me she had got a note from Tim, asking her to meet him for a few minutes that night, in one of the little arbor things on the hotel grounds. He said if she didn't he would kill himself. That was a laugh for us—the big false alarm. I tried to talk Myrtle out of going, but she had just enough booze in her to feel gay and she said she was going to give him an earful.

"We were all dancing in the hotel that night. Max was there for a while, and then I didn't see him any more. Myrtle was dancing with a fellow named Rutgers, a lawyer here in town. After a while she left him and went out one of the side doors. She winked at me when she passed, so I knew she was going down to see Tim. She had just got out when I heard the shot. Nobody else paid any attention to it. I suppose I wouldn't have noticed it either if I hadn't known about Myrtle and Tim.

"I told Holly I wanted to see Myrtle, and went out after her, by myself. I must have been about five minutes behind her in getting out. When I got outside I saw lights down by one of the summer houses, and people. I went down there, and— This talking is thirsty work."

I poured out a couple of hookers of gin. She went into the kitchen for another siphon and more ice. We mixed them up, drank, and she settled down to her tale again:

"There was Tim Noonan, dead, with a hole in his temple and his gun lying beside him. Perhaps a dozen people were standing around, hotel people, visitors, one of Noonan's men, a dick named MacSwain. As soon as Myrtle saw me she took me away from the crowd, back in the shade of some trees.

" 'Max killed him,' she said. 'What'll I do?'

"I asked her about it. She told me she had seen the flash of the gun and at first she thought Tim had killed himself after all. She was too far away and it was too dark for her to see anything else. When she ran down to him, he was rolling around, moaning, 'He didn't have to kill me over her. I'd have—' She couldn't make out the rest of it. He was rolling around, bleeding from the hole in his temple.

"Myrtle was afraid Max had done it, but she had to be sure, so she knelt down and tried to pick up Tim's head, asking: 'Who did it, Tim?'

"He was almost gone, but before he passed out he got enough strength to tell her, 'Max!'

"She kept asking me, 'What'll I do?' I asked her if anybody else had heard Tim, and she said the dick had. He came running up while she was trying to lift Tim's head. She didn't think anybody else had been near enough to hear, but the dick had.

"I didn't want Max to get in a jam over killing a mutt like Tim Noonan. Max didn't mean anything to me then, except that I liked him, and I didn't like any of the Noonans. I knew the dick—MacSwain. I used to know his wife. He had been a pretty good guy, straight as ace-deuce-trey-four-five, till he got on the force. Then he went the way of the rest of them. His wife stood as much of it as she could and then left him.

"Knowing this dick, I told Myrtle I thought we could fix things. A little jack would ruin MacSwain's memory, or, if he didn't like that, Max could have him knocked off. She had Tim's note threatening suicide. If the dick would play along, the hole in Tim's head from his own gun and the note would smooth everything over pretty.

"I left Myrtle under the trees and went out to hunt for Max. He wasn't around. There weren't many people there, and I could hear the hotel orchestra still playing dance music. I couldn't find Max, so I went back to Myrtle. She was all worked up over another idea. She didn't want Max to know that she had found out that he had killed Tim. She was afraid of him.

"See what I mean? She was afraid that if she and Max ever broke off he'd put her out of the way if he knew she had enough on him to swing him. I know how she felt. I got the same notion later, and kept just as quiet as she did. So we figured that if it could be fixed up without his knowing about it, so much the better. I didn't want to show in it either.

"Myrtle went back alone to the group around Tim and got hold of MacSwain. She took him off a little way and made the deal with him. She had some dough on her. She gave him two hundred and a diamond ring that had cost a fellow named Boyle a thousand. I thought he'd be back for more later, but he didn't. He shot square with her. With the help of the letter he put over the suicide story.

"Noonan knew there was something fishy about the layout, but he could never peg it. I think he suspected Max of having something to do with it. But Max had an air-tight alibi—trust him for that—and I think even Noonan finally counted him out. But Noonan never believed it happened the way it was made to look. He broke MacSwain—kicked him off the force.

"Max and Myrtle slid apart a little while after that. No row or anything—they just slid apart. I don't think she ever felt easy around him again, though so far as I know he never suspected her of knowing anything. She's sick now, as I told you, and hasn't got long to live. I think she'd not so much mind telling the truth if she were asked. MacSwain's still hanging around town. He'd talk if there was something in it for him. Those two have got the stuff on Max—and wouldn't Noonan eat it up! Is that good enough to give your stirring-up a start?"

"Couldn't it have been suicide?" I asked. "With Tim Noonan getting a last-minute bright idea to stick it on Max?"

"That four-flusher shoot himself? Not a chance."

"Could Myrtle have shot him?"

"Noonan didn't overlook that one. But she couldn't have been a third of the distance down the slope when the shot was fired. Tim had powder-marks on his head, and hadn't been shot and rolled down the slope. Myrtle's out."

"But Max had an alibi?"

"Yes, indeed. He always has. He was in the hotel bar, on the other side of the building, all the time. Four men said so. As I remember it, they said it openly and often, long before anybody asked them. There were other men in the bar who didn't remember whether Max had been there or not, but those four remembered. They'd remember anything Max wanted remembered."

Her eyes got large and then narrowed to black-fringed slits. She leaned toward me, upsetting her glass with an elbow.

"Peak Murry was one of the four. He and Max are on the outs now. Peak might tell it straight now. He's got a pool room on Broadway."

"This MacSwain, does he happen to be named Bob?" I asked. "A bow-legged man with a long jaw like a hog's?"

"Yes. You know him?"

"By sight. What does he do now?"

"A small-time grifter. What do you think of the stack-up?"

"Not bad. Maybe I can use it."

"Then let's talk scratch."

I grinned at the greed in her eyes and said:

"Not just yet, sister. We'll have to see how it works out before we start scattering pennies around."

She called me a damned nickel-nurser and reached for the gin.

"No more for me, thanks," I told her, looking at my watch. "It's getting along toward five a.m. and I've got a busy day ahead."

She decided she was hungry again. That reminded me that I was. It took half an hour or more to get waffles, ham and coffee off the stove. It took some more time to get them into our stomachs and to smoke some cigarettes over extra cups of coffee. It was quite a bit after six when I got ready to leave.

I went back to my hotel and got into a tub of cold water. It braced me a lot, and I needed bracing. At forty I could get along on gin as a substitute for sleep, but not comfortably.

When I had dressed I sat down and composed a document:

> Just before he died, Tim Noonan told me he had
> been shot by Max Thaler. Detective Bob MacSwain
> heard him tell me. I gave Detective MacSwain $200 and
> a diamond ring worth $1,000 to keep quiet and make it
> look like suicide.

With this document in my pocket I went downstairs, had another breakfast that was mostly coffee, and went up to the City Hospital.

Visiting hours were in the afternoon, but by flourishing my Continental Detective Agency credentials and giving everybody to understand that an hour's delay might cause thousands of deaths, or words to that effect, I got to see Myrtle Jennison.

She was in a ward on the third floor, alone. The other four beds were empty. She could have been a girl of twenty-five or a woman of fifty-five. Her face was a bloated spotty mask. Lifeless yellow hair in two stringy braids lay on the pillow beside her.

I waited until the nurse who had brought me up left. Then I held my document out to the invalid and said:

"Will you sign this, please, Miss Jennison?"

She looked at me with ugly eyes that were shaded into no particular dark color by the pads of flesh around them, then at the document, and finally brought a shapeless fat hand from under the covers to take it.

She pretended it took her nearly five minutes to read the forty-two words I had written. She let the document fall down on the covers and asked:

"Where'd you get that?" Her voice was tinny, irritable.

"Dinah Brand sent me to you."

She asked eagerly:

"Has she broken off with Max?"

"Not that I know of," I lied. "I imagine she just wants to have this on hand in case it should come in handy."

"And get her fool throat slit. Give me a pencil."

I gave her my fountain pen and held my notebook under the document, to stiffen it while she scribbled her signature at the bottom, and to have it in my hands as soon as she had finished. While I fanned the paper dry she said:

"If that's what she wants it's all right with me. What do I care what anybody does now? I'm done. Hell with them all!" She sniggered and suddenly threw the bedclothes down to her knees, showing me a horrible swollen body in a coarse white nightgown. "How do you like me? See, I'm done."

I pulled the covers up over her again and said:

"Thanks for this, Miss Jennison."

"That's all right. It's nothing to me any more. Only"—her puffy chin quivered—"it's hell to die ugly as this."

CHAPTER XII

A New Deal

I WENT OUT to hunt for MacSwain. Neither city directory nor telephone book told me anything. I did the pool rooms, cigar stores, speakeasies, looking around first, then asking cautious questions. That got me nothing. I walked the streets, looking for bowed legs. That got me nothing. I decided to go back to my hotel, grab a nap, and resume the hunting at night.

In a far corner of the lobby a man stopped hiding behind a newspaper and came out to meet me. He had bowed legs, a hog jaw, and was MacSwain.

I nodded carelessly at him and walked on toward the elevators. He followed me, mumbling:

"Hey, you got a minute?"

"Yeah, just about." I stopped, pretending indifference.

"Let's get out of sight," he said nervously.

I took him up to my room. He straddled a chair and put a match in his mouth. I sat on the side of the bed and waited for him to say something. He chewed his match a while and began:

"I'm going to come clean with you, brother. I'm—"

"You mean you're going to tell me you knew me when you braced me yesterday?" I asked. "And you're going to tell me Bush hadn't told you to bet on him? And you didn't until afterwards? And you knew about his record because you used to be a bull? And you thought if you could get me to put it to him you could clean up a little dough playing him?"

"I'll be damned if I was going to come through with that much," he said "but since it's been said I'll put a yes to it."

"Did you clean up?"

"I win myself six hundred iron men." He pushed his hat back and scratched his forehead with the chewed end of his match. "And then I lose myself that and my own two hundred and some in a crap game. What do you think of that? I pick up six hundred berries like shooting fish, and have to bum four bits for breakfast."

I said it was a tough break but that was the kind of a world we lived in.

He said, "Uh-huh," put the match back in his mouth, ground it some more, and added: "That's why I thought I'd come to see you. I used to be in the racket myself and—"

"What did Noonan put the skids under you for?"

"Skids? What skids? I quit. I come into a piece of change when the wife got killed in an automobile accident—insurance—and I quit."

"I heard he kicked you out the time his brother shot himself."

"Well, then you heard wrong. It was just after that, but you can ask him if I didn't quit."

"It's not that much to me. Go on telling me why you came to see me."

"I'm busted, flat. I know you're a Continental op, and I got a pretty good hunch what you're up to here. I'm close to a lot that's going on on both sides of things in this burg. There's things I could do for you, being an ex-dick, knowing the ropes both ways."

"You want to stool-pigeon for me?"

He looked me straight in the eye and said evenly:

"There's no sense in a man picking out the worst name he can find for everything."

"I'll give you something to do, MacSwain." I took out Myrtle Jennison's document and passed it to him. "Tell me about that."

He read it through carefully, his lips framing the words, the match wavering up and down in his mouth. He got up, put the paper on the bed beside me, and scowled down at it.

"There's something I'll have to find out about first," he said, very solemnly. "I'll be back in a little while and give you the whole story."

I laughed and told him:

"Don't be silly. You know I'm not going to let you walk out on me."

"I don't know that." He shook his head, still solemn. "Neither do you. All you know is whether you're going to try to stop me."

"The answer's yeah," I said while I considered that he was

fairly hard and strong, six or seven years younger than I, and twenty or thirty pounds lighter.

He stood at the foot of the bed and looked at me with solemn eyes. I sat on the side of the bed and looked at him with whatever kind of eyes I had at the time. We did this for nearly three minutes.

I used part of the time measuring the distance between us, figuring out how, by throwing my body back on the bed and turning on my hip, I could get my heels in his face if he jumped me. He was too close for me to pull the gun. I had just finished this mental map-making when he spoke:

"That lousy ring wasn't worth no grand. I did swell to get two centuries for it."

"Sit down and tell me about it."

He shook his head again and said:

"First I want to know what you're meaning to do about it."

"Cop Whisper."

"I don't mean that. I mean with me."

"You'll have to go over to the Hall with me."

"I won't."

"Why not? You're only a witness."

"I'm only a witness that Noonan can hang a bribe-taking, or an accomplice after the act rap on, or both. And he'd be tickled simple to have the chance."

This jaw-wagging didn't seem to be leading anywhere. I said:

"That's too bad. But you're going to see him."

"Try and take me."

I sat up straighter and slid my right hand back to my hip.

He grabbed for me. I threw my body back on the bed, did the hip-spin, swung my feet at him. It was a good trick, only it didn't work. In his hurry to get at me he bumped the bed aside just enough to spill me off on the floor.

I landed all sprawled out on my back. I kept dragging at my gun while I tried to roll under the bed.

Missing me, his lunge carried him over the low footboard, over the side of the bed. He came down beside me, on the back of his neck, his body somersaulting over.

I put the muzzle of my gun in his left eye and said:

"You're making a fine pair of clowns of us. Be still while I get up or I'll make an opening in your head for brains to leak in."

I got up, found and pocketed my document, and let him get up.

"Knock the dents out of your hat and put your necktie in front, so you won't disgrace me going through the streets," I ordered after I had run a hand over his clothes and found nothing that felt like a weapon. "You can suit yourself about remembering that this gat is going to be in my overcoat pocket, with a hand on it."

He straightened his hat and tie and said:

"Hey, listen: I'm in this, I guess, and cutting up won't get me nothing. Suppose I be good. Could you forget about the tussle? See—maybe it'd be smoother for me if they thought I come along without being dragged."

"O.K."

"Thanks, brother."

Noonan was out eating. We had to wait half an hour in his outer office. When he came in he greeted me with the usual *How are you? . . . That certainly is fine . . .* and the rest of it. He didn't say anything to MacSwain—simply eyed him sourly.

We went into the chief's private office. He pulled a chair over to his desk for me and then sat in his own, ignoring the ex-dick.

I gave Noonan the sick girl's document.

He gave it one glance, bounced out of his chair, and smashed a fist the size of a cantaloup into MacSwain's face.

The punch carried MacSwain across the room until a wall stopped him. The wall creaked under the strain, and a framed photograph of Noonan and other city dignitaries welcoming somebody in spats dropped down to the floor with the hit man.

The fat chief waddled over, picked up the picture and beat it to splinters on MacSwain's head and shoulders.

Noonan came back to his desk, puffing, smiling, saying cheerfully to me:

"That fellow's a rat if there ever was one."

MacSwain sat up and looked around, bleeding from nose, mouth and head.

Noonan roared at him:

"Come here, you."

MacSwain said, "Yes, chief," scrambled up and ran over to the desk.

Noonan said: "Come through or I'll kill you."

MacSwain said:

"Yes, chief. It was like she said, only that rock wasn't worth no grand. But she give me it and the two hundred to keep my mouth shut, because I got there just when she asks him, 'Who did it, Tim?' and he says, 'Max!' He says it kind of loud and sharp, like he wanted to get it out before he died, because he died right then, almost before he'd got it out. That's the way it was, chief, but the rock wasn't worth no—"

"Damn the rock," Noonan barked. "And stop bleeding on my rug."

MacSwain hunted in his pocket for a dirty handkerchief, mopped his nose and mouth with it, and jabbered on:

"That's the way it was, chief. Everything else was like I said at the time, only I didn't say anything about hearing him say Max done it. I know I hadn't ought to—"

"Shut up," Noonan said, and pressed one of the buttons on his desk.

A uniformed copper came in. The chief jerked a thumb at MacSwain and said:

"Take this baby down cellar and let the wrecking crew work on him before you lock him up."

MacSwain started a desperate plea, "Aw, chief!" but the copper took him away before he could get any farther.

Noonan stuck a cigar at me, tapped the document with another and asked:

"Where's this broad?"

"In the City Hospital, dying. You'll have the 'cuter get a stiff out of her? That one's not so good legally—I framed it for effect. Another thing—I hear that Peak Murry and Whisper aren't playmates any more. Wasn't Murry one of his alibis?"

The chief said, "He was," picked up one of his phones, said, "McGraw," and then: "Get hold of Peak Murry and ask him to drop in. And have Tony Agosti picked up for that knife-throwing."

He put the phone down, stood up, made a lot of cigar smoke, and said through it:

"I haven't always been on the up-and-up with you."

I thought that was putting it mildly, but I didn't say anything while he went on:

"You know your way around. You know what these jobs are. There's this one and that one that's got to be listened to. Just because a man's chief of police doesn't mean he's chief. Maybe you're a lot of trouble to somebody that can be a lot of trouble to me. Don't make any difference if I think you're a right guy. I got to play with them that play with me. See what I mean?"

I wagged my head to show I did.

"That's the way it was," he said. "But no more. This is something else, a new deal. When the old woman kicked off Tim was just a lad. She said to me, 'Take care of him, John,' and I promised I would. And then Whisper murders him on account of that tramp." He reached down and took my hand. "See what I'm getting at? That's a year and a half ago, and you give me my first chance to hang it on him. I'm telling you there's no man in Personville that's got a voice big enough to talk you down. Not after today."

That pleased me and I said so. We purred at each other until a lanky man with an extremely up-turned nose in the middle of a round and freckled face was ushered in. It was Peak Murry.

"We were just wondering about the time when Tim died," the chief said when Murry had been given a chair and a cigar, "where Whisper was. You were out to the Lake that night, weren't you?"

"Yep," Murry said and the end of his nose got sharper.

"With Whisper?"

"I wasn't with him all the time."

"Were you with him at the time of the shooting?"

"Nope."

The chief's greenish eyes got smaller and brighter. He asked softly:

"You know where he was?"

"Nope."

The chief sighed in a thoroughly satisfied way and leaned back in his chair.

"Damn it, Peak," he said, "you told us before that you were with him at the bar."

"Yep, I did," the lanky man admitted. "But that don't mean nothing except that he asked me to and I didn't mind helping out a friend."

"Meaning you don't mind standing a perjury rap?"

"Don't kid me." Murry spit vigorously at the cuspidor. "I didn't say nothing in no court rooms."

"How about Jerry and George Kelly and O'Brien?" the chief asked. "Did they say they were with him just because he asked them to?"

"O'Brien did. I don't know nothing about the others. I was going out of the bar when I run into Whisper, Jerry and Kelly, and went back to have a shot with them. Kelly told me Tim had been knocked off. Then Whisper says, 'It never hurts anybody to have an alibi. We were here all the time, weren't we?' and he looks at O'Brien, who's behind the bar. O'Brien says, 'Sure you was,' and when Whisper looks at me I say the same thing. But I don't know no reasons why I've got to cover him up nowadays."

"And Kelly said Tim had been knocked off? Didn't say he had been found dead?"

" 'Knocked off' was the words he used."

The chief said:

"Thanks, Peak. You oughtn't to have done like you did, but what's done is done. How are the kids?"

Murry said they were doing fine, only the baby wasn't as fat as he'd like to have him. Noonan phoned the prosecuting attorney's office and had Dart and a stenographer take Peak's story before he left.

Noonan, Dart and the stenographer set out for the City Hospital to get a complete statement from Myrtle Jennison. I didn't go along. I decided I needed sleep, told the chief I would see him later, and returned to the hotel.

CHAPTER XIII

—*$200.10*—

I HAD my vest unbuttoned when the telephone bell rang. It was Dinah Brand, complaining that she had been trying to get me since ten o'clock.

"Have you done anything on what I told you?" she asked.

"I've been looking it over. It seems pretty good. I think maybe I'll crack it this afternoon."

"Don't. Hold it till I see you. Can you come up now?"

I looked at the vacant white bed and said, "Yes," without much enthusiasm.

Another tub of cold water did me so little good that I almost fell asleep in it.

Dan Rolff let me in when I rang the girl's bell. He looked and acted as if nothing out of the ordinary had happened the night before. Dinah Brand came into the hall to help me off with my overcoat. She had on a tan woolen dress with a two-inch rip in one shoulder seam.

She took me into the living room. She sat on the Chesterfield beside me and said:

"I'm going to ask you to do something for me. You like me enough, don't you?"

I admitted that. She counted the knuckles of my left hand with a warm forefinger and explained:

"I want you to not do anything more about what I told you last night. Now wait a minute. Wait till I get through. Dan was right. I oughtn't sell Max out like that. It would be utterly filthy. Besides, it's Noonan you chiefly want, isn't it? Well, if you'll be a nice darling and lay off Max this time, I'll give you enough on Noonan to nail him forever. You'd like that better, wouldn't you? And you like me too much to want to take advantage of me by using information I gave you when I was mad at what Max had said, don't you?"

"What is the dirt on Noonan?" I asked.

She kneaded my biceps and murmured: "You promise?"

"Not yet."

She pouted at me and said:

"I'm off Max for life, on the level. You've got no right to make me turn rat."

"What about Noonan?"

"Promise first."

"No."

She dug fingers into my arm and asked sharply:

"You've already gone to Noonan?"

"Yeah."

She let go my arm, frowned, shrugged, and said gloomily:

"Well, how can I help it?"

I stood up and a voice said:

"Sit down."

It was a hoarse whispering voice—Thaler's.

I turned to see him standing in the dining room doorway, a big gun in one of his little hands. A red-faced man with a scarred cheek stood behind him.

The other doorway—opening to the hall—filled as I sat down. The loose-mouthed chinless man I had heard Whisper call Jerry came a step through it. He had a couple of guns. The more angular one of the blond kids who had been in the King Street joint looked over his shoulder.

Dinah Brand got up from the Chesterfield, put her back to Thaler, and addressed me. Her voice was husky with rage.

"This is none of my doing. He came here by himself, said he was sorry for what he had said, and showed me how we could make a lot of coin by turning Noonan up for you. The whole thing was a plant, but I fell for it. Honest to Christ! He was to wait upstairs while I put it to you. I didn't know anything about the others. I didn't—"

Jerry's casual voice drawled:

"If I shoot a pin from under her, she'll sure sit down, and maybe shut up. O.K.?"

I couldn't see Whisper. The girl was between us. He said:

"Not now. Where's Dan?"

The angular blond youngster said:

"Up on the bathroom floor. I had to sap him."

Dinah Brand turned around to face Thaler. Stocking seams made s's up the ample backs of her legs. She said:

"Max Thaler, you're a lousy little—"

He whispered, very deliberately:

"Shut up and get out of the way."

She surprised me by doing both, and she kept quiet while he spoke to me:

"So you and Noonan are trying to paste his brother's death on me?"

"It doesn't need pasting. It's a natural."

He curved his thin lips at me and said:

"You're as crooked as he is."

I said:

"You know better. I played your side when he tried to frame you. This time he's got you copped to rights."

Dinah Brand flared up again, waving her arms in the center of the room, storming:

"Get out of here, the whole lot of you. Why should I give a God-damn about your troubles? Get out."

The blond kid who had sapped Rolff squeezed past Jerry and came grinning into the room. He caught one of the girl's flourished arms and bent it behind her.

She twisted toward him, socked him in the belly with her other fist. It was a very respectable wallop—man-size. It broke his grip on her arm, sent him back a couple of steps.

The kid gulped a wide mouthful of air, whisked a blackjack from his hip, and stepped in again. His grin was gone.

Jerry laughed what little chin he had out of sight.

Thaler whispered harshly: "Lay off!"

The kid didn't hear him. He was snarling at the girl.

She watched him with a face hard as a silver dollar. She was standing with most of her weight on her left foot. I guessed blondy was going to stop a kick when he closed in.

The kid feinted a grab with his empty left hand, started the blackjack at her face.

Thaler whispered, "Lay off," again, and fired.

The bullet smacked blondy under the right eye, spun him around, and dropped him backwards into Dinah Brand's arms.

This looked like the time, if there was to be any.

In the excitement I had got my hand to my hip. Now I yanked the gun out and snapped a cap at Thaler, trying for his shoulder.

That was wrong. If I had tried for a bulls-eye I would have winged him. Chinless Jerry hadn't laughed himself blind. He beat me to the shot. His shot burnt my wrist, throwing me off the target. But, missing Thaler, my slug crumpled the red-faced man behind him.

Not knowing how badly my wrist was nicked, I switched the gun to my left hand.

Jerry had another try at me. The girl spoiled it by heaving the corpse at him. The dead yellow head banged into his knees. I jumped for him while he was off-balance.

The jump took me out of the path of Thaler's bullet. It also tumbled me and Jerry out into the hall, all tangled up together.

Jerry wasn't tough to handle, but I had to work quick. There was Thaler behind me. I socked Jerry twice, kicked him, butted him at least once, and was hunting for a place to bite when he went limp under me. I poked him again where his chin should have been—just to make sure he wasn't faking—and went away on hands and knees, down the hall a bit, out of line with the door.

I sat on my heels against the wall, held my gun level at Thaler's part of the premises, and waited. I couldn't hear anything for the moment except blood singing in my head.

Dinah Brand stepped out of the door I had tumbled through, looked at Jerry, then at me. She smiled with her tongue between her teeth, beckoned with a jerk of her head, and returned to the living room. I followed her cautiously.

Whisper stood in the center of the floor. His hands were empty and so was his face. Except for his vicious little mouth he looked like something displaying suits in a clothing store window.

Dan Rolff stood behind him, with a gun-muzzle tilted to the little gambler's left kidney. Rolff's face was mostly blood. The blond kid—now dead on the floor between Rolff and me—had sapped him plenty.

I grinned at Thaler and said, "Well, this is nice," before I saw that Rolff had another gun, centered on my chubby middle. That wasn't so nice. But my gun was reasonably level in my hand. I didn't have much worse than an even break.

Rolff said:

"Put down your pistol."

I looked at Dinah, looked puzzled, I suppose. She shrugged and told me:

"It seems to be Dan's party."

"Yeah? Somebody ought to tell him I don't like to play this way."

Rolff repeated: "Put down your pistol."

I said disagreeably:

"I'm damned if I will. I've shed twenty pounds trying to nab this bird, and I can spare twenty more for the same purpose."

Rolff said:

"I'm not interested in what is between you two, and I have no intention of giving either of you—"

Dinah Brand had wandered across the room. When she was behind Rolff, I interrupted his speech by telling her:

"If you upset him now you're sure of making two friends— Noonan and me. You can't trust Thaler any more, so there's no use helping him."

She laughed and said:

"Talk money, darling."

"Dinah!" Rolff protested. He was caught. She was behind him and she was strong enough to handle him. It wasn't likely that he would shoot her, and it wasn't likely that anything else would keep her from doing whatever she decided to do.

"A hundred dollars," I bid.

"My God!" she exclaimed, "I've actually got a cash offer out of you. But not enough."

"Two hundred."

"You're getting reckless. But I still can't hear you."

"Try," I said. "It's worth that to me not to have to shoot Rolff's gun out of his hand, but no more than that."

"You got a good start. Don't weaken. One more bid, anyway."

"Two hundred dollars and ten cents and that's all."

"You big bum," she said, "I won't do it."

"Suit yourself." I made a face at Thaler and cautioned him: "When what happens happens be damned sure you keep still."

Dinah cried:

"Wait! Are you really going to start something?"

"I'm going to take Thaler out with me, regardless."

"Two hundred and a dime?"

"Yeah."

"Dinah," Rolff called without turning his face from me, "you won't—"

But she laughed, came close to his back, and wound her strong arms around him, pulling his arms down, pinning them to his sides.

I shoved Thaler out of the way with my right arm, and kept my gun on him while I yanked Rolff's weapons out of his hands. Dinah turned the lunger loose.

He took two steps toward the dining room door, said wearily, "There is no—" and collapsed on the floor.

Dinah ran to him. I pushed Thaler through the hall door, past the still sleeping Jerry, and to the alcove beneath the front stairs, where I had seen a phone.

I called Noonan, told him I had Thaler, and where.

"Mother of God!" he said. "Don't kill him till I get there."

CHAPTER XIV

Max

THE NEWS of Whisper's capture spread quickly.
When Noonan, the coppers he had brought along, and I took the gambler and the now conscious Jerry into the City Hall there were at least a hundred people standing around watching us.

All of them didn't look pleased. Noonan's coppers—a shabby lot at best—moved around with whitish strained faces. But Noonan was the most triumphant guy west of the Mississippi. Even the bad luck he had trying to third-degree Whisper couldn't spoil his happiness.

Whisper stood up under all they could give him. He would talk to his lawyer, he said, and to nobody else, and he stuck to it. And, as much as Noonan hated the gambler, here was a prisoner he didn't give the works, didn't turn over to the wrecking crew. Whisper had killed the chief's brother, and the chief hated his guts, but Whisper was still too much somebody in Poisonville to be roughed around.

Noonan finally got tired of playing with his prisoner, and sent him up—the prison was on the City Hall's top floor—to be stowed away. I lit another of the chief's cigars and read the detailed statement he had got from the woman in the hospital. There was nothing in it that I hadn't learned from Dinah and MacSwain.

The chief wanted me to come out to his house for dinner, but I lied out of it, pretending that my wrist—now in a bandage—was bothering me. It was really little more than a burn.

While we were talking about it, a pair of plain-clothes men brought in the red-faced bird who had stopped the slug I had missed Whisper with. It had broken a rib for him, and he had taken a back-door sneak while the rest of us were busy. Noonan's men had picked him up in a doctor's office. The chief failed to get any information out of him, and sent him off to the hospital.

I got up and prepared to leave, saying:

"The Brand girl gave me the tip-off on this. That's why I asked you to keep her and Rolff out of it."

The chief took hold of my left hand for the fifth or sixth time in the past couple of hours.

"If you want her taken care of, that's enough for me," he assured me. "But if she had a hand in turning that bastard up, you can tell her for me that any time she wants anything, all she's got to do is name it."

I said I'd tell her that, and went over to my hotel, thinking about that neat white bed. But it was nearly eight o'clock, and my stomach needed attention. I went into the hotel dining room and had that fixed up.

Then a leather chair tempted me into stopping in the lobby while I burnt a cigar. That led to conversation with a traveling railroad auditor from Denver, who knew a man I knew in St. Louis. Then there was a lot of shooting in the street.

We went to the door and decided that the shooting was in the vicinity of the City Hall. I shook the auditor and moved up that way.

I had done two-thirds of the distance when an automobile came down the street toward me, moving fast, leaking gunfire from the rear.

I backed into an alley entrance and slid my gun loose. The car came abreast. An arc-light brightened two faces in the front of the car. The driver's meant nothing to me. The upper part of the other's was hidden by a pulled-down hat. The lower part was Whisper's.

Across the street was the entrance to another block of my alley, lighted at the far end. Between the light and me, somebody moved just as Whisper's car roared past. The somebody had dodged from behind one shadow that might have been an ash-can to another.

What made me forget Whisper was that the somebody's legs had a bowed look.

A load of coppers buzzed past, throwing lead at the first car.

I skipped across the street, into the section of alley that held a man who might have bowed legs.

If he was my man, it was a fair bet he wasn't armed. I played it that way, moving straight up the slimy middle of the alley, looking into shadows with eyes, ears and nose.

Three-quarters of a block of this, and a shadow broke away from another shadow—a man going pell-mell away from me.

"Stop!" I bawled, pounding my feet after him. "Stop, or I'll plug you, MacSwain."

He ran half a dozen strides farther and stopped, turning.

"Oh, it's you," he said, as if it made any difference who took him back to the hoosegow.

"Yeah," I confessed. "What are all you people doing wandering around loose?"

"I don't know nothing about it. Somebody dynamited the floor out of the can. I dropped through the hole with the rest of them. There was some mugs standing off the bulls. I made the back-trotters with one bunch. Then we split, and I was figuring on cutting over and making the hills. I didn't have nothing to do with it. I just went along when she blew open."

"Whisper was pinched this evening," I told him.

"Hell! Then that's it. Noonan had ought to know he'd never keep that guy screwed up—not in this burg."

We were standing still in the alley where MacSwain had stopped running.

"You know what he was pinched for?" I asked.

"Uh-huh, for killing Tim."

"You know who killed Tim?"

"Huh? Sure, he did."

"You did."

"Huh? What's the matter? You simple?"

"There's a gun in my left hand," I warned him.

"But look here—didn't he tell the broad that Whisper done it? What's the matter with you?"

"He didn't say *Whisper*. I've heard women call Thaler *Max*, but I've never heard a man here call him anything but *Whisper*. Tim didn't say *Max*. He said *MacS*—the first part of *MacSwain*—and died before he could finish it. Don't forget about the gun."

"What would I have killed him for? He was after Whisper's—"

"I haven't got around to that yet," I admitted, "but let's see: You and your wife had busted up. Tim was a ladies' man, wasn't he? Maybe there's something there. I'll have to look it up. What started me thinking about you was that you never tried to get any more money out of the girl."

"Cut it out," he begged. "You know there ain't any sense to it. What would I have hung around afterwards for? I'd have been out getting an alibi, like Whisper."

"Why? You were a dick then. Close by was the spot for you—to see that everything went right—handle it yourself."

"You know damned well it don't hang together, don't make sense. Cut it out, for God's sake."

"I don't mind how goofy it is," I said. "It's something to put to Noonan when we get back. He's likely all broken up over Whisper's crush-out. This will take his mind off it."

MacSwain got down on his knees in the muddy alley and cried:

"Oh, Christ, no! He'd croak me with his hands."

"Get up and stop yelling," I growled. "Now will you give it to me straight?"

He whined: "He'd croak me with his hands."

"Suit yourself. If you won't talk, I will, to Noonan. If you'll come through to me, I'll do what I can for you."

"What can you do?" he asked hopelessly, and started sniveling again. "How do I know you'll try to do anything?"

I risked a little truth on him:

"You said you had a hunch what I'm up to here in Poisonville. Then you ought to know that it's my play to keep Noonan and Whisper split. Letting Noonan think Whisper killed Tim will keep them split. But if you don't want to play with me, come on, we'll play with Noonan."

"You mean you won't tell him?" he asked eagerly. "You promise?"

"I promise you nothing," I said. "Why should I? I've got you with your pants down. Talk to me or Noonan. And make up your mind quick. I'm not going to stand here all night."

He made up his mind to talk to me.

"I don't know how much you know, but it was like you said, my wife fell for Tim. That's what put me on the tramp. You can ask anybody if I wasn't a good guy before that. I was this way: what she wanted I wanted her to have. Mostly what she wanted was tough on me. But I couldn't be any other way. We'd have been a damned sight better off if I could. So I let her move out and put in divorce papers, so she could marry him, thinking he meant to.

"Pretty soon I begin to hear he's chasing this Myrtle Jennison. I couldn't go that. I'd given him his chance with Helen, fair and square. Now he was giving her the air for this Myrtle. I wasn't going to stand for that. Helen wasn't no hanky-panky. It was accidental, though, running into him at the Lake that night. When I saw him go down to them summer houses I went after him. That looked like a good quiet place to have it out.

"I guess we'd both had a little something to drink. Anyway, we had it hot and heavy. When it got too hot for him, he pulled the gun. He was yellow. I grabbed it, and in the tussle it went off. I swear to God I didn't shoot him except like that. It went off while the both of us had our hands on it. I beat it back in some bushes. But when I got in the bushes I could hear him moaning and talking. There was people coming—a girl running down from the hotel, that Myrtle Jennison.

"I wanted to go back and hear what Tim was saying, so I'd know where I stood, but I was leary of being the first one there. So I had to wait till the girl got to him, listening all the time to his squawking, but too far away to make it out. When she got to him, I ran over and got there just as he died trying to say my name.

"I didn't think about that being Whisper's name till she propositioned me with the suicide letter, the two hundred, and the rock. I'd just been stalling around, pretending to get the job lined up—being on the force then—and trying to find out where I stood. Then she makes the play and I know I'm sitting pretty. And that's the way it went till you started digging it up again."

He slopped his feet up and down in the mud and added:

"Next week my wife got killed—an accident. Uh-huh, an accident. She drove the Ford square in front of No. 6 where it comes down the long grade from Tanner and stopped it there."

"Is Mock Lake in this county?" I asked.

"No, Boulder County."

"That's out of Noonan's territory. Suppose I take you over there and hand you to the sheriff?"

"No. He's Senator Keefer's son-in-law—Tom Cook. I might as well be here. Noonan could get to me through Keefer."

"If it happened the way you say, you've got at least an even chance of beating the rap in court."

"They won't give me a chance. I'd have stood it if there'd been a chance in the world of getting an even break—but not with them."

"We're going back to the Hall," I said. "Keep your mouth shut."

Noonan was waddling up and down the floor, cursing the half a dozen bulls who stood around wishing they were somewhere else.

"Here's something I found roaming around," I said, pushing MacSwain forward.

Noonan knocked the ex-detective down, kicked him, and told one of the coppers to take him away.

Somebody called Noonan on the phone. I slipped out without saying, "Good-night," and walked back to the hotel.

Off to the north some guns popped.

A group of three men passed me, shifty-eyed, walking pigeon-toed.

A little farther along, another man moved all the way over to the curb to give me plenty of room to pass. I didn't know him and didn't suppose he knew me.

A lone shot sounded not far away.

As I reached the hotel, a battered black touring car went down the street, hitting fifty at least, crammed to the curtains with men.

I grinned after it. Poisonville was beginning to boil out under the lid, and I felt so much like a native that even the memory of my very un-nice part in the boiling didn't keep me from getting twelve solid end-to-end hours of sleep.

CHAPTER XV

Cedar Hill Inn

Mickey Linehan used the telephone to wake me a little
after noon.

"We're here," he told me. "Where's the reception committee?"

"Probably stopped to get a rope. Check your bags and
come up to the hotel. Room 537. Don't advertise your visit."

I was dressed when they arrived.

Mickey Linehan was a big slob with sagging shoulders and
a shapeless body that seemed to be coming apart at all its
joints. His ears stood out like red wings, and his round red
face usually wore the meaningless smirk of a half-wit. He
looked like a comedian and was.

Dick Foley was a boy-sized Canadian with a sharp irritable
face. He wore high heels to increase his height, perfumed his
handkerchiefs and saved all the words he could.

They were both good operatives.

"What did the Old Man tell you about the job?" I asked
when we had settled into seats. The Old Man was the manager of the Continental's San Francisco branch. He was also
known as Pontius Pilate, because he smiled pleasantly when
he sent us out to be crucified on suicidal jobs. He was a gentle, polite, elderly person with no more warmth in him than a
hangman's rope. The Agency wits said he could spit icicles in
July.

"He didn't seem to know much what it was all about,"
Mickey said, "except that you had wired for help. He said he
hadn't got any reports from you for a couple of days."

"The chances are he'll wait a couple more. Know anything
about this Personville?"

Dick shook his head. Mickey said:

"Only that I've heard parties call it Poisonville like they
meant it."

I told them what I knew and what I had done. The telephone bell interrupted my tale in the last quarter.

Dinah Brand's lazy voice:

"Hello! How's the wrist?"

"Only a burn. What do you think of the crush-out?"

"It's not my fault," she said. "I did my part. If Noonan couldn't hold him, that's just too bad. I'm coming downtown to buy a hat this afternoon. I thought I'd drop in and see you for a couple of minutes if you're going to be there."

"What time?"

"Oh, around three."

"Right, I'll expect you, and I'll have that two hundred and a dime I owe you."

"Do," she said. "That's what I'm coming in for. Ta-ta."

I went back to my seat and my story.

When I had finished, Mickey Linehan whistled and said:

"No wonder you're scared to send in any reports. The Old Man wouldn't do much if he knew what you've been up to, would he?"

"If it works out the way I want it to, I won't have to report all the distressing details," I said. "It's right enough for the Agency to have rules and regulations, but when you're out on a job you've got to do it the best way you can. And anybody that brings any ethics to Poisonville is going to get them all rusty. A report is no place for the dirty details, anyway, and I don't want you birds to send any writing back to San Francisco without letting me see it first."

"What kind of crimes have you got for us to pull?" Mickey asked.

"I want you to take Pete the Finn. Dick will take Lew Yard. You'll have to play it the way I've been playing—do what you can when you can. I've an idea that the pair of them will try to make Noonan let Whisper alone. I don't know what he'll do. He's shifty as hell and he does want to even up his brother's killing."

"After I take this Finnish gent," Mickey said, "what do I do with him? I don't want to brag about how dumb I am, but this job is plain as astronomy to me. I understand everything about it except what you have done and why, and what you're trying to do and how."

"You can start off by shadowing him. I've got to have a wedge that can be put between Pete and Yard, Yard and Noonan, Pete and Noonan, Pete and Thaler, or Yard and

Thaler. If we can smash things up enough—break the combination—they'll have their knives in each other's backs, doing our work for us. The break between Thaler and Noonan is a starter. But it'll sag on us if we don't help it along.

"I could buy more dope on the whole lot from Dinah Brand. But there's no use taking anybody into court, no matter what you've got on them. They own the courts, and, besides, the courts are too slow for us now. I've got myself tangled up in something and as soon as the Old Man smells it—and San Francisco isn't far enough away to fool his nose—he's going to be sitting on the wire, asking for explanations. I've got to have results to hide the details under. So evidence won't do. What we've got to have is dynamite."

"What about our respected client, Mr. Elihu Willsson?" Mickey asked. "What are you planning to do with or to him?"

"Maybe ruin him, maybe club him into backing us up. I don't care which. You'd better stay at the Hotel Person, Mickey, and Dick can go to the National. Keep apart, and, if you want to keep me from being fired, burn the job up before the Old Man tumbles. Better write these down."

I gave them names, descriptions, and addresses when I had them, of Elihu Willsson; Stanley Lewis, his secretary; Dinah Brand; Dan Rolff; Noonan; Max Thaler, alias Whisper; his right-hand man, the chinless Jerry; Mrs. Donald Willsson; Lewis' daughter, who had been Donald Willsson's secretary; and Bill Quint, Dinah's radical ex-boy-friend.

"Now hop to it," I said. "And don't kid yourselves that there's any law in Poisonville except what you make for yourself."

Mickey said I'd be surprised how many laws he could get along without. Dick said: "So long," and they departed.

After breakfast I went over to the City Hall.

Noonan's greenish eyes were bleary, as if they hadn't been sleeping, and his face had lost some of its color. He pumped my hand up and down as enthusiastically as ever, and the customary amount of cordiality was in his voice and manner.

"Any line on Whisper?" I asked when we had finished the glad-handing.

"I think I've got something." He looked at the clock on

the wall and then at his phone. "I'm expecting word any minute. Sit down."

"Who else got away?"

"Jerry Hooper and Tony Agosti are the only other ones still out. We picked up the rest. Jerry is Whisper's man-Friday, and the wop's one of his mob. He's the bozo that put the knife in Ike Bush the night of the fight."

"Any more of Whisper's mob in?"

"No. We just had the three of them, except Buck Wallace, the fellow you potted. He's in the hospital."

The chief looked at the wall clock again, and at his watch. It was exactly two o'clock. He turned to the phone. It rang. He grabbed it, said:

"Noonan talking. . . . Yes. . . . Yes. . . . Yes. . . . Right."

He pushed the phone aside and played a tune on the row of pearl buttons on his desk. The office filled up with coppers.

"Cedar Hill Inn," he said. "You follow me out with your detail, Bates. Terry, shoot out Broadway and hit the dump from behind. Pick up the boys on traffic duty as you go along. It's likely we'll need everybody we can get. Duffy, take yours out Union street and around by the old mine road. McGraw will hold headquarters down. Get hold of everybody you can and send them after us. Jump!"

He grabbed his hat and went after them, calling over his thick shoulder to me:

"Come on, man, this is the kill."

I followed him down to the department garage, where the engines of half a dozen cars were roaring. The chief sat beside his driver. I sat in back with four detectives.

Men scrambled into the other cars. Machine guns were unwrapped. Arm-loads of rifles and riot-guns were distributed, and packages of ammunition.

The chief's car got away first, off with a jump that hammered our teeth together. We missed the garage door by half an inch, chased a couple of pedestrians diagonally across the sidewalk, bounced off the curb into the roadway, missed a truck as narrowly as we had missed the door, and dashed out King Street with our siren wide open.

Panicky automobiles darted right and left, regardless of traffic rules, to let us through. It was a lot of fun.

I looked back, saw another police car following us, a third turning into Broadway. Noonan chewed a cold cigar and told the driver:

"Give her a bit more, Pat."

Pat twisted us around a frightened woman's coupé, put us through a slot between street car and laundry wagon—a narrow slot that we couldn't have slipped through if our car hadn't been so smoothly enameled—and said:

"All right, but the brakes ain't no good."

"That's nice," the gray-mustached sleuth on my left said. He didn't sound sincere.

Out of the center of the city there wasn't much traffic to bother us, but the paving was rougher. It was a nice half-hour's ride, with everybody getting a chance to sit in everybody else's lap. The last ten minutes of it was over an uneven road that had hills enough to keep us from forgetting what Pat had said about the brakes.

We wound up at a gate topped by a shabby electric sign that had said *Cedar Hill Inn* before it lost its globes. The roadhouse, twenty feet behind the gate, was a squat wooden building painted a moldly green and chiefly surrounded by rubbish. Front door and windows were closed, blank.

We followed Noonan out of the car. The machine that had been trailing us came into sight around a bend in the road, slid to rest beside ours, and unloaded its cargo of men and weapons.

Noonan ordered this and that.

A trio of coppers went around each side of the building. Three others, including a machine-gunner, remained by the gate. The rest of us walked through tin cans, bottles, and ancient newspaper to the front of the house.

The gray-mustached detective who had sat beside me in the car carried a red ax. We stepped up on the porch.

Noise and fire came out under a window sill.

The gray-mustached detective fell down, hiding the ax under his corpse.

The rest of us ran away.

I ran with Noonan. We hid in the ditch on the Inn side of the road. It was deep enough, and banked high enough, to let us stand almost erect without being targets.

The chief was excited.

"What luck!" he said happily. "He's here, by God, he's here!"

"That shot came from under the sill," I said. "Not a bad trick."

"We'll spoil it, though," he said cheerfully. "We'll sieve the dump. Duffy ought to be pulling up on the other road by now, and Terry Shane won't be many minutes behind him. Hey, Donner!" he called to a man who was peeping around a boulder. "Swing around back and tell Duffy and Shane to start closing in as soon as they come, letting fly with all they got. Where's Kimble?"

The peeper jerked a thumb toward a tree beyond him. We could see only the upper part of it from our ditch.

"Tell him to set up his mill and start grinding," Noonan ordered. "Low, across the front, ought to do it like cutting cheese."

The peeper disappeared.

Noonan went up and down the ditch, risking his noodle over the top now and then for a look around, once in a while calling or gesturing to his men.

He came back, sat on his heels beside me, gave me a cigar, and lit one for himself.

"It'll do," he said complacently. "Whisper won't have a chance. He's done."

The machine-gun by the tree fired, haltingly, experimentally, eight or ten shots. Noonan grinned and let a smoke ring float out of his mouth. The machine-gun settled down to business, grinding out metal like the busy little death factory it was. Noonan blew another smoke ring and said:

"That's exactly what'll do it."

I agreed that it ought to. We leaned against the clay bank and smoked while, farther away, another machine-gun got going, and then a third. Irregularly, rifles, pistols, shot-guns joined in. Noonan nodded approvingly and said:

"Five minutes of that will let him know there's a hell."

When the five minutes were up I suggested a look at the re-mains. I gave him a boost up the bank and scrambled up after him.

The roadhouse was as bleak and empty-looking as before, but more battered. No shots came from it. Plenty were going into it.

"What do you think?" Noonan asked.

"If there's a cellar there might be a mouse alive in it."

"Well, we could finish him afterwards."

He took a whistle out of his pocket and made a lot of noise. He waved his fat arms, and the gun-fire began dwindling. We had to wait for the word to go all the way around.

Then we crashed the door.

The first floor was ankle-deep with booze that was still gur-gling from bullet holes in the stacked-up cases and barrels that filled most of the house.

Dizzy with the fumes of spilled hooch, we waded around until we had found four dead bodies and no live ones. The four were swarthy foreign-looking men in laborers' clothes. Two of them were practically shot to pieces.

Noonan said:

"Leave them here and get out."

His voice was cheerful, but in a flashlight's glow his eyes showed white-ringed with fear.

We went out gladly, though I did hesitate long enough to pocket an unbroken bottle labeled *Dewar*.

A khaki-dressed copper was tumbling off a motorcycle at the gate. He yelled at us:

"The First National's been stuck up."

Noonan cursed savagely, bawled:

"He's foxed us, damn him! Back to town, everybody."

Everybody except us who had ridden with the chief beat it for the machines. Two of them took the dead detective with them.

Noonan looked at me out of his eye-corners and said:

"This is a tough one, no fooling."

I said, "Well," shrugged, and sauntered over to his car, where the driver was sitting at the wheel. I stood with my back to the house, talking to Pat. I don't remember what we talked about. Presently Noonan and the other sleuths joined us.

Only a little flame showed through the open roadhouse door before we passed out of sight around the bend in the road.

CHAPTER XVI

Exit Jerry

THERE WAS a mob around the First National Bank. We pushed through it to the door, where we found sour-faced McGraw.

"Was six of them, masked," he reported to the chief as we went inside. "They hit it about two-thirty. Five of them got away clean with the jack. The watchman here dropped one of them, Jerry Hooper. He's over on the bench, cold. We got the roads blocked, and I wired around, if it ain't too late. Last seen of them was when they made the turn into King Street, in a black Lincoln."

We went over to look at the dead Jerry, lying on one of the lobby benches with a brown robe over him. The bullet had gone in under his left shoulder blade.

The bank watchman, a harmless looking old duffer, pushed up his chest and told us about it:

"There wasn't no chance to do nothing at first. They were in 'fore anybody knew anything. And maybe they didn't work fast. Right down the line, scooping it up. No chance to do anything then. But I says to myself, 'All righty, young fellows, you've got it all your own way now, but wait till you try to leave.'

"And I was as good as my word, you bet you. I runs right to the door after them and cut loose with the old firearm. I got that fellow just as he was stepping into the car. I bet you I'd of got more of them if I'd of had more cartridges, because it's kind of hard shooting down like that, standing in the—"

Noonan stopped the monologue by patting the old duffer's back till his lungs were empty, telling him, "That certainly is fine. That certainly is fine."

McGraw pulled the robe up over the dead man again and growled:

"Nobody can identify anybody. But with Jerry on it, it's a cinch it was Whisper's caper."

The chief nodded happily and said:

"I'll leave it in your hands, Mac. Going to poke around here, or going back to the Hall with me?" he asked me.

"Neither. I've got a date, and I want to get into dry shoes."

Dinah Brand's little Marmon was standing in front of the hotel. I didn't see her. I went up to my room, leaving the door unlocked. I had got my hat and coat off when she came in without knocking.

"My God, you keep a boozy smelling room," she said.

"It's my shoes. Noonan took me wading in rum."

She crossed to the window, opened it, sat on the sill, and asked:

"What was that for?"

"He thought he was going to find your Max out in a dump called Cedar Hill Inn. So we went out there, shot the joint silly, murdered some dagoes, spilled gallons of liquor, and left the place burning."

"Cedar Hill Inn? I thought it had been closed up for a year or more."

"It looked it, but it was somebody's warehouse."

"But you didn't find Max there?" she asked.

"While we were there he seems to have been knocking over Elihu's First National Bank."

"I saw that," she said. "I had just come out of Bengren's, the store two doors away. I had just got in my car when I saw a big boy backing out of the bank, carrying a sack and a gun, with a black handkerchief over his face."

"Was Max with them?"

"No, he wouldn't be. He'd send Jerry and the boys. That's what he has them for. Jerry was there. I knew him as soon as he got out of the car, in spite of the black handkerchief. They all had black ones. Four of them came out of the bank, running down to the car at the curb. Jerry and another fellow were in the car. When the four came across the sidewalk, Jerry jumped out and went to meet them. That's when the shooting started and Jerry dropped. The others jumped in the bus and lit out. How about that dough you owe me?"

I counted out ten twenty-dollar bills and a dime. She left the window to come for them.

"That's for pulling Dan off, so you could cop Max," she

said when she had stowed the money away in her bag. "Now how about what I was to get for showing you where you could turn up the dope on his killing Tim Noonan?"

"You'll have to wait till he's indicted. How do I know the dope's any good?"

She frowned and asked:

"What do you do with all the money you don't spend?" Her face brightened. "You know where Max is now?"

"No."

"What's it worth to know?"

"Nothing."

"I'll tell you for a hundred bucks."

"I wouldn't want to take advantage of you that way."

"I'll tell you for fifty bucks."

I shook my head.

"Twenty-five."

"I don't want him," I said. "I don't care where he is. Why don't you peddle the news to Noonan?"

"Yes, and try to collect. Do you only perfume yourself with booze, or is there any for drinking purposes?"

"Here's a bottle of so-called Dewar that I picked up at Cedar Hill this afternoon. There's a bottle of King George in my bag. What's your choice?"

She voted for King George. We had a drink apiece, straight, and I said:

"Sit down and play with it while I change clothes."

When I came out of the bathroom twenty-five minutes later she was sitting at the secretary, smoking a cigarette and studying a memoranda book that had been in a side pocket of my gladstone bag.

"I guess these are the expenses you've charged up on other cases," she said without looking up. "I'm damned if I can see why you can't be more liberal with me. Look, here's a six-hundred-dollar item marked *Inf.* That's information you bought from somebody, isn't it? And here's a hundred and fifty below it—*Top*—whatever that is. And here's another day when you spent nearly a thousand dollars."

"They must be telephone numbers," I said, taking the book from her. "Where were you raised? Fanning my baggage!"

"I was raised in a convent," she told me. "I won the good

behavior prize every year I was there. I thought little girls who put extra spoons of sugar in their chocolate went to hell for gluttony. I didn't even know there was such a thing as profanity until I was eighteen. The first time I heard any I damned near fainted." She spit on the rug in front of her, tilted her chair back, put her crossed feet on my bed, and asked: "What do you think of that?"

I pushed her feet off the bed and said:

"I was raised in a water-front saloon. Keep your saliva off my floor or I'll toss you out on your neck."

"Let's have another drink first. Listen, what'll you give me for the inside story of how the boys didn't lose anything building the City Hall—the story that was in the papers I sold Donald Willsson?"

"That doesn't click with me. Try another."

"How about why the first Mrs. Lew Yard was sent to the insane asylum?"

"No."

"King, our sheriff, eight thousand dollars in debt four years ago, now the owner of as nice a collection of downtown business blocks as you'd want to see. I can't give you all of it, but I can show you where to get it."

"Keep trying," I encouraged her.

"No. You don't want to buy anything. You're just hoping you'll pick up something for nothing. This isn't bad Scotch. Where'd you get it?"

"Brought it from San Francisco with me."

"What's the idea of not wanting any of this information I'm offering? Think you can get it cheaper?"

"Information of that kind's not much good to me now. I've got to move quick. I need dynamite—something to blow them apart."

She laughed and jumped up, her big eyes sparkling.

"I've got one of Lew Yard's cards. Suppose we sent the bottle of Dewar you copped to Pete with the card. Wouldn't he take it as a declaration of war? If Cedar Hill was a liquor cache, it was Pete's. Wouldn't the bottle and Lew's card make him think Noonan had knocked the place over under orders?"

I considered it and said:

"Too crude. It wouldn't fool him. Besides, I'd just as leave have Pete and Lew both against the chief at this stage."

She pouted and said:

"You think you know everything. You're just hard to get along with. Take me out tonight? I've got a new outfit that'll knock them cockeyed."

"Yeah."

"Come up for me around eight."

She patted my cheek with a warm hand, said, "Ta-ta," and went out as the telephone bell began jingling.

"My chinch and Dick's are together at your client's joint," Mickey Linehan reported over the wire. "Mine's been generally busier than a hustler with two bunks, though I don't know what the score is yet. Anything new?"

I said there wasn't and went into conference with myself across the bed, trying to guess what would come of Noonan's attack on Cedar Hill Inn and Whisper's on the First National Bank. I would have given something for ability to hear what was being said up at old Elihu's house by him, Pete the Finn, and Lew Yard. But I hadn't that ability, and I was never much good at guessing, so after half an hour I stopped tormenting my brain and took a nap.

It was nearly seven o'clock when I came out of the nap. I washed, dressed, loaded my pockets with a gun and a pint flask of Scotch, and went up to Dinah's.

CHAPTER XVII

Reno

S HE TOOK me into her living room, backed away from me, revolved, and asked me how I liked the new dress. I said I liked it. She explained that the color was rose beige and that the dinguses on the side were something or other, winding up:

"And you really think I look good in it?"

"You always look good," I said. "Lew Yard and Pete the Finn went calling on old Elihu this afternoon."

She made a face at me and said:

"You don't give a damn about my dress. What did they do there?"

"A pow-wow, I suppose."

She looked at me through her lashes and asked:

"Don't you really know where Max is?"

Then I did. There was no use admitting I hadn't known all along. I said:

"At Willsson's, probably, but I haven't been interested enough to make sure."

"That's goofy of you. He's got reasons for not liking you and me. Take mama's advice and nail him quick, if you like living and like having mama live too."

I laughed and said:

"You don't know the worst of it. Max didn't kill Noonan's brother. Tim didn't say *Max*. He tried to say *MacSwain*, and died before he could finish."

She grabbed my shoulders and tried to shake my hundred and ninety pounds. She was almost strong enough to do it.

"God damn you!" Her breath was hot in my face. Her face was white as her teeth. Rouge stood out sharply like red labels pasted on her mouth and cheeks. "If you've framed him and made me frame him, you've got to kill him—now."

I don't like being manhandled, even by young women who look like something out of mythology when they're steamed up. I took her hands off my shoulders, and said:

"Stop bellyaching. You're still alive."

"Yes, still. But I know Max better than you do. I know how much chance anybody that frames him has got of staying alive long. It would be bad enough if we had got him right, but—"

"Don't make so much fuss over it. I've framed my millions and nothing's happened to me. Get your hat and coat and we'll feed. You'll feel better then."

"You're crazy if you think I'm going out. Not with that—"

"Stop it, sister. If he's that dangerous he's just as likely to get you here as anywhere. So what difference does it make?"

"It makes a— You know what you're going to do? You're going to stay here until Max is put out of the way. It's your fault and you've got to look out for me. I haven't even got Dan. He's in the hospital."

"I can't," I said. "I've got work to do. You're all burnt up over nothing. Max has probably forgotten all about you by now. Get your hat and coat. I'm starving."

She put her face close to mine again, and her eyes looked as if they had found something horrible in mine.

"Oh, you're rotten!" she said. "You don't give a damn what happens to me. "You're using me as you use the others—that dynamite you wanted. I trusted you."

"You're dynamite, all right, but the rest of it's kind of foolish. You look a lot better when you're happy. Your features are heavy. Anger makes them downright brutal. I'm starving, sister."

"You'll eat here," she said. "You're not going to get me out after dark."

She meant it. She swapped the rose beige dress for an apron, and took inventory of the ice box. There were potatoes, lettuce, canned soup and half a fruit cake. I went out and got a couple of steaks, rolls, asparagus, and tomatoes.

When I came back she was mixing gin, vermouth and orange bitters in a quart shaker, not leaving a lot of space for them to move around in.

"Did you see anything?" she asked.

I sneered at her in a friendly way. We carried the cocktails into the dining room and played bottoms-up while the meal cooked. The drinks cheered her a lot. By the time we sat down to the food she had almost forgotten her fright. She wasn't a very good cook, but we ate as if she were.

We put a couple of gin-gingerales in on top the dinner.

She decided she wanted to go places and do things. No lousy little runt could keep her cooped up, because she had been as square with him as anybody could be until he got nasty over nothing, and if he didn't like what she did he could go climb trees or jump in lakes, and we'd go out to the Silver Arrow where she had meant to take me, because she had promised Reno she'd show up at his party, and by God she would, and anybody who thought she wouldn't was crazy as a pet cuckoo, and what did I think of that?

"Who's Reno?" I asked while she tied herself tighter in the apron by pulling the strings the wrong way.

"Reno Starkey. You'll like him. He's a right guy. I promised him I'd show at his celebration and that's just what I'll do."

"What's he celebrating?"

"What the hell's the matter with this lousy apron? He was sprung this afternoon."

"Turn around and I'll unwind you. What was he in for? Stand still."

"Blowing a safe six or seven months ago—Turlock's, the jeweler. Reno, Put Collings, Blackie Whalen, Hank O'Marra, and a little lame guy called Step-and-a-Half. They had plenty of cover—Lew Yard—but the jewelers' association dicks tied the job to them last week. So Noonan had to go through the motions. It doesn't mean anything. They got out on bail at five o'clock this afternoon, and that's the last anybody will ever hear about it. Reno's used to it. He was already out on bail for three other capers. Suppose you mix another little drink while I'm inserting myself in the dress."

The Silver Arrow was half-way between Personville and Mock Lake.

"It's not a bad dump," Dinah told me as her little Marmon carried us toward it. "Polly De Voto is a good scout and any-thing she sells you is good, except maybe the Bourbon. That always tastes a little bit like it had been drained off a corpse. You'll like her. You can get away with anything out here so long as you don't get noisy. She won't stand for noise. There it is. See the red and blue lights through the trees?"

We rode out of the woods into full view of the roadhouse, a very electric-lighted imitation castle set close to the road.

"What do you mean she won't stand for noise?" I asked, listening to the chorus of pistols singing *Bang-bang-bang.*

"Something up," the girl muttered, stopping the car.

Two men dragging a woman between them ran out of the roadhouse's front door, ran away into the darkness. A man sprinted out a side door, away. The guns sang on. I didn't see any flashes.

Another man broke out and vanished around the back.

A man leaned far out a front second-story window, a black gun in his hand.

Dinah blew her breath out sharply.

From a hedge by the road, a flash of orange pointed briefly up at the man in the window. His gun flashed downward. He leaned farther out. No second flash came from the hedge.

The man in the window put a leg over the sill, bent, hung by his hands, dropped.

Our car jerked forward. Dinah's lower lip was between her teeth.

The man who had dropped from the window was gathering himself up on hands and knees.

Dinah put her face in front of mine and screamed: "Reno!"

The man jumped up, his face to us. He made the road in three leaps, as we got to him.

Dinah had the little Marmon wide open before Reno's feet were on the running board beside me. I wrapped my arms around him, and damned near dislocated them holding him on. He made it as tough as he could for me by leaning out to try for a shot at the guns that were tossing lead all around us.

Then it was all over. We were out of range, sight and sound of the Silver Arrow, speeding away from Personville.

Reno turned around and did his own holding on. I took my arms in and found that all the joints still worked. Dinah was busy with the car.

Reno said:

"Thanks, kid. I needed pulling out."

"That's all right," she told him. "So that's the kind of parties you throw?"

"We had guests that wasn't invited. You know the Tanner road?"

"Yes."

"Take it. It'll put us over to Mountain Boulevard, and we can get back to town that-a-way."

The girl nodded, slowed up a little, and asked:

"Who were the uninvited guests?"

"Some plugs that don't know enough to leave me alone."

"Do I know them?" she asked, too casually, as she turned the car into a narrower and rougher road.

"Let it alone, kid," Reno said. "Better get as much out of the heap as it's got."

She prodded another fifteen miles an hour out of the Marmon. She had plenty to do now holding the car to the road, and Reno had plenty holding himself to the car. Neither of them made any more conversation until the road brought us into one that had more and better paving.

Then he asked:

"So you paid Whisper off?"

"Um-hmm."

"They're saying you turned rat on him."

"They would. What do you think?"

"Ditching him was all right. But throwing in with a dick and cracking the works to him is kind of sour. Damned sour, if you ask me."

He looked at me while he said it. He was a man of thirty-four or -five, fairly tall, broad and heavy without fat. His eyes were large, brown, dull, and set far apart in a long, slightly sallow horse face. It was a humorless face, stolid, but somehow not unpleasant. I looked at him and said nothing.

The girl said: "If that's the way you feel about it, you can—"

"Look out," Reno grunted.

We had swung around a curve. A long black car was straight across the road ahead of us—a barricade.

Bullets flew around us. Reno and I threw bullets around while the girl made a polo pony of the little Marmon.

She shoved it over to the left of the road, let the left wheels ride the bank high, crossed the road again with Reno's and my weight on the inside, got the right bank under the left wheels just as our side of the car began to lift in spite of our weight, slid us down in the road with our backs to the enemy, and took us out of the neighborhood by the time we had emptied our guns.

A lot of people had done a lot of shooting, but so far as we could tell nobody's bullets had hurt anybody.

Reno, holding to the door with his elbows while he pushed another clip into his automatic, said:

"Nice work, kid. You handle the bus like you meant it."

Dinah asked: "Where now?"

"Far away first. Just follow the road. We'll have to figure it out. Looks like they got the burg closed up on us. Keep your dog on it."

We put ten or twelve more miles between Personville and us. We passed a few cars, saw nothing to show we were being chased. A short bridge rumbled under us. Reno said:

"Take the right turn at the top of the hill."

We took it, into a dirt road that wound between trees down the side of a rock-ridged hill. Ten miles an hour was fast going here. After five minutes of creeping along Reno ordered a halt. We heard nothing, saw nothing, during the half-hour we sat in darkness. Then Reno said:

"There's an empty shack a mile down the way. We'll camp there, huh? There's no sense trying to crash the city line again tonight."

Dinah said she would prefer anything to being shot at again. I said it was all right with me, though I would rather have tried to find some path back to the city.

We followed the dirt track cautiously until our headlights settled on a small clapboard building that badly needed the paint it had never got.

"Is this it?" Dinah asked Reno.

"Uh-huh. Stay here till I look it over."

He left us, appearing soon in the beam of our lights at the shack door. He fumbled with keys at the padlock, got it off, opened the door, and went in. Presently he came to the door and called:

"All right. Come in and make yourselves to home."

Dinah cut off the engine and got out of the car.

"Is there a flashlight in the car?" I asked.

She said, "Yes," gave it to me, yawned, "My God, I'm tired. I hope there's something to drink in the hole."

I told her I had a flask of Scotch. The news cheered her up.

The shack was a one-room affair that held an army cot covered with brown blankets, a deal table with a deck of cards and some gummy poker chips on it, a brown iron stove, four chairs, an oil lamp, dishes, pots, pans and buckets, three shelves with canned food on them, a pile of firewood and a wheelbarrow.

Reno was lighting the lamp when we came in. He said:

"Not so tough. I'll hide the heap and then we'll be all set till daylight."

Dinah went over to the cot, turned back the covers, and reported:

"Maybe there's things in it, but anyway it's not alive with them. Now let's have that drink."

I unscrewed the flask and passed it to her while Reno went out to hide the car. When she had finished, I took a shot.

The purr of the Marmon's engine got fainter. I opened the door and looked out. Downhill, through trees and bushes, I could see broken chunks of white light going away. When I lost them for good I returned indoors and asked the girl:

"Have you ever had to walk home before?"

"What?"

"Reno's gone with the car."

"The lousy tramp! Thank God he left us where there's a bed, anyway."

"That'll get you nothing."

"No?"

"No. Reno had a key to this dump. Ten to one the birds after him know about it. That's why he ditched us here. We're supposed to argue with them, hold them off his trail a while."

She got up wearily from the cot, cursed Reno, me, all men from Adam on, and said disagreeably:

"You know everything. What do we do next?"

"We find a comfortable spot in the great open spaces, not too far away, and wait to see what happens."

"I'm going to take the blankets."

"Maybe one won't be missed, but you'll tip our mitts if you take more than that."

"Damn your mitts," she grumbled, but she took only one blanket.

I blew out the lamp, padlocked the door behind us, and with the help of the flashlight picked a way through the undergrowth.

On the hillside above we found a little hollow from which road and shack could be not too dimly seen through foliage thick enough to hide us unless we showed a light.

I spread the blanket there and we settled down.

The girl leaned against me and complained that the ground was damp, that she was cold in spite of her fur coat, that she had a cramp in her leg, and that she wanted a cigarette.

I gave her another drink from the flask. That bought me ten minutes of peace.

Then she said:

"I'm catching cold. By the time anybody comes, if they ever do, I'll be sneezing and coughing loud enough to be heard in the city."

"Just once," I told her. "Then you'll be all strangled."

"There's a mouse or something crawling under the blanket."

"Probably only a snake."

"Are you married?"

"Don't start that."

"Then you are?"

"No."

"I'll bet your wife's glad of it."

I was trying to find a suitable come-back to that wise-crack when a distant light gleamed up the road. It disappeared as I sh-sh'd the girl.

"What is it?" she asked.

"A light. It's gone now. Our visitors have left their car and are finishing the trip afoot."

A lot of time went by. The girl shivered with her cheek warm against mine. We heard footsteps, saw dark figures moving on the road and around the shack, without being sure whether we did or didn't.

A flashlight ended our doubt by putting a bright circle on the shack's door. A heavy voice said:

"We'll let the broad come out."

There was a half-minute of silence while they waited for a reply from indoors. Then the same heavy voice asked: "Coming?" Then more silence.

Gunfire, a familiar sound tonight, broke the silence. Something hammered boards.

"Come on," I whispered to the girl. "We'll have a try at their car while they're making a racket."

"Let them alone," she said, pulling my arm down as I started up. "I've had enough of it for one night. We're all right here."

"Come on," I insisted.

She said, "I won't," and she wouldn't, and presently, while we argued, it was too late. The boys below had kicked in the door, found the hut empty, and were bellowing for their car.

It came, took eight men aboard, and followed Reno's track downhill.

"We might as well move in again," I said. "It's not likely they'll be back this way tonight."

"I hope to God there's some Scotch left in that flask," she said as I helped her stand up.

CHAPTER XVIII

Painter Street

THE SHACK'S supply of canned goods didn't include anything that tempted us for breakfast. We made the meal of coffee cooked in very stale water from a galvanized pail.

A mile of walking brought us to a farmhouse where there was a boy who didn't mind earning a few dollars by driving us to town in the family Ford. He had a lot of questions, to which we gave him phoney answers or none. He set us down in front of a little restaurant in upper King Street, where we ate quantities of buckwheat cakes and bacon.

A taxi put us at Dinah's door a little before nine o'clock. I searched the place for her, from roof to cellar, and found no signs of visitors.

"When will you be back?" she asked as she followed me to the door.

"I'll try to pop in between now and midnight, if only for a few minutes. Where does Lew Yard live?"

"1622 Painter Street. Painter's three blocks over. 1622's four blocks up. What are you going to do there?" Before I could answer, she put her hands on my arm and begged: "Get Max, will you? I'm afraid of him."

"Maybe I'll sic Noonan on him a little later. It depends on how things work out."

She called me a damned double-crossing something or other who didn't care what happened to her as long as his dirty work got done.

I went over to Painter Street. 1622 was a red brick house with a garage under the front porch.

A block up the street I found Dick Foley in a hired drive-yourself Buick. I got in beside him, asking:

"What's doing?"

"Spot two. Out three-thirty, office to Willsson's. Mickey. Five. Home. Busy. Kept plant. Off three, seven. Nothing yet."

That was supposed to inform me that he had picked up Lew Yard at two the previous afternoon; had shadowed him to Willsson's at three-thirty, where Mickey had tailed Pete; had followed Yard away at five, to his residence; had seen people going in and out of the house, but had not shadowed any of them; had watched the house until three this morning, and had returned to the job at seven; and since then had seen nobody go in or out.

"You'll have to drop this and take a plant on Willsson's," I said. "I hear Whisper Thaler's holing-up there, and I'd like an eye kept on him till I make up my mind whether to turn him up for Noonan or not."

Dick nodded and started the engine grinding. I got out and returned to the hotel.

There was a telegram from the Old Man:

SEND BY FIRST MAIL FULL EXPLANATION OF PRESENT OPERATION AND CIRCUMSTANCES UNDER WHICH YOU ACCEPTED IT WITH DAILY REPORTS TO DATE

I put the telegram in my pocket and hoped things would keep on breaking fast. To have sent him the dope he wanted at that time would have been the same as sending in my resignation.

I bent a fresh collar around my neck and trotted over to the City Hall.

"Hello," Noonan greeted me. "I was hoping you'd show up. Tried to get you at your hotel but they told me you hadn't been in."

He wasn't looking well this morning, but under his glad-handing he seemed, for a change, genuinely glad to see me.

As I sat down one of his phones rang. He put the receiver to his ear, said, "Yes?" listened for a moment, said, "You better go out there yourself, Mac," and had to make two attempts to get the receiver back on its prong before he succeeded. His face had gone a little doughy, but his voice was almost normal as he told me:

"Lew Yard's been knocked off—shot coming down his front steps just now."

"Any details?" I asked while I cursed myself for having pulled Dick Foley away from Painter Street an hour too soon. That was a tough break.

Noonan shook his head, staring at his lap.

"Shall we go out and look at the remains?" I suggested, getting up.

He neither got up nor looked up.

"No," he said wearily to his lap. "To tell the truth, I don't want to. I don't know as I could stand it just now. I'm getting sick of this killing. It's getting to me—on my nerves, I mean."

I sat down again, considered his low spirits, and asked:

"Who do you guess killed him?"

"God knows," he mumbled. "Everybody's killing everybody. Where's it going to end?"

"Think Reno did it?"

Noonan winced, started to look up at me, changed his mind, and repeated:

"God knows."

I went at him from another angle:

"Anybody knocked off in the battle at the Silver Arrow last night?"

"Only three."

"Who were they?"

"A pair of Johnson-brothers named Blackie Whalen and Put Collings that only got out on bail around five yesterday, and Dutch Jake Wahl, a guerrilla."

"What was it all about?"

"Just a roughhouse, I guess. It seems that Put and Blackie and the others that got out with them were celebrating with a lot of friends, and it wound up in smoke."

"All of them Lew Yard's men?"

"I don't know anything about that," he said.

I got up, said, "Oh, all right," and started for the door.

"Wait," he called. "Don't run off like that. I guess they were."

I came back to my chair. Noonan watched the top of his desk. His face was gray, flabby, damp, like fresh putty.

"Whisper's staying at Willsson's," I told him.

He jerked his head up. His eyes darkened. Then his mouth twitched, and he let his head sag again. His eyes faded.

"I can't go through with it," he mumbled. "I'm sick of this butchering. I can't stand any more of it."

"Sick enough to give up the idea of evening the score for Tim's killing, if it'll make peace?" I asked.

"I am."

"That's what started it," I reminded him. "If you're willing to call it off, it ought to be possible to stop it."

He raised his face and looked at me with eyes that were like a dog's looking at a bone.

"The others ought to be as sick of it as you are," I went on. "Tell them how you feel about it. Have a get-together and make peace."

"They'd think I was up to some kind of a trick," he objected miserably.

"Have the meeting at Willsson's. Whisper's camping there. You'd be the one risking tricks going there. Are you afraid of that?"

He frowned and asked:

"Will you go with me?"

"If you want me."

"Thanks," he said. "I—I'll try it."

CHAPTER XIX

The Peace Conference

ALL THE OTHER delegates to the peace conference were on hand when Noonan and I arrived at Willsson's home at the appointed time, nine o'clock that night. Everybody nodded to us, but the greetings didn't go any further than that.

Pete the Finn was the only one I hadn't met before. The bootlegger was a big-boned man of fifty with a completely bald head. His forehead was small, his jaws enormous—wide, heavy, bulging with muscle.

We sat around Willsson's library table.

Old Elihu sat at the head. The short-clipped hair on his round pink skull was like silver in the light. His round blue eyes were hard, domineering, under their bushy white brows. His mouth and chin were horizontal lines.

On his right Pete the Finn sat watching everybody with tiny black eyes that never moved. Reno Starkey sat next to the bootlegger. Reno's sallow horse face was as stolidly dull as his eyes.

Max Thaler was tilted back in a chair on Willsson's left. The little gambler's carefully pressed pants legs were carelessly crossed. A cigarette hung from one corner of his tight-lipped mouth.

I sat next to Thaler. Noonan sat on my other side.

Elihu Willsson opened the meeting.

He said things couldn't go on the way they were going. We were all sensible men, reasonable men, grown men who had seen enough of the world to know that a man couldn't have everything his own way, no matter who he was. Compromises were things everybody had to make sometimes. To get what he wanted, a man had to give other people what they wanted. He said he was sure that what we all most wanted now was to stop this insane killing. He said he was sure that everything could be frankly discussed and settled in an‑hour without turning Personville into a slaughter-house.

It wasn't a bad oration.

When it was over there was a moment of silence. Thaler looked past me, at Noonan, as if he expected something of him. The rest of us followed his example, looking at the chief of police.

Noonan's face turned red and he spoke huskily:

"Whisper, I'll forget you killed Tim." He stood up and held out a beefy paw. "Here's my hand on it."

Thaler's thin mouth curved into a vicious smile.

"Your bastard of a brother needed killing, but I didn't kill him," he whispered coldly.

Red became purple in the chief's face.

I said loudly:

"Wait, Noonan. We're going at this wrong. We won't get anywhere unless everybody comes clean. Otherwise we'll all be worse off than before. MacSwain killed Tim, and you know it."

He stared at me with dumbfounded eyes. He gaped. He couldn't understand what I had done to him.

I looked at the others, tried to look virtuous as hell, asked:

"That's settled, isn't it? Let's get the rest of the kicks squared." I addressed Pete the Finn: "How do you feel about yesterday's accident to your warehouse and the four men?"

"One hell of an accident," he rumbled.

I explained:

"Noonan didn't know you were using the joint. He went there thinking it empty, just to clear the way for a job in town. Your men shot first, and then he really thought he had stumbled into Thaler's hideout. When he found he'd been stepping in your puddle he lost his head and touched the place off."

Thaler was watching me with a hard small smile in eyes and mouth. Reno was all dull stolidity. Elihu Willsson was leaning toward me, his old eyes sharp and wary. I don't know what Noonan was doing. I couldn't afford to look at him. I was in a good spot if I played my hand right, and in a terrible one if I didn't.

"The men, they get paid for taking chances," Pete the Finn said. "For the other, twenty-five grand will make it right."

Noonan spoke quickly, eagerly:

"All right, Pete, all right, I'll give it to you."

I pushed my lips together to keep from laughing at the panic in his voice.

I could look at him safely now. He was licked, broken, willing to do anything to save his fat neck, or to try to. I looked at him.

He wouldn't look at me. He sat down and looked at nobody. He was busy trying to look as if he didn't expect to be carved apart before he got away from these wolves to whom I had handed him.

I went on with the work, turning to Elihu Willsson:

"Do you want to squawk about your bank being knocked over, or do you like it?"

Max Thaler touched my arm and suggested:

"We could tell better maybe who's entitled to beef if you'd give us what you've got first."

I was glad to.

"Noonan wanted to nail you," I told him, "but he either got word, or expected to get word, from Yard and Willsson here to let you alone. So he thought if he had the bank looted and framed you for it, your backers would ditch you, and let him go after you right. Yard, I understand, was supposed to put his O.K. on all the capers in town. You'd be cutting into his territory, and gyping Willsson. That's how it would look. And that was supposed to make them hot enough that they'd help Noonan cop you. He didn't know you were here.

"Reno and his mob were in the can. Reno was Yard's pup, but he didn't mind crossing up his head-man. He already had the idea that he was about ready to take the burg away from Lew." I turned to Reno and asked: "Isn't that it?"

He looked at me woodenly and said:

"You're telling it."

I continued telling it:

"Noonan fakes a tip that you're at Cedar Hill, and takes all the coppers he can't trust out there with him, even cleaning the traffic detail out of Broadway, so Reno would have a clear road. McGraw and the bulls that are in on the play let Reno and his mob sneak out of the hoosegow, pull the job, and duck back in. Nice thing in alibis. Then they got sprung on bail a couple of hours later.

"It looks as if Lew Yard tumbled. He sent Dutch Jake Wahl and some other boys out to the Silver Arrow last night to teach Reno and his pals not to take things in their own hands like that. But Reno got away, and got back to the city. It was either him or Lew then. He made sure which it would be by being in front of Lew's house with a gun when Lew came out this morning. Reno seems to have had the right dope, because I notice that right now he's holding down a chair that would have been Lew Yard's if Lew hadn't been put on ice."

Everybody was sitting very still, as if to call attention to how still they were sitting. Nobody could count on having any friends among those present. It was no time for careless motions on anybody's part.

If what I had said meant anything one way or the other to Reno he didn't show it.

Thaler whispered softly:

"Didn't you skip some of it?"

"You mean the part about Jerry?" I kept on being the life of the party: "I was coming back to that. I don't know whether he got away from the can when you crushed out, and was caught later, or whether he didn't get away, or why. And I don't know how willingly he went along on the bank caper. But he did go along, and he was dropped and left in front of the bank because he was your right bower, and his being killed there would pin the trick to you. He was kept in the car till the get-away was on. Then he was pushed out, and was shot in the back. He was facing the bank, with his back to the car, when he got his."

Thaler looked at Reno and whispered:

"Well?"

Reno looked with dull eyes at Thaler and asked calmly:

"What of it?"

Thaler stood up, said, "Deal me out," and walked to the door.

Pete the Finn stood up, leaning on the table with big bony hands, speaking from deep in his chest:

"Whisper." And when Thaler had stopped and turned to face him: "I'm telling you this. You, Whisper, and all of you. That damn gun-work is out. All of you understand it. You've got no brains to know what is best for yourselves. So I'll tell you. This busting the town open is no good for business. I won't have it any more. You be nice boys or I'll make you.

"I got one army of young fellows that know what to do on

any end of a gun. I got to have them in my racket. If I got to use them on you I'll use them on you. You want to play with gunpowder and dynamite? I'll show you what playing is. You like to fight? I'll give you fighting. Mind what I tell you. That's all."

Pete the Finn sat down.

Thaler looked thoughtful for a moment, and went away without saying or showing what he had thought.

His going made the others impatient. None wanted to remain until anybody else had time to accumulate a few guns in the neighborhood.

In a very few minutes Elihu Willsson and I had the library to ourselves.

We sat and looked at one another.

Presently he said:

"How would you like to be chief of police?"

"No. I'm a rotten errand boy."

"I don't mean with this bunch. After we've got rid of them."

"And got another just like them."

"Damn you," he said, "it wouldn't hurt to take a nicer tone to a man old enough to be your father."

"Who curses me and hides behind his age."

Anger brought a vein out blue in his forehead. Then he laughed.

"You're a nasty talking lad," he said, "but I can't say you haven't done what I paid you to do."

"A swell lot of help I've got from you."

"Did you need wet-nursing? I gave you the money and a free hand. That's what you asked for. What more did you want?"

"You old pirate," I said, "I blackmailed you into it, and you played against me all the way till now, when even you can see that they're hell-bent on gobbling each other up. Now you talk about what you did for me."

"Old pirate," he repeated. "Son, if I hadn't been a pirate I'd still be working for the Anaconda for wages, and there'd be no Personville Mining Corporation. You're a damned little woolly lamb yourself, I suppose. I was had, son, where the hair was short. There were things I didn't like—worse things that I didn't know about until tonight—but I was caught and had to bide my time. Why since that Whisper Thaler has been here I've been a prisoner in my own home, a damned hostage!"

"Tough. Where do you stand now?" I demanded. "Are you behind me?"

"If you win."

I got up and said:

"I hope to Christ you get caught with them."

He said:

"I reckon you do, but I won't." He squinted his eyes merrily at me. "I'm financing you. That shows I mean well, don't it? Don't be too hard on me, son, I'm kind of—"

I said "Go to hell," and walked out.

CHAPTER XX

Laudanum

D ICK FOLEY in his hired car was at the next corner. I had him drive me over to within a block of Dinah Brand's house, and walked the rest of the way.

"You look tired," she said when I had followed her into the living room. "Been working?"

"Attending a peace conference out of which at least a dozen killings ought to grow."

The telephone rang. She answered it and called me.

Reno Starkey's voice:

"I thought maybe you'd like to hear about Noonan being shot to hell and gone when he got out of his heap in front of his house. You never saw anybody that was deader. Must have had thirty pills pumped in him."

"Thanks."

Dinah's big blue eyes asked questions.

"First fruits of the peace conference, plucked by Whisper Thaler," I told her. "Where's the gin?"

"Reno talking, wasn't it?"

"Yeah. He thought I'd like to hear about Poisonville being all out of police chiefs."

"You mean—?"

"Noonan went down tonight, according to Reno. Haven't you got any gin? Or do you like making me ask for it?"

"You know where it is. Been up to some of your cute tricks?"

I went back into the kitchen, opened the top of the refrigerator, and attacked the ice with an ice pick that had a six-inch awl-sharp blade set in a round blue and white handle. The girl stood in the doorway and asked questions. I didn't answer them while I put ice, gin, lemon juice and seltzer together in two glasses.

"What have you been doing?" she demanded as we carried our drinks into the dining room. "You look ghastly."

I put my glass on the table, sat down facing it, and complained:

"This damned burg's getting me. If I don't get away soon I'll be going blood-simple like the natives. There's been what? A dozen and a half murders since I've been here. Donald Willsson; Ike Bush; the four wops and the dick at Cedar Hill; Jerry; Lew Yard; Dutch Jake, Blackie Whalen and Put Collings at the Silver Arrow; Big Nick, the copper I potted; the blond kid Whisper dropped here; Yakima Shorty, old Elihu's prowler; and now Noonan. That's sixteen of them in less than a week, and more coming up."

She frowned at me and said sharply:

"Don't look like that."

I laughed and went on:

"I've arranged a killing or two in my time, when they were necessary. But this is the first time I've ever got the fever. It's this damned burg. You can't go straight here. I got myself tangled at the beginning. When old Elihu ran out on me there was nothing I could do but try to set the boys against each other. I had to swing the job the best way I could. How could I help it if the best way was bound to lead to a lot of killing? The job couldn't be handled any other way without Elihu's backing."

"Well, if you couldn't help it, what's the use of making a lot of fuss over it? Drink your drink."

I drank half of it and felt the urge to talk some more.

"Play with murder enough and it gets you one of two ways. It makes you sick, or you get to like it. It got Noonan the first way. He was green around the gills after Yard was knocked off, all the stomach gone out of him, willing to do anything to make peace. I took him in, suggested that he and the other survivors get together and patch up their differences.

"We had the meeting at Willsson's tonight. It was a nice party. Pretending I was trying to clear away everybody's mis-understandings by coming clean all around, I stripped Noonan naked and threw him to them—him and Reno. That broke up the meeting. Whisper declared himself out. Pete told everybody where they stood. He said battling was bad for his bootlegging racket, and anybody who started anything from then on could expect to have his booze guards turned loose on them. Whisper didn't look impressed. Neither did Reno."

"They wouldn't be," the girl said. "What did you do to Noonan? I mean how did you strip him and Reno?"

"I told the others that he had known all along that MacSwain killed Tim. That was the only lie I told them. Then I told them about the bank stick-up being turned by Reno and the chief, with Jerry taken along and dropped on the premises to tie the job to Whisper. I knew that's the way it was if what you told me was right, about Jerry getting out of the car, starting toward the bank and being shot. The hole was in his back. Fitting in with that, McGraw said the last seen of the stick-up car was when it turned into King Street. The boys would be returning to the City Hall, to their jail alibi."

"But didn't the bank watchman say he shot Jerry? That's the way it was in the papers."

"He said so, but he'd say anything and believe it. He probably emptied his gun with his eyes shut, and anything that fell was his. Didn't you see Jerry drop?"

"Yes, I did, and he was facing the bank, but it was all too confused for me to see who shot him. There were a lot of men shooting, and—"

"Yeah. They'd see to that. I also advertised the fact—at least, it looks like a fact to me—that Reno plugged Lew Yard. This Reno is a tough egg, isn't he? Noonan went watery, but all they got out of Reno was a 'What of it?' It was all nice and gentlemanly. They were evenly divided—Pete and Whisper against Noonan and Reno. But none of them could count on his partner backing him up if he made a play, and by the time the meeting was over the pairs had been split. Noonan was out of the count, and Reno and Whisper, against each other, had Pete against them. So everybody sat around and behaved and watched everybody else while I juggled death and destruction.

"Whisper was the first to leave, and he seems to have had time to collect some rods in front of Noonan's house by the time the chief reached home. The chief was shot down. If Pete the Finn meant what he said—and he has the look of a man who would—he'll be out after Whisper. Reno was as much to blame for Jerry's death as Noonan, so Whisper ought to be gunning for him. Knowing it, Reno will be out to get

Whisper first, and that will set Pete on his trail. Besides that, Reno will likely have his hands full standing off those of the late Lew Yard's underlings who don't fancy Reno as boss. All in all it's one swell dish."

Dinah Brand reached across the table and patted my hand. Her eyes were uneasy. She said:

"It's not your fault, darling. You said yourself that there was nothing else you could do. Finish your drink and we'll have another."

"There was plenty else I could do," I contradicted her. "Old Elihu ran out on me at first simply because these birds had too much on him for him to risk a break unless he was sure they could be wiped out. He couldn't see how I could do it, so he played with them. He's not exactly their brand of cut-throat, and, besides, he thinks the city is his personal property, and he doesn't like the way they've taken it away from him.

"I could have gone to him this afternoon and showed him that I had them ruined. He'd have listened to reason. He'd have come over to my side, have given me the support I needed to swing the play legally. I could have done that. But it's easier to have them killed off, easier and surer, and, now that I'm feeling this way, more satisfying. I don't know how I'm going to come out with the Agency. The Old Man will boil me in oil if he ever finds out what I've been doing. It's this damned town. Poisonville is right. It's poisoned me.

"Look. I sat at Willsson's table tonight and played them like you'd play trout, and got just as much fun out of it. I looked at Noonan and knew he hadn't a chance in a thousand of living another day because of what I had done to him, and I laughed, and felt warm and happy inside. That's not me. I've got hard skin all over what's left of my soul, and after twenty years of messing around with crime I can look at any sort of a murder without seeing anything in it but my bread and butter, the day's work. But this getting a rear out of planning deaths is not natural to me. It's what this place has done to me."

She smiled too softly and spoke too indulgently:

"You exaggerate so, honey. They deserve all they get. I wish you wouldn't look like that. You make me feel creepy."

I grinned, picked up the glasses, and went out to the kitchen for more gin. When I came back she frowned at me over anxious dark eyes and asked:

"Now what did you bring the ice pick in for?"

"To show you how my mind's running. A couple of days ago, if I thought about it at all, it was as a good tool to pry off chunks of ice." I ran a finger down its half-foot of round steel blade to the needle point. "Not a bad thing to pin a man to his clothes with. That's the way I'm betting, on the level. I can't even see a mechanical cigar lighter without thinking of filling one with nitroglycerine for somebody you don't like. There's a piece of copper wire lying in the gutter in front of your house—thin, soft, and just long enough to go around a neck with two ends to hold on. I had one hell of a time to keep from picking it up and stuffing it in my pocket, just in case—"

"You're crazy."

"I know it. That's what I've been telling you. I'm going blood-simple."

"Well, I don't like it. Put that thing back in the kitchen and sit down and be sensible."

I obeyed two-thirds of the order.

"The trouble with you is," she scolded me, "your nerves are shot. You've been through too much excitement in the last few days. Keep it up and you're going to have the heebie-jeebies for fair, a nervous breakdown."

I held up a hand with spread fingers. It was steady enough. She looked at it and said:

"That doesn't mean anything. It's inside you. Why don't you sneak off for a couple of days' rest? You've got things here so they'll run themselves. Let's go down to Salt Lake. It'll do you good."

"Can't, sister. Somebody's got to stay here to count the dead. Besides, the whole program is based on the present combination of people and events. Our going out of town would change that, and the chances are the whole thing would have to be gone over again."

"Nobody would have to know you were gone, and I've got nothing to do with it."

"Since when?"

She leaned forward, made her eyes small, and asked:

"Now what are you getting at?"

"Nothing. Just wondering how you got to be a disinterested bystander all of a sudden. Forgotten that Donald Willsson was killed because of you, starting the whole thing? Forgotten that it was the dope you gave me on Whisper that kept the job from petering out in the middle?"

"You know just as well as I do that none of that was my fault," she said indignantly. "And it's all past, anyway. You're just bringing it up because you're in a rotten humor and want to argue."

"It wasn't past last night, when you were scared stiff Whisper was going to kill you."

"Will you stop talking about killing!"

"Young Albury once told me Bill Quint had threatened to kill you," I said.

"Stop it."

"You seem to have a gift for stirring up murderous notions in your boy friends. There's Albury waiting trial for killing Willsson. There's Whisper who's got you shivering in corners. Even I haven't escaped your influence. Look at the way I've turned. And I've always had a private notion that Dan Rolff's going to have a try at you some day."

"Dan! You're crazy. Why, I—"

"Yeah. He was a lunger and down and out, and you took him in. You gave him a home and all the laudanum he wants. You use him for errand boy, you slap his face in front of me, and slap him around in front of others. He's in love with you. One of these mornings you're going to wake up and find he's whittled your neck away."

She shivered, got up and laughed.

"I'm glad one of us knows what you're talking about, if you do," she said as she carried our empty glasses through the kitchen door.

I lit a cigarette and wondered why I felt the way I did, wondered if I were getting psychic, wondered whether there was anything in this presentiment business or whether my nerves were just ragged.

"The next best thing for you to do if you won't go away," the girl advised me when she returned with full glasses, "is to get plastered and forget everything for a few hours. I put a double slug of gin in yours. You need it."

"It's not me," I said, wondering why I was saying it, but somehow enjoying it. "It's you. Every time I mention killing, you jump on me. You're a woman. You think if nothing's said about it, maybe none of the God only knows how many people in town who might want to will kill you. That's silly. Nothing we say or don't say is going to make Whisper, for instance—"

"Please, please stop! I am silly. I am afraid of the words. I'm afraid of him. I— Oh, why didn't you put him out of the way when I asked you?"

"Sorry," I said, meaning it.

"Do you think he—?"

"I don't know," I told her, "and I reckon you're right. There's no use talking about it. The thing to do is drink, though there doesn't seem to be much body to this gin."

"That's you, not the gin. Do you want an honest to God rear?"

"I'd drink nitroglycerine tonight."

"That's just about what you're going to get," she promised me.

She rattled bottles in the kitchen and brought me in a glass of what looked like the stuff we had been drinking. I sniffed at it and said:

"Some of Dan's laudanum, huh? He still in the hospital?"

"Yes. I think his skull is fractured. There's your kick, mister, if that's what you want."

I put the doped gin down my throat. Presently I felt more comfortable. Time went by as we drank and talked in a world that was rosy, cheerful, and full of fellowship and peace on earth.

Dinah stuck to gin. I tried that for a while too, and then had another gin and laudanum.

For a while after that I played a game, trying to hold my eyes open as if I were awake, even though I couldn't see anything out of them. When the trick wouldn't fool her any more I gave it up.

The last thing I remembered was her helping me on to the living room Chesterfield.

CHAPTER XXI

The Seventeenth Murder

I DREAMED I was sitting on a bench, in Baltimore, facing the tumbling fountain in Harlem Park, beside a woman who wore a veil. I had come there with her. She was somebody I knew well. But I had suddenly forgotten who she was. I couldn't see her face because of the long black veil.

I thought that if I said something to her I would recognize her voice when she answered. But I was very embarrassed and was a long time finding anything to say. Finally I asked her if she knew a man named Carroll T. Harris.

She answered me, but the roar and swish of the tumbling fountain smothered her voice, and I could hear nothing.

Fire engines went out Edmondson Avenue. She left me to run after them. As she ran she cried, "Fire! Fire!" I recognized her voice then and knew who she was, and knew she was someone important to me. I ran after her, but it was too late. She and the fire engines were gone.

I walked streets hunting for her, half the streets in the United States, Gay Street and Mount Royal Avenue in Baltimore, Colfax Avenue in Denver, Aetna Road and St. Clair Avenue in Cleveland, McKinney Avenue in Dallas, Lemartine and Cornell and Amory Streets in Boston, Berry Boulevard in Louisville, Lexington Avenue in New York, until I came to Victoria Street in Jacksonville, where I heard her voice again, though I still could not see her.

I walked more streets, listening to her voice. She was calling a name, not mine, one strange to me, but no matter how fast I walked or in what direction, I could get no nearer her voice. It was the same distance from me in the street that runs past the Federal Building in El Paso as in Detroit's Grand Circus Park. Then the voice stopped.

Tired and discouraged, I went into the lobby of the hotel that faces the railroad station in Rocky Mount, North Carolina, to rest. While I sat there a train came in. She got off it and came into the lobby, over to me, and began kissing me. I was very uncomfortable because everybody stood around looking at us and laughing.

That dream ended there.

I dreamed I was in a strange city hunting for a man I hated. I had an open knife in my pocket and meant to kill him with it when I found him. It was Sunday morning. Church bells were ringing, crowds of people were in the streets, going to and from church. I walked almost as far as in the first dream, but always in this same strange city.

Then the man I was after yelled at me, and I saw him. He was a small brown man who wore an immense sombrero. He was standing on the steps of a tall building on the far side of a wide plaza, laughing at me. Between us, the plaza was crowded with people, packed shoulder to shoulder.

Keeping one hand on the open knife in my pocket, I ran toward the little brown man, running on the heads and shoulders of the people in the plaza. The heads and shoulders were of unequal heights and not evenly spaced. I slipped and floundered over them.

The little brown man stood on the steps and laughed until I had almost reached him. Then he ran into the tall building. I chased him up miles of spiral stairway, always just an inch more than a hand's reach behind him. We came to the roof. He ran straight across to the edge and jumped just as one of my hands touched him.

His shoulder slid out of my fingers. My hand knocked his sombrero off, and closed on his head. It was a smooth hard round head no larger than a large egg. My fingers went all the way around it. Squeezing his head in one hand, I tried to bring the knife out of my pocket with the other—and realized that I had gone off the edge of the roof with him. We dropped giddily down toward the millions of upturned faces in the plaza, miles down.

I opened my eyes in the dull light of morning sun filtered through drawn blinds.

I was lying face down on the dining room floor, my head resting on my left forearm. My right arm was stretched straight out. My right hand held the round blue and white handle of

Dinah Brand's ice pick. The pick's six-inch needle-sharp blade was buried in Dinah Brand's left breast.

She was lying on her back, dead. Her long muscular legs were stretched out toward the kitchen door. There was a run down the front of her right stocking.

Slowly, gently, as if afraid of awakening her, I let go the ice pick, drew in my arm, and got up.

My eyes burned. My throat and mouth were hot, woolly. I went into the kitchen, found a bottle of gin, tilted it to my mouth, and kept it there until I had to breathe. The kitchen clock said seven-forty-one.

With the gin in me I returned to the dining room, switched on the lights, and looked at the dead girl.

Not much blood was in sight: a spot the size of a silver dollar around the hole the ice pick made in her blue silk dress. There was a bruise on her right cheek, just under the cheek bone. Another bruise, finger-made, was on her right wrist. Her hands were empty. I moved her enough to see that nothing was under her.

I examined the room. So far as I could tell, nothing had been changed in it. I went back to the kitchen and found no recognizable changes there.

The spring lock on the back door was fastened, and had no marks to show it had been monkeyed with. I went to the front door and failed to find any marks on it. I went through the house from top to bottom, and learned nothing. The windows were all right. The girl's jewelry, on her dressing table (except the two diamond rings on her hands), and four hundred odd dollars in her handbag, on a bedroom chair, were undisturbed.

In the dining room again, I knelt beside the dead girl and used my handkerchief to wipe the ice pick handle clean of any prints my fingers had left on it. I did the same to glasses, bottles, doors, light buttons, and the pieces of furniture I had touched, or was likely to have touched.

Then I washed my hands, examined my clothes for blood, made sure I was leaving none of my property behind, and went to the front door. I opened it, wiped the inner knob, closed it behind me, wiped the outer knob, and went away.

* * *

From a drug store in upper Broadway I telephoned Dick Foley and asked him to come over to my hotel. He arrived a few minutes after I got there.

"Dinah Brand was killed in her house last night or early this morning," I told him. "Stabbed with an ice pick. The police don't know it yet. I've told you enough about her for you to know that there are any number of people who might have had reason for killing her. There are three I want looked up first—Whisper, Dan Rolff and Bill Quint, the radical fellow. You've got their descriptions. Rolff is in the hospital with a dented skull. I don't know which hospital. Try the City first. Get hold of Mickey Linehan—he's still camped on Pete the Finn's trail—and have him let Pete rest while he gives you a hand on this. Find out where those three birds were last night. And time means something."

The little Canadian op had been watching me curiously while I talked. Now he started to say something, changed his mind, grunted, "Righto," and departed.

I went out to look for Reno Starkey. After an hour of searching I located him, by telephone, in a Ronney Street rooming house.

"By yourself?" he asked when I had said I wanted to see him.

"Yeah."

He said I could come out, and told me how to get there. I took a taxi. It was a dingy two-story house near the edge of town.

A couple of men loitered in front of a grocer's on the corner above. Another pair sat on the low wooden steps of the house down at the next corner. None of the four was conspicuously refined in appearance.

When I rang the bell two men opened the door. They weren't so mild looking either.

I was taken upstairs to a front room where Reno, collarless and in shirt-sleeves and vest, sat tilted back in a chair with his feet on the window sill.

He nodded his sallow horse face and said:

"Pull a chair over."

The men who had brought me up went away, closing the door. I sat down and said:

"I want an alibi. Dinah Brand was killed last night after I left her. There's no chance of my being copped for it, but with Noonan dead I don't know how I'm hitched up with the department. I don't want to give them any openings to even try to hang anything on me. If I've got to I can prove where I was last night, but you can save me a lot of trouble if you will."

Reno looked at me with dull eyes and asked:

"Why pick on me?"

"You phoned me there last night. You're the only person who knows I was there the first part of the night. I'd have to fix it with you even if I got the alibi somewhere else, wouldn't I?"

He asked:

"You didn't croak her, did you?"

I said, "No," casually.

He stared out the window a little while before he spoke. He asked:

"What made you think I'd give you the lift? Do I owe you anything for what you done to me at Willsson's last night?"

I said:

"I didn't hurt you any. The news was half-out anyhow. Whisper knew enough to guess the rest. I only gave you a show-down. What do you care? You can take care of yourself."

"I aim to try," he agreed. "All right. You was at the Tanner House in Tanner. That's a little burg twenty-thirty miles up the hill. You went up there after you left Willsson's and stayed till morning. A guy named Ricker that hangs around Murry's with a hire heap drove you up and back. You ought to know what you was doing up there. Give me your sig and I'll have it put on the register."

"Thanks," I said as I unscrewed my fountain pen.

"Don't say them. I'm doing this because I need all the friends I can get. When the time comes that you sit in with me and Whisper and Pete, I don't expect the sour end of it."

"You won't get it," I promised. "Who's going to be chief of police?"

"McGraw's acting chief. He'll likely cinch it."

"How'll he play?"

"With the Finn. Rough stuff will hurt his shop just like it does Pete's. It'll have to be hurt some. I'd be a swell mutt to sit still while a guy like Whisper is on the loose. It's me or him. Think he croaked the broad?"

"He had reason enough," I said as I gave him the slip of paper on which I had written my name. "She double-crossed him, sold him out, plenty."

"You and her was kind of thick, wasn't you?" he asked.

I let the question alone, lighting a cigarette. Reno waited a while and then said:

"You better hunt up Ricker and let him get a look at you so's he'll know how to describe you if he's asked."

A long-legged youngster of twenty-two or so with a thin freckled face around reckless eyes opened the door and came into the room. Reno introduced him to me as Hank O'Marra. I stood up to shake his hand, and then asked Reno:

"Can I reach you here if I need to?"

"Know Peak Murry?"

"I've met him, and I know his joint."

"Anything you give him will get to me," he said. "We're getting out of here. It's not so good. That Tanner lay is all set."

"Right. Thanks." I went out of the house.

CHAPTER XXII

The Ice Pick

D OWNTOWN, I went first to police headquarters.
McGraw was holding down the chief's desk. His
blond-lashed eyes looked suspiciously at me, and the lines in
his leathery face were even deeper and sourer than usual.

"When'd you see Dinah Brand last?" he asked without any
preliminaries, not even a nod. His voice rasped disagreeably
through his bony nose.

"Ten-forty last night, or thereabout," I said. "Why?"

"Where?"

"Her house."

"How long were you there?"

"Ten minutes, maybe fifteen."

"Why?"

"Why what?"

"Why didn't you stay any longer than that?"

"What," I asked, sitting down in the chair he hadn't offered me, "makes it any of your business?"

He glared at me while he filled his lungs so he could yell,
"Murder!" in my face.

I laughed and said:

"You don't think she had anything to do with Noonan's
killing?"

I wanted a cigarette, but cigarettes were too well known as
first aids to the nervous for me to take a chance on one just
then.

McGraw was trying to look through my eyes. I let him
look, having all sorts of confidence in my belief that, like a lot
of people, I looked most honest when I was lying. Presently
he gave up the eye-study and asked:

"Why not?"

That was weak enough. I said, "All right, why not?" indifferently, offered him a cigarette, and took one myself. Then I
added: "My guess is that Whisper did it."

"Was he there?" For once McGraw cheated his nose, snapping the words off his teeth.

"Was he where?"

"At Brand's?"

"No," I said, wrinkling my forehead. "Why should he be—
if he was off killing Noonan?"

"Damn Noonan!" the acting chief exclaimed irritably.
"What do you keep dragging him in for?"

I tried to look at him as if I thought him crazy.

He said:

"Dinah Brand was murdered last night."

I said: "Yeah?"

"Now will you answer my questions?"

"Of course. I was at Willsson's with Noonan and the others. After I left there, around ten-thirty, I dropped in at her
house to tell her I had to go up to Tanner. I had a half-way
date with her. I stayed there about ten minutes, long enough
to have a drink. There was nobody else there, unless they
were hiding. When was she killed? And how?"

McGraw told me he had sent a pair of his dicks—Shepp
and Vanaman—to see the girl that morning, to see how much
help she could and would give the department in copping
Whisper for Noonan's murder. The dicks got to her house at
nine-thirty. The front door was ajar. Nobody answered their
ringing. They went in and found the girl lying on her back in
the dining room, dead, with a stab wound in her left breast.

The doctor who examined the body said she had been
killed with a slender, round, pointed blade about six inches in
length, at about three o'clock in the morning. Bureaus, closets, trunks, and so on, had apparently been skilfully and thoroughly ransacked. There was no money in the girl's handbag,
or elsewhere in the house. The jewel case on her dressing
table was empty. Two diamond rings were on her fingers.

The police hadn't found the weapon with which she had
been stabbed. The fingerprint experts hadn't turned up anything they could use. Neither doors nor windows seemed to
have been forced. The kitchen showed that the girl had been
drinking with a guest or guests.

"Six inches, round, slim, pointed," I repeated the weapon's
description. "That sounds like her ice pick."

McGraw reached for the phone and told somebody to send
Shepp and Vanaman in. Shepp was a stoop-shouldered tall

man whose wide mouth had a grimly honest look that probably came from bad teeth. The other detective was short, stocky, with purplish veins in his nose and hardly any neck.

McGraw introduced us and asked them about the ice pick. They had not seen it, were positive it hadn't been there. They wouldn't have overlooked an article of its sort.

"Was it there last night?" McGraw asked me.

"I stood beside her while she chipped off pieces of ice with it."

I described it. McGraw told the dicks to search her house again, and then to try to find the pick in the vicinity of the house.

"You knew her," he said when Shepp and Vanaman had gone. "What's your slant on it?"

"Too new for me to have one," I dodged the question. "Give me an hour or two to think it over. What do you think?"

He fell back into sourness, growling, "How the hell do I know?"

But the fact that he let me go away without asking me any more questions told me he had already made up his mind that Whisper had killed the girl.

I wondered if the little gambler had done it, or if this was another of the wrong raps that Poisonville police chiefs liked to hang on him. It didn't seem to make much difference now. It was a cinch he had—personally or by deputy—put Noonan out, and they could only hang him once.

There were a lot of men in the corridor when I left McGraw. Some of these men were quite young—just kids— quite a few were foreigners, and most of them were every bit as tough looking as any men should be.

Near the street door I met Donner, one of the coppers who had been on the Cedar Hill expedition.

"Hello," I greeted him. "What's the mob? Emptying the can to make room for more?"

"Them's our new specials," he told me, speaking as if he didn't think much of them. "We're going to have a argumented force."

"Congratulations," I said and went on out.

In his pool room I found Peak Murry sitting at a desk behind the cigar counter talking to three men. I sat down on the other side of the room and watched two kids knock balls around. In a few minutes the lanky proprietor came over to me.

"If you see Reno some time," I told him, "you might let him know that Pete the Finn's having his mob sworn in as special coppers."

"I might," Murry agreed.

Mickey Linehan was sitting in the lobby when I got back to my hotel. He followed me up to my room, and reported:

"Your Dan Rolff pulled a sneak from the hospital somewhere after midnight last night. The croakers are kind of steamed up about it. Seems they were figuring on pulling a lot of little pieces of bone out of his brain this morning. But him and his duds were gone. We haven't got a line on Whisper yet. Dick's out now trying to place Bill Quint. What's what on this girl's carving? Dick tells me you got it before the coppers."

"It—"

The telephone bell rang.

A man's voice, carefully oratorical, spoke my name with a question mark after it.

I said: "Yeah."

The voice said:

"This is Mr. Charles Proctor Dawn speaking. I think you will find it well worth your while to appear at my offices at your earliest convenience."

"Will I? Who are you?"

"Mr. Charles Proctor Dawn, attorney-at-law. My suite is in the Rutledge Block, 310 Green Street. I think you will find it well—"

"Mind telling me part of what it's about?" I asked.

"There are affairs best not discussed over the telephone. I think you will find—"

"All right," I interrupted him again. "I'll be around to see you this afternoon if I get a chance."

"You will find it very, very advisable," he assured me.

I hung up on that.

Mickey said:

"You were going to give me the what's what on the Brand slaughter."

I said:

"I wasn't. I started to say it oughtn't to be hard to trace Rolff—running around with a fractured skull and probably a lot of bandages. Suppose you try it. Give Hurricane Street a play first."

Mickey grinned all the way across his comedian's red face, said, "Don't tell me anything that's going on—I'm only working with you," picked up his hat, and left me.

I spread myself on the bed, smoked cigarettes end to end, and thought about last night—my frame of mind, my passing out, my dreams, and the situation into which I woke. The thinking was unpleasant enough to make me glad when it was interrupted.

Fingernails scratched the outside of my door. I opened the door.

The man who stood there was a stranger to me. He was young, thin, and gaudily dressed. He had heavy eyebrows and a small mustache that were coal-black against a very pale, nervous, but not timid, face.

"I'm Ted Wright," he said, holding out a hand as if I were glad to meet him. "I guess you've heard Whisper talk about me."

I gave him my hand, let him in, closed the door, and asked:

"You're a friend of Whisper's?"

"You bet." He held up two thin fingers pressed tightly together. "Just like that, me and him."

I didn't say anything. He looked around the room, smiled nervously, crossed to the open bathroom door, peeped in, came back to me, rubbed his lips with his tongue, and made his proposition:

"I'll knock him off for you for half a grand."

"Whisper?"

"Yep, and it's dirt cheap."

"Why do I want him killed?" I asked.

"He un-womaned you, didn't he?"

"Yeah?"

"You ain't that dumb."

A notion stirred in my noodle. To give it time to crawl around I said: "Sit down. This needs talking over."

"It don't need nothing," he said, looking at me sharply, not moving toward either chair. "You either want him knocked off or you don't."

"Then I don't."

He said something I didn't catch, down in his throat, and turned to the door. I got between him and it. He stopped, his eyes fidgeting.

I said:

"So Whisper's dead?"

He stepped back and put a hand behind him. I poked his jaw, leaning my hundred and ninety pounds on the poke.

He got his legs crossed and went down.

I pulled him up by the wrists, yanked his face close to mine, and growled:

"Come through. What's the racket?"

"I ain't done nothing to you."

"Let me catch you. Who got Whisper?"

"I don't know nothing a—"

I let go of one of his wrists, slapped his face with my open hand, caught his wrist again, and tried my luck at crunching both of them while I repeated:

"Who got Whisper?"

"Dan Rolff," he whined. "He walked up to him and stuck him with the same skewer Whisper had used on the twist. That's right."

"How do you know it was the one Whisper killed the girl with?"

"Dan said so."

"What did Whisper say?"

"Nothing. He looked funny as hell, standing there with the butt of the sticker sticking out his side. Then he flashes the rod and puts two pills in Dan just like one, and the both of them go down together, cracking heads, Dan's all bloody through the bandages."

"And then what?"

"Then nothing. I roll them over, and they're a pair of stiffs. Every word I'm telling you is gospel."

"Who else was there?"

"Nobody else. Whisper was hiding out, with only me to go between him and the mob. He killed Noonan hisself, and he didn't want to have to trust nobody for a couple of days, till he could see what was what, excepting me."

"So you, being a smart boy, thought you could run around to his enemies and pick up a little dough for killing him after he was dead?"

"I was clean, and this won't be no place for Whisper's pals when the word gets out that he's croaked," Wright whined. "I had to raise a get-away stake."

"How'd you make out so far?"

"I got a century from Pete and a century and a half from Peak Murry—for Reno—with more promised from both when I turn the trick." The whine changed into boasting as he talked. "I bet you I could get McGraw to come across too, and I thought you'd kick in with something."

"They must be high in the air to toss dough at a woozy racket like that."

"I don't know," he said superiorly. "It ain't such a lousy one at that." He became humble again. "Give me a chance, chief. Don't gum it on me. I'll give you fifty bucks now and a split of whatever I get from McGraw if you'll keep your clam shut till I can put it over and grab a rattler."

"Nobody but you knows where Whisper is?"

"Nobody else, except Dan, that's as dead as he is."

"Where are they?"

"The old Redman warehouse down on Porter Street. In the back, upstairs, Whisper had a room fixed up with a bed, stove, and some grub. Give me a chance. Fifty bucks now and a cut on the rest."

I let go of his arm and said:

"I don't want the dough, but go ahead. I'll lay off for a couple of hours. That ought to be long enough."

"Thanks, chief. Thanks, thanks," and he hurried away from me.

I put on my coat and hat, went out, found Green Street and the Rutledge Block. It was a wooden building a long while past any prime it might ever have had. Mr. Charles Proctor Dawn's establishment was on the second floor. There was no elevator. I climbed a worn and rickety flight of wooden steps.

The lawyer had two rooms, both dingy, smelly, and poorly lighted. I waited in the outer one while a clerk who went well with the rooms carried my name in to the lawyer. Half a minute later the clerk opened the door and beckoned me in.

Mr. Charles Proctor Dawn was a little fat man of fifty-something. He had prying triangular eyes of a very light color, a short fleshy nose, and a fleshier mouth whose greediness was only partly hidden between a ragged gray mustache and a ragged gray Vandyke beard. His clothes were dark and unclean looking without actually being dirty.

He didn't get up from his desk, and throughout my visit he kept his right hand on the edge of a desk drawer that was some six inches open.

He said:

"Ah, my dear sir, I am extremely gratified to find that you had the good judgment to recognize the value of my counsel."

His voice was even more oratorical than it had been over the wire.

I didn't say anything.

Nodding his whiskers as if my not saying anything was another exhibition of good judgment, he continued:

"I may say, in all justice, that you will find it the invariable part of sound judgment to follow the dictates of my counsel in all cases. I may say this, my dear sir, without false modesty, appreciating with both fitting humility and a deep sense of true and lasting values, my responsibilities as well as my prerogatives as a—and why should I stoop to conceal the fact that there are those who feel justified in preferring to substitute the definite article for the indefinite?—recognized and accepted leader of the bar in this thriving state."

He knew a lot of sentences like those, and he didn't mind using them on me. Finally he got along to:

"Thus, that conduct which in a minor practitioner might seem irregular, becomes, when he who exercises it occupies such indisputable prominence in his community—and, I might say, not merely the immediate community—as serves to place him above fear of reproach, simply that greater ethic which scorns the pettier conventionalities when confronted with an opportunity to serve mankind through one of its individual representatives. Therefore, my dear sir, I have not hesitated to brush aside scornfully all trivial considerations of accepted precedent, to summon you, to say to you frankly and candidly, my dear sir, that your interests will best be served by and through retaining me as your legal representative."

I asked:

"What'll it cost?"

"That," he said loftily, "is of but secondary importance. However, it is a detail which has its deserved place in our relationship, and must be not overlooked or neglected. We shall say, a thousand dollars now. Later, no doubt—"

He ruffled his whiskers and didn't finish the sentence.

I said I hadn't, of course, that much money on me.

"Naturally, my dear sir. Naturally. But that is of not the least importance in any degree. None whatever. Any time will do for that, any time up to ten o'clock tomorrow morning."

"At ten tomorrow," I agreed. "Now I'd like to know why I'm supposed to need legal representatives."

He made an indignant face.

"My dear sir, this is no matter for jesting, of that I assure you."

I explained that I hadn't been joking, that I really was puzzled.

He cleared his throat, frowned more or less importantly, said:

"It may well be, my dear sir, that you do not fully comprehend the peril that surrounds you, but it is indubitably preposterous that you should expect me to suppose that you are without any inkling of the difficulties—the legal difficulties, my dear sir—with which you are about to be confronted, growing, as they do, out of occurrences that took place at no more remote time than last night, my dear sir, last night. However, there is no time to go into that now. I have a pressing appointment with Judge Leffner. On the morrow I shall be glad to go more thoroughly into each least ramification of the situation—and I assure you they are many—with you. I shall expect you at ten tomorrow morning."

I promised to be there, and went out. I spent the evening in my room, drinking unpleasant whiskey, thinking unpleasant thoughts, and waiting for reports that didn't come from Mickey and Dick. I went to sleep at midnight.

CHAPTER XXIII

Mr. Charles Proctor Dawn

I WAS half dressed the next morning when Dick Foley came in. He reported, in his word-saving manner, that Bill Quint had checked out of the Miners' Hotel at noon the previous day, leaving no forwarding address.

A train left Personville for Ogden at twelve-thirty-five. Dick had wired the Continental's Salt Lake branch to send a man up to Ogden to try to trace Quint.

"We can't pass up any leads," I said, "but I don't think Quint's the man we want. She gave him the air long ago. If he had meant to do anything about it he would have done it before this. My guess is that when he heard she had been killed he decided to duck, being a discarded lover who had threatened her."

Dick nodded and said:

"Gun play out the road last night. Hijacking. Four trucks of hooch nailed, burned."

That sounded like Reno Starkey's answer to the news that the big bootlegger's mob had been sworn in as special coppers.

Mickey Linehan arrived by the time I had finished dressing.

"Dan Rolff was at the house, all right," he reported. "The Greek grocer on the corner saw him come out around nine yesterday morning. He went down the street wobbling and talking to himself. The Greek thought he was drunk."

"How come the Greek didn't tell the police? Or did he?"

"Wasn't asked. A swell department this burg's got. What do we do: find him for them and turn him in with the job all tacked up?"

"McGraw has decided Whisper killed her," I said, "and he's not bothering himself with any leads that don't lead that way. Unless he came back later for the ice pick, Rolff didn't turn the trick. She was killed at three in the morning. Rolff wasn't there at eight-thirty, and the pick was still sticking in her. It was—"

Dick Foley came over to stand in front of me and ask:

"How do you know?"

I didn't like the way he looked or the way he spoke. I said: "You know because I'm telling you."

Dick didn't say anything. Mickey grinned his halfwit's grin and asked:

"Where do we go from here? Let's get this thing polished off."

"I've got a date for ten," I told them. "Hang around the hotel till I get back. Whisper and Rolff are probably dead—so we won't have to hunt for them." I scowled at Dick and said: "I was told that. I didn't kill either of them."

The little Canadian nodded without lowering his eyes from mine.

I ate breakfast alone, and then set out for the lawyer's office.

Turning off King Street, I saw Hank O'Marra's freckled face in an automobile that was going up Green Street. He was sitting beside a man I didn't know. The long-legged youngster waved an arm at me and stopped the car. I went over to him.

He said:

"Reno wants to see you."

"Where will I find him?"

"Jump in."

"I can't go now," I said. "Probably not till afternoon."

"See Peak when you're ready."

I said I would. O'Marra and his companion drove on up Green Street. I walked half a block south to the Rutledge Block.

With a foot on the first of the rickety steps that led up to the lawyer's floor, I stopped to look at something.

It was barely visible back in a dim corner of the first floor. It was a shoe. It was lying in a position that empty shoes don't lie in.

I took my foot off the step and went toward the shoe. Now I could see an ankle and the cuff of a black pants-leg above the shoe-top.

That prepared me for what I found.

I found Mr. Charles Proctor Dawn huddled among two brooms, a mop and a bucket, in a little alcove formed by the back of the stairs and a corner of the wall. His Vandyke beard was red with blood from a cut that ran diagonally across his forehead. His head was twisted sidewise and backward at an angle that could only be managed with a broken neck.

I quoted Noonan's, "What's got to be done has got to be done," to myself, and, gingerly pulling one side of the dead man's coat out of the way, emptied his inside coat pocket, transferring a black book and a sheaf of papers to my own pocket. In two of his other pockets I found nothing I wanted. The rest of his pockets couldn't be got at without moving him, and I didn't care to do that.

Five minutes later I was back in the hotel, going in through a side door, to avoid Dick and Mickey in the lobby, and walking up to the mezzanine to take an elevator.

In my room I sat down and examined my loot.

I took the book first, a small imitation-leather memoranda book of the sort that sells for not much money in any stationery store. It held some fragmentary notes that meant nothing to me, and thirty-some names and addresses that meant as little, with one exception:

Helen Albury
1229A Hurricane St.

That was interesting because, first, a young man named Robert Albury was in prison, having confessed that he shot and killed Donald Willsson in a fit of jealousy aroused by Willsson's supposed success with Dinah Brand; and, second, Dinah Brand had lived, and had been murdered, at 1232 Hurricane Street, across the street from 1229A.

I did not find my name in the book.

I put the book aside and began unfolding and reading the papers I had taken with it. Here too I had to wade through a lot that didn't mean anything to find something that did.

This find was a group of four letters held together by a rubber band.

The letters were in slitted envelopes that had postmarks dated a week apart, on the average. The latest was a little more than six months old. The letters were addressed to Dinah Brand. The first—that is, the earliest—wasn't so bad, for a love letter. The second was a bit goofier. The third and fourth were swell examples of how silly an ardent and unsuccessful wooer can be, especially if he's getting on in years. The four letters were signed by Elihu Willsson.

I had not found anything to tell me definitely why Mr. Charles Proctor Dawn had thought he could blackmail me out of a thousand dollars, but I had found plenty to think about. I encouraged my brain with two Fatimas, and then went downstairs.

"Go out and see what you can raise on a lawyer named Charles Proctor Dawn," I told Mickey. "He's got offices in Green Street. Stay away from them. Don't put in a lot of time on him. I just want a rough line quick."

I told Dick to give me a five-minute start and then follow me out to the neighborhood of 1229A Hurricane Street.

1229A was the upper flat in a two-story building almost directly opposite Dinah's house. 1229 was divided into two flats, with a private entrance for each. I rang the bell at the one I wanted.

The door was opened by a thin girl of eighteen or nineteen with dark eyes set close together in a shiny yellowish face under short-cut brown hair that looked damp.

She opened the door, made a choked, frightened, sound in her throat, and backed away from me, holding both hands to her open mouth.

"Miss Helen Albury?" I asked.

She shook her head violently from side to side. There was no truthfulness in it. Her eyes were crazy.

I said:

"I'd like to come in and talk to you a few minutes," going in as I spoke, closing the door behind me.

She didn't say anything. She went up the steps in front of me, her head twisted around so she could watch me with her scary eyes.

We went into a scantily furnished living room. Dinah's house could be seen from its windows.

The girl stood in the center of the floor, her hands still to her mouth.

I wasted time and words trying to convince her that I was

harmless. It was no good. Everything I said seemed to increase her panic. It was a damned nuisance. I quit trying, and got down to business.

"You are Robert Albury's sister?" I asked.

No reply, nothing but the senseless look of utter fear.

I said:

"After he was arrested for killing Donald Willsson you took this flat so you could watch her. What for?"

Not a word from her. I had to supply my own answer:

"Revenge. You blamed Dinah Brand for your brother's trouble. You watched for your chance. It came the night before last. You sneaked into her house, found her drunk, stabbed her with the ice pick you found there."

She didn't say anything. I hadn't succeeded in jolting the blankness out of her frightened face. I said:

"Dawn helped you, engineered it for you. He wanted Elihu Willsson's letters. Who was the man he sent to get them, the man who did the actual killing? Who was he?"

That got me nothing. No change in her expression, or lack of expression. No word. I thought I would like to spank her. I said:

"I've given you your chance to talk. I'm willing to listen to your side of the story. But suit yourself."

She suited herself by keeping quiet. I gave it up. I was afraid of her, afraid she would do something even crazier than her silence if I pressed her further. I went out of the flat not sure that she had understood a single word I had said.

At the corner I told Dick Foley:

"There's a girl in there, Helen Albury, eighteen, five six, skinny, not more than a hundred, if that, eyes close together, brown, yellow skin, brown short hair, straight, got on a gray suit now. Tail her. If she cuts up on you throw her in the can. Be careful—she's crazy as a bedbug."

I set out for Peak Murry's dump, to locate Reno and see what he wanted. Half a block from my destination I stepped into an office building doorway to look the situation over.

A police patrol wagon stood in front of Murry's. Men were being led, dragged, carried, from pool room to wagon. The leaders, draggers, and carriers did not look like regular coppers. They were, I supposed, Pete the Finn's crew, now special officers. Pete, with McGraw's help, apparently was making good his threat to give Whisper and Reno all the war they wanted.

While I watched, an ambulance arrived, was loaded, and drove away. I was too far away to recognize anybody or any bodies. When the height of the excitement seemed past I circled a couple of blocks and returned to my hotel.

Mickey Linehan was there with information about Mr. Charles Proctor Dawn.

"He's the guy that the joke was wrote about: 'Is he a criminal lawyer?' 'Yes, very.' This fellow Albury that you nailed, some of his family hired this bird Dawn to defend him. Albury wouldn't have anything to do with him when Dawn came to see him. This three-named shyster nearly went over himself last year, on a blackmail rap, something to do with a parson named Hill, but squirmed out of it. Got some property out on Libert Street, wherever that is. Want me to keep digging?"

"That'll do. We'll stick around till we hear from Dick."

Mickey yawned and said that was all right with him, never being one that had to run around a lot to keep his blood circulating, and asked if I knew we were getting nationally famous.

I asked him what he meant by that.

"I just ran into Tommy Robins," he said. "The Consolidated Press sent him here to cover the doings. He tells me some of the other press associations and a big-city paper or two are sending in special correspondents, beginning to play our troubles up."

I was making one of my favorite complaints—that newspapers were good for nothing except to hash things up so nobody could unhash them—when I heard a boy chanting my name. For a dime he told me I was wanted on the phone.

Dick Foley:

"She showed right away. To 310 Green Street. Full of coppers. Mouthpiece named Dawn killed. Police took her to the Hall."

"She still there?"

"Yes, in the chief's office."

"Stick, and get anything you pick up to me quick."

I went back to Mickey Linehan and gave him my room key and instructions:

"Camp in my room. Take anything that comes for me and pass it on. I'll be at the Shannon around the corner, registered as J. W. Clark. Tell Dick and nobody."

Mickey asked, "What the hell?" got no answer, and moved his loose-jointed bulk toward the elevators.

CHAPTER XXIV

Wanted

I WENT around to the Shannon Hotel, registered my alias, paid my day's rent, and was taken to room 321.

An hour passed before the phone rang.

Dick Foley said he was coming up to see me.

He arrived within five minutes. His thin worried face was not friendly. Neither was his voice. He said:

"Warrants out for you. Murder. Two counts—Brand and Dawn. I phoned. Mickey said he'd stick. Told me you were here. Police got him. Grilling him now."

"Yeah, I expected that."

"So did I," he said sharply.

I said, making myself drawl the words:

"You think I killed them, don't you, Dick?"

"If you didn't, it's a good time to say so."

"Going to put the finger on me?" I asked.

He pulled his lips back over his teeth. His face changed from tan to buff.

I said:

"Go back to San Francisco, Dick. I've got enough to do without having to watch you."

He put his hat on very carefully and very carefully closed the door behind him when he went out.

At four o'clock I had some lunch, cigarettes, and an *Evening Herald* sent up to me.

Dinah Brand's murder, and the newer murder of Charles Proctor Dawn, divided the front page of the *Herald*, with Helen Albury connecting them.

Helen Albury was, I read, Robert Albury's sister, and she was, in spite of his confession, thoroughly convinced that her brother was not guilty of murder, but the victim of a plot. She had retained Charles Proctor Dawn to defend him. (I could guess that the late Charles Proctor had hunted her up, and not she him.) The brother refused to have Dawn or any other lawyer, but the girl (properly encouraged by Dawn, no doubt) had not given up the fight.

Finding a vacant flat across the street from Dinah Brand's house, Helen Albury had rented it, and had installed herself therein with a pair of field glasses and one idea—to prove that Dinah and her associates were guilty of Donald Willsson's murder.

I, it seems, was one of the "associates." The *Herald* called me "a man supposed to be a private detective from San Francisco, who has been in the city for several days, apparently on intimate terms with Max ('Whisper') Thaler, Daniel Rolff, Oliver ('Reno') Starkey, and Dinah Brand." We were the plotters who had framed Robert Albury.

The night that Dinah had been killed, Helen Albury, peeping through her window, had seen things that were, according to the *Herald*, extremely significant when considered in connection with the subsequent finding of Dinah's dead body. As soon as the girl heard of the murder, she took her important knowledge to Charles Proctor Dawn. He, the police learned from his clerks, immediately sent for me, and had been closeted with me that afternoon. He had later told his clerks that I was to return the next—this—morning at ten. This morning I had not appeared to keep my appointment. At twenty-five minutes past ten, the janitor of the Rutledge Block had found Charles Proctor Dawn's body in a corner behind the staircase, murdered. It was believed that valuable papers had been taken from the dead man's pockets.

At the very moment that the janitor was finding the dead lawyer, I, it seems, was in Helen Albury's flat, having forced an entrance, and was threatening her. After she succeeded in throwing me out, she hurried to Dawn's offices, arriving while the police were there, telling them her story. Police sent to my hotel had not found me there, but in my room they had found one Michael Linehan, who also represented himself to be a San Francisco private detective. Michael Linehan was still being questioned by the police. Whisper, Reno, Rolff and I were being hunted by the police, charged with murder. Important developments were expected.

Page two held an interesting half-column. Detectives Shepp and Vanaman, the discoverers of Dinah Brand's body, had mysteriously vanished. Foul play on the part of us "associates" was feared.

There was nothing in the paper about last night's hijacking, nothing about the raid on Peak Murry's joint.

I went out after dark. I wanted to get in touch with Reno. From a drug store I phoned Peak Murry's pool room.

"Is Peak there?" I asked.

"This is Peak," said a voice that didn't sound anything at all like his. "Who's talking?"

I said disgustedly, "This is Lillian Gish," hung up the receiver, and removed myself from the neighborhood.

I gave up the idea of finding Reno and decided to go calling on my client, old Elihu, and try to blackjack him into good behavior with the love letters he had written Dinah Brand, and which I had stolen from Dawn's remains.

I walked, keeping to the darker side of the darkest streets. It was a fairly long walk for a man who sneers at exercise. By the time I reached Willsson's block I was in bad enough humor to be in good shape for the sort of interviews he and I usually had. But I wasn't to see him for a little while yet.

I was two pavements from my destination when somebody *S-s-s-s-s'd* at me.

I probably didn't jump twenty feet.

" 'S all right," a voice whispered.

It was dark there. Peeping out under my bush—I was on my hands and knees in somebody's front yard—I could make out the form of a man crouching close to a hedge, on my side of it.

My gun was in my hand now. There was no special reason why I shouldn't take his word for it that it was all right.

I got up off my knees and went to him. When I got close enough I recognized him as one of the men who had let me into the Ronney Street house the day before.

I sat on my heels beside him and asked:

"Where'll I find Reno? Hank O'Marra said he wanted to see me."

"He does that. Know where Kid McLeod's place is at?"

"No."

"It's on Martin Street above King, corner the alley. Ask for the Kid. Go back that-away three blocks, and then down. You can't miss it."

I said I'd try not to, and left him crouching behind his hedge, watching my client's place, waiting, I guessed, for a shot at Pete the Finn, Whisper, or any of Reno's other un-friends who might happen to call on old Elihu.

Following directions, I came to a soft drink and rummy es-tablishment with red and yellow paint all over it. Inside I asked for Kid McLeod. I was taken into a back room, where a fat man with a dirty collar, a lot of gold teeth, and only one ear, admitted he was McLeod.

"Reno sent for me," I said. "Where'll I find him?"

"And who does that make you?" he asked.

I told him who I was. He went out without saying any-thing. I waited ten minutes. He brought a boy back with him, a kid of fifteen or so with a vacant expression on a pimply red face.

"Go with Sonny," Kid McLeod told me.

I followed the boy out a side door, down two blocks of back street, across a sandy lot, through a ragged gate, and up to the back door of a frame house.

The boy knocked on the door and was asked who he was.

"Sonny, with a guy the Kid sent," he replied.

The door was opened by long-legged O'Marra. Sonny went away. I went into a kitchen where Reno Starkey and four other men sat around a table that had a lot of beer on it. I no-ticed that two automatic pistols hung on nails over the top of the door through which I had come. They would be handy if any of the house's occupants opened the door, found an en-emy with a gun there, and were told to put up their hands.

Reno poured me a glass of beer and led me through the dining room into a front room. A man lay on his belly there, with one eye to the crack between the drawn blind and the bottom of the window, watching the street.

"Go back and get yourself some beer," Reno told him.

He got up and went away. We made ourselves comfortable in adjoining chairs.

"When I fixed up that Tanner alibi for you," Reno said, "I told you I was doing it because I needed all the friends I could get."

"You got one."

"Crack the alibi yet?" he asked.

"Not yet."

"It'll hold," he assured me, "unless they got too damned much on you. Think they have?"

I did think so. I said:

"No. McGraw's just feeling playful. That'll take care of itself. How's your end holding up?"

He emptied his glass, wiped his mouth on the back of a hand, and said:

"I'll make out. But that's what I wanted to see you about. Here's how she stacks up. Pete's throwed in with McGraw. That lines coppers and beer mob up against me and Whisper. But hell! Me and Whisper are busier trying to put the chive in each other than bucking the combine. That's a sour racket. While we're tangling, them bums will eat us up."

I said I had been thinking the same thing. He went on:

"Whisper'll listen to you. Find him, will you? Put it to him. Here's the proposish: he means to get me for knocking off Jerry Hooper, and I mean to get him first. Let's forget that for a couple of days. Nobody won't have to trust nobody else. Whisper don't ever show in any of his jobs anyways. He just sends the boys. I'll do the same this time. We'll just put the mobs together to swing the caper. We run them together, rub out that damned Finn, and then we'll have plenty of time to go gunning among ourselves.

"Put it to him cold. I don't want him to get any ideas that I'm dodging a rumpus with him or any other guy. Tell him I say if we put Pete out of the way we'll have more room to do our own scrapping in. Pete's holed-up down in Whiskeytown. I ain't got enough men to go down there and pull him out. Neither has Whisper. The two of us together has. Put it to him."

"Whisper," I said, "is dead."

Reno said, "Is that so?" as if he thought it wasn't.

"Dan Rolff killed him yesterday morning, down in the old Redman warehouse, stuck him with the ice pick Whisper had used on the girl."

Reno asked:

"You know this? You're not just running off at the head?"

"I know it."

"Damned funny none of his mob act like he was gone," he said, but he was beginning to believe me.

"They don't know it. He was hiding out, with Ted Wright the only one in on the where. Ted knew it. He cashed in on it. He told me he got a hundred or a hundred and fifty from you, through Peak Murry."

"I'd have given the big umpchay twice that for the straight dope," Reno grumbled. He rubbed his chin and said: "Well, that settles the Whisper end."

I said: "No."

"What do you mean, no?"

"If his mob don't know where he is," I suggested, "let's tell them. They blasted him out of the can when Noonan copped him. Think they'd try it again if the news got around that McGraw had picked him up on the quiet?"

"Keep talking," Reno said.

"If his friends try to crack the hoosegow again, thinking he's in it, that'll give the department, including Pete's specials, something to do. While they're doing it, you could try your luck in Whiskeytown."

"Maybe," he said slowly, "maybe we'll try just that thing."

"It ought to work," I encouraged him, standing up. "I'll see you—"

"Stick around. This is as good a spot as any while there's a reader out for you. And we'll need a good guy like you on the party."

I didn't like that so much. I knew enough not to say so. I sat down again.

Reno got busy arranging the rumor. The telephone was worked over-time. The kitchen door was worked as hard, letting men in and out. More came in than went out. The house filled with men, smoke, tension.

CHAPTER XXV

Whiskeytown

A T HALF-PAST one Reno turned from answering a phone call to say:

"Let's take a ride."

He went upstairs. When he came down he carried a black valise. Most of the men had gone out the kitchen door by then.

Reno gave me the black valise, saying:

"Don't wrastle it around too much."

It was heavy.

The seven of us left in the house went out the front door and got into a curtained touring car that O'Marra had just driven up to the curb. Reno sat beside O'Marra. I was squeezed in between men in the back seat, with the valise squeezed between my legs.

Another car came out of the first cross street to run ahead of us. A third followed us. Our speed hung around forty, fast enough to get us somewhere, not fast enough to get us a lot of attention.

We had nearly finished the trip before we were bothered.

The action started in a block of one-story houses of the shack type, down in the southern end of the city.

A man put his head out of a door, put his fingers in his mouth, and whistled shrilly.

Somebody in the car behind us shot him down.

At the next corner we ran through a volley of pistol bullets.

Reno turned around to tell me:

"If they pop the bag, we'll all of us hit the moon. Get it open. We got to work fast when we get there."

I had the fasteners unsnapped by the time we came to rest at the curb in front of a dark three-story brick building.

Men crawled all over me, opening the valise, helping themselves to the contents, bombs made of short sections of two-inch pipe, packed in sawdust in the bag. Bullets bit chunks out of the car's curtains.

Reno reached back for one of the bombs, hopped out to

the sidewalk, paid no attention to a streak of blood that suddenly appeared in the middle of his left cheek, and heaved his piece of stuffed pipe at the brick building's door.

A sheet of flame was followed by deafening noise. Hunks of things pelted us while we tried to keep from being knocked over by the concussion. Then there was no door to keep anybody out of the red brick building.

A man ran forward, swung his arm, let a pipeful of hell go through the doorway. The shutters came off the downstairs windows, fire and glass flying behind them.

The car that had followed us was stationary up the street, trading shots with the neighborhood. The car that had gone ahead of us had turned into a side street. Pistol shots from behind the red brick building, between the explosions of our cargo, told us that our advance car was covering the back door.

O'Marra, out in the middle of the street, bent far over, tossed a bomb to the brick building's roof. It didn't explode. O'Marra put one foot high in the air, clawed at his throat, and fell solidly backward.

Another of our party went down under the slugs that were cutting at us from a wooden building next to the brick one.

Reno cursed stolidly and said:

"Burn them out, Fat."

Fat spit on a bomb, ran around the back of our car, and swung his arm.

We picked ourselves up off the sidewalk, dodged flying things, and saw that the frame house was all out of whack, with flames climbing its torn edges.

"Any left?" Reno asked as we looked around, enjoying the novelty of not being shot at.

"Here's the last one," Fat said, holding out a bomb.

Fire was dancing inside the upper windows of the brick house. Reno looked at it, took the bomb from Fat, and said:

"Back off. They'll be coming out."

We moved away from the front of the house.

A voice indoors yelled:

"Reno!"

Reno slipped into the shadow of our car before he called back:

"Well?"

"We're done," a heavy voice shouted. "We're coming out. Don't shoot."

Reno asked: "Who's we're?"

"This is Pete," the heavy voice said. "There's four left of us."

"You come first," Reno ordered, "with your mitts on the top of your head. The others come out one at a time, same way, after you. And half a minute apart is close enough. Come on."

We waited a moment, and then Pete the Finn appeared in the dynamited doorway, his hands holding the top of his bald head. In the glare from the burning next-door house we could see that his face was cut, his clothes almost all torn off.

Stepping over wreckage, the bootlegger came slowly down the steps to the sidewalk.

Reno called him a lousy fish-eater and shot him four times in face and body.

Pete went down. A man behind me laughed.

Reno hurled the remaining bomb through the doorway.

We scrambled into our car. Reno took the wheel. The engine was dead. Bullets had got to it.

Reno worked the horn while the rest of us piled out.

The machine that had stopped at the corner came for us. Waiting for it, I looked up and down the street that was bright with the glow of two burning buildings. There were a few faces at windows, but whoever besides us was in the street had taken to cover. Not far away, firebells sounded.

The other machine slowed up for us to climb aboard. It was already full. We packed it in layers, with the overflow hanging on the running boards.

We bumped over dead Hank O'Marra's legs and headed for home. We covered one block of the distance with safety if not comfort. After that we had neither.

A limousine turned into the street ahead of us, came half a block toward us, put its side to us, and stopped. Out of the side, gun-fire.

Another car came around the limousine and charged us. Out of it, gun-fire.

We did our best, but we were too damned amalgamated for

good fighting. You can't shoot straight holding a man in your lap, another hanging on your shoulder, while a third does his shooting from an inch behind your ear.

Our other car—the one that had been around at the building's rear—came up and gave us a hand. But by then two more had joined the opposition. Apparently Thaler's mob's attack on the jail was over, one way or the other, and Pete's army, sent to help there, had returned in time to spoil our get-away. It was a sweet mess.

I leaned over a burning gun and yelled in Reno's ear:

"This is the bunk. Let's us extras get out and do our wrangling from the street."

He thought that a good idea, and gave orders:

"Pile out, some of you hombres, and take them from the pavements."

I was the first man out, with my eye on a dark alley entrance.

Fat followed me to it. In my shelter, I turned on him and growled:

"Don't pile up on me. Pick your own hole. There's a cellarway that looks good."

He agreeably trotted off toward it, and was shot down at his third step.

I explored my alley. It was only twenty feet long, and ended against a high board fence with a locked gate.

A garbage can helped me over the gate into a brick-paved yard. The side fence of that yard let me into another, and from that I got into another, where a fox terrier raised hell at me.

I kicked the pooch out of the way, made the opposite fence, untangled myself from a clothes line, crossed two more yards, got yelled at from a window, had a bottle thrown at me, and dropped into a cobble-stoned back street.

The shooting was behind me, but not far enough. I did all I could to remedy that. I must have walked as many streets as I did in my dreams the night Dinah was killed.

My watch said it was three-thirty a.m. when I looked at it on Elihu Willsson's front steps.

CHAPTER XXVI

Blackmail

I HAD to push my client's doorbell a lot before I got any play on it.

Finally the door was opened by the tall sun-burned chauffeur. He was dressed in undershirt and pants, and had a billiard cue in one fist.

"What do you want?" he demanded, and then, when he got another look at me: "It's you, is it? Well, what do you want?"

"I want to see Mr. Willsson."

"At four in the morning? Go on with you," and he started to close the door.

I put a foot against it. He looked from my foot to my face, hefted the billiard cue, and asked:

"You after getting your kneecap cracked?"

"I'm not playing," I insisted. "I've got to see the old man. Tell him."

"I don't have to tell him. He told me no later than this afternoon that if you come around he didn't want to see you."

"Yeah?" I took the four love letters out of my pocket, picked out the first and least idiotic of them, held it out to the chauffeur, and said: "Give him that and tell him I'm sitting on the steps with the rest of them. Tell him I'll sit here five minutes and then carry the rest of them to Tommy Robins of the Consolidated Press."

The chauffeur scowled at the letter, said, "To hell with Tommy Robins and his blind aunt!" took the letter, and closed the door.

Four minutes later he opened the door again and said:

"Inside, you."

I followed him upstairs to old Elihu's bedroom.

My client sat up in bed with his love letter crushed in one round pink fist, its envelope in the other.

His short white hair bristled. His round eyes were as much red as blue. The parallel lines of his mouth and chin almost touched. He was in a lovely humor.

As soon as he saw me he shouted:

"So after all your brave talking you had to come back to the old pirate to have your neck saved, did you?"

I said I didn't anything of the sort. I said if he was going to talk like a sap he ought to lower his voice so the people in Los Angeles wouldn't learn what a sap he was.

The old boy let his voice out another notch, bellowing:

"Because you've stolen a letter or two that don't belong to you, you needn't think you—"

I put fingers in my ears. They didn't shut out the noise, but they insulted him into cutting the bellowing short.

I took the fingers out and said:

"Send the flunkey away so we can talk. You won't need him. I'm not going to hurt you."

He said, "Get out," to the chauffeur.

The chauffeur, looking at me without fondness, left us, closing the door.

Old Elihu gave me the rush act, demanding that I surrender the rest of the letters immediately, wanting to know loudly and profanely where I had got them, what I was doing with them, threatening me with this, that, and the other, but mostly just cursing me.

I didn't surrender the letters. I said:

"I took them from the man you hired to recover them. A tough break for you that he had to kill the girl."

Enough red went out of the old man's face to leave it normally pink. He worked his lips over his teeth, screwed up his eyes at me, and said:

"Is that the way you're going to play it?"

His voice came comparatively quiet from his chest. He had settled down to fight.

I pulled a chair over beside the bed, sat down, put as much amusement as I could in a grin, and said:

"That's one way."

He watched me, working his lips, saying nothing. I said:

"You're the damndest client I ever had. What do you do? You hire me to clean town, change your mind, run out on me, work against me until I begin to look like a winner, then get on the fence, and now when you think I'm licked again, you don't even want to let me in the house. Lucky for me I happened to run across those letters."

He said: "Blackmail."

I laughed and said:

"Listen who's naming it. All right, call it that." I tapped the edge of the bed with a forefinger. "I'm not licked, old top. I've won. You came crying to me that some naughty men had taken your little city away from you. Pete the Finn, Lew Yard, Whisper Thaler, and Noonan. Where are they now?

"Yard died Tuesday morning, Noonan the same night, Whisper Wednesday morning, and the Finn a little while ago. I'm giving your city back to you whether you want it or not. If that's blackmail, O.K. Now here's what you're going to do. You're going to get hold of your mayor, I suppose the lousy village has got one, and you and he are going to phone the governor— Keep still until I get through.

"You're going to tell the governor that your city police have got out of hand, what with bootleggers sworn in as officers, and so on. You're going to ask him for help—the national guard would be best. I don't know how various ruckuses around town have come out, but I do know the big boys—the ones you were afraid of—are dead. The ones that had too much on you for you to stand up to them. There are plenty of busy young men working like hell right now, trying to get into the dead men's shoes. The more, the better. They'll make it easier for the white-collar soldiers to take hold while everything is disorganized. And none of the substitutes are likely to have enough on you to do much damage.

"You're going to have the mayor, or the governor, whichever it comes under, suspend the whole Personville police department, and let the mail-order troops handle things till you can organize another. I'm told that the mayor and the governor are both pieces of your property. They'll do what you tell them. And that's what you're going to tell them. It can be done, and it's got to be done.

"Then you'll have your city back, all nice and clean and ready to go to the dogs again. If you don't do it, I'm going to turn these love letters of yours over to the newspaper buzzards, and I don't mean your *Herald* crew—the press associations. I got the letters from Dawn. You'll have a lot of fun proving that you didn't hire him to recover them, and that he didn't kill the girl doing it. But the fun you'll have is nothing to the fun people will have reading these letters. They're hot. I haven't laughed so much over anything since the hogs ate my kid brother."

I stopped talking.

The old man was shaking, but there was no fear in his shaking. His face was purple again. He opened his mouth and roared:

"Publish them and be damned!"

I took them out of my pocket, dropped them on his bed, got up from my chair, put on my hat, and said:

"I'd give my right leg to be able to believe that the girl was killed by somebody you sent to get the letters. By God, I'd like to top off the job by sending you to the gallows!"

He didn't touch the letters. He said:

"You told me the truth about Thaler and Pete?"

"Yeah. But what difference does it make? You'll only be pushed around by somebody else."

He threw the bedclothes aside and swung his stocky pajamaed legs and pink feet over the edge of the bed.

"Have you got the guts," he barked, "to take the job I offered you once before—chief of police?"

"No. I lost my guts out fighting your fights while you were hiding in bed and thinking up new ways of disowning me. Find another wet nurse."

He glared at me. Then shrewd wrinkles came around his eyes.

He nodded his old head and said:

"You're afraid to take the job. So you did kill the girl?"

I left him as I had left him the last time, saying, "Go to hell!" and walking out.

The chauffeur, still toting his billiard cue, still regarding me without fondness, met me on the ground floor and took me to the door, looking as if he hoped I would start something. I didn't. He slammed the door after me.

The street was grey with the beginning of daylight.

Up the street a black coupé stood under some trees. I couldn't see if anyone was in it. I played safe by walking in the opposite direction. The coupé moved after me.

There is nothing in running down streets with automobiles

in pursuit. I stopped, facing this one. It came on. I took my hand away from my side when I saw Mickey Linehan's red face through the windshield.

He swung the door open for me to get in.

"I thought you might come up here," he said as I sat beside him, "but I was a second or two too late. I saw you go in, but was too far away to catch you."

"How'd you make out with the police?" I asked. "Better keep driving while we talk."

"I didn't know anything, couldn't guess anything, didn't have any idea of what you were working on, just happened to hit town and meet you. Old friends—that line. They were still trying when the riot broke. They had me in one of the little offices across from the assembly room. When the circus cut loose I back-windowed them."

"How'd the circus wind up?" I asked.

"The coppers shot hell out of them. They got the tip-off half an hour ahead of time, and had the whole neighborhood packed with specials. Seems it was a juicy row while it lasted— no duck soup for the coppers at that. Whisper's mob, I hear."

"Yeah. Reno and Pete the Finn tangled tonight. Hear anything about it?"

"Only that they'd had it."

"Reno killed Pete and ran into an ambush on the get-away. I don't know what happened after that. Seen Dick?"

"I went up to his hotel and was told he'd checked out to catch the evening train."

"I sent him back home," I explained. "He seemed to think I'd killed Dinah Brand. He was getting on my nerves with it."

"Well?"

"You mean, did I kill her? I don't know, Mickey. I'm trying to find out. Want to keep riding with me, or want to follow Dick back to the Coast?"

Mickey said:

"Don't get so cocky over one lousy murder that maybe didn't happen. But what the hell? You know you didn't lift her dough and pretties."

"Neither did the killer. They were still there after eight that morning, when I left. Dan Rolff was in and out between then and nine. He wouldn't have taken them. The— I've got it!

The coppers that found the body—Shepp and Vanaman—got there at nine-thirty. Besides the jewelry and money, some letters old Willsson had written the girl were—must have been—taken. I found them later in Dawn's pocket. The two dicks disappeared just about then. See it?

"When Shepp and Vanaman found the girl dead they looted the joint before they turned in the alarm. Old Willsson being a millionaire, his letters looked good to them, so they took them along with the other valuables, and turned them—the letters—over to the shyster to peddle back to Elihu. But Dawn was killed before he could do anything on that end. I took the letters. Shepp and Vanaman, whether they did or didn't know that the letters were not found in the dead man's possession, got cold feet. They were afraid the letters would be traced to them. They had the money and jewelry. They lit out."

"Sounds fair enough," Mickey agreed, "but it don't seem to put any fingers on any murderers."

"It clears the way some. We'll try to clear it some more. See if you can find Porter Street and an old Warehouse called Redman. The way I got it, Rolff killed Whisper there, walked up to him and stabbed him with the ice pick he had found in the girl. If he did it that way, then Whisper hadn't killed her. Or he would have been expecting something of the sort, and wouldn't have let the lunger get that close to him. I'd like to look at their remains and check up."

"Porter's over beyond King," Mickey said. "We'll try the south end first. It's nearer and more likely to have warehouses. Where do you set this Rolff guy?"

"Out. If he killed Whisper for killing the girl, that marks him off. Besides, she had bruises on her wrist and cheek, and he wasn't strong enough to rough her. My notion is that he left the hospital, spent the night God knows where, showed up at the girl's house after I left that morning, let himself in with his key, found her, decided Whisper had done the trick, took the sticker out of her, and went hunting Whisper."

"So?" Mickey said. "Now where do you get the idea that you might be the boy who put it over?"

"Stop it," I said grouchily as we turned into Porter Street. "Let's find our warehouse."

CHAPTER XXVII

Warehouses

W E RODE down the street, jerking our eyes around, hunting for buildings that looked like deserted warehouses. It was light enough by now to see well.

Presently I spotted a big square rusty-red building set in the center of a weedy lot. Disuse stuck out all over lot and building. It had the look of a likely candidate.

"Pull up at the next corner," I said. "That looks like the dump. You stick with the heap while I scout it."

I walked two unnecessary blocks so I could come into the lot behind the building. I crossed the lot carefully, not sneaking, but not making any noises I could avoid.

I tried the back door cautiously. It was locked, of course. I moved over to a window, tried to look in, couldn't because of gloom and dirt, tried the window, and couldn't budge it.

I went to the next window with the same luck. I rounded the corner of the building and began working my way along the north side. The first window had me beaten. The second went up slowly with my push, and didn't make much noise doing it.

Across the inside of the window frame, from top to bottom, boards were nailed. They looked solid and strong from where I stood.

I cursed them, and remembered hopefully that the window hadn't made much noise when I raised it. I climbed up on the sill, put a hand against the boards, and tried them gently.

They gave.

I put more weight behind my hand. The boards went away from the left side of the frame, showing me a row of shiny nail points.

I pushed them back farther, looked past them, saw nothing but darkness, heard nothing.

With my gun in my right fist, I stepped over the sill, down into the building. Another step to the left put me out of the window's gray light.

I switched my gun to my left hand and used my right to push the boards back over the window.

A full minute of breathless listening got me nothing. Holding my gun-arm tight to my side, I began exploring the joint. Nothing but the floor came under my feet as I inch-by-inched them forward. My groping left hand felt nothing until it touched a rough wall. I seemed to have crossed a room that was empty.

I moved along the wall, hunting for a door. Half a dozen of my under-sized steps brought me to one. I leaned an ear against it, and heard no sound.

I found the knob, turned it softly, eased the door back.

Something swished.

I did four things all together: let go the knob, jumped, pulled trigger, and had my left arm walloped with something hard and heavy as a tombstone.

The flare of my gun showed me nothing. It never does, though it's easy to think you've seen things. Not knowing what else to do, I fired again, and once more.

An old man's voice pleaded:

"Don't do that, partner. You don't have to do that."

I said: "Make a light."

A match spluttered on the floor, kindled, and put flickering yellow light on a battered face. It was an old face of the useless, characterless sort that goes well with park benches. He was sitting on the floor, his stringy legs sprawled far apart. He didn't seem hurt anywhere. A table-leg lay beside him.

"Get up and make a light," I ordered, "and keep matches burning until you've done it."

He struck another match, sheltered it carefully with his hands as he got up, crossed the room, and lit a candle on a three-legged table.

I followed him, keeping close. My left arm was numb or I would have taken hold of him for safety.

"What are you doing here?" I asked when the candle was burning.

I didn't need his answer. One end of the room was filled with wooden cases piled six high, branded *Perfection Maple Syrup*.

While the old man explained that as God was his keeper he

didn't know nothing about it, that all he knew was that a man named Yates had two days ago hired him as night watchman, and if anything was wrong he was as innocent as innocent, I pulled part of the top off one case.

The bottles inside had Canadian Club labels that looked as if they had been printed with a rubber stamp.

I left the cases and, driving the old man in front of me with the candle, searched the building. As I expected, I found nothing to indicate that this was the warehouse Whisper had occupied.

By the time we got back to the room that held the liquor my left arm was strong enough to lift a bottle. I put it in my pocket and gave the old man some advice:

"Better clear out. You were hired to take the place of some of the men Pete the Finn turned into special coppers. But Pete's dead now and his racket has gone blooey."

When I climbed out the window the old man was standing in front of the cases, looking at them with greedy eyes while he counted on his fingers.

"Well?" Mickey asked when I returned to him and his coupé.

I took out the bottle of anything but Canadian Club, pulled the cork, passed it to him, and then put a shot into my own system.

He asked, "Well?" again.

I said: "Let's try to find the old Redman warehouse."

He said: "You're going to ruin yourself some time telling people too much," and started the car moving.

Three blocks farther up the street we saw a faded sign, *Redman & Company.* The building under the sign was long, low, and narrow, with corrugated iron roof and few windows.

"We'll leave the boat around the corner," I said. "And you'll go with me this time. I didn't have a whole lot of fun by myself last trip."

When we climbed out of the coupé, an alley ahead promised a path to the warehouse's rear. We took it.

A few people were wandering through the streets, but it was still too early for the factories that filled most of this part of town to come to life.

At the rear of our building we found something interesting. The back door was closed. Its edge, and the edge of the frame, close to the lock, were scarred. Somebody had worked there with a jimmy.

Mickey tried the door. It was unlocked. Six inches at a time, with pauses between, he pushed it far enough back to let us squeeze in.

When we squeezed in we could hear a voice. We couldn't make out what the voice was saying. All we could hear was the faint rumble of a distant man's voice, with a suggestion of quarrelsomeness in it.

Mickey pointed a thumb at the door's scar and whispered: "Not coppers."

I took two steps inside, keeping my weight on my rubber heels. Mickey followed, breathing down the back of my neck.

Ted Wright had told me Whisper's hiding place was in the back, upstairs. The distant rumbling voice could have been coming from there.

I twisted my face around to Mickey and asked:

"Flashlight?"

He put it in my left hand. I had my gun in my right. We crept forward.

The door, still a foot open, let in enough light to show us the way across this room to a doorless doorway. The other side of the doorway was black.

I flicked the light across the blackness, found a door, shut off the light, and went forward. The next squirt of light showed us steps leading up.

We went up the steps as if we were afraid they would break under our feet.

The rumbling voice had stopped. There was something else in the air. I didn't know what. Maybe a voice not quite loud enough to be heard, if that means anything.

I had counted nine steps when a voice spoke clearly above us. It said:

"Sure, I killed the bitch."

A gun said something, the same thing four times, roaring like a 16-inch rifle under the iron roof.

The first voice said: "All right."

By that time Mickey and I had put the rest of the steps

behind us, had shoved a door out of the way, and were trying to pull Reno Starkey's hands away from Whisper's throat.

It was a tough job and a useless one. Whisper was dead.

Reno recognized me and let his hands go limp.

His eyes were as dull, his horse face as wooden, as ever.

Mickey carried the dead gambler to the cot that stood in one end of the room, spreading him on it.

The room, apparently once an office, had two windows. In their light I could see a body stowed under the cot—Dan Rolff. A Colt's service automatic lay in the middle of the floor.

Reno bent his shoulders, swaying.

"Hurt?" I asked.

"He put all four in me," he said calmly, bending to press both forearms against his lower body.

"Get a doc," I told Mickey.

"No good," Reno said. "I got no more belly left than Peter Collins."

I pulled a folding chair over and sat him down on it, so he could lean forward and hold himself together.

Mickey ran out and down the stairs.

"Did you know he wasn't croaked?" Reno asked.

"No. I gave it to you the way I got it from Ted Wright."

"Ted left too soon," he said. "I was leary of something like that, and came to make sure. He trapped me pretty, playing dead till I was under the gun." He stared dully at Whisper's corpse. "Game at that, damn him. Dead, but wouldn't lay down, bandaging hisself, laying here waiting by hisself." He smiled, the only smile I had ever seen him use. "But he's just meat and not much of it now."

His voice was thickening. A little red puddle formed under the edge of his chair. I was afraid to touch him. Only the pressure of his arms, and his bent-forward position, were keeping him from falling apart.

He stared at the puddle and asked:

"How the hell did you figure you didn't croak her?"

"I had to take it out in hoping I hadn't, till just now," I said. "I had you pegged for it, but couldn't be sure. I was all hopped up that night, and had a lot of dreams, with bells ringing and voices calling, and a lot of stuff like that. I got an idea maybe it wasn't straight dreaming so much as hop-head nightmares stirred up by things that were happening around me.

"When I woke up, the lights were out. I didn't think I killed her, turned off the light, and went back to take hold of the ice pick. But it could have happened other ways. You knew I was there that night. You gave me my alibi without stalling. That got me thinking. Dawn tried blackmailing me after he heard Helen Albury's story. The police, after hearing her story, tied you, Whisper, Rolff and me together. I found Dawn dead after seeing O'Marra half a block away. It looked like the shyster had tried blackmailing you. That and the police tying us together started me thinking the police had as much on the rest of you as on me. What they had on me was that Helen Albury had seen me go in or out or both that night. It was a good guess they had the same on the rest of you. There were reasons for counting Whisper and Rolff out. That left you—and me. But why you killed her's got me puzzled."

"I bet you," he said, watching the red puddle grow on the floor. "It was her own damned fault. She calls me up, tells me Whisper's coming to see her, and says if I get there first I can bushwack him. I'd like that. I go over there, stick around, but he don't show."

He stopped, pretending interest in the shape the red puddle was taking. I knew pain had stopped him, but I knew he would go on talking as soon as he got himself in hand. He meant to die as he had lived, inside the same tough shell. Talking could be torture, but he wouldn't stop on that account, not while anybody was there to see him. He was Reno Starkey who could take anything the world had without batting an eye, and he would play it out that way to the end.

"I got tired of waiting," he went on after a moment. "I hit her door and asked howcome. She takes me in, telling me there's nobody there. I'm doubtful, but she swears she's alone, and we go back in the kitchen. Knowing her, I'm beginning to think maybe it's me and not Whisper that's being trapped."

Mickey came in, telling us he had phoned for an ambulance.

Reno used the interruption to rest his voice, and then continued with his story:

"Later, I find that Whisper did phone her he was coming, and got there before me. You were coked. She was afraid to let him in, so he beat it. She don't tell me that, scared I'll go and leave her. You're hopped and she wants protection against Whisper coming back. I don't know none of that then. I'm leary that I've walked into something, knowing her. I think I'll take hold of her and slap the truth out of her. I try it, and she grabs the pick and screams. When she squawks, I hear a man's feet hitting the floor. The trap's sprung, I think."

He spoke slower, taking more time and pains to turn each word out calmly and deliberately, as talking became harder. His voice had become blurred, but if he knew it he pretended he didn't.

"I don't mean to be the only one that's hurt. I twist the pick out of her hand and stick it in her. You gallop out, coked to the edges, charging at the whole world with both eyes shut. She tumbles into you. You go down, roll around till your hand hits the butt of the pick. Holding on to that, you go to sleep, peaceful as she is. I see it then, what I've done. But hell! she's croaked. There's nothing to do about it. I turn off the lights and go home. When you—"

A tired looking ambulance crew—Poisonville gave them plenty of work—brought a litter into the room, ending Reno's tale. I was glad of it. I had all the information I wanted, and sitting there listening to and watching him talk himself to death wasn't pleasant.

I took Mickey over to a corner of the room and muttered in his ear:

"The job's yours from now on. I'm going to duck. I ought to be in the clear, but I know my Poisonville too well to take any chances. I'll drive your car to some way station where I can catch a train for Ogden. I'll be at the Roosevelt Hotel there, registered as P. F. King. Stay with the job, and let me know when it's wise to either take my own name again or a trip to Honduras."

I spent most of my week in Ogden trying to fix up my reports so they would not read as if I had broken as many Agency rules, state laws and human bones as I had.

Mickey arrived on the sixth night.

He told me that Reno was dead, that I was no longer officially a criminal, that most of the First National Bank stick-up
loot had been recovered, that MacSwain had confessed killing
Tim Noonan, and that Personville, under martial law, was developing into a sweet-smelling and thornless bed of roses.

Mickey and I went back to San Francisco.

I might just as well have saved the labor and sweat I had
put into trying to make my reports harmless. They didn't fool
the Old Man. He gave me merry hell.

THE DAIN CURSE

To
Albert S. Samuels

CONTENTS

PART ONE: THE DAINS

CHAPTER I

Eight Diamonds

IT WAS a diamond all right, shining in the grass half a dozen feet from the blue brick walk. It was small, not more than a quarter of a carat in weight, and unmounted. I put it in my pocket and began searching the lawn as closely as I could without going at it on all fours.

I had covered a couple of square yards of sod when the Leggetts' front door opened.

A woman came out on the broad stone top step and looked down at me with good-humored curiosity.

She was a woman of about my age, forty, with darkish blond hair, a pleasant plump face, and dimpled pink cheeks. She had on a lavender-flowered white house-dress.

I stopped poking at the grass and went up to her, asking: "Is Mr. Leggett in?"

"Yes." Her voice was placid as her face. "You wish to see him?"

I said I did.

She smiled at me and at the lawn.

"You're another detective, aren't you?"

I admitted that.

She took me up to a green, orange, and chocolate room on the second floor, put me in a brocaded chair, and went to call her husband from his laboratory. While I waited, I looked around the room, deciding that the dull orange rug under my feet was probably both genuinely oriental and genuinely ancient, that the walnut furniture hadn't been ground out by machinery, and that the Japanese pictures on the wall hadn't been selected by a prude.

Edgar Leggett came in saying: "I'm sorry to have kept you waiting, but I couldn't break off till now. Have you learned something?"

His voice was unexpectedly harsh, rasping, though his manner was friendly enough. He was a dark-skinned erect man in his middle forties, muscularly slender and of medium height. He would have been handsome if his brown face hadn't been so deeply marked with sharp, hard lines across the forehead and from nostrils down across mouth-corners. Dark hair, worn rather long, curled above and around the broad, grooved forehead. Red-brown eyes were abnormally bright behind horn-rimmed spectacles. His nose was long, thin, and high-bridged. His lips were thin, sharp, nimble, over a small, bony chin. His black and white clothes were well made and cared for.

"Not yet," I said to his question. "I'm not a police detective—Continental Agency—for the insurance company—and I'm just starting."

"Insurance company?" He seemed surprised, raising dark eyebrows above the dark tops of his spectacles.

"Yeah. Didn't—?"

"Surely," he said, smiling, stopping my words with a small flourish of one hand. It was a long, narrow hand with over-developed finger-tips, ugly as most trained hands are. "Surely. They would have been insured. I hadn't thought of that. They weren't my diamonds, you know; they were Halstead's."

"Halstead and Beauchamp? I didn't get any details from the insurance company. You had the diamonds on approval?"

"No. I was using them experimentally. Halstead knew of my work with glass—coloring it, staining or dyeing it, after its manufacture—and he became interested in the possibility of the process being adapted to diamonds, particularly in improving off-color stones, removing yellowish and brownish tinges, emphasizing blues. He asked me to try it and five weeks ago gave me those diamonds to work on. There were eight of them, none especially valuable. The largest weighed only a trifle more than half a carat, some of the others only a quarter, and except for two they were all of poor color. They're the stones the burglar got."

"Then you hadn't succeeded?" I asked.

"Frankly," he said, "I hadn't made the slightest progress. This was a more delicate matter, and on more obdurate material."

"Where'd you keep them?"

"Usually they were left lying around in the open—always in the laboratory, of course—but for several days now they had

been locked in the cabinet—since my last unsuccessful experiment."

"Who knew about the experiments?"

"Anyone, everyone—there was no occasion for secrecy."

"They were stolen from the cabinet?"

"Yes. This morning we found our front door open, the cabinet drawer forced, and the diamonds gone. The police found
marks on the kitchen door. They say the burglar came in that
way and left by the front door. We heard nothing last night.
And nothing else was taken."

"The front door was ajar when I came downstairs this
morning," Mrs. Leggett said from the doorway. "I went upstairs and awakened Edgar, and we searched the house and
found the diamonds gone. The police think the man I saw
must have been the burglar."

I asked about the man she had seen.

"It was last night, around midnight, when I opened the
bedroom windows before going to bed. I saw a man standing
upon the corner. I can't say, even now, that there was anything very suspicious-looking about him. He was standing
there as if waiting for somebody. He was looking down this
way, but not in a way to make me think he was watching this
house. He was a man past forty, I should say, rather short and
broad—somewhat of your build—but he had a bristly brown
mustache and was pale. He wore a soft hat and overcoat—
dark—I think they were brown. The police think that's the
same man Gabrielle saw."

"Who?"

"My daughter Gabrielle," she said. "Coming home late one
night—Saturday night, I think it was—she saw a man and
thought he had come from our steps; but she wasn't sure and
didn't think anything more of it until after the burglary."

"I'd like to talk to her. Is she home?"

Mrs. Leggett went out to get her.

I asked Leggett: "Were the diamonds loose?"

"They were unset, of course, and in small manila envelopes
—Halstead and Beauchamp's—each in a separate envelope,
with a number and the weight of the stone written in pencil.
The envelopes are missing too."

Mrs. Leggett returned with her daughter, a girl of twenty

or less in a sleeveless white silk dress. Of medium height, she looked more slender than she actually was. She had hair as curly as her father's, and no longer, but of a much lighter brown. She had a pointed chin and extremely white, smooth skin, and of her features only the green-brown eyes were large: forehead, mouth, and teeth were remarkably small. I stood up to be introduced to her, and asked about the man she had seen.

"I'm not positive that he came from the house," she said, "or even from the lawn." She was sullen, as if she didn't like being questioned. "I thought he might have, but I only saw him walking up the street."

"What sort of looking man was he?"

"I don't know. It was dark. I was in the car, he was walking up the street. I didn't examine him closely. He was about your size. It might have been you, for all I know."

"It wasn't. That was Saturday night?"

"Yes—that is, Sunday morning."

"What time?"

"Oh, three o'clock or after," she said impatiently.

"Were you alone?"

"Hardly."

I asked her who was with her and finally got a name: Eric Collinson had driven her home. I asked where I could find Eric Collinson. She frowned, hesitated, and said he was employed by Spear, Camp and Duffy, stock-brokers. She also said she had a putrid headache and she hoped I would excuse her now, as she knew I couldn't have any more questions to ask her. Then, without waiting for any reply I might have made to that, she turned and went out of the room. Her ears, I noticed when she turned, had no lobes, and were queerly pointed at the top.

"How about your servants?" I asked Mrs. Leggett.

"We've only one—Minnie Hershey, a Negress. She doesn't sleep here, and I'm sure she had nothing to do with it. She's been with us for nearly two years and I can vouch for her honesty."

I said I'd like to talk to Minnie, and Mrs. Leggett called her in. The servant was a small, wiry mulatto girl with the straight black hair and brown features of an Indian. She was very polite and very insistent that she had nothing to do with the theft of the diamonds and had known nothing about the burglary until she arrived at the house that morning. She gave me her home address, in San Francisco's darktown.

Leggett and his wife took me up to the laboratory, a large room that covered all but a small fifth of the third story. Charts hung between the windows on the whitewashed wall. The wooden floor was uncovered. An X-ray machine—or something similar—four or five smaller machines, a forge, a wide sink, a large zinc table, some smaller porcelain ones, stands, racks of glassware, siphon-shaped metal tanks—that sort of stuff filled most of the room.

The cabinet the diamonds had been taken from was a green-painted steel affair with six drawers all locking together. The second drawer from the top—the one the diamonds had been in—was open. Its edge was dented where a jimmy or chisel had been forced between it and the frame. The other drawers were still locked. Leggett said the forcing of the diamond drawer had jammed the locking mechanism so that he would have to get a mechanic to open the others.

We went downstairs, through a room where the mulatto was walking around behind a vacuum cleaner, and into the kitchen. The back door and its frame were marked much as the cabinet was, apparently by the same tool.

When I had finished looking at the door, I took the diamond out of my pocket and showed it to the Leggetts, asking: "Is this one of them?"

Leggett picked it out of my palm with forefinger and thumb, held it up to the light, turned it from side to side, and said: "Yes. It has that cloudy spot down at the culet. Where did you get it?"

"Out front, in the grass."

"Ah, our burglar dropped some of his spoils in his haste."

I said I doubted it.

Leggett pulled his brows together behind his glasses, looked at me with smaller eyes, and asked sharply: "What do you think?"

"I think it was planted there. Your burglar knew too much. He knew which drawer to go to. He didn't waste time on anything else. Detectives always say: 'Inside job,' because it saves work if they can find a victim right on the scene; but I can't see anything else here."

Minnie came to the door, still holding the vacuum cleaner, and began to cry that she was an honest girl, and nobody had any right to accuse her of anything, and they could search her and her home if they wanted to, and just because she was a colored girl was no reason, and so on and so on; and not all of it could be made out, because the vacuum cleaner was still humming in her hand and she sobbed while she talked. Tears ran down her cheeks.

Mrs. Leggett went to her, patted her shoulder, and said: "There, there. Don't cry, Minnie. I know you hadn't any-thing to do with it, and so does everybody else. There, there." Presently she got the girl's tears turned off and sent her upstairs.

Leggett sat on a corner of the kitchen table and asked: "You suspect someone in this house?"

"Somebody who's been in it, yeah."

"Whom?"

"Nobody yet."

"That"—he smiled, showing white teeth almost as small as his daughter's—"means everybody—all of us?"

"Let's take a look at the lawn," I suggested. "If we find any more diamonds I'll say maybe I'm mistaken about the inside angle."

Half-way through the house, as we went towards the front door, we met Minnie Hershey in a tan coat and violet hat, coming to say good-bye to her mistress. She wouldn't, she said tearfully, work anywhere where anybody thought she had stolen anything. She was just as honest as anybody else, and more than some, and just as much entitled to respect, and if she couldn't get it one place she could another, because she knew places where people wouldn't accuse her of stealing things after she had worked for them for two long years with-out ever taking so much as a slice of bread.

Mrs. Leggett pleaded with her, reasoned with her, scolded her, and commanded her, but none of it was any good. The brown girl's mind was made up, and away she went.

Mrs. Leggett looked at me, making her pleasant face as

severe as she could, and said reprovingly: "Now see what you've done."

I said I was sorry, and her husband and I went out to examine the lawn. We didn't find any more diamonds.

CHAPTER II

Long-nose

I PUT in a couple of hours canvassing the neighborhood, trying to place the man Mrs. and Miss Leggett had seen. I didn't have any luck with that one, but I picked up news of another. A Mrs. Priestly—a pale semi-invalid who lived three doors below the Leggetts—gave me the first line on him.

Mrs. Priestly often sat at a front window at night when she couldn't sleep. On two of these nights she had seen the man. She said he was a tall man, and young, she thought, and he walked with his head thrust forward. The street was too poorly lighted for her to describe his coloring and clothes.

She had first seen him a week before. He had passed up and down on the other side of the street five or six times, at intervals of fifteen or twenty minutes, with his face turned as if watching something—or looking for something—on Mrs. Priestly's—and the Leggetts'—side of the street. She thought it was between eleven and twelve o'clock that she had seen him the first time that night, and around one o'clock the last. Several nights later—Saturday—she had seen him again, not walking this time, but standing on the corner below, looking up the street, at about midnight. He went away after half an hour, and she had not seen him again.

Mrs. Priestly knew the Leggetts by sight, but knew very little about them, except that the daughter was said to be a bit wild. They seemed to be nice people, but kept to themselves. He had moved into the house in 1921, alone except for the housekeeper—a Mrs. Begg, who, Mrs. Priestly understood, was now with a family named Freemander in Berkeley. Mrs. Leggett and Gabrielle had not come to live with Leggett until 1923.

Mrs. Priestly said she had not been at her window the previous night and therefore had not seen the man Mrs. Leggett had seen on the corner.

A man named Warren Daley, who lived on the opposite side of the street, down near the corner where Mrs. Priestly had seen her man, had, when locking up the house Sunday night, surprised a man—apparently the same man—in the vestibule. Daley was not at home when I called, but, after telling me this much, Mrs. Daley got him on the phone for me.

Daley said the man had been standing in the vestibule, either hiding from or watching someone up the street. As soon as Daley opened the door, the man ran away, down the street, paying no attention to Daley's "What are you doing there?" Daley said he was a man of thirty-two or three, fairly well dressed in dark clothes, and had a long, thin, and sharp nose.

That was all I could shake the neighborhood down for. I went to the Montgomery Street offices of Spear, Camp and Duffy and asked for Eric Collinson.

He was young, blond, tall, broad, sunburned, and dressy, with the good-looking unintelligent face of one who would know everything about polo, or shooting, or flying, or something of that sort—maybe even two things of that sort—but not much about anything else. We sat on a fatted leather seat in the customers' room, now, after market hours, empty except for a weedy boy juggling numbers on the board. I told Collinson about the burglary and asked him about the man he and Miss Leggett had seen Saturday night.

"He was an ordinary-looking chap, as far as I could see. It was dark. Short and chunky. You think he took them?"

"Did he come from the Leggett house?" I asked.

"From the lawn, at least. He seemed jumpy—that's why I thought perhaps he'd been nosing around where he shouldn't. I suggested I go after him and ask him what he was up to, but Gaby wouldn't have it. Might have been a friend of her father's. Did you ask him? He goes in for odd eggs."

"Wasn't that late for a visitor to be leaving?"

He looked away from me, so I asked: "What time was it?"

"Midnight, I dare say."

"Midnight?"

"That's the word. The time when the graves give up their dead, and ghosts walk."

"Miss Leggett said it was after three o'clock."

"You see how it is!" he exclaimed, blandly triumphant, as if he had demonstrated something we had been arguing about. "She's half blind and won't wear glasses for fear of losing beauty. She's always making mistakes like that. Plays abominable bridge—takes deuces for aces. It was probably a quarter after twelve, and she looked at the clock and got the hands mixed."

I said: "That's too bad," and "Thanks," and went up to Halstead and Beauchamp's store in Geary Street.

Watt Halstead was a suave, pale, bald, fat man, with tired eyes and a too tight collar. I told him what I was doing and asked him how well he knew Leggett.

"I know him as a desirable customer and by reputation as a scientist. Why do you ask?"

"His burglary's sour—in spots anyway."

"Oh, you're mistaken. That is, you're mistaken if you think a man of his caliber would be mixed up in anything like that. A servant, of course; yes, that's possible: it often happens, doesn't it? But not Leggett. He is a scientist of some standing—he has done some remarkable work with color—and, unless our credit department has been misinformed, a man of more than moderate means. I don't mean that he is wealthy in the modern sense of the word, but too wealthy for a thing of that sort. And, confidentially, I happen to know that his present balance in the Seaman's National Bank is in excess of ten thousand dollars. Well—the eight diamonds were worth no more than a thousand or twelve or thirteen hundred dollars."

"At retail? Then they cost you five or six hundred?"

"Well," smiling, "seven fifty would be nearer."

"How'd you come to give him the diamonds?"

"He's a customer of ours, as I've told you, and when I learned what he had done with glass, I thought what a wonderful thing it would be if the same method could be applied to diamonds. Fitzstephan—it was largely through him that I learned of Leggett's work with glass—was skeptical, but I thought it worth trying—still think so—and persuaded Leggett to try."

Fitzstephan was a familiar name. I asked: "Which Fitzstephan was that?"

"Owen, the writer. You know him?"

"Yeah, but I didn't know he was on the coast. We used to drink out of the same bottle. Do you know his address?"

Halstead found it in the telephone book for me, a Nob Hill apartment.

From the jeweler's I went to the vicinity of Minnie Hershey's home. It was a Negro neighborhood, which made the getting of reasonably accurate information twice as unlikely as it always is.

What I managed to get added up to this: The girl had come to San Francisco from Winchester, Virginia, four or five years ago, and for the last half-year had been living with a Negro called Rhino Tingley. One told me Rhino's first name was Ed, another Bill, but they agreed that he was young, big, and black and could easily be recognized by the scar on his chin. I was also told that he depended for his living on Minnie and pool; that he was not bad except when he got mad—then he was supposed to be a holy terror; and that I could get a look at him the early part of almost any evening in either Bunny Mack's barber-shop or Big-foot Gerber's cigar-store.

I learned where these joints were and then went downtown again, to the police detective bureau in the Hall of Justice. Nobody was in the pawnshop detail office. I crossed the corridor and asked Lieutenant Duff whether anybody had been put on the Leggett job.

He said: "See O'Gar."

I went into the assembly room, looking for O'Gar and wondering what he—a homicide detail detective-sergeant—had to do with my job. Neither O'Gar nor Pat Reddy, his partner, was in. I smoked a cigarette, tried to guess who had been killed, and decided to phone Leggett.

"Any police detectives been in since I left?" I asked when his harsh voice was in my ear.

"No, but the police called up a little while ago and asked my wife and daughter to come to a place in Golden Gate Avenue to see if they could identify a man there. They left a few minutes ago. I didn't accompany them, not having seen the supposed burglar."

"Whereabouts in Golden Gate Avenue?"

He didn't remember the number, but he knew the block—above Van Ness Avenue. I thanked him and went out there.

In the designated block I found a uniformed copper stand-ing in the doorway of a small apartment house. I asked him if O'Gar was there.

"Up in three ten," he said.

I rode up in a rickety elevator. When I got out on the third floor, I came face to face with Mrs. Leggett and her daughter, leaving.

"Now I hope you're satisfied that Minnie had nothing to do with it," Mrs. Leggett said chidingly.

"The police found your man?"

"Yes."

I said to Gabrielle Leggett: "Eric Collinson says it was only midnight, or a few minutes later, that you got home Saturday night."

"Eric," she said irritably, passing me to enter the elevator, "is an ass."

Her mother, following her into the elevator, reprimanded her amiably: "Now, dear."

I walked down the hall to a doorway where Pat Reddy stood talking to a couple of reporters, said hello, squeezed past them into a short passage-way, and went through that to a shabbily furnished room where a dead man lay on a wall bed.

Phels, of the police identification bureau, looked up from his magnifying glass to nod at me and then went on with his examination of a mission table's edge.

O'Gar pulled his head and shoulders in the open window and growled: "So we got to put up with you again?"

O'Gar was a burly, stolid man of fifty, who wore wide-brimmed black hats of the movie-sheriff sort. There was a lot of sense in his hard bullet-head, and he was comfortable to work with.

I looked at the corpse—a man of forty or so, with a heavy, pale face, short hair touched with gray, a scrubby, dark mus-tache, and stocky arms and legs. There was a bullet hole just over his navel, and another high on the left side of his chest.

"It's a man," O'Gar said as I put the blankets over him again. "He's dead."

"What else did somebody tell you?" I asked.

"Looks like him and another guy glaumed the ice, and then

the other guy decided to take a one-way split. The envelopes are here"—O'Gar took them out of his pocket and ruffled them with a thumb—"but the diamonds ain't. They went down the fire-escape with the other guy a little while back. People spotted him making the sneak, but lost him when he cut through the alley. Tall guy with a long nose. This one"— he pointed the envelopes at the bed—"has been here a week. Name of Louis Upton, with New York labels. We don't know him. Nobody in the dump'll say they ever saw him with anybody else. Nobody'll say they know Long-nose."

Pat Reddy came in. He was a big, jovial youngster, with almost brains enough to make up for his lack of experience. I told him and O'Gar what I had turned up on the job so far.

"Long-nose and this bird taking turns watching Leggett's?" Reddy suggested.

"Maybe," I said, "but there's an inside angle. How many envelopes have you got there, O'Gar?"

"Seven."

"Then the one for the planted diamond is missing."

"How about the yellow girl?" Reddy asked.

"I'm going out for a look at her man tonight," I said. "You people trying New York on this Upton?"

"Uh-huh," O'Gar said.

CHAPTER III

Something Black

A T THE Nob Hill address Halstead had given me, I told my
name to the boy at the switchboard and asked him to
pass it on to Fitzstephan. I remembered Fitzstephan as a long,
lean, sorrel-haired man of thirty-two, with sleepy gray eyes, a
wide, humorous mouth, and carelessly worn clothes; a man
who pretended to be lazier than he was, would rather talk
than do anything else, and had a lot of what seemed to be
accurate information and original ideas on any subject that
happened to come up, as long as it was a little out of the
ordinary.

I had met him five years before, in New York, where I was
digging dirt on a chain of fake mediums who had taken a
coal-and-ice dealer's widow for a hundred thousand dollars.
Fitzstephan was plowing the same field for literary material.
We became acquainted and pooled forces. I got more out of
the combination than he did, since he knew the spook racket
inside and out; and, with his help, I cleaned up my job in a
couple of weeks. We were fairly chummy for a month or two
after that, until I left New York.

"Mr. Fitzstephan says to come right up," the switchboard
boy said.

His apartment was on the sixth floor. He was standing at its
door when I got out of the elevator.

"By God," he said, holding out a lean hand, "it *is* you!"

"None other."

He hadn't changed any. We went into a room where half a
dozen bookcases and four tables left little room for anything
else. Magazines and books in various languages, papers, clippings, proof sheets, were scattered everywhere—all just as it
used to be in his New York rooms.

We sat down, found places for our feet between table-legs,
and accounted roughly for our lives since we had last seen one
another. He had been in San Francisco for a little more than
a year—except, he said, for week-ends, and two months
hermiting in the country, finishing a novel. I had been

there nearly five years. He liked San Francisco, he said, but wouldn't oppose any movement to give the West back to the Indians.

"How's the literary grift go?" I asked.

He looked at me sharply, demanding: "You haven't been reading me?"

"No. Where'd you get that funny idea?"

"There was something in your tone, something proprietary, as in the voice of one who has bought an author for a couple of dollars. I haven't met it often enough to be used to it. Good God! Remember once I offered you a set of my books as a present?" He had always liked to talk that way.

"Yeah. But I never blamed you. You were drunk."

"On sherry—Elsa Donne's sherry. Remember Elsa? She showed us a picture she had just finished, and you said it was pretty. Sweet God, wasn't she furious! You said it so vapidly and sincerely and as if you were so sure that she would like your saying it. Remember? She put us out, but we'd both already got plastered on her sherry. But you weren't tight enough to take the books."

"I was afraid I'd read them and understand them," I explained, "and then you'd have felt insulted."

A Chinese boy brought us cold white wine.

Fitzstephan said: "I suppose you're still hounding the unfortunate evil-doer?"

"Yeah. That's how I happened to locate you. Halstead tells me you know Edgar Leggett."

A gleam pushed through the sleepiness in his gray eyes, and he sat up a little in his chair, asking: "Leggett's been up to something?"

"Why do you say that?"

"I didn't say it. I asked it." He made himself limp in the chair again, but the gleam didn't go out of his eyes. "Come on, out with it. Don't try to be subtle with me, my son; that's not your style at all. Try it and you're sunk. Out with it: what's Leggett been up to?"

"We don't do it that way," I said. "You're a story-writer. I can't trust you not to build up on what I tell you. I'll save mine till after you've spoken your piece, so yours won't be twisted to fit mine. How long have you known him?"

"Since shortly after I came here. He's always interested me. There's something obscure in him, something dark and inviting. He is, for instance, physically ascetic—neither smoking or drinking, eating meagerly, sleeping, I'm told, only three or four hours a night—but mentally, or spiritually, sensual—does that mean anything to you?—to the point of decadence. You used to think I had an abnormal appetite for the fantastic. You should know him. His friends—no, he hasn't any—his choice companions are those who have the most outlandish ideas to offer: Marquard and his insane figures that aren't figures, but the boundaries of areas in space that are the figures; Denbar Curt and his algebraism; the Haldorns and their Holy Grail sect; crazy Laura Joines; Farnham—"

"And you," I put in, "with explanations and descriptions that explain and describe nothing. I hope you don't think any of what you've said means anything to me."

"I remember you now: you were always like that." He grinned at me, running thin fingers through his sorrel hair. "Tell me what's up while I try to find one-syllable words for you."

I asked him if he knew Eric Collinson. He said he did; there was nothing to know about him except that he was engaged to Gabrielle Leggett, that his father was the lumber Collinson, and that Eric was Princeton, stocks and bonds, and hand-ball, a nice boy.

"Maybe," I said, "but he lied to me."

"Isn't that like a sleuth?" Fitzstephan shook his head, grinning. "You must have had the wrong fellow—somebody impersonating him. The Chevalier Bayard doesn't lie, and, besides, lying requires imagination. You've—or wait! Was a woman involved in your question?"

I nodded.

"You're correct, then," Fitzstephan assured me. "I apologize. The Chevalier Bayard always lies when a woman is involved, even if it's unnecessary and puts her to a lot of trouble. It's one of the conventions of Bayardism, something to do with guarding her honor or the like. Who was the woman?"

"Gabrielle Leggett," I said, and told him all I knew about the Leggetts, the diamonds, and the dead man in Golden

Gate Avenue. Disappointment deepened in his face while I talked.

"That's trivial, dull," he complained when I had finished. "I've been thinking of Leggett in terms of Dumas, and you bring me a piece of gimcrackery out of O. Henry. You've let me down, you and your shabby diamonds. But"—his eyes brightened again—"this may lead to something. Leggett may or may not be criminal, but there's more to him than a twopenny insurance swindle."

"You mean," I asked, "that he's one of these master minds? So you read newspapers? What do you think he is? King of the bootleggers? Chief of an international crime syndicate? A white-slave magnate? Head of a dope ring? Or queen of the counterfeiters in disguise?"

"Don't be an idiot," he said. "But he's got brains, and there's something black in him. There's something he doesn't want to think about, but must not forget. I've told you that he's thirsty for all that's dizziest in thought, yet he's cold as a fish, but with a bitter-dry coldness. He's a neurotic who keeps his body fit and sensitive and ready—for what?—while he drugs his mind with lunacies. Yet he's cold and sane. If a man has a past that he wants to forget, he can easiest drug his mind against memory through his body, with sensuality if not with narcotics. But suppose the past is not dead, and this man must keep himself fit to cope with it should it come into the present. Well, then he would be wisest to anæsthetize his mind directly, letting his body stay strong and ready."

"And this past?"

Fitzstephan shook his head, saying: "If I don't know—and I don't—it isn't my fault. Before you're through, you'll know how difficult it is to get information out of that family."

"Did you try?"

"Certainly. I'm a novelist. My business is with souls and what goes on in them. He's got one that attracts me, and I've always considered myself unjustly treated by his not turning himself inside out for me. You know, I doubt if Leggett's his name. He's French. He told me once he came from Atlanta, but he's French in outlook, in quality of mind, in everything except admission."

"What of the rest of the family?" I asked. "Gabrielle's cuckoo, isn't she?"

"I wonder." Fitzstephan looked curiously at me. "Are you saying that carelessly, or do you really think she's off?"

"I don't know. She's odd, an uncomfortable sort of person. And, then, she's got animal ears, hardly any forehead; and her eyes shift from green to brown and back without ever settling on one color. How much of her affairs have you turned up in your snooping around?"

"Are you—who make your living snooping—sneering at my curiosity about people and my attempts to satisfy it?"

"We're different," I said. "I do mine with the object of putting people in jail, and I get paid for it, though not as much as I should."

"That's not different," he said. "I do mine with the object of putting people in books, and I get paid for it, though not as much as I should."

"Yeah, but what good does that do?"

"God knows. What good does putting them in jail do?"

"Relieves congestion," I said. "Put enough people in jail, and cities wouldn't have traffic problems. What do you know about this Gabrielle?"

"She hates her father. He worships her."

"How come the hate?"

"I don't know; perhaps because he worships her."

"There's no sense to that," I complained. "You're just being literary. What about Mrs. Leggett?"

"You've never eaten one of her meals, I suppose? You'd have no doubts if you had. None but a serene, sane soul ever achieved such cooking. I've often wondered what she thinks of the weird creatures who are her husband and daughter, though I imagine she simply accepts them as they are without even being conscious of their weirdness."

"All this is well enough in its way," I said, "but you still haven't told me anything definite."

"No, I haven't," he replied, "and that, my boy, is it. I've told you what I know and what I imagine, and none of it is definite. That's the point—in a year of trying I've learned nothing definite about Leggett. Isn't that—remembering my curiosity and my usual skill in satisfying it—enough to convince you that the man is hiding something and knows how to hide it?"

"Is it? I don't know. But I know I've wasted enough time learning nothing that anybody can be jailed for. Dinner to-morrow night? Or the next?"

"The next. About seven o'clock?"

I said I would stop for him, and went out. It was then af-ter five o'clock. Not having had any luncheon, I went up to Blanco's for food, and then to darktown for a look at Rhino Tingley.

I found him in Big-foot Gerber's cigar-store, rolling a fat cigar around in his mouth, telling something to the other Negroes—four of them—in the place.

". . . says to him: 'Nigger, you talking yourself out of skin,' and I reaches out my hand for him, and, 'fore God, there weren't none of him there excepting his footprints in the ce-ment pavement, eight feet apart and leading home."

Buying a package of cigarettes, I weighed him in while he talked. He was a chocolate man of less than thirty years, close to six feet tall and weighing two hundred pounds plus, with big yellow-balled pop eyes, a broad nose, a big blue-lipped and blue-gummed mouth, and a ragged black scar running from his lower lip down behind his blue and white striped collar. His clothes were new enough to look new, and he wore them sportily. His voice was a heavy bass that shook the glass of the show-cases when he laughed with his audience.

I went out of the store while they were laughing, heard the laughter stop short behind me, resisted the temptation to look back, and moved down the street towards the building where he and Minnie lived. He came abreast of me when I was half a block from the flat.

I said nothing while we took seven steps side by side.

Then he said: "You the man that been inquirying around about me?"

The sour odor of Italian wine was thick enough to be seen.

I considered, and said: "Yeah."

"What you got to do with me?" he asked, not disagreeably, but as if he wanted to know.

Across the street Gabrielle Leggett, in brown coat and brown and yellow hat, came out of Minnie's building and walked south, not turning her face towards us. She walked swiftly and her lower lip was between her teeth.

I looked at the Negro. He was looking at me. There was nothing in his face to show that he had seen Gabrielle Leggett, or that the sight of her meant anything to him.

I said: "You've got nothing to hide, have you? What do you care who asks about you?"

"All the same, I'm the party to come to if you wants to know about me. You the man that got Minnie fired?"

"She wasn't fired. She quit."

"Minnie don't have to take nobody's lip. She—"

"Let's go over and talk to her," I suggested, leading the way across the street. At the front door he went ahead, up a flight of stairs, down a dark hall to a door which he opened with one of the twenty or more keys on his ring.

Minnie Hershey, in a pink kimono trimmed with yellow ostrich feathers that looked like little dead ferns, came out of the bedroom to meet us in the living-room. Her eyes got big when she saw me.

Rhino said: "You know this gentleman, Minnie."

Minnie said: "Y-yes."

I said: "You shouldn't have left the Leggetts' that way. Nobody thinks you had anything to do with the diamonds. What did Miss Leggett want here?"

"There been no Miss Leggetts here," she told me. "I don't know what you talking about."

"She came out as we were coming in."

"Oh! *Miss* Leggett. I thought you said *Mrs.* Leggett. I beg your pardon. Yes, sir. Miss Gabrielle was sure enough here. She wanted to know if I wouldn't come back there. She thinks a powerful lot of me, Miss Gabrielle does."

"That," I said, "is what you ought to do. It was foolish, leaving like that."

Rhino took the cigar out of his mouth and pointed the red end at the girl.

"You away from them," he boomed, "and you stay away from them. You don't have to take nothing from nobody." He put a hand in his pants pocket, lugged out a thick bundle of paper money, thumped it down on the table, and rumbled: "What for you have to work for folks?"

He was talking to the girl, but looking at me, grinning, gold teeth shining against purplish mouth. The girl looked at him scornfully, said: "Lead him around, *vino*," and turned to me again, her brown face tense, anxious to be believed, saying earnestly: "Rhino got that money in a crap game, mister. Hope to die if he didn't."

Rhino said: "Ain't nobody's business where I got my money. I got it. I got—" He put his cigar on the edge of the table, picked up the money, wet a thumb as big as a heel on a tongue like a bath-mat, and counted his roll bill by bill down on the table. "Twenty—thirty—eighty—hundred—hundred and ten—two hundred and ten—three hundred and ten—three hundred and thirty—three hundred and thirty-five—four hundred and thirty-five—five hundred and thirty-five—five hundred and eighty-five—six hundred and five—six hundred and ten—six hundred and twenty—seven hundred and twenty—seven hundred and seventy—eight hundred and twenty—eight hundred and thirty—eight hundred and forty—nine hundred and forty—nine hundred and sixty—nine hundred and seventy—nine hundred and seventy-five—nine hundred and ninety-five—ten hundred and fifteen—ten hundred and twenty—eleven hundred and twenty—eleven hundred and seventy. Anybody want to know what I got, that's what I got—eleven hundred and seventy dollars. Anybody want to know where I get it, maybe I tell them, maybe I don't. Just depend on how I feel about it."

Minnie said: "He won it in a crap game, mister, up the Happy Day Social Club. Hope to die if he didn't."

"Maybe I did," Rhino said, still grinning widely at me. "But supposing I didn't?"

"I'm no good at riddles," I said, and, after again advising Minnie to return to the Leggetts, left the flat. Minnie closed the door behind me. As I went down the hall I could hear her voice scolding and Rhino's chesty bass laughter.

In a downtown Owl drug-store I turned to the Berkeley section of the telephone directory, found only one Freemander listed, and called the number. Mrs. Begg was there and consented to see me if I came over on the next ferry.

The Freemander house was set off a road that wound up-hill towards the University of California.

Mrs. Begg was a scrawny, big-boned woman, with not much gray hair packed close around a bony skull, hard gray eyes, and hard, capable hands. She was sour and severe, but plain-spoken enough to let us talk turkey without a lot of preliminary hemming and hawing.

I told her about the burglary and my belief that the thief had been helped, at least with information, by somebody who knew the Leggett household, winding up: "Mrs. Priestly told me you had been Leggett's housekeeper, and she thought you could help me."

Mrs. Begg said she doubted whether she could tell me anything that would pay me for my trip from the city, but she was willing to do what she could, being an honest woman and having nothing to conceal from anybody. Once started, she told me a great deal, damned near talking me earless. Throwing out the stuff that didn't interest me, I came away with this information:

Mrs. Begg had been hired by Leggett, through an employment agency, as housekeeper in the spring of 1921. At first she had a girl to help her, but there wasn't enough work for two, so, at Mrs. Begg's suggestion, they let the girl go. Leggett was a man of simple tastes and spent nearly all his time on the top floor, where he had his laboratory and a cubbyhole bedroom. He seldom used the rest of the house except when he had friends in for an evening. Mrs. Begg didn't like his friends, though she could say nothing against them except that the way they talked was a shame and a disgrace. Edgar Leggett was as nice a man as a person could want to know, she said, only so secretive that it made a person nervous. She was never allowed to go up on the third floor, and the door of the laboratory was always kept locked. Once a month a Jap would come in to clean it up under Leggett's supervision. Well, she supposed he had a lot of scientific secrets, and maybe dangerous chemicals, that he didn't want people poking into, but just the same it made a person uneasy. She didn't know anything about her employer's personal or family affairs and knew her place too well to ask him any questions.

In August 1923—it was a rainy morning, she remembered— a woman and a girl of fifteen, with a lot of suit-cases, had come to the house. She let them in and the woman asked for

Mr. Leggett. Mrs. Begg went up to the laboratory door and told him, and he came down. Never in all her born days had she seen such a surprised man as he was when he saw them. He turned absolutely white, and she thought he was going to fall down, he shook that bad. She didn't know what Leggett and the woman and the girl said to one another that morning, because they jabbered away in some foreign language, though the lot of them could talk English as good as anybody else, and better than most, especially that Gabrielle when she got to cursing. Mrs. Begg had left them and gone on about her business. Pretty soon Leggett came out to the kitchen and told her his visitors were a Mrs. Dain, his sister-in-law, and her daughter, neither of whom he had seen for ten years; and that they were going to stay there with him. Mrs. Dain later told Mrs. Begg that they were English, but had been living in New York for several years. Mrs. Begg said she liked Mrs. Dain, who was a sensible woman and a first-rate housewife, but that Gabrielle was a tartar. Mrs. Begg always spoke of the girl as "that Gabrielle."

With the Dains there, and with Mrs. Dain's ability as a housekeeper, there was no longer any place for Mrs. Begg. They had been very liberal, she said, helping her find a new place and giving her a generous bonus when she left. She hadn't seen any of them since, but, thanks to the careful watch she habitually kept on the marriage, death, and birth notices in the morning papers, she had learned, a week after she left, that a marriage license had been issued to Edgar Leggett and Alice Dain.

CHAPTER IV

The Vague Harpers

WHEN I arrived at the agency at nine the next morning, Eric Collinson was sitting in the reception room. His sunburned face was dingy without pinkness, and he had forgotten to put stickum on his hair.

"Do you know anything about Miss Leggett?" he asked, jumping up and meeting me at the door. "She wasn't home last night, and she's not home yet. Her father wouldn't say he didn't know where she was, but I'm sure he didn't. He told me not to worry, but how can I help worrying? Do you know anything about it?"

I said I didn't and told him about seeing her leave Minnie Hershey's the previous evening. I gave him the mulatto's address and suggested that he ask her. He jammed his hat on his head and hurried off.

Getting O'Gar on the phone, I asked him if he had heard from New York yet.

"Uh-huh," he said. "Upton—that's his right name—was once one of you private dicks—had a agency of his own—till '23, when him and a guy named Harry Ruppert were sent over for trying to fix a jury. How'd you make out with the shine?"

"I don't know. This Rhino Tingley's carrying an eleven-hundred-case roll. Minnie says he got it with the rats and mice. Maybe he did: it's twice what he could have peddled Leggett's stuff for. Can you try to have it checked? He's supposed to have got it at the Happy Day Social Club."

O'Gar promised to do what he could and hung up.

I sent a wire to our New York branch, asking for more dope on Upton and Ruppert, and then went up to the county clerk's office in the municipal building, where I dug into the August and September 1923 marriage-license file. The application I wanted was dated August 26 and bore Edgar Leggett's statement that he was born in Atlanta, Georgia, on March 6, 1883, and that this was his second marriage; and Alice Dain's statement that she was born in London, England, on October 22, 1888, and that she had not been married before.

When I returned to the agency, Eric Collinson, his yellow hair still further disarranged, was again lying in wait for me.

"I saw Minnie," he said excitedly, "and she couldn't tell me anything. She said Gaby was there last night to ask her to come back to work, but that's all she knew about her. But she —she's wearing an emerald ring that I'm positive is Gaby's."

"Did you ask her about it?"

"Who? Minnie? No. How could I? It would have been— you know."

"That's right," I agreed, thinking of Fitzstephan's Chevalier Bayard, "we must always be polite. Why did you lie to me about the time you and Miss Leggett got home the other night?"

Embarrassment made his face more attractive-looking and less intelligent.

"That was silly of me," he stammered, "but I didn't—you know—I thought you—I was afraid—"

He wasn't getting anywhere. I suggested: "You thought that was a late hour and didn't want me to get wrong notions about her?"

"Yes, that's it."

I shooed him out and went into the operatives' room, where Mickey Linehan—big, loose-hung, red-faced—and Al Mason—slim, dark, sleek—were swapping lies about the times they had been shot at, each trying to pretend he had been more frightened than the other. I told them who was who and what was what on the Leggett job—as far as my knowledge went, and it didn't go far when I came to putting it in words—and sent Al out to keep an eye on the Leggetts' house, Mickey to see how Minnie and Rhino behaved.

Mrs. Leggett, her pleasant face shadowed, opened the door when I rang the bell an hour later. We went into the green, orange, and chocolate room, where we were joined by her husband. I passed on to them the information about Upton that O'Gar had received from New York and told them I had wired for more dope on Ruppert.

"Some of your neighbors saw a man who was not Upton loitering around," I said, "and a man who fits the same description ran down the fire-escape from the room Upton was killed in. We'll see what Ruppert looks like."

I was watching Leggett's face. Nothing changed in it. His too bright red-brown eyes held interest and nothing else.

I asked: "Is Miss Leggett in?"

He said: "No."

"When will she be in?"

"Probably not for several days. She's gone out of town."

"Where can I find her?" I asked, turning to Mrs. Leggett. "I've some questions to ask her."

Mrs. Leggett avoided my gaze, looking at her husband.

His metallic voice answered my question: "We don't know, exactly. Friends of hers, a Mr. and Mrs. Harper, drove up from Los Angeles and asked her to go along on a trip up in the mountains. I don't know which route they intended taking, and doubt if they had any definite destination."

I asked questions about the Harpers. Leggett admitted knowing very little about them. Mrs. Harper's first name was Carmel, he said, and everybody called the man Bud, but Leggett wasn't sure whether his name was Frank or Walter. Nor did he know the Harpers' Los Angeles address. He thought they had a house somewhere in Pasadena, but wasn't sure, having, in fact, heard something about their selling the house, or perhaps only intending to. While he told me this nonsense, his wife sat staring at the floor, lifting her blue eyes twice to look swiftly, pleadingly, at her husband.

I asked her: "Don't you know anything more about them than that?"

"No," she said weakly, darting another glance at her husband's face, while he, paying no attention to her, stared levelly at me.

"When did they leave?" I asked.

"Early this morning," Leggett said. "They were staying at one of the hotels—I don't know which—and Gabrielle spent the night with them so they could start early."

I had enough of the Harpers. I asked: "Did either of you— any of you—know anything about Upton—have any dealings with him of any sort—before this affair?"

Leggett said: "No."

I had other questions, but the kind of replies I was drawing didn't mean anything, so I stood up to go. I was tempted to tell him what I thought of him, but there was no profit in that.

He got up too, smiling politely, and said: "I'm sorry to have caused the insurance company all this trouble through what was, after all, probably my carelessness. I should like to ask your opinion: do you really think I should accept responsibility for the loss of the diamonds and make it good?"

"The way it stands," I said, "I think you should; but that wouldn't stop the investigation."

Mrs. Leggett put her handkerchief to her mouth quickly.

Leggett said: "Thanks." His voice was casually polite. "I'll have to think it over."

On my way back to the agency I dropped in on Fitzstephan for half an hour. He was writing, he told me, an article for the *Psychopathological Review*—that's probably wrong, but it was something on that order—condemning the hypothesis of an unconscious or subconscious mind as a snare and a delusion, a pitfall for the unwary and a set of false whiskers for the charlatan, a gap in psychology's roof that made it impossible, or nearly, for the sound scholar to smoke out such faddists as, for example, the psychoanalyst and the behaviorist, or words to that effect. He went on like that for ten minutes or more, finally coming back to the United States with: "But how are you getting along with the problem of the elusive diamonds?"

"This way and that way," I said, and told him what I had learned and done so far.

"You've certainly," he congratulated me when I finished, "got it all as tangled and confused as possible."

"It'll be worse before it's better," I predicted. "I'd like to have ten minutes alone with Mrs. Leggett. Away from her husband, I imagine things could be done with her. Could you get anything out of her? I'd like to know why Gabrielle has gone, even if I can't learn where."

"I'll try," Fitzstephan said willingly. "Suppose I go out there tomorrow afternoon—to borrow a book. Waite's *Rosy Cross* will do it. They know I'm interested in that sort of stuff. He'll be working in the laboratory, and I'll refuse to disturb him. I'll have to go at it in an offhand way, but maybe I can get something out of her."

"Thanks," I said. "See you tomorrow night."

I spent most of the afternoon putting my findings and guesses on paper and trying to fit them together in some sort of order. Eric Collinson phoned twice to ask if I had any news of his Gabrielle. Neither Mickey Linehan nor Al Mason reported anything. At six o'clock I called it a day.

CHAPTER V

Gabrielle

THE NEXT DAY brought happenings.

Early in the morning there was a telegram from our New York office. Decoded, it read:

LOUIS UPTON FORMER PROPRIETOR DETECTIVE AGENCY HERE STOP ARRESTED SEPTEMBER FIRST ONE NINE TWO THREE FOR BRIBING TWO JURORS IN SEXTON MURDER TRIAL STOP TRIED TO SAVE HIMSELF BY IMPLICATING HARRY RUPPERT OPERATIVE IN HIS EMPLOY STOP BOTH MEN CONVICTED STOP BOTH RELEASED FROM SING SING FEBRUARY SIX THIS YEAR STOP RUPPERT SAID TO HAVE THREATENED TO KILL UPTON STOP RUPPERT THIRTY TWO YEARS FIVE FEET ELEVEN INCHES HUNDRED FIFTY POUNDS BROWN HAIR AND EYES SALLOW COMPLEXION THIN FACE LONG THIN NOSE WALKS WITH STOOP AND CHIN OUT STOP MAILING PHOTOGRAPHS

That placed Ruppert definitely enough as the man Mrs. Priestly and Daley had seen and the man who had probably killed Upton.

O'Gar called me on the phone to tell me: "That dinge of yours—Rhino Tingley—was picked up in a hock shop last night trying to unload some jewelry. None of it was loose diamonds. We haven't been able to crack him yet, just got him identified. I sent a man out to Leggett's with some of the stuff, thinking it might be theirs, but they said no."

That didn't fit in anywhere. I suggested: "Try Halstead and Beauchamp. Tell them you think the stuff is Leggett's. Don't tell them he said it wasn't."

Half an hour later the detective-sergeant phoned me again, from the jewelers', to tell me that Halstead had positively identified two pieces—a string of pearls and a topaz brooch—as articles Leggett had purchased there for his daughter.

"That's swell," I said. "Now will you do this? Go out to Rhino's flat and put the screws on his woman, Minnie Hershey. Frisk the joint, rough her up; the more you scare her, the better. She may be wearing an emerald ring. If she is, or if it—or any other jewelry that might be the Leggetts'—is there, you can take it away with you; but don't stay too long and don't bother her afterwards. I've got her covered. Just stir her up and beat it."

"I'll turn her white," O'Gar promised.

Dick Foley was in the operatives' room, writing his report on a warehouse robbery that had kept him up all night. I chased him out to help Mickey with the mulatto.

"Both of you tail her if she leaves her joint after the police are through," I said, "and as soon as you put her in anywhere, one of you get to a phone and let me know."

I went back to my office and burned cigarettes. I was ruining the third one when Eric Collinson phoned to ask if I had found his Gabrielle yet.

"Not quite, but I've got prospects. If you aren't busy, you might come over and go along with me—if it so happens that there turns out to be some place to go."

He said, very eagerly, that he would do that.

A few minutes later Mickey Linehan phoned: "The high yellow's gone visiting," and gave me a Pacific Avenue address.

The phone rang again before I got it out of my hand.

"This is Watt Halstead," a voice said. "Can you come down to see me for a minute or two?"

"Not now. What is it?"

"It's about Edgar Leggett, and it's quite puzzling. The police brought some jewelry in this morning, asking whether we knew whose it was. I recognized a string of pearls and a brooch that Edgar Leggett bought from us for his daughter last year—the brooch in the spring, the pearls at Christmas. After the police had gone, I, quite naturally, phoned Leggett; and he took the most peculiar attitude. He waited until I had told him about it, then said: 'I thank you very much for your interference in my affairs,' and hung up. What do you suppose is the matter with him?"

"God knows. Thanks. I've got to run now, but I'll stop in when I get a chance."

I hunted up Owen Fitzstephan's number, called it, and heard his drawled: "Hello."

"You'd better get busy on your book-borrowing if any good's to come of it," I said.

"Why? Are things taking place?"

"Things are."

"Such as?" he asked.

"This and that, but it's no time for anybody who wants to poke his nose into the Leggett mysteries to be dilly-dallying with pieces about unconscious minds."

"Right," he said; "I'm off to the front now."

Eric Collinson had come in while I was talking to the novelist.

"Come on," I said, leading the way out towards the elevators. "This might not be a false alarm."

"Where are we going?" he asked impatiently. "Have you found her? Is she all right?"

I replied to the only one of his questions that I had the answer to by giving him the Pacific Avenue address Mickey had given me. It meant something to Collinson. He said: "That's Joseph's place."

We were in the elevator with half a dozen other people. I held my response down to a "Yeah?"

He had a Chrysler roadster parked around the corner. We got into it and began bucking traffic and traffic signals towards Pacific Avenue.

I asked: "Who is Joseph?"

"Another cult. He's the head of it. He calls his place the Temple of the Holy Grail. It's the fashionable one just now. You know how they come and go in California. I don't like having Gabrielle there, if that's where she is—though—I don't know—they may be all right. He's one of Mr. Leggett's queer friends. Do you know that she's there?"

"Maybe. Is she a member of the cult?"

"She goes there, yes. I've been there with her."

"What sort of a layout is it?"

"Oh, it seems to be all right," he said somewhat reluctantly. "The right sort of people: Mrs. Payson Laurence, and the Ralph Colemans, and Mrs. Livingston Rodman, people like that. And the Haldorns—that's Joseph and his wife Aaronia—seem to be quite all right, but—but I don't like the idea of Gabrielle going there like this." He missed the end of a cable car with the Chrysler's right wheel. "I don't think it's good for her to come too much under their influence."

"You've been there; what is their brand of hocus-pocus?" I asked.

"It isn't hocus-pocus, really," he replied, wrinkling his forehead. "I don't know very much about their creed, or anything like that, but I've been to their services with Gabrielle, and they're quite as dignified, as beautiful even, as either Episcopalian or Catholic services. You mustn't think that this is the Holy Roller or House of David sort of thing. It isn't at all. Whatever it is, it is quite first-rate. The Haldorns are people of—of—well, more culture than I."

"Then what's the matter with them?"

He shook his head gloomily. "I honestly don't know that anything is. I don't like it. I don't like having Gabrielle go off like this without letting anybody know where she's gone. Do you think her parents knew where she had gone?"

"No."

"I don't think so either," he said.

From the street the Temple of the Holy Grail looked like what it had originally been, a six-story yellow brick apartment building. There was nothing about its exterior to show that it wasn't still that. I made Collinson drive past it to the corner where Mickey Linehan was leaning his lop-sided bulk against a stone wall. He came to the car as it stopped at the curb.

"The dark meat left ten minutes ago," he reported, "with Dick behind her. Nobody else that looks like anybody you listed has been out."

"Camp here in the car and watch the door," I told him. "We're going in," I said to Collinson. "Let me do most of the talking."

When we reached the Temple door I had to caution him: "Try not breathing so hard. Everything will probably be oke."

I rang the bell. The door was opened immediately by a broad-shouldered, meaty woman of some year close to fifty. She was a good three inches taller than my five feet six. Flesh hung in little bags on her face, but there was neither softness nor looseness in her eyes and mouth. Her long upper lip had been shaved. She was dressed in black, black clothes that covered her from chin and ear-lobes to within less than an inch of the floor.

"We want to see Miss Leggett," I said.

She pretended she hadn't understood me.

"We want to see Miss Leggett," I repeated, "Miss Gabrielle Leggett."

"I don't know." Her voice was bass. "But come in."

She took us not very cheerfully into a small, dimly lighted reception room to one side of the foyer, told us to wait there, and went away.

"Who's the village blacksmith?" I asked Collinson.

He said he didn't know her. He fidgeted around the room. I sat down. Drawn blinds let in too little light for me to make out much of the room, but the rug was soft and thick, and what I could see of the furniture leaned towards luxury rather than severity.

Except for Collinson's fidgeting, no sound came from anywhere in the building. I looked at the open door and saw that we were being examined. A small boy of twelve or thirteen stood there staring at us with big dark eyes that seemed to have lights of their own in the semi-darkness.

I said: "Hello, son."

Collinson jumped around at the sound of my voice.

The boy said nothing. He stared at me for at least another minute with the blank, unblinking, embarrassing stare that only children can manage completely, then turned his back on me and walked away, making no more noise going than he had made coming.

"Who's that?" I asked Collinson.

"It must be the Haldorns' son Manuel. I've never seen him before."

Collinson walked up and down. I sat and watched the door. Presently a woman, walking silently on the thick carpet, appeared there and came into the reception room. She was tall, graceful; and her dark eyes seemed to have lights of their own, like the boy's. That was all I could see clearly then.

I stood up.

She addressed Collinson: "How do you do? This is Mr. Collinson, isn't it?" Her voice was the most musical I had ever heard.

Collinson mumbled something or other and introduced me to the woman, calling her Mrs. Haldorn. She gave me a warm, firm hand and then crossed the room to raise a blind, letting in a fat rectangle of afternoon sun. While I blinked at her in the sudden brightness, she sat down and motioned us into chairs.

I saw her eyes first. They were enormous, almost black, warm, and heavily fringed with almost black lashes. They were the only live, human, real, things in her face. There was warmth and there was beauty in her oval, olive-skinned face, but, except for the eyes, it was warmth and beauty that didn't seem to have anything to do with reality. It was as if her face were not a face, but a mask that she had worn until it had almost become a face. Even her mouth, which was a mouth to talk about, looked not so much like flesh as like a too perfect imitation of flesh, softer and redder and maybe warmer than genuine flesh, but not genuine flesh. Above this face, or mask, uncut black hair was tied close to her head, parted in the middle, and drawn across temples and upper ears to end in a knot on the nape of her neck. Her neck was long, strong, slender; her body tall, fully fleshed, supple; her clothes dark and silky, part of her body.

I said: "We want to see Miss Leggett, Mrs. Haldorn."

She asked curiously: "Why do you think she is here?"

"That doesn't make any difference, does it?" I replied quickly, before Collinson could say something wrong. "She is. We'd like to see her."

"I don't think you can," she said slowly. "She isn't well, and she came here to rest, particularly to get away from people for a while."

"Sorry," I said, "but it's a case of have to. We wouldn't have come like this if it hadn't been important."

"It is important?"

"Yeah."

She hesitated, said: "Well, I'll see," excused herself, and left us.

"I wouldn't mind moving in here myself," I told Collinson.

He didn't know what I was talking about. His face was flushed and excited.

"Gabrielle may not like our coming here like this," he said.

I said that would be too bad.

Aaronia Haldorn returned to us.

"I'm really very sorry," she said, standing in the doorway, smiling politely, "but Miss Leggett doesn't wish to see you."

"I'm sorry she doesn't," I said, "but we'll have to see her."

She drew herself up straight and her smile went away.

"I beg your pardon?" she said.

"We'll have to see her," I repeated, keeping my voice amiable. "It's important, as I told you."

"I am sorry." Even the iciness she got into her voice didn't keep it from being beautiful. "You cannot see her."

I said: "Miss Leggett's an important witness, as you probably know, in a robbery and murder job. Well, we've got to see her. If it suits you better, I'm willing to wait half an hour till we can get a policeman up here with whatever authority you make necessary. We're going to see her."

Collinson said something unintelligible, though it sounded apologetic.

Aaronia Haldorn made the slightest of bows.

"You may do as you see fit," she said coldly. "I do not approve of your disturbing Miss Leggett against her wishes, and so far as my permission is concerned, I do not give it. If you insist, I cannot prevent you."

"Thanks. Where is she?"

"Her room is on the fifth floor, just beyond the stairs, to the left."

She bent her head a little once more and went away.

Collinson put a hand on my arm, mumbling: "I don't know whether I—whether we ought to do this. Gabrielle's not going to like it. She won't—"

"Suit yourself," I growled, "but I'm going up. Maybe she won't like it, but neither do I like having people running away and hiding when I want to ask them about stolen diamonds."

He frowned, chewed his lips, and made uncomfortable faces, but he went along with me. We found an automatic elevator, rode to the fifth floor, and went down a purple-carpeted corridor to the door just beyond the stairs on the left-hand side.

I tapped the door with the back of my hand. There was no answer from inside. I tapped again, louder.

A voice sounded inside the room. It might have been anybody's voice, though probably a woman's. It was too faint for us to know what it said and too smothered for us to know who was saying it.

I poked Collinson with my elbow and ordered: "Call her."

He pulled at his collar with a forefinger and called hoarsely: "Gaby, it's Eric."

That didn't bring an answer.

I thumped the wood again, calling: "Open the door."

The voice inside said something that was nothing to me. I repeated my thumping and calling. Down the corridor a door opened and a sallow thin-haired old man's head stuck out and asked: "What's the matter?" I said: "None of your damned business," and pounded the door again.

The inside voice came strong enough now to let us know that it was complaining, though no words could be made out yet. I rattled the knob and found that the door was unlocked. Rattling the knob some more, I worked the door open an inch or so. Then the voice was clearer. I heard soft feet on the floor. I heard a choking sob. I pushed the door open.

Eric Collinson made a noise in his throat that was like somebody very far away yelling horribly.

Gabrielle Leggett stood beside the bed, swaying a little, holding the white foot-rail of the bed with one hand. Her face was white as lime. Her eyes were all brown, dull, focused on nothing, and her small forehead was wrinkled. She looked as if she knew there was something in front of her and was wondering what it was. She had on one yellow stocking, a brown velvet skirt that had been slept in, and a yellow chemise. Scattered around the room were a pair of brown slippers, the other stocking, a brown and gold blouse, a brown coat, and a brown and yellow hat.

Everything else in the room was white: white-papered walls and white-painted ceiling; white-enameled chairs, bed, table, fixtures—even to the telephone—and woodwork; white felt on the floor. None of the furniture was hospital furniture, but solid whiteness gave it that appearance. There were two windows, and two doors besides the one I had opened. The door on the left opened into a bathroom, the one on the right into a small dressing-room.

I pushed Collinson into the room, followed him, and

closed the door. There was no key in it, and no place for a key, no lock of any fixable sort. Collinson stood gaping at the girl, his jaw sagging, his eyes as vacant as hers; but there was more horror in his face. She leaned against the foot of the bed and stared at nothing with dark, blank eyes in a ghastly, puzzled face.

I put an arm around her and sat her on the side of the bed, telling Collinson: "Gather up her clothes." I had to tell him twice before he came out of his trance.

He brought me her things and I began dressing her. He dug his fingers into my shoulder and protested in a voice that would have been appropriate if I had been robbing a poor-box:

"No! You can't—"

"What the hell?" I asked, pushing his hand away. "You can have the job if you want it."

He was sweating. He gulped and stuttered: "No, no! I couldn't—it—" He broke off and walked to the window.

"She told me you were an ass," I said to his back, and discovered I was putting the brown and gold blouse on her backwards. She might as well have been a wax figure, for all the help she gave me, but at least she didn't struggle when I wrestled her around, and she stayed where I shoved her.

By the time I had got her into coat and hat, Collinson had come away from the window and was spluttering questions at me. What was the matter with her? Oughtn't we to get a doctor? Was it safe to take her out? And when I stood up, he took her away from me, supporting her with his long, thick arms, babbling: "It's Eric, Gaby. Don't you know me? Speak to me. What is the matter, dear?"

"There's nothing the matter except that she's got a skinful of dope," I said. "Don't try to bring her out of it. Wait till we get her home. You take this arm and I'll take that. She can walk all right. If we run into anybody, just keep going and let me handle them. Let's go."

We didn't meet anybody. We went out to the elevator, down in it to the ground floor, across the foyer, and into the street without seeing a single person.

We went down to the corner where we had left Mickey in the Chrysler.

"That's all for you," I told him.

He said: "Right, so long," and went away.

Collinson and I wedged the girl between us in the roadster, and he put it in motion.

We rode three blocks. Then he asked: "Are you sure home's the best place for her?"

I said I was. He didn't say anything for five more blocks and then repeated his question, adding something about a hospital.

"Why not a newspaper office?" I sneered.

Three blocks of silence, and he started again: "I know a doctor who—"

"I've got work to do," I said; "and Miss Leggett home now, in the shape she's in now, will help me get it done. So she goes home."

He scowled, accusing me angrily: "You'd humiliate her, disgrace her, endanger her life, for the sake of—"

"Her life's in no more danger than yours or mine. She's simply got a little more of the junk in her than she can stand up under. And she took it. I didn't give it to her."

The girl we were talking about was alive and breathing between us—even sitting up with her eyes open—but knowing no more of what was going on than if she had been in Finland.

We should have turned to the right at the next corner. Collinson held the car straight and stepped it up to forty-five miles an hour, staring ahead, his face hard and lumpy.

"Take the next turn," I commanded.

"No," he said, and didn't. The speedometer showed a 50, and people on the sidewalks began looking after us as we whizzed by.

"Well?" I asked, wriggling an arm loose from the girl's side.

"We're going down the peninsula," he said firmly. "She's not going home in her condition."

I grunted: "Yeah?" and flashed my free hand at the controls. He knocked it aside, holding the wheel with one hand, stretching the other out to block me if I tried again.

"Don't do that," he cautioned me, increasing our speed another half-dozen miles. "You know what will happen to all of us if you—"

I cursed him, bitterly, fairly thoroughly, and from the heart.

His face jerked around to me, full of righteous indignation because, I suppose, my language wasn't the kind one should use in a lady's company.

And that brought it about.

A blue sedan came out of a cross-street a split second before we got there. Collinson's eyes and attention got back to his driving in time to twist the roadster away from the sedan, but not in time to make a neat job of it. We missed the sedan by a couple of inches, but as we passed behind it our rear wheels started sliding out of line. Collinson did what he could, giving the roadster its head, going with the skid, but the corner curb wouldn't co-operate. It stood stiff and hard where it was. We hit it sidewise and rolled over on the lamp-post behind it. The lamp-post snapped, crashed down on the sidewalk. The roadster, over on its side, spilled us out around the lamp-post. Gas from the broken post roared up at our feet.

Collinson, most of the skin scraped from one side of his face, crawled back on hands and knees to turn off the roadster's engine. I sat up, raising the girl, who was on my chest, with me. My right shoulder and arm were out of whack, dead. The girl was making whimpering noises in her chest, but I couldn't see any marks on her except a shallow scratch on one cheek. I had been her cushion, had taken the jolt for her. The soreness of my chest, belly, and back, the lameness of my shoulder and arm, told me how much I had saved her.

People helped us up. Collinson stood with his arms around the girl, begging her to say she wasn't dead, and so on. The smash had jarred her into semi-consciousness, but she still didn't know whether there had been an accident or what. I went over and helped Collinson hold her up—though neither needed help—saying earnestly to the gathering crowd: "We've got to get her home. Who can—?"

A pudgy man in plus fours offered his services. Collinson and I got in the back of his car with the girl, and I gave the pudgy man her address. He said something about a hospital, but I insisted that home was the place for her. Collinson was too upset to say anything. Twenty minutes later we took the girl out of the car in front of her house. I thanked the pudgy man profusely, giving him no opportunity to follow us indoors.

CHAPTER VI

The Man From Devil's Island

A FTER some delay—I had to ring twice—the Leggetts' door was opened by Owen Fitzstephan. There was no sleepiness in his eyes: they were hot and bright, as they were when he found life interesting. Knowing the sort of things that interested him, I wondered what had happened.

"What have you been doing?" he asked, looking at our clothes, at Collinson's bloody face, at the girl's scratched cheek.

"Automobile accident," I said. "Nothing serious. Where's everybody?"

"Everybody," he said, with peculiar emphasis on the word, "is up in the laboratory;" and then to me: "Come here."

I followed him across the reception hall to the foot of the stairs, leaving Collinson and the girl standing just inside the street door. Fitzstephan put his mouth close to my ear and whispered:

"Leggett's committed suicide."

I was more annoyed than surprised. I asked: "Where is he?"

"In the laboratory. Mrs. Leggett and the police are up there. It happened only half an hour ago."

"We'll all go up," I said.

"Isn't it rather unnecessary," he asked, "taking Gabrielle up there?"

"Might be tough on her," I said irritably, "but it's necessary enough. Anyway, she's coked-up and better able to stand the shock than she will be later, when the stuff's dying out in her." I turned to Collinson. "Come on, we'll go up to the laboratory."

I went ahead, letting Fitzstephan help Collinson with the girl. There were six people in the laboratory: a uniformed copper—a big man with a red mustache—standing beside the door; Mrs. Leggett, sitting on a wooden chair in the far end of the room, her body bent forward, her hands holding a handkerchief to her face, sobbing quietly; O'Gar and Reddy, standing by one of the windows, close together, their heads rubbing over a sheaf of papers that the detective-sergeant held in his thick fists; a gray-faced, dandified man in dark clothes, standing beside the zinc table, twiddling eye-glasses on a black ribbon in his hand; and Edgar Leggett, seated on a chair at the table, his head and upper body resting on the table, his arms sprawled out.

O'Gar and Reddy looked up from their reading as I came in. Passing the table on my way to join them at the window, I saw blood, a small black automatic pistol lying close to one of Leggett's hands, and seven unset diamonds grouped by his head.

O'Gar said, "Take a look," and handed me part of his sheaf of paper—four stiff white sheets covered with very small, precise, and regular handwriting in black ink. I was getting interested in what was written there when Fitzstephan and Collinson came in with Gabrielle Leggett.

Collinson looked at the dead man at the table. Collinson's face went white. He put his big body between the girl and her father.

"Come in," I said.

"This is no place for Miss Leggett now," he said hotly, turning to take her away.

"We ought to have everybody in here," I told O'Gar. He nodded his bullet head at the policeman. The policeman put a hand on Collinson's shoulder and said: "You'll have to come in, the both of you."

Fitzstephan placed a chair by one of the end windows for the girl. She sat down and looked around the room—at the dead man, at Mrs. Leggett, at all of us—with eyes that were dull but no longer completely blank. Collinson stood beside her, glaring at me. Mrs. Leggett hadn't looked up from her handkerchief.

I spoke to O'Gar, clearly enough for the others to hear: "Let's read the letter out loud."

He screwed up his eyes, hesitated, then thrust the rest of his sheaf at me, saying: "Fair enough. You read it."

I read:

"To the police:—

"My name is Maurice Pierre de Mayenne. I was born in Fécamp, department of Seine-Inférieure, France, on March 6,

1883, but was chiefly educated in England. In 1903 I went to Paris to study painting, and there, four years later, I made the acquaintance of Alice and Lily Dain, orphan daughters of a British naval officer. I married Lily the following year, and in 1909 our daughter Gabrielle was born.

"Shortly after my marriage I had discovered that I had made a most horrible mistake, that it was Alice, and not my wife Lily, whom I really loved. I kept this discovery to myself until the child was past the most difficult baby years; that is, until she was nearly five, and then told my wife, asking that she divorce me so I could marry Alice. She refused.

"On June 6, 1913, I murdered Lily and fled with Alice and Gabrielle to London, where I was soon arrested and returned to Paris, to be tried, found guilty, and sentenced to life imprisonment on the Iles du Salut. Alice, who had had no part in the murder, no knowledge of it until after it was done, and who had accompanied us to London only because of her love for Gabrielle, was also tried, but justly acquitted. All this is a matter of record in Paris.

"In 1918 I escaped from the islands with a fellow convict named Jacques Labaud, on a flimsy raft. I do not know—we never knew—how long we were adrift on the ocean, nor, toward the last, how long we went without food and water. Then Labaud could stand no more, and died. He died of starvation and exposure. I did not kill him. No living creature could have been feeble enough for me to have killed it, no matter what my desire. But when Labaud was dead there was enough food for one, and I lived to be washed ashore in the Golfo Triste.

"Calling myself Walter Martin, I secured employment with a British copper mining company at Aroa, and within a few months had become private secretary to Philip Howart, the resident manager. Shortly after this promotion I was approached by a cockney named John Edge, who outlined to me a plan by which we could defraud the company of a hundred-odd pounds monthly. When I refused to take part in the fraud, Edge revealed his knowledge of my identity, and threatened exposure unless I assisted him. That Venezuela had no extradition treaty with France might save me from being returned to the islands, Edge said; but that was not my chief danger: Labaud's body had been cast ashore, undecomposed enough to show what had happened to him, and I, an escaped murderer, would be under the necessity of proving to a Venezuelan court that I had not killed Labaud in Venezuelan waters to keep from starving.

"I still refused to join Edge in his fraud, and prepared to go away. But while I was making my preparations he killed Howart and looted the company safe. He urged me to flee with him, arguing that I could not face the police investigation even if he did not expose me. That was true enough: I went with him. Two months later, in Mexico City, I learned why Edge had been so desirous of my company. He had a firm hold on me, through his knowledge of my identity, and a great—an unjustified—opinion of my ability; and he intended using me to commit crimes that were beyond his grasp. I was determined, no matter what happened, no matter what became necessary, never to return to the Iles du Salut; but neither did I intend becoming a professional criminal. I attempted to desert Edge in Mexico City; he found me; we fought; and I killed him. I killed him in self-defense: he struck me first.

"In 1920 I came to the United States, to San Francisco, changed my name once more—to Edgar Leggett—and began making a new place for myself in the world, developing experiments with color that I had attempted as a young artist in Paris. In 1923, believing that Edgar Leggett could never now be connected with Maurice de Mayenne, I sent for Alice and Gabrielle, who were then living in New York, and Alice and I were married. But the past was not dead, and there was no unbridgeable chasm between Leggett and Mayenne. Alice, not hearing from me after my escape, not knowing what had happened to me, employed a private detective to find me, a Louis Upton. Upton sent a man named Ruppert to South America, and Ruppert succeeded in tracing me step by step from my landing in the Golfo Triste up to, but no farther than, my departure from Mexico City after Edge's death. In doing this, Ruppert of course learned of the deaths of Lebaud, Howart and Edge; three deaths of which I was guiltless, but of which—or at least of one or more of which—I most certainly, my record being what it is, would be convicted if tried.

"I do not know how Upton found me in San Francisco. Possibly he traced Alice and Gabrielle to me. Late last Saturday night he called upon me and demanded money as the price of silence. Having no money available at the time, I put him off until Tuesday, when I gave him the diamonds as part payment. But I was desperate. I knew what being at Upton's mercy would mean, having experienced the same thing with Edge. I determined to kill him. I decided to pretend the diamonds had been stolen, and to so inform you, the police. Upton, I was confident, would thereupon immediately communicate with me. I would make an appointment with him and shoot him down in cold blood, confident that I would have no difficulty in arranging a story that would make me seem justified in having killed this known burglar, in whose possession, doubtless, the stolen diamonds would be found.

"I think the plan would have been successful. However, Ruppert—pursuing Upton with a grudge of his own to settle —saved me from killing Upton by himself killing him. Ruppert, the man who had traced my course from Devil's Island to Mexico City, had also, either from Upton or by spying on Upton, learned that Mayenne was Leggett, and, with the police after him for Upton's murder, he came here, demanding that I shelter him, returning the diamonds, claiming money in their stead.

"I killed him. His body is in the cellar. Out front, a detective is watching my house. Other detectives are busy elsewhere inquiring into my affairs. I have not been able satisfactorily to explain certain of my actions, nor to avoid contradictions, and, now that I am actually suspect, there is little chance of the past's being kept secret. I have always known—have known it most surely when I would not admit it to myself—that this would one day happen. I am not going back to Devil's Island. My wife and daughter had neither knowledge of nor part in Ruppert's death.

"Maurice de Mayenne."

CHAPTER VII

The Curse

NOBODY said anything for some minutes after I had finished reading. Mrs. Leggett had taken her handkerchief from her face to listen, sobbing softly now and then. Gabrielle Leggett was looking jerkily around the room, light fighting cloudiness in her eyes, her lips twitching as if she was trying to get words out but couldn't.

I went to the table, bent over the dead man, and ran my hand over his pockets. The inside coat pocket bulged. I reached under his arm, unbuttoned and pulled open his coat, taking a brown wallet from the pocket. The wallet was thick with paper money—fifteen thousand dollars when we counted it later.

Showing the others the wallet's contents, I asked:

"Did he leave any message besides the one I read?"

"None that's been found," O'Gar said. "Why?"

"Any that you know of, Mrs. Leggett?" I asked.

She shook her head.

"Why?" O'Gar asked again.

"He didn't commit suicide," I said. "He was murdered."

Gabrielle Leggett screamed shrilly and sprang out of her chair, pointing a sharp-nailed white finger at Mrs. Leggett.

"She killed him," the girl shrieked. "She said, 'Come back here,' and held the kitchen door open with one hand, and picked up the knife from the drain-board with the other, and when he went past her she pushed it in his back. I saw her do it. She killed him. I wasn't dressed, and when I heard them coming I hid in the pantry, and I saw her do it."

Mrs. Leggett got to her feet. She staggered, and would have fallen if Fitzstephan hadn't gone over to steady her. Amazement washed her swollen face empty of grief.

The gray-faced dandified man by the table—Doctor Riese, I learned later—said, in a cold, crisp voice:

"There is no stab wound. He was shot through the temple by a bullet from this pistol, held close, slanting up. Clearly suicide, I should say."

Collinson forced Gabrielle down to her chair again, trying to calm her. She was working her hands together and moaning.

I disagreed with the doctor's last statement, and said so while turning something else over in my mind:

"Murder. He had this money in his pocket. He was going away. He wrote that letter to the police to clear his wife and daughter, so they wouldn't be punished for complicity in his crimes. Did it," I asked O'Gar, "sound to you like the dying statement of a man who was leaving a wife and daughter he loved? No message, no word, to them—all to the police."

"Maybe you're right," the bullet-headed man said; "but supposing he was going away, he still didn't leave them any——"

"He would have told them—either on paper or talking—something before he went, if he had lived long enough. He was winding up his affairs, preparing to go away, and—— Maybe he *was* going to commit suicide, though the money and the tone of the letter make me doubt it; but even in that case my guess is that he didn't, that he was killed before he had finished his preparations—maybe because he was taking too long a time. How was he found?"

"I heard," Mrs. Leggett sobbed; "I heard the shot, and ran up here, and he——he was like that. And I went down to the telephone, and the bell—the doorbell—rang, and it was Mr. Fitzstephan, and I told him. It couldn't——there was nobody else in the house to——to kill him."

"You killed him," I said to her. "He was going away. He wrote this statement, shouldering your crimes. You killed Ruppert down in the kitchen. That's what the girl was talking about. Your husband's letter sounded enough like a suicide letter to pass for one, you thought; so you murdered him—murdered him because you thought his confession and death would hush up the whole business, keep us from poking into it any further."

Her face didn't tell me anything. It was distorted, but in a way that might have meant almost anything. I filled my lungs and went on, not exactly bellowing, but getting plenty of noise out:

"There are half a dozen lies in your husband's statement—

half a dozen that I can peg now. He didn't send for you and his daughter. You traced him here. Mrs. Begg said he was the most surprised man she had ever seen when you arrived from New York. He didn't give Upton the diamonds. His account of why he gave them to Upton and of what he intended doing afterwards is ridiculous: it's simply the best story he could think of on short notice to cover you up. Leggett would have given him money or he would have given him nothing; he wouldn't have been foolish enough to give him somebody else's diamonds and have all this stink raised.

"Upton traced you here and he came to you with his demand—not to your husband. You had hired Upton to find Leggett; you were the one he knew; he and Ruppert had traced Leggett for you, not only to Mexico City, but all the way here. They'd have squeezed you before this if they hadn't been sent to Sing Sing for another trick. When they got out, Upton came here and made his play. You framed the burglary; you gave Upton the diamonds; and you didn't tell your husband anything about it. Your husband thought the burglary was on the level. Otherwise, would he—a man with his record—have risked reporting it to the police?

"Why didn't you tell him about Upton? Didn't you want him to know that you had had him traced step by step from Devil's Island to San Francisco? Why? His southern record was a good additional hold on him, if you needed one? You didn't want him to know you knew about Labaud and Howart and Edge?"

I didn't give her a chance to answer any of these questions, but sailed ahead, turning my voice loose:

"Maybe Ruppert, following Upton here, got in touch with you, and you had him kill Upton, a job he was willing to do on his own hook. Probably, because he did kill him and he did come to you afterwards, and you thought it necessary to put the knife into him down in the kitchen. You didn't know the girl, hiding in the pantry, saw you; but you did know that you were getting out of your depth. You knew that your chances of getting away with Ruppert's murder were slim. Your house was too much in the spotlight. So you played your only out. You went to your husband with the whole

story—or as much of it as could be arranged to persuade him
—and got him to shoulder it for you. And then you handed
him this—here at the table.

"He shielded you. He had always shielded you. *You*," I
thundered, my voice in fine form by now, "killed your sister
Lily, his first wife, and let him take the fall for you. *You* went
to London with him after that. Would you have gone with
your sister's murderer if you had been innocent? *You* had him
traced here, and *you* came here after him, and *you* married
him. *You* were the one who decided he had married the
wrong sister, and *you* killed her."

"She did! She did!" cried Gabrielle Leggett, trying to
get up from the chair in which Collinson was holding her.
"She——"

Mrs. Leggett drew herself up straight, and smiled, showing
strong yellowish teeth set edge to edge. She took two steps
towards the center of the room. One hand was on her hip,
the other hanging loosely at her side. The housewife—
Fitzstephan's serene sane soul—was suddenly gone. This was
a blonde woman whose body was rounded, not with the
plumpness of contented, well-cared-for early middle age, but
with the cushioned, soft-sheathed muscles of the hunting
cats, whether in jungle or alley.

I picked up the pistol from the table and put it in my
pocket.

"You wish to know who killed my sister?" Mrs. Leggett
asked softly, speaking to me, her teeth clicking together between words, her mouth smiling, her eyes burning. "She, the
dope fiend, Gabrielle—she killed her mother. She is the one
he shielded."

The girl cried out something unintelligible.

"Nonsense," I said. "She was a baby."

"Oh, but it is not nonsense," the woman said. "She was
nearly five, a child of five playing with a pistol that she had
taken from a drawer while her mother slept. The pistol went
off and Lily died. An accident, of course, but Maurice was too
sensitive a soul to bear the thought of her growing up knowing that she had killed her mother. Besides, it was likely that
Maurice would have been convicted in any event. It was
known that he and I were intimate, that he wanted his free-

dom from Lily; and he was at the door of Lily's bedroom when the shot was fired. But that was a slight matter to him: his one desire was to save the child from memory of what she had done, so her life might not be blackened by the knowledge that she had, however accidentally, killed her mother."

What made this especially nasty was the niceness with which the woman smiled as she talked, and the care—almost fastidious—with which she selected her words, mouthing them daintily. She went on:

"Gabrielle was always, even before she became addicted to drugs, a child of, one might say, limited mentality; and so, by the time the London police had found us, we had succeeded in quite emptying her mind of the last trace of memory, that is, of this particular memory. This is, I assure you, the entire truth. She killed her mother; and her father, to use your expression, took the fall for her."

"Fairly plausible," I conceded, "but it doesn't hang together right. There's a chance that you made Leggett believe that, but I doubt it. I think you're trying to hurt your stepdaughter because she's told us of seeing you knife Ruppert downstairs."

She pulled her lips back from her teeth and took a quick step toward me, her eyes wide and white-ringed; then she checked herself, laughed sharply, and the glare went from her eyes—or maybe went back through them, to smolder behind them. She put her hands on her hips and smiled playfully, airily, at me and spoke playfully to me, while mad hatred glowed behind eyes, smile, and voice.

"Am I? Then I must tell you this, which I should not tell you unless it was true. I taught her to kill her mother. Do you understand? I taught her, trained her, drilled her, rehearsed her. Do you understand that? Lily and I were true sisters, inseparable, hating one another poisonously. Maurice, he wished to marry neither of us—why should he?—though he was intimate enough with both. You are to try to understand that literally. But we were poverty-ridden and he was not, and, because we were and he wasn't, Lily wished to marry him. And I, I wished to marry him because she did. We were true sisters, like that in all things. But Lily got him, first—trapped him—that is crude but exact—into matrimony.

"Gabrielle was born six or seven months later. What a happy little family we were. I lived with them—weren't Lily and I inseparable?—and from the first Gabrielle had more love for me than for her mother. I saw to that: there was nothing her Aunt Alice wouldn't do for her dear niece; because her preferring me infuriated Lily, not that Lily herself loved the child so much, but that we were sisters; and whatever one wanted the other wanted, not to share, but exclusively.

"Gabrielle had hardly been born before I began planning what I should some day do; and when she was nearly five I did it. Maurice's pistol, a small one, was kept in a locked drawer high in a chiffonier. I unlocked the drawer, unloaded the pistol, and taught Gabrielle an amusing little game. I would lie on Lily's bed, pretending to sleep. The child would push a chair to the chiffonier, climb up on it, take the pistol from the drawer, creep over to the bed, put the muzzle of the pistol to my head, and press the trigger. When she did it well, making little or no noise, holding the pistol correctly in her tiny hands, I would reward her with candy, cautioning her against saying anything about the game to her mother or to anyone else, as we were going to surprise her mother with it.

"We did. We surprised her completely one afternoon when, having taken aspirin for a headache, Lily was sleeping in her bed. That time I unlocked the drawer but did not unload the pistol. Then I told the child she might play the game with her mother; and I went to visit friends on the floor below, so no one would think I had had any part in my dear sister's demise. I thought Maurice would be away all afternoon. I intended, when I heard the shot, to rush upstairs with my friends and find with them that the child playing with the pistol had killed her mother.

"I had little fear of the child's talking afterwards. Of, as I have said, limited mentality, loving and trusting me as she did, and in my hands both before and during any official inquiry that might be made, I knew I could very easily control her, make sure that she said nothing to reveal my part in the—ah—enterprise. But Maurice very nearly spoiled the whole thing. Coming home unexpectedly, he reached the bedroom door just as Gabrielle pressed the trigger. The tiniest fraction of a second earlier, and he would have been in time to save his wife's life.

"Well, that was unfortunate in that it led to his being convicted; but it certainly prevented his ever suspecting me; and his subsequent desire to wipe from the child's mind all remembrance of the deed relieved me of any further anxiety or effort. I did follow him to this country after his escape from Devil's Island, and I did follow him to San Francisco when Upton had found him for me; and I used Gabrielle's love for me and her hatred of him—I had carefully cultivated that with skilfully clumsy attempts to persuade her to forgive him for murdering her mother—and the necessity of keeping her in ignorance of the truth, and my record of faithfulness to him and her, to make him marry me, to make him think that marrying me would in some sense salvage our ruined lives. The day he married Lily I swore I would take him away from her. And I did. And I hope my dear sister in hell knows it."

The smile was gone. Mad hatred was no longer *behind* eyes and voice: it was *in* them, and in the set of her features, the pose of her body. This mad hatred—and she as part of it—seemed the only live thing in the room. The eight of us who looked at and listened to her didn't, for the moment, count: we were alive to her, but not to each other, nor to anything but her.

She turned from me to fling an arm out at the girl on the other side of the room; and now her voice was throaty, vibrant, with savage triumph in it; and her words were separated into groups by brief pauses, so that she seemed to be chanting them.

"You're her daughter," she cried; "and you're cursed with the same black soul and rotten blood that she and I and all the Dains have had; and you're cursed with your mother's blood on your hands in babyhood; and with the twisted mind and the need for drugs that are my gifts to you; and your life will be black as your mother's and mine were black; and the lives of those you touch will be black as Maurice's was black; and your——"

"Stop!" Eric Collinson gasped. "Make her stop."

Gabrielle Leggett, both hands to her ears, her face twisted

with terror, screamed once—horribly—and fell forward out of her chair.

Pat Reddy was young at manhunting, but O'Gar and I should have known better than to stop watching Mrs. Leggett even for a half-second, no matter how urgently the girl's scream and fall pulled at our attention. But we did look at the girl—if for less than half a second—and that was long enough. When we looked at Mrs. Leggett again, she had a gun in her hand, and she had taken her first step towards the door.

Nobody was between her and the door: the uniformed copper had gone to help Collinson with Gabrielle Leggett. Nobody was behind her: her back was to the door and by turning she had brought Fitzstephan into her field of vision. She glared over the black gun, burning eyes darting from one to another of us, taking another step backward, snarling: "Don't you move."

Pat Reddy shifted his weight to the balls of his feet. I frowned at him, shaking my head. The hall and stairs were better places in which to catch her: in here somebody would die.

She backed over the sill, blew breath between her teeth with a hissing, spitting, sound, and was gone down the hall.

Owen Fitzstephan was first through the door after her. The policeman got in my way, but I was second out. The woman had reached the head of the stairs, at the other end of the dim hall, with Fitzstephan, not far behind, rapidly overtaking her.

He caught her on the between-floors landing, just as I reached the top of the stairs. He pinned one of her arms to her body, but the other, with the gun, was free. He grabbed at it and missed. She twisted the muzzle in to his body as I— with my head bent to miss the edge of the floor—leaped down at them.

I landed on them just in time, crashing into them, smashing them into the corner of the wall, sending her bullet, meant for the sorrel-haired man, into a step.

We weren't standing up. I caught with both hands at the flash of her gun, missed, and had her by the waist. Close to my chin Fitzstephan's lean fingers closed on her gun-hand wrist.

She twisted her body against my right arm. My right arm was still lame from our spill out of the Chrysler. It wouldn't hold. Her thick body went up, turning over on me.

Gunfire roared in my ear, burnt my cheek.

The woman's body went limp.

When O'Gar and Reddy pulled us apart she lay still. The second bullet had gone through her throat.

I went up to the laboratory. Gabrielle Leggett, with the doctor and Collinson kneeling beside her, was lying on the floor.

I told the doctor: "Better take a look at Mrs. Leggett. She's on the stairs. Dead, I think, but you'd better take a look."

The doctor went out. Collinson, chafing the unconscious girl's hands, looked at me as if I were something there ought to be a law against, and said:

"I hope you're satisfied with the way your work got done."

"It got done," I said.

CHAPTER VIII

But and If

FITZSTEPHAN and I ate one of Mrs. Schindler's good dinners that evening in her low-ceilinged basement, and drank her husband's good beer. The novelist in Fitzstephan was busy trying to find what he called Mrs. Leggett's psychological basis.

"The killing of her sister is plain enough, knowing her character as we now do," he said, "and so are the killing of her husband, her attempt to ruin her niece's life when she was exposed, and even her determination to kill herself on the stairs rather than be caught. But the quiet years in between—where do they fit in?"

"It's Leggett's murder that doesn't fit in," I argued. "The rest is all one piece. She wanted him. She killed her sister—or had her killed—in a way to tie him to her; but the law pulled them apart. There was nothing she could do about that, except wait and hope for the chance that always existed, that he would be freed some day. We don't know of anything else she wanted then. Why shouldn't she be quiet, holding Gabrielle as her hostage against the chance she hoped for, living comfortably enough, no doubt, on his money? When she heard of his escape, she came to America and set about finding him. When her detectives located him here she came to him. He was willing to marry her. She had what she wanted. Why should she be anything but quiet? She wasn't a trouble-maker for the fun of it—one of these people who act out of pure mischief. She was simply a woman who wanted what she wanted and was willing to go to any length to get it. Look how patiently, and for how many years, she hid her hatred from the girl. And her wants weren't even very extravagant. You won't find the key to her in any complicated derangements. She was simple as an animal, with an animal's simple ignorance of right and wrong, dislike for being thwarted, and spitefulness when trapped."

Fitzstephan drank beer and asked:

"You'd reduce the Dain curse, then, to a primitive strain in the blood?"

"To less than that, to words in an angry woman's mouth."

"It's fellows like you that take all the color out of life." He sighed behind cigarette smoke. "Doesn't Gabrielle's being made the tool of her mother's murder convince you of the necessity—at least the poetic necessity—of the curse?"

"Not even if she *was* the tool, and that's something I wouldn't bet on. Apparently Leggett didn't doubt it. He stuffed his letter with those ancient details to keep her covered up. But we've only got Mrs. Leggett's word that he actually saw the child kill her mother. On the other hand, Mrs. Leggett said, in front of Gabrielle, that Gabrielle had been brought up to believe her father the murderer—so we can believe that. And it isn't likely—though it's possible—that he would have gone that far except to save her from knowlege of her own guilt. But, from that point on, one guess at the truth is about as good as another. Mrs. Leggett wanted him and she got him. Then why in hell did she kill him?"

"You jump around so," Fitzstephan complained. "You answered that back in the laboratory. Why don't you stick to your answer? You said she killed him because the letter sounded enough like a pre-suicide statement to pass, and she thought it and his death would ensure her safety."

"That was good enough to say then," I admitted; "but not now, in cold blood, with more facts to fit in. She had worked and waited for years to get him. He must have had some value to her."

"But she didn't love him, or there is no reason to suppose she did. He hadn't that value to her. He was to her no more than a trophy of the hunt; and that's a value not affected by death—one has the head embalmed and nailed on the wall."

"Then why did she keep Upton away from him? Why did she kill Ruppert? Why should she have carried the load for him there? It was his danger. Why did she make it hers if he had no value to her? Why did she risk all that to keep him from learning that the past had come to life again?"

"I think I see what you're getting at," Fitzstephan said slowly. "You think——"

"Wait—here's another thing. I talked to Leggett and his wife together a couple of times. Neither of them addressed a word to the other either time, though the woman did a lot of acting to make me think she would have told me something about her daughter's disappearance if it had not been for him."

"Where did you find Gabrielle?"

"After seeing Ruppert murdered, she beat it to the Haldorn's with what money she had and her jewelry, turning the jewelry over to Minnie Hershey to raise money on. Minnie bought a couple of pieces for herself—her man had picked himself up a lot of dough in a crap game a night or two before: the police checked that—and sent the man out to peddle the rest. He was picked up in a hock-shop, just on general suspicion."

"Gabrielle was leaving home for good?" he asked.

"You can't blame her—thinking her father a murderer, and now catching her step-mother in the act. Who'd want to live in a home like that?"

"And you think Leggett and his wife were on bad terms? That may be: I hadn't seen much of them lately, and wasn't intimate enough with them to have been let in on a condition of that sort if it had existed. Do you think he had perhaps learned something—some of the truth about her?"

"Maybe, but not enough to keep him from taking the fall for her on Ruppert's murder; and what he had learned wasn't connected with this recent affair, because the first time I saw him he really believed in the burglary. But then——"

"Aw, shut up! You're never satisfied until you've got two buts and an if attached to everything. I don't see any reason for doubting Mrs. Leggett's story. She told us the whole thing quite gratuitously. Why should we suppose that she'd lie to implicate herself?"

"You mean in her sister's murder? She'd been acquitted of that, and I suppose the French system's like ours in that she couldn't be tried again for it, no matter what she confessed. She didn't give anything away, brother."

"Always belittling," he said. "You need more beer to expand your soul."

At the Leggett-Ruppert inquests I saw Gabrielle Leggett

again, but was not sure that she even recognized me. She was with Madison Andrews, who had been Leggett's attorney and was now his estate's executor. Eric Collinson was there, but, peculiarly, apparently not with Gabrielle. He gave me nods and nothing else.

The newspapers got hold of what Mrs. Leggett had said happened in Paris in 1913, and made a couple-day fuss over it. The recovery of Halstead and Beauchamp's diamonds let the Continental Detective Agency out: we wrote *Discontinued* at the bottom of the Leggett record. I went up in the mountains to snoop around for a gold-mine-owner who thought his employes were gypping him.

I expected to be in the mountains for at least a month: inside jobs of that sort take time. On the evening of my tenth day there I had a long-distance call from the Old Man, my boss.

"I'm sending Foley up to relieve you," he said. "Don't wait for him. Catch tonight's train back. The Leggett matter is active again."

CHAPTER IX

Tad's Blind Man

MADISON ANDREWS was a tall gaunt man of sixty with ragged white hair, eyebrows, and mustache that exaggerated the ruddiness of his bony hard-muscled face. He wore his clothes loose, chewed tobacco, and had twice in the past ten years been publicly named co-respondent in divorce suits.

"I dare say young Collinson has babbled all sorts of nonsense to you," he said. "He seems to think I'm in my second childhood, as good as told me so."

"I haven't seen him," I said. "I've only been back in town a couple of hours, long enough to go to the office and then come here."

"Well," he said, "he is her fiancé, but I am responsible for her, and I preferred following Doctor Riese's counsel. He is her physician. He said that letting her go to the Temple for a short stay would do more to restore her to mental health than anything else we could do. I couldn't disregard his advice. The Haldorns may be, probably are, charlatans, but Joseph Haldorn is certainly the only person to whom Gabrielle has willingly talked, and in whose company she has seemed at peace, since her parents' deaths. Doctor Riese said that to cross her in her desire to go to the Temple would be to send her mind deeper into its illness. Could I snap my fingers at his opinion because young Collinson didn't like it?"

I said: "No."

"I have no illusions concerning the cult," he went on defending himself. "It is probably as full of quackery as any other. But we are not concerned with its religious aspect. We're interested in it as therapeutics, as a cure for Gabrielle's mind. Even if the character of its membership were not such that I could count with certainty on Gabrielle's safety, I should still have been tempted to let her go. Her recovery is, as I see it, the thing with which we should be most concerned, and nothing else should be allowed to interfere with that."

He was worried. I nodded and kept quiet, waiting to learn what was worrying him. I got it little by little as he went on talking around in circles.

On Doctor Riese's advice and over Collinson's protests he had let Gabrielle Leggett go to the Temple of the Holy Grail to stay awhile. She had wanted to go, no less prominently respectable a person than Mrs. Livingston Rodman was staying there at the time, the Haldorns had been Edgar Leggett's friends: Andrews let her go. That had been six days ago. She had taken the mulatto, Minnie Hershey, with her as maid. Doctor Riese had gone to see her each day. On four days he had found her improved. On the fifth day her condition had alarmed him. Her mind was more completely dazed than it had ever been, and she had the symptoms of one who had been subjected to some sort of shock. He couldn't get anything out of her. He couldn't get anything out of Minnie. He couldn't get anything out of the Haldorns. He had no way of learning what had happened, or if anything had happened.

Eric Collinson had held Riese up for daily reports on Gabrielle. Riese told him the truth about his last visit. Collinson hit the ceiling. He wanted the girl taken away from the Temple immediately: the Haldorns were preparing to murder her, according to his notion. He and Andrews had a swell row. Andrews thought that the girl has simply suffered a relapse from which she would most speedily recover if left where she wished to stay. Riese was inclined to agree with Andrews. Collinson didn't. He threatened to create a stink if they didn't yank her away *pronto.*

That worried Andrews. It wouldn't look so good for him, the hard-headed lawyer, letting his ward go to such a place, if anything happened to her. On the other hand, he said he really believed it was for her benefit to stay there. And he didn't want anything to happen to her. He finally reached a compromise with Collinson. Gabrielle should be allowed to remain in the Temple for a few more days at least, but somebody should be put in there to keep an eye on her, and to see that the Haldorns weren't playing any tricks on her.

Riese had suggested me: my luck in hitting on the manner of Leggett's death had impressed him. Collinson had objected that my brutality was largely responsible for Gabrielle's present condition, but he had finally given in. I already knew Gabrielle and her history, and I hadn't made such a total mess of that first job: my efficiency offset my brutality, or words to that effect. So Andrews had phoned the Old Man, offered him a high enough rate to justify pulling me off another job, and there I was.

"The Haldorns know you are coming," Andrews wound up. "It doesn't matter what they think about it. I simply told them that Doctor Riese and I had decided that, until Gabrielle's mind became more settled, it would be best to have a competent man on hand in case of emergency, as much perhaps to safeguard others as her. There is no need of my giving you instructions. It is simply a matter of taking every precaution."

"Does Miss Leggett know I'm coming?"

"No, and I don't think we need say anything to her about it. You'll make your watch over her as unobtrusive as possible, of course, and I doubt that she will, in her present state of mind, pay enough attention to your presence to resent it. If she does—well, we'll see."

Andrews gave me a note to Aaronia Haldorn.

An hour and a half later I was sitting opposite her in the Temple reception room while she read it. She put it aside and offered me long Russian cigarettes in a white jade box. I apologized for sticking to my Fatimas, and worked the lighter on the smoking stand she pushed out between us. When our cigarettes were burning, she said:

"We shall try to make you as comfortable as possible. We are neither barbarians nor fanatics. I explain this because so many people are surprised to find us neither. This is a temple, but none of us supposes that happiness, comfort, or any of the ordinary matters of civilized living, will desecrate it. You are not one of us. Perhaps—I hope—you will become one of us. However—do not squirm—you won't, I assure you, be annoyed. You may attend our services or not, as you choose, and you may come and go as you wish. You will show us, I am sure, the same consideration we show you, and I am equally sure that you will not interfere in any way with anything you may see—no matter how peculiar you may think it—so long as it does not promise to affect your—patient."

"Of course not," I promised.

She smiled, as if to thank me, rubbed her cigarette's end in the ash tray, and stood up, saying: "I'll show you your room."

Not a word had been said by either of us about my previous visit.

Carrying my hat and gladstone bag, I followed her to the elevator. We got out at the fifth floor.

"That is Miss Leggett's room," Aaronia Haldorn said, indicating the door that Collinson and I had taken turns knocking a couple of weeks before. "And this is yours." She opened the door that faced Gabrielle's across the corridor.

My room was a duplicate of hers, except that it was without a dressing-room. My door, like hers, had no lock.

"Where does her maid sleep?" I asked.

"In one of the servant's rooms on the top floor. Doctor Riese is with Miss Leggett now, I think. I'll tell him you have arrived."

I thanked her. She went out of my room, closing the door.

Fifteen minutes later Doctor Riese knocked and came in.

"I am glad you are here," he said, shaking hands. He had a crisp, precise way of turning out his words, sometimes emphasizing them by gesturing with the black-ribboned glasses in his hand. I never saw the glasses on his nose. "We shan't need your professional skill, I trust, but I am glad you are here."

"What's wrong?" I asked in what was meant for a tone that invited confidences.

He looked sharply at me, tapped his glasses on his left thumb-nail, and said:

"What is wrong is, so far as I know, altogether in my sphere. I know of nothing else wrong." He shook my hand again. "You'll find your part quite boring, I hope."

"But yours isn't?" I suggested.

He stopped turning away towards the door, frowned, tapped his glasses with his thumb-nail again, and said:

"No, it is not." He hesitated, as if deciding whether to say something more, decided not to, and moved to the door.

"I've a right to know what you honestly think about it," I said.

He looked sharply at me again. "I don't know what I

honestly think about it." A pause. "I am not satisfied." He didn't look satisfied. "I'll be in again this evening."

He went out and shut the door. Half a minute later he opened the door, said, "Miss Leggett is extremely ill," shut the door again and went away.

I grumbled, "This is going to be a lot of fun," to myself, sat down at a window and smoked a cigarette.

A maid in black and white knocked on the door and asked me what I wanted for luncheon. She was a hearty pink and plump blonde somewhere in the middle twenties, with blue eyes that looked curiously at me and had jokes in them. I took a shot of Scotch from the bottle in my bag, ate the luncheon the maid presently returned with, and spent the afternoon in my room.

By keeping my ears open I managed to catch Minnie as she came out of her mistress's room at a little after four. The mulatto's eyes jerked wide when she saw me standing in my doorway.

"Come in," I said. "Didn't Doctor Riese tell you I was here?"

"No, sir. Are—are you——? You're not wanting anything with Miss Gabrielle?"

"Just looking out for her, seeing that nothing happens to her. And if you'll keep me wised up, let me know what she says and does, and what others say and do, you'll be helping me, and helping her; because then I won't have to bother her."

The mulatto said, "Yes, yes," readily enough, but, as far as I could learn from her brown face, my coöperative idea wasn't getting across any too well.

"How is she this afternoon?" I asked.

"She's right cheerful this afternoon, sir. She like this place."

"How'd she spend the afternoon?"

"She——I don't know, sir. She just kind of spent it—quiet like."

Not much news there. I said:

"Doctor Reise thinks she'll be better off not knowing I'm here, so you needn't say anything to her about me."

"No, sir, I sure won't," she promised, but it sounded more polite than sincere.

In the early evening Aaronia Haldorn came in and invited me down to dinner. The dining-room was paneled and furnished in dark walnut. There were ten of us at the table.

Joseph Haldorn was tall, built like a statue, and wore a black silk robe. His hair was thick, long, white, and glossy. His thick beard, trimmed round, was white and glossy. Aaronia Haldorn introduced me to him, calling him, "Joseph," as if he had no last name. All the others addressed him in the same way. He gave me a white even-toothed smile and a warm strong hand. His face, healthily pink, was without line or wrinkle. It was a tranquil face, especially the clear brown eyes, somehow making you feel at peace with the world. The same soothing quality was in his baritone voice.

He said: "We are happy to have you here."

The words were merely polite, meaningless, yet, as he said them, I actually believed that for some reason he was happy. Now I understood Gabrielle Leggett's desire to come to this place. I said that I, too, was happy to be there, and while I was saying it I actually thought I was.

Besides Joseph and his wife and their son at the table there was Mrs. Rodman, a tall frail woman with transparent skin, faded eyes, and a voice that never rose above a murmur; a man named Fleming, who was young, dark, very thin, and wore a dark mustache and the detached air of one busy with his own thoughts; Major Jeffries, a well-tailored, carefully mannered man, stout and bald and sallow; his wife, a pleasant sort of person in spite of a kittenishness thirty years too young for her; a Miss Hillen, sharp of chin and voice, with an intensely eager manner; and Mrs. Pavlov, who was quite young, had a high-cheek-boned dark face, and avoided everybody's eyes.

The food, served by two Filipino boys, was good. There was not much conversation and none of it was religious. It wasn't so bad.

After dinner I returned to my room. I listened at Gabrielle Leggett's door for a few minutes, but heard nothing. In my room I fidgeted and smoked and waited for Doctor Riese to show up as he had promised. He didn't show up. I supposed that one of the emergencies that are regular parts of doctors' lives had kept him elsewhere, but his not coming made me irritable. Nobody went in or out of Gabrielle's room. I tiptoed over to listen at her door a couple of times. Once I heard nothing. Once I heard faint meaningless rustling sounds.

At a little after ten o'clock I heard some of the inmates going past my door, probably on their way to their rooms for the night.

At five minutes past eleven I heard Gabrielle's door open. I opened mine. Minnie Hershey was going down the corridor toward the rear of the building. I was tempted to call her, but didn't. My last attempt to get anything out of her had been a flop, and I wasn't feeling tactful enough now to stand much chance of having better luck.

By this time I had given up hopes of seeing Riese before the following day.

I switched off my lights, left my door open, and sat there in the dark, looking at the girl's door and cursing the world. I thought of Tad's blind man in a dark room hunting for a black hat that wasn't there, and knew how he felt.

At a little before midnight Minnie Hershey, in hat and coat as if she had just come in from the street, returned to Gabrielle's room. She didn't seem to see me. I stood up silently and tried to peep past her when she opened the door, but didn't have any luck.

Minnie remained there until nearly one o'clock, and when she came out she closed the door very softly, walking tiptoe. That was an unnecessary precaution on the thick carpet. Because it was unnecessary it made me nervous. I went to my door and called in a low voice:

"Minnie."

Maybe she didn't hear me. She went on tiptoeing down the corridor. That increased my jumpiness. I went after her quickly and stopped her by catching one of her wiry wrists.

Her Indian face was expressionless.

"How is she?" I asked.

"Miss Gabrielle's all right, sir. You just leave her alone," she mumbled.

"She's not all right. What's she doing now?"

"She's sleeping."

"Coked?"

She raised angry maroon eyes and let them drop again, saying nothing.

"She sent you out to get dope?" I demanded, tightening my grip on her wrist.

"She sent me out to get some—some medicine—yes, sir."

"And took some and went to sleep?"

"Y-yes, sir."

"We'll go back and take a look at her," I said.

The mulatto tried to jerk her wrist free. I held it. She said:

"You leave me alone, Mister, or else I'll yell."

"I'll leave you alone after we've had our look, maybe," I said, turning her around with my other hand on her shoulder. "So if you're going to yell you can get started right now."

She wasn't willing to go back to her mistress's room, but she didn't make me drag her. Gabrielle Leggett was lying on her side in bed, sleeping quietly, the bed-clothes stirring gently with her breathing. Her small white face, at rest, with brown curls falling over it, looked like a sick child's.

I turned Minnie loose and went back to my room. Sitting there in the dark I understood why people bit their finger-nails. I sat there for an hour or more, and then, God-damning myself for an old woman, I took off my shoes, picked the most comfortable chair, put my feet on another, hung a blanket over me, and went to sleep facing Gabrielle Leggett's door through my open doorway.

CHAPTER X

Dead Flowers

I OPENED my eyes drowsily, decided that I had dozed off for only a moment, closed my eyes, drifted back into slumber, and then roused myself sluggishly again. Something wasn't right.

I forced my eyes open, then closed them, and opened them again. Whatever wasn't right had to do with that. Blackness was there when they were open and when they were closed. That should have been reasonable enough: the night was dark, and my windows were out of the street lights' range. That should have been reasonable enough, but it wasn't: I remembered that I had left my door open, and the corridor lights had been on. Facing me was no pale rectangle of light framed by my doorway, with Gabrielle's door showing through.

I was too awake by now to jump up suddenly. I held my breath and listened, hearing nothing but the tick of my wristwatch. Cautiously moving my hand, I looked at the luminous dial—3:17. I had been asleep longer than I had supposed, and the corridor light had been put out.

My head was numb, my body stiff and heavy, and there was a bad taste in my mouth. I got out from under the blanket, and out of my chairs, moving awkwardly, my muscles stubborn. I crept on stockinged feet to the door, and bumped into the door. It had been closed. When I opened it the corridor light was burning as before. The air that came in from the corridor seemed surprisingly fresh, sharp, pure.

I turned my face back into the room, sniffing. There was an odor of flowers, faint, stuffy, more the odor of a closed place in which flowers had died than of flowers themselves. Lilies of the valley, moonflowers, perhaps another one or two. I spent time trying to divide the odor into its parts, seriously trying to determine whether a trace of honeysuckle was actually present. Then I vaguely remembered having dreamed of a funeral. Trying to recall exactly what I had dreamed, I leaned against the door-frame and let sleep come into me again.

The jerking up of my neck muscles when my head had sunk too low aroused me. I wrestled my eyes open, standing there on legs that weren't part of me, stupidly wondering why I didn't go to bed. While I drowsed over the idea that there might be some reason why I shouldn't sleep, if I could only think of it, I put a hand against the wall to steady myself. The hand touched the light button. I had sense enough to push it.

Light scorched my eyes. Squinting, I could see a world that was real to me, and could remember that I had work to do. I made for the bathroom, where cold water on head and face left me still stupid and muddled, but at least partly conscious.

I turned off my lights, crossed to Gabrielle's door, listened, and heard nothing. I opened the door, stepped inside, and closed the door. My flashlight showed me an empty bed with covers thrown down across the foot. I put a hand in the hollow her body had made in the bed—cold. There was nobody in bathroom or dressing-alcove. Under the edge of the bed lay a pair of green mules, and a green dressing-gown, or something of the sort, was hanging over the back of a chair.

I went to my room for my shoes, and then walked down the front stairs, intending to go through the house from bottom to top. I would go silently first, and then, if, as was likely enough, I ran across nothing, I could start kicking in doors, turning people out of bed, and raising hell till I turned up the girl. I wanted to find her as soon as possible, but she had too long a start for a few minutes to make much difference now; so if I didn't waste any time, neither did I run.

I was half-way between the second and first floors when I saw something move below—or, rather, saw the movement of something without actually seeing it. It moved from the direction of the street-door towards the interior of the house. I was looking towards the elevator at the time as I walked down the stairs. The banister shut off my view of the street-door. What I saw was a flash of movement across half a dozen of the spaces between the banister's uprights. By the time I had brought my eyes into focus there, there was nothing to see. I thought I had seen a face, but that's what anybody would have thought in my position, and all I had actually seen was the movement of something pale.

The lobby, and what I could see of the corridors, were

vacant when I reached the ground-floor. I started towards the rear of the building, and stopped. I heard, for the first time since I had awakened, a noise that I hadn't made. A shoe-sole had scuffed on the stone steps the other side of the street-door.

I walked to the front door, got one hand on the bolt, the other hand on the latch, snapped them back together, and yanked the door open with my left hand, letting my right hand hang within a twist of my gun.

Eric Collinson stood on the top step.

"What the hell are you doing here?" I asked sourly.

It was a long story, and he was too excited to make it a clear one. As nearly as I could untangle it from his words, he had been in the habit of phoning Doctor Riese daily for reports on Gabrielle's progress. Today—or rather yesterday—and last night, he had failed to get the doctor on the wire. He had called up as late as two o'clock this morning. Doctor Riese was not at home, he had been told, and none of the household knew where he was or why he was not at home. Collinson had then, after the two-o'clock call, come to the neighborhood of the Temple, on the chance that he might see me and get some word of the girl. He hadn't intended, he said, coming to the door until he saw me looking out.

"Until you did what?" I asked.

"Saw you."

"When?"

"A minute ago, when you looked out."

"You didn't see me," I said. "What did you see?"

"Somebody looking out, peeping out. I thought it was you, and came up from the corner where I was sitting in the car. Is Gabrielle all right?"

"Sure," I said. There was no use telling him I was hunting for her, and have him blow up on me. "Don't talk so loud. Riese's people don't know where he is?"

"No—they seem worried. But that's all right if Gabrielle's all right." He put a hand on my upper arm. "Could—could I see her? Just for a second? I won't say anything. She needn't even know I've seen her. I don't mean now—but can't you arrange it?"

This bird was young, tall, strong, and perfectly willing to

have himself broken into pieces for Gabrielle Leggett. I knew something was wrong. I didn't know what. I didn't know what I would have to do to make it right, and how much help I would need. I couldn't afford to turn him away. On the other hand, I couldn't give him the low-down on the racket —that would have turned him into a wild man. I said:

"Come in. I'm on an inspection trip. You can go along if you keep quiet, and afterwards we'll see what we can do."

He came in, looking and acting as if I were St. Peter letting him into Heaven. I closed the door and led him through the lobby, down the main corridor. So far as we could see we had the joint to ourselves. And then we didn't.

Gabrielle Leggett came around a corner just ahead of us. She was barefooted. Her only clothing was a yellow silk nightgown that was splashed with dark stains. In both hands, held out in front of her as she walked, she carried a large dagger, almost a sword. It was red and wet. Her hands and bare arms were red and wet. There was a dab of blood on one of her cheeks. Her eyes were clear, bright, and calm. Her small forehead was smooth, her mouth and chin firmly set.

She walked up to me, her untroubled gaze holding my probably troubled one, and said evenly, just as if she had expected to find me there, had come there to find me:

"Take it. It is evidence. I killed him."

I said: "Huh?"

Still looking straight into my eyes, she said:

"You are a detective. Take me to where they will hang me."

It was easier to move my hand than my tongue. I took the bloody dagger from her. It was a broad, thick-bladed weapon, double-edged, with a bronze hilt like a cross.

Eric Collinson pushed past me, babbling words that nobody could have made out, going for the girl with shaking outstretched hands. She shrank over against the wall, away from him, fear in her face.

"Don't let him touch me," she begged.

"Gabrielle," he cried, reaching for her.

"No, no," she panted.

I walked into his arms, my body between him and her, facing him, pressing him back with a hand against his chest, growling at him: "Be still, you."

He took my shoulders in his big brown hands and began pushing me out of the way. I got ready to rap him on the chin with the heavy bronze dagger hilt. But we didn't have to go that far: looking over me at the girl he forgot his intentions of forcing me out of his path, and his hands went loose on my shoulders. I leaned on the hand that I had on his chest, moving him back until he was against the wall; and then stepped away from him, a little to one side, so I could see both him and her facing each other from opposite walls.

"Be still till we see what's happened," I told him, and turned to the girl, pointing the dagger at her. "What's happened?"

She was calm again.

"Come," she said. "I'll show you. Don't let Eric come, please."

"He won't bother you," I promised.

She nodded at that, gravely, and led us back down the corridor, around the corner, and up to a small iron door that stood ajar. She went through first. I followed her. Collinson was at my heels. Fresh air hit us when we went through the door. I looked up and saw dim stars in a dark sky. I looked down again. In the light that came through the open door behind us I saw that we were walking on a floor of white marble, or pentagonal tiles that imitated white marble. The place was dark except for the light from behind us. I took my flashlight out.

Walking unhurriedly on bare feet that must have found the tiled floor chilly, she led us straight to a square grayish shape that loomed up ahead. When she halted close to it and said, "There," I clicked on my light.

The light glittered and glistened on a wide altar of brilliant white, crystal, and silver.

On the lowest of the three altar steps Doctor Riese lay dead on his back.

His face was composed, as if he were sleeping. His arms were straight down at his sides. His clothes were not rumpled, though his coat and vest were unbuttoned. His shirt was all blood. There were four holes in his shirt-front, all alike, all the size and shape that the weapon the girl had given me would have made. No blood was coming from his wounds now, but when I put a hand on his forehead I found it not quite cold. There was blood on the altar steps, and on the floor below, where his noseglasses, unbroken, on the end of their black ribbon, lay.

I straightened up and swung the beam of my light into the girl's face. She blinked and squinted, but her face showed nothing except that physical discomfort.

"You killed him?" I asked.

Young Collinson came out of his trance to bawl: "No."

"Shut up," I told him, stepping closer to the girl, so he couldn't wedge himself between us. "Did you?" I asked her again.

"Are you surprised?" she inquired quietly. "You were there when my step-mother told of the cursed Dain blood in me, and of what it had done and would do to me and those who touched me. Is this," she asked, pointing at the dead man, "anything you should not have expected?"

"Don't be silly," I said while I tried to figure out her calmness. I had seen her coked to the ears before, but this wasn't that. I didn't know what this was. "Why did you kill him?"

Collinson grabbed my arm and yanked me around to face him. He was all on fire.

"We can't stand here talking," he cried. "We've got to get her out of here, away from this. We've got to hide the body, or put it some place where they'll think somebody else did it. You know how those things are done. I'll take her home. You fix it."

"Yeah?" I asked. "What'll I do? Frame it on one of the Filipino boys, so they'll hang him instead of her?"

"Yes, that's it. You know how to——"

"Like hell that's it," I said. "You've got nice ideas."

His face got redder. He stammered: "I didn't——didn't mean so they'll hang anybody, really. I wouldn't want you to do that. But couldn't it be fixed for him to get away? I—— I'd make it worth his while. He could——"

"Turn it off," I growled. "You're wasting our time."

"But you've got to," he insisted. "You came here to see that nothing happened to Gabrielle and you've got to go through with it."

"Yeah? You're a smart boy."

"I know it's a lot to ask, but I'll pay——"

"Stop it." I took my arm out of his hands and turned to the girl again, asking: "Who else was here when it happened?"

"No one."

I played my light around, on the corpse and altar, all over the floor, on the walls, and saw nothing I hadn't seen before. The walls were white, smooth, and unbroken except for the door we had come through and another, exactly like it, on the other side. These four straight whitewashed walls, undecorated, rose six stories to the sky.

I put the dagger beside Riese's body, snapped off the light, and told Collinson: "We'll take Miss Leggett up to her room."

"For God's sake let's get her out of here—out of this house—now, while there's time!"

I said she'd look swell running through the streets barefooted and with nothing on but a bloodstained nightie.

I turned on the light again when I heard him making noises. He was jerking his arms out of his overcoat. He said: "I've got the car at the corner, and I can carry her to it," and started towards her with the coat held out.

She ran around to the other side of me, moaning: "Oh, don't let him touch me."

I put out an arm to stop him. It wasn't strong enough. The girl got behind me. Collinson pursued her and she came around in front. I felt like the center of a merry-go-round, and didn't like the feel of it. When Collinson came in front of me, I drove my shoulder into his side, sending him staggering over against the side of the altar. Following him, I planted myself in front of the big sap and blew off steam: "Stop it. If you want to play with us you've got to stop cutting up, and do what you're told, and let her alone. Yes or no?"

He straightened his legs under him and began: "But, man, you can't——"

"Let her alone," I said. "Let me alone. The next break you make I'm going to sock your jaw with the flat of a gun. If you want it now, say so. Will you behave?"

He muttered: "All right."

I turned around to see the girl, a gray shadow, running towards the open door, her bare feet making little noise on the tiles. My shoes made an ungodly racket as I went after her. Just inside the door I caught her with an arm around her waist. The next moment my arm was jerked away, and I was flung aside, smacking into the wall, slipping down on one knee. Collinson, looking eight feet tall in the darkness, stood close to me, storming down at me, but all I could pick out of his many words was a "damn you."

I was in a swell mood when I got up from my knee. Playing nurse-maid to a crazy girl wasn't enough: I had to be chucked around by her boy friend. I put all the hypocrisy I had into my voice when I said casually, "You oughtn't to do that," to him and went over to where the girl was standing by the door.

"We'll go up to your room now," I told her.

"Not Eric," she protested.

"He won't bother you," I promised again, hoping there'd be more truth to it this time. "Go ahead."

She hesitated, then went through the doorway. Collinson, looking partly sheepish, partly savage, and altogether discontented, followed me through. I closed the door, asking the girl if she had the key. "No," she said, as if she hadn't known there was a key.

We rode up in the elevator, the girl keeping me always between her and her fiancé, if that's what he still was. He stared fixedly at nothing. I studied her face, still trying to dope her out, to decide whether she had been shocked back into sanity or farther away from it. Looking at her, the first guess seemed likely, but I had a hunch it wasn't. We saw nobody between the altar and her room. I switched on her lights and we went in. I closed the door and put my back against it. Collinson put his overcoat and hat on a chair and stood beside them, folding his arms, looking at Gabrielle. She sat on the edge of the bed and looked at my feet.

"Tell us the whole thing, quick," I commanded.

She looked up at my face and said: "I should like to go to sleep now."

That settled the question of her sanity, so far as I was concerned: she hadn't any. But now I had another thing to worry me. This room was not exactly as it had been before. Something had been changed in it since I had been there not many minutes ago. I shut my eyes, trying to shake up my memory for a picture of it then; I opened my eyes, looking at it now.

"Can't I?" she asked.

I let her question wait while I put my gaze around the room, checking it up item by item, as well as I could. The only change I could put my finger on was Collinson's coat and hat on the chair. There was no mystery to their presence; and the chair, I decided, was what had bothered me. It still did. I went to it and picked up his coat. There was nothing under it. That's what was wrong: a green dressing-gown, or something of the sort, had been there before, and was not there now. I didn't see it elsewhere in the room, and didn't have enough confidence in its being there to search for it. The green mules were under the bed.

I said to the girl:

"Not now. Go in the bathroom and wash the blood off, and then get dressed. Take your clothes in there with you. When you're dressed, give your nightgown to Collinson." I turned to him. "Put it in your pocket and keep it there. Don't go out of the room until I come back, and don't let anybody in. I won't be gone long. Got a gun?"

"No," he said, "but I——"

The girl got up from the bed, came over to stand close in front of me, and interrupted him.

"You can't leave me here with him," she said earnestly. "I won't have it. Isn't it enough that I've killed one man tonight? Don't make me kill another." She was earnest, but not excited, speaking as if her words were quite reasonable.

"I've got to go out for a while," I said. "And you can't stay alone. Do what I tell you."

"Do you know what you're doing?" she asked in a thin, tired voice. "You can't know, or you wouldn't do it." Her back was to Collinson. She lifted her face so that I saw rather than heard the nearly soundless words her lips formed: "Not Eric. Let him go."

She had me woozy: a little more of it and I would have been ready for the cell next to hers: I was actually tempted to let her have her way. I jerked a thumb at the bathroom and said: "You can stay in there till I come back, if you want, but he'll have to stay here."

She nodded hopelessly and went into the dressing-alcove. When she crossed from there to the bathroom, carrying clothes in her arms, a tear was shiny beneath each eye.

I gave my gun to Collinson. The hand in which he took it was tight and shaky. He was making a lot of noise with his breath. I said: "Now don't be a sap. Give me some help instead of trouble for once. Nobody in or out: if you have to shoot, shoot."

He tried to say something, couldn't, grabbed my nearest hand, and did his best to disable it. I took it away from him and went down to the scene of Doctor Riese's murder. I had some difficulty in getting there. The iron door through which we had passed a few minutes ago was now locked. The lock seemed simple enough. I went at it with the fancy attachments on my pocket-knife, and presently had the door open.

I didn't find the green gown inside. I didn't find Riese's body on the altar steps. It was nowhere in sight. The dagger was gone. Every trace of blood, except where the pool on the white floor had left a faintly yellow stain, was gone. Somebody had been tidying up.

CHAPTER XI

God

I WENT BACK to the lobby, to a recess where I had seen a telephone. The phone was there, but dead. I put it down and set out for Minnie Hershey's room on the sixth floor. I hadn't been able to do much with the mulatto so far, but she was apparently devoted to her mistress, and, with the telephone useless, I needed a messenger.

I opened the mulatto's door—lockless as the others—and went in, closing it behind me. Holding a hand over the lens of my flashlight, I snapped it on. Enough light leaked through my fingers to show me the brown girl in her bed, sleeping. The windows were closed, the atmosphere heavy, with a faint stuffiness that was familiar, the odor of a place where flowers had died.

I looked at the girl in bed. She was on her back, breathing through open mouth, her face more like an Indian's than ever with the heaviness of sleep on it. Looking at her, I felt drowsy myself. It seemed a shame to turn her out. Perhaps she was dreaming of—I shook my head, trying to clear it of the muddle settling there. Lilies of the valley, moonflowers—flowers that had died—was honeysuckle one of the flowers? The question seemed to be important. The flashlight was heavy in my hand, too heavy. Hell with it: I let it drop. It hit my foot, puzzling me: who had touched my foot? Gabrielle Leggett, asking to be saved from Eric Collinson? That didn't make sense, or did it? I tried to shake my head again, tried desperately. It weighed a ton, and would barely move from side to side. I felt myself swaying; put out a foot to steady myself. The foot and leg were weak, limber, doughy. I had to take another step or fall, took it, forced my head up and my eyes open, hunting for a place to fall, and saw the window six inches from my face.

I swayed forward till the sill caught my thighs, holding me up. My hands were on the sill. I tried to find the handles on the bottom of the window, wasn't sure that I had found them, but put everything I had into an upward heave. The window didn't budge. My hands seemed nailed down. I think I sobbed then; and, holding the sill with my right hand, I beat the glass from the center of the pane with my open left.

Air that stung like ammonia came through the opening. I put my face to it, hanging to the sill with both hands, sucking air in through mouth, nose, eyes, ears, and pores, laughing, with water from my stinging eyes trickling down into my mouth. I hung there drinking air until I was reasonably sure of my legs under me again, and of my eyesight, until I knew myself able to think and move again, though neither speedily nor surely. I couldn't afford to wait longer. I put a handkerchief over my mouth and nose and turned away from the window.

Not more than three feet away, there in the black room, a pale bright thing like a body, but not like flesh, stood writhing before me.

It was tall, yet not so tall as it seemed, because it didn't stand on the floor, but hovered with its feet a foot or more above the floor. Its feet——it had feet, but I don't know what their shape was. They had no shape, just as the thing's legs and torso, arms and hands, head and face, had no shape, no fixed form. They writhed, swelling and contracting, stretching and shrinking, not greatly, but without pause. An arm drifted into the body, was swallowed by the body, came out again as if poured out. The nose stretched down over the gaping shapeless mouth, shrank back up into the face till it was flush with the pulpy cheeks, grew out again. Eyes spread until they were one gigantic eye that blotted out the whole upper face, diminished until there was no eye, and opened in their places again. The legs were now one leg like a twisting, living, pedestal, and then three, and then two. No feature or member ever stopped twisting, quivering, writhing long enough for its average outline, its proper shape, to be seen. The thing was a thing like a man who floated above the floor, with a horrible grimacing greenish face and pale flesh that was not flesh, that was visible in the dark, and that was as fluid and as unresting and as transparent as tidal water.

I knew—then—that I was off-balance from breathing the dead-flower stuff, but I couldn't—though I tried to—tell myself that I did not see this thing. It was there. It was there within reach of my hand if I leaned forward, shivering, writhing, between me and the door. I didn't believe in the supernatural—but what of that? The thing was there. It was there and it was not, I knew, a trick of luminous paint, a man with a sheet over him. I gave it up. I stood there with my handkerchief jammed to my nose and mouth, not stirring, not breathing, possibly not even letting my blood run through me. I was there, and the thing was there, and I stayed where I was.

The thing spoke, though I could not say that I actually heard the words: it was as if I simply became, through my entire body, conscious of the words:

"Down, enemy of the Lord God; down on your knees."

I stirred then, to lick my lips with a tongue drier than they were.

"Down, accursed of the Lord God, before the blow falls."

An argument was something I understood. I moved my handkerchief sufficiently to say: "Go to hell." It had a silly sound, especially in the creaking voice I had used.

The thing's body twisted convulsively, swayed, and bent towards me.

I dropped my handkerchief and reached for the thing with both hands. I got hold of the thing, and I didn't. My hands were on it, *in* it to the wrists, into the center of it, and shut on it. And there was nothing in my hands but dampness without temperature, neither warm nor cold.

That same dampness came into my face when the thing's face floated into mine. I bit at its face—yes—and my teeth closed on nothing, though I could see and feel that my face was *in* its face. And in my hands, on my arms, against my body, the thing squirmed and writhed, shuddered and shivered, swirling wildly now, breaking apart, reuniting madly in the black air.

Through the thing's transparent flesh I could see my hands clenched in the center of its damp body. I opened them, struck up and down inside it with stiff crooked fingers, trying to gouge it open; and I could see it being torn apart, could see it flowing together after my clawing fingers had passed; but all I could feel was its dampness.

Now another feeling came to me, growing quickly once it

had started—of an immense suffocating weight bearing me
down. This thing that had no solidity had weight, weight that
was pressing me down, smothering me. My knees were going
soft. I spit its face out of my mouth, tore my right hand free
from its body and struck up at its face, and felt nothing but
its dampness brushing my fist.

I clawed at its insides again with my left hand, tearing at
this substance that was so plainly seen, so faintly felt. And
then on my left hand I saw something else—blood. Blood
that was dark and thick and real covered my hand, dripped
from it, running out between my fingers.

I laughed and got strength to straighten my back against
the monstrous weight on me, wrenching at the thing's insides
again, croaking: "I'll gut you plenty." More blood came
through my fingers. I tried to laugh again, triumphantly, and
couldn't, choking instead. The thing's weight on me was
twice what it had been. I staggered back, sagging against the
wall, flattening myself against it to keep from sliding down it.

Air from the broken window, cold, pure, bitter, came over
my shoulder to sting my nostrils, to tell me—by its difference
from the air I had been breathing—that not the thing's
weight, but the poisonous flower-smelling stuff, had been
bearing me down.

The thing's greenish pale dampness squirmed over my face
and body. Coughing, I stumbled through the thing, to the
door, got the door open, and sprawled out in the corridor
that was now as dark as the room I had just left.

As I fell, somebody fell over me. But this was no indescribable thing. It was human. The knees that hit my back were
human, sharp. The grunt that blew hot breath in my ear was
human, surprised. The arm my fingers caught was human,
thin. I thanked God for its thinness. The corridor air was doing me a lot of good, but I was in no shape to do battle with
an athlete.

I put what strength I had into my grip on the thin arm,
dragging it under me as I rolled over on as much of the rest
of its owner as I could cover. My other hand, flung out across
the man's thin body as I rolled, struck something that was
hard and metallic on the floor. Bending my wrist, I got my
fingers on it, and recognized its feel: it was the over-size

dagger with which Riese had been killed. The man I was lolling on had, I guessed, stood beside the door of Minnie's room, waiting to carve me when I came out; and my fall had saved me, making him miss me with the blade, tripping him. Now he was kicking, jabbing, and butting up at me from his face-down position on the floor, with my hundred and ninety pounds anchoring him there.

Holding on to the dagger, I took my right hand from his arm and spread it over the back of his head, grinding his face into the carpet, taking it easy, waiting for more of the strength that was coming back into me with each breath. A minute or two more and I would be ready to pick him up and get words out of him.

But I wasn't allowed to wait that long. Something hard pounded my right shoulder, then my back, and then struck the carpet close to our heads. Somebody was swinging a club at me.

I rolled off the skinny man. The club-swinger's feet stopped my rolling. I looped my right arm above the feet, took another rap on the back, missed the legs with my circling arm, and felt skirts against my hand. Surprised, I pulled my hand back. Another chop of the club—on my side this time—reminded me that this was no place for gallantry. I made a fist of my hand and struck back at the skirt. It folded around my fist: a meaty shin stopped my fist. The shin's owner snarled above me and backed off before I could hit out again.

Scrambling up on hands and knees, I bumped my head into wood—a door. A hand on the knob helped me up. Somewhere inches away in the dark the club swished again. The knob turned in my hand. I went in with the door, into the room, and made as little noise as I could, practically none, shutting the door.

Behind me in the room a voice said, very softly, but also very earnestly:

"Go right out of here or I'll shoot you."

It was the plump blonde maid's voice, frightened. I turned, bending low in case she did shoot. Enough of the dull gray of approaching daylight came into this room to outline a shadow sitting up in bed, holding something small and dark in one outstretched hand.

"It's me," I whispered.

"Oh, you!" She didn't lower the thing in her hand.

"You in on the racket?" I asked, risking a slow step towards the bed.

"I do what I'm told and I keep my mouth shut, but I'm not going in for strong-arm work, not for the money they're paying me."

"Swell," I said, taking more and quicker steps towards the bed. "Could I get down through this window to the floor below if I tied a couple of sheets together?"

"I don't know—— Ouch! Stop!"

I had her gun—a .32 automatic—in my right hand, her wrist in my left, and was twisting them. "Let go," I ordered, and she did. Releasing her hand, I stepped back, picking up the dagger I had dropped on the foot of the bed.

I tiptoed to the door and listened. I couldn't hear anything. I opened the door slowly, and couldn't hear anything, couldn't see anything in the dim grayness that went through the door. Minnie Hershey's door was open, as I had left it when I tumbled out. The thing I had fought wasn't there. I went into Minnie's room, switching on the lights. She was lying as she had lain before, sleeping heavily. I pocketed my gun, pulled down the covers, picked Minnie up, and carried her over to the maid's room.

"See if you can bring her to life," I told the maid, dumping the mulatto on the bed beside her.

"She'll come around all right in a little while: they always do."

I said, "Yeah?" and went out, down to the fifth floor, to Gabrielle Leggett's room.

Gabrielle's room was empty. Collinson's hat and overcoat were gone; so were the clothes she had taken into the bathroom; and so was the bloody nightgown.

I cursed the pair of them, trying to show no favoritism, but probably concentrating most on Collinson; snapped off the lights; and ran down the front stairs, feeling as violent as I must have looked, battered and torn and bruised, with a red dagger in one hand, a gun in the other. For four flights of down-going I heard nothing, but when I reached the second floor a noise like small thunder was audible below me.

Dashing down the remaining flight, I identified it as some-body's knocking on the front door. I hoped the somebody wore a uniform. I went to the door, unlocked it, and pulled it open.

Eric Collinson was there, wild-eyed, white-faced, and frantic.

"Where's Gaby?" he gasped.

"God damn you," I said and hit him in the face with the gun.

He drooped, bending forward, stopped himself with hands on the vestibule's opposite walls, hung there a moment, and slowly pulled himself upright again. Blood leaked from a corner of his mouth.

"Where's Gaby?" he repeated doggedly.

"Where'd you leave her?"

"Here. I was taking her away. She asked me to. She sent me out first to see if anybody was in the street. Then the door closed."

"You're a smart boy," I grumbled. "She tricked you, still trying to save you from that lousy curse. Why in hell couldn't you do what I told you? But come on; we'll have to find her."

She wasn't in any of the reception rooms off the lobby. We left the lights on in them and hurried down the main corridor.

A small figure in white pajamas sprang out of a doorway and fastened itself on me, tangling itself in my legs, all but up-setting me. Unintelligible words came out of it. I pulled it loose from me and saw that it was the boy Manuel. Tears wet his panic-stricken face and crying ruined all the words he was trying to speak.

"Take it easy, son," I said. "I can't understand a word you're saying."

I understood, "Don't let him kill her."

"Who kill who?" I asked. "And take your time."

He didn't take his time, but I managed to hear "father" and "mama."

"Your father's trying to kill your mother?" I asked, since that seemed the most likely combination.

His head went up and down.

"Where?" I asked.

He fluttered a hand at the iron door ahead. I started towards it, and stopped.

"Listen, son," I bargained. "I'd like to help your mother, but I've got to know where Miss Leggett is first. Do you know where she is?"

"In there with them," he cried. "Oh, hurry, do hurry!"

"Right. Come on, Collinson," and we raced for the iron door.

The door was closed, but not locked. I yanked it open. The altar was glaring white, crystal, and silver in an immense beam of blue-white light that slanted down from an edge of the roof.

At one end of the altar Gabrielle crouched, her face turned up into the beam of light. Her face was ghastly white and expressionless in the harsh light. Aaronia Haldorn lay on the altar step where Riese had lain. There was a dark bruise on her forehead. Her hands and feet were tied with broad white bands of cloth, her arms tied to her body. Most of her clothes had been torn off.

Joseph, white-robed, stood in front of the altar, and of his wife. He stood with both arms held high and wide-spread, his back and neck bent so that his bearded face was lifted to the sky. In his right hand he held an ordinary horn-handled carving knife, with a long curved blade. He was talking to the sky, but his back was to us, and we couldn't hear his words. As we came through the door, he lowered his arms and bent over his wife. We were still a good thirty feet from him. I bellowed:

"Joseph!"

He straightened again, turning, and when the knife came into view I saw that it was still clean, shiny.

"Who calls Joseph, a name that is no more?" he asked, and I'd be a liar if I didn't admit that, standing there—for I had halted ten feet from him, with Collinson beside me—looking at him, listening to his voice, I didn't begin to feel that perhaps, after all, nothing very terrible had been about to happen. "There is no Joseph," he went on, not waiting for an answer to his question. "You may now know, as the world shall soon know, that he who went among you as Joseph was not Joseph, but God Himself. Now that you know, go."

I should have said, "Bunk," and jumped him. To any other man, I would have. To this one I didn't. I said:

"I'll have to take Miss Leggett and Mrs. Haldorn with me," and said it indecisively, almost apologetically.

He drew himself up taller, and his white-bearded face was stern.

"Go," he commanded; "go from me before your defiance leads to destruction."

Aaronia Haldorn spoke from where she lay tied on the step, spoke to me:

"Shoot. Shoot now—quick. Shoot."

I said to the man:

"I don't care what your right name is. You're going to the can. Now put your knife down."

"Blasphemer," he thundered, and took a step towards me. "Now you will die."

That should have been funny. It wasn't.

I yelled, "Stop," at him. He wouldn't stop. I was afraid. I fired. The bullet hit his cheek. I saw the hole it made. No muscle twitched in his face; not even his eyes blinked. He walked deliberately, not hurrying, towards me.

I worked the automatic's trigger, pumping six more bullets into his face and body. I saw them go in. And he came on steadily, showing in no way that he was conscious of them. His eyes and face were stern, but not angry. When he was close to me the knife in his hand went up high above his head. That's no way to fight with a knife; but he wasn't fighting: he was bringing retribution to me, and he paid as little attention to my attempts to stop him as a parent does to those of a small child he's punishing.

I was fighting. When the knife, shining over our heads, started down I went in under it, bending my right forearm against his knife-arm, driving the dagger in my left hand at his throat. I drove the heavy blade into his throat, in till the hilt's cross stopped it. Then I was through.

I didn't know I had closed my eyes until I found myself opening them. The first thing I saw was Eric Collinson kneeling beside Gabrielle Leggett, turning her face from the glaring light-beam, trying to rouse her. Next I saw Aaronia Haldorn, apparently unconscious on the altar step, with the boy Manuel crying on her and pulling with too nervous hands at her bonds. Then I saw that I was standing with my legs apart, and that Joseph was lying between my feet, dead, with the dagger through his neck.

"Thank God he wasn't really God," I mumbled to myself.

A brown body in white brushed past me, and Minnie Hershey was throwing herself down in front of Gabrielle Leggett, crying:

"Oh, Miss Gabrielle, I thought that devil had come alive and was after you again."

I went over to the mulatto and took her by the shoulder, lifting her up, asking her: "How could he? Didn't you kill him dead?"

"Yes, sir, but—"

"But you thought he might have come back in another shape?"

"Y-yes, sir. I thought he was—" She stopped and worked her lips together.

"Me?" I asked.

She nodded, not looking at me.

CHAPTER XII

The Unholy Grail

O WEN FITZSTEPHAN and I ate another of Mrs. Schindler's good dinners that evening, though my eating was a matter of catching bites between words. His curiosity poked at me with questions, requests to have this or that point made clear, and orders to keep talking whenever I stopped for breath or food.

"You could have got me in on it," he had complained before our soup was in front of us. "I knew the Haldorns, you know, or, at least, had met them once or twice at Leggett's. You could have used that as an excuse for somehow letting me in on the affair, so that I'd now have first-hand knowledge of what happened, and why; instead of having to depend on what I can get out of you and what the newspapers imagine their readers would like to think had happened."

"I had," I said, "enough grief with the one guy I did let in on it—Eric Collinson."

"Whatever trouble you had with him was your own fault, for selecting the wrong assistant, when such a better one was available. But come, my boy, I'm listening. Let's have the story, and then I can tell you where you erred."

"Sure," I agreed, "you'll be able to do that. Well, the Haldorns were originally actors. Most of what I can tell you comes from her, so a lot of maybes will have to be hung on it in spots. Fink won't talk at all; and the other help—maids, Filipino boys, Chinese cook, and the like—don't seem to know anything that helps much. None of them seems to have been let in on the trick stuff.

"As actors, Aaronia Haldorn says, she and Joseph were just pretty good, not getting on as well as they wanted to. About a year ago she ran into an old acquaintance—a one-time trouper—who had chucked the stage for the pulpit, and had made a go of it, now riding in Packards instead of day-coaches. That gave her something to think about. Thinking in that direction meant, pretty soon, thinking about Aimee, Buchman, Jeddu what's-his-name, and the other headliners.

And in the end her thinking came to, why not us? They—or she: Joseph was a lightweight—rigged up a cult that pretended to be the revival of an old Gaelic church, dating from King Arthur's time, or words to that effect."

"Yes," said Fitzstephan; "Arthur Machen's. But go on."

"They brought their cult to California because everybody does, and picked San Francisco because it held less competition than Los Angeles. With them they brought a little fellow named Tom Fink who had at one time or another been in charge of the mechanical end of most of the well-known stage magicians' and illusionists' acts; and Fink's wife, a big village-smith of a woman.

"They didn't want a mob of converts: they wanted them few but wealthy. The racket got away to a slow start—until they landed Mrs. Rodman. She fell plenty. They took her for one of her apartment buildings, and she also footed the remodeling bill. The stage mechanic Fink was in charge of the remodeling, and did a neat job. They didn't need the kitchens that were dotted, one to an apartment, through the building, and Fink knew how to use part of that scattered kitchen-space for concealed rooms and cabinets; and he knew how to adapt the gas and water pipes, and the electric wiring, to his hocus-pocus.

"I can't give you the mechanical details now; not till we've had time to take the joint apart. It's going to be interesting. I saw some of their work—mingled right in with it—a ghost made by an arrangement of lights thrown up on steam rising from a padded pipe that had been pushed into a dark room through a concealed opening in the wainscoting under a bed. The part of the steam that wasn't lighted was invisible in the darkness, showing only a man-shape that quivered and writhed, and that was damp and real to the touch, without any solidity. You can take my word for its being a weird stunt, especially when you've been filled up with the stuff they pumped into the room before they turned their spook loose on you. I don't know whether they used ether or chloroform or what: its odor was nicely disguised with some sort of flower perfume. This spook—I fought with it, on the level, and even thought I had it bleeding, not knowing I had cut my hand breaking a window to let air in. It was a beaut: it made a few minutes seem like a lot of hours to me.

"Till the very last, when Haldorn went wild, there wasn't anything crude about their work. They kept the services—the whole public end of the cult—as dignified and orderly and restrained as possible. The hocus-pocusing was all done in the privacy of the victim's bedroom. First the perfumed gas was pumped in. Then the illuminated steam spook was sicked on him, with a voice coming out of the same pipe—or maybe there was another arrangement for that—to give him his orders, or whatever was to be given. The gas kept him from being too sharp-eyed and suspicious, and also weakened his will, so he'd be more likely to do what he was told. It was slick enough; and I imagine they squeezed themselves out a lot of pennies that way.

"Happening in the victim's room, when he was alone, these visions had a lot of authority, and the Haldorns gave them more by the attitude they took towards them. Discussion of these visions was not absolutely prohibited, but was discouraged. They were supposed—these spook sessions—to be confidential between the victim and his God, to be too sacred to be bragged about. Mentioning them, even to Joseph, unless there was some special reason for having to mention them, was considered in bad taste, indelicate. See how nicely that would work out? The Haldorns seemed to be *not* trying to capitalize on these spook sessions, seemed not to know what took place in them, and therefore to have no interest in whether the victim carried out his spook-given instructions or not. Their stand was that that was simply and strictly a concern of the victim's and his God's."

"That's very good," Fitzstephan said, smiling delightedly, "a neat reversal of the usual cult's—the usual sect's, for that matter—insistence on confession, public testimony, or some other form of advertising the mysteries. Go on."

I tried to eat. He said:

"What of the members, the customers? How do they like their cult now? You've talked to some of them, haven't you?"

"Yeah," I said; "but what can you do with people like them? Half of them are still willing to string along with Aaronia Haldorn. I showed Mrs. Rodman one of the pipes that the spooks came out of. When she had gasped once and gulped twice she offered to take us to the cathedral and show us that the images there, including the one on the cross, were made out of even more solid and earthly materials than steam; and asked us if we would arrest the bishop on proof that no actual flesh and blood—whether divine or not—was in the monstrance. I thought O'Gar, who's a good Catholic, would blackjack her."

"The Colemans weren't there, were they? The Ralph Colemans?"

"No."

"Too bad," he said, grinning. "I must look Ralph up and question him. He'll be in hiding by now, of course, but he's worth hunting out. He always has the most consistently logical and creditable reasons for having done the most idiotic things. He is"—as if that explained it—"an advertising man." Fitzstephan frowned at the discovery that I was eating again, and said impatiently: "Talk, my boy, talk."

"You've met Haldorn," I said. "What did you think of him?"

"I saw him twice, I think. He was, undoubtedly, impressive."

"He was," I agreed. "He had what he needed. Ever talk to him?"

"No; that is, not except to exchange the polite equivalents of 'pleased to meet you.' "

"Well, he looked at you and spoke to you, and things happened inside you. I'm not the easiest guy in the world to dazzle, I hope; but he had me going. I came damned near to believing he was God toward the last. He was quite young—in his thirties: they'd had the coloring—the pigment—in his hair and beard killed to give him that Father Joseph front. His wife says she used to hypnotize him before he went into action, and that without being hynotized he wasn't so effective on people. Later he got so that he could hypnotize himself without her help, and toward the last it became a permanent condition with him.

"She didn't know her husband had fallen for Gabrielle till after the girl had come to stay in the Temple. Until then she thought that Gabrielle was to him, as to her, just another customer—one whose recent troubles made her a very likely prospect. But Joseph had fallen for her, and wanted her. I don't know how far he had worked on her, nor even how he had worked on her, but I suppose he was sewing her up by using his hocus-pocus against her fear of the Dain curse. Anyway, Doctor Riese finally discovered that everything wasn't going well with her. Yesterday morning he told me he was coming back to see her that evening, and he did come back, but he didn't see her; and I didn't see him—not then.

"He went back to see Joseph before he came up to the girl's room, and managed to overhear Joseph giving instructions to the Finks. That should have been fine, but wasn't. Riese was foolish enough to let Joseph know he had overheard him. Joseph locked Riese up—a prisoner.

"They had cut loose on Minnie from the very beginning. She was a mulatto, and therefore susceptible to that sort of game, and she was devoted to Gabrielle Leggett. They had chucked visions and voices at the poor girl until she was dizzy. Now they decided to make her kill Riese. They drugged him and put him on the altar. They ghosted her into thinking that he was Satan—this is serious: they did this—come up from hell to carry Gabrielle down and keep her from becoming a saint. Minnie was ripe for it—poor boogie—and when the spirit told her that she had been selected to save her mistress, that she'd find the annointed weapon on her table, she followed the instructions the spirit gave her. She got out of bed, picked up the dagger that had been put on her table, went down to the altar, and killed Riese.

"To play safe, they pumped some of the gas into my room, to keep me slumbering while Minnie was at work. But I had been nervous, jumpy, and was sleeping in a chair in the center of the room, instead of on the bed, close to the gas-pipe; so I came out of the dope before the night was far gone.

"By this time, Aaronia Haldorn had made a couple of discoveries: first, that her husband's interest in the girl wasn't altogether financial; and second, that he had gone off center, was a dangerous maniac. Going around hypnotized all the time, what brains he had—not a whole lot to start with, she says—had become completely scrambled. His success in flimflamming his followers had gone to his head. He thought he could do anything, get away with anything. He had dreams, she says, of the entire world deluded into belief in his divinity: he didn't see why that would be any—or much—more difficult than fooling the handful that he had fooled. She thinks he actually had insane notions of his own divinity. I don't go that far. I think he knew well enough that he wasn't divine, but thought he could kid the rest of the world. These details don't make much difference: the thing is that he was a nut who saw no limit to his power.

"Aaronia Haldorn had, she says, no knowledge of Riese's murder until after it was done. Joseph, using the vision-and-voice trick, sent Gabrielle down to see the corpse on the altar step. That would fit in, you see, with his original scheme to tie her to him by playing his divinity against her curse. Apparently, he intended joining her there, and putting on an act of some sort for her. But Collinson and I interrupted that. Joseph and Gabrielle heard us talking at the door, so Joseph held back, not joining her at the altar, and she came to meet us. Joseph's plan was successful this far: the girl actually believed the curse had been responsible for Riese's death. She told us she had killed him and ought to be hanged for it.

"As soon as I saw Riese's body I knew she hadn't killed him. He was lying in an orderly position. It was plain he had been doped before being killed. Then the door leading to the altar, which I imagined was kept locked, was open, and she didn't know anything about the key. There was a chance that she had been in on the killing, but none that she had done it alone as she confessed.

"The place was scientifically equipped for eavesdropping: both of the Haldorns heard her confession. Aaronia got busy manufacturing evidence to fit the confession. She went up to Gabrielle's room and got her dressing-gown; got the bloody dagger from where I had dropped it beside the body after taking it from the girl; wrapped the dagger in the dressing-gown, and stuck them in a corner where the police could find them easy enough. Meanwhile, Joseph is working in another direction. He doesn't—as his wife does—want Gabrielle carried off to jail or the booby-hatch. He wants her. He wants her belief in her guilt and responsibility to tie her to him, not take her away. He remove's Riese's remains—tucking them in one of the concealed cabinets—and has the Finks clean up the mess.

He's overheard Collinson trying to persuade me to hush up the doings, and so he knows he can count on the boy—the only other exactly sane witness—to keep quiet if I'm taken care of.

"Kill yourself into a hole, and the chances are a time comes when you have to kill yourself out. To this nut Joseph now, 'taking care of' me is simply a matter of another murder. He and the Finks—though I don't think we're going to prove their part—went to work on Minnie with the spooks again. She had killed Riese docilely enough: why not me? You see, they were handicapped by not being equipped for this whole-sale murdering into which they had all of a sudden plunged. For instance, except for my gun and one of the maids'— which they didn't know anything about—there wasn't a fire-arm in the place; and the dagger was the only other weapon —until they got to dragging in carving sets and plumber's helpers. Then, too, I suppose, there were the sleeping cus-tomers to consider—Mrs. Rodman's probable dislike for be-ing roused by the noise of her spiritual guides ganging up on a roughneck sleuth. Anyway, the idea was that Minnie could be induced to walk up to me and stick the dagger into me in a quiet way.

"They had found the dagger again, in the dressing-gown, where Aaronia had stuck it; and Joseph began suspecting that his wife was double-crossing him. When he caught her in the act of turning on the dead-flower stuff so strong in Minnie's room that it knocked her completely out—put her so soundly asleep that a dozen ghosts couldn't have stirred her into ac-tion—he was sure of her treachery; and, up to his neck now, decided to kill *her*."

"His wife?" Fitzstephan asked.

"Yeah, but what difference does that make? It might as well have been anybody else for all the sense it makes. I hope you're not trying to keep this nonsense straight in your mind. You know damned well all this didn't happen."

"Then what," he asked, looking puzzled, "did happen?"

"I don't know. I don't think anybody knows. I'm telling you what I saw plus the part of what Aaronia Haldorn told me which fits in with what I saw. To fit in with what I saw, most of it must have happened very nearly as I've told you. If you want to believe that it did, all right. I don't. I'd rather believe I saw things that weren't there."

"Not now," he pleaded. "Later, after you've finished the story, you can attach your ifs and buts to it, distorting and twisting it, making it as cloudy and confusing and generally hopeless as you like. But first please finish it, so I'll see it at least once in its original state before you start improving it."

"You actually believe what I've told you so far?" I asked.

He nodded, grinning, and said that he not only believed it but liked it.

"What a childish mind you've got," I said. "Let me tell you the story about the wolf that went to the little girl's grandmother's house and—"

"I always liked that one, too; but finish this one now. Joseph had decided to kill his wife."

"All right. There's not much more. While Minnie was being worked on, I popped into her room, intending to rouse her and send her for help. Before I did any rousing, I was needing some myself: I had a couple of lungfuls of the gas. The Finks must have turned the ghost loose on me, because Joseph was probably on his way downstairs with his wife at that time. He had faith enough in his divinity-shield, or he was nutty enough, to take her down and tie her on the altar before he carved her. Or maybe he had a way of fitting that stunt into his scheme, or maybe he simply had a liking for bloody theatricals. Anyway, he probably took her down there while I was up in Minnie's room going around and around with the ghost.

"The ghost had me sweating ink, and when I finally left him and tottered out into the corridor, the Finks jumped me. I say they did, and know it; but it was too dark for me to see them. I beat them off, got a gun, and went downstairs. Collinson and Gabrielle were gone from where I had left them. I found Collinson: Gabrielle had put him outside and shut the door on him. The Haldorns' son—a kid of thirteen or so—came to us with the news that Papa was about to kill Mama, and that Gabrielle was with them. I killed Haldorn, but I almost didn't. I put seven bullets in him. Hard-coated .32's go in clean, without much of a thump, true enough; but I put seven of them in him—in his face and body—standing close and firing pointblank—and he didn't even know it. That's how completely he had himself hypnotized. I finally got him down by driving the dagger through his neck."

I stopped. Fitzstephan asked: "Well?"

"Well what?"

"What happened after that?"

"Nothing," I said. "That's the kind of a story it is. I warned you there was no sense to it."

"But what was Gabrielle doing there?"

"Crouching beside the altar, looking up at the pretty spotlight."

"But why was she there? What was her reason for being there? Had she been called there again? Or was she there of her own free will? How did she come to be there? What was she there for?"

"I don't know. She didn't know. I asked her. She didn't know she was there."

"But surely you could learn something from the others?"

"Yeah," I said; "what I've told you, chiefly from Aaronia Haldorn. She and her husband ran a cult, and he went crazy and began murdering people, and how could she help it? Fink won't talk. He's a mechanic, yes; and he put in his trick-machinery for the Haldorns and operated it; but he doesn't know what happened last night. He heard a lot of noises, but it was none of his business to go poking his nose out to see what it was: the first he knew anything was wrong was when some police came and started giving him hell. Mrs. Fink's gone. The other employes probably don't really know anything, though it's a gut they could make some good guesses. Manuel, the little boy, is too frightened to talk—and will be sure to know nothing when he gets over his fright. What we're up against is this: if Joseph went crazy and committed some murders on his own hook, the others, even though they unknowingly helped him, are in the clear. The worst any of them can draw is a light sentence for taking part in the cult swindle. But if any of them admits knowing anything, then he lets himself in for trouble as an accomplice in the murder. Nobody's likely to do that."

"I see," Fitzstephan said slowly. "Joseph is dead, so Joseph did everything. How will you get around that?"

"I won't," I said; "though the police will at least try to. My end's done, so Madison Andrews told me a couple of hours ago."

"But if, as you say, you aren't satisfied that you've learned the whole truth of the affair, I should think you—"

"It's not me," I said. "There's a lot I'd like to do yet, but I was hired, this time, by Andrews, to guard her while she was in the Temple. She isn't there now, and Andrews doesn't think there's anything further to be learned about what happened there. And, as far as guarding her is necessary, her husband ought to be able to do that."

"Her what?"

"Husband."

Fitzstephan thumped his stein down on the table so that beer sloshed over the sides.

"Now there you are," he said accusingly. "You didn't tell me anything about that. God only knows how much else there is that you've not told me."

"Collinson took advantage of the confusion to carry her off to Reno, where they won't have to wait the Californian three days for their license. I didn't know they'd gone till Andrews jumped on my neck three or four hours later. He was kind of unpleasant about it, which is one of the ways we came to stop being client and operative."

"I didn't know he was opposed to Collinson as a husband for her."

"I don't know that he is, but he didn't think this the time, nor that the way, for their wedding."

"I can understand that," he said as we got up from the table. "Andrews likes to have his way in most things."

PART THREE: QUESADA

CHAPTER XIII

The Cliff Road

Eric Collinson wired me from Quesada:

COME IMMEDIATELY STOP NEED YOU STOP TROUBLE DANGER STOP MEET ME AT SUNSET HOTEL STOP DO NOT COMMUNICATE STOP GABRIELLE MUST NOT KNOW STOP HURRY

ERIC CARTER

The telegram came to the agency on Friday morning.

I wasn't in San Francisco that morning. I was up in Martinez dickering with a divorced wife of Phil Leach, alias a lot of names. We wanted him for spreading reams of orphan paper through the Northwest, and we wanted him badly. This ex-wife—a sweet-looking little blonde telephone operator—had a fairly recent photograph of Phil, and was willing to sell it.

"He never thought enough of me to risk passing any bum checks so I could have things," she complained. "I had to bring in my own share of the nut. So why shouldn't I make something out of him now, when I guess some tramp's getting plenty? Now how much will you give for it?"

She had an exaggerated idea of how much the photograph was worth to us, of course, but I finally made the deal with her. But it was after six when I returned to the city, too late for a train that would put me in Quesada that night. I packed a bag, got my car from the garage, and drove down.

Quesada was a one-hotel town pasted on the rocky side of a young mountain that sloped into the Pacific Ocean some eighty miles from San Francisco. Quesada's beach was too abrupt and hard and jagged for bathing, so Quesada had never got much summer-resort money. For a while it had been a hustling rum-running port, but that racket was dead now: bootleggers had learned there was more profit and less worry in handling domestic hooch than imported. Quesada had gone back to sleep.

I got there at eleven-something that night, garaged my car, and crossed the street to the Sunset Hotel. It was a low, sprawled-out, yellow building. The night clerk was alone in the lobby, a small effeminate man well past sixty who went to a lot of trouble to show me that his fingernails were rosy and shiny.

When he had read my name on the register he gave me a sealed envelope—hotel stationery—addressed to me in Eric Collinson's handwriting. I tore it open and read:

> *Do not leave the hotel until I have seen you.*
> *E. C.*

"How long has this been here?" I asked.

"Since about eight o'clock. Mr. Carter waited for you for more than an hour, until after the last stage came in from the railroad."

"He isn't staying here?"

"Oh, dear, no. He and his bride have got the Tooker place, down in the cove."

Collinson wasn't the sort of person to whose instructions I'd pay a whole lot of attention. I asked:

"How do you get there?"

"You'd never be able to find it at night," the clerk assured me, "unless you went all the way around by the East road, and not then, I'm sure, unless you knew the country."

"Yeah? How do you get there in the daytime?"

"You go down this street to the end, take the fork of the road on the ocean side, and follow that up along the cliff. It isn't really a road, more of a path. It's about three miles to the house, a brown house, shingled all over, on a little hill. It's easily enough found in the daytime if you remember to keep to the right, to the ocean side, all the way down. But you'd never, never in the world, be able to find—"

"Thanks," I said, not wanting to hear the story all over again.

He led me up to a room, promised to call me at five, and I was asleep by midnight.

The morning was dull, ugly, foggy, and cold when I climbed out of bed to say, "All right, thanks," into the phone. It hadn't improved much by the time I had got dressed and gone downstairs. The clerk said there was not a chance in the world of getting anything to eat in Quesada before seven o'clock.

I went out of the hotel, down the street until it became a dirt road, kept to the dirt road until it forked, and turned into the branch that bent toward the ocean. This branch was never really a road from its beginning, and soon was nothing but a rocky path climbing along the side of a rocky ledge that kept pushing closer to the water's edge. The side of the ledge became steeper and steeper, until the path was simply an irregular shelf on the face of a cliff—a shelf eight or ten feet wide in places, no more than four or five in others. Above and behind the path, the cliff rose sixty or seventy feet; below and in front, it slanted down a hundred or more to ravel out in the ocean. A breeze from the general direction of China was pushing fog over the top of the cliff, making noisy lather of sea water at its bottom.

Rounding a corner where the cliff was steepest—was, in fact, for a hundred yards or so, straight up and down—I stopped to look at a small ragged hole in the path's outer rim. The hole was perhaps six inches across, with fresh loose earth piled in a little semicircular mound on one side, scattered on the other. It wasn't exciting to look at, but it said plainly to even such a city man as I was: here a bush was uprooted not so long ago.

There was no uprooted bush in sight. I chucked my cigarette away and got down on hands and knees, putting my head out over the path's rim, looking down. I saw the bush twenty feet below. It was perched on the top of a stunted tree that grew almost parallel to the cliff, fresh brown earth sticking to the bush's roots. The next thing that caught my eye was also brown—a soft hat lying upside down between two pointed gray rocks, half-way down to the water. I looked at the bottom of the cliff and saw the feet and legs.

They were a man's feet and legs, in black shoes and dark trousers. The feet lay on the top of a water-smoothed boulder, lay on their sides, six inches apart, both pointing to the left. From the feet, dark-trousered legs slanted down into the water, disappearing beneath the surface a few inches above the knees. That was all I could see from the cliff road.

I went down the cliff, though not at that point. It was a lot too steep there to be tackled by a middle-aged fat man. A couple of hundred yards back, the path had crossed a crooked ravine that creased the cliff diagonally from top to bottom. I returned to the ravine and went down it, stumbling, sliding, sweating and swearing, but reaching the bottom all in one piece, with nothing more serious the matter with me than torn fingers, dirty clothes, and ruined shoes.

The fringe of rock that lay between cliff and ocean wasn't meant to be walked on, but I managed to travel over it most of the way, having to wade only once or twice, and then not up to my knees. But when I came to the spot where the feet and legs were I had to go waist-deep into the Pacific to lift the body, which rested on its back on the worn slanting side of a mostly submerged boulder, covered from thighs up by frothing water. I got my hands under the armpits, found solid ground for my feet, and lifted.

It was Eric Collinson's body. Bones showed through flesh and clothing on his shattered back. The back of his head—that half of it—was crushed. I dragged him out of the water and put him down on dry rocks. His dripping pockets contained a hundred and fifty-four dollars and eighty-two cents, a watch, a knife, a gold pen and pencil, papers, a couple of letters, and a memoranda book. I spread out the papers, letters, and book; and read them; and learned nothing except that what was written in them hadn't anything to do with his death. I couldn't find anything else—on him or near him—to tell me more about his death than the uprooted bush, the hat caught between rocks, and the position of his body had told me.

I left him there and went back to the ravine, panting and heaving myself up it to the cliff path, returning to where the bush had grown. I didn't find anything there in the way of significant marks, footprints, or the like. The path was chiefly hard rock. I went on along it. Presently the cliff began to bend away from the ocean, lowering the path along its side. After another half-mile there was no cliff at all, merely a bush-grown ridge at whose foot the path ran. There was no sun yet. My pants stuck disagreeably to my chilly legs. Water squunched in my torn shoes. I hadn't had any breakfast. My cigarettes had got wet. My left knee ached from a twist it had got sliding down the ravine. I cursed the detective business and slopped on along the path.

The path took me away from the sea for a while, across the neck of a wooded point that pushed the ocean back, down into a small valley, up the side of a low hill; and then I saw the house the night clerk had described.

It was a rather large two-story building, roof and walls brown-shingled, set on a hump in the ground close to where the ocean came in to take a quarter-mile u-shaped bite out of the coast. The house faced the water. I was behind it. There was nobody in sight. The ground-floor windows were closed, with drawn blinds. The second-story windows were open. Off to one side were some smaller farm buildings.

I went around to the front of the house. Wicker chairs and a table were on the screened front porch. The screened porch-door was hooked on the inside. I rattled it noisily. I rattled it off and on for at least five minutes, and got no response. I went around to the rear again, and knocked on the back door. My knocking knuckles pushed the door open half a foot. Inside was a dark kitchen and silence. I opened the door wider, knocking on it again, loudly. More silence.

I called: "Mrs. Collinson."

When no answer came I went through the kitchen and a darker dining room, found a flight of stairs, climbed them, and began poking my head into rooms.

There was nobody in the house.

In one bedroom, a .38 automatic pistol lay in the center of the floor. There was an empty shell close to it, another under a chair across the room, and a faint odor of burnt gunpowder in the air. In one corner of the ceiling was a hole that a .38 bullet could have made, and, under it on the floor, a few crumbs of plaster. The bed-clothes were smooth and undisturbed. Clothes in the closet, things on and in table and bureau, told me this was Eric Collinson's bedroom.

Next to it, according to the same sort of evidence, was Gabrielle's bedroom. Her bed had not been slept in, or had been made since being slept in. On the floor of her closet I found a black satin dress, a once-white handkerchief, and a pair of black suede slippers, all wet and muddy—the handkerchief also wet with blood. In her bathroom—in the tub—were a bath-towel and a face-towel, both stained with mud and blood, and still damp. On her dressing-table was a small piece of thick white paper that had been folded. White powder clung to one crease. I touched it with the end of my tongue—morphine.

I went back to Quesada, changed my shoes and socks, got breakfast and a supply of dry cigarettes, and asked the clerk—a dapper boy, this one—who was responsible for law and order there.

"The marshal's Dick Cotton," he told me; "but he went up to the city last night. Ben Rolly's deputy sheriff. You can likely find him over at his old man's office."

"Where's that?"

"Next door to the garage."

I found it, a one-story red brick building with wide glass windows labeled *J. King Rolly, Real Estate, Mortgages, Loans, Stocks and Bonds, Insurance, Notes, Employment Agency, Notary Public, Moving and Storage*, and a lot more that I've forgotten.

Two men were inside, sitting with their feet on a battered desk behind a battered counter. One was a man of fifty-and, with hair, eyes, and skin of indefinite, washed-out tan shades—an amiable, aimless-looking man in shabby clothes. The other was twenty years younger and in twenty years would look just like him.

"I'm hunting," I said, "for the deputy sheriff."

"Me," the younger man said, easing his feet from desk to floor. He didn't get up. Instead, he put a foot out, hooked a chair by its rounds, pulled it from the wall, and returned his feet to the desk-top. "Set down. This is Pa," wiggling a thumb at the other man. "You don't have to mind him."

"Know Eric Carter?" I asked.

"The fellow honeymooning down to the Tooker place? I didn't know his front name was Eric."

"Eric Carter," the elder Rolly said; "that's the way I made out the rent receipt for him."

"He's dead," I told them. "He fell off the cliff road last night or this morning. It could have been an accident."

The father looked at the son with round tan eyes. The son

looked at me with questioning tan eyes and said: "Tch, tch, tch."

I gave him a card. He read it carefully, turning it over to see that there was nothing on its back, and passed it to his father.

"Go down and take a look at him?" I suggested.

"I guess I ought to," the deputy sheriff agreed, getting up from his chair. He was a larger man than I had supposed—as big as the dead Collinson boy—and, in spite of his slouchiness, he had a nicely muscled body.

I followed him out to a dusty car in front of the office. Rolly senior didn't go with us.

"Somebody told you about it?" the deputy sheriff asked when we were riding.

"I stumbled on him. Know who the Carters are?"

"Somebody special?"

"You heard about the Riese murder in the San Francisco temple?"

"Uh-huh, I read the papers."

"Mrs. Carter was the Gabrielle Leggett mixed up in that, and Carter was the Eric Collinson."

"Tch, tch, tch," he said.

"And her father and step-mother were killed a couple of weeks before that."

"Tch, tch, tch," he said. "What's the matter with them?"

"A family curse."

"Sure enough?"

I didn't know how seriously he meant that question, though he seemed serious enough. I hadn't got him sized up yet. However, clown or not, he was the deputy sheriff stationed at Quesada, and this was his party. He was entitled to the facts. I gave them to him as we bounced over the lumpy road, gave him all I had, from Paris in 1913 to the cliff road a couple of hours ago.

"When they came back from being married in Reno, Collinson dropped in to see me. They had to stick around for the Haldorn bunch's trial, and he wanted a quiet place to take the girl: she was still in a daze. You know Owen Fitzstephan?"

"The writer fellow that was down here a while last year? Uh-huh."

"Well, he suggested this place."

"I know. The old man mentioned it. But what'd they take them aliases for?"

"To dodge publicity, and, partly, to try to dodge something like this."

He frowned vaguely and asked:

"You mean they expected something like this?"

"Well, it's easy to say, 'I told you so,' after things happen, but I've never thought we had the answer to either of the two mix-ups she's been in. And not having the answer—how could you tell what to expect? I didn't think so much of their going off into seclusion like this while whatever was hanging over her—if anything was—was still hanging over her, but Collinson was all for it. I made him promise to wire me if he saw anything funny. Well, he did."

Rolly nodded three or four times, then asked:

"What makes you think he didn't fall off the cliff?"

"He sent for me. Something was wrong. Outside of that, too many things have happened around his wife for me to believe in accidents."

"There's the curse, though," he said.

"Yeah," I agreed, studying his indefinite face, still trying to figure him out. "But the trouble with it is it's worked out too well, too regularly. It's the first one I ever ran across that did."

He frowned over my opinion for a couple of minutes, and then stopped the car. "We'll have to get out here: the road ain't so good the rest of the way." None of it had been. "Still and all, you do hear of them working out. There's things that happen that makes a fellow think there's things in the world—in life—that he don't know much about." He frowned again as we set off afoot, and found a word he liked. "It's inscrutable," he wound up.

I let that go at that.

He went ahead up the cliff path, stopping of his own accord where the bush had been torn up, a detail I hadn't mentioned. I didn't say anything while he stared down at Collinson's body, looked searchingly up and down the face of the cliff, and then went up and down the path, bent far over, his tan eyes intent on the ground.

He wandered around for ten minutes or more, then

straightened up and said: "There's nothing here that I can find. Let's go down."

I started back toward the ravine, but he said there was a better way ahead. There was. We went down it to the dead man.

Rolly looked from the corpse to the edge of the path high above us, and complained: "I don't hardly see how he could have landed just thataway."

"He didn't. I pulled him out of the water," I said, showing the deputy exactly where I had found the body.

"That would be more like it," he decided.

I sat on a rock and smoked a cigarette while he went around examining, touching, moving rocks, pebbles, and sand. He didn't seem to have any luck.

CHAPTER XIV

The Crumpled Chrysler

WE CLIMBED to the path again and went on to the Collinsons' house. I showed Rolly the stained towels, handkerchief, dress, and slippers; the paper that had held morphine; the gun on Collinson's floor, the hole in the ceiling, and the empty shells on the floor.

"That shell under the chair is where it was," I said; "but the other—the one in the corner—was here, close to the gun, when I saw it before."

"You mean it's been moved since you were here?"

"Yeah."

"But what good would that do anybody?" he objected.

"None that I know of, but it's been moved."

He had lost interest. He was looking at the ceiling. He said:

"Two shots and one hole. I wonder. Maybe the other went out the window."

He went back to Gabrielle Collinson's bedroom and examined the black velvet gown. There were some torn places in it—down near the bottom—but no bullet-holes. He put the dress down and picked up the morphine paper from the dressing table.

"What do you suppose this is doing here?" he asked.

"She uses it. It's one of the things her step-mother taught her."

"Tch, tch, tch. Kind of looks like she might have done it."

"Yeah?"

"You know it does. She's a dope fiend, ain't she? They had had trouble, and he sent for you, and—" He broke off, pursed his lips, then asked: "What time do you reckon he was killed?"

"I don't know. Maybe last night, on his way home from waiting for me."

"You were in the hotel all night?"

"From eleven-something till five this morning. Of course I could have sneaked out for long enough to pull a murder between those hours."

"I didn't mean nothing like that," he said. "I was just wondering. What kind of looking woman is this Mrs. Collinson-Carter? I never saw her."

"She's about twenty; five feet four or five; looks thinner than she really is; light brown hair, short and curly; big eyes that are sometimes brown and sometimes green; white skin; hardly any forehead; small mouth and teeth; pointed chin; no lobes on her ears, and they're pointed on top; been sick for a couple of months and looks it."

"Oughtn't be hard to pick her up," he said, and began poking into drawers, closets, trunks, and so on. I had poked into them on my first visit, and hadn't found anything interesting either.

"Don't look like she did any packing or took much of anything with her," he decided when he came back to where I was sitting by the dressing-table. He pointed a thick finger at the monogrammed silver toilet-set on the table. "What's the G.D.L. for?"

"Her name was Gabrielle Something Leggett before she was married."

"Oh, yes. She went away in the car, I reckon. Huh?"

"Did they have one down here?" I asked.

"He used to come to town in a Chrysler roadster when he didn't walk. She could only have took it out by the East road. We'll go out thataway and see."

Outside, I waited while he made circles around the house, finding nothing. In front of a shed where a car obviously had been kept he pointed at some tracks, and said, "Drove out this morning." I took his word for it.

We walked along a dirt road to a gravel one, and along that perhaps a mile to a gray house that stood in a group of red farm buildings. A small-boned, high-shouldered man who limped slightly was oiling a pump behind the house. Rolly called him Debro.

"Sure, Ben," he replied to Rolly's question. "She went by here about seven this morning, going like a bat out of hell. There wasn't anybody else in the car."

"How was she dressed?" I asked.

"She didn't have on any hat and a tan coat."

I asked him what he knew about the Carters: he was their

nearest neighbor. He didn't know anything about them. He had talked to Carter two or three times, and thought him an agreeable enough young fellow. Once he had taken the missus over to call on Mrs. Carter, but Carter told them she was lying down, not feeling well. None of the Debros had ever seen her except at a distance, walking or riding with her husband.

"I don't guess there's anybody around here that's talked to her," he wound up, "except of course Mary Nunez."

"Mary working for them?" the deputy asked.

"Yes. What's the matter, Ben? Something the matter over there?"

"He fell off the cliff last night, and she's gone away without saying anything to anybody."

Debro whistled.

Rolly went into the house to use Debro's phone, reporting to the sheriff. I stayed outside with Debro, trying to get more—if only his opinions—out of him. All I got were expressions of amazement.

"We'll go over and see Mary," the deputy said when he came from the phone; and then, when we had left Debro, had crossed the road, and were walking through a field towards a cluster of trees: "Funny she wasn't there."

"Who is she?"

"A Mex. Lives down in the hollow with the rest of them. Her man, Pedro Nunez, is doing a life-stretch in Folsom for killing a bootlegger named Dunne in a hijacking two-three years back."

"Local killing?"

"Uh-huh. It happened down in the cove in front of the Tooker place."

We went through the trees and down a slope to where half a dozen shacks—shaped, sized, and red-leaded to resemble box-cars—lined the side of a stream, with vegetable gardens spread out behind them. In front of one of the shacks a shapeless Mexican woman in a pink-checkered dress sat on an empty canned-soup box smoking a corncob pipe and nursing a brown baby. Ragged and dirty children played between the buildings, with ragged and dirty mongrels helping them make noise. In one of the gardens a brown man in overalls that had once been blue was barely moving a hoe.

The children stopped playing to watch Rolly and me cross the stream on conveniently placed stones. The dogs came yapping to meet us, snarling and snapping around us until one of the boys chased them. We stopped in front of the woman with the baby. The deputy grinned down at the baby and said:

"Well, well, ain't he getting to be a husky son-of-a-gun!"

The woman took the pipe from her mouth long enough to complain stolidly:

"Colic all the time."

"Tch, tch, tch. Where's Mary Nunez?"

The pipe-stem pointed at the next shack.

"I thought she was working for them people at the Tooker place," he said.

"Sometimes," the woman replied indifferently.

We went to the next shack. An old woman in a gray wrapper had come to the door, watching us while stirring something in a yellow bowl.

"Where's Mary?" the deputy asked.

She spoke over her shoulder into the shack's interior, and moved aside to let another woman take her place in the doorway. This other woman was short and solidly built, somewhere in her early thirties, with intelligent dark eyes in a wide, flat face. She held a dark blanket together at her throat. The blanket hung to the floor all around her.

"Howdy, Mary," Rolly greeted her. "Why ain't you over to the Carters'?"

"I'm sick, Mr. Rolly." She spoke without accent. "Chills—so I just stayed home today."

"Tch, tch, tch. That's too bad. Have you had the doc?"

She said she hadn't. Rolly said she ought to. She said she didn't need him: she had chills often. Rolly said that might be so, but that was all the more reason for having him: it was best to play safe and have things like that looked after. She said yes but doctors took so much money, and it was bad enough being sick without having to pay for it. He said in the long run it was likely to cost folks more not having a doctor than having him. I had begun to think they were going to keep it up all day when Rolly finally brought the talk around to the Carters again, asking the woman about her work there.

She told us she had been hired two weeks ago, when they took the house. She went there each morning at nine—they never got up before ten—cooked their meals, did the housework, and left after washing the dinner dishes in the evening—usually somewhere around seven-thirty. She seemed surprised at the news that Collinson—Carter to her—had been killed and his wife had gone away. She told us that Collinson had gone out by himself, for a walk, he said, right after dinner the previous night. That was at about half-past six, dinner having been, for no especial reason, a little early. When she left for home, at a few minutes past seven, Mrs. Carter had been reading a book in the front second-story room.

Mary Nunez couldn't, or wouldn't, tell us anything on which I could base a reasonable guess at Collinson's reason for sending for me. She knew, she insisted, nothing about them except that Mrs. Carter didn't seem happy—wasn't happy. She—Mary Nunez—had figured it all out to her own satisfaction: Mrs. Carter loved someone else, but her parents had made her marry Carter; and so, of course, Carter had been killed by the other man, with whom Mrs. Carter had now run away. I couldn't get her to say that she had any grounds for this belief other than her woman's intuition, so I asked her about the Carters' visitors.

She said she had never seen any.

Rolly asked her if the Carters ever quarreled. She started to say, "No," and then, rapidly, said they did, often, and were never on good terms. Mrs. Carter didn't like to have her husband near her, and several times had told him, in Mary's hearing, that if he didn't go away from her and stay away she would kill him. I tried to pin Mary down to details, asking what had led up to these threats, how they had been worded, but she wouldn't be pinned down. All she remembered positively, she told us, was that Mrs. Carter had threatened to kill Mr. Carter if he didn't go away from her.

"That pretty well settles that," Rolly said contentedly when we had crossed the stream again and were climbing the slope toward Debro's.

"What settles what?"

"That his wife killed him."

"Think she did?"

"So do you."

I said: "No."

Rolly stopped walking and looked at me with vague worried eyes.

"Now how can you say that?" he remonstrated. "Ain't she a dope fiend? And cracked in the bargain, according to your own way of telling it? Didn't she run away? Wasn't them things she left behind torn and dirty and bloody? Didn't she threaten to kill him so much that he got scared and sent for you?"

"Mary didn't hear threats," I said. "They were warnings—about the curse. Gabrielle Collinson really believed in it, and thought enough of him to try to save him from it. I've been through that before with her. That's why she wouldn't have married him if he hadn't carried her off while she was too rattled to know what she was doing. And she was afraid on that account afterwards."

"But who's going to believe—?"

"I'm not asking anybody to believe anything," I growled, walking on again. "I'm telling you what I believe. And while I'm at it I'll tell you I believe Mary Nunez is lying when she says she didn't go to the house this morning. Maybe she didn't have anything to do with Collinson's death. Maybe she simply went there, found the Collinsons gone, saw the bloody things and the gun—kicking that shell across the floor without knowing it—and then beat it back to her shack, fixing up that chills story to keep herself out of it; having had enough of that sort of trouble when her husband was sent over. Maybe not. Anyway, that would be how nine out of ten women of her sort in her place would have played it; and I want more proof before I believe her chills just happened to hit her this morning."

"Well," the deputy sheriff asked; "if she didn't have nothing to do with it, what difference does all that make anyway?"

The answers I thought up to that were profane and insulting. I kept them to myself.

At Debro's again, we borrowed a loose-jointed touring car of at least three different makes, and drove down the East road, trying to trace the girl in the Chrysler. Our first stop was at the house of a man named Claude Baker. He was a lanky sallow person with an angular face three or four days behind the razor. His wife was probably younger than he, but looked older—a tired and faded thin woman who might have been pretty at one time. The oldest of their six children was a bow-legged, freckled girl of ten; the youngest was a fat and noisy infant in its first year. Some of the in-betweens were boys and some girls, but they all had colds in their heads. The whole Baker family came out on the porch to receive us. They hadn't seen her, they said: they were never up as early as seven o'clock. They knew the Carters by sight, but knew nothing about them. They asked more questions than Rolly and I did.

Shortly beyond the Baker house the road changed from gravel to asphalt. What we could see of the Chrysler's tracks seemed to show that it had been the last car over the road. Two miles from Baker's we stopped in front of a small bright green house surrounded by rose bushes. Rolly bawled:

"Harve! Hey, Harve!"

A big-boned man of thirty-five or so came to the door, said, "Hullo, Ben," and walked between the rose bushes to our car. His features, like his voice, were heavy, and he moved and spoke deliberately. His last name was Whidden. Rolly asked him if he had seen the Chrysler.

"Yes, Ben, I saw them," he said. "They went past around a quarter after seven this morning, hitting it up."

"They?" I asked, while Rolly asked: "Them?"

"There was a man and a woman—or a girl—in it. I didn't get a good look at them—just saw them whizz past. She was driving, a kind of small woman she looked like from here, with brown hair."

"What did the man look like?"

"Oh, he was maybe forty, and didn't look like he was very big either. A pinkish face, he had, and gray coat and hat."

"Ever see Mrs. Carter?" I asked.

"The bride living down the cove? No. I seen him, but not her. Was that her?"

I said we thought it was.

"The man wasn't him," he said. "He was somebody I never seen before."

"Know him again if you saw him?"

"I reckon I would—if I saw him going past like that."

Four miles beyond Whidden's we found the Chrysler. It was a foot or two off the road, on the left-hand side, standing on all fours with its radiator jammed into a eucalyptus tree. All its glass was shattered, and the front third of its metal was pretty well crumpled. It was empty. There was no blood in it. The deputy sheriff and I seemed to be the only people in the vicinity.

We ran around in circles, straining our eyes at the ground, and when we got through we knew what we had known at the beginning—the Chrysler had run into a eucalyptus tree. There were tire-marks on the road, and marks that could have been footprints on the ground by the car; but it was possible to find the same sort of marks in a hundred places along that, or any other, road. We got into our borrowed car again and drove on, asking questions wherever we found someone to question; and all the answers were: No, we didn't see her or them.

"What about this fellow Baker?" I asked Rolly as we turned around to go back. "Debro saw her alone. There was a man with her when she passed Whidden's. The Bakers saw nothing, and it was in their territory that the man must have joined her."

"Well," he said, argumentatively; "it could of happened that way, couldn't it?"

"Yeah, but it might be a good idea to do some more talking to them."

"If you want to," he consented without enthusiasm. "But don't go dragging me into any arguments with them. He's my wife's brother."

That made a difference. I asked:

"What sort of man is he?"

"Claude's kind of shiftless, all right. Like the old man says, he don't manage to raise nothing much but kids on that farm of his, but I never heard tell that he did anybody any harm."

"If you say he's all right, that's enough for me," I lied. "We won't bother him."

CHAPTER XV

I've Killed Him

S HERIFF FEENEY, fat, florid, and with a lot of brown mustache, and district attorney Vernon, sharp-featured, aggressive, and hungry for fame, came over from the county seat. They listened to our stories, looked the ground over, and agreed with Rolly that Gabrielle Collinson had killed her husband. When Marshal Dick Cotton—a pompous, unintelligent man in his forties—returned from San Francisco, he added his vote to the others. The coroner and his jury came to the same opinion, though officially they limited themselves to the usual "person or persons unknown," with recommendations involving the girl.

The time of Collinson's death was placed between eight and nine o'clock Friday night. No marks not apparently caused by his fall had been found on him. The pistol found in his room had been identified as his. No fingerprints were on it. I had an idea that some of the county officials half suspected me of having seen to that, though nobody said anything of that sort. Mary Nunez stuck to her story of being kept home by chills. She had a flock of Mexican witnesses to back it up. I couldn't find any to knock holes in it. We found no further trace of the man Whidden had seen. I tried the Bakers again, by myself, with no luck. The marshal's wife, a frail youngish woman with a weak pretty face and nice shy manners, who worked in the telegraph office, said Collinson had sent off his wire to me early Friday morning. He was pale and shaky, she said, with dark-rimmed, bloodshot eyes. She had supposed he was drunk, though she hadn't smelled alcohol on his breath.

Collinson's father and brother came down from San Francisco. Hubert Collinson, the father, was a big calm man who looked capable of taking as many more millions out of Pacific Coast lumber as he wanted. Laurence Collinson was a year or two older than his dead brother, and much like him in appearance. Both Collinson's were careful to say nothing that could be interpreted as suggesting they thought Gabrielle had

305

been responsible for Eric's death, but there was little doubt that they did think so.

Hubert Collinson said quietly to me, "Go ahead; get to the bottom of it;" and thus became the fourth client for whom the agency had been concerned with Gabrielle's affairs.

Madison Andrews came down from San Francisco. He and I talked in my hotel room. He sat on a chair by the window, cut a cube of tobacco from a yellowish plug, put it in his mouth, and decided that Collinson had committed suicide.

I sat on the side of the bed, set fire to a Fatima, and contradicted him:

"He wouldn't have torn up the bush if he'd gone over willingly."

"Then it was an accident. That was a dangerous road to be walked in the dark."

"I've stopped believing in accidents," I said. "And he had sent me an SOS. And there was the gun that had been fired in his room."

He leaned forward in his chair. His eyes were hard and watchful. He was a lawyer cross-examining a witness.

"You think Gabrielle was responsible?"

I wouldn't go that far. I said:

"He was murdered. He was murdered by—— I told you two weeks ago that we weren't through with that damned curse, and that the only way to get through with it was to have the Temple business sifted to the bottom."

"Yes, I remember," he said without quite sneering. "You advanced the theory that there was some connecting link between her parents' deaths and the trouble she had at the Haldorns'; but, as I recall it, you had no idea what the link might be. Don't you think that deficiency has a tendency to make your theory a little—say—vaporous?"

"Does it? Her father, step-mother, physician, and husband have been killed, one after the other, in less than two months; and her maid jailed for murder. All the people closest to her. Doesn't that look like a program? And"—I grinned at him—"are you sure it's not going further? And if it does, aren't you the next closest person to her?"

"Preposterous!" He was very much annoyed now. "We know about her parents' deaths, and about Riese's, and that

there was no link between them. We know that those responsible for Riese's murder are now either dead or in prison.
There's no getting around that. It's simply preposterous to
say there are links between one and another of these crimes
when we know there's none."

"We don't know anything of the kind," I insisted. "All we
know is that we haven't found the links. Who profits—or
could hope to profit—by what has happened?"

"Not a single person so far as I know."

"Suppose she died? Who'd get the estate?"

"I don't know. There are distant relations in England or
France, I dare say."

"That doesn't get us very far," I growled. "Anyway, nobody's tried to kill her. It's her friends who get the knock-
off."

The lawyer reminded me sourly that we couldn't say that
nobody had tried to kill her—or had succeeded—until we
found her. I couldn't argue with him about that. Her trail still
ended where the eucalyptus tree had stopped the Chrysler.

I gave him a piece of advice before he left:

"Whatever you believe, there's no sense in your taking unnecessary chances: remember that there might be a program,
and you might be next on it. It won't hurt to be careful."

He didn't thank me. He suggested, unpleasantly, that
doubtless I thought he should hire private detectives to guard
him.

Madison Andrews had offered a thousand-dollar reward for
information leading to discovery of the girl's whereabouts.
Hubert Collinson had offered another thousand, with an additional twenty-five hundred for the arrest and conviction of
his son's murderer. Half the population of the county had
turned bloodhound. Anywhere you went you found men
walking, or even crawling, around, searching fields, paths,
hills, and valleys for clues, and in the woods you were likely to
find more amateur gumshoes than trees.

Her photographs had been distributed and published
widely. The newspapers, from San Diego to Vancouver, gave
us a tremendous play, whooping it up in all the colored ink
they had. All the San Francisco and Los Angeles Continental
operatives who could be pulled off other jobs were checking

Quesada's exits, hunting, questioning, finding nothing. Radio broadcasters helped. The police everywhere, all the agency's branches, were stirred up.

And by Monday all this hubbub had brought us exactly nothing.

Monday afternoon I went back to San Francisco and told all my troubles to the Old Man. He listened politely, as if to some moderately interesting story that didn't concern him personally, smiled his meaningless smile, and, instead of any assistance, gave me his pleasantly expressed opinion that I'd eventually succeed in working it all out to a satisfactory conclusion.

Then he told me that Fitzstephan had phoned, trying to get in touch with me. "It may be important. He would have gone down to Quesada to find you if I hadn't told him I expected you."

I called Fitzstephan's number.

"Come up," he said. "I've got something. I don't know whether it's a fresh puzzle, or the key to a puzzle; but it's something."

I rode up Nob Hill on a cable car and was in his apartment within fifteen minutes.

"All right, spring it," I said as we sat down in his paper-, magazine-, and book-littered living room.

"Any trace of Gabrielle yet?" he asked.

"No. But spring the puzzle. Don't be literary with me, building up to climaxes and the like. I'm too crude for that— it'd only give me a bellyache. Just spread it out for me."

"You'll always be what you are," he said, trying to seem disappointed and disgusted, but not succeeding because he was—inwardly—too excited over something. "Somebody—a man—called me up early Saturday morning—half-past one— on the phone. He asked: 'Is this Fitzstephan?' I said: 'Yes;' and then the voice said: 'Well, I've killed him.' He said it just like that. I'm sure of those exact words, though they weren't very clear. There was a lot of noise on the line, and the voice seemed distant.

"I didn't know who it was—what he was talking about. I asked: 'Killed who? Who is this?' I couldn't understand any of his answer except the word 'money.' He said something about money, repeating it several times, but I could understand only that one word. There were some people here—the Marquards, Laura Joines with some man she'd brought, Ted and Sue Van Slack—and we had been in the middle of a literary free-for-all. I had a wisecrack on my tongue—something about Cabell being a romanticist in the same sense that the wooden horse was Trojan—and didn't want to be robbed of my opportunity to deliver it by this drunken joker, or whoever he was, on the phone. I couldn't make heads or tails of what he was saying, so I hung up and went back to my guests.

"It never occurred to me that the phone conversation could have had any meaning until yesterday morning, when I read about Collinson's death. I was at the Colemans', up in Ross. I went up there Saturday morning, for the week-end, having finally run Ralph to earth." He grinned. "And I made him glad enough to see me leave this morning." He became serious again. "Even after hearing of Collinson's death, I wasn't convinced that my phone call was of any importance, had any meaning. It was such a silly sort of thing. But of course I meant to tell you about it. But look—this was in my mail when I got home this morning."

He took an envelope from his pocket and tossed it over to me. It was a cheap and shiny white envelope of the kind you can buy anywhere. Its corners were dark and curled, as if it had been carried in a pocket for some time. Fitzstephan's name and address had been printed on it, with a hard pencil, by someone who was a rotten printer, or who wanted to be thought so. It was postmarked San Francisco, nine o'clock Saturday morning. Inside was a soiled and crookedly torn piece of brown wrapping paper, with one sentence—as poorly printed with pencil as the address—on it:

ANY BODY THAT WANTS MRS. CARTER
CAN HAVE SAME BY PAYING $10000——

There was no date, no salutation, no signature.

"She was seen driving away alone as late as seven Saturday morning," I said. "This was mailed here, eighty miles away, in time to be postmarked at nine—taken from the box in the first morning collection, say. That's one to get wrinkles over. But even that's not as funny as its coming to you instead of to Andrews, who's in charge of her affairs, or her father-in-law, who's got the most money."

"It is funny and it isn't," Fitzstephan replied. His lean face was eager. "There may be a point of light there. You know I recommended Quesada to Collinson, having spent a couple of months there last spring finishing *The Wall of Ashdod*, and gave him a card to a real estate dealer named Rolly—the deputy sheriff's father—there, introducing him as Eric Carter. A native of Quesada might not know she was Gabrielle Collinson, née Leggett. In that case he wouldn't know how to reach her people except through me, who had sent her and her husband there. So the letter is sent to me, but starts off *Anybody that*, to be passed on to the interested persons."

"A native might have done that," I said slowly; "or a kidnapper who wanted us to think he was a native, didn't want us to think he knew the Collinsons."

"Exactly. And as far as I know none of the natives knew my address here."

"How about Rolly?"

"Not unless Collinson gave it to him. I simply scribbled the introduction on the back of a card."

"Said anything to anybody else about the phone call and this letter?" I asked.

"I mentioned the call to the people who were here Friday night—when I thought it was a joke or a mistake. I haven't shown this to anybody else. In fact," he said, "I was a little doubtful about showing it at all—and still am. Is it going to make trouble for me?"

"Yeah, it will. But you oughtn't mind that. I thought you liked first-hand views of trouble. Better give me the names and addresses of your guests. If they and Coleman account for your whereabouts Friday night and over the week-end, nothing serious will happen to you; though you'll have to go down to Quesada and let the county officials third-degree you."

"Shall we go now?"

"I'm going back tonight. Meet me at the Sunset Hotel there in the morning. That'll give me time to work on the officials—so they won't throw you in the dungeon on sight."

I went back to the agency and put in a Quesada call. I

couldn't get hold of Vernon or the sheriff, but Cotton was reachable. I gave him the information I had got from Fitzstephan, promising to produce the novelist for questioning the next morning.

The marshal said the search for the girl was still going on without results. Reports had come in that she had been seen—practically simultaneously—in Los Angeles, Eureka, Carson City, Denver, Portland, Tijuana, Ogden, San Jose, Vancouver, Porterville, and Hawaii. All except the most ridiculous reports were being run out.

The telephone company could tell me that Owen Fitzstephan's Saturday morning phone-call had not been a long distance call, and that nobody in Quesada had called a San Francisco number either Friday night or Saturday morning.

Before I left the agency I visited the Old Man again, asking him if he would try to persuade the district attorney to turn Aaronia Haldorn and Tom Fink loose on bail.

"They're not doing us any good in jail," I explained, "and, loose, they might lead us somewhere if we shadowed them. He oughtn't to mind: he knows he hasn't a chance in the world of hanging murder-raps on them as things now stack up."

The Old Man promised to do his best, and to put an operative behind each of our suspects if they were sprung.

I went over to Madison Andrews' office. When I had told him about Fitzstephan's messages, and had given him our explanation of them, the lawyer nodded his bony white-thatched head and said:

"And whether that's the true explanation or not, the county authorities will now have to give up their absurd theory that Gabrielle killed her husband."

I shook my head sidewise.

"What?" he asked explosively.

"They're going to think the messages were cooked up to clear her," I predicted.

"Is that what you think?" His jaws got lumpy in front of his ears, and his tangled eyebrows came down over his eyes.

"I hope they weren't," I said; "because if it's a trick it's a damned childish one."

"How could it be?" he demanded loudly. "Don't talk nonsense. None of us knew anything then. The body hadn't been found when—"

"Yeah," I agreed; "and that's why, if it turns out to have been a stunt, it'll hang Gabrielle."

"I don't understand you," he said disagreeably. "One minute you're talking about somebody persecuting the girl, and the next minute you're talking as if you thought she was the murderer. Just what do you think?"

"Both can be true," I replied, no less disagreeably. "And what difference does it make what I think? It'll be up to the jury when she's found. The question now is: what are you going to do about the ten-thousand-dollar demand—if it's on the level?"

"What I'm going to do is increase the reward for her recovery, with an additional reward for the arrest of her abductor."

"That's the wrong play," I said. "Enough reward money has been posted. The only way to handle a kidnapping is to come across. I don't like it any more than you do, but it's the only way. Uncertainty, nervousness, fear, disappointment, can turn even a mild kidnapper into a maniac. Buy the girl free, and then do your fighting. Pay what's asked when it's asked."

He tugged at his ragged mustache, his jaw set obstinately, his eyes worried. But the jaw won out.

"I'm damned if I'll knuckle down," he said.

"That's your business." I got up and reached for my hat. "Mine's finding Collinson's murderer, and having her killed is more likely to help me than not."

He didn't say anything.

I went down to Hubert Collinson's office. He wasn't in, but I told Laurence Collinson my story, winding up:

"Will you urge your father to put up the money? And to have it ready to pass over as soon as the kidnapper's instructions come?"

"It won't be necessary to urge him," he said immediately. "Of course we shall pay whatever is required to ensure her safety."

CHAPTER XVI

The Night Hunt

I CAUGHT the 5:25 train south. It put me in Poston, a dusty town twice Quesada's size, at 7:30; and a rattle-trap stage, in which I was the only passenger, got me to my destination half an hour later. Rain was beginning to fall as I was leaving the stage across the street from the hotel.

Jack Santos, a San Francisco reporter, came out of the telegraph office and said: "Hello. Anything new?"

"Maybe, but I'll have to give it to Vernon first."

"He's in his room in the hotel, or was ten minutes ago. You mean the ransom letter that somebody got?"

"Yeah. He's already given it out?"

"Cotton started to, but Vernon headed him off, told us to let it alone."

"Why?"

"No reason at all except that it was Cotton giving it to us." Santos pulled the corners of his thin lips down. "It's been turned into a contest between Vernon, Feeney, and Cotton to see which can get his name and picture printed most."

"They been doing anything except that?"

"How can they?" he asked disgustedly. "They spend ten hours a day trying to make the front page, ten more trying to keep the others from making it, and they've got to sleep some time."

In the hotel I gave "nothing new" to some more reporters, registered again, left my bag in my room, and went down the hall to 204. Vernon opened the door when I had knocked. He was alone, and apparently had been reading the newspapers that made a pink, green, and white pile on the bed. The room was blue-gray with cigar smoke.

This district attorney was a thirty-year-old dark-eyed man who carried his chin up and out so that it was more prominent than nature had intended, bared all his teeth when he talked, and was very conscious of being a go-getter. He shook my hand briskly and said:

"I'm glad you're back. Come in. Sit down. Are there any new developments?"

"Cotton pass you the dope I gave him?"

"Yes." Vernon posed in front of me, hands in pockets, feet far apart. "What importance do you attach to it?"

"I advised Andrews to get the money ready. He won't. The Collinsons will."

"They will," he said, as if confirming a guess I had made. "And?" He held his lips back so that his teeth remained exposed.

"Here's the letter." I gave it to him. "Fitzstephan will be down in the morning."

He nodded emphatically, carried the letter closer to the light, and examined it and its envelope minutely. When he had finished he tossed it contemptuously to the table.

"Obviously a fraud," he said. "Now what, exactly, is this Fitzstephan's—is that the name?—story?"

I told him, word for word. When that was done, he clicked his teeth together, turned to the telephone, and told someone to tell Feeney that he—Mr. Vernon, district attorney—wished to see him immediately. Ten minutes later the sheriff came in wiping rain off his big brown mustache.

Vernon jerked a thumb at me and ordered: "Tell him."

I repeated what Fitzstephan had told me. The sheriff listened with an attentiveness that turned his florid face purple and had him panting. As the last word left my mouth, the district attorney snapped his fingers and said:

"Very well. He claims there were people in his apartment when the phone call came. Make a note of their names. He claims to have been in Ross over the week-end, with the—who were they? Ralph Coleman? Very well. Sheriff, see that those things are checked up. We'll learn how much truth there is to it."

I gave the sheriff the names and addresses Fitzstephan had given me. Feeney wrote them on the back of a laundry list and puffed out to get the county's crime-detecting machinery going on them.

Vernon hadn't anything to tell me. I left him to his newspapers and went downstairs. The effeminate night clerk beckoned me over to the desk and said:

"Mr. Santos asked me to tell you that services are being held in his room tonight."

I thanked the clerk and went up to Santos' room. He, three other newshounds, and a photographer were there. The game was stud. I was sixteen dollars ahead at twelve-thirty, when I was called to the phone to listen to the district attorney's aggressive voice:

"Will you come to my room immediately?"

"Yeah." I gathered up my hat and coat, telling Santos: "Cash me in. Important call. I always have one when I get a little ahead of the game."

"Vernon?" he asked as he counted my chips.

"Yeah."

"It can't be much," he sneered, "or he'd 've sent for Red too," nodding at the photographer, "so tomorrow's readers could see him holding it in his hand."

Cotton, Feeney, and Rolly were with the district attorney. Cotton—a medium-sized man with a round dull face dimpled in the chin—was dressed in black rubber boots, slicker, and hat that were wet and muddy. He stood in the middle of the room, his round eyes looking quite proud of their owner. Feeney, straddling a chair, was playing with his mustache; and his florid face was sulky. Rolly, standing beside him, rolling a cigarette, looked vaguely amiable as usual.

Vernon closed the door behind me and said irritably:

"Cotton thinks he's discovered something. He thinks——"

Cotton came forward, chest first, interrupting:

"I don't think nothing. I know durned well——"

Vernon snapped his fingers between the marshal and me, saying, just as snappishly:

"Never mind that. We'll go out there and see."

I stopped at my room for raincoat, gun, and flashlight. We went downstairs and climbed into a muddy car. Cotton drove. Vernon sat beside him. The rest of us sat in back. Rain beat on top and curtains, trickling in through cracks.

"A hell of a night to be chasing pipe dreams," the sheriff grumbled, trying to dodge a leak.

"Dick'd do a sight better minding his own business," Rolly agreed. "What's he got to do with what don't happen in Quesada?"

"If he'd take more care of what does happen there, he wouldn't have to worry about what's down the shore," Feeney said, and he and his deputy sniggered together.

Whatever point there was to this conversation was over my head. I asked:

"What's he up to?"

"Nothing," the sheriff told me. "You'll see that it's nothing, and, by God! I'm going to give him a piece of my mind. I don't know what's the matter with Vernon, paying any attention to him at all."

That didn't mean anything to me. I peeped out between curtains. Rain and darkness shut out the scenery, but I had an idea that we were headed for some point on the East road. It was a rotten ride—wet, noisy, and bumpy. It ended in as dark, wet, and muddy a spot as any we had gone through.

Cotton switched off the lights and got out, the rest of us following, slipping and slopping in wet clay up to our ankles.

"This is too damned much," the sheriff complained.

Vernon started to say something, but the marshal was walking away, down the road. We plodded after him, keeping together more by the sound of our feet squashing in the mud than by sight. It was black.

Presently we left the road, struggled over a high wire fence, and went on with less mud under our feet, but slippery grass. We climbed a hill. Wind blew rain down it into our faces. The sheriff was panting. I was sweating. We reached the top of the hill and went down its other side, with the rustle of sea-water on rocks ahead of us. Boulders began crowding grass out of our path as the descent got steeper. Once Cotton slipped to his knees, tripping Vernon, who saved himself by grabbing me. The sheriff's panting sounded like groaning now. We turned to the left, going along in single file, the surf close beside us. We turned to the left again, climbed a slope, and halted under a low shed without walls—a wooden roof propped on a dozen posts. Ahead of us a larger building made a black blot against the almost black sky.

Cotton whispered: "Wait till I see if his car's here."

He went away. The sheriff blew out his breath and grunted: "Damn such a expedition!" Rolly sighed.

The marshal returned jubilant.

"It ain't there, so he ain't here," he said. "Come on, it'll get us out of the wet anyways."

We followed him up a muddy path between bushes to the black house, up on its back porch. We stood there while he got a window open, climbed through, and unlocked the door. Our flashlights, used for the first time now, showed us a small neat kitchen. We went in, muddying the floor.

Cotton was the only member of the party who showed any enthusiasm. His face, from hat-brim to dimpled chin, was the face of a master of ceremonies who is about to spring what he is sure will be a delightful surprise. Vernon regarded him skeptically, Feeney disgustedly, Rolly indifferently, and I—who didn't know what we were there for—no doubt curiously.

It developed that we were there to search the house. We did it, or at least Cotton did it while the rest of us pretended to help him. It was a small house. There was only one room on the ground-floor besides the kitchen, and only one—an unfinished bedroom—above. A grocer's bill and a tax-receipt in a table-drawer told me whose house it was—Harvey Whidden's. He was the big-boned deliberate man who had seen the stranger in the Chrysler with Gabrielle Collinson.

We finished the ground-floor with a blank score, and went upstairs. There, after ten minutes of poking around, we found something. Rolly pulled it out from between bed-slats and mattress. It was a small flat bundle wrapped in a white linen towel.

Cotton dropped the mattress, which he had been holding up for the deputy to look under, and joined us as we crowded around Rolly's package. Vernon took it from the deputy sheriff and unrolled it on the bed. Inside the towel were a package of hair-pins, a lace-edged white handkerchief, a silver hair-brush and comb engraved G.D.L., and a pair of black kid gloves, small and feminine.

I was more surprised than anyone else could have been.

"G.D.L.," I said, to be saying something, "could be Gabrielle Something Leggett—Mrs. Collinson's name before she was married."

Cotton said triumphantly: "You're durned right it could."

A heavy voice said from the doorway:

"Have you got a search-warrant? What the hell are you doing here if you haven't? It's burglary, and you know it."

Harvey Whidden was there. His big body, in a yellow slicker, filled the doorway. His heavy-featured face was dark and angry.

Vernon began: "Whidden, I——"

The marshal screamed, "It's him!" and pulled a gun from under his coat.

I pushed his arm as he fired at the man in the doorway. The bullet hit the wall.

Whidden's face was now more astonished than angry. He jumped back through the doorway and ran downstairs. Cotton, upset by my push, straightened himself up, cursed me, and ran out after Whidden. Vernon, Feeney, and Rolly stood staring after them.

I said: "This is good clean sport, but it makes no sense to me. What's it all about?"

Nobody told me. I said: "This comb and brush were on Mrs. Collinson's table when we searched the house, Rolly."

The deputy sheriff nodded uncertainly, still staring at the door. No noise came through it now. I asked:

"Would there be any special reason for Cotton framing Whidden?"

The sheriff said: "They ain't good friends." (I had noticed that.) "What do you think, Vern?"

The district attorney took his gaze from the door, rolled the things in their towel again, and stuffed the bundle in his pocket. "Come on," he snapped, and strode downstairs.

The front door was open. We saw nothing, heard nothing, of Cotton and Whidden. A Ford—Whidden's—stood at the front gate soaking up rain. We got into it. Vernon took the wheel, and drove to the house in the cove. We hammered at its door until it was opened by an old man in gray underwear, put there as caretaker by the sheriff.

The old man told us that Cotton had been there at eight o'clock that night, just, he said, to look around again. He, the caretaker, didn't know no reason why the marshal had to be watched, so he hadn't bothered him, letting him do what he wanted, and, so far as he knew, the marshal hadn't taken any of the Collinsons' property, though of course he might of.

Vernon and Feeney gave the old man hell, and we went back to Quesada.

Rolly was with me on the back seat. I asked him:

"Who is this Whidden? Why should Cotton pick on him?"

"Well, for one thing, Harve's got kind of a bad name, from being mixed up in the rum-running that used to go on here, and from being in trouble now and then."

"Yeah? And for another thing?"

The deputy sheriff frowned, hesitating, hunting for words; and before he had found them we were stopping in front of a vine-covered cottage on a dark street corner. The district attorney led the way to its front porch and rang the bell.

After a little while a woman's voice sounded overhead:

"Who's there?"

We had to retreat to the steps to see her—Mrs. Cotton at a second-story window.

"Dick got home yet?" Vernon asked.

"No, Mr. Vernon, he hasn't. I was getting worried. Wait a minute; I'll come down."

"Don't bother," he said. "We won't wait. I'll see him in the morning."

"No. Wait," she said urgently and vanished from the window.

A moment later she opened the front door. Her blue eyes were dark and excited. She had on a rose bathrobe.

"You needn't have bothered," the district attorney said. "There was nothing special. We got separated from him a little while ago, and just wanted to know if he'd got back yet. He's all right."

"Was——?" Her hands worked folds of her bathrobe over her thin breasts. "Was he after——after Harvey——Harvey Whidden?"

Vernon didn't look at her when he said, "Yes;" and he said it without showing his teeth. Feeney and Rolly looked as uncomfortable as Vernon.

Mrs. Cotton's face turned pink. Her lower lip trembled, blurring her words.

"Don't believe him, Mr. Vernon. Don't believe a word he tells you. Harve didn't have anything to do with those

Collinsons, with neither one of them. Don't let Dick tell you he did. He didn't."

Vernon looked at his feet and didn't say anything. Rolly and Feeney were looking intently out through the open door—we were standing just inside it—at the rain. Nobody seemed to have any intention of speaking.

I asked, "No?" putting more doubt in my voice than I actually felt.

"No, he didn't," she cried, turning her face to me. "He couldn't. He couldn't have had anything to do with it." The pink went out of her face, leaving it white and desperate. "He—he was here that night—all night—from before seven until daylight."

"Where was your husband?"

"Up in the city, at his mother's."

"What's her address?"

She gave it to me, a Noe Street number.

"Did anybody——?"

"Aw, come on," the sheriff protested, still staring at the rain. "Ain't that enough?"

Mrs. Cotton turned from me to the district attorney again, taking hold of one of his arms.

"Don't tell it on me, please, Mr. Vernon," she begged. "I don't know what I'd do if it came out. But I had to tell you. I couldn't let him put it on Harve. Please, you won't tell anybody else?"

The district attorney swore that under no circumstances would he, or any of us, repeat what she had told us to anybody; and the sheriff and his deputy agreed with vigorous red-faced nods.

But when we were in the Ford again, away from her, they forgot their embarrassment and became manhunters again. Within ten minutes they had decided that Cotton, instead of going to San Francisco to his mother's Friday night, had remained in Quesada, had killed Collinson, had gone to the city to phone Fitzstephan and mail the letter, and then had returned to Quesada in time to kidnap Mrs. Collinson; planning from the first to plant the evidence against Whidden, with whom he had long been on bad terms, having always suspected what everybody else knew—that Whidden was Mrs. Cotton's lover.

The sheriff—he whose chivalry had kept me from more thoroughly questioning the woman a few minutes ago—now laughed his belly up and down.

"That's rich," he gurgled. "Him out framing Harve, and Harve getting himself a alibi in *his* bed. Dick's face ought to be a picture for Puck when we spring that on him. Let's find him tonight."

"Better wait," I advised. "It won't hurt to check up his San Francisco trip before we put it to him. All we've got on him so far is that he tried to frame Whidden. If he's the murderer and kidnapper he seems to have gone to a lot of unnecessary foolishness."

Feeney scowled at me and defended their theory:

"Maybe he was more interested in framing Harve than anything else."

"Maybe," I said; "but it won't hurt to give him a little more rope and see what he does with it."

Feeney was against that. He wanted to grab the marshal *pronto*; but Vernon reluctantly backed me up. We dropped Rolly at his house and returned to the hotel.

In my room, I put in a phone-call for the agency in San Francisco. While I was waiting for the connection knuckles tapped my door. I opened it and let in Jack Santos, pajamaed, bathrobed, and slippered.

"Have a nice ride?" he asked, yawning.

"Swell."

"Anything break?"

"Not for publication, but—under the hat—the new angle is that our marshal is trying to hang the job on his wife's boy friend—with home-made evidence. The other big officials think Cotton turned the trick himself."

"That ought to get them all on the front page." Santos sat on the foot of my bed and lit a cigarette. "Ever happen to hear that Feeney was Cotton's rival for the telegraphing hand of the present Mrs. Cotton, until she picked the marshal—the triumph of dimples over mustachios?"

"No," I admitted. "What of it?"

"How do I know? I just happened to pick it up. A fellow in the garage told me."

"How long ago?"

"That they were rival suitors? Less than a couple of years."

I got my San Francisco call, and told Field—the agency night-man—to have somebody check up the marshal's Noe Street visit. Santos yawned and went out while I was talking. I went to bed when I had finished.

CHAPTER XVII

Below Dull Point

THE TELEPHONE BELL brought me out of sleep a little before ten the following morning. Mickey Linehan, talking from San Francisco, told me Cotton had arrived at his mother's house at between seven and seven-thirty Saturday morning. The marshal had slept for five or six hours—telling his mother he had been up all night laying for a burglar—and had left for home at six that evening.

Cotton was coming in from the street when I reached the lobby. He was red-eyed and weary, but still determined.

"Catch Whidden?" I asked.

"No, durn him, but I will. Say, I'm glad you jiggled my arm, even if it did let him get away. I——well, sometimes a fellow's enthusiasm gets the best of his judgment."

"Yeah. We stopped at your house on our way back, to see how you'd made out."

"I ain't been home yet," he said. "I put in the whole durned night hunting for that fellow. Where's Vern and Feeney?"

"Pounding their ears. Better get some sleep yourself," I suggested. "I'll ring you up if anything happens."

He set off for home. I went into the café for breakfast. I was half through when Vernon joined me there. He had telegrams from the San Francisco police department and the Marin County sheriff's office, confirming Fitzstephan's alibis.

"I got my report on Cotton," I said. "He reached his mother's at seven or a little after Saturday morning, and left at six that evening."

"Seven or a little after?" Vernon didn't like that. If the marshal had been in San Francisco at that time he could hardly have been abducting the girl. "Are you sure?"

"No, but that's the best we've been able to do so far. There's Fitzstephan now." Looking through the café door, I had seen the novelist's lanky back at the hotel desk. "Excuse me a moment."

I went over and got Fitzstephan, bringing him back to the

table with me, and introducing him to Vernon. The district attorney stood up to shake hands with him, but was too busy with thoughts of Cotton to bother now with anything else. Fitzstephan said he had had breakfast before leaving the city, and ordered a cup of coffee. Just then I was called to the phone.

Cotton's voice, but excited almost beyond recognition:

"For God's sake get Vernon and Feeney and come up here."

"What's the matter?" I asked.

"Hurry! Something awful's happened. Hurry!" he cried, and hung up.

I went back to the table and told Vernon about it. He jumped up, upsetting Fitzstephan's coffee. Fitzstephan got up too, but hesitated, looking at me.

"Come on," I invited him. "Maybe this'll be one of the things you like."

Fitzstephan's car was in front of the hotel. The marshal's house was only seven blocks away. Its front door was open. Vernon knocked on the frame as we went in, but we didn't wait for an answer.

Cotton met us in the hall. His eyes were round and blood-shot in a face as hard-white as marble. He tried to say something, but couldn't get the words past his tight-set teeth. He gestured towards the door behind him with a fist that was clenched on a piece of brown paper.

Through the doorway we saw Mrs. Cotton. She was lying on the blue-carpeted floor. She had on a pale blue dress. Her throat was covered with dark bruises. Her lips and tongue—the tongue, swollen, hung out—were darker than the bruises. Her eyes were wide open, bulging, up-turned, and dead. Her hand, when I touched it, was still warm.

Cotton, following us into the room, held out the brown paper in his hand. It was an irregularly torn piece of wrapping paper, covered on both sides with writing—nervously, un-evenly, hastily scribbled in pencil. A softer pencil had been used than on Fitzstephan's message, and the paper was a darker brown.

I was closest to Cotton. I took the paper, and read it aloud hurriedly, skipping unnecessary words:

"Whidden came last night . . . said husband after him . . . frame him for Collinson trouble . . . I hid him in garret . . . he said only way to save him was to say he was here Friday night . . . said if I didn't they'd hang him . . . when Mr. Vernon came Harve said he'd kill me if I didn't . . . so I said it . . . but he wasn't here that night . . . I didn't know he was guilty then . . . told me afterwards . . . tried to kidnap her Thursday night . . . husband nearly caught him . . . came in office after Collinson sent telegram and saw it . . . followed him and killed him . . . went to San Francisco, drinking whiskey . . . decided to go through with kidnapping anyway . . . phoned man who knew her to try to learn who he could get money from . . . too drunk to talk good . . . wrote letter and came back . . . met her on road . . . took her to old bootleggers' hiding place somewhere below Dull Point . . . goes in boat . . . afraid he'll kill me . . . locked in garret . . . writing while he's down getting food . . . murderer . . . I won't help him . . . Daisy Cotton."

The sheriff and Rolly had arrived while I was reading it. Feeney's face was as white and set as Cotton's.

Vernon bared his teeth at the marshal, snarling:

"You wrote that."

Feeney grabbed it from my hands, looked at it, shook his head, and said hoarsely:

"No, that's her writing, all right."

Cotton was babbling:

"No, before God, I didn't. I planted that stuff on him, I'll admit that, but that was all. I come home and find her like this. I swear to God!"

"Where were you Friday night?" Vernon asked.

"Here, watching the house. I thought—I thought he might—— But he wasn't here that night. I watched till daybreak and then went to the city. I didn't——"

The sheriff's bellow drowned the rest of Cotton's words. The sheriff was waving the dead woman's letter. He bellowed:

"Below Dull Point! What are we waiting for?"

He plunged out of the house, the rest of us following. Cotton and Rolly rode to the waterfront in the deputy's car. Vernon, the sheriff, and I rode with Fitzstephan. The sheriff cried throughout the short trip, tears splashing on the automatic pistol he held in his lap.

At the waterfront we changed from the cars to a green and white motor boat run by a pink-cheeked, tow-headed youngster called Tim. Tim said he didn't know anything about any bootleggers' hiding places below Dull Point, but if there was one there he could find it. In his hands the boat produced a lot of speed, but not enough for Feeney and Cotton. They stood together in the bow, guns in their fists, dividing their time between straining forward and yelling back for more speed.

Half an hour from the dock, we rounded a blunt promontory that the others called Dull Point, and Tim cut down our speed, putting the boat in closer to the rocks that jumped up high and sharp at the water's edge. We were now all eyes—eyes that soon ached from staring under the noon sun but kept on staring. Twice we saw clefts in the rock-walled shore, pushed hopefully in to them, saw that they were blind, leading nowhere, opening into no hiding-places.

The third cleft was even more hopeless-looking at first sight, but, now that Dull Point was some distance behind us, we couldn't pass up anything. We slid in to the cleft, got close enough to decide that it was another blind one, gave it up, and told Tim to go on. We were washed another couple of feet nearer before the tow-headed boy could bring the boat around.

Cotton, in the bow, bent forward from the waist and yelled:

"Here it is."

He pointed his gun at one side of the cleft. Tim let the boat drift in another foot or so. Craning our necks, we could see that what we had taken for the shore-line on that side was actually a high, thin, saw-toothed ledge of rock, separated from the cliff at this end by twenty feet of water.

"Put her in," Feeney ordered.

Tim frowned at the water, hesitated, said: "She can't make it."

The boat backed him up by shuddering suddenly under our feet, with an unpleasant rasping noise.

"That be damned!" the sheriff bawled. "Put her in."

Tim took a look at the sheriff's wild face, and put her in.

The boat shuddered under our feet again, more violently, and now there was a tearing sound in with the rasping, but we went through the opening and turned down behind the saw-tooth ledge.

We were in a v-shaped pocket, twenty feet wide where we had come in, say eighty feet long, high-walled, inaccessible by land, accessible by sea only as we had come. The water that floated us—and was coming in rapidly to sink us—ran a third of the way down the pocket. White sand paved the other two thirds. A small boat was resting its nose on the edge of the sand. It was empty. Nobody was in sight. There didn't seem to be anywhere for anybody to hide. There were footprints, large and small, in the sand, empty tin cans, and the remains of a fire.

"Harve's," Rolly said, nodding at the boat.

Our boat grounded beside it. We jumped, splashed, ashore —Cotton ahead, the others spread out behind him.

As suddenly as if he had sprung out of the air, Harvey Whidden appeared in the far end of the v, standing in the sand, a rifle in his hands. Anger and utter astonishment were mixed in his heavy face, and in his voice when he yelled:

"You God-damned double-crossing——" The noise his rifle made blotted out the rest of his words.

Cotton had thrown himself down sideways. The rifle bullet missed him by inches, sang between Fitzstephan and me, nicking his hat-brim, and splattered on the rocks behind. Four of our guns went off together, some more than once.

Whidden went over backwards, his feet flying in the air. He was dead when we got to him—three bullets in his chest, one in his head.

We found Gabrielle Collinson cowering back in the corner of a narrow-mouthed hole in the rock wall—a long triangular cave whose mouth had been hidden from our view by the slant at which it was set. There were blankets in there, spread over a pile of dried seaweed, some canned goods, a lantern, and another rifle.

The girl's small face was flushed and feverish, and her voice was hoarse: she had a cold in her chest. She was too frightened at first to tell us anything coherent, and apparently recognized neither Fitzstephan nor me.

The boat we had come in was out of commission. Whidden's boat couldn't be trusted to carry more than three with safety through the surf. Tim and Rolly set off for Quesada in it, to get us a larger vessel. It was an hour-and-a-half's round trip. While they were gone we worked on the girl, soothing her, assuring her that she was among friends, that there was nothing to be afraid of now. Her eyes gradually became less scary, her breathing easier, and her nails less tightly pressed into her palms. At the end of an hour she was answering our questions.

She said she knew nothing of Whidden's attempt to kidnap her Thursday night, nothing of the telegram Eric had sent me. She sat up all Friday night waiting for him to return from his walk, and at daylight, frantic at his failure to return, had gone to look for him. She found him—as I had. Then she went back to the house and tried to commit suicide—to put an end to the curse by shooting herself.

"I tried twice," she whispered; "but I couldn't. I couldn't. I was too much a coward. I couldn't keep the pistol pointing at myself while I did it. I tried the first time to shoot myself in the temple, and then in the breast; but I hadn't the courage. Each time I jerked it away just before I fired. And after the second time I couldn't even get courage to try again."

She changed her clothes then—evening clothes, now muddy and torn from her search—and drove away from the house. She didn't say where she had intended going. She didn't seem to know. Probably she hadn't had any destination—was simply going away from the place where the curse had settled on her husband.

She hadn't driven far when she had seen a machine coming towards her, driven by the man who had brought her here. He had turned his car across the road in front of her, blocking the road. Trying to avoid hitting his car, she had run into a tree—and hadn't known anything else until she had awakened in the cave. She had been here since then. The man had left her here alone most of the time. She had neither strength nor courage to escape by swimming, and there was no other way out.

The man had told her nothing, had asked her nothing, had addressed no words to her except to say, "Here's some food," or, "Till I bring you some water, you'll have to get along on canned tomatoes when you're thirsty," or other things of that sort. She never remembered having seen him before. She didn't know his name. He was the only man she had seen since her husband's death.

"What did he call you?" I asked. "Mrs. Carter? Or Mrs. Collinson?"

She frowned thoughtfully, then shook her head, saying:

"I don't think he ever called me by name. He never spoke unless he had to, and he wasn't here very much. I was usually alone."

"How long had he been here this time?"

"Since before daylight. The noise of his boat woke me up."

"Sure? This is important. Are you sure he's been here since daylight?"

"Yes."

I was sitting on my heels in front of her. Cotton was standing on my left, beside the sheriff. I looked up at the marshal and said:

"That puts it up to you, Cotton. Your wife was still warm when we saw her—after eleven."

He goggled at me, stammering: "Wh-what's that you say?"

On the other side of me I heard Vernon's teeth click together sharply.

I said:

"Your wife was afraid Whidden would kill her, and wrote that statement. But he didn't kill her. He's been here since daylight. You found the statement, learned from it that they *had* been too friendly. Well, what did you do then?"

"That's a lie," he cried. "There ain't a word of truth in it. She was dead there when I found her. I never—"

"You killed her," Vernon barked at him over my head. "You choked her, counting on that statement to throw suspicion on Whidden."

"That's a lie," the marshal cried again, and made the mistake of trying to get his gun out.

Feeney slugged him, dropping him, and had hand-cuffs on his wrists before he could get up again.

CHAPTER XVIII

The Pineapple

I T DOESN'T make sense," I said. "It's dizzy. When we grab our man—or woman—we're going to find it's a goof, and Napa will get it instead of the gallows."

"That," Owen Fitzstephan said, "is characteristic of you. You're stumped, bewildered, flabbergasted. Do you admit you've met your master, have run into a criminal too wily for you? Not you. He's outwitted you: therefore he's an idiot or a lunatic. Now really. Of course there's a certain unexpected modesty to that attitude."

"But he's got to be goofy," I insisted. "Look: Mayenne marries——"

"Are you," he asked disgustedly, "going to recite that catalogue again?"

"You've got a flighty mind. That's no good in this business. You don't catch murderers by amusing yourself with interesting thoughts. You've got to sit down to all the facts you can get and turn them over and over till they click."

"If that's your technic, you'll have to put up with it," he said; "but I'm damned if I see why I should suffer. You recited the Mayenne-Leggett-Collinson history step by step last night at least half a dozen times. You've done nothing else since breakfast this morning. I'm getting enough of it. Nobody's mysteries ought to be as tiresome as you're making this one."

"Hell," I said; "I sat up half the night after you went to bed and recited it to myself. You got to turn them over and over, my boy, till they click."

"I like the Nick Carter school better. Aren't you even threatened with any of the conclusions that this turning-them-over-and-over is supposed to lead to?"

"Yeah, I've got one. It's that Vernon and Feeney are wrong in thinking that Cotton was working with Whidden on the kidnapping, and double-crossed him. According to them, Cotton thought up the plan and persuaded Whidden to do the rough stuff while the marshal used his official position to cover him up. Collinson stumbled on the plan and was killed.

330

Then Cotton made his wife write that statement—it's phony, right enough, was dictated to her—killed her, and led us to Whidden. Cotton was the first man ashore when we got to the hiding place—to make sure Whidden was killed resisting arrest before he could talk."

Fitzstephan ran long fingers through his sorrel hair and asked:

"Don't you think jealousy would have given Cotton motive enough?"

"Yeah. But where's Whidden's motive for putting himself in Cotton's hands? Besides, where does that layout fit in with the Temple racket?"

"Are you sure," Fitzstephan asked, "that you're right in thinking there must be a connection?"

"Yeah. Gabrielle's father, step-mother, physician, and husband have been slaughtered in less than a handful of weeks—all the people closest to her. That's enough to tie it all together for me. If you want more links, I can point them out to you. Upton and Ruppert were the apparent instigators of the first trouble, and got killed. Haldorn of the second, and got killed. Whidden of the third, and got killed. Mrs. Leggett killed her husband; Cotton apparently killed his wife; and Haldorn would have killed his if I hadn't blocked him. Gabrielle, as a child, was made to kill her mother; Gabrielle's maid was made to kill Riese, and nearly me. Leggett left behind him a statement explaining—not altogether satisfactorily—everything, and was killed. So did and was Mrs. Cotton. Call any of these pairs coincidences. Call any couple of pairs coincidences. You'll still have enough left to point at somebody who's got a system he likes, and sticks to it."

Fitzstephan squinted thoughtfully at me, agreeing:

"There may be something in that. It does, as you put it, look like the work of one mind."

"And a goofy one."

"Be obstinate about it," he said. "But even your goof must have a motive."

"Why?"

"Damn your sort of mind," he said with good-natured impatience. "If he had no motive connected with Gabrielle, why should his crimes be connected with her?"

"We don't know that all of them are," I pointed out. "We only know of the ones that are."

He grinned and said:

"You'll go any distance to disagree, won't you?"

I said:

"Then again, maybe the goof's crimes are connected with Gabrielle because he is."

Fitzstephan let his gray eyes go sleepy over that, pursing his mouth, looking at the door closed between my room and Gabrielle's.

"All right," he said, looking at me again. "Who's your maniac close to Gabrielle?"

"The closest and goofiest person to Gabrielle is Gabrielle herself."

Fitzstephan got up and crossed the hotel room—I was sitting on the edge of the bed—to shake my hand with solemn enthusiasm.

"You're wonderful," he said. "You amaze me. Ever have night sweats? Put out your tongue and say, 'Ah.'"

"Suppose," I began, but was interrupted by a feeble tapping on the corridor door.

I went to the door and opened it. A thin man of my own age and height in wrinkled black clothes stood in the corridor. He was breathing heavily through a red-veined nose, and his small brown eyes were timid.

"You know me," he said apologetically.

"Yeah. Come in." I introduced him to Fitzstephan: "This is the Tom Fink who was one of Haldorn's helpers in the Temple of the Holy Grail."

Fink looked reproachfully at me, then dragged his crumpled hat from his head and crossed the room to shake Fitzstephan's hand. That done, he returned to me and said, almost whispering:

"I come down to tell you something."

"Yeah?"

He fidgeted, turning his hat around and around in his hands. I winked at Fitzstephan and went out with Fink. In the corridor, I closed the door and stopped, saying: "Let's have it."

Fink rubbed his lips with his tongue and then with the back of one scrawny hand. He said, in his half-whisper:

"I come down to tell you something I thought you ought to know."

"Yeah?"

"It's about this fellow Whidden that was killed."

"Yeah?"

"He was——"

The door to my room split open. Floors, walls, and ceiling wriggled under, around, and over us. There was too much noise to be heard—a roar that was felt bodily. Tom Fink was carried away from me, backward. I had sense enough to throw myself down as I was blown in the opposite direction, and got nothing worse out of it than a bruised shoulder when I hit the wall. A door-frame stopped Fink, wickedly, its edge catching the back of his head. He came forward again, folding over to lie face-down on the floor, still except for blood running from his head.

I got up and made for my room. Fitzstephan was a mangled pile of flesh and clothing in the center of the floor. My bed was burning. There was neither glass nor wire netting left in the window. I saw these things mechanically as I staggered toward Gabrielle's room. The connecting door was open—perhaps blown open.

She was crouching on all fours in bed, facing the foot, her feet on the pillows. Her nightdress was torn at one shoulder. Her green-brown eyes—glittering under brown curls that had tumbled down to hide her forehead—were the eyes of an animal gone trap-crazy. Saliva glistened on her pointed chin. There was nobody else in the room.

"Where's the nurse?" My voice was choked.

The girl said nothing. Her eyes kept their crazy terror focused on me.

"Get under the covers," I ordered. "Want to get pneumonia?"

She didn't move. I walked around to the side of the bed, lifting an end of the covers with one hand, reaching out the other to help her, saying:

"Come on, get inside."

She made a queer noise deep in her chest, dropped her head, and put her sharp teeth into the back of my hand. It hurt. I put her under the covers, returned to my room, and was pushing my burning mattress through the window when people began to arrive.

"Get a doctor," I called to the first of them; "and stay out of here."

I had got rid of the mattress by the time Mickey Linehan pushed through the crowd that was now filling the corridor. Mickey blinked at what was left of Fitzstephan, at me, and asked:

"What the hell?"

His big loose mouth sagged at the ends, looking like a grin turned upside down.

I licked burnt fingers and asked unpleasantly:

"What the hell does it look like?"

"More trouble, sure." The grin turned right side up on his red face. "Sure—you're here."

Ben Rolly came in. "Tch, tch, tch," he said, looking around. "What do you suppose happened?"

"Pineapple," I said.

"Tch, tch, tch."

Doctor George came in and knelt beside the wreck of Fitzstephan. George had been Gabrielle's physician since her return from the cave the previous day. He was a short, chunky, middle-aged man with a lot of black hair everywhere except on his lips, cheeks, chin, and nose-bridge. His hairy hands moved over Fitzstephan.

"What's Fink been doing?" I asked Mickey.

"Hardly any. I got on his tail when they sprung him yesterday noon. He went from the hoosgow to a hotel on Kearny Street and got himself a room. He spent most of the afternoon in the Public Library, reading the newspaper files on the girl's troubles, from beginning to date. He ate after that, and went back to the hotel. He could have back-doored me. If he didn't, he camped in his room all night. It was dark at midnight when I knocked off so I could be on the job again at six a.m. He showed at seven-something, got breakfast, and grabbed a rattler for Poston, changed to the stage for here, and came straight to the hotel, asking for you. That's the crop."

"Damn my soul!" the kneeling doctor exclaimed. "The man's not dead."

I didn't believe him. Fitzstephan's right arm was gone, and most of his right leg. His body was too twisted to see what was left of it, but there was only one side to his face. I said:

"There's another one out in the hall, with his head knocked in."

"Oh, he's all right," the doctor muttered without looking up. "But this one—well, damn my soul!"

He scrambled to his feet and began ordering this and that. He was excited. A couple of men came in from the corridor. The woman who had been nursing Gabrielle Collinson—a Mrs. Herman—joined them, and another man with a blanket. They took Fitzstephan away.

"That fellow out in the hall Fink?" Rolly asked.

"Yeah." I told him what Fink had told me, adding: "He hadn't finished when the blow-up came."

"Suppose the bomb was meant for him, meant to keep him from finishing?"

Mickey said: "Nobody followed him down from the city, except me."

"Maybe," I said. "Better see what they're doing with him, Mick."

Mickey went out.

"This window was closed," I told Rolly. "There was no noise as of something being thrown through the glass just before the explosion; and there's no broken window-glass inside the room. The screen was over it, too, so we can say the pineapple wasn't chucked in through the window."

Rolly nodded vaguely, looking at the door to Gabrielle's room.

"Fink and I were in the corridor talking," I went on. "I ran straight back through here to her room. Nobody could have got out of her room after the explosion without my seeing them—or hearing them. There wasn't finger-snapping time between my losing sight of her corridor-door from the outside, and seeing it again from the inside. The screen over her window is still OK."

"Mrs. Herman wasn't in there with her?" Rolly asked.

"She was supposed to be, but wasn't. We'll find out about

that. There's no use thinking Mrs. Collinson chucked the bomb. She's been in bed since we brought her back from Dull Point yesterday. She couldn't have had the bomb planted there because she had no way of knowing that she was going to occupy the room. Nobody's been in there since except you, Feeney, Vernon, the doctor, the nurse, and me."

"I wasn't going to say she had anything to do with it," the deputy sheriff mumbled. "What does she say?"

"Nothing yet. We'll try her now, though I doubt if it'll get us much."

It didn't. Gabrielle lay in the middle of the bed, the covers gathered close to her chin as if she was prepared to duck down under them at the first alarm, and shook her head No to everything we asked, whether the answer fit or didn't.

The nurse came in, a big-breasted, red-haired woman of forty-something with a face that seemed honest because it was homely, freckled, and blue-eyed. She swore on the Gideon Bible that she had been out of the room for less than five minutes, just going downstairs for some stationery, intending to write a letter to her nephew in Vallejo while her patient was sleeping; and that was the only time she had been out of the room all day. She had met nobody in the corridor, she said.

"You left the door unlocked?" I asked.

"Yes, so I wouldn't be as likely to wake her when I came back."

"Where's the stationery you got?"

"I didn't get it. I heard the explosion and ran back up-stairs." Fear came into her face, turning the freckles to ghastly spots. "You don't think——!"

"Better look after Mrs. Collinson," I said gruffly.

CHAPTER XIX

The Degenerate

ROLLY and I went back to my room, closing the connecting door. He said:

"Tch, tch, tch. I'd of thought Mrs. Herman was the last person in the world to——"

"You ought to've," I grumbled. "You recommended her. Who is she?"

"She's Tod Herman's wife. He's got the garage. She used to be a trained nurse before she married Tod. I thought she was all right."

"She got a nephew in Vallejo?"

"Uh-huh; that would be the Schultz kid that works at Mare Island. How do you suppose she come to get mixed up in——?"

"Probably didn't, or she would have had the writing paper she went after. Put somebody here to keep people out till we can borrow a San Francisco bomb-expert to look it over."

The deputy called one of the men in from the corridor, and we left him looking important in the room. Mickey Linehan was in the lobby when we got there.

"Fink's got a cracked skull. He's on his way to the county hospital with the other wreck."

"Fitzstephan dead yet?" I asked.

"Nope, and the doc thinks if they get him over where they got the right kind of implements they can keep him from dying. God knows what for—the shape he's in! But that's just the kind of stuff a croaker thinks is a lot of fun."

"Was Aaronia Haldorn sprung with Fink?" I asked.

"Yes. Al Mason's tailing her."

"Call up the Old Man and see if Al's reported anything on her. Tell the Old Man what's happened here, and see if they've found Andrews."

"Andrews?" Rolly asked as Mickey headed for the phone. "What's the matter with him?"

"Nothing that I know of; only we haven't been able to find him to tell him Mrs. Collinson has been rescued. His office hasn't seen him since yesterday morning, and nobody will say they know where he is."

"Tch, tch, tch. Is there any special reason for wanting him?"

"I don't want her on my hands the rest of my life," I said. "He's in charge of her affairs, he's responsible for her, and I want to turn her over to him."

Rolly nodded vaguely.

We went outside and asked all the people we could find all the questions we could think of. None of the answers led anywhere, except to repeated assurance that the bomb hadn't been chucked through the window. We found six people who had been in sight of that side of the hotel immediately before, and at the time of, the explosion; and none of them had seen anything that could be twisted into bearing on the bomb-throwing.

Mickey came away from the phone with the information that Aaronia Haldorn, when released from the city prison, had gone to the home of a family named Jeffries in San Mateo, and had been there ever since; and that Dick Foley, hunting for Andrews, had hopes of locating him in Sausalito.

District attorney Vernon and sheriff Feeney, with a horde of reporters and photographers close behind them, arrived from the county seat. They went through a lot of detecting motions that got them nowhere except on the front pages of all the San Francisco and Los Angeles papers—the place they liked best.

I had Gabrielle Collinson moved into another room in the hotel, and posted Mickey Linehan next door, with the connecting door unlocked. Gabrielle talked now, to Vernon, Feeney, Rolly, and me. What she said didn't help us much. She had been asleep, she said; had been awakened by a terrible noise and a terrible jarring of her bed; and then I had come in. That was all she knew.

Late in the afternoon McCracken, a San Francisco police department bomb-expert, arrived. After examining all the fragments of this and that which he could sweep up, he gave us a preliminary verdict that the bomb had been a small one, of aluminum, charged with a low-grade nitroglycerine, and exploded by a crude friction device.

"Amateur or professional job?" I asked.

McCracken spit out loose shreds of tobacco—he was one of the men who chew their cigarettes—and said:

"I'd say it was made by a guy that knew his stuff, but had to work with what he could get his hands on. I'll tell you more when I've worked this junk over in the lab."

"No timer on it?" I asked.

"No signs of one."

Doctor George returned from the county seat with the news that what was left of Fitzstephan still breathed. The doctor was tickled pink. I had to yell at him to make him hear my questions about Fink and Gabrielle. Then he told me Fink's life wasn't in danger, and the girl's cold was enough better that she might get out of bed if she wished. I asked about her nerves, but he was in too much of a hurry to get back to Fitzstephan to pay much attention to anything else.

"Hm-m-m, yes, certainly," he muttered, edging past me towards his car. "Quiet, rest, freedom from anxiety," and he was gone.

I ate dinner with Vernon and Feeney in the hotel café that evening. They didn't think I had told them all I knew about the bombing, and kept me on the witness stand throughout the meal, though neither of them accused me pointblank of holding out.

After dinner I went up to my new room. Mickey was sprawled on the bed reading a newspaper.

"Go feed yourself," I said. "How's our baby?"

"She's up. How do you figure her—only fifty cards to her deck?"

"Why?" I asked. "What's she been doing?"

"Nothing. I was just thinking."

"That's from having an empty stomach. Better go eat."

"Aye, aye, Mr. Continental," he said and went out.

The next room was quiet. I listened at the door and then tapped it. Mrs. Herman's voice said: "Come in."

She was sitting beside the bed making gaudy butterflies on a piece of yellowish cloth stretched on hoops. Gabrielle Collinson sat in a rocking chair on the other side of the room, frowning at hands clasped in her lap—clasped hard enough to whiten the knuckles and spread the finger-ends. She had on the tweed clothes in which she had been kidnapped. They were still rumpled, but had been brushed clean of mud. She didn't look up when I came in. The nurse did, pushing her freckles together in an uneasy smile.

"Good evening," I said, trying to make a cheerful entrance. "Looks like we're running out of invalids."

That brought no response from the girl, too much from the nurse.

"Yes, indeed," Mrs. Herman exclaimed with exaggerated enthusiasm. "We can't call Mrs. Collinson an invalid now—now that she's up and about—and I'm almost sorry that she is—he-he-he—because I certainly never did have such a nice patient in every way; but that's what we girls used to say at the hospital when we were in training: the nicer the patient was, the shorter the time we'd have him, while you take a disagreeable one and she'd live—I mean, be there—forever and a day, it seems like. I remember once when——"

I made a face at her and wagged my head at the door. She let the rest of her words die inside her open mouth. Her face turned red, then white. She dropped her embroidery and got up, saying idiotically: "Yes, yes, that's the way it always is. Well, I've got to go see about those—you know—what do you call them. Pardon me for a few minutes, please." She went out quickly, sidewise, as if afraid I'd sneak up behind her and kick her.

When the door had closed, Gabrielle looked up from her hands and said:

"Owen is dead."

She didn't ask, she said it; but there was no way of treating it except as a question.

"No." I sat down in the nurse's chair and fished out cigarettes. "He's alive."

"Will he live?" Her voice was still husky from her cold.

"The doctors think so," I exaggerated.

"If he lives, will he——?" She left the question unfinished, but her husky voice seemed impersonal enough.

"He'll be pretty badly maimed."

She spoke more to herself than to me:

"That should be even more satisfactory."

I grinned. If I was as good an actor as I thought, there was nothing in the grin but good-humored amusement.

"Laugh," she said gravely. "I wish you could laugh it away. But you can't. It's there. It will always be there." She looked down at her hands and whispered: "Cursed."

Spoken in any other tone, that last word would have been melodramatic, ridiculously stagey. But she said it automatically, without any feeling, as if saying it had become a habit. I could see her lying in bed in the dark, whispering it to herself hour after hour, whispering it to her body when she put on her clothes, to her face reflected in mirrors, day after day.

I squirmed in my chair and growled:

"Stop it. Just because a bad-tempered woman works off her hatred and rage in a ten-twenty-thirty speech about——"

"No, no; my step-mother merely put in words what I have always known. I hadn't known it was in the Dain blood, but I knew it was in mine. How could I help knowing? Hadn't I the physical marks of degeneracy?" She crossed the room to stand in front of me, turning her head sidewise, holding back her curls with both hands. "Look at my ears—without lobes, pointed tops. People don't have ears like that. Animals do." She turned her face to me again, still holding back her hair. "Look at my forehead—its smallness, its shape—animal. My teeth." She bared them—white, small, pointed. "The shape of my face." Her hands left her hair and slid down her cheeks, coming together under her oddly pointed small chin.

"Is that all?" I asked. "Haven't you got cloven hoofs? All right. Say these things are as peculiar as you seem to think they are. What of it? Your step-mother was a Dain, and she was poison, but where were her physical marks of degeneracy? Wasn't she as normal, as wholesome-looking as any woman you're likely to find?"

"But that's no answer." She shook her head impatiently. "She didn't have the physical marks perhaps. I have, and the mental ones too. I——" She sat down on the side of the bed close to me, elbows on knees, tortured white face between hands. "I've not ever been able to think clearly, as other people do, even the simplest thoughts. Everything is always so confused in my mind. No matter what I try to think about, there's a fog that gets between me and it, and other thoughts get between us, so I barely catch a glimpse of the thought I want before I lose it again, and have to hunt through the fog, and at last find it, only to have the same thing happen again and again and again. Can you understand how horrible that can become: going through life like that—year after year—knowing you will always be like that—or worse?"

"I can't," I said. "It sounds normal as hell to me. Nobody thinks clearly, no matter what they pretend. Thinking's a dizzy business, a matter of catching as many of those foggy glimpses as you can and fitting them together the best you can. That's why people hang on so tight to their beliefs and opinions; because, compared to the haphazard way in which they're arrived at, even the goofiest opinion seems wonderfully clear, sane, and self-evident. And if you let it get away from you, then you've got to dive back into that foggy muddle to wangle yourself out another to take its place."

She took her face out of her hands and smiled shyly at me, saying:

"It's funny I didn't like you before." Her face became serious again. "But——"

"But nothing," I said. "You're old enough to know that everybody except very crazy people and very stupid people suspect themselves now and then—or whenever they happen to think about it—of not being exactly sane. Evidence of goofiness is easily found: the more you dig into yourself, the more you turn up. Nobody's mind could stand the sort of examination you've been giving yours. Going around trying to prove yourself cuckoo! It's a wonder you haven't driven yourself nuts."

"Perhaps I have."

"No. Take my word for it, you're sane. Or don't take my word for it. Look. You got a hell of a start in life. You got into bad hands at the very beginning. Your step-mother was plain poison, and did her best to ruin you, and in the end succeeded in convincing you that you were smeared with a very special family curse. In the past couple of months—the time I've known you—all the calamities known to man have been piled up on you, and your belief in your curse has made you hold yourself responsible for every item in the pile. All right. How's it affected you? You've been dazed a lot of the time, hysterical part of the time, and when your husband was killed you tried to kill yourself, but weren't unbalanced enough to face the shock of the bullet tearing through your flesh.

"Well, good God, sister! I'm only a hired man with only a hired man's interest in your troubles, and some of them have had me groggy. Didn't I try to bite a ghost back in that Temple? And I'm supposed to be old and toughened to crime. This morning—after all you'd been through—somebody touches off a package of nitroglycerine almost beside your bed. Here you are this evening, up and dressed, arguing with me about your sanity.

"If you aren't normal, it's because you're tougher, saner, cooler than normal. Stop thinking about your Dain blood and think about the Mayenne blood in you. Where do you suppose you got your toughness, except from him? It's the same toughness that carried him through Devil's Island, Central America, and Mexico, and kept him standing up till the end. You're more like him than like the one Dain I saw. Physically, you take after your father, and if you've got any physical marks of degeneracy—whatever that means—you got them from him."

She seemed to like that. Her eyes were almost happy. But I had talked myself out of words for the moment, and while I was hunting for more behind a cigarette the shine went out of her eyes.

"I'm glad—I'm grateful to you for what you've said, if you've meant it." Hopelessness was in her tone again, and her face was back between her hands. "But, whatever I am, she was right. You can't say she wasn't. You can't deny that my life has been cursed, blackened, and the lives of everyone who's touched me."

"I'm one answer to that," I said. "I've been around you a lot recently, and I've mixed into your affairs enough, and nothing's happened to me that a night's sleep wouldn't fix up."

"But in a different way," she protested slowly, wrinkling her forehead. "There's no personal relationship with you. It's professional with you—your work. That makes a difference."

I laughed and said:

"That won't do. There's Fitzstephan. He knew your family, of course, but he was here through me, on my account, and was actually, then, a step further removed from you than I.

Why shouldn't I have gone down first? Maybe the bomb was meant for me? Maybe. But that brings us to a human mind behind it—one that can bungle—and not your infallible curse."

"You are mistaken," she said, staring at her knees. "Owen loved me."

I decided not to appear surprised. I asked:

"Had you——?"

"No, please! Please don't ask me to talk about it. Not now—after what happened this morning." She jerked her shoulders up high and straight, said crisply: "You said something about an infallible curse. I don't know whether you misunderstand me, or are pretending to, to make me seem foolish. But I don't believe in an infallible curse, one coming from the devil or God, like Job's, say." She was earnest now, no longer talking to change the conversation. "But can't there be—aren't there people who are so thoroughly—fundamentally—evil that they poison—bring out the worst in—everybody they touch? And can't that——?"

"There are people who can," I half-agreed, "when they want to."

"No, no! Whether they want to or not. When they desperately don't want to. It is so. It is. I loved Eric because he was clean and fine. You know he was. You knew him well enough, and you know men well enough, to know he was. I loved him that way, wanted him that way. And then, when we were married——"

She shuddered and gave me both of her hands. The palms were dry and hot, the ends of her fingers cold. I had to hold them tight to keep the nails out of my flesh. I asked:

"You were a virgin when you married him?"

"Yes, I was. I am. I——"

"It's nothing to get excited about," I said. "You are, and have the usual silly notions. And you use dope, don't you?"

She nodded. I went on:

"That would cut your own interest in sex to below normal, so that a perfectly natural interest in it on somebody else's part would seem abnormal. Eric was too young, too much in love with you, maybe too inexperienced, to keep from being clumsy. You can't make anything horrible out of that."

"But it wasn't only Eric," she explained. "Every man I've

known. Don't think me conceited. I know I'm not beautiful. But I don't want to be evil. I don't. Why do men——? Why have all the men I've——?"

"Are you," I asked, "talking about me?"

"No—you know I'm not. Don't make fun of me, please."

"Then there are exceptions? Any others? Madison Andrews, for instance?"

"If you know him at all well, or have heard much about him, you don't have to ask that."

"No," I agreed. "But you can't blame the curse with him—it's habit. Was he very bad?"

"He was very funny," she said bitterly.

"How long ago was it?"

"Oh, possibly a year and a half. I didn't say anything to my father and step-mother. I was—I was ashamed that men were like that to me, and that——"

"How do you know," I grumbled, "that most men aren't like that to most women? What makes you think your case is so damned unique? If your ears were sharp enough, you could listen now and hear a thousand women in San Francisco making the same complaint, and—God knows—maybe half of them would be thinking themselves sincere."

She took her hands away from me and sat up straight on the bed. Some pink came into her face.

"Now you *have* made me feel silly," she said.

"Not much sillier than I do. I'm supposed to be a detective. Since this job began, I've been riding around on a merry-go-round, staying the same distance behind your curse, suspecting what it'd look like if I could get face to face with it, but never getting there. I will now. Can you stand another week or two?"

"You mean——?"

"I'm going to show you that your curse is a lot of hooey, but it'll take a few days, maybe a couple of weeks."

She was round-eyed and trembling, wanting to believe me, afraid to. I said:

"That's settled. What are you going to do now?"

"I—I don't know. Do you mean what you've said? That this can be ended? That I'll have no more——? That you can——?"

"Yeah. Could you go back to the house in the cove for a while? It might help things along, and you'll be safe enough there. We could take Mrs. Herman with us, and maybe an op or two."

"I'll go," she said.

I looked at my watch and stood up saying:

"Better go back to bed. We'll move down tomorrow. Good night."

She chewed her lower lip, wanting to say something, not wanting to say it, finally blurting it out:

"I'll have to have morphine down there."

"Sure. What's your day's ration?"

"Five—ten grains."

"That's mild enough," I said, and then, casually: "Do you like using the stuff?"

"I'm afraid it's too late for my liking or not liking it to matter."

"You've been reading the Hearst papers," I said. "If you want to break off, and we've a few days to spare down there, we'll use them weaning you. It's not so tough."

She laughed shakily, with a queer twitching of her mouth.

"Go away," she cried. "Don't give me any more assurances, any more of your promises, please. I can't stand any more tonight. I'm drunk on them now. Please go away."

"All right. Night."

"Good night—and thanks."

I went into my room, closing the door. Mickey was unscrewing the top of a flask. His knees were dusty. He turned his half-wit's grin on me and said:

"What a swell dish you are. What are you trying to do? Win yourself a home?"

"Sh-h-h. Anything new?"

"The master minds have gone back to the county seat. The red-head nurse was getting a load at the keyhole when I came back from feeding. I chased her."

"And took her place?" I asked, nodding at his dusty knees. You couldn't embarrass Mickey. He said:

"Hell, no. She was at the other door, in the hall."

CHAPTER XX

The House in the Cove

I GOT Fitzstephan's car from the garage and drove Gabrielle and Mrs. Herman down to the house in the cove late the following morning. The girl was in low spirits. She made a poor job of smiling when spoken to, and had nothing to say on her own account. I thought she might be depressed by the thought of returning to the house she had shared with Collinson, but when we got there she went in with no appearance of reluctance, and being there didn't seem to increase her depression.

After luncheon—Mrs. Herman turned out to be a good cook—Gabrielle decided she wanted to go outdoors, so she and I walked over to the Mexican settlement to see Mary Nunez. The Mexican woman promised to come back to work the next day. She seemed fond of Gabrielle, but not of me.

We returned home by way of the shore, picking a path between scattered rocks. We walked slowly. The girl's forehead was puckered between her eyebrows. Neither of us said anything until we were within a quarter of a mile of the house. Then Gabrielle sat down on the rounded top of a boulder that was warm in the sun.

"Can you remember what you told me last night?" she asked, running her words together in her hurry to get them out. She looked frightened.

"Yeah."

"Tell me again," she begged, moving over to one end of her boulder. "Sit down and tell me again—all of it."

I did. According to me, it was as foolish to try to read character from the shape of ears as from the position of stars, tea-leaves, or spit in the sand; anybody who started hunting for evidence of insanity in himself would certainly find plenty, because all but stupid minds were jumbled affairs; she was, as far as I could see, too much like her father to have much Dain blood in her, or to have been softened much by what she had, even if you wanted to believe that things like that could be handed down; there was nothing to show that her influence on people was any worse than anybody else's, it being doubtful that many people had a very good influence on those of the opposite sex, and, anyway, she was too young, inexperienced, and self-centered to judge how she varied from the normal in this respect; I would show her in a few days that there was for her difficulties a much more tangible, logical, and jailable answer than any curse; and she wouldn't have much trouble breaking away from morphine, since she was a fairly light user of the stuff and had a temperament favorable to a cure.

I spent three-quarters of an hour working these ideas over for her, and didn't make such a lousy job of it. The fear went out of her eyes as I talked. Toward the last she smiled to herself. When I had finished she jumped up, laughing, working her fingers together.

"Thank you. Thank you," she babbled. "Please don't let me ever stop believing you. Make me believe you even if—— No. It *is* true. Make me believe it always. Come on. Let's walk some more."

She almost ran me the rest of the way to the house, chattering all the way. Mickey Linehan was on the porch. I stopped there with him while the girl went in.

"Tch, tch, tch, as Mr. Rolly says." He shook his grinning face at me. "I ought to tell her what happened to that poor girl up in Poisonville that got so she thought she could trust you."

"Bring any news down from the village with you?" I asked.

"Andrews has turned up. He was at the Jeffries' place in San Mateo, where Aaronia Haldorn's staying. She's still there. Andrews was there from Tuesday afternoon till last night. Al was watching the place and saw him go in, but didn't peg him till he came out. The Jeffries are away—San Diego. Dick's tailing Andrews now. Al says the Haldorn broad hasn't been off the place. Rolly tells me Fink's awake, but don't know anything about the bomb. Fitzstephan's still hanging on to life."

"I think I'll run over and talk to Fink this afternoon," I said. "Stick around here. And—oh, yeah—you'll have to act respectful to me when Mrs. Collinson's around. It's important that she keep on thinking I'm hot stuff."

"Bring back some booze," Mickey said. "I can't do it sober."

Fink was propped up in bed when I got to him, looking out under bandages. He insisted that he knew nothing about the bomb, that all he had come down for was to tell me that Harvey Whidden was his step-son, the missing village-blacksmith's son by a former marriage.

"Well, what of it?" I asked.

"I don't know what of it, except that he was, and I thought you'd want to know about it."

"Why should I?"

"The papers said you said there was some kind of connection between what happened here and what happened up there, and that heavy-set detective said you said I knew more about it than I let on. And I don't want any more trouble, so I thought I'd just come down and tell you, so you couldn't say I hadn't told all I knew."

"Yeah? Then tell me what you know about Madison Andrews."

"I don't know anything about him. I don't know him. He's her guardian or something, ain't he? I read that in the newspapers. But I don't know him."

"Aaronia Haldorn does."

"Maybe she does, mister, but I don't. I just worked for the Haldorns. It wasn't anything to me but a job."

"What was it to your wife?"

"The same thing, a job."

"Where is she?"

"I don't know."

"Why'd she run away from the Temple?"

"I told you before, I don't know. Didn't want to get in trouble, I—— Who wouldn't of run away if they got a chance?"

The nurse who had been fluttering around became a nuisance by this time, so I left the hospital for the district attorney's office in the court house. Vernon pushed aside a stack of papers with a the-world-can-wait gesture, and said, "Glad to see you; sit down," nodding vigorously, showing me all his teeth.

I sat down and said:

"Been talking to Fink. I couldn't get anything out of him, but he's our meat. The bomb couldn't have got in there except by him."

Vernon frowned for a moment, then shook his chin at me, and snapped:

"What was his motive? And you were there. You say you were looking at him all the time he was in the room. You say you saw nothing."

"What of that?" I asked. "He could outsmart me there. He was a magician's mechanic. He'd know how to make a bomb, and how to put it down without my seeing it. That's his game. We don't know what Fitzstephan saw. They tell me he'll pull through. Let's hang on to Fink till he does."

Vernon clicked his teeth together and said: "Very well, we'll hold him."

I went down the corridor to the sheriff's office. Feeney wasn't in, but his chief deputy—a lanky, pockmarked man named Sweet—said he knew from the way Feeney had spoken of me that he—Feeney—would want me to be given all the help I asked for.

"That's fine," I said. "What I'm interested in now is picking up a couple of bottles of—well, gin, Scotch—whatever happens to be best in this part of the country."

Sweet scratched his Adam's apple and said:

"I wouldn't know about that. Maybe the elevator boy. I guess his gin would be safest. Say, Dick Cotton's crying his head off wanting to see you. Want to talk to him?"

"Yeah, though I don't know what for."

"Well, come back in a couple of minutes."

I went out and rang for the elevator. The boy—he had an age-bent back and a long yellow-gray mustache—was alone in it.

"Sweet said maybe you'd know where I could get a gallon of the white," I said.

"He's crazy," the boy grumbled, and then, when I kept quiet: "You'll be going out this way?"

"Yeah, in a little while."

He closed the door. I went back to Sweet. He took me down an inclosed walk that connected the court house with the prison behind, and left me alone with Cotton in a small boiler-plate cell. Two days in jail hadn't done the marshal of Quesada any good. He was gray-faced and jumpy, and the dimple in his chin kept squirming as he talked. He hadn't anything to tell me except that he was innocent.

All I could think of to say to him was: "Maybe, but you brought it on yourself. What evidence there is is against you. I don't know whether it's enough to convict you or not—depends on your lawyer."

"What did he want?" Sweet asked when I had gone back to him.

"To tell me that he's innocent."

The deputy scratched his Adam's apple again and asked:

"It's supposed to make any difference to you?"

"Yeah, it's been keeping me awake at night. See you later."

I went out to the elevator. The boy pushed a newspaper-wrapped gallon jug at me and said: "Ten bucks." I paid him, stowed the jug in Fitzstephan's car, found the local telephone office, and put in a call for Vic Dallas's drug-store in San Francisco's Mission district.

"I want," I told Vic, "fifty grains of M. and eight of those calomel-ipecac-atropine-strychnine-cascara shots. I'll have somebody from the agency pick up the package tonight or in the morning. Right?"

"If you say so, but if you kill anybody with it don't tell them where you got the stuff."

"Yeah," I said; "they'll die just because I haven't got a lousy pill-roller's diploma."

I put in another San Francisco call, for the agency, talking to the Old Man.

"Can you spare me another op?" I asked.

"MacMan is available, or he can relieve Drake. Whichever you prefer."

"MacMan'll do. Have him stop at Dallas's drug-store for a package on the way down. He knows where it is."

The Old Man said he had no new reports on Aaronia Haldorn and Andrews.

I drove back to the house in the cove. We had company. Three strange cars were standing empty in the driveway, and half a dozen newshounds were sitting and standing around Mickey on the porch. They turned their questions on me.

"Mrs. Collinson's here for a rest," I said. "No interviews, no posing for pictures. Let her alone. If anything breaks here I'll see that you get it, those of you who lay off her. The only thing I can tell you now is that Fink's being held for the bombing."

"What did Andrews come down for?" Jack Santos asked.

That wasn't a surprise to me: I had expected him to turn up now that he had come out of seclusion.

"Ask him," I suggested. "He's administering Mrs. Collinson's estate. You can't make a mystery out of his coming down to see her."

"Is it true that they're on bad terms?"

"No."

"Then why didn't he show up before this—yesterday, or the day before?"

"Ask him."

"Is it true that he's up to his tonsils in debt, or was before the Leggett estate got into his hands?"

"Ask him."

Santos smiled with thinned lips and said:

"We don't have to: we asked some of his creditors. Is there anything to the report that Mrs. Collinson and her husband had quarreled over her being too friendly with Whidden, a couple of days before her husband was killed?"

"Anything but the truth," I said. "Tough. You could do a lot with a story like that."

"Maybe we will," Santos said. "Is it true that she and her husband's family are on the outs, that old Hubert has said he's willing to spend all he's got to see that she pays for any part she had in his son's death?"

I didn't know. I said:

"Don't be a chump. We're working for Hubert now, taking care of her."

"Is it true that Mrs. Haldorn and Tom Fink were released because they had threatened to tell all they knew if they were held for trial?"

"Now you're kidding me, Jack," I said. "Is Andrews still here?"

"Yes."

I went indoors and called Mickey in, asking him: "Seen Dick?"

"He drove past a couple of minutes after Andrews came."

"Sneak away and find him. Tell him not to let the newspaper gang make him, even if he has to risk losing Andrews for a while. They'd go crazy all over their front pages if they learned we were shadowing him, and I don't want them to go that crazy."

Mrs. Herman was coming down the stairs. I asked her where Andrews was.

"Up in the front room."

I went up there. Gabrielle, in a low-cut dark silk gown, was sitting stiff and straight on the edge of a leather rocker. Her face was white and sullen. She was looking at a handkerchief stretched between her hands. She looked up at me as if glad I had come in. Andrews stood with his back to the fireplace. His white hair, eyebrows, and mustache stood out every which way from his bony pink face. He shifted his scowl from the girl to me, and didn't seem glad I had come in.

I said, "Hullo," and found a table-corner to prop myself on.

He said: "I've come to take Mrs. Collinson back to San Francisco."

She didn't say anything. I said:

"Not to San Mateo?"

"What do you mean by that?" The white tangles of his brows came down to hide all but the bottom halves of his blue eyes.

"God knows. Maybe my mind's been corrupted by the questions the newspapers have been asking me."

He didn't quite wince. He said, slowly, deliberately:

"Mrs. Haldorn sent for me professionally. I went to see her to explain how impossible it would be, in the circumstances, for me to advise or represent her."

"That's all right with me," I said. "And if it took you thirty hours to explain that to her, it's nobody's business."

"Precisely."

"But—I'd be careful how I told the reporters waiting downstairs that. You know how suspicious they are—for no reason at all."

He turned to Gabrielle again, speaking quietly, but with some impatience:

"Well, Gabrielle, are you going with me?"

"Should I?" she asked me.

"Not unless you especially want to."

"I—I don't."

"Then that's settled," I said.

Andrews nodded and went forward to take her hand, saying:

"I'm sorry, but I must get back to the city now, my dear. You should have a phone put in, so you can reach me in case you need to."

He declined her invitation to stay to dinner, said, "Good evening," not unpleasantly, to me, and went out. Through a window I could see him presently getting into his car, giving as little attention as possible to the newspaper men gathered around him.

Gabrielle was frowning at me when I turned away from the window.

"What did you mean by what you said about San Mateo?" she asked.

"How friendly are he and Aaronia Haldorn?" I asked.

"I haven't any idea. Why? Why did you talk to him as you did?"

"Detective business. For one thing, there's a rumor that getting control of the estate may have helped him keep his own head above water. Maybe there's nothing in it. But it won't hurt to give him a little scare, so he'll get busy straightening things out—if he has done any juggling—between now and clean-up day. No use of you losing money along with the rest of your troubles."

"Then he——?" she began.

"He's got a week—several days at least—to unjuggle in. That ought to be enough."

"But——"

Mrs. Herman, calling us to dinner, ended the conversation.

Gabrielle ate very little. She and I had to do most of the talking until I got Mickey started telling about a job he had been on up in Eureka, where he posed as a foreigner who knew no English. Since English was the only language he did know, and Eureka normally held at least one specimen of every nationality there is, he'd had a hell of a time keeping people from finding out just what he was supposed to be. He made a long and laughable story of it. Maybe some of it was the truth: he always got a lot of fun out of acting like the other half of a half-wit.

After the meal he and I strolled around outside while the spring night darkened the grounds.

"MacMan will be down in the morning," I told him. "You and he will have to do the watchdog. Divide it between you anyway you want, but one will have to be on the job all the time."

"Don't give yourself any of the worst of it," he complained. "What's this supposed to be down here—a trap?"

"Maybe."

"Maybe. Uh-huh. You don't know what the hell you're doing. You're stalling around waiting for the horseshoe in your pocket to work."

"The outcome of successful planning always looks like luck to saps. Did Dick have any news?"

"No. He tailed Andrews straight here from his house."

The front door opened, throwing yellow light across the porch. Gabrielle, a dark cape on her shoulders, came into the yellow light, shut the door, and came down the gravel walk.

"Take a nap now if you want," I told Mickey. "I'll call you when I turn in. You'll have to stand guard till morning."

"You're a darb." He laughed in the dark. "By God, you're a darb."

"There's a gallon of gin in the car."

"Huh? Why didn't you say so instead of wasting my time just talking?" The lawn grass swished against his shoes as he walked away.

I moved towards the gravel walk, meeting the girl.

"Isn't it a lovely night?" she said.

"Yeah. But you're not supposed to go roaming around alone in the dark, even if your troubles are practically over."

"I didn't intend to," she said, taking my arm. "And what does practically over mean?"

"That there are a few details to be taken care of—the morphine, for instance."

She shivered and said:

"I've only enough left for tonight. You promised to——"

"Fifty grains coming in the morning."

She kept quiet, as if waiting for me to say something else. I didn't say anything else. Her fingers wriggled on my sleeve.

"You said it wouldn't be hard to cure me." She spoke half-questioningly, as if expecting me to deny having said anything of the sort.

"It wouldn't."

"You said, perhaps . . ." letting the words fade off.

"We'd do it while we were here?"

"Yes."

"Want to?" I asked. "It's no go if you don't."

"Do I want to?" She stood still in the road, facing me. "I'd give——" A sob ended that sentence. Her voice came again, high-pitched, thin: "Are you being honest with me? Are you? Is what you've told me—all you told me last night and this afternoon—as true as you made it sound? Do I believe in you because you're sincere? Or because you've learned how—as a trick of your business—to make people believe in you?"

She might have been crazy, but she wasn't so stupid. I gave her the answer that seemed best at the time:

"Your belief in me is built on mine in you. If mine's unjustified, so is yours. So let me ask you a question first: were you lying when you said, 'I don't want to be evil'?"

"Oh, I don't. I don't."

"Well, then," I said with an air of finality, as if that settled it. "Now if you want to get off the junk, off we'll get you."

"How—how long will it take?"

"Say a week, to be safe. Maybe less."

"Do you mean that? No longer than that?"

"That's all for the part that counts. You'll have to take care of yourself for some time after, till your system's hitting on all eight again, but you'll be off the junk."

"Will I suffer—much?"

"A couple of bad days; but they won't be as bad as you'll think they are, and your father's toughness will carry you through them."

"If," she said slowly, "I should find out in the middle of it that I can't go through with it, can I——?"

"There'll be nothing you can do about it," I promised cheerfully. "You'll stay in till you come out the other end."

She shivered again and asked:

"When shall we start?"

"Day after tomorrow. Take your usual snort tomorrow, but don't try to stock up. And don't worry about it. It'll be tougher on me than on you: I'll have to put up with you."

"And you'll make allowances—you'll understand—if I'm not always nice while I'm going through it? Even if I'm nasty?"

"I don't know." I didn't want to encourage her to cut up on me. "I don't think so much of niceness that can be turned into nastiness by a little grief."

"Oh, but——" She stopped, wrinkled her forehead, said: "Can't we send Mrs. Herman away? I don't want to——I don't want her looking at me."

"I'll get rid of her in the morning."

"And if I'm——you won't let anybody else see me——if I'm not——if I'm too terrible?"

"No," I promised. "But look here: you're preparing to put on a show for me. Stop thinking about that end of it. You're going to behave. I don't want a lot of monkey-business out of you."

She laughed suddenly, asking:

"Will you beat me if I'm bad?"

I said she might still be young enough for a spanking to do her good.

CHAPTER XXI

Aaronia Haldorn

M ARY NUNEZ arrived at half-past seven the next morning. Mickey Linehan drove Mrs. Herman to Quesada, leaving her there, returning with MacMan and a load of groceries.

MacMan was a square-built, stiff-backed ex-soldier. Ten years of the islands had baked his tight-mouthed, solid-jawed, grim face a dark oak. He was the perfect soldier: he went where you sent him, stayed where you put him, and had no ideas of his own to keep him from doing exactly what you told him.

He gave me the druggist's package. I took ten grains of morphine up to Gabrielle. She was eating breakfast in bed. Her eyes were watery, her face damp and grayish. When she saw the bindles in my hand she pushed her tray aside and held her hands out eagerly, wriggling her shoulders.

"Come back in five minutes?" she asked.

"You can take your jolt in front of me. I won't blush."

"But I would," she said, and did.

I went out, shut the door, and leaned against it, hearing the crackle of paper and the clink of a spoon on the water-glass. Presently she called:

"All right."

I went in again. A crumpled ball of white paper in the tray was all that remained of one bindle. The others weren't in sight. She was leaning back against her pillows, eyes half closed, as comfortable as a cat full of goldfish. She smiled lazily at me and said:

"You're a dear. Know what I'd like to do today? Take some lunch and go out on the water—spend the whole day floating in the sun."

"That ought to be good for you. Take either Linehan or MacMan with you. You're not to go out alone."

"What are you going to do?"

"Ride up to Quesada, over to the county seat, maybe as far as the city."

"Mayn't I go with you?"

I shook my head, saying: "I've got work to do, and you're supposed to be resting."

She said, "Oh," and reached for her coffee. I turned to the door. "The rest of the morphine." She spoke over the edge of her cup. "You've put it in a safe place, where nobody will find it?"

"Yeah," I said, grinning at her, patting my coat-pocket.

In Quesada I spent half an hour talking to Rolly and reading the San Francisco papers. They were beginning to poke at Andrews with hints and questions that stopped just short of libel. That was so much to the good. The deputy sheriff hadn't anything to tell me.

I went over to the county seat. Vernon was in court. Twenty minutes of the sheriff's conversation didn't add anything to my education. I called up the agency and talked to the Old Man. He said Hubert Collinson, our client, had expressed some surprise at our continuing the operation, having supposed that Whidden's death had cleared up the mystery of his son's murder.

"Tell him it didn't," I said. "Eric's murder was tied up with Gabrielle's troubles, and we can't get to the bottom of one except through the other. It'll probably take another week. Collinson's all right," I assured the Old Man. "He'll stand for it when it's explained to him."

The Old Man said, "I certainly hope so," rather coldly, not enthusiastic over having five operatives at work on a job that the supposed client might not want to pay for.

I drove up to San Francisco, had dinner at the St. Germain, stopped at my rooms to collect another suit and a bagful of clean shirts and the like, and got back to the house in the cove a little after midnight. MacMan came out of the darkness while I was tucking the car—we were still using Fitz-stephan's—under the shed. He said nothing had happened in my absence. We went into the house together. Mickey was in the kitchen, yawning and mixing himself a drink before relieving MacMan on sentry duty.

"Mrs. Collinson gone to bed?" I asked.

"Her light's still on. She's been in her room all day."

MacMan and I had a drink with Mickey and then went upstairs. I knocked at the girl's door.

"Who is it?" she asked. I told her. She said: "Yes?"

"No breakfast in the morning."

"Really?" Then, as if it were something she had almost for-gotten: "Oh, I've decided not to put you to all the trouble of curing me." She opened the door and stood in the opening, smiling too pleasantly at me, a finger holding her place in a book. "Did you have a nice ride?"

"All right," I said, taking the rest of the morphine from my pocket and holding it out to her. "There's no use of my car-rying this around."

She didn't take it. She laughed in my face and said:

"You *are* a brute, aren't you?"

"Well, it's your cure, not mine." I put the stuff back in my pocket. "If you——" I broke off to listen. A board had creaked down the hall. Now there was a soft sound, as of a bare foot dragging across the floor.

"That's Mary watching over me," Gabrielle whispered gaily. "She made a bed in the attic and refused to go home. She doesn't think I'm safe with you and your friends. She warned me against you, said you were—what was it?—oh, yes—wolves. Are you?"

"Practically. Don't forget—no breakfast in the morning."

The following afternoon I gave her the first dose of Vic Dallas's mixture, and three more at two-hour intervals. She spent that day in her room. That was Saturday.

On Sunday she had ten grains of morphine and was in high spirits all day, considering herself as good as cured already.

On Monday she had the remainder of Vic's concoction, and the day was pretty much like Saturday. Mickey Linehan returned from the county seat with the news that Fitzstephan was conscious, but too weak and too bandaged to have talked if the doctors had let him; that Andrews had been to San Mateo to see Aaronia Haldorn again; and that she had been to the hospital to see Fink, but had been refused permission by the sheriff's office.

Tuesday was a more exciting day.

Gabrielle was up and dressed when I carried her orange-juice breakfast in. She was bright-eyed, restless, talkative, and laughed easily and often until I mentioned—off-hand—that she was to have no more morphine.

"Ever, you mean?" Her face and voice were panicky. "No, you don't mean that?"

"Yeah."

"But I'll die." Tears filled her eyes, ran down her small white face, and she wrung her hands. It was childishly pathetic. I had to remind myself that tears were one of the symptoms of morphine withdrawal. "You know that's not the way. I don't expect as much as usual. I know I'll get less and less each day. But you can't stop it like this. You're joking. That would kill me." She cried some more at the thought of being killed.

I made myself laugh as if I were sympathetic but amused.

"Nonsense," I said cheerfully. "The chief trouble you're going to have is in being too alive. A couple of days of that, and you'll be all set."

She bit her lips, finally managed a smile, holding out both hands to me.

"I'm going to believe you," she said. "I do believe you. I'm going to believe you no matter what you say."

Her hands were clammy. I squeezed them and said:

"That'll be swell. Now back to bed. I'll look in every now and then, and if you want anything in between, sing out."

"You're not going off today?"

"No," I promised.

She stood the gaff pretty well all afternoon. Of course, there wasn't much heartiness in the way she laughed at herself between attacks when the sneezing and yawning hit her, but the thing was that she tried to laugh.

Madison Andrews came between five and half-past. Having seen him drive in, I met him on the porch. The ruddiness of his face had been washed out to a weak orange.

"Good evening," he said politely. "I wish to see Mrs. Collinson."

"I'll deliver any message to her," I offered.

He pulled his white eyebrows down and some of his normal ruddiness came back.

"I wish to see her." It was a command.

"She doesn't wish to see you. Is there any message?"

All of his ruddiness was back now. His eyes were hot. I was standing between him and the door. He couldn't go in while

I stood there. For a moment he seemed about to push me out of the way. That didn't worry me: he was carrying a handicap of twenty pounds and twenty years.

He pulled his jaw into his neck and spoke in the voice of authority:

"Mrs. Collinson must return to San Francisco with me. She cannot stay here. This is a preposterous arrangement."

"She's not going to San Francisco," I said. "If necessary, the district attorney can hold her here as a material witness. Try upsetting that with any of your court orders, and we'll give you something else to worry about. I'm telling you this so you'll know how we stand. We'll prove that she might be in danger from you. How do we know you haven't played marbles with the estate? How do we know you don't mean to take advantage of her present upset condition to shield yourself from trouble over the estate? Why, man, you might even be planning to send her to an insane-asylum so the estate will stay under your control."

He was sick behind his eyes, though the rest of him stood up well enough under this broadside. When he had got his breath and had swallowed, he demanded:

"Does Gabrielle believe this?" His face was magenta.

"Who said anybody believed it?" I was trying to be bland. "I'm just telling you what we'll go into court with. You're a lawyer. You know there's not necessarily any connection between what's true and what you go into court with—or into the newspapers."

The sickness spread from behind his eyes, pushing the color from his face, the stiffness from his bones; but he held himself tall and he found a level voice.

"You may tell Mrs. Collinson," he said, "that I shall return my letters testamentary to the court this week, with an accounting of the estate, and a request that I be relieved."

"That'll be swell," I said, but I felt sorry for the old boy shuffling down to his car, climbing slowly into it.

I didn't tell Gabrielle he had been there.

She was whining a little now between her yawning and sneezing, and her eyes were running water. Face, body, and hands were damp with sweat. She couldn't eat. I kept her full of orange juice. Noises and odors—no matter how faint, how

pleasant—were becoming painful to her, and she twitched
and jerked continually in her bed.

"Will it get much worse than this?" she asked.

"Not much. There'll be nothing you can't stand."

Mickey Linehan was waiting for me when I got downstairs.

"The spick's got herself a chive," he said pleasantly.

"Yeah?"

"Yeah. It's the one I've been using to shuck lemons to take
the stink out of that bargain-counter gin you bought—or did
you just borrow it, the owner knowing you'd return it because nobody could drink it? It's a paring knife—four or five
inches of stainless steel blade—so you won't get rust-marks
on your undershirt when she sticks it in your back. I couldn't
find it, and asked her about it, and she didn't look at me like
I was a well-poisoner when she said she didn't know anything
about it, and that's the first time she never looked at me that
way, so I knew she had it."

"Smart of you," I said. "Well, keep an eye on her. She
don't like us much."

"I'm to do that?" Mickey grinned. "My idea would be for
everybody to look out for himself, seeing that you're the lad
she dog-eyes most, and it's most likely you that'll get whittled
on. What'd you ever do to her? You haven't been dumb
enough to fool with a Mex lady's affections, have you?"

I didn't think he was funny, though he may have been.

Aaronia Haldorn arrived just before dark, in a Lincoln limousine driven by a negro who turned the siren loose when he
brought the car into the drive. I was in Gabrielle's room
when the thing howled. She all but jumped out of bed, utterly terrorized by what must have been an ungodly racket to
her too sensitive ears.

"What was it? What was it?" she kept crying between rattling teeth, her body shaking the bed.

"Sh-h-h," I soothed her. I was acquiring a pretty fair bedside manner. "Just an automobile horn. Visitors. I'll go down
and head them off."

"You won't let anybody see me?" she begged.

"No. Be a good girl till I get back."

Aaronia Haldorn was standing beside the limousine talking
to MacMan when I came out. In the dim light, her face was

a dusky oval mask between black hat and black fur coat—but her luminous eyes were real enough.

"How do you do?" she said, holding out a hand. Her voice was a thing to make warm waves run up your back. "I'm glad for Mrs. Collinson's sake that you're here. She and I have had excellent proof of your protective ability, both owing our lives to it."

That was all right, but it had been said before. I made a gesture that was supposed to indicate modest distaste for the subject, and beat her to the first tap with:

"I'm sorry she can't see you. She isn't well."

"Oh, but I should so like to see her, if only for a moment. Don't you think it might be good for her?"

I said I was sorry. She seemed to accept that as final, though she said: "I came all the way from the city to see her."

I tried that opening with:

"Didn't Mr. Andrews tell you . . . ?" letting it ravel out.

She didn't say whether he had. She turned and began walking slowly across the grass. There was nothing for me to do but walk along beside her. Full darkness was only a few minutes away. Presently, when we had gone thirty or forty feet from the car, she said:

"Mr. Andrews thinks you suspect him."

"He's right."

"Of what do you suspect him?"

"Juggling the estate. Mind, I don't know, but I do suspect him."

"Really?"

"Really," I said; "and not of anything else."

"Oh, I should suppose that was quite enough."

"It's enough for me. I didn't think it was enough for you."

"I beg your pardon?"

I didn't like the ground I was on with this woman. I was afraid of her. I piled up what facts I had, put some guesses on them, and took a jump from the top of the heap into space:

"When you got out of prison, you sent for Andrews, pumped him for all he knew, and then, when you learned he was playing with the girl's pennies, you saw what looked to you like a chance to confuse things by throwing suspicion on him. The old boy's woman-crazy: he'd be duck-soup for a woman like you. I don't know what you're planning to do with him, but you've got him started, and have got the papers started after him. I take it you gave them the tip-off on his high financing? It's no good, Mrs. Haldorn. Chuck it. It won't work. You can stir him up, all right, and make him do something criminal, get him into a swell jam: he's desperate enough now that he's being poked at. But whatever he does now won't hide what somebody else did in the past. He's promised to get the estate in order and hand it over. Let him alone. It won't work."

She didn't say anything while we took another dozen steps. A path came under our feet. I said:

"This is the path that runs up the cliff, the one Eric Collinson was pushed from. Did you know him?"

She drew in her breath sharply, with almost a sob in her throat, but her voice was steady, quiet and musical, when she replied:

"You know I did. Why should you ask?"

"Detectives like questions they already know the answers to. Why did you come down here, Mrs. Haldorn?"

"Is that another whose answer you know?"

"I know you came for one or both of two reasons."

"Yes?"

"First, to learn how close we were to our riddle's answer. Right?"

"I've my share of curiosity, naturally," she confessed.

"I don't mind making that much of your trip a success. I know the answer."

She stopped in the path, facing me, her eyes phosphorescent in the deep twilight. She put a hand on my shoulder: she was taller than I. The other hand was in her coat-pocket. She put her face nearer mine. She spoke very slowly, as if taking great pains to be understood:

"Tell me truthfully. Don't pretend. I don't want to do an unnecessary wrong. Wait, wait—think before you speak—and believe me when I say this isn't the time for pretending, for lying, for bluffing. Now tell me the truth: do you know the answer?"

"Yeah."

She smiled faintly, taking her hand from my shoulder, saying:

"Then there's no use of our fencing."

I jumped at her. If she had fired from her pocket she might have plugged me. But she tried to get the gun out. By then I had a hand on her wrist. The bullet went into the ground between our feet. The nails of her free hand put three red ribbons down the side of my face. I tucked my head under her chin, turned my hip to her before her knee came up, brought her body hard against mine with one arm around her, and bent her gun-hand behind her. She dropped the gun as we fell. I was on top. I stayed there until I had found the gun. I was getting up when McMan arrived.

"Everything's eggs in the coffee," I told him, having trouble with my voice.

"Have to plug her?" he asked, looking at the woman lying still on the ground.

"No, she's all right. See that the chauffeur's behaving."

MacMan went away. The woman sat up, tucked her legs under her, and rubbed her wrist. I said:

"That's the second reason for your coming, though I thought you meant it for Mrs. Collinson."

She got up, not saying anything. I didn't help her up, not wanting her to know how shaky I was. I said:

"Since we've gone this far, it won't do any harm and it might do some good to talk."

"I don't think anything will do any good now." She set her hat straight. "You say you know. Then lies are worthless, and only lies would help." She shrugged. "Well, what now?"

"Nothing now, if you'll promise to remember that the time for being desperate is past. This kind of thing splits up in three parts—being caught, being convicted, and being punished. Admit it's too late to do anything about the first, and —well, you know what California courts and prison boards are."

She looked curiously at me and asked: "Why do you tell me this?"

"Because being shot at's no treat to me, and because when a job's done I like to get it cleaned up and over with. I'm not interested in trying to convict you for your part in the racket, and it's a nuisance having you horning in now, trying to muddy things up. Go home and behave."

Neither of us said anything more until we had walked back to the limousine. Then she turned, put out her hand to me, and said:

"I think—I don't know yet—I think I owe you even more now than before."

I didn't say anything and I didn't take her hand. Perhaps it was because she was holding her hand out that she asked:

"May I have my pistol now?"

"No."

"Will you give my best wishes to Mrs. Collinson, and tell her I'm so sorry I couldn't see her?"

"Yeah."

She said, "Goodbye," and got into the car; I took off my hat and she rode away.

CHAPTER XXII

Confessional

MICKEY LINEHAN opened the front door for me. He looked at my scratched face and laughed:

"You do have one hell of a time with your women. Why don't you ask them instead of trying to take it away from them? It'd save you a lot of skin." He poked a thumb at the ceiling. "Better go up and negotiate with that one. She's been raising hell."

I went up to Gabrielle's room. She was sitting in the middle of the wallowed-up bed. Her hands were in her hair, tugging at it. Her soggy face was thirty-five years old. She was making hurt-animal noises in her throat.

"It's a fight, huh?" I said from the door.

She took her hands out of her hair.

"I won't die?" The question was a whimper between edge-to-edge teeth.

"Not a chance."

She sobbed and lay down. I straightened the covers over her. She complained that there was a lump in her throat, that her jaws and the hollows behind her knees ached.

"Regular symptoms," I assured her. "They won't bother you much, and you'll miss the cramps."

Fingernails scratched the door. Gabrielle jumped up in bed, crying:

"Don't go away again."

"No farther than the door," I promised, and went to it.

MacMan was there.

"That Mexican Mary," he whispered, "was hiding in the bushes watching you and the woman. I spotted her when she came out, and tailed her across to the road below. She stopped the limousine and talked with the woman—five-ten minutes. I couldn't get near enough to hear any of it."

"Where is she now?"

"In the kitchen. She came back. The woman in the heap went on. Mickey says the Mex is packing a knife and is going to make grief for us. Reckon he's right?"

"He generally is," I said. "She's strong for Mrs. Collinson, and doesn't think we mean her any good. Why in hell can't she mind her own business? It adds up that she peeped and saw Mrs. Haldorn wasn't for us, figured she was for Mrs. Collinson, and braced her. I hope Mrs. Haldorn had sense enough to tell her to behave. Anyway, there's nothing we can do but watch her. No use giving her the gate: we've got to have a cook."

When MacMan had gone Gabrielle remembered we had had a visitor, and asked me about it, and about the shot she had heard and my scratched face.

"It was Aaronia Haldorn," I told her; "and she lost her head. No harm done. She's gone now."

"She came here to kill me," the girl said, not excitedly, but as if she knew certainly.

"Maybe. She wouldn't admit anything. Why should she kill you?"

I didn't get an answer to that.

It was a long bad night. I spent most of it in the girl's room, in a leather rocker dragged in from the front room. She got perhaps an hour and a half of sleep, in three instalments. Nightmares brought her screaming out of all three. I dozed when she let me. Off and on through the night I heard stealthy sounds in the hall—Mary Nunez watching over her mistress, I supposed.

Wednesday was a longer and worse day. By noon my jaws were as sore as Gabrielle's, from going around holding my back teeth together. She was getting the works now. Light was positive, active, pain to her eyes, sound to her ears, odors of any sort to her nostrils. The weight of her silk nightgown, the touch of sheets over and under her, tortured her skin. Every nerve she had yanked every muscle she had, continually. Promises that she wasn't going to die were no good now: life wasn't nice enough.

"Stop fighting it, if you want," I said. "Let yourself go. I'll take care of you."

She took me at my word, and I had a maniac on my hands. Once her shrieks brought Mary Nunez to the door, snarling and spitting at me in Mex-Spanish. I was holding Gabrielle down in bed by the shoulders, sweating as much as she was.

"Get out of here," I snarled back at the Mexican woman.

She put a brown hand into the bosom of her dress and came a step into the room. Mickey Linehan came up behind her, pulled her back into the hall, and shut the door.

Between the high spots, Gabrielle lay on her back, panting, twitching, staring at the ceiling with hopeless suffering eyes. Sometimes her eyes closed, but the jerking of her body didn't stop.

Rolly came down from Quesada that afternoon with word that Fitzstephan had come sufficiently alive to be questioned by Vernon. Fitzstephan had told the district attorney that he had not seen the bomb, had seen nothing to show when, where, and how it came into the room; but that he had an indistinct memory of hearing a tinkling, as of broken glass falling, and a thud on the floor close to him just after Fink and I had left the room.

I told Rolly to tell Vernon I'd try to get over to see him the next day, and to hang on to Fink. The deputy sheriff promised to deliver the message, and left. Mickey and I were standing on the porch. We didn't have anything to say to each other, hadn't all day. I was lighting a cigarette when the girl's voice came from indoors. Mickey turned away, saying something with the name of God in it.

I scowled at him and asked angrily:

"Well, am I right or wrong?"

He glared back at me, said, "I'd a damned sight rather be wrong," and walked away.

I cursed him and went inside. Mary Nunez, starting up the front stairs, retreated towards the kitchen when she saw me, walking backwards, her eyes watching me crazily. I cursed her and went upstairs to where I had left MacMan at the girl's door. He wouldn't look at me, so I made it unanimous by cursing him.

Gabrielle spent the balance of the afternoon shrieking, begging, and crying for morphine. That evening she made a complete confession:

"I told you I didn't want to be evil," she said, wadding the bedclothes in feverish hands. "That was a lie. I did. I've always wanted to, always have been. I wanted to do to you what I did to the others; but now I don't want you: I want morphine. They won't hang me: I know that. And I don't care what else they do to me, if I get morphine."

She laughed viciously and went on:

"You were right when you said I brought out the worst in men because I wanted to. I did want to; and I did——except, I failed with Doctor Riese, and with Eric. I don't know what was the matter with them. But I failed with both of them, and in failing let them learn too much about me. And that's why they were killed. Joseph drugged Doctor Riese, and I killed him myself, and then we made Minnie think she had. And I persuaded Joseph to kill Aaronia, and he would have done it —he would have done anything I asked—if you hadn't interfered. I got Harvey to kill Eric for me. I was tied to Eric— legally—a good man who wanted to make a good woman of me."

She laughed again, licking her lips.

"Harvey and I had to have money, and I couldn't—I was too afraid of being suspected—get enough from Andrews; so we pretended I had been kidnapped, to get it that way. It was a shame you killed Harvey: he was a glorious beast. I had that bomb, had had it for months. I took it from father's laboratory, when he was making some experiments for a moving picture company. It wasn't very large, and I always carried it with me—just in case. I meant it for you in the hotel room. There was nothing between Owen and me—that was another lie—he didn't love me. I meant it for you, because you were——because I was afraid you were getting at the truth. I was feverish, and when I heard two men go out, leaving one in your room, I was sure the one was you. I didn't see that it was Owen till too late—till I had opened the door a little and thrown the bomb in. Now you've got what you want. Give me morphine. There's no reason for your playing with me any longer. Give me morphine. You've succeeded. Have what I've told you written out: I'll sign it. You can't pretend now I'm worth curing, worth saving. Give me morphine."

Now it was my turn to laugh, asking:

"And aren't you going to confess to kidnapping Charlie Ross and blowing up the *Maine*?"

We had some more hell—a solid hour of it—before she exhausted herself again. The night dragged through. She got a little more than two hours' sleep, a half-hour gain over the previous night. I dozed in the chair when I could.

Sometime before daylight I woke to the feel of a hand on my coat. Keeping my breathing regular, I pushed my eye-lids far enough apart to squint through the lashes. We had a very dim light in the room, but I thought Gabrielle was in bed, though I couldn't see whether she was asleep or awake. My head was tilted back to rest on the back of the chair. I couldn't see the hand that was exploring my inside coat-pocket, nor the arm that came down over my shoulder; but they smelled of the kitchen, so I knew they were brown.

The Mexican woman was standing behind me. Mickey had told me she had a knife. Imagination told me she was holding it in her other hand. Good judgment told me to let her alone. I did that, closing my eyes again. Paper rustled between her fingers, and her hand left my pocket.

I moved my head sleepily then, and changed a foot's posi-tion. When I heard the door close quietly behind me, I sat up and looked around. Gabrielle was sleeping. I counted the bindles in my pocket and found that eight of them had been taken.

Presently Gabrielle opened her eyes. This was the first time since the cure started that she had awakened quietly. Her face was haggard, but not wild-eyed. She looked at the window and asked:

"Isn't day coming yet?"

"It's getting light." I gave her some orange juice. "We'll get some solid food in you today."

"I don't want food. I want morphine."

"Don't be silly. You'll get food. You won't get morphine. Today won't be like yesterday. You're over the hump, and the rest of it's downhill going, though you may hit a couple of rough spots. It's silly to ask for morphine now. What do you want to do? Have nothing to show for the hell you've been through? You've got it licked now: stay with it."

"Have I——have I really got it licked?"

"Yeah. All you've got to buck now is nervousness, and the memory of how nice it felt to have a skinful of hop."

"I can do it," she said. "I can do it because you say I can."

She got along fine till late in the morning, when she blew

up for an hour or two. But it wasn't so bad, and I got her straightened out again. When Mary brought up her luncheon I left them together and went downstairs for my own.

Mickey and MacMan were already at the dining room table. Neither of them spoke a word—to one another or to me—during the meal. Since they kept quiet, I did.

When I went back upstairs, Gabrielle, in a green bathrobe, was sitting in the leather rocker that had been my bed for two nights. She had brushed her hair and powdered her face. Her eyes were mostly green, with a lift to the lower lids as if she was hiding a joke. She said with mock solemnity:

"Sit down. I want to talk seriously to you."

I sat down.

"Why did you go through all this with——for me?" She was really serious now. "You didn't have to, and it couldn't have been pleasant. I was——I don't know how bad I was." She turned red from forehead to chest. "I know I was revolting, disgusting. I know how I must seem to you now. Why ——why did you?"

I said:

"I'm twice your age, sister; an old man. I'm damned if I'll make a chump of myself by telling you why I did it, why it was neither revolting nor disgusting, why I'd do it again and be glad of the chance."

She jumped out of her chair, her eyes round and dark, her mouth trembling.

"You mean——?"

"I don't mean anything that I'll admit," I said; "and if you're going to parade around with that robe hanging open you're going to get yourself some bronchitis. You ex-hop-heads have to be careful about catching cold."

She sat down again, put her hands over her face, and began crying. I let her cry. Presently she giggled through her fingers and asked:

"Will you go out and let me be alone all afternoon?"

"Yeah, if you'll keep warm."

I drove over to the county seat, went to the county hospital, and argued with people until they let me into Fitz-stephan's room.

He was ninety per cent bandages, with only an eye, an ear,

and one side of his mouth peeping out. The eye and the half-mouth smiled through linen at me, and a voice came through:

"No more of your hotel rooms for me." It wasn't a clear voice because it had to come out sidewise, and he couldn't move his jaw; but there was plenty of vitality in it. It was the voice of a man who meant to keep on living.

I smiled at him and said:

"No hotel rooms this time, unless you think San Quentin's a hotel. Strong enough to stand up under a third-degree, or shall we wait a day or two?"

"I ought to be at my best now," he said. "Facial expressions won't betray me."

"Good. Now here's the first point: Fink handed you that bomb when he shook hands with you. That's the only way it could have got in without my seeing it. His back was to me then. You didn't know what he was handing you, but you had to take it, just as you have to deny it now, or tip us off that you were tied up with the Holy Grail mob, and that Fink had reasons for killing you."

Fitzstephan said: "You say the most remarkable things. I'm glad he had reasons, though."

"You engineered Riese's murder. The others were your accomplices. When Joseph died the blame was put all on him, the supposed madman. That's enough to let the others out, or ought to be. But here you are killing Collinson and planning God knows what else. Fink knows that if you keep it up you're going to let the truth out about the Temple murder, and he'll swing with you. So, scared panicky, he tries to stop you."

Fitzstephan said: "Better and better. So I killed Collinson?"

"You had him killed—hired Whidden and then didn't pay him. He kidnapped the girl then, holding her for his money, knowing she was what you wanted. It was you his bullet came closest to when we cornered him."

Fitzstephan said: "I'm running out of exclamatory phrases. So I was after her? I wondered about my motive."

"You must have been pretty rotten with her. She'd had a bad time with Andrews, and even with Eric, but she didn't mind talking about them. But when I tried to learn the details of your wooing she shuddered and shut up. I suppose she slammed you down so hard you bounced, and you're the sort of egoist to be driven to anything by that."

Fitzstephan said: "I suppose. You know, I've had more than half an idea at times that you were secretly nursing some exceptionally idiotic theory."

"Well, why shouldn't I? You were standing beside Mrs. Leggett when she suddenly got that gun. Where'd she get it? Chasing her out of the laboratory and down the stairs wasn't in character—not for you. Your hand was on her gun when that bullet hit her neck. Was I supposed to be deaf, dumb, and blind? There was, as you agreed, one mind behind all Gabrielle's troubles. You're the one person who has that sort of a mind, whose connection with each episode can be traced, and who has the necessary motive. The motive held me up: I couldn't be sure of it till I'd had my first fair chance to pump Gabrielle—after the explosion. And another thing that held me up was my not being able to tie you to the Temple crowd till Fink and Aaronia Haldorn did it for me."

Fitzstephan said: "Ah, Aaronia helped tie me? What has she been up to?" He said it absent-mindedly, and his one visible gray eye was small, as if he was busy with other thoughts behind it.

"She's done her best to cover you up by gumming the works, creating confusion, setting us after Andrews, even trying to shoot me. I mentioned Collinson just after she'd learned that the Andrews false-trail was no good. She gave me a half-concealed gasp and sob, just on the off-chance that it'd lead me astray, overlooking no bets. I like her: she's shifty."

"She's so headstrong," Fitzstephan said lightly, not having listened to half I had said, busy with his own thoughts. He turned his head on the pillow so that his eye looked at the ceiling, narrow and brooding.

I said: "And so ends the Great Dain Curse."

He laughed then, as well as he could with one eye and a fraction of a mouth, and said:

"Suppose, my boy, I were to tell you I'm a Dain?"

I said: "Huh?"

He said: "My mother and Gabrielle's maternal grandfather were brother and sister."

I said: "I'll be damned."

"You'll have to go away and let me think," he said. "I don't know yet what I shall do. Understand, at present I admit nothing. But the chances are I shall insist on the curse, shall use it to save my dear neck. In that event, my son, you're going to see a most remarkable defense, a circus that will send the nation's newspapers into happy convulsions. I shall be a Dain, with the cursed Dain blood in me, and the crimes of Cousin Alice and Cousin Lily and Second-cousin Gabrielle and the Lord knows how many other criminal Dains shall be evidence in my behalf. The number of my own crimes will be to my advantage, on the theory that nobody but a lunatic could have committed so many. And won't they be many? I'll produce crimes and crimes, dating from the cradle.

"Even literature shall help me. Didn't most reviewers agree that *The Pale Egyptian* was the work of a sub-Mongolian? And, as I remember, the consensus was that my *Eighteen Inches* bore all the better known indications of authorial degeneracy. Evidence, son, to save my sweet neck. And I shall wave my mangled body at them—an arm gone, a leg gone, parts of my torso and face—a ruin whose crimes and high Heaven have surely brought sufficient punishment upon him. And perhaps the bomb shocked me into sanity again, or, at least, out of criminal insanity. Perhaps I'll even have become religious. It'll be a splendid circus. It tempts me. But I must think before I commit myself."

He panted through the uncovered half of his mouth, exhausted by his speech, looking at me with a gray eye that held triumphant mirth.

"You'll probably make a go of it," I said as I prepared to leave. "And I'm satisfied if you do. You've taken enough of a licking. And, legally, you're entitled to beat the jump if ever anybody was."

"Legally entitled?" he repeated, the mirth going out of his eye. He looked away, and then at me again, uneasily. "Tell me the truth. Am I?"

I nodded.

"But, damn it, that spoils it," he complained, fighting to keep the uneasiness out of his eye, fighting to retain his usual lazily amused manner, and not making such a poor job of it. "It's no fun if I'm really cracked."

When I got back to the house in the cove, Mickey and MacMan were sitting on the front steps. MacMan said, "Hello," and Mickey said: "Get any fresh woman-scars while you were away? Your little playmate's been asking for you." I supposed from this—from my being readmitted to the white race—that Gabrielle had had a good afternoon.

She was sitting up in bed with pillows behind her back, her face still—or again—powdered, her eyes shining happily.

"I didn't mean for you to go away forever," she scolded. "It was nasty of you. I've got a surprise for you and I've nearly burst waiting."

"Well, here I am. What is it?"

"Shut your eyes."

I shut them.

"Open your eyes."

I opened them. She was holding out to me the eight bindles that Mary Nunez had picked my pocket for.

"I've had them since noon," she said proudly; "and they've got finger-marks and tear-marks on them, but not one of them has been opened. It—honestly—it wasn't so hard not to."

"I knew it wouldn't be, for you," I said. "That's why I didn't take them away from Mary."

"You knew? You trusted me that much—to go away and leave me with them?"

Nobody but an idiot would have confessed that for two days the folded papers had held powdered sugar instead of the original morphine.

"You're the nicest man in the world." She caught one of my hands and rubbed her cheek into it, then dropped it quickly, frowned her face out of shape, and said: "Except! You sat there this noon and deliberately tried to make me think you were in love with me."

"Well?" I asked, trying to keep my face straight.

"You hypocrite. You deceiver of young girls. It would serve you right if I made you marry me—or sued you for breach of promise. I honestly believed you all afternoon—and it *did* help me. I believed you until you came in just now, and then I saw——" She stopped.

"Saw what?"

"A monster. A nice one, an especially nice one to have around when you're in trouble, but a monster just the same, without any human foolishness like love in him, and—— What's the matter? Have I said something I shouldn't?"

"I don't think you should have," I said. "I'm not sure I wouldn't trade places with Fitzstephan now—if that big-eyed woman with the voice was part of the bargain."

"Oh, dear!" she said.

CHAPTER XXIII

The Circus

OWEN FITZSTEPHAN never spoke to me again. He refused to see me, and when, as a prisoner, he couldn't help himself there, he shut his mouth and kept it shut. This sudden hatred of me—for it amounted to that—had grown, I supposed, out of his knowing I thought him insane. He wanted the rest of the world, or at least the dozen who would represent the world on his jury, to think he had been crazy—and did make them think so—but he didn't want me to agree with them. As a sane man who, by pretending to be a lunatic, had done as he pleased and escaped punishment, he had a joke—if you wanted to call it that—on the world. But if he was a lunatic who, ignorant of his craziness, thought he was pretending to be a lunatic, then the joke—if you wanted to call it that—was on him. And my having such a joke on him was more than his egotism could stomach, even though it's not likely he ever admitted to himself that he was, or might be, actually crazy. Whatever he thought, he never spoke to me after the hospital interview in which I had said he was legally entitled to escape hanging.

His trial, when he was well enough to appear in court some months later, was every bit of the circus he had promised, and the newspapers had their happy convulsions. He was tried in the county court house for Mrs. Cotton's murder. Two new witnesses had been found, who had seen him walking away from the rear of the Cotton house that morning, and a third who identified his car as the one that had been parked four blocks away all—or all the latter part of—the previous night. The city and county district attorneys agreed that this evidence made the Cotton case the strongest against him.

Fitzstephan's plea was *Not guilty by reason of insanity*, or whatever the legal wording was. Since Mrs. Cotton's murder had been the last of his crimes, his lawyers could, and did, introduce, as proof of his insanity, all that he had done in the others. They made a high, wide, and handsome job of it, carrying out his original idea that the best way to prove him crazy was to show he had committed more crimes than any sane man could have. Well, it was plain enough that he had.

He had known Alice Dain, his cousin, in New York when she and Gabrielle, then a child, were living there. Gabrielle couldn't corroborate this: we had only Fitzstephan's word for it; but it may have been so. He said they concealed his relationship from the others because they did not want the girl's father—for whom Alice was then searching—to know that she was bringing with her any links with the dangerous past. Fitzstephan said Alice had been his mistress in New York: that could have been true, but didn't matter.

After Alice and Gabrielle left New York for San Francisco, Fitzstephan and the woman exchanged letters occasionally, but with no definite purpose. Fitzstephan then met the Haldorns. The cult was his idea: he organized it, financed it, and brought it to San Francisco, though he kept his connection with it a secret, since everyone who knew him knew his skepticism; and his interest in it would have advertised it as the fake it was. To him, he said, the cult was a combination of toy and meal-ticket: he liked influencing people, especially in obscure ways, and people didn't seem to like buying his books.

Aaronia Haldorn was his mistress. Joseph was a puppet, in the family as in the Temple.

In San Francisco Fitzstephan and Alice arranged so that he became acquainted with her husband and Gabrielle through other friends of the family. Gabrielle was now a young woman. Her physical peculiarities, which he interpreted pretty much as she had, fascinated him; and he tried his luck with her. He didn't have any. That made him doubly determined to land her: he was that way. Alice was his ally. She knew him and she hated the girl—so she wanted him to have her. Alice had told Fitzstephan the family history. The girl's father did not know at this time that she had been taught to think him her mother's murderer. He knew she had a deep aversion to him, but did not know on what it was based. He thought that what he had gone through in prison and since had marked him with a hardness naturally enough repellant to a young girl who was, in spite of their relationship, actually only a recent acquaintance.

He learned the truth about it when, surprising Fitzstephan in further attempts to make Gabrielle—as Fitzstephan put it—listen to reason, he had got into a three-cornered row with the pair of them. Leggett now began to understand what sort of a woman he was married to. Fitzstephan was no longer invited to the Leggett house, but kept in touch with Alice and waited his time.

His time came when Upton arrived with his demand for blackmail. Alice went to Fitzstephan for advice. He gave it to her—poisonously. He urged her to handle Upton herself, concealing his demand—his knowledge of the Leggett past—from Leggett. He told her she should above all else continue to keep her knowledge of Leggett's Central American and Mexican history concealed from him—a valuable hold on him now that he hated her because of what she'd taught the girl. Giving Upton the diamonds, and faking the burglary evidence, were Fitzstephan's ideas. Poor Alice didn't mean anything to him: he didn't care what happened to her so long as he could ruin Leggett and get Gabrielle.

He succeeded in the first of those aims: guided by him, Alice completely demolished the Leggett household, thinking, until the very last, when he pursued her after giving her the pistol in the laboratory, that he had a clever plan by which they would be saved; that is, she and he would: her husband didn't count with her any more than she with Fitzstephan. Fitzstephan had had to kill her, of course, to keep her from exposing him when she found that his clever plan was a trap for her.

Fitzstephan said he killed Leggett himself. When Gabrielle left the house after seeing Ruppert's murder, she left a note saying she had gone for good. That broke up the arrangement as far as Leggett was concerned. He told Alice he was through, was going away, and offered of his own accord to write a statement assuming responsibility for what she had done. Fitzstephan tried to persuade Alice to kill him, but she wouldn't. He did. He wanted Gabrielle, and he didn't think a live Leggett, even though a fugitive from justice, would let him have her.

Fitzstephan's success in getting rid of Leggett, and in escaping detection by killing Alice, encouraged him. He went

blithely on with his plan to get the girl. The Haldorns had
been introduced to the Leggetts some months before, and already had her nibbling at their hook. She had gone to them
when she ran away from home. Now they persuaded her to
come to the Temple again. The Haldorns didn't know what
Fitzstephan was up to, what he had done to the Leggetts:
they thought that the girl was only another of the likely
prospects he fed them. But Doctor Riese, hunting for Joseph
in Joseph's part of the Temple the day I got there, opened a
door that should have been locked, and saw Fitzstephan and
the Haldorns in conference.

That was dangerous: Riese couldn't be kept quiet, and,
once Fitzstephan's connection with the Temple was known,
as likely as not the truth about his part in the Leggett riot
would come out. He had two easily handled tools—Joseph
and Minnie. He had Riese killed. But that woke Aaronia up
to his true interest in Gabrielle. Aaronia, jealous, could and
would either make him give up the girl or ruin him. He persuaded Joseph that none of them was safe from the gallows
while Aaronia lived. When I saved Aaronia by killing her husband, I also saved Fitzstephan for the time: Aaronia and Fink
had to keep quiet about Riese's death if they wanted to save
themselves from being charged with complicity in it.

By this time Fitzstephan had hit his stride. He looked on
Gabrielle now as his property, bought with the deaths he had
caused. Each death had increased her price, her value to
him. When Eric carried her off and married her, Fitzstephan
hadn't hesitated. Eric was to be killed.

Nearly a year before, Fitzstephan had wanted a quiet place
where he could go to finish a novel. Mrs. Fink, my village-
blacksmith, had recommended Quesada. She was a native of
the village, and her son by a former marriage, Harvey
Whidden, was living there. Fitzstephan went to Quesada for a
couple of months, and became fairly well acquainted with
Whidden. Now that there was another murder to be done,
Fitzstephan remembered Whidden as a man who might do it,
for a price.

When Fitzstephan heard that Collinson wanted a quiet
place where his wife could rest and recuperate while they were
waiting for the Haldorns' trial, he suggested Quesada. Well, it

was a quiet place, probably the quietest in California. Then Fitzstephan went to Whidden with an offer of a thousand dollars for Eric's murder. Whidden refused at first, but he wasn't nimble-witted, and Fitzstephan could be persuasive enough, so the bargain had been made.

Whidden bungled a try at it Thursday night, frightening Collinson into wiring me, saw the wire in the telegraph office, and thought he had to go through with it then to save himself. So he fortified himself with whiskey, followed Collinson Friday night, and shoved him off the cliff. Then he took some more whiskey and came to San Francisco, considering himself by this time a hell of a desperate guy. He phoned his employer, saying: "Well, I killed him easy enough and dead enough. Now I want my money."

Fitzstephan's phone came through the house switchboard: he didn't know who might have heard Whidden talking. He decided to play safe. He pretended he didn't know who was talking nor what he was talking about. Thinking Fitzstephan was double-crossing him, knowing what the novelist wanted, Whidden decided to take the girl and hold her for, not his original thousand dollars, but ten thousand. He had enough drunken cunning to disguise his handwriting when he wrote his note to Fitzstephan, not to sign it, and to so word it that Fitzstephan couldn't tell the police who had sent it without explaining how he knew who had sent it.

Fitzstephan wasn't sitting any too pretty. When he got Whidden's note, he decided to play his hand boldly, pushing his thus-far-solid luck. He told me about the phone-call and gave me the letter. That entitled him to show himself in Quesada with an excellent reason for being there. But he came down ahead of time, the night before he joined me, and went to the marshal's house to ask Mrs. Cotton—whose relation to Whidden he knew—where he could find the man. Whidden was there, hiding from the marshal. Whidden wasn't nimble-witted, and Fitzstephan was persuasive enough when he wanted to be: Fitzstephan explained how Whidden's recklessness had forced him to pretend to not understand the phone-call. Fitzstephan had a scheme by which Whidden could now collect his ten thousand dollars in safety, or so he made Whidden think.

Whidden went back to his hiding-place. Fitzstephan remained with Mrs. Cotton. She, poor woman, now knew too
much, and didn't like what she knew. She was doomed: killing people was the one sure and safe way of keeping them
quiet: his whole recent experience proved it. His experience
with Leggett told him that if he could get her to leave behind
a statement in which various mysterious points were satisfactorily—and not too truthfully—explained, his situation would
be still further improved. She suspected his intentions, and
didn't want to help him carry them out. She finally wrote the
statement he dictated, but not until late in the morning. His
description of how he finally got it from her wasn't pleasant;
but he got it, and then strangled her, barely finishing when
her husband arrived home from his all-night hunt.

Fitzstephan escaped by the back door—the witnesses who
had seen him go away from the house didn't come forward
until his photograph in the papers jogged their memories—
and joined Vernon and me at the hotel. He went with us to
Whidden's hiding-place below Dull Point. He knew Whidden,
knew the dull man's probable reaction to this second betrayal.
He knew that neither Cotton nor Feeney would be sorry to
have to shoot Whidden. Fitzstephan believed he could trust to
his luck and what gamblers call the percentage of the situation. That failing, he meant to stumble when he stepped from
the boat, accidentally shooting Whidden with the gun in his
hand. (He remembered how neatly he had disposed of Mrs.
Leggett.) He might have been blamed for that, might even
have been suspected, but he could hardly have been convicted
of anything.

Once again his luck held. Whidden, seeing Fitzstephan
with us, had flared up and tried to shoot him, and we had
killed Whidden.

That was the story with which this crazy man, thinking
himself sane, tried to establish his insanity, and succeeded.
The other charges against him were dropped. He was sent to
the state asylum at Napa. A year later he was discharged. I
don't suppose the asylum officials thought him cured: they
thought he was too badly crippled ever to be dangerous again.

Aaronia Haldorn carried him off to an island in Puget
Sound, I've heard.

She testified at his trial, as one of his witnesses, but was not herself tried for anything. The attempt of her husband and Fitzstephan to kill her had, for all practical purposes, removed her from among the guilty.

We never found Mrs. Fink.

Tom Fink drew a five-to-fifteen-years jolt in San Quentin for what he had done to Fitzstephan. Neither of them seemed to blame the other now, and each tried to cover the other up on the witness stand. Fink's professed motive for the bombing was to avenge his step-son's death, but nobody swallowed that. He had tried to check Fitzstephan's activities before Fitzstephan brought the whole works down on their ears.

Released from prison, finding himself shadowed, Fink had seen both reason for fear and a means to safety in that shadow. He *had* back-doored Mickey that night, slipping out to get the material for his bomb, and then in again, working all night on the bomb. The news he had brought me was supposed to account for his presence in Quesada. The bomb wasn't large—its outer cover was an aluminum soap container wrapped in white paper—and neither he nor Fitzstephan had had any difficulty in concealing it from me when it passed between them during their handshaking. Fitzstephan had thought it something Aaronia was sending him, something important enough to justify the risk in sending it. He couldn't have refused to take it without attracting my attention, without giving away the connection between him and Fink. He had concealed it until we had left the room, and then had opened it—to wake up in the hospital. Tom Fink had thought himself safe, with Mickey to testify that he had shadowed him from the time he had left the prison, and me to account for his behavior on the scene of the bombing.

Fitzstephan said that he did not think Alice Leggett's account of the killing of her sister Lily was the truth, that he thought she—Alice—had done the killing herself and had lied to hurt Gabrielle. Everybody took it for granted that he was right—everybody, including Gabrielle—though he didn't have any evidence to support what was after all only his guess. I was tempted to have the agency's Paris correspondent see what he could dig up on that early affair, but decided not to.

It was nobody's business except Gabrielle's, and she seemed happy enough with what had already been dug up.

She was in the Collinsons' hands now. They had come to Quesada for her as soon as the newspapers put out their first extra accusing Fitzstephan of Eric's murder. The Collinsons hadn't had to be crude about it—to admit that they'd ever suspected her of anything: when Andrews had surrendered his letters testamentary, and another administrator—Walter Fielding—had been appointed, the Collinsons had simply seemed to pick her up, as was their right as her closest relations, where Andrews had put her down.

Two months in the mountains topped off her cure, and she came back to the city looking like nothing that she had been. The difference was not only in appearance.

"I can't really make myself believe that all that actually happened to me," she told me one noon when she, Laurence Collinson, and I were lunching together between morning and afternoon court-sessions. "Is it, do you think, because there was so much of it that I became callous?"

"No. Remember you were going around coked up most of the time. That saved you from the sharp edge. Lucky for you you were. Stay away from the morphine now and it'll always be a hazy sort of dream. Any time you want to bring it back clear and vivid, take a jolt."

"I won't, I won't, ever," she said; "not even to give you the —the fun of bullying me through a cure again. He enjoyed himself awfully," she told Laurence Collinson. "He used to curse me, ridicule me, threaten me with the most terrible things, and then, at the last, I think he tried to seduce me. And if I'm uncouth at times, Laurence, you'll have to blame him: he positively hadn't a refining influence."

She seemed to have come back far enough.

Laurence Collinson laughed with us, but not from any farther down than his chin. I had an idea he thought I hadn't a refining influence.

THE MALTESE FALCON

To
Jose

CONTENTS

CHAPTER I

Spade & Archer

S AMUEL SPADE'S jaw was long and bony, his chin a jutting v under the more flexible v of his mouth. His nostrils curved back to make another, smaller, v. His yellow-grey eyes were horizontal. The v *motif* was picked up again by thickish brows rising outward from twin creases above a hooked nose, and his pale brown hair grew down—from high flat temples— in a point on his forehead. He looked rather pleasantly like a blond satan.

He said to Effie Perine: "Yes, sweetheart?"

She was a lanky sunburned girl whose tan dress of thin woolen stuff clung to her with an effect of dampness. Her eyes were brown and playful in a shiny boyish face. She finished shutting the door behind her, leaned against it, and said: "There's a girl wants to see you. Her name's Wonderly."

"A customer?"

"I guess so. You'll want to see her anyway: she's a knock-out."

"Shoo her in, darling," said Spade. "Shoo her in."

Effie Perine opened the door again, following it back into the outer office, standing with a hand on the knob while saying: "Will you come in, Miss Wonderly?"

A voice said, "Thank you," so softly that only the purest articulation made the words intelligible, and a young woman came through the doorway. She advanced slowly, with tentative steps, looking at Spade with cobalt-blue eyes that were both shy and probing.

She was tall and pliantly slender, without angularity anywhere. Her body was erect and high-breasted, her legs long, her hands and feet narrow. She wore two shades of blue that had been selected because of her eyes. The hair curling from under her blue hat was darkly red, her full lips more brightly red. White teeth glistened in the crescent her timid smile made.

Spade rose bowing and indicating with a thick-fingered hand the oaken armchair beside his desk. He was quite six feet tall. The steep rounded slope of his shoulders made his body seem almost conical—no broader than it was thick—and kept his freshly pressed grey coat from fitting very well.

Miss Wonderly murmured, "Thank you," softly as before and sat down on the edge of the chair's wooden seat.

Spade sank into his swivel-chair, made a quarter-turn to face her, smiled politely. He smiled without separating his lips. All the v's in his face grew longer.

The tappity-tap-tap and the thin bell and muffled whir of Effie Perine's typewriting came through the closed door. Somewhere in a neighboring office a power-driven machine vibrated dully. On Spade's desk a limp cigarette smoldered in a brass tray filled with the remains of limp cigarettes. Ragged grey flakes of cigarette-ash dotted the yellow top of the desk and the green blotter and the papers that were there. A buff-curtained window, eight or ten inches open, let in from the court a current of air faintly scented with ammonia. The ashes on the desk twitched and crawled in the current.

Miss Wonderly watched the grey flakes twitch and crawl. Her eyes were uneasy. She sat on the very edge of the chair. Her feet were flat on the floor, as if she were about to rise. Her hands in dark gloves clasped a flat dark handbag in her lap.

Spade rocked back in his chair and asked: "Now what can I do for you, Miss Wonderly?"

She caught her breath and looked at him. She swallowed and said hurriedly: "Could you—? I thought—I—that is—" Then she tortured her lower lip with glistening teeth and said nothing. Only her dark eyes spoke now, pleading.

Spade smiled and nodded as if he understood her, but pleasantly, as if nothing serious were involved. He said: "Suppose you tell me about it, from the beginning, and then we'll know what needs doing. Better begin as far back as you can."

"That was in New York."

"Yes."

"I don't know where she met him. I mean I don't know where in New York. She's five years younger than I—only seventeen—and we didn't have the same friends. I don't suppose we've ever been as close as sisters should be. Mama and Papa are in Europe. It would kill them. I've got to get her back before they come home."

"Yes," he said.

"They're coming home the first of the month."

Spade's eyes brightened. "Then we've two weeks," he said.

"I didn't know what she had done until her letter came. I was frantic." Her lips trembled. Her hands mashed the dark handbag in her lap. "I was too afraid she had done something like this to go to the police, and the fear that something had happened to her kept urging me to go. There wasn't anyone I could go to for advice. I didn't know what to do. What could I do?"

"Nothing, of course," Spade said, "but then her letter came?"

"Yes, and I sent her a telegram asking her to come home. I sent it to General Delivery here. That was the only address she gave me. I waited a whole week, but no answer came, not another word from her. And Mama and Papa's return was drawing nearer and nearer. So I came to San Francisco to get her. I wrote her I was coming. I shouldn't have done that, should I?"

"Maybe not. It's not always easy to know what to do. You haven't found her?"

"No, I haven't. I wrote her that I would go to the St. Mark, and I begged her to come and let me talk to her even if she didn't intend to go home with me. But she didn't come. I waited three days, and she didn't come, didn't even send me a message of any sort."

Spade nodded his blond satan's head, frowned sympathetically, and tightened his lips together.

"It was horrible," Miss Wonderly said, trying to smile. "I couldn't sit there like that—waiting—not knowing what had happened to her, what might be happening to her." She stopped trying to smile. She shuddered. "The only address I had was General Delivery. I wrote her another letter, and yesterday afternoon I went to the Post Office. I stayed there until after dark, but I didn't see her. I went there again this morning, and still didn't see Corinne, but I saw Floyd Thursby."

Spade nodded again. His frown went away. In its place came a look of sharp attentiveness.

"He wouldn't tell me where Corinne was," she went on,

hopelessly. "He wouldn't tell me anything, except that she was well and happy. But how can I believe that? That is what he would tell me anyhow, isn't it?"

"Sure," Spade agreed. "But it might be true."

"I hope it is. I do hope it is," she exclaimed. "But I can't go back home like this, without having seen her, without even having talked to her on the phone. He wouldn't take me to her. He said she didn't want to see me. I can't believe that. He promised to tell her he had seen me, and to bring her to see me—if she would come—this evening at the hotel. He said he knew she wouldn't. He promised to come himself if she wouldn't. He—"

She broke off with a startled hand to her mouth as the door opened.

The man who had opened the door came in a step, said, "Oh, excuse me!" hastily took his brown hat from his head, and backed out.

"It's all right, Miles," Spade told him. "Come in. Miss Wonderly, this is Mr. Archer, my partner."

Miles Archer came into the office again, shutting the door behind him, ducking his head and smiling at Miss Wonderly, making a vaguely polite gesture with the hat in his hand. He was of medium height, solidly built, wide in the shoulders, thick in the neck, with a jovial heavy-jawed red face and some grey in his close-trimmed hair. He was apparently as many years past forty as Spade was past thirty.

Spade said: "Miss Wonderly's sister ran away from New York with a fellow named Floyd Thursby. They're here. Miss Wonderly has seen Thursby and has a date with him tonight. Maybe he'll bring the sister with him. The chances are he won't. Miss Wonderly wants us to find the sister and get her away from him and back home." He looked at Miss Wonderly. "Right?"

"Yes," she said indistinctly. The embarrassment that had gradually been driven away by Spade's ingratiating smiles and nods and assurances was pinkening her face again. She looked at the bag in her lap and picked nervously at it with a gloved finger.

Spade winked at his partner.

Miles Archer came forward to stand at a corner of the desk. While the girl looked at her bag he looked at her. His little brown eyes ran their bold appraising gaze from her lowered face to her feet and up to her face again. Then he looked at Spade and made a silent whistling mouth of appreciation.

Spade lifted two fingers from the arm of his chair in a brief warning gesture and said:

"We shouldn't have any trouble with it. It's simply a matter of having a man at the hotel this evening to shadow him away when he leaves, and shadow him until he leads us to your sister. If she comes with him, and you persuade her to return with you, so much the better. Otherwise—if she doesn't want to leave him after we've found her—well, we'll find a way of managing that."

Archer said: "Yeh." His voice was heavy, coarse.

Miss Wonderly looked up at Spade, quickly, puckering her forehead between her eyebrows.

"Oh, but you must be careful!" Her voice shook a little, and her lips shaped the words with nervous jerkiness. "I'm deathly afraid of him, of what he might do. She's so young and his bringing her here from New York is such a serious— Mightn't he—mightn't he do—something to her?"

Spade smiled and patted the arms of his chair.

"Just leave that to us," he said. "We'll know how to handle him."

"But mightn't he?" she insisted.

"There's always a chance." Spade nodded judicially. "But you can trust us to take care of that."

"I do trust you," she said earnestly, "but I want you to know that he's a dangerous man. I honestly don't think he'd stop at anything. I don't believe he'd hesitate to—to kill Corinne if he thought it would save him. Mightn't he do that?"

"You didn't threaten him, did you?"

"I told him that all I wanted was to get her home before Mama and Papa came so they'd never know what she had done. I promised him I'd never say a word to them about it if he helped me, but if he didn't Papa would certainly see that he was punished. I—I don't suppose he believed me, altogether."

"Can he cover up by marrying her?" Archer asked.

The girl blushed and replied in a confused voice: "He has a wife and three children in England. Corinne wrote me that, to explain why she had gone off with him."

"They usually do," Spade said, "though not always in England." He leaned forward to reach for pencil and pad of paper. "What does he look like?"

"Oh, he's thirty-five years old, perhaps, and as tall as you, and either naturally dark or quite sunburned. His hair is dark too, and he has thick eyebrows. He talks in a rather loud, blustery way and has a nervous, irritable manner. He gives the impression of being—of violence."

Spade, scribbling on the pad, asked without looking up: "What color eyes?"

"They're blue-grey and watery, though not in a weak way. And—oh, yes—he has a marked cleft in his chin."

"Thin, medium, or heavy build?"

"Quite athletic. He's broad-shouldered and carries himself erect, has what could be called a decidedly military carriage. He was wearing a light grey suit and a grey hat when I saw him this morning."

"What does he do for a living?" Spade asked as he laid down his pencil.

"I don't know," she said. "I haven't the slightest idea."

"What time is he coming to see you?"

"After eight o'clock."

"All right, Miss Wonderly, we'll have a man there. It'll help if—"

"Mr. Spade, could, either you or Mr. Archer?" She made an appealing gesture with both hands. "Could either of you look after it personally? I don't mean that the man you'd send wouldn't be capable, but—oh!—I'm so afraid of what might happen to Corrine. I'm afraid of him. Could you? I'd be—I'd expect to be charged more, of course." She opened her handbag with nervous fingers and put two hundred-dollar bills on Spade's desk. "Would that be enough?"

"Yeh," Archer said, "and I'll look after it myself."

Miss Wonderly stood up, impulsively holding a hand out to him.

"Thank you! Thank you!" she exclaimed, and then gave Spade her hand, repeating: "Thank you!"

"Not at all," Spade said over it. "Glad to. It'll help some if you either meet Thursby downstairs or let yourself be seen in the lobby with him at some time."

"I will," she promised, and thanked the partners again.

"And don't look for me," Archer cautioned her. "I'll see you all right."

Spade went to the corridor-door with Miss Wonderly. When he returned to his desk Archer nodded at the hundred-dollar bills there, growled complacently, "They're right enough," picked one up, folded it, and tucked it into a vest-pocket. "And they had brothers in her bag."

Spade pocketed the other bill before he sat down. Then he said: "Well, don't dynamite her too much. What do you think of her?"

"Sweet! And you telling me not to dynamite her." Archer guffawed suddenly without merriment. "Maybe you saw her first, Sam, but I spoke first." He put his hands in his trousers-pockets and teetered on his heels.

"You'll play hell with her, you will." Spade grinned wolfishly, showing the edges of teeth far back in his jaw. "You've got brains, yes you have." He began to make a cigarette.

CHAPTER II

Death in the Fog

A TELEPHONE-BELL rang in darkness. When it had rung three times bed-springs creaked, fingers fumbled on wood, something small and hard thudded on a carpeted floor, the springs creaked again, and a man's voice said:

"Hello. . . . Yes, speaking. . . . Dead? . . . Yes. . . . Fifteen minutes. Thanks."

A switch clicked and a white bowl hung on three gilded chains from the ceiling's center filled the room with light. Spade, barefooted in green and white checked pajamas, sat on the side of his bed. He scowled at the telephone on the table while his hands took from beside it a packet of brown papers and a sack of Bull Durham tobacco.

Cold steamy air blew in through two open windows, bringing with it half a dozen times a minute the Alcatraz foghorn's dull moaning. A tinny alarm-clock, insecurely mounted on a corner of Duke's *Celebrated Criminal Cases of America*—face down on the table—held its hands at five minutes past two.

Spade's thick fingers made a cigarette with deliberate care, sifting a measured quantity of tan flakes down into curved paper, spreading the flakes so that they lay equal at the ends with a slight depression in the middle, thumbs rolling the paper's inner edge down and up under the outer edge as forefingers pressed it over, thumbs and fingers sliding to the paper cylinder's ends to hold it even while tongue licked the flap, left forefinger and thumb pinching their end while right forefinger and thumb smoothed the damp seam, right forefinger and thumb twisting their end and lifting the other to Spade's mouth.

He picked up the pigskin and nickel lighter that had fallen to the floor, manipulated it, and with the cigarette burning in a corner of his mouth stood up. He took off his pajamas. The smooth thickness of his arms, legs, and body, the sag of his big rounded shoulders, made his body like a bear's. It was like a shaved bear's: his chest was hairless. His skin was childishly soft and pink.

He scratched the back of his neck and began to dress. He put on a thin white union-suit, grey socks, black garters, and dark brown shoes. When he had fastened his shoes he picked up the telephone, called Graystone 4500, and ordered a taxicab. He put on a green-striped white shirt, a soft white collar, a green necktie, the grey suit he had worn that day, a loose tweed overcoat, and a dark grey hat. The street-door-bell rang as he stuffed tobacco, keys, and money into his pockets.

Where Bush Street roofed Stockton before slipping downhill to Chinatown, Spade paid his fare and left the taxicab. San Francisco's night-fog, thin, clammy, and penetrant, blurred the street. A few yards from where Spade had dismissed the taxicab a small group of men stood looking up an alley. Two women stood with a man on the other side of Bush Street, looking at the alley. There were faces at windows.

Spade crossed the sidewalk between iron-railed hatchways that opened above bare ugly stairs, went to the parapet, and, resting his hands on the damp coping, looked down into Stockton Street.

An automobile popped out of the tunnel beneath him with a roaring swish, as if it had been blown out, and ran away. Not far from the tunnel's mouth a man was hunkered on his heels before a billboard that held advertisements of a moving picture and a gasoline across the front of a gap between two store-buildings. The hunkered man's head was bent almost to the sidewalk so he could look under the billboard. A hand flat on the paving, a hand clenched on the billboard's green frame, held him in this grotesque position. Two other men stood awkwardly together at one end of the billboard, peeping through the few inches of space between it and the building at that end. The building at the other end had a blank grey sidewall that looked down on the lot behind the billboard. Lights flickered on the sidewall, and the shadows of men moving among lights.

Spade turned from the parapet and walked up Bush Street to the alley where men were grouped. A uniformed policeman chewing gum under an enameled sign that said *Burritt St.* in white against dark blue put out an arm and asked:

"What do you want here?"

"I'm Sam Spade. Tom Polhaus phoned me."

"Sure you are." The policeman's arm went down. "I didn't know you at first. Well, they're back there." He jerked a thumb over his shoulder. "Bad business."

"Bad enough," Spade agreed, and went up the alley.

Half-way up it, not far from the entrance, a dark ambulance stood. Behind the ambulance, to the left, the alley was bounded by a waist-high fence, horizontal strips of rough boarding. From the fence dark ground fell away steeply to the billboard on Stockton Street below.

A ten-foot length of the fence's top rail had been torn from a post at one end and hung dangling from the other. Fifteen feet down the slope a flat boulder stuck out. In the notch between boulder and slope Miles Archer lay on his back. Two men stood over him. One of them held the beam of an electric torch on the dead man. Other men with lights moved up and down the slope.

One of them hailed Spade, "Hello, Sam," and clambered up to the alley, his shadow running up the slope before him. He was a barrel-bellied tall man with shrewd small eyes, a thick mouth, and carelessly shaven dark jowls. His shoes, knees, hands, and chin were daubed with brown loam.

"I figured you'd want to see it before we took him away," he said as he stepped over the broken fence.

"Thanks, Tom," Spade said. "What happened?" He put an elbow on a fence-post and looked down at the men below, nodding to those who nodded to him.

Tom Polhaus poked his own left breast with a dirty finger. "Got him right through the pump—with this." He took a fat revolver from his coat-pocket and held it out to Spade. Mud inlaid the depressions in the revolver's surface. "A Webley. English, ain't it?"

Spade took his elbow from the fence-post and leaned down to look at the weapon, but he did not touch it.

"Yes," he said, "Webley-Fosbery automatic revolver. That's it. Thirty-eight, eight shot. They don't make them any more. How many gone out of it?"

"One pill." Tom poked his breast again. "He must've been dead when he cracked the fence." He raised the muddy revolver. "Ever seen this before?"

Spade nodded. "I've seen Webley-Fosberys," he said without interest, and then spoke rapidly: "He was shot up here, huh? Standing where you are, with his back to the fence. The man that shot him stands here." He went around in front of Tom and raised a hand breast-high with leveled forefinger. "Lets him have it and Miles goes back, taking the top off the fence and going on through and down till the rock catches him. That it?"

"That's it," Tom replied slowly, working his brows together. "The blast burnt his coat."

"Who found him?"

"The man on the beat, Shilling. He was coming down Bush, and just as he got here a machine turning threw head-lights up here, and he saw the top off the fence. So he came up to look at it, and found him."

"What about the machine that was turning around?"

"Not a damned thing about it, Sam. Shilling didn't pay any attention to it, not knowing anything was wrong then. He says nobody didn't come out of here while he was coming down from Powell or he'd've seen them. The only other way out would be under the billboard on Stockton. Nobody went that way. The fog's got the ground soggy, and the only marks are where Miles slid down and where this here gun rolled."

"Didn't anybody hear the shot?"

"For the love of God, Sam, we only just got here. Somebody must've heard it, when we find them." He turned and put a leg over the fence. "Coming down for a look at him before he's moved?"

Spade said: "No."

Tom halted astride the fence and looked back at Spade with surprised small eyes.

Spade said: "You've seen him. You'd see everything I could."

Tom, still looking at Spade, nodded doubtfully and withdrew his leg over the fence.

"His gun was tucked away on his hip," he said. "It hadn't been fired. His overcoat was buttoned. There's a hundred and sixty-some bucks in his clothes. Was he working, Sam?"

Spade, after a moment's hesitation, nodded.

Tom asked: "Well?"

"He was supposed to be tailing a fellow named Floyd Thursby," Spade said, and described Thursby as Miss Wonderly had described him.

"What for?"

Spade put his hands into his overcoat-pockets and blinked sleepy eyes at Tom.

Tom repeated impatiently: "What for?"

"He was an Englishman, maybe. I don't know what his game was, exactly. We were trying to find out where he lived." Spade grinned faintly and took a hand from his pocket to pat Tom's shoulder. "Don't crowd me." He put the hand in his pocket again. "I'm going out to break the news to Miles's wife." He turned away.

Tom, scowling, opened his mouth, closed it without having said anything, cleared his throat, put the scowl off his face, and spoke with a husky sort of gentleness:

"It's tough, him getting it like that. Miles had his faults same as the rest of us, but I guess he must've had some good points too."

"I guess so," Spade agreed in a tone that was utterly mean-ingless, and went out of the alley.

In an all-night drug-store on the corner of Bush and Taylor Streets, Spade used a telephone.

"Precious," he said into it a little while after he had given a number, "Miles has been shot. . . . Yes, he's dead. . . . Now don't get excited. . . . Yes. . . . You'll have to break it to Iva. . . . No, I'm damned if I will. You've got to do it. . . . That's a good girl. . . . And keep her away from the office. . . . Tell her I'll see her—uh—some time. . . . Yes, but don't tie me up to anything. . . . That's the stuff. You're an angel. 'Bye."

Spade's tinny alarm-clock said three-forty when he turned on the light in the suspended bowl again. He dropped his hat and overcoat on the bed and went into his kitchen, returning to the bedroom with a wine-glass and a tall bottle of Bacardi. He poured a drink and drank it standing. He put bottle and glass on the table, sat on the side of the bed facing them, and rolled a cigarette. He had drunk his third glass of Bacardi and was lighting his fifth cigarette when the street-door-bell rang. The hands of the alarm-clock registered four-thirty.

Spade sighed, rose from the bed, and went to the telephone-box beside his bathroom door. He pressed the button that released the street-door-lock. He muttered, "Damn her," and stood scowling at the black telephone-box, breathing irregularly while a dull flush grew in his cheeks.

The grating and rattling of the elevator-door opening and closing came from the corridor. Spade sighed again and moved towards the corridor-door. Soft heavy footsteps sounded on the carpeted floor outside, the footsteps of two men. Spade's face brightened. His eyes were no longer harassed. He opened the door quickly.

"Hello, Tom," he said to the barrel-bellied tall detective with whom he had talked in Burritt Street, and, "Hello, Lieutenant," to the man beside Tom. "Come in."

They nodded together, neither saying anything, and came in. Spade shut the door and ushered them into his bedroom. Tom sat on an end of the sofa by the windows. The Lieutenant sat on a chair beside the table.

The Lieutenant was a compactly built man with a round head under short-cut grizzled hair and a square face behind a short-cut grizzled mustache. A five-dollar-gold-piece was pinned to his necktie and there was a small elaborate diamond-set secret-society-emblem on his lapel.

Spade brought two wine-glasses in from the kitchen, filled them and his own with Bacardi, gave one to each of his visitors, and sat down with his on the side of the bed. His face was placid and uncurious. He raised his glass, and said, "Success to crime," and drank it down.

Tom emptied his glass, set it on the floor beside his feet, and wiped his mouth with a muddy forefinger. He stared at the foot of the bed as if trying to remember something of which it vaguely reminded him.

The Lieutenant looked at his glass for a dozen seconds, took a very small sip of its contents, and put the glass on the table at his elbow. He examined the room with hard deliberate eyes, and then looked at Tom.

Tom moved uncomfortably on the sofa and, not looking up, asked: "Did you break the news to Miles's wife, Sam?"

Spade said: "Uh-huh."

"How'd she take it?"

Spade shook his head. "I don't know anything about women."

Tom said softly: "The hell you don't."

The Lieutenant put his hands on his knees and leaned forward. His greenish eyes were fixed on Spade in a peculiarly rigid stare, as if their focus were a matter of mechanics, to be changed only by pulling a lever or pressing a button.

"What kind of gun do you carry?" he asked.

"None. I don't like them much. Of course there are some in the office."

"I'd like to see one of them," the Lieutenant said. "You don't happen to have one here?"

"No."

"You sure of that?"

"Look around." Spade smiled and waved his empty glass a little. "Turn the dump upside-down if you want. I won't squawk—if you've got a search-warrant."

Tom protested: "Oh, hell, Sam!"

Spade set his glass on the table and stood up facing the Lieutenant.

"What do you want, Dundy?" he asked in a voice hard and cold as his eyes.

Lieutenant Dundy's eyes had moved to maintain their focus on Spade's. Only his eyes had moved.

Tom shifted his weight on the sofa again, blew a deep breath out through his nose, and growled plaintively: "We're not wanting to make any trouble, Sam."

Spade, ignoring Tom, said to Dundy: "Well, what do you want? Talk turkey. Who in hell do you think you are, coming in here trying to rope me?"

"All right," Dundy said in his chest, "sit down and listen."

"I'll sit or stand as I damned please," said Spade, not moving.

"For Christ's sake be reasonable," Tom begged. "What's the use of us having a row? If you want to know why we didn't talk turkey it's because when I asked you who this Thursby was you as good as told me it was none of my business. You can't treat us that way, Sam. It ain't right and it won't get you anywheres. We got our work to do."

Lieutenant Dundy jumped up, stood close to Spade, and thrust his square face up at the taller man's.

"I've warned you your foot was going to slip one of these days," he said.

Spade made a depreciative mouth, raising his eyebrows. "Everybody's foot slips sometime," he replied with derisive mildness.

"And this is yours."

Spade smiled and shook his head. "No, I'll do nicely, thank you." He stopped smiling. His upper lip, on the left side, twitched over his eyetooth. His eyes became narrow and sultry. His voice came out deep as the Lieutenant's. "I don't like this. What are you sucking around for? Tell me, or get out and let me go to bed."

"Who's Thursby?" Dundy demanded.

"I told Tom what I knew about him."

"You told Tom damned little."

"I knew damned little."

"Why were you tailing him?"

"I wasn't. Miles was—for the swell reason that we had a client who was paying good United States money to have him tailed."

"Who's the client?"

Placidity came back to Spade's face and voice. He said reprovingly: "You know I can't tell you that until I've talked it over with the client."

"You'll tell it to me or you'll tell it in court," Dundy said hotly. "This is murder and don't you forget it."

"Maybe. And here's something for you to not forget, sweetheart. I'll tell it or not as I damned please. It's a long while since I burst out crying because policemen didn't like me."

Tom left the sofa and sat on the foot of the bed. His carelessly shaven mud-smeared face was tired and lined.

"Be reasonable, Sam," he pleaded. "Give us a chance. How can we turn up anything on Miles's killing if you won't give us what you've got?"

"You needn't get a headache over that," Spade told him. "I'll bury my dead."

Lieutenant Dundy sat down and put his hands on his knees again. His eyes were warm green discs.

"I thought you would," he said. He smiled with grim content. "That's just exactly why we came to see you. Isn't it, Tom?"

Tom groaned, but said nothing articulate.

Spade watched Dundy warily.

"That's just exactly what I said to Tom," the Lieutenant went on. "I said: 'Tom, I've got a hunch that Sam Spade's a man to keep the family-troubles in the family.' That's just what I said to him."

The wariness went out of Spade's eyes. He made his eyes dull with boredom. He turned his face around to Tom and asked with great carelessness: "What's itching your boy-friend now?"

Dundy jumped up and tapped Spade's chest with the ends of two bent fingers.

"Just this," he said, taking pains to make each word distinct, emphasizing them with his tapping finger-ends: "Thursby was shot down in front of his hotel just thirty-five minutes after you left Burritt Street."

Spade spoke, taking equal pains with his words: "Keep your God-damned paws off me."

Dundy withdrew the tapping fingers, but there was no change in his voice: "Tom says you were in too much of a hurry to even stop for a look at your partner."

Tom growled apologetically: "Well, damn it, Sam, you did run off like that."

"And you didn't go to Archer's house to tell his wife," the Lieutenant said. "We called up and that girl in your office was there, and she said you sent her."

Spade nodded. His face was stupid in its calmness.

Lieutenant Dundy raised his two bent fingers towards Spade's chest, quickly lowered them, and said: "I give you ten minutes to get to a phone and do your talking to the girl. I give you ten minutes to get to Thursby's joint—Geary near Leavenworth—you could do it easy in that time, or fifteen at the most. And that gives you ten or fifteen minutes of waiting before he showed up."

"I knew where he lived?" Spade asked. "And I knew he hadn't gone straight home from killing Miles?"

"You knew what you knew," Dundy replied stubbornly. "What time did you get home?"

"Twenty minutes to four. I walked around thinking things over."

The Lieutenant wagged his round head up and down. "We knew you weren't home at three-thirty. We tried to get you on the phone. Where'd you do your walking?"

"Out Bush Street a way and back."

"Did you see anybody that—?"

"No, no witnesses," Spade said and laughed pleasantly. "Sit down, Dundy. You haven't finished your drink. Get your glass, Tom."

Tom said: "No, thanks, Sam."

Dundy sat down, but paid no attention to his glass of rum.

Spade filled his own glass, drank, set the empty glass on the table, and returned to his bedside-seat.

"I know where I stand now," he said, looking with friendly eyes from one of the police-detectives to the other. "I'm sorry I got up on my hind legs, but you birds coming in and trying to put the work on me made me nervous. Having Miles knocked off bothered me, and then you birds cracking foxy. That's all right now, though, now that I know what you're up to."

Tom said: "Forget it."

The Lieutenant said nothing.

Spade asked: "Thursby die?"

While the Lieutenant hesitated Tom said: "Yes."

Then the Lieutenant said angrily: "And you might just as well know it—if you don't—that he died before he could tell anybody anything."

Spade was rolling a cigarette. He asked, not looking up: "What do you mean by that? You think I did know it?"

"I meant what I said," Dundy replied bluntly.

Spade looked up at him and smiled, holding the finished cigarette in one hand, his lighter in the other.

"You're not ready to pinch me yet, are you, Dundy?" he asked.

Dundy looked with hard green eyes at Spade and did not answer him.

"Then," said Spade, "there's no particular reason why I should give a damn what you think, is there, Dundy?"

Tom said: "Aw, be reasonable, Sam."

Spade put the cigarette in his mouth, set fire to it, and laughed smoke out.

"I'll be reasonable, Tom," he promised. "How did I kill this Thursby? I've forgotten."

Tom grunted disgust. Lieutenant Dundy said: "He was shot four times in the back, with a forty-four or forty-five, from across the street, when he started to go in the hotel. Nobody saw it, but that's the way it figures."

"And he was wearing a Luger in a shoulder-holster," Tom added. "It hadn't been fired."

"What do the hotel-people know about him?" Spade asked.

"Nothing except that he'd been there a week."

"Alone?"

"Alone."

"What did you find on him? or in his room?"

Dundy drew his lips in and asked: "What'd you think we'd find?"

Spade made a careless circle with his limp cigarette. "Something to tell you who he was, what his story was. Did you?"

"We thought you could tell us that."

Spade looked at the Lieutenant with yellow-grey eyes that held an almost exaggerated amount of candor. "I've never seen Thursby, dead or alive."

Lieutenant Dundy stood up looking dissatisfied. Tom rose yawning and stretching.

"We've asked what we came to ask," Dundy said, frowning over eyes hard as green pebbles. He held his mustached upper lip tight to his teeth, letting his lower lip push the words out. "We've told you more than you've told us. That's fair enough. You know me, Spade. If you did or you didn't you'll get a square deal out of me, and most of the breaks. I don't know that I'd blame you a hell of a lot—but that wouldn't keep me from nailing you."

"Fair enough," Spade replied evenly. "But I'd feel better about it if you'd drink your drink."

Lieutenant Dundy turned to the table, picked up his glass, and slowly emptied it. Then he said, "Good night," and held out his hand. They shook hands ceremoniously. Tom and Spade shook hands ceremoniously. Spade let them out. Then he undressed, turned off the lights, and went to bed.

Three Women

WHEN Spade reached his office at ten o'clock the follow-ing morning Effie Perine was at her desk opening the morning's mail. Her boyish face was pale under its sunburn. She put down the handful of envelopes and the brass paper-knife she held and said: "She's in there." Her voice was low and warning.

"I asked you to keep her away," Spade complained. He too kept his voice low.

Effie Perine's brown eyes opened wide and her voice was ir-ritable as his: "Yes, but you didn't tell me how." Her eyelids went together a little and her shoulders drooped. "Don't be cranky, Sam," she said wearily. "I had her all night."

Spade stood beside the girl, put a hand on her head, and smoothed her hair away from its parting. "Sorry, angel, I haven't—" He broke off as the inner door opened. "Hello, Iva," he said to the woman who had opened it.

"Oh, Sam!" she said.

She was a blonde woman of a few more years than thirty. Her facial prettiness was perhaps five years past its best mo-ment. Her body for all its sturdiness was finely modeled and exquisite. She wore black clothes from hat to shoes. They had as mourning an impromptu air. Having spoken, she stepped back from the door and stood waiting for Spade.

He took his hand from Effie Perine's head and entered the inner office, shutting the door. Iva came quickly to him, raising her sad face for his kiss. Her arms were around him before his held her. When they had kissed he made a little movement as if to release her, but she pressed her face to his chest and began sobbing.

He stroked her round back, saying: "Poor darling." His voice was tender. His eyes, squinting at the desk that had been his partner's, across the room from his own, were angry. He drew his lips back over his teeth in an impatient grimace and turned his chin aside to avoid contact with the crown of her hat. "Did you send for Miles's brother?" he asked.

"Yes, he came over this morning." The words were blurred by her sobbing and his coat against her mouth.

He grimaced again and bent his head for a surreptitious look at the watch on his wrist. His left arm was around her, the hand on her left shoulder. His cuff was pulled back far enough to leave the watch uncovered. It showed ten-ten.

The woman stirred in his arms and raised her face again. Her blue eyes were wet, round, and white-ringed. Her mouth was moist.

"Oh, Sam," she moaned, "did you kill him?"

Spade stared at her with bulging eyes. His bony jaw fell down. He took his arms from her and stepped back out of her arms. He scowled at her and cleared his throat.

She held her arms up as he had left them. Anguish clouded her eyes, partly closed them under eyebrows pulled up at the inner ends. Her soft damp red lips trembled.

Spade laughed a harsh syllable, "Ha!" and went to the buff-curtained window. He stood there with his back to her looking through the curtain into the court until she started towards him. Then he turned quickly and went to his desk. He sat down, put his elbows on the desk, his chin between his fists, and looked at her. His yellowish eyes glittered between narrowed lids.

"Who," he asked coldly, "put that bright idea in your head?"

"I thought—" She lifted a hand to her mouth and fresh tears came to her eyes. She came to stand beside the desk, moving with easy sure-footed grace in black slippers whose smallness and heel-height were extreme. "Be kind to me, Sam," she said humbly.

He laughed at her, his eyes still glittering. "You killed my husband, Sam, be kind to me." He clapped his palms together and said: "Jesus Christ."

She began to cry audibly, holding a white handkerchief to her face.

He got up and stood close behind her. He put his arms around her. He kissed her neck between ear and coat-collar. He said: "Now, Iva, don't." His face was expressionless. When she had stopped crying he put his mouth to her ear and murmured: "You shouldn't have come here today, precious. It wasn't wise. You can't stay. You ought to be home."

She turned around in his arms to face him and asked: "You'll come tonight?"

He shook his head gently. "Not tonight."

"Soon?"

"Yes."

"How soon?"

"As soon as I can."

He kissed her mouth, led her to the door, opened it, said, "Good-bye, Iva," bowed her out, shut the door, and returned to his desk.

He took tobacco and cigarette-papers from his vest-pockets, but did not roll a cigarette. He sat holding the papers in one hand, the tobacco in the other, and looked with brooding eyes at his dead partner's desk.

Effie Perine opened the door and came in. Her brown eyes were uneasy. Her voice was careless. She asked: "Well?"

Spade said nothing. His brooding gaze did not move from his partner's desk.

The girl frowned and came around to his side. "Well," she asked in a louder voice, "how did you and the widow make out?"

"She thinks I shot Miles," he said. Only his lips moved.

"So you could marry her?"

Spade made no reply to that.

The girl took his hat from his head and put it on the desk. Then she leaned over and took the tobacco-sack and the papers from his inert fingers.

"The police think I shot Thursby," he said.

"Who is he?" she asked, separating a cigarette-paper from the packet, sifting tobacco into it.

"Who do you think I shot?" he asked.

When she ignored that question he said: "Thursby's the guy Miles was supposed to be tailing for the Wonderly girl."

Her thin fingers finished shaping the cigarette. She licked it, smoothed it, twisted its ends, and placed it between Spade's lips. He said, "Thanks, honey," put an arm around her slim waist, and rested his cheek wearily against her hip, shutting his eyes.

"Are you going to marry Iva?" she asked, looking down at his pale brown hair.

"Don't be silly," he muttered. The unlighted cigarette bobbed up and down with the movement of his lips.

"She doesn't think it's silly. Why should she—the way you've played around with her?"

He sighed and said: "I wish to Christ I'd never seen her."

"Maybe you do now." A trace of spitefulness came into the girl's voice. "But there was a time."

"I never know what to do or say to women except that way," he grumbled, "and then I didn't like Miles."

"That's a lie, Sam," the girl said. "You know I think she's a louse, but I'd be a louse too if it would give me a body like hers."

Spade rubbed his face impatiently against her hip, but said nothing.

Effie Perine bit her lip, wrinkled her forehead, and, bending over for a better view of his face, asked: "Do you suppose she could have killed him?"

Spade sat up straight and took his arm from her waist. He smiled at her. Her smile held nothing but amusement. He took out his lighter, snapped on the flame, and applied it to the end of his cigarette. "You're an angel," he said tenderly through smoke, "a nice rattle-brained angel."

She smiled a bit wryly. "Oh, am I? Suppose I told you that your Iva hadn't been home many minutes when I arrived to break the news at three o'clock this morning?"

"Are you telling me?" he asked. His eyes had become alert though his mouth continued to smile.

"She kept me waiting at the door while she undressed or finished undressing. I saw her clothes where she had dumped them on a chair. Her hat and coat were underneath. Her singlette, on top, was still warm. She said she had been asleep, but she hadn't. She had wrinkled up the bed, but the wrinkles weren't mashed down."

Spade took the girl's hand and patted it. "You're a detective, darling, but"—he shook his head—"she didn't kill him."

Effie Perine snatched her hand away. "That louse wants to marry you, Sam," she said bitterly.

He made an impatient gesture with his head and one hand.

She frowned at him and demanded: "Did you see her last night?"

"No."

"Honestly?"

"Honestly. Don't act like Dundy, sweetheart. It ill becomes you."

"Has Dundy been after you?"

"Uh-huh. He and Tom Polhaus dropped in for a drink at four o'clock."

"Do they really think you shot this what's-his-name?"

"Thursby." He dropped what was left of his cigarette into the brass tray and began to roll another.

"Do they?" she insisted.

"God knows." His eyes were on the cigarette he was making. "They did have some such notion. I don't know how far I talked them out of it."

"Look at me, Sam."

He looked at her and laughed so that for the moment merriment mingled with the anxiety in her face.

"You worry me," she said, seriousness returning to her face as she talked. "You always think you know what you're doing, but you're too slick for your own good, and some day you're going to find it out."

He sighed mockingly and rubbed his cheek against her arm. "That's what Dundy says, but you keep Iva away from me, sweet, and I'll manage to survive the rest of my troubles." He stood up and put on his hat. "Have the *Spade & Archer* taken off the door and *Samuel Spade* put on. I'll be back in an hour, or phone you."

Spade went through the St. Mark's long purplish lobby to the desk and asked a red-haired dandy whether Miss Wonderly was in. The red-haired dandy turned away, and then back shaking his head. "She checked out this morning, Mr. Spade."

"Thanks."

Spade walked past the desk to an alcove off the lobby where a plump young-middle-aged man in dark clothes sat at a flat-topped mahogany desk. On the edge of the desk facing the lobby was a triangular prism of mahogany and brass inscribed *Mr. Freed.*

The plump man got up and came around the desk holding out his hand.

"I was awfully sorry to hear about Archer, Spade," he said in the tone of one trained to sympathize readily without intrusiveness. "I've just seen it in the *Call*. He was in here last night, you know."

"Thanks, Freed. Were you talking to him?"

"No. He was sitting in the lobby when I came in early in the evening. I didn't stop. I thought he was probably working and I know you fellows like to be left alone when you're busy. Did that have anything to do with his—?"

"I don't think so, but we don't know yet. Anyway, we won't mix the house up in it if it can be helped."

"Thanks."

"That's all right. Can you give me some dope on an ex-guest, and then forget that I asked for it?"

"Surely."

"A Miss Wonderly checked out this morning. I'd like to know the details."

"Come along," Freed said, "and we'll see what we can learn."

Spade stood still, shaking his head. "I don't want to show in it."

Freed nodded and went out of the alcove. In the lobby he halted suddenly and came back to Spade.

"Harriman was the house-detective on duty last night," he said. "He's sure to have seen Archer. Shall I caution him not to mention it?"

Spade looked at Freed from the corners of his eyes. "Better not. That won't make any difference as long as there's no connection shown with this Wonderly. Harriman's all right, but he likes to talk, and I'd as lief not have him think there's anything to be kept quiet."

Freed nodded again and went away. Fifteen minutes later he returned.

"She arrived last Tuesday, registering from New York. She hadn't a trunk, only some bags. There were no phone-calls charged to her room, and she doesn't seem to have received much, if any, mail. The only one anybody remembers having seen her with was a tall dark man of thirty-six or so. She went out at half-past nine this morning, came back an hour later, paid her bill, and had her bags carried out to a car. The boy who carried them says it was a Nash touring car, probably a hired one. She left a forwarding address—the Ambassador, Los Angeles."

Spade said, "Thanks a lot, Freed," and left the St. Mark.

When Spade returned to his office Effie Perine stopped typing a letter to tell him: "Your friend Dundy was in. He wanted to look at your guns."

"And?"

"I told him to come back when you were here."

"Good girl. If he comes back again let him look at them."

"And Miss Wonderly called up."

"It's about time. What did she say?"

"She wants to see you." The girl picked up a slip of paper from her desk and read the memorandum penciled on it: "She's at the Coronet, on California Street, apartment one thousand and one. You're to ask for Miss Leblanc."

Spade said, "Give me," and held out his hand. When she had given him the memorandum he took out his lighter, snapped on the flame, set it to the slip of paper, held the paper until all but one corner was curling black ash, dropped it on the linoleum floor, and mashed it under his shoe-sole.

The girl watched him with disapproving eyes.

He grinned at her, said, "That's just the way it is, dear," and went out again.

CHAPTER IV

The Black Bird

M ISS WONDERLY, in a belted green crêpe silk dress, opened the door of apartment 1001 at the Coronet. Her face was flushed. Her dark red hair, parted on the left side, swept back in loose waves over her right temple, was somewhat tousled.

Spade took off his hat and said: "Good morning."

His smile brought a fainter smile to her face. Her eyes, of blue that was almost violet, did not lose their troubled look. She lowered her head and said in a hushed, timid, voice: "Come in, Mr. Spade."

She led him past open kitchen-, bathroom-, and bedroom-doors into a cream and red living-room, apologizing for its confusion: "Everything is upside-down. I haven't even finished unpacking."

She laid his hat on a table and sat down on a walnut settee. He sat on a brocaded oval-backed chair facing her.

She looked at her fingers, working them together, and said: "Mr. Spade, I've a terrible, terrible confession to make."

Spade smiled a polite smile, which she did not lift her eyes to see, and said nothing.

"That—that story I told you yesterday was all—a story," she stammered, and looked up at him now with miserable frightened eyes.

"Oh, that," Spade said lightly. "We didn't exactly believe your story."

"Then—?" Perplexity was added to the misery and fright in her eyes.

"We believed your two hundred dollars."

"You mean—?" She seemed to not know what he meant.

"I mean that you paid us more than if you'd been telling the truth," he explained blandly, "and enough more to make it all right."

Her eyes suddenly lighted up. She lifted herself a few inches from the settee, settled down again, smoothed her skirt, leaned forward, and spoke eagerly: "And even now you'd be willing to—?"

Spade stopped her with a palm-up motion of one hand. The upper part of his face frowned. The lower part smiled. "That depends," he said. "The hell of it is, Miss—— Is your name Wonderly or Leblanc?"

She blushed and murmured: "It's really O'Shaughnessy— Brigid O'Shaughnessy."

"The hell of it is, Miss O'Shaughnessy, that a couple of murders"—she winced—"coming together like this get everybody stirred up, make the police think they can go the limit, make everybody hard to handle and expensive. It's not—"

He stopped talking because she had stopped listening and was waiting for him to finish.

"Mr. Spade, tell me the truth." Her voice quivered on the verge of hysteria. Her face had become haggard around desperate eyes. "Am I to blame for—for last night?"

Spade shook his head. "Not unless there are things I don't know about," he said. "You warned us that Thursby was dangerous. Of course you lied to us about your sister and all, but that doesn't count: we didn't believe you." He shrugged his sloping shoulders. "I wouldn't say it was your fault."

She said, "Thank you," very softly, and then moved her head from side to side. "But I'll always blame myself." She put a hand to her throat. "Mr. Archer was so—so alive yesterday afternoon, so solid and hearty and—"

"Stop it," Spade commanded. "He knew what he was doing. They're the chances we take."

"Was—was he married?"

"Yes, with ten thousand insurance, no children, and a wife who didn't like him."

"Oh, please don't!" she whispered.

Spade shrugged again. "That's the way it was." He glanced at his watch and moved from his chair to the settee beside her. "There's no time for worrying about that now." His voice was pleasant but firm. "Out there a flock of policemen and assistant district attorneys and reporters are running around with their noses to the ground. What do you want to do?"

"I want you to save me from—from it all," she replied in a thin tremulous voice. She put a timid hand on his sleeve. "Mr. Spade, do they know about me?"

"Not yet. I wanted to see you first."

"What—what would they think if they knew about the way I came to you—with those lies?"

"It would make them suspicious. That's why I've been stalling them till I could see you. I thought maybe we wouldn't have to let them know all of it. We ought to be able to fake a story that will rock them to sleep, if necessary."

"You don't think I had anything to do with the—the murders—do you?"

Spade grinned at her and said: "I forgot to ask you that. Did you?"

"No."

"That's good. Now what are we going to tell the police?"

She squirmed on her end of the settee and her eyes wavered between heavy lashes, as if trying and failing to free their gaze from his. She seemed smaller, and very young and oppressed.

"Must they know about me at all?" she asked. "I think I'd rather die than that, Mr. Spade. I can't explain now, but can't you somehow manage so that you can shield me from them, so I won't have to answer their questions? I don't think I could stand being questioned now. I think I would rather die. Can't you, Mr. Spade?"

"Maybe," he said, "but I'll have to know what it's all about."

She went down on her knees at his knees. She held her face up to him. Her face was wan, taut, and fearful over tight-clasped hands.

"I haven't lived a good life," she cried. "I've been bad—worse than you could know—but I'm not all bad. Look at me, Mr. Spade. You know I'm not all bad, don't you? You can see that, can't you? Then can't you trust me a little? Oh, I'm so alone and afraid, and I've got nobody to help me if you won't help me. I know I've no right to ask you to trust me if I won't trust you. I do trust you, but I can't tell you. I can't tell you now. Later I will, when I can. I'm afraid, Mr. Spade. I'm afraid of trusting you. I don't mean that. I do trust you, but—I trusted Floyd and— I've nobody else, nobody else, Mr. Spade. You can help me. You've said you can help me. If I hadn't believed you could save me I would have run away today instead of sending for you. If I thought anybody else could save me would I be down on my knees like this? I know this isn't fair of me. But be generous, Mr. Spade, don't ask me to be fair. You're strong, you're resourceful, you're brave. You can spare me some of that strength and resourcefulness and courage, surely. Help me, Mr. Spade. Help me because I need help so badly, and because if you don't where will I find anyone who can, no matter how willing? Help me. I've no right to ask you to help me blindly, but I do ask you. Be generous, Mr. Spade. You can help me. Help me."

Spade, who had held his breath through much of this speech, now emptied his lungs with a long sighing exhalation between pursed lips and said: "You won't need much of anybody's help. You're good. You're very good. It's chiefly your eyes, I think, and that throb you get into your voice when you say things like 'Be generous, Mr. Spade.'"

She jumped up on her feet. Her face crimsoned painfully, but she held her head erect and she looked Spade straight in the eyes.

"I deserve that," she said. "I deserve it, but—oh!—I did want your help so much. I do want it, and need it, so much. And the lie was in the way I said it, and not at all in what I said." She turned away, no longer holding herself erect. "It is my own fault that you can't believe me now."

Spade's face reddened and he looked down at the floor, muttering: "Now you are dangerous."

Brigid O'Shaughnessy went to the table and picked up his hat. She came back and stood in front of him holding the hat, not offering it to him, but holding it for him to take if he wished. Her face was white and thin.

Spade looked at his hat and asked: "What happened last night?"

"Floyd came to the hotel at nine o'clock, and we went out for a walk. I suggested that so Mr. Archer could see him. We stopped at a restaurant in Geary Street, I think it was, for supper and to dance, and came back to the hotel at about half-past twelve. Floyd left me at the door and I stood inside and watched Mr. Archer follow him down the street, on the other side."

"Down? You mean towards Market Street?"

"Yes."

"Do you know what they'd be doing in the neighborhood of Bush and Stockton, where Archer was shot?"

"Isn't that near where Floyd lived?"

"No. It would be nearly a dozen blocks out of his way if he was going from your hotel to his. Well, what did you do after they had gone?"

"I went to bed. And this morning when I went out for breakfast I saw the headlines in the papers and read about—you know. Then I went up to Union Square, where I had seen automobiles for hire, and got one and went to the hotel for my luggage. After I found my room had been searched yesterday I knew I would have to move, and I had found this place yesterday afternoon. So I came up here and then telephoned your office."

"Your room at the St. Mark was searched?" he asked.

"Yes, while I was at your office." She bit her lip. "I didn't mean to tell you that."

"That means I'm not supposed to question you about it?"

She nodded shyly.

He frowned.

She moved his hat a little in her hands.

He laughed impatiently and said: "Stop waving the hat in my face. Haven't I offered to do what I can?"

She smiled contritely, returned the hat to the table, and sat beside him on the settee again.

He said: "I've got nothing against trusting you blindly except that I won't be able to do you much good if I haven't some idea of what it's all about. For instance, I've got to have some sort of a line on your Floyd Thursby."

"I met him in the Orient." She spoke slowly, looking down at a pointed finger tracing eights on the settee between them. "We came here from Hongkong last week. He was—he had promised to help me. He took advantage of my helplessness and dependence on him to betray me."

"Betray you how?"

She shook her head and said nothing.

Spade, frowning with impatience, asked: "Why did you want him shadowed?"

"I wanted to learn how far he had gone. He wouldn't even let me know where he was staying. I wanted to find out what he was doing, whom he was meeting, things like that."

"Did he kill Archer?"

She looked up at him, surprised. "Yes, certainly," she said.

"He had a Luger in a shoulder-holster. Archer wasn't shot with a Luger."

"He had a revolver in his overcoat-pocket," she said.

"You saw it?"

"Oh, I've seen it often. I know he always carries one there. I didn't see it last night, but I know he never wears an overcoat without it."

"Why all the guns?"

"He lived by them. There was a story in Hongkong that he had come out there, to the Orient, as bodyguard to a gambler who had had to leave the States, and that the gambler had since disappeared. They said Floyd knew about his disappearing. I don't know. I do know that he always went heavily armed and that he never went to sleep without covering the floor around his bed with crumpled newspaper so nobody could come silently into his room."

"You picked a nice sort of playmate."

"Only that sort could have helped me," she said simply, "if he had been loyal."

"Yes, if." Spade pinched his lower lip between finger and thumb and looked gloomily at her. The vertical creases over his nose deepened, drawing his brows together. "How bad a hole are you actually in?"

"As bad," she said, "as could be."

"Physical danger?"

"I'm not heroic. I don't think there's anything worse than death."

"Then it's that?"

"It's that as surely as we're sitting here"—she shivered—"unless you help me."

He took his fingers away from his mouth and ran them through his hair. "I'm not Christ," he said irritably. "I can't work miracles out of thin air." He looked at his watch. "The day's going and you're giving me nothing to work with. Who killed Thursby?"

She put a crumpled handkerchief to her mouth and said, "I don't know," through it.

"Your enemies or his?"

"I don't know. His, I hope, but I'm afraid—I don't know."

"How was he supposed to be helping you? Why did you bring him here from Hongkong?"

She looked at him with frightened eyes and shook her head in silence. Her face was haggard and pitifully stubborn.

Spade stood up, thrust his hands into the pockets of his jacket, and scowled down at her. "This is hopeless," he said savagely. "I can't do anything for you. I don't know what you want done. I don't even know if you know what you want."

She hung her head and wept.

He made a growling animal noise in his throat and went to the table for his hat.

"You won't," she begged in a small choked voice, not looking up, "go to the police?"

"Go to them!" he exclaimed, his voice loud with rage. "They've been running me ragged since four o'clock this morning. I've made myself God knows how much trouble standing them off. For what? For some crazy notion that I could help you. I can't. I won't try." He put his hat on his head and pulled it down tight. "Go to them? All I've got to do is stand still and they'll be swarming all over me. Well, I'll tell them what I know and you'll have to take your chances."

She rose from the settee and held herself straight in front of him though her knees were trembling, and she held her white panic-stricken face up high though she couldn't hold the twitching muscles of mouth and chin still. She said: "You've been patient. You've tried to help me. It is hopeless, and useless, I suppose." She stretched out her right hand. "I thank you for what you have done. I—I'll have to take my chances."

Spade made the growling animal noise in his throat again and sat down on the settee. "How much money have you got?" he asked.

The question startled her. Then she pinched her lower lip between her teeth and answered reluctantly: "I've about five hundred dollars left."

"Give it to me."

She hesitated, looking timidly at him. He made angry gestures with mouth, eyebrows, hands, and shoulders. She went into her bedroom, returning almost immediately with a sheaf of paper money in one hand.

He took the money from her, counted it, and said: "There's only four hundred here."

"I had to keep some to live on," she explained meekly, putting a hand to her breast.

"Can't you get any more?"

"No."

"You must have something you can raise money on," he insisted.

"I've some rings, a little jewelry."

"You'll have to hock them," he said, and held out his hand. "The Remedial's the best place—Mission and Fifth."

She looked pleadingly at him. His yellow-grey eyes were hard and implacable. Slowly she put her hand inside the neck of her dress, brought out a slender roll of bills, and put them in his waiting hand.

He smoothed the bills out and counted them—four twenties, four tens, and a five. He returned two of the tens and the five to her. The others he put in his pocket. Then he stood up and said: "I'm going out and see what I can do for you. I'll be back as soon as I can with the best news I can manage. I'll ring four times—long, short, long, short—so you'll know it's me. You needn't go to the door with me. I can let myself out."

He left her standing in the center of the floor looking after him with dazed blue eyes.

Spade went into a reception-room whose door bore the legend *Wise, Merican & Wise*. The red-haired girl at the switchboard said: "Oh, hello, Mr. Spade."

"Hello, darling," he replied. "Is Sid in?"

He stood beside her with a hand on her plump shoulder while she manipulated a plug and spoke into the mouthpiece: "Mr. Spade to see you, Mr. Wise." She looked up at Spade. "Go right in."

He squeezed her shoulder by way of acknowledgment,

crossed the reception-room to a dully lighted inner corridor, and passed down the corridor to a frosted glass door at its far end. He opened the frosted glass door and went into an office where a small olive-skinned man with a tired oval face under thin dark hair dotted with dandruff sat behind an immense desk on which bales of paper were heaped.

The small man flourished a cold cigar-stub at Spade and said: "Pull a chair around. So Miles got the big one last night?" Neither his tired face nor his rather shrill voice held any emotion.

"Uh-huh, that's what I came in about." Spade frowned and cleared his throat. "I think I'm going to have to tell a coroner to go to hell, Sid. Can I hide behind the sanctity of my clients' secrets and identities and what-not, all the same priest or lawyer?"

Sid Wise lifted his shoulders and lowered the ends of his mouth. "Why not? An inquest is not a court-trial. You can try, anyway. You've gotten away with more than that before this."

"I know, but Dundy's getting snotty, and maybe it is a little bit thick this time. Get your hat, Sid, and we'll go see the right people. I want to be safe."

Sid Wise looked at the papers massed on his desk and groaned, but he got up from his chair and went to the closet by the window. "You're a son of a gun, Sammy," he said as he took his hat from its hook.

Spade returned to his office at ten minutes past five that evening. Effie Perine was sitting at his desk reading *Time*. Spade sat on the desk and asked: "Anything stirring?"

"Not here. You look like you'd swallowed the canary."

He grinned contentedly. "I think we've got a future. I always had an idea that if Miles would go off and die somewhere we'd stand a better chance of thriving. Will you take care of sending flowers for me?"

"I did."

"You're an invaluable angel. How's your woman's intuition today?"

"Why?"

"What do you think of Wonderly?"

"I'm for her," the girl replied without hesitation.

"She's got too many names," Spade mused, "Wonderly, Leblanc, and she says the right one's O'Shaughnessy."

"I don't care if she's got all the names in the phone-book. That girl is all right, and you know it."

"I wonder." Spade blinked sleepily at Effie Perine. He chuckled. "Anyway she's given up seven hundred smacks in two days, and that's all right."

Effie Perine sat up straight and said: "Sam, if that girl's in trouble and you let her down, or take advantage of it to bleed her, I'll never forgive you, never have any respect for you, as long as I live."

Spade smiled unnaturally. Then he frowned. The frown was unnatural. He opened his mouth to speak, but the sound of someone's entrance through the corridor-door stopped him.

Effie Perine rose and went into the outer office. Spade took off his hat and sat in his chair. The girl returned with an engraved card—*Mr. Joel Cairo.*

"This guy is queer," she said.

"In with him, then, darling," said Spade.

Mr. Joel Cairo was a small-boned dark man of medium height. His hair was black and smooth and very glossy. His features were Levantine. A square-cut ruby, its sides paralleled by four baguette diamonds, gleamed against the deep green of his cravat. His black coat, cut tight to narrow shoulders, flared a little over slightly plump hips. His trousers fitted his round legs more snugly than was the current fashion. The uppers of his patent-leather shoes were hidden by fawn spats. He held a black derby hat in a chamois-gloved hand and came towards Spade with short, mincing, bobbing steps. The fragrance of *chypre* came with him.

Spade inclined his head at his visitor and then at a chair, saying: "Sit down, Mr. Cairo."

Cairo bowed elaborately over his hat, said, "I thank you," in a high-pitched thin voice and sat down. He sat down primly, crossing his ankles, placing his hat on his knees, and began to draw off his yellow gloves.

Spade rocked back in his chair and asked: "Now what can I do for you, Mr. Cairo?" The amiable negligence of his tone, his motion in the chair, were precisely as they had been when he had addressed the same question to Brigid O'Shaughnessy on the previous day.

Cairo turned his hat over, dropping his gloves into it, and placed it bottom-up on the corner of the desk nearest him. Diamonds twinkled on the second and fourth fingers of his left hand, a ruby that matched the one in his tie even to the surrounding diamonds on the third finger of his right hand. His hands were soft and well cared for. Though they were not large their flaccid bluntness made them seem clumsy. He rubbed his palms together and said over the whispering sound they made: "May a stranger offer condolences for your partner's unfortunate death?"

"Thanks."

"May I ask, Mr. Spade, if there was, as the newspapers inferred, a certain—ah—relationship between that unfortunate happening and the death a little later of the man Thursby?"

Spade said nothing in a blank-faced definite way.

Cairo rose and bowed. "I beg your pardon." He sat down and placed his hands side by side, palms down, on the corner of the desk. "More than idle curiosity made me ask that, Mr. Spade. I am trying to recover an—ah—ornament that has been—shall we say?—mislaid. I thought, and hoped, you could assist me."

Spade nodded with eyebrows lifted to indicate attentiveness.

"The ornament is a statuette," Cairo went on, selecting and mouthing his words carefully, "the black figure of a bird."

Spade nodded again, with courteous interest.

"I am prepared to pay, on behalf of the figure's rightful owner, the sum of five thousand dollars for its recovery." Cairo raised one hand from the desk-corner and touched a spot in the air with the broad-nailed tip of an ugly forefinger. "I am prepared to promise that—what is the phrase?—no questions will be asked." He put his hand on the desk again beside the other and smiled blandly over them at the private detective.

"Five thousand is a lot of money," Spade commented, looking thoughtfully at Cairo. "It—"

Fingers drummed lightly on the door.

When Spade had called, "Come in," the door opened far enough to admit Effie Perine's head and shoulders. She had put on a small dark felt hat and a dark coat with a grey fur collar.

"Is there anything else?" she asked.

"No. Good night. Lock the door when you go, will you?"

"Good night," she said and disappeared behind the closing door.

Spade turned in his chair to face Cairo again, saying: "It's an interesting figure."

The sound of the corridor-door's closing behind Effie Perine came to them.

Cairo smiled and took a short compact flat black pistol out of an inner pocket. "You will please," he said, "clasp your hands together at the back of your neck."

CHAPTER V

The Levantine

SPADE did not look at the pistol. He raised his arms and, leaning back in his chair, intertwined the fingers of his two hands behind his head. His eyes, holding no particular expression, remained focused on Cairo's dark face.

Cairo coughed a little apologetic cough and smiled nervously with lips that had lost some of their redness. His dark eyes were humid and bashful and very earnest. "I intend to search your offices, Mr. Spade. I warn you that if you attempt to prevent me I shall certainly shoot you."

"Go ahead." Spade's voice was as empty of expression as his face.

"You will please stand," the man with the pistol instructed him at whose thick chest the pistol was aimed. "I shall have to make sure that you are not armed."

Spade stood up pushing his chair back with his calves as he straightened his legs.

Cairo went around behind him. He transferred the pistol from his right hand to his left. He lifted Spade's coat-tail and looked under it. Holding the pistol close to Spade's back, he put his right hand around Spade's side and patted his chest. The Levantine face was then no more than six inches below and behind Spade's right elbow.

Spade's elbow dropped as Spade spun to the right. Cairo's face jerked back not far enough: Spade's right heel on the patent-leathered toes anchored the smaller man in the elbow's path. The elbow struck him beneath the cheek-bone, staggering him so that he must have fallen had he not been held by Spade's foot on his foot. Spade's elbow went on past the astonished dark face and straightened when Spade's hand struck down at the pistol. Cairo let the pistol go the instant that Spade's fingers touched it. The pistol was small in Spade's hand.

Spade took his foot off Cairo's to complete his about-face. With his left hand Spade gathered together the smaller man's coat-lapels—the ruby-set green tie bunching out over his knuckles—while his right hand stowed the captured weapon away in a coat-pocket. Spade's yellow-grey eyes were somber. His face was wooden, with a trace of sullenness around the mouth.

Cairo's face was twisted by pain and chagrin. There were tears in his dark eyes. His skin was the complexion of polished lead except where the elbow had reddened his cheek.

Spade by means of his grip on the Levantine's lapels turned him slowly and pushed him back until he was standing close in front of the chair he had lately occupied. A puzzled look replaced the look of pain in the lead-colored face. Then Spade smiled. His smile was gentle, even dreamy. His right shoulder raised a few inches. His bent right arm was driven up by the shoulder's lift. Fist, wrist, forearm, crooked elbow, and upper arm seemed all one rigid piece, with only the limber shoulder giving them motion. The fist struck Cairo's face, covering for a moment one side of his chin, a corner of his mouth, and most of his cheek between cheek-bone and jaw-bone.

Cairo shut his eyes and was unconscious.

Spade lowered the limp body into the chair, where it lay with sprawled arms and legs, the head lolling back against the chair's back, the mouth open.

Spade emptied the unconscious man's pockets one by one, working methodically, moving the lax body when necessary, making a pile of the pockets' contents on the desk. When the last pocket had been turned out he returned to his own chair, rolled and lighted a cigarette, and began to examine his spoils. He examined them with grave unhurried thoroughness.

There was a large wallet of dark soft leather. The wallet contained three hundred and sixty-five dollars in United States bills of several sizes; three five-pound notes; a much-visaed Greek passport bearing Cairo's name and portrait; five folded sheets of pinkish onion-skin paper covered with what seemed to be Arabic writing; a raggedly clipped newspaper-account of the finding of Archer's and Thursby's bodies; a post-card-photograph of a dusky woman with bold cruel eyes and a tender drooping mouth; a large silk handkerchief, yellow with age and somewhat cracked along its folds; a thin sheaf of Mr. Joel Cairo's engraved cards; and a ticket for an orchestra seat at the Geary Theatre that evening.

Besides the wallet and its contents there were three gaily colored silk handkerchiefs fragrant of *chypre*; a platinum Longines watch on a platinum and red gold chain, attached at the other end to a small pear-shaped pendant of some white metal; a handful of United States, British, French, and Chinese coins; a ring holding half a dozen keys; a silver and onyx fountain-pen; a metal comb in a leatherette case; a nail-file in a leatherette case; a small street-guide to San Francisco; a Southern Pacific baggage-check; a half-filled package of violet pastilles; a Shanghai insurance-broker's business-card; and four sheets of Hotel Belvedere writing paper, on one of which was written in small precise letters Samuel Spade's name and the addresses of his office and his apartment.

Having examined these articles carefully—he even opened the back of the watch-case to see that nothing was hidden inside—Spade leaned over and took the unconscious man's wrist between finger and thumb, feeling his pulse. Then he dropped the wrist, settled back in his chair, and rolled and lighted another cigarette. His face while he smoked was, except for occasional slight and aimless movements of his lower lip, so still and reflective that it seemed stupid; but when Cairo presently moaned and fluttered his eyelids Spade's face became bland, and he put the beginning of a friendly smile into his eyes and mouth.

Joel Cairo awakened slowly. His eyes opened first, but a full minute passed before they fixed their gaze on any definite part of the ceiling. Then he shut his mouth and swallowed, exhaling heavily through his nose afterward. He drew in one foot and turned a hand over on his thigh. Then he raised his head from the chair-back, looked around the office in confusion, saw Spade, and sat up. He opened his mouth to speak, started, clapped a hand to his face where Spade's fist had struck and where there was now a florid bruise.

Cairo said through his teeth, painfully: "I could have shot you, Mr. Spade."

"You could have tried," Spade conceded.

"I did not try."

"I know."

"Then why did you strike me after I was disarmed?"

"Sorry," Spade said, and grinned wolfishly, showing his

jaw-teeth, "but imagine my embarrassment when I found that five-thousand-dollar offer was just hooey."

"You are mistaken, Mr. Spade. That was, and is, a genuine offer."

"What the hell?" Spade's surprise was genuine.

"I am prepared to pay five thousand dollars for the figure's return." Cairo took his hand away from his bruised face and sat up prim and business-like again. "You have it?"

"No."

"If it is not here"—Cairo was very politely skeptical—"why should you have risked serious injury to prevent my searching for it?"

"I should sit around and let people come in and stick me up?" Spade flicked a finger at Cairo's possessions on the desk. "You've got my apartment-address. Been up there yet?"

"Yes, Mr. Spade. I am ready to pay five thousand dollars for the figure's return, but surely it is natural enough that I should try first to spare the owner that expense if possible."

"Who is he?"

Cairo shook his head and smiled. "You will have to forgive my not answering that question."

"Will I?" Spade leaned forward smiling with tight lips. "I've got you by the neck, Cairo. You've walked in and tied yourself up, plenty strong enough to suit the police, with last night's killings. Well, now you'll have to play with me or else."

Cairo's smile was demure and not in any way alarmed. "I made somewhat extensive inquiries about you before taking any action," he said, "and was assured that you were far too reasonable to allow other considerations to interfere with profitable business relations."

Spade shrugged. "Where are they?" he asked.

"I have offered you five thousand dollars for—"

Spade thumped Cairo's wallet with the backs of his fingers and said: "There's nothing like five thousand dollars here. You're betting your eyes. You could come in and say you'd pay me a million for a purple elephant, but what in hell would that mean?"

"I see, I see," Cairo said thoughtfully, screwing up his eyes. "You wish some assurance of my sincerity." He brushed his red lower lip with a fingertip. "A retainer, would that serve?"

"It might."

Cairo put his hand out towards his wallet, hesitated, withdrew the hand, and said: "You will take, say, a hundred dollars?"

Spade picked up the wallet and took out a hundred dollars. Then he frowned, said, "Better make it two hundred," and did.

Cairo said nothing.

"Your first guess was that I had the bird," Spade said in a crisp voice when he had put the two hundred dollars into his pocket and had dropped the wallet on the desk again. "There's nothing in that. What's your second?"

"That you know where it is, or, if not exactly that, that you know it is where you can get it."

Spade neither denied nor affirmed that: he seemed hardly to have heard it. He asked: "What sort of proof can you give me that your man is the owner?"

"Very little, unfortunately. There is this, though: nobody else can give you any authentic evidence of ownership at all. And if you know as much about the affair as I suppose—or I should not be here—you know that the means by which it was taken from him shows that his right to it was more valid than anyone else's—certainly more valid than Thursby's."

"What about his daughter?" Spade asked.

Excitement opened Cairo's eyes and mouth, turned his face red, made his voice shrill. "*He* is not the owner!"

Spade said, "Oh," mildly and ambiguously.

"Is he here, in San Francisco, now?" Cairo asked in a less shrill, but still excited, voice.

Spade blinked his eyes sleepily and suggested: "It might be better all around if we put our cards on the table."

Cairo recovered composure with a little jerk. "I do not think it would be better." His voice was suave now. "If you know more than I, I shall profit by your knowledge, and so will you to the extent of five thousand dollars. If you do not then I have made a mistake in coming to you, and to do as you suggest would be simply to make that mistake worse."

Spade nodded indifferently and waved his hand at the

articles on the desk, saying: "There's your stuff"; and then, when Cairo was returning them to his pockets: "It's understood that you're to pay my expenses while I'm getting this black bird for you, and five thousand dollars when it's done?"

"Yes, Mr. Spade; that is, five thousand dollars less whatever moneys have been advanced to you—five thousand in all."

"Right. And it's a legitimate proposition." Spade's face was solemn except for wrinkles at the corners of his eyes. "You're not hiring me to do any murders or burglaries for you, but simply to get it back if possible in an honest and lawful way."

"If possible," Cairo agreed. His face also was solemn except for the eyes. "And in any event with discretion." He rose and picked up his hat. "I am at the Hotel Belvedere when you wish to communicate with me—room six-thirty-five. I confidently expect the greatest mutual benefit from our association, Mr. Spade." He hesitated. "May I have my pistol?"

"Sure. I'd forgotten it."

Spade took the pistol out of his coat-pocket and handed it to Cairo.

Cairo pointed the pistol at Spade's chest.

"You will please keep your hands on the top of the desk," Cairo said earnestly. "I intend to search your offices."

Spade said: "I'll be damned." Then he laughed in his throat and said: "All right. Go ahead. I won't stop you."

CHAPTER VI

The Undersized Shadow

F OR HALF AN HOUR after Joel Cairo had gone Spade sat alone, still and frowning, at his desk. Then he said aloud in the tone of one dismissing a problem, "Well, they're paying for it," and took a bottle of Manhattan cocktail and a paper drinking-cup from a desk-drawer. He filled the cup two-thirds full, drank, returned the bottle to the drawer, tossed the cup into the wastebasket, put on his hat and overcoat, turned off the lights, and went down to the night-lit street.

An undersized youth of twenty or twenty-one in neat grey cap and overcoat was standing idly on the corner below Spade's building.

Spade walked up Sutter Street to Kearny, where he entered a cigar-store to buy two sacks of Bull Durham. When he came out the youth was one of four people waiting for a street-car on the opposite corner.

Spade ate dinner at Herbert's Grill in Powell Street. When he left the Grill, at a quarter to eight, the youth was looking into a nearby haberdasher's window.

Spade went to the Hotel Belvedere, asking at the desk for Mr. Cairo. He was told that Cairo was not in. The youth sat in a chair in a far corner of the lobby.

Spade went to the Geary Theatre, failed to see Cairo in the lobby, and posted himself on the curb in front, facing the theatre. The youth loitered with other loiterers before Marquard's restaurant below.

At ten minutes past eight Joel Cairo appeared, walking up Geary Street with his little mincing bobbing steps. Apparently he did not see Spade until the private detective touched his shoulder. He seemed moderately surprised for a moment, and then said: "Oh, yes, of course you saw the ticket."

"Uh-huh. I've got something I want to show you." Spade drew Cairo back towards the curb a little away from the other waiting theatre-goers. "The kid in the cap down by Marquard's."

Cairo murmured, "I'll see," and looked at his watch. He

looked up Geary Street. He looked at a theatre-sign in front of him on which George Arliss was shown costumed as Shylock, and then his dark eyes crawled sidewise in their sockets until they were looking at the kid in the cap, at his cool pale face with curling lashes hiding lowered eyes.

"Who is he?" Spade asked.

Cairo smiled up at Spade. "I do not know him."

"He's been tailing me around town."

Cairo wet his lower lip with his tongue and asked: "Do you think it was wise, then, to let him see us together?"

"How do I know?" Spade replied. "Anyway, it's done."

Cairo removed his hat and smoothed his hair with a gloved hand. He replaced his hat carefully on his head and said with every appearance of candor: "I give you my word I do not know him, Mr. Spade. I give you my word I have nothing to do with him. I have asked nobody's assistance except yours, on my word of honor."

"Then he's one of the others?"

"That may be."

"I just wanted to know, because if he gets to be a nuisance I may have to hurt him."

"Do as you think best. He is not a friend of mine."

"That's good. There goes the curtain. Good night," Spade said, and crossed the street to board a westbound streetcar.

The youth in the cap boarded the same car.

Spade left the car at Hyde Street and went up to his apartment. His rooms were not greatly upset, but showed unmistakable signs of having been searched. When Spade had washed and had put on a fresh shirt and collar he went out again, walked up to Sutter Street, and boarded a westbound car. The youth boarded it also.

Within half a dozen blocks of the Coronet Spade left the car and went into the vestibule of a tall brown apartment-building. He pressed three bell-buttons together. The street-door-lock buzzed. He entered, passed the elevator and stairs, went down a long yellow-walled corridor to the rear of the building, found a back door fastened by a Yale lock, and let himself out into a narrow court. The court led to a dark back street, up which Spade walked for two blocks. Then he crossed over to California Street and went to the Coronet. It was not quite half-past nine o'clock.

The eagerness with which Brigid O'Shaughnessy welcomed Spade suggested that she had been not entirely certain of his coming. She had put on a satin gown of the blue shade called Artoise that season, with chalcedony shoulder-straps, and her stockings and slippers were Artoise.

The red and cream sitting-room had been brought to order and livened with flowers in squat pottery vases of black and silver. Three small rough-barked logs burned in the fireplace. Spade watched them burn while she put away his hat and coat.

"Do you bring me good news?" she asked when she came into the room again. Anxiety looked through her smile, and she held her breath.

"We won't have to make anything public that hasn't already been made public."

"The police won't have to know about me?"

"No."

She sighed happily and sat on the walnut settee. Her face relaxed and her body relaxed. She smiled up at him with admiring eyes. "However did you manage it?" she asked more in wonder than in curiosity.

"Most things in San Francisco can be bought, or taken."

"And you won't get into trouble? Do sit down." She made room for him on the settee.

"I don't mind a reasonable amount of trouble," he said with not too much complacence.

He stood beside the fireplace and looked at her with eyes that studied, weighed, judged her without pretense that they were not studying, weighing, judging her. She flushed slightly under the frankness of his scrutiny, but she seemed more sure of herself than before, though a becoming shyness had not left her eyes. He stood there until it seemed plain that he meant to ignore her invitation to sit beside her, and then crossed to the settee.

"You aren't," he asked as he sat down, "exactly the sort of person you pretend to be, are you?"

"I'm not sure I know what you mean," she said in her hushed voice, looking at him with puzzled eyes.

"Schoolgirl manner," he explained, "stammering and blushing and all that."

She blushed and replied hurriedly, not looking at him: "I told you this afternoon that I've been bad—worse than you could know."

"That's what I mean," he said. "You told me that this afternoon in the same words, same tone. It's a speech you've practiced."

After a moment in which she seemed confused almost to the point of tears she laughed and said: "Very well, then, Mr. Spade, I'm not at all the sort of person I pretend to be. I'm eighty years old, incredibly wicked, and an iron-molder by trade. But if it's a pose it's one I've grown into, so you won't expect me to drop it entirely, will you?"

"Oh, it's all right," he assured her. "Only it wouldn't be all right if you were actually that innocent. We'd never get anywhere."

"I won't be innocent," she promised with a hand on her heart.

"I saw Joel Cairo tonight," he said in the manner of one making polite conversation.

Gaiety went out of her face. Her eyes, focused on his profile, became frightened, then cautious. He had stretched his legs out and was looking at his crossed feet. His face did not indicate that he was thinking about anything.

There was a long pause before she asked uneasily:

"You—you know him?"

"I saw him tonight." Spade did not look up and he maintained his light conversational tone. "He was going to see George Arliss."

"You mean you talked to him?"

"Only for a minute or two, till the curtain-bell rang."

She got up from the settee and went to the fireplace to poke the fire. She changed slightly the position of an ornament on the mantelpiece, crossed the room to get a box of cigarettes from a table in a corner, straightened a curtain, and returned to her seat. Her face now was smooth and unworried.

Spade grinned sidewise at her and said: "You're good. You're very good."

Her face did not change. She asked quietly: "What did he say?"

"About what?"

She hesitated. "About me."

"Nothing." Spade turned to hold his lighter under the end of her cigarette. His eyes were shiny in a wooden satan's face.

"Well, what did he say?" she asked with half-playful petulance.

"He offered me five thousand dollars for the black bird."

She started, her teeth tore the end of her cigarette, and her eyes, after a swift alarmed glance at Spade, turned away from him.

"You're not going to go around poking at the fire and straightening up the room again, are you?" he asked lazily.

She laughed a clear merry laugh, dropped the mangled cigarette into a tray, and looked at him with clear merry eyes. "I won't," she promised. "And what did you say?"

"Five thousand dollars is a lot of money."

She smiled, but when, instead of smiling, he looked gravely at her, her smile became faint, confused, and presently vanished. In its place came a hurt, bewildered look. "Surely you're not really considering it," she said.

"Why not? Five thousand dollars is a lot of money."

"But, Mr. Spade, you promised to help me." Her hands were on his arm. "I trusted you. You can't—" She broke off, took her hands from his sleeve and worked them together.

Spade smiled gently into her troubled eyes. "Don't let's try to figure out how much you've trusted me," he said. "I promised to help you—sure—but you didn't say anything about any black birds."

"But you must've known or—or you wouldn't have mentioned it to me. You do know now. You won't—you can't—treat me like that." Her eyes were cobalt-blue prayers.

"Five thousand dollars is," he said for the third time, "a lot of money."

She lifted her shoulders and hands and let them fall in a gesture that accepted defeat. "It is," she agreed in a small dull voice. "It is far more than I could ever offer you, if I must bid for your loyalty."

Spade laughed. His laughter was brief and somewhat bitter. "That is good," he said, "coming from you. What have you given me besides money? Have you given me any of your confidence? any of the truth? any help in helping you? Haven't you tried to buy my loyalty with money and nothing else? Well, if I'm peddling it, why shouldn't I let it go to the highest bidder?"

"I've given you all the money I have." Tears glistened in her white-ringed eyes. Her voice was hoarse, vibrant. "I've thrown myself on your mercy, told you that without your help I'm utterly lost. What else is there?" She suddenly moved close to him on the settee and cried angrily: "Can I buy you with my body?"

Their faces were few inches apart. Spade took her face between his hands and he kissed her mouth roughly and contemptuously. Then he sat back and said: "I'll think it over." His face was hard and furious.

She sat still holding her numb face where his hands had left it.

He stood up and said: "Christ! there's no sense to this." He took two steps towards the fireplace and stopped, glowering at the burning logs, grinding his teeth together.

She did not move.

He turned to face her. The two vertical lines above his nose were deep clefts between red wales. "I don't give a damn about your honesty," he told her, trying to make himself speak calmly. "I don't care what kind of tricks you're up to, what your secrets are, but I've got to have something to show that you know what you're doing."

"I do know. Please believe that I do, and that it's all for the best, and—"

"Show me," he ordered. "I'm willing to help you. I've done what I could so far. If necessary I'll go ahead blindfolded, but I can't do it without more confidence in you than I've got now. You've got to convince me that you know what it's all about, that you're not simply fiddling around by guess and by God, hoping it'll come out all right somehow in the end."

"Can't you trust me just a little longer?"

"How much is a little? And what are you waiting for?"

She bit her lip and looked down. "I must talk to Joel Cairo," she said almost inaudibly.

"You can see him tonight," Spade said, looking at his watch. "His show will be out soon. We can get him on the phone at his hotel."

She raised her eyes, alarmed. "But he can't come here. I can't let him know where I am. I'm afraid."

"My place," Spade suggested.

She hesitated, working her lips together, then asked: "Do you think he'd go there?"

Spade nodded.

"All right," she exclaimed, jumping up, her eyes large and bright. "Shall we go now?"

She went into the next room. Spade went to the table in the corner and silently pulled the drawer out. The drawer held two packs of playing-cards, a pad of score-cards for bridge, a brass screw, a piece of red string, and a gold pencil. He had shut the drawer and was lighting a cigarette when she returned wearing a small dark hat and a grey kidskin coat, carrying his hat and coat.

Their taxicab drew up behind a dark sedan that stood directly in front of Spade's street-door. Iva Archer was alone in the sedan, sitting at the wheel. Spade lifted his hat to her and went indoors with Brigid O'Shaughnessy. In the lobby he halted beside one of the benches and asked: "Do you mind waiting here a moment? I won't be long."

"That's perfectly all right," Brigid O'Shaughnessy said, sitting down. "You needn't hurry."

Spade went out to the sedan. When he had opened the sedan's door Iva spoke quickly: "I've got to talk to you, Sam. Can't I come in?" Her face was pale and nervous.

"Not now."

Iva clicked her teeth together and asked sharply: "Who is she?"

"I've only a minute, Iva," Spade said patiently. "What is it?"

"Who is she?" she repeated, nodding at the street-door.

He looked away from her, down the street. In front of a garage on the next corner an undersized youth of twenty or twenty-one in neat grey cap and overcoat loafed with his back against a wall. Spade frowned and returned his gaze to Iva's insistent face. "What is the matter?" he asked. "Has anything happened? You oughtn't to be here at this time of night."

"I'm beginning to believe that," she complained. "You told me I oughtn't to come to the office, and now I oughtn't to come here. Do you mean I oughtn't to chase after you? If that's what you mean why don't you say it right out?"

"Now, Iva, you've got no right to take that attitude."

"I know I haven't. I haven't any rights at all, it seems, where you're concerned. I thought I did. I thought your pretending to love me gave me—"

Spade said wearily: "This is no time to be arguing about that, precious. What was it you wanted to see me about?"

"I can't talk to you here, Sam. Can't I come in?"

"Not now."

"Why can't I?"

Spade said nothing.

She made a thin line of her mouth, squirmed around straight behind the wheel, and started the sedan's engine, staring angrily ahead.

When the sedan began to move Spade said, "Good night, Iva," shut the door, and stood at the curb with his hat in his hand until it had been driven away. Then he went indoors again.

Brigid O'Shaughnessy rose smiling cheerfully from the bench and they went up to his apartment.

CHAPTER VII

G in the Air

IN HIS BEDROOM that was a living-room now the wall-bed was up, Spade took Brigid O'Shaughnessy's hat and coat, made her comfortable in a padded rocking chair, and telephoned the Hotel Belvedere. Cairo had not returned from the theatre. Spade left his telephone-number with the request that Cairo call him as soon as he came in.

Spade sat down in the armchair beside the table and without any preliminary, without an introductory remark of any sort, began to tell the girl about a thing that had happened some years before in the Northwest. He talked in a steady matter-of-fact voice that was devoid of emphasis or pauses, though now and then he repeated a sentence slightly rearranged, as if it were important that each detail be related exactly as it had happened.

At the beginning Brigid O'Shaughnessy listened with only partial attentiveness, obviously more surprised by his telling the story than interested in it, her curiosity more engaged with his purpose in telling the story than with the story he told; but presently, as the story went on, it caught her more and more fully and she became still and receptive.

A man named Flitcraft had left his real-estate-office, in Tacoma, to go to luncheon one day and had never returned. He did not keep an engagement to play golf after four that afternoon, though he had taken the initiative in making the engagement less than half an hour before he went out to luncheon. His wife and children never saw him again. His wife and he were supposed to be on the best of terms. He had two children, boys, one five and the other three. He owned his house in a Tacoma suburb, a new Packard, and the rest of the appurtenances of successful American living.

Flitcraft had inherited seventy thousand dollars from his father, and, with his success in real estate, was worth something in the neighborhood of two hundred thousand dollars at the time he vanished. His affairs were in order, though there were enough loose ends to indicate that he had not been setting them in order preparatory to vanishing. A deal that would have brought him an attractive profit, for instance, was to have been concluded the day after the one on which he disappeared. There was nothing to suggest that he had more than fifty or sixty dollars in his immediate possession at the time of his going. His habits for months past could be accounted for too thoroughly to justify any suspicion of secret vices, or even of another woman in his life, though either was barely possible.

"He went like that," Spade said, "like a fist when you open your hand."

When he had reached this point in his story the telephone-bell rang.

"Hello," Spade said into the instrument. "Mr. Cairo? . . . This is Spade. Can you come up to my place—Post Street—Now? . . . Yes, I think it is." He looked at the girl, pursed his lips, and then said rapidly: "Miss O'Shaughnessy is here and wants to see you."

Brigid O'Shaughnessy frowned and stirred in her chair, but did not say anything.

Spade put the telephone down and told her: "He'll be up in a few minutes. Well, that was in 1922. In 1927 I was with one of the big detective agencies in Seattle. Mrs. Flitcraft came in and told us somebody had seen a man in Spokane who looked a lot like her husband. I went over there. It was Flitcraft, all right. He had been living in Spokane for a couple of years as Charles—that was his first name—Pierce. He had an automobile-business that was netting him twenty or twenty-five thousand a year, a wife, a baby son, owned his home in a Spokane suburb, and usually got away to play golf after four in the afternoon during the season."

Spade had not been told very definitely what to do when he found Flitcraft. They talked in Spade's room at the Davenport. Flitcraft had no feeling of guilt. He had left his first family well provided for, and what he had done seemed to him perfectly reasonable. The only thing that bothered him was a doubt that he could make that reasonableness clear to Spade. He had never told anybody his story before, and thus had not had to attempt to make its reasonableness explicit. He tried now.

"I got it all right," Spade told Brigid O'Shaughnessy, "but Mrs. Flitcraft never did. She thought it was silly. Maybe it was. Anyway, it came out all right. She didn't want any scandal, and, after the trick he had played on her—the way she looked at it—she didn't want him. So they were divorced on the quiet and everything was swell all around.

"Here's what had happened to him. Going to lunch he passed an office-building that was being put up—just the skeleton. A beam or something fell eight or ten stories down and smacked the sidewalk alongside him. It brushed pretty close to him, but didn't touch him, though a piece of the sidewalk was chipped off and flew up and hit his cheek. It only took a piece of skin off, but he still had the scar when I saw him. He rubbed it with his finger—well, affectionately—when he told me about it. He was scared stiff of course, he said, but he was more shocked than really frightened. He felt like somebody had taken the lid off life and let him look at the works."

Flitcraft had been a good citizen and a good husband and father, not by any outer compulsion, but simply because he was a man who was most comfortable in step with his surroundings. He had been raised that way. The people he knew were like that. The life he knew was a clean orderly sane responsible affair. Now a falling beam had shown him that life was fundamentally none of these things. He, the good citizen-husband-father, could be wiped out between office and restaurant by the accident of a falling beam. He knew then that men died at haphazard like that, and lived only while blind chance spared them.

It was not, primarily, the injustice of it that disturbed him: he accepted that after the first shock. What disturbed him was the discovery that in sensibly ordering his affairs he had got out of step, and not into step, with life. He said he knew before he had gone twenty feet from the fallen beam that he would never know peace again until he had adjusted himself to this new glimpse of life. By the time he had eaten his luncheon he had found his means of adjustment. Life could be ended for him at random by a falling beam: he would change his life at random by simply going away. He loved his family, he said, as much as he supposed was usual, but he knew he was leaving them adequately provided for, and his love for them was not of the sort that would make absence painful.

"He went to Seattle that afternoon," Spade said, "and from there by boat to San Francisco. For a couple of years he wandered around and then drifted back to the Northwest, and settled in Spokane and got married. His second wife didn't look like the first, but they were more alike than they were different. You know, the kind of women that play fair games of golf and bridge and like new salad-recipes. He wasn't sorry for what he had done. It seemed reasonable enough to him. I don't think he even knew he had settled back naturally into the same groove he had jumped out of in Tacoma. But that's the part of it I always liked. He adjusted himself to beams falling, and then no more of them fell, and he adjusted himself to them not falling."

"How perfectly fascinating," Brigid O'Shaughnessy said. She left her chair and stood in front of him, close. Her eyes were wide and deep. "I don't have to tell you how utterly at a disadvantage you'll have me, with him here, if you choose."

Spade smiled slightly without separating his lips. "No, you don't have to tell me," he agreed.

"And you know I'd never have placed myself in this position if I hadn't trusted you completely." Her thumb and forefinger twisted a black button on his blue coat.

Spade said, "That again!" with mock resignation.

"But you know it's so," she insisted.

"No, I don't know it." He patted the hand that was twisting the button. "My asking for reasons why I should trust you brought us here. Don't let's confuse things. You don't have to trust me, anyhow, as long as you can persuade me to trust you."

She studied his face. Her nostrils quivered.

Spade laughed. He patted her hand again and said: "Don't worry about that now. He'll be here in a moment. Get your business with him over, and then we'll see how we'll stand."

"And you'll let me go about it—with him—in my own way?"

"Sure."

She turned her hand under his so that her fingers pressed his. She said softly: "You're a God-send."

Spade said: "Don't overdo it."

She looked reproachfully at him, though smiling, and returned to the padded rocker.

Joel Cairo was excited. His dark eyes seemed all irises and his high-pitched thin-voiced words were tumbling out before Spade had the door half-open.

"That boy is out there watching the house, Mr. Spade, that boy you showed me, or to whom you showed me, in front of the theatre. What am I to understand from that, Mr. Spade? I came here in good faith, with no thought of tricks or traps."

"You were asked in good faith." Spade frowned thoughtfully. "But I ought to've guessed he might show up. He saw you come in?"

"Naturally. I could have gone on, but that seemed useless, since you had already let him see us together."

Brigid O'Shaughnessy came into the passageway behind Spade and asked anxiously: "What boy? What is it?"

Cairo removed his black hat from his head, bowed stiffly, and said in a prim voice: "If you do not know, ask Mr. Spade. I know nothing about it except through him."

"A kid who's been trying to tail me around town all evening," Spade said carelessly over his shoulder, not turning to face the girl. "Come on in, Cairo. There's no use standing here talking for all the neighbors."

Brigid O'Shaughnessy grasped Spade's arm above the elbow and demanded: "Did he follow you to my apartment?"

"No. I shook him before that. Then I suppose he came back here to try to pick me up again."

Cairo, holding his black hat to his belly with both hands, had come into the passageway. Spade shut the corridor-door behind him and they went into the living-room. There Cairo bowed stiffly over his hat once more and said: "I am delighted to see you again, Miss O'Shaughnessy."

"I was sure you would be, Joe," she replied, giving him her hand.

He made a formal bow over her hand and released it quickly.

She sat in the padded rocker she had occupied before. Cairo sat in the armchair by the table. Spade, when he had hung Cairo's hat and coat in the closet, sat on an end of the sofa in front of the windows and began to roll a cigarette.

Brigid O'Shaughnessy said to Cairo: "Sam told me about your offer for the falcon. How soon can you have the money ready?"

Cairo's eyebrows twitched. He smiled. "It is ready." He continued to smile at the girl for a little while after he had spoken, and then looked at Spade.

Spade was lighting his cigarette. His face was tranquil.

"In cash?" the girl asked.

"Oh, yes," Cairo replied.

She frowned, put her tongue between her lips, withdrew it, and asked: "You are ready to give us five thousand dollars, now, if we give you the falcon?"

Cairo held up a wriggling hand. "Excuse me," he said. "I expressed myself badly. I did not mean to say that I have the money in my pockets, but that I am prepared to get it on a very few minutes' notice at any time during banking hours."

"Oh!" She looked at Spade.

Spade blew cigarette-smoke down the front of his vest and said: "That's probably right. He had only a few hundred in his pockets when I frisked him this afternoon."

When her eyes opened round and wide he grinned.

The Levantine bent forward in his chair. He failed to keep eagerness from showing in his eyes and voice. "I can be quite prepared to give you the money at, say, half-past ten in the morning. Eh?"

Brigid O'Shaughnessy smiled at him and said: "But I haven't got the falcon."

Cairo's face was darkened by a flush of annoyance. He put an ugly hand on either arm of his chair, holding his small-boned body erect and stiff between them. His dark eyes were angry. He did not say anything.

The girl made a mock-placatory face at him. "I'll have it in a week at the most, though," she said.

"Where is it?" Cairo used politeness of mien to express skepticism.

"Where Floyd hid it."

"Floyd? Thursby?"

She nodded.

"And you know where that is?" he asked.

"I think I do."

"Then why must we wait a week?"

"Perhaps not a whole week. Whom are you buying it for, Joe?"

Cairo raised his eyebrows. "I told Mr. Spade. For its owner."

Surprise illuminated the girl's face. "So you went back to him?"

"Naturally I did."

She laughed softly in her throat and said: "I should have liked to have seen that."

Cairo shrugged. "That was the logical development." He rubbed the back of one hand with the palm of the other. His upper lids came down to shade his eyes. "Why, if I in turn may ask a question, are you willing to sell to me?"

"I'm afraid," she said simply, "after what happened to Floyd. That's why I haven't it now. I'm afraid to touch it except to turn it over to somebody else right away."

Spade, propped on an elbow on the sofa, looked at and listened to them impartially. In the comfortable slackness of his body, in the easy stillness of his features, there was no indication of either curiosity or impatience.

"Exactly what," Cairo asked in a low voice, "happened to Floyd?"

The tip of Brigid O'Shaughnessy's right forefinger traced a swift G in the air.

Cairo said, "I see," but there was something doubting in his smile. "Is he here?"

"I don't know." She spoke impatiently. "What difference does it make?"

The doubt in Cairo's smile deepened. "It might make a world of difference," he said, and rearranged his hands in his lap so that, intentionally or not, a blunt forefinger pointed at Spade.

The girl glanced at the pointing finger and made an impatient motion with her head. "Or me," she said, "or you."

"Exactly, and shall we add more certainly the boy outside?"

"Yes," she agreed and laughed. "Yes, unless he's the one you had in Constantinople."

Sudden blood mottled Cairo's face. In a shrill enraged voice he cried: "The one you couldn't make?"

Brigid O'Shaughnessy jumped up from her chair. Her lower lip was between her teeth. Her eyes were dark and wide in a tense white face. She took two quick steps towards Cairo. He started to rise. Her right hand went out and cracked sharply against his cheek, leaving the imprint of fingers there.

Cairo grunted and slapped her cheek, staggering her side-wise, bringing from her mouth a brief muffled scream.

Spade, wooden of face, was up from the sofa and close to them by then. He caught Cairo by the throat and shook him. Cairo gurgled and put a hand inside his coat. Spade grasped the Levantine's wrist, wrenched it away from the coat, forced it straight out to the side, and twisted it until the clumsy flaccid fingers opened to let the black pistol fall down on the rug.

Brigid O'Shaughnessy quickly picked up the pistol.

Cairo, speaking with difficulty because of the fingers on his throat, said: "This is the second time you've put your hands on me." His eyes, though the throttling pressure on his throat made them bulge, were cold and menacing.

"Yes," Spade growled. "And when you're slapped you'll take it and like it." He released Cairo's wrist and with a thick open hand struck the side of his face three times, savagely.

Cairo tried to spit in Spade's face, but the dryness of the Levantine's mouth made it only an angry gesture. Spade slapped the mouth, cutting the lower lip.

The door-bell rang.

Cairo's eyes jerked into focus on the passageway that led to the corridor-door. His eyes had become unangry and wary. The girl had gasped and turned to face the passageway. Her face was frightened. Spade stared gloomily for a moment at the blood trickling from Cairo's lip, and then stepped back, taking his hand from the Levantine's throat.

"Who is it?" the girl whispered, coming close to Spade; and Cairo's eyes jerked back to ask the same question.

Spade gave his answer irritably: "I don't know."

The bell rang again, more insistently.

"Well, keep quiet," Spade said, and went out of the room, shutting the door behind him.

Spade turned on the light in the passageway and opened the door to the corridor. Lieutenant Dundy and Tom Polhaus were there.

"Hello, Sam," Tom said. "We thought maybe you wouldn't've gone to bed yet."

Dundy nodded, but said nothing.

Spade said good-naturedly: "Hello. You guys pick swell hours to do your visiting in. What is it this time?"

Dundy spoke then, quietly: "We want to talk to you, Spade."

"Well?" Spade stood in the doorway, blocking it. "Go ahead and talk."

Tom Polhaus advanced saying: "We don't have to do it standing here, do we?"

Spade stood in the doorway and said: "You can't come in." His tone was very slightly apologetic.

Tom's thick-featured face, even in height with Spade's, took on an expression of friendly scorn, though there was a bright gleam in his small shrewd eyes. "What the hell, Sam?" he protested and put a big hand playfully on Spade's chest.

Spade leaned against the pushing hand, grinned wolfishly, and asked: "Going to strong-arm me, Tom?"

Tom grumbled, "Aw, for God's sake," and took his hand away.

Dundy clicked his teeth together and said through them: "Let us in."

Spade's lip twitched over his eyetooth. He said: "You're not coming in. What do you want to do about it? Try to get in? Or do your talking here? Or go to hell?"

Tom groaned.

Dundy, still speaking through his teeth, said: "It'd pay you to play along with us a little, Spade. You've got away with this and you've got away with that, but you can't keep it up forever."

"Stop me when you can," Spade replied arrogantly.

"That's what I'll do." Dundy put his hands behind him and thrust his hard face up towards the private detective's.

"There's talk going around that you and Archer's wife were cheating on him."

Spade laughed. "That sounds like something you thought up yourself."

"Then there's not anything to it?"

"Not anything."

"The talk is," Dundy said, "that she tried to get a divorce out of him so's she could put in with you, but he wouldn't give it to her. Anything to that?"

"No."

"There's even talk," Dundy went on stolidly, "that that's why he was put on the spot."

Spade seemed mildly amused. "Don't be a hog," he said. "You oughtn't try to pin more than one murder at a time on me. Your first idea that I knocked Thursby off because he'd killed Miles falls apart if you blame me for killing Miles too."

"You haven't heard me say you killed anybody," Dundy replied. "You're the one that keeps bringing that up. But suppose I did. You could have blipped them both. There's a way of figuring it."

"Uh-huh. I could've butchered Miles to get his wife, and then Thursby so I could hang Miles's killing on him. That's a hell of a swell system, or will be when I can give somebody else the bump and hang Thursby's on them. How long am I supposed to keep that up? Are you going to put your hand on my shoulder for all the killings in San Francisco from now on?"

Tom said: "Aw, cut the comedy, Sam. You know damned well we don't like this any more than you do, but we got our work to do."

"I hope you've got something to do besides pop in here early every morning with a lot of damned fool questions."

"And get damned lying answers," Dundy added deliberately.

"Take it easy," Spade cautioned him.

Dundy looked him up and down and then looked him straight in the eyes. "If you say there was nothing between you and Archer's wife," he said, "you're a liar, and I'm telling you so."

A startled look came into Tom's small eyes.

Spade moistened his lips with the tip of his tongue and asked: "Is that the hot tip that brought you here at this ungodly time of night?"

"That's one of them."

"And the others?"

Dundy pulled down the corners of his mouth. "Let us in." He nodded significantly at the doorway in which Spade stood.

Spade frowned and shook his head.

Dundy's mouth-corners lifted in a smile of grim satisfaction. "There must've been something to it," he told Tom.

Tom shifted his feet and, not looking at either man, mumbled: "God knows."

"What's this?" Spade asked. "Charades?"

"All right, Spade, we're going." Dundy buttoned his overcoat. "We'll be in to see you now and then. Maybe you're right in bucking us. Think it over."

"Uh-huh," Spade said, grinning. "Glad to see you any time, Lieutenant, and whenever I'm not busy I'll let you in."

A voice in Spade's living-room screamed: "Help! Help! Police! Help!" The voice, high and thin and shrill, was Joel Cairo's.

Lieutenant Dundy stopped turning away from the door, confronted Spade again, and said decisively: "I guess we're going in."

The sounds of a brief struggle, of a blow, of a subdued cry, came to them.

Spade's face twisted into a smile that held little joy. He said, "I guess you are," and stood out of the way.

When the police-detectives had entered he shut the corridor-door and followed them back to the living-room.

CHAPTER VIII

Horse Feathers

B RIGID O'SHAUGHNESSY was huddled in the armchair by the table. Her forearms were up over her cheeks, her knees drawn up until they hid the lower part of her face. Her eyes were white-circled and terrified.

Joel Cairo stood in front of her, bending over her, holding in one hand the pistol Spade had twisted out of his hand. His other hand was clapped to his forehead. Blood ran through the fingers of that hand and down under them to his eyes. A smaller trickle from his cut lip made three wavy lines across his chin.

Cairo did not heed the detectives. He was glaring at the girl huddled in front of him. His lips were working spasmodically, but no coherent sound came from between them.

Dundy, the first of the three into the living-room, moved swiftly to Cairo's side, put a hand on his own hip under his overcoat, a hand on the Levantine's wrist, and growled: "What are you up to here?"

Cairo took the red-smeared hand from his head and flourished it close to the Lieutenant's face. Uncovered by the hand, his forehead showed a three-inch ragged tear. "This is what she has done," he cried. "Look at it."

The girl put her feet down on the floor and looked warily from Dundy, holding Cairo's wrist, to Tom Polhaus, standing a little behind them, to Spade, leaning against the door-frame. Spade's face was placid. When his gaze met hers his yellow-grey eyes glinted for an instant with malicious humor and then became expressionless again.

"Did you do that?" Dundy asked the girl, nodding at Cairo's cut head.

She looked at Spade again. He did not in any way respond to the appeal in her eyes. He leaned against the door-frame and observed the occupants of the room with the polite detached air of a disinterested spectator.

The girl turned her eyes up to Dundy's. Her eyes were wide and dark and earnest. "I had to," she said in a low throbbing voice. "I was all alone in here with him when he attacked me. I couldn't—I tried to keep him off. I—I couldn't make myself shoot him."

"Oh, you liar!" Cairo cried, trying unsuccessfully to pull the arm that held his pistol out of Dundy's grip. "Oh, you dirty filthy liar!" He twisted himself around to face Dundy. "She's lying awfully. I came here in good faith and was attacked by both of them, and when you came he went out to talk to you, leaving her here with this pistol, and then she said they were going to kill me after you left, and I called for help, so you wouldn't leave me here to be murdered, and then she struck me with the pistol."

"Here, give me this thing," Dundy said, and took the pistol from Cairo's hand. "Now let's get this straight. What'd you come here for?"

"He sent for me." Cairo twisted his head around to stare defiantly at Spade. "He called me up on the phone and asked me to come here."

Spade blinked sleepily at the Levantine and said nothing.

Dundy asked: "What'd he want you for?"

Cairo withheld his reply until he had mopped his bloody forehead and chin with a lavender-barred silk handkerchief. By then some of the indignation in his manner had been replaced by caution. "He said he wanted—they wanted—to see me. I didn't know what about."

Tom Polhaus lowered his head, sniffed the odor of *chypre* that the mopping handkerchief had released in the air, and turned his head to scowl interrogatively at Spade. Spade winked at him and went on rolling a cigarette.

Dundy asked: "Well, what happened then?"

"Then they attacked me. She struck me first, and then he choked me and took the pistol out of my pocket. I don't know what they would have done next if you hadn't arrived at that moment. I dare say they would have murdered me then and there. When he went out to answer the bell he left her here with the pistol to watch over me."

Brigid O'Shaughnessy jumped out of the armchair crying, "Why don't you make him tell the truth?" and slapped Cairo on the cheek.

Cairo yelled inarticulately.

Dundy pushed the girl back into the chair with the hand that was not holding the Levantine's arm and growled: "None of that now."

Spade, lighting his cigarette, grinned softly through smoke and told Tom: "She's impulsive."

"Yeah," Tom agreed.

Dundy scowled down at the girl and asked: "What do you want us to think the truth is?"

"Not what he said," she replied. "Not anything he said." She turned to Spade. "Is it?"

"How do I know?" Spade responded. "I was out in the kitchen mixing an omelette when it all happened, wasn't I?"

She wrinkled her forehead, studying him with eyes that perplexity clouded.

Tom grunted in disgust.

Dundy, still scowling at the girl, ignored Spade's speech and asked her: "If he's not telling the truth, how come he did the squawking for help, and not you?"

"Oh, he was frightened to death when I struck him," she replied, looking contemptuously at the Levantine.

Cairo's face flushed where it was not blood-smeared. He exclaimed: "Pfoo! Another lie!"

She kicked his leg, the high heel of her blue slipper striking him just below the knee. Dundy pulled him away from her while big Tom came to stand close to her, rumbling: "Behave, sister. That's no way to act."

"Then make him tell the truth," she said defiantly.

"We'll do that all right," he promised. "Just don't get rough."

Dundy, looking at Spade with green eyes hard and bright and satisfied, addressed his subordinate: "Well, Tom, I don't guess we'll go wrong pulling the lot of them in."

Tom nodded gloomily.

Spade left the door and advanced to the center of the room, dropping his cigarette into a tray on the table as he passed it. His smile and manner were amiably composed. "Don't be in a hurry," he said. "Everything can be explained."

"I bet you," Dundy agreed, sneering.

Spade bowed to the girl. "Miss O'Shaughnessy," he said, "may I present Lieutenant Dundy and Detective-sergeant

Polhaus." He bowed to Dundy. "Miss O'Shaughnessy is an operative in my employ."

Joel Cairo said indignantly: "That isn't so. She—"

Spade interrupted him in a quite loud, but still genial, voice: "I hired her just recently, yesterday. This is Mr. Joel Cairo, a friend—an acquaintance, at any rate—of Thursby's. He came to me this afternoon and tried to hire me to find something Thursby was supposed to have on him when he was bumped off. It looked funny, the way he put it to me, so I wouldn't touch it. Then he pulled a gun—well, never mind that unless it comes to a point of laying charges against each other. Anyway, after talking it over with Miss O'Shaughnessy, I thought maybe I could get something out of him about Miles's and Thursby's killings, so I asked him to come up here. Maybe we put the questions to him a little rough, but he wasn't hurt any, not enough to have to cry for help. I'd already had to take his gun away from him again."

As Spade talked anxiety came into Cairo's reddened face. His eyes moved jerkily up and down, shifting their focus uneasily between the floor and Spade's bland face.

Dundy confronted Cairo and bruskly demanded: "Well, what've you got to say to that?"

Cairo had nothing to say for nearly a minute while he stared at the Lieutenant's chest. When he lifted his eyes they were shy and wary. "I don't know what I should say," he murmured. His embarrassment seemed genuine.

"Try telling the facts," Dundy suggested.

"The facts?" Cairo's eyes fidgeted, though their gaze did not actually leave the Lieutenant's. "What assurance have I that the facts will be believed?"

"Quit stalling. All you've got to do is swear to a complaint that they took a poke at you and the warrant-clerk will believe you enough to issue a warrant that'll let us throw them in the can."

Spade spoke in an amused tone: "Go ahead, Cairo. Make him happy. Tell him you'll do it, and then we'll swear to one against you, and he'll have the lot of us."

Cairo cleared his throat and looked nervously around the room, not into the eyes of anyone there.

Dundy blew breath through his nose in a puff that was not quite a snort and said: "Get your hats."

Cairo's eyes, holding worry and a question, met Spade's mocking gaze. Spade winked at him and sat on the arm of the padded rocker. "Well, boys and girls," he said, grinning at the Levantine and at the girl with nothing but delight in his voice and grin, "we put it over nicely."

Dundy's hard square face darkened the least of shades. He repeated peremptorily: "Get your hats."

Spade turned his grin on the Lieutenant, squirmed into a more comfortable position on the chair-arm, and asked lazily: "Don't you know when you're being kidded?"

Tom Polhaus's face became red and shiny.

Dundy's face, still darkening, was immobile except for lips moving stiffly to say: "No, but we'll let that wait till we get down to the Hall."

Spade rose and put his hands in his trousers-pockets. He stood erect so he might look that much farther down at the Lieutenant. His grin was a taunt and self-certainty spoke in every line of his posture.

"I dare you to take us in, Dundy," he said. "We'll laugh at you in every newspaper in San Francisco. You don't think any of us is going to swear to any complaints against the others, do you? Wake up. You've been kidded. When the bell rang I said to Miss O'Shaughnessy and Cairo: 'It's those damned bulls again. They're getting to be nuisances. Let's play a joke on them. When you hear them going one of you scream, and then we'll see how far we can string them along before they tumble.' And—"

Brigid O'Shaughnessy bent forward in her chair and began to laugh hysterically.

Cairo started and smiled. There was no vitality in his smile, but he held it fixed on his face.

Tom, glowering, grumbled: "Cut it out, Sam."

Spade chuckled and said: "But that's the way it was. We—"

"And the cut on his head and mouth?" Dundy asked scornfully. "Where'd they come from?"

"Ask him," Spade suggested. "Maybe he cut himself shaving."

Cairo spoke quickly, before he could be questioned, and the muscles of his face quivered under the strain of holding his smile in place while he spoke. "I fell. We intended to be struggling for the pistol when you came in, but I fell. I tripped on the end of the rug and fell while we were pretending to struggle."

Dundy said: "Horse feathers."

Spade said: "That's all right, Dundy, believe it or not. The point is that that's our story and we'll stick to it. The newspapers will print it whether they believe it or not, and it'll be just as funny one way as the other, or more so. What are you going to do about it? It's no crime to kid a copper, is it? You haven't got anything on anybody here. Everything we told you was part of the joke. What are you going to do about it?"

Dundy put his back to Spade and gripped Cairo by the shoulders. "You can't get away with that," he snarled, shaking the Levantine. "You belched for help and you've got to take it."

"No, sir," Cairo sputtered. "It was a joke. He said you were friends of his and would understand."

Spade laughed.

Dundy pulled Cairo roughly around, holding him now by one wrist and the nape of his neck. "I'll take you along for packing the gun, anyway," he said. "And I'll take the rest of you along to see who laughs at the joke."

Cairo's alarmed eyes jerked sidewise to focus on Spade's face.

Spade said: "Don't be a sap, Dundy. The gun was part of the plant. It's one of mine." He laughed. "Too bad it's only a thirty-two, or maybe you could find it was the one Thursby and Miles were shot with."

Dundy released Cairo, spun on his heel, and his right fist clicked on Spade's chin.

Brigid O'Shaughnessy uttered a short cry.

Spade's smile flickered out at the instant of the impact, but returned immediately with a dreamy quality added. He steadied himself with a short backward step and his thick sloping shoulders writhed under his coat. Before his fist could come up Tom Polhaus had pushed himself between the two men, facing Spade, encumbering Spade's arms with the closeness of his barrel-like belly and his own arms.

"No, no, for Christ's sake!" Tom begged.

After a long moment of motionlessness Spade's muscles relaxed. "Then get him out of here quick," he said. His smile had gone away again, leaving his face sullen and somewhat pale.

Tom, staying close to Spade, keeping his arms on Spade's arms, turned his head to look over his shoulder at Lieutenant Dundy. Tom's small eyes were reproachful.

Dundy's fists were clenched in front of his body and his feet were planted firm and a little apart on the floor, but the truculence in his face was modified by thin rims of white showing between green irises and upper eyelids.

"Get their names and addresses," he ordered.

Tom looked at Cairo, who said quickly: "Joel Cairo, Hotel Belvedere."

Spade spoke before Tom could question the girl. "You can always get in touch with Miss O'Shaughnessy through me."

Tom looked at Dundy. Dundy growled: "Get her address."

Spade said: "Her address is in care of my office."

Dundy took a step forward, halting in front of the girl. "Where do you live?" he asked.

Spade addressed Tom: "Get him out of here. I've had enough of this."

Tom looked at Spade's eyes—hard and glittering—and mumbled: "Take it easy, Sam." He buttoned his coat and turned to Dundy, asking, in a voice that aped casualness, "Well, is that all?" and taking a step towards the door.

Dundy's scowl failed to conceal indecision.

Cairo moved suddenly towards the door, saying: "I'm going too, if Mr. Spade will be kind enough to give me my hat and coat."

Spade asked: "What's the hurry?"

Dundy said angrily: "It was all in fun, but just the same you're afraid to be left here with them."

"Not at all," the Levantine replied, fidgeting, looking at neither of them, "but it's quite late and—and I'm going. I'll go out with you if you don't mind."

Dundy put his lips together firmly and said nothing. A light was glinting in his green eyes.

Spade went to the closet in the passageway and fetched Cairo's hat and coat. Spade's face was blank. His voice held the same blankness when he stepped back from helping the Levantine into his coat and said to Tom: "Tell him to leave the gun."

Dundy took Cairo's pistol from his overcoat-pocket and put it on the table. He went out first, with Cairo at his heels. Tom halted in front of Spade, muttering, "I hope to God you know what you're doing," got no response, sighed, and followed the others out. Spade went after them as far as the bend in the passageway, where he stood until Tom had closed the corridor-door.

CHAPTER IX

Brigid

S PADE returned to the living-room and sat on an end of the sofa, elbows on knees, cheeks in hands, looking at the floor and not at Brigid O'Shaughnessy smiling weakly at him from the armchair. His eyes were sultry. The creases between brows over his nose were deep. His nostrils moved in and out with his breathing.

Brigid O'Shaughnessy, when it became apparent that he was not going to look up at her, stopped smiling and regarded him with growing uneasiness.

Red rage came suddenly into his face and he began to talk in a harsh guttural voice. Holding his maddened face in his hands, glaring at the floor, he cursed Dundy for five minutes without break, cursed him obscenely, blasphemously, repetitiously, in a harsh guttural voice.

Then he took his face out of his hands, looked at the girl, grinned sheepishly, and said: "Childish, huh? I know, but, by God, I do hate being hit without hitting back." He touched his chin with careful fingers. "Not that it was so much of a sock at that." He laughed and lounged back on the sofa, crossing his legs. "A cheap enough price to pay for winning." His brows came together in a fleeting scowl. "Though I'll remember it."

The girl, smiling again, left her chair and sat on the sofa beside him. "You're absolutely the wildest person I've ever known," she said. "Do you always carry on so high-handed?"

"I let him hit me, didn't I?"

"Oh, yes, but a police official."

"It wasn't that," Spade explained. "It was that in losing his head and slugging me he overplayed his hand. If I'd mixed it with him then he couldn't've backed down. He'd've had to go through with it, and we'd've had to tell that goofy story at headquarters." He stared thoughtfully at the girl, and asked: "What did you do to Cairo?"

"Nothing." Her face became flushed. "I tried to frighten

him into keeping still until they had gone and he either got too frightened or stubborn and yelled."

"And then you smacked him with the gun?"

"I had to. He attacked me."

"You don't know what you're doing." Spade's smile did not hide his annoyance. "It's just what I told you: you're fumbling along by guess and by God."

"I'm sorry," she said, face and voice soft with contrition, "Sam."

"Sure you are." He took tobacco and papers from his pockets and began to make a cigarette. "Now you've had your talk with Cairo. Now you can talk to me."

She put a fingertip to her mouth, staring across the room at nothing with widened eyes, and then, with narrower eyes, glanced quickly at Spade. He was engrossed in the making of his cigarette. "Oh, yes," she began, "of course—" She took the finger away from her mouth and smoothed her blue dress over her knees. She frowned at her knees.

Spade licked his cigarette, sealed it, and asked, "Well?" while he felt for his lighter.

"But I didn't," she said, pausing between words as if she were selecting them with great care, "have time to finish talking to him." She stopped frowning at her knees and looked at Spade with clear candid eyes. "We were interrupted almost before we had begun."

Spade lighted his cigarette and laughed his mouth empty of smoke. "Want me to phone him and ask him to come back?"

She shook her head, not smiling. Her eyes moved back and forth between her lids as she shook her head, maintaining their focus on Spade's eyes. Her eyes were inquisitive.

Spade put an arm across her back, cupping his hand over the smooth bare white shoulder farthest from him. She leaned back into the bend of his arm. He said: "Well, I'm listening."

She twisted her head around to smile up at him with playful insolence, asking: "Do you need your arm there for that?"

"No." He removed his hand from her shoulder and let his arm drop down behind her.

"You're altogether unpredictable," she murmured.

He nodded and said amiably: "I'm still listening."

"Look at the time!" she exclaimed, wriggling a finger at the alarm-clock perched atop the book saying two-fifty with its clumsily shaped hands.

"Uh-huh, it's been a busy evening."

"I must go." She rose from the sofa. "This is terrible."

Spade did not rise. He shook his head and said: "Not until you've told me about it."

"But look at the time," she protested, "and it would take hours to tell you."

"It'll have to take them then."

"Am I a prisoner?" she asked gaily.

"Besides, there's the kid outside. Maybe he hasn't gone home to sleep yet."

Her gaiety vanished. "Do you think he's still there?"

"It's likely."

She shivered. "Could you find out?"

"I could go down and see."

"Oh, that's—will you?"

Spade studied her anxious face for a moment and then got up from the sofa saying: "Sure." He got a hat and overcoat from the closet. "I'll be gone about ten minutes."

"Do be careful," she begged as she followed him to the corridor-door.

He said, "I will," and went out.

Post Street was empty when Spade issued into it. He walked east a block, crossed the street, walked west two blocks on the other side, recrossed it, and returned to his building without having seen anyone except two mechanics working on a car in a garage.

When he opened his apartment-door Brigid O'Shaughnessy was standing at the bend in the passageway, holding Cairo's pistol straight down at her side.

"He's still there," Spade said.

She bit the inside of her lip and turned slowly, going back into the living-room. Spade followed her in, put his hat and overcoat on a chair, said, "So we'll have time to talk," and went into the kitchen.

He had put the coffee-pot on the stove when she came to the door, and was slicing a slender loaf of French bread. She stood in the doorway and watched him with preoccupied eyes. The fingers of her left hand idly caressed the body and barrel of the pistol her right hand still held.

"The table-cloth's in there," he said, pointing the bread-knife at a cupboard that was one breakfast-nook partition.

She set the table while he spread liverwurst on, or put cold corned beef between, the small ovals of bread he had sliced. Then he poured the coffee, added brandy to it from a squat bottle, and they sat at the table. They sat side by side on one of the benches. She put the pistol down on the end of the bench nearer her.

"You can start now, between bites," he said.

She made a face at him, complained, "You're the most insistent person," and bit a sandwich.

"Yes, and wild and unpredictable. What's this bird, this falcon, that everybody's all steamed up about?"

She chewed the beef and bread in her mouth, swallowed it, looked attentively at the small crescent its removal had made in the sandwich's rim, and asked: "Suppose I wouldn't tell you? Suppose I wouldn't tell you anything at all about it? What would you do?"

"You mean about the bird?"

"I mean about the whole thing."

"I wouldn't be too surprised," he told her, grinning so that the edges of his jaw-teeth were visible, "to know what to do next."

"And that would be?" She transferred her attention from the sandwich to his face. "That's what I wanted to know: what would you do next?"

He shook his head.

Mockery rippled in a smile on her face. "Something wild and unpredictable?"

"Maybe. But I don't see what you've got to gain by covering up now. It's coming out bit by bit anyhow. There's a lot of it I don't know, but there's some of it I do, and some more that I can guess at, and, give me another day like this, I'll soon be knowing things about it that you don't know."

"I suppose you do now," she said, looking at her sandwich again, her face serious. "But—oh!—I'm so tired of it, and I do so hate having to talk about it. Wouldn't it—wouldn't it be just as well to wait and let you learn about it as you say you will?"

Spade laughed. "I don't know. You'll have to figure that out for yourself. My way of learning is to heave a wild and unpredictable monkey-wrench into the machinery. It's all right with me, if you're sure none of the flying pieces will hurt you."

She moved her bare shoulders uneasily, but said nothing. For several minutes they ate in silence, he phlegmatically, she thoughtfully. Then she said in a hushed voice: "I'm afraid of you, and that's the truth."

He said: "That's not the truth."

"It is," she insisted in the same low voice. "I know two men I'm afraid of and I've seen both of them tonight."

"I can understand your being afraid of Cairo," Spade said. "He's out of your reach."

"And you aren't?"

"Not that way," he said and grinned.

She blushed. She picked up a slice of bread encrusted with grey liverwurst. She put it down on her plate. She wrinkled her white forehead and she said: "It's a black figure, as you know, smooth and shiny, of a bird, a hawk or falcon, about that high." She held her hands a foot apart.

"What makes it important?"

She sipped coffee and brandy before she shook her head. "I don't know," she said. "They'd never tell me. They promised me five hundred pounds if I helped them get it. Then Floyd said afterward, after we'd left Joe, that he'd give me seven hundred and fifty."

"So it must be worth more than seventy-five hundred dollars?"

"Oh, much more than that," she said. "They didn't pretend that they were sharing equally with me. They were simply hiring me to help them."

"To help them how?"

She lifted her cup to her lips again. Spade, not moving the domineering stare of his yellow-grey eyes from her face, began to make a cigarette. Behind them the percolator bubbled on the stove.

"To help them get it from the man who had it," she said slowly when she had lowered her cup, "a Russian named Kemidov."

"How?"

"Oh, but that's not important," she objected, "and wouldn't help you"—she smiled impudently—"and is certainly none of your business."

"This was in Constantinople?"

She hesitated, nodded, and said: "Marmora."

He waved his cigarette at her, saying: "Go ahead, what happened then?"

"But that's all. I've told you. They promised me five hundred pounds to help them and I did and then we found that Joe Cairo meant to desert us, taking the falcon with him and leaving us nothing. So we did exactly that to him, first. But then I wasn't any better off than I had been before, because Floyd hadn't any intention at all of paying me the seven hundred and fifty pounds he had promised me. I had learned that by the time we got here. He said we would go to New York, where he would sell it and give me my share, but I could see he wasn't telling me the truth." Indignation had darkened her eyes to violet. "And that's why I came to you to get you to help me learn where the falcon was."

"And suppose you'd got it? What then?"

"Then I'd have been in a position to talk terms with Mr. Floyd Thursby."

Spade squinted at her and suggested: "But you wouldn't have known where to take it to get more money than he'd give you, the larger sum that you knew he expected to sell it for?"

"I did not know," she said.

Spade scowled at the ashes he had dumped on his plate. "What makes it worth all that money?" he demanded. "You must have some idea, at least be able to guess."

"I haven't the slightest idea."

He directed the scowl at her. "What's it made of?"

"Porcelain or black stone. I don't know. I've never touched it. I've only seen it once, for a few minutes. Floyd showed it to me when we'd first got hold of it."

Spade mashed the end of his cigarette in his plate and made one draught of the coffee and brandy in his cup. His scowl had gone away. He wiped his lips with his napkin, dropped it crumpled on the table, and spoke casually: "You *are* a liar."

She got up and stood at the end of the table, looking down at him with dark abashed eyes in a pinkening face. "I am a liar," she said. "I have always been a liar."

"Don't brag about it. It's childish." His voice was good-humored. He came out from between table and bench. "Was there any truth at all in that yarn?"

She hung her head. Dampness glistened on her dark lashes. "Some," she whispered.

"How much?"

"Not—not very much."

Spade put a hand under her chin and lifted her head. He laughed into her wet eyes and said: "We've got all night before us. I'll put some more brandy in some more coffee and we'll try again."

Her eyelids drooped. "Oh, I'm so tired," she said tremulously, "so tired of it all, of myself, of lying and thinking up lies, and of not knowing what is a lie and what is the truth. I wish I—"

She put her hands up to Spade's cheeks, put her open mouth hard against his mouth, her body flat against his body.

Spade's arms went around her, holding her to him, muscles bulging his blue sleeves, a hand cradling her head, its fingers half lost among red hair, a hand moving groping fingers over her slim back. His eyes burned yellowly.

CHAPTER X

The Belvedere Divan

BEGINNING DAY had reduced night to a thin smokiness when Spade sat up. At his side Brigid O'Shaughnessy's soft breathing had the regularity of utter sleep. Spade was quiet leaving bed and bedroom and shutting the bedroom-door. He dressed in the bathroom. Then he examined the sleeping girl's clothes, took a flat brass key from the pocket of her coat, and went out.

He went to the Coronet, letting himself into the building and into her apartment with the key. To the eye there was nothing furtive about his going in: he entered boldly and directly. To the ear his going in was almost unnoticeable: he made as little sound as might be.

In the girl's apartment he switched on all the lights. He searched the place from wall to wall. His eyes and thick fingers moved without apparent haste, and without ever lingering or fumbling or going back, from one inch of their fields to the next, probing, scrutinizing, testing with expert certainty. Every drawer, cupboard, cubbyhole, box, bag, trunk—locked or unlocked—was opened and its contents subjected to examination by eyes and fingers. Every piece of clothing was tested by hands that felt for telltale bulges and ears that listened for the crinkle of paper between pressing fingers. He stripped the bed of bedclothes. He looked under rugs and at the under side of each piece of furniture. He pulled down blinds to see that nothing had been rolled up in them for concealment. He leaned through windows to see that nothing hung below them on the outside. He poked with a fork into powder and cream-jars on the dressing-table. He held atomizers and bottles up against the light. He examined dishes and pans and food and food-containers. He emptied the garbage-can on spread sheets of newspaper. He opened the top of the flush-box in the bathroom, drained the box, and peered down into it. He examined and tested the metal screens over the drains of bathtub, wash-bowl, sink, and laundry-tub.

He did not find the black bird. He found nothing that

seemed to have any connection with a black bird. The only piece of writing he found was a week-old receipt for the month's apartment-rent Brigid O'Shaughnessy had paid. The only thing he found that interested him enough to delay his search while he looked at it was a double-handful of rather fine jewelry in a polychrome box in a locked dressing-table-drawer.

When he had finished he made and drank a cup of coffee. Then he unlocked the kitchen-window, scarred the edge of its lock a little with his pocket-knife, opened the window—over a fire-escape—got his hat and overcoat from the settee in the living-room, and left the apartment as he had come.

On his way home he stopped at a store that was being opened by a puffy-eyed shivering plump grocer and bought oranges, eggs, rolls, butter, and cream.

Spade went quietly into his apartment, but before he had shut the corridor-door behind him Brigid O'Shaughnessy cried: "Who is that?"

"Young Spade bearing breakfast."

"Oh, you frightened me!"

The bedroom-door he had shut was open. The girl sat on the side of the bed, trembling, with her right hand out of sight under a pillow.

Spade put his packages on the kitchen-table and went into the bedroom. He sat on the bed beside the girl, kissed her smooth shoulder, and said: "I wanted to see if that kid was still on the job, and to get stuff for breakfast."

"Is he?"

"No."

She sighed and leaned against him. "I awakened and you weren't here and then I heard someone coming in. I was terrified."

Spade combed her red hair back from her face with his fingers and said: "I'm sorry, angel. I thought you'd sleep through it. Did you have that gun under your pillow all night?"

"No. You know I didn't. I jumped up and got it when I was frightened."

He cooked breakfast—and slipped the flat brass key into her coat-pocket again—while she bathed and dressed.

She came out of the bathroom whistling *En Cuba*. "Shall I make the bed?" she asked.

"That'd be swell. The eggs need a couple of minutes more."

Their breakfast was on the table when she returned to the kitchen. They sat where they had sat the night before and ate heartily.

"Now about the bird?" Spade suggested presently as they ate.

She put her fork down and looked at him. She drew her eyebrows together and made her mouth small and tight. "You can't ask me to talk about that this morning of all mornings," she protested. "I don't want to and I won't."

"It's a stubborn damned hussy," he said sadly and put a piece of roll into his mouth.

The youth who had shadowed Spade was not in sight when Spade and Brigid O'Shaughnessy crossed the sidewalk to the waiting taxicab. The taxicab was not followed. Neither the youth nor another loiterer was visible in the vicinity of the Coronet when the taxicab arrived there.

Brigid O'Shaughnessy would not let Spade go in with her. "It's bad enough to be coming home in evening dress at this hour without bringing company. I hope I don't meet anybody."

"Dinner tonight?"

"Yes."

They kissed. She went into the Coronet. He told the chauffeur: "Hotel Belvedere."

When he reached the Belvedere he saw the youth who had shadowed him sitting in the lobby on a divan from which the elevators could be seen. Apparently the youth was reading a newspaper.

At the desk Spade learned that Cairo was not in. He frowned and pinched his lower lip. Points of yellow light began to dance in his eyes. "Thanks," he said softly to the clerk and turned away.

Sauntering, he crossed the lobby to the divan from which the elevators could be seen and sat down beside—not more than a foot from—the young man who was apparently reading a newspaper.

The young man did not look up from his newspaper. Seen at this scant distance, he seemed certainly less than twenty years old. His features were small, in keeping with his stature, and regular. His skin was very fair. The whiteness of his cheeks was as little blurred by any considerable growth of beard as by the glow of blood. His clothing was neither new nor of more than ordinary quality, but it, and his manner of wearing it, was marked by a hard masculine neatness.

Spade asked casually, "Where is he?" while shaking tobacco down into a brown paper curved to catch it.

The boy lowered his paper and looked around, moving with a purposeful sort of slowness, as of a more natural swiftness restrained. He looked with small hazel eyes under somewhat long curling lashes at Spade's chest. He said, in a voice as colorless and composed and cold as his young face: "What?"

"Where is he?" Spade was busy with his cigarette.

"Who?"

"The fairy."

The hazel eyes' gaze went up Spade's chest to the knot of his maroon tie and rested there. "What do you think you're doing, Jack?" the boy demanded. "Kidding me?"

"I'll tell you when I am." Spade licked his cigarette and smiled amiably at the boy. "New York, aren't you?"

The boy stared at Spade's tie and did not speak. Spade nodded as if the boy had said yes and asked: "Baumes rush?"

The boy stared at Spade's tie for a moment longer, then raised his newspaper and returned his attention to it. "Shove off," he said from the side of his mouth.

Spade lighted his cigarette, leaned back comfortably on the divan, and spoke with good-natured carelessness: "You'll have to talk to me before you're through, sonny—some of you will—and you can tell G. I said so."

The boy put his paper down quickly and faced Spade, staring at his necktie with bleak hazel eyes. The boy's small hands were spread flat over his belly. "Keep asking for it and you're going to get it," he said, "plenty." His voice was low and flat and menacing. "I told you to shove off. Shove off."

Spade waited until a bespectacled pudgy man and a thin-legged blonde girl had passed out of hearing. Then he chuckled and said: "That would go over big back on Seventh Avenue. But you're not in Romeville now. You're in my burg." He inhaled cigarette-smoke and blew it out in a long pale cloud. "Well, where is he?"

The boy spoke two words, the first a short guttural verb, the second "you."

"People lose teeth talking like that." Spade's voice was still amiable though his face had become wooden. "If you want to hang around you'll be polite."

The boy repeated his two words.

Spade dropped his cigarette into a tall stone jar beside the divan and with a lifted hand caught the attention of a man who had been standing at an end of the cigar-stand for several minutes. The man nodded and came towards them. He was a middle-aged man of medium height, round and sallow of face, compactly built, tidily dressed in dark clothes.

"Hello, Sam," he said as he came up.

"Hello, Luke."

They shook hands and Luke said: "Say, that's too bad about Miles."

"Uh-huh, a bad break." Spade jerked his head to indicate the boy on the divan beside him. "What do you let these cheap gunmen hang out in your lobby for, with their tools bulging their clothes?"

"Yes?" Luke examined the boy with crafty brown eyes set in a suddenly hard face. "What do you want here?" he asked.

The boy stood up. Spade stood up. The boy looked at the two men, at their neckties, from one to the other. Luke's necktie was black. The boy looked like a schoolboy standing in front of them.

Luke said: "Well, if you don't want anything, beat it, and don't come back."

The boy said, "I won't forget you guys," and went out.

They watched him go out. Spade took off his hat and wiped his damp forehead with a handkerchief.

The hotel-detective asked: "What is it?"

"Damned if I know," Spade replied. "I just happened to spot him. Know anything about Joel Cairo—six-thirty-five?"

"Oh, that one!" The hotel detective leered.

"How long's he been here?"

"Four days. This is the fifth."

"What about him?"

"Search me, Sam. I got nothing against him but his looks."

"Find out if he came in last night?"

"Try to," the hotel-detective promised and went away. Spade sat on the divan until he returned. "No," Luke reported, "he didn't sleep in his room. What is it?"

"Nothing."

"Come clean. You know I'll keep my clam shut, but if there's anything wrong we ought to know about it so's we can collect our bill."

"Nothing like that," Spade assured him. "As a matter of fact, I'm doing a little work for him. I'd tell you if he was wrong."

"You'd better. Want me to kind of keep an eye on him?"

"Thanks, Luke. It wouldn't hurt. You can't know too much about the men you're working for these days."

It was twenty-one minutes past eleven by the clock over the elevator-doors when Joel Cairo came in from the street. His forehead was bandaged. His clothes had the limp unfreshness of too many hours' consecutive wear. His face was pasty, with sagging mouth and eyelids.

Spade met him in front of the desk. "Good morning," Spade said easily.

Cairo drew his tired body up straight and the drooping lines of his face tightened. "Good morning," he responded without enthusiasm.

There was a pause.

Spade said: "Let's go some place where we can talk."

Cairo raised his chin. "Please excuse me," he said. "Our conversations in private have not been such that I am anxious to continue them. Pardon my speaking bluntly, but it is the truth."

"You mean last night?" Spade made an impatient gesture with head and hands. "What in hell else could I do? I thought you'd see that. If you pick a fight with her, or let her pick one with you, I've got to throw in with her. I don't know where that damned bird is. You don't. She does. How in hell are we going to get it if I don't play along with her?"

Cairo hesitated, said dubiously: "You have always, I must say, a smooth explanation ready."

Spade scowled. "What do you want me to do? Learn to stutter? Well, we can talk over here." He led the way to the divan. When they were seated he asked: "Dundy take you down to the Hall?"

"Yes."

"How long did they work on you?"

"Until a very little while ago, and very much against my will." Pain and indignation were mixed in Cairo's face and voice. "I shall certainly take the matter up with the Consulate General of Greece and with an attorney."

"Go ahead, and see what it gets you. What did you let the police shake out of you?"

There was prim satisfaction in Cairo's smile. "Not a single thing. I adhered to the course you indicated earlier in your rooms." His smile went away. "Though I certainly wished you had devised a more reasonable story. I felt decidedly ridiculous repeating it."

Spade grinned mockingly. "Sure," he said, "but its goofiness is what makes it good. You sure you didn't give them anything?"

"You may rely upon it, Mr. Spade, I did not."

Spade drummed with his fingers on the leather seat between them. "You'll be hearing from Dundy again. Stay dummied-up on him and you'll be all right. Don't worry about the story's goofiness. A sensible one would've had us all in the cooler." He rose to his feet. "You'll want sleep if you've been standing up under a police-storm all night. See you later."

Effie Perine was saying, "No, not yet," into the telephone when Spade entered his outer office. She looked around at him and her lips shaped a silent word: "Iva." He shook his head. "Yes, I'll have him call you as soon as he comes in," she said aloud and replaced the receiver on its prong. "That's the third time she's called up this morning," she told Spade.

He made an impatient growling noise.

The girl moved her brown eyes to indicate the inner office. "Your Miss O'Shaughnessy's in there. She's been waiting since a few minutes after nine."

Spade nodded as if he had expected that and asked: "What else?"

"Sergeant Polhaus called up. He didn't leave any message."

"Get him for me."

"And G. called up."

Spade's eyes brightened. He asked: "Who?"

"G. That's what he said." Her air of personal indifference to the subject was flawless. "When I told him you weren't in he said: 'When he comes in, will you please tell him that G., who got his message, phoned and will phone again?'."

Spade worked his lips together as if tasting something he liked. "Thanks, darling," he said. "See if you can get Tom Polhaus." He opened the inner door and went into his private office, pulling the door to behind him.

Brigid O'Shaughnessy, dressed as on her first visit to the office, rose from a chair beside his desk and came quickly towards him. "Somebody has been in my apartment," she exclaimed. "It is all upside-down, every which way."

He seemed moderately surprised. "Anything taken?"

"I don't think so. I don't know. I was afraid to stay. I changed as fast as I could and came down here. Oh, you must've let that boy follow you there!"

Spade shook his head. "No, angel." He took an early copy of an afternoon paper from his pocket, opened it, and showed her a quarter-column headed SCREAM ROUTS BURGLAR.

A young woman named Carolin Beale, who lived alone in a Sutter Street apartment, had been awakened at four that morning by the sound of somebody moving in her bedroom. She had screamed. The mover had run away. Two other women who lived alone in the same building had discovered, later in the morning, signs of the burglar's having visited their apartments. Nothing had been taken from any of the three.

"That's where I shook him," Spade explained. "I went into that building and ducked out the back door. That's why all three were women who lived alone. He tried the apartments that had women's names in the vestibule-register, hunting for you under an alias."

"But he was watching your place when we were there," she objected.

Spade shrugged. "There's no reason to think he's working

alone. Or maybe he went to Sutter Street after he had begun to think you were going to stay all night in my place. There are a lot of maybes, but I didn't lead him to the Coronet."

She was not satisfied. "But he found it, or somebody did."

"Sure." He frowned at her feet. "I wonder if it could have been Cairo. He wasn't at his hotel all night, didn't get in till a few minutes ago. He told me he had been standing up under a police-grilling all night. I wonder." He turned, opened the door, and asked Effie Perine: "Got Tom yet?"

"He's not in. I'll try again in a few minutes."

"Thanks." Spade shut the door and faced Brigid O'Shaughnessy.

She looked at him with cloudy eyes. "You went to see Joe this morning?" she asked.

"Yes."

She hesitated. "Why?"

"Why?" He smiled down at her. "Because, my own true love, I've got to keep in some sort of touch with all the loose ends of this dizzy affair if I'm ever going to make heads or tails of it." He put an arm around her shoulders and led her over to his swivel-chair. He kissed the tip of her nose lightly and set her down in the chair. He sat on the desk in front of her. He said: "Now we've got to find a new home for you, haven't we?"

She nodded with emphasis. "I won't go back there."

He patted the desk beside his thighs and made a thoughtful face. "I think I've got it," he said presently. "Wait a minute." He went into the outer office, shutting the door.

Effie Perine reached for the telephone, saying: "I'll try again."

"Afterwards. Does your woman's intuition still tell you that she's a madonna or something?"

She looked sharply up at him. "I still believe that no matter what kind of trouble she's gotten into she's all right, if that's what you mean."

"That's what I mean," he said. "Are you strong enough for her to give her a lift?"

"How?"

"Could you put her up for a few days?"

"You mean at home?"

"Yes. Her joint's been broken into. That's the second burglary she's had this week. It'd be better for her if she wasn't alone. It would help a lot if you could take her in."

Effie Perine leaned forward, asking earnestly: "Is she really in danger, Sam?"

"I think she is."

She scratched her lip with a fingernail. "That would scare Ma into a green hemorrhage. I'll have to tell her she's a surprise-witness or something that you're keeping under cover till the last minute."

"You're a darling," Spade said. "Better take her out there now. I'll get her key from her and bring whatever she needs over from her apartment. Let's see. You oughtn't to be seen leaving here together. You go home now. Take a taxi, but make sure you aren't followed. You probably won't be, but make sure. I'll send her out in another in a little while, making sure she isn't followed."

CHAPTER XI

The Fat Man

THE TELEPHONE-BELL was ringing when Spade returned to his office after sending Brigid O'Shaughnessy off to Effie Perine's house. He went to the telephone.

"Hello. . . . Yes, this is Spade. . . . Yes, I got it. I've been waiting to hear from you. . . . Who? . . . Mr. Gutman? Oh, yes, sure! . . . Now—the sooner the better. . . . Twelve C. . . . Right. Say fifteen minutes. . . . Right."

Spade sat on the corner of his desk beside the telephone and rolled a cigarette. His mouth was a hard complacent v. His eyes, watching his fingers make the cigarette, smoldered over lower lids drawn up straight.

The door opened and Iva Archer came in.

Spade said, "Hello, honey," in a voice as lightly amiable as his face had suddenly become.

"Oh, Sam, forgive me! forgive me!" she cried in a choked voice. She stood just inside the door, wadding a black-bordered handkerchief in her small gloved hands, peering into his face with frightened red and swollen eyes.

He did not get up from his seat on the desk-corner. He said: "Sure. That's all right. Forget it."

"But, Sam," she wailed, "I sent those policemen there. I was mad, crazy with jealousy, and I phoned them that if they'd go there they'd learn something about Miles's murder."

"What made you think that?"

"Oh, I didn't! But I was mad, Sam, and I wanted to hurt you."

"It made things damned awkward." He put his arm around her and drew her nearer. "But it's all right now, only don't get any more crazy notions like that."

"I won't," she promised, "ever. But you weren't nice to me last night. You were cold and distant and wanted to get rid of me, when I had come down there and waited so long to warn you, and you—"

"Warn me about what?"

"About Phil. He's found out about—about you being in

478

love with me, and Miles had told him about my wanting a divorce, though of course *he* never knew what for, and now Phil thinks we—you killed his brother because he wouldn't give me the divorce so we could get married. He told me he believed that, and yesterday he went and told the police."

"That's nice," Spade said softly. "And you came to warn me, and because I was busy you got up on your ear and helped this damned Phil Archer stir things up."

"I'm sorry," she whimpered, "I know you won't forgive me. I—I'm sorry, sorry, sorry."

"You ought to be," he agreed, "on your own account as well as mine. Has Dundy been to see you since Phil did his talking? Or anybody from the bureau?"

"No." Alarm opened her eyes and mouth.

"They will," he said, "and it'd be just as well to not let them find you here. Did you tell them who you were when you phoned?"

"Oh, no! I simply told them that if they'd go to your apartment right away they'd learn something about the murder and hung up."

"Where'd you phone from?"

"The drug-store up above your place. Oh, Sam, dearest, I—"

He patted her shoulder and said pleasantly: "It was a dumb trick, all right, but it's done now. You'd better run along home and think up things to tell the police. You'll be hearing from them. Maybe it'd be best to say 'no' right across the board." He frowned at something distant. "Or maybe you'd better see Sid Wise first." He removed his arm from around her, took a card out of his pocket, scribbled three lines on its back, and gave it to her. "You can tell Sid everything." He frowned. "Or almost everything. Where were you the night Miles was shot?"

"Home," she replied without hesitating.

He shook his head, grinning at her.

"I was," she insisted.

"No," he said, "but if that's your story it's all right with me. Go see Sid. It's up on the next corner, the pinkish building, room eight-twenty-seven."

Her blue eyes tried to probe his yellow-grey ones. "What makes you think I wasn't home?" she asked slowly.

"Nothing except that I know you weren't."

"But I was, I was." Her lips twisted and anger darkened her eyes. "Effie Perine told you that," she said indignantly. "I saw her looking at my clothes and snooping around. You know she doesn't like me, Sam. Why do you believe things she tells you when you know she'd do anything to make trouble for me?"

"Jesus, you women," Spade said mildly. He looked at the watch on his wrist. "You'll have to trot along, precious. I'm late for an appointment now. You do what you want, but if I were you I'd tell Sid the truth or nothing. I mean leave out the parts you don't want to tell him, but don't make up anything to take its place."

"I'm not lying to you, Sam," she protested.

"Like hell you're not," he said and stood up.

She strained on tiptoe to hold her face nearer his. "You don't believe me?" she whispered.

"I don't believe you."

"And you won't forgive me for—for what I did?"

"Sure I do." He bent his head and kissed her mouth. "That's all right. Now run along."

She put her arms around him. "Won't you go with me to see Mr. Wise?"

"I can't, and I'd only be in the way." He patted her arms, took them from around his body, and kissed her left wrist between glove and sleeve. He put his hands on her shoulders, turned her to face the door, and released her with a little push. "Beat it," he ordered.

The mahogany door of suite 12-C at the Alexandria Hotel was opened by the boy Spade had talked to in the Belvedere lobby. Spade said, "Hello," good-naturedly. The boy did not say anything. He stood aside holding the door open.

Spade went in. A fat man came to meet him.

The fat man was flabbily fat with bulbous pink cheeks and lips and chins and neck, with a great soft egg of a belly that was all his torso, and pendant cones for arms and legs. As he advanced to meet Spade all his bulbs rose and shook and fell separately with each step, in the manner of clustered soap-bubbles not yet released from the pipe through which they had been blown. His eyes, made small by fat puffs around them, were dark and sleek. Dark ringlets thinly covered his broad scalp. He wore a black cutaway coat, black vest, black satin Ascot tie holding a pinkish pearl, striped grey worsted trousers, and patent-leather shoes.

His voice was a throaty purr. "Ah, Mr. Spade," he said with enthusiasm and held out a hand like a fat pink star.

Spade took the hand and smiled and said: "How do you do, Mr. Gutman?"

Holding Spade's hand, the fat man turned beside him, put his other hand to Spade's elbow, and guided him across a green rug to a green plush chair beside a table that held a siphon, some glasses, and a bottle of Johnnie Walker whiskey on a tray, a box of cigars—Coronas del Ritz—two newspapers, and a small and plain yellow soapstone box.

Spade sat in the green chair. The fat man began to fill two glasses from bottle and siphon. The boy had disappeared. Doors set in three of the room's walls were shut. The fourth wall, behind Spade, was pierced by two windows looking out over Geary Street.

"We begin well, sir," the fat man purred, turning with a proffered glass in his hand. "I distrust a man that says when. If he's got to be careful not to drink too much it's because he's not to be trusted when he does."

Spade took the glass and, smiling, made the beginning of a bow over it.

The fat man raised his glass and held it against a window's light. He nodded approvingly at the bubbles running up in it. He said: "Well, sir, here's to plain speaking and clear under-standing."

They drank and lowered their glasses.

The fat man looked shrewdly at Spade and asked: "You're a close-mouthed man?"

Spade shook his head. "I like to talk."

"Better and better!" the fat man exclaimed. "I distrust a close-mouthed man. He generally picks the wrong time to talk and says the wrong things. Talking's something you can't do judiciously unless you keep in practice." He beamed over his glass. "We'll get along, sir, that we will." He set his glass on the table and held the box of Coronas del Ritz out to Spade. "A cigar, sir."

Spade took a cigar, trimmed the end of it, and lighted it. Meanwhile the fat man pulled another green plush chair around to face Spade's within convenient distance and placed a smoking-stand within reach of both chairs. Then he took his glass from the table, took a cigar from the box, and lowered himself into his chair. His bulbs stopped jouncing and settled into flabby rest. He sighed comfortably and said: "Now, sir, we'll talk if you like. And I'll tell you right out that I'm a man who likes talking to a man that likes to talk."

"Swell. Will we talk about the black bird?"

The fat man laughed and his bulbs rode up and down on his laughter. "Will we?" he asked and, "We will," he replied. His pink face was shiny with delight. "You're the man for me, sir, a man cut along my own lines. No beating about the bush, but right to the point. 'Will we talk about the black bird?' We will. I like that, sir. I like that way of doing business. Let us talk about the black bird by all means, but first, sir, answer me a question, please, though maybe it's an unnecessary one, so we'll understand each other from the beginning. You're here as Miss O'Shaughnessy's representative?"

Spade blew smoke above the fat man's head in a long slanting plume. He frowned thoughtfully at the ash-tipped end of his cigar. He replied deliberately: "I can't say yes or no. There's nothing certain about it either way, yet." He looked up at the fat man and stopped frowning. "It depends."

"It depends on—?"

Spade shook his head. "If I knew what it depends on I could say yes or no."

The fat man took a mouthful from his glass, swallowed it, and suggested: "Maybe it depends on Joel Cairo?"

Spade's prompt "Maybe" was noncommittal. He drank.

The fat man leaned forward until his belly stopped him. His smile was ingratiating and so was his purring voice. "You could say, then, that the question is which one of them you'll represent?"

"You could put it that way."

"It will be one or the other?"

"I didn't say that."

The fat man's eyes glistened. His voice sank to a throaty whisper asking: "Who else is there?"

Spade pointed his cigar at his own chest. "There's me," he said.

The fat man sank back in his chair and let his body go flaccid. He blew his breath out in a long contented gust. "That's wonderful, sir," he purred. "That's wonderful. I do like a man that tells you right out he's looking out for himself. Don't we all? I don't trust a man that says he's not. And the man that's telling the truth when he says he's not I distrust most of all, because he's an ass and an ass that's going contrary to the laws of nature."

Spade exhaled smoke. His face was politely attentive. He said: "Uh-huh. Now let's talk about the black bird."

The fat man smiled benevolently. "Let's," he said. He squinted so that fat puffs crowding together left nothing of his eyes but a dark gleam visible. "Mr. Spade, have you any conception of how much money can be made out of that black bird?"

"No."

The fat man leaned forward again and put a bloated pink hand on the arm of Spade's chair. "Well, sir, if I told you—by Gad, if I told you half!—you'd call me a liar."

Spade smiled. "No," he said, "not even if I thought it. But if you won't take the risk just tell me what it is and I'll figure out the profits."

The fat man laughed. "You couldn't do it, sir. Nobody could do it that hadn't had a world of experience with things of that sort, and"—he paused impressively—"there aren't any other things of that sort." His bulbs jostled one another as he laughed again. He stopped laughing, abruptly. His fleshy lips hung open as laughter had left them. He stared at Spade with an intentness that suggested myopia. He asked: "You mean you don't know what it is?" Amazement took the throatiness out of his voice.

Spade made a careless gesture with his cigar. "Oh, hell," he said lightly, "I know what it's supposed to look like. I know the value in life you people put on it. I don't know what it is."

"She didn't tell you?"

"Miss O'Shaughnessy?"

"Yes. A lovely girl, sir."

"Uh-huh. No."

The fat man's eyes were dark gleams in ambush behind pink puffs of flesh. He said indistinctly, "She must know," and then, "And Cairo didn't either?"

"Cairo is cagey. He's willing to buy it, but he won't risk telling me anything I don't know already."

The fat man moistened his lips with his tongue. "How much is he willing to buy it for?" he asked.

"Ten thousand dollars."

The fat man laughed scornfully. "Ten thousand, and dollars, mind you, not even pounds. That's the Greek for you. Humph! And what did you say to that?"

"I said if I turned it over to him I'd expect the ten thousand."

"Ah, yes, *if!* Nicely put, sir." The fat man's forehead squirmed in a flesh-blurred frown. "They must know," he said only partly aloud, then: "Do they? Do they know what the bird is, sir? What was your impression?"

"I can't help you there," Spade confessed. "There's not much to go by. Cairo didn't say he did and he didn't say he didn't. She said she didn't, but I took it for granted that she was lying."

"That was not an injudicious thing to do," the fat man said, but his mind was obviously not on his words. He scratched his head. He frowned until his forehead was marked by raw red creases. He fidgeted in his chair as much as his size and the size of the chair permitted fidgeting. He shut his eyes, opened them suddenly—wide—and said to Spade: "Maybe they don't." His bulbous pink face slowly lost its worried frown and then, more quickly, took on an expression of ineffable happiness. "If they don't," he cried, and again: "If they don't I'm the only one in the whole wide sweet world who does!"

Spade drew his lips back in a tight smile. "I'm glad I came to the right place," he said.

The fat man smiled too, but somewhat vaguely. Happiness had gone out of his face, though he continued to smile, and caution had come into his eyes. His face was a watchful-eyed smiling mask held up between his thoughts and Spade. His eyes, avoiding Spade's, shifted to the glass at Spade's elbow. His face brightened. "By Gad, sir," he said, "your glass is empty." He got up and went to the table and clattered glasses and siphon and bottle mixing two drinks.

Spade was immobile in his chair until the fat man, with a flourish and a bow and a jocular "Ah, sir, this kind of medicine will never hurt you!" had handed him his refilled glass. Then Spade rose and stood close to the fat man, looking down at him, and Spade's eyes were hard and bright. He raised his glass. His voice was deliberate, challenging: "Here's to plain speaking and clear understanding."

The fat man chuckled and they drank. The fat man sat down. He held his glass against his belly with both hands and smiled up at Spade. He said: "Well, sir, it's surprising, but it well may be a fact that neither of them does know exactly what that bird is, and that nobody in all this whole wide sweet world knows what it is, saving and excepting only your humble servant, Casper Gutman, Esquire."

"Swell." Spade stood with legs apart, one hand in his trousers-pocket, the other holding his glass. "When you've told me there'll only be two of us who know."

"Mathematically correct, sir"—the fat man's eyes twinkled—"but"—his smile spread—"I don't know for certain that I'm going to tell you."

"Don't be a damned fool," Spade said patiently. "You know what it is. I know where it is. That's why we're here."

"Well, sir, where is it?"

Spade ignored the question.

The fat man bunched his lips, raised his eyebrows, and cocked his head a little to the left. "You see," he said blandly, "I must tell you what I know, but you will not tell me what you know. That is hardly equitable, sir. No, no, I do not think we can do business along those lines."

Spade's face became pale and hard. He spoke rapidly in a low furious voice: "Think again and think fast. I told that punk of yours that you'd have to talk to me before you got through. I'll tell you now that you'll do your talking today or you are through. What are you wasting my time for? You and your lousy secret! Christ! I know exactly what that stuff is that they keep in the subtreasury vaults, but what good does that do me? I can get along without you. God damn you! Maybe you could have got along without me if you'd kept clear of me. You can't now. Not in San Francisco. You'll come in or you'll get out—and you'll do it today."

He turned and with angry heedlessness tossed his glass at the table. The glass struck the wood, burst apart, and splashed its contents and glittering fragments over table and floor. Spade, deaf and blind to the crash, wheeled to confront the fat man again.

The fat man paid no more attention to the glass's fate than Spade did: lips pursed, eyebrows raised, head cocked a little to the left, he had maintained his pink-faced blandness through-out Spade's angry speech, and he maintained it now.

Spade, still furious, said: "And another thing, I don't want—"

The door to Spade's left opened. The boy who had admit-ted Spade came in. He shut the door, stood in front of it with his hands flat against his flanks, and looked at Spade. The boy's eyes were wide open and dark with wide pupils. Their gaze ran over Spade's body from shoulders to knees, and up again to settle on the handkerchief whose maroon border peeped from the breast-pocket of Spade's brown coat.

"Another thing," Spade repeated, glaring at the boy: "Keep that gunsel away from me while you're making up your mind. I'll kill him. I don't like him. He makes me nervous. I'll kill him the first time he gets in my way. I won't give him an even break. I won't give him a chance. I'll kill him."

The boy's lips twitched in a shadowy smile. He neither raised his eyes nor spoke.

The fat man said tolerantly: "Well, sir, I must say you have a most violent temper."

"Temper?" Spade laughed crazily. He crossed to the chair on which he had dropped his hat, picked up the hat, and set it on his head. He held out a long arm that ended in a thick forefinger pointing at the fat man's belly. His angry voice filled the room. "Think it over and think like hell. You've got till five-thirty to do it in. Then you're either in or out, for keeps." He let his arm drop, scowled at the bland fat man for a moment, scowled at the boy, and went to the door through which he had entered. When he opened the door he turned and said harshly: "Five-thirty—then the curtain."

The boy, staring at Spade's chest, repeated the two words he had twice spoken in the Belvedere lobby. His voice was not loud. It was bitter.

Spade went out and slammed the door.

CHAPTER XII

Merry-Go-Round

SPADE rode down from Gutman's floor in an elevator. His lips were dry and rough in a face otherwise pale and damp. When he took out his handkerchief to wipe his face he saw his hand trembling. He grinned at it and said, "Whew!" so loudly that the elevator-operator turned his head over his shoulder and asked: "Sir?"

Spade walked down Geary Street to the Palace Hotel, where he ate luncheon. His face had lost its pallor, his lips their dryness, and his hand its trembling by the time he had sat down. He ate hungrily without haste, and then went to Sid Wise's office.

When Spade entered, Wise was biting a fingernail and staring at the window. He took his hand from his mouth, screwed his chair around to face Spade, and said: "'Lo. Push a chair up."

Spade moved a chair to the side of the big paper-laden desk and sat down. "Mrs. Archer come in?" he asked.

"Yes." The faintest of lights flickered in Wise's eyes. "Going to marry the lady, Sammy?"

Spade sighed irritably through his nose. "Christ, now you start that!" he grumbled.

A brief tired smile lifted the corners of the lawyer's mouth. "If you don't," he said, "you're going to have a job on your hands."

Spade looked up from the cigarette he was making and spoke sourly: "You mean you are? Well, that's what you're for. What did she tell you?"

"About you?"

"About anything I ought to know."

Wise ran fingers through his hair, sprinkling dandruff down on his shoulders. "She told me she had tried to get a divorce from Miles so she could—"

"I know all that," Spade interrupted him. "You can skip it. Get to the part I don't know."

"How do I know how much she—?"

488

"Quit stalling, Sid." Spade held the flame of his lighter to the end of his cigarette. "What did she tell you that she wanted kept from me?"

Wise looked reprovingly at Spade. "Now, Sammy," he began, "that's not—"

Spade looked heavenward at the ceiling and groaned: "Dear God, he's my own lawyer that's got rich off me and I have to get down on my knees and beg him to tell me things!" He lowered at Wise. "What in hell do you think I sent her to you for?"

Wise made a weary grimace. "Just one more client like you," he complained, "and I'd be in a sanatarium—or San Quentin."

"You'd be with most of your clients. Did she tell you where she was the night he was killed?"

"Yes."

"Where?"

"Following him."

Spade sat up straight and blinked. He exclaimed incredulously: "Jesus, these women!" Then he laughed, relaxed, and asked: "Well, what did she see?"

Wise shook his head. "Nothing much. When he came home for dinner that evening he told her he had a date with a girl at the St. Mark, ragging her, telling her that was her chance to get the divorce she wanted. She thought at first he was just trying to get under her skin. He knew—"

"I know the family history," Spade said. "Skip it. Tell me what she did."

"I will if you'll give me a chance. After he had gone out she began to think that maybe he might have had that date. You know Miles. It would have been like him to—"

"You can skip Miles's character too."

"I oughtn't to tell you a damned thing," the lawyer said. "So she got their car from the garage and drove down to the St. Mark, sitting in the car across the street. She saw him come out of the hotel and she saw that he was shadowing a man and a girl—she says she saw the same girl with you last night—who had come out just ahead of him. She knew then that he was working, had been kidding her. I suppose she was disappointed, and mad—she sounded that way when she told me about it. She followed Miles long enough to make sure he was shadowing the pair, and then she went up to your apartment. You weren't home."

"What time was that?" Spade asked.

"When she got to your place? Between half-past nine and ten the first time."

"The first time?"

"Yes. She drove around for half an hour or so and then tried again. That would make it, say, ten-thirty. You were still out, so she drove back downtown and went to a movie to kill time until after midnight, when she thought she'd be more likely to find you in."

Spade frowned. "She went to a movie at ten-thirty?"

"So she says—the one on Powell Street that stays open till one in the morning. She didn't want to go home, she said, because she didn't want to be there when Miles came. That always made him mad, it seems, especially if it was around midnight. She stayed in the movie till it closed." Wise's words came out slower now and there was a sardonic glint in his eye. "She says she had decided by then not to go back to your place again. She says she didn't know whether you'd like having her drop in that late. So she went to Tait's—the one on Ellis Street—had something to eat and then went home—alone." Wise rocked back in his chair and waited for Spade to speak.

Spade's face was expressionless. He asked: "You believe her?"

"Don't you?" Wise replied.

"How do I know? How do I know it isn't something you fixed up between you to tell me?"

Wise smiled. "You don't cash many checks for strangers, do you, Sammy?"

"Not basketfuls. Well, what then? Miles wasn't home. It was at least two o'clock by then—must've been—and he was dead."

"Miles wasn't home," Wise said. "That seems to have made her mad again—his not being home first to be made mad by her not being home. So she took the car out of the garage again and went back to your place."

"And I wasn't home. I was down looking at Miles's corpse.

Jesus, what a swell lot of merry-go-round riding. Then what?"

"She went home, and her husband still wasn't there, and while she was undressing your messenger came with the news of his death."

Spade didn't speak until he had with great care rolled and lighted another cigarette. Then he said: "I think that's an all right spread. It seems to click with most of the known facts. It ought to hold."

Wise's fingers, running through his hair again, combed more dandruff down on his shoulders. He studied Spade's face with curious eyes and asked: "But you don't believe it?"

Spade plucked his cigarette from between his lips. "I don't believe it or disbelieve it, Sid. I don't know a damned thing about it."

A wry smile twisted the lawyer's mouth. He moved his shoulders wearily and said: "That's right—I'm selling you out. Why don't you get an honest lawyer—one you can trust?"

"That fellow's dead." Spade stood up. He sneered at Wise. "Getting touchy, huh? I haven't got enough to think about: now I've got to remember to be polite to you. What did I do? Forget to genuflect when I came in?"

Sid Wise smiled sheepishly. "You're a son of a gun, Sammy," he said.

Effie Perine was standing in the center of Spade's outer office when he entered. She looked at him with worried brown eyes and asked: "What happened?"

Spade's face grew stiff. "What happened where?" he demanded.

"Why didn't she come?"

Spade took two long steps and caught Effie Perine by the shoulders. "She didn't get there?" he bawled into her frightened face.

She shook her head violently from side to side. "I waited and waited and she didn't come, and I couldn't get you on the phone, so I came down."

Spade jerked his hands away from her shoulders, thrust them far down in his trousers-pockets, said, "Another merry-go-round," in a loud enraged voice, and strode into his private office. He came out again. "Phone your mother," he commanded. "See if she's come yet."

He walked up and down the office while the girl used the telephone. "No," she said when she had finished. "Did—did you send her out in a taxi?"

His grunt probably meant yes.

"Are you sure she— Somebody must have followed her!"

Spade stopped pacing the floor. He put his hands on his hips and glared at the girl. He addressed her in a loud savage voice: "Nobody followed her. Do you think I'm a God-damned schoolboy? I made sure of it before I put her in the cab, I rode a dozen blocks with her to be more sure, and I checked her another half-dozen blocks after I got out."

"Well, but—"

"But she didn't get there. You've told me that. I believe it. Do you think I think she did get there?"

Effie Perine sniffed. "You certainly act like a God-damned schoolboy," she said.

Spade made a harsh noise in his throat and went to the corridor-door. "I'm going out and find her if I have to dig up sewers," he said. "Stay here till I'm back or you hear from me. For Christ's sake let's do something right."

He went out, walked half the distance to the elevators, and retraced his steps. Effie Perine was sitting at her desk when he opened the door. He said: "You ought to know better than to pay any attention to me when I talk like that."

"If you think I pay any attention to you you're crazy," she replied, "only"—she crossed her arms and felt her shoulders, and her mouth twitched uncertainly—"I won't be able to wear an evening gown for two weeks, you big brute."

He grinned humbly, said, "I'm no damned good, darling," made an exaggerated bow, and went out again.

Two yellow taxicabs were at the corner-stand to which Spade went. Their chauffeurs were standing together talking. Spade asked: "Where's the red-faced blond driver that was here at noon?"

"Got a load," one of the chauffeurs said.

"Will he be back here?"

"I guess so."

The other chauffeur ducked his head to the east. "Here he comes now."

Spade walked down to the corner and stood by the curb until the red-faced blond chauffeur had parked his cab and got out. Then Spade went up to him and said: "I got into your cab with a lady at noontime. We went out Stockton Street and up Sacramento to Jones, where I got out."

"Sure," the red-faced man said, "I remember that."

"I told you to take her to a Ninth-Avenue-number. You didn't take her there. Where did you take her?"

The chauffeur rubbed his cheek with a grimy hand and looked doubtfully at Spade. "I don't know about this."

"It's all right," Spade assured him, giving him one of his cards. "If you want to play safe, though, we can ride up to your office and get your superintendent's OK."

"I guess it's all right. I took her to the Ferry Building."

"By herself?"

"Yeah. Sure."

"Didn't take her anywhere else first?"

"No. It was like this: after we dropped you I went on out Sacramento, and when we got to Polk she rapped on the glass and said she wanted to get a newspaper, so I stopped at the corner and whistled for a kid, and she got her paper."

"Which paper?"

"The *Call*. Then I went on out Sacramento some more, and just after we'd crossed Van Ness she knocked on the glass again and said take her to the Ferry Building."

"Was she excited or anything?"

"Not so's I noticed."

"And when you got to the Ferry Building?"

"She paid me off, and that was all."

"Anybody waiting for her there?"

"I didn't see them if they was."

"Which way did she go?"

"At the Ferry? I don't know. Maybe upstairs, or towards the stairs."

"Take the newspaper with her?"

"Yeah, she had it tucked under her arm when she paid me."

"With the pink sheet outside, or one of the white?"

"Hell, Cap, I don't remember that."

Spade thanked the chauffeur, said, "Get yourself a smoke," and gave him a silver dollar.

Spade bought a copy of the *Call* and carried it into an office-building-vestibule to examine it out of the wind.

His eyes ran swiftly over the front-page-headlines and over those on the second and third pages. They paused for a moment under SUSPECT ARRESTED AS COUNTERFEITER on the fourth page, and again on page five under BAY YOUTH SEEKS DEATH WITH BULLET. Pages six and seven held nothing to interest him. On eight 3 BOYS ARRESTED AS S.F. BURGLARS AFTER SHOOTING held his attention for a moment, and after that nothing until he reached the thirty-fifth page, which held news of the weather, shipping, produce, finance, divorce, births, marriages, and deaths. He read the list of dead, passed over pages thirty-six and thirty-seven—financial news—found nothing to stop his eyes on the thirty-eighth and last page, sighed, folded the newspaper, put it in his coat-pocket, and rolled a cigarette.

For five minutes he stood there in the office-building-vestibule smoking and staring sulkily at nothing. Then he walked up to Stockton Street, hailed a taxicab, and had himself driven to the Coronet.

He let himself into the building and into Brigid O'Shaughnessy's apartment with the key she had given him. The blue gown she had worn the previous night was hanging across the foot of her bed. Her blue stockings and slippers were on the bedroom floor. The polychrome box that had held jewelry in her dressing-table-drawer now stood empty on the dressing-table-top. Spade frowned at it, ran his tongue across his lips, strolled through the rooms, looking around but not touching anything, then left the Coronet and went downtown again.

In the doorway of Spade's office-building he came face to face with the boy he had left at Gutman's. The boy put himself in Spade's path, blocking the entrance, and said: "Come on. He wants to see you."

The boy's hands were in his overcoat-pockets. His pockets bulged more than his hands need have made them bulge.

Spade grinned and said mockingly: "I didn't expect you till five-twenty-five. I hope I haven't kept you waiting."

The boy raised his eyes to Spade's mouth and spoke in the strained voice of one in physical pain: "Keep on riding me and you're going to be picking iron out of your navel."

Spade chuckled. "The cheaper the crook, the gaudier the patter," he said cheerfully. "Well, let's go."

They walked up Sutter Street side by side. The boy kept his hands in his overcoat-pockets. They walked a little more than a block in silence. Then Spade asked pleasantly: "How long have you been off the gooseberry lay, son?"

The boy did not show that he had heard the question.

"Did you ever—?" Spade began, and stopped. A soft light began to glow in his yellowish eyes. He did not address the boy again.

They went into the Alexandria, rode up to the twelfth floor, and walked down the corridor towards Gutman's suite. Nobody else was in the corridor.

Spade lagged a little, so that, when they were within fifteen feet of Gutman's door, he was perhaps a foot and a half behind the boy. He leaned sidewise suddenly and grasped the boy from behind by both arms, just beneath the boy's elbows. He forced the boy's arms forward so that the boy's hands, in his overcoat-pockets, lifted the overcoat up before him. The boy struggled and squirmed, but he was impotent in the big man's grip. The boy kicked back, but his feet went between Spade's spread legs.

Spade lifted the boy straight up from the floor and brought him down hard on his feet again. The impact made little noise on the thick carpet. At the moment of impact Spade's hands slid down and got a fresh grip on the boy's wrists. The boy, teeth set hard together, did not stop straining against the man's big hands, but he could not tear himself loose, could not keep the man's hands from crawling down over his own hands. The boy's teeth ground together audibly, making a noise that mingled with the noise of Spade's breathing as Spade crushed the boy's hands.

They were tense and motionless for a long moment. Then the boy's arms became limp. Spade released the boy and stepped back. In each of Spade's hands, when they came out of the boy's overcoat-pockets, there was a heavy automatic pistol.

The boy turned and faced Spade. The boy's face was a ghastly white blank. He kept his hands in his overcoat-pockets. He looked at Spade's chest and did not say anything.

Spade put the pistols in his own pockets and grinned derisively. "Come on," he said. "This will put you in solid with your boss."

They went to Gutman's door and Spade knocked.

CHAPTER XIII

The Emperor's Gift

GUTMAN opened the door. A glad smile lighted his fat face. He held out a hand and said: "Ah, come in, sir! Thank you for coming. Come in."

Spade shook the hand and entered. The boy went in behind him. The fat man shut the door. Spade took the boy's pistols from his pockets and held them out to Gutman. "Here. You shouldn't let him run around with these. He'll get himself hurt."

The fat man laughed merrily and took the pistols. "Well, well," he said, "what's this?" He looked from Spade to the boy.

Spade said: "A crippled newsie took them away from him, but I made him give them back."

The white-faced boy took the pistols out of Gutman's hands and pocketed them. The boy did not speak.

Gutman laughed again. "By Gad, sir," he told Spade, "you're a chap worth knowing, an amazing character. Come in. Sit down. Give me your hat."

The boy left the room by the door to the right of the entrance.

The fat man installed Spade in a green plush chair by the table, pressed a cigar upon him, held a light to it, mixed whiskey and carbonated water, put one glass in Spade's hand, and, holding the other, sat down facing Spade.

"Now, sir," he said, "I hope you'll let me apologize for—"

"Never mind that," Spade said. "Let's talk about the black bird."

The fat man cocked his head to the left and regarded Spade with fond eyes. "All right, sir," he agreed. "Let's." He took a sip from the glass in his hand. "This is going to be the most astounding thing you've ever heard of, sir, and I say that knowing that a man of your caliber in your profession must have known some astounding things in his time."

Spade nodded politely.

The fat man screwed up his eyes and asked: "What do you

t the Order of the Hospital of St. John of
called the Knights of Rhodes and other

s cigar. "Not much—only what I remember
ᴗ y in school—Crusaders or something."

"Very good. Now you don't remember that Suleiman the
Magnificent chased them out of Rhodes in 1523?"

"No."

"Well, sir, he did, and they settled in Crete. And they stayed
there for seven years, until 1530 when they persuaded the
Emperor Charles V to give them"—Gutman held up three
puffy fingers and counted them—"Malta, Gozo, and Tripoli."

"Yes?"

"Yes, sir, but with these conditions: they were to pay the
Emperor each year the tribute of one"—he held up a finger—
"falcon in acknowledgment that Malta was still under Spain,
and if they ever left the island it was to revert to Spain.
Understand? He was giving it to them, but not unless they
used it, and they couldn't give or sell it to anybody else."

"Yes."

The fat man looked over his shoulders at the three closed
doors, hunched his chair a few inches nearer Spade's, and reduced his voice to a husky whisper: "Have you any conception of the extreme, the immeasurable, wealth of the Order at
that time?"

"If I remember," Spade said, "they were pretty well fixed."

Gutman smiled indulgently. "Pretty well, sir, is putting it
mildly." His whisper became lower and more purring. "They
were rolling in wealth, sir. You've no idea. None of us has any
idea. For years they had preyed on the Saracens, had taken
nobody knows what spoils of gems, precious metals, silks,
ivories—the cream of the cream of the East. That is history,
sir. We all know that the Holy Wars to them, as to the
Templars, were largely a matter of loot.

"Well, now, the Emperor Charles has given them Malta,
and all the rent he asks is one insignificant bird per annum,
just as a matter of form. What could be more natural than for
these immeasurably wealthy Knights to look around for some
way of expressing their gratitude? Well, sir, that's exactly what
they did, and they hit on the happy thought of sending

Charles for the first year's tribute, not an insignificant live bird, but a glorious golden falcon encrusted from head to foot with the finest jewels in their coffers. And—remember, sir—they had fine ones, the finest out of Asia." Gutman stopped whispering. His sleek dark eyes examined Spade's face, which was placid. The fat man asked: "Well, sir, what do you think of that?"

"I don't know."

The fat man smiled complacently. "These are facts, historical facts, not schoolbook history, not Mr. Wells's history, but history nevertheless." He leaned forward. "The archives of the Order from the twelfth century on are still at Malta. They are not intact, but what is there holds no less than three"—he held up three fingers—"references that can't be to anything else but this jeweled falcon. In J. Delaville Le Roulx's *Les Archives de l'Ordre de Saint-Jean* there is a reference to it—oblique to be sure, but a reference still. And the unpublished—because unfinished at the time of his death—supplement to Paoli's *Dell' origine ed instituto del sacro militar ordine* has a clear and unmistakable statement of the facts I am telling you."

"All right," Spade said.

"All right, sir. Grand Master Villiers de l'Isle d'Adam had this foot-high jeweled bird made by Turkish slaves in the castle of St. Angelo and sent it to Charles, who was in Spain. He sent it in a galley commanded by a French knight named Cormier or Corvere, a member of the Order." His voice dropped to a whisper again. "It never reached Spain." He smiled with compressed lips and asked: "You know of Barbarossa, Redbeard, Khair-ed-Din? No? A famous admiral of buccaneers sailing out of Algiers then. Well, sir, he took the Knights' galley and he took the bird. The bird went to Algiers. That's a fact. That's a fact that the French historian Pierre Dan put in one of his letters from Algiers. He wrote that the bird had been there for more than a hundred years, until it was carried away by Sir Francis Verney, the English adventurer who was with the Algerian buccaneers for a while. Maybe it wasn't, but Pierre Dan believed it was, and that's good enough for me.

"There's nothing said about the bird in Lady Frances Verney's *Memoirs of the Verney Family during the Seventeenth*

Century, to be sure. I looked. And it's pretty certain that Sir Francis didn't have the bird when he died in a Messina hospital in 1615. He was stony broke. But, sir, there's no denying that the bird *did* go to Sicily. It was there and it came into the possession there of Victor Amadeus II some time after he became king in 1713, and it was one of his gifts to his wife when he married in Chambéry after abdicating. That is a fact, sir. Carutti, the author of *Storia del Regno di Vittorio Amadeo II*, himself vouched for it.

"Maybe they—Amadeo and his wife—took it along with them to Turin when he tried to revoke his abdication. Be that as it may, it turned up next in the possession of a Spaniard who had been with the army that took Naples in 1734—the father of Don José Monino y Redondo, Count of Floridablanca, who was Charles III's chief minister. There's nothing to show that it didn't stay in that family until at least the end of the Carlist War in '40. Then it appeared in Paris at just about the time that Paris was full of Carlists who had had to get out of Spain. One of them must have brought it with him, but, whoever he was, it's likely he knew nothing about its real value. It had been—no doubt as a precaution during the Carlist trouble in Spain—painted or enameled over to look like nothing more than a fairly interesting black statuette. And in that disguise, sir, it was, you might say, kicked around Paris for seventy years by private owners and dealers too stupid to see what it was under the skin."

The fat man paused to smile and shake his head regretfully. Then he went on: "For seventy years, sir, this marvelous item was, as you might say, a football in the gutters of Paris—until 1911 when a Greek dealer named Charilaos Konstantinides found it in an obscure shop. It didn't take Charilaos long to learn what it was and to acquire it. No thickness of enamel could conceal value from his eyes and nose. Well, sir, Charilaos was the man who traced most of its history and who identified it as what it actually was. I got wind of it and finally forced most of the history out of him, though I've been able to add a few details since.

"Charilaos was in no hurry to convert his find into money at once. He knew that—enormous as its intrinsic value was—a far higher, a terrific, price could be obtained for it once its authenticity was established beyond doubt. Possibly he planned to do business with one of the modern descendents of the old Order—the English Order of St. John of Jerusalem, the Prussian Johanniterorden, or the Italian or German *langues* of the Sovereign Order of Malta—all wealthy orders."

The fat man raised his glass, smiled at its emptiness, and rose to fill it and Spade's. "You begin to believe me a little?" he asked as he worked the siphon.

"I haven't said I didn't."

"No," Gutman chuckled. "But how you looked." He sat down, drank generously, and patted his mouth with a white handkerchief. "Well, sir, to hold it safe while pursuing his researches into its history, Charilaos had re-enamelled the bird, apparently just as it is now. One year to the very day after he had acquired it—that was possibly three months after I'd made him confess to me—I picked up the *Times* in London and read that his establishment had been burglarized and him murdered. I was in Paris the next day." He shook his head sadly. "The bird was gone. By Gad, sir, I was wild. I didn't believe anybody else knew what it was. I didn't believe he had told anybody but me. A great quantity of stuff had been stolen. That made me think that the thief had simply taken the bird along with the rest of his plunder, not knowing what it was. Because I assure you that a thief who knew its value would not burden himself with anything else—no, sir—at least not anything less than crown jewels."

He shut his eyes and smiled complacently at an inner thought. He opened his eyes and said: "That was seventeen years ago. Well, sir, it took me seventeen years to locate that bird, but I did it. I wanted it, and I'm not a man that's easily discouraged when he wants something." His smile grew broad. "I wanted it and I found it. I want it and I'm going to have it." He drained his glass, dried his lips again, and returned his handkerchief to his pocket. "I traced it to the home of a Russian general—one Kemidov—in a Constantinople suburb. He didn't know a thing about it. It was nothing but a black enameled figure to him, but his natural contrariness—the natural contrariness of a Russian general—kept him from selling it to me when I made him an offer. Perhaps in my eagerness I was a little unskillful, though not very. I don't know about that. But I did know I wanted it and I was afraid this stupid soldier might begin to investigate his property, might chip off some of the enamel. So I sent some—ah—agents to get it. Well, sir, they got it and I haven't got it." He stood up and carried his empty glass to the table. "But I'm going to get it. Your glass, sir."

"Then the bird doesn't belong to any of you?" Spade asked, "but to a General Kemidov?"

"Belong?" the fat man said jovially. "Well, sir, you might say it belonged to the King of Spain, but I don't see how you can honestly grant anybody else clear title to it—except by right of possession." He clucked. "An article of that value that has passed from hand to hand by such means is clearly the property of whoever can get hold of it."

"Then it's Miss O'Shaughnessy's now?"

"No, sir, except as my agent."

Spade said, "Oh," ironically.

Gutman, looking thoughtfully at the stopper of the whiskey-bottle in his hand, asked: "There's no doubt that she's got it now?"

"Not much."

"Where?"

"I don't know exactly."

The fat man set the bottle on the table with a bang. "But you said you did," he protested.

Spade made a careless gesture with one hand. "I meant to say I know where to get it when the time comes."

The pink bulbs of Gutman's face arranged themselves more happily. "And you do?" he asked.

"Yes."

"Where?"

Spade grinned and said: "Leave that to me. That's my end."

"When?"

"When I'm ready."

The fat man pursed his lips and, smiling with only slight uneasiness, asked: "Mr. Spade, where is Miss O'Shaughnessy now?"

"In my hands, safely tucked away."

Gutman smiled with approval. "Trust you for that, sir," he

said. "Well now, sir, before we sit down to talk prices, answer me this: how soon can you—or how soon are you willing to—produce the falcon?"

"A couple of days."

The fat man nodded. "That is satisfactory. We— But I forget our nourishment." He turned to the table, poured whiskey, squirted charged water into it, set a glass at Spade's elbow and held his own aloft. "Well, sir, here's to a fair bargain and profits large enough for both of us."

They drank. The fat man sat down. Spade asked: "What's your idea of a fair bargain?"

Gutman held his glass up to the light, looked affectionately at it, took another long drink, and said: "I have two proposals to make, sir, and either is fair. Take your choice. I will give you twenty-five thousand dollars when you deliver the falcon to me, and another twenty-five thousand as soon as I get to New York; or I will give you one quarter—twenty-five per cent—of what I realize on the falcon. There you are, sir: an almost immediate fifty thousand dollars or a vastly greater sum within, say, a couple of months."

Spade drank and asked: "How much greater?"

"Vastly," the fat man repeated. "Who knows how much greater? Shall I say a hundred thousand, or a quarter of a million? Will you believe me if I name the sum that seems the probable minimum?"

"Why not?"

The fat man smacked his lips and lowered his voice to a purring murmur. "What would you say, sir, to half a million?"

Spade narrowed his eyes. "Then you think the dingus is worth two million?"

Gutman smiled serenely. "In your own words, why not?" he asked.

Spade emptied his glass and set it on the table. He put his cigar in his mouth, took it out, looked at it, and put it back in. His yellow-grey eyes were faintly muddy. He said: "That's a hell of a lot of dough."

The fat man agreed: "That's a hell of a lot of dough." He leaned forward and patted Spade's knee. "That is the absolute rock-bottom minimum—or Charilaos Konstantinides was a blithering idiot—and he wasn't."

Spade removed the cigar from his mouth again, frowned at it with distaste, and put it on the smoking-stand. He shut his eyes hard, opened them again. Their muddiness had thickened. He said: "The—the minimum, huh? And the maximum?" An unmistakable *sh* followed the x in maximum as he said it.

"The maximum?" Gutman held his empty hand out, palm up. "I refuse to guess. You'd think me crazy. I don't know. There's no telling how high it could go, sir, and that's the one and only truth about it."

Spade pulled his sagging lower lip tight against the upper. He shook his head impatiently. A sharp frightened gleam awoke in his eyes—and was smothered by the deepening muddiness. He stood up, helping himself up with his hands on the arms of his chair. He shook his head again and took an uncertain step forward. He laughed thickly and muttered: "God damn you."

Gutman jumped up and pushed his chair back. His fat globes jiggled. His eyes were dark holes in an oily pink face.

Spade swung his head from side to side until his dull eyes were pointed at—if not focused on—the door. He took another uncertain step.

The fat man called sharply: "Wilmer!"

A door opened and the boy came in.

Spade took a third step. His face was grey now, with jaw-muscles standing out like tumors under his ears. His legs did not straighten again after his fourth step and his muddy eyes were almost covered by their lids. He took his fifth step.

The boy walked over and stood close to Spade, a little in front of him, but not directly between Spade and the door. The boy's right hand was inside his coat over his heart. The corners of his mouth twitched.

Spade essayed his sixth step.

The boy's leg darted out across Spade's leg, in front. Spade tripped over the interfering leg and crashed face-down on the floor. The boy, keeping his right hand under his coat, looked down at Spade. Spade tried to get up. The boy drew his right foot far back and kicked Spade's temple. The kick rolled Spade over on his side. Once more he tried to get up, could not, and went to sleep.

CHAPTER XIV

La Paloma

SPADE, coming around the corner from the elevator at a few minutes past six in the morning, saw yellow light glowing through the frosted glass of his office-door. He halted abruptly, set his lips together, looked up and down the corridor, and advanced to the door with swift quiet strides.

He put his hand on the knob and turned it with care that permitted neither rattle nor click. He turned the knob until it would turn no farther: the door was locked. Holding the knob still, he changed hands, taking it now in his left hand. With his right hand he brought his keys out of his pocket, carefully, so they could not jingle against one another. He separated the office-key from the others and, smothering the others together in his palm, inserted the office-key in the lock. The insertion was soundless. He balanced himself on the balls of his feet, filled his lungs, clicked the door open, and went in.

Effie Perine sat sleeping with her head on her forearms, her forearms on her desk. She wore her coat and had one of Spade's overcoats wrapped cape-fashion around her.

Spade blew his breath out in a muffled laugh, shut the door behind him, and crossed to the inner door. The inner office was empty. He went over to the girl and put a hand on her shoulder.

She stirred, raised her head drowsily, and her eyelids fluttered. Suddenly she sat up straight, opening her eyes wide. She saw Spade, smiled, leaned back in her chair, and rubbed her eyes with her fingers. "So you finally got back?" she said. "What time is it?"

"Six o'clock. What are you doing here?"

She shivered, drew Spade's overcoat closer around her, and yawned. "You told me to stay till you got back or phoned."

"Oh, you're the sister of the boy who stood on the burning deck?"

"I wasn't going to—" She broke off and stood up, letting his coat slide down on the chair behind her. She looked with dark excited eyes at his temple under the brim of his hat and exclaimed: "Oh, your head! What happened?"

His right temple was dark and swollen.

"I don't know whether I fell or was slugged. I don't think it amounts to much, but it hurts like hell." He barely touched it with his fingers, flinched, turned his grimace into a grim smile, and explained: "I went visiting, was fed knockout-drops, and came to twelve hours later all spread out on a man's floor."

She reached up and removed his hat from his head. "It's terrible," she said. "You'll have to get a doctor. You can't walk around with a head like that."

"It's not as bad as it looks, except for the headache, and that might be mostly from the drops." He went to the cabinet in the corner of the office and ran cold water on a handkerchief. "Anything turn up after I left?"

"Did you find Miss O'Shaughnessy, Sam?"

"Not yet. Anything turn up after I left?"

"The District Attorney's office phoned. He wants to see you."

"Himself?"

"Yes, that's the way I understood it. And a boy came in with a message—that Mr. Gutman would be delighted to talk to you before five-thirty."

Spade turned off the water, squeezed the handkerchief, and came away from the cabinet holding the handkerchief to his temple. "I got that," he said. "I met the boy downstairs, and talking to Mr. Gutman got me this."

"Is that the G. who phoned, Sam?"

"Yes."

"And what—?"

Spade stared through the girl and spoke as if using speech to arrange his thoughts: "He wants something he thinks I can get. I persuaded him I could keep him from getting it if he didn't make the deal with me before five-thirty. Then—uh-huh—sure—it was after I'd told him he'd have to wait a couple of days that he fed me the junk. It's not likely he thought I'd die. He'd know I'd be up and around in ten or twelve hours. So maybe the answer's that he figured he could get it without my help in that time if I was fixed so I couldn't butt in." He scowled. "I hope to Christ he was wrong." His stare became less distant. "You didn't get any word from the O'Shaughnessy?"

The girl shook her head no and asked: "Has this got anything to do with her?"

"Something."

"This thing he wants belongs to her?"

"Or to the King of Spain. Sweetheart, you've got an uncle who teaches history or something over at the University?"

"A cousin. Why?"

"If we brightened his life with an alleged historical secret four centuries old could we trust him to keep it dark awhile?"

"Oh, yes, he's good people."

"Fine. Get your pencil and book."

She got them and sat in her chair. Spade ran more cold water on his handkerchief and, holding it to his temple, stood in front of her and dictated the story of the falcon as he had heard it from Gutman, from Charles V's grant to the Hospitallers up to—but no further than—the enameled bird's arrival in Paris at the time of the Carlist influx. He stumbled over the names of authors and their works that Gutman had mentioned, but managed to achieve some sort of phonetic likeness. The rest of the history he repeated with the accuracy of a trained interviewer.

When he had finished the girl shut her notebook and raised a flushed smiling face to him. "Oh, isn't this thrilling?" she said. "It's—"

"Yes, or ridiculous. Now will you take it over and read it to your cousin and ask him what he thinks of it? Has he ever run across anything that might have some connection with it? Is it probable? Is it possible—even barely possible? Or is it the bunk? If he wants more time to look it up, OK, but get some sort of opinion out of him now. And for God's sake make him keep it under his hat."

"I'll go right now," she said, "and you go see a doctor about that head."

"We'll have breakfast first."

"No, I'll eat over in Berkeley. I can't wait to hear what Ted thinks of this."

"Well," Spade said, "don't start boo-hooing if he laughs at you."

After a leisurely breakfast at the Palace, during which he read both morning papers, Spade went home, shaved, bathed, rubbed ice on his bruised temple, and put on fresh clothes.

He went to Brigid O'Shaughnessy's apartment at the Coronet. Nobody was in the apartment. Nothing had been changed in it since his last visit.

He went to the Alexandria Hotel. Gutman was not in. None of the other occupants of Gutman's suite was in. Spade learned that these other occupants were the fat man's secretary, Wilmer Cook, and his daughter Rhea, a brown-eyed fair-haired smallish girl of seventeen whom the hotel-staff said was beautiful. Spade was told that the Gutman party had arrived at the hotel, from New York, ten days before, and had not checked out.

Spade went to the Belvedere and found the hotel-detective eating in the hotel-café.

"Morning, Sam. Set down and bite an egg." The hotel-detective stared at Spade's temple. "By God, somebody maced you plenty!"

"Thanks, I've had mine," Spade said as he sat down, and then, referring to his temple: "It looks worse than it is. How's my Cairo's conduct?"

"He went out not more than half an hour behind you yesterday and I ain't seen him since. He didn't sleep here again last night."

"He's getting bad habits."

"Well, a fellow like that alone in a big city. Who put the slug to you, Sam?"

"It wasn't Cairo." Spade looked attentively at the small silver dome covering Luke's toast. "How's chances of giving his room a casing while he's out?"

"Can do. You know I'm willing to go all the way with you all the time." Luke pushed his coffee back, put his elbows on the table, and screwed up his eyes at Spade. "But I got a hunch you ain't going all the way with me. What's the honest-to-God on this guy, Sam? You don't have to kick back on me. You know I'm regular."

Spade lifted his eyes from the silver dome. They were clear and candid. "Sure, you are," he said. "I'm not holding out. I gave you it straight. I'm doing a job for him, but he's got some friends that look wrong to me and I'm a little leery of him."

"The kid we chased out yesterday was one of his friends."

"Yes, Luke, he was."

"And it was one of them that shoved Miles across."

Spade shook his head. "Thursby killed Miles."

"And who killed him?"

Spade smiled. "That's supposed to be a secret, but, confidentially, I did," he said, "according to the police."

Luke grunted and stood up saying: "You're a tough one to figure out, Sam. Come on, we'll have that look-see."

They stopped at the desk long enough for Luke to "fix it so we'll get a ring if he comes in," and went up to Cairo's room. Cairo's bed was smooth and trim, but paper in wastebasket, unevenly drawn blinds, and a couple of rumpled towels in the bathroom showed that the chambermaid had not yet been in that morning.

Cairo's luggage consisted of a square trunk, a valise, and a gladstone bag. His bathroom-cabinet was stocked with cosmetics—boxes, cans, jars, and bottles of powders, creams, unguents, perfumes, lotions, and tonics. Two suits and an overcoat hung in the closet over three pairs of carefully treed shoes.

The valise and smaller bag were unlocked. Luke had the trunk unlocked by the time Spade had finished searching elsewhere.

"Blank so far," Spade said as they dug down into the trunk.

They found nothing there to interest them.

"Any particular thing we're supposed to be looking for?" Luke asked as he locked the trunk again.

"No. He's supposed to have come here from Constantinople. I'd like to know if he did. I haven't seen anything that says he didn't."

"What's his racket?"

Spade shook his head. "That's something else I'd like to know." He crossed the room and bent down over the wastebasket. "Well, this is our last shot."

He took a newspaper from the basket. His eyes brightened

when he saw it was the previous day's *Call*. It was folded with the classified-advertising-page outside. He opened it, examined that page, and nothing there stopped his eyes.

He turned the paper over and looked at the page that had been folded inside, the page that held financial and shipping news, the weather, births, marriages, divorces, and deaths. From the lower left-hand corner, a little more than two inches of the bottom of the second column had been torn out.

Immediately above the tear was a small caption *Arrived Today* followed by:

> 12:20 A.M.—Capac from Astoria.
> 5:05 A.M.—Helen P. Drew from Greenwood.
> 5:06 A.M.—Albarado from Bandon.

The tear passed through the next line, leaving only enough of its letters to make *from Sydney* inferable.

Spade put the *Call* down on the desk and looked into the wastebasket again. He found a small piece of wrapping-paper, a piece of string, two hosiery tags, a haberdasher's sale-ticket for half a dozen pairs of socks, and, in the bottom of the basket, a piece of newspaper rolled into a tiny ball.

He opened the ball carefully, smoothed it out on the desk, and fitted it into the torn part of the *Call*. The fit at the sides was exact, but between the top of the crumpled fragment and the inferable *from Sydney* half an inch was missing, sufficient space to have held announcement of six or seven boats' arrival. He turned the sheet over and saw that the other side of the missing portion could have held only a meaningless corner of a stock-broker's advertisement.

Luke, leaning over his shoulder, asked: "What's this all about?"

"Looks like the gent's interested in a boat."

"Well, there's no law against that, or is there?" Luke said while Spade was folding the torn page and the crumpled fragment together and putting them into his coat-pocket. "You all through here now?"

"Yes. Thanks a lot, Luke. Will you give me a ring as soon as he comes in?"

"Sure."

*

Spade went to the Business Office of the *Call*, bought a copy of the previous day's issue, opened it to the shipping-news-page, and compared it with the page taken from Cairo's wastebasket. The missing portion had read:

> 5:17 A.M.—Tahiti from Sydney and Papeete.
> 6:05 A.M.—Admiral Peoples from Astoria.
> 8:07 A.M.—Caddopeak from San Pedro.
> 8:17 A.M.—Silverado from San Pedro.
> 8:05 A.M.—La Paloma from Hongkong.
> 9:03 A.M.—Daisy Gray from Seattle.

He read the list slowly and when he had finished he under-scored *Hongkong* with a fingernail, cut the list of arrivals from the paper with his pocket-knife, put the rest of the paper and Cairo's sheet into the wastebasket, and returned to his office.

He sat down at his desk, looked up a number in the tele-phone-book, and used the telephone.

"Kearny one four o one, please. . . . Where is the *Paloma*, in from Hongkong yesterday morning, docked?" He repeated the question. "Thanks."

He held the receiver-hook down with his thumb for a moment, released it, and said: "Davenport two o two o, please. . . . Detective bureau, please. . . . Is Sergeant Polhaus there? . . . Thanks. . . . Hello, Tom, this is Sam Spade. . . . Yes, I tried to get you yesterday afternoon. . . . Sure, suppose you go to lunch with me. . . . Right."

He kept the receiver to his ear while his thumb worked the hook again.

"Davenport o one seven o, please. . . . Hello, this is Samuel Spade. My secretary got a phone-message yesterday that Mr. Bryan wanted to see me. Will you ask him what time's the most convenient for him? . . . Yes, Spade, S-p-a-d-e." A long pause. "Yes. . . . Two-thirty? All right. Thanks."

He called a fifth number and said: "Hello, darling, let me talk to Sid? . . . Hello, Sid—Sam. I've got a date with the District Attorney at half-past two this afternoon. Will you give me a ring—here or there—around four, just to see that I'm not in trouble? . . . Hell with your Saturday afternoon golf: your job's to keep me out of jail. . . . Right, Sid. 'Bye."

He pushed the telephone away, yawned, stretched, felt his bruised temple, looked at his watch, and rolled and lighted a cigarette. He smoked sleepily until Effie Perine came in.

Effie Perine came in smiling, bright-eyed and rosy-faced. "Ted says it could be," she reported, "and he hopes it is. He says he's not a specialist in that field, but the names and dates are all right, and at least none of your authorities or their works are out-and-out fakes. He's all excited over it."

"That's swell, as long as he doesn't get too enthusiastic to see through it if it's phoney."

"Oh, he wouldn't—not Ted! He's too good at his stuff for that."

"Uh-huh, the whole damned Perine family's wonderful," Spade said, "including you and the smudge of soot on your nose."

"He's not a Perine, he's a Christy." She bent her head to look at her nose in her vanity-case-mirror. "I must've got that from the fire." She scrubbed the smudge with the corner of a handkerchief.

"The Perine-Christy enthusiasm ignite Berkeley?" he asked.

She made a face at him while patting her nose with a powdered pink disc. "There was a boat on fire when I came back. They were towing it out from the pier and the smoke blew all over our ferry-boat."

Spade put his hands on the arms of his chair. "Were you near enough to see the name of the boat?" he asked.

"Yes. *La Paloma*. Why?"

Spade smiled ruefully. "I'm damned if I know why, sister," he said.

CHAPTER XV

Every Crackpot

S PADE and Detective-sergeant Polhaus ate pickled pigs' feet at one of big John's tables at the States Hof Brau.

Polhaus, balancing pale bright jelly on a fork half-way between plate and mouth, said: "Hey, listen, Sam! Forget about the other night. He was dead wrong, but you know anybody's liable to lose their head if you ride them thataway."

Spade looked thoughtfully at the police-detective. "Was that what you wanted to see me about?" he asked.

Polhaus nodded, put the forkful of jelly into his mouth, swallowed it, and qualified his nod: "Mostly."

"Dundy send you?"

Polhaus made a disgusted mouth. "You know he didn't. He's as bullheaded as you are."

Spade smiled and shook his head. "No, he's not, Tom," he said. "He just thinks he is."

Tom scowled and chopped at his pig's foot with a knife. "Ain't you ever going to grow up?" he grumbled. "What've you got to beef about? He didn't hurt you. You came out on top. What's the sense of making a grudge of it? You're just making a lot of grief for yourself."

Spade placed his knife and fork carefully together on his plate, and put his hands on the table beside his plate. His smile was faint and devoid of warmth. "With every bull in town working overtime trying to pile up grief for me a little more won't hurt. I won't even know it's there."

Polhaus's ruddiness deepened. He said: "That's a swell thing to say to me."

Spade picked up his knife and fork and began to eat. Polhaus ate.

Presently Spade asked: "See the boat on fire in the bay?"

"I saw the smoke. Be reasonable, Sam. Dundy was wrong and he knows it. Why don't you let it go at that?"

"Think I ought to go around and tell him I hope my chin didn't hurt his fist?"

Polhaus cut savagely into his pig's foot.

Spade said: "Phil Archer been in with any more hot tips?"

"Aw, hell! Dundy didn't think you shot Miles, but what else could he do except run the lead down? You'd've done the same thing in his place, and you know it."

"Yes?" Malice glittered in Spade's eyes. "What made him think I didn't do it? What makes you think I didn't? Or don't you?"

Polhaus's ruddy face flushed again. He said: "Thursby shot Miles."

"You think he did."

"He did. That Webley was his, and the slug in Miles came out of it."

"Sure?" Spade demanded.

"Dead sure," the police-detective replied. "We got hold of a kid—a bellhop at Thursby's hotel—that had seen it in his room just that morning. He noticed it particular because he'd never saw one just like it before. I never saw one. You say they don't make them any more. It ain't likely there'd be another around and—anyway—if that wasn't Thursby's what happened to his? And that's the gun the slug in Miles come out of." He started to put a piece of bread into his mouth, withdrew it, and asked: "You say you've seen them before: where was that at?" He put the bread into his mouth.

"In England before the war."

"Sure, there you are."

Spade nodded and said: "Then that leaves Thursby the only one I killed."

Polhaus squirmed in his chair and his face was red and shiny. "Christ's sake, ain't you never going to forget that?" he complained earnestly. "That's out. You know it as well as I do. You'd think you wasn't a dick yourself the way you bellyache over things. I suppose you don't never pull the same stuff on anybody that we pulled on you?"

"You mean that you tried to pull on me, Tom—just tried."

Polhaus swore under his breath and attacked the remainder of his pig's foot.

Spade said: "All right. You know it's out and I know it's out. What does Dundy know?"

"He knows it's out."

"What woke him up?"

"Aw, Sam, he never really thought you'd—" Spade's smile checked Polhaus. He left the sentence incomplete and said: "We dug up a record on Thursby."

"Yes? Who was he?"

Polhaus's shrewd small brown eyes studied Spade's face. Spade exclaimed irritably: "I wish to God I knew half as much about this business as you smart guys think I do!"

"I wish we all did," Polhaus grumbled. "Well, he was a St. Louis gunman the first we hear of him. He was picked up a lot of times back there for this and that, but he belonged to the Egan mob, so nothing much was ever done about any of it. I don't know howcome he left that shelter, but they got him once in New York for knocking over a row of stuss-games —his twist turned him up—and he was in a year before Fallon got him sprung. A couple of years later he did a short hitch in Joliet for pistol-whipping another twist that had given him the needle, but after that he took up with Dixie Monahan and didn't have any trouble getting out whenever he happened to get in. That was when Dixie was almost as big a shot as Nick the Greek in Chicago gambling. This Thursby was Dixie's bodyguard and he took the run-out with him when Dixie got in wrong with the rest of the boys over some debts he couldn't or wouldn't pay off. That was a couple of years back —about the time the Newport Beach Boating Club was shut up. I don't know if Dixie had any part in that. Anyways, this is the first time him or Thursby's been seen since."

"Dixie's been seen?" Spade asked.

Polhaus shook his head. "No." His small eyes became sharp, prying. "Not unless you've seen him or know somebody's seen him."

Spade lounged back in his chair and began to make a cigarette. "I haven't," he said mildly. "This is all new stuff to me."

"I guess it is," Polhaus snorted.

Spade grinned at him and asked: "Where'd you pick up all this news about Thursby?"

"Some of it's on the records. The rest—well—we got it here and there."

"From Cairo, for instance?" Now Spade's eyes held the prying gleam.

Polhaus put down his coffee-cup and shook his head. "Not a word of it. You poisoned that guy for us."

Spade laughed. "You mean a couple of high-class sleuths like you and Dundy worked on that lily-of-the-valley all night and couldn't crack him?"

"What do you mean—all night?" Polhaus protested. "We worked on him for less than a couple of hours. We saw we wasn't getting nowhere, and let him go."

Spade laughed again and looked at his watch. He caught John's eye and asked for the check. "I've got a date with the D.A. this afternoon," he told Polhaus while they waited for his change.

"He send for you?"

"Yes."

Polhaus pushed his chair back and stood up, a barrel-bellied tall man, solid and phlegmatic. "You won't be doing me any favor," he said, "by telling him I've talked to you like this."

A lathy youth with salient ears ushered Spade into the District Attorney's office. Spade went in smiling easily, saying easily: "Hello, Bryan!"

District Attorney Bryan stood up and held his hand out across his desk. He was a blond man of medium stature, perhaps forty-five years old, with aggressive blue eyes behind black-ribboned nose-glasses, the over-large mouth of an orator, and a wide dimpled chin. When he said, "How do you do, Spade?" his voice was resonant with latent power.

They shook hands and sat down.

The District Attorney put his finger on one of the pearl buttons in a battery of four on his desk, said to the lathy youth who opened the door again, "Ask Mr. Thomas and Healy to come in," and then, rocking back in his chair, addressed Spade pleasantly: "You and the police haven't been hitting it off so well, have you?"

Spade made a negligent gesture with the fingers of his right hand. "Nothing serious," he said lightly. "Dundy gets too enthusiastic."

The door opened to admit two men. The one to whom Spade said, "Hello, Thomas!" was a sunburned stocky man of thirty in clothing and hair of a kindred unruliness. He clapped Spade on the shoulder with a freckled hand, asked, "How's tricks?" and sat down beside him. The second man was younger and colorless. He took a seat a little apart from the others and balanced a stenographer's notebook on his knee, holding a green pencil over it.

Spade glanced his way, chuckled, and asked Bryan: "Anything I say will be used against me?"

The District Attorney smiled. "That always holds good." He took his glasses off, looked at them, and set them on his nose again. He looked through them at Spade and asked: "Who killed Thursby?"

Spade said: "I don't know."

Bryan rubbed his black eyeglass-ribbon between thumb and fingers and said knowingly: "Perhaps you don't, but you certainly could make an excellent guess."

"Maybe, but I wouldn't."

The District Attorney raised his eyebrows.

"I wouldn't," Spade repeated. He was serene. "My guess might be excellent, or it might be crummy, but Mrs. Spade didn't raise any children dippy enough to make guesses in front of a district attorney, an assistant district attorney, and a stenographer."

"Why shouldn't you, if you've nothing to conceal?"

"Everybody," Spade responded mildly, "has something to conceal."

"And you have—?"

"My guesses, for one thing."

The District Attorney looked down at his desk and then up at Spade. He settled his glasses more firmly on his nose. He said: "If you'd prefer not having the stenographer here we can dismiss him. It was simply as a matter of convenience that I brought him in."

"I don't mind him a damned bit," Spade replied. "I'm willing to have anything I say put down and I'm willing to sign it."

"We don't intend asking you to sign anything," Bryan assured him. "I wish you wouldn't regard this as a formal inquiry at all. And please don't think I've any belief—much less confidence—in those theories the police seem to have formed."

"No?"

"Not a particle."

Spade sighed and crossed his legs. "I'm glad of that." He felt in his pockets for tobacco and papers. "What's your theory?"

Bryan leaned forward in his chair and his eyes were hard and shiny as the lenses over them. "Tell me who Archer was shadowing Thursby for and I'll tell you who killed Thursby."

Spade's laugh was brief and scornful. "You're as wrong as Dundy," he said.

"Don't misunderstand me, Spade," Bryan said, knocking on the desk with his knuckles. "I don't say your client killed Thursby or had him killed, but I do say that, knowing who your client is, or was, I'll mighty soon know who killed Thursby."

Spade lighted his cigarette, removed it from his lips, emptied his lungs of smoke, and spoke as if puzzled: "I don't exactly get that."

"You don't? Then suppose I put it this way: where is Dixie Monahan?"

Spade's face retained its puzzled look. "Putting it that way doesn't help much," he said. "I still don't get it."

The District Attorney took his glasses off and shook them for emphasis. He said: "We know Thursby was Monahan's bodyguard and went with him when Monahan found it wise to vanish from Chicago. We know Monahan welshed on something like two-hundred-thousand-dollars' worth of bets when he vanished. We don't know—not yet—who his creditors were." He put the glasses on again and smiled grimly. "But we all know what's likely to happen to a gambler who welshes, and to his bodyguard, when his creditors find him. It's happened before."

Spade ran his tongue over his lips and pulled his lips back over his teeth in an ugly grin. His eyes glittered under pulled-down brows. His reddening neck bulged over the rim of his collar. His voice was low and hoarse and passionate. "Well, what do you think? Did I kill him for his creditors? Or just find him and let them do their own killing?"

"No, no!" the District Attorney protested. "You misunderstand me."

"I hope to Christ I do," Spade said.

"He didn't mean that," Thomas said.

"Then what did he mean?"

Bryan waved a hand. "I only mean that you might have been involved in it without knowing what it was. That could—"

"I see," Spade sneered. "You don't think I'm naughty. You just think I'm dumb."

"Nonsense," Bryan insisted: "Suppose someone came to you and engaged you to find Monahan, telling you they had reasons for thinking he was in the city. The someone might give you a completely false story—any one of a dozen or more would do—or might say he was a debtor who had run away, without giving you any of the details. How could you tell what was behind it? How would you know it wasn't an ordinary piece of detective work? And under those circumstances you certainly couldn't be held responsible for your part in it unless"—his voice sank to a more impressive key and his words came out spaced and distinct—"you made yourself an accomplice by concealing your knowledge of the murderer's identity or information that would lead to his apprehension."

Anger was leaving Spade's face. No anger remained in his voice when he asked: "That's what you meant?"

"Precisely."

"All right. Then there's no hard feelings. But you're wrong."

"Prove it."

Spade shook his head. "I can't prove it to you now. I can tell you."

"Then tell me."

"Nobody ever hired me to do anything about Dixie Monahan."

Bryan and Thomas exchanged glances. Bryan's eyes came back to Spade and he said: "But, by your own admission, somebody did hire you to do something about his bodyguard Thursby."

"Yes, about his ex-bodyguard Thursby."

"Ex?"

"Yes, ex."

"You know that Thursby was no longer associated with Monahan? You know that positively?"

Spade stretched out his hand and dropped the stub of his cigarette into an ashtray on the desk. He spoke carelessly: "I don't know anything positively except that my client wasn't interested in Monahan, had never been interested in Monahan. I heard that Thursby took Monahan out to the Orient and lost him."

Again the District Attorney and his assistant exchanged glances.

Thomas, in a tone whose matter-of-factness did not quite hide excitement, said: "That opens another angle. Monahan's friends could have knocked Thursby off for ditching Monahan."

"Dead gamblers don't have any friends," Spade said.

"It opens up two new lines," Bryan said. He leaned back and stared at the ceiling for several seconds, then sat upright quickly. His orator's face was alight. "It narrows down to three things. Number one: Thursby was killed by the gamblers Monahan had welshed on in Chicago. Not knowing Thursby had sloughed Monahan—or not believing it—they killed him because he had been Monahan's associate, or to get him out of the way so they could get to Monahan, or because he had refused to lead them to Monahan. Number two: he was killed by friends of Monahan. Or number three: he sold Monahan out to his enemies and then fell out with them and they killed him."

"Or number four," Spade suggested with a cheerful smile: "he died of old age. You folks aren't serious, are you?"

The two men stared at Spade, but neither of them spoke. Spade turned his smile from one to the other of them and shook his head in mock pity. "You've got Arnold Rothstein on the brain," he said.

Bryan smacked the back of his left hand down into the palm of his right. "In one of those three categories lies the solution." The power in his voice was no longer latent. His right hand, a fist except for protruding forefinger, went up and then down to stop with a jerk when the finger was leveled at Spade's chest. "And you can give us the information that will enable us to determine the category."

Spade said, "Yes?" very lazily. His face was somber. He touched his lower lip with a finger, looked at the finger, and then scratched the back of his neck with it. Little irritable lines had appeared in his forehead. He blew his breath out heavily through his nose and his voice was an ill-humored growl. "You wouldn't want the kind of information I could give you, Bryan. You couldn't use it. It'd poop this gambler's-revenge-scenario for you."

Bryan sat up straight and squared his shoulders. His voice was stern without blustering. "You are not the judge of that. Right or wrong, I am nonetheless the District Attorney."

Spade's lifted lip showed his eyetooth. "I thought this was an informal talk."

"I am a sworn officer of the law twenty-four hours a day," Bryan said, "and neither formality nor informality justifies your withholding from me evidence of crime, except of course"—he nodded meaningly—"on certain constitutional grounds."

"You mean if it might incriminate me?" Spade asked. His voice was placid, almost amused, but his face was not. "Well, I've got better grounds than that, or grounds that suit me better. My clients are entitled to a decent amount of secrecy. Maybe I can be made to talk to a Grand Jury or even a Coroner's Jury, but I haven't been called before either yet, and it's a cinch I'm not going to advertise my clients' business until I have to. Then again, you and the police have both accused me of being mixed up in the other night's murders. I've had trouble with both of you before. As far as I can see, my best chance of clearing myself of the trouble you're trying to make for me is by bringing in the murderers—all tied up. And my only chance of ever catching them and tying them up and bringing them in is by keeping away from you and the police, because neither of you show any signs of knowing what in hell it's all about." He rose and turned his head over his shoulder to address the stenographer: "Getting this all right, son? Or am I going too fast for you?"

The stenographer looked at him with startled eyes and replied: "No, sir, I'm getting it all right."

"Good work," Spade said and turned to Bryan again. "Now if you want to go to the Board and tell them I'm obstructing justice and ask them to revoke my license, hop to it. You've tried it before and it didn't get you anything but a good laugh all around." He picked up his hat.

Bryan began: "But look here—"

Spade said: "And I don't want any more of these informal talks. I've got nothing to tell you or the police and I'm God-damned tired of being called things by every crackpot on the city payroll. If you want to see me pinch me or subpœna me or something and I'll come down with my lawyer." He put his hat on his head, said, "See you at the inquest, maybe," and stalked out.

CHAPTER XVI

The Third Murder

S PADE went into the Hotel Sutter and telephoned the Alexandria. Gutman was not in. No member of Gutman's party was in. Spade telephoned the Belvedere. Cairo was not in, had not been in that day.

Spade went to his office.

A swart greasy man in notable clothes was waiting in the outer room. Effie Perine, indicating the swart man, said: "This gentleman wishes to see you, Mr. Spade."

Spade smiled and bowed and opened the inner door. "Come in." Before following the man in Spade asked Effie Perine: "Any news on that other matter?"

"No, sir."

The swart man was the proprietor of a moving-picture-theater in Market Street. He suspected one of his cashiers and a doorman of colluding to defraud him. Spade hurried him through the story, promised to "take care of it," asked for and received fifty dollars, and got rid of him in less than half an hour.

When the corridor-door had closed behind the showman Effie Perine came into the inner office. Her sunburned face was worried and questioning. "You haven't found her yet?" she asked.

He shook his head and went on stroking his bruised temple lightly in circles with his fingertips.

"How is it?" she asked.

"All right, but I've got plenty of headache."

She went around behind him, put his hand down, and stroked his temple with her slender fingers. He leaned back until the back of his head over the chair-top rested against her breast. He said: "You're an angel."

She bent her head forward over his and looked down into his face. "You've got to find her, Sam. It's more than a day and she—"

He stirred and impatiently interrupted her: "I haven't got

to do anything, but if you'll let me rest this damned head a minute or two I'll go out and find her."

She murmured, "Poor head," and stroked it in silence awhile. Then she asked: "You know where she is? Have you any idea?"

The telephone-bell rang. Spade picked up the telephone and said: "Hello. . . . Yes, Sid, it came out all right, thanks. . . . No. . . . Sure. He got snotty, but so did I. . . . He's nursing a gambler's-war pipe-dream. . . . Well, we didn't kiss when we parted. I declared my weight and walked out on him. . . . That's something for you to worry about. . . . Right. 'Bye." He put the telephone down and leaned back in his chair again.

Effie Perin came from behind him and stood at his side. She demanded: "Do you think you know where she is, Sam?"

"I know where she went," he replied in a grudging tone.

"Where?" She was excited.

"Down to the boat you saw burning."

Her eyes opened until their brown was surrounded by white. "You went down there." It was not a question.

"I did not," Spade said.

"Sam," she cried angrily, "she may be—"

"She went down there," he said in a surly voice. "She wasn't taken. She went down there instead of to your house when she learned the boat was in. Well, what the hell? Am I supposed to run around after my clients begging them to let me help them?"

"But, Sam, when I told you the boat was on fire!"

"That was at noon and I had a date with Polhaus and another with Bryan."

She glared at him between tightened lids. "Sam Spade," she said, "you're the most contemptible man God ever made when you want to be. Because she did something without confiding in you you'd sit here and do nothing when you know she's in danger, when you know she might be—"

Spade's face flushed. He said stubbornly: "She's pretty capable of taking care of herself and she knows where to come for help when she thinks she needs it, and when it suits her."

"That's spite," the girl cried, "and that's all it is! You're sore because she did something on her own hook, without telling you. Why shouldn't she? You're not so damned honest, and you haven't been so much on the level with her, that she should trust you completely."

Spade said: "That's enough of that."

His tone brought a brief uneasy glint into her hot eyes, but she tossed her head and the glint vanished. Her mouth was drawn taut and small. She said: "If you don't go down there this very minute, Sam, I will and I'll take the police down there." Her voice trembled, broke, and was thin and wailing. "Oh, Sam, go!"

He stood up cursing her. Then he said: "Christ! It'll be easier on my head than sitting here listening to you squawk." He looked at his watch. "You might as well lock up and go home."

She said: "I won't. I'm going to wait right here till you come back."

He said, "Do as you damned please," put his hat on, flinched, took it off, and went out carrying it in his hand.

An hour and a half later, at twenty minutes past five, Spade returned. He was cheerful. He came in asking: "What makes you so hard to get along with, sweetheart?"

"Me?"

"Yes, you." He put a finger on the tip of Effie Perine's nose and flattened it. He put his hands under her elbows, lifted her straight up, and kissed her chin. He set her down on the floor again and asked: "Anything doing while I was gone?"

"Luke—what's his name?—at the Belvedere called up to tell you Cairo has returned. That was about half an hour ago."

Spade snapped his mouth shut, turned with a long step, and started for the door.

"Did you find her?" the girl called.

"Tell you about it when I'm back," he replied without pausing and hurried out.

A taxicab brought Spade to the Belvedere within ten minutes of his departure from his office. He found Luke in the lobby. The hotel-detective came grinning and shaking his head to meet Spade. "Fifteen minutes late," he said. "Your bird has fluttered."

Spade cursed his luck.

"Checked out—gone bag and baggage," Luke said. He took a battered memorandum-book from a vest-pocket, licked his thumb, thumbed pages, and held the book out open to Spade. "There's the number of the taxi that hauled him. I got that much for you."

"Thanks." Spade copied the number on the back of an envelope. "Any forwarding address?"

"No. He just come in carrying a big suitcase and went upstairs and packed and come down with his stuff and paid his bill and got a taxi and went without anybody being able to hear what he told the driver."

"How about his trunk?"

Luke's lower lip sagged. "By God," he said, "I forgot that! Come on."

They went up to Cairo's room. The trunk was there. It was closed, but not locked. They raised the lid. The trunk was empty.

Luke said: "What do you know about that!"

Spade did not say anything.

Spade went back to his office. Effie Perine looked up at him, inquisitively.

"Missed him," Spade grumbled and passed into his private room.

She followed him in. He sat in his chair and began to roll a cigarette. She sat on the desk in front of him and put her toes on a corner of his chair-seat.

"What about Miss O'Shaughnessy?" she demanded.

"I missed her too," he replied, "but she had been there."

"On the *La Paloma*?"

"*The La* is a lousy combination," he said.

"Stop it. Be nice, Sam. Tell me."

He set fire to his cigarette, pocketed his lighter, patted her shins, and said: "Yes, *La Paloma*. She got down there at a little after noon yesterday." He pulled his brows down. "That means she went straight there after leaving the cab at the Ferry Building. It's only a few piers away. The Captain wasn't aboard. His name's Jacobi and she asked for him by name. He was uptown on business. That would mean he didn't expect her, or not at that time anyway. She waited there till he came back at four o'clock. They spent the time from then till meal-time in his cabin and she ate with him."

He inhaled and exhaled smoke, turned his head aside to spit a yellow tobacco-flake off his lip, and went on: "After the meal Captain Jacobi had three more visitors. One of them was Gutman and one was Cairo and one was the kid who delivered Gutman's message to you yesterday. Those three came together while Brigid was there and the five of them did a lot of talking in the Captain's cabin. It's hard to get anything out of the crew, but they had a row and somewhere around eleven o'clock that night a gun went off there, in the Captain's cabin. The watchman beat it down there, but the Captain met him outside and told him everything was all right. There's a fresh bullet-hole in one corner of the cabin, up high enough to make it likely that the bullet didn't go through anybody to get there. As far as I could learn there was only the one shot. But as far as I could learn wasn't very far."

He scowled and inhaled smoke again. "Well, they left around midnight—the Captain and his four visitors all together—and all of them seem to have been walking all right. I got that from the watchman. I haven't been able to get hold of the Custom-House-men who were on duty there then. That's all of it. The Captain hasn't been back since. He didn't keep a date he had this noon with some shipping-agents, and they haven't found him to tell him about the fire."

"And the fire?" she asked.

Spade shrugged. "I don't know. It was discovered in the hold, aft—in the rear basement—late this morning. The chances are it got started some time yesterday. They got it out all right, though it did damage enough. Nobody liked to talk about it much while the Captain's away. It's the—"

The corridor-door opened. Spade shut his mouth. Effie Perine jumped down from the desk, but a man opened the connecting door before she could reach it.

"Where's Spade?" the man asked.

His voice brought Spade up erect and alert in his chair. It was a voice harsh and rasping with agony and with the strain of keeping two words from being smothered by the liquid bubbling that ran under and behind them.

Effie Perine, frightened, stepped out of the man's way.

He stood in the doorway with his soft hat crushed between his head and the top of the door-frame: he was nearly seven feet tall. A black overcoat cut long and straight and like a sheath, buttoned from throat to knees, exaggerated his leanness. His shoulders stuck out, high, thin, angular. His bony face—weather-coarsened, age-lined—was the color of wet sand and was wet with sweat on cheeks and chin. His eyes were dark and bloodshot and mad above lower lids that hung down to show pink inner membrane. Held tight against the left side of his chest by a black-sleeved arm that ended in a yellowish claw was a brown-paper-wrapped parcel bound with thin rope—an ellipsoid somewhat larger than an American football.

The tall man stood in the doorway and there was nothing to show that he saw Spade. He said, "You know—" and then the liquid bubbling came up in his throat and submerged whatever else he said. He put his other hand over the hand that held the ellipsoid. Holding himself stiffly straight, not putting his hands out to break his fall, he fell forward as a tree falls.

Spade, wooden-faced and nimble, sprang from his chair and caught the falling man. When Spade caught him the man's mouth opened and a little blood spurted out, and the brown-wrapped parcel dropped from the man's hands and rolled across the floor until a foot of the desk stopped it. Then the man's knees bent and he bent at the waist and his thin body became limber inside the sheathlike overcoat, sagging in Spade's arms so that Spade could not hold it up from the floor.

Spade lowered the man carefully until he lay on the floor on his left side. The man's eyes—dark and bloodshot, but not now mad—were wide open and still. His mouth was open as when blood had spurted from it, but no more blood came from it, and all his long body was as still as the floor it lay on.

Spade said: "Lock the door."

While Effie Perine, her teeth chattering, fumbled with the corridor-door's lock Spade knelt beside the thin man, turned him over on his back, and ran a hand down inside his over-coat. When he withdrew the hand presently it came out smeared with blood. The sight of his bloody hand brought not the least nor briefest of changes to Spade's face. Holding that hand up where it would touch nothing, he took his lighter out of his pocket with his other hand. He snapped on the flame and held the flame close to first one and then the other of the thin man's eyes. The eyes—lids, balls, irises, and pupils—remained frozen, immobile.

Spade extinguished the flame and returned the lighter to his pocket. He moved on his knees around to the dead man's side and, using his one clean hand, unbuttoned and opened the tubular overcoat. The inside of the overcoat was wet with blood and the double-breasted blue jacket beneath it was sod-den. The jacket's lapels, where they crossed over the man's chest, and both sides of his coat immediately below that point, were pierced by soggy ragged holes.

Spade rose and went to the washbowl in the outer office.

Effie Perine, wan and trembling and holding herself up-right by means of a hand on the corridor-door's knob and her back against its glass, whispered: "Is—is he—?"

"Yes. Shot through the chest, maybe half a dozen times." Spade began to wash his hands.

"Oughtn't we—?" she began, but he cut her short: "It's too late for a doctor now and I've got to think before we do anything." He finished washing his hands and began to rinse the bowl. "He couldn't have come far with those in him. If he— Why in hell couldn't he have stood up long enough to say something?" He frowned at the girl, rinsed his hands again, and picked up a towel. "Pull yourself together. For Christ's sake don't get sick on me now!" He threw the towel down and ran fingers through his hair. "We'll have a look at that bundle."

He went into the inner office again, stepped over the dead man's legs, and picked up the brown-paper-wrapped parcel. When he felt its weight his eyes glowed. He put it on his desk, turning it over so that the knotted part of the rope was uppermost. The knot was hard and tight. He took out his pocket-knife and cut the rope.

The girl had left the door and, edging around the dead man with her face turned away, had come to Spade's side. As she stood there—hands on a corner of the desk—watching him pull the rope loose and push aside brown paper, excitement began to supplant nausea in her face. "Do you think it is?" she whispered.

"We'll soon know," Spade said, his big fingers busy with the inner husk of coarse grey paper, three sheets thick, that the brown paper's removal had revealed. His face was hard and dull. His eyes were shining. When he had put the grey paper out of the way he had an egg-shaped mass of pale excelsior, wadded tight. His fingers tore the wad apart and then he had the foot-high figure of a bird, black as coal and shiny where its polish was not dulled by wood-dust and fragments of excelsior.

Spade laughed. He put a hand down on the bird. His widespread fingers had ownership in their curving. He put his other arm around Effie Perine and crushed her body against his. "We've got the damned thing, angel," he said.

"Ouch!" she said, "you're hurting me."

He took his arm away from her, picked the black bird up in both hands, and shook it to dislodge clinging excelsior. Then he stepped back holding it up in front of him and blew dust off it, regarding it triumphantly.

Effie Perine made a horrified face and screamed, pointing at his feet.

He looked down at his feet. His last backward step had brought his left heel into contact with the dead man's hand, pinching a quarter-inch of flesh at a side of the palm between heel and floor. Spade jerked his foot away from the hand.

The telephone-bell rang.

He nodded at the girl. She turned to the desk and put the receiver to her ear. She said: "Hello. . . . Yes. . . . Who? . . . Oh, yes!" Her eyes became large. "Yes. . . . Yes. . . . Hold the line. . . ." Her mouth suddenly stretched wide and fearful. She cried: "Hello! Hello! Hello!" She rattled the prong up and down and cried, "Hello!" twice. Then she sobbed and spun around to face Spade, who was close beside her by now. "It was Miss O'Shaughnessy," she said wildly. "She wants you. She's at the Alexandria—in danger. Her voice was—oh, it was awful, Sam!—and something happened to her before she could finish. Go help her, Sam!"

Spade put the falcon down on the desk and scowled gloomily. "I've got to take care of this fellow first," he said, pointing his thumb at the thin corpse on the floor.

She beat his chest with her fists, crying: "No, no—you've got to go to her. Don't you see, Sam? He had the thing that was hers and he came to you with it. Don't you see? He was helping her and they killed him and now she's— Oh, you've got to go!"

"All right." Spade pushed her away and bent over his desk, putting the black bird back into its nest of excelsior, bending the paper around it, working rapidly, making a larger and clumsy package. "As soon as I've gone phone the police. Tell them how it happened, but don't drag any names in. You don't know. I got the phone-call and I told you I had to go out, but I didn't say where." He cursed the rope for being tangled, yanked it into straightness, and began to bind the package. "Forget this thing. Tell it as it happened, but forget he had a bundle." He chewed his lower lip. "Unless they pin you down. If they seem to know about it you'll have to admit it. But that's not likely. If they do then I took the bundle away with me, unopened." He finished tying the knot and straightened up with the parcel under his left arm. "Get it straight, now. Everything happened the way it did happen, but without this dingus unless they already know about it. Don't deny it—just don't mention it. And I got the phone-call—not you. And you don't know anything about anybody else having any connection with this fellow. You don't know anything about him and you can't talk about my business until you see me. Got it?"

"Yes, Sam. Who—do you know who he is?"

He grinned wolfishly. "Uh-uh," he said, "but I'd guess he was Captain Jacobi, master of *La Paloma*." He picked up his hat and put it on. He looked thoughtfully at the dead man and then around the room.

"Hurry, Sam," the girl begged.

"Sure," he said absent-mindedly, "I'll hurry. Might not hurt to get those few scraps of excelsior off the floor before the police come. And maybe you ought to try to get hold of

Sid. No." He rubbed his chin. "We'll leave him out of it awhile. It'll look better. I'd keep the door locked till they come." He took his hand from his chin and rubbed her cheek. "You're a damned good man, sister," he said and went out.

CHAPTER XVII

Saturday Night

C ARRYING the parcel lightly under his arm, walking briskly, with only the ceaseless shifting of his eyes to denote wariness, Spade went, partly by way of an alley and a narrow court, from his office-building to Kearny and Post Streets, where he hailed a passing taxicab.

The taxicab carried him to the Pickwick Stage terminal in Fifth Street. He checked the bird at the Parcel Room there, put the check into a stamped envelope, wrote *M. F. Holland* and a San Francisco Post Office box-number on the envelope, sealed it, and dropped it into a mail-box. From the stage-terminal another taxi-cab carried him to the Alexandria Hotel.

Spade went up to suite 12-C and knocked on the door. The door was opened, when he had knocked a second time, by a small fair-haired girl in a shimmering yellow dressing-gown—a small girl whose face was white and dim and who clung desperately to the inner doorknob with both hands and gasped: "Mr. Spade?"

Spade said, "Yes," and caught her as she swayed.

Her body arched back over his arm and her head dropped straight back so that her short fair hair hung down her scalp and her slender throat was a firm curve from chin to chest.

Spade slid his supporting arm higher up her back and bent to get his other arm under her knees, but she stirred then, resisting, and between parted lips that barely moved blurred words came: "No! Ma' me wa'!"

Spade made her walk. He kicked the door shut and he walked her up and down the green-carpeted room from wall to wall. One of his arms around her small body, that hand under her armpit, his other hand gripping her other arm, held her erect when she stumbled, checked her swaying, kept urging her forward, but made her tottering legs bear all her weight they could bear. They walked across and across the floor, the girl falteringly, with incoördinate steps, Spade surely on the balls of his feet with balance unaffected by her staggering. Her face was chalk-white and eyeless, his sullen, with eyes hardened to watch everywhere at once.

He talked to her monotonously: "That's the stuff. Left, right, left, right. That's the stuff. One, two, three, four, one, two, three, now we turn." He shook her as they turned from the wall. "Now back again. One, two, three, four. Hold your head up. That's the stuff. Good girl. Left, right, left, right. Now we turn again." He shook her again. "That's the girl. Walk, walk, walk, walk. One, two, three, four. Now we go around." He shook her, more roughly, and increased their pace. "That's the trick. Left, right, left, right. We're in a hurry. One, two, three. . . ."

She shuddered and swallowed audibly. Spade began to chafe her arm and side and he put his mouth nearer her ear. "That's fine. You're doing fine. One, two, three, four. Faster, faster, faster, faster. That's it. Step, step, step, step. Pick them up and lay them down. That's the stuff. Now we turn. Left, right, left, right. What'd they do—dope you? The same stuff they gave me?"

Her eyelids twitched up then for an instant over dulled golden-brown eyes and she managed to say all of "Yes" except the final consonant.

They walked the floor, the girl almost trotting now to keep up with Spade, Spade slapping and kneading her flesh through yellow silk with both hands, talking and talking while his eyes remained hard and aloof and watchful. "Left, right, left, right, left, right, turn. That's the girl. One, two, three, four, one, two, three, four. Keep the chin up. That's the stuff. One, two . . ."

Her lids lifted again a bare fraction of an inch and under them her eyes moved weakly from side to side.

"That's fine," he said in a crisp voice, dropping his monotone. "Keep them open. Open them wide—wide!" He shook her.

She moaned in protest, but her lids went farther up, though her eyes were without inner light. He raised his hand and slapped her cheek half a dozen times in quick succession. She moaned again and tried to break away from him. His arm held her and swept her along beside him from wall to wall.

"Keep walking," he ordered in a harsh voice, and then: "Who are you?"

Her "Rhea Gutman" was thick but intelligible.

"The daughter?"

"Yes." Now she was no farther from the final consonant than *sh*.

"Where's Brigid?"

She twisted convulsively around in his arms and caught at one of his hands with both of hers. He pulled his hand away quickly and looked at it. Across its back was a thin red scratch an inch and a half or more in length.

"What the hell?" he growled and examined her hands. Her left hand was empty. In her right hand, when he forced it open, lay a three-inch jade-headed steel bouquet-pin. "What the hell?" he growled again and held the pin up in front of her eyes.

When she saw the pin she whimpered and opened her dressing-gown. She pushed aside the cream-colored pajama-coat under it and showed him her body below her left breast—white flesh crisscrossed with thin red lines, dotted with tiny red dots, where the pin had scratched and punctured it. "To stay awake . . . walk . . . till you came. . . . She said you'd come . . . were so long." She swayed.

Spade tightened his arm around her and said: "Walk."

She fought against his arm, squirming around to face him again. "No . . . tell you . . . sleep . . . save her . . ."

"Brigid?" he demanded.

"Yes . . . took her . . . Bur-Burlingame . . . twenty-six Ancho . . . hurry . . . too late . . ." Her head fell over on her shoulder.

Spade pushed her head up roughly. "Who took her there? Your father?"

"Yes . . . Wilmer . . . Cairo." She writhed and her eyelids twitched but did not open. ". . . kill her." Her head fell over again and again he pushed it up.

"Who shot Jacobi?"

She did not seem to hear the question. She tried pitifully to hold her head up, to open her eyes. She mumbled: "Go . . . she . . ."

He shook her brutally. "Stay awake till the doctor comes."

Fear opened her eyes and pushed for a moment the cloudiness from her face. "No, no," she cried thickly, "father . . . kill me . . . swear you won't . . . he'd know . . . I did . . . for her . . . promise . . . won't . . . sleep . . . all right . . . morning . . ."

He shook her again. "You're sure you can sleep the stuff off all right?"

"Ye'." Her head fell down again.

"Where's your bed?"

She tried to raise a hand, but the effort had become too much for her before the hand pointed at anything except the carpet. With the sigh of a tired child she let her whole body relax and crumple.

Spade caught her up in his arms—scooped her up as she sank—and, holding her easily against his chest, went to the nearest of the three doors. He turned the knob far enough to release the catch, pushed the door open with his foot, and went into a passageway that ran past an open bathroom-door to a bedroom. He looked into the bathroom, saw it was empty, and carried the girl into the bedroom. Nobody was there. The clothing that was in sight and things on the chiffonier said it was a man's room.

Spade carried the girl back to the green-carpeted room and tried the opposite door. Through it he passed into another passageway, past another empty bathroom, and into a bedroom that was feminine in its accessories. He turned back the bedclothes and laid the girl on the bed, removed her slippers, raised her a little to slide the yellow dressing-gown off, fixed a pillow under her head, and put the covers up over her.

Then he opened the room's two windows and stood with his back to them staring at the sleeping girl. Her breathing was heavy but not troubled. He frowned and looked around, working his lips together. Twilight was dimming the room. He stood there in the weakening light for perhaps five minutes. Finally he shook his thick sloping shoulders impatiently and went out, leaving the suite's outer door unlocked.

Spade went to the Pacific Telephone and Telegraph Company's station in Powell Street and called Davenport 2020.

"Emergency Hospital, please. . . . Hello, there's a girl in suite twelve C at the Alexandria Hotel who has been drugged. . . . Yes, you'd better send somebody to take a look at her. . . . This is Mr. Hooper of the Alexandria."

He put the receiver on its prong and laughed. He called another number and said: "Hello, Frank. This is Sam Spade. . . . Can you let me have a car with a driver who'll keep his mouth shut? . . . To go down the peninsula right away. . . . Just a couple of hours. . . . Right. Have him pick me up at John's, Ellis Street, as soon as he can make it."

He called another number—his office's—held the receiver to his ear for a little while without saying anything, and replaced it on its hook.

He went to John's Grill, asked the waiter to hurry his order of chops, baked potato, and sliced tomatoes, ate hurriedly, and was smoking a cigarette with his coffee when a thick-set youngish man with a plaid cap set askew above pale eyes and a tough cheery face came into the Grill and to his table.

"All set, Mr. Spade. She's full of gas and rearing to go."

"Swell." Spade emptied his cup and went out with the thick-set man. "Know where Ancho Avenue, or Road, or Boulevard, is in Burlingame?"

"Nope, but if she's there we can find her."

"Let's do that," Spade said as he sat beside the chauffeur in the dark Cadillac sedan. "Twenty-six is the number we want, and the sooner the better, but we don't want to pull up at the front door."

"Correct."

They rode half a dozen blocks in silence. The chauffeur said: "Your partner got knocked off, didn't he, Mr. Spade?"

"Uh-huh."

The chauffeur clucked. "She's a tough racket. You can have it for mine."

"Well, hack-drivers don't live forever."

"Maybe that's right," the thick-set man conceded, "but, just the same, it'll always be a surprise to me if I don't."

Spade stared ahead at nothing and thereafter, until the chauffeur tired of making conversation, replied with uninterested yeses and noes.

*

At a drug-store in Burlingame the chauffeur learned how to reach Ancho Avenue. Ten minutes later he stopped the sedan near a dark corner, turned off the lights, and waved his hand at the block ahead. "There she is," he said. "She ought to be on the other side, maybe the third or fourth house."

Spade said, "Right," and got out of the car. "Keep the engine going. We may have to leave in a hurry."

He crossed the street and went up the other side. Far ahead a lone street-light burned. Warmer lights dotted the night on either side where houses were spaced half a dozen to a block. A high thin moon was cold and feeble as the distant street-light. A radio droned through the open windows of a house on the other side of the street.

In front of the second house from the corner Spade halted. On one of the gateposts that were massive out of all proportion to the fence flanking them a 2 and a 6 of pale metal caught what light there was. A square white card was nailed over them. Putting his face close to the card, Spade could see that it was a *For Sale or Rent* sign. There was no gate between the posts. Spade went up the cement walk to the house. He stood still on the walk at the foot of the porch-steps for a long moment. No sound came from the house. The house was dark except for another pale square card nailed on its door.

Spade went up to the door and listened. He could hear nothing. He tried to look through the glass of the door. There was no curtain to keep his gaze out, but inner darkness. He tiptoed to a window and then to another. They, like the door, were uncurtained except by inner darkness. He tried both windows. They were locked. He tried the door. It was locked.

He left the porch and, stepping carefully over dark unfamiliar ground, walked through weeds around the house. The side-windows were too high to be reached from the ground. The back door and the one back window he could reach were locked.

Spade went back to the gatepost and, cupping the flame between his hands, held his lighter up to the *For Sale or Rent* sign. It bore the printed name and address of a San Mateo real-estate-dealer and a line penciled in blue: *Key at 31.*

Spade returned to the sedan and asked the chauffeur: "Got a flashlight?"

"Sure." He gave it to Spade. "Can I give you a hand at anything?"

"Maybe." Spade got into the sedan. "We'll ride up to number thirty-one. You can use your lights."

Number 31 was a square grey house across the street from, but a little farther up than, 26. Lights glowed in its downstairs-windows. Spade went up on the porch and rang the bell. A dark-haired girl of fourteen or fifteen opened the door. Spade, bowing and smiling, said: "I'd like to get the key to number twenty-six."

"I'll call Papa," she said and went back into the house calling: "Papa!"

A plump red-faced man, bald-headed and heavily mustached, appeared, carrying a newspaper.

Spade said: "I'd like to get the key to twenty-six."

The plump man looked doubtful. He said: "The juice is not on. You couldn't see anything."

Spade patted his pocket. "I've a flashlight."

The plump man looked more doubtful. He cleared his throat uneasily and crumpled the newspaper in his hand.

Spade showed him one of his business-cards, put it back in his pocket, and said in a low voice: "We got a tip that there might be something hidden there."

The plump man's face and voice were eager. "Wait a minute," he said. "I'll go over with you."

A moment later he came back carrying a brass key attached to a black and red tag. Spade beckoned to the chauffeur as they passed the car and the chauffeur joined them.

"Anybody been looking at the house lately?" Spade asked.

"Not that I know of," the plump man replied. "Nobody's been to me for the key in a couple of months."

The plump man marched ahead with the key until they had gone up on the porch. Then he thrust the key into Spade's hand, mumbled, "Here you are," and stepped aside.

Spade unlocked the door and pushed it open. There was silence and darkness. Holding the flashlight—dark—in his left hand, Spade entered. The chauffeur came close behind him and then, at a little distance, the plump man followed them.

They searched the house from bottom to top, cautiously at first, then, finding nothing, boldly. The house was empty—unmistakably—and there was nothing to indicate that it had been visited in weeks.

Saying, "Thanks, that's all," Spade left the sedan in front of the Alexandria. He went into the hotel, to the desk, where a tall young man with a dark grave face said: "Good evening, Mr. Spade."

"Good evening." Spade drew the young man to one end of the desk. "These Gutmans—up in twelve C—are they in?"

The young man replied, "No," darting a quick glance at Spade. Then he looked away, hesitated, looked at Spade again, and murmured: "A funny thing happened in connection with them this evening, Mr. Spade. Somebody called the Emergency Hospital and told them there was a sick girl up there."

"And there wasn't?"

"Oh, no, there was nobody up there. They went out earlier in the evening."

Spade said: "Well, these practical-jokers have to have their fun. Thanks."

He went to a telephone-booth, called a number, and said: "Hello. . . . Mrs. Perine? . . . Is Effie there? . . . Yes, please. . . . Thanks.

"Hello, angel! What's the good word? . . . Fine, fine! Hold it. I'll be out in twenty minutes. . . . Right."

Half an hour later Spade rang the doorbell of a two-story brick building in Ninth Avenue. Effie Perine opened the door. Her boyish face was tired and smiling. "Hello, boss," she said. "Enter." She said in a low voice: "If Ma says anything to you, Sam, be nice to her. She's all up in the air."

Spade grinned reassuringly and patted her shoulder.

She put her hands on his arm. "Miss O'Shaughnessy?"

"No," he growled. "I ran into a plant. Are you sure it was her voice?"

"Yes."

He made an unpleasant face. "Well, it was hooey."

She took him into a bright living-room, sighed, and slumped down on one end of a Chesterfield, smiling cheerfully up at him through her weariness.

He sat beside her and asked: "Everything went OK? Nothing said about the bundle?"

"Nothing. I told them what you told me to tell them, and they seemed to take it for granted that the phone-call had something to do with it, and that you were out running it down."

"Dundy there?"

"No. Hoff and O'Gar and some others I didn't know. I talked to the Captain too."

"They took you down to the Hall?"

"Oh, yes, and they asked me loads of questions, but it was all—you know—routine."

Spade rubbed his palms together. "Swell," he said and then frowned, "though I guess they'll think up plenty to put to me when we meet. That damned Dundy will, anyway, and Bryan." He moved his shoulders. "Anybody you know, outside of the police, come around?"

"Yes." She sat up straight. "That boy—the one who brought the message from Gutman—was there. He didn't come in, but the police left the corridor-door open while they were there and I saw him standing there."

"You didn't say anything?"

"Oh, no. You had said not to. So I didn't pay any attention to him and the next time I looked he was gone."

Spade grinned at her. "Damned lucky for you, sister, that the coppers got there first."

"Why?"

"He's a bad egg, that lad—poison. Was the dead man Jacobi?"

"Yes."

He pressed her hands and stood up. "I'm going to run along. You'd better hit the hay. You're all in."

She rose. "Sam, what is—?"

He stopped her words with his hand on her mouth. "Save it till Monday," he said. "I want to sneak out before your mother catches me and gives me hell for dragging her lamb through gutters."

*

Midnight was a few minutes away when Spade reached his home. He put his key into the street-door's lock. Heels clicked rapidly on the sidewalk behind him. He let go the key and wheeled. Brigid O'Shaughnessy ran up the steps to him. She put her arms around him and hung on him, panting: "Oh, I thought you'd never come!" Her face was haggard, distraught, shaken by the tremors that shook her from head to foot.

With the hand not supporting her he felt for the key again, opened the door, and half lifted her inside. "You've been waiting?" he asked.

"Yes." Panting spaced her words. "In a—doorway—up the —street."

"Can you make it all right?" he asked. "Or shall I carry you?"

She shook her head against his shoulder. "I'll be—all right —when I—get where—I can—sit down."

They rode up to Spade's floor in the elevator and went around to his apartment. She left his arm and stood beside him—panting, both hands to her breast—while he unlocked his door. He switched on the passageway light. They went in. He shut the door and, with his arm around her again, took her back towards the living-room. When they were within a step of the living-room-door the light in the living-room went on.

The girl cried out and clung to Spade.

Just inside the living-room-door fat Gutman stood smiling benevolently at them. The boy Wilmer came out of the kitchen behind them. Black pistols were gigantic in his small hands. Cairo came from the bathroom. He too had a pistol.

Gutman said: "Well, sir, we're all here, as you can see for yourself. Now let's come in and sit down and be comfortable and talk."

CHAPTER XVIII

The Fall-Guy

S PADE, with his arms around Brigid O'Shaughnessy, smiled
meagerly over her head and said: "Sure, we'll talk."

Gutman's bulbs jounced as he took three waddling backward steps away from the door.

Spade and the girl went in together. The boy and Cairo followed them in. Cairo stopped in the doorway. The boy put
away one of his pistols and came up close behind Spade.

Spade turned his head far around to look down over his
shoulder at the boy and said: "Get away. You're not going to
frisk me."

The boy said: "Stand still. Shut up."

Spade's nostrils went in and out with his breathing. His
voice was level. "Get away. Put your paw on me and I'm going to make you use the gun. Ask your boss if he wants me
shot up before we talk."

"Never mind, Wilmer," the fat man said. He frowned indulgently at Spade. "You are certainly a most headstrong individual. Well, let's be seated."

Spade said, "I told you I didn't like that punk," and took
Brigid O'Shaughnessy to the sofa by the windows. They sat
close together, her head against his left shoulder, his left
arm around her shoulders. She had stopped trembling, had
stopped panting. The appearance of Gutman and his companions seemed to have robbed her of that freedom of personal movement and emotion that is animal, leaving her alive,
conscious, but quiescent as a plant.

Gutman lowered himself into the padded rocking chair.
Cairo chose the armchair by the table. The boy Wilmer did
not sit down. He stood in the doorway where Cairo had
stood, letting his one visible pistol hang down at his side,
looking under curling lashes at Spade's body. Cairo put his
pistol on the table beside him.

Spade took off his hat and tossed it to the other end of the
sofa. He grinned at Gutman. The looseness of his lower lip
and the droop of his upper eyelids combined with the v's in

his face to make his grin lewd as a satyr's. "That daughter of yours has a nice belly," he said, "too nice to be scratched up with pins."

Gutman's smile was affable if a bit oily.

The boy in the doorway took a short step forward, raising his pistol as far as his hip. Everybody in the room looked at him. In the dissimilar eyes with which Brigid O'Shaughnessy and Joel Cairo looked at him there was, oddly, something identically reproving. The boy blushed, drew back his advanced foot, straightened his legs, lowered the pistol and stood as he had stood before, looking under lashes that hid his eyes at Spade's chest. The blush was pale enough and lasted for only an instant, but it was startling on his face that habitually was so cold and composed.

Gutman turned his sleek-eyed fat smile on Spade again. His voice was a suave purring. "Yes, sir, that was a shame, but you must admit that it served its purpose."

Spade's brows twitched together. "Anything would've," he said. "Naturally I wanted to see you as soon as I had the falcon. Cash customers—why not? I went to Burlingame expecting to run into this sort of a meeting. I didn't know you were blundering around, half an hour late, trying to get me out of the way so you could find Jacobi again before he found me."

Gutman chuckled. His chuckle seemed to hold nothing but satisfaction. "Well, sir," he said, "in any case, here we are having our little meeting, if that's what you wanted."

"That's what I wanted. How soon are you ready to make the first payment and take the falcon off my hands?"

Brigid O'Shaughnessy sat up straight and looked at Spade with surprised blue eyes. He patted her shoulder inattentively. His eyes were steady on Gutman's. Gutman's twinkled merrily between sheltering fat-puffs. He said: "Well, sir, as to that," and put a hand inside the breast of his coat.

Cairo, hands on thighs, leaned forward in his chair, breathing between parted soft lips. His dark eyes had the surface-shine of lacquer. They shifted their focus warily from Spade's face to Gutman's, from Gutman's to Spade's.

Gutman repeated, "Well, sir, as to that," and took a white envelope from his pocket. Ten eyes—the boy's now only half obscured by his lashes—looked at the envelope. Turning the envelope over in his swollen hands, Gutman studied for a moment its blank white front and then its back, unsealed, with the flap tucked in. He raised his head, smiled amiably, and scaled the envelope at Spade's lap.

The envelope, though not bulky, was heavy enough to fly true. It struck the lower part of Spade's chest and dropped down on his thighs. He picked it up deliberately and opened it deliberately, using both hands, having taken his left arm from around the girl. The contents of the envelope were thousand-dollar bills, smooth and stiff and new. Spade took them out and counted them. There were ten of them. Spade looked up smiling. He said mildly: "We were talking about more money than this."

"Yes, sir, we were," Gutman agreed, "but we were talking then. This is actual money, genuine coin of the realm, sir. With a dollar of this you can buy more than with ten dollars of talk." Silent laughter shook his bulbs. When their commotion stopped he said more seriously, yet not altogether seriously: "There are more of us to be taken care of now." He moved his twinkling eyes and his fat head to indicate Cairo. "And—well, sir, in short—the situation has changed."

While Gutman talked Spade had tapped the edges of the ten bills into alignment and had returned them to their envelope, tucking the flap in over them. Now, with forearms on knees, he sat hunched forward, dangling the envelope from a corner held lightly by finger and thumb down between his legs. His reply to the fat man was careless: "Sure. You're together now, but I've got the falcon."

Joel Cairo spoke. Ugly hands grasping the arms of his chair, he leaned forward and said primly in his high-pitched thin voice: "I shouldn't think it would be necessary to remind you, Mr. Spade, that though you may have the falcon yet we certainly have you."

Spade grinned. "I'm trying to not let that worry me," he said. He sat up straight, put the envelope aside—on the sofa —and addressed Gutman: "We'll come back to the money later. There's another thing that's got to be taken care of first. We've got to have a fall-guy."

The fat man frowned without comprehension, but before

he could speak Spade was explaining: "The police have got to have a victim—somebody they can stick for those three murders. We—"

Cairo, speaking in a brittle excited voice, interrupted Spade. "Two—only two—murders, Mr. Spade. Thursby undoubtedly killed your partner."

"All right, two," Spade growled. "What difference does that make? The point is we've got to feed the police some—"

Now Gutman broke in, smiling confidently, talking with good-natured assurance: "Well, sir, from what we've seen and heard of you I don't think we'll have to bother ourselves about that. We can leave the handling of the police to you, all right. You won't need any of our inexpert help."

"If that's what you think," Spade said, "you haven't seen or heard enough."

"Now come, Mr. Spade. You can't expect us to believe at this late date that you are the least bit afraid of the police, or that you are not quite able to handle—"

Spade snorted with throat and nose. He bent forward, resting forearms on knees again, and interrupted Gutman irritably: "I'm not a damned bit afraid of them and I know how to handle them. That's what I'm trying to tell you. The way to handle them is to toss them a victim, somebody they can hang the works on."

"Well, sir, I grant you that's one way of doing it, but—"

" 'But' hell!" Spade said. "It's the only way." His eyes were hot and earnest under a reddening forehead. The bruise on his temple was liver-colored. "I know what I'm talking about. I've been through it all before and expect to go through it again. At one time or another I've had to tell everybody from the Supreme Court down to go to hell, and I've got away with it. I got away with it because I never let myself forget that a day of reckoning was coming. I never forget that when the day of reckoning comes I want to be all set to march into headquarters pushing a victim in front of me, saying: 'Here, you chumps, is your criminal.' As long as I can do that I can put my thumb to my nose and wriggle my fingers at all the laws in the book. The first time I can't do it my name's Mud. There hasn't been a first time yet. This isn't going to be it. That's flat."

Gutman's eyes flickered and their sleekness became dubious, but he held his other features in their bulbous pink smiling complacent cast and there was nothing of uneasiness in his voice. He said: "That's a system that's got a lot to recommend it, sir—by Gad, it has! And if it was anyway practical this time I'd be the first to say: 'Stick to it by all means, sir.' But this just happens to be a case where it's not possible. That's the way it is with the best of systems. There comes a time when you've got to make exceptions, and a wise man just goes ahead and makes them. Well, sir, that's just the way it is in this case and I don't mind telling you that I think you're being very well paid for making an exception. Now maybe it will be a little more trouble to you than if you had your victim to hand over to the police, but"—he laughed and spread his hands—"you're not a man that's afraid of a little bit of trouble. You know how to do things and you know you'll land on your feet in the end, no matter what happens." He pursed his lips and partly closed one eye. "You'll manage that, sir."

Spade's eyes had lost their warmth. His face was dull and lumpy. "I know what I'm talking about," he said in a low, consciously patient, tone. "This is my city and my game. I could manage to land on my feet—sure—this time, but the next time I tried to put over a fast one they'd stop me so fast I'd swallow my teeth. Hell with that. You birds'll be in New York or Constantinople or some place else. I'm in business here."

"But surely," Gutman began, "you can—"

"I can't," Spade said earnestly. "I won't. I mean it." He sat up straight. A pleasant smile illuminated his face, erasing its dull lumpishness. He spoke rapidly in an agreeable, persuasive, tone: "Listen to me, Gutman. I'm telling you what's best for all of us. If we don't give the police a fall-guy it's ten to one they'll sooner or later stumble on information about the falcon. Then you'll have to duck for cover with it—no matter where you are—and that's not going to help you make a fortune off it. Give them a fall-guy and they'll stop right there."

"Well, sir, that's just the point," Gutman replied, and still only in his eyes was uneasiness faintly apparent. "Will they stop right there? Or won't the fall-guy be a fresh clew that as likely as not will lead them to information about the falcon? And, on the other hand, wouldn't you say they were stopped right now, and that the best thing for us to do is leave well enough alone?"

A forked vein began to swell in Spade's forehead. "Jesus! you don't know what it's all about either," he said in a restrained tone. "They're not asleep, Gutman. They're lying low, waiting. Try to get that. I'm in it up to my neck and they know it. That's all right as long as I do something when the time comes. But it won't be all right if I don't." His voice became persuasive again. "Listen, Gutman, we've absolutely got to give them a victim. There's no way out of it. Let's give them the punk." He nodded pleasantly at the boy in the doorway. "He actually did shoot both of them—Thursby and Jacobi —didn't he? Anyway, he's made to order for the part. Let's pin the necessary evidence on him and turn him over to them."

The boy in the doorway tightened the corners of his mouth in what may have been a minute smile. Spade's proposal seemed to have no other effect on him. Joel Cairo's dark face was open-mouthed, open-eyed, yellowish, and amazed. He breathed through his mouth, his round effeminate chest rising and falling, while he gaped at Spade. Brigid O'Shaughnessy had moved away from Spade and had twisted herself around on the sofa to stare at him. There was a suggestion of hysterical laughter behind the startled confusion in her face.

Gutman remained still and expressionless for a long moment. Then he decided to laugh. He laughed heartily and lengthily, not stopping until his sleek eyes had borrowed merriment from his laughter. When he stopped laughing he said: "By Gad, sir, you're a character, that you are!" He took a white handkerchief from his pocket and wiped his eyes. "Yes, sir, there's never any telling what you'll do or say next, except that it's bound to be something astonishing."

"There's nothing funny about it." Spade did not seem offended by the fat man's laughter, nor in any way impressed. He spoke in the manner of one reasoning with a recalcitrant, but not altogether unreasonable, friend. "It's our best bet. With him in their hands, the police will—"

"But, my dear man," Gutman objected, "can't you see? If I even for a moment thought of doing it— But that's ridiculous too. I feel towards Wilmer just exactly as if he were my own son. I really do. But if I even for a moment thought of doing what you propose, what in the world do you think would keep Wilmer from telling the police every last detail about the falcon and all of us?"

Spade grinned with stiff lips. "If we had to," he said softly, "we could have him killed resisting arrest. But we won't have to go that far. Let him talk his head off. I promise you nobody'll do anything about it. That's easy enough to fix."

The pink flesh on Gutman's forehead crawled in a frown. He lowered his head, mashing his chins together over his collar, and asked: "How?" Then, with an abruptness that set all his fat bulbs to quivering and tumbling against one another, he raised his head, squirmed around to look at the boy, and laughed uproariously. "What do you think of this, Wilmer? It's funny, eh?"

The boy's eyes were cold hazel gleams under his lashes. He said in a low distinct voice: "Yes, it's funny—the son of a bitch."

Spade was talking to Brigid O'Shaughnessy: "How do you feel now, angel? Any better?"

"Yes, much better, only"—she reduced her voice until the last words would have been unintelligible two feet away— "I'm frightened."

"Don't be," he said carelessly and put a hand on her greystockinged knee. "Nothing very bad's going to happen. Want a drink?"

"Not now, thanks." Her voice sank again. "Be careful, Sam."

Spade grinned and looked at Gutman, who was looking at him. The fat man smiled genially, saying nothing for a moment, and then asked: "How?"

Spade was stupid. "How what?"

The fat man considered more laughter necessary then, and an explanation: "Well, sir, if you're really serious about this— this suggestion of yours, the least we can do in common politeness is to hear you out. Now how are you going about fixing it so that Wilmer"—he paused here to laugh again— "won't be able to do us any harm?"

Spade shook his head. "No," he said, "I wouldn't want to take advantage of anybody's politeness, no matter how common, like that. Forget it."

The fat man puckered up his facial bulbs. "Now come, come," he protested, "you make me decidedly uncomfortable. I shouldn't have laughed, and I apologize most humbly and sincerely. I wouldn't want to seem to ridicule anything you'd suggest, Mr. Spade, regardless of how much I disagreed with you, for you must know that I have the greatest respect and admiration for your astuteness. Now mind you, I don't see how this suggestion of yours can be in any way practical—even leaving out the fact that I couldn't feel any different towards Wilmer if he was my own flesh and blood—but I'll consider it a personal favor as well as a sign that you've accepted my apologies, sir, if you'll go ahead and outline the rest of it."

"Fair enough," Spade said. "Bryan is like most district attorneys. He's more interested in how his record will look on paper than in anything else. He'd rather drop a doubtful case than try it and have it go against him. I don't know that he ever deliberately framed anybody he believed innocent, but I can't imagine him letting himself believe them innocent if he could scrape up, or twist into shape, proof of their guilt. To be sure of convicting one man he'll let half a dozen equally guilty accomplices go free—if trying to convict them all might confuse his case.

"That's the choice we'll give him and he'll gobble it up. He wouldn't want to know about the falcon. He'll be tickled pink to persuade himself that anything the punk tells him about it is a lot of chewing-gum, an attempt to muddle things up. Leave that end to me. I can show him that if he starts fooling around trying to gather up everybody he's going to have a tangled case that no jury will be able to make heads or tails of, while if he sticks to the punk he can get a conviction standing on his head."

Gutman wagged his head sidewise in a slow smiling gesture of benign disapproval. "No, sir," he said, "I'm afraid that won't do, won't do at all. I don't see how even this District Attorney of yours can link Thursby and Jacobi and Wilmer together without having to—"

"You don't know district attorneys," Spade told him. "The Thursby angle is easy. He was a gunman and so's your punk. Bryan's already got a theory about that. There'll be no catch there. Well, Christ! they can only hang the punk once. Why try him for Jacobi's murder after he's been convicted of Thursby's? They simply close the record by writing it up against him and let it go at that. If, as is likely enough, he used the same gun on both, the bullets will match up. Everybody will be satisfied."

"Yes, but—" Gutman began, and stopped to look at the boy.

The boy advanced from the doorway, walking stiff-legged, with his legs apart, until he was between Gutman and Cairo, almost in the center of the floor. He halted there, leaning forward slightly from the waist, his shoulders raised towards the front. The pistol in his hand still hung at his side, but his knuckles were white over its grip. His other hand was a small hard fist down at his other side. The indelible youngness of his face gave an indescribably vicious—and inhuman—turn to the white-hot hatred and the cold white malevolence in his face. He said to Spade in a voice cramped by passion: "You bastard, get up on your feet and go for your heater!"

Spade smiled at the boy. His smile was not broad, but the amusement in it seemed genuine and unalloyed.

The boy said: "You bastard, get up and shoot it out if you've got the guts. I've taken all the riding from you I'm going to take."

The amusement in Spade's smile deepened. He looked at Gutman and said: "Young Wild West." His voice matched his smile. "Maybe you ought to tell him that shooting me before you get your hands on the falcon would be bad for business."

Gutman's attempt at a smile was not successful, but he kept the resultant grimace on his mottled face. He licked dry lips with a dry tongue. His voice was too hoarse and gritty for the paternally admonishing tone it tried to achieve. "Now, now, Wilmer," he said, "we can't have any of that. You shouldn't let yourself attach so much importance to these things. You—"

The boy, not taking his eyes from Spade, spoke in a choked voice out the side of his mouth: "Make him lay off me then.

I'm going to fog him if he keeps it up and there won't be anything that'll stop me from doing it."

"Now, Wilmer," Gutman said and turned to Spade. His face and voice were under control now. "Your plan is, sir, as I said in the first place, not at all practical. Let's not say anything more about it."

Spade looked from one of them to the other. He had stopped smiling. His face held no expression at all. "I say what I please," he told them.

"You certainly do," Gutman said quickly, "and that's one of the things I've always admired in you. But this matter is, as I say, not at all practical, so there's not the least bit of use of discussing it any further, as you can see for yourself."

"I can't see it for myself," Spade said, "and you haven't made me see it, and I don't think you can." He frowned at Gutman. "Let's get this straight. Am I wasting time talking to you? I thought this was your show. Should I do my talking to the punk? I know how to do that."

"No, sir," Gutman replied, "you're quite right in dealing with me."

Spade said: "All right. Now I've got another suggestion. It's not as good as the first, but it's better than nothing. Want to hear it?"

"Most assuredly."

"Give them Cairo."

Cairo hastily picked up his pistol from the table beside him. He held it tight in his lap with both hands. Its muzzle pointed at the floor a little to one side of the sofa. His face had become yellowish again. His black eyes darted their gaze from face to face. The opaqueness of his eyes made them seem flat, two-dimensional.

Gutman, looking as if he could not believe he had heard what he had heard, asked: "Do what?"

"Give the police Cairo."

Gutman seemed about to laugh, but he did not laugh. Finally he exclaimed: "Well, by Gad, sir!" in an uncertain tone.

"It's not as good as giving them the punk," Spade said. "Cairo's not a gunman and he carries a smaller gun than Thursby and Jacobi were shot with. We'll have to go to more trouble framing him, but that's better than not giving the police anybody."

Cairo cried in a voice shrill with indignation: "Suppose we give them you, Mr. Spade, or Miss O'Shaughnessy? How about that if you're so set on giving them somebody?"

Spade smiled at the Levantine and answered him evenly: "You people want the falcon. I've got it. A fall-guy is part of the price I'm asking. As for Miss O'Shaughnessy"—his dispassionate glance moved to her white perplexed face and then back to Cairo and his shoulders rose and fell a fraction of an inch—"if you think she can be rigged for the part I'm perfectly willing to discuss it with you."

The girl put her hands to her throat, uttered a short strangled cry, and moved farther away from him.

Cairo, his face and body twitching with excitement, exclaimed: "You seem to forget that you are not in a position to insist on anything."

Spade laughed, a harsh derisive snort.

Gutman said, in a voice that tried to make firmness ingratiating: "Come now, gentlemen, let's keep our discussion on a friendly basis; but there certainly is"—he was addressing Spade—"something in what Mr. Cairo says. You must take into consideration the—"

"Like hell I must." Spade flung his words out with a brutal sort of carelessness that gave them more weight than they could have got from dramatic emphasis or from loudness. "If you kill me, how are you going to get the bird? If I know you can't afford to kill me till you have it, how are you going to scare me into giving it to you?"

Gutman cocked his head to the left and considered these questions. His eyes twinkled between puckered lids. Presently he gave his genial answer: "Well, sir, there are other means of persuasion besides killing and threatening to kill."

"Sure," Spade agreed, "but they're not much good unless the threat of death is behind them to hold the victim down. See what I mean? If you try anything I don't like I won't stand for it. I'll make it a matter of your having to call it off or kill me, knowing you can't afford to kill me."

"I see what you mean." Gutman chuckled. "That is an attitude, sir, that calls for the most delicate judgment on both sides, because, as you know, sir, men are likely to forget in the heat of action where their best interest lies and let their emotions carry them away."

Spade too was all smiling blandness. "That's the trick, from my side," he said, "to make my play strong enough that it ties you up, but yet not make you mad enough to bump me off against your better judgment."

Gutman said fondly: "By Gad, sir, you are a character!"

Joel Cairo jumped up from his chair and went around behind the boy and behind Gutman's chair. He bent over the back of Gutman's chair and, screening his mouth and the fat man's ear with his empty hand, whispered. Gutman listened attentively, shutting his eyes.

Spade grinned at Brigid O'Shaughnessy. Her lips smiled feebly in response, but there was no change in her eyes; they did not lose their numb stare. Spade turned to the boy: "Two to one they're selling you out, son."

The boy did not say anything. A trembling in his knees began to shake the knees of his trousers.

Spade addressed Gutman: "I hope you're not letting yourself be influenced by the guns these pocket-edition desperadoes are waving."

Gutman opened his eyes. Cairo stopped whispering and stood erect behind the fat man's chair.

Spade said: "I've practiced taking them away from both of them, so there'll be no trouble there. The punk is—"

In a voice choked horribly by emotion the boy cried, "All right!" and jerked his pistol up in front of his chest.

Gutman flung a fat hand out at the boy's wrist, caught the wrist, and bore it and the gun down while Gutman's fat body was rising in haste from the rocking chair. Joel Cairo scurried around to the boy's other side and grasped his other arm. They wrestled with the boy, forcing his arms down, holding them down, while he struggled futilely against them. Words came out of the struggling group: fragments of the boy's incoherent speech—"right . . . go . . . bastard . . . smoke"—Gutman's "Now, now, Wilmer!" repeated many times; Cairo's "No, please, don't" and "Don't do that, Wilmer."

Wooden-faced, dreamy-eyed, Spade got up from the sofa and went over to the group. The boy, unable to cope with the

weight against him, had stopped struggling. Cairo, still holding the boy's arm, stood partly in front of him, talking to him
soothingly. Spade pushed Cairo aside gently and drove his left
fist against the boy's chin. The boy's head snapped back as far
as it could while his arms were held, and then came forward.
Gutman began a desperate "Here, what—?" Spade drove his
right fist against the boy's chin.

Cairo dropped the boy's arm, letting him collapse against
Gutman's great round belly. Cairo sprang at Spade, clawing at
his face with the curved stiff fingers of both hands. Spade
blew his breath out and pushed the Levantine away. Cairo
sprang at him again. Tears were in Cairo's eyes and his red
lips worked angrily, forming words, but no sound came from
between them.

Spade laughed, grunted, "Jesus, you're a pip!" and cuffed
the side of Cairo's face with an open hand, knocking him over
against the table. Cairo regained his balance and sprang at
Spade the third time. Spade stopped him with both palms
held out on long rigid arms against his face. Cairo, failing to
reach Spade's face with his shorter arms, thumped Spade's
arms.

"Stop it," Spade growled. "I'll hurt you."

Cairo cried, "Oh, you big coward!" and backed away from
him.

Spade stooped to pick up Cairo's pistol from the floor, and
then the boy's. He straightened up holding them in his left
hand, dangling them upside-down by their trigger-guards
from his forefinger.

Gutman had put the boy in the rocking chair and stood
looking at him with troubled eyes in an uncertainly puckered
face. Cairo went down on his knees beside the chair and began to chafe one of the boy's limp hands.

Spade felt the boy's chin with his fingers. "Nothing
cracked," he said. "We'll spread him on the sofa." He put his
right arm under the boy's arm and around his back, put his
left forearm under the boy's knees, lifted him without apparent effort, and carried him to the sofa.

Brigid O'Shaughnessy got up quickly and Spade laid the
boy there. With his right hand Spade patted the boy's clothes,
found his second pistol, added it to the others in his left hand,

and turned his back on the sofa. Cairo was already sitting beside the boy's head.

Spade clinked the pistols together in his hand and smiled cheerfully at Gutman. "Well," he said, "there's our fall-guy."

Gutman's face was grey and his eyes were clouded. He did not look at Spade. He looked at the floor and did not say anything.

Spade said: "Don't be a damned fool again. You let Cairo whisper to you and you held the kid while I pasted him. You can't laugh that off and you're likely to get yourself shot trying to."

Gutman moved his feet on the rug and said nothing.

Spade said: "And the other side of it is that you'll either say yes right now or I'll turn the falcon and the whole Goddamned lot of you in."

Gutman raised his head and muttered through his teeth: "I don't like that, sir."

"You won't like it," Spade said. "Well?"

The fat man sighed and made a wry face and replied sadly: "You can have him."

Spade said: "That's swell."

CHAPTER XIX

The Russian's Hand

THE BOY lay on his back on the sofa, a small figure that was—except for its breathing—altogether corpselike to the eye. Joel Cairo sat beside the boy, bending over him, rubbing his cheeks and wrists, smoothing his hair back from his forehead, whispering to him, and peering anxiously down at his white still face.

Brigid O'Shaughnessy stood in an angle made by table and wall. One of her hands was flat on the table, the other to her breast. She pinched her lower lip between her teeth and glanced furtively at Spade whenever he was not looking at her. When he looked at her she looked at Cairo and the boy.

Gutman's face had lost its troubled cast and was becoming rosy again. He had put his hands in his trousers-pockets. He stood facing Spade, watching him without curiosity.

Spade, idly jingling his handful of pistols, nodded at Cairo's rounded back and asked Gutman: "It'll be all right with him?"

"I don't know," the fat man replied placidly. "That part will have to be strictly up to you, sir."

Spade's smile made his v-shaped chin more salient. He said: "Cairo."

The Levantine screwed his dark anxious face around over his shoulder.

Spade said: "Let him rest awhile. We're going to give him to the police. We ought to get the details fixed before he comes to."

Cairo asked bitterly: "Don't you think you've done enough to him without that?"

Spade said: "No."

Cairo left the sofa and went close to the fat man. "Please don't do this thing, Mr. Gutman," he begged. "You must realize that—"

Spade interrupted him: "That's settled. The question is, what are you going to do about it? Coming in? Or getting out?"

Though Gutman's smile was a bit sad, even wistful in its way, he nodded his head. "I don't like it either," he told the Levantine, "but we can't help ourselves now. We really can't."

Spade asked: "What are you doing, Cairo? In or out?"

Cairo wet his lips and turned slowly to face Spade. "Suppose," he said, and swallowed. "Have I—? Can I choose?"

"You can," Spade assured him seriously, "but you ought to know that if the answer is *out* we'll give you to the police with your boy-friend."

"Oh, come, Mr. Spade," Gutman protested, "that is not—"

"Like hell we'll let him walk out on us," Spade said. "He'll either come in or he'll go in. We can't have a lot of loose ends hanging around." He scowled at Gutman and burst out irritably: "Jesus God! is this the first thing you guys ever stole? You're a fine lot of lollipops! What are you going to do next—get down and pray?" He directed his scowl at Cairo. "Well? Which?"

"You give me no choice." Cairo's narrow shoulders moved in a hopeless shrug. "I come in."

"Good," Spade said and looked at Gutman and at Brigid O'Shaughnessy. "Sit down."

The girl sat down gingerly on the end of the sofa by the unconscious boy's feet. Gutman returned to the padded rocking chair, and Cairo to the armchair. Spade put his handful of pistols on the table and sat on the table-corner beside them. He looked at the watch on his wrist and said: "Two o'clock. I can't get the falcon till daylight, or maybe eight o'clock. We've got plenty of time to arrange everything."

Gutman cleared his throat. "Where is it?" he asked and then added in haste: "I don't really care, sir. What I had in mind was that it would be best for all concerned if we did not get out of each other's sight until our business has been transacted." He looked at the sofa and at Spade again, sharply. "You have the envelope?"

Spade shook his head, looking at the sofa and then at the girl. He smiled with his eyes and said: "Miss O'Shaughnessy has it."

"Yes, I have it," she murmured, putting a hand inside her coat. "I picked it up. . . ."

"That's all right," Spade told her. "Hang on to it." He addressed Gutman: "We won't have to lose sight of each other. I can have the falcon brought here."

"That will be excellent," Gutman purred. "Then, sir, in exchange for the ten thousand dollars and Wilmer you will give us the falcon and an hour or two of grace—so we won't be in the city when you surrender him to the authorities."

"You don't have to duck," Spade said. "It'll be air-tight."

"That may be, sir, but nevertheless we'll feel safer well out of the city when Wilmer is being questioned by your District Attorney."

"Suit yourself," Spade replied. "I can hold him here all day if you want." He began to roll a cigarette. "Let's get the details fixed. Why did he shoot Thursby? And why and where and how did he shoot Jacobi?"

Gutman smiled indulgently, shaking his head and purring: "Now come, sir, you can't expect that. We've given you the money and Wilmer. That is our part of the agreement."

"I do expect it," Spade said. He held his lighter to his cigarette. "A fall-guy is what I asked for, and he's not a fall-guy unless he's a cinch to take the fall. Well, to cinch that I've got to know what's what." He pulled his brows together. "What are you bellyaching about? You're not going to be sitting so damned pretty if you leave him with an out."

Gutman leaned forward and wagged a fat finger at the pistols on the table beside Spade's legs. "There's ample evidence of his guilt, sir. Both men were shot with those weapons. It's a very simple matter for the police-department-experts to determine that the bullets that killed the men were fired from those weapons. You know that; you've mentioned it yourself. And that, it seems to me, is ample proof of his guilt."

"Maybe," Spade agreed, "but the thing's more complicated than that and I've got to know what happened so I can be sure the parts that won't fit in are covered up."

Cairo's eyes were round and hot. "Apparently you've forgotten that you assured us it would be a very simple affair," Cairo said. He turned his excited dark face to Gutman. "You see! I advised you not to do this. I don't think—"

"It doesn't make a damned bit of difference what either of you think," Spade said bluntly. "It's too late for that now and you're in too deep. Why did he kill Thursby?"

Gutman interlaced his fingers over his belly and rocked his chair. His voice, like his smile, was frankly rueful. "You are an uncommonly difficult person to get the best of," he said. "I begin to think that we made a mistake in not letting you alone from the very first. By Gad, I do, sir!"

Spade moved his hand carelessly. "You haven't done so bad. You're staying out of jail and you're getting the falcon. What do you want?" He put his cigarette in a corner of his mouth and said around it: "Anyhow you know where you stand now. Why did he kill Thursby?"

Gutman stopped rocking. "Thursby was a notorious killer and Miss O'Shaughnessy's ally. We knew that removing him in just that manner would make her stop and think that perhaps it would be best to patch up her differences with us after all, besides leaving her without so violent a protector. You see, sir, I am being candid with you?"

"Yes. Keep it up. You didn't think he might have the falcon?"

Gutman shook his head so that his round cheeks wabbled. "We didn't think that for a minute," he replied. He smiled benevolently. "We had the advantage of knowing Miss O'Shaughnessy far too well for that and, while we didn't know then she had given the falcon to Captain Jacobi in Hongkong to be brought over on the *Paloma* while they took a faster boat, still we didn't for a minute think that, if only one of them knew where it was, Thursby was the one."

Spade nodded thoughtfully and asked: "You didn't try to make a deal with him before you gave him the works?"

"Yes, sir, we certainly did. I talked to him myself that night. Wilmer had located him two days before and had been trying to follow him to wherever he was meeting Miss O'Shaughnessy, but Thursby was too crafty for that even if he didn't know he was being watched. So that night Wilmer went to his hotel, learned he wasn't in, and waited outside for him. I suppose Thursby returned immediately after killing your partner. Be that as it may, Wilmer brought him to see me. We could do nothing with him. He was quite determinedly loyal to Miss O'Shaughnessy. Well, sir, Wilmer followed him back to his hotel and did what he did."

Spade thought for a moment. "That sounds all right. Now Jacobi."

Gutman looked at Spade with grave eyes and said: "Captain Jacobi's death was entirely Miss O'Shaughnessy's fault."

The girl gasped, "Oh!" and put a hand to her mouth.

Spade's voice was heavy and even. "Never mind that now. Tell me what happened."

After a shrewd look at Spade, Gutman smiled. "Just as you say, sir," he said. "Well, Cairo, as you know, got in touch with me—I sent for him—after he left police headquarters the night—or morning—he was up here. We recognized the mutual advantage of pooling forces." He directed his smile at the Levantine. "Mr. Cairo is a man of nice judgment. The *Paloma* was his thought. He saw the notice of its arrival in the papers that morning and remembered that he had heard in Hongkong that Jacobi and Miss O'Shaughnessy had been seen together. That was when he had been trying to find her there, and he thought at first that she had left on the *Paloma*, though later he learned that she hadn't. Well, sir, when he saw the notice of arrival in the paper he guessed just what had happened: she had given the bird to Jacobi to bring here for her. Jacobi did not know what it was, of course. Miss O'Shaughnessy is too discreet for that."

He beamed at the girl, rocked his chair twice, and went on: "Mr. Cairo and Wilmer and I went to call on Captain Jacobi and were fortunate enough to arrive while Miss O'Shaughnessy was there. In many ways it was a difficult conference, but finally, by midnight we had persuaded Miss O'Shaughnessy to come to terms, or so we thought. We then left the boat and set out for my hotel, where I was to pay Miss O'Shaughnessy and receive the bird. Well, sir, we mere men should have known better than to suppose ourselves capable of coping with her. *En route*, she and Captain Jacobi and the falcon slipped completely through our fingers." He laughed merrily. "By Gad, sir, it was neatly done."

Spade looked at the girl. Her eyes, large and dark with pleading, met his. He asked Gutman: "You touched off the boat before you left?"

"Not intentionally, no, sir," the fat man replied, "though I dare say we—or Wilmer at least—were responsible for the fire. He had been out trying to find the falcon while the rest of us were talking in the cabin and no doubt was careless with matches."

"That's fine," Spade said. "If any slip-up makes it necessary for us to try him for Jacobi's murder we can also hang an arson-rap on him. All right. Now about the shooting."

"Well, sir, we dashed around town all day trying to find them and we found them late this afternoon. We weren't sure at first that we'd found them. All we were sure of was that we'd found Miss O'Shaughnessy's apartment. But when we listened at the door we heard them moving around inside, so we were pretty confident we had them and rang the bell. When she asked us who we were and we told her—through the door—we heard a window going up.

"We knew what that meant, of course; so Wilmer hurried downstairs as fast as he could and around to the rear of the building to cover the fire-escape. And when he turned into the alley he ran right plumb smack into Captain Jacobi running away with the falcon under his arm. That was a difficult situation to handle, but Wilmer did every bit as well as he could. He shot Jacobi—more than once—but Jacobi was too tough to either fall or drop the falcon, and he was too close for Wilmer to keep out of his way. He knocked Wilmer down and ran on. And this was in broad daylight, you understand, in the afternoon. When Wilmer got up he could see a policeman coming up from the block below. So he had to give it up. He dodged into the open back door of the building next the Coronet, through into the street, and then up to join us—and very fortunate he was, sir, to make it without being seen.

"Well, sir, there we were—stumped again. Miss O'Shaughnessy had opened the door for Mr. Cairo and me after she had shut the window behind Jacobi, and she—" He broke off to smile at a memory. "We persuaded—that is the word, sir—her to tell us that she had told Jacobi to take the falcon to you. It seemed very unlikely that he'd live to go that far, even if the police didn't pick him up, but that was the only chance we had, sir. And so, once more, we persuaded Miss O'Shaughnessy to give us a little assistance. We—well—persuaded her to phone your office in an attempt to draw you away before Jacobi got there, and we sent Wilmer after him. Unfortunately it had taken us too long to decide and to persuade Miss O'Shaughnessy to—"

The boy on the sofa groaned and rolled over on his side. His eyes opened and closed several times. The girl stood up and moved into the angle of table and wall again.

"—coöperate with us," Gutman concluded hurriedly, "and so you had the falcon before we could reach you."

The boy put one foot on the floor, raised himself on an elbow, opened his eyes wide, put the other foot down, sat up, and looked around. When his eyes focused on Spade bewilderment went out of them.

Cairo left his armchair and went over to the boy. He put his arm on the boy's shoulders and started to say something. The boy rose quickly to his feet, shaking Cairo's arm off. He glanced around the room once and then fixed his eyes on Spade again. His face was set hard and he held his body so tense that it seemed drawn in and shrunken.

Spade, sitting on the corner of the table, swinging his legs carelessly, said: "Now listen, kid. If you come over here and start cutting up I'm going to kick you in the face. Sit down and shut up and behave and you'll last longer."

The boy looked at Gutman.

Gutman smiled benignly at him and said: "Well, Wilmer, I'm sorry indeed to lose you, and I want you to know that I couldn't be any fonder of you if you were my own son; but—well, by Gad!—if you lose a son it's possible to get another—and there's only one Maltese falcon."

Spade laughed.

Cairo moved over and whispered in the boy's ear. The boy, keeping his cold hazel eyes on Gutman's face, sat down on the sofa again. The Levantine sat beside him.

Gutman's sigh did not affect the benignity of his smile. He said to Spade: "When you're young you simply don't understand things."

Cairo had an arm around the boy's shoulders again and was whispering to him. Spade grinned at Gutman and addressed Brigid O'Shaughnessy: "I think it'd be swell if you'd see what you can find us to eat in the kitchen, with plenty of coffee. Will you? I don't like to leave my guests."

"Surely," she said and started towards the door.

Gutman stopped rocking. "Just a moment, my dear." He held up a thick hand. "Hadn't you better leave the envelope in here? You don't want to get grease-spots on it."

The girl's eyes questioned Spade. He said in an indifferent tone: "It's still his."

She put her hand inside her coat, took out the envelope, and gave it to Spade. Spade tossed it into Gutman's lap, saying: "Sit on it if you're afraid of losing it."

"You misunderstand me," Gutman replied suavely. "It's not that at all, but business should be transacted in a business-like manner." He opened the flap of the envelope, took out the thousand-dollar bills, counted them, and chuckled so that his belly bounced. "For instance there are only nine bills here now." He spread them out on his fat knees and thighs. "There were ten when I handed it to you, as you very well know." His smile was broad and jovial and triumphant.

Spade looked at Brigid O'Shaughnessy and asked: "Well?"

She shook her head sidewise with emphasis. She did not say anything, though her lips moved slightly, as if she had tried to. Her face was frightened.

Spade held his hand out to Gutman and the fat man put the money into it. Spade counted the money—nine thousand-dollar bills—and returned it to Gutman. Then Spade stood up and his face was dull and placid. He picked up the three pistols on the table. He spoke in a matter-of-fact voice. "I want to know about this. We"—he nodded at the girl, but without looking at her—"are going in the bathroom. The door will be open and I'll be facing it. Unless you want a three-story drop there's no way out of here except past the bathroom door. Don't try to make it."

"Really, sir," Gutman protested, "it's not necessary, and certainly not very courteous of you, to threaten us in this manner. You must know that we've not the least desire to leave."

"I'll know a lot when I'm through." Spade was patient but resolute. "This trick upsets things. I've got to find the answer. It won't take long." He touched the girl's elbow. "Come on."

*

In the bathroom Brigid O'Shaughnessy found words. She put her hands up flat on Spade's chest and her face up close to his and whispered: "I did not take that bill, Sam."

"I don't think you did," he said, "but I've got to know. Take your clothes off."

"You won't take my word for it?"

"No. Take your clothes off."

"I won't."

"All right. We'll go back to the other room and I'll have them taken off."

She stepped back with a hand to her mouth. Her eyes were round and horrified. "You would?" she asked through her fingers.

"I will," he said. "I've got to know what happened to that bill and I'm not going to be held up by anybody's maidenly modesty."

"Oh, it isn't that." She came close to him and put her hands on his chest again. "I'm not ashamed to be naked before you, but—can't you see?—not like this. Can't you see that if you make me you'll—you'll be killing something?"

He did not raise his voice. "I don't know anything about that. I've got to know what happened to the bill. Take them off."

She looked at his unblinking yellow-grey eyes and her face became pink and then white again. She drew herself up tall and began to undress. He sat on the side of the bathtub watching her and the open door. No sound came from the living-room. She removed her clothes swiftly, without fumbling, letting them fall down on the floor around her feet. When she was naked she stepped back from her clothing and stood looking at him. In her mien was pride without defiance or embarrassment.

He put his pistols on the toilet-seat and, facing the door, went down on one knee in front of her garments. He picked up each piece and examined it with fingers as well as eyes. He did not find the thousand-dollar bill. When he had finished he stood up holding her clothes out in his hands to her. "Thanks," he said. "Now I know."

She took the clothing from him. She did not say anything. He picked up his pistols. He shut the bathroom door behind him and went into the living-room.

Gutman smiled amiably at him from the rocking chair. "Find it?" he asked.

Cairo, sitting beside the boy on the sofa, looked at Spade with questioning opaque eyes. The boy did not look up. He was leaning forward, head between hands, elbows on knees, staring at the floor between his feet.

Spade told Gutman: "No, I didn't find it. You palmed it."

The fat man chuckled. "I palmed it?"

"Yes," Spade said, jingling the pistols in his hand. "Do you want to say so or do you want to stand for a frisk?"

"Stand for—?"

"You're going to admit it," Spade said, "or I'm going to search you. There's no third way."

Gutman looked up at Spade's hard face and laughed outright. "By Gad, sir, I believe you would. I really do. You're a character, sir, if you don't mind my saying so."

"You palmed it," Spade said.

"Yes, sir, that I did." The fat man took a crumpled bill from his vest-pocket, smoothed it on a wide thigh, took the envelope holding the nine bills from his coat-pocket, and put the smoothed bill in with the others. "I must have my little joke every now and then and I was curious to know what you'd do in a situation of that sort. I must say that you passed the test with flying colors, sir. It never occurred to me that you'd hit on such a simple and direct way of getting at the truth."

Spade sneered at him without bitterness. "That's the kind of thing I'd expect from somebody the punk's age."

Gutman chuckled.

Brigid O'Shaughnessy, dressed again except for coat and hat, came out of the bathroom, took a step towards the living-room, turned around, went to the kitchen, and turned on the light.

Cairo edged closer to the boy on the sofa and began whispering in his ear again. The boy shrugged irritably.

Spade, looking at the pistols in his hand and then at Gutman, went out into the passageway, to the closet there. He opened the door, put the pistols inside on the top of a trunk, shut the door, locked it, put the key in his trousers-pocket, and went to the kitchen door.

Brigid O'Shaughnessy was filling an aluminum percolator.

"Find everything?" Spade asked.

"Yes," she replied in a cool voice, not raising her head. Then she set the percolator aside and came to the door. She blushed and her eyes were large and moist and chiding. "You shouldn't have done that to me, Sam," she said softly.

"I had to find out, angel." He bent down, kissed her mouth lightly, and returned to the living-room.

Gutman smiled at Spade and offered him the white envelope, saying: "This will soon be yours; you might as well take it now."

Spade did not take it. He sat in the armchair and said: "There's plenty of time for that. We haven't done enough talking about the money-end. I ought to have more than ten thousand."

Gutman said: "Ten thousand dollars is a lot of money."

Spade said: "You're quoting me, but it's not all the money in the world."

"No, sir, it's not. I grant you that. But it's a lot of money to be picked up in as few days and as easily as you're getting it."

"You think it's been so damned easy?" Spade asked, and shrugged. "Well, maybe, but that's my business."

"It certainly is," the fat man agreed. He screwed up his eyes, moved his head to indicate the kitchen, and lowered his voice. "Are you sharing with her?"

Spade said: "That's my business too."

"It certainly is," the fat man agreed once more, "but"—he hesitated—"I'd like to give you a word of advice."

"Go ahead."

"If you don't—I dare say you'll give her some money in any event, but—if you don't give her as much as she thinks she ought to have, my word of advice is—be careful."

Spade's eyes held a mocking light. He asked: "Bad?"

"Bad," the fat man replied.

Spade grinned and began to roll a cigarette.

Cairo, still muttering in the boy's ear, had put his arm around the boy's shoulders again. Suddenly the boy pushed his arm away and turned on the sofa to face the Levantine. The boy's face held disgust and anger. He made a fist of one small hand and struck Cairo's mouth with it. Cairo cried out as a woman might have cried and drew back to the very end of the sofa. He took a silk handkerchief from his pocket and put it to his mouth. It came away daubed with blood. He put it to his mouth once more and looked reproachfully at the boy. The boy snarled, "Keep away from me," and put his face between his hands again. Cairo's handkerchief released the fragrance of *chypre* in the room.

Cairo's cry had brought Brigid O'Shaughnessy to the door. Spade, grinning, jerked a thumb at the sofa and told her: "The course of true love. How's the food coming along?"

"It's coming," she said and went back to the kitchen.

Spade lighted his cigarette and addressed Gutman: "Let's talk about money."

"Willingly, sir, with all my heart," the fat man replied, "but I might as well tell you frankly right now that ten thousand is every cent I can raise."

Spade exhaled smoke. "I ought to have twenty."

"I wish you could. I'd give it to you gladly if I had it, but ten thousand dollars is every cent I can manage, on my word of honor. Of course, sir, you understand that is simply the first payment. Later—"

Spade laughed. "I know you'll give me millions later," he said, "but let's stick to this first payment now. Fifteen thousand?"

Gutman smiled and frowned and shook his head. "Mr. Spade, I've told you frankly and candidly and on my word of honor as a gentleman that ten thousand dollars is all the money I've got—every penny—and all I can raise."

"But you didn't say positively."

Gutman laughed and said: "Positively."

Spade said gloomily: "That's not any too good, but if it's the best you can do—give it to me."

Gutman handed him the envelope. Spade counted the bills and was putting them in his pocket when Brigid O'Shaughnessy came in carrying a tray.

The boy would not eat. Cairo took a cup of coffee. The girl, Gutman, and Spade ate the scrambled eggs, bacon, toast, and marmalade she had prepared, and drank two cups of coffee apiece. Then they settled down to wait the rest of the night through.

Gutman smoked a cigar and read *Celebrated Criminal Cases of America*, now and then chuckling over or commenting on the parts of its contents that amused him. Cairo nursed his mouth and sulked on his end of the sofa. The boy sat with his head in his hands until a little after four o'clock. Then he lay down with his feet towards Cairo, turned his face to the window, and went to sleep. Brigid O'Shaughnessy, in the armchair, dozed, listened to the fat man's comments, and carried on wide-spaced desultory conversations with Spade.

Spade rolled and smoked cigarettes and moved, without fidgeting or nervousness, around the room. He sat sometimes on an arm of the girl's chair, on the table-corner, on the floor at her feet, on a straight-backed chair. He was wide-awake, cheerful, and full of vigor.

At half-past five he went into the kitchen and made more coffee. Half an hour later the boy stirred, awakened, and sat up yawning. Gutman looked at his watch and questioned Spade: "Can you get it now?"

"Give me another hour."

Gutman nodded and went back to his book.

At seven o'clock Spade went to the telephone and called Effie Perine's number. "Hello, Mrs. Perine? . . . This is Mr. Spade. Will you let me talk to Effie, please? . . . Yes, it is. . . . Thanks." He whistled two lines of *En Cuba*, softly. "Hello, angel. Sorry to get you up. . . . Yes, very. Here's the plot: in our Holland box at the Post Office you'll find an envelope addressed in my scribble. There's a Pickwick Stage parcel-room-check in it—for the bundle we got yesterday. Will you get the bundle and bring it to me—p.d.q.? . . . Yes, I'm home. . . . That's the girl—hustle. . . . 'Bye."

The street-door-bell rang at ten minutes of eight. Spade went to the telephone-box and pressed the button that released the lock. Gutman put down his book and rose smiling. "You don't mind if I go to the door with you?" he asked.

"OK," Spade told him.

Gutman followed him to the corridor-door. Spade opened it. Presently Effie Perine, carrying the brown-wrapped parcel, came from the elevator. Her boyish face was gay and bright and she came forward quickly, almost trotting. After one glance she did not look at Gutman. She smiled at Spade and gave him the parcel.

He took it saying: "Thanks a lot, lady. I'm sorry to spoil your day of rest, but this—"

"It's not the first one you've spoiled," she replied, laughing, and then, when it was apparent that he was not going to invite her in, asked: "Anything else?"

He shook his head. "No, thanks."

She said, "Bye-bye," and went back to the elevator.

Spade shut the door and carried the parcel into the living-room. Gutman's face was red and his cheeks quivered. Cairo and Brigid O'Shaughnessy came to the table as Spade put the parcel there. They were excited. The boy rose, pale and tense, but he remained by the sofa, staring under curling lashes at the others.

Spade stepped back from the table saying: "There you are."

Gutman's fat fingers made short work of cord and paper and excelsior, and he had the black bird in his hands. "Ah," he said huskily, "now, after seventeen years!" His eyes were moist.

Cairo licked his red lips and worked his hands together. The girl's lower lip was between her teeth. She and Cairo, like Gutman, and like Spade and the boy, were breathing heavily. The air in the room was chilly and stale, and thick with tobacco smoke.

Gutman set the bird down on the table again and fumbled at a pocket. "It's it," he said, "but we'll make sure." Sweat glistened on his round cheeks. His fingers twitched as he took out a gold pocket-knife and opened it.

Cairo and the girl stood close to him, one on either side. Spade stood back a little where he could watch the boy as well as the group at the table.

Gutman turned the bird upside-down and scraped an edge of its base with his knife. Black enamel came off in tiny curls, exposing blackened metal beneath. Gutman's knife-blade bit into the metal, turning back a thin curved shaving. The inside of the shaving, and the narrow plane its removal had left, had the soft grey sheen of lead.

Gutman's breath hissed between his teeth. His face became turgid with hot blood. He twisted the bird around and hacked at its head. There too the edge of his knife bared lead. He let knife and bird bang down on the table while he wheeled to confront Spade. "It's a fake," he said hoarsely.

Spade's face had become somber. His nod was slow, but there was no slowness in his hand's going out to catch Brigid O'Shaughnessy's wrist. He pulled her to him and grasped her chin with his other hand, raising her face roughly. "All right," he growled into her face. "You've had *your* little joke. Now tell us about it."

She cried: "No, Sam, no! That is the one I got from Kemidov. I swear—"

Joel Cairo thrust himself between Spade and Gutman and began to emit words in a shrill spluttering stream: "That's it! That's it! It was the Russian! I should have known! What a fool we thought him, and what fools he made of us!" Tears ran down the Levantine's cheeks and he danced up and down. "You bungled it!" he screamed at Gutman. "You and your stupid attempt to buy it from him! You fat fool! You let him know it was valuable and he found out how valuable and made a duplicate for us! No wonder we had so little trouble stealing it! No wonder he was so willing to send me off around the world looking for it! You imbecile! You bloated idiot!" He put his hands to his face and blubbered.

Gutman's jaw sagged. He blinked vacant eyes. Then he shook himself and was—by the time his bulbs had stopped jouncing—again a jovial fat man. "Come, sir," he said good-naturedly, "there's no need of going on like that. Everybody errs at times and you may be sure this is every bit as severe a blow to me as to anyone else. Yes, that is the Russian's hand, there's no doubt of it. Well, sir, what do you suggest? Shall we stand here and shed tears and call each other names? Or shall we"—he paused and his smile was a cherub's—"go to Constantinople?"

Cairo took his hands from his face and his eyes bulged. He stammered: "You are—?" Amazement coming with full comprehension made him speechless.

Gutman patted his fat hands together. His eyes twinkled. His voice was a complacent throaty purring: "For seventeen

years I have wanted that little item and have been trying to
get it. If I must spend another year on the quest—well, sir—
that will be an additional expenditure in time of only"—his
lips moved silently as he calculated—"five and fifteen-seven-
teenths per cent."

The Levantine giggled and cried: "I go with you!"

Spade suddenly released the girl's wrist and looked around
the room. The boy was not there. Spade went into the passageway. The corridor-door stood open. Spade made a dissatisfied mouth, shut the door, and returned to the living-room.
He leaned against the door-frame and looked at Gutman and
Cairo. He looked at Gutman for a long time, sourly. Then he
spoke, mimicking the fat man's throaty purr: "Well, sir, I
must say you're a swell lot of thieves!"

Gutman chuckled. "We've little enough to boast about,
and that's a fact, sir," he said. "But, well, we're none of us
dead yet and there's not a bit of use thinking the world's
come to an end just because we've run into a little setback."
He brought his left hand from behind him and held it out towards Spade, pink smooth hilly palm up. "I'll have to ask you
for that envelope, sir."

Spade did not move. His face was wooden. He said: "I held
up my end. You got your dingus. It's your hard luck, not
mine, that it wasn't what you wanted."

"Now come, sir," Gutman said persuasively, "we've all
failed and there's no reason for expecting any one of us to
bear the brunt of it, and—" He brought his right hand from
behind him. In the hand was a small pistol, an ornately engraved and inlaid affair of silver and gold and mother-of-pearl.
"In short, sir, I must ask you to return my ten thousand
dollars."

Spade's face did not change. He shrugged and took the envelope from his pocket. He started to hold it out to Gutman,
hesitated, opened the envelope, and took out one thousand-
dollar bill. He put that bill into his trousers-pocket. He
tucked the envelope's flap in over the other bills and held
them out to Gutman. "That'll take care of my time and expenses," he said.

Gutman, after a little pause, imitated Spade's shrug and accepted the envelope. He said: "Now, sir, we will say good-bye

to you, unless"—the fat puffs around his eyes crinkled—"you care to undertake the Constantinople expedition with us. You don't? Well, sir, frankly I'd like to have you along. You're a man to my liking, a man of many resources and nice judgment. Because we know you're a man of nice judgment we know we can say good-bye with every assurance that you'll hold the details of our little enterprise in confidence. We know we can count on you to appreciate the fact that, as the situation now stands, any legal difficulties that come to us in connection with these last few days would likewise and equally come to you and the charming Miss O'Shaughnessy. You're too shrewd not to recognize that, sir, I'm sure."

"I understand that," Spade replied.

"I was sure you would. I'm also sure that, now there's no alternative, you'll somehow manage the police without a fall-guy."

"I'll make out all right," Spade replied.

"I was sure you would. Well, sir, the shortest farewells are the best. Adieu." He made a portly bow. "And to you, Miss O'Shaughnessy, adieu. I leave you the *rara avis* on the table as a little memento."

CHAPTER XX

If They Hang You

F OR ALL of five minutes after the outer door had closed behind Casper Gutman and Joel Cairo, Spade, motionless,
stood staring at the knob of the open living-room-door. His
eyes were gloomy under a forehead drawn down. The clefts at
the root of his nose were deep and red. His lips protruded
loosely, pouting. He drew them in to make a hard v and went
to the telephone. He had not looked at Brigid O'Shaughnessy,
who stood by the table looking with uneasy eyes at him.

He picked up the telephone, set it on its shelf again, and
bent to look into the telephone-directory hanging from a corner of the shelf. He turned the pages rapidly until he found
the one he wanted, ran his finger down a column, straightened up, and lifted the telephone from the shelf again. He
called a number and said:

"Hello, is Sergeant Polhaus there? . . . Will you call him,
please? This is Samuel Spade. . . ." He stared into space,
waiting. "Hello, Tom, I've got something for you. . . . Yes,
plenty. Here it is: Thursby and Jacobi were shot by a kid
named Wilmer Cook." He described the boy minutely. "He's
working for a man named Casper Gutman." He described
Gutman. "That fellow Cairo you met here is in with them
too. . . . Yes, that's it. . . . Gutman's staying at the
Alexandria, suite twelve C, or was. They've just left here and
and they're blowing town, so you'll have to move fast, but I
don't think they're expecting a pinch. . . . There's a girl in it
too—Gutman's daughter." He described Rhea Gutman.
"Watch yourself when you go up against the kid. He's supposed to be pretty good with the gun. . . . That's right,
Tom, and I've got some stuff here for you. I think I've got
the guns he used. . . . That's right. Step on it—and luck to
you!"

Spade slowly replaced receiver on prong, telephone on
shelf. He wet his lips and looked down at his hands. Their
palms were wet. He filled his deep chest with air. His eyes

were glittering between straightened lids. He turned and took three long swift steps into the living-room.

Brigid O'Shaughnessy, startled by the suddenness of his approach, let her breath out in a little laughing gasp.

Spade, face to face with her, very close to her, tall, big-boned and thick-muscled, coldly smiling, hard of jaw and eye, said: "They'll talk when they're nailed—about us. We're sitting on dynamite, and we've only got minutes to get set for the police. Give me all of it—fast. Gutman sent you and Cairo to Constantinople?"

She started to speak, hesitated, and bit her lip.

He put a hand on her shoulder. "God damn you, talk!" he said. "I'm in this with you and you're not going to gum it. Talk. He sent you to Constantinople?"

"Y-yes, he sent me. I met Joe there and—and asked him to help me. Then we—"

"Wait. You asked Cairo to help you get it from Kemidov?"

"Yes."

"For Gutman?"

She hesitated again, squirmed under the hard angry glare of his eyes, swallowed, and said: "No, not then. We thought we would get it for ourselves."

"All right. Then?"

"Oh, then I began to be afraid that Joe wouldn't play fair with me, so—so I asked Floyd Thursby to help me."

"And he did. Well?"

"Well, we got it and went to Hongkong."

"With Cairo? Or had you ditched him before that?"

"Yes. We left him in Constantinople, in jail—something about a check."

"Something you fixed up to hold him there?"

She looked shamefacedly at Spade and whispered: "Yes."

"Right. Now you and Thursby are in Hongkong with the bird."

"Yes, and then—I didn't know him very well—I didn't know whether I could trust him. I thought it would be safer —anyway, I met Captain Jacobi and I knew his boat was coming here, so I asked him to bring a package for me—and that was the bird. I wasn't sure I could trust Thursby, or that Joe or—or somebody working for Gutman might not be on the boat we came on—and that seemed the safest plan."

"All right. Then you and Thursby caught one of the fast boats over. Then what?"

"Then—then I was afraid of Gutman. I knew he had people—connections—everywhere, and he'd soon know what we had done. And I was afraid he'd have learned that we had left Hongkong for San Francisco. He was in New York and I knew if he heard that by cable he would have plenty of time to get here by the time we did, or before. He did. I didn't know that then, but I was afraid of it, and I had to wait here until Captain Jacobi's boat arrived. And I was afraid Gutman would find me—or find Floyd and buy him over. That's why I came to you and asked you to watch him for—"

"That's a lie," Spade said. "You had Thursby hooked and you knew it. He was a sucker for women. His record shows that—the only falls he took were over women. And once a chump, always a chump. Maybe you didn't know his record, but you'd know you had him safe."

She blushed and looked timidly at him.

He said: "You wanted to get him out of the way before Jacobi came with the loot. What was your scheme?"

"I—I knew he'd left the States with a gambler after some trouble. I didn't know what it was, but I thought that if it was anything serious and he saw a detective watching him he'd think it was on account of the old trouble, and would be frightened into going away. I didn't think—"

"You told him he was being shadowed," Spade said confidently. "Miles hadn't many brains, but he wasn't clumsy enough to be spotted the first night."

"I told him, yes. When we went out for a walk that night I pretended to discover Mr. Archer following us and pointed him out to Floyd." She sobbed. "But please believe, Sam, that I wouldn't have done it if I had thought Floyd would kill him. I thought he'd be frightened into leaving the city. I didn't for a minute think he'd shoot him like that."

Spade smiled wolfishly with his lips, but not at all with his eyes. He said: "If you thought he wouldn't you were right, angel."

The girl's upraised face held utter astonishment.

Spade said: "Thursby didn't shoot him."

Incredulity joined astonishment in the girl's face.

Spade said: "Miles hadn't many brains, but, Christ! he had too many years' experience as a detective to be caught like that by the man he was shadowing. Up a blind alley with his gun tucked away on his hip and his overcoat buttoned? Not a chance. He was as dumb as any man ought to be, but he wasn't quite that dumb. The only two ways out of the alley could be watched from the edge of Bush Street over the tunnel. You'd told us Thursby was a bad actor. He couldn't have tricked Miles into the alley like that, and he couldn't have driven him in. He was dumb, but not dumb enough for that."

He ran his tongue over the inside of his lips and smiled affectionately at the girl. He said: "But he'd've gone up there with you, angel, if he was sure nobody else was up there. You were his client, so he would have had no reason for not dropping the shadow on your say-so, and if you caught up with him and asked him to go up there he'd've gone. He was just dumb enough for that. He'd've looked you up and down and licked his lips and gone grinning from ear to ear—and then you could've stood as close to him as you liked in the dark and put a hole through him with the gun you had got from Thursby that evening."

Brigid O'Shaughnessy shrank back from him until the edge of the table stopped her. She looked at him with terrified eyes and cried: "Don't—don't talk to me like that, Sam! You know I didn't! You know—"

"Stop it." He looked at the watch on his wrist. "The police will be blowing in any minute now and we're sitting on dynamite. Talk!"

She put the back of a hand on her forehead. "Oh, why do you accuse me of such a terrible—?"

"Will you stop it?" he demanded in a low impatient voice. "This isn't the spot for the schoolgirl-act. Listen to me. The pair of us are sitting under the gallows." He took hold of her wrists and made her stand up straight in front of him. "Talk!"

"I—I— How did you know he—he licked his lips and looked—?"

Spade laughed harshly. "I knew Miles. But never mind that. Why did you shoot him?"

She twisted her wrists out of Spade's fingers and put her hands up around the back of his neck, pulling his head down until his mouth all but touched hers. Her body was flat against his from knees to chest. He put his arms around her, holding her tight to him. Her dark-lashed lids were half down over velvet eyes. Her voice was hushed, throbbing: "I didn't mean to, at first. I didn't, really. I meant what I told you, but when I saw Floyd couldn't be frightened I—"

Spade slapped her shoulder. He said: "That's a lie. You asked Miles and me to handle it ourselves. You wanted to be sure the shadower was somebody you knew and who knew you, so they'd go with you. You got the gun from Thursby that day—that night. You had already rented the apartment at the Coronet. You had trunks there and none at the hotel and when I looked the apartment over I found a rent-receipt dated five or six days before the time you told me you rented it."

She swallowed with difficulty and her voice was humble. "Yes, that's a lie, Sam. I did intend to if Floyd— I—I can't look at you and tell you this, Sam." She pulled his head farther down until her cheek was against his cheek, her mouth by his ear, and whispered: "I knew Floyd wouldn't be easily frightened, but I thought that if he knew somebody was shadowing him either he'd— Oh, I can't say it, Sam!" She clung to him, sobbing.

Spade said: "You thought Floyd would tackle him and one or the other of them would go down. If Thursby was the one then you were rid of him. If Miles was, then you could see that Floyd was caught and you'd be rid of him. That it?"

"S-something like that."

"And when you found that Thursby didn't mean to tackle him you borrowed the gun and did it yourself. Right?"

"Yes—though not exactly."

"But exact enough. And you had that plan up your sleeve from the first. You thought Floyd would be nailed for the killing."

"I—I thought they'd hold him at least until after Captain Jacobi had arrived with the falcon and—"

"And you didn't know then that Gutman was here hunting for you. You didn't suspect that or you wouldn't have shaken your gunman. You knew Gutman was here as soon as you heard Thursby had been shot. Then you knew you needed another protector, so you came back to me. Right?"

"Yes, but—oh, sweetheart!—it wasn't only that. I would have come back to you sooner or later. From the first instant I saw you I knew—"

Spade said tenderly: "You angel! Well, if you get a good break you'll be out of San Quentin in twenty years and you can come back to me then."

She took her cheek away from his, drawing her head far back to stare up without comprehension at him.

He was pale. He said tenderly: "I hope to Christ they don't hang you, precious, by that sweet neck." He slid his hands up to caress her throat.

In an instant she was out of his arms, back against the table, crouching, both hands spread over her throat. Her face was wild-eyed, haggard. Her dry mouth opened and closed. She said in a small parched voice: "You're not—" She could get no other words out.

Spade's face was yellow-white now. His mouth smiled and there were smile-wrinkles around his glittering eyes. His voice was soft, gentle. He said: "I'm going to send you over. The chances are you'll get off with life. That means you'll be out again in twenty years. You're an angel. I'll wait for you." He cleared his throat. "If they hang you I'll always remember you."

She dropped her hands and stood erect. Her face became smooth and untroubled except for the faintest of dubious glints in her eyes. She smiled back at him, gently. "Don't, Sam, don't say that even in fun. Oh, you frightened me for a moment! I really thought you— You know you do such wild and unpredictable things that—" She broke off. She thrust her face forward and stared deep into his eyes. Her cheeks and the flesh around her mouth shivered and fear came back into her eyes. "What—? Sam!" She put her hands to her throat again and lost her erectness.

Spade laughed. His yellow-white face was damp with sweat and though he held his smile he could not hold softness in his voice. He croaked: "Don't be silly. You're taking the fall. One of us has got to take it, after the talking those birds will do. They'd hang me sure. You're likely to get a better break. Well?"

"But—but, Sam, you can't! Not after what we've been to each other. You can't—"

"Like hell I can't."

She took a long trembling breath. "You've been playing with me? Only pretending you cared—to trap me like this? You didn't—care at all? You didn't—don't—l-love me?"

"I think I do," Spade said. "What of it?" The muscles holding his smile in place stood out like wales. "I'm not Thursby. I'm not Jacobi. I won't play the sap for you."

"That is not just," she cried. Tears came to her eyes. "It's unfair. It's contemptible of you. You know it was not that. You can't say that."

"Like hell I can't," Spade said. "You came into my bed to stop me asking questions. You led me out yesterday for Gutman with that phoney call for help. Last night you came here with them and waited outside for me and came in with me. You were in my arms when the trap was sprung—I couldn't have gone for a gun if I'd had one on me and couldn't have made a fight of it if I had wanted to. And if they didn't take you away with them it was only because Gutman's got too much sense to trust you except for short stretches when he has to and because he thought I'd play the sap for you and—not wanting to hurt you—wouldn't be able to hurt him."

Brigid O'Shaughnessy blinked her tears away. She took a step towards him and stood looking him in the eyes, straight and proud. "You called me a liar," she said. "Now you are lying. You're lying if you say you don't know down in your heart that, in spite of anything I've done, I love you."

Spade made a short abrupt bow. His eyes were becoming bloodshot, but there was no other change in his damp and yellowish fixedly smiling face. "Maybe I do," he said. "What of it? I should trust you? You who arranged that nice little trick for—for my predecessor, Thursby? You who knocked off Miles, a man you had nothing against, in cold blood, just like swatting a fly, for the sake of double-crossing Thursby? You who double-crossed Gutman, Cairo, Thursby—one, two, three? You who've never played square with me for half an hour at a stretch since I've known you? I should trust you? No, no, darling. I wouldn't do it even if I could. Why should I?"

Her eyes were steady under his and her hushed voice was steady when she replied: "Why should you? If you've been playing with me, if you do not love me, there is no answer to that. If you did, no answer would be needed."

Blood streaked Spade's eyeballs now and his long-held smile had become a frightful grimace. He cleared his throat huskily and said: "Making speeches is no damned good now." He put a hand on her shoulder. The hand shook and jerked. "I don't care who loves who. I'm not going to play the sap for you. I won't walk in Thursby's and Christ knows who else's footsteps. You killed Miles and you're going over for it. I could have helped you by letting the others go and standing off the police the best way I could. It's too late for that now. I can't help you now. And I wouldn't if I could."

She put a hand on his hand on her shoulder. "Don't help me then," she whispered, "but don't hurt me. Let me go away now."

"No," he said. "I'm sunk if I haven't got you to hand over to the police when they come. That's the only thing that can keep me from going down with the others."

"You won't do that for me?"

"I won't play the sap for you."

"Don't say that, please." She took his hand from her shoulder and held it to her face. "Why must you do this to me, Sam? Surely Mr. Archer wasn't as much to you as—"

"Miles," Spade said hoarsely, "was a son of a bitch. I found that out the first week we were in business together and I meant to kick him out as soon as the year was up. You didn't do me a damned bit of harm by killing him."

"Then what?"

Spade pulled his hand out of hers. He no longer either smiled or grimaced. His wet yellow face was set hard and deeply lined. His eyes burned madly. He said: "Listen. This isn't a damned bit of good. You'll never understand me, but I'll try once more and then we'll give it up. Listen. When a man's partner is killed he's supposed to do something about it. It doesn't make any difference what you thought of him. He was your partner and you're supposed to do something about it. Then it happens we were in the detective business. Well, when one of your organization gets killed it's bad business to let the killer get away with it. It's bad all around—bad for that one organization, bad for every detective everywhere. Third, I'm a detective and expecting me to run criminals down and then let them go free is like asking a dog to catch a rabbit and let it go. It can be done, all right, and sometimes it is done, but it's not the natural thing. The only way I could have let you go was by letting Gutman and Cairo and the kid go. That's—"

"You're not serious," she said. "You don't expect me to think that these things you're saying are sufficient reason for sending me to the—"

"Wait till I'm through and then you can talk. Fourth, no matter what I wanted to do now it would be absolutely impossible for me to let you go without having myself dragged to the gallows with the others. Next, I've no reason in God's world to think I can trust you and if I did this and got away with it you'd have something on me that you could use whenever you happened to want to. That's five of them. The sixth would be that, since I've also got something on you, I couldn't be sure you wouldn't decide to shoot a hole in *me* some day. Seventh, I don't even like the idea of thinking that there might be one chance in a hundred that you'd played me for a sucker. And eighth—but that's enough. All those on one side. Maybe some of them are unimportant. I won't argue about that. But look at the number of them. Now on the other side we've got what? All we've got is the fact that maybe you love me and maybe I love you."

"You know," she whispered, "whether you do or not."

"I don't. It's easy enough to be nuts about you." He looked hungrily from her hair to her feet and up to her eyes again. "But I don't know what that amounts to. Does anybody ever? But suppose I do? What of it? Maybe next month I won't. I've been through it before—when it lasted that long. Then what? Then I'll think I played the sap. And if I did it and got sent over then I'd be sure I was the sap. Well, if I send you over I'll be sorry as hell—I'll have some rotten nights—but that'll pass. Listen." He took her by the shoulders and bent her back, leaning over her. "If that doesn't mean anything to you forget it and we'll make it this: I won't because all of me wants to—wants to say to hell with the consequences and do it—and because—God damn you—you've counted on that with me the same as you counted on that with the others." He took his hands from her shoulders and let them fall to his sides.

She put her hands up to his cheeks and drew his face down again. "Look at me," she said, "and tell me the truth. Would you have done this to me if the falcon had been real and you had been paid your money?"

"What difference does that make now? Don't be too sure I'm as crooked as I'm supposed to be. That kind of reputation might be good business—bringing in high-priced jobs and making it easier to deal with the enemy."

She looked at him, saying nothing.

He moved his shoulders a little and said: "Well, a lot of money would have been at least one more item on the other side of the scales."

She put her face up to his face. Her mouth was slightly open with lips a little thrust out. She whispered: "If you loved me you'd need nothing more on that side."

Spade set the edges of his teeth together and said through them: "I won't play the sap for you."

She put her mouth to his, slowly, her arms around him, and came into his arms. She was in his arms when the door-bell rang.

Spade, left arm around Brigid O'Shaughnessy, opened the corridor-door. Lieutenant Dundy, Detective-sergeant Tom Polhaus, and two other detectives were there.

Spade said: "Hello, Tom. Get them?"

Polhaus said: "Got them.'

"Swell. Come in. Here's another one for you." Spade pressed the girl forward. "She killed Miles. And I've got some exhibits—the boy's guns, one of Cairo's, a black statuette that all the hell was about, and a thousand-dollar bill that I was supposed to be bribed with." He looked at Dundy, drew his brows together, leaned forward to peer into the Lieutenant's face, and burst out laughing. "What in hell's the matter with your little playmate, Tom? He looks heartbroken." He laughed again. "I bet, by God! when he heard Gutman's story he thought he had me at last."

"Cut it out, Sam," Tom grumbled. "We didn't think—"

"Like hell he didn't," Spade said merrily. "He came up here with his mouth watering, though you'd have sense enough to know I'd been stringing Gutman."

"Cut it out," Tom grumbled again, looking uneasily side-wise at his superior. "Anyways we got it from Cairo. Gutman's dead. The kid had just finished shooting him up when we got there."

Spade nodded. "He ought to have expected that," he said.

Effie Perine put down her newspaper and jumped out of Spade's chair when he came into the office at a little after nine o'clock Monday morning.

He said: "Morning, angel."

"Is that—what the papers have—right?" she asked.

"Yes, ma'am." He dropped his hat on the desk and sat down. His face was pasty in color, but its lines were strong and cheerful and his eyes, though still somewhat red-veined, were clear.

The girl's brown eyes were peculiarly enlarged and there was a queer twist to her mouth. She stood beside him, staring down at him.

He raised his head, grinned, and said mockingly: "So much for your woman's intuition."

Her voice was queer as the expression on her face. "You did that, Sam, to her?"

He nodded. "Your Sam's a detective." He looked sharply at her. He put his arm around her waist, his hand on her hip. "She did kill Miles, angel," he said gently, "offhand, like that." He snapped the fingers of his other hand.

She escaped from his arm as if it had hurt her. "Don't, please, don't touch me," she said brokenly. "I know—I know you're right. You're right. But don't touch me now—not now."

Spade's face became pale as his collar.

The corridor-door's knob rattled. Effie Perine turned

quickly and went into the outer office, shutting the door behind her. When she came in again she shut it behind her.

She said in a small flat voice: "Iva is here."

Spade, looking down at his desk, nodded almost impercep-
tibly. "Yes," he said, and shivered. "Well, send her in."

THE GLASS KEY

CONTENTS

CHAPTER I

The Body in China Street

GREEN DICE rolled across the green table, struck the rim together, and bounced back. One stopped short holding six white spots in two equal rows uppermost. The other tumbled out to the center of the table and came to rest with a single spot on top.

Ned Beaumont grunted softly—"Uhn!"—and the winners cleared the table of money.

Harry Sloss picked up the dice and rattled them in a pale broad hairy hand. "Shoot two bits." He dropped a twenty-dollar bill and a five-dollar bill on the table.

Ned Beaumont stepped back saying: "Get on him, gamblers, I've got to refuel." He crossed the billiard-room to the door. There he met Walter Ivans coming in. He said, "'Lo, Walt," and would have gone on, but Ivans caught his elbow as he passed and turned to face him.

"D-d-did you t-talk to P-p-paul?" When Ivans said "P-p-paul" a fine spray flew out between his lips.

"I'm going up to see him now." Ivans's china-blue eyes brightened in his round fair face until Ned Beaumont, narrow of eye, added: "Don't expect much. If you could wait awhile."

Ivans's chin twitched. "B-b-but she's going to have the b-b-baby next month."

A startled look came into Ned Beaumont's dark eyes. He took his arm out of the shorter man's hand and stepped back. Then a corner of his mouth twitched under his dark mustache and he said: "It's a bad time, Walt, and—well—you'll save yourself disappointment by not looking for much before November." His eyes were narrow again and watchful.

"B-b-but if you t-tell him—"

"I'll put it to him as hot as I can and you ought to know he'll go the limit, but he's in a tough spot right now." He moved his shoulders and his face became gloomy except for the watchful brightness of his eyes.

Ivans wet his lips and blinked his eyes many times. He drew

in a long breath and patted Ned Beaumont's chest with both hands. "G-g-go up now," he said in an urgent pleading voice. "I-I'll wait here f-for you."

II

Ned Beaumont went upstairs lighting a thin green-dappled cigar. At the second-floor landing, where the Governor's portrait hung, he turned towards the front of the building and knocked on the broad oaken door that shut off the corridor at that end.

When he heard Paul Madvig's "All right" he opened the door and went in.

Paul Madvig was alone in the room, standing at the window, with his hands in his trousers-pockets, his back to the door, looking through the screen down into dark China Street.

He turned around slowly and said: "Oh, here you are." He was a man of forty-five, tall as Ned Beaumont, but forty pounds heavier without softness. His hair was light, parted in the middle, and brushed flat to his head. His face was handsome in a ruddy stout-featured way. His clothes were saved from flashiness by their quality and by his manner of wearing them.

Ned Beaumont shut the door and said: "Lend me some money."

From his inner coat-pocket Madvig took a large brown wallet. "What do you want?"

"Couple of hundred."

Madvig gave him a hundred-dollar bill and five twenties, asking: "Craps?"

"Thanks." Ned Beaumont pocketed the money. "Yes."

"It's a long time since you've done any winning, isn't it?" Madvig asked as he returned his hands to his trousers-pockets.

"Not so long—a month or six weeks."

Madvig smiled. "That's a long time to be losing."

"Not for me." There was a faint note of irritation in Ned Beaumont's voice.

Madvig rattled coins in his pocket. "Much of a game

tonight?" He sat on a corner of the table and looked down at his glistening brown shoes.

Ned Beaumont looked curiously at the blond man, then shook his head and said: "Peewee." He walked to the window. Above the buildings on the opposite side of the street the sky was black and heavy. He went behind Madvig to the telephone and called a number. "Hello, Bernie. This is Ned. What's the price on Peggy O'Toole? . . . Is that all? . . . Well, give me five hundred of each. . . . Sure. . . . I'm betting it's going to rain and if it does she'll beat Incinerator. . . . All right, give me a better price then. . . . Right." He put the receiver on its prong and came around in front of Madvig again.

Madvig asked: "Why don't you try laying off awhile when you hit one of these sour streaks?"

Ned Beaumont scowled. "That's no good, only spreads it out. I ought to've put that fifteen hundred on the nose instead of spreading it across the board. Might as well take your punishment and get it over with."

Madvig chuckled and raised his head to say: "If you can stand the gaff."

Ned Beaumont drew down the ends of his mouth, the ends of his mustache following them down. "I can stand anything I've got to stand," he said as he moved towards the door.

He had his hand on the door-knob when Madvig said, earnestly: "I guess you can, at that, Ned."

Ned Beaumont turned around and asked, "Can what?" fretfully.

Madvig transferred his gaze to the window. "Can stand anything," he said.

Ned Beaumont studied Madvig's averted face. The blond man stirred uncomfortably and moved coins in his pockets again. Ned Beaumont made his eyes blank and asked in an utterly puzzled tone: "Who?"

Madvig's face flushed. He rose from the table and took a step towards Ned Beaumont. "You go to hell," he said.

Ned Beaumont laughed.

Madvig grinned sheepishly and wiped his face with a green-bordered handkerchief. "Why haven't you been out to the house?" he asked. "Mom was saying last night she hadn't seen you for a month."

"Maybe I'll drop in some night this week."

"You ought to. You know how Mom likes you. Come for supper." Madvig put his handkerchief away.

Ned Beaumont moved towards the door again, slowly, watching the blond man from the ends of his eyes. With his hand on the knob he asked: "Was that what you wanted to see me about?"

Madvig frowned. "Yes, that is—" He cleared his throat. "Uh—oh—there's something else." Suddenly his diffidence was gone, leaving him apparently tranquil and self-possessed. "You know more about this stuff than I do. Miss Henry's birthday's Thursday. What do you think I ought to give her?"

Ned Beaumont took his hand from the door-knob. His eyes, by the time he was facing Madvig squarely again, had lost their shocked look. He blew cigar-smoke out and asked: "They're having some kind of birthday doings, aren't they?"

"Yes."

"You invited?"

Madvig shook his head. "But I'm going there to dinner to-morrow night."

Ned Beaumont looked down at his cigar, then up at Madvig's face again, and asked: "Are you going to back the Senator, Paul?"

"I think we will."

Ned Beaumont's smile was mild as his voice when he put his next question: "Why?"

Madvig smiled. "Because with us behind him he'll snow Roan under and with his help we can put over the whole ticket just like nobody was running against us."

Ned Beaumont put his cigar in his mouth. He asked, still mildly: "Without you"—he stressed the pronoun—"behind him could the Senator make the grade this time?"

Madvig was calmly positive. "Not a chance."

Ned Beaumont, after a little pause, asked: "Does he know that?"

"He ought to know it better than anybody else. And if he didn't know it— What the hell's the matter with you?"

Ned Beaumont's laugh was a sneer. "If he didn't know it,"

he suggested, "you wouldn't be going there to dinner to-morrow night?"

Madvig, frowning, asked again: "What the hell's the matter with you?"

Ned Beaumont took the cigar from his mouth. His teeth had bitten the end of it into shredded ruin. He said: "There's nothing the matter with me." He put thoughtful-ness on his face: "You don't think the rest of the ticket needs his support?"

"Support's something no ticket can get too much of," Madvig replied carelessly, "but without his help we could manage to hold up our end all right."

"Have you promised him anything yet?"

Madvig pursed his lips. "It's pretty well settled."

Ned Beaumont lowered his head until he was looking up under his brows at the blond man. His face had become pale. "Throw him down, Paul," he said in a low husky voice. "Sink him."

Madvig put his fists on his hips and exclaimed softly and in-credulously: "Well, I'll be damned!"

Ned Beaumont walked past Madvig and with unsteady thin fingers mashed the burning end of his cigar in the hammered copper basin on the table.

Madvig stared at the younger man's back until he straight-ened and turned. Then the blond man grinned at him with affection and exasperation. "What gets into you, Ned?" he complained. "You go along fine for just so long and then for no reason at all you throw an ing-bing. I'll be a dirty so-and-so if I can make you out!"

Ned Beaumont made a grimace of distaste. He said, "All right, forget it," and immediately returned to the attack with a skeptical question: "Do you think he'll play ball with you after he's re-elected?"

Madvig was not worried. "I can handle him."

"Maybe, but don't forget he's never been licked at any-thing in his life."

Madvig nodded in complete agreement. "Sure, and that's one of the best reasons I know for throwing in with him."

"No, it isn't, Paul," Ned Beaumont said earnestly. "It's the very worst. Think that over even if it hurts your head. How far has this dizzy blonde daughter of his got her hooks into you?"

Madvig said: "I'm going to marry Miss Henry."

Ned Beaumont made a whistling mouth, though he did not whistle. He made his eyes smaller and asked: "Is that part of the bargain?"

Madvig grinned boyishly. "Nobody knows it yet," he replied, "except you and me."

Spots of color appeared in Ned Beaumont's lean cheeks. He smiled his nicest smile and said: "You can trust me not to go around bragging about it and here's a piece of advice. If that's what you want, make them put it in writing and swear to it before a notary and post a cash bond, or, better still, insist on the wedding before election-day. Then you'll at least be sure of your pound of flesh, or she'll weigh around a hundred and ten, won't she?"

Madvig shifted his feet. He avoided Ned Beaumont's gaze while saying: "I don't know why you keep talking about the Senator like he was a yegg. He's a gentleman and—"

"Absolutely. Read about it in the *Post*—one of the few aristocrats left in American politics. And his daughter's an aristocrat. That's why I'm warning you to sew your shirt on when you go to see them, or you'll come away without it, because to them you're a lower form of animal life and none of the rules apply."

Madvig sighed and began: "Aw, Ned, don't be so damned—"

But Ned Beaumont had remembered something. His eyes were shiny with malice. He said: "And we oughtn't to forget that young Taylor Henry's an aristocrat too, which is probably why you made Opal stop playing around with him. How's that going to work out when you marry his sister and he's your daughter's uncle-in-law or something? Will that entitle him to begin playing around with her again?"

Madvig yawned. "You didn't understand me right, Ned," he said. "I didn't ask for all this. I just asked you what kind of present I ought to give Miss Henry."

Ned Beaumont's face lost its animation, became a slightly sullen mask. "How far have you got with her?" he asked in a voice that expressed nothing of what he might have been thinking.

"Nowhere. I've been there maybe half a dozen times to talk to the Senator. Sometimes I see her and sometimes I don't, but only to say 'How do you do' or something with other people around. You know, I haven't had a chance to say anything to her yet."

Amusement glinted for a moment in Ned Beaumont's eyes and vanished. He brushed back one side of his mustache with a thumb-nail and asked: "Tomorrow's your first dinner there?"

"Yes, though I don't expect it to be the last."

"And you didn't get a bid to the birthday party?"

"No." Madvig hesitated. "Not yet."

"Then the answer's one you won't like."

Madvig's face was impassive. "Such as?" he asked.

"Don't give her anything."

"Oh, hell, Ned!"

Ned Beaumont shrugged. "Do whatever you like. You asked me."

"But why?"

"You're not supposed to give people things unless you're sure they'd like to get them from you."

"But everybody likes to—"

"Maybe, but it goes deeper than that. When you give somebody something, you're saying out loud that you know they'd like to have you give—"

"I got you," Madvig said. He rubbed his chin with fingers of his right hand. He frowned and said: "I guess you're right." His face cleared. He said: "But I'll be damned if I'll pass up the chance."

Ned Beaumont said quickly: "Well, flowers then, or something like that, might be all right."

"Flowers? Jesus! I wanted—"

"Sure, you wanted to give her a roadster or a couple of yards of pearls. You'll get your chance at that later. Start little and grow."

Madvig made a wry face. "I guess you're right, Ned. You know more about this kind of stuff than I do. Flowers it is."

"And not too many of them." Then, in the same breath: "Walt Ivans's telling the world you ought to spring his brother."

Madvig pulled the bottom of his vest down. "The world can tell him Tim's going to stay indoors till after election."

"You're going to let him stand trial?"

"I am," Madvig replied, and added with more heat: "You know damned well I can't help it, Ned. With everybody up for re-election and the woman's clubs on the war-path it would be jumping in the lake to have Tim's case squared now."

Ned Beaumont grinned crookedly at the blond man and made his voice drawl. "We didn't have to do much worrying about women's clubs before we joined the aristocracy."

"We do now." Madvig's eyes were opaque.

"Tim's wife's going to have a baby next month," Ned Beaumont said.

Madvig blew breath out in an impatient gust. "Anything to make it tougher," he complained. "Why don't they think of those things before they get in trouble? They've got no brains, none of them."

"They've got votes."

"That's the hell of it," Madvig growled. He glowered at the floor for a moment, then raised his head. "We'll take care of him as soon as the votes are counted, but nothing doing till then."

"That's not going over big with the boys," Ned Beaumont said, looking obliquely at the blond man. "Brains or no brains, they're used to being taken care of."

Madvig thrust his chin out a little. His eyes, round and opaquely blue, were fixed on Ned Beaumont's. In a soft voice he asked: "Well?"

Ned Beaumont smiled and kept his voice matter-of-fact. "You know it won't take a lot of this to start them saying it was different in the old days before you put in with the Senator."

"Yes?"

Ned Beaumont stood his ground with no change in voice or smile. "You know how little of this can start them saying Shad O'Rory still takes care of his boys."

Madvig, who had listened with an air of complete attentiveness, now said in a very deliberately quiet voice: "I know you won't start them talking like that, Ned, and I know I can count on you to do your best to stop any of that kind of talk you happen to hear."

For a moment after that they stood silent, looking eye into eye, and there was no change in the face of either. Ned Beaumont ended the silence. He said: "It might help some if we took care of Tim's wife and the kid."

"That's the idea." Madvig drew his chin back and his eyes lost their opaqueness. "Look after it, will you? Give them everything."

III

Walter Ivans was waiting for Ned Beaumont at the foot of the stairs, bright-eyed and hopeful. "Wh-what did he s-say?"

"It's what I told you: no can do. After election Tim's to have anything he needs to get out, but nothing stirring till then."

Walter Ivans hung his head and made a low growling noise in his chest.

Ned Beaumont put a hand on the shorter man's shoulder and said: "It's a tough break and nobody knows it better than Paul, but he can't help himself. He wants you to tell her not to pay any bills. Send them to him—rent, grocer, doctor, and hospital."

Walter Ivans jerked his head up and caught Ned Beaumont's hand in both of his. "B-by G-god that's white of him!" The china-blue eyes were wet. "B-b-but I wish he could g-get Tim out."

Ned Beaumont said, "Well, there's always a chance that something will come up to let him," freed his hand, said, "I'll be seeing you," and went around Ivans to the billiard-room door.

The billiard-room was deserted.

He got his hat and coat and went to the front door. Long oyster-colored lines of rain slanted down into China Street. He smiled and addressed the rain under his breath: "Come down, you little darlings, thirty-two hundred and fifty dollars' worth of you."

He went back and called a taxicab.

IV

Ned Beaumont took his hands away from the dead man and stood up. The dead man's head rolled a little to the left, away from the curb, so that his face lay fully in the light from the corner street-lamp. It was a young face and its expression of anger was increased by the dark ridge that ran diagonally across the forehead from the edge of the curly fair hair to an eyebrow.

Ned Beaumont looked up and down China Street. As far up the street as the eye could see no person was there. Two blocks down the street, in front of the Log Cabin Club, two men were getting out of an automobile. They left the automobile standing in front of the Club, facing Ned Beaumont, and went into the Club.

Ned Beaumont, after staring down at the automobile for several seconds, suddenly twisted his head around to look up the street again and then, with a swiftness that made both movements one continuous movement, whirled and sprang upon the sidewalk in the shadow of the nearest tree. He was breathing through his mouth and though tiny points of sweat had glistened on his hands in the light he shivered now and turned up the collar of his overcoat.

He remained in the tree's shadow with one hand on the tree for perhaps half a minute. Then he straightened abruptly and began to walk towards the Log Cabin Club. He walked with increasing swiftness, leaning forward, and was moving at something more than a half-trot when he spied a man coming up the other side of the street. He immediately slackened his pace and made himself walk erect. The man entered a house before he came opposite Ned Beaumont.

By the time Ned Beaumont reached the Club he had stopped breathing through his mouth. His lips were still somewhat faded. He looked at the empty automobile without pausing, climbed the Club's steps between the two lanterns, and went indoors.

Harry Sloss and another man were crossing the foyer from the cloak-room. They halted and said together: "Hello, Ned." Sloss added: "I hear you had Peggy O'Toole today."

"Yes."

"For much?"

"Thirty-two hundred."

Sloss ran his tongue over his lower lip. "That's nice. You ought to be set for a game tonight."

"Later, maybe. Paul in?"

"I don't know. We just got in. Don't make it too late: I promised the girl I'd be home early."

Ned Beaumont said, "Right," and went over to the cloak-room. "Paul in?" he asked the attendant.

"Yes, about ten minutes ago."

Ned Beaumont looked at his wrist-watch. It was half past ten. He went up to the front second-story room. Madvig in dinner clothes was sitting at the table with a hand stretched out towards the telephone when Ned Beaumont came in.

Madvig withdrew his hand and said: "How are you, Ned?" His large handsome face was ruddy and placid.

Ned Beaumont said, "I've been worse," while shutting the door behind him. He sat on a chair not far from Madvig's. "How'd the Henry dinner go?"

The skin at the corners of Madvig's eyes crinkled. "I've been at worse," he said.

Ned Beaumont was clipping the end of a pale spotted cigar. The shakiness of his hands was incongruous with the steadiness of his voice asking: "Was Taylor there?" He looked up at Madvig without raising his head.

"Not for dinner. Why?"

Ned Beaumont stretched out crossed legs, leaned back in his chair, moved the hand holding his cigar in a careless arc, and said: "He's dead in a gutter up the street."

Madvig, unruffled, asked: "Is that so?"

Ned Beaumont leaned forward. Muscles tightened in his lean face. The wrapper of his cigar broke between his fingers with a thin crackling sound. He asked irritably: "Did you understand what I said?"

Madvig nodded slowly.

"Well?"

"Well what?"

"He was killed."

"All right," Madvig said. "Do you want me to get hysterical about it?"

Ned Beaumont sat up straight in his chair and asked: "Shall I call the police?"

Madvig raised his eyebrows a little. "Don't they know it?"

Ned Beaumont was looking steadily at the blond man. He replied: "There was nobody around when I saw him. I wanted to see you before I did anything. Is it all right for me to say I found him?"

Madvig's eyebrows came down. "Why not?" he asked blankly.

Ned Beaumont rose, took two steps towards the telephone, halted, and faced the blond man again. He spoke with slow emphasis: "His hat wasn't there."

"He won't need it now." Then Madvig scowled and said: "You're a God-damned fool, Ned."

Ned Beaumont said, "One of us is," and went to the telephone.

v

TAYLOR HENRY MURDERED
BODY OF SENATOR'S SON FOUND IN CHINA STREET

Believed to have been the victim of a hold-up, Taylor Henry, 26, son of Senator Ralph Bancroft Henry, was found dead in China Street near the corner of Pamela Avenue at a few minutes after 10 o'clock last night.

Coroner William J. Hoops stated that young Henry's death was due to a fracture of the skull and concussion of the brain caused by hitting the back of his head against the edge of the curb after having been knocked down by a blow from a blackjack or other blunt instrument on his forehead.

The body is believed to have been first discovered by Ned Beaumont, 914 Randall Avenue, who went to the Log Cabin Club, two blocks away, to telephone the police; but before he had succeeded in getting Police Headquarters on the wire, the body had been found and reported by Patrolman Michael Smitt.

Chief of Police Frederick M. Rainey immediately ordered a wholesale round-up of all suspicious characters in the city and issued a statement to the effect that no stone will be left unturned in his effort to apprehend the murderer or murderers at once.

Members of Taylor Henry's family stated that he left his home on Charles Street at about half past nine o'clock to . . .

Ned Beaumont put the newspaper aside, swallowed the coffee that remained in his cup, put cup and saucer on the table beside his bed, and leaned back against the pillows. His face was tired and sallow. He pulled the covers up to his neck, clasped his hands together behind his head, and stared with dissatisfied eyes at the etching that hung between his bedroom-windows.

For half an hour he lay there with only his eyelids moving. Then he picked up the newspaper and reread the story. As he read, dissatisfaction spread from his eyes to all his face. He put the paper aside again, got out of bed, slowly, wearily, wrapped his lean white-pajamaed body in a small-figured brown and black kimono, thrust his feet into brown slippers, and, coughing a little, went into his living-room.

It was a large room in the old manner, high of ceiling and wide of window, with a tremendous mirror over the fireplace and much red plush on the furnishings. He took a cigar from a box on the table and sat in a wide red chair. His feet rested in a parallelogram of late morning sun and the smoke he blew out became suddenly full-bodied as it drifted into the sunlight. He frowned now and chewed a finger-nail when the cigar was not in his mouth.

Knocking sounded on his door. He sat up straight, keen of eye and alert. "Come in."

A white-jacketed waiter came in.

Ned Beaumont said, "Oh, all right," in a disappointed tone and relaxed again against the red plush of his chair.

The waiter passed through to the bedroom, came out with a tray of dishes, and went away. Ned Beaumont threw what was left of his cigar into the fireplace and went into his bathroom. By the time he had shaved, bathed, and dressed, his face had lost its sallowness, his carriage most of its weariness.

VI

It was not quite noon when Ned Beaumont left his rooms and walked eight blocks to a pale grey apartment-building in Link Street. He pressed a button in the vestibule, entered the building when the door-lock clicked, and rode to the sixth floor in a small automatic elevator.

He pressed the bell-button set in the frame of a door marked 611. The door was opened immediately by a diminutive girl who could have been only a few months out of her teens. Her eyes were dark and angry, her face white, except around her eyes, and angry. She said, "Oh, hello," and with a smile and a vaguely placatory motion of one hand apologized for her anger. Her voice had a metallic thinness. She wore a brown fur coat, but not a hat. Her short-cut hair—it was nearly black—lay smooth and shiny as enamel on her round head. The gold-set stones pendant from her ear-lobes were carnelian. She stepped back pulling the door back with her.

Ned Beaumont advanced through the doorway asking: "Bernie up yet?"

Anger burned in her face again. She said in a shrill voice: "The crummy bastard!"

Ned Beaumont shut the door behind him without turning around.

The girl came close to him, grasped his arms above the elbows, and tried to shake him. "You know what I did for that bum?" she demanded. "I left the best home any girl ever had and a mother and father that thought I was the original Miss Jesus. They told me he was no good. Everybody told me that and they were right and I was too dumb to know it. Well, I hope to tell you I know it now, the . . ." The rest was shrill obscenity.

Ned Beaumont, motionless, listened gravely. His eyes were not a well man's now. He asked, when breathlessness had stopped her words for the moment: "What's he done?"

"Done? He's taken a run-out on me, the . . ." The rest of that sentence was obscenity.

Ned Beaumont flinched. The smile into which he pushed his lips was watery. He asked: "I don't suppose he left anything for me?"

The girl clicked her teeth together and pushed her face nearer his. Her eyes widened. "Does he owe you anything?"

"I won—" He coughed. "I'm supposed to have won thirty-two hundred and fifty bucks on the fourth race yesterday."

She took her hands from his arms and laughed scornfully. "Try and get it. Look." She held out her hands. A carnelian ring was on the little finger of her left hand. She raised her hands and touched her carnelian ear-rings. "That's every stinking piece of my jewelry he left me and he wouldn't've left me that if I hadn't had them on."

Ned Beaumont asked, in a queer detached voice: "When does this happen?"

"Last night, though I didn't find it out till this morning, but don't think I'm not going to make Mr. Son-of-a-bitch wish to God he'd never seen me." She put a hand inside her dress and brought it out a fist. She held the fist up close to Ned Beaumont's face and opened it. Three small crumpled pieces of paper lay in her hand. When he reached for them she closed her fingers over them again, stepping back and snatching her hand away.

He moved the corners of his mouth impatiently and let his hand fall down at his side.

She said excitedly: "Did you see the paper this morning about Taylor Henry?"

Ned Beaumont's reply, "Yes," was calm enough, but his chest moved out and in with a quick breath.

"Do you know what these are?" She held the three crumpled bits of paper out in her open hand once more.

Ned Beaumont shook his head. His eyes were narrow, shiny.

"They're Taylor Henry's IOUs," she said triumphantly, "twelve hundred dollars' worth of them."

Ned Beaumont started to say something, checked himself, and when he spoke his voice was lifeless. "They're not worth a nickel now he's dead."

She thrust them inside her dress again and came close to Ned Beaumont. "Listen," she said: "they never were worth a nickel and that's why he's dead."

"Is that a guess?"

"It's any damned thing you want to call it," she told him. "But let me tell you something: Bernie called Taylor up last Friday and told him he'd give him just three days to come across."

Ned Beaumont brushed a side of his mustache with a thumb-nail. "You're not just being mad, are you?" he asked cautiously.

She made an angry face. "Of course I'm mad," she said.

"I'm just mad enough to take them to the police and that's what I'm going to do. But if you think it didn't happen you're just a plain damned fool."

He seemed still unconvinced. "Where'd you get them?"

"Out of the safe." She gestured with her sleek head towards the interior of the apartment.

He asked: "What time last night did he blow?"

"I don't know. I got home at half past nine and sat around most of the night expecting him. It wasn't till morning that I began to suspect something and looked around and saw he'd cleaned house of every nickel in money and every piece of my jewelry that I wasn't wearing."

He brushed his mustache with his thumb-nail again and asked: "Where do you think he'd go?"

She stamped her foot and, shaking both fists up and down, began to curse the missing Bernie again in a shrill enraged voice.

Ned Beaumont said: "Stop it." He caught her wrists and held them still. He said: "If you're not going to do anything about it but yell, give me those markers and I'll do something about it."

She tore her wrists out of his hands, crying: "I'll give you nothing. I'll give them to the police and not to another damned soul."

"All right, then do it. Where do you think he'd go, Lee?"

Lee said bitterly that she didn't know where he would go, but she knew where she would like to have him go.

Ned Beaumont said wearily: "That's the stuff. Wisecracking is going to do us a lot of good. Think he'd go back to New York?"

"How do I know?" Her eyes had suddenly become wary.

Annoyance brought spots of color into Ned Beaumont's cheeks. "What are you up to now?" he asked suspiciously.

Her face was an innocent mask. "Nothing. What do you mean?"

He leaned down towards her. He spoke with considerable earnestness, shaking his head slowly from side to side with his words. "Don't think you're not going to the police with them, Lee, because you are."

She said: "Of course I am."

VII

In the drug-store that occupied part of the ground-floor of the apartment-building Ned Beaumont used a telephone. He called the Police Department's number, asked for Lieutenant Doolan, and said: "Hello. Lieutenant Doolan? . . . I'm speaking for Miss Lee Wilshire. She's in Bernie Despain's apartment at 1666 Link Street. He seems to have suddenly disappeared last night, leaving some of Taylor Henry's IOUs behind him. . . . That's right, and she says she heard him threaten him a couple of days ago. . . . Yes, and she wants to see you as soon as possible. . . . No, you'd better come up or send and as soon as you can. . . . Yes. . . . That doesn't make any difference. You don't know me. I'm just speaking for her because she didn't want to phone from his apartment. . . ." He listened a moment longer, then, without having said anything else, put the receiver on its prong and went out of the drug-store.

VIII

Ned Beaumont went to a neat red brick house in a row of neat red brick houses in upper Thames Street. The door was opened to his ring by a young negress who smiled with her whole brown face, said, "How do you do, Mr. Beaumont?" and made the opening of the door a hearty invitation.

Ned Beaumont said: "'Lo, June. Anybody home?"

"Yes, sir, they still at the dinner-table."

He walked back to the dining-room where Paul Madvig and his mother sat facing one another across a red-and-white-clothed table. There was a third chair at the table, but it was not occupied and the plate and silver in front of it had not been used.

Paul Madvig's mother was a tall gaunt woman whose blondness had been faded not quite white by her seventy-some years. Her eyes were as blue and clear and young as her son's—younger than her son's when she looked up at Ned Beaumont entering the room. She deepened the lines in her forehead, however, and said: "So here you are at last. You're a worthless boy to neglect an old woman like this."

Ned Beaumont grinned impudently at her and said: "Aw, Mom, I'm a big boy now and I've got my work to look after." He flirted a hand at Madvig. "'Lo, Paul."

Madvig said: "Sit down and June'll scrape you up something to eat."

Ned Beaumont was bending to kiss the scrawny hand Mrs. Madvig had held out to him. She jerked it away and scolded him: "Wherever do you learn such tricks?"

"I told you I was getting to be a big boy now." He addressed Madvig: "Thanks, I'm only a few minutes past breakfast." He looked at the vacant chair. "Where's Opal?"

Mrs. Madvig replied: "She's laying down. She's not feeling good."

Ned Beaumont nodded, waited a moment, and asked politely: "Nothing serious?" He was looking at Madvig.

Madvig shook his head. "Headache or something. I think the kid dances too much."

Mrs. Madvig said: "You certainly are a fine father not to know when your daughter has headaches."

Skin crinkled around Madvig's eyes. "Now, Mom, don't be indecent," he said and turned to Ned Beaumont. "What's the good word?"

Ned Beaumont went around Mrs. Madvig to the vacant chair. He sat down and said: "Bernie Despain blew town last night with my winnings on Peggy O'Toole."

The blond man opened his eyes.

Ned Beaumont said: "He left behind him twelve hundred dollars' worth of Taylor Henry's IOUs."

The blond man's eyes jerked narrow.

Ned Beaumont said: "Lee says he called Taylor Friday and gave him three days to make good."

Madvig touched his chin with the back of a hand. "Who's Lee?"

"Bernie's girl."

"Oh." Then, when Ned Beaumont said nothing, Madvig asked: "What'd he say he was going to do about it if Taylor didn't come across?"

"I didn't hear." Ned Beaumont put a forearm on the table and leaned over it towards the blond man. "Have me made a deputy sheriff or something, Paul."

"For Christ's sake!" Madvig exclaimed, blinking. "What do you want anything like that for?"

"It'll make it easier for me. I'm going after this guy and having a buzzer may keep me from getting in a jam."

Madvig looked through worried eyes at the younger man. "What's got you all steamed up?" he asked slowly.

"Thirty-two hundred and fifty dollars."

"That's all right," Madvig said, still speaking slowly, "but something was itching you last night before you knew you'd been welshed on."

Ned Beaumont moved an impatient arm. "Do you expect me to stumble over corpses without batting an eye?" he asked. "But forget that. That doesn't count now. This does. I've got to get this guy. I've got to." His face was pale, set hard, and his voice was desperately earnest. "Listen, Paul: it's not only the money, though thirty-two hundred is a lot, but it would be the same if it was five bucks. I go two months without winning a bet and that gets me down. What good am I if my luck's gone? Then I cop, or think I do, and I'm all right again. I can take my tail out from between my legs and feel that I'm a person again and not just something that's being kicked around. The money's important enough, but it's not the real thing. It's what losing and losing and losing does to me. Can you get that? It's getting me licked. And then, when I think I've worn out the jinx, this guy takes a Mickey Finn on me. I can't stand for it. If I stand for it I'm licked, my nerve's gone. I'm not going to stand for it. I'm going after him. I'm going regardless, but you can smooth the way a lot by fixing me up."

Madvig put out a big open hand and roughly pushed Ned Beaumont's drawn face. "Oh, hell, Ned!" he said, "sure I'll fix you up. The only thing is I don't like you getting mixed up in things, but—hell!—if it's like that—I guess the best shot would be to make you a special investigator in the District Attorney's office. That way you'll be under Farr and he won't be poking his nose in."

Mrs. Madvig stood up with a plate in each bony hand. "If I didn't make a rule of not ever meddling in men's affairs," she said severely, "I certainly would have something to say to the pair of you, running around with the good Lord only knows what kind of monkey-business afoot that's likely as not to get you into the Lord only knows what kind of trouble."

Ned Beaumont grinned until she had left the room with the plates. Then he stopped grinning and said: "Will you fix it up now so everything'll be ready this afternoon?"

"Sure," Madvig agreed, rising. "I'll phone Farr. And if there's anything else I can do, you know."

Ned Beaumont said, "Sure," and Madvig went out.

Brown June came in and began to clear the table.

"Is Miss Opal sleeping now, do you think?" Ned Beaumont asked.

"No, sir, I just now took her up some tea and toast."

"Run up and ask her if I can pop in for a minute?"

"Yes, sir, I sure will."

After the negress had gone out Ned Beaumont got up from the table and began to walk up and down the room. Spots of color made his lean cheeks warm just beneath his cheek-bones. He stopped walking when Madvig came in.

"Oke," Madvig said. "If Farr's not in see Barbero. He'll fix you up and you don't have to tell him anything."

Ned Beaumont said, "Thanks," and looked at the brown girl in the doorway.

She said: "She says to come right up."

IX

Opal Madvig's room was chiefly blue. She, in a blue and silver wrapper, was propped up on pillows in her bed when Ned Beaumont came in. She was blue-eyed as her father and grandmother, long-boned as they and firm-featured, with fair pink skin still childish in texture. Her eyes were reddened now.

She dropped a piece of toast on the tray in her lap, held her hand out to Ned Beaumont, showed him strong white teeth in a smile, and said: "Hello, Ned." Her voice was not steady.

He did not take her hand. He slapped the back of it lightly, said, "'Lo, snip," and sat on the foot of her bed. He crossed his long legs and took a cigar from his pocket. "Smoke hurt the head?"

"Oh, no," she said.

He nodded as if to himself, returned the cigar to his pocket, and dropped his careless air. He twisted himself around on the bed to look more directly at her. His eyes were humid with sympathy. His voice was husky. "I know, youngster, it's tough."

She stared baby-eyed at him. "No, really, most of the headache's gone and it wasn't so awfully wretched anyway." Her voice was no longer unsteady.

He smiled at her with thinned lips and asked: "So I'm an outsider now?"

She put a small frown between her brows. "I don't know what you mean, Ned."

Hard of mouth and eye, he replied: "I mean Taylor."

Though the tray moved a little on her knees, nothing in her face changed. She said: "Yes, but—you know—I hadn't seen him for months, since Dad made—"

Ned Beaumont stood up abruptly. He said, "All right," over his shoulder as he moved towards the door.

The girl in the bed did not say anything.

He went out of the room and down the stairs.

Paul Madvig, putting on his coat in the lower hall, said: "I've got to go down to the office to see about those sewer-contracts. I'll drop you at Farr's office if you want."

Ned Beaumont had said, "Fine," when Opal's voice came to them from upstairs: "Ned, oh, Ned!"

"Righto," he called back and then to Madvig: "Don't wait if you're in a hurry."

Madvig looked at his watch. "I ought to run along. See you at the Club tonight?"

Ned Beaumont said, "Uh-huh," and went upstairs again.

Opal had pushed the tray down to the foot of the bed. She said: "Close the door." When he had shut the door she moved over in bed to make a place for him to sit beside her. Then she asked: "What makes you act like that?"

"You oughtn't to lie to me," he said gravely as he sat down.

"But, Ned!" Her blue eyes tried to probe his brown ones.

He asked: "How long since you saw Taylor?"

"You mean to talk to?" Her face and voice were candid. "It's been weeks and—"

He stood up abruptly. He said, "All right," over his shoulder while walking towards the door.

She let him get within a step of the door before she called: "Oh, Ned, don't make it so hard for me."

He turned around slowly, his face blank.

"Aren't we friends?" she asked.

"Sure," he replied readily without eagerness, "but it's hard to remember it when we're lying to each other."

She turned sidewise in bed, laying her cheek against the topmost pillow, and began to cry. She made no sound. Her tears fell down on the pillow and made a greyish spot there.

He returned to the bed, sat down beside her again, and moved her head from the pillow to his shoulder.

She cried there silently for several minutes. Then muffled words came from where her mouth was pressed against his coat: "Did—did you know I had been meeting him?"

"Yes."

She sat up straight, alarmed. "Did Dad know it?"

"I don't think so. I don't know."

She lowered her head to his shoulder so that her next words were muffled. "Oh, Ned, I was with him only yesterday afternoon, all afternoon!"

He tightened his arm around her, but did not say anything.

After another pause she asked: "Who—who do you think could have done it to him?"

He winced.

She raised her head suddenly. There was no weakness in her now. "Do you know, Ned?"

He hesitated, wet his lips, mumbled: "I think I do."

"Who?" she asked fiercely.

He hesitated again, evading her eyes, then put a slow question to her: "Will you promise to keep it to yourself till the time comes?"

"Yes," she replied quickly, but when he would have spoken she stopped him by grabbing his nearer shoulder with both hands. "Wait. I won't promise unless you'll promise me that they won't get off, that they'll be caught and punished."

"I can't promise that. Nobody can."

She stared at him, biting her lip, then said: "All right, then, I'll promise anyway. Who?"

"Did he ever tell you that he owed a gambler named Bernie Despain more money than he could pay?"

"Did—did this Despain—?"

"I think so, but did he ever say anything to you about owing—?"

"I knew he was in trouble. He told me that, but he didn't say what it was except that he and his father had had a row about some money and that he was—'desperate' is what he said."

"Didn't mention Despain?"

"No. What was it? Why do you think this Despain did it?"

"He had over a thousand dollars' worth of Taylor's IOUs and couldn't collect. He left town last night in a hurry. The police are looking for him now." He lowered his voice, looking a little sidewise at her. "Would you do something to help them catch and convict him?"

"Yes. What?"

"I mean something a bit off-color. You see, it's going to be hard to convict him, but, if he's guilty, would you do something that might be a little bit—well—off-color to make sure of nailing him?"

"Anything," she replied.

He sighed and rubbed his lips together.

"What is it you want done?" she asked eagerly.

"I want you to get me one of his hats."

"What?"

"I want one of Taylor's hats," Ned Beaumont said. His face had flushed. "Can you get me one?"

She was bewildered. "But what for, Ned?"

"To make sure of nailing Despain. That's all I can tell you now. Can you get it for me or can't you?"

"I—I think I can, but I wish you'd—"

"How soon?"

"This afternoon, I think," she said, "but I wish—"

He interrupted her again. "You don't want to know anything about it. The fewer know about it the better and the same thing goes for your getting the hat." He put his arm around her and drew her to him. "Did you really love him, snip, or was it just because your father—"

"I did really love him," she sobbed. "I'm pretty sure—I'm sure I did."

CHAPTER II

The Hat Trick

N ED BEAUMONT, wearing a hat that did not quite fit him, followed the porter carrying his bags through Grand Central Terminal to a Forty-second Street exit, and thence to a maroon taxicab. He tipped the porter, climbed into the taxicab, gave its driver the name of a hotel off Broadway in the Forties, and settled back lighting a cigar. He chewed the cigar more than he smoked it as the taxicab crawled through theater-bound traffic towards Broadway.

At Madison Avenue a green taxicab, turning against the light, ran full tilt into Ned Beaumont's maroon one, driving it over against a car that was parked by the curb, hurling him into a corner in a shower of broken glass.

He pulled himself upright and climbed out into the gathering crowd. He was not hurt, he said. He answered a policeman's questions. He found the hat that did not quite fit him and put it on his head. He had his bags transferred to another taxicab, gave the hotel's name to the second driver, and huddled back in a corner, white-faced and shivering, while the ride lasted.

When he had registered at the hotel he asked for his mail and was given two telephone-memorandum-slips and two sealed envelopes without postage stamps.

He asked the bellboy who took him to his room to get him a pint of rye whisky. When the boy had gone he turned the key in the door and read the telephone-memoranda. Both slips were dated that day, one marked *4:50* P.M., the other *8:05* P.M. He looked at his wrist-watch. It was 8:45 P.M.

The earlier slip read: *At the Gargoyle.* The later read: *At Tom & Jerry's. Will phone later.* Both were signed: *Jack.*

He opened one of the envelopes. It contained two sheets of paper covered by bold masculine handwriting, dated the previous day.

She is staying at the Matin, room 1211, registered as Eileen Dale, Chicago. She did some phoning from the depot and con-

nected with a man and girl who live E. 30th. They went to a lot
of places, mostly speakies, probably hunting him, but don't seem
to have much luck. My room is 734. Man and girl named Brook.

The sheet of paper in the other envelope, covered by the
same handwriting, was dated that day.

I saw Deward this morning, but he says he did not know
Bernie was in town. Will phone later.

Both of these messages were signed: *Jack.*

Ned Beaumont washed, put on fresh linen from his bags,
and was lighting a cigar when the bellboy brought him his
pint of whisky. He paid the boy, got a tumbler from the bathroom, and drew a chair up to the bedroom-window. He sat
there smoking, drinking, and staring down at the other side
of the street until his telephone-bell rang.

"Hello," he said into the telephone. "Yes, Jack. . . . Just
now. . . . Where? . . . Sure . . . . Sure, on my way."

He took another drink of whisky, put on the hat that did
not quite fit him, picked up the overcoat he had dropped
across a chair-back, put it on, patted one of its pockets,
switched off the lights, and went out.

It was then ten minutes past nine o'clock.

II

Through double swinging glazed doors under an electric
sign that said *Tom & Jerry's* down the front of a building
within sight of Broadway, Ned Beaumont passed into a narrow corridor. A single swinging door in the corridor's left wall
let him into a small restaurant.

A man at a corner-table stood up and raised a forefinger at
him. The man was of medium height, young and dapper, with
a sleek dark rather good-looking face.

Ned Beaumont went over to him. "'Lo, Jack," he said as
they shook hands.

"They're upstairs, the girl and those Brook people," Jack
told him. "You ought to be all right sitting here with your
back to the stairs. I can spot them if they go out, or him coming in, and there's enough people in the way to keep him
from making you."

Ned Beaumont sat down at Jack's table. "They waiting for him?"

Jack moved his shoulders. "I don't know, but they're doing some stalling about something. Want something to eat? You can't get anything to drink downstairs here."

Ned Beaumont said: "I want a drink. Can't we find a place upstairs where they won't see us?"

"It's not a very big joint," Jack protested. "There's a couple of booths up there where we might be hidden from them, but if he comes in he's likely to spot us."

"Let's risk it. I want a drink and I might as well talk to him right here if he does show up."

Jack looked curiously at Ned Beaumont, then turned his eyes away and said: "You're the boss. I'll see if one of the booths is empty." He hesitated, moved his shoulders again, and left the table.

Ned Beaumont twisted himself around in his chair to watch the dapper young man go back to the stairs and mount them. He watched the foot of the stairs until the young man came down again. From the second step Jack beckoned. He said, when Ned Beaumont had joined him there: "The best of them's empty and her back's this way, so you can get a slant at the Brooks as you go over."

They went upstairs. The booths—tables and benches set within breast-high wooden stalls—were to the right of the stair-head. They had to turn and look through a wide arch and down past the bar to see into the second-floor dining-room.

Ned Beaumont's eyes focused on the back of Lee Wilshire in sleeveless fawn gown and brown hat. Her brown fur coat was hanging over the back of her chair. He looked at her companions. At her left was a hawk-nosed long-chinned pale man, a predatory animal of forty or so. Facing her sat a softly fleshed red-haired girl with eyes set far apart. She was laughing.

Ned Beaumont followed Jack to their stall. They sat down with the table between them. Ned Beaumont sat with his back to the dining-room, close to the end of his bench to take full advantage of the wooden wing's shelter. He took off his hat, but not his overcoat.

A waiter came. Ned Beaumont said: "Rye." Jack said: "Rickey."

Jack opened a package of cigarettes, took one out, and, staring at it, said: "It's your game and I'm working for you, but this isn't a hell of a good spot to go up against him if he's got friends here."

"Has he?"

Jack put the cigarette in a corner of his mouth so it moved batonwise with his words. "If they're waiting here for him, it might be one of his hang-outs."

The waiter came with their drinks. Ned Beaumont drained his glass immediately and complained: "Cut to nothing."

"Yes, I guess it is," Jack said and took a sip from his glass. He set fire to the end of his cigarette and took another sip.

"Well," Ned Beaumont said, "I'm going up against him as soon as he shows."

"Fair enough." Jack's good-looking dark face was inscrutable. "What do I do?"

Ned Beaumont said, "Leave it to me," and caught their waiter's attention.

He ordered a double Scotch, Jack another rickey. Ned Beaumont emptied his glass as soon as it arrived. Jack let his first drink be carried away no more than half consumed and sipped at his second. Presently Ned Beaumont had another double Scotch and another while Jack had time to finish none of his drinks.

Then Bernie Despain came upstairs.

Jack, watching the head of the stairs, saw the gambler and put a foot on Ned Beaumont's under the table. Ned Beaumont, looking up from his empty glass, became suddenly hard and cold of eye. He put his hands flat on the table and stood up. He stepped out of the stall and faced Despain. He said: "I want my money, Bernie."

The man who had come upstairs behind Despain now walked around him and struck Ned Beaumont very hard in the body with his left fist. He was not a tall man, but his shoulders were heavy and his fists were large globes.

Ned Beaumont was knocked back against a stall-partition. He bent forward and his knees gave, but he did not fall. He hung there for a moment. His eyes were glassy and his skin had taken on a greenish tinge. He said something nobody could have understood and went to the head of the stairs.

He went down the stairs, loose-jointed, pallid, and bare-headed. He went through the downstairs dining-room to the street and out to the curb, where he vomited. When he had vomited, he went to a taxicab that stood a dozen feet away, climbed into it, and gave the driver an address in Greenwich Village.

III

Ned Beaumont left the taxicab in front of a house whose open basement-door, under brown stone steps, let noise and light out into a dark street. He went through the basement-doorway into a narrow room where two white-coated bar-tenders served a dozen men and women at a twenty-foot bar and two waiters moved among tables at which other people sat.

The balder bar-tender said, "For Christ's sake, Ned!" put down the pink mixture he was shaking in a tall glass, and stuck a wet hand out across the bar.

Ned Beaumont said, "'Lo, Mack," and shook the wet hand.

One of the waiters came up to shake Ned Beaumont's hand and then a round and florid Italian whom Ned Beaumont called Tony. When these greetings were over Ned Beaumont said he would buy a drink.

"Like hell you will," Tony said. He turned to the bar and rapped on it with an empty cocktail-glass. "This guy can't buy so much as a glass of water tonight," he said when he had the bar-tenders' attention. "What he wants is on the house."

Ned Beaumont said: "That's all right for me, so I get it. Double Scotch."

Two girls at a table in the other end of the room stood up and called together: "Yoo-hoo, Ned!"

He told Tony, "Be back in a minute," and went to the girls' table. They embraced him, asked him questions, introduced him to the men with them, and made a place for him at their table.

He sat down and replied to their questions that he was

back in New York only for a short visit and not to stay and that his was double Scotch.

At a little before three o'clock they rose from their table, left Tony's establishment, and went to another almost exactly like it three blocks away, where they sat at a table that could hardly have been told from the first and drank the same sort of liquor they had been drinking.

One of the men went away at half past three. He did not say good-by to the others, nor they to him. Ten minutes later Ned Beaumont, the other man, and the two girls left. They got into a taxicab at the corner and went to a hotel near Washington Square, where the other man and one of the girls got out.

The remaining girl took Ned Beaumont, who called her Fedink, to an apartment in Seventy-third Street. The apartment was very warm. When she opened the door warm air came out to meet them. When she was three steps inside the living-room she sighed and fell down on the floor.

Ned Beaumont shut the door and tried to awaken her, but she would not wake. He carried and dragged her difficultly into the next room and put her on a chintz-covered day-bed. He took off part of her clothing, found some blankets to spread over her, and opened a window. Then he went into the bathroom and was sick. After that he returned to the living-room, lay down on the sofa in all his clothes, and went to sleep.

IV

A telephone-bell, ringing close to Ned Beaumont's head, awakened him. He opened his eyes, put his feet down on the floor, turned on his side, and looked around the room. When he saw the telephone he shut his eyes and relaxed.

The bell continued to ring. He groaned, opened his eyes again, and squirmed until he had freed his left arm from beneath his body. He put his wrist close to his eyes and looked at his watch, squinting. The watch's crystal was gone and its hands had stopped at twelve minutes to twelve.

Ned Beaumont squirmed again on the sofa until he was leaning on his left elbow, holding his head up on his left hand. The telephone-bell was still ringing. He looked around the room with miserably dull eyes. The lights were burning. Through an open doorway he could see Fedink's blanket-covered feet on an end of the day-bed.

He groaned again and sat up, running fingers through his tousled dark hair, squeezing his temples between the heels of his palms. His lips were dry and brownly encrusted. He ran his tongue over them and made a distasteful face. Then he rose, coughing a little, took off his gloves and overcoat, dropped them on the sofa, and went into the bathroom.

When he came out he went to the day-bed and looked down at Fedink. She was sleeping heavily, face down, one blue-sleeved arm crooked above her head. The telephone-bell had stopped ringing. He pulled his tie straight and returned to the living-room.

Three Murad cigarettes were in an open box on the table between two chairs. He picked up one of the cigarettes, muttered, "Nonchalant," without humor, found a paper of matches, lit the cigarette, and went into the kitchen. He squeezed the juice of four oranges into a tall glass and drank it. He made and drank two cups of coffee.

As he came out of the kitchen Fedink asked in a woefully flat voice: "Where's Ted?" Her one visible eye was partially open.

Ned Beaumont went over to her. "Who's Ted?" he asked.

"That fellow I was with."

"Were you with somebody? How do I know?"

She opened her mouth and made an unpleasant clucking sound shutting it. "What time is it?"

"I don't know that either. Somewhere around daylight."

She rubbed her face into the chintz cushion under it and said: "A swell guy I turned out to be, promising to marry him yesterday and then leaving him to take the first tramp I run into home with me." She opened and shut the hand that was above her head. "Or am I home?"

"You had a key to the place, anyway," Ned Beaumont told her. "Want some orange-juice and coffee?"

"I don't want a damned thing except to die. Will you go away, Ned, and not ever come back?"

"It's going to be hard on me," he said ill-naturedly, "but I'll try."

He put on his overcoat and gloves, took a dark wrinkled cap from one overcoat-pocket, put the cap on, and left the house.

V

Half an hour later Ned Beaumont was knocking on the door of room 734 at his hotel. Presently Jack's voice, drowsy, came through the door: "Who's that?"

"Beaumont."

"Oh," without enthusiasm, "all right."

Jack opened the door and turned on the lights. He was in green-spotted pajamas. His feet were bare. His eyes were dull, his face flushed, with sleepiness. He yawned, nodded, and went back to bed, where he stretched himself out on his back and stared at the ceiling. Then he asked, with not much interest: "How are you this morning?"

Ned Beaumont had shut the door. He stood between door and bed looking sullenly at the man in the bed. He asked: "What happened after I left?"

"Nothing happened." Jack yawned again. "Or do you mean what did I do?" He did not wait for a reply. "I went out and took a plant across the street till they came out. Despain and the girl and the guy that slugged you came out. They went to the Buckman, Forty-eighth Street. That's where Despain's holing up—apartment 938—name of Barton Dewey. I hung around there till after three and then knocked off. They were all still in there unless they were fooling me." He jerked his head slightly in the direction of a corner of the room. "Your hat's on the chair there. I thought I might as well save it for you."

Ned Beaumont went over to the chair and picked up the hat that did not quite fit him. He stuffed the wrinkled dark cap in his overcoat-pocket and put the hat on his head.

Jack said: "There's some gin on the table if you want a shot."

Ned Beaumont said: "No, thanks. Have you got a gun?"

Jack stopped staring at the ceiling. He sat up in bed, stretched his arms out wide, yawned for the third time, and asked: "What are you figuring on doing?" His voice held nothing beyond polite curiosity.

"I'm going to see Despain."

Jack had drawn his knees up, had clasped his hands around them, and was sitting hunched forward a little staring at the foot of the bed. He said slowly: "I don't think you ought to, not right now."

"I've got to, right now," Ned Beaumont said.

His voice made Jack look at him. Ned Beaumont's face was an unhealthy yellowish grey. His eyes were muddy, red-rimmed, not sufficiently open to show any of the whites. His lips were dry and somewhat thicker than usual.

"Been up all night?" Jack asked.

"I got some sleep."

"Unkdray?"

"Yes, but how about the gun?"

Jack swung his legs out from beneath the covers and down over the side of the bed. "Why don't you get some sleep first? Then we can go after them. You're in no shape now."

Ned Beaumont said: "I'm going now."

Jack said: "All right, but you're wrong. You know they're no babies to go up against shaky. They mean it."

"Where's the gun?" Ned Beaumont asked.

Jack stood up and began to unbutton his pajama-coat.

Ned Beaumont said: "Give me the gun and get back in bed. I'm going."

Jack fastened the button he had just unfastened and got into bed. "The gun's in the top bureau-drawer," he said. "There are extra cartridges in there too if you want them." He turned over on his side and shut his eyes.

Ned Beaumont found the pistol, put it in a hip-pocket, said, "See you later," switched off the lights, and went out.

VI

The Buckman was a square-built yellow apartment-building that filled most of the block it stood in. Inside, Ned Beaumont said he wanted to see Mr. Dewey. When asked for his name he said: "Ned Beaumont."

Five minutes later he was walking away from an elevator down a long corridor towards an open door where Bernie Despain stood.

Despain was a small man, short and stringy, with a head too

large for his body. The size of his head was exaggerated until it seemed a deformity by long thick fluffy waved hair. His face was swarthy, large-featured except for the eyes, and strongly lined across the forehead and down from nostrils past the mouth. He had a faintly reddish scar on one cheek. His blue suit was carefully pressed and he wore no jewelry.

He stood in the doorway, smiling sardonically, and said: "Good morning, Ned."

Ned Beaumont said: "I want to talk to you, Bernie."

"I guessed you did. As soon as they phoned your name up I said to myself: 'I bet you he wants to talk to me.'"

Ned Beaumont said nothing. His yellow face was tight-lipped.

Despain's smile became looser. He said: "Well, my boy, you don't have to stand here. Come on in." He stepped aside.

The door opened into a small vestibule. Through an opposite door that stood open Lee Wilshire and the man who had struck Ned Beaumont could be seen. They had stopped packing two traveling-bags to look at Ned Beaumont.

He went into the vestibule.

Despain followed him in, shut the corridor-door, and said: "The Kid's kind of hasty and when you come up to me like that he thought maybe you were looking for trouble, see? I give him hell about it and maybe if you ask him he'll apologize."

The Kid said something in an undertone to Lee Wilshire, who was glaring at Ned Beaumont. She laughed a vicious little laugh and replied: "Yes, a sportsman to the last."

Bernie Despain said: "Go right in, Mr. Beaumont. You've already met the folks, haven't you?"

Ned Beaumont advanced into the room where Lee and the Kid were.

The Kid asked: "How's the belly?"

Ned Beaumont did not say anything.

Bernie Despain exclaimed: "Jesus! For a guy that says he came up here to talk you've done less of it than anybody I ever heard of."

"I want to talk to you," Ned Beaumont said. "Do we have to have all these people around?"

"I do," Despain replied. "You don't. You can get away from them just by walking out and going about your own business."

"I've got business here."

"That's right, there was something about money." Despain grinned at the Kid. "Wasn't there something about money, Kid?"

The Kid had moved to stand in the doorway through which Ned Beaumont had come into the room. "Something," he said in a rasping voice, "but I forget what."

Ned Beaumont took off his overcoat and hung it on the back of a brown easy-chair. He sat down in the chair and put his hat behind him. He said: "That's not my business this time. I'm—let's see." He took a paper from his inner coat-pocket, unfolded it, glanced at it, and said: "I'm here as special investigator for the District Attorney's office."

For a small fraction of a second the twinkle in Despain's eyes was blurred, but he said immediately: "Ain't you getting up in the world! The last time I saw you you were just punking around for Paul."

Ned Beaumont refolded the paper and returned it to his pocket.

Despain said: "Well, go ahead, investigate something for us—anything—just to show us how it's done." He sat down facing Ned Beaumont, wagging his too-large head. "You ain't going to tell me you came all the way to New York to ask me about killing Taylor Henry?"

"Yes."

"That's too bad. I could've saved you the trip." He flourished a hand at the traveling-bags on the floor. "As soon as Lee told me what it was all about I started packing up to go back and laugh at your frame-up."

Ned Beaumont lounged back comfortably in his chair. One of his hands was behind him. He said: "If it's a frame-up it's Lee's. The police got their dope from her."

"Yes," she said angrily, "when I had to because you sent them there, you bastard."

Despain said: "Uh-huh, Lee's a dumb cluck, all right, but those markers don't mean anything. They—"

"I'm a dumb cluck, am I?" Lee cried indignantly. "Didn't I come all the way here to warn you after you'd run off with every stinking piece of—"

"Yes," Despain agreed pleasantly, "and coming here shows

just what a dumb cluck you are, because you led this guy right to me."

"If that's the way you feel about it I'm damned glad I did give the police those IOUs, and what do you think of that?"

Despain said: "I'll tell you just exactly what I think of it after our company's gone." He turned to Ned Beaumont. "So honest Paul Madvig's letting you drop the shuck on me, huh?"

Ned Beaumont smiled. "You're not being framed, Bernie, and you know it. Lee gave us the lead-in and the rest that we got clicked with it."

"There's some more besides what she gave you?"

"Plenty."

"What?"

Ned Beaumont smiled again. "There are lots of things I could say to you, Bernie, that I wouldn't want to say in front of a crowd."

Despain said: "Nuts!"

The Kid spoke from the doorway to Despain in his rasping voice: "Let's chuck this sap out on his can and get going."

"Wait," Despain said. Then he frowned and put a question to Ned Beaumont: "Is there a warrant out for me?"

"Well, I don't—"

"Yes or no?" Despain's bantering humor was gone.

Ned Beaumont said slowly: "Not that I know of."

Despain stood up and pushed his chair back. "Then get the hell out of here and make it quick, or I'll let the Kid take another poke at you."

Ned Beaumont stood up. He picked up his overcoat. He took his cap out of his overcoat-pocket and, holding it in one hand, his overcoat over the other arm, said seriously: "You'll be sorry." Then he walked out in a dignified manner. The Kid's rasping laughter and Lee's shriller hooting followed him out.

VII

Outside the Buckman Ned Beaumont started briskly down the street. His eyes were glowing in his tired face and his dark mustache twitched above a flickering smile.

At the first corner he came face to face with Jack. He asked: "What are you doing here?"

Jack said: "I'm still working for you, far as I know, so I came along to see if I could find anything to do."

"Swell. Find us a taxi quick. They're sliding out."

Jack said, "Ay, ay," and went down the street.

Ned Beaumont remained on the corner. The front and side entrances of the Buckman could be seen from there.

In a little while Jack returned in a taxicab. Ned Beaumont got into it and they told the driver where to park it.

"What did you do to them?" Jack asked when they were sitting still.

"Things."

"Oh."

Ten minutes passed and Jack, saying, "Look," was pointing a forefinger at a taxicab drawing up to the Buckman's side door.

The Kid, carrying two traveling-bags, left the building first, then, when he was in the taxicab, Despain and the girl ran out to join him. The taxicab ran away.

Jack leaned forward and told his driver what to do. They ran along in the other cab's wake. They wound through streets that were bright with morning sunlight, going by a devious route finally to a battered brown stone house in west Forty-ninth Street.

Despain's cab stopped in front of the house and, once more, the Kid was the first of the trio out on the sidewalk. He looked up and down the street. He went up to the front door of the house and unlocked it. Then he returned to the taxicab. Despain and the girl jumped out and went indoors hurriedly. The Kid followed with the bags.

"Stick here with the cab," Ned Beaumont told Jack.

"What are you going to do?"

"Try my luck."

Jack shook his head. "This is another wrong neighborhood to look for trouble in," he said.

Ned Beaumont said: "If I come out with Despain, you beat it. Get another taxi and go back to watch the Buckman. If I don't come out, use your own judgment."

He opened the cab-door and stepped out. He was shivering. His eyes were shiny. He ignored something that Jack leaned out to say and hurried across the street to the house into which the two men and the girl had gone.

He went straight up the front steps and put a hand on the door-knob. The knob turned in his hand. The door was not locked. He pushed it open and, after peering into the dim hallway, went in.

The door slammed shut behind him and one of the Kid's fists struck his head a glancing blow that carried his cap away and sent him crashing into the wall. He sank down a little, giddily, almost to one knee, and the Kid's other fist struck the wall over his head.

He pulled his lips back over his teeth and drove a fist into the Kid's groin, a short sharp blow that brought a snarl from the Kid and made him fall back so that Ned Beaumont could pull himself up straight before the Kid was upon him again.

Up the hallway a little, Bernie Despain was leaning against the wall, his mouth stretched wide and thin, his eyes narrowed to dark points, saying over and over in a low voice: "Sock him, Kid, sock him. . . ." Lee Wilshire was not in sight.

The Kid's next two blows landed on Ned Beaumont's chest, mashing him against the wall, making him cough. The third, aimed at his face, he avoided. Then he pushed the Kid away from him with a forearm against his throat and kicked the Kid in the belly. The Kid roared angrily and came in with both fists going, but forearm and foot had carried him away from Ned Beaumont and had given Ned Beaumont time to get his right hand to his hip-pocket and to get Jack's revolver out of his pocket. He had not time to level the revolver, but, holding it at a downward angle, he pulled the trigger and managed to shoot the Kid in the right thigh. The Kid yelped and fell down on the hallway floor. He lay there looking up at Ned Beaumont with frightened blood-shot eyes.

Ned Beaumont stepped back from him, put his left hand in his trousers-pocket, and addressed Bernie Despain: "Come on out with me. I want to talk to you." His face was sullenly determined.

Footsteps ran overhead, somewhere back in the building a door opened, and down the hallway excited voices were audible, but nobody came into sight.

Despain stared for a long moment at Ned Beaumont as if horribly fascinated. Then, without a word, he stepped over the man on the floor and went out of the building ahead of Ned Beaumont. Ned Beaumont put the revolver in his jacket-pocket before he went down the street-steps, but he kept his hand on it.

"Up to that taxi," he told Despain, indicating the car out of which Jack was getting. When they reached the taxicab he told the chauffeur to drive them anywhere, "just around till I tell you where to go."

They were in motion when Despain found his voice. He said: "This is a hold-up. I'll give you anything you want because I don't want to be killed, but it's just a hold-up."

Ned Beaumont laughed disagreeably and shook his head. "Don't forget I've risen in the world to be something or other in the District Attorney's office."

"But there's no charge against me. I'm not wanted. You said—"

"I was spoofing you, Bernie, for reasons. You're wanted."

"For what?"

"Killing Taylor Henry."

"That? Hell, I'll go back and face that. What've you got against me? I had some of his markers, sure. And I left the night he was killed, sure. And I gave him hell because he wouldn't make them good, sure. What kind of case is that for a first-class lawyer to beat? Jesus, if I left the markers behind in my safe at some time before nine-thirty—to go by Lee's story—don't that show I wasn't trying to collect that night?"

"No, and that isn't all the stuff we've got on you."

"That's all there could be," Despain said earnestly.

Ned Beaumont sneered. "Wrong, Bernie. Remember I had a hat on when I came to see you this morning?"

"Maybe. I think you did."

"Remember I took a cap out of my overcoat-pocket and put it on when I left?"

Bewilderment, fear, began to come into the swarthy man's small eyes. "By Jesus! Well? What are you getting at?"

"I'm getting at the evidence. Do you remember the hat didn't fit me very well?"

Bernie Despain's voice was hoarse: "I don't know, Ned. For Christ's sake, what do you mean?"

"I mean it didn't fit me because it wasn't my hat. Do you remember that the hat Taylor was wearing when he was murdered wasn't found?"

"I don't know. I don't know anything about him."

"Well, I'm trying to tell you the hat I had this morning was Taylor's hat and it's now planted down between the cushion-seat and the back of that brown easy-chair in the apartment you had at the Buckman. Do you think that, with the rest, would be enough to set you on the hot seat?"

Despain would have screamed in terror if Ned Beaumont had not clapped a hand over his mouth and growled, "Shut up," in his ear.

Sweat ran down the swarthy face. Despain fell over on Ned Beaumont, seizing the lapels of his coat with both hands, babbling: "Listen, don't you do that to me, Ned. You can have every cent I owe you, every cent with interest, if you won't do that. I never meant to rob you, Ned, honest to God. It was just that I was caught short and thought I'd treat it like a loan. Honest to God, Ned. I ain't got much now, but I'm fixed to get the money for Lee's rocks that I'm selling to-day and I'll give you your dough, every nickel of it, out of that. How much was it, Ned? I'll give you all of it right away, this morning."

Ned Beaumont pushed the swarthy man over to his own side of the taxicab and said: "It was thirty-two hundred and fifty dollars."

"Thirty-two hundred and fifty dollars. You'll get it, every cent of it, this morning, right away." Despain looked at his watch. "Yes, sir, right this minute as soon as we can get there. Old Stein will be at his place before this. Only say you'll let me go, Ned, for old times' sake."

Ned Beaumont rubbed his hands together thoughtfully. "I can't exactly let you go. Not right now, I mean. I've got to remember the District Attorney connection and that you're wanted for questioning. So all we can dicker about is the hat. Here's the proposition: give me my money and I'll see that

I'm alone when I turn up the hat and nobody else will ever know about it. Otherwise I'll see that half the New York police are with me and— There you are. Take it or leave it."

"Oh, God!" Bernie Despain groaned. "Tell him to drive us to old Stein's place. It's on . . ."

CHAPTER III

The Cyclone Shot

NED BEAUMONT leaving the train that had brought him
back from New York was a clear-eyed erect tall man.
Only the flatness of his chest hinted at any constitutional
weakness. In color and line his face was hale. His stride was
long and elastic. He went nimbly up the concrete stairs that
connected train-shed with street-level, crossed the waiting-
room, waved a hand at an acquaintance behind the information counter, and passed out of the station through one of the
street-doors.

While waiting on the sidewalk for the porter with his bags
to come he bought a newspaper. He opened it when he was
in a taxicab riding towards Randall Avenue with his luggage.
He read a half-column on the front page:

SECOND BROTHER KILLED
FRANCIS F. WEST MURDERED CLOSE TO
SPOT WHERE BROTHER MET DEATH

For the second time within two weeks tragedy came to the West
family of 1342 N. Achland Avenue last night when Francis F. West,
31, was shot to death in the street less than a block from the corner
where he had seen his brother Norman run down and killed by an
alleged bootleg car last month.

Francis West, who was employed as waiter at the Rockaway Café,
was returning from work at a little after midnight, when, according
to those who witnessed the tragedy, he was overtaken by a black
touring car that came down Achland Avenue at high speed. The car
swung in to the curb as it reached West, and more than a score of
shots are said to have been fired from it. West fell with eight bullets
in his body, dying before anybody could reach him. The death car,
which is said not to have stopped, immediately picked up speed
again and vanished around the corner of Bowman Street. The police
are hampered in their attempt to find the car by conflicting descriptions given by witnesses, none of whom claims to have seen any of
the men in the automobile.

Boyd West, the surviving brother, who also witnessed Norman's
death last month, could ascribe no reason for Francis's murder. He said

631

he knew of no enemies his brother had made. Miss Marie Shepperd, 1917 Baker Avenue, to whom Francis West was to have been married next week, was likewise unable to name anyone who might have desired her fiancé's death.

Timothy Ivans, alleged driver of the car that accidentally ran down and killed Norman West last month, refused to talk to reporters in his cell at the City Prison, where he is held without bail, awaiting trial for manslaughter.

Ned Beaumont folded the newspaper with careful slowness and put it in one of his overcoat-pockets. His lips were drawn a little together and his eyes were bright with thinking. Otherwise his face was composed. He leaned back in a corner of the taxicab and played with an unlighted cigar.

In his rooms he went, without pausing to remove hat or coat, to the telephone and called four numbers, asking each time whether Paul Madvig was there and whether it was known where he could be found. After the fourth call he gave up trying to find Madvig.

He put the telephone down, picked his cigar up from where he had laid it on the table, lighted the cigar, laid it on the edge of the table again, picked up the telephone, and called the City Hall's number. He asked for the District Attorney's office. While he waited he dragged a chair, by means of a foot hooked under one of its rounds, over to the telephone, sat down, and put the cigar in his mouth.

Then he said into the telephone: "Hello. Is Mr. Farr in? . . . Ned Beaumont. . . . Yes, thanks." He inhaled and exhaled smoke slowly. "Hello, Farr? . . . Just got in a couple of minutes ago. . . . Yes. Can I see you now? . . . That's right. Has Paul said anything to you about the West killing? . . . Don't know where he is, do you? . . . Well, there's an angle I'd like to talk to you about. . . . Yes, say half an hour. . . . Right."

He put the telephone aside and went across the room to look at the mail on a table by the door. There were some magazines and nine letters. He looked rapidly at the envelopes, dropped them on the table again without having opened any, and went into his bedroom to undress, then into his bathroom to shave and bathe.

II

District Attorney Michael Joseph Farr was a stout man of forty. His hair was a florid stubble above a florid pugnacious face. His walnut desk-top was empty except for a telephone and a large desk-set of green onyx whereon a nude metal figure holding aloft an airplane stood on one foot between two black and white fountain-pens that slanted off to either side at rakish angles.

He shook Ned Beaumont's hand in both of his and pressed him down into a leather-covered chair before returning to his own seat. He rocked back in his chair and asked: "Have a nice trip?" Inquisitiveness gleamed through the friendliness in his eyes.

"It was all right," Ned Beaumont replied. "About this Francis West: with him out of the way how does the case against Tim Ivans stand?"

Farr started, then made that startled motion part of a deliberate squirming into a more comfortable position in his chair.

"Well, it won't make such a lot of difference there," he said, "that is, not a whole lot, since there's still the other brother to testify against Ivans." He very noticeably did not watch Ned Beaumont's face, but looked at a corner of the walnut desk. "Why? What'd you have on your mind?"

Ned Beaumont was looking gravely at the man who was not looking at him. "I was just wondering. I suppose it's all right, though, if the other brother can and will identify Tim."

Farr, still not looking up, said: "Sure." He rocked his chair back and forth gently, an inch or two each way half a dozen times. His fleshy cheeks moved in little ripples where they covered his jaw-muscles. He cleared his throat and stood up. He looked at Ned Beaumont now with friendly eyes. "Wait a minute," he said. "I've got to go see about something. They forget everything if I don't keep right on their tails. Don't go. I want to talk to you about Despain."

Ned Beaumont murmured, "Don't hurry," as the District Attorney left the office, and sat and smoked placidly all the fifteen minutes he was gone.

Farr returned frowning. "Sorry to leave you like that," he said as he sat down, "but we're fairly smothered under work. If it keeps up like this—" He completed the sentence by making a gesture of hopelessness with his hands.

"That's all right. Anything new on the Taylor Henry killing?"

"Nothing here. That's what I wanted to ask you about—Despain." Again Farr was definitely not watching Ned Beaumont's face.

A thin mocking smile that the other man could not see twitched for an instant the corners of Ned Beaumont's mouth. He said: "There's not much of a case against him when you come to look at it closely."

Farr nodded slowly at the corner of his desk. "Maybe, but his blowing town that same night don't look so damned good."

"He had another reason for that," Ned Beaumont said, "a pretty good one." The shadowy smile came and went.

Farr nodded again in the manner of one willing to be convinced. "You don't think there's a chance that he really killed him?"

Ned Beaumont's reply was given carelessly: "I don't think he did it, but there's always a chance and you've got plenty to hold him awhile on if you want to."

The District Attorney raised his head and looked at Ned Beaumont. He smiled with a mixture of diffidence and good-fellowship and said: "Tell me to go to hell if it's none of my business, but why in the name of God did Paul send you to New York after Bernie Despain?"

Ned Beaumont withheld his reply for a thoughtful moment. Then he moved his shoulders a little and said: "He didn't send me. He let me go."

Farr did not say anything.

Ned Beaumont filled his lungs with cigar-smoke, emptied them, and said: "Bernie welshed on a bet with me. That's why he took the run-out. It just happened that Taylor Henry was killed the night of the day Peggy O'Toole came in in front with fifteen hundred of my dollars on her."

The District Attorney said hastily: "That's all right, Ned. It's none of my business what you and Paul do. I'm—you see, it's just that I'm not so damned sure that maybe Despain didn't happen to run into young Henry on the street by luck and take a crack at him. I think maybe I'll hold him awhile to be safe." His blunt undershot mouth curved in a smile that was somewhat ingratiating. "Don't think I'm pushing my snoot into Paul's affairs, or yours, but—" His florid face was turgid and shiny. He suddenly bent over and yanked a desk-drawer open. Paper rattled under his fingers. His hand came out of the drawer and went across the desk towards Ned Beaumont. In his hand was a small white envelope with a slit edge. "Here." His voice was thick. "Look at this and see what you think of it, or is it only damned foolishness?"

Ned Beaumont took the envelope, but did not immediately look at it. He kept his eyes, now cold and bright, focused on the District Attorney's red face.

Farr's face became a darker red under the other man's stare and he raised a beefy hand in a placatory gesture. His voice was placatory: "I don't attach any importance to it, Ned, but—I mean we always get a lot of junk like that on every case that comes up and—well, read it and see."

After another considerable moment Ned Beaumont shifted his gaze from Farr to the envelope. The address was typewritten:

> *M. J. Farr, Esq.*
> *District Attorney*
> *City Hall*
> *City*

Personal

The postmark was dated the previous Saturday. Inside was a single sheet of white paper on which three sentences with neither salutation nor signature were typewritten:

Why did Paul Madvig steal one of Taylor Henry's hats after he was murdered?

What became of the hat that Taylor Henry was wearing when he was murdered?

Why was the man who claimed to have first found Taylor Henry's body made a member of your staff?

Ned Beaumont folded this communication, returned it to its envelope, dropped it down on the desk, and brushed his mustache with a thumb-nail from center to left and from center to right, looking at the District Attorney with level eyes, addressing him in a level tone: "Well?"

Farr's cheeks rippled again where they covered his jaw-muscles. He frowned over pleading eyes. "For God's sake, Ned," he said earnestly, "don't think I'm taking that seriously. We get bales of that kind of crap every time anything happens. I only wanted to show it to you."

Ned Beaumont said: "That's all right as long as you keep on feeling that way about it." He was still level of eye and voice. "Have you said anything to Paul about it?"

"About the letter? No. I haven't seen him since it came this morning."

Ned Beaumont picked the envelope up from the desk and put it in his inner coat-pocket. The District Attorney, watching the letter go into the pocket, seemed uncomfortable, but he did not say anything.

Ned Beaumont said, when he had stowed the letter away and had brought a thin dappled cigar out of another pocket: "I don't think I'd say anything to him about it if I were you. He's got enough on his mind."

Farr was saying, "Sure, whatever you say, Ned," before Ned Beaumont had finished his speech.

After that neither of them said anything for a while during which Farr resumed his staring at the desk-corner and Ned Beaumont stared thoughtfully at Farr. This period of silence was ended by a soft buzzing that came from under the District Attorney's desk.

Farr picked up his telephone and said: "Yes. . . . Yes." His undershot lip crept out over the edge of the upper lip and his florid face became mottled. "The hell he's not!" he snarled. "Bring the bastard in and put him up against him and then if he don't we'll do some work on him. . . . Yes. . . . Do it." He slammed the receiver on its prong and glared at Ned Beaumont.

Ned Beaumont had paused in the act of lighting his cigar. It was in one hand. His lighter, alight, was in the other. His face was thrust forward a little between them. His eyes glittered. He put the tip of his tongue between his lips, withdrew it, and moved his lips in a smile that had nothing to do with pleasure. "News?" he asked in a low persuasive voice.

The District Attorney's voice was savage: "Boyd West, the other brother that identified Ivans. I got to thinking about it when we were talking and sent out to see if he could still identify him. He says he's not sure, the bastard."

Ned Beaumont nodded as if this news was not unexpected. "How'll that fix things?"

"He can't get away with it," Farr snarled. "He identified him once and he'll stick to it when he gets in front of a jury. I'm having him brought in now and by the time I get through with him he'll be a good boy."

Ned Beaumont said: "Yes? And suppose he doesn't?"

The District Attorney's desk trembled under a blow from the District Attorney's fist. "He will."

Apparently Ned Beaumont was unimpressed. He lighted his cigar, extinguished and pocketed his lighter, blew smoke out, and asked in a mildly amused tone: "Sure he will, but suppose he doesn't? Suppose he looks at Tim and says: 'I'm not sure that's him'?"

Farr smote his desk again. "He won't—not when I'm through with him—he won't do anything but get up in front of the jury and say: 'That's him.' "

Amusement went out of Ned Beaumont's face and he spoke a bit wearily: "He's going to back down on the identification and you know he is. Well, what can you do about it? There's nothing you can do about it, is there? It means your case against Tim Ivans goes blooey. You found the carload of booze where he left it, but the only proof you've got that he was driving it when it ran down Norman West was the eye-witness testimony of his two brothers. Well, if Francis is dead and Boyd's afraid to talk you've got no case and you know it."

In a loud enraged voice Farr began: "If you think I'm going to sit on my—"

But with an impatient motion of the hand holding his cigar Ned Beaumont interrupted him. "Sitting, standing, or riding a bicycle," he said, "you're licked and you know it."

"Do I? I'm District Attorney of this city and county and I—" Abruptly Farr stopped blustering. He cleared his throat

and swallowed. Belligerence went out of his eyes, to be replaced first by confusion and then by something akin to fear.
He leaned across the desk, too worried to keep worry from
showing in his florid face. He said: "Of course you know if
you—if Paul—I mean if there's any reason why I shouldn't—
you know—we can let it go at that."

The smile that had nothing to do with pleasure was lifting
the ends of Ned Beaumont's lips again and his eyes glittered
through cigar-smoke. He shook his head slowly and spoke
slowly in an unpleasantly sweet tone: "No, Farr, there isn't
any reason, or none of that kind. Paul promised to spring
Ivans after election, but, believe it or not, Paul never had anybody killed and, even if he did, Ivans wasn't important
enough to have anybody killed for. No, Farr, there isn't any
reason and I wouldn't like to think you were going around
thinking there was."

"For God's sake, Ned, get me right," Farr protested. "You
know damned well there's nobody in the city any stronger for
Paul and for you than me. You ought to know that. I didn't
mean anything by what I said except that—well, that you can
always count on me."

Ned Beaumont said, "That's fine," without much enthusiasm and stood up.

Farr rose and came around the desk with a red hand out.
"What's your hurry?" he asked. "Why don't you stick around
and see how this West acts when they bring him in? Or"—he
looked at his watch—"what are you doing tonight? How
about going to dinner with me?"

"Sorry I can't," Ned Beaumont replied. "I've got to run
along."

He let Farr pump his hand up and down, murmured a
"Yes, I will" in response to the District Attorney's insistence
that he drop in often and that they get together some night,
and went out.

III

Walter Ivans was standing beside one of a row of men
operating nailing-machines in the box-factory where he was
employed as foreman, when Ned Beaumont came in. He saw

Ned Beaumont at once and, hailing him with an uplifted hand, came down the center aisle, but in Ivans's china-blue eyes and round fair face there was somewhat less pleasure than he seemed to be trying to put there.

Ned Beaumont said, "'Lo, Walt," and by turning slightly towards the door escaped the necessity of either taking or pointedly ignoring the shorter man's proffered hand. "Let's get out of this racket."

Ivans said something that was blurred by the din of metal driving metal into wood and they went to the open door by which Ned Beaumont had entered. Outside was a wide platform of solid timber. A flight of wooden steps ran down twenty feet to the ground.

They stood on the wooden platform and Ned Beaumont asked: "You know one of the witnesses against your brother was knocked off last night?"

"Y-yes, I saw it in the p-p-paper."

Ned Beaumont asked: "You know the other one's not sure now he can identify Tim?"

"N-no, I didn't know that, N-ned."

Ned Beaumont said: "You know if he doesn't Tim'll get off."

"Y-yes."

Ned Beaumont said: "You don't look as happy about it as you ought to."

Ivans wiped his forehead with his shirt-sleeve. "B-b-but I am, N-ned, b-by God I am!"

"Did you know West? The one that was killed."

"N-no, except that I went to s-see him once, t-to ask him to g-go kind of easy on T-tim."

"What'd he say?"

"He wouldn't."

"When was that?"

Ivans shifted his feet and wiped his face with his sleeve again. "T-t-two or three d-days ago."

Ned Beaumont asked softly: "Any idea who could have killed him, Walt?"

Ivans shook his head violently from side to side.

"Any idea who could've had him killed, Walt?"

Ivans shook his head.

For a moment Ned Beaumont stared reflectively over Ivans's shoulder. The clatter of the nailing-machines came through the door ten feet away and from another story came the whirr of saws. Ivans drew in and expelled a long breath.

Ned Beaumont's mien had become sympathetic when he transferred his gaze to the shorter man's china-blue eyes again. He leaned down a little and asked: "Are you all right, Walt? I mean there are going to be people who'll think maybe you might have shot West to save your brother. Have you got—?"

"I-I-I was at the C-club all last night, from eight o'clock t-t-till after t-two this morning," Walter Ivans replied as rapidly as the impediment in his speech permitted. "Harry Sloss and B-ben Ferriss and Brager c-c-can tell you."

Ned Beaumont laughed. "That's a lucky break for you, Walt," he said gaily.

He turned his back on Walter Ivans and went down the wooden steps to the street. He paid no attention to Walter Ivans's very friendly "Good-by, Ned."

IV

From the box-factory Ned Beaumont walked four blocks to a restaurant and used a telephone. He called the four numbers he had called earlier in the day, asking again for Paul Madvig and, not getting him on the wire, left instructions for Madvig to call him. Then he got a taxicab and went home.

Additional pieces of mail had been put with those already on the table by his door. He hung up his hat and overcoat, lighted a cigar, and sat down with his mail in the largest of the red-plush chairs. The fourth envelope he opened was similar to the one the District Attorney had shown him. It contained a single sheet of paper bearing three typewritten sentences without salutation or signature:

Did you find Taylor Henry's body after he was dead or were you present when he was murdered?

Why did you not report his death until after the police had found the body?

Do you think you can save the guilty by manufacturing evidence against the innocent?

Ned Beaumont screwed up his eyes and wrinkled his forehead over this message and drew much smoke from his cigar. He compared it with the one the District Attorney had received. Paper and typing were alike, as were the manner in which each paper's three sentences were arranged and the time of the postmarks.

Scowling, he returned each to its envelope and put them in his pocket, only to take them out again immediately to reread and re-examine them. Too rapid smoking made his cigar burn irregularly down one side. He put the cigar on the edge of the table beside him with a grimace of distaste and picked at his mustache with nervous fingers. He put the messages away once more and leaned back in his chair, staring at the ceiling and biting a finger-nail. He ran fingers through his hair. He put the end of a finger between his collar and his neck. He sat up and took the envelopes out of his pocket again, but put them back without having looked at them. He chewed his lower lip. Finally he shook himself impatiently and began to read the rest of his mail. He was reading it when the telephone-bell rang.

He went to the telephone. "Hello. . . . Oh, 'lo, Paul, where are you? . . . How long will you be there? . . . Yes, fine, drop in on your way. . . . Right, I'll be here."

He returned to his mail.

V

Paul Madvig arrived at Ned Beaumont's rooms as the bells in the grey church across the street were ringing the Angelus. He came in saying heartily: "Howdy, Ned. When'd you get back?" His big body was clothed in grey tweeds.

"Late this morning," Ned Beaumont replied as they shook hands.

"Make out all right?"

Ned Beaumont showed the edges of his teeth in a contented smile. "I got what I went after—all of it."

"That's great." Madvig threw his hat on a chair and sat on another beside the fireplace.

Ned Beaumont returned to his chair. "Anything happen while I was gone?" he asked as he picked up the half-filled cocktail-glass standing beside the silver shaker on the table at his elbow.

"We got the muddle on the sewer-contract straightened out."

Ned Beaumont sipped his cocktail and asked: "Have to make much of a cut?"

"Too much. There won't be anything like the profit there ought to be, but that's better than taking a chance on stirring things up this close to election. We'll make it up on the street-work next year when the Salem and Chestnut extensions go through."

Ned Beaumont nodded. He was looking at the blond man's outstretched crossed ankles. He said: "You oughtn't to wear silk socks with tweeds."

Madvig raised a leg straight out to look at the ankle. "No? I like the feel of silk."

"Then lay off tweeds. Taylor Henry buried?"

"Friday."

"Go to the funeral?"

"Yes," Madvig replied and added a little self-consciously: "The Senator suggested it."

Ned Beaumont put his glass on the table and touched his lips with a white handkerchief taken from the outer breast-pocket of his coat. "How is the Senator?" He looked obliquely at the blond man and did not conceal the amusement in his eyes.

Madvig replied, still somewhat self-consciously: "He's all right. I spent most of this afternoon up there with him."

"At his house?"

"Uh-huh."

"Was the blonde menace there?"

Madvig did not quite frown. He said: "Janet was there."

Ned Beaumont, putting his handkerchief away, made a choked gurgling sound in his throat and said: "M-m-m. It's Janet now. Getting anywhere with her?"

Composure came back to Madvig. He said evenly: "I still think I'm going to marry her."

"Does she know yet that—that your intentions are honor-able?"

"For Christ's sake, Ned!" Madvig protested. "How long are you going to keep me on the witness-stand?"

Ned Beaumont laughed, picked up the silver shaker, shook it, and poured himself another drink. "How do you like the Francis West killing?" he asked when he was sitting back with the glass in his hand.

Madvig seemed puzzled for a moment. Then his face cleared and he said: "Oh, that's the fellow that got shot on Achland Avenue last night."

"That's the fellow."

A fainter shade of puzzlement returned to Madvig's blue eyes. He said: "Well, I didn't know him."

Ned Beaumont said: "He was one of the witnesses against Walter Ivans's brother. Now the other witness, Boyd West, is afraid to testify, so the rap falls through."

"That's swell," Madvig said, but by the time the last word had issued from his mouth a doubtful look had come into his eyes. He drew his legs in and leaned forward. "Afraid?" he asked.

"Yes, unless you like scared better."

Madvig's face hardened into attentiveness and his eyes became stony blue disks. "What are you getting at, Ned?" he asked in a crisp voice.

Ned Beaumont emptied his glass and set it on the table. "After you told Walt Ivans you couldn't spring Tim till election was out of the way he took his troubles to Shad O'Rory," he said in a deliberate monotone, as if reciting a lesson. "Shad sent some of his guerrillas around to scare the two Wests out of appearing against Tim. One of them wouldn't scare and they bumped him off."

Madvig, scowling, objected: "What the hell does Shad care about Tim Ivans's troubles?"

Ned Beaumont, reaching for the cocktail-shaker, said irritably: "All right, I'm just guessing. Forget it."

"Cut it out, Ned. You know your guesses are good enough for me. If you've got anything on your mind, spill it."

Ned Beaumont set the shaker down without having poured a drink and said: "It might be just a guess, at that, Paul, but this is the way it looks to me. Everybody knows Walt Ivans's been working for you down in the Third Ward and is a member of the Club and everything and that you'd do anything you could to get his brother out of a jam if he asked you. Well, everybody, or a lot of them, is going to start wondering whether you didn't have the witnesses against his brother shot and frightened into silence. That goes for the outsiders, the women's clubs you're getting so afraid of these days, and the respectable citizens. The insiders—the ones that mostly wouldn't care if you had done that—are going to get something like the real news. They're going to know that one of your boys had to go to Shad to get fixed up and that Shad fixed him up. Well, that's the hole Shad's put you in—or don't you think he'd go that far to put you in a hole?"

Madvig growled through his teeth: "I know damned well he would, the louse." He was lowering down at a green leaf worked in the rug at his feet.

Ned Beaumont, after looking intently at the blond man, went on: "And there's another angle to look for. Maybe it won't happen, but you're open to it if Shad wants to work it."

Madvig looked up to ask: "What?"

"Walt Ivans was at the Club all last night, till two this morning. That's about three hours later than he ever stayed there before except on election- or banquet-nights. Understand? He was making himself an alibi—in our Club. Suppose"—Ned Beaumont's voice sank to a lower key and his dark eyes were round and grave—"Shad jobs Walt by planting evidence that he killed West? Your women's clubs and all the people who like to squawk about things like that are going to think that Walt's alibi is phony—that we fixed it up to shield him."

Madvig said: "The louse." He stood up and thrust his hands into his trousers-pockets. "I wish to Christ the election was either over or further away."

"None of this would've happened then."

Madvig took two steps into the center of the room. He muttered, "God damn him," and stood frowning at the telephone on the stand beside the bedroom-door. His huge chest moved with his breathing. He said from the side of his mouth, without looking at Ned Beaumont: "Figure out a way of blocking that angle." He took a step towards the telephone and halted. "Never mind," he said and turned to face Ned Beaumont. "I think I'll knock Shad loose from our little city. I'm tired of having him around. I think I'll knock him loose right away, starting tonight."

Ned Beaumont asked: "For instance?"

Madvig grinned. "For instance," he replied, "I think I'll have Rainey close up the Dog House and Paradise Gardens and every dive that we know Shad or any of his friends are interested in. I think I'll have Rainey smack them over in one long row, one after the other, this very same night."

Ned Beaumont spoke hesitantly: "You're putting Rainey in a tough spot. Our coppers aren't used to bothering with Prohibition-enforcement. They're not going to like it very much."

"They can do it once for me," Madvig said, "without feeling that they've paid all their debts."

"Maybe." Ned Beaumont's face and voice were dubious still. "But this wholesale stuff is too much like using a cyclone shot to blow off a safe-door when you could get it off without any fuss by using a come-along."

"Have you got something up your sleeve, Ned?"

Ned Beaumont shook his head. "Nothing I'm sure of, but it wouldn't hurt to wait a couple of days till—"

Now Madvig shook his head. "No," he said. "I want action. I don't know a damned thing about opening safes, Ned, but I do know fighting—my kind—going in with both hands working. I never could learn to box and the only times I ever tried I got licked. We'll give Mr. O'Rory the cyclone shot."

VI

The stringy man in horn-rimmed spectacles said: "So you don't have to worry none about that." He sat complacently back in his chair.

The man on his left—a raw-boned man with a bushy brown mustache and not much hair on his head—said to the man on his left: "It don't sound so God-damned swell to me."

"No?" The stringy man turned to glare through his spectacles at the raw-boned man. "Well, Paul don't never have to come down to my ward hisself to—"

The raw-boned man said: "Aw, nurts!"

Madvig addressed the raw-boned man: "Did you see Parker, Breen?"

Breen said: "Yes, I saw him and he says five, but I think we can get a couple more out of him."

The bespectacled man said contemptuously: "My God, I'd think so!"

Breen sneered sidewise at him. "Yes? And who'd you ever get that much out of?"

Three knocks sounded on the broad oaken door.

Ned Beaumont rose from the chair he was straddling and went to the door. He opened it less than a foot.

The man who had knocked was a small-browed dark man in blue clothes that needed pressing. He did not try to enter the room and he tried to speak in an undertone, but excitement made his words audible to everyone in the room. "Shad O'Rory's downstairs. He wants to see Paul."

Ned Beaumont shut the door and turned with his back against it to look at Paul Madvig. Only those two of the ten men in the room seemed undisturbed by the small-browed man's announcement. All the others did not show their excitement frankly—in some it could be seen in their suddenly acquired stoniness—but there was none whose respiration was exactly as it had been before.

Ned Beaumont, pretending he did not know repetition was unnecessary, said, in a tone that expressed suitable interest in his words: "O'Rory wants to see you. He's downstairs."

Madvig looked at his watch. "Tell him I'm tied up right now, but if he'll wait a little while I'll see him."

Ned Beaumont nodded and opened the door. "Tell him Paul's busy now," he instructed the man who had knocked, "but if he'll stick around awhile Paul'll see him." He shut the door.

Madvig was questioning a square-faced yellowish man about their chances of getting more votes on the other side of Chestnut Street. The square-faced man replied that he thought they would get more than last time "by a hell of a sight," but still not enough to make much of a dent in the opposition. While he talked his eyes kept crawling sidewise to the door.

Ned Beaumont sat astride his chair by the window again smoking a cigar.

Madvig addressed to another man a question having to do with the size of the campaign-contribution to be expected from a man named Hartwick. This other man kept his eyes from the door, but his reply lacked coherence.

Neither Madvig's and Ned Beaumont's calmness of mien nor their business-like concentration on campaign-problems could check the growth of tension in the room.

After fifteen minutes Madvig rose and said: "Well, we're not on Easy Street yet, but she's shaping up. Keep hard at it and we'll make the grade." He went to the door and shook each man's hand as they went out. They went out somewhat hurriedly.

Ned Beaumont, who had not left his chair, asked, when he and Madvig were the only ones in the room: "Do I stick around or beat it?"

"Stick around." Madvig crossed to the window and looked down into sunny China Street.

"Both hands working?" Ned Beaumont asked after a little pause.

Madvig turned from the window nodding. "I don't know anything else"—he grinned boyishly at the man straddling the chair—"except maybe the feet too."

Ned Beaumont started to say something, but was interrupted by the noise the turning door-knob made.

A man opened the door and came in. He was a man of little more than medium height, trimly built with a trimness that gave him a deceptively frail appearance. Though his hair was a sheer sleek white he was probably not much past his thirty-fifth year. His eyes were a notable clear grey-blue set in a rather long and narrow, but very finely sculptured, face. He wore a dark blue overcoat over a dark blue suit and carried a black derby hat in a black-gloved hand.

The man who came in behind him was a bow-legged ruffian of the same height, a swarthy man with something apish in the slope of his big shoulders, the length of his thick arms, and the flatness of his face. This one's hat—a grey fedora—was on his head. He shut the door and leaned against it, putting his hands in the pockets of his plaid overcoat.

The first man, having advanced by then some four or five steps into the room, put his hat on a chair and began to take off his gloves.

Madvig, hands in trousers-pockets, smiled amiably and said: "How are you, Shad?"

The white-haired man said: "Fine, Paul. How's yourself?" His voice was a musical barytone. The faintest of brogues colored his words.

Madvig indicated with a small jerk of his head the man on the chair and asked: "You know Beaumont?"

O'Rory said: "Yes."

Ned Beaumont said: "Yes."

Neither nodded to the other and Ned Beaumont did not get up from his chair.

Shad O'Rory had finished taking off his gloves. He put them in an overcoat-pocket and said: "Politics is politics and business is business. I've been paying my way and I'm willing to go on paying my way, but I want what I'm paying for." His modulated voice was no more than pleasantly earnest.

"What do you mean by that?" Madvig asked as if he did not greatly care.

"I mean that half the coppers in town are buying their cakes and ale with dough they're getting from me and some of my friends."

Madvig sat down by the table. "Well?" he asked, carelessly as before.

"I want what I'm paying for. I'm paying to be let alone. I want to be let alone."

Madvig chuckled. "You don't mean, Shad, that you're complaining to me because your coppers won't stay bought?"

"I mean that Doolan told me last night that the orders to shut up my places came straight from you."

Madvig chuckled again and turned his head to address Ned Beaumont: "What do you think of that, Ned?"

Ned Beaumont smiled thinly, but said nothing.

Madvig said: "You know what I think of it? I think Captain Doolan's been working too hard. I think somebody ought to give Captain Doolan a nice long leave of absence. Don't let me forget it."

O'Rory said: "I bought protection, Paul, and I want it.

Business is business and politics is politics. Let's keep them apart."

Madvig said: "No."

Shad O'Rory's blue eyes looked dreamily at some distant thing. He smiled a little sadly and there was a note of sadness in his musical slightly Irish voice when he spoke. He said: "It's going to mean killing."

Madvig's blue eyes were opaque and his voice was as difficultly read as his eyes. He said: "If you make it mean killing."

The white-haired man nodded. "It'll have to mean killing," he said, still sadly. "I'm too big to take the boot from you now."

Madvig leaned back in his chair and crossed his legs. His tone attached little importance to his words. He said: "Maybe you're too big to take it laying down, but you'll take it." He pursed his lips and added as an afterthought: "You are taking it."

Dreaminess and sadness went swiftly out of Shad O'Rory's eyes. He put his black hat on his head. He adjusted his coat-collar to his neck. He pointed a long white finger at Madvig and said: "I'm opening the Dog House again tonight. I don't want to be bothered. Bother me and I'll bother you."

Madvig uncrossed his legs and reached for the telephone on the table. He called the Police Department's number, asked for the Chief, and said to him: "Hello, Rainey. . . . Yes, fine. How are the folks? . . . That's good. Say, Rainey, I hear Shad's thinking of opening up again tonight. . . . Yes. . . . Yes, slam it down so hard it bounces. . . . Right. . . . Sure. Good-by." He pushed the telephone back and addressed O'Rory: "Now do you understand how you stand? You're through, Shad. You're through here for good."

O'Rory said softly, "I understand," turned, opened the door, and went out.

The bow-legged ruffian paused to spit—deliberately—on the rug in front of him and to stare with bold challenging eyes at Madvig and Ned Beaumont. Then he went out.

Ned Beaumont wiped the palms of his hands with a handkerchief. He said nothing to Madvig, who was looking at him with questioning eyes. Ned Beaumont's eyes were gloomy.

After a moment Madvig asked: "Well?"

Ned Beaumont said: "Wrong, Paul."

Madvig rose and went to the window. "Jesus Christ!" he complained over his shoulder, "don't anything ever suit you?"

Ned Beaumont got up from his chair and walked towards the door.

Madvig, turning from the window, asked angrily: "Some more of your God-damned foolishness?"

Ned Beaumont said, "Yes," and went out of the room. He went downstairs, got his hat, and left the Log Cabin Club. He walked seven blocks to the railroad station, bought a ticket for New York, and made reservations on a night train. Then he took a taxicab to his rooms.

VII

A stout shapeless woman in grey clothes and a chubby half-grown boy were packing Ned Beaumont's trunk and three leather bags under his supervision when the door-bell rang.

The woman rose grunting from her knees and went to the door. She opened it wide. "My goodness, Mr. Madvig," she said. "Come right on in."

Madvig came in saying: "How are you, Mrs. Duveen? You get younger-looking every day." His gaze passed over the trunk and bags to the boy. "Hello, Charley. Ready for the job running the cement-mixer yet?"

The boy grinned bashfully and said: "How do you do, Mr. Madvig?"

Madvig's smile came around to Ned Beaumont. "Going places?"

Ned Beaumont smiled politely. "Yes," he said.

The blond man looked around the room, at the bags and trunk again, at the clothes piled on chairs and the drawers standing open. The woman and the boy went back to their work. Ned Beaumont found two somewhat faded shirts in a pile on a chair and put them aside.

Madvig asked: "Got half an hour to spare, Ned?"

"I've got plenty of time."

Madvig said: "Get your hat."

Ned Beaumont got his hat and overcoat. "Get as much of it in as you can," he told the woman as he and Madvig moved towards the door, "and what's left over can be sent on with the other stuff."

He and Madvig went downstairs to the street. They walked south a block. Then Madvig asked: "Where're you going, Ned?"

"New York."

They turned into an alley.

Madvig asked: "For good?"

Ned Beaumont shrugged. "I'm leaving here for good."

They opened a green wooden door set in the red brick rear wall of a building and went down a passageway and through another door into a bar-room where half a dozen men were drinking. They exchanged greetings with the bar-tender and three of the drinkers as they passed through to a small room where there were four tables. Nobody else was there. They sat at one of the tables.

The bar-tender put his head in and asked: "Beer as per usual, gents?"

Madvig said, "Yes," and then, when the bar-tender had withdrawn: "Why?"

Ned Beaumont said: "I'm tired of hick-town stuff."

"Meaning me?"

Ned Beaumont did not say anything.

Madvig did not say anything for a while. Then he sighed and said: "This is a hell of a time to be throwing me down."

The bar-tender came in with two seidels of pale beer and a bowl of pretzels. When he had gone out again, shutting the door behind him, Madvig exclaimed: "Christ, you're hard to get along with, Ned!"

Ned Beaumont moved his shoulders. "I never said I wasn't." He lifted his seidel and drank.

Madvig was breaking a pretzel into small bits. "Do you really want to go, Ned?" he asked.

"I'm going."

Madvig dropped the fragments of pretzel on the table and took a check-book from his pocket. He tore out a check, took a fountain-pen from another pocket, and filled in the check. Then he fanned it dry and dropped it on the table in front of Ned Beaumont.

Ned Beaumont, looking down at the check, shook his head

and said: "I don't need money and you don't owe me anything."

"I do. I owe you more than that, Ned. I wish you'd take it."

Ned Beaumont said, "All right, thanks," and put the check in his pocket.

Madvig drank beer, ate a pretzel, started to drink again, set his seidel down on the table, and asked: "Was there anything on your mind—any kick—besides that back in the Club this afternoon?"

Ned Beaumont shook his head. "You don't talk to me like that. Nobody does."

"Hell, Ned, I didn't say anything."

Ned Beaumont did not say anything.

Madvig drank again. "Mind telling me why you think I handled O'Rory wrong?"

"It wouldn't do any good."

"Try."

Ned Beaumont said: "All right, but it won't do any good." He tilted his chair back, holding his seidel in one hand, some pretzels in the other. "Shad'll fight. He's got to. You've got him in a corner. You've told him he's through here for good. There's nothing he can do now but play the long shot. If he can upset you this election he'll be fixed to square anything he has to do to win. If you win the election he's got to drift anyhow. You're using the police on him. He'll have to fight back at the police and he will. That means you're going to have something that can be made to look like a crime-wave. You're trying to re-elect the whole city administration. Well, giving them a crime-wave—and one it's an even bet they're not going to be able to handle—just before election isn't going to make them look any too efficient. They—"

"You think I ought to've laid down to him?" Madvig demanded, scowling.

"I don't think that. I think you should have left him an out, a line of retreat. You shouldn't have got him with his back to the wall."

Madvig's scowl deepened. "I don't know anything about your kind of fighting. He started it. All I know is when you got somebody cornered you go in and finish them. That system's worked all right for me so far." He blushed a little. "I don't mean I think I'm Napoleon or something, Ned, but I came up from running errands for Packy Flood in the old Fifth to where I'm sitting kind of pretty today."

Ned Beaumont emptied his seidel and let the front legs of his chair come down on the floor. "I told you it wouldn't do any good," he said. "Have it your own way. Keep on thinking that what was good enough for the old Fifth is good enough anywhere."

In Madvig's voice there was something of resentment and something of humility when he asked: "You don't think much of me as a big-time politician, do you, Ned?"

Now Ned Beaumont's face flushed. He said: "I didn't say that, Paul."

"But that's what it amounts to, isn't it?" Madvig insisted.

"No, but I do think you've let yourself be outsmarted this time. First you let the Henrys wheedle you into backing the Senator. There was your chance to go in and finish an enemy who was cornered, but that enemy happened to have a daughter and social position and what not, so you—"

"Cut it out, Ned," Madvig grumbled.

Ned Beaumont's face became empty of expression. He stood up saying, "Well, I must be running along," and turned to the door.

Madvig was up behind him immediately, with a hand on his shoulder, saying: "Wait, Ned."

Ned Beaumont said: "Take your hand off me." He did not look around.

Madvig put his other hand on Ned Beaumont's arm and turned him around. "Look here, Ned," he began.

Ned Beaumont said: "Let go." His lips were pale and stiff.

Madvig shook him. He said: "Don't be a God-damned fool. You and I—"

Ned Beaumont struck Madvig's mouth with his left fist.

Madvig took his hands away from Ned Beaumont and fell back two steps. While his pulse had time to beat perhaps three times his mouth hung open and astonishment was in his face. Then his face darkened with anger and he shut his mouth tight, so his jaw was hard and lumpy. He made fists of his hands, hunched his shoulders, and swayed forward.

Ned Beaumont's hand swept out to the side to grasp one of the heavy glass seidels on the table, though he did not lift it from the table. His body leaned a little to that side as he had leaned to get the seidel. Otherwise he stood squarely confronting the blond man. His face was drawn thin and rigid, with white lines of strain around the mouth. His dark eyes glared fiercely into Madvig's blue ones.

They stood thus, less than a yard apart—one blond, tall and powerfully built, leaning far forward, big shoulders hunched, big fists ready; the other dark of hair and eye, tall and lean, body bent a little to one side with an arm slanting down from that side to hold a heavy glass seidel by its handle—and except for their breathing there was no sound in the room. No sound came in from the bar-room on the other side of the thin door, the rattling of glasses nor the hum of talk nor the splash of water.

When quite two minutes had passed Ned Beaumont took his hand away from the seidel and turned his back to Madvig. Nothing changed in Ned Beaumont's face except that his eyes, when no longer focused on Madvig's, became hard and cold instead of angrily glaring. He took an unhurried step towards the door.

Madvig spoke hoarsely from deep down in him. "Ned."

Ned Beaumont halted. His face became paler. He did not turn around.

Madvig said: "You crazy son of a bitch."

Then Ned Beaumont turned around, slowly.

Madvig put out an open hand and pushed Ned Beaumont's face sidewise, shoving him off balance so he had to put a foot out quickly to that side and put a hand on one of the chairs at the table.

Madvig said: "I ought to knock hell out of you."

Ned Beaumont grinned sheepishly and sat down on the chair he had staggered against. Madvig sat down facing him and knocked on the top of the table with his seidel.

The bar-tender opened the door and put his head in.

"More beer," Madvig said.

From the bar-room, through the open door, came the sound of men talking and the sound of glasses rattling against glasses and against wood.

CHAPTER IV

The Dog House

NED BEAUMONT, at breakfast in bed, called, "Come in," and then, when the outer door had opened and closed: "Yes?"

A low-pitched rasping voice in the living-room asked: "Where are you, Ned?" Before Ned Beaumont could reply the rasping voice's owner had come to the bedroom-door and was saying: "Pretty soft for you." He was a sturdy young man with a square-cut sallow face, a wide thick-lipped mouth, from a corner of which a cigarette dangled, and merry dark squinting eyes.

"'Lo, Whisky," Ned Beaumont said to him. "Treat yourself to a chair."

Whisky looked around the room. "Pretty good dump you've got here," he said. He removed the cigarette from his lips and, without turning his head, used the cigarette to point over his shoulder at the living-room behind him. "What's all the keysters for? Moving out?"

Ned Beaumont thoroughly chewed and swallowed the scrambled eggs in his mouth before replying: "Thinking of it."

Whisky said, "Yes?" while moving towards a chair that faced the bed. He sat down. "Where to?"

"New York maybe."

"What do you mean maybe?"

Ned Beaumont said: "Well, I've got a ducat that reads to there, anyway."

Whisky knocked cigarette-ash on the floor and returned the cigarette to the left side of his mouth. He snuffled. "How long you going to be gone?"

Ned Beaumont held a coffee-cup half-way between the tray and his mouth. He looked thoughtfully over it at the sallow young man. Finally he said, "It's a one-way ticket," and drank.

Whisky squinted at Ned Beaumont now until one of his dark eyes was entirely shut and the other was no more than a thin black gleam. He took the cigarette from his mouth and knocked more ash on the floor. His rasping voice held a persuasive note. "Why don't you see Shad before you go?" he suggested.

Ned Beaumont put his cup down and smiled. He said: "Shad and I aren't good enough friends that his feelings'll be hurt if I go away without saying good-by."

Whisky said: "That ain't the point."

Ned Beaumont moved the tray from his lap to the bedside-table. He turned on his side, propping himself up on an elbow on the pillows. He pulled the bed-clothes higher up over his chest. Then he asked: "What is the point?"

"The point is you and Shad ought to be able to do business together."

Ned Beaumont shook his head. "I don't think so."

"Can't you be wrong?" Whisky demanded.

"Sure," the man in bed confessed. "Once back in 1912 I was. I forget what it was about."

Whisky rose to mash his cigarette in one of the dishes on the tray. Standing beside the bed, close to the table, he said: "Why don't you try it, Ned?"

Ned Beaumont frowned. "Looks like a waste of time, Whisky. I don't think Shad and I could get along together."

Whisky sucked a tooth noisily. The downward curve of his thick lips gave the noise a scornful cast. "Shad thinks you could," he said.

Ned Beaumont opened his eyes. "Yes?" he asked. "He sent you here?"

"Hell, yes," Whisky said. "You don't think I'd be here talking like this if he hadn't."

Ned Beaumont narrowed his eyes again and asked: "Why?"

"Because he thought him and you could do business together."

"I mean," Ned Beaumont explained, "why did he think I'd want to do business with him?"

Whisky made a disgusted face. "Are you trying to kid me, Ned?" he asked.

"No."

"Well, for the love of Christ, don't you think everybody in town knows about you and Paul having it out at Pip Carson's yesterday?"

Ned Beaumont nodded. "So that's it," he said softly, as if to himself.

"That's it," the man with the rasping voice assured him, "and Shad happens to know you fell out over thinking Paul hadn't ought to've had Shad's joints smeared. So you're sitting pretty with Shad now if you use your head."

Ned Beaumont said thoughtfully: "I don't know. I'd like to get out of here, get back to the big city."

"Use your head," Whisky rasped. "The big city'll still be there after election. Stick around. You know Shad's dough-heavy and's putting it out in chunks to beat Madvig. Stick around and get yourself a slice of it."

"Well," Ned Beaumont said slowly, "it wouldn't hurt to talk it over with him."

"You're damned right it wouldn't," Whisky said heartily. "Pin your diapers on and we'll go now."

Ned Beaumont said, "Right," and got out of bed.

II

Shad O'Rory rose and bowed. "Glad to see you, Beaumont," he said. "Drop your hat and coat anywhere." He did not offer to shake hands.

Ned Beaumont said, "Good morning," and began to take off his overcoat.

Whisky, in the doorway, said: "Well, I'll be seeing you guys later."

O'Rory said, "Yes, do," and Whisky, drawing the door shut as he backed out, left them.

Ned Beaumont dropped his overcoat on the arm of a sofa, put his hat on the overcoat, and sat down beside them. He looked without curiosity at O'Rory.

O'Rory had returned to his chair, a deeply padded squat affair of dull wine and gold. He crossed his knees and put his hands together—tips of fingers and thumbs touching—atop his uppermost knee. He let his finely sculptured head sink down towards his chest so that his grey-blue eyes looked upward under his brows at Ned Beaumont. He said, in his pleasantly modulated Irish voice: "I owe you something for trying to talk Paul out of—"

"You don't," Ned Beaumont said.

O'Rory asked: "I don't?"

"No. I was with him then. What I told him was for his own good. I thought he was making a bad play."

O'Rory smiled gently. "And he'll know it before he's through," he said.

Silence was between them awhile then. O'Rory sat half-buried in his chair smiling at Ned Beaumont. Ned Beaumont sat on the sofa looking, with eyes that gave no indication of what he thought, at O'Rory.

The silence was broken by O'Rory asking: "How much did Whisky tell you?"

"Nothing. He said you wanted to see me."

"He was right enough as far as he went," O'Rory said. He took his finger-tips apart and patted the back of one slender hand with the palm of the other. "Is it so that you and Paul have broken for good and all?"

"I thought you knew it," Ned Beaumont replied. "I thought that's why you sent for me."

"I heard it," O'Rory said, "but that's not always the same thing. What were you thinking you might do now?"

"There's a ticket for New York in my pocket and my clothes are packed."

O'Rory raised a hand and smoothed his sleek white hair. "You came here from New York, didn't you?"

"I never told anybody where I came from."

O'Rory took his hand from his hair and made a small gesture of protestation. "You don't think I'm one to give a damn where any man comes from, do you?" he asked.

Ned Beaumont did not say anything.

The white-haired man said: "But I do care about where you go and if I have my way as much as I'd like you won't be going off to New York yet awhile. Did you never happen to think that maybe you could still do yourself a lot of good right here?"

"No," Ned Beaumont said, "that is, not till Whisky came."

"And what do you think now?"

"I don't know anything about it. I'm waiting to hear what you've got to say."

O'Rory put his hand to his hair again. His blue-grey eyes were friendly and shrewd. He asked: "How long have you been here?"

"Fifteen months."

"And you and Paul have been close as a couple of fingers how long?"

"Year."

O'Rory nodded. "And you ought to know a lot of things about him," he said.

"I do."

O'Rory said: "You ought to know a lot of things I could use."

Ned Beaumont said evenly: "Make your proposition."

O'Rory got up from the depths of his chair and went to a door opposite the one through which Ned Beaumont had come. When he opened the door a huge English bulldog waddled in. O'Rory went back to his chair. The dog lay on the rug in front of the wine and gold chair staring with morose eyes up at its master.

O'Rory said: "One thing I can offer you is a chance to pay Paul back plenty."

Ned Beaumont said: "That's nothing to me."

"It is not?"

"Far as I'm concerned we're quits."

O'Rory raised his head. He asked softly: "And you wouldn't want to do anything to hurt him?"

"I didn't say that," Ned Beaumont replied a bit irritably. "I don't mind hurting him, but I can do it any time I want to on my own account and I don't want you to think you're giving me anything when you give me a chance to."

O'Rory wagged his head up and down, pleasantly. "Suits me," he said, "so he's hurt. Why did he bump off young Henry?"

Ned Beaumont laughed. "Take it easy," he said. "You haven't made your proposition yet. That's a nice pooch. How old is he?"

"Just about the limit, seven." O'Rory put out a foot and rubbed the dog's nose with the tip of it. The dog moved its tail sluggishly. "How does this hit you? After election I'll stake you to the finest gambling-house this state's ever seen and let you run it to suit yourself with all the protection you ever heard of."

"That's an *if* offer," Ned Beaumont said in a somewhat bored manner, "*if* you win. Anyhow, I'm not sure I want to stay here after election, or even that long."

O'Rory stopped rubbing the dog's nose with his shoe-tip. He looked up at Ned Beaumont again, smiled dreamily, and asked: "Don't you think we're going to win the election?"

Ned Beaumont smiled. "You won't bet even money on it."

O'Rory, still smiling dreamily, asked another question: "You're not so God-damned hot for putting in with me, are you, Beaumont?"

"No." Ned Beaumont rose and picked up his hat. "It wasn't any idea of mine." His voice was casual, his face politely expressionless. "I told Whisky it'd just be wasting time." He reached for his overcoat.

The white-haired man said: "Sit down. We can still talk, can't we? And maybe we'll get somewhere before we're through."

Ned Beaumont hesitated, moved his shoulders slightly, took off his hat, put it and his overcoat on the sofa, and sat down beside them.

O'Rory said: "I'll give you ten grand in cash right now if you'll come in and ten more election-night if we beat Paul and I'll keep that house-offer open for you to take or leave."

Ned Beaumont pursed his lips and stared gloomily at O'Rory under brows drawn together. "You want me to rat on him, of course," he said.

"I want you to go into the *Observer* with the low-down on everything you know about him being mixed up in—the sewer-contracts, the how and why of killing Taylor Henry, that Shoemaker junk last winter, the dirt on how he's running the city."

"There's nothing in the sewer-business now," Ned Beaumont said, speaking as if his mind was more fully occupied with other thoughts. "He let his profits go to keep from raising a stink."

"All right," O'Rory conceded, blandly confident, "but there is something in the Taylor Henry business."

"Yes, we'd have him there," Ned Beaumont said, frowning,

"but I don't know whether we could use the Shoemaker stuff"—he hesitated—"without making trouble for me."

"Hell, we don't want that," O'Rory said quickly. "That's out. What else have we got?"

"Maybe we can do something with the street-car-franchise extension and with that trouble last year in the County Clerk's office. We'll have to do some digging first, though."

"It'll be worth it for both of us," O'Rory said. "I'll have Hinkle—he's the *Observer* guy—put the stuff in shape. You just give him the dope and let him write it. We can start off with the Taylor Henry thing. That's something that's right on tap."

Ned Beaumont brushed his mustache with a thumb-nail and murmured: "Maybe."

Shad O'Rory laughed. "You mean we ought to start off first with the ten thousand dollars?" he asked. "There's something in that." He got up and crossed the room to the door he had opened for the dog. He opened it and went out, shutting it behind him. The dog did not get up from in front of the wine and gold chair.

Ned Beaumont lit a cigar. The dog turned his head and watched him.

O'Rory came back with a thick sheaf of green hundred-dollar bills held together by a band of brown paper on which was written in blue ink: *$10,000*. He thumped the sheaf down on the hand not holding it and said: "Hinkle's out there now. I told him to come in."

Ned Beaumont frowned. "I ought to have a little time to straighten it out in my mind."

"Give it to Hinkle any way it comes to you. He'll put it in shape."

Ned Beaumont nodded. He blew cigar-smoke out and said: "Yes, I can do that."

O'Rory held out the sheaf of paper money.

Saying, "Thanks," Ned Beaumont took it and put it in his inside coat-pocket. It made a bulge there in the breast of his coat over his flat chest.

Shad O'Rory said, "The thanks go both ways," and went back to his chair.

Ned Beaumont took the cigar out of his mouth. "Here's

something I want to tell you while I think of it," he said. "Framing Walt Ivans for the West killing won't bother Paul as much as leaving it as is."

O'Rory looked curiously at Ned Beaumont for a moment before asking: "Why?"

"Paul's not going to let him have the Club alibi."

"You mean he's going to give the boys orders to forget Ivans was there?"

"Yes."

O'Rory made a clucking noise with his tongue, asked: "How'd he get the idea I was going to play tricks on Ivans?"

"Oh, we figured it out."

O'Rory smiled. "You mean you did," he said. "Paul's not that shifty."

Ned Beaumont made a modest grimace and asked: "What kind of job did you put up on him?"

O'Rory chuckled. "We sent the clown over to Braywood to buy the guns that were used." His grey-blue eyes suddenly became hard and sharp. Then amusement came back into them and he said: "Oh, well, none of that's big stuff now, now that Paul's hell-bent on making a row of it. But that's what started him picking on me, isn't it?"

"Yes," Ned Beaumont told him, "though it was likely to come sooner or later anyhow. Paul thinks he gave you your start here and you ought to stay under his wing and not grow big enough to buck him."

O'Rory smiled gently. "And I'm the boy that'll make him sorry he ever gave me that start," he promised. "He can—"

A door opened and a man came in. He was a young man in baggy grey clothes. His ears and nose were very large. His indefinitely brown hair needed trimming and his rather grimy face was too deeply lined for his years.

"Come in, Hinkle," O'Rory said. "This is Beaumont. He'll give you the dope. Let me see it when you've shaped it up and we'll get the first shot in tomorrow's paper."

Hinkle smiled with bad teeth and muttered something unintelligibly polite to Ned Beaumont.

Ned Beaumont stood up saying: "Fine. We'll go over to my place now and get to work on it."

O'Rory shook his head. "It'll be better here," he said.

Ned Beaumont, picking up hat and overcoat, smiled and said: "Sorry, but I'm expecting some phone-calls and things. Get your hat, Hinkle."

Hinkle, looking frightened, stood still and dumb.

O'Rory said: "You'll have to stay here, Beaumont. We can't afford to have anything happen to you. Here you'll have plenty of protection."

Ned Beaumont smiled his nicest smile. "If it's the money you're worried about"—he put his hand inside his coat and brought it out holding the money—"you can hang on to it till I've turned in the stuff."

"I'm not worried about anything," O'Rory said calmly. "But you're in a tough spot if Paul gets the news you've come over to me and I don't want to take any chances on having you knocked off."

"You'll have to take them," Ned Beaumont said. "I'm going."

O'Rory said: "No."

Ned Beaumont said: "Yes."

Hinkle turned quickly and went out of the room.

Ned Beaumont turned around and started for the other door, the one through which he had come into the room, walking erectly without haste.

O'Rory spoke to the bulldog at his feet. The dog got up in cumbersome haste and waddled around Ned Beaumont to the door. He stood on wide-spread legs in front of the door and stared morosely at Ned Beaumont.

Ned Beaumont smiled with tight lips and turned to face O'Rory again. The package of hundred-dollar bills was in Ned Beaumont's hand. He raised the hand, said, "You know where you can stick it," and threw the package of bills at O'Rory.

As Ned Beaumont's arm came down the bulldog, leaping clumsily, came up to meet it. His jaws shut over Ned Beaumont's wrist. Ned Beaumont was spun to the left by the impact and he sank on one knee with his arm down close to the floor to take the dog's weight off his arm.

Shad O'Rory rose from his chair and went to the door through which Hinkle had retreated. He opened it and said: "Come in a minute." Then he approached Ned Beaumont who, still down on one knee, was trying to let his arm yield to the strain of the dog's pulling. The dog was almost flat on the floor, all four feet braced, holding the arm.

Whisky and two other men came into the room. One of the others was the apish bow-legged man who had accompanied Shad O'Rory to the Log Cabin Club. One was a sandy-haired boy of nineteen or twenty, stocky, rosy-cheeked, and sullen. The sullen boy went around behind Ned Beaumont, between him and the door. The bow-legged ruffian put his right hand on Ned Beaumont's left arm, the arm the dog was not holding. Whisky halted half-way between Ned Beaumont and the other door.

Then O'Rory said, "Patty," to the dog.

The dog released Ned Beaumont's wrist and waddled over to its master.

Ned Beaumont stood up. His face was pallid and damp with sweat. He looked at his torn coat-sleeve and wrist and at the blood running down his hand. His hand was trembling.

O'Rory said in his musical Irish voice: "You would have it."

Ned Beaumont looked up from his wrist at the white-haired man. "Yes," he said, "and it'll take some more of it to keep me from going out of here."

III

Ned Beaumont opened his eyes and groaned.

The rosy-cheeked boy with sandy hair turned his head over his shoulder to growl: "Shut up, you bastard."

The apish dark man said: "Let him alone, Rusty. Maybe he'll try to get out again and we'll have some more fun." He grinned down at his swollen knuckles. "Deal the cards."

Ned Beaumont mumbled something about Fedink and sat up. He was in a narrow bed without sheets or bed-clothes of any sort. The bare mattress was blood-stained. His face was swollen and bruised and blood-smeared. Dried blood glued his shirt-sleeve to the wrist the dog had bitten and that hand was caked with drying blood. He was in a small yellow and white bedroom furnished with two chairs, a table, a chest of drawers, a wall-mirror, and three white-framed French prints, besides the bed. Facing the foot of the bed was a door that stood open to show part of the interior of a white-tiled bathroom. There was another door, shut. There were no windows.

The apish dark man and the rosy-cheeked boy with sandy hair sat on the chairs playing cards on the table. There was about twenty dollars in paper and silver on the table.

Ned Beaumont looked, with brown eyes wherein hate was a dull glow that came from far beneath the surface, at the card-players and began to get out of bed. Getting out of bed was a difficult task for him. His right arm hung useless. He had to push his legs over the side of the bed one at a time with his left hand and twice he fell over on his side and had to push himself upright again in bed with his left arm.

Once the apish man leered up at him from his cards to ask humorously: "How're you making out, brother?" Otherwise the two at the table let him alone.

He stood finally, trembling, on his feet beside the bed. Steadying himself with his left hand on the bed he reached its end. There he drew himself erect and, staring fixedly at his goal, lurched towards the closed door. Near it he stumbled and went down on his knees, but his left hand, thrown desperately out, caught the knob and he pulled himself up on his feet again.

Then the apish man laid his cards carefully down on the table and said: "Now." His grin, showing remarkably beautiful white teeth, was wide enough to show that the teeth were not natural. He went over and stood beside Ned Beaumont.

Ned Beaumont was tugging at the door-knob.

The apish man said, "Now there, Houdini," and with all his weight behind the blow drove his right fist into Ned Beaumont's face.

Ned Beaumont was driven back against the wall. The back of his head struck the wall first, then his body crashed flat against the wall, and he slid down the wall to the floor.

Rosy-cheeked Rusty, still holding his cards at the table, said gloomily, but without emotion: "Jesus, Jeff, you'll croak him."

Jeff said: "Him?" He indicated the man at his feet by kicking him not especially hard on the thigh. "You can't croak him. He's tough. He's a tough baby. He likes this." He bent down, grasped one of the unconscious man's lapels in each hand, and dragged him to his knees. "Don't you like it, baby?" he asked and, holding Ned Beaumont up on his knees with one hand, struck his face with the other fist.

The door-knob was rattled from the outside.

Jeff called: "Who's that?"

Shad O'Rory's pleasant voice: "Me."

Jeff dragged Ned Beaumont far enough from the door to let it open, dropped him there, and unlocked the door with a key taken from his pocket.

O'Rory and Whisky came in. O'Rory looked at the man on the floor, then at Jeff, and finally at Rusty. His blue-grey eyes were clouded. When he spoke it was to ask Rusty: "Jeff been slapping him down for the fun of it?"

The rosy-cheeked boy shook his head. "This Beaumont is a son of a bitch," he said sullenly. "Every time he comes to he gets up and starts something."

"I don't want him killed, not yet," O'Rory said. He looked down at Ned Beaumont. "See if you can bring him around again. I want to talk to him."

Rusty got up from the table. "I don't know," he said. "He's pretty far gone."

Jeff was more optimistic. "Sure we can," he said. "I'll show you. Take his feet, Rusty." He put his hands under Ned Beaumont's armpits.

They carried the unconscious man into the bathroom and put him in the tub. Jeff put the stopper in and turned on cold water from both the faucet below and the shower above. "That'll have him up and singing in no time," he predicted.

Five minutes later, when they hauled him dripping from the tub and set him on his feet, Ned Beaumont could stand. They took him into the bedroom again. O'Rory was sitting on one of the chairs smoking a cigarette. Whisky had gone.

"Put him on the bed," O'Rory ordered.

Jeff and Rusty led their charge to the bed, turned him around, and pushed him down on it. When they took their hands away from him he fell straight back on the bed. They pulled him into a sitting position again and Jeff slapped his battered face with an open hand, saying: "Come on, Rip Van Winkle, come to life."

"A swell chance of him coming to life," the sullen Rusty grumbled.

"You think he won't?" Jeff asked cheerfully and slapped Ned Beaumont again.

Ned Beaumont opened the one eye not too swollen to be opened.

O'Rory said: "Beaumont."

Ned Beaumont raised his head and tried to look around the room, but there was nothing to show he could see Shad O'Rory.

O'Rory got up from his chair and stood in front of Ned Beaumont, bending down until his face was few inches from the other man's. He asked: "Can you hear me, Beaumont?"

Ned Beaumont's open eye looked dull hate into O'Rory's eyes.

O'Rory said: "This is O'Rory, Beaumont. Can you hear what I say?"

Moving his swollen lips with difficulty, Ned Beaumont uttered a thick "Yes."

O'Rory said: "Good. Now listen to what I tell you. You're going to give me the dope on Paul." He spoke very distinctly without raising his voice, without his voice losing any of its musical quality. "Maybe you think you won't, but you will. I'll have you worked on from now till you do. Do you understand me?"

Ned Beaumont smiled. The condition of his face made the smile horrible. He said: "I won't."

O'Rory stepped back and said: "Work on him."

While Rusty hesitated, the apish Jeff knocked aside Ned Beaumont's upraised hand and pushed him down on the bed. "I got something to try." He scooped up Ned Beaumont's legs and tumbled them on the bed. He leaned over Ned Beaumont, his hands busy on Ned Beaumont's body.

Ned Beaumont's body and arms and legs jerked convulsively and three times he groaned. After that he lay still.

Jeff straightened up and took his hands away from the man on the bed. He was breathing heavily through his ape's mouth. He growled, half in complaint, half in apology: "It ain't no good now. He's throwed another joe."

IV

When Ned Beaumont recovered consciousness he was alone in the room. The lights were on. As laboriously as before he got himself out of bed and across the room to the door. The door was locked. He was fumbling with the knob when the door was thrown open, pushing him back against the wall.

Jeff in his underwear, barefoot, came in. "Ain't you a pip?" he said. "Always up to some kind of tricks. Don't you never get tired of being bounced on the floor?" He took Ned Beaumont by the throat with his left hand and struck him in the face with his right fist, twice, but not so hard as he had hit him before. Then he pushed him backwards over to the bed and threw him on it. "And stay put awhile this time," he growled.

Ned Beaumont lay still with closed eyes.

Jeff went out, locking the door behind him.

Painfully Ned Beaumont climbed out of bed and made his way to the door. He tried it. Then he withdrew two steps and tried to hurl himself against it, succeeding only in lurching against it. He kept trying until the door was flung open again by Jeff.

Jeff said: "I never seen a guy that liked being hit so much or that I liked hitting so much." He leaned far over to one side and swung his fist up from below his knee.

Ned Beaumont stood blindly in the fist's path. It struck his cheek and knocked him the full length of the room. He lay still where he fell. He was lying there two hours later when Whisky came into the room.

Whisky awakened him with water from the bathroom and helped him to the bed. "Use your head," Whisky begged him. "These mugs'll kill you. They've got no sense."

Ned Beaumont looked dully at Whisky through a dull and bloody eye. "Let 'em," he managed to say.

He slept then until he was awakened by O'Rory, Jeff, and Rusty. He refused to tell O'Rory anything about Paul Madvig's affairs. He was dragged out of bed, beaten into unconsciousness, and flung into bed again.

This was repeated a few hours later. No food was brought to him.

Going on hands and knees into the bathroom when he had regained consciousness after the last of these beatings, he saw, on the floor behind the wash-stand's pedestal, a narrow safety-razor-blade red with the rust of months. Getting it out from behind the pedestal was a task that took him all of ten minutes and his nerveless fingers failed a dozen times before they succeeded in picking it up from the tiled floor. He tried to cut his throat with it, but it fell out of his hand after he had no more than scratched his chin in three places. He lay down on the bathroom-floor and sobbed himself to sleep.

When he awakened again he could stand, and did. He doused his head in cold water and drank four glasses of water. The water made him sick and after that he began to shake with a chill. He went into the bedroom and lay down on the bare blood-stained mattress, but got up almost immediately to go stumbling and staggering in haste back to the bathroom, where he got down on hands and knees and searched the floor until he had found the rusty razor-blade. He sat on the floor and put the razor-blade into his vest-pocket. Putting it in, his fingers touched his lighter. He took the lighter out and looked at it. A cunning gleam came into his one open eye as he looked at the lighter. The gleam was not sane.

Shaking so that his teeth rattled together, he got up from the bathroom-floor and went into the bedroom again. He laughed harshly when he saw the newspaper under the table where the apish dark man and the sullen rosy-cheeked boy had played cards. Tearing and rumpling and wadding the paper in his hands, he carried it to the door and put it on the floor there. In each of the drawers in the chest of drawers he found a piece of wrapping-paper folded to cover the bottom. He rumpled them and put them with the newspaper against the door. With the razor-blade he made a long gash in the mattress, pulled out big handfuls of the coarse grey cotton with which the mattress was stuffed, and carried them to the door. He was not shaking now, nor stumbling, and he used both hands dexterously, but presently he tired of gutting the mattress and dragged what was left of it—tick and all—to the door.

He giggled then and, after the third attempt, got his lighter ignited. He set fire to the bottom of the heap against the door. At first he stood close to the heap, crouching over it, but as the smoke increased it drove him back step by step, reluctantly, coughing as he retreated. Presently he went into the bathroom, soaked a towel with water, and wrapped it around his head, covering eyes, nose, and mouth. He came stumbling back into the bedroom, a dim figure in the smoky room, fell against the bed, and sat down on the floor beside it.

Jeff found him there when he came in.

Jeff came in cursing and coughing through the rag he held against nose and mouth. In opening the door he had pushed most of the burning heap back a little. He kicked some more out of the way and stamped through the rest to reach Ned Beaumont. He took Ned Beaumont by the back of the collar and dragged him out of the room.

Outside, still holding Ned Beaumont by the back of the collar, Jeff kicked him to his feet and ran him down to the far end of the corridor. There he pushed him through an open doorway, bawled, "I'm going to eat one of your ears when I come back, you bastard," at him, kicked him again, stepped back into the corridor, slammed the door, and turned the key in its lock.

Ned Beaumont, kicked into the room, saved himself from a fall by catching hold of a table. He pushed himself up a little nearer straight and looked around. The towel had fallen down muffler-fashion around his neck and shoulders. The room had two windows. He went to the nearer window and tried to raise it. It was locked. He unfastened the lock and raised the window. Outside was night. He put a leg over the sill, then the other, turned so that he was lying belly-down across the sill, lowered himself until he was hanging by his hands, felt with his feet for some support, found none, and let himself drop.

CHAPTER V

The Hospital

A NURSE was doing something to Ned Beaumont's face. "Where am I?" he asked.

"St. Luke's Hospital." She was a small nurse with very large bright hazel eyes, a breathless sort of hushed voice, and an odor of mimosa.

"What day?"

"It's Monday."

"What month and year?" he asked. When she frowned at him he said: "Oh, never mind. How long have I been here?"

"This is the third day."

"Where's the telephone?" He tried to sit up.

"Stop that," she said. "You can't use the telephone and you mustn't get yourself excited."

"You use it, then. Call Hartford six one one six and tell Mr. Madvig that I've got to see him right away."

"Mr. Madvig's here every afternoon," she said, "but I don't think Doctor Tait will let you talk to anybody yet. As a matter of fact you've done a whole lot more talking now than you ought to."

"What is it now? Morning or afternoon?"

"Morning."

"That's too long to wait," he said. "Call him now."

"Doctor Tait will be in in a little while."

"I don't want any Doctor Taits," he said irritably. "I want Paul Madvig."

"You'll do what you're told," she replied. "You'll lie there and be quiet till Doctor Tait comes."

He scowled at her. "What a swell nurse you are. Didn't anybody ever tell you it's not good for patients to be quarreled with?"

She ignored his question.

He said: "Besides, you're hurting my jaw."

She said: "If you'd keep it still it wouldn't get hurt."

He was quiet for a moment. Then he asked: "What's supposed to have happened to me? Or didn't you get far enough in your lessons to know?"

"Probably a drunken brawl," she told him, but she could not keep her face straight after that. She laughed and said: "But honestly you shouldn't talk so much and you can't see anybody till the doctor says so."

II

Paul Madvig arrived early in the afternoon. "Christ, I'm glad to see you alive again!" he said. He took the invalid's un-bandaged left hand in both of his.

Ned Beaumont said: "I'm all right. But here's what we've got to do: grab Walt Ivans and have him taken over to Bray-wood and shown to the gun-dealers there. He—"

"You told me all that," Madvig said. "That's done."

Ned Beaumont frowned. "I told you?"

"Sure—the morning you were picked up. They took you to the Emergency Hospital and you wouldn't let them do any-thing to you till you'd seen me and I came down there and you told me about Ivans and Braywood and passed out cold."

"It's a blank to me," Ned Beaumont said. "Did you nail them?"

"We got the Ivanses, all right, and Walt Ivans talked after he was identified in Braywood and the Grand Jury indicted Jeff Gardner and two John Does, but we're not going to be able to nail Shad on it. Gardner's the man Ivans dickered with and anybody knows he wouldn't do anything without Shad's say-so, but proving it's another thing."

"Jeff's the monkey-looking guy, huh? Has he been picked up yet?"

"No. Shad took him into hiding with him after you got away, I guess. They had you, didn't they?"

"Uh-huh. In the Dog House, upstairs. I went there to lay a trap for the gent and he out-trapped me." He scowled. "I remember going there with Whisky Vassos and being bitten by the dog and knocked around by Jeff and a blond kid. Then there was something about a fire and—that's about all. Who found me? and where?"

"A copper found you crawling on all fours up the middle of

Colman Street at three in the morning leaving a trail of blood behind you."

"I think of funny things to do," Ned Beaumont said.

III

The small nurse with large eyes opened the door cautiously and put her head in.

Ned Beaumont addressed her in a tired voice: "All right—peekaboo! But don't you think you're a little old for that?"

The nurse opened the door wider and stood on the sill holding the edge of the door with one hand. "No wonder people beat you up," she said. "I wanted to see if you were awake. Mr. Madvig and"—the breathless quality became more pronounced in her voice and her eyes became brighter—"a lady are here."

Ned Beaumont looked at her curiously and a bit mockingly. "What kind of lady?"

"It's Miss Janet Henry," she replied in the manner of one revealing some unexpected pleasant thing.

Ned Beaumont turned on his side, his face away from the nurse. He shut his eyes. A corner of his mouth twitched, but his voice was empty of expression: "Tell them I'm still asleep."

"You can't do that," she said. "They know you're not asleep—even if they haven't heard you talking—or I'd've been back before this."

He groaned dramatically and propped himself up on his elbow. "She'd only come back again some other time," he grumbled. "I might as well get it over with."

The nurse, looking at him with contemptuous eyes, said sarcastically: "We've had to keep policemen in front of the hospital to fight off all the women that've been trying to see you."

"That's all right for you to say," he told her. "Maybe you're impressed by senators' daughters who are in the roto all the time, but you've never been hounded by them the way I have. I tell you they've made my life miserable, them and their brown roto-sections. Senators' daughters, always senators' daughters, never a representative's daughter or a cabinet minister's daughter or an alderman's daughter for the sake of variety—never anything but— Do you suppose senators are more prolific than—"

"You're not really funny," the nurse said. "It's the way you comb your hair. I'll bring them in." She left the room.

Ned Beaumont took a long breath. His eyes were shiny. He moistened his lips and then pressed them together in a tight secretive smile, but when Janet Henry came into the room his face was a mask of casual politeness.

She came straight to his bed and said: "Oh, Mr. Beaumont, I was so glad to hear that you were recovering so nicely that I simply had to come." She put a hand in his and smiled down at him. Though her eyes were not a dark brown her otherwise pure blondness made them seem dark. "So if you didn't want me to come you're not to blame Paul. I made him bring me."

Ned Beaumont smiled back at her and said: "I'm awfully glad you did. It's terribly kind of you."

Paul Madvig, following Janet Henry into the room, had gone around to the opposite side of the bed. He grinned affectionately from her to Ned Beaumont and said: "I knew you'd be, Ned. I told her so. How's it go today?"

"Nobly. Pull some chairs up."

"We can't stay," the blond man replied. "I've got to meet M'Laughlin at the Grandcourt."

"But I don't," Janet Henry said. She directed her smile at Ned Beaumont again. "Mayn't I stay—a little while?"

"I'd love that," Ned Beaumont assured her while Madvig, coming around the bed to place a chair for her, beamed delightedly upon each of them in turn and said: "That's fine." When the girl was sitting beside the bed and her black coat had been laid back over the back of the chair, Madvig looked at his watch and growled: "I've got to run." He shook Ned Beaumont's hand. "Anything I can get for you?"

"No, thanks, Paul."

"Well, be good." The blond man turned towards Janet Henry, stopped, and addressed Ned Beaumont again: "How far do you think I ought to go with M'Laughlin this first time?"

Ned Beaumont moved his shoulders a little. "As far as you want, so long as you don't put anything in plain words. They scare him. But you could hire him to commit murders if you put it to him in a long-winded way, like: 'If there was a man named Smith who lived in such and such a place and he got sick or something and didn't get well and you happened to drop in to see me some time and just by luck an envelope addressed to you had been sent there in care of me, how would I know it had five hundred dollars in it?'."

Madvig nodded. "I don't want any murders," he said, "but we do need that railroad vote." He frowned. "I wish you were up, Ned."

"I will be in a day or two. Did you see the *Observer* this morning?"

"No."

Ned Beaumont looked around the room. "Somebody's run off with it. The dirt was in an editorial in a box in the middle of the front page. *What are our city officials going to do about it?* A list of six weeks' crimes to show we're having a crime-wave. A lot smaller list of who's been caught to show the police aren't able to do much about it. Most of the squawking done about Taylor Henry's murder."

When her brother was named, Janet Henry winced and her lips parted in a little silent gasp. Madvig looked at her and then quickly at Ned Beaumont to move his head in a brief warning gesture.

Ned Beaumont, ignoring the effect of his words on the others, continued: "They were brutal about that. Accused the police of deliberately keeping their hands off the murder for a week so a gambler high in political circles could use it to square a grievance with another gambler—meaning my going after Despain to collect my money. Wondered what Senator Henry thought of his new political allies' use of his son's murder for this purpose."

Madvig, red of face, fumbling for his watch, said hastily: "I'll get a copy and read it. I've got to—"

"Also," Ned Beaumont went on serenely, "they accuse the police of raiding—after having protected them for years—those joints whose owners wouldn't come across with enormous campaign-contributions. That's what they make of your fight with Shad O'Rory. And they promise to print a list of the places that are still running because their owners did come across."

Madvig said, "Well, well," uncomfortably, said, "Good-by, have a nice visit," to Janet Henry, "See you later," to Ned Beaumont, and went out.

Janet Henry leaned forward in her chair. "Why don't you like me?" she asked Ned Beaumont.

"I think maybe I do," he said.

She shook her head. "You don't. I know it."

"You can't go by my manners," he told her. "They're always pretty bad."

"You don't like me," she insisted, not answering his smile, "and I want you to."

He was modest. "Why?"

"Because you are Paul's best friend," she replied.

"Paul," he said, looking obliquely at her, "has a lot of friends: he's a politician."

She moved her head impatiently. "You're his best friend." She paused, then added: "He thinks so."

"What do you think?" he asked with incomplete seriousness.

"I think you are," she said gravely, "or you would not be here now. You would not have gone through that for him."

His mouth twitched in a meager smile. He did not say anything.

When it became manifest that he was not going to speak she said earnestly: "I wish you would like me, if you can."

He repeated: "I think maybe I do."

She shook her head. "You don't."

He smiled at her. His smile was very young and engaging, his eyes shy, his voice youthfully diffident and confiding, as he said: "I'll tell you what makes you think that, Miss Henry. It's—you see, Paul picked me up out of the gutter, as you might say, just a year or so ago, and so I'm kind of awkward and clumsy when I'm around people like you who belong to another world altogether—society and roto-sections and all— and you mistake that—uh—*gaucherie* for enmity, which it isn't at all."

She rose and said, "You're ridiculing me," without resentment.

When she had gone Ned Beaumont lay back on his pillows and stared at the ceiling with glittering eyes until the nurse came in.

The nurse came in and asked: "What have you been up to now?"

Ned Beaumont raised his head to look sullenly at her, but he did not speak.

The nurse said: "She went out of here as near crying as anybody could without crying."

Ned Beaumont lowered his head to the pillow again. "I must be losing my grip," he said. "I usually make senators' daughters cry."

IV

A man of medium size, young and dapper, with a sleek dark rather good-looking face, came in.

Ned Beaumont sat up in bed and said: "'Lo, Jack."

Jack said, "You don't look as bad as I thought you would," and advanced to the side of the bed.

"I'm still all in one piece. Grab a chair."

Jack sat down and took out a package of cigarettes.

Ned Beaumont said: "I've got another job for you." He put a hand under his pillows and brought out an envelope.

Jack lit his cigarette before he took the envelope from Ned Beaumont's hand. It was a plain white envelope addressed to Ned Beaumont at St. Luke's Hospital and bore the local postmark dated two days before. Inside was a single type-written sheet of paper which Jack took out and read.

What do you know about Paul Madvig that Shad O'Rory was so anxious to learn?

Has it anything to do with the murder of Taylor Henry?

If not, why should you have gone to such lengths to keep it secret?

Jack refolded the sheet of paper and returned it to the envelope before he raised his head. Then he asked: "Does it make sense?"

"Not that I know of. I want you to find out who wrote it."

Jack nodded. "Do I keep it?"

"Yes."

Jack put the envelope in his pocket. "Any ideas about who might have done it?"

"None at all."

Jack studied the lighted end of his cigarette. "It's a job, you know," he said presently.

"I know it," Ned Beaumont agreed, "and all I can tell you is that there's been a lot of them—or several of them—in the past week. That's my third. I know Farr got at least one. I don't know who else has been getting them."

"Can I see some of the others?"

Ned Beaumont said: "That's the only one I kept. They're all pretty much alike, though—same paper, same typewriting, three questions in each, all on the same subject."

Jack regarded Ned Beaumont with inquisitive eyes. "But not exactly the same questions?" he asked.

"Not exactly, but all getting to the same point."

Jack nodded and smoked his cigarette.

Ned Beaumont said: "You understand this is to be strictly on the qt."

"Sure." Jack took the cigarette from his mouth. "The 'same point' you mentioned is Madvig's connection with the murder?"

"Yes," Ned Beaumont replied, looking with level eyes at the sleek dark young man, "and there isn't any connection."

Jack's dark face was inscrutable. "I don't see how there could be," he said as he stood up.

v

The nurse came in carrying a large basket of fruit. "Isn't it lovely?" she said as she set it down.

Ned Beaumont nodded cautiously.

The nurse took a small stiff envelope from the basket. "I bet you it's from her," she said, giving Ned Beaumont the envelope.

"What'll you bet?"

"Anything you want."

Ned Beaumont nodded as if some dark suspicion had been confirmed. "You looked," he said.

"Why, you—" Her words stopped when he laughed, but indignation remained in her mien.

He took Janet Henry's card from the envelope. One word

was written on it: *Please!* Frowning at the card, he told the nurse, "You win," and tapped the card on a thumb-nail. "Help yourself to that gunk and take enough of it so it'll look as if I'd been eating it."

Later that afternoon he wrote:

MY DEAR MISS HENRY—

You've quite overwhelmed me with your kindness—first your coming to see me, and then the fruit. I don't at all know how to thank you, but I hope I shall some day be able to more clearly show my gratitude.

Sincerely yours,
NED BEAUMONT

When he had finished he read what he had written, tore it up, and rewrote it on another sheet of paper, using the same words, but rearranging them to make the ending of the second sentence read: "be able some day to show my gratitude more clearly."

VI

Ned Beaumont, in bathrobe and slippers this morning, was reading a copy of the *Observer* over his breakfast at a table by the window of his hospital-room when Opal Madvig came in. He folded the newspaper, put it face-down on the table beside his tray, and rose saying, "'Lo, snip," cordially. He was pale.

"Why didn't you call me up when you got back from New York?" she demanded in an accusing tone. She too was pale. Pallor accentuated the childlike texture of her skin, yet made her face seem less young. Her blue eyes were wide open and dark with emotion, but not to be read easily. She held herself tall without stiffness, in the manner of one more sure of his balance than of stability underfoot. Ignoring the chair he moved out from the wall for her, she repeated, imperatively as before: "Why didn't you?"

He laughed at her, softly, indulgently, and said: "I like you in that shade of brown."

"Oh, Ned, please—"

"That's better," he said. "I intended coming out to the house, but—well—there were lots of things happening when

I got back and a lot of loose ends of things that had happened while I was gone, and by the time I finished with those I ran into Shad O'Rory and got sent here." He waved an arm to indicate the hospital.

Her gravity was not affected by the lightness of his tone.

"Are they going to hang this Despain?" she asked curtly.

He laughed again and said: "We're not going to get very far talking like this."

She frowned, but said, "Are they, Ned?" with less haughtiness.

"I don't think so," he told her, shaking his head a little. "The chances are he didn't kill Taylor after all."

She did not seem surprised. "Did you know that when you asked me to—to help you get—or fix up—evidence against him?"

He smiled reproachfully. "Of course not, snip. What do you think I am?"

"You did know it." Her voice was cold and scornful as her blue eyes. "You only wanted to get the money he owed you and you made me help you use Taylor's murder for that."

"Have it your own way," he replied indifferently.

She came a step closer to him. The faintest of quivers disturbed her chin for an instant, then her young face was firm and bold again. "Do you know who killed him?" she asked, her eyes probing his.

He shook his head slowly from side to side.

"Did Dad?"

He blinked. "You mean did Paul know who killed him?"

She stamped a foot. "I mean did Dad kill him?" she cried.

He put a hand over her mouth. His eyes had jerked into focus on the closed door. "Shut up," he muttered.

She stepped back from his hand as one of her hands pushed it away from her face. "Did he?" she insisted.

In a low angry voice he said: "If you must be a nit-wit at least don't go around with a megaphone. Nobody cares what kind of idiotic notions you have as long as you keep them to yourself, but you've got to keep them to yourself."

Her eyes opened wide and dark. "Then he did kill him," she said in a small flat voice, but with utter certainty.

He thrust his face down towards hers. "No, my dear," he said in an enraged sugary voice, "he didn't kill him." He held his face near hers. A vicious smile distorted his features.

Firm of countenance and voice, not drawing back from him, she said: "If he didn't I can't understand what difference it makes what I say or how loud."

An end of his mouth twitched up in a sneer. "You'd be surprised how many things there are you can't understand," he said angrily, "and never will if you keep on like this." He stepped back from her, a long step, and put his fists in the pockets of his bathrobe. Both corners of his mouth were pulled down now and there were grooves in his forehead. His narrowed eyes stared at the floor in front of her feet. "Where'd you get this crazy idea?" he growled.

"It's not a crazy idea. You know it's not."

He moved his shoulders impatiently and demanded: "Where'd you get it?"

She too moved her shoulders. "I didn't get it anywhere. I—I suddenly saw it."

"Nonsense," he said sharply, looking up at her under his brows. "Did you see the *Observer* this morning?"

"No."

He stared at her with hard skeptical eyes.

Annoyance brought a little color into her face. "I did not," she said. "Why do you ask?"

"No?" he asked in a tone that said he did not believe her, but the skeptical gleam had gone out his eyes. They were dull and thoughtful. Suddenly they brightened. He took his right hand from his bathrobe-pocket. He held it out towards her, palm up. "Let me see the letter," he said.

She stared at him with round eyes. "What?"

"The letter," he said, "the typewritten letter—three questions and no signature."

She lowered her eyes to avoid his and embarrassment disturbed, very slightly, her features. After a moment of hesitation she asked, "How did you know?" and opened her brown hand-bag.

"Everybody in town's had at least one," he said carelessly. "Is this your first?"

"Yes." She gave him a crumpled sheet of paper. He straightened it out and read:

Are you really too stupid to know that your father murdered your lover?

If you do not know it, why did you help him and Ned Beaumont in their attempt to fasten the crime on an innocent man?

Do you know that by helping your father escape justice you are making yourself an accomplice in his crime?

Ned Beaumont nodded and smiled lightly. "They're all pretty much alike," he said. He wadded the paper in a loose ball and tossed it at the waste-basket beside the table. "You'll probably get some more of them now you're on the mailing-list."

Opal Madvig drew her lower lip in between her teeth. Her blue eyes were bright without warmth. They studied Ned Beaumont's composed face.

He said: "O'Rory's trying to make campaign-material out of it. You know about my trouble with him. That was because he thought I'd broken with your father and could be paid to help frame him for the murder—enough at least to beat him at the polls—and I wouldn't."

Her eyes did not change. "What did you and Dad fight about?" she asked.

"That's nobody's business but ours, snip," he said gently, "if we did fight."

"You did," she said, "in Carson's speakeasy." She put her teeth together with a click and said boldly: "You quarreled when you found out that he really had—had killed Taylor."

He laughed and asked in a mocking tone: "Hadn't I known that all along?"

Her expression was not affected by his humor. "Why did you ask if I had seen the *Observer*?" she demanded. "What was in it?"

"Some more of the same sort of nonsense," he told her evenly. "It's there on the table if you want to see it. There'll be plenty of it before the campaign's over: this is going to be that kind. And you'll be giving your father a swell break by swallowing—" He broke off with an impatient gesture because she was no longer listening to him.

She had gone to the table and was picking up the newspaper he had put down when she came in.

He smiled pleasantly at her back and said: "It's on the front page, *An Open Letter to the Mayor*."

As she read she began to tremble—her knees, her hands, her mouth—so that Ned Beaumont frowned anxiously at her, but when she had finished and had dropped the newspaper on the table and had turned to face him directly her tall body and fair face were statue-like in their immobility. She addressed him in a low voice between lips that barely moved to let the words out: "They wouldn't dare say such things if they were not true."

"That's nothing to what'll be said before they're through," he drawled lazily. He seemed amused, though there was a suggestion of anger difficultly restrained in the glitter of his eyes.

She looked at him for a long moment, then, saying nothing, turned towards the door.

He said: "Wait."

She halted and confronted him again. His smile was friendly now, ingratiating. Her face was a tinted statue's.

He said: "Politics is a tough game, snip, the way it's being played here this time. The *Observer* is on the other side of the fence and they're not worrying much about the truth of anything that'll hurt Paul. They—"

"I don't believe that," she said. "I know Mr. Mathews—his wife was only a few years ahead of me at school and we were friends—and I don't believe he'd say anything like that about Dad unless it was true, or unless he had good reason for thinking it true."

Ned Beaumont chuckled. "You know a lot about it. Mathews is up to his ears in debt. The State Central Trust Company holds both mortgages on his plant—one on his house too, for that matter. The State Central belongs to Bill Roan. Bill Roan is running for the Senate against Henry. Mathews does what he's told to do and prints what he's told to print."

Opal Madvig did not say anything. There was nothing to indicate that she had been at all convinced by Ned Beaumont's argument.

He went on, speaking in an amiable, persuasive, tone: "This"—he flicked a finger at the paper on the table—"is nothing to what'll come later. They're going to rattle Taylor Henry's bones till they think up something worse and we're going to have this sort of stuff to read till election's over. We might just as well get used to it now and you, of all people, oughtn't to let yourself be bothered by it. Paul doesn't mind it much. He's a politician and—"

"He's a murderer," she said in a low distinct voice.

"And his daughter's a chump," he exclaimed irritably. "Will you stop that foolishness?"

"My father is a murderer," she said.

"You're crazy. Listen to me, snip. Your father had absolutely nothing to do with Taylor's murder. He—"

"I don't believe you," she said gravely. "I'll never believe you again."

He scowled at her.

She turned and went to the door.

"Wait," he said. "Let me—"

She went out and shut the door behind her.

VII

Ned Beaumont's face, after a grimace of rage at the closed door, became heavily thoughtful. Lines came into his forehead. His dark eyes grew narrow and introspective. His lips puckered up under his mustache. Presently he put a finger to his mouth and bit its nail. He breathed regularly, but with more depth than usual.

Footsteps sounded outside his door. He dropped his appearance of thoughtfulness and walked idly towards the window, humming *Little Lost Lady*. The footsteps went on past his door. He stopped humming and bent to pick up the sheet of paper holding the three questions that had been addressed to Opal Madvig. He did not smooth the paper, but thrust it, crumpled in a loose ball as it was, into one of his bathrobe-pockets.

He found and lit a cigar then and, with it between his teeth burning, stood by the table and squinted down through smoke at the front page of the *Observer* lying there.

AN OPEN LETTER TO THE MAYOR

SIR:

The *Observer* has come into possession of certain information which it believes to be of paramount importance in clearing up the mystery surrounding the recent murder of Taylor Henry.

This information is incorporated in several affidavits now in the *Observer's* safety-deposit box. The substance of these affidavits is as follows:

1. That Paul Madvig quarreled with Taylor Henry some months ago over the young man's attentions to his daughter and forbade his daughter to see Henry again.

2. That Paul Madvig's daughter nevertheless continued to meet Taylor Henry in a furnished room he had rented for that purpose.

3. That they were together in this furnished room the afternoon of the very day on which he was killed.

4. That Paul Madvig went to Taylor Henry's home that evening, supposedly to remonstrate with the young man, or his father, again.

5. That Paul Madvig appeared angry when he left the Henry residence a few minutes before Taylor Henry was murdered.

6. That Paul Madvig and Taylor Henry were seen within half a block of each other, less than a block from the spot where the young man's body was found, not more than fifteen minutes before his body was found.

7. That the Police Department has not at present a single detective engaged in trying to find Taylor Henry's murderer.

The *Observer* believes that you should know these things and that the voters and taxpayers should know them. The *Observer* has no ax to grind, no motive except the desire to see justice done. The *Observer* will welcome an opportunity to hand these affidavits, as well as all other information it has, to you or to any qualified city or state official and, if such a course can be shown an aid to justice, to refrain from publishing any or all of the details of these affidavits.

But the *Observer* will not permit the information incorporated in these affidavits to be ignored. If the officials elected and appointed to enforce law and order in this city and state do not consider these affidavits of sufficient importance to be acted upon, the *Observer* will carry the matter to that higher tribunal, the People of this City, by publishing them in full.

H. K. MATHEWS, Publisher

Ned Beaumont grunted derisively and blew cigar-smoke down at this declaration, but his eyes remained somber.

VIII

Early that afternoon Paul Madvig's mother came to see Ned Beaumont.

He put his arms around her and kissed her on both cheeks until she pushed him away with a mock-severe "Do stop it. You're worse than the Airedale Paul used to have."

"I'm part Airedale," he said, "on my father's side," and went behind her to help her out of her sealskin coat.

Smoothing her black dress, she went to the bed and sat on it.

He hung the coat on the back of a chair and stood—legs apart, hands in bathrobe-pockets—before her.

She studied him critically. "You don't look so bad," she said presently, "nor yet so good. How do you feel?"

"Swell. I'm only hanging around here on account of the nurses."

"That wouldn't surprise me much, neither," she told him. "But don't stand there ogling me like a Cheshire cat. You make me nervous. Sit down." She patted the bed beside her.

He sat down beside her.

She said: "Paul seems to think you did something very grand and noble by doing whatever it was you did, but you can't tell me that if you had behaved yourself you would ever have got into whatever scrape you got into at all."

"Aw, Mom," he began.

She cut him off. The gaze of her blue eyes that were young as her son's bored into Ned Beaumont's brown ones. "Look here, Ned, Paul didn't kill that whipper-snapper, did he?"

Surprise opened Ned Beaumont's eyes and mouth. "No."

"I didn't think so," the old woman said. "He's always been a good boy, but I've heard that there's some nasty hints going around and the Lord only knows what goes on in this politics. I'm sure I haven't any idea."

Amazement tinged with humor was in the eyes with which Ned Beaumont looked at her bony face.

She said: "Well, goggle at me, but I haven't got any way of knowing what you men are up to, or what you do without thinking anything of it. It was a long while before ever you were born that I gave up trying to find out."

He patted her shoulder. "You're a humdinger, Mom," he said admiringly.

She drew away from his hand and fixed him with severe penetrant eyes again. "Would you tell me if he had killed him?" she demanded.

He shook his head no.

"Then how do I know he didn't?"

He laughed. "Because," he explained, "if he had I'd still say, 'No,' but then, if you asked me if I'd tell you the truth if he had, I'd say, 'Yes.'" Merriment went out of his eyes and voice. "He didn't do it, Mom." He smiled at her. He smiled with his lips only and they were thin against his teeth. "It would be nice if somebody in town besides me thought he didn't do it and it would be especially nice if that other one was his mother."

IX

An hour after Mrs. Madvig's departure Ned Beaumont received a package containing four books and Janet Henry's card. He was writing her a note of thanks when Jack arrived.

Jack, letting cigarette-smoke come out with his words, said: "I think I've got something, though I don't know how you're going to like it."

Ned Beaumont looked thoughtfully at the sleek young man and smoothed the left side of his mustache with a forefinger. "If it's what I hired you to get I'll like it well enough." His voice was matter-of-fact as Jack's. "Sit down and tell me about it."

Jack sat down carefully, crossed his legs, put his hat on the floor, and looked from his cigarette to Ned Beaumont. He said: "It looks like those things were written by Madvig's daughter."

Ned Beaumont's eyes widened a little, but only for a moment. His face lost some of its color and his breathing became irregular. There was no change in his voice. "What makes it look like that?"

From an inner pocket Jack brought two sheets of paper similar in size and make, folded alike. He gave them to Ned Beaumont who, when he had unfolded them, saw that on each were three typewritten questions, the same three questions on each sheet.

"One of them's the one you gave me yesterday," Jack said. "Could you tell which?"

Ned Beaumont shook his head slowly from side to side.

"There's no difference," Jack said. "I wrote the other one on Charter Street where Taylor Henry had a room that Madvig's daughter used to come to—with a Corona typewriter that was there and on paper that was there. So far as anybody seems to know there were only two keys to the place. He had one and she had one. She's been back there at least a couple of times since he was killed."

Ned Beaumont, scowling now at the sheets of paper in his hands, nodded without looking up.

Jack lit a fresh cigarette from the one he had been smoking, rose and went to the table to mash the old cigarette in the ash-tray there, and returned to his seat. There was nothing in his face or manner to show that he had any interest in Ned Beaumont's reaction to their discovery.

After another minute of silence Ned Beaumont raised his head a little and asked: "How'd you get this?"

Jack put his cigarette in a corner of his mouth where it wagged with his words. "The *Observer* tip on the place this morning gave me the lead. That's where the police got theirs too, but they got there first. I got a pretty good break, though: the copper left in charge was a friend of mine—Fred Hurley—and for a ten-spot he let me do all the poking around I wanted."

Ned Beaumont rattled the papers in his hand. "Do the police know this?" he asked.

Jack shrugged. "I didn't tell them. I pumped Hurley, but he didn't know anything—just put there to watch things till they decide what they're going to do. Maybe they know, maybe they don't." He shook cigarette-ash on the floor. "I could find out."

"Never mind that. What else did you turn up?"

"I didn't look for anything else."

Ned Beaumont, after a quick glance at the dark young man's inscrutable face, looked down at the sheets of paper again. "What kind of dump is it?"

"Thirteen twenty-four. They had a room and bath under the name of French. The woman that runs the place claims she didn't know who they really were till the police came to-day. Maybe she didn't. It's the kind of joint where not much is asked. She says they used to be there a lot, mostly in the af-ternoons, and that the girl's been back a couple of times in the last week or so that she knows of, though she could pop in and out without being seen easily enough."

"Sure it's her?"

Jack made a noncommittal gesture with one hand. "The description's right." He paused, then added carelessly as he exhaled smoke: "She's the only one the woman saw since he was killed."

Ned Beaumont raised his head again. His eyes were hard. "Taylor had others coming there?" he asked.

Jack made the noncommittal gesture once more. "The woman wouldn't say so. She said she didn't know, but from the way she said it I'd say it was a safe bet she was lying."

"Couldn't tell by what's in the place?"

Jack shook his head. "No. There's not much woman stuff there—just a kimono and toilet things and pajamas and stuff like that."

"Much of his stuff there?"

"Oh, a suit and a pair of shoes and some underwear and pajamas and socks and so on."

"Any hats?"

Jack smiled. "No hats," he said.

Ned Beaumont got up and went to the window. Outside darkness was almost complete. A dozen raindrops clung to the glass and as many more struck it lightly while Ned Beaumont stood there. He turned to face Jack again. "Thanks a lot, Jack," he said slowly. His eyes were focused on Jack's face in a dully absent-minded stare. "I think maybe I'll have another job for you soon—maybe tonight. I'll give you a ring."

Jack said, "Right," and rose and went out.

Ned Beaumont went to the closet for his clothes, carried them into the bathroom, and put them on. When he came out a nurse was in his room, a tall full-bodied woman with a shiny pale face.

"Why, you're dressed!" she exclaimed.

"Yes, I've got to go out."

Alarm joined astonishment in her mien. "But you can't, Mr. Beaumont," she protested. "It's night and it's beginning to rain and Doctor Tait would—"

"I know, I know," he said impatiently, and went around her to the door.

CHAPTER VI

The Observer

M RS. MADVIG opened her front door. "Ned!" she cried, "are you crazy? Running around on a night like this, and you just out of the hospital."

"The taxi didn't leak," he said, but his grin lacked virility. "Paul in?"

"He went out not more than half an hour ago, I think to the Club. But come in, come in."

"Opal home?" he asked as he shut the door and followed her down the hall.

"No. She's been off somewhere since morning."

Ned Beaumont halted in the living-room-doorway. "I can't stay," he said. "I'll run on down to the Club and see Paul there." His voice was not quite steady.

The old woman turned quickly towards him. "You'll do no such thing," she said in a scolding voice. "Look at you, you're just about to have a chill. You'll sit right down there by the fire and let me get you something hot to drink."

"Can't, Mom," he told her. "I've got to go places."

Her blue eyes wherein age did not show became bright and keen. "When did you leave the hospital?" she demanded.

"Just now."

She put her lips together hard, then opened them a little to say accusingly: "You walked out." A shadow disturbed the clear blueness of her eyes. She came close to Ned Beaumont and held her face close to his: she was nearly as tall as he. Her voice was harsh now as if coming from a parched throat. "Is it something about Paul?" The shadow in her eyes became recognizable as fear. "And Opal?"

His voice was barely audible. "It's something I've got to see them about."

She touched one of his cheeks somewhat timidly with bony fingers. "You're a good boy, Ned," she said.

He put an arm around her. "Don't worry, Mom. None of it's bad as it could be. Only—if Opal comes home make her stay—if you can."

"Is it anything you can tell me, Ned?" she asked.

"Not now and—well—it might be just as well not to let either of them know you think anything's wrong."

II

Ned Beaumont walked five blocks through the rain to a drug-store. He used a telephone there first to order a taxicab and then to call two numbers and ask for Mr. Mathews. He did not get Mr. Mathews on the wire.

He called another number and asked for Mr. Rumsen. A moment later he was saying: "'Lo, Jack, this is Ned Beaumont. Busy? . . . Fine. Here it is. I want to know if the girl we were talking about went to see Mathews of the *Observer* today and what she did afterwards, if she did. . . . That's right, Hal Mathews. I tried to get him by phone, there and home, but no luck. . . . Well, on the quiet if you can, but get it and get it quick. . . . No, I'm out of the hospital. I'll be home waiting. You know my number. . . . Yes, Jack. Fine, thanks, and ring me as often as you can. . . . 'By."

He went out to the waiting taxicab, got into it, and gave the driver his address, but after half a dozen blocks he tapped the front window with his fingers and gave the driver another address.

Presently the taxicab came to rest in front of a squat greyish house set in the center of a steeply sloping smooth lawn. "Wait," he told the driver as he got out.

The greyish house's front door was opened to his ring by a red-haired maid.

"Mr. Farr in?" he asked her.

"I'll see. Who shall I tell him?"

"Mr. Beaumont."

The District Attorney came into the reception-hall with both hands out. His florid pugnacious face was all smiling. "Well, well, Beaumont, this is a real pleasure," he said as he rushed up to his visitor. "Here, give me your coat and hat."

Ned Beaumont smiled and shook his head. "I can't stay," he said. "I just dropped in for a second on my way home from the hospital."

"All shipshape again? Splendid!"

"Feeling pretty good," Ned Beaumont said. "Anything new?"

"Nothing very important. The birds who manhandled you are still loose—in hiding somewhere—but we'll get them."

Ned Beaumont made a depreciatory mouth. "I didn't die and they weren't trying to kill me: you could only stick them with an assault-charge." He looked somewhat drowsily at Farr. "Had any more of those three-question epistles?"

The District Attorney cleared his throat. "Uh—yes, come to think of it, there were one or two more of them."

"How many?" Ned Beaumont asked. His voice was politely casual. The ends of his lips were raised a little in an idle smile. Amusement glinted in his eyes, but his eyes held Farr's.

The District Attorney cleared his throat. "Three," he said reluctantly. Then his eyes brightened. "Did you hear about the splendid meeting we had at—?"

Ned Beaumont interrupted him. "All along the same line?" he asked.

"Uh—more or less." The District Attorney licked his lips and a pleading expression began to enter his eyes.

"How much more—or less?"

Farr's eyes slid their gaze down from Ned Beaumont's eyes to his necktie and sidewise to his left shoulder. He moved his lips vaguely, but did not utter a sound.

Ned Beaumont's smile was openly malicious now. "All saying Paul killed Taylor Henry?" he asked in a sugary voice.

Farr jumped, his face faded to a light orange, and in his excitement he let his startled eyes focus on Ned Beaumont's eyes again. "Christ, Ned!" he gasped.

Ned Beaumont laughed. "You're getting nerves, Farr," he said, still sugary of voice. "Better watch yourself or you'll be going to pieces." He made his face grave. "Has Paul said anything to you about it? About your nerves, I mean."

"N-no."

Ned Beaumont smiled again. "Maybe he hasn't noticed it—yet." He raised an arm, glanced at his wrist-watch, then at Farr. "Found out who wrote them yet?" he asked sharply.

The District Attorney stammered: "Look here, Ned, I don't—you know—it's not—" floundered and stopped.

Ned Beaumont asked: "Well?"

The District Attorney gulped and said desperately: "We've got something, Ned, but it's too soon to say. Maybe there's nothing to it. You know how these things are."

Ned Beaumont nodded. There was nothing but friendliness in his face now. His voice was level and cool without chilliness saying: "You've learned where they were written and you've found the machine they were written on, but that's all you've got so far. You haven't got enough to even guess who wrote them."

"That's right, Ned," Farr blurted out with a great air of relief.

Ned Beaumont took Farr's hand and shook it cordially. "That's the stuff," he said. "Well, I've got to run along. You can't go wrong taking things slowly, being sure you're right before you go ahead. You can take my word for that."

The District Attorney's face and voice were warm with emotion. "Thanks, Ned, thanks!"

III

At ten minutes past nine o'clock that evening the tele-phone-bell in Ned Beaumont's living-room rang. He went quickly to the telephone. "Hello. . . . Yes, Jack. . . . Yes. . . . Yes. . . . Where? . . . Yes, that's fine. . . . That'll be all tonight. Thanks a lot."

When he rose from the telephone he was smiling with pale lips. His eyes were shiny and reckless. His hands shook a little.

The telephone-bell rang again before he had taken his third step. He hesitated, went back to the telephone. "Hello. . . . Oh, hello, Paul. . . . Yes, I got tired of playing invalid. . . . Nothing special—just thought I'd drop in and see you. . . . No, I'm afraid I can't. I'm not feeling as strong as I thought I was, so I think I'd better go to bed. . . . Yes, tomorrow, sure. . . . 'By."

He put on rain-coat and hat going downstairs. Wind drove rain in at him when he opened the street-door, drove it into his face as he walked half a block to the garage on the corner.

In the garage's glass-walled office a lanky brown-haired man in once-white overalls was tilted back on a wooden chair, his feet on a shelf above an electric heater, reading a newspaper. He lowered the newspaper when Ned Beaumont said: "'Lo, Tommy."

The dirtiness of Tommy's face made his teeth seem whiter than they were. He showed many of them in a grin and said: "Kind of weatherish tonight."

"Yes. Got an iron I can have? One that'll carry me over country roads tonight?"

Tommy said: "Jesus! Lucky for you you could pick your night. You might've had to go on a bad one. Well, I got a Buick that I don't care what happens to."

"Will it get me there?"

"It's just as likely to as anything else," Tommy said, "tonight."

"All right. Fill it up for me. What's the best road up Lazy Creek way on a night like this?"

"How far up?"

Ned Beaumont looked thoughtfully at the garage-man, then said: "Along about where it runs into the river."

Tommy nodded. "The Mathews place?" he asked.

Ned Beaumont did not say anything.

Tommy said: "It makes a difference which place you're going to."

"Yes? The Mathews place." Ned Beaumont frowned. "This is under the hat, Tommy."

"Did you come to me because you thought I'd talk or because you knew I wouldn't?" Tommy demanded argumentatively.

Ned Beaumont said: "I'm in a hurry."

"Then you take the New River Road as far as Barton's, take the dirt road over the bridge there—if you can make it at all—and then the first cross-road back east. That'll bring you in behind Mathews's place along about the top of the hill. If you can't make the dirt road in this weather you'll have to go on up the New River Road to where it crosses and then cut back along the old one."

"Thanks."

When Ned Beaumont was getting into the Buick Tommy said to him in a markedly casual tone: "There's an extra gun in the side-pocket."

Ned Beaumont stared at the lanky man. "Extra?" he asked blankly.

"Pleasant trip," Tommy said.

Ned Beaumont shut the door and drove away.

IV

The clock in the dashboard said ten-thirty-two. Ned Beaumont switched off the lights and got somewhat stiffly out of the Buick. Wind-driven rain hammered tree, bush, ground, man, car with incessant wet blows. Downhill, through rain and foliage, irregular small patches of yellow light glowed faintly. Ned Beaumont shivered, tried to draw his rain-coat closer around him, and began to stumble downhill through drenched underbrush towards the patches of light.

Wind and rain on his back pushed him downhill towards the patches. As he went downhill stiffness gradually left him so that, though he stumbled often and staggered, and was tripped by obstacles underfoot, he kept his feet under him and moved nimbly enough, if erratically, towards his goal.

Presently a path came under his feet. He turned into it, holding it partly by its sliminess under his feet, partly by the feel of the bushes whipping his face on either side, and not at all by sight. The path led him off to the left for a little distance, but then, swinging in a broad curve, brought him to the brink of a small gorge through which water rushed noisily and from there, in another curve, to the front door of the building where the yellow light glowed.

Ned Beaumont went straight up to the door and knocked.

The door was opened by a grey-haired bespectacled man. His face was mild and greyish and the eyes that peered anxiously through the pale-tortoise-shell-encircled lenses of his spectacles were grey. His brown suit was neat and of good quality, but not fashionably cut. One side of his rather high stiff white collar had been blistered in four places by drops of water. He stood aside holding the door open and said, "Come in, sir, come in out of the rain," in a friendly if not hearty voice. "A wretched night to be out in."

Ned Beaumont lowered his head no more than two inches in the beginning of a bow and stepped indoors. He was in a large room that occupied all the building's ground-floor. The sparseness and simplicity of the room's furnishings gave it a primitive air that was pleasantly devoid of ostentation. It was a kitchen, a dining-room, and a living-room.

Opal Madvig rose from the footstool on which she had been sitting at one end of the fireplace and, holding herself tall and straight, stared with hostile bleak eyes at Ned Beaumont.

He took off his hat and began to unbutton his rain-coat. The others recognized him then.

The man who had opened the door said, "Why, it's Beaumont!" in an incredulous voice and looked wide-eyed at Shad O'Rory.

Shad O'Rory was sitting in a wooden chair in the center of the room facing the fireplace. He smiled dreamily at Ned Beaumont, saying, in his musical faintly Irish barytone, "And so it is," and, "How are you, Ned?"

Jeff Gardner's apish face broadened in a grin that showed his beautiful false teeth and almost completely hid his little red eyes. "By Jesus, Rusty!" he said to the sullen rosy-cheeked boy who lounged on the bench beside him, "little Rubber Ball has come back to us. I told you he liked the way we bounced him around."

Rusty lowered at Ned Beaumont and growled something that did not carry across the room.

The thin girl in red sitting not far from Opal Madvig looked at Ned Beaumont with bright interested dark eyes.

Ned Beaumont took off his coat. His lean face, still bearing the marks of Jeff's and Rusty's fists, was tranquil except for the recklessness aglitter in his eyes. He put his coat and hat on a long unpainted chest that was against one wall near the door. He smiled politely at the man who had admitted him and said: "My car broke down as I was passing. It's very kind of you to give me shelter, Mr. Mathews."

Mathews said, "Not at all—glad to," somewhat vaguely. Then his frightened eyes looked pleadingly at O'Rory again.

O'Rory stroked his smooth white hair with a slender pale hand and smiled pleasantly at Ned Beaumont, but did not say anything.

Ned Beaumont advanced to the fireplace. "'Lo, snip," he said to Opal Madvig.

She did not respond to his greeting. She stood there and looked at him with hostile bleak eyes.

He directed his smile at the thin girl in red. "This is Mrs. Mathews, isn't it?"

She said, "It is," in a soft, almost cooing, voice and held out her hand.

"Opal told me you were a schoolmate of hers," he said as he took her hand. He turned from her to face Rusty and Jeff. "'Lo, boys," he said carelessly. "I was hoping I'd see you some time soon."

Rusty said nothing.

Jeff's face became an ugly mask of grinning delight. "Me and you both," he said heartily, "now that my knuckles are all healed up again. What do you guess it is that makes me get such a hell of a big kick out of slugging you?"

Shad O'Rory gently addressed the apish man without turning to look at him: "You talk too much with your mouth, Jeff. Maybe if you didn't you'd still have your own teeth."

Mrs. Mathews spoke to Opal in an undertone. Opal shook her head and sat down on the stool by the fire again.

Mathews, indicating a wooden chair at the other end of the fireplace, said nervously: "Sit down, Mr. Beaumont, and dry your feet and—and get warm."

"Thanks." Ned Beaumont pulled the chair out more directly in the fire's glow and sat down.

Shad O'Rory was lighting a cigarette. When he had finished he took it from between his lips and asked: "How are you feeling, Ned?"

"Pretty good, Shad."

"That's fine." O'Rory turned his head a little to speak to the two men on the bench: "You boys can go back to town tomorrow." He turned back to Ned Beaumont, explaining blandly: "We were playing safe as long as we didn't know for sure you weren't going to die, but we don't mind standing an assault-rap."

Ned Beaumont nodded. "The chances are I won't go to the trouble of appearing against you, anyhow, on that, but don't forget our friend Jeff's wanted for West's murder." His voice was light, but into his eyes, fixed on the log burning in the fireplace, came a brief evil glint. There was nothing in his eyes but mockery when he moved them to the left to focus on Mathews. "Though of course I might so I could make trouble for Mathews for helping you hide out."

Mathews said hastily: "I didn't, Mr. Beaumont. I didn't even know they were here until we came up today and I was as surprised as—" He broke off, his face panicky, and addressed Shad O'Rory, whining: "You know you are welcome. You know that, but the point I'm trying to make"—his face was illuminated by a sudden glad smile—"is that by helping you without knowing it I didn't do anything I could be held legally responsible for."

O'Rory said softly: "Yes, you helped me without knowing it." His notable clear blue-grey eyes looked without interest at the newspaper-publisher.

Mathews's smile lost its gladness, flickered out entirely. He fidgeted with fingers at his necktie and presently evaded O'Rory's gaze.

Mrs. Mathews spoke to Ned Beaumont, sweetly: "Everybody's been so dull this evening. It was simply ghastly until you came."

He looked at her curiously. Her dark eyes were bright, soft, inviting. Under his appraising look she lowered her head a little and pursed her lips a little, coquettishly. Her lips were thin, too dark with rouge, but beautiful in form. He smiled at her and, rising, went over to her.

Opal Madvig stared at the floor before her. Mathews, O'Rory, and the two men on the bench watched Ned Beaumont and Mathews's wife.

He asked, "What makes them so dull?" and sat down on the floor in front of her, cross-legged, not facing her directly, his back to the fire, leaning on a hand on the floor behind him, his face turned up to one side towards her.

"I'm sure I don't know," she said, pouting. "I thought it was going to be fun when Hal asked me if I wanted to come up here with him and Opal. And then, when we got here, we found these—" she paused a moment—said, "friends of Hal's," with poorly concealed dubiety—and went on: "here and everybody's been sitting around hinting at some secret they've all got between them that I don't know anything about and it's been unbearably stupid. Opal's been as bad as the rest. She—"

Her husband said, "Now, Eloise," in an ineffectually authoritative tone and, when she raised her eyes to meet his, got more embarrassment than authority in his gaze.

"I don't care," she told him petulantly. "It's true and Opal is as bad as the rest of you. Why, you and she haven't even talked about whatever business it was you were coming up here to discuss in the first place. Don't think I'd've stayed here this long if it hadn't been for the storm. I wouldn't."

Opal Madvig's face had flushed, but she did not raise her eyes.

Eloise Mathews bent her head down towards Ned Beaumont again and the petulance in her face became playful. "That's what you've got to make up for," she assured him, "and that and not because you're beautiful is why I was so glad to see you."

He frowned at her in mock indignation.

She frowned at him. Her frown was genuine. "Did your car really break down?" she demanded, "or did you come here to see them on the same dull business that's making them so stupidly mysterious? You did. You're another one of them."

He laughed. He asked: "It wouldn't make any difference why I came if I changed my mind after seeing you, would it?"

"No—o—o"—she was suspicious—"but I'd have to be awfully sure you had changed it."

"And anyway," he promised lightly, "I won't be mysterious about anything. Haven't you really got an idea of what they're all eating their hearts out about?"

"Not the least," she replied spitefully, "except that I'm pretty sure it must be something very stupid and probably political."

He put his free hand up and patted one of hers. "Smart girl, right on both counts." He turned his head to look at O'Rory and Mathews. When his eyes came back to hers they were shiny with merriment. "Want me to tell you about it?"

"No."

"First," he said, "Opal thinks her father murdered Taylor Henry."

Opal Madvig made a horrible strangling noise in her throat and sprang up from the footstool. She put the back of one hand over her mouth. Her eyes were open so wide the whites showed all around the irises and they were glassy and dreadful.

Rusty lurched to his feet, his face florid with anger, but Jeff, leering, caught the boy's arm. "Let him alone," he rasped good-naturedly. "He's all right." The boy stood straining against the apish man's grip on his arm, but did not try to free himself.

Eloise Mathews sat frozen in her chair, staring without comprehension at Opal.

Mathews was trembling, a shrunken grey-faced sick man whose lower lip and lower eyelids sagged.

Shad O'Rory was sitting forward in his chair, finely modeled long face pale and hard, eyes like blue-grey ice, hands gripping chair-arms, feet flat on the floor.

"Second," Ned Beaumont said, his poise nowise disturbed by the agitation of the others, "she—"

"Ned, don't!" Opal Madvig cried.

He screwed himself around on the floor then to look up at her.

She had taken her hand from her mouth. Her hands were knotted together against her chest. Her stricken eyes, her whole haggard face, begged mercy of him.

He studied her gravely awhile. Through window and wall came the sound of rain dashing against the building in wild gusts and between gusts the bustling of the near-by river. His eyes, studying her, were cool, deliberate. Presently he spoke to her in a voice kind enough but aloof: "Isn't that why you're here?"

"Please don't," she said hoarsely.

He moved his lips in a thin smile that his eyes had nothing to do with and asked: "Nobody's supposed to go around talking about it except you and your father's other enemies?"

She put her hands—fists—down at her sides, raised her face angrily, and said in a hard ringing voice: "He did murder Taylor."

Ned Beaumont leaned back against his hand again and looked up at Eloise Mathews. "That's what I was telling you," he drawled. "Thinking that, she went to your husband after she saw the junk he printed this morning. Of course he didn't think Paul had done any killing: he's just in a tough spot—with his mortgages held by the State Central, which is owned by Shad's candidate for the Senate—and he has to do what he's told. What she—"

Mathews interrupted him. The publisher's voice was thin and desperate. "Now you stop that, Beaumont. You—"

O'Rory interrupted Mathews. O'Rory's voice was quiet, musical. "Let him talk, Mathews," he said. "Let him say his say."

"Thanks, Shad," Ned Beaumont said carelessly, not looking around, and went on: "She went to your husband to have him confirm her suspicion, but he couldn't give her anything that would do that unless he lied to her. He doesn't know anything. He's simply throwing mud wherever Shad tells him to throw it. But here's what he can do and does. He can print in tomorrow's paper the story about her coming in and telling him she believes her father killed her lover. That'll be a lovely wallop. 'Opal Madvig Accuses Father of Murder; Boss's Daughter Says He Killed Senator's Son!' Can't you see that in black ink all across the front of the *Observer?*"

Eloise Mathews, her eyes large, her face white, was listening breathlessly, bending forward, her face above his. Wind-flung rain beat walls and windows. Rusty filled and emptied his lungs with a long sighing breath.

Ned Beaumont put the tip of his tongue between smiling lips, withdrew it, and said: "That's why he brought her up here, to keep her under cover till the story breaks. Maybe he knew Shad and the boys were here, maybe not. It doesn't make any difference. He's getting her off where nobody can find out what she's done till the papers are out. I don't mean that he'd've brought her here, or would hold her here, against her will—that wouldn't be very bright of him the way things stack up now—but none of that's necessary. She's willing to go to any lengths to ruin her father."

Opal Madvig said, in a whisper, but distinctly: "He did kill him."

Ned Beaumont sat up straight and looked at her. He

looked solemnly at her for a moment, then smiled, shook his head in a gesture of amused resignation, and leaned back on his elbows.

Eloise Mathews was staring with dark eyes wherein wonder was predominant at her husband. He had sat down. His head was bowed. His hands hid his face.

Shad O'Rory recrossed his legs and took out a cigarette. "Through?" he asked mildly.

Ned Beaumont's back was to O'Rory. He did not turn to reply: "You'd hardly believe how through I am." His voice was level, but his face was suddenly tired, spent.

O'Rory lit his cigarette. "Well," he said when he had done that, "what the hell does it all amount to? It's our turn to hang a big one on you and we're doing it. The girl came in with the story on her own hook. She came here because she wanted to. So did you. She and you and anybody else can go wherever they want to go whenever they want to." He stood up. "Personally, I'm wanting to go to bed. Where do I sleep, Mathews?"

Eloise Mathews spoke, to her husband: "This is not true, Hal." It was not a question.

He was slow taking his hands from his face. He achieved dignity saying: "Darling, there is a dozen times enough evidence against Madvig to justify us in insisting that the police at least question him. That is all we have done."

"I did not mean that," his wife said.

"Well, darling, when Miss Madvig came—" He faltered, stopped, a grey-faced man who shivered before the look in his wife's eyes and put his hands over his face again.

v

Eloise Mathews and Ned Beaumont were alone in the large ground-floor room, sitting, in chairs a few feet apart, with the fireplace in front of them. She was bent forward, looking with tragic eyes at the last burning log. His legs were crossed. One of his arms was hooked over the back of his chair. He smoked a cigar and watched her surreptitiously.

The stairs creaked and her husband came half-way down them. He was fully clothed except that he had taken off his collar. His necktie, partially loosened, hung outside his vest. He said: "Darling, won't you come to bed? It's midnight."

She did not move.

He said: "Mr. Beaumont, will you—?"

Ned Beaumont, when his name was spoken, turned his face towards the man on the stairs, a face cruelly placid. When Mathews's voice broke, Ned Beaumont returned his attention to his cigar and Mathews's wife.

After a little while Mathews went upstairs again.

Eloise Mathews spoke without taking her gaze from the fire. "There is some whisky in the chest. Will you get it?"

"Surely." He found the whisky and brought it to her, then found some glasses. "Straight?" he asked.

She nodded. Her round breasts were moving the red silk of her dress irregularly with her breathing.

He poured two large drinks.

She did not look up from the fire until he had put one glass in her hand. When she looked up she smiled, crookedly, twisting her heavily rouged exquisite thin lips sidewise. Her eyes, reflecting red light from the fire, were too bright.

He smiled down at her.

She lifted her glass and said, cooing: "To my husband!"

Ned Beaumont said, "No," casually and tossed the contents of his glass into the fireplace, where it spluttered and threw dancing flames up.

She laughed in delight and jumped to her feet. "Pour another," she ordered.

He picked the bottle up from the floor and refilled his glass.

She lifted hers high over her head. "To you!"

They drank. She shuddered.

"Better take something with it or after it," he suggested.

She shook her head. "I want it that way." She put a hand on his arm and turned her back to the fire, standing close beside him. "Let's bring that bench over here."

"That's an idea," he agreed.

They moved the chairs from in front of the fireplace and brought the bench there, he carrying one end, she the other. The bench was broad, low, backless.

"Now turn off the lights," she said.

He did so. When he returned to the bench she was sitting on it pouring whisky into their glasses.

"To you, this time," he said and they drank and she shuddered.

He sat beside her. They were rosy in the glow from the fireplace.

The stairs creaked and her husband came down them. He halted on the bottom step and said: "Please, darling!"

She whispered in Ned Beaumont's ear, savagely: "Throw something at him."

Ned Beaumont chuckled.

She picked up the whisky-bottle and said: "Where's your glass?"

While she was filling their glasses Mathews went upstairs.

She gave Ned Beaumont his glass and touched it with her own. Her eyes were wild in the red glow. A lock of dark hair had come loose and was down across her brow. She breathed through her mouth, panting softly. "To us!" she said.

They drank. She let her empty glass fall and came into his arms. Her mouth was to his when she shuddered. The fallen glass broke noisily on the wooden floor. Ned Beaumont's eyes were narrow, crafty. Hers were shut tight.

They had not moved when the stairs creaked. Ned Beaumont did not move then. She tightened her thin arms around him. He could not see the stairs. Both of them were breathing heavily now.

Then the stairs creaked again and, shortly afterwards, they drew their heads apart, though they kept their arms about one another. Ned Beaumont looked at the stairs. Nobody was there.

Eloise Mathews slid her hand up the back of his head, running her fingers through his hair, digging her nails into his scalp. Her eyes were not now altogether closed. They were laughing dark slits. "Life's like that," she said in a small bitter mocking voice, leaning back on the bench, drawing him with her, drawing his mouth to hers.

They were in that position when they heard the shot.

Ned Beaumont was out of her arms and on his feet immediately. "His room?" he asked sharply.

She blinked at him in dumb terror.

"His room?" he repeated.

She moved a feeble hand. "In front," she said thickly.

He ran to the stairs and went up in long leaps. At the head of the stairs he came face to face with the apish Jeff, dressed except for his shoes, blinking sleep out of his swollen eyes. Jeff put a hand to his hip, put the other hand out to stop Ned Beaumont, and growled: "Now what's all this?"

Ned avoided the outstretched hand, slid past it, and drove his left fist into the apish muzzle. Jeff staggered back snarling. Ned Beaumont sprang past him and ran towards the front of the building. O'Rory came out of another room and ran behind him.

From downstairs came Mrs. Mathews's scream.

Ned Beaumont flung a door open and stopped. Mathews lay on his back on a bedroom-floor under a lamp. His mouth was open and a little blood had trickled from it. One of his arms was thrown out across the floor. The other lay on his chest. Over against the wall, where the outstretched arm seemed to be pointing at it, was a dark revolver. On a table by the window was a bottle of ink—its stopper upside down beside it—a pen, and a sheet of paper. A chair stood close to the table, facing it.

Shad O'Rory pushed past Ned Beaumont and knelt beside the man on the floor. While he was there Ned Beaumont, behind him, swiftly glanced at the paper on the table, then thrust it into his pocket.

Jeff came in, followed by Rusty, naked.

O'Rory stood up and spread his hands apart in a little gesture of finality. "Shot himself through the roof of the mouth," he said. "Finis."

Ned Beaumont turned and went out of the room. In the hall he met Opal Madvig.

"What, Ned?" she asked in a frightened voice.

"Mathews has shot himself. I'll go down and stay with her till you get some clothes on. Don't go in there. There's nothing to see." He went downstairs.

Eloise Mathews was a dim shape lying on the floor beside the bench.

He took two quick steps towards her, halted, and looked around the room with shrewd cold eyes. Then he walked over to the woman, went down on a knee beside her, and felt her pulse. He looked at her as closely as he could in the dull light of the dying fire. She gave no sign of consciousness. He pulled the paper he had taken from her husband's table out of his pocket and moved on his knees to the fireplace, where, in the red embers' glow, he read:

I, Howard Keith Mathews, being of sound mind and memory, declare this to be my last will and testament:

I give and bequeath to my beloved wife, Eloise Braden Mathews, her heirs and assigns, all my real and personal property, of whatever nature or kind.

I hereby appoint the State Central Trust Company the sole executor of this will.

In witness whereof I have hereunto subscribed my name this . . .

Ned Beaumont, smiling grimly, stopped reading and tore the will three times across. He stood up, reached over the fire-screen, and dropped the torn pieces of paper into the glowing embers. The fragments blazed brightly a moment and were gone. With the wrought-iron shovel that stood beside the fire he mashed the paper-ash into the wood-coals.

Then he returned to Mrs. Mathews's side, poured a little whisky into the glass he had drunk from, raised her head, and forced some of the liquor between her lips. She was partly awake, coughing, when Opal Madvig came downstairs.

VI

Shad O'Rory came down the stairs. Jeff and Rusty were behind him. All of them were dressed. Ned Beaumont was standing by the door, in rain-coat and hat.

"Where are you going, Ned?" Shad asked.

"To find a phone."

O'Rory nodded. "That's a good enough idea," he said, "but there's something I want to ask you about." He came the rest of the way down the stairs, his followers close behind him.

Ned Beaumont said: "Yes?" He took his hand out of his pocket. The hand was visible to O'Rory and the men behind him, but Ned Beaumont's body concealed it from the bench where Opal sat with arms around Eloise Mathews. A square pistol was in the hand. "Just so there won't be any foolishness. I'm in a hurry."

O'Rory did not seem to see the pistol, though he came no nearer. He said, reflectively: "I was thinking that with an open ink-bottle and a pen on the table and a chair up to it it's kind of funny we didn't find any writing up there."

Ned Beaumont smiled in mock astonishment. "What, no writing?" He took a step backwards, towards the door. "That's a funny one, all right. I'll discuss it with you for hours when I come back from phoning."

"Now would be better," O'Rory said.

"Sorry." Ned Beaumont backed swiftly to the door, felt behind him for the knob, found it, and had the door open. "I won't be gone long." He jumped out and slammed the door.

The rain had stopped. He left the path and ran through tall grass around the other side of the house. From the house came the sound of another door slamming in the rear. The river was audible not far to Ned Beaumont's left. He worked his way through underbrush towards it.

A high-pitched sharp whistle, not loud, sounded somewhere behind him. He floundered through an area of soft mud to a clump of trees and turned away from the river among them. The whistle came again, on his right. Beyond the trees were shoulder-high bushes. He went among them, bending forward from the waist for concealment, though the night's blackness was all but complete.

His way was uphill, up a hill frequently slippery, always uneven, through brush that tore his face and hands, caught his clothing. Three times he fell. He stumbled many times. The whistle did not come again. He did not find the Buick. He did not find the road along which he had come.

He dragged his feet now and stumbled where there were no obstructions and when presently he had topped the hill and was going down its other slope he began to fall more often. At the bottom of the hill he found a road and turned to the right on it. Its clay stuck to his feet in increasing bulk so that he had to stop time after time to scrape it off. He used his pistol to scrape it off.

When he heard a dog bark behind him he stopped and

turned drunkenly to look back. Close to the road, fifty feet behind him, was the vague outline of a house he had passed. He retraced his steps and came to a tall gate. The dog—a shapeless monster in the night—hurled itself at the other side of the gate and barked terrifically.

Ned Beaumont fumbled along an end of the gate, found the catch, unfastened it, and staggered in. The dog backed away, circling, feinting attacks it never made, filling the night with clamor.

A window screeched up and a heavy voice called: "What the hell are you doing to that dog?"

Ned Beaumont laughed weakly. Then he shook himself and replied in not too thin a voice: "This is Beaumont of the District Attorney's office. I want to use your phone. There's a dead man down there."

The heavy voice roared: "I don't know what you're talking about. Shut up, Jeanie!" The dog barked three times with increased energy and became silent. "Now what is it?"

"I want to phone. District Attorney's office. There's a dead man down there."

The heavy voice exclaimed: "The hell you say!" The window screeched shut.

The dog began its barking and circling and feinting again. Ned Beaumont threw his muddy pistol at it. It turned and ran out of sight behind the house.

The front door was opened by a red-faced barrel-bodied short man in a long blue night-shirt. "Holy Maria, you're a mess!" he gasped when Ned Beaumont came into the light from the doorway.

"Phone," Ned Beaumont said.

The red-faced man caught him as he swayed. "Here," he said gruffly, "tell me who to call and what to say. You can't do anything."

"Phone," Ned Beaumont said.

The red-faced man steadied him along a hallway, opened a door, said: "There she is and it's a damned good thing for you the old woman ain't home or you'd never get in with all that mud on you."

Ned Beaumont fell into the chair in front of the telephone, but he did not immediately reach for the telephone. He scowled at the man in the blue night-shirt and said thickly: "Go out and shut the door."

The red-faced man had not come into the room. He shut the door.

Ned Beaumont picked up the receiver, leaned forward so that he was propped against the table by his elbows on it, and called Paul Madvig's number. Half a dozen times while he waited his eyelids closed, but each time he forced them open again and when, at last, he spoke into the telephone it was clearly.

"'Lo, Paul—Ned. . . . Never mind that. Listen to me. Mathews's committed suicide at his place on the river and didn't leave a will. . . . Listen to me. This is important. With a lot of debts and no will naming an executor it'll be up to the courts to appoint somebody to administer the estate. Get that? . . . Yes. See that it comes up before the right judge— Phelps, say—and we can keep the *Observer* out of the fight— except on our side—till after election. Got that? . . . All right, all right, now listen. That's only part of it. This is what's got to be done now. The *Observer* is loaded with dynamite for the morning. You've got to stop it. I'd say get Phelps out of bed and get an injunction out of him—anything to stop it till you can show the *Observer's* hired men where they stand now that the paper's going to be bossed for a month or so by our friends. . . . I can't tell you now, Paul, but it's dynamite and you've got to keep it from going on sale. Get Phelps out of bed and go down and look at it your-selves. You've got maybe three hours before it's out on the streets. . . . That's right. . . . What? . . . Opal? Oh, she's all right. She's with me. . . . Yes, I'll bring her home. . . . And will you phone the county people about Mathews? I'm going back there now. Right."

He laid the receiver on the table and stood up, staggered to the door, got it open after the second attempt, and fell out into the hallway, where the wall kept him from tumbling down on the floor.

The red-faced man came hurrying to him. "Just lean on me, brother, and I'll make you comfortable. I got a blanket spread over the davenport so we won't have to worry about the mud and—"

Ned Beaumont said: "I want to borrow a car. I've got to go back to Mathews's."

"Is it him that's dead?"

"Yes."

The red-faced man raised his eyebrows and made a squeaky whistling sound.

"Will you lend me the car?" Ned Beaumont demanded.

"My God, brother, be reasonable! How could you drive a car?"

Ned Beaumont backed away from the other, unsteadily. "I'll walk," he said.

The red-faced man glared at him. "You won't neither. If you'll keep your hair on till I get my pants I'll drive you back, though likely enough you'll die on me on the way."

Opal Madvig and Eloise Mathews were together in the large ground-floor room when Ned Beaumont was carried rather than led into it by the red-faced man. The men had come in without knocking. The two girls were standing close together, wide-eyed, startled.

Ned Beaumont pulled himself out of his companion's arms and looked dully around the room. "Where's Shad?" he mumbled.

Opal answered him: "He's gone. All of them have gone."

"All right," he said, speaking difficultly. "I want to talk to you alone."

Eloise Mathews ran over to him. "You killed him!" she cried.

He giggled idiotically and tried to put his arms around her.

She screamed, struck him in the face with an open hand.

He fell straight back without bending. The red-faced man tried to catch him, but could not. He did not move at all after he struck the floor.

CHAPTER VII

The Henchmen

SENATOR HENRY put his napkin on the table and stood up. Rising, he seemed taller than he was and younger. His somewhat small head, under its thin covering of grey hair, was remarkably symmetrical. Aging muscles sagged in his patrician face, accentuating its vertical lines, but slackness had not yet reached his lips, nor was it apparent that the years had in any way touched his eyes: they were a greenish grey, deep-set, not large but brilliant, and their lids were firm. He spoke with studied grave courtesy: "You'll forgive me if I carry Paul off upstairs for a little while?"

His daughter replied: "Yes, if you'll leave me Mr. Beaumont and if you'll promise not to stay up there all evening."

Ned Beaumont smiled politely, inclining his head.

He and Janet Henry went into a white-walled room where coal burned sluggishly in a grate under a white mantelpiece and put somber red gleams on the mahogany furniture.

She turned on a lamp beside the piano and sat down there with her back to the keyboard, her head between Ned Beaumont and the lamp. Her blond hair caught lamplight and held it in a nimbus around her head. Her black gown was of some suèdelike material that reflected no light and she wore no jewelry.

Ned Beaumont leaned over to knock ash from his cigar down on the burning coal. A dark pearl in his shirt-bosom, twinkling in the fire's glow as he moved, was like a red eye winking. When he straightened, he asked: "You'll play something?"

"Yes, if you wish—though I don't play exceptionally well— but later. I'd like to talk to you now while I've an opportunity." Her hands were together in her lap. Her arms, held straight, forced her shoulders up and in towards her neck.

Ned Beaumont nodded politely, but did not say anything. He left the fireplace and sat not far from her on a sofa with lyre ends. Though he was attentive, there was no curiosity in his mien.

Turning on the piano-bench to face him directly, she asked: "How is Opal?" Her voice was low, intimate.

His voice was casual: "Perfectly all right as far as I know, though I haven't seen her since last week." He lifted his cigar half a foot towards his mouth, lowered it, and as if the question had just come to his mind asked: "Why?"

She opened her brown eyes wide. "Isn't she in bed with a nervous break-down?"

"Oh, that!" he said carelessly, smiling. "Didn't Paul tell you?"

"Yes, he told me she was in bed with a nervous break-down." She stared at him, perplexed. "He told me that."

Ned Beaumont's smile became gentle. "I suppose he's sensitive about it," he said slowly, looking at his cigar. Then he looked up at her and moved his shoulders a little. "There's nothing the matter with her that way. It's simply that she got the foolish idea that he had killed your brother and—still more foolishly—was going around talking about it. Well, Paul couldn't have his daughter running around accusing him of murder, so he had to keep her home till she gets the notion out of her head."

"You mean she's—" she hesitated: her eyes were bright "—she's—well—a prisoner?"

"You make it sound melodramatic," he protested carelessly. "She's only a child. Isn't making children stay in their rooms one of the usual ways of disciplining them?"

Janet Henry replied hastily: "Oh, yes! Only—" She looked at her hands in her lap, up at his face again. "But why did she think that?"

Ned Beaumont's voice was tepid as his smile. "Who doesn't?" he asked.

She put her hands on the edge of the piano-bench beside her and leaned forward. Her white face was earnestly set. "That's what I wanted to ask you, Mr. Beaumont. Do people think that?"

He nodded. His face was placid.

Her knuckles were white over the bench-edge. Her voice was parched asking: "Why?"

He rose from the sofa and crossed to the fireplace to drop the remainder of his cigar into the fire. When he returned to his seat he crossed his long legs and leaned back at ease. "The other side thinks it's good politics to make people think that," he said. There was nothing in his voice, his face, his manner to show that he had any personal interest in what he was talking about.

She frowned. "But, Mr. Beaumont, why should people think it unless there's some sort of evidence, or something that can be made to look like evidence?"

He looked curiously and amusedly at her. "There is, of course," he said. "I thought you knew that." He combed a side of his mustache with a thumb-nail. "Didn't you get any of the anonymous letters that've been going around?"

She stood up quickly. Excitement distorted her face. "Yes, today!" she exclaimed. "I wanted to show it to you, to—"

He laughed softly and raised a hand, palm out in an arresting gesture. "Don't bother. They all seem to be pretty much alike and I've seen plenty of them."

She sat down again, slowly, reluctantly.

He said: "Well, those letters, the stuff the *Observer* was printing till we pulled it out of the fight, the talk the others have been circulating"—he shrugged his thin shoulders—"they've taken what facts there are and made a pretty swell case against Paul."

She took her lower lip from between her teeth to ask: "Is—is he actually in danger?"

Ned Beaumont nodded and spoke with calm certainty: "If he loses the election, loses his hold on the city and state government, they'll electrocute him."

She shivered and asked in a voice that shook: "But he's safe if he wins?"

Ned Beaumont nodded again. "Sure."

She caught her breath. Her lips trembled so that her words came out jerkily: "Will he win?"

"I think so."

"And it won't make any difference then no matter how much evidence there is against him, he'll—" her voice broke "—he'll not be in danger?"

"He won't be tried," Ned Beaumont told her. Abruptly he sat up straight. He shut his eyes tight, opened them, and stared at her tense pale face. A glad light came into his eyes, gladness spread over his face. He laughed—not loud but in complete delight—and stood up exclaiming: "Judith herself!"

Janet Henry sat breathlessly still, looking at him with un-comprehending brown eyes in a blank white face.

He began to walk around the room in an irregular route, talking happily—not to her—though now and then he turned his head over his shoulder to smile at her. "That's the game, of course," he said. "She could put up with Paul—be polite to him—for the sake of the political backing her father needed, but that would have its limits. Or that's all that would be nec-essary, Paul being so much in love with her. But when she de-cided Paul had killed her brother and was going to escape punishment unless she— That's splendid! Paul's daughter and his sweetheart both trying to steer him to the electric chair. He certainly has a lot of luck with women." He had a slender pale green-spotted cigar in one hand now. He halted in front of Janet Henry, clipped the end of the cigar, and said, not ac-cusingly, but as if sharing a discovery with her: "You sent those anonymous letters around. Certainly you did. They were written on the typewriter in the room where your brother and Opal used to meet. He had a key and she had a key. She didn't write them because she was stirred up by them. You did. You took his key when it was turned over to you and your father with the rest of his stuff by the police, sneaked into the room, and wrote them. That's fine." He began to walk again. He said: "Well, we'll have to make the Senator get in a squad of good able-bodied nurses and lock you in your room with a nervous break-down. It's getting to be epidemic among our politicians' daughters, but we've got to make sure of the elec-tion even if every house in town has to have its patient." He turned his head over his shoulder to smile amiably at her.

She put a hand to her throat. Otherwise she did not move. She did not speak.

He said: "The Senator won't give us much trouble, luckily. He doesn't care about anything—not you or his dead son—as much as he does about being re-elected and he knows he can't do that without Paul." He laughed. "That's what drove you into the Judith rôle, huh? You knew your father wouldn't split with Paul—even if he thought him guilty—till the election was won. Well, that's a comforting thing to know—for us."

When he stopped talking to light his cigar she spoke. She had taken her hand down from her throat. Her hands were in her lap. She sat erect without stiffness. Her voice was cool and composed. She said: "I am not good at lying. I know Paul killed Taylor. I wrote the letters."

Ned Beaumont took the burning cigar from his mouth, came back to the lyre-end sofa, and sat down facing her. His face was grave, but without hostility. He said: "You hate Paul, don't you? Even if I proved to you that he didn't kill Taylor you'd still hate him, wouldn't you?"

"Yes," she replied, her light brown eyes steady on his darker ones, "I think I should."

"That's it," he said. "You don't hate him because you think he killed your brother. You think he killed your brother because you hate him."

She moved her head slowly from side to side. "No," she said.

He smiled skeptically. Then he asked: "Have you talked it over with your father?"

She bit her lip and her face flushed a little.

Ned Beaumont smiled again. "And he told you it was ridiculous," he said.

Pink deepened in her cheeks. She started to say something, but did not.

He said: "If Paul killed your brother your father knows it."

She looked down at her hands in her lap and said dully, miserably: "My father should know it, but he will not believe it."

Ned Beaumont said: "He ought to know." His eyes became narrower. "Did Paul say anything at all to him that night about Taylor and Opal?"

She raised her head, astonished. "Don't you know what happened that night?" she asked.

"No."

"It hadn't anything to do with Taylor and Opal," she said, word tumbling over word in her eagerness to get them spoken. "It—" She jerked her face towards the door and shut her mouth with a click. Deep-chested rumbling laughter had come through the door, and the sound of approaching steps. She faced Ned Beaumont again, hastily, lifting her hands in an appealing gesture. "I've got to tell you," she whispered, desperately earnest. "Can I see you tomorrow?"

"Yes."

"Where?"

"My place?" he suggested.

She nodded quickly. He had time to mutter his address, she to whisper, "After ten?" and he to nod before Senator Henry and Paul Madvig came into the room.

II

Paul Madvig and Ned Beaumont said good-night to the Henrys at half past ten o'clock and got into a brown sedan which Madvig drove down Charles Street. When they had ridden a block and a half Madvig blew his breath out in a satisfied gust and said: "Jesus, Ned, you don't know how tickled I am that you and Janet are hitting it off so nice."

Ned Beaumont, looking obliquely at the blond man's profile, said: "I can get along with anybody."

Madvig chuckled. "Yes you can," he said indulgently, "like hell."

Ned Beaumont's lips curved in a thin secretive smile. He said: "I've got something I want to talk to you about tomorrow. Where'll you be, say, in the middle of the afternoon?"

Madvig turned the sedan into China Street. "At the office," he said. "It's the first of the month. Why don't you do your talking now? There's a lot of night left yet."

"I don't know it all now. How's Opal?"

"She's all right," Madvig said gloomily, then exclaimed: "Christ! I wish I could be sore at the kid. It'd make it a lot easier." They passed a street-light. He blurted out: "She's not pregnant."

Ned Beaumont did not say anything. His face was expressionless.

Madvig reduced the sedan's speed as they approached the Log Cabin Club. His face was red. He asked huskily: "What do you think, Ned? Was she"—he cleared his throat noisily—"his mistress? Or was it just boy and girl stuff?"

Ned Beaumont said: "I don't know. I don't care. Don't ask her, Paul."

Madvig stopped the sedan and sat for a moment at the wheel staring straight ahead. Then he cleared his throat again and spoke in a low hoarse voice: "You're not the worst guy in the world, Ned."

"Uh-uh," Ned Beaumont agreed as they got out of the sedan.

They entered the Club, separating casually under the Governor's portrait at the head of the stairs on the second floor.

Ned Beaumont went into a rather small room in the rear where five men were playing stud poker and three were watching them play. The players made a place for him at the table and by three o'clock, when the game broke up, he had won some four hundred dollars.

III

It was nearly noon when Janet Henry arrived at Ned Beaumont's rooms. He had been pacing the floor, alternately biting his finger-nails and puffing at cigars, for more than an hour. He went without haste to the door when she rang, opened it, and, smiling with an air of slight but pleasant surprise, said: "Good morning."

"I'm awfully sorry to be late," she began, "but—"

"But you're not," he assured her. "It was to have been any time after ten."

He ushered her into his living-room.

"I like this," she said, turning around slowly, examining the old-fashioned room, the height of its ceiling, the width of its windows, the tremendous mirror over the fireplace, the red plush of the furniture. "It's delightful." She turned her brown eyes towards a half-open door. "Is that your bedroom?"

"Yes. Would you like to see it?"

"I'd love to."

He showed her the bedroom, then the kitchen and bathroom.

"It's perfect," she said as they returned to the living-room. "I didn't know there could be any more of these left in a city as horribly up to date as ours has become."

He made a little bow to acknowledge her approval. "I think it's rather nice and, as you can see, there's no one here to eavesdrop on us unless they're stowed away in a closet, which isn't likely."

She drew herself up and looked straight into his eyes. "I did not think of that. We may not agree, may even become— or now be—enemies, but I know you're a gentleman, or I shouldn't be here."

He asked in an amused tone: "You mean I've learned not to wear tan shoes with blue suits? Things like that?"

"I don't mean things like that."

He smiled. "Then you're wrong. I'm a gambler and a politician's hanger-on."

"I'm not wrong." A pleading expression came into her eyes. "Please don't let us quarrel, at least not until we must."

"I'm sorry." His smile was apologetic now. "Won't you sit down?"

She sat down. He sat in another wide red chair facing her. He said: "Now you were going to tell me what happened at your house the night your brother was killed."

"Yes," issuing from her mouth, was barely audible. Her face became pink and she transferred her gaze to the floor. When she raised her eyes again they were shy. Embarrassment clogged her voice: "I wanted you to know. You are Paul's friend and that—that may make you my enemy, but— I think when you know what happened—when you know the truth— you'll not be—at least not be my enemy. I don't know. Perhaps you'll— But you ought to know. Then you can decide. And he hasn't told you." She looked intently at him so that shyness went out of her eyes. "Has he?"

"I don't know what happened at your house that night," he said. "He didn't tell me."

She leaned towards him quickly to ask: "Doesn't that show it's something he wants to conceal, something he has to conceal?"

He moved his shoulders. "Suppose it does?" His voice was unexcited, uneager.

She frowned. "But you must see— Never mind that now. I'll tell you what happened and you can see it for yourself." She continued to lean far forward, staring at his face with intent brown eyes. "He came to dinner, the first time we'd had him to dinner."

"I knew that," Ned Beaumont said, "and your brother wasn't there."

"Taylor wasn't at the dinner-table," she corrected him earnestly, "but he was up in his room. Only Father, Paul, and I were at the table. Taylor was going out to dinner. He—he wouldn't eat with Paul because of the trouble they'd had about Opal."

Ned Beaumont nodded attentively without warmth.

"After dinner Paul and I were alone for a little while in—in the room where you and I talked last night and he suddenly put his arms around me and kissed me."

Ned Beaumont laughed, not loudly, but with abrupt irrepressible merriment.

Janet Henry looked at him in surprise.

He modified his laugh to a smile and said: "I'm sorry. Go on. I'll tell you later why I laughed." But when she would have gone on he said: "Wait. Did he say anything when he kissed you?"

"No. That is, he may have, but nothing I understood." Perplexity was deepening in her face. "Why?"

Ned Beaumont laughed again. "He ought to've said something about his pound of flesh. It was probably my fault. I had been trying to persuade him not to support your father in the election, had told him that your father was using you as bait to catch his support, and had advised him that if he was willing to be bought that way he ought to be sure and collect his pound of flesh ahead of the election or he'd never get it."

She opened her eyes wide and there was less perplexity in them.

He said: "That was that afternoon, though I didn't think I'd had much luck putting it over." He wrinkled his forehead. "What did you do to him? He was meaning to marry you and was chock-full of respect and what not for you and you must have rubbed him pretty thoroughly the wrong way to make him jump at you like that."

"I didn't do anything to him," she replied slowly, "though it had been a difficult evening. None of us was comfortable. I thought—I tried not to show that—well—that I resented having to entertain him. He wasn't at ease, I know, and I suppose that—his embarrassment—and perhaps a suspicion that you had been right made him—" She finished the sentence with a brief quick outward motion of both hands.

Ned Beaumont nodded. "What happened then?" he asked.

"I was furious, of course, and left him."

"Didn't you say anything to him?" Ned Beaumont's eyes twinkled with imperfectly hidden mirth.

"No, and he didn't say anything I could hear. I went upstairs and met Father coming down. While I was telling him what had happened—I was as angry with Father as with Paul, because it was Father's fault that Paul was there—we heard Paul going out the front door. And then Taylor came down from his room." Her face became white and tense, her voice husky with emotion. "He had heard me talking to Father and he asked me what had happened, but I left him there with Father and went on to my room, too angry to talk any more about it. And I didn't see either of them again until Father came to my room and told me Taylor had—had been killed." She stopped talking and looked white-faced at Ned Beaumont, twisting her fingers together, awaiting his response to her story.

His response was a cool question: "Well, what of it?"

"What of it?" she repeated in amazement. "Don't you see? How could I help knowing then that Taylor had run out after Paul and had caught up with him and had been killed by him? He was furious and—" Her face brightened. "You know his hat wasn't found. He was too much in a hurry—too angry—to stop for his hat. He—"

Ned Beaumont shook his head slowly from side to side and interrupted her. His voice held nothing but certainty. "No," he said. "That won't do. Paul wouldn't've had to kill Taylor and he wouldn't've done it. He could have managed him with one hand and he doesn't lose his head in a fight. I know that. I've seen Paul fight and I've fought with him. That won't do." He drew eyelids closer together around eyes that had become stony. "But suppose he did? I mean accidentally, though I can't believe even that. But could you make anything out of it except self-defense?"

She raised her head scornfully. "If it were self-defense, why should he hide it?"

Ned Beaumont seemed unimpressed. "He wants to marry you," he explained. "It wouldn't help him much to admit he'd killed your brother even—" He chuckled. "I'm getting as bad as you are. Paul didn't kill him, Miss Henry."

Her eyes were stony as his had been. She looked at him and did not speak.

His expression became thoughtful. He asked: "You've only"—he wriggled the fingers of one hand—"the two and two you think you've put together to tell you that your brother ran out after Paul that night?"

"That is enough," she insisted. "He did. He must've. Otherwise—why, otherwise what would he have been doing down there in China Street bare-headed?"

"Your father didn't see him go out?"

"No. He didn't know it either until we heard—"

He interrupted her. "Does he agree with you?"

"He must," she cried. "It's unmistakable. He must, no matter what he says, just as you must." Tears were in her eyes now. "You can't expect me to believe that you don't, Mr. Beaumont. I don't know what you knew before. You found Taylor dead. I don't know what else you found, but now you must know the truth."

Ned Beaumont's hands began to tremble. He slumped farther down in his chair so he could thrust his hands into his trousers-pockets. His face was tranquil except for hard lines of strain around his mouth. He said: "I found him dead. There was nobody else there. I didn't find anything else."

"You have now," she said.

His mouth twitched under his dark mustache. His eyes became hot with anger. He spoke in a low, harsh, deliberately bitter, voice: "I know whoever killed your brother did the world a favor."

She shrank back in her chair with a hand thrown up to her throat, at first, but almost immediately the horror went out of her face and she sat upright and looked compassionately at him. She said softly: "I know. You're Paul's friend. It hurts."

He lowered his head a little and muttered: "It was a rotten thing to say. It was silly." He smiled wryly. "You see I was right about not being a gentleman." He stopped smiling and shame went out of his eyes leaving them clear and steady. He said in a quiet voice: "You're right about my being Paul's friend. I'm that no matter who he killed."

After a long moment of earnest staring at him she spoke in a small flat voice: "Then this is useless? I thought if I could show you the truth—" She broke off with a hopeless gesture in which hands, shoulders, and head took part.

He moved his head slowly from side to side.

She sighed and stood up holding out her hand. "I'm sorry and disappointed, but we needn't be enemies, need we?"

He rose facing her, but did not take her hand. He said: "The part of you that's tricked Paul and is trying to trick him is my enemy."

She held her hand there while asking: "And the other part of me, the part that hasn't anything to do with that?"

He took her hand and bowed over it.

IV

When Janet Henry had gone Ned Beaumont went to his telephone, called a number, and said: "Hello, this is Mr. Beaumont. Has Mr. Madvig come in yet? . . . When he comes will you tell him I called and will be in to see him? . . . Yes, thanks."

He looked at his wrist-watch. It was a little after one o'clock. He lit a cigar and sat down at a window, smoking and staring at the grey church across the street. Out-blown cigar-smoke recoiled from the window-panes in grey clouds over his head. His teeth crushed the end of his cigar. He sat there for ten minutes, until his telephone-bell rang.

He went to the telephone. "Hello. . . . Yes, Harry. . . . Sure. Where are you? . . . I'm coming downtown. Wait there for me. . . . Half an hour. . . . Right."

He threw his cigar into the fireplace, put on his hat and overcoat, and went out. He walked six blocks to a restaurant, ate a salad and rolls, drank a cup of coffee, walked four blocks to a small hotel named Majestic, and rode to the fourth floor in an elevator operated by an undersized youth who called him Ned and asked what he thought of the third race.

Ned Beaumont thought and said: "Lord Byron ought to do it."

The elevator-operator said: "I hope you're wrong. I got Pipe-organ."

Ned Beaumont shrugged. "Maybe, but he's carrying a lot of weight." He went to room 417 and knocked on the door.

Harry Sloss, in his shirt-sleeves, opened the door. He was a thickset pale man of thirty-five, broad-faced and partially bald. He said: "On the dot. Come on in."

When Sloss had shut the door Ned Beaumont asked: "What's the diffugalty?"

The thickset man went over to the bed and sat down. He scowled anxiously at Ned Beaumont. "It don't look so damned good to me, Ned."

"What don't?"

"This thing of Ben going to the Hall with it."

Ned Beaumont said irritably: "All right. Any time you're ready to tell me what you're talking about's soon enough for me."

Sloss raised a pale broad hand. "Wait, Ned, I'll tell you what it's about. Just listen." He felt in his pocket for cigarettes, bringing out a package mashed limp. "You remember the night the Henry kid was pooped?"

Ned Beaumont's "Uh-huh" was carelessly uttered.

"Remember me and Ben had just come in when you got there, at the Club?"

"Yes."

"Well, listen: we saw Paul and the kid arguing up there under the trees."

Ned Beaumont brushed a side of his mustache with a thumb-nail, once, and spoke slowly, looking puzzled: "But I saw you get out of the car in front of the Club—that was just after I found him—and you came up the other way." He moved a forefinger. "And Paul was already in the Club ahead of you."

Sloss nodded his broad head vigorously. "That's all right," he said, "but we'd drove on down China Street to Pinky Klein's place and he wasn't there and we turned around and drove back to the Club."

Ned Beaumont nodded. "Just what did you see?"

"We saw Paul and the kid standing there under the trees arguing."

"You could see that as you rode past?"

Sloss nodded vigorously again.

"It was a dark spot," Ned Beaumont reminded him. "I don't see how you could've made out their faces riding past like that, unless you slowed up or stopped."

"No, we didn't, but I'd know Paul anywhere," Sloss insisted.

"Maybe, but how'd you know it was the kid with him?"

"It was. Sure, it was. We could see enough of him to know that."

"And you could see they were arguing? What do you mean by that? Fighting?"

"No, but standing like they were having an argument. You know how you can tell when people are arguing sometimes by the way they stand."

Ned Beaumont smiled mirthlessly. "Yes, if one of them's standing on the other's face." His smile vanished. "And that's what Ben went to the Hall with?"

"Yes. I don't know whether he went in with it on his own account or whether Farr got hold of it somehow and sent for him, but anyhow he spilled it to Farr. That was yesterday."

"How'd you hear about it, Harry?"

"Farr's hunting for me," Sloss said. "That's the way I heard about it. Ben'd told him I was with him and Farr sent word for me to drop in and see him, but I don't want any part of it."

"I hope you don't, Harry," Ned Beaumont said. "What are you going to say if Farr catches you?"

"I'm not going to let him catch me if I can help it. That's what I wanted to see you about." He cleared his throat and moistened his lips. "I thought maybe I ought to get out of town for a week or two, till it kind of blows over, and that'd take a little money."

Ned Beaumont smiled and shook his head. "That's not the thing to do," he told the thickset man. "If you want to help Paul go tell Farr you couldn't recognize the two men under the trees and that you don't think anybody in your car could."

"All right, that's what I'll do," Sloss said readily, "but, listen, Ned, I ought to get something out of it. I'm taking a chance and—well—you know how it is."

Ned Beaumont nodded. "We'll pick you out a soft job after election, one you'll have to show up on maybe an hour a day."

"That'll be—" Sloss stood up. His green-flecked palish eyes were urgent. "I'll tell you, Ned, I'm broke as hell. Couldn't you make it a little dough now instead? It'd come in damned handy."

"Maybe. I'll talk it over with Paul."

"Do that, Ned, and give me a ring."

"Sure. So long."

v

From the Majestic Hotel Ned Beaumont went to the City Hall, to the District Attorney's office, and said he wanted to see Mr. Farr.

The round-faced youth to whom he said it left the outer office, returning a minute later apologetic of mien. "I'm sorry, Mr. Beaumont, but Mr. Farr is not in."

"When will he be back?"

"I don't know. His secretary says he didn't leave word."

"I'll take a chance. I'll wait awhile in his office."

The round-faced youth stood in his way. "Oh, you can't do—"

Ned Beaumont smiled his nicest smile at the youth and asked softly: "Don't you like this job, son?"

The youth hesitated, fidgeted, and stepped out of Ned Beaumont's way. Ned Beaumont walked down the inner corridor to the District Attorney's door and opened it.

Farr looked up from his desk, sprang to his feet. "Was that you?" he cried. "Damn that boy! He never gets anything right. A Mr. Bauman, he said."

"No harm done," Ned Beaumont said mildly. "I got in."

He let the District Attorney shake his hand up and down and lead him to a chair. When they were seated he asked idly: "Anything new?"

"Nothing." Farr rocked back in his chair, thumbs hooked

in lower vest-pockets. "Just the same old grind, though God knows there's enough of that."

"How's the electioneering going?"

"It could be better"—a shadow passed over the District Attorney's pugnacious red face—"but I guess we'll manage all right."

Ned Beaumont kept idleness in his voice. "What's the matter?"

"This and that. Things always come up. That's politics, I guess."

"Anything I can do—or Paul—to help?" Ned Beaumont asked and then, when Farr had shaken his red-stubble-covered head: "This talk that Paul's got something to do with the Henry killing the worst thing you're up against?"

A frightened gleam came into Farr's eyes, disappeared as he blinked. He sat up straight in his chair. "Well," he said cautiously, "there's a lot of feeling that we ought to've cleared the murder up before this. That is one of the things—maybe one of the biggest."

"Made any progress since I saw you last? Turned up anything new on it?"

Farr shook his head. His eyes were wary.

Ned Beaumont smiled without warmth. "Still taking it slow on some of the angles?"

The District Attorney squirmed in his chair. "Well, yes, of course, Ned."

Ned Beaumont nodded approvingly. His eyes were shiny with malice. His voice was a taunt: "Is the Ben Ferriss angle one of them that you're taking it slow on?"

Farr's blunt undershot mouth opened and shut. He rubbed his lips together. His eyes, after their first startled widening, became devoid of expression. He said: "I don't know whether there's anything at all in Ferriss's story or not, Ned. I don't guess there is. I didn't even think enough of it to tell you about it."

Ned Beaumont laughed derisively.

Farr said: "You know I wouldn't hold out anything on you and Paul, anything that was important. You know me well enough for that."

"We knew you before you got nerves," Ned Beaumont

replied. "But that's all right. If you want the fellow that was in the car with Ferriss you can pick him up right now in room 417 at the Majestic."

Farr was staring at his green desk-set, at the dancing nude figure holding an airplane aloft between two slanting pens. His face was lumpy. He said nothing.

Ned Beaumont rose from his chair smiling with thin lips. He said: "Paul's always glad to help the boys out of holes. Do you think it would help if he'd let himself be arrested and tried for the Henry murder?"

Farr did not move his eyes from the green desk-set. He said doggedly: "It's not for me to tell Paul what to do."

"There's a thought!" Ned Beaumont exclaimed. He leaned over the side of the desk until his face was near the District Attorney's ear and lowered his voice to a confidential key. "And here's another one that goes with it. It's not for you to do much Paul wouldn't tell you to do."

He went out grinning, but stopped grinning when he was outside.

CHAPTER VIII

The Kiss-Off

NED BEAUMONT opened a door marked *East State Construction & Contracting Company* and exchanged good-afternoons with the two young ladies at desks inside, then he passed through a larger room in which there were half a dozen men to whom he spoke and opened a door marked *Private.* He went into a square room where Paul Madvig sat at a battered desk looking at papers placed in front of him by a small man who hovered respectfully over his shoulder.

Madvig raised his head and said: "Hello, Ned." He pushed the papers aside and told the small man: "Bring this junk back after while."

The small man gathered up his papers and, saying, "Certainly, sir," and, "How do you do, Mr. Beaumont?" left the room.

Madvig said: "You look like you'd had a tough night, Ned. What'd you do? Sit down."

Ned Beaumont had taken off his overcoat. He put it on a chair, put his hat on it, and took out a cigar. "No, I'm all right. What's new in your life?" He sat on a corner of the battered desk.

"I wish you'd go see M'Laughlin," the blond man said. "You can handle him if anybody can."

"All right. What's the matter with him?"

Madvig grimaced. "Christ knows! I thought I had him lined up, but he's going shifty on us."

A somber gleam came into Ned Beaumont's dark eyes. He looked down at the blond man and said: "Him too, huh?"

Madvig asked slowly, after a moment's deliberation: "What do you mean by that, Ned?"

Ned Beaumont's reply was another question: "Is everything going along to suit you?"

Madvig moved his big shoulders impatiently, but his eyes did not lose their surveying stare. "Nor so damned bad either," he said. "We can get along without M'Laughlin's batch of votes if we have to."

729

"Maybe," Ned Beaumont's lips had become thin, "but we can't keep on losing them and come out all right." He put his cigar in a corner of his mouth and said around it: "You know we're not as well off as we were two weeks ago."

Madvig grinned indulgently at the man on his desk. "Jesus, you like to sing them, Ned! Don't anything ever look right to you?" He did not wait for a reply, but went on placidly: "I've never been through a campaign yet that didn't look like it was going to hell at some time or other. They don't, though."

Ned Beaumont was lighting his cigar. He blew smoke out and said: "That doesn't mean they never will." He pointed the cigar at Madvig's chest. "If Taylor Henry's killing isn't cleared up pronto you won't have to worry about the campaign. You'll be sunk whoever wins."

Madvig's blue eyes became opaque. There was no other change in his face. His voice was unchanged. "Just what do you mean by that, Ned?"

"Everybody in town thinks you killed him."

"Yes?" Madvig put a hand up to his chin, rubbed it thoughtfully. "Don't let that worry you. I've had things said about me before."

Ned Beaumont smiled tepidly and asked with mock admiration: "Is there anything you haven't been through before? Ever been given the electric cure?"

The blond man laughed. "And don't think I ever will," he said.

"You're not very far from it right now, Paul," Ned Beaumont said softly.

Madvig laughed again. "Jesus Christ!" he scoffed.

Ned Beaumont shrugged. "You're not busy?" he asked. "I'm not taking up your time with my nonsense?"

"I'm listening to you," Madvig told him quietly. "I never lost anything listening to you."

"Thank you, sir. Why do you suppose M'Laughlin's wiggling out from under?"

Madvig shook his head.

"He figures you're licked," Ned Beaumont said. "Everybody knows the police haven't tried to find Taylor's murderer and everybody thinks it's because you killed him. M'Laughlin figures that's enough to lick you at the polls this time."

"Yes? He figures they'd rather have Shad running the city than me? He figures being suspected of one murder makes my rep worse than Shad's?"

Ned Beaumont scowled at the blond man. "You're either kidding yourself or trying to kid me. What's Shad's reputation got to do with it? He's not out in the open behind his candidates. You are and it's your candidates who're responsible for nothing being done about the murder."

Madvig put his hand to his chin again and leaned his elbow on the desk. His handsome ruddy face was unlined. He said: "We've been talking a lot about what other people figure, Ned. Let's talk about what you figure. Figure I'm licked?"

"You probably are," Ned Beaumont said in a low sure voice. "It's a cinch you are if you sit still." He smiled. "But your candidates ought to come out all right."

"That," Madvig said phlegmatically, "ought to be explained."

Ned Beaumont leaned over and carefully knocked cigar-ash into the brass spittoon beside the desk. Then he said, unemotionally: "They're going to cross you up."

"Yes?"

"Why not? You've let Shad take most of the riff-raff from behind you. You're counting on the respectable people, the better element, to carry the election. They're getting leery. Well, your candidates make a grand-stand-play, arrest you for murder, and the respectable citizens—delighted with these noble officials who are brave enough to jail their own acknowledged boss when he breaks the law—trample each other to death in their hurry to get to the polls and elect the heroes to four more years of city-administering. You can't blame the boys much. They know they're sitting pretty if they do it and out of work if they don't."

Madvig took his hand from his chin to ask: "You don't count much on their loyalty, do you, Ned?"

Ned Beaumont smiled. "Just as much as you do," he replied. His smile went away. "I'm not guessing, Paul. I went in to see Farr this afternoon. I had to walk in, crash the gate —he tried to dodge me. He pretended he hadn't been digging into the killing. He tried to stall me on what he'd found out. In the end he dummied up on me." He made a disdainful mouth. "Farr, the guy I could always make jump through hoops."

"Well, that's only Farr," Madvig began.

Ned Beaumont cut him short. "Only Farr, and that's the tip-off. Rutlege or Brody or even Rainey might clip you on their own, but if Farr's doing anything it's a pipe he knows the others are with him." He frowned at the blond man's stolid face. "You can stop believing me any time you want to, Paul."

Madvig made a careless gesture with the hand he had held to his chin. "I'll let you know when I stop," he said. "How'd you happen to drop in on Farr?"

"Harry Sloss called me up today. It seems he and Ben Ferriss saw you arguing with Taylor in China Street the night of the murder, or claim they did." Ned Beaumont was looking with eyes that held no particular expression at the blond man and his voice was matter-of-fact. "Ben had gone to Farr with it. Harry wanted to be paid for not going. There's a couple of your Club-members reading the signs. I've been watching Farr lose his nerve for some time, so I went in to check him up."

Madvig nodded. "And you're sure he's knifing me?"

"Yes."

Madvig got up from his chair and went to the window. He stood there, hands in trousers-pockets, looking through the glass for perhaps three minutes while Ned Beaumont, sitting on the desk, smoked and looked at the blond man's wide back. Then, not turning his head, Madvig asked: "What'd you say to Harry?"

"Stalled him."

Madvig left the window and came back to the desk, but he did not sit down. His ruddiness had deepened. Otherwise no change had come into his face. His voice was level. "What do you think we ought to do?"

"About Sloss? Nothing. The other monkey's already gone to Farr. It doesn't make much difference what Sloss does."

"I didn't mean that. I meant about the whole thing."

Ned Beaumont dropped his cigar into the spittoon. "I've told you. If Taylor Henry's murder isn't cleared up pronto you're sunk. That's the whole thing. That's the only thing worth doing anything about."

Madvig stopped looking at Ned Beaumont. He looked at a wide vacant space on the wall. He pressed his full lips together. Moisture appeared on his temples. He said from deep in his chest: "That won't do. Think up something else."

Ned Beaumont's nostrils moved with his breathing and the brown of his eyes seemed dark as the pupils. He said: "There isn't anything else, Paul. Any other way plays into the hands of either Shad or Farr and his crew and either of them will ruin you."

Madvig said somewhat hoarsely: "There must be an out, Ned. Think."

Ned Beaumont left the desk and stood close in front of the blond man. "There isn't. That's the only way. You're going to take it whether you like it or not, or I'm going to take it for you."

Madvig shook his head violently. "No. Lay off."

Ned Beaumont said: "That's one thing I won't do for you, Paul."

Then Madvig looked Ned Beaumont in the eyes and said in a harsh whisper: "I killed him, Ned."

Ned Beaumont drew breath in and let it out in a long sigh.

Madvig put his hands on Ned Beaumont's shoulders and his words came out thick and blurred. "It was an accident, Ned. He ran down the street after me when I left, with a cane he'd picked up on the way out. We'd had—there'd been some trouble there and he caught up with me and tried to hit me with the stick. I don't know how it happened, but pulling it away from him I hit him on the head with it—not hard—it couldn't've been very hard—but he fell back and smashed his head on the curb."

Ned Beaumont nodded. His face had suddenly become empty of all expression except hard concentration on Madvig's words. He asked in a crisp voice that matched his face: "What happened to the cane?"

"I took it away under my overcoat and burned it. After I knew he was dead I found it in my hand, when I was walking down to the Club, so I put it under my overcoat and then burned it."

"What kind of cane was it?"

"A rough brown one, heavy."

"And his hat?"

"I don't know, Ned. I guess it was knocked off and some-body picked it up."

"He had one on?"

"Yes, sure."

Ned Beaumont brushed a side of his mustache with a thumb-nail. "You remember Sloss's and Ferriss's car passing you?"

Madvig shook his head. "No, though they may have."

Ned Beaumont frowned at the blond man. "You gummed things up plenty by running off with the stick and burning it and keeping quiet all this time," he grumbled. "You had a clear self-defense plea."

"I know, but I didn't want that, Ned," Madvig said hoarsely. "I want Janet Henry more than I ever wanted anything in my life and what chance would I have then, even if it was an accident?"

Ned Beaumont laughed in Madvig's face. It was a low laugh and bitter. He said: "You'd have more chance than you've got now."

Madvig, staring at him, said nothing.

Ned Beaumont said: "She's always thought you killed her brother. She hates you. She's been trying to play you into the electric chair. She's responsible for first throwing suspicion on you with anonymous letters sent around to everybody that might be interested. She's the one that turned Opal against you. She was in my rooms this morning telling me this, try-ing to turn me. She—"

Madvig said: "That's enough." He stood erect, a big blond man whose eyes were cold blue disks. "What is it, Ned? Do you want her yourself or is it—" He broke off contemptu-ously. "It doesn't make any difference." He jerked a thumb carelessly at the door. "Get out, you heel, this is the kiss-off."

Ned Beaumont said: "I'll get out when I've finished talking."

Madvig said: "You'll get out when you're told to. You can't say anything I'll believe. You haven't said anything I believe. You never will now."

Ned Beaumont said: "Oke." He picked up his hat and overcoat and went out.

II

Ned Beaumont went home. His face was pale and sullen. He slouched down in one of the big red chairs with a bottle of Bourbon whisky and a glass on the table beside him, but he did not drink. He stared gloomily at his black-shod feet and bit a finger-nail. His telephone-bell rang. He did not answer it. Twilight began to displace day in the room. The room was dusky when he rose and went to the telephone.

He called a number. Then: "Hello, I'd like to speak to Miss Henry, please." After a pause that he spent whistling tunelessly under his breath, he said: "Hello, Miss Henry? . . . Yes. . . . I've just come from telling Paul all about it, about you. . . . Yes, and you were right. He did what you counted on his doing. . . ." He laughed. "You did. You knew he'd call me a liar, refuse to listen to me, and throw me out, and he did all of it. . . . No, no, that's all right. It had to happen. . . . No, really. . . . Oh, it's probably permanent enough. Things were said that can't easily be unsaid. . . . Yes, all evening, I think. . . . That'll be fine. . . . All right. 'By."

He poured out a glass of whisky then and drank it. After that he went into his darkening bedroom, set his alarm-clock for eight o'clock, and lay down fully clothed on his back on the bed. For a while he looked at the ceiling. Then he slept, breathing irregularly, until the alarm rang.

He got up sluggishly from his bed and, switching on lights, went into the bathroom, washed his face and hands, put on a fresh collar, and started a fire in the living-room-fireplace. He read a newspaper until Janet Henry arrived.

She was excited. Though she at once began to assure Ned Beaumont that she had not foreseen the result of his telling Paul about her visit, had not counted on it, elation danced frankly in her eyes and she could not keep smiles from curving her lips while they shaped the apologetic words.

He said: "It doesn't matter. I'd've had to do it if I'd known how it was going to turn out. I suppose I did know down underneath. It's one of those things. And if you'd told me it would happen I'd only've taken that for a challenge and would've jumped to it."

She held her hands out to him. "I'm glad," she said. "I won't pretend I'm not."

"I'm sorry," he told her as he took her hands, "but I wouldn't have gone a step out of my way to avoid it."

She said: "And now you know I'm right. He did kill Taylor." Her eyes were inquisitive.

He nodded. "He told me he did."

"And you'll help me now?" Her hands pressed his. She came closer to him.

He hesitated, frowning down at her eager face. "It was self-defense, or an accident," he said slowly. "I can't—"

"It was murder!" she cried. "Of course he'd say it was self-defense!" She shook her head impatiently. "And even if it was self-defense or an accident, shouldn't he be made to go into court and prove it like anybody else?"

"He's waited too long. This month he's kept quiet would be against him."

"Well, whose fault was that?" she demanded. "And do you think he would have kept quiet so long if it had been self-defense?"

He nodded with slow emphasis. "That was on your account. He's in love with you. He didn't want you to know he'd killed your brother."

"I do know it!" she cried fiercely. "And everybody's going to know it!"

He moved his shoulders a little. His face was gloomy.

"You won't help me?" she asked.

"No."

"Why? You've quarreled with him."

"I believe his story. I know it's too late for him to put it across in court. We're through, but I won't do that to him." He moistened his lips. "Let him alone. It's likely they'll do it to him without your help or mine."

"I won't," she said. "I won't let him alone until he's been punished as he deserves." She caught her breath and her eyes darkened. "Do you believe him enough to risk finding proof that he lied to you?"

"What do you mean?" he asked cautiously.

"Will you help me find proof of the truth, whether he's

lying or not? There must be positive proof somewhere, some proof that we can find. If you really believe him you won't be afraid to help me find it."

He studied her face awhile before asking: "If I do and we find your positive proof, will you promise to accept it whichever way it stacks up?"

"Yes," she said readily, "if you will too."

"And you'll keep what we find to yourself till we've finished the job—found our positive proof—won't use what we find against him till we've got it all?"

"Yes."

"It's a bargain," he said.

She sobbed happily and tears came to her eyes.

He said: "Sit down." His face was lean and hard, his voice curt. "We've got to get schemes rigged. Have you heard from him this afternoon or evening, since he and I had our row?"

"No."

"Then we can't be sure how you stand with him. There's a chance he may have decided later that I was right. That won't make any difference between him and me now—we're done —but we've got to find out as soon as we can." He scowled at her feet and brushed his mustache with a thumb-nail. "You'll have to wait till he comes to you. You can't afford to call him up. If he's shaky about you that might decide him. How sure of him are you?"

She was sitting in the chair by the table. She said: "I'm as sure of him as a woman can be of a man." She uttered a little embarrassed laugh. "I know that sounds— But I am, Mr. Beaumont."

He nodded. "Then that's probably all right, but you ought to know definitely by tomorrow. Have you ever tried to pump him?"

"Not yet, not really. I was waiting—"

"Well, that's out for the time being. No matter how sure you are of him you'll have to be careful now. Have you picked up anything you haven't told me about?"

"No," she said, shaking her head. "I haven't known very well how to go about it. That's why I so wanted you to—"

He interrupted her again: "Didn't it occur to you to hire a private detective?"

"Yes, but I was afraid, afraid I'd go to one who'd tell Paul. I didn't know who to go to, who I could trust."

"I've got one we can use." He ran fingers through his dark hair. "Now there are two things I want you to find out, if you don't know them now. Are any of your brother's hats missing? Paul says he had a hat on. There was none there when I found him. See if you can find out how many he had and if they're all accounted for"—he smiled obliquely—"except the one I borrowed."

She paid no attention to his smile. She shook her head and raised her hands a little, dispiritedly. "I can't," she said. "We got rid of all his things some time ago and I doubt if anybody knew exactly what he had anyway."

Ned Beaumont shrugged. "I didn't think we'd get anywhere on that," he told her. "The other thing's a walking-stick, whether any of them—his or your father's—are missing, particularly a rough heavy brown one."

"It would be Father's," she said eagerly, "and I think it's there."

"Check it up." He bit his thumb-nail. "That'll be enough for you to do between now and tomorrow, that and maybe find out how you stand with Paul."

"What is it?" she asked. "I mean about the stick." She stood up, excited.

"Paul says your brother attacked him with it and was struck by it while Paul was taking it away from him. He says he carried the stick away and burned it."

"Oh, I'm sure Father's sticks are all there," she cried. Her face was white, her eyes wide.

"Didn't Taylor have any?"

"Only a silver-headed black one." She put a hand on his wrist. "If they're all there it will mean that—"

"It might mean something," he said and put a hand on her hand. "But no tricks," he warned her.

"I won't," she promised. "If you only knew how happy I am to have your help, how much I've wanted it, you'd know you could trust me."

"I hope so." He took his hand from hers.

III

Alone in his rooms Ned Beaumont walked the floor awhile, his face pinched, his eyes shiny. At twenty minutes to ten he looked at his wrist-watch. Then he put on his overcoat and went down to the Majestic Hotel, where he was told that Harry Sloss was not in. He left the hotel, found a taxicab, got into it, and said: "West Road Inn."

The West Road Inn was a square white building—grey in the night—set among trees back from the road some three miles beyond the city limits. Its ground-floor was brightly lighted and half a dozen automobiles stood in front of it. Others were in a long dark shed off to the left.

Ned Beaumont, nodding familiarly at the doorman, went into a large dining-room where a three-man orchestra was playing extravagantly and eight or ten people were dancing. He passed down an aisle between tables, skirted the dance-floor, and stopped in front of the bar that occupied one corner of the room. He was alone on the customers' side of the bar.

The bar-tender, a fat man with a spongy nose, said: "Evening, Ned. We ain't been seeing you much lately."

"'Lo, Jimmy. Been behaving. Manhattan."

The bar-tender began to mix the cocktail. The orchestra finished its piece. A woman's voice rose thin and shrill: "I won't stay in the same place with that Beaumont bastard."

Ned Beaumont turned around, leaning back against the edge of the bar. The bar-tender became motionless with the cocktail-shaker in his hand.

Lee Wilshire was standing in the center of the dance-floor glaring at Ned Beaumont. One of her hands was on the fore-arm of a bulky youth in a blue suit a bit too tight for him. He too was looking at Ned Beaumont, rather stupidly. She said: "He's a no-good bastard and if you don't throw him out I'm going out."

Everyone else in the place was attentively silent.

The youth's face reddened. His attempt at a scowl increased his appearance of embarrassment.

The girl said: "I'll go over and slap him myself if you don't."

Ned Beaumont, smiling, said: "'Lo, Lee. Seen Bernie since he got out?"

Lee cursed him and took an angry step forward.

The bulky youth put out a hand and stopped her. "I'll fix him," he said, "the bastard." He adjusted his coat-collar to his neck, pulled the front of his coat down, and stalked off the dance-floor to face Ned Beaumont. "What's the idea?" he demanded. "What's the idea of talking to the little lady like that?"

Ned Beaumont, staring soberly at the youth, stretched his right arm out to the side and laid his hand palm-up on the bar. "Give me something to tap him with, Jimmy," he said. "I don't feel like fist-fighting."

One of the bar-tender's hands was already out of sight beneath the bar. He brought it up holding a small bludgeon and put the bludgeon in Ned Beaumont's hand. Ned Beaumont let it lie there while he said: "She gets called a lot of things. The last guy I saw her with was calling her a dumb cluck."

The youth drew himself up straight, his eyes shifting from side to side. He said: "I won't forget you and some day me and you will meet when there's nobody around." He turned on his heel and addressed Lee Wilshire. "Come on, let's blow out of this dump."

"Go ahead and blow," she said spitefully. "I'll be God-damned if I'm going with you. I'm sick of you."

A thick-bodied man with nearly all gold teeth came up and said: "Yes you will, the both of you. Get."

Ned Beaumont laughed and said: "The—uh—little lady's with me, Corky."

Corky said, "Fair enough," and then to the youth: "Outside, bum."

The youth went out.

Lee Wilshire had returned to her table. She sat there with her cheeks between her fists, staring at the cloth.

Ned Beaumont sat down facing her. He said to the waiter: "Jimmy's got a Manhattan that belongs to me. And I want some food. Eaten yet, Lee?"

"Yes," she said without looking up. "I want a silver fizz."

Ned Beaumont said: "Fine. I want a minute steak with mushrooms, whatever vegetable Tony's got that didn't come out of a can, some lettuce and tomatoes with Roquefort dressing, and coffee."

When the waiter had gone Lee said bitterly: "Men are no good, none of them. That big false alarm!" She began to cry silently.

"Maybe you pick the wrong kind," Ned Beaumont suggested.

"You should tell me that," she said, looking up angrily at him, "after the lousy trick you played me."

"I didn't play you any lousy trick," he protested. "If Bernie had to hock your pretties to pay back the money he'd gypped me out of it wasn't my fault."

The orchestra began to play.

"Nothing's ever a man's fault," she complained. "Come on and dance."

"Oh, all right," he said reluctantly.

When they returned to the table his cocktail and her fizz were there.

"What's Bernie doing these days?" he asked as they drank.

"I don't know. I haven't seen him since he got out and I don't want to see him. Another swell guy! What breaks I've been getting this year! Him and Taylor and this bastard!"

"Taylor Henry?" he asked.

"Yes, but I didn't have much to do with him," she explained quickly, "because that's while I was living with Bernie."

Ned Beaumont finished his cocktail before he said: "You were just one of the girls who used to meet him in his Charter Street place now and then."

"Yes," she said, looking warily at him.

He said: "I think we ought to have a drink."

She powdered her face while he caught their waiter's attention and ordered their drinks.

IV

The door-bell awakened Ned Beaumont. He got drowsily out of bed, coughing a little, and put on kimono and slippers. It was a few minutes after nine by his alarm-clock. He went to the door.

Janet Henry came in apologizing. "I know it's horribly

early, but I simply couldn't wait another minute. I tried and tried to get you on the phone last night and hardly slept a wink because I couldn't. All of Father's sticks are there. So, you see, he lied."

"Has he got a heavy rough brown one?"

"Yes, that's the one Major Sawbridge brought him from Scotland. He never uses it, but it's there." She smiled triumphantly at Ned Beaumont.

He blinked sleepily and ran fingers through his tousled hair. "Then he lied, right enough," he said.

"And," she said gaily, "he was there when I got home last night."

"Paul?"

"Yes. And he asked me to marry him."

Sleepiness went out of Ned Beaumont's eyes. "Did he say anything about our battle?"

"Not a word."

"What did you say?"

"I said it was too soon after Taylor's death for me even to engage myself to him, but I didn't say I wouldn't a little later, so we've got what I believe is called an understanding."

He looked curiously at her.

Gaiety went out of her face. She put a hand on his arm. Her voice broke a little. "Please don't think I'm altogether heartless," she said, "but—oh!—I do so want to—to do what we set out to do that everything else seems—well—not important at all."

He moistened his lips and said in a grave gentle voice: "What a spot he'd be in if you loved him as much as you hate him."

She stamped her foot and cried: "Don't say that! Don't ever say that again!"

Irritable lines appeared in his forehead and his lips tightened together.

She said, "Please," contritely, "but I can't bear that."

"Sorry," he said. "Had breakfast yet?"

"No. I was too anxious to bring my news to you."

"Fine. You'll eat with me. What do you like?" He went to the telephone.

After he had ordered breakfast he went into the bathroom

to wash his teeth, face, and hands and brush his hair. When he returned to the living-room she had removed her hat and coat and was standing by the fireplace smoking a cigarette. She started to say something, but stopped when the telephone-bell rang.

He went to the telephone. "Hello. . . . Yes, Harry, I stopped in, but you were out. . . . I wanted to ask you about—you know—the chap you saw with Paul that night. Did he have a hat? . . . He did? Sure? . . . And did he have a stick in his hand? . . . Oke. . . . No, I couldn't do anything with Paul on that, Harry. Better see him yourself. . . . Yes. . . . 'By."

Janet Henry's eyes questioned him as he got up from the telephone.

He said: "That was one of a couple of fellows who claim they saw Paul talking to your brother in the street that night. He says he saw the hat, but not the stick. It was dark, though, and this pair were riding past in a car. I wouldn't bet they saw anything very clearly."

"Why are you so interested in the hat? Is it so important?"

He shrugged. "I don't know. I'm only an amateur detective, but it looks like a thing that might have some meaning, one way or another."

"Have you learned anything else since yesterday?"

"No. I spent part of the evening buying drinks for a girl Taylor used to play around with, but there wasn't anything there."

"Anyone I know?" she asked.

He shook his head, then looked sharply at her and said: "It wasn't Opal, if that's what you're getting at."

"Don't you think we might be able to—to get some information from her?"

"Opal? No. She thinks her father killed Taylor, but she thinks it was on her account. It wasn't anything she knew that sent her off—not any inside stuff—it was your letters and the *Observer* and things like that."

Janet Henry nodded, but seemed unconvinced.

Their breakfast arrived.

The telephone-bell rang while they were eating. Ned Beaumont went to the telephone and said: "Hello. . . . Yes,

Mom. . . . What?" He listened, frowning, for several seconds, then said: "There isn't much you can do about it except let them and I don't think it'll do any harm. . . . No, I don't know where he is. . . . I don't think I will. . . . Well, don't worry about it, Mom, it'll be all right. . . . Sure, that's right. . . . 'By." He returned to the table smiling. "Farr's got the same idea you had," he said as he sat down. "That was Paul's mother. A man from the District Attorney's office is there to question Opal." A bright gleam awakened in his eyes. "She can't help them any, but they're closing in on him."

"Why did she call you?" Janet Henry asked.

"Paul had gone out and she didn't know where to find him."

"Doesn't she know that you and Paul have quarreled?"

"Apparently not." He put down his fork. "Look here. Are you sure you want to go through with this thing?"

"I want to go through with it more than I ever wanted to do anything in my life," she told him.

Ned Beaumont laughed bitterly, said: "They're practically the same words Paul used telling me how much he wanted you."

She shuddered, her face hardened, and she looked coldly at him.

He said: "I don't know about you. I'm not sure of you. I had a dream I don't much like."

She smiled then. "Surely you don't believe in dreams?"

He did not smile. "I don't believe in anything, but I'm too much of a gambler not to be affected by a lot of things."

Her smile became less mocking. She asked: "What was this dream that makes you mistrust me?" She held up a finger, pretending seriousness. "And then I'll tell you one I had about you."

"I was fishing," he said, "and I caught an enormous fish— a rainbow trout, but enormous—and you said you wanted to look at it and you picked it up and threw it back in the water before I could stop you."

She laughed merrily. "What did you do?"

"That was the end of the dream."

"It was a lie," she said. "I won't throw your trout back.

Now I'll tell you mine. I was—" Her eyes widened. "When was yours? The night you came to dinner?"

"No. Last night."

"Oh, that's too bad. It would be nicer in an impressive way if we'd done our dreaming on the same night and the same hour and the same minute. Mine was the night you were there. We were—this is in the dream—we were lost in a forest, you and I, tired and starving. We walked and walked till we came to a little house and we knocked on the door, but nobody answered. We tried the door. It was locked. Then we peeped through a window and inside we could see a great big table piled high with all imaginable kinds of food, but we couldn't get in through either of the windows because they had iron bars over them. So we went back to the door and knocked and knocked again and still nobody answered. Then we thought that sometimes people left their keys under doormats and we looked and there it was. But when we opened the door we saw hundreds and hundreds of snakes on the floor where we hadn't been able to see them through the window and they all came sliding and slithering towards us. We slammed the door shut and locked it and stood there frightened to death listening to them hissing and knocking their heads against the inside of the door. Then you said that perhaps if we opened the door and hid from the snakes they'd come out and go away, so we did. You helped me climb up on the roof—it was low in this part of the dream: I don't remember what it was like before—and you climbed up after me and leaned down and unlocked the door, and all the snakes came slithering out. We lay holding our breath on the roof until the last of the hundreds and hundreds of them had slithered out of sight into the forest. Then we jumped down and ran inside and locked the door and ate and ate and ate and I woke sitting up in bed clapping my hands and laughing."

"I think you made that up," Ned Beaumont said after a little pause.

"Why?"

"It starts out to be a nightmare and winds up something else and all the dreams I ever had about food ended before I got a chance to do any actual eating."

Janet Henry laughed. "I didn't make all of it up," she said, "but you needn't ask which part is true. You've accused me of lying and I'll tell you nothing now."

"Oh, all right." He picked up his fork again, but did not eat. He asked, with an air of just having the thought: "Does your father know anything? Do you think we could get anything out of him if we went to him with what we know?"

"Yes," she said eagerly, "I do."

He scowled thoughtfully. "The only trouble is he might go up in the air and explode the works before we're ready. He's hot-headed, isn't he?"

Her answer was given reluctantly: "Yes, but"—her face brightened, pleadingly—"I'm sure if we showed him why it's important to wait until we've— But we are ready now, aren't we?"

He shook his head. "Not yet."

She pouted.

"Maybe tomorrow," he said.

"Really?"

"That's not a promise," he cautioned her, "but I think we will be."

She put a hand across the table to take one of his hands. "But you will promise to let me know the very minute we're ready, no matter what time of day or night it is?"

"Sure, I'll promise you that." He looked obliquely at her. "You're not very anxious to be in at the death, are you?"

His tone brought a flush to her face, but she did not lower her eyes. "I know you think I'm a monster," she said. "Perhaps I am."

He looked down at his plate and muttered: "I hope you like it when you get it."

CHAPTER IX

The Heels

AFTER Janet Henry had gone Ned Beaumont went to his telephone, called Jack Rumsen's number, and when he had that one on the wire said: "Can you drop in to see me, Jack? . . . Fine. 'By."

He was dressed by the time Jack arrived. They sat in facing chairs, each with a glass of Bourbon whisky and mineral water, Ned Beaumont smoking a cigar, Jack a cigarette.

Ned Beaumont asked: "Heard anything about the split between Paul and me?"

Jack said, "Yes," casually.

"What do you think of it?"

"Nothing. I remember the last time it was supposed to happen it turned out to be a trick on Shad O'Rory."

Ned Beaumont smiled as if he had expected that reply. "Is that what everybody thinks it is this time?"

The dapper young man said: "A lot of them do."

Ned Beaumont inhaled cigar-smoke slowly, asked: "Suppose I told you it was on the level this time?"

Jack said nothing. His face told nothing of his thoughts.

Ned Beaumont said: "It is." He drank from his glass. "How much do I owe you?"

"Thirty bucks for that job on the Madvig girl. You settled for the rest."

Ned Beaumont took a roll of paper money from a trousers-pocket, separated three ten-dollar bills from the roll, and gave them to Jack.

Jack said: "Thanks."

Ned Beaumont said: "Now we're quits." He inhaled smoke and blew it out while saying: "I've got another job I want done. I'm after Paul's scalp on the Taylor Henry killing. He told me he did it, but I need a little more proof. Want to work on it for me?"

Jack said: "No."

"Why not?"

The dark young man rose to put his empty glass on

747

the table. "Fred and I are building up a nice little private-detective business here," he said. "A couple of years more and we'll be sitting pretty. I like you, Beaumont, but not enough to monkey with the man that runs the city."

Ned Beaumont said evenly: "He's on the chutes. The whole crew's getting ready to ditch him. Farr and Rainey are—"

"Let them do it. I don't want in on that racket and I'll believe they can do it when it's done. Maybe they'll give him a bump or two, but making it stick's another thing. You know him better than I do. You know he's got more guts than all the rest of them put together."

"He has and that's what's licking him. Well, if you won't, you won't."

Jack said, "I won't," and picked up his hat. "Anything else I'll be glad to do, but—" He moved one hand in a brief gesture of finality.

Ned Beaumont stood up. There was no resentment in his manner, none in his voice when he said: "I thought you might feel that way about it." He brushed a side of his mustache with a thumb and stared thoughtfully past Jack. "Maybe you can tell me this: any idea where I can find Shad?"

Jack shook his head. "Since the third time they knocked his place over—when the two coppers were killed—he's been laying low, though they don't seem to have a hell of a lot on him personally." He took his cigarette from his mouth. "Know Whisky Vassos?"

"Yes."

"You might find out from him if you know him well enough. He's around town. You can usually find him some time during the night at Tim Walker's place on Smith Street."

"Thanks, Jack, I'll try that."

"That's all right," Jack said. He hesitated. "I'm sorry as hell you and Madvig split. I wish you—" He broke off and turned towards the door. "You know what you're doing."

II

Ned Beaumont went down to the District Attorney's office. This time there was no delay in ushering him into Farr's presence.

Farr did not get up from his desk, did not offer to shake hands. He said: "How do you do, Beaumont? Sit down." His voice was coldly polite. His pugnacious face was not so red as usual. His eyes were level and hard.

Ned Beaumont sat down, crossed his legs comfortably, and said: "I wanted to tell you about what happened when I went to see Paul after I left here yesterday."

Farr's "Yes?" was cold and polite.

"I told him how I'd found you—panicky." Ned Beaumont, smiling his nicest smile, went on in the manner of one telling a fairly amusing but unimportant anecdote: "I told him I thought you were trying to get up enough nerve to hang the Taylor Henry murder on him. He believed me at first, but when I told him the only way to save himself was by turning up the real murderer, he said that was no good. He said he was the real murderer, though he called it an accident or self-defense or something."

Farr's face had become paler and was stiff around the mouth, but he did not speak.

Ned Beaumont raised his eyebrows. "I'm not boring you, am I?" he asked.

"Go on, continue," the District Attorney said coldly.

Ned Beaumont tilted his chair back. His smile was mocking. "You think I'm kidding, don't you? You think it's a trick we're playing on you." He shook his head and murmured: "You're a timid soul, Farr."

Farr said: "I'm glad to listen to any information you can give me, but I'm very busy, so I'll have to ask you—"

Ned Beaumont laughed then and replied: "Oke. I thought maybe you'd like to have this information in an affidavit or something."

"Very well." Farr pressed one of the pearl buttons on his desk.

A grey-haired woman in green came in.

"Mr. Beaumont wants to dictate a statement," Farr told her.

She said, "Yes, sir," sat at the other side of Farr's desk, put her note-book on the desk, and, holding a silver pencil over the book, looked at Ned Beaumont with blank brown eyes.

He said: "Yesterday afternoon in his office in the Nebel Building, Paul Madvig told me that he had been to dinner at

Senator Henry's house the night Taylor Henry was killed; that he and Taylor Henry had some sort of trouble there; that after he left the house Taylor Henry ran after him and caught up with him and tried to hit him with a rough heavy brown walking-stick; that in trying to take the stick from Taylor Henry he accidentally struck him on the forehead with it, knocking him down; and that he carried the stick away with him and burned it. He said his only reason for concealing his part in Taylor Henry's death was his desire to keep it from Janet Henry. That's all of it."

Farr addressed the stenographer: "Transcribe that right away."

She left the office.

Ned Beaumont said: "I thought I was bringing you news that would get you all excited." He sighed. "I thought you'd fairly tear your hair over it."

The District Attorney looked steadily at him.

Ned Beaumont, unabashed, said: "I thought at least you'd have Paul dragged in and confronted with this"—he waved a hand—"'damaging disclosure' is a good phrase."

The District Attorney spoke in a restrained tone: "Please permit me to run my own office."

Ned Beaumont laughed again and relapsed into silence until the grey-haired stenographer returned with a typed copy of his statement. Then he asked: "Do I swear to it?"

"No," Farr said, "just sign it. That will be sufficient."

Ned Beaumont signed the paper. "This isn't nearly so much fun as I thought it was going to be," he complained cheerfully.

Farr's undershot jaw tightened. "No," he said with grim satisfaction, "I don't suppose it is."

"You're a timid soul, Farr," Ned Beaumont repeated. "Be careful about taxis when you cross streets." He bowed. "See you later."

Outside, he grimaced angrily.

III

That night Ned Beaumont rang the door-bell of a dark three-story house in Smith Street. A short man who had a small head and thick shoulders opened the door half a foot, said, "All right," and opened it the rest of the way.

Ned Beaumont, saying, "'Lo," entered, walked twenty feet down a dim hallway past two closed doors on the right, opened a door on the left, and went down a wooden flight of steps into a basement where there was a bar and where a radio was playing softly.

Beyond the bar was a frosted glass door marked *Toilet*. This door opened and a man came out, a swarthy man with something apish in the slope of his big shoulders, the length of his thick arms, the flatness of his face, and the curve of his bowed legs—Jeff Gardner.

He saw Ned Beaumont and his reddish small eyes glistened. "Well, blind Christ, if it ain't Sock-me-again Beaumont!" he roared, showing his beautiful teeth in a huge grin.

Ned Beaumont said, "'Lo, Jeff," while everyone in the place looked at them.

Jeff swaggered over to Ned Beaumont, threw his left arm roughly around his shoulders, seized Ned Beaumont's right hand with his right hand, and addressed the company jovially: "This is the swellest guy I ever skinned a knuckle on and I've skinned them on plenty." He dragged Ned Beaumont to the bar. "We're all going to have a little drink and then I'll show you how it's done. By Jesus, I will!" He leered into Ned Beaumont's face. "What do you say to that, my lad?"

Ned Beaumont, looking stolidly at the ugly dark face so close to, though lower than, his, said: "Scotch."

Jeff laughed delightedly and addressed the company again: "You see, he likes it. He's a—" he hesitated, frowning, wet his lips "—a God-damned massacrist, that's what he is." He leered at Ned Beaumont. "You know what a massacrist is?"

"Yes."

Jeff seemed disappointed. "Rye," he told the bar-tender. When their drinks were set before them he released Ned Beaumont's hand, though he kept his arm across his shoulders. They drank. Jeff set down his glass and put his hand on Ned Beaumont's wrist. "I got just the place for me and you upstairs," he said, "a room that's too little for you to fall down in. I can bounce you around off the walls. That way we won't be wasting a lot of time while you're getting up off the floor."

Ned Beaumont said: "I'll buy a drink."

"That ain't a dumb idea," Jeff agreed.

They drank again.

When Ned Beaumont had paid for the drinks Jeff turned him towards the stairs. "Excuse us, gents," he said to the others at the bar, "but we got to go up and rehearse our act." He patted Ned Beaumont's shoulder. "Me and my sweetheart."

They climbed two flights of steps and went into a small room in which a sofa, two tables, and half a dozen chairs were crowded. There were some empty glasses and plates holding the remains of sandwiches on one table.

Jeff peered near-sightedly around the room and demanded: "Now where in hell did she go?" He released Ned Beaumont's wrist, took the arm from around his shoulders, and asked: "You don't see no broad here, do you?"

"No."

Jeff wagged his head up and down emphatically. "She's gone," he said. He took an uncertain step backwards and jabbed the bell-button beside the door with a dirty finger. Then, flourishing his hand, he made a grotesque bow and said: "Set down."

Ned Beaumont sat down at the less disorderly of the two tables.

"Set in any God-damned chair you want to set in," Jeff said with another large gesture. "If you don't like that one, take another. I want you to consider yourself my guest and the hell with you if you don't like it."

"It's a swell chair," Ned Beaumont said.

"It's a hell of a chair," Jeff said. "There ain't a chair in the dump that's worth a damn. Look." He picked up a chair and tore one of its front legs out. "You call that a swell chair? Listen, Beaumont, you don't know a damned thing about chairs." He put the chair down, tossed the leg on the sofa. "You can't fool me. I know what you're up to. You think I'm drunk, don't you?"

Ned Beaumont grinned. "No, you're not drunk."

"The hell I'm not drunk. I'm drunker than you are. I'm drunker than anybody in this dump. I'm drunk as hell and don't think I'm not, but—" He held up a thick unclean forefinger.

A waiter came in the doorway asking: "What is it, gents?"

Jeff turned to confront him. "Where've you been? Sleeping? I rung for you one hour ago."

The waiter began to say something.

Jeff said: "I bring the best friend I got in the world up here for a drink and what the hell happens? We have to sit around a whole God-damned hour waiting for a lousy waiter. No wonder he's sore at me."

"What do you want?" the waiter asked indifferently.

"I want to know where in hell the girl that was in here went to."

"Oh, her? She's gone."

"Gone where?"

"I don't know."

Jeff scowled. "Well, you find out, and God-damned quick. What's the idea of not knowing where she went? If this ain't a swell joint where nobody—" A shrewd light came into his red eyes. "I'll tell you what to do. You go up to the ladies' toilet and see if she's there."

"She ain't there," the waiter said. "She went out."

"The dirty bastard!" Jeff said and turned to Ned Beaumont. "What'd you do to a dirty bastard like that? I bring you up here because I want you to meet her because I know you'll like her and she'll like you and she's too God-damned snotty to meet my friends and out she goes."

Ned Beaumont was lighting a cigar. He did not say anything.

Jeff scratched his head, growled, "Well, bring us something to drink, then," sat down across the table from Ned Beaumont, and said savagely: "Mine's rye."

Ned Beaumont said: "Scotch."

The waiter went away.

Jeff glared at Ned Beaumont. "Don't get the idea that I don't know what you're up to, either," he said angrily.

"I'm not up to anything," Ned Beaumont replied carelessly. "I'd like to see Shad and I thought maybe I'd find Whisky Vassos here and he'd send me to Shad."

"Don't you think I know where Shad is?"

"You ought to."

"Then why didn't you ask me?"

"All right. Where is he?"

Jeff slapped the table mightily with an open hand and bawled: "You're a liar. You don't give a God-damn where Shad is. It's me you're after."

Ned Beaumont smiled and shook his head.

"It is," the apish man insisted. "You know God-damned well that—"

A young-middle-aged man with plump red lips and round eyes came to the door. He said: "Cut it out, Jeff. You're making more noise than everybody else in the place."

Jeff screwed himself around in his chair. "It's this bastard," he told the man in the doorway, indicating Ned Beaumont with a jerk of his thumb. "He thinks I don't know what he's up to. I know what he's up to. He's a heel and that's what he is. And I'm going to beat hell out of him and that's what I'm going to do."

The man in the doorway said reasonably, "Well, you don't have to make so much noise about it," winked at Ned Beaumont, and went away.

Jeff said gloomily: "Tim's turning into a heel too." He spit on the floor.

The waiter came in with their drinks.

Ned Beaumont raised his glass, said, "Looking at you," and drank.

Jeff said: "I don't want to look at you. You're a heel." He stared somberly at Ned Beaumont.

"You're crazy."

"You're a liar. I'm drunk. But I ain't so drunk that I don't know what you're up to." He emptied his glass, wiped his mouth with the back of his hand. "And I say you're a heel."

Ned Beaumont, smiling amiably, said: "All right. Have it your way."

Jeff thrust his apish muzzle forward a little. "You think you're smart as hell, don't you?"

Ned Beaumont did not say anything.

"You think it's a damned smart trick coming in here and trying to get me plastered so you can turn me up."

"That's right," Ned Beaumont said carelessly, "there is a

murder-charge against you for bumping off Francis West, isn't there?"

Jeff said: "Hell with Francis West."

Ned Beaumont shrugged. "I didn't know him."

Jeff said: "You're a heel."

Ned Beaumont said: "I'll buy a drink."

The apish man nodded solemnly and tilted his chair back to reach the bell-button. With his finger on the button he said: "But you're still a heel." His chair swayed back under him, turning. He got his feet flat on the floor and brought the chair down on all fours before it could spill him. "The bastard!" he snarled, pulling it around to the table again. He put his elbows on the table and propped his chin up on one fist. "What the hell do I care who turns me up? You don't think they'd ever fry me, do you?"

"Why not?"

"Why not? Jesus! I wouldn't have to stand the rap till after election and then it's all Shad's."

"Maybe."

"Maybe hell!"

The waiter came in and they ordered their drinks.

"Maybe Shad would let you take the fall anyhow," Ned Beaumont said idly when they were alone again. "Things like that have happened."

"A swell chance," Jeff scoffed, "with all I've got on him."

Ned Beaumont exhaled cigar-smoke. "What've you got on him?"

The apish man laughed, boisterously, scornfully, and pounded the table with an open hand. "Christ!" he roared, "he thinks I'm drunk enough to tell him."

From the doorway came a quiet voice, a musical slightly Irish barytone: "Go on, Jeff, tell him." Shad O'Rory stood in the doorway. His grey-blue eyes looked somewhat sadly at Jeff.

Jeff squinted his eyes merrily at the man in the doorway and said: "How are you, Shad? Come in and set down to a drink. Meet Mr. Beaumont. He's a heel."

O'Rory said softly: "I told you to stay under cover."

"But, Jesus, Shad, I was getting so's I was afraid I'd bite myself! And this joint's under cover, ain't it? It's a speakeasy."

O'Rory looked a moment longer at Jeff, then at Ned Beaumont. "Good evening, Beaumont."

" 'Lo, Shad."

O'Rory smiled gently and, indicating Jeff with a tiny nod, asked: "Get much out of him?"

"Not much I didn't already know," Ned Beaumont replied. "He makes a lot of noise, but all of it doesn't make sense."

Jeff said: "I think you're a pair of heels."

The waiter arrived with their drinks. O'Rory stopped him. "Never mind. They've had enough." The waiter carried their drinks away. Shad O'Rory came into the room and shut the door. He stood with his back against it. He said: "You talk too much, Jeff. I've told you that before."

Ned Beaumont deliberately winked at Jeff.

Jeff said angrily to him: "What the hell's the matter with you?"

Ned Beaumont laughed.

"I'm talking to you, Jeff," O'Rory said.

"Christ, don't I know it?"

O'Rory said: "We're coming to the place where I'm going to stop talking to you."

Jeff stood up. "Don't be a heel, Shad," he said. "What the hell?" He came around the table. "Me and you've been pals a long time. You always were my pal and I'll always be yours." He put his arms out to embrace O'Rory, lurching towards him. "Sure, I'm smoked, but—"

O'Rory put a white hand on the apish man's chest and thrust him back. "Sit down." He did not raise his voice.

Jeff's left fist whipped out at O'Rory's face.

O'Rory's head moved to the right, barely enough to let the fist whip past his cheek. O'Rory's long finely sculptured face was gravely composed. His right hand dropped down behind his hip.

Ned Beaumont flung from his chair at O'Rory's right arm, caught it with both hands, going down on his knees.

Jeff, thrown against the wall by the impetus behind his left fist, now turned and took Shad O'Rory's throat in both hands. The apish face was yellow, distorted, hideous. There was no longer any drunkenness in it.

"Got the roscoe?" Jeff panted.

"Yes." Ned Beaumont stood up, stepped back holding a black pistol leveled at O'Rory.

O'Rory's eyes were glassy, protuberant, his face mottled, turgid. He did not struggle against the man holding his throat.

Jeff turned his head over his shoulder to grin at Ned Beaumont. The grin was wide, genuine, idiotically bestial. Jeff's little red eyes glinted merrily. He said in a hoarse good-natured voice: "Now you see what we got to do. We got to give him the works."

Ned Beaumont said: "I don't want anything to do with it." His voice was steady. His nostrils quivered.

"No?" Jeff leered at him. "I expect you think Shad's a guy that'll forget what we done." He ran his tongue over his lips. "He'll forget. I'll fix that."

Grinning from ear to ear at Ned Beaumont, not looking at the man whose throat he held in his hands, Jeff began to take in and let out long slow breaths. His coat became lumpy over his shoulders and back and along his arms. Sweat appeared on his ugly dark face.

Ned Beaumont was pale. He too was breathing heavily and moisture filmed his temples. He looked over Jeff's lumpy shoulder at O'Rory's face.

O'Rory's face was liver-colored. His eyes stood far out, blind. His tongue came out blue between bluish lips. His slender body writhed. One of his hands began to beat the wall behind him, mechanically, without force.

Grinning at Ned Beaumont, not looking at the man whose throat he held, Jeff spread his legs a little wider and arched his back. O'Rory's hand stopped beating the wall. There was a muffled crack, then, almost immediately, a sharper one. O'Rory did not writhe now. He sagged in Jeff's hands.

Jeff laughed in his throat. "That's keno," he said. He kicked a chair out of the way and dropped O'Rory's body on the sofa. O'Rory's body fell there face down, one hand and his feet hanging down to the floor. Jeff rubbed his hands on his hips and faced Ned Beaumont. "I'm just a big good-natured slob," he said. "Anybody can kick me around all they want to and I never do nothing about it."

Ned Beaumont said: "You were afraid of him."

Jeff laughed. "I hope to tell you I was. So was anybody that was in their right mind. I suppose you wasn't?" He laughed again, looked around the room, said: "Let's screw before anybody pops in." He held out his hand. "Give me the roscoe. I'll ditch it."

Ned Beaumont said: "No." He moved his hand sidewise until the pistol was pointed at Jeff's belly. "We can say this was self-defense. I'm with you. We can beat it at the inquest."

"Jesus, that's a bright idea!" Jeff exclaimed. "Me with a murder-rap hanging over me for that West guy!" His small red eyes kept shifting their focus from Ned Beaumont's face to the pistol in his hand.

Ned Beaumont smiled with thin pale lips. "That's what I was thinking about," he said softly.

"Don't be a God-damned sap," Jeff blustered, taking a step forward. "You—"

Ned Beaumont backed away, around one of the tables. "I don't mind plugging you, Jeff," he said. "Remember I owe you something."

Jeff stood still and scratched the back of his head. "What kind of a heel are you?" he asked perplexedly.

"Just a pal." Ned Beaumont moved the pistol forward suddenly. "Sit down."

Jeff, after a moment's glowering hesitation, sat down.

Ned Beaumont put out his left hand and pressed the bell-button.

Jeff stood up.

Ned Beaumont said: "Sit down."

Jeff sat down.

Ned Beaumont said: "Keep your hands on the table."

Jeff shook his head lugubriously. "What a half-smart bastard you turned out to be," he said. "You don't think they're going to let you drag me out of here, do you?"

Ned Beaumont went around the table again and sat on a chair facing Jeff and facing the door.

Jeff said: "The best thing for you to do is give me that gun and hope I'll forget you made the break. Jesus, Ned, this is one of my hang-outs! You ain't got a chance in the world of pulling a fast one here."

Ned Beaumont said: "Keep your hand away from the catchup-bottle."

The waiter opened the door, goggled at them.

"Tell Tim to come up," Ned Beaumont said, and then, to the apish man when he would have spoken: "Shut up."

The waiter shut the door and hurried away.

Jeff said: "Don't be a sap, Neddy. This can't get you anything but a rub-out. What good's it going to do you to try to turn me up? None." He wet his lips with his tongue. "I know you're kind of sore about the time we were rough with you, but—hell!—that wasn't my fault. I was just doing what Shad told me, and ain't I evened that up now by knocking him off for you?"

Ned Beaumont said: "If you don't keep your hand away from that catchup-bottle I'm going to shoot a hole in it."

Jeff said: "You're a heel."

The young-middle-aged man with plump lips and round eyes opened the door, came in quickly, and shut it behind him.

Ned Beaumont said: "Jeff's killed O'Rory. Phone the police. You'll have time to clear the place before they get here. Better get a doctor, too, in case he's not dead."

Jeff laughed scornfully. "If he ain't dead I'm the Pope." He stopped laughing and addressed the plump-mouthed man with careless familiarity: "What do you think of this guy thinking you're going to let him get away with that? Tell him what a fat chance he has of getting away with it, Tim."

Tim looked at the dead man on the sofa, at Jeff, and at Ned Beaumont. His round eyes were sober. He spoke to Ned Beaumont, slowly: "This is a tough break for the house. Can't we drag him out in the street and let him be found there?"

Ned Beaumont shook his head. "Get your place cleaned up before the coppers get here and you'll be all right. I'll do what I can for you."

While Tim hesitated Jeff said: "Listen, Tim, you know me. You know—"

Tim said without especial warmth: "For Christ's sake pipe down."

Ned Beaumont smiled. "Nobody knows you, Jeff, now Shad's dead."

"No?" The apish man sat back more comfortably in his chair and his face cleared. "Well, turn me up. Now I know what kind of sons of bitches you are I'd rather take the fall than ask a God-damned thing of either of you."

Tim, ignoring Jeff, asked: "Have to play it that way?"

Ned Beaumont nodded.

"I guess I can stand it," Tim said and put his hand on the door-knob.

"Mind seeing if Jeff's got a gun on him?" Ned Beaumont asked.

Tim shook his head. "It happened here, but I've got nothing to do with it and I'm going to have nothing to do with it," he said and went out.

Jeff, slouching back comfortably in his chair, his hands idle on the edge of the table before him, talked to Ned Beaumont until the police came. He talked cheerfully, calling Ned Beaumont numerous profane and obscene and merely insulting names, accusing him of a long and varied list of vices.

Ned Beaumont listened with polite interest.

A raw-boned white-haired man in a lieutenant's uniform was the first policeman to come in. Half a dozen police detectives were behind him.

Ned Beaumont said: "'Lo, Brett. I think he's got a gun on him."

"What's it all about?" Brett asked, looking at the body on the sofa while two of the detectives, squeezing past him, took hold of Jeff Gardner.

Ned Beaumont told Brett what had happened. His story was truthful except in giving the impression that O'Rory had been killed in the heat of their struggle and not after he had been disarmed.

While Ned Beaumont was talking a doctor came in, turned Shad O'Rory's body over on the sofa, examined him briefly, and stood up. The Lieutenant looked at the doctor. The doctor said, "Gone," and went out of the small crowded room.

Jeff was jovially cursing the two detectives who held him. Every time he cursed, one of the detectives struck him in the face with his fist. Jeff laughed and kept on cursing them. His false teeth had been knocked out. His mouth bled.

Ned Beaumont gave the dead man's pistol to Brett and

stood up. "Want me to come along to headquarters now? Or will tomorrow do?"

"Better come along now," Brett replied.

IV

It was long past midnight when Ned Beaumont left police headquarters. He said good-night to the two reporters who had come out with him and got into a taxicab. The address he gave the driver was Paul Madvig's.

Lights were on in the ground-floor of Madvig's house and as Ned Beaumont climbed the front steps the door was opened by Mrs. Madvig. She was dressed in black and had a shawl over her shoulders.

He said: "'Lo, Mom. What are you doing up so late?"

She said, "I thought it was Paul," though she looked at him without disappointment.

"Isn't he home? I wanted to see him." He looked sharply at her. "What's the matter?"

The old woman stepped back, pulling the door back with her. "Come in, Ned."

He went in.

She shut the door and said: "Opal tried to commit suicide."

He lowered his eyes and mumbled: "What? What do you mean?"

"She had cut one of her wrists before the nurse could stop her. She didn't lose much blood, though, and she's all right if she doesn't try it again." There was as little of weakness in her voice as in her mien.

Ned Beaumont's voice was not steady. "Where's Paul?"

"I don't know. We haven't been able to find him. He ought to be home before this. I don't know where he is." She put a bony hand on Ned Beaumont's upper arm and now her voice shook a little. "Are you—are you and Paul—?" She stopped, squeezing his arm.

He shook his head. "That's done for good."

"Oh, Ned, boy, isn't there anything you can do to patch it up? You and he—" Again she broke off.

He raised his head and looked at her. His eyes were wet.

He said gently: "No, Mom, that's done for good. Did he tell you about it?"

"He only told me, when I said I'd phoned you about that man from the District Attorney's office being here, that I wasn't ever to do anything like that again, that you—that you were not friends now."

Ned Beaumont cleared his throat. "Listen, Mom, tell him I came to see him. Tell him I'm going home and will wait there for him, will be waiting all night." He cleared his throat again and added lamely: "Tell him that."

Mrs. Madvig put her bony hands on his shoulders. "You're a good boy, Ned. I don't want you and Paul to quarrel. You're the best friend he ever had, no matter what's come between you. What is it? Is it that Janet—?"

"Ask Paul," he said in a low bitter voice. He moved his head impatiently. "I'm going to run along, Mom, unless there's something I can do for you or Opal. Is there?"

"Not unless you'd go up to see her. She's not sleeping yet and maybe it would do some good to talk to her. She used to listen to you."

He shook his head. "No," he said, "she wouldn't want to see me"—he swallowed—"either."

CHAPTER X

The Shattered Key

NED BEAUMONT went home. He drank coffee, smoked, read a newspaper, a magazine, and half a book. Now and then he stopped reading to walk, fidgeting, around his rooms. His door-bell did not ring. His telephone-bell did not ring.

At eight o'clock in the morning he bathed, shaved, and put on fresh clothes. Then he had breakfast sent in and ate it.

At nine o'clock he went to the telephone, called Janet Henry's number, asked for her, and said: "Good morning. . . . Yes, fine, thanks. . . . Well, we're ready for the fireworks. . . . Yes. . . . If your father's there suppose we let him in on the whole thing first. . . . Fine, but not a word till I get there. . . . As soon as I can make it. I'm leaving now. . . . Right. See you in minutes."

He got up from the telephone staring into space, clapped his hands together noisily, and rubbed their palms together. His mouth was a sullen line under his mustache, his eyes hot brown points. He went to the closet and briskly put on his overcoat and hat. He left his room whistling *Little Lost Lady* between his teeth and took long steps through the streets.

"Miss Henry's expecting me," he said to the maid who opened the Henrys' door.

She said, "Yes, sir," and guided him to a sunny bright-papered room where the Senator and his daughter were at breakfast.

Janet Henry jumped up immediately and came to him with both hands out, crying excitedly: "Good morning!"

The Senator rose in more leisurely manner, looking with polite surprise at his daughter, then holding his hand out to Ned Beaumont, saying: "Good morning, Mr. Beaumont. I'm very glad to see you. Won't you—?"

"Thanks, no, I've had breakfast."

Janet Henry was trembling. Excitement had drained her skin of color, had darkened her eyes, giving her the appearance of one drugged. "We have something to tell you, Father," she

763

said in a strained uneven voice, "something that—" She turned abruptly to Ned Beaumont. "Tell him! Tell him!"

Ned Beaumont glanced obliquely at her, drawing his brows together, then looked directly at her father. The Senator had remained standing by his place at the table. Ned Beaumont said: "What we've got is pretty strong evidence—including a confession—that Paul Madvig killed your son."

The Senator's eyes became narrower and he put a hand flat on the table in front of him. "What is this pretty strong evidence?" he asked.

"Well, sir, the chief thing is the confession, of course. He says your son ran out after him that night and tried to hit him with a rough brown walking-stick and that in taking the stick away from your son he accidentally struck him with it. He says he took the stick away and burned it, but your daughter" —he made a little bow at Janet Henry—"says it's still here."

"It is," she said. "It's the one Major Sawbridge brought you."

The Senator's face was pale as marble and as firm. "Proceed," he said.

Ned Beaumont made a small gesture with one hand. "Well, sir, that would blow up his story about its being an accident or self-defense—your son's not having the stick." He moved his shoulders a little. "I told Farr this yesterday. He's apparently afraid to take many chances—you know what he is—but I don't see how he can keep from picking Paul up today."

Janet Henry frowned at Ned Beaumont, obviously perplexed by something, started to speak, but pressed her lips together instead.

Senator Henry touched his lips with the napkin he held in his left hand, dropped the napkin on the table, and asked: "Is there—ah—any other evidence?"

Ned Beaumont's reply was another question carelessly uttered: "Isn't that enough?"

"But there is still more, isn't there?" Janet demanded.

"Stuff to back this up," Ned Beaumont said depreciatively. He addressed the Senator: "I can give you more details, but you've got the main story now. That's enough, isn't it?"

"Quite enough," the Senator said. He put a hand to his forehead. "I cannot believe it, yet it is so. If you'll excuse me for a moment and"—to his daughter—"you too, my dear, I should like to be alone, to think, to adjust myself to— No, no, stay here. I should like to go to my room." He bowed gracefully. "Please remain, Mr. Beaumont. I shall not be long —merely a moment to—to adjust myself to the knowledge that this man with whom I've worked shoulder to shoulder is my son's murderer."

He bowed again and went out, carrying himself rigidly erect.

Ned Beaumont put a hand on Janet Henry's wrist and asked in a low tense voice: "Look here, is he likely to fly off the handle?"

She looked at him, startled.

"Is he likely to go dashing off hunting for Paul?" he explained. "We don't want that. There's no telling what would happen."

"I don't know," she said.

He grimaced impatiently. "We can't let him do it. Can't we go somewhere near the front door so we can stop him if he tries it?"

"Yes." She was frightened.

She led him to the front of the house, into a small room that was dim behind heavily curtained windows. Its door was within a few feet of the street-door. They stood close together in the dim room, close to the door that stood some six inches ajar. Both of them were trembling. Janet Henry tried to whisper to Ned Beaumont, but he sh-h-hed her into silence.

They were not there long before soft footfalls sounded on the hall-carpet and Senator Henry, wearing hat and overcoat, hurried towards the street-door.

Ned Beaumont stepped out and said: "Wait, Senator Henry."

The Senator turned. His face was hard and cold, his eyes imperious. "You will please excuse me," he said. "I must go out."

"That's no good," Ned Beaumont said. He went up close to the Senator. "Just more trouble."

Janet Henry went to her father's side. "Don't go, Father," she begged. "Listen to Mr. Beaumont."

"I have listened to Mr. Beaumont," the Senator said. "I'm

perfectly willing to listen to him again if he has any more information to give me. Otherwise I must ask you to excuse
me." He smiled at Ned Beaumont. "It is on what you told
me that I'm acting now."

Ned Beaumont regarded him with level eyes. "I don't think
you ought to go to see him," he said.

The Senator looked haughtily at Ned Beaumont.

Janet said, "But, Father," before the look in his eyes
stopped her.

Ned Beaumont cleared his throat. Spots of color were in
his cheeks. He put his left hand out quickly and touched
Senator Henry's right-hand overcoat-pocket.

Senator Henry stepped back indignantly.

Ned Beaumont nodded as if to himself. "That's no good at
all," he said earnestly. He looked at Janet Henry. "He's got a
gun in his pocket."

"Father!" she cried and put a hand to her mouth.

Ned Beaumont pursed his lips. "Well," he told the Senator,
"it's a cinch we can't let you go out of here with a gun in
your pocket."

Janet Henry said: "Don't let him, Ned."

The Senator's eyes burned scornfully at them. "I think
both of you have quite forgotten yourselves," he said. "Janet,
you will please go to your room."

She took two reluctant steps away, then halted and cried: "I
won't! I won't let you do it. Don't let him, Ned."

Ned Beaumont moistened his lips. "I won't," he promised.

The Senator, staring coldly at him, put his right hand on
the street-door's knob.

Ned Beaumont leaned forward and put a hand over the
Senator's. "Look here, sir," he said respectfully, "I can't let
you do this. I'm not just interfering." He took his hand off
the Senator's, felt in the inside pocket of his coat, and
brought out a torn, creased, and soiled piece of folded paper.
"Here's my appointment as special investigator for the
District Attorney's office last month." He held it out to the
Senator. "It's never been cancelled as far as I know, so"—he
shrugged—"I can't let you go off to shoot somebody."

The Senator did not look at the paper. He said contemptuously: "You are trying to save your murderous friend's life."

"You know that isn't so."

The Senator drew himself up. "Enough of this," he said and turned the door-knob.

Ned Beaumont said: "Step on the sidewalk with that gun in your pocket and I'll arrest you."

Janet Henry wailed: "Oh, Father!"

The Senator and Ned Beaumont stood staring into each other's eyes, both breathing audibly.

The Senator was the first to speak. He addressed his daughter: "Will you leave us for a few minutes, my dear? There are things I should like to say to Mr. Beaumont."

She looked questioningly at Ned Beaumont. He nodded. "Yes," she told her father, "if you won't go out before I've seen you again."

He smiled and said: "You shall see me."

The two men watched her walk away down the hall, turn to the left with a glance thrown back at them, and vanish through a doorway.

The Senator said ruefully: "I'm afraid you've not had so good an influence on my daughter as you should. She isn't usually so—ah—headstrong."

Ned Beaumont smiled apologetically, but did not speak.

The Senator asked: "How long has this been going on?"

"You mean our digging into the murder? Only a day or two for me. Your daughter's been at it from the beginning. She's always thought Paul did it."

"What?" The Senator's mouth remained open.

"She's always thought he did it. Didn't you know? She hates him like poison—always has."

"Hates him?" the Senator gasped. "My God, no!"

Ned Beaumont nodded and smiled curiously at the man against the door. "Didn't you know that?"

The Senator blew his breath out sharply. "Come in here," he said and led the way into the dim room where Ned Beaumont and Janet Henry had hidden. The Senator switched on the lights while Ned Beaumont was shutting the door. Then they faced one another, both standing.

"I want to talk to you as man to man, Mr. Beaumont," the Senator began. "We can forget your"—he smiled—"official connections, can't we?"

Ned Beaumont nodded. "Yes. Farr's probably forgotten them too."

"Exactly. Now, Mr. Beaumont, I am not a blood-thirsty man, but I'm damned if I can bear the thought of my son's murderer walking around free and unpunished when—"

"I told you they'll have to pick him up. They can't get out of it. The evidence is too strong and everybody knows it."

The Senator smiled again, icily. "You are surely not trying to tell me, as one practicing politician to another, that Paul Madvig is in any danger of being punished for anything he might do in this city?"

"I am. Paul's sunk. They're double-crossing him. The only thing that's holding them up is that they're used to jumping when he cracks the whip and they need a little time to gather courage."

Senator Henry smiled and shook his head. "You'll allow me to disagree with you? And to point out the fact that I've been in politics more years than you've lived?"

"Sure."

"Then I can assure you that they never will get the necessary amount of courage, no matter how much time they're given. Paul is their boss and, despite possible temporary rebellions, he will remain their boss."

"It doesn't look like we'll agree on that," Ned Beaumont said. "Paul's sunk." He frowned. "Now about this gun business. That's no good. You'd better give it to me." He held out his hand.

The Senator put his right hand in his overcoat-pocket.

Ned Beaumont stepped close to the Senator and put his left hand on the Senator's wrist. "Give me it."

The Senator glared angrily at him.

"All right," Ned Beaumont said, "if I've got to do that," and, after a brief struggle in which a chair was upset, took the weapon—an old-fashioned nickeled revolver—away from the Senator. He was thrusting the revolver into one of his hip-pockets when Janet Henry, wild of eye, white of face, came in.

"What is it?" she cried.

"He won't listen to reason," Ned Beaumont grumbled. "I had to take the gun away from him."

The Senator's face was twitching and he panted hoarsely.

He took a step towards Ned Beaumont. "Get out of my house," he ordered.

"I won't," Ned Beaumont said. The ends of his lips jerked. Anger began to burn in his eyes. He put a hand out and touched Janet Henry's arm roughly. "Sit down and listen to this. You asked for it and you're going to get it." He spoke to the Senator: "I've got a lot to say, so maybe you'd better sit down too."

Neither Janet Henry nor her father sat down. She looked at Ned Beaumont with wide panic-stricken eyes, he with hard wary ones. Their faces were similarly white.

Ned Beaumont said to the Senator: "You killed your son."

Nothing changed in the Senator's face. He did not move.

For a long moment Janet Henry was still as her father. Then a look of utter horror came into her face and she sat down slowly on the floor. She did not fall. She slowly bent her knees and sank down on the floor in a sitting position, leaning to the right, her right hand on the floor for support, her horrified face turned up to her father and Ned Beaumont.

Neither of the men looked at her.

Ned Beaumont said to the Senator: "You want to kill Paul now so he can't say you killed your son. You know you can kill him and get away with it—dashing gentleman of the old school stuff—if you can put over on the world the attitude you tried to put over on us." He stopped.

The Senator said nothing.

Ned Beaumont went on: "You know he's going to stop covering you up if he's arrested, because he's not going to have Janet thinking he killed her brother if he can help it." He laughed bitterly. "And what a swell joke on him that is!" He ran fingers through his hair. "What happened is something like this: when Taylor heard about Paul kissing Janet he ran after him, taking the stick with him and wearing a hat, though that's not as important. When you thought of what might happen to your chances of being re-elected—"

The Senator interrupted him in a hoarse angry tone: "This is nonsense! I will not have my daughter subjected—"

Ned Beaumont laughed brutally. "Sure it's nonsense," he said. "And your bringing the stick you killed him with back home, and wearing his hat because you'd run out bare-headed after him, is nonsense too, but it's nonsense that'll nail you to the cross."

Senator Henry said in a low scornful voice: "And what of Paul's confession?"

Ned Beaumont grinned. "Plenty of it," he said. "I tell you what let's do. Janet, you phone him and ask him to come over right away. Then we'll tell him about your father starting after him with a gun and see what he says."

Janet stirred, but did not rise from the floor. Her face was blank.

Her father said: "That is ridiculous. We will do nothing of the sort."

Ned Beaumont said peremptorily: "Phone him, Janet."

She got up on her feet, still blank of face, and, paying no attention to the Senator's sharp "Janet!" went to the door.

The Senator changed his tone then and said, "Wait, dear," to her and, "I should like to speak to you alone again," to Ned Beaumont.

"All right," Ned Beaumont said, turning to the girl hesitating in the doorway.

Before he could speak to her she was saying stubbornly: "I want to hear it. I've a right to hear it."

He nodded, looked at her father again, and said: "She has."

"Janet, dear," the Senator said, "I'm trying to spare you. I—"

"I don't want to be spared," she said in a small flat voice. "I want to know."

The Senator turned his palms out in a defeated gesture. "Then I shall say nothing."

Ned Beaumont said: "Phone Paul, Janet."

Before she could move the Senator spoke: "No. This is more difficult than it should be made for me, but—" He took out a handkerchief and wiped his hands. "I am going to tell you exactly what happened and then I am going to ask a favor of you, one I think you cannot refuse. However—" He broke off to look at his daughter. "Come in, my dear, and close the door, if you must hear it."

She shut the door and sat on a chair near it, leaning forward, her body stiff, her face tense.

The Senator put his hands behind him, the handkerchief

still in them, and, looking without enmity at Ned Beaumont, said: "I ran out after Taylor that night because I did not care to lose Paul's friendship through my son's hot-headedness. I caught up with them in China Street. Paul had taken the stick from him. They were, or at least Taylor was, quarreling hotly. I asked Paul to leave us, to leave me to deal with my son, and he did so, giving me the stick. Taylor spoke to me as no son should speak to a father and tried to thrust me out of his way so he could pursue Paul again. I don't know exactly how it happened—the blow—but it happened and he fell and struck his head on the curb. Paul came back then—he hadn't gone far—and we found that Taylor had died instantly. Paul insisted that we leave him there and not admit our part in his death. He said no matter how unavoidable it was a nasty scandal could be made of it in the coming campaign and—well—I let him persuade me. It was he who picked up Taylor's hat and gave it to me to wear home—I had run out bare-headed. He assured me that the police investigation would be stopped if it threatened to come too near us. Later—last week, in fact—when I had become alarmed by the rumors that he had killed Taylor, I went to him and asked him if we hadn't better make a clean breast of it. He laughed at my fears and assured me he was quite able to take care of himself." He brought his hands from behind him, wiped his face with the handkerchief, and said: "That is what happened."

His daughter cried out in a choking voice: "You let him lie there, like that, in the street!"

He winced, but did not say anything.

Ned Beaumont, after a moment's frowning silence, said: "A campaign-speech—some truth gaudied up." He grimaced. "You had a favor to ask."

The Senator looked down at the floor, then up at Ned Beaumont again. "But that is for your ear alone."

Ned Beaumont said: "No."

"Forgive me, dear," the Senator said to his daughter, then to Ned Beaumont: "I have told you the truth, but I realize fully the position I have put myself in. The favor I ask is the return of my revolver and five minutes—a minute—alone in this room."

Ned Beaumont said: "No."

The Senator swayed with a hand to his breast, the handkerchief hanging down from his hand.

Ned Beaumont said: "You'll take what's coming to you."

II

Ned Beaumont went to the street-door with Farr, his grey-haired stenographer, two police-detectives, and the Senator.

"Not going along?" Farr asked.

"No, but I'll be seeing you."

Farr pumped his hand up and down with enthusiasm. "Make it sooner and oftener, Ned," he said. "You play tricks on me, but I don't hold that against you when I see what comes of them."

Ned Beaumont grinned at him, exchanged nods with the detectives, bowed to the stenographer, and shut the door. He walked upstairs to the white-walled room where the piano was. Janet Henry rose from the lyre-end sofa when he came in.

"They've gone," he said in a consciously matter-of-fact voice.

"Did—did they—?"

"They got a pretty complete statement out of him—more details than he told us."

"Will you tell me the truth about it?"

"Yes," he promised.

"What—" She broke off. "What will they do to him, Ned?"

"Probably not a great deal. His age and prominence and so on will help him. The chances are they'll convict him of manslaughter and then set the sentence aside or suspend it."

"Do you think it was an accident?"

Ned Beaumont shook his head. His eyes were cold. He said bluntly: "I think he got mad at the thought of his son interfering with his chances of being re-elected and hit him."

She did not protest. She was twining her fingers together. When she asked her next question it was with difficulty. "Was—was he going to—to shoot Paul?"

"He was. He could get away with the grand-old-man-avenging-the-death-the-law-couldn't-avenge line. He knew Paul wasn't going to stay dummied up if he was arrested. Paul was doing it, just as he was supporting your father for re-election, because he wanted you. He couldn't get you by pretending he'd killed your brother. He didn't care what any-body else thought, but he didn't know you thought he had and he would have cleared himself in a second if he had."

She nodded miserably. "I hated him," she said, "and I wronged him and I still hate him." She sobbed. "Why is that, Ned?"

He made an impatient gesture with one hand. "Don't ask me riddles."

"And you," she said, "tricked me and made a fool of me and brought this on me and I don't hate you."

"More riddles," he said.

"How long, Ned," she asked, "how long have you known —known about Father?"

"I don't know. It's been in the back of my head for a long time. That was about the only thing that'd fit in with Paul's foolishness. If he'd killed Taylor he'd've let me know before this. There was no reason why he should hide that from me. There was a reason why he'd hide your father's crimes from me. He knew I didn't like your father. I'd made that plain enough. He didn't think he could trust me not to knife your father. He knew I wouldn't knife *him*. So, when I'd told him I was going to clear up the killing regardless of what he said, he gave me that phony confession to stop me."

She asked: "Why didn't you like Father?"

"Because," he said hotly, "I don't like pimps."

Her face became red, her eyes abashed. She asked in a dry constricted voice: "And you don't like me because—?"

He did not say anything.

She bit her lip and cried: "Answer me!"

"You're all right," he said, "only you're not all right for Paul, not the way you've been playing him. Neither of you were anything but poison for him. I tried to tell him that. I tried to tell him you both considered him a lower form of animal life and fair game for any kind of treatment. I tried to tell him your father was a man all his life used to winning without much trouble and that in a hole he'd either lose his head or turn wolf. Well, he was in love with you, so—" He snapped his teeth together and walked over to the piano.

"You despise me," she said in a low hard voice. "You think I'm a whore."

"I don't despise you," he said irritably, not turning to face her. "Whatever you've done you've paid for and been paid for and that goes for all of us."

There was silence between them then until she said: "Now you and Paul will be friends again."

He turned from the piano with a movement as if he were about to shake himself and looked at the watch on his wrist. "I'll have to say good-by now."

A startled light came into her eyes. "You're not going away?"

He nodded. "I can catch the four-thirty."

"You're not going away for good?"

"If I can dodge being brought back for some of these trials and I don't think that'll be so hard."

She held her hands out impulsively. "Take me with you."

He blinked at her. "Do you really want to go or are you just being hysterical?" he asked. Her face was crimson by then. Before she could speak he said: "It doesn't make any difference. I'll take you if you want to go." He frowned. "But all this"—he waved a hand to indicate the house—"who'll take care of that?"

She said bitterly: "I don't care—our creditors."

"There's another thing you ought to think about," he said slowly. "Everybody's going to say you deserted your father as soon as he got in trouble."

"I am deserting him," she said, "and I want people to say that. I don't care what they say—if you'll take me away." She sobbed. "If—I wouldn't if only he hadn't gone away and left him lying there alone in that dark street."

Ned Beaumont said brusquely: "Never mind that now. If you're going get packed. Only what you can get in a couple of bags. We can send for the other stuff later, maybe."

She uttered a high-pitched unnatural laugh and ran out of the room. He lit a cigar, sat down at the piano, and played softly until she returned. She had put on a black hat and black coat and was carrying two traveling-bags.

III

They rode in a taxicab to his rooms. For most of the ride they were silent. Once she said suddenly: "In that dream—

I didn't tell you—the key was glass and shattered in our hands just as we got the door open, because the lock was stiff and we had to force it."

He looked sidewise at her and asked: "Well?"

She shivered. "We couldn't lock the snakes in and they came out all over us and I woke up screaming."

"That was only a dream," he said. "Forget it." He smiled without merriment. "You threw my trout back—in the dream."

The taxicab stopped in front of his house. They went up to his rooms. She offered to help him pack, but he said: "No, I can do it. Sit down and rest. We've got an hour before the train leaves."

She sat in one of the red chairs. "Where are you—we going?" she asked timidly.

"New York, first anyhow."

He had one bag packed when the door-bell rang. "You'd better go into the bedroom," he told her and carried her bags in there. He shut the connecting door when he came out.

He went to the outer door and opened it.

Paul Madvig said: "I came to tell you you were right and I know it now."

"You didn't come last night."

"No, I didn't know it then. I got home right after you left."

Ned Beaumont nodded. "Come in," he said, stepping out of the doorway.

Madvig went into the living-room. He looked immediately at the bags, but let his glance roam around the room for a while before asking: "Going away?"

"Yes."

Madvig sat in the chair Janet Henry had occupied. His age showed in his face and he sat down wearily.

"How's Opal?" Ned Beaumont asked.

"She's all right, poor kid. She'll be all right now."

"You did it to her."

"I know, Ned. Jesus, I know it!" Madvig stretched his legs out and looked at his shoes. "I hope you don't think I'm feeling proud of myself." After a pause Madvig added: "I think—I know Opal'd like to see you before you go."

"You'll have to say good-by to her for me and to Mom too. I'm leaving on the four-thirty."

Madvig raised blue eyes clouded by anguish. "You're right, of course, Ned," he said huskily, "but—well—Christ knows you're right!" He looked down at his shoes again.

Ned Beaumont asked: "What are you going to do with your not quite faithful henchmen? Kick them back in line? Or have they kicked themselves back?"

"Farr and the rest of those rats?"

"Uh-huh."

"I'm going to teach them something." Madvig spoke with determination, but there was no enthusiasm in his voice and he did not look up from his shoes. "It'll cost me four years, but I can use those four years cleaning house and putting together an organization that will stay put."

Ned Beaumont raised his eyebrows. "Going to knife them at the polls?"

"Knife them, hell, dynamite them! Shad's dead. I'm going to let his crew run things for the next four years. There's none of them that can build anything solid enough for me to worry about. I'll get the city back next time and by then I'll have done my house-cleaning."

"You could win now," Ned Beaumont said.

"Sure, but I don't want to win with those bastards."

Ned Beaumont nodded. "It takes patience and guts, but it's the best way to play it, I reckon."

"They're all I've got," Madvig said miserably. "I'll never have any brains." He shifted the focus of his eyes from his feet to the fireplace. "Have you got to go, Ned?" he asked almost inaudibly.

"Got to."

Madvig cleared his throat violently. "I don't want to be a God-damned fool," he said, "but I'd like to think that whether you went or stayed you weren't holding anything against me, Ned."

"I'm not holding anything against you, Paul."

Madvig raised his head quickly. "Shake hands with me?"

"Certainly."

Madvig jumped up. His hand caught Ned Beaumont's, crushed it. "Don't go, Ned. Stick it out with me. Christ knows

I need you now. Even if I didn't—I'll do my damndest to make up for all that."

Ned Beaumont shook his head. "You haven't got anything to make up for with me."

"And you'll—?"

Ned Beaumont shook his head again. "I can't. I've got to go."

Madvig released the other's hand and sat down again, morosely, saying: "Well, it serves me right."

Ned Beaumont made an impatient gesture. "That's got nothing to do with it." He stopped and bit his lip. Then he said bluntly: "Janet's here."

Madvig stared at him.

Janet Henry opened the bedroom-door and came into the living-room. Her face was pale and drawn, but she held it high. She went straight up to Paul Madvig and said: "I've done you a lot of harm, Paul. I've—"

His face had become pale as hers. Now blood rushed into it. "Don't, Janet," he said hoarsely. "Nothing you could do . . ." The rest of his speech was unintelligibly mumbled.

She stepped back, flinching.

Ned Beaumont said: "Janet is going away with me."

Madvig's lips parted. He looked dumbly at Ned Beaumont and as he looked the blood went out of his face again. When his face was quite bloodless he mumbled something of which only the word "luck" could be understood, turned clumsily around, went to the door, opened it, and went out, leaving it open behind him.

Janet Henry looked at Ned Beaumont. He stared fixedly at the door.

THE THIN MAN

To
Lillian

I

I WAS leaning against the bar in a speakeasy on Fifty-second Street, waiting for Nora to finish her Christmas shopping, when a girl got up from the table where she had been sitting with three other people and came over to me. She was small and blonde, and whether you looked at her face or at her body in powder-blue sports clothes the result was satisfactory. "Aren't you Nick Charles?" she asked.

I said: "Yes."

She held out her hand. "I'm Dorothy Wynant. You don't remember me, but you ought to remember my father, Clyde Wynant. You—"

"Sure," I said, "and I remember you now, but you were only a kid of eleven or twelve then, weren't you?"

"Yes, that was eight years ago. Listen: remember those stories you told me? Were they true?"

"Probably not. How is your father?"

She laughed. "I was going to ask you. Mamma divorced him, you know, and we never hear from him—except when he gets in the newspapers now and then with some of his carryings on. Don't you ever see him?"

My glass was empty. I asked her what she would have to drink, she said Scotch and soda, I ordered two of them and said: "No, I've been living in San Francisco."

She said slowly: "I'd like to see him. Mamma would raise hell if she found it out, but I'd like to see him."

"Well?"

"He's not where we used to live, on Riverside Drive, and he's not in the phone book or city directory."

"Try his lawyer," I suggested.

Her face brightened. "Who is he?"

"It used to be a fellow named Mac-something-or-other—Macaulay, that's it, Herbert Macaulay. He was in the Singer Building."

"Lend me a nickel," she said, and went out to the telephone. She came back smiling. "I found him. He's just round the corner on Fifth Avenue."

"Your father?"

"The lawyer. He says my father's out of town. I'm going round to see him." She raised her glass to me. "Family reunions. Look, why don't—"

Asta jumped up and punched me in the belly with her front feet. Nora, at the other end of the leash, said: "She's had a swell afternoon—knocked over a table of toys at Lord & Taylor's, scared a fat woman silly by licking her leg in Saks's, and's been patted by three policemen."

I made introductions. "My wife, Dorothy Wynant. Her father was once a client of mine, when she was only so high. A good guy, but screwy."

"I was fascinated by him," Dorothy said, meaning me, "a real live detective, and used to follow him around making him tell me about his experiences. He told me awful lies, but I believed every word."

I said: "You look tired, Nora."

"I am. Let's sit down."

Dorothy Wynant said she had to go back to her table. She shook hands with Nora; we must drop in for cocktails, they were living at the Courtland, her mother's name was Jorgensen now. We would be glad to and she must come see us some time, we were at the Normandie and would be in New York for another week or two. Dorothy patted the dog's head and left us.

We found a table. Nora said: "She's pretty."

"If you like them like that."

She grinned at me. "You got types?"

"Only you, darling—lanky brunettes with wicked jaws."

"And how about the red-head you wandered off with at the Quinns' last night?"

"That's silly," I said. "She just wanted to show me some French etchings."

2

THE NEXT DAY Herbert Macaulay telephoned me. "Hello. I didn't know you were back in town till Dorothy Wynant told me. How about lunch?"

"What time is it?"

"Half past eleven. Did I wake you up?"

"Yes," I said, "but that's all right. Suppose you come up here for lunch: I've got a hangover and don't feel like running around much. . . . O.K., say one o'clock."

I had a drink with Nora, who was going out to have her hair washed, then another after a shower, and was feeling better by the time the telephone rang again.

A female voice asked: "Is Mr. Macaulay there?"

"Not yet."

"Sorry to trouble you, but would you mind asking him to call his office as soon as he gets there? It's important."

I promised to do that.

Macaulay arrived about ten minutes later. He was a big curly-haired, rosy-cheeked, rather good-looking chap of about my age—forty-one—though he looked younger. He was supposed to be a pretty good lawyer. I had worked on several jobs for him when I was living in New York and we had always got along nicely.

Now we shook hands and patted each other's backs, and he asked me how the world was treating me, and I said, "Fine," and asked him and he said, "Fine," and I told him to call his office.

He came away from the telephone frowning. "Wynant's back in town," he said, "and wants me to meet him."

I turned around with the drinks I had poured. "Well, the lunch can—"

"Let him wait," he said, and took one of the glasses from me.

"Still as screwy as ever?"

"That's no joke," Macaulay said solemnly. "You heard they had him in a sanatorium for nearly a year back in '29?"

"No."

He nodded. He sat down, put his glass on a table beside his

chair, and leaned towards me a little. "What's Mimi up to, Charles?"

"Mimi? Oh, the wife—the ex-wife. I don't know. Does she have to be up to something?"

"She usually is," he said dryly, and then very slowly, "and I thought you'd know."

So that was it. I said: "Listen, Mac, I haven't been a detective for six years, since 1927."

He stared at me.

"On the level," I assured him, "a year after I got married, my wife's father died and left her a lumber mill and a narrow-gauge railroad and some other things and I quit the Agency to look after them. Anyway I wouldn't be working for Mimi Wynant, or Jorgensen, or whatever her name is—she never liked me and I never liked her."

"Oh, I didn't think you—" Macaulay broke off with a vague gesture and picked up his glass. When he took it away from his mouth, he said: "I was just wondering. Here Mimi phones me three days ago—Tuesday—trying to find Wynant; then yesterday Dorothy phones, saying you told her to, and comes around, and—I thought you were still sleuthing, so I was wondering what it was all about."

"Didn't they tell you?"

"Sure—they wanted to see him for old times' sake. That means a lot."

"You lawyers are a suspicious crew," I said. "Maybe they did—that and money. But what's the fuss about? Is he in hiding?"

Macaulay shrugged. "You know as much about it as I do. I haven't seen him since October." He drank again. "How long are you going to be in town?"

"Till after New Year's," I told him and went to the telephone to ask room service for menus.

3

NORA AND I went to the opening of *Honeymoon* at the Little Theatre that night and then to a party given by some people named Freeman or Fielding or something. I felt pretty low when she called me the next morning. She gave me a newspaper and a cup of coffee and said: "Read that."

I patiently read a paragraph or two, then put the paper down and took a sip of coffee. "Fun's fun," I said, "but right now I'd swap you all the interviews with Mayor-elect O'Brien ever printed—and throw in the Indian picture—for a slug of whis—"

"Not that, stupid." She put a finger on the paper. "That."

INVENTOR'S SECRETARY
MURDERED IN APARTMENT
JULIA WOLF'S BULLET-RIDDLED BODY FOUND;
POLICE SEEK HER EMPLOYER, CLYDE WYNANT

The bullet-riddled body of Julia Wolf, thirty-two-year-old confidential secretary to Clyde Miller Wynant, well-known inventor, was discovered late yesterday afternoon in the dead woman's apartment at 411 East Fifty-fourth St. by Mrs. Christian Jorgensen, divorced wife of the inventor, who had gone there in an attempt to learn her former husband's present address.

Mrs. Jorgensen, who returned Monday after a six-year stay in Europe, told police that she heard feeble groans when she rang the murdered woman's door-bell, whereupon she notified an elevator boy, Mervin Holly, who called Walter Meany, apartment-house superintendent. Miss Wolf was lying on the bedroom floor with four .32-calibre bullet-wounds in her chest when they entered the apartment, and died without having recovered consciousness before police and medical aid arrived.

Herbert Macaulay, Wynant's attorney, told the police that he had not seen the inventor since October. He stated that Wynant called him on the telephone yesterday and made an appointment, but failed to keep it; and disclaimed any knowledge of his client's whereabouts. Miss Wolf, Macaulay stated, had been in the inventor's employ for the past eight years. The attorney said he knew nothing about the dead woman's family or private affairs and could throw no light on her murder.

The bullet-wounds could not have been self-inflicted, according to . . .

The rest of it was the usual police department hand-out.

"Do you suppose he killed her?" Nora asked when I put the paper down again.

"Wynant? I wouldn't be surprised. He's batty as hell."

"Did you know her?"

"Yes. How about a drop of something to cut the phlegm?"

"What was she like?"

"Not bad," I said. "She wasn't bad-looking and she had a lot of sense and a lot of nerve—and it took both to live with that guy."

"She lived with him?"

"Yes. I want a drink, please. That is, it was like that when I knew them."

"Why don't you have some breakfast first? Was she in love with him or was it just business?"

"I don't know. It's too early for breakfast."

When Nora opened the door to go out, the dog came in and put her front feet on the bed, her face in my face. I rubbed her head and tried to remember something Wynant had once said to me, something about women and dogs. It was not the woman-spaniel-walnut-tree line. I could not remember what it was, but there seemed to be some point in trying to remember.

Nora returned with two drinks and another question: "What's he like?"

"Tall—over six feet—and one of the thinnest men I've ever seen. He must be about fifty now, and his hair was almost white when I knew him. Usually needs a haircut, ragged brindle mustache, bites his fingernails." I pushed the dog away to reach for my drink.

"Sounds lovely. What were you doing with him?"

"A fellow who'd worked for him accused him of stealing some kind of idea or invention from him. Rosewater was his name. He tried to shake Wynant down by threatening to shoot him, bomb his house, kidnap his children, cut his wife's throat—I don't know what all—if he didn't come across. We never caught him—must've scared him off. Anyway, the threats stopped and nothing happened."

Nora stopped drinking to ask: "Did Wynant really steal it?"

"Tch, tch, tch," I said. "This is Christmas Eve: try to think good of your fellow man."

4

T HAT AFTERNOON I took Asta for a walk, explained to two people that she was a Schnauzer and not a cross between a Scottie and an Irish terrier, stopped at Jim's for a couple of drinks, ran into Larry Crowley, and brought him back to the Normandie with me. Nora was pouring cocktails for the Quinns, Margot Innes, a man whose name I did not catch, and Dorothy Wynant.

Dorothy said she wanted to talk to me, so we carried our cocktails into the bedroom.

She came to the point right away. "Do you think my father killed her, Nick?"

"No," I said. "Why should I?"

"Well, the police have— Listen, she was his mistress, wasn't she?"

I nodded. "When I knew them."

She stared at her glass while saying, "He's my father. I never liked him. I never liked Mamma." She looked up at me. "I don't like Gilbert." Gilbert was her brother.

"Don't let that worry you. Lots of people don't like their relatives."

"Do you like them?"

"My relatives?"

"Mine." She scowled at me. "And stop talking to me as if I was still twelve."

"It's not that," I explained. "I'm getting tight."

"Well, do you?"

I shook my head. "You were all right, just a spoiled kid. I could get along without the rest of them."

"What's the matter with us?" she asked, not argumentatively, but as if she really wanted to know.

"Different things. Your—"

Harrison Quinn opened the door and said: "Come on over and play some ping-pong, Nick."

"In a little while."

"Bring beautiful along." He leered at Dorothy and went away.

She said: "I don't suppose you know Jorgensen."

"I know a Nels Jorgensen."

"Some people have all the luck. This one's named Christian. He's a honey. That's Mamma—divorces a lunatic and marries a gigolo." Her eyes became wet. She caught her breath in a sob and asked: "What am I going to do, Nick?" Her voice was a frightened child's.

I put an arm around her and made what I hoped were comforting sounds. She cried on my lapel. The telephone beside the bed began to ring. In the next room *Rise and Shine* was coming through the radio. My glass was empty. I said: "Walk out on them."

She sobbed again. "You can't walk out on yourself."

"Maybe I don't know what you're talking about."

"Please don't tease me," she said humbly.

Nora, coming in to answer the telephone, looked questioningly at me. I made a face at her over the girl's head.

When Nora said "Hello" into the telephone, the girl stepped quickly back away from me and blushed. "I—I'm sorry," she stammered, "I didn't—"

Nora smiled sympathetically at her. I said: "Don't be a dope." The girl found her handkerchief and dabbed at her eyes with it.

Nora spoke into the telephone: "Yes. . . . I'll see if he's in. Who's calling, please?" She put a hand over the mouthpiece and addressed me: "It's a man named Norman. Do you want to talk to him?"

I said I didn't know and took the telephone. "Hello."

A somewhat harsh voice said: "Mr. Charles? . . . Mr. Charles, I understand that you were formerly connected with the Trans-American Detective Agency."

"Who is this?" I asked.

"My name is Albert Norman, Mr. Charles, which probably means nothing to you, but I would like to lay a proposition before you. I am sure you will—"

"What kind of a proposition?"

"I can't discuss it over the phone, Mr. Charles, but if you will give me half an hour of your time, I can promise—"

"Sorry," I said. "I'm pretty busy and—"

"But, Mr. Charles, this is—" Then there was a loud noise: it could have been a shot or something falling or anything else that would make a loud noise. I said, "Hello," a couple of times, got no answer, and hung up.

Nora had Dorothy over in front of a looking-glass soothing her with powder and rouge. I said, "A guy selling insurance," and went into the living-room for a drink.

Some more people had come in. I spoke to them. Harrison Quinn left the sofa where he had been sitting with Margot Innes and said: "Now ping-pong." Asta jumped up and punched me in the belly with her front feet. I shut off the radio and poured myself a cocktail. The man whose name I had not caught was saying: "Comes the revolution and we'll all be lined up against the wall—first thing." He seemed to think it was a good idea.

Quinn came over to refill his glass. He looked towards the bedroom door. "Where'd you find the little blonde?"

"Used to bounce it on my knee."

"Which knee?" he asked. "Could I touch it?"

Nora and Dorothy came out of the bedroom. I saw an afternoon paper on the radio and picked it up. Headlines said:

JULIA WOLF ONCE RACKETEER'S GIRL;
ARTHUR NUNHEIM IDENTIFIES BODY;
WYNANT STILL MISSING

Nora, at my elbow, spoke in a low voice: "I asked her to have dinner with us. Be nice to the child"—Nora was twenty-six—"she's all upset."

"Whatever you say." I turned around. Dorothy, across the room, was laughing at something Quinn was telling her. "But if you get mixed up in people's troubles, don't expect me to kiss you where you're hurt."

"I won't. You're a sweet old fool. Don't read that here now." She took the newspaper away from me and stuck it out of sight behind the radio.

5

NORA COULD NOT sleep that night. She read Chaliapin's memoirs until I began to doze and then woke me up by asking: "Are you asleep?"

I said I was.

She lit a cigarette for me, one for herself. "Don't you ever think you'd like to go back to detecting once in a while just for the fun of it? You know, when something special comes up, like the Lindb—"

"Darling," I said, "my guess is that Wynant killed her, and the police'll catch him without my help. Anyway, it's nothing in my life."

"I didn't mean just that, but—"

"But besides I haven't the time: I'm too busy trying to see that you don't lose any of the money I married you for." I kissed her. "Don't you think maybe a drink would help you to sleep?"

"No, thanks."

"Maybe it would if I took one." When I brought my Scotch and soda back to bed, she was frowning into space. I said: "She's cute, but she's cuckoo. She wouldn't be his daughter if she wasn't. You can't tell how much of what she says is what she thinks and you can't tell how much of what she thinks ever really happened. I like her, but I think you're letting—"

"I'm not sure I like her," Nora said thoughtfully, "she's probably a little bastard, but if a quarter of what she told us is true, she's in a tough spot."

"There's nothing I can do to help her."

"She thinks you can."

"And so do you, which shows that no matter what you think, you can always get somebody else to go along with you."

Nora sighed. "I wish you were sober enough to talk to." She leaned over to take a sip of my drink. "I'll give you your Christmas present now if you'll give me mine."

I shook my head. "At breakfast."

"But it's Christmas now."

"Breakfast."

"Whatever you're giving me," she said, "I hope I don't like it."

"You'll have to keep them anyway, because the man at the Aquarium said he positively wouldn't take them back. He said they'd already bitten the tails off the—"

"It wouldn't hurt you any to find out if you can help her, would it? She's got so much confidence in you, Nicky."

"Everybody trusts Greeks."

"Please."

"You just want to poke your nose into things that—"

"I meant to ask you: did his wife know the Wolf girl was his mistress?"

"I don't know. She didn't like her."

"What's the wife like?"

"I don't know—a woman."

"Good-looking?"

"Used to be very."

"She old?"

"Forty, forty-two. Cut it out, Nora. You don't want any part of it. Let the Charleses stick to the Charleses' troubles and the Wynants stick to the Wynants'."

She pouted. "Maybe that drink would help me."

I got out of bed and mixed her a drink. As I brought it into the bedroom, the telephone began to ring. I looked at my watch on the table. It was nearly five o'clock.

Nora was talking into the telephone: "Hello. . . . Yes, speaking." She looked sidewise at me. I shook my head no. "Yes. . . . Why, certainly. . . . Yes, certainly." She put the telephone down and grinned at me.

"You're wonderful," I said. "Now what?"

"Dorothy's coming up. I think she's tight."

"That's great." I picked up my bathrobe. "I was afraid I was going to have to go to sleep."

She was bending over looking for her slippers. "Don't be such an old fuff. You can sleep all day." She found her slippers and stood up in them. "Is she really as afraid of her mother as she says?"

"If she's got any sense. Mimi's poison."

Nora screwed up her dark eyes at me and asked slowly: "What are you holding out on me?"

"Oh, dear," I said, "I was hoping I wouldn't have to tell you. Dorothy is really my daughter. I didn't know what I was doing, Nora. It was spring in Venice and I was so young and there was a moon over the—"

"Be funny. Don't you want something to eat?"

"If you do. What do you want?"

"Raw chopped beef sandwich with a lot of onion and some coffee."

Dorothy arrived while I was telephoning an all-night delicatessen. When I went into the living-room, she stood up with some difficulty and said: "I'm awfully sorry, Nick, to keep bothering you and Nora like this, but I can't go home this way tonight. I can't. I'm afraid to. I don't know what'd happen to me, what I'd do. Please don't make me." She was very drunk. Asta sniffed at her ankles.

I said: "Sh-h-h. You're all right here. Sit down. There'll be some coffee in a little while. Where'd you get the snoutful?"

She sat down and shook her head stupidly. "I don't know. I've been everywhere since I left you. I've been everywhere except home because I can't go home this way. Look what I got." She stood up again and took a battered automatic pistol out of her coat pocket. "Look at that." She waved it at me while Asta, wagging her tail, jumped happily at it.

Nora made a noise with her breathing. The back of my neck was cold. I pushed the dog aside and took the pistol away from Dorothy. "What kind of clowning is this? Sit down." I dropped the pistol into a bathrobe pocket and pushed Dorothy down in her chair.

"Don't be mad at me, Nick," she whined. "You can keep it. I don't want to make a nuisance of myself."

"Where'd you get it?" I asked.

"In a speakeasy on Tenth Avenue. I gave a man my bracelet—the one with the emeralds and diamonds—for it."

"And then won it back from him in a crap game," I said. "You've still got it on."

She stared at her bracelet. "I thought I did."

I looked at Nora and shook my head. Nora said: "Aw, don't bully her, Nick. She's—"

"He's not bullying me, Nora, he's really not," Dorothy said quickly. "He—he's the only person I got in the world to turn to."

I remembered Nora had not touched her Scotch and soda, so I went into the bedroom and drank it. When I came back, Nora was sitting on the arm of Dorothy's chair with an arm around the girl. Dorothy was sniffling; Nora was saying: "But

Nick's not mad, dear. He likes you." She looked up at me. "You're not mad, are you, Nicky?"

"No, I'm just hurt." I sat on the sofa. "Where'd you get the gun, Dorothy?"

"From a man—I told you."

"What man?"

"I told you—a man in a speakeasy."

"And you gave him a bracelet for it."

"I thought I did, but—look—I've still got my bracelet."

"I noticed that."

Nora patted the girl's shoulder. "Of course you've still got your bracelet."

I said: "When the boy comes with that coffee and stuff, I'm going to bribe him to stick around. I'm not going to stay alone with a couple of—"

Nora scowled at me, told the girl: "Don't mind him. He's been like that all night."

The girl said: "He thinks I'm a silly little drunken fool."

Nora patted her shoulder some more.

I asked: "But what'd you want a gun for?"

Dorothy sat up straight and stared at me with wide drunken eyes. "Him," she whispered excitedly, "if he bothered me. I was afraid because I was drunk. That's what it was. And then I was afraid of that, too, so I came here."

"You mean your father?" Nora asked, trying to keep excitement out of her voice.

The girl shook her head. "Clyde Wynant's my father. My stepfather." She leaned against Nora's breast.

Nora said, "Oh," in a tone of very complete understanding. Then she said, "You poor child," and looked significantly at me.

I said: "Let's all have a drink."

"Not me." Nora was scowling at me again. "And I don't think Dorothy wants one."

"Yes, she does. It'll help her sleep." I poured her a terrific dose of Scotch and saw that she drank it. It worked nicely: she was sound asleep by the time our coffee and sandwiches came.

Nora said: "Now you're satisfied."

"Now I'm satisfied. Shall we tuck her in before we eat?"

I carried her into the bedroom and helped Nora undress her. She had a beautiful little body.

We went back to our food. I took the pistol out of my pocket and examined it. It had been kicked around a lot. There were two cartridges in it, one in the chamber, one in the magazine.

"What are you going to do with it?" Nora asked.

"Nothing till I find out if it's the one Julia Wolf was killed with. It's a .32."

"But she said—"

"She got it in a speakeasy—from a man—for a bracelet. I heard her."

Nora leaned over her sandwich at me. Her eyes were very shiny and almost black. "Do you suppose she got it from her stepfather?"

"I do," I said, but I said it too earnestly.

Nora said: "You're a Greek louse. But maybe she did; you don't know. And you don't believe her story."

"Listen, darling, tomorrow I'll buy you a whole lot of detective stories, but don't worry your pretty little head over mysteries tonight. All she was trying to tell you was that she was afraid Jorgensen was waiting to try to make her when she got home and she was afraid she was drunk enough to give in."

"But her mother!"

"This family's a family. You can—"

Dorothy Wynant, standing unsteadily in the doorway in a nightgown much too long for her, blinked at the light and said: "Please, can I come in for a little while? I'm afraid in there alone."

"Sure."

She came over and curled up beside me on the sofa while Nora went to get something to put around her.

6

THE THREE of us were at breakfast early that afternoon when the Jorgensens arrived. Nora answered the telephone and came away from it trying to pretend she was not tickled. "It's your mother," she told Dorothy. "She's down-stairs. I told her to come up."

Dorothy said: "Damn it. I wish I hadn't phoned her."

I said: "We might just as well be living in the lobby."

Nora said: "He doesn't mean that." She patted Dorothy's shoulder.

The doorbell rang. I went to the door.

Eight years had done no damage to Mimi's looks. She was a little riper, showier, that was all. She was larger than her daughter, and her blondness was more vivid. She laughed and held her hands out to me. "Merry Christmas. It's awfully good to see you after all these years. This is my husband. Mr. Charles, Chris."

I said, "I'm glad to see you, Mimi," and shook hands with Jorgensen. He was probably five years younger than his wife, a tall thin erect dark man, carefully dressed and sleek, with smooth hair and a waxed mustache.

He bowed from the waist. "How do you do, Mr. Charles?" His accent was heavy, Teutonic, his hand was lean and mus-cular.

We went inside.

Mimi, when the introductions were over, apologized to Nora for popping in on us. "But I did want to see your husband again, and then I know the only way to get this brat of mine anywhere on time is to carry her off bodily." She turned her smile on Dorothy. "Better get dressed, honey."

Honey grumbled through a mouthful of toast that she didn't see why she had to waste an afternoon at Aunt Alice's even if it was Christmas. "I bet Gilbert's not going."

Mimi said Asta was a lovely dog and asked me if I had *any* idea where that ex-husband of hers might be.

"No."

She went on playing with the dog. "He's crazy, absolutely crazy, to disappear at a time like this. No wonder the police at first thought he had something to do with it."

"What do they think now?" I asked.

She looked up at me. "Haven't you seen the papers?"

"No."

"It's a man named Morelli—a gangster. He killed her. He was her lover."

"They caught him?"

"Not yet, but he did it. I wish I could find Clyde. Macaulay won't help me at all. He says he doesn't know where he is, but that's ridiculous. He has powers of attorney from him and everything and I know very well he's in touch with Clyde. Do you think Macaulay's trustworthy?"

"He's Wynant's lawyer," I said. "There's no reason why you should trust him."

"Just what I thought." She moved over a little on the sofa. "Sit down. I've got millions of things to ask you."

"How about a drink first?"

"Anything but egg-nog," she said. "It makes me bilious."

When I came out of the pantry, Nora and Jorgensen were trying their French on each other, Dorothy was still pretending to eat, and Mimi was playing with the dog again. I distributed the drinks and sat down beside Mimi.

She said: "Your wife's lovely."

"I like her."

"Tell me the truth, Nick: do you think Clyde's really crazy? I mean crazy enough that something ought to be done about it."

"How do I know?"

"I'm worried about the children," she said. "I've no claim on him any more—the settlement he made when I divorced him took care of all that—but the children have. We're absolutely penniless now and I'm worried about them. If he is crazy he's just as likely as not to throw away everything and leave them without a cent. What do you think I ought to do?"

"Thinking about putting him in the booby-hatch?"

"No-o," she said slowly, "but I would like to talk to him." She put a hand on my arm. "You could find him."

I shook my head.

"Won't you help me, Nick? We used to be friends." Her big blue eyes were soft and appealing.

Dorothy, at the table, was watching us suspiciously.

"For Christ's sake, Mimi," I said, "there's a thousand detectives in New York. Hire one of them. I'm not working at it any more."

"I know, but— Was Dorry very drunk last night?"

"Maybe I was. She seemed all right to me."

"Don't you think she's gotten to be a pretty little thing?"

"I always thought she was."

She thought that over for a moment, then said: "She's only a child, Nick."

"What's that got to do with what?" I asked.

She smiled. "How about getting some clothes on, Dorry?"

Dorothy sulkily repeated that she didn't see why she had to waste an afternoon at Aunt Alice's.

Jorgensen turned to address his wife: "Mrs. Charles has the great kindness to suggest that we do not—"

"Yes," Nora said, "why don't you stay awhile? There'll be some people coming in. It won't be very exciting, but—" She waved her glass a little to finish the sentence.

"I'd love to," Mimi replied slowly, "but I'm afraid Alice—"

"Make our apologies to her by telephone," Jorgensen suggested.

"I'll do it," Dorothy said.

Mimi nodded. "Be nice to her."

Dorothy went into the bedroom. Everybody seemed much brighter. Nora caught my eye and winked merrily and I had to take it and like it because Mimi was looking at me then.

Mimi asked me: "You really didn't want us to stay, did you?"

"Of course."

"Chances are you're lying. Weren't you sort of fond of poor Julia?"

" 'Poor Julia' sounds swell from you. I liked her all right."

Mimi put her hand on my arm again. "She broke up my life with Clyde. Naturally I hated her—then—but that's a long time ago. I had no feeling against her when I went to see her Friday. And, Nick, I saw her die. She didn't deserve to die. It was horrible. No matter what I'd felt, there'd be nothing left but pity now. I meant 'poor Julia' when I said it."

"I don't know what you're up to," I said. "I don't know what any of you are up to."

"Any of us," she repeated. "Has Dorry been—"

Dorothy came in from the bedroom. "I squared it." She kissed her mother on the mouth and sat down beside her.

Mimi, looking in her compact-mirror to see her mouth had not been smeared, asked: "She wasn't peevish about it?"

"No, I squared it. What do you have to do to get a drink?"

I said: "You have to walk over to that table where the ice and bottles are and pour it."

Mimi said: "You drink too much."

"I don't drink as much as Nick." She went over to the table.

Mimi shook her head. "These children! I mean you were pretty fond of Julia Wolf, weren't you?"

Dorothy called: "You want one, Nick?"

"Thanks," I said; then to Mimi, "I liked her well enough."

"You're the damnedest evasive man," she complained. "Did you like her as much as you used to like me, for instance?"

"You mean those couple of afternoons we killed?"

Her laugh was genuine. "That's certainly an answer." She turned to Dorothy, carrying glasses towards us. "You'll have to get a robe that shade of blue, darling. It's very becoming to you."

I took one of the glasses from Dorothy and said I thought I had better get dressed.

7

WHEN I came out of the bathroom, Nora and Dorothy were in the bedroom, Nora combing her hair, Dorothy sitting on the side of the bed dangling a stocking.

Nora made a kiss at me in the dressing-table mirror. She looked very happy.

"You like Nick a lot, don't you, Nora?" Dorothy asked.

"He's an old Greek fool, but I'm used to him."

"Charles isn't a Greek name."

"It's Charalambides," I explained. "When the old man came over, the mugg that put him through Ellis Island said Charalambides was too long—too much trouble to write— and whittled it down to Charles. It was all right with the old man; they could have called him X so they let him in."

Dorothy stared at me. "I never know when you're lying." She started to put on the stocking, stopped. "What's Mamma trying to do to you?"

"Nothing. Pump me. She'd like to know what you did and said last night."

"I thought so. What'd you tell her?"

"What could I tell her? You didn't do or say anything."

She wrinkled her forehead over that, but when she spoke again it was about something else: "I never knew there was anything between you and Mamma. Of course I was only a kid then and wouldn't have known what it was all about even if I'd noticed anything, but I didn't even know you called each other by your first names."

Nora turned from the mirror laughing. "Now we're getting somewhere." She waved the comb at Dorothy. "Go on, dear."

Dorothy said earnestly: "Well, I didn't know."

I was taking laundry pins out of a shirt. "What do you know now?" I asked.

"Nothing," she said slowly, and her face began to grow pink, "but I can guess." She bent over her stocking.

"Can and do," I growled. "You're a dope, but don't look so embarrassed. You can't help it if you've got a dirty mind."

She raised her head and laughed, but when she asked, "Do you think I take after Mamma much?" she was serious.

"I wouldn't be surprised."

"But do you?"

"You want me to say no. No."

"That's what I have to live with," Nora said cheerfully. "You can't do anything with him."

I finished dressing first and went out to the living-room. Mimi was sitting on Jorgensen's knees. She stood up and asked: "What'd you get for Christmas?"

"Nora gave me a watch." I showed it to her.

She said it was lovely, and it was. "What'd you give her?"

"Necklace."

Jorgensen said, "May I?" and rose to mix himself a drink.

The doorbell rang. I let the Quinns and Margot Innes in, introduced them to the Jorgensens. Presently Nora and Dorothy finished dressing and came out of the bedroom, and

Quinn attached himself to Dorothy. Larry Crowley arrived, with a girl named Denis, and a few minutes later the Edges. I won thirty-two dollars—on the cuff—from Margot at backgammon. The Denis girl had to go into the bedroom and lie down awhile. Alice Quinn, with Margot's help, tore her husband away from Dorothy at a little after six and carried him off to keep a date they had. The Edges left. Mimi put on her coat, got her husband and daughter into their coats.

"It's awful short notice," she said, "but can't you come to dinner tomorrow night?"

Nora said: "Certainly."

We shook hands and made polite speeches all around and they went away.

Nora shut the door after them and leaned her back against it. "Jesus, he's a handsome guy," she said.

8

SO FAR I had known just where I stood on the Wolf-Wynant-Jorgensen troubles and what I was doing—the answers were, respectively, nowhere and nothing—but when we stopped at Reuben's for coffee on our way home at four the next morning, Nora opened a newspaper and found a line in one of the gossip columns: "Nick Charles, former Trans-American Detective Agency ace, on from Coast to sift the Julia Wolf murder mystery"; and when I opened my eyes and sat up in bed some six hours later Nora was shaking me and a man with a gun in his hand was standing in the bedroom doorway.

He was a plump dark youngish man of medium height, broad through the jaws, narrow between the eyes. He wore a black derby hat, a black overcoat that fitted him very snugly, a dark suit, and black shoes, all looking as if he had bought them within the past fifteen minutes. The gun, a blunt black .38-calibre automatic, lay comfortably in his hand, not pointing at anything.

Nora was saying: "He made me let him in, Nick. He said he had to—"

"I got to talk to you," the man with the gun said. "That's all, but I got to do that." His voice was low, rasping.

I had blinked myself awake by then. I looked at Nora. She was excited, but apparently not frightened: she might have been watching a horse she had a bet on coming down the stretch with a nose lead.

I said: "All right, talk, but do you mind putting the gun away? My wife doesn't care, but I'm pregnant and I don't want the child to be born with—"

He smiled with his lower lip. "You don't have to tell me you're tough. I heard about you." He put the pistol in his overcoat pocket. "I'm Shep Morelli."

"I never heard about you," I said.

He took a step into the room and began to shake his head from side to side. "I didn't knock Julia off."

"Maybe you didn't, but you're bringing the news to the wrong place. I got nothing to do with it."

"I haven't seen her in three months," he said. "We were washed up."

"Tell the police."

"I wouldn't have any reason to hurt her: she was always on the up and up with me."

"That's all swell," I said, "only you're peddling your fish in the wrong market."

"Listen." He took another step towards the bed. "Studsy Burke tells me you used to be O.K. That's why I'm here. Do the—"

"How is Studsy?" I asked. "I haven't seen him since the time he went up the river in '23 or '24."

"He's all right. He'd like to see you. He's got a joint on West Forty-ninth, the Pigiron Club. But listen, what's the law doing to me? Do they think I did it? Or is it just something else to pin on me?"

I shook my head. "I'd tell you if I knew. Don't let newspapers fool you: I'm not in this. Ask the police."

"That'd be very smart." He smiled with his lower lip again. "That'd be the smartest thing I ever did. Me that a police captain's been in a hospital three weeks on account we had an argument. The boys would like me to come in and ask 'em questions. They'd like it right down to the end of their blackjacks." He turned a hand over, palm up. "I come to you on the level. Studsy says you're on the level. Be on the level."

"I'm being on the level," I assured him. "If I knew anything I'd—"

Knuckles drummed on the corridor door, three times, sharply. Morelli's gun was in his hand before the noise stopped. His eyes seemed to move in all directions at once. His voice was a metallic snarl deep in his chest: "Well?"

"I don't know." I sat up a little higher in bed and nodded at the gun in his hand. "That makes it your party." The gun pointed very accurately at my chest. I could hear the blood in my ears, and my lips felt swollen. I said: "There's no fire-escape." I put my left hand out towards Nora, who was sitting on the far side of the bed.

The knuckles hit the door again, and a deep voice called: "Open up. Police."

Morelli's lower lip crawled up to lap the upper, and the whites of his eyes began to show under the irises. "You son of a bitch," he said slowly, almost as if he were sorry for me. He moved his feet the least bit, flattening them against the floor.

A key touched the outer lock.

I hit Nora with my left hand, knocking her down across the room. The pillow I chucked with my right hand at Morelli's gun seemed to have no weight; it drifted slow as a piece of tissue paper. No noise in the world, before or after, was ever as loud as Morelli's gun going off. Something pushed my left side as I sprawled across the floor. I caught one of his ankles and rolled over with it, bringing him down on me, and he clubbed my back with the gun until I got a hand free and began to hit him as low in the body as I could.

Men came in and dragged us apart.

It took us five minutes to bring Nora to.

She sat up holding her cheek and looked around the room until she saw Morelli, nippers on one wrist, standing between two detectives. Morelli's face was a mess: the coppers had worked him over a little just for the fun of it. Nora glared at me. "You damned fool," she said, "you didn't have to knock me cold. I knew you'd take him, but I wanted to see it."

One of the coppers laughed. "Jesus," he said admiringly, "there's a woman with hair on her chest."

She smiled at him and stood up. When she looked at me she stopped smiling. "Nick, you're—"

I said I didn't think it was much and opened what was left of my pyjama-coat. Morelli's bullet had scooped out a gutter perhaps four inches long under my left nipple. A lot of blood was running out of it, but it was not very deep.

Morelli said: "Tough luck. A couple of inches over would make a lot of difference the right way."

The copper who had admired Nora—he was a big sandy man of forty-eight or fifty in a gray suit that did not fit him very well—slapped Morelli's mouth.

Keyser, the Normandie's manager, said he would get a doctor and went to the telephone. Nora ran to the bathroom for towels.

I put a towel over the wound and lay down on the bed. "I'm all right. Don't let's fuss over it till the doctor comes. How'd you people happen to pop in?"

The copper who had slapped Morelli said: "We happen to hear this is getting to be kind of a meeting-place for Wynant's family and his lawyer and everybody, so we think we'll kind of keep an eye on it in case he happens to show up, and this morning when Mack here, who was the eye we were kind of keeping on it at the time, sees this bird duck in, he gives us a ring and we get hold of Mr. Keyser and come on up, and pretty lucky for you."

"Yes, pretty lucky for me, or maybe I wouldn't've got shot."

He eyed me suspiciously. His eyes were pale gray and watery. "This bird a friend of yours?"

"I never saw him before."

"What'd he want of you?"

"Wanted to tell me he didn't kill the Wolf girl."

"What's that to you?"

"Nothing."

"What'd he think it was to you?"

"Ask him. I don't know."

"I'm asking you."

"Keep on asking."

"I'll ask you another one: you're going to swear to the complaint on him shooting you?"

"That's another one I can't answer right now. Maybe it was an accident."

"Oke. There's plenty of time. I guess we got to ask you a lot more things than we'd figured on." He turned to one of his companions: there were four of them. "We'll frisk the joint."

"Not without a warrant," I told him.

"So you say. Come on, Andy." They began to search the place.

The doctor—a colorless whisp of a man with the snuffles—came in, clucked and sniffed over my side, got the bleeding stopped and a bandage on, and told me I would have nothing to worry about if I lay still for a couple of days. Nobody would tell the doctor anything. The police would not let him touch Morelli. He went away looking even more colorless and vague.

The big sandy man had returned from the living-room holding one hand behind him. He waited until the doctor had gone, then asked: "Have you got a pistol permit?"

"No."

"Then what are you doing with this?" He brought from behind him the gun I had taken from Dorothy Wynant.

There was nothing I could say.

"You've heard about the Sullivan Act?" he asked.

"Yes."

"Then you know where you stand. This gun yours?"

"No."

"Whose is it?"

"I'll have to try to remember."

He put the pistol in his pocket and sat down on a chair beside the bed. "Listen, Mr. Charles," he said. "I guess we're both of us doing this wrong. I don't want to get tough with you and I don't guess you really want to get tough with me. That hole in your side can't be making you feel any too good, so I ain't going to bother you any more till you've had a little rest. Then maybe we can get together the way we ought to."

"Thanks," I said and meant it. "We'll buy a drink."

Nora said, "Sure," and got up from the edge of the bed.

The big sandy man watched her go out of the room. He

shook his head solemnly. His voice was solemn: "By God, sir, you're a lucky man." He suddenly held out his hand. "My name's Guild, John Guild."

"You know mine." We shook hands.

Nora came back with a siphon, a bottle of Scotch, and some glasses on a tray. She tried to give Morelli a drink, but Guild stopped her. "It's mighty kind of you, Mrs. Charles, but it's against the law to give a prisoner drinks or drugs except on a doctor's say-so." He looked at me. "Ain't that right?"

I said it was. The rest of us drank.

Presently Guild set down his empty glass and stood up. "I got to take this gun along with me, but don't you worry about that. We got plenty of time to talk when you're feeling better." He took Nora's hand and made an awkward bow over it. "I hope you didn't mind what I said back there awhile ago, but I meant it in a—"

Nora can smile very nicely. She gave him one of her nicest smiles. "Mind? I liked it."

She let the policemen and their prisoner out. Keyser had gone a few minutes before.

"He's sweet," she said when she came back from the door. "Hurt much?"

"No."

"It's pretty much my fault, isn't it?"

"Nonsense. How about another drink?"

She poured me one. "I wouldn't take too many of these today."

"I won't," I promised. "I could do with some kippers for breakfast. And, now our troubles seem to be over for a while, you might have them send up our absentee watchdog. And tell the operator not to give us any calls; there'll probably be reporters."

"What are you going to tell the police about Dorothy's pistol? You'll have to tell them something, won't you?"

"I don't know yet."

"Tell me the truth, Nick: have I been too silly?"

I shook my head. "Just silly enough."

She laughed, said, "You're a Greek louse," and went around to the telephone.

9

Nora said: "You're just showing off, that's all it is. And what for? I know bullets bounce off you. You don't have to prove it to me."

"It's not going to hurt me to get up."

"And it's not going to hurt you to stay in bed at least one day. The doctor said—"

"If he knew anything he'd cure his own snuffles." I sat up and put my feet on the floor. Asta tickled them with her tongue.

Nora brought me slippers and robe. "All right, hard guy, get up and bleed on the rugs."

I stood up cautiously and seemed to be all right as long as I went easy with my left arm and kept out of the way of Asta's front feet.

"Be reasonable," I said. "I didn't want to get mixed up with these people—still don't—but a fat lot of good that's doing me. Well, I can't just blunder out of it. I've got to see."

"Let's go away," she suggested. "Let's go to Bermuda or Havana for a week or two, or back to the Coast."

"I'd still have to tell the police some kind of story about that gun. And suppose it turns out to be the gun she was killed with? If they don't know already they're finding out."

"Do you really think it is?"

"That's guessing. We'll go there for dinner tonight and—"

"We'll do nothing of the kind. Have you gone completely nuts? If you want to see anybody have them come here."

"It's not the same thing." I put my arms around her. "Stop worrying about this scratch. I'm all right."

"You're showing off," she said. "You want to let people see you're a hero who can't be stopped by bullets."

"Don't be nasty."

"I will be nasty. I'm not going to have you—"

I shut her mouth with a hand over it. "I want to see the Jorgensens together at home, I want to see Macaulay, and I want to see Studsy Burke. I've been pushed around too much. I've got to see about things."

"You're so damned pig-headed," she complained. "Well, it's only five o'clock. Lie down till it's time to dress."

I made myself comfortable on the living-room sofa. We had the afternoon papers sent up. Morelli, it seemed, had shot me—twice for one of the papers and three times for another—when I tried to arrest him for Julia Wolf's murder, and I was too near death to see anybody or to be moved to a hospital. There were pictures of Morelli and a thirteen-year-old one of me in a pretty funny-looking hat, taken, I remembered, when I was working on the Wall Street explosion. Most of the follow-up stories on the murder of Julia Wolf were rather vague. We were reading them when our little constant visitor, Dorothy Wynant, arrived.

I could hear her at the door when Nora opened it: "They wouldn't send my name up, so I sneaked up. Please don't send me away. I can help you nurse Nick. I'll do anything. Please, Nora."

Nora had a chance then to say: "Come on in."

Dorothy came in. She goggled at me. "B-but the papers said you—"

"Do I look like I'm dying? What's happened to you?" Her lower lip was swollen and cut near one corner, there was a bruise on one cheek-bone and two fingernail scratches down the other cheek, and her eyes were red and swollen.

"Mamma beat me," she said. "Look." She dropped her coat on the floor, tore off a button unbuttoning her dress, took an arm out of its sleeve, and pushed the dress down to show her back. There were dark bruises on her arm, and her back was criss-crossed by long red welts. She was crying now. "See?"

Nora put an arm around her. "You poor kid."

"What'd she beat you for?" I asked.

She turned from Nora and knelt on the floor beside my sofa. Asta came over and nuzzled her. "She thought I came—came to see you about Father and Julia Wolf." Sobs broke up her sentences. "That's why she came over here—to find out—and you made her think I didn't. You—you made her think you didn't care anything about what happened—just like you made me—and she was all right till she saw the papers this afternoon. Then she knew—she knew you'd been lying about not having anything to do with it. She beat me to try to make me tell her what I'd told you."

"What'd you tell her?"

"I couldn't tell her anything. I—I couldn't tell her about Chris. I couldn't tell her anything."

"Was he there?"

"Yes."

"And he let her beat you like this?"

"But he—he never makes her stop."

I said to Nora: "For God's sake, let's have a drink."

Nora said, "Sure," picked up Dorothy's coat, laid it across the back of a chair, and went into the pantry.

Dorothy said: "Please let me stay here, Nick. I won't be any trouble, honestly, and you told me yourself I ought to walk out on them. You know you did, and I've got nowhere else to go. Please."

"Take it easy. This thing needs a little figuring out. I'm as much afraid of Mimi as you are, you know. What did she think you'd told me?"

"She must know something—something about the murder that she thinks I know—but I don't, Nick. Honest to God, I don't."

"That helps a lot," I complained. "But listen, sister: there are things you know and we're going to start with those. You come clean at and from the beginning—or we don't play."

She made a movement as if she were about to cross her heart. "I swear I will," she said.

"That'll be swell. Now let's drink." We took a glass apiece from Nora. "Tell her you were leaving for good?"

"No, I didn't say anything. Maybe she doesn't know yet I'm not in my room."

"That helps some."

"You're not going to make me go back?" she cried.

Nora said over her glass: "The child can't stay and be beaten like that, Nick."

I said: "Sh-h-h. I don't know. I was just thinking that if we're going there for dinner maybe it's better for Mimi not to know—"

Dorothy stared at me with horrified eyes while Nora said: "Don't think you're going to take me there now."

Then Dorothy spoke rapidly: "But Mamma doesn't expect

you. I don't even know whether she'll be there. The papers said you were dying. She doesn't think you're coming."

"So much the better," I said. "We'll surprise them."

She put her face, white now, close to mine, spilling some of her drink on my sleeve in her excitement. "Don't go. You can't go there now. Listen to me. Listen to Nora. You can't go." She turned her white face around to look up at Nora. "Can he? Tell him he can't."

Nora, not shifting the focus of her dark eyes from my face, said: "Wait, Dorothy. He ought to know what's best. What is it, Nick?"

I made a face at her. "I'm just fumbling around. If you say Dorothy stays here, she stays. I guess she can sleep with Asta. But you've got to leave me alone on the rest of it. I don't know what I'm going to do because I don't know what's being done to me. I've got to find out. I've got to find out in my own way."

"We won't interfere," Dorothy said. "Will we, Nora?"

Nora continued to look at me, saying nothing.

I asked Dorothy: "Where'd you get that gun? And nothing out of books this time."

She moistened her lower lip and her face became pinker. She cleared her throat.

"Careful," I said. "If it's another piece of chewing-gum, I'll phone Mimi to come get you."

"Give her a chance," Nora said.

Dorothy cleared her throat again. "Can—can I tell you something that happened to me when I was a little child?"

"Has it got anything to do with the gun?"

"Not exactly, but it'll help you understand why I—"

"Not now. Some other time. Where'd you get the gun?"

"I wish you'd let me." She hung her head.

"Where'd you get the gun?"

Her voice was barely audible. "From a man in a speakeasy."

I said: "I knew we'd get the truth at last." Nora frowned and shook her head at me. "All right, say you did. What speakeasy?"

Dorothy raised her head. "I don't know. It was on Tenth Avenue, I think. Your friend Mr. Quinn would know. He took me there."

"You met him after you left us that night?"

"Yes."

"By accident, I suppose."

She looked reproachfully at me. "I'm trying to tell you the truth, Nick. I'd promised to meet him at a place called the Palma Club. He wrote the address down for me. So after I said good-night to you and Nora, I met him there and we went to a lot of places, winding up in this place where I got the gun. It was an awful tough place. You can ask him if I'm not telling the truth."

"Quinn get the gun for you?"

"No. He'd passed out then. He was sleeping with his head on the table. I left him there. They said they'd get him home all right."

"And the gun?"

"I'm coming to it." She began to blush. "He told me it was a gunman's hang-out. That's why I'd said let's go there. And after he went to sleep I got to talking to a man there, an awful tough-looking man. I was fascinated. And all the time I didn't want to go home, I wanted to come back here, but I didn't know if you'd let me." Her face was quite red now and in her embarrassment she blurred her words. "So I thought perhaps if I—if you thought I was in a terrible fix—and, besides, that way I wouldn't feel so silly. Anyhow, I asked this awful tough-looking gangster, or whatever he was, if he would sell me a pistol or tell me where I could buy one. He thought I was kidding and laughed at first, but I told him I wasn't, and then he kept on grinning, but he said he'd see, and when he came back he said yes, he could get me one and asked how much I would pay for it. I didn't have much money, but I offered him my bracelet, but I guess he didn't think it was any good, because he said no, he'd have to have cash, so finally I gave him twelve dollars—all I had but a dollar for the taxi—and he gave me the pistol and I came over here and made up that about being afraid to go home because of Chris." She finished so rapidly her words ran together, and she sighed as if very glad to have finished.

"Then Chris hasn't been making passes at you?"

She bit her lip. "Yes, but not—not that bad." She put both

hands on my arm, and her face almost touched mine. "You've got to believe me. I couldn't tell you all that, couldn't make myself out such a cheap little lying fool, if it wasn't the truth."

"It makes more sense if I don't believe you," I said. "Twelve bucks isn't enough money. We'll let that rest for a minute, though. Did you know Mimi was going to see Julia Wolf that afternoon?"

"No. I didn't even know she was trying to find my father then. They didn't say where they were going that afternoon."

"They?"

"Yes, Chris left the apartment with her."

"What time was that?"

She wrinkled her forehead. "It must've been pretty close to three o'clock—after two thirty, anyway—because I remember I was late for a date to go shopping with Elsie Hamilton and was hurrying into my clothes."

"They come back together?"

"I don't know. They were both home before I came."

"What time was that?"

"Some time after six. Nick, you don't think they— Oh, I remember something she said while she was dressing. I don't know what Chris said, but she said: 'When I ask her she'll tell me,' in that Queen-of-France way she talks sometimes. You know. I didn't hear anything else. Does that mean anything?"

"What'd she tell you about the murder when you came home?"

"Oh, just about finding her and how upset she was and about the police and everything."

"She seem very shocked?"

Dorothy shook her head. "No, just excited. You know Mamma." She stared at me for a moment, asked slowly: "You don't think she had anything to do with it?"

"What do you think?"

"I hadn't thought. I just thought about my father." A little later she said gravely: "If he did it, it's because he's crazy, but she'd kill somebody if she wanted to."

"It doesn't have to be either of them," I reminded her.

"The police seem to have picked Morelli. What'd she want to find your father for?"

"For money. We're broke: Chris spent it all." She pulled down the corners of her mouth. "I suppose we all helped, but he spent most of it. Mamma's afraid he'll leave her if she hasn't any money."

"How do you know that?"

"I've heard them talk."

"Do you think he will?"

She nodded with certainty. "Unless she has money."

I looked at my watch and said: "The rest of it'll have to wait till we get back. You can stay here tonight, anyhow. Make yourself comfortable and have the restaurant send up your dinner. It's probably better if you don't go out."

She stared miserably at me and said nothing.

Nora patted her shoulder. "I don't know what he's doing, Dorothy, but if he says we ought to go there for dinner he probably knows what he's talking about. He wouldn't—"

Dorothy smiled and jumped up from the floor. "I believe you. I won't be silly any more."

I called the desk on the telephone and asked them to send up our mail. There were a couple of letters for Nora, one for me, some belated Christmas cards (including one from Larry Crowley, which was a copy of Haldeman-Julius Little Blue Book Number 1534, with "and a Merry Christmas," followed by Larry's name enclosed in a holly wreath, all printed in red under the book's title, *How to Test Your Urine at Home*), a number of telephone-call memoranda slips, and a telegram from Philadelphia:

NICK CHARLES
THE NORMANDIE   NEW YORK N Y
WILL YOU COMMUNICATE WITH HERBERT MACAULAY TO
DISCUSS TAKING CHARGE OF INVESTIGATION OF WOLF
MURDER STOP AM GIVING HIM FULL INSTRUCTIONS STOP
BEST REGARDS
                              CLYDE MILLER WYNANT

I put the telegram in an envelope with a note saying it had just reached me and sent it by messenger to the Police Department Homicide Bureau.

10

IN THE TAXICAB Nora asked: "You're sure you feel all right?"

"Sure."

"And this isn't going to be too much for you?"

"I'm all right. What'd you think of the girl's story?"

She hesitated. "You don't believe her, do you?"

"God forbid—at least till I've checked it up."

"You know more about this kind of thing than I do," she said, "but I think she was at least trying to tell the truth."

"A lot of the fancier yarns come from people who are trying to do that. It's not easy once you're out of the habit."

She said: "I bet you know a lot about human nature, Mr. Charles. Now don't you? Some time you must tell me about your experiences as a detective."

I said: "Buying a gun for twelve bucks in a speakeasy. Well, maybe, but . . ."

We rode a couple of blocks in silence. Then Nora asked: "What's really the matter with her?"

"Her old man's crazy: she thinks she is."

"How do you know?"

"You asked me. I'm telling you."

"You mean you're guessing?"

"I mean that's what's wrong with her; I don't know whether Wynant's actually nuts and I don't know whether she inherited any of it if he is, but she thinks both answers are yes, and it's got her doing figure eights."

When we stopped in front of the Courtland she said: "That's horrible, Nick. Somebody ought to—"

I said I didn't know: maybe Dorothy was right. "Likely as not she's making doll clothes for Asta right now."

We sent our names up to the Jorgensens and, after some delay, were told to go up. Mimi met us in the corridor when we stepped out of the elevator, met us with open arms and many words. "Those wretched newspapers. They had me frantic with their nonsense about your being at death's door. I phoned twice, but they wouldn't give me your apartment, wouldn't tell me how you were." She had both of my hands. "I'm so glad, Nick, that it was just a pack of lies, even if you will have to take pot luck with us tonight. Naturally I didn't expect you and— But you're pale. You really have been hurt."

"Not much," I said. "A bullet scraped my side, but it doesn't amount to anything."

"And you came to dinner in spite of that! That is flattering, but I'm afraid it's foolish too." She turned to Nora. "Are you sure it was wise to let him—"

"I'm not sure," Nora said, "but he wanted to come."

"Men are such idiots," Mimi said. She put an arm around me. "They either make mountains out of nothing or utterly neglect things that may— But come in. Here, let me help you."

"It's not that bad," I assured her, but she insisted on leading me to a chair and packing me in with half a dozen cushions.

Jorgensen came in, shook hands with me, and said he was glad to find me more alive than the newspapers had said. He bowed over Nora's hand. "If I may be excused one little minute more I will finish the cocktails." He went out.

Mimi said: "I don't know where Dorry is. Off sulking somewhere, I suppose. You haven't any children, have you?"

Nora said: "No."

"You're missing a lot, though they can be a great trial sometimes." Mimi sighed. "I suppose I'm not strict enough. When I do have to scold Dorry she seems to think I'm a complete monster." Her face brightened. "Here's my other tot. You remember Mr. Charles, Gilbert. And this is Mrs. Charles."

Gilbert Wynant was two years younger than his sister, a gangling pale blond boy of eighteen with not too much chin under a somewhat slack mouth. The size of his remarkably clear blue eyes, and the length of the lashes, gave him a slightly effeminate look. I hoped he had stopped being the whining little nuisance he was as a kid.

Jorgensen brought in his cocktails, and Mimi insisted on being told about the shooting. I told her, making it even more meaningless than it had been.

"But why should he have come to you?" she asked.

"God knows. I'd like to know. The police'd like to know."

Gilbert said: "I read somewhere that when habitual criminals are accused of things they didn't do—even little things—they're much more upset by it than other people would be. Do you think that's so, Mr. Charles?"

"It's likely."

"Except," Gilbert added, "when it's something big, you know, something they would like to've done."

I said again it was likely.

Mimi said: "Don't be polite to Gil if he starts talking nonsense, Nick. His head's so cluttered up with reading. Get us another cocktail, darling."

He went over to get the shaker. Nora and Jorgensen were in a corner sorting phonograph records.

I said: "I had a wire from Wynant today."

Mimi looked warily around the room, then leaned forward, and her voice was almost a whisper: "What did he say?"

"Wanted me to find out who killed her. It was sent from Philadelphia this afternoon."

She was breathing heavily. "Are you going to do it?"

I shrugged. "I turned it over to the police."

Gilbert came back with the shaker. Jorgensen and Nora had put Bach's *Little Fugue* on the phonograph. Mimi quickly drank her cocktail and had Gilbert pour her another.

He sat down and said: "I want to ask you: can you tell dope-addicts by looking at them?" He was trembling.

"Very seldom. Why?"

"I was wondering. Even if they're confirmed addicts?"

"The further along they are, the better the chances of noticing that something's wrong, but you can't often be sure it's dope."

"Another thing," he said, "Gross says when you're stabbed you only feel a sort of push at the time and it's not until afterwards that it begins to hurt. Is that so?"

"Yes, if you're stabbed reasonably hard with a reasonably sharp knife. A bullet's the same way: you only feel the blow—and with a small-calibre steel-jacketed bullet not much of that—at first. The rest comes when the air gets to it."

Mimi drank her third cocktail and said: "I think you're both being indecently gruesome, especially after what happened to Nick today. Do try to find Dorry, Gil. You must know some of her friends. Phone them. I suppose she'll be along presently, but I worry about her."

"She's over at our place," I said.

"At your place?" Her surprise may have been genuine.

"She came over this afternoon and asked if she could stay with us awhile."

She smiled tolerantly and shook her head. "These young-sters!" She stopped smiling. "Awhile?"

I nodded.

Gilbert, apparently waiting to ask me another question, showed no interest in this conversation between his mother and me.

Mimi smiled again and said: "I'm sorry she's bothering you and your wife, but it's a relief to know she's there instead of off the Lord only knows where. She'll have finished her pout-ing by the time you get back. Send her along home, will you?" She poured me a cocktail. "You've been awfully nice to her."

I did not say anything.

Gilbert began: "Mr. Charles, do criminals—I mean profes-sional criminals—usually—"

"Don't interrupt, Gil," Mimi said. "You will send her along home, won't you?" She was pleasant, but she was Dorothy's Queen of France.

"She can stay if she wants. Nora likes her."

She shook a crooked finger at me. "But I won't have you spoiling her like that. I suppose she told you all sorts of non-sense about me."

"She did say something about a beating."

"There you are," Mimi said complacently, as if that proved her point. "No, you'll have to send her home, Nick."

I finished my cocktail.

"Well?" she asked.

"She can stay with us if she wants, Mimi. We like having her."

"That's ridiculous. Her place is at home. I want her here." Her voice was a little sharp. "She's only a baby. You shouldn't encourage her foolish notions."

"I'm not doing anything. If she wants to stay, she stays."

Anger was a very pretty thing in Mimi's blue eyes. "She's

my child and she's a minor. You've been very kind to her, but this isn't being kind to her or to me, and I won't have it. If you won't send her home, I'll take steps to bring her home. I'd rather not be disagreeable about it, but"—she leaned forward and deliberately spaced her words—"she's coming home."

I said: "You don't want to pick a fight with me, Mimi."

She looked at me as if she were going to say I love you, and asked: "Is that a threat?"

"All right," I said, "have me arrested for kidnapping, contributing to the delinquency of a minor, and mopery."

She said suddenly in a harsh enraged voice: "And tell your wife to stop pawing my husband."

Nora, looking for another phonograph record with Jorgensen, had a hand on his sleeve. They turned to look at Mimi in surprise.

I said: "Nora, Mrs. Jorgensen wants you to keep your hands off Mr. Jorgensen."

"I'm awfully sorry." Nora smiled at Mimi, then looked at me, put a very artificial expression of concern on her face, and in a somewhat singsong voice, as if she were a schoolchild reciting a piece, said: "Oh, Nick, you're pale. I'm sure you have exceeded your strength and will have a relapse. I'm sorry, Mrs. Jorgensen, but I think I should get him home and to bed right away. You will forgive us, won't you?"

Mimi said she would. Everybody was the soul of politeness to everybody else. We went downstairs and got a taxicab.

"Well," Nora said, "so you talked yourself out of a dinner. What do you want to do now? Go home and eat with Dorothy?"

I shook my head. "I can do without Wynants for a little while. Let's go to Max's: I'd like some snails."

"Right. Did you find out anything?"

"Nothing."

She said meditatively: "It's a shame that guy's so handsome."

"What's he like?"

"Just a big doll. It's a shame."

We had dinner and went back to the Normandie. Dorothy was not there. I felt as if I had expected that.

Nora went through the rooms, called up the desk. No note, no message had been left for us.

"So what?" she asked.

It was not quite ten o'clock. "Maybe nothing," I said. "Maybe anything. My guess is she'll show up about three in the morning, tight, with a machine-gun she bought in Childs'."

Nora said: "To hell with her. Get into pyjamas and lie down."

I I

MY SIDE felt a lot better when Nora called me at noon the next day. "My nice policeman wants to see you," she said. "How do you feel?"

"Terrible. I must've gone to bed sober." I pushed Asta out of the way and got up.

Guild rose with a drink in his hand when I entered the living-room, and smiled all across his broad sandy face. "Well, well, Mr. Charles, you look spry enough this morning."

I shook hands with him and said yes I felt pretty good, and we sat down.

He frowned good-naturedly. "Just the same, you oughtn't've played that trick on me."

"Trick?"

"Sure, running off to see people when I'd put off asking you questions to give you a chance to rest up. I kind of figured that ought to give me first call on you, as you might say."

"I didn't think," I said. "I'm sorry. See that wire I got from Wynant?"

"Uh-huh. We're running it out in Philly."

"Now about that gun," I began, "I—"

He stopped me. "What gun? That ain't a gun any more. The firing pin's busted off, the guts are rusted and jammed. If anybody's fired it in six months—or could—I'm the Pope of Rome. Don't let's waste any time talking about that piece of junk."

I laughed. "That explains a lot. I took it away from a drunk who said he'd bought it in a speakeasy for twelve bucks. I believe him now."

"Somebody'll sell him the City Hall one of these days. Man to man, Mr. Charles, are you working on the Wolf job or ain't you?"

"You saw the wire from Wynant."

"I did. Then you ain't working for him. I'm still asking you."

"I'm not a private detective any more. I'm not any kind of a detective."

"I heard that. I'm still asking you."

"All right. No."

He thought for a moment, said: "Then let me put it another way: are you interested in the job?"

"I know the people, naturally I'm interested."

"And that's all?"

"Yes."

"And you don't expect to be working on it?"

The telephone rang and Nora went to answer it.

"To be honest with you, I don't know. If people keep on pushing me into it, I don't know how far they'll carry me."

Guild wagged his head up and down. "I can see that. I don't mind telling you I'd like to have you in on it—on the right side."

"You mean not on Wynant's side. Did he do it?"

"That I couldn't say, Mr. Charles, but I don't have to tell you he ain't helping us any to find out who did it."

Nora appeared in the doorway. "Telephone, Nick."

Herbert Macaulay was on the wire. "Hello, Charles. How's the wounded?"

"I'm all right, thanks."

"Did you hear from Wynant?"

"Yes."

"I got a letter from him saying he had wired you. Are you too sick to—"

"No, I'm up and around. If you'll be in your office late this afternoon I'll drop in."

"Swell," he said. "I'll be here till six."

I returned to the living-room. Nora was inviting Guild to

have lunch while we had breakfast. He said it was mighty kind of her. I said I ought to have a drink before breakfast. Nora went to order meals and pour drinks.

Guild shook his head and said: "She's a mighty fine woman, Mr. Charles."

I nodded solemnly.

He said: "Suppose you should get pushed into this thing, as you say, I'd like it a lot more to feel you were working with us than against us."

"So would I."

"That's a bargain then," he said. He hunched his chair around a little. "I don't guess you remember me, but back when you were working this town I was walking beat on Forty-third Street."

"Of course," I said, lying politely. "I knew there was something familiar about— Being out of uniform makes a difference."

"I guess it does. I'd like to be able to take it as a fact that you're not holding out anything we don't already know."

"I don't mean to. I don't know what you know. I don't know very much. I haven't seen Macaulay since the murder and I haven't even been following it in the newspapers."

The telephone was ringing again. Nora gave us our drinks and went to answer it.

"What we know ain't much of a secret," Guild said, "and if you want to take the time to listen I don't mind giving it to you." He tasted his drink and nodded approvingly. "Only there's a thing I'd like to ask first. When you went to Mrs. Jorgensen's last night, did you tell her about getting the telegram from him?"

"Yes, and I told her I'd turned it over to you."

"What'd she say?"

"Nothing. She asked questions. She's trying to find him."

He put his head a little to one side and partly closed one eye. "You don't think there's any chance of them being in cahoots, do you?" He held up a hand. "Understand I don't know why they would be or what it'd be all about if they were, but I'm just asking."

"Anything's possible," I said, "but I'd say it was pretty safe they aren't working together. Why?"

"I guess you're right." Then he added vaguely: "But there's a couple of points." He sighed. "There always is. Well, Mr. Charles, here's just about all we know for certain and if you can give us a little something more here and there as we go along I'll be mighty thankful to you."

I said something about doing my best.

"Well, along about the 3rd of last October Wynant tells Macaulay he's got to leave town for a while. He don't tell Macaulay where he's going or what for, but Macaulay gets the idea that he's off to work on some invention or other that he wants to keep quiet—and he gets it out of Julia Wolf later that he's right—and he guesses Wynant's gone off to hide somewhere in the Adirondacks, but when he asks her about that later she says she don't know any more about it than he does."

"She know what the invention was?"

Guild shook his head. "Not according to Macaulay, only that it was probably something that he needed room for and machinery or things that cost money, because that's what he was fixing up with Macaulay. He was fixing it so Macaulay could get hold of his stocks and bonds and other things he owned and turn 'em into money when he wanted it and take care of his banking and everything just like Wynant himself."

"Power of attorney covering everything, huh?"

"Exactly. And listen, when he wanted money, he wanted it in cash."

"He was always full of screwy notions," I said.

"That's what everybody says. The idea seems to be he don't want to take any chances on anybody tracing him through checks, or anybody up there knowing he's Wynant. That's why he didn't take the girl along with him—didn't even let her know where he was, if she was telling the truth—and let his whiskers grow." With his left hand he stroked an imaginary beard.

" 'Up there,' " I quoted. "So he was in the Adirondacks?"

Guild moved one shoulder. "I just said that because that and Philadelphia are the only ideas anybody's give us. We're trying the mountains, but we don't know. Maybe Australia."

"And how much of this money in cash did Wynant want?"

"I can tell you that exactly." He took a wad of soiled bent

and dog-eared papers out of his pocket, selected an envelope
that was a shade dirtier than most of the others, and stuffed
the others back in his pocket. "The day after he talked to
Macaulay he drew five thousand out of the bank himself, in
cash. On the 28th—this is October, you understand—he had
Macaulay get another five for him, and twenty-five hundred
on the 6th of November, and a thousand on the 15th, and
seventy-five hundred on the 30th, and fifteen hundred on the
6th—that would be December—and a thousand on the 18th,
and five thousand on the 22nd, which was the day before she
was killed."

"Nearly thirty thou," I said. "A nice bank balance he had."

"Twenty-eight thousand five hundred, to be exact." Guild
returned the envelope to his pocket. "But you understand it
wasn't all in there. After the first call Macaulay would sell
something every time to raise the dough." He felt in his
pocket again. "I got a list of the stuff he sold, if you want to
see it."

I said I didn't. "How'd he turn the money over to
Wynant?"

"Wynant would write the girl when he wanted it, and she'd
get it from Macaulay. He's got her receipts."

"And how'd she get it to Wynant?"

Guild shook his head. "She told Macaulay she used to meet
him places he told her, but he thinks she knew where he was,
though she always said she didn't."

"And maybe she still had that last five thousand on her
when she was killed, huh?"

"Which might make it robbery, unless"—Guild's watery
gray eyes were almost shut—"he killed her when he came
there to get it."

"Or unless," I suggested, "somebody else who killed her
for some other reason found the money there and thought
they might as well take it along."

"Sure," he agreed. "Things like that happen all the time.
It even happens sometimes that the first people that find a
body like that pick up a little something before they turn in
the alarm." He held up a big hand. "Of course, with Mrs.
Jorgensen—a lady like that—I hope you don't think I'm—"

"Besides," I said, "she wasn't alone, was she?"

"For a little while. The phone in the apartment was out of whack, and the elevator boy rode the superintendent down to phone from the office. But get me right on this, I'm not saying Mrs. Jorgensen did anything funny. A lady like that wouldn't be likely—"

"What was the matter with the phone?" I asked.

The doorbell rang.

"Well," Guild said, "I don't know just what to make of it. The phone had—"

He broke off as a waiter came in and began to set a table.

"About the phone," Guild said when we were sitting at the table, "I don't know just what to make of it, as I said. It had a bullet right smack through the mouthpiece of it."

"Accidental or—?"

"I'd just as lief ask you. It was from the same gun as the four that hit her, of course, but whether he missed her with that one or did it on purpose I don't know. It seems like a kind of noisy way to put a phone on the bum."

"That reminds me," I said, "didn't anybody hear all this shooting? A .32's not a shotgun, but somebody ought to've heard it."

"Sure," he said disgustedly. "The place is lousy with people that think they heard things now, but nobody did anything about it then, and God knows they don't get together much on what they think they heard."

"It's always like that," I said sympathetically.

"Don't I know it." He put a forkful of food in his mouth. "Where was I? Oh, yes, about Wynant. He gave up his apartment when he went away, and put his stuff in storage. We been looking through it—the stuff—but ain't found anything yet to show where he went or even what he was working on, which we thought maybe might help. We didn't have any better luck in his shop on First Avenue. It's been locked up too since he went away, except that she used to go down there for an hour or two once or twice a week to take care of his mail and things. There's nothing to tell us anything in the mail that's come since she got knocked off. We didn't find anything in her place to help." He smiled at Nora. "I guess this must be pretty dull to you, Mrs. Charles."

"Dull?" She was surprised. "I'm sitting on the edge of my chair."

"Ladies usually like more color," he said, and coughed, "kind of glamour. Anyways, we got nothing to show where he's been, only he phones Macaulay last Friday and says to meet him at two o'clock in the Plaza lobby. Macaulay wasn't in, so he just left the message."

"Macaulay was here," I said, "for lunch."

"He told me. Well, Macaulay don't get to the Plaza till nearly three and he don't find any Wynant there and Wynant ain't registered there. He tries describing him, with and without a beard, but nobody at the Plaza remembers seeing him. He phones his office, but Wynant ain't called up again. And then he phones Julia Wolf and she tells him she don't even know Wynant's in town, which he figures is a lie, because he had just give her five thousand dollars for Wynant yesterday and figures Wynant's come for it, but he just says all right and hangs up and goes on about his business."

"His business such as what?" I asked.

Guild stopped chewing the piece of roll he had just bitten off. "I guess it wouldn't hurt to know, at that. I'll find out. There didn't seem to be anything pointing at him, so we didn't bother with that, but it don't ever hurt any to know who's got an alibi and who ain't."

I shook my head no at the question he had decided not to ask. "I don't see anything pointing at him, except that he's Wynant's lawyer and probably knows more than he's telling."

"Sure. I understand. Well, that's what people have lawyers for, I guess. Now about the girl: maybe Julia Wolf wasn't her real name at all. We ain't been able to find out for sure yet, but we have found out she wasn't the kind of dame you'd expect him to be trusting to handle all that dough—I mean if he knew about her."

"Had a record?"

He wagged his head up and down. "This is elegant stew. A couple of years before she went to work for him she did six months on a badger-game charge out West, in Cleveland, under the name of Rhoda Stewart."

"You suppose Wynant knew that?"

"Search me. Don't look like he'd turned her loose with that dough if he did, but you can't tell. They tell me he was kind of nuts about her, and you know how guys can go. She was running around off and on with this Shep Morelli and his boys too."

"Have you really got anything on him?" I asked.

"Not on this," he said regretfully, "but we wanted him for a couple of other things." He drew his sandy brows together a little. "I wish I knew what sent him here to see you. Of course these junkies are likely to do anything, but I wish I knew."

"I told you all I knew."

"I'm not doubting that," he assured me. He turned to Nora. "I hope you don't think we were too rough with him, but you see you got to—"

Nora smiled and said she understood perfectly and filled his cup with coffee.

"Thank you, ma'am."

"What's a junkie?" she asked.

"Hop-head."

She looked at me. "Was Morelli—?"

"Primed to the ears," I said.

"Why didn't you tell me?" she complained. "I miss everything." She left the table to answer the telephone.

Guild asked: "You going to prosecute him for shooting you?"

"Not unless you need it."

He shook his head. His voice was casual, though there was some curiosity in his eyes. "I guess we got enough on him for a while."

"You were telling me about the girl."

"Yes," he said. "Well, we found out she's been spending a lot of nights away from her apartment—two or three days at a stretch sometimes. Maybe that's when she was meeting Wynant. I don't know. We ain't been able to knock any holes in Morelli's story of not seeing her for three months. What do you make of that?"

"The same thing you do," I replied. "It's just about three months since Wynant went off. Maybe it means something, maybe not."

Nora came in and said Harrison Quinn was on the telephone. He told me he had sold some bonds I was writing off losses on and gave me the prices.

"Have you seen Dorothy Wynant?" I asked.

"Not since I left her in your place, but I'm meeting her at the Palma for cocktails this afternoon. Come to think of it, she told me not to tell you. How about that gold, Nick? You're missing something if you don't get in on it. Those wild men from the West are going to give us some kind of inflation as soon as Congress meets, that's certain, and even if they don't, everybody expects them to. As I told you last week, there's already talk of a pool being—"

"All right," I said and gave him an order to buy some Dome Mines at 12½.

He remembered then that he had seen something in the newspapers about my having been shot. He was pretty vague about it and paid very little attention to my assurances that I was all right. "I suppose that means no ping-pong for a couple of days," he said with what seemed genuine regret. "Listen: you've got tickets for the opening tonight. If you can't use them I'll be—"

"We're going to use them. Thanks just the same."

He laughed and said good-by.

A waiter was carrying away the table when I returned to the living-room. Guild had made himself comfortable on the sofa. Nora was telling him: ". . . have to go away over the Christmas holidays every year because what's left of my family make a fuss over them and if we're home they come to visit us or we have to visit them, and Nick doesn't like it." Asta was licking her paws in a corner.

Guild looked at his watch. "I'm taking up a lot of you folks' time. I didn't mean to impose—"

I sat down and said: "We were just about up to the murder, weren't we?"

"Just about." He relaxed on the sofa again. "That was on Friday the 23rd at some time before twenty minutes after three in the afternoon, which was the time Mrs. Jorgensen got there and found her. It's kind of hard to say how long she'd been laying there dying before she was found. The only thing we know is that she was all right and answered the phone—and the phone was all right—at about half past two, when Mrs. Jorgensen called her up and was still all right around three, when Macaulay phoned."

"I didn't know Mrs. Jorgensen phoned."

"It's a fact." Guild cleared his throat. "We didn't suspect anything there, you understand, but we checked it up just as a matter of course and found out from the girl at the switchboard at the Courtland that she put the call through for Mrs. J. about two thirty."

"What did Mrs. J. say?"

"She said she called up to ask where she could find Wynant, but this Julia Wolf said she didn't know, so Mrs. J., thinking she's lying and maybe she can get her to tell the truth if she sees her, asks if she can drop in for a minute, and she says sure." He frowned at my right knee. "Well, she went there and found her. The apartment-house people don't remember seeing anybody going in or out of the Wolf apartment, but that's easy. A dozen people could do it without being seen. The gun wasn't there. There wasn't any signs of anybody busting in, and things in the place hadn't been disturbed any more than I've told you. I mean the place didn't look like it had been frisked. She had on a diamond ring that must've been worth a few hundred and there was thirty-some bucks in her bag. The people there know Wynant and Morelli—both of 'em have been in and out enough—but claim they ain't seen either for some time. The fire-escape window was locked and the fire-escape didn't look like it had been walked on recently." He turned his hands over, palms up. "I guess that's the crop."

"No fingerprints?"

"Hers, some belonging to the people that clean up the place, near as we can figure. Nothing any good to us."

"Nothing out of her friends?"

"She didn't seem to have any—not any close ones."

"How about the—what was his name?—Nunheim who identified her as a friend of Morelli's?"

"He just knew her by sight through seeing her around with Morelli and recognized her picture when he saw it in the paper."

"Who is he?"

"He's all right. We know all about him."

"You wouldn't hold out on me, would you," I asked, "after getting me to promise not to hold out on you?"

Guild said: "Well, if it don't go any further, he's a fellow that does some work for the department now and then."

"Oh."

He stood up. "I hate to say it, but that's just about as far as we've got. You got anything you can help with?"

"No."

He looked at me steadily for a moment. "What do you think of it?"

"That diamond ring, was it an engagement ring?"

"She had it on that finger." After a pause he asked: "Why?"

"It might help to know who bought it for her. I'm going to see Macaulay this afternoon. If anything turns up I'll give you a ring. It looks like Wynant, all right, but—"

He growled good-naturedly, "Uh-huh, but," shook hands with Nora and me, thanked us for our whisky, our lunch, our hospitality, and our kindness in general, and went away.

I told Nora: "I'm not one to suggest that your charm wouldn't make any man turn himself inside out for you, but don't be too sure that guy isn't kidding us."

"So it's come to that," she said. "You're jealous of policemen."

12

MACAULAY'S letter from Clyde Wynant was quite a document. It was very badly typewritten on plain white paper and dated Philadelphia, Pa., December 26, 1932. It read:

Dear Herbert:

I am telegraphing Nick Charles who worked for me you will remember some years ago and who is in New York to get in touch with you about the terrible death of poor Julia. I want you to do everything in your power to [a line had been x'd and m'd out here so that it was impossible to make anything at all of it]

persuade him to find her murderer. I don't care what it costs—
pay him!

Here are some facts I want you to give him outside of all you
know about it yourself. I don't think he should tell these facts to
the police, but he will know what is best and I want him to have
a completely free hand as I have got the utmost confidence in
him. Perhaps you had better just show him this letter, after which
I must ask you to carefully destroy it.

Here are the facts.

When I met Julia Thursday night to get that $1000 from her
she told me she wanted to quit her job. She said she hadn't been
at all well for some time and her doctor had told her she ought
to go away and rest and now that her uncle's estate had been set-
tled she could afford to and wanted to do it. She had never said
anything about bad health before and I thought she was hiding
her real reason and tried to get it out of her, but she stuck to
what she had said. I didn't know anything about her uncle
dying either. She said it was her Uncle John in Chicago. I sup-
pose that could be looked up if it's important. I couldn't per-
suade her to change her mind, so she was to leave the last day of
the month. She seemed worried or frightened, but she said she
wasn't. I was sorry at first that she was going, but then I wasn't,
because I had always been able to trust her and now I wouldn't
be if she was lying, as I thought she was.

The next fact I want Charles to know is that whatever any-
body may think or whatever was true some time ago Julia and I
["are now" was x'd out lightly] *were at the time of her murder*
and had been for more than a year *not anything more to each*
other than employee and employer. This relationship was the re-
sult of mutual agreement.

Next, I believe some attempt should be made to learn the
present whereabouts of the Victor Rosewater with whom we had
trouble some years ago inasmuch as the experiments I am now
engaged in are in line with those he claimed I cheated him out
of and I consider him quite insane enough to have killed Julia
in a rage at her refusal to tell him where I could be found.

Fourth, and most important, *has my divorced wife been in*
communication with Rosewater? How did she learn I was car-
rying out the experiments with which he once assisted me?

Fifth, the police must be convinced at once that I can tell them nothing about the murder so that they will take no steps to find me—steps that might lead to a discovery of and a premature exposure of my experiments, which I would consider very *dangerous* at this time. This can best be avoided by clearing up the mystery of her murder immediately, and that is what I wish to have done.

I will communicate with you from time to time and if in the meanwhile anything should arise to make communication with me imperative *insert the following advertisement in the Times:*

Abner. Yes. Bunny.

I will thereupon arrange to get in touch with you.

I hope you sufficiently understand the necessity of persuading Charles to act for me, since he is already acquainted with the Rosewater trouble and knows most of the people concerned.

Yours truly,
Clyde Miller Wynant

I put the letter down on Macaulay's desk and said: "It makes a lot of sense. Do you remember what his row with Rosewater was about?"

"Something about changes in the structure of crystals. I can look it up." Macaulay picked up the first sheet of the letter and frowned at it. "He says he got a thousand dollars from her that night. I gave her five thousand for him; she told me that's what he wanted."

"Four thousand from Uncle John's estate?" I suggested.

"Looks like it. That's funny: I never thought she'd gyp him. I'll have to find out about the other money I turned over to her."

"Did you know she'd done a jail sentence in Cleveland on a badger-game charge?"

"No. Had she really?"

"According to the police—under the name of Rhoda Stewart. Where'd Wynant find her?"

He shook his head. "I've no idea."

"Know anything about where she came from originally, relatives, things like that?"

He shook his head again.

"Who was she engaged to?" I asked.

"I didn't know she was engaged."

"She was wearing a diamond ring on that finger."

"That's news to me," he said. He shut his eyes and thought. "No, I can't remember ever noticing an engagement ring." He put his forearms on his desk and grinned over them at me. "Well, what are the chances of getting you to do what he wants?"

"Slim."

"I thought so." He moved a hand to touch the letter. "You know as much about how he feels as I do. What would make you change your mind?"

"I don't—"

"Would it help any if I could persuade him to meet you? Maybe if I told him that was the only way you'd take it—"

"I'm willing to talk to him," I said, "but he'd have to talk a lot straighter than he's writing."

Macaulay asked slowly: "You mean you think he may have killed her?"

"I don't know anything about that," I said. "I don't know as much as the police do, and it's a cinch they haven't got enough on him to make the pinch even if they could find him."

Macaulay sighed. "Being a goof's lawyer is not much fun. I'll try to make him listen to reason, but I know he won't."

"I meant to ask, how are his finances these days? Is he as well fixed as he used to be?"

"Almost. The depression's hurt him some, along with the rest of us, and the royalties from his smelting process have gone pretty much to hell now that the metals are dead, but he can still count on fifty or sixty thousand a year from his glassine and soundproofing patents, with a little more coming in from odds and ends like—" He broke off to ask: "You're not worrying about his ability to pay whatever you'd ask?"

"No, I was just wondering." I thought of something else: "Has he any relatives outside of his ex-wife and children?"

"A sister, Alice Wynant, that hasn't been on speaking terms with him for—it must be four or five years now."

I supposed that was the Aunt Alice the Jorgensens had not gone to see Christmas afternoon. "What'd they fall out about?" I asked.

"He gave an interview to one of the papers saying he didn't

think the Russian Five Year Plan was necessarily doomed to failure. Actually he didn't make it much stronger than that."

I laughed. "They're a—"

"She's even better than he is. She can't remember things. The time her brother had his appendix out, she and Mimi were in a taxi going to see him the first afternoon and they passed a hearse coming from the direction of the hospital. Miss Alice turned pale and grabbed Mimi by the arm and said: 'Oh, dear! If that should be what's-his-name!' "

"Where does she live?"

"On Madison Avenue. It's in the phone book." He hesitated. "I don't think—"

"I'm not going to bother her." Before I could say anything else his telephone began to ring.

He put the receiver to his ear and said: "Hello. . . . Yes, speaking. . . . Who? . . . Oh, yes. . . ." Muscles tightened around his mouth, and his eyes opened a little wider. "Where?" He listened some more. "Yes, surely. Can I make it?" He looked at the watch on his left wrist. "Right. See you on the train." He put the telephone down. "That was Lieutenant Guild," he told me. "Wynant's tried to commit suicide in Allentown, Pennsylvania."

13

DOROTHY and Quinn were at the bar when I went into the Palma Club. They did not see me until I came up beside Dorothy and said: "Hello, folks." Dorothy had on the same clothes I had last seen her in.

She looked at me and at Quinn and her face flushed. "You had to tell him."

"The girl's in a pet," Quinn said cheerfully. "I got that stock for you. You ought to pick up some more and what are you drinking?"

"Old-fashioned. You're a swell guest—ducking out without leaving a word behind you."

Dorothy looked at me again. The scratches on her face

were pale, the bruise barely showed, and her mouth was no longer swollen. "I trusted you," she said. She seemed about to cry.

"What do you mean by that?"

"You know what I mean. Even when you went to dinner at Mamma's I trusted you."

"And why not?"

Quinn said: "She's been in a pet all afternoon. Don't bait her." He put a hand on one of hers. "There, there, darling, don't you—"

"Please shut up." She took her hand away from him. "You know very well what I mean," she told me. "You and Nora both made fun of me to Mamma and—"

I began to see what had happened. "She told you that and you believed it?" I laughed. "After twenty years you're still a sucker for her lies? I suppose she phoned you after we left: we had a row and didn't stay long."

She hung her head and said, "Oh, I am a fool," in a low miserable voice. Then she grabbed me by both arms and said: "Listen, let's go over and see Nora now. I've got to square myself with her. I'm such an ass. It'd serve me right if she never—"

"Sure. There's plenty of time. Let's have this drink first."

Quinn said: "Brother Charles, I'd like to shake your hand. You've brought sunshine back into the life of our little tot and joy to—" He emptied his glass. "Let's go over and see Nora. The booze there is just as good and costs us less."

"Why don't you stay here?" she asked him.

He laughed and shook his head. "Not me. Maybe you can get Nick to stay here, but I'm going with you. I've put up with your snottiness all afternoon: now I'm going to bask in the sunshine."

Gilbert Wynant was with Nora when we reached the Normandie. He kissed his sister and shook hands with me and, when he had been introduced, Harrison Quinn.

Dorothy immediately began to make long and earnest and none too coherent apologies to Nora.

Nora said: "Stop it. There's nothing to forgive. If Nick's told you I was sore or hurt or anything of the sort he's just a Greek liar. Let me take your coat."

Quinn turned on the radio. At the stroke of the gong it was five thirty-one and one quarter, Eastern Standard Time.

Nora told Quinn, "Play bar-tender: you know where the stuff is," and followed me into the bathroom. "Where'd you find her?"

"In a speak. What's Gilbert doing here?"

"He came over to see her, so he said. She didn't go home last night and he thought she was still here." She laughed. "He wasn't surprised at not finding her, though. He said she was always wandering off somewhere, she has dromomania, which comes from a mother fixation and is very interesting. He said Stekel claims people who have it usually show klepto-maniac impulses too, and he's left things around to see if she'd steal them, but she never has yet that he knows of."

"He's quite a lad. Did he say anything about his father?"

"No."

"Maybe he hadn't heard. Wynant tried to commit suicide down in Allentown. Guild and Macaulay have gone down to see him. I don't know whether to tell the youngsters or not. I wonder if Mimi had a hand in his coming over here."

"I wouldn't think so, but if you do—"

"I'm just wondering," I said. "Has he been here long?"

"About an hour. He's a funny kid. He's studying Chinese and writing a book on Knowledge and Belief—not in Chinese—and thinks Jack Oakie's very good."

"So do I. Are you tight?"

"Not very."

When we returned to the living-room, Dorothy and Quinn were dancing to *Eadie Was a Lady*.

Gilbert put down the magazine he was looking at and po-litely said he hoped I was recovering from my injury.

I said I was.

"I've never been hurt, really hurt," he went on, "that I can remember. I've tried hurting myself, of course, but that's not the same thing. It just made me uncomfortable and irritable and sweat a lot."

"That's pretty much the same thing," I said.

"Really? I thought there'd be more—well, more to it." He moved a little closer to me. "It's things like that I don't know. I'm so horribly young I haven't had a chance to— Mr.

Charles, if you're too busy or don't want to, I hope you'll say so, but I'd appreciate it very much if you'd let me talk to you some time when there aren't a lot of people around to interrupt us. There are so many things I'd like to ask you, things I don't know anybody else could tell me and—"

"I'm not so sure about that," I said, "but I'll be glad to try any time you want."

"You really don't mind? You're not just being polite?"

"No, I mean it, only I'm not sure you'll get as much help as you expect. It depends on what you want to know."

"Well, things like cannibalism," he said. "I don't mean in places like Africa and New Guinea—in the United States, say. Is there much of it?"

"Not nowadays. Not that I know of."

"Then there was once?"

"I don't know how much, but it happened now and then before the country was completely settled. Wait a minute: I'll give you a sample." I went over to the bookcase and got the copy of Duke's *Celebrated Criminal Cases of America* that Nora had picked up in a second-hand-book store, found the place I wanted, and gave it to him. "It's only three or four pages."

ALFRED G. PACKER, THE "MANEATER," WHO MURDERED HIS FIVE COMPANIONS IN THE MOUNTAINS OF COLORADO, ATE THEIR BODIES AND STOLE THEIR MONEY.

In the fall of 1873 a party of twenty daring men left Salt Lake City, Utah, to prospect in the San Juan country. Having heard glowing accounts of the fortunes to be made, they were light-hearted and full of hope as they started on their journey, but as the weeks rolled by and they beheld nothing but barren wastes and snowy mountains, they grew despondent. The further they proceeded, the less inviting appeared the country, and they finally became desperate when it appeared that their only reward would be starvation and death.

Just as the prospectors were about to give up in despair, they saw an Indian camp in the distance, and while they had no assurance as to what treatment they would receive at the hands of the "Reds," they decided that any death was preferable to starvation, so they agreed to take a chance.

When they approached the camp they were met by an Indian who appeared to be friendly and escorted them to Chief Ouray. To their great surprise, the Indians treated them with every consideration and insisted upon their remaining in the camp until they had fully recuperated from their hardships.

Finally the party decided to make another start, with the Los Pinos Agency as their goal. Ouray attempted to dissuade them from continuing the journey, and did succeed in influencing ten of the party to abandon the trip and return to Salt Lake. The other ten determined to continue, so Ouray supplied them with provisions and admonished them to follow the Gunnison River, which was named after Lieutenant Gunnison, who was murdered in 1852. (See life of Joe Smith, the Mormon.)

Alfred G. Packer, who appeared as the leader of the party which continued the journey, boasted of his knowledge of the topography of the country and expressed confidence in his ability to find his way without difficulty. When his party had traveled a short distance, Packer told them that rich mines had recently been discovered near the headwaters of the Rio Grande River, and he offered to guide the party to the mines.

Four of the party insisted that they follow Ouray's instructions, but Packer persuaded five men, named Swan, Miller, Noon, Bell and Humphreys, to accompany him to the mines, while the other four proceeded along the river.

Of the party of four, two died from starvation and exposure, but the other two finally reached the Los Pinos Agency in February, 1874, after enduring indescribable hardships. General Adams was in command of this agency, and the unfortunate men were treated with every consideration. When they regained their strength they started back to civilization.

In March, 1874, General Adams was called to Denver on business, and one cold, blizzardy morning, while he was still away, the employees of the agency, who were seated at the breakfast table, were startled by the appearance at the door of a wild-looking man who begged piteously for food and shelter. His face was frightfully bloated but otherwise he appeared to be in fairly good condition, although his stomach would not retain the food given him. He stated that his name was Packer and claimed that his five companions had deserted him while he was ill, but had left a rifle with him which he brought into the Agency.

After partaking of the hospitality of the employees at the Agency for ten days, Packer proceeded to a place called Saquache, claiming that he intended to work his way to Pennsylvania, where he had a brother. At Saquache, Packer drank heavily and appeared to be well supplied with money. While intoxicated, he told many conflicting stories regarding the fate of his companions, and it was suspected that he had disposed of his erstwhile associates by foul means.

At this time General Adams stopped at Saquache on his return from Denver to the Agency, and while at the home of Otto Mears he was advised to arrest Packer and investigate his movements. The General decided to take him back to the Agency, and while en route they stopped at the cabin of Major Downey, where they met the ten men who listened to the Indian chief and abandoned the trip. It was then proven that a great part of Packer's statement was false, so the General decided that the matter required a complete investigation, and Packer was bound and taken to the Agency, where he was held in close confinement.

On April 2, 1874, two wildly excited Indians ran into the Agency, holding strips of flesh in their hands which they called "white man's meat," and which they stated they found just outside the agency. As it had been lying on the snow and the weather had been extremely cold, it was still in good condition.

When Packer caught sight of the exhibits, his face became livid, and with a low moan he sank to the floor. Restoratives were administered and after pleading for mercy, he made a statement substantially as follows:

"When I and five others left Ouray's camp, we estimated that we had sufficient provisions for the long and arduous journey before us, but our food rapidly disappeared and we were soon on the verge of starvation. We dug roots from the ground upon which we subsisted for some days, but as they were not nutritious and as the extreme cold had driven all animals and birds to shelter, the situation became desperate. Strange looks came into the eyes of each of the party and they all became suspicious of each other. One day I went out to gather wood for the fire and when I returned I found that Mr. Swan, the oldest man in the party, had been struck on the head and killed, and the remainder of the party were in the act of cutting up the body preparatory to eating it. His money, amounting to $2000.00, was divided among the remainder of the party.

"This food only lasted a few days, and I suggested that Miller be the next victim because of the large amount of flesh he carried. His skull was split open with a hatchet as he was in the act of picking up a piece of wood. Humphreys and Noon were the next victims. Bell and I then entered into a solemn compact that as we were the only ones left we would stand by each other whatever befell, and rather than harm each other we would die of starvation. One day Bell said, 'I can stand it no longer,' and he rushed at me like a famished tiger, at the same time attempting to strike me with his gun. I parried the blow and killed him with a hatchet. I then cut his flesh into strips which I carried with me as I pursued my journey. When I espied the Agency from the top of the hill, I threw away the strips I had left, and I confess I did so reluctantly as I had grown fond of human flesh, especially that portion around the breast."

After relating this grewsome story, Packer agreed to guide a party in charge of H. Lauter to the remains of the murdered men. He led them to some high, inaccessible mountains, and as he claimed to be bewildered, it was decided to abandon the search and start back the next day.

That night Packer and Lauter slept side by side, and during the night Packer assaulted him with the intent to commit murder and escape, but he was overpowered, bound, and after the party reached the Agency, he was turned over to the Sheriff.

Early in June of that year, an artist named Reynolds, from Peoria, Ill., while sketching along the shores of Lake Christoval, discovered the remains of the five men lying in a grove of hemlocks. Four of the bodies were lying together in a row, and the fifth, minus the head, was found a short distance away. The bodies of Bell, Swan, Humphreys and Noon had rifle bullet wounds in the back of the head, and when Miller's head was found it was crushed in, evidently by a blow from a rifle which was lying near by, the stock being broken from the barrel.

The appearance of the bodies clearly indicated that Packer had been guilty of cannibalism as well as murder. He probably spoke the truth when he stated his preference for the breast of man, as in each instance the entire breast was cut away to the ribs.

A beaten path was found leading from the bodies to a near-by cabin, where blankets and other articles belonging to the murdered men were discovered, and everything indicated that Packer lived in this cabin for many days after the murders, and that he made frequent trips to the bodies for his supply of human meat.

After these discoveries the Sheriff procured warrants charging Packer with five murders, but during his absence the prisoner escaped.

Nothing was heard of him again until January 29, 1883, nine years later, when General Adams received a letter from Cheyenne, Wyoming, in which a Salt Lake prospector stated that he had met Packer face to face in that locality. The informant stated that the fugitive was known as John Schwartze, and was suspected of being engaged in operations with a gang of outlaws.

Detectives began an investigation, and on March 12, 1883, Sheriff Sharpless of Laramie County arrested Packer, and on the 17th inst.

Sheriff Smith of Hinsdale County brought the prisoner back to Lake City, Col.

His trial on the charge of murdering Israel Swan in Hinsdale County on March 1, 1874, was begun on April 3, 1883. It was proven that each member of the party except Packer possessed considerable money. The defendant repeated his former statement, wherein he claimed that he had only killed Bell, and had done so in self-defense.

On April 13, the jury found the defendant guilty with the death penalty attached. A stay of execution was granted to Packer, who immediately appealed to the Supreme Court. In the meantime he was transferred to the Gunnison jail to save him from mob violence.

In October, 1885, the Supreme Court granted a new trial and it was then decided to bring him to trial on five charges of manslaughter. He was found guilty on each charge and was sentenced to serve eight years for each offense, making a total of forty years.

He was pardoned on January 1, 1901, and died on a ranch near Denver on April 24, 1907.

While Gilbert was reading this, I got myself a drink. Dorothy stopped dancing to join me. "Do you like him?" she asked, jerking her head to indicate Quinn.

"He's all right."

"Maybe, but he can be terribly silly. You didn't ask me where I stayed last night. Don't you care?"

"It's none of my business."

"But I found out something for you."

"What?"

"I stayed at Aunt Alice's. She's not exactly right in the head, but she's awfully sweet. She told me she had a letter from my father today warning her against Mamma."

"Warning her how? Just what did he say?"

"I didn't see it. Aunt Alice has been mad with him for several years and she tore it up. She says he's become a Communist and she's sure the Communists killed Julia Wolf and will kill him in the end. She thinks it's all over some secret they betrayed."

I said: "Oh my God!"

"Well, don't blame me. I'm just telling you what she told me. I told you she wasn't exactly right in the head."

"Did she tell you that junk was in the letter?"

Dorothy shook her head. "No. She only said the warning

was. As near as I remember she said he wrote her not to trust Mamma under any circumstances and not to trust anybody connected with her, which I suppose means all of us."

"Try to remember more."

"But there wasn't any more. That's all she told me."

"Where was the letter from?" I asked.

"She didn't know—except that it had come air-mail. She said she wasn't interested."

"What did she think of it? I mean, did she take the warning seriously?"

"She said he was a dangerous radical—they're her very words—and she wasn't interested in anything he had to say."

"How seriously do you take it?"

She stared at me for a long moment and she moistened her lips before she spoke. "I think he—"

Gilbert, book in hand, came over to us. He seemed disappointed in the story I had given him. "It's very interesting," he said, "but, if you know what I mean, it's not a pathological case." He put an arm around his sister's waist. "It was more a matter of that or starving."

"Not unless you want to believe him," I said.

Dorothy asked: "What is it?"

"A thing in the book," Gilbert replied.

"Tell him about the letter your aunt got," I said to Dorothy.

She told him.

When she had finished, he grimaced impatiently. "That's silly. Mamma's not really dangerous. She's just a case of arrested development. Most of us have outgrown ethics and morals and so on. Mamma's just not grown up to them yet." He frowned and corrected himself thoughtfully: "She might be dangerous, but it would be like a child playing with matches."

Nora and Quinn were dancing.

"And what do you think of your father?" I asked.

Gilbert shrugged. "I haven't seen him since I was a child. I've got a theory about him, but a lot of it's guess-work. I'd like—the chief thing I'd like to know is if he's impotent."

I said: "He tried to kill himself today, down in Allentown."

Dorothy cried, "He didn't," so sharply that Quinn and

Nora stopped dancing, and she turned and thrust her face up at her brother's. "Where's Chris?" she demanded.

Gilbert looked from her face to mine and quickly back to her's. "Don't be an ass," he said coldly. "He's off with that girl of his, that Fenton girl."

Dorothy did not look as if she believed him.

"She's jealous of him," he explained to me. "It's that mother fixation."

I asked: "Did either of you ever see the Victor Rosewater your father had trouble with back when I first knew you?"

Dorothy shook her head. Gilbert said: "No. Why?"

"Just an idea I had. I never saw him either, but the description they gave me, with some easy changes, could be made to fit your Chris Jorgensen."

14

THAT NIGHT Nora and I went to the opening of the Radio City Music Hall, decided we had had enough of the performance after an hour, and left. "Where to?" Nora asked.

"I don't care. Want to hunt up that Pigiron Club that Morelli told us about? You'll like Studsy Burke. He used to be a safe-burglar. He claims to've cracked the safe in the Hagerstown jail while he was doing thirty days there for disorderly conduct."

"Let's," she said.

We went down to Forty-ninth Street and, after asking two taxi-drivers, two newsboys, and a policeman, found the place. The doorman said he didn't know about any Burkes, but he'd see. Studsy came to the door. "How are you, Nick?" he said. "Come on in."

He was a powerfully built man of medium height, a little fat now, but not soft. He must have been at least fifty, but looked ten years younger than that. He had a broad, pleasantly ugly, pockmarked face under not much hair of no particular color, and even his baldness could not make his forehead seem large. His voice was a deep bass growl.

I shook hands with him and introduced him to Nora.

"A wife," he said. "Think of that. By God, you'll drink champagne or you'll fight me."

I said we wouldn't fight and we went inside. His place had a comfortably shabby look. It was between hours: there were only three customers in the place. We sat at a table in a corner and Studsy told the waiter exactly which bottle of wine to bring. Then he examined me carefully and nodded. "Marriage done you good." He scratched his chin. "It's a long time I don't see you."

"A long time," I agreed.

"He sent me up the river," he told Nora.

She clucked sympathetically. "Was he a good detective?"

Studsy wrinkled what forehead he had. "Folks say, but I don't know. The once he caught me was a accident: I led with my right."

"How come you sicked this wild man Morelli on me?" I asked.

"You know how foreigners are," he said; "they're hysterical. I don't know he's going to do nothing like that. He's worrying about the coppers trying to hang that Wolf dame's killing on him and we see in the paper you got something to do with it and I say to him, 'Nick might not maybe sell his own mother out and you feel like you got to talk to somebody,' so he says he will. What'd you do, make faces at him?"

"He let himself be spotted sneaking in and then blamed me for it. How'd he find me?"

"He's got friends and you wasn't hiding, was you?"

"I'd only been in town a week and there was nothing in the paper saying where I was staying."

"Is that so?" Studsy asked with interest. "Where you been?"

"I live in San Francisco now. How'd he find me?"

"That's a swell town. I ain't been there in years, but it's one swell town. I oughtn't tell you, Nick. Ask him. It's his business."

"Except that you sent him to me."

"Well, yes," he said, "except that, of course; but then, see, I was putting in a boost for you." He said it seriously.

I said: "My pal."

"How did I know he was going to blow his top? Anyways, he didn't hurt you much, did he?"

"Maybe not, but it didn't do me any good and I—" I stopped as the waiter arrived with the champagne. We tasted it and said it was swell. It was pretty bad. "Think he killed the girl?" I asked.

Studsy shook his head sidewise with certainty. "No chance."

"He's a fellow you can persuade to shoot," I said.

"I know—these foreigners are hysterical—but he was around here all that afternoon."

"All?"

"All. I'll take my oath to it. Some of the boys and girls were celebrating upstairs and I know for a fact he wasn't off his hip, let alone out of here, all afternoon. No kidding, that's a thing he can prove."

"Then what was he worried about?"

"Do I know? Ain't that what I been asking him myself? But you know how these foreigners are."

I said: "Uh-huh. They're hysterical. He wouldn't've sent a friend around to see her, would he?"

"I think you got the boy wrong," Studsy said. "I knew the dame. She used to come in here with him sometimes. They was just playing. He wasn't nuts enough about her that he'd have any reason for weighting her down like that. On the level."

"Was she on the stuff too?"

"I don't know. I seen her take it sometimes, but maybe she was just being sociable, taking a shot because he did."

"Who else did she play around with?"

"Nobody I know," Studsy replied indifferently. "There was a rat named Nunheim used to come in here that was on the make for her, but he didn't get nowhere that I could see."

"So that's where Morelli got my address."

"Don't be silly. All Morelli'd want of him would be a crack at him. What's it to him telling the police Morelli knew the dame? A friend of yours?"

I thought it over and said: "I don't know him. I hear he does chores for the police now and then."

"M-m-m. Thanks."

"Thanks for what? I haven't said anything."

"Fair enough. Now you tell me something: what's all this fiddlededee about, huh? That guy Wynant killed her, didn't he?"

"A lot of people think so," I said, "but fifty bucks'll get you a hundred he didn't."

He shook his head. "I don't bet with you in your own racket"—his face brightened—"but I tell you what I will do and we can put some dough on it if you want. You know that time you copped me, I did lead with my right like I said, and I always wondered if you could do it again. Some time when you're feeling well I'd like—"

I laughed and said: "No, I'm all out of condition."

"I'm hog-fat myself," he insisted.

"Besides, that was a fluke: you were off balance and I was set."

"You're just trying to let me down easy," he said, and then more thoughtfully, "though I guess you did get the breaks at that. Well, if you won't— Here, let me fill your glasses."

Nora decided that she wanted to go home early and sober, so we left Studsy and his Pigiron Club at a little after eleven o'clock. He escorted us to a taxicab and shook our hands vigorously. "This has been a fine pleasure," he told us.

We said equally polite things and rode away.

Nora thought Studsy was marvelous. "Half his sentences I can't understand at all."

"He's all right."

"You didn't tell him you'd quit gum-shoeing."

"He'd've thought I was trying to put something over on him," I explained. "To a mugg like him, once a sleuth always a sleuth, and I'd rather lie to him than have him think I'm lying. Have you got a cigarette? He really trusts me, in a way."

"Were you telling the truth when you said Wynant didn't kill her?"

"I don't know. My guess is I was."

At the Normandie there was a telegram for me from Macaulay in Allentown:

MAN HERE IS NOT WYNANT AND DID NOT TRY TO
COMMIT SUICIDE

15

I HAD a stenographer in the next morning and got rid of most of the mail that had been accumulating; had a telephone conversation with our lawyer in San Francisco—we were trying to keep one of the mill's customers from being thrown into bankruptcy; spent an hour going over a plan we had for lowering our state taxes; was altogether the busy business man, and felt pretty virtuous by two o'clock, when I knocked off work for the day and went out to lunch with Nora.

She had a date to play bridge after lunch. I went down to see Guild: I had talked to him on the telephone earlier in the day.

"So it was a false alarm?" I said after we had shaken hands and made ourselves comfortable in chairs.

"That's what it was. He wasn't any more Wynant than I am. You know how it is: we told the Philly police he'd sent a wire from there and broadcasted his description, and for the next week anybody that's skinny and maybe got whiskers is Wynant to half of the State of Pennsylvania. This was a fellow named Barlow, a carpenter out of work as near as we can figure out, that got shot by a nigger trying to stick him up. He can't talk much yet."

"He couldn't've been shot by somebody who made the same mistake the Allentown police did?" I asked.

"You mean thought he was Wynant? I guess that could be—if it helps any. Does it?"

I said I didn't know. "Did Macaulay tell you about the letter he got from Wynant?"

"He didn't tell me what was in it."

I told him. I told him what I knew about Rosewater.

He said: "Now, that's interesting."

I told him about the letter Wynant had sent his sister.

He said: "He writes a lot of people, don't he?"

"I thought of that." I told him Victor Rosewater's description with a few easy changes would fit Christian Jorgensen.

He said: "It don't hurt any to listen to a man like you. Don't let me stop you."

I told him that was the crop.

He rocked back in his chair and screwed his pale gray eyes up at the ceiling. "There's some work to be done there," he said presently.

"Was this fellow in Allentown shot with a .32?" I asked.

Guild stared curiously at me for a moment, then shook his head. "A .44. You got something on your mind?"

"No. Just chasing the set-up around in my head."

He said, "I know what that is," and leaned back to look at the ceiling some more. When he spoke again it was as if he was thinking of something else. "That alibi of Macaulay's you was asking about is all right. He was late for a date then and we know for a fact he was in a fellow's office named Hermann on Fifty-seventh Street from five minutes after three till twenty after, the time that counts."

"What's the five minutes after three?"

"That's right, you don't know about that. Well, we found a fellow named Caress with a cleaning and dyeing place on First Avenue that called her up at five minutes after three to ask her if she had any work for him, and she said no and told him she was liable to go away. So that narrows the time down to from three five to three twenty. You ain't really suspicious of Macaulay?"

"I'm suspicious of everybody," I said. "Where were you between three five and three twenty?"

He laughed. "As a matter of fact," he said, "I'm just about the only one of the lot that ain't got an alibi. I was at the moving pictures."

"The rest of them have?"

He wagged his head up and down. "Jorgensen left his place with Mrs. Jorgensen—that was about five minutes to three— and sneaked over on West Seventy-third Street to see a girl named Olga Fenton—we promised not to tell his wife—and stayed there till about five. We know what Mrs. Jorgensen did. The daughter was dressing when they left and she took a taxi at a quarter past and went straight to Bergdorf-Goodman's. The son was in the Public Library all afternoon— Jesus, he reads funny books. Morelli was in a joint over in the Forties." He laughed. "And where was you?"

"I'm saving mine till I really need it. None of those look

too air-tight, but legitimate alibis seldom do. How about Nunheim?"

Guild seemed surprised. "What makes you think of him?"

"I hear he had a yen for the girl."

"And where'd you hear it?"

"I heard it."

He scowled. "Would you say it was reliable?"

"Yes."

"Well," he said slowly, "he's one guy we can check up on. But look here, what do you care about these people? Don't you think Wynant done it?"

I gave him the same odds I had given Studsy: "Twenty-five'll get you fifty he didn't."

He scowled at me over that for a long silent moment, then said: "That's an idea, anyways. Who's your candidate?"

"I haven't got that far yet. Understand, I don't know anything. I'm not saying Wynant didn't do it. I'm just saying everything doesn't point at him."

"And saying it two to one. What don't point at him?"

"Call it a hunch, if you want," I said, "but—"

"I don't want to call it anything," he said. "I think you're a smart detective. I want to listen to what you got to say."

"Mostly I've got questions to say. For instance, how long was it from the time the elevator boy let Mrs. Jorgensen off at the Wolf girl's floor until she rang for him and said she heard groans?"

Guild pursed his lips, opened them to ask, "You think she might've—?" and left the rest of the question hanging in the air.

"I think she might've. I'd like to know where Nunheim was. I'd like to know the answers to the questions in Wynant's letter. I'd like to know where the four-thousand-dollar difference between what Macaulay gave the girl and what she seems to have given Wynant went. I'd like to know where her engagement ring came from."

"We're doing the best we can," Guild said. "Me—just now I'd like to know why, if he didn't do it, Wynant don't come in and answer questions for us."

"One reason might be that Mrs. Jorgensen'd like to slam

him in the squirrel cage again." I thought of something. "Herbert Macaulay's working for Wynant: you didn't just take Macaulay's word for it that the man in Allentown wasn't him?"

"No. He was a younger man than Wynant, with damned little gray in his hair and no dye, and he didn't look like the pictures we got." He seemed positive. "You got anything to do the next hour or so?"

"No."

"That's fine." He stood up. "I'll get some of the boys working on these things we been discussing and then maybe me and you will pay some visits."

"Swell," I said, and he went out of the office.

There was a copy of the *Times* in his wastebasket. I fished it out and turned to the Public Notices columns. Macaulay's advertisement was there:

"Abner. Yes. Bunny."

When Guild returned I asked: "How about Wynant's help, whoever he had working in the shop? Have they been looked up?"

"Uh-huh, but they don't know anything. They was laid off at the end of the week that he went away—there's two of them—and haven't seen him since."

"What were they working on when the shop was closed?"

"Some kind of paint or something—something about a permanent green. I don't know. I'll find out if you want."

"I don't suppose it matters. Is it much of a shop?"

"Looks like a pretty good lay-out, far as I can tell. You think the shop might have something to do with it?"

"Anything might."

"Uh-huh. Well, let's run along."

16

FIRST THING," Guild said as we left his office, "we'll go see Mr. Nunheim. He ought to be home: I told him to stick around till I phoned him."

Mr. Nunheim's home was on the fourth floor of a dark, damp, and smelly building made noisy by the Sixth Avenue elevated. Guild knocked on the door.

There were sounds of hurried movement inside, then a voice asked: "Who is it?" The voice was a man's, nasal, somewhat irritable.

Guild said: "John."

The door was hastily opened by a small sallow man of thirty-five or -six whose visible clothes were an undershirt, blue pants, and black silk stockings. "I wasn't expecting you, Lieutenant," he whined. "You said you'd phone." He seemed frightened. His dark eyes were small and set close together; his mouth was wide, thin, and loose; and his nose was peculiarly limber, a long, drooping nose, apparently boneless.

Guild touched my elbow with his hand and we went in. Through an open door to the left an unmade bed could be seen. The room we entered was a living-room, shabby and dirty, with clothing, newspapers, and dirty dishes sitting around. In an alcove to the right there was a sink and a stove. A woman stood between them holding a sizzling skillet in her hand. She was a big-boned, full-fleshed, red-haired woman of perhaps twenty-eight, handsome in a rather brutal, sloppy way. She wore a rumpled pink kimono and frayed pink mules with lopsided bows on them. She stared sullenly at us.

Guild did not introduce me to Nunheim and he paid no attention to the woman. "Sit down," he said, and pushed some clothing out of the way to make a place for himself on an end of the sofa.

I removed part of a newspaper from a rocking-chair and sat down. Since Guild kept his hat on I did the same with mine.

Nunheim went over to the table, where there was about two inches of whisky in a pint bottle and a couple of tumblers, and said: "Have a shot?"

Guild made a face. "Not that vomit. What's the idea of telling me you just knew the Wolf girl by sight?"

"That's all I did, Lieutenant, that's the Christ's truth." Twice his eyes slid sidewise towards me and he jerked them back. "Maybe I said hello to her or how are you or something like that when I saw her, but that's all I knew her. That's the Christ's truth."

The woman in the alcove laughed, once, derisively, and there was no merriment in her face.

Nunheim twisted himself around to face her. "All right," he told her, his voice shrill with rage, "put your mouth in and I'll pop a tooth out of it."

She swung her arm and let the skillet go at his head. It missed, crashing into the wall. Grease and egg-yolks made fresher stains on wall, floor, and furniture.

He started for her. I did not have to rise to put out a foot and trip him. He tumbled down on the floor. The woman had picked up a paring knife.

"Cut it out," Guild growled. He had not stood up either. "We come here to talk to you, not to watch this rough-house comedy. Get up and behave yourself."

Nunheim got slowly to his feet. "She drives me nuts when she's drinking," he said. "She been ragging me all day." He moved his right hand back and forth. "I think I sprained my wrist."

The woman walked past us without looking at any of us, went into the bedroom, and shut the door.

Guild said: "Maybe if you'd quit sucking around after other women you wouldn't have so much trouble with this one."

"What do you mean, Lieutenant?" Nunheim was surprised and innocent and perhaps pained.

"Julia Wolf."

The little sallow man was indignant now. "That's a lie, Lieutenant. Anybody that say I ever—"

Guild interrupted him by addressing me: "If you want to take a poke at him, I wouldn't stop on account of his bum wrist: he couldn't ever hit hard anyhow."

Nunheim turned to me with both hands out. "I didn't mean you were a liar. I meant maybe somebody made a mistake if they—"

Guild interrupted him again: "You wouldn't've taken her if you could've gotten her?"

Nunheim moistened his lower lip and looked warily at the bedroom door. "Well," he said slowly in a cautiously low voice, "of course she was a classy number. I guess I wouldn't've turned it down."

"But you never tried to make her?"

Nunheim hesitated, then moved his shoulders and said: "You know how it is. A fellow knocking around tries most everything he runs into."

Guild looked sourly at him. "You'd done better to tell me that in the beginning. Where were you the afternoon she was knocked off?"

The little man jumped as if he had been stuck with a pin. "For Christ's sake, Lieutenant, you don't think I had anything to do with that. What would I want to hurt her for?"

"Where were you?"

Nunheim's loose lips twitched nervously. "What day was she—" He broke off as the bedroom door opened.

The big woman came out carrying a suitcase. She had put on street clothes.

"Miriam," Nunheim said.

She stared at him dully and said: "I don't like crooks, and even if I did, I wouldn't like crooks that are stool-pigeons, and if I liked crooks that are stool-pigeons, I still wouldn't like you." She turned to the outer door.

Guild, catching Nunheim's arm to keep him from following the woman, repeated: "Where were you?"

Nunheim called: "Miriam. Don't go. I'll behave, I'll do anything. Don't go, Miriam."

She went out and shut the door.

"Let me go," he begged Guild. "Let me bring her back. I can't get along without her. I'll bring her right back and tell you anything you want to know. Let me go. I've got to have her."

Guild said: "Nuts. Sit down." He pushed the little man down in a chair. "We didn't come here to watch you and that broad dance around a maypole. Where were you the afternoon the girl was killed?"

Nunheim put his hands over his face and began to cry.

"Keep on stalling," Guild said, "and I'm going to slap you silly."

I poured some whisky in a tumbler and gave it to Nunheim.

"Thank you, sir, thank you." He drank it, coughed, and brought out a dirty handkerchief to wipe his face with. "I can't remember offhand, Lieutenant," he whined. "Maybe I was over at Charlie's shooting pool, maybe I was here. Miriam would remember if you'll let me go bring her back."

Guild said: "The hell with Miriam. How'd you like to be thrown in the can on account of not remembering?"

"Just give me a minute. I'll remember. I'm not stalling, Lieutenant. You know I always come clean with you. I'm just upset now. Look at my wrist." He held up his right wrist to let us see it was swelling. "Just one minute." He put his hands over his face again.

Guild winked at me and we waited for the little man's memory to work.

Suddenly he took his hands down from his face and laughed. "Holy hell! It would serve me right if you had pinched me. That's the afternoon I was— Wait, I'll show you." He went into the bedroom.

After a few minutes Guild called: "Hey, we haven't got all night. Shake it up."

There was no answer.

The bedroom was empty when we went into it and when we opened the bathroom door the bathroom was empty. There was an open window and a fire-escape.

I said nothing, tried to look nothing.

Guild pushed his hat back a little from his forehead and said: "I wish he hadn't done that." He went to the telephone in the living-room.

While he was telephoning, I poked around in drawers and closets, but found nothing. My search was not very thorough and I gave it up as soon as he had finished putting the police machinery in action.

"I guess we'll find him, all right," he said. "I got some news. We've identified Jorgensen as Rosewater."

"Who made the identification?"

"I sent a man over to talk to the girl that gave him his alibi, this Olga Fenton, and he finally got it out of her. He says he couldn't shake her on the alibi, though. I'm going over and have a try at her. Want to come along?"

I looked at my watch and said: "I'd like to, but it's too late. Picked him up yet?"

"The order's out." He looked thoughtfully at me. "And will that baby have to do some talking!"

I grinned at him. "Now who do you think killed her?"

"I'm not worrying," he said. "Just let me have things to squeeze enough people with and I'll turn up the right one before the whistle blows."

In the street he promised to let me know what happened, and we shook hands and separated. He ran after me a couple of seconds later to send his very best regards to Nora.

17

HOME, I delivered Guild's message to Nora and told her the day's news.

"I've got a message for you, too," she said. "Gilbert Wynant dropped in and was quite disappointed at missing you. He asked me to tell you he has something of the 'utmost importance' to tell you."

"He's probably discovered that Jorgensen has a mother fixation."

"Do you think Jorgensen killed her?" she asked.

"I thought I knew who did it," I said, "but it's too mixed up right now for anything but guesses."

"And what's your guess?"

"Mimi, Jorgensen, Wynant, Nunheim, Gilbert, Dorothy, Aunt Alice, Morelli, you, me, or Guild. Maybe Studsy did it. How about shaking up a drink?"

She mixed some cocktails. I was on my second or third when she came back from answering the telephone and said: "Your friend Mimi wants to talk to you."

I went to the telephone. "Hello, Mimi."

"I'm awfully sorry I was so rude the other night, Nick, but I was so upset and I just simply lost my temper and made a show of myself. Please forgive me." She ran through this very rapidly, as if anxious to get it over with.

"That's all right," I said.

She hardly let me get my three words out before she was speaking again, but slower and more earnestly now: "Can I see you, Nick? Something horrible has happened, something —I don't know what to do, which way to turn."

"What is it?"

"I can't tell you over the phone, but you've got to tell me what to do. I've got to have somebody's advice. Can't you come over?"

"You mean now?"

"Yes. Please."

I said, "All right," and went back to the living-room. "I'm going to run over and see Mimi. She says she's in a jam and needs help."

Nora laughed. "Keep your legs crossed. She apologize to you? She did to me."

"Yes, all in one breath. Is Dorothy home or still at Aunt Alice's?"

"Still at Auntie's, according to Gilbert. How long will you be?"

"No longer than I have to. The chances are they've copped Jorgensen and she wants to know if it can be fixed."

"Can they do anything to him? I mean if he didn't kill the Wolf girl."

"I suppose the old charges against him—threats by mail, attempted extortion—could be raked up." I stopped drinking to ask Nora and myself a question: "I wonder if he and Nunheim know each other." I thought that over, but could make nothing more than a possibility of it. "Well, I'm on my way."

18

MIMI received me with both hands. "It's awfully, awfully nice of you to forgive me, Nick, but then you've always been awfully nice. I don't know what got into me Monday night."

I said: "Forget it."

Her face was somewhat pinker than usual and the firmness of its muscles made it seem younger. Her blue eyes were very bright. Her hands had been cold on mine. She was tense with excitement, but I could not figure out what kind of excitement it was.

She said: "It was awfully sweet of your wife, too, to—"

"Forget it."

"Nick, what can they do to you for concealing evidence that somebody's guilty of a murder?"

"Make you an accomplice—accomplice after the fact is the technical term—if they want."

"Even if you voluntarily change your mind and give them the evidence?"

"They can. Usually they don't."

She looked around the room as if to make sure there was nobody else there and said: "Clyde killed Julia. I found the proof and hid it. What'll they do to me?"

"Probably nothing except give you hell—if you turn it in. He was once your husband: you and he are close enough together that no jury'd be likely to blame you for trying to cover him up—unless, of course, they had reason to think you had some other motive."

She asked coolly, deliberately: "Do you?"

"I don't know," I said. "My guess would be that you had intended to use this proof of his guilt to shake him down for some dough as soon as you could get in touch with him, and that now something else has come up to make you change your mind."

She made a claw of her right hand and struck at my face with her pointed nails. Her teeth were together, her lips drawn far back over them.

I caught her wrist. "Women are getting tough," I said, trying to sound wistful. "I just left one that heaved a skillet at a guy."

She laughed, though her eyes did not change. "You're such a bastard. You always think the worst of me, don't you?"

I took my hand away from her wrist and she rubbed the marks my fingers had left on it.

"Who was the woman who threw the skillet?" she asked. "Anyone I know?"

"It wasn't Nora, if that's what you mean. Have they arrested Victor-Christian Rosewater-Jorgensen yet?"

"What?"

I believed in her bewilderment, though both it and my

belief in it surprised me. "Jorgensen is Rosewater," I said. "You remember him. I thought you knew."

"You mean that horrible man who—?"

"Yes."

"I won't believe it." She stood up working her fingers together. "I won't. I won't." Her face was sick with fear, her voice strained, unreal as a ventriloquist's. "I won't believe it."

"That'll help a lot," I said.

She was not listening to me. She turned her back to me and went to a window, where she stood with her back to me.

I said: "There's a couple of men in a car out front who look like they might be coppers waiting to pick him up when he—"

She turned around and asked sharply: "Are you sure he's Rosewater?" Most of the fear had already gone out of her face and her voice was at least human again.

"The police are."

We stared at each other, both of us busy thinking. I was thinking she had not been afraid that Jorgensen killed Julia Wolf, or even that he might be arrested: she was afraid his only reason for marrying her had been as a move in some plot against Wynant.

When I laughed—not because the idea was funny, but because it had come to me so suddenly—she started and smiled uncertainly. "I won't believe it," she said, and her voice was very soft now, "until he tells me himself."

"And when he does—then what?"

She moved her shoulders a little, and her lower lip quivered. "He is my husband."

That should have been funny, but it annoyed me. I said: "Mimi, this is Nick. You remember me, N-i-c-k."

"I know you never think any good of me," she said gravely. "You think I'm—"

"All right. All right. Let it pass. Let's get back to the dope on Wynant you found."

"Yes, that," she said, and turned away from me. When she turned back her lip was quivering again. "That was a lie, Nick. I didn't find anything." She came close to me. "Clyde had no right to send those letters to Alice and Macaulay trying to make everybody suspicious of me and I thought it would serve him right if I made up something against him, because I really did think—I mean, I do think—he killed her and it was only—"

"What'd you make up?" I asked.

"I—I hadn't made it up yet. I wanted to find out about what they could do—you know, the things I asked you—first. I might've pretended she came to a little when I was alone with her, while the others were phoning, and told me he did it."

"You didn't say you heard something and kept quiet, you said you found something and hid it."

"But I hadn't really made up my mind what I—"

"When'd you hear about Wynant's letter to Macaulay?"

"This afternoon," she said, "there was a man here from the police."

"Didn't he ask you anything about Rosewater?"

"He asked me if I knew him or had ever known him, and I thought I was telling the truth when I said no."

"Maybe you did," I said, "and for the first time I now believe you were telling the truth when you said you found some sort of evidence against Wynant."

She opened her eyes wider. "I don't understand."

"Neither do I, but it could be like this: you could've found something and decided to hold it out, probably with the idea of selling it to Wynant; then when his letters started people looking you over, you decided to give up the money idea and both pay him back and protect yourself by turning it over to the police; and, finally, when you learn that Jorgensen is Rosewater, you make another about-face and hold it out, not for money this time, but to leave Jorgensen in as bad a spot as possible as punishment for having married you as a trick in his game against Wynant and not for love."

She smiled calmly and asked: "You really think me capable of anything, don't you?"

"That doesn't matter," I said. "What ought to matter to you is that you'll probably wind up your life in prison somewhere."

Her scream was not loud, but it was horrible, and the fear that had been in her face before was as nothing to that there now. She caught my lapels and clung to them, babbling: "Don't say that, please don't. Say you don't think it." She was trembling so I put an arm around her to keep her from falling.

We did not hear Gilbert until he coughed and asked: "Aren't you well, Mamma?"

She slowly took her hands down from my lapels and moved back a step and said: "Your mother's a silly woman." She was still trembling, but she smiled at me and she made her voice playful: "You're a brute to frighten me like that."

I said I was sorry.

Gilbert put his coat and hat on a chair and looked from one to the other of us with polite interest. When it became obvious that neither of us was going to tell him anything he coughed again, said, "I'm awfully glad to see you," and came over to shake hands with me.

I said I was glad to see him.

Mimi said: "Your eyes look tired. I bet you've been reading all afternoon without your glasses again." She shook her head and told me: "He's as unreasonable as his father."

"Is there any news of Father?" he asked.

"Not since that false alarm about his suicide," I said. "I suppose you heard it was a false alarm."

"Yes." He hesitated. "I'd like to see you for a few minutes before you go."

"Sure."

"But you're seeing him now, darling," Mimi said. "Are there secrets between you that I'm not supposed to know about?" Her tone was light enough. She had stopped trembling.

"It would bore you." He picked up his hat and coat, nodded at me, and left the room.

Mimi shook her head again and said: "I don't understand that child at all. I wonder what he made of our tableau." She did not seem especially worried. Then, more seriously: "What made you say that, Nick?"

"About you winding up in—?"

"No, never mind." She shuddered. "I don't want to hear it. Can't you stay for dinner? I'll probably be all alone."

"I'm sorry I can't. Now how about this evidence you found?"

"I didn't really find anything. That was a lie." She frowned earnestly. "Don't look at me like that. It really was a lie."

"So you sent for me just to lie to me?" I asked. "Then why'd you change your mind?"

She chuckled. "You must really like me, Nick, or you wouldn't always be so disagreeable."

I could not follow that line of reasoning. I said: "Well, I'll see what Gilbert wants and run along."

"I wish you could stay."

"I'm sorry I can't," I said again. "Where'll I find him?"

"The second door to the— Will they really arrest Chris?"

"That depends," I told her, "on what kind of answers he gives them. He'll have to talk pretty straight to stay out."

"Oh, he'll—" she broke off, looked sharply at me, asked, "You're not playing a trick on me? He's really that Rosewater?"

"The police are sure enough of it."

"But the man who was here this afternoon didn't ask a single question about Chris," she objected. "He only asked me if I knew—"

"They weren't sure then," I explained. "It was just a half-idea."

"But they're sure now?"

I nodded.

"How'd they find out?"

"From a girl he knows," I said.

"Who?" Her eyes darkened a little, but her voice was under control.

"I can't remember her name." Then I went back to the truth: "The one that gave him his alibi for the afternoon of the murder."

"Alibi?" she asked indignantly. "Do you mean to tell me the police would take the word of a girl like that?"

"Like what?"

"You know what I mean."

"I don't. Do you know the girl?"

"No," she said as if I had insulted her. She narrowed her eyes and lowered her voice until it was not much more than a whisper: "Nick, do you suppose he killed Julia?"

"What would he do that for?"

"Suppose he married me to get revenge on Clyde," she said, "and— You know he did urge me to come over here and try to get some money from Clyde. Maybe I suggested it—I don't know—but he did urge me. And then suppose he happened to run into Julia. She knew him, of course, because they worked for Clyde at the same time. And he knew I was going over to see her that afternoon and was afraid if I made her mad she might expose him to me and so— Couldn't that be?"

"That doesn't make any sense at all. Besides, you and he left here together that afternoon. He wouldn't've had time to—"

"But my taxicab was awfully slow," she said, "and then I may have stopped somewhere on— I think I did. I think I stopped at a drug store to get some aspirin." She nodded energetically. "I remember I did."

"And he knew you were going to stop, because you had told him," I suggested. "You can't go on like this, Mimi. Murder's serious. It's nothing to frame people for just because they played tricks on you."

"Tricks?" she asked, glaring at me. "Why, that . . ." She called Jorgensen all the usual profane, obscene, and otherwise insulting names, her voice gradually rising until towards the end she was screaming into my face.

When she stopped for breath I said: "That's pretty cursing, but it—"

"He even had the nerve to hint that I might've killed her," she told me. "He didn't have nerve enough to ask me, but he kept leading up to it until I told him positively that—well, that I didn't do it."

"That's not what you started to say. You told him positively what?"

She stamped her foot. "Stop heckling me."

"All right and to hell with you," I said. "Coming here wasn't my idea." I started towards my hat and coat.

She ran after me, caught my arm. "Please, Nick, I'm sorry. It's this rotten temper of mine. I don't know what I—"

Gilbert came in and said: "I'll go along part of the way with you."

Mimi scowled at him. "You were listening."

"How could I help it, the way you screamed?" he asked. "Can I have some money?"

"And we haven't finished talking," she said.

I looked at my watch. "I've got to run, Mimi. It's late."

"Will you come back after you get through with your date?"

"If it's not too late. Don't wait for me."

"I'll be here," she said. "It doesn't matter how late it is."

I said I would try to make it. She gave Gilbert his money. He and I went downstairs.

19

"I WAS LISTENING," Gilbert told me as we left the building. "I think it's silly not to listen whenever you get a chance if you're interested in studying people, because they're never exactly the same as when you're with them. People don't like it when they know about it, of course, but"—he smiled—"I don't suppose birds and animals like having naturalists spying on them either."

"Hear much of it?" I asked.

"Oh, enough to know I didn't miss any of the important part."

"And what'd you think of it?"

He pursed his lips, wrinkled his forehead, said judicially: "It's hard to say exactly. Mamma's good at hiding things sometimes, but she's never much good at making them up. It's a funny thing—I suppose you've noticed it—the people who lie the most are nearly always the clumsiest at it, and they're easier to fool with lies than most people, too. You'd think they'd be on the look-out for lies, but they seem to be the very ones that will believe almost anything at all. I suppose you've noticed that, haven't you?"

"Yes."

He said: "What I wanted to tell you: Chris didn't come home last night. That's why Mamma's more upset than usual, and when I got the mail this morning there was a letter for him that I thought might have something in it, so I steamed it open." He took a letter from his pocket and held it out to me. "You'd better read it and then I'll seal it again and put it with tomorrow's mail in case he comes back, though I don't think he will."

"Why don't you?" I asked as I took the letter.

"Well, he's really Rosewater. . . ."

"You say anything to him about it?"

"I didn't have a chance. I haven't seen him since you told me."

I looked at the letter in my hand. The envelope was postmarked Boston, Massachusetts, December 27, 1932, and addressed in a slightly childish feminine hand to Mr. Christian Jorgensen, Courtland Apts., New York, N.Y. "How'd you happen to open it?" I asked, taking the letter out of the envelope.

"I don't believe in intuition," he said, "but there are probably odors, sounds, maybe something about the handwriting, that you can't analyze, maybe aren't even conscious of, that influence you sometimes. I don't know what it was: I just felt there might be something important in it."

"You often feel that way about the family's mail?"

He glanced quickly at me as if to see whether I was spoofing, then said: "Not often, but I have opened their mail before. I told you I was interested in studying people."

I read the letter:

Dear Vic—

Olga wrote me about you being back in the U.S. married to another woman and using the name of Christian Jorgensen. That is not right Vic as you very well know the same as leaving me without word of any kind all these years. And no money. I know that you had to go away on account of that trouble you had with Mr. Wynant but am sure he has long since forgot all about that and I do think you might have written to me as you know very well I have always been your friend and am willing to do anything within my power for you at any time. I do not want to scold you Vic but I have to see you. I will be off from the store Sunday and Monday on account of New Years and will come down to N.Y. Saturday night and must have a talk with you. Write me where you will meet me and what time as I do not want to make any trouble for you. Be sure and write me right away so I will get it in time.

Your true wife,
Georgia

There was a street address.

I said, "Well, well, well," and put the letter back in its envelope. "And you resisted the temptation to tell your mother about this?"

"Oh, I knew what her reaction would be. You saw how she carried on with just what you told her. What do you think I ought to do about it?"

"You ought to let me tell the police."

He nodded immediately. "If you think that's the best thing. You can show it to them if you want."

I said, "Thanks," and put the letter in my pocket.

He said: "Now there's another thing: I had some morphine I was experimenting with and somebody stole it, about twenty grains."

"Experimenting how?"

"Taking it. I wanted to study the effects."

"And how'd you like them?" I asked.

"Oh, I didn't expect to like it. I just wanted to know about it. I don't like things that dull my mind. That's why I don't very often drink, or even smoke. I want to try cocaine, though, because that's supposed to sharpen the brain, isn't it?"

"It's supposed to. Who do you think copped the stuff?"

"I suspect Dorothy, because I have a theory about her. That's why I'm going over to Aunt Alice's for dinner: Dorry's still there and I want to find out. I can make her tell me anything."

"Well, if she's been over there," I asked, "how could she—"

"She was home for a little while last night," he said, "and, besides, I don't know exactly when it was taken. Today was the first time I opened the box it was in for three or four days."

"Did she know you had it?"

"Yes. That's one of the reasons I suspect her. I don't think anybody else did. I experimented on her too."

"How'd she like it?"

"Oh, she liked it all right, but she'd have taken it anyhow. But what I want to ask you is could she have become an addict in a little time like that?"

"Like what?"

"A week—no—ten days."

"Hardly, unless she thought herself into it. Did you give her much?"

"No."

"Let me know if you find out," I said. "I'm going to grab a taxi here. Be seeing you."

"You're coming over later tonight, aren't you?"

"If I can make it. Maybe I'll see you then."

"Yes," he said, "and thanks awfully."

At the first drug store I stopped to telephone Guild, not expecting to catch him in his office, but hoping to learn how to reach him at his home. He was still there, though.

"Working late," I said.

His "That's what" sounded very cheerful.

I read Georgia's letter to him, gave him her address.

"Good pickings," he said.

I told him Jorgensen had not been home since the day before.

"Think we'll find him in Boston?" he asked.

"Either there," I guessed, "or as far south as he could manage to get by this time."

"We'll try 'em both," he said, still cheerful. "Now I got a bit of news for you. Our friend Nunheim was filled full of .32s just about an hour after he copped the sneak on us—deader'n hell. The pills look like they come from the same gun that cut down the Wolf dame. The experts are matching 'em up now. I guess he wishes he'd stayed and talked to us."

20

NORA was eating a piece of cold duck with one hand and working on a jig-saw puzzle with the other when I got home.

"I thought you'd gone to live with her," she said. "You used to be a detective: find me a brownish piece shaped something like a snail with a long neck."

"Piece of duck or puzzle? Don't let's go to the Edges' tonight: they're dull folk."

"All right, but they'll be sore."

"We wouldn't be that lucky," I complained. "They'd get sore at the Quinns and—"

"Harrison called you up. He told me to tell you now's the time to buy some McIntyre Porcupine—I think that's right—to go with your Dome stock. He said it closed at twenty and a quarter." She put a finger on her puzzle. "The piece I want goes in there."

I found the piece she wanted and told her, almost word for word, what had been done and said at Mimi's.

"I don't believe it," she said. "You made it up. There aren't any people like that. What's the matter with them? Are they the first of a new race of monsters?"

"I just tell you what happens; I don't explain it."

"How would you explain it? There doesn't seem to be a single one in the family—now that Mimi's turned against her Chris—who has even the slightest reasonably friendly feeling for any of the others, and yet there's something very alike in all of them."

"Maybe that explains it," I suggested.

"I'd like to see Aunt Alice," she said. "Are you going to turn that letter over to the police?"

"I've already phoned Guild," I replied, and told her about Nunheim.

"What does that mean?" she asked.

"For one thing, if Jorgensen's out of town, as I think he is, and the bullets are from the same gun that was used on Julia Wolf, and they probably are, then the police'll have to find his accomplice if they want to hang anything on him."

"I'm sure if you were a good detective you'd be able to make it much clearer to me than it is." She went to work on her puzzle again. "Are you going back to see Mimi?"

"I doubt it. How about letting that dido rest while we get some dinner?"

The telephone rang and I said I would get it. It was Dorothy Wynant. "Hello. Nick?"

"The same. How are you, Dorothy?"

"Gil just got here and asked me about that you-know, and I wanted to tell you I did take it, but I only took it to try to keep him from becoming a dope-fiend."

"What'd you do with it?" I asked.

"He made me give it back to him and he doesn't believe me, but, honestly, that's the only reason I took it."

"I believe you."

"Will you tell Gil, then? If you believe me, he will, because he thinks you know all about things like that."

"I'll tell him as soon as I see him," I promised.

There was a pause, then she asked: "How's Nora?"

"Looks all right to me. Want to talk to her?"

"Well, yes, but there's something I want to ask you. Did—did Mamma say anything about me when you were over there today?"

"Not that I remember. Why?"

"And did Gil?"

"Only about the morphine."

"Are you sure?"

"Pretty sure," I said. "Why?"

"It's nothing, really—if you're sure. It's just silly."

"Right. I'll call Nora." I went into the living-room. "Dorothy wants to talk to you. Don't ask her to eat with us."

When Nora returned from the telephone she had a look in her eye.

"Now what's up?" I asked.

"Nothing. Just 'How are you' and all that."

I said: "If you're lying to the old man, God'll punish you."

We went over to a Japanese place on Fifty-eighth Street for dinner and then I let Nora talk me into going to the Edges' after all.

Halsey Edge was a tall scrawny man of fifty-something with a pinched yellow face and no hair at all. He called himself "a ghoul by profession and inclination"—his only joke, if that is what it was—by which he meant he was an archæologist, and he was very proud of his collection of battle-axes. He was not so bad once you had resigned yourself to the fact that you were in for occasional cataloguings of his armory—stone axes, copper axes, bronze axes, double-bladed axes, faceted axes, polygonal axes, scalloped axes, hammer axes, adze axes, Mesopotamian axes, Hungarian axes, Nordic axes, and all of them looking pretty moth-eaten. It was his wife we objected to. Her name was Leda, but he called her Tip. She was very

small and her hair, eyes, and skin, though naturally of different shades, were all muddy. She seldom sat—she perched on
things—and liked to cock her head a little to one side. Nora
had a theory that once when Edge opened an antique grave,
Tip ran out of it, and Margot Innes always spoke of her as the
gnome, pronouncing all the letters. She once told me that she
did not think any literature of twenty years ago would live,
because it had no psychiatry in it. They lived in a pleasant old
three-story house on the edge of Greenwich Village and their
liquor was excellent.

A dozen or more people were there when we arrived. Tip
introduced us to the ones we did not know and then backed
me into a corner. "Why didn't you tell me that those people
I met at your place Christmas were mixed up in a murder
mystery?" she asked, tilting her head to the left until her ear
was practically resting on her shoulder.

"I don't know that they are. Besides, what's one murder
mystery nowadays?"

She tilted her head to the right. "You didn't even tell me
you had taken the case."

"I had done what? Oh, I see what you mean. Well, I hadn't
and haven't. My getting shot ought to prove I was an innocent bystander."

"Does it hurt much?"

"It itches. I forgot to have the dressing changed this afternoon."

"Wasn't Nora utterly terrified?"

"So was I and so was the guy that shot me. There's Halsey.
I haven't spoken to him yet."

As I slid around her to escape she said: "Harrison promised
to bring the daughter tonight."

I talked to Edge for a few minutes—chiefly about a place in
Pennsylvania he was buying—then found myself a drink and
listened to Larry Crowley and Phil Thames swap dirty stories
until some woman came over and asked Phil—he taught at
Columbia—one of the questions about technocracy that people were asking that week. Larry and I moved away.

We went over to where Nora was sitting. "Watch yourself,"
she told me. "The gnome's hell-bent on getting the inside
story of Julia Wolf's murder out of you."

"Let her get it out of Dorothy," I said. "She's coming with Quinn."

"I know."

Larry said: "He's nuts over that girl, isn't he? He told me he was going to divorce Alice and marry her."

Nora said, "Poor Alice," sympathetically. She did not like Alice.

Larry said: "That's according to how you look at it." He liked Alice. "I saw that fellow who's married to the girl's mother yesterday. You know, the tall fellow I met at your house."

"Jorgensen?"

"That's it. He was coming out of a pawnshop on Sixth Avenue near Forty-sixth."

"Talk to him?"

"I was in a taxi. It's probably polite to pretend you don't see people coming out of pawnshops, anyhow."

Tip said, "Sh-h-h," in all directions, and Levi Oscant began to play the piano. Quinn and Dorothy arrived while he was playing. Quinn was drunk as a lord and Dorothy seemed to have something better than a glow.

She came over to me and whispered: "I want to leave when you and Nora do."

I said: "You won't be here for breakfast."

Tip said, "Sh-h-h," in my direction.

We listened to some more music.

Dorothy fidgeted beside me for a minute and whispered again: "Gil says you're going over to see Mamma later. Are you?"

"I doubt it."

Quinn came unsteadily around to us. "How're you, boy? How're you, Nora? Give him my message?" (Tip said, "Sh-h-h," at him. He paid no attention to her. Other people looked relieved and began to talk.) "Listen, boy, you bank at the Golden Gate Trust in San Francisco, don't you?"

"Got a little money there."

"Get it out, boy. I heard tonight they're plenty shaky."

"All right. I haven't got much there, though."

"No? What do you do with all your money?"

"Me and the French hoard gold."

He shook his head solemnly. "It's fellows like you that put the country on the bum."

"And it's fellows like me that don't go on the bum with it," I said. "Where'd you get the skinful?"

"It's Alice. She's been sulking for a week. If I didn't drink I'd go crazy."

"What's she sulking about?"

"About my drinking. She thinks—" He leaned forward and lowered his voice confidentially. "Listen. You're all my friends and I'm going to tell you what I'm going to do. I'm going to get a divorce and marry—"

He had tried to put an arm around Dorothy. She pushed it away and said: "You're silly and you're tiresome. I wish you'd leave me alone."

"She thinks I'm silly and tiresome," he told me. "You know why she don't want to marry me? I bet you don't. It's because she's in—"

"Shut up! Shut up, you drunken fool!" Dorothy began to beat his face with both hands. Her face was red, her voice shrill. "If you say that again I'll kill you!"

I pulled Dorothy away from Quinn; Larry caught him, kept him from falling. He whimpered: "She hit me, Nick." Tears ran down his cheeks.

Dorothy had her face against my coat and seemed to be crying.

We had what audience there was. Tip came running, her face bright with curiosity. "What is it, Nick?"

I said: "Just a couple of playful drunks. They're all right. I'll see that they get home all right."

Tip was not for that: she wanted them to stay at least until she had a chance to discover what had happened. She urged Dorothy to lie down awhile, offered to get something—whatever she meant by that—for Quinn, who was having trouble standing up now.

Nora and I took them out. Larry offered to go along, but we decided that was not necessary. Quinn slept in a corner of the taxicab during the ride to his apartment, and Dorothy sat stiff and silent in the other corner, with Nora between them. I clung to a folding seat and thought that anyway we had not stayed long at the Edges'.

Nora and Dorothy remained in the taxicab while I took Quinn upstairs. He was pretty limp.

Alice opened the door when I rang. She had on green pyjamas and held a hairbrush in one hand. She looked wearily at Quinn and spoke wearily: "Bring it in."

I took it in and spread it on a bed. It mumbled something I could not make out and moved one hand feebly back and forth, but its eyes stayed shut.

"I'll tuck him in," I said and loosened his tie.

Alice leaned on the foot of the bed. "If you want to. I've given up doing it."

I took off his coat, vest, and shirts.

"Where'd he pass out this time?" she asked with not much interest. She was still standing at the foot of the bed, brushing her hair now.

"The Edges'." I unbuttoned his pants.

"With that little Wynant bitch?" The question was casual.

"There were a lot of people there."

"Yes," she said. "He wouldn't pick a secluded spot." She brushed her hair a couple of times. "So you don't think it's clubby to tell me anything."

Her husband stirred a little and mumbled: "Dorry."

I took off his shoes.

Alice sighed. "I can remember when he had muscles." She stared at her husband until I took off the last of his clothes and rolled him under the covers. Then she sighed again and said: "I'll get you a drink."

"You'll have to make it short: Nora's waiting in the cab."

She opened her mouth as if to speak, shut it, opened it again to say: "Righto."

I went into the kitchen with her.

Presently she said: "It's none of my business, Nick, but what do people think of me?"

"You're like everybody else: some people like you, some people don't, and some have no feeling about it one way or the other."

She frowned. "That's not exactly what I meant. What do people think about my staying with Harrison with him chasing everything that's hot and hollow?"

"I don't know, Alice."

"What do you think?"

"I think you probably know what you're doing and whatever you do is your own business."

She looked at me with dissatisfaction. "You'll never talk yourself into any trouble, will you?" She smiled bitterly. "You know I'm only staying with him for his money, don't you? It may not be a lot to you, but it is to me—the way I was raised."

"There's always divorce and alimony. You ought to have—"

"Drink your drink and get to hell out of here," she said wearily.

21

NORA MADE a place for me between her and Dorothy in the taxicab. "I want some coffee," she said. "Reuben's?"

I said, "All right," and gave the driver the address.

Dorothy asked timidly: "Did his wife say anything?"

"She sent her love to you."

Nora said: "Stop being nasty."

Dorothy said: "I don't really like him, Nick. I won't ever see him again—honestly." She seemed pretty sober now. "It was—well, I was lonesome and he was somebody to run around with."

I started to say something, but stopped when Nora poked me in the side.

Nora said: "Don't worry about it. Harrison's always been a simpleton."

"I don't want to stir things up," I said, "but I think he's really in love with the girl."

Nora poked me in the side again.

Dorothy peered at my face in the dim light. "You're—you're not— You're not making fun of me, Nick?"

"I ought to be."

"I heard a new story about the gnome tonight," Nora said in the manner of one who did not mean to be interrupted, and explained to Dorothy, "That's Mrs. Edge. Levi says . . ."

The story was funny enough if you knew Tip. Nora went on talking about her until we got out of the taxicab at Reuben's.

Herbert Macaulay was in the restaurant, sitting at a table with a plump dark-haired girl in red. I waved at him and, after we had ordered some food, went over to speak to him.

"Nick Charles, Louise Jacobs," he said. "Sit down. What's news?"

"Jorgensen's Rosewater," I told him.

"The hell he is!"

I nodded. "And he seems to have a wife in Boston."

"I'd like to see him," he said slowly. "I knew Rosewater. I'd like to make sure."

"The police seem sure enough. I don't know whether they've found him yet. Think he killed Julia?"

Macaulay shook his head with emphasis. "I can't see Rosewater killing anybody—not as I knew him—in spite of those threats he made. You remember I didn't take them very seriously at the time. What else has happened?" When I hesitated, he said: "Louise is all right. You can talk."

"It's not that. I've got to go back to my folks and food. I came over to ask if you'd got an answer to your ad in this morning's *Times*."

"Not yet. Sit down, Nick, there's a lot I want to ask you. You told the police about Wynant's letter, didn't—"

"Come up to lunch tomorrow and we'll bat it around. I've got to get back to my folks."

"Who is the little blonde girl?" Louise Jacobs asked. "I've seen her places with Harrison Quinn."

"Dorothy Wynant."

"You know Quinn?" Macaulay asked me.

"Ten minutes ago I was putting him to bed."

Macaulay grinned. "I hope you keep his acquaintance like that—social."

"Meaning what?"

Macaulay's grin became rueful. "He used to be my broker, and his advice led me right up to the poorhouse steps."

"That's sweet," I said. "He's my broker now and I'm following his advice."

Macaulay and the girl laughed. I pretended I was laughing and returned to my table.

Dorothy said: "It's not midnight yet and Mamma said she'd be expecting you. Why don't we all go to see her?"

Nora was very carefully pouring coffee into her cup.

"What for?" I asked. "What are you two up to now?"

It would have been hard to find two more innocent faces than theirs.

"Nothing, Nick," Dorothy said. "We thought it would be nice. It's early and—"

"And we all love Mimi."

"No—o, but—"

"It's too early to go home," Nora said.

"There are speakeasies," I suggested, "and nightclubs and Harlem."

Nora made a face. "All your ideas are alike."

"Want to go over to Barry's and try our luck at faro?"

Dorothy started to say yes, but stopped when Nora made another face.

"That's the way I feel about seeing Mimi again," I said. "I've had enough of her for one day."

Nora sighed to show she was being patient. "Well, if we're going to wind up in a speakeasy as usual, I'd rather go to your friend Studsy's, if you won't let him give us any more of that awful champagne. He's cute."

"I'll do my best," I promised and asked Dorothy, "Did Gilbert tell you he caught Mimi and me in a compromising position?"

She tried to exchange glances with Nora, but Nora's glance was occupied with a cheese blintz on her plate. "He—he didn't exactly say that."

"Did he tell you about the letter?"

"From Chris's wife? Yes." Her blue eyes glittered. "Won't Mamma be furious!"

"You like it, though."

"Suppose I do? What of it? What did she ever do to make me—"

Nora said: "Nick, stop bullying the child."

I stopped.

2 2

Business was good at the Pigiron Club. The place was full of people, noise, and smoke. Studsy came from behind the cash register to greet us. "I was hoping you'd come in." He shook my hand and Nora's and grinned broadly at Dorothy.

"Anything special?" I asked.

He made a bow. "Everything's special with ladies like these."

I introduced him to Dorothy.

He bowed to her and said something elaborate about any friend of Nick's and stopped a waiter. "Pete, put a table up here for Mr. Charles."

"Pack them in like this every night?" I asked.

"I got no kick," he said. "They come once, they come back again. Maybe I ain't got no black marble cuspidors, but you don't have to spit out what you buy here. Want to lean against the bar whilst they're putting up that table?"

We said we did and ordered drinks.

"Hear about Nunheim?" I asked.

He looked at me for a moment before making up his mind to say: "Uh-huh, I heard. His girl's down there"—he moved his head to indicate the other end of the room—"celebrating, I guess."

I looked past Studsy down the room and presently picked out big red-haired Miriam sitting at a table with half a dozen men and women. "Hear who did it?" I asked.

"She says the police done it—he knew too much."

"That's a laugh," I said.

"That's a laugh," he agreed. "There's your table. Set right down. I'll be back in a minute."

We carried our glasses over to a table that had been squeezed in between two tables which had occupied a space large enough for one and made ourselves as nearly comfortable as we could.

Nora tasted her drink and shuddered. "Do you suppose this could be the 'bitter vetch' they used to put in cross-word puzzles?"

Dorothy said: "Oh, look."

We looked and saw Shep Morelli coming towards us. His face had attracted Dorothy's attention. Where it was not dented it was swollen and its coloring ranged from deep purple around one eye to the pale pink of a piece of court-plaster on his chin.

He came to our table and leaned over a little to put both fists on it. "Listen," he said, "Studsy says I ought to apologize."

Nora murmured, "Old Emily Post Studsy," while I asked, "Well?"

Morelli shook his battered head. "I don't apologize for what I do—people've got to take it or leave it—but I don't mind telling you I'm sorry I lost my noodle and cracked down on you and I hope it ain't bothering you much and if there's anything I can do to square it I—"

"Forget it. Sit down and have a drink. This is Mr. Morelli, Miss Wynant."

Dorothy's eyes became wide and interested.

Morelli found a chair and sat down. "I hope you won't hold it against me, neither," he told Nora.

She said: "It was fun."

He looked at her suspiciously.

"Out on bail?" I asked.

"Uh-huh, this afternoon." He felt his face gingerly with one hand. "That's where the new ones come from. They had me resisting some more arrest just for good measure before they turned me loose."

Nora said indignantly: "That's horrible. You mean they really—"

I patted her hand.

Morelli said: "You got to expect it." His swollen lower lip moved in what was meant for a scornful smile. "It's all right as long as it takes two or three of 'em to do it."

Nora turned to me. "Did you do things like that?"

"Who? Me?"

Studsy came over to us carrying a chair. "They lifted his face, huh?" he said, nodding at Morelli. We made room for him and he sat down. He grinned complacently at Nora's drink and at Nora. "I guess you don't get no better than that in your fancy Park Avenue joints—and you pay four bits a slug for it here."

Nora's smile was weak, but it was a smile. She put her foot on mine under the table.

I asked Morelli: "Did you know Julia Wolf in Cleveland?"

He looked sidewise at Studsy, who was leaning back in his chair, gazing around the room, watching his profits mount.

"When she was Rhoda Stewart," I added.

He looked at Dorothy.

I said: "You don't have to be cagey. She's Clyde Wynant's daughter."

Studsy stopped gazing around the room and beamed on Dorothy. "So you are? And how is your pappy?"

"But I haven't seen him since I was a little girl," she said.

Morelli wet the end of a cigarette and put it between his swollen lips. "I come from Cleveland." He struck a match. His eyes were dull—he was trying to keep them dull. "She wasn't Rhoda Stewart except once—Nancy Kane." He looked at Dorothy again. "Your father knows it."

"Do you know my father?"

"We had some words once."

"What about?" I asked.

"Her." The match in his hand had burned down to his fingers. He dropped it, struck another, and lit his cigarette. He raised his eyebrows at me, wrinkling his forehead. "Is this O.K.?"

"Sure. There's nobody here you can't talk in front of."

"O.K. He was jealous as hell. I wanted to take a poke at him, but she wouldn't let me. That was all right: he was her bank-roll."

"How long ago was this?"

"Six months, eight months."

"Have you seen him since she got knocked off?"

He shook his head. "I never seen him but a couple of times, and this time I'm telling you about is the last."

"Was she gypping him?"

"She don't say she is. I figure she is."

"Why?"

"She's a wise head—plenty smart. She was getting dough somewheres. Once I wanted five grand." He snapped his fingers. "Cash."

I decided against asking if he had paid her back. "Maybe he gave it to her."

"Sure—maybe."

"Did you tell any of this to the police?" I asked.

He laughed once, contemptuously. "They thought they could smack it out of me. Ask 'em what they think now. You're a right guy, I don't—" He broke off, took the cigarette from between his lips. "The earysipelas kid," he said and put out a hand to touch the ear of a man who, sitting at one of the tables we had been squeezed in between, had been leaning further and further back towards us.

The man jumped and turned a startled pale pinched face around over his shoulder at Morelli.

Morelli said: "Pull in that lug—it's getting in our drinks."

The man stammered, "I d-didn't mean nothing, Shep," and rammed his belly into his table trying to get as far as possible from us, which still did not take him out of ear-shot.

Morelli said, "You won't ever mean nothing, but that don't keep you from trying," and returned his attention to me. "I'm willing to go all the way with you—the kid's dead, it's not going to hurt her any—but Mulrooney ain't got a wrecking crew that can get it out of me."

"Swell," I said. "Tell me about her, where you first ran into her, what she did before she tied up with Wynant, where he found her."

"I ought to have a drink." He twisted himself around in his chair and called: "Hey, garsong—you with the boy on your back!"

The somewhat hunchbacked waiter Studsy had called Pete pushed through people to our table and grinned affectionately down at Morelli. "What'll it be?" He sucked a tooth noisily.

We gave our orders and the waiter went away.

Morelli said: "Me and Nancy lived in the same block. Old man Kane had a candy store on the corner. She used to pinch cigarettes for me." He laughed. "Her old man kicked hell out of me once for showing her how to get nickels out of the telephone with a piece of wire. You know, the old style ones. Jesus, we couldn't've been more than in the third grade." He laughed again, low in his throat. "I wanted to glaum some fixtures from a row of houses they were building around the corner and plant 'em in his cellar and tell Schultz, the cop on the beat, to pay him back, but she wouldn't let me."

Nora said: "You must've been a little darling."

"I was that," he said fondly. "Listen. Once when I was no more'n five or—"

A feminine voice said: "I thought that was you."

I looked up and saw it was red-haired Miriam speaking to me. I said: "Hello."

She put her hands on her hips and stared somberly at me. "So he knew too much for you."

"Maybe, but he took it on the lam down the fire-escape with his shoes in his hand before he told us any of it."

"Balls!"

"All right. What do you think he knew that was too much for us?"

"Where Wynant is," she said.

"So? Where is he?"

"I don't know. Art knew."

"I wish he'd told us. We—"

"Balls!" she said again. "You know and the police know. Who do you think you're kidding?"

"I'm not kidding. I don't know where Wynant is."

"You're working for him and the police are working with you. Don't kid me. Art thought knowing was going to get him a lot of money, poor sap. He didn't know what it was going to get him."

"Did he tell you he knew?" I asked.

"I'm not as dumb as you think. He told me he knew something that was going to get him big dough and I've seen how it worked out. I guess I can put two and two together."

"Sometimes the answer's four," I said, "and sometimes it's twenty-two. I'm not working for Wynant. Now don't say, 'Balls,' again. Do you want to help—"

"No. He was a rat and he held out on the people he was ratting for. He asked for what he got, only don't expect me to forget that I left him with you and Guild, and the next time anybody saw him he was dead."

"I don't want you to forget anything. I'd like you to remember whether—"

"I've got to go to the can," she said and walked away. Her carriage was remarkably graceful.

"I don't know as I'd want to be mixed up with that dame," Studsy said thoughtfully. "She's mean medicine."

Morelli winked at me.

Dorothy touched my arm. "I don't understand, Nick."

I told her that was all right and addressed Morelli: "You were telling us about Julia Wolf."

"Uh-huh. Well, old man Kane booted her out when she was fifteen or sixteen and got in some kind of a jam with a high-school teacher and she took up with a guy called Face Peppler, a smart kid if he didn't talk too much. I remember once me and Face were—" He broke off and cleared his throat. "Anyways, Face and her stuck together—what the hell—it must be five, six years, throwing out the time he was in the army and she was living with some guy that I can't remember his name—a cousin of Dick O'Brien's, a skinny dark-headed guy that liked his liquor. But she went back to Face when he come out of the army, and they stuck together till they got nailed trying to shake down some bird from Toronto. Face took it and got her off with six months—they give him the business. Last I heard he was still in. I saw her when she came out—she touched me for a couple hundred to blow town. I hear from her once, when she sends it back to me and tells me Julia Wolf's her name now and she likes the big city fine, but I know Face is hearing from her right along. So when I move here in '28, I look her up. She's—"

Miriam came back and stood with her hands on her hips as before. "I've been thinking over what you said. You must think I'm pretty dumb."

"No," I said, not very truthfully.

"It's a cinch I'm not dumb enough to fall for that song and dance you tried to give me. I can see things when they're right in front of me."

"All right."

"It's not all right. You killed Art and—"

"Not so loud, girlie." Studsy rose and took her arm. His voice was soothing. "Come along. I want to talk to you." He led her towards the bar.

Morelli winked again. "He likes that. Well, I was saying I

looked her up when I moved here, and she told me she had this job with Wynant and he was nuts about her and she was sitting pretty. It seems they learned her shorthand in Ohio when she was doing her six months and she figures maybe it'll be an in to something—you know, maybe she can get a job somewheres where they'll go out and leave the safe open. A agency had sent her over to do a couple days' work for Wynant and she figured maybe he'd be worth more for a long pull than for a quick tap and a get-away, so she give him the business and wound up with a steady connection. She was smart enough to tell him she had a record and was trying to go straight now and all that, so's not to have the racket spoiled if he found out anyhow, because she said his lawyer was a little leery of her and might have her looked up. I don't know just what she was doing, you understand, because it's her game and she don't need my help, and even if we are pals in a way, there's no sense in telling me anything I might want to go to her boss with. Understand, she wasn't my girl or anything—we was just a couple old friends, been kids playing together. Well, I used to see her ever once in a while—we used to come here a lot—till he kicked up too much of a fuss and then she said she was going to cut it out, she wasn't going to lose a soft bed over a few drinks with me. So that was that. That was October, I guess, and she stuck to it. I haven't seen her since."

"Who else did she run around with?" I asked.

Morelli shook his head. "I don't know. She don't do much talking about people."

"She was wearing a diamond engagement ring. Know anything about it?"

"Nothing except she didn't get it from me. She wasn't wearing it when I see her."

"Do you think she meant to throw in with Peppler again when he got out?"

"Maybe. She didn't seem to worry much about him being in, but she liked to work with him all right and I guess they'd've teamed up again."

"And how about the cousin of Dick O'Brien, the skinny dark-headed lush? What became of him?"

Morelli looked at me in surprise. "Search me."

Studsy returned alone. "Maybe I'm wrong," he said as he sat down, "but I think somebody could do something with that cluck if they took hold of her right."

Morelli said: "By the throat."

Studsy grinned good-naturedly. "No. She's trying to get somewhere. She works hard at her singing lessons and—"

Morelli looked at his empty glass and said: "This tiger milk of yours must be doing her pipes a lot of good." He turned his head to yell at Pete: "Hey, you with the knapsack, some more of the same. We got to sing in the choir tomorrow."

Pete said: "Coming up, Sheppy." His lined gray face lost its dull apathy when Morelli spoke to him.

An immensely fat blond man—so blond he was nearly albino—who had been sitting at Miriam's table came over and said to me in a thin, tremulous, effeminate voice: "So you're the party who put it to little Art Nunheim—"

Morelli hit the fat man in his fat belly, as hard as he could without getting up. Studsy, suddenly on his feet, leaned over Morelli and smashed a big fist into the fat man's face. I noticed, foolishly, that he still led with his right. Hunchbacked Pete came up behind the fat man and banged his empty tray down with full force on the fat man's head. The fat man fell back, upsetting three people and a table. Both bar-tenders were with us by then. One of them hit the fat man with a blackjack as he tried to get up, knocking him forward on hands and knees, the other put a hand down inside the fat man's collar in back, twisting the collar to choke him. With Morelli's help they got the fat man to his feet and hustled him out.

Pete looked after them and sucked a tooth. "That goddamned Sparrow," he explained to me, "you can't take no chances on him when he's drinking."

Studsy was at the next table, the one that had been upset, helping people pick up themselves and their possessions. "That's bad," he was saying, "bad for business, but where you going to draw the line? I ain't running a dive, but I ain't trying to run a young ladies' seminary neither."

Dorothy was pale, frightened; Nora wide-eyed and amazed. "It's a madhouse," she said. "What'd they do that for?"

"You know as much about it as I do," I told her.

Morelli and the bar-tenders came in again, looking pretty pleased with themselves. Morelli and Studsy returned to their seats at our table.

"You boys are impulsive," I said.

Studsy repeated, "Impulsive," and laughed, "Ha-ha-ha."

Morelli was serious. "Any time that guy starts anything, you got to start it first. It's too late when he gets going. We seen him like that before, ain't we, Studsy?"

"Like what?" I asked. "He hadn't done anything."

"He hadn't, all right," Morelli said slowly, "but it's a kind of feeling you get about him sometimes. Ain't that right, Studsy?"

Studsy said: "Uh-huh, he's hysterical."

23

I T WAS about two o'clock when we said good-night to Studsy and Morelli and left the Pigiron Club.

Dorothy slumped down in her corner of the taxicab and said: "I'm going to be sick. I know I am." She sounded as if she was telling the truth.

Nora said: "That booze." She put her head on my shoulder. "Your wife is drunk, Nicky. Listen, you've got to tell me what happened—everything. Not now, tomorrow. I don't understand a thing that was said or a thing that was done. They're marvelous."

Dorothy said: "Listen, I can't go to Aunt Alice's like this. She'd have a fit."

Nora said: "They oughtn't've hit that fat man like that, though it must've been funny in a cruel way."

Dorothy said: "I suppose I'd better go to Mamma's."

Nora said: "Erysipelas hasn't got anything to do with ears. What's a lug, Nicky?"

"An ear."

Dorothy said: "Aunt Alice would have to see me because I forgot the key and I'd have to wake her up."

Nora said: "I love you, Nicky, because you smell nice and know such fascinating people."

Dorothy said: "It's not much out of your way to drop me at Mamma's, is it?"

I said, "No," and gave the driver Mimi's address.

Nora said: "Come home with us."

Dorothy said: "No—o, I'd better not."

Nora asked, "Why not?" and Dorothy said, "Well, I don't think I ought to," and that kind of thing went on until the taxicab stopped at the Courtland.

I got out and helped Dorothy out. She leaned heavily on my arm. "Please come up, just for a minute."

Nora said, "Just for a minute," and got out of the taxicab.

I told the driver to wait. We went upstairs. Dorothy rang the bell. Gilbert, in pyjamas and bathrobe, opened the door. He raised one hand in a warning gesture and said in a low voice: "The police are here."

Mimi's voice came from the living-room: "Who is it, Gil?"

"Mr. and Mrs. Charles and Dorothy."

Mimi came to meet us as we went in. "I never was so glad to see anybody. I just didn't know which way to turn." She had on a pinkish satin robe over a pinkish silk nightgown, and her face was pink and by no means unhappy. She ignored Dorothy, squeezed one of Nora's hands, one of mine. "Now I'm going to stop worrying and leave it all up to you, Nick. You'll have to tell the foolish little woman what to do."

Dorothy, behind me, said, "Balls!" under her breath, but with a lot of feeling.

Mimi did not show that she had heard her daughter. Still holding our hands, she drew us back towards the living-room, chattering: "You know Lieutenant Guild. He's been very nice, but I'm sure I must have tried his patience. I've been so—well—I mean I've been so bewildered. But now you're here and—"

We went into the living-room.

Guild said, "Hello," to me and, "Good evening, ma'am," to Nora. The man with him, the one he had called Andy and who had helped him search our rooms the morning of Morelli's visit, nodded and grunted at us.

"What's up?" I asked.

Guild looked at Mimi out the corners of his eyes, then at me, and said: "The Boston police found Jorgensen or Rosewater or whatever you want to call him at his first wife's place and asked him some questions for us. The chief answer seems to be he don't have anything to do with Julia Wolf getting killed or not getting killed and Mrs. Jorgensen can prove it because she's been holding out what amounts to the goods on Wynant." His eyes slid sidewise in their sockets to focus on Mimi again. "The lady kind of don't want to say yes and kind of don't want to say no. To tell you the truth, Mr. Charles, I don't know what to make of her in a lot of ways."

I could understand that. I said, "She's probably frightened," and Mimi tried to look frightened. "Has he been divorced from the first wife?"

"Not according to the first wife."

Mimi said: "She's lying, I bet."

I said: "Sh-h-h. Is he coming back to New York?"

"It looks like he's going to make us extradite him if we want him. Boston says he's squawking his head off for a lawyer."

"Do you want him that bad?"

Guild moved his big shoulders. "If bringing him back'll help us on this murder. I don't care much about any of the old charges or the bigamy. I never believe in hounding a man over things that are none of my business."

I asked Mimi: "Well?"

"Can I talk to you alone?"

I looked at Guild, who said: "Anything that'll help."

Dorothy touched my arm. "Nick, listen to me first. I—" She broke off. Everybody was staring at her.

"What?" I asked.

"I—I want to talk to you first."

"Go ahead."

"I mean alone," she said.

I patted her hand. "Afterwards."

Mimi led me into her bedroom and carefully shut the door. I sat on the bed and lit a cigarette. Mimi leaned back against the door and smiled at me very gently and trustingly. Half a minute passed that way.

Then she said, "You do like me, Nick," and when I said nothing she asked, "Don't you?"

"No."

She laughed and came away from the door. "You mean you don't approve of me." She sat on the bed beside me. "But you do like me well enough to help me?"

"That depends."

"Depends on wha—"

The door opened and Dorothy came in. "Nick, I've got to—"

Mimi jumped up and confronted her daughter. "Get out of here," she said through her teeth.

Dorothy flinched, but she said: "I won't. You're not going to make a—"

Mimi slashed Dorothy across the mouth with the back of her right hand. "Get out of here."

Dorothy screamed and put a hand to her mouth. Holding it there, holding her wide frightened eyes on Mimi's face, she backed out of the room.

Mimi shut the door again.

I said: "You must come over to our place some time and bring your little white whips."

She did not seem to hear me. Her eyes were heavy, brooding, and her lips were thrust out a little in a half-smile, and when she spoke, her voice seemed heavier, throatier, than usual. "My daughter's in love with you."

"Nonsense."

"She is and she's jealous of me. She has absolute spasms whenever I get within ten feet of you." She spoke as if thinking of something else.

"Nonsense. Maybe she's got a little hangover from that crush she had on me when she was twelve, but that's all it is."

Mimi shook her head. "You're wrong, but never mind." She sat down on the bed beside me again. "You've got to help me out of this. I—"

"Sure," I said. "You're a delicate *fleur* that needs a great big man's protection."

"Oh, that?" She waved a hand at the door through which Dorothy had gone. "You're surely not getting— Why, it's nothing you haven't heard about before—and seen and done, for that matter. It's nothing to worry you." She smiled as before, with heavy, brooding eyes, and lips thrust out a little. "If you want Dorry, take her, but don't get sentimental about it.

But never mind that. Of course I'm not a delicate *fleur*. You never thought I was."

"No," I agreed.

"Well, then," she said with an air of finality.

"Well then what?"

"Stop being so damned coquettish," she said. "You know what I mean. You understand me as well as I understand you."

"Just about, but you've been doing the coquetting ever since—"

"I know. That was a game. I'm not playing now. That son of a bitch made a fool of me, Nick, an out and out fool, and now he's in trouble and expects me to help him. I'll help him." She put a hand on my knee and her pointed nails dug into my flesh. "The police, they don't believe me. How can I make them believe that he's lying, that I know nothing more than I've told them about the murder?"

"You probably can't," I said slowly, "especially since Jorgensen's only repeating what you told me a few hours ago."

She caught her breath, and her nails dug into me again. "Did you tell them that?"

"Not yet." I took her hand off my knee.

She sighed with relief. "And of course you won't tell them now, will you?"

"Why not?"

"Because it's a lie. He lied and I lied. I didn't find anything, anything at all."

I said: "We're back where we were earlier, and I believe you just as much now as I did then. What happened to those new terms we were on? You understanding me, me understanding you, no coquetting, no games, no playing."

She slapped my hand lightly. "All right. I did find something—not much, but something—and I'm not going to give it up to help that son of a bitch. You can understand how I feel about it, Nick. You'd feel the same—"

"Maybe," I said, "but the way it stands, I've got no reason for putting in with you. Your Chris is no enemy of mine. I've got nothing to gain by helping you frame him."

She sighed. "I've been thinking about that a lot. I don't

suppose what money I could give you would mean much to you now"—she smiled crookedly—"nor my beautiful white body. But aren't you interested in saving Clyde?"

"Not necessarily."

She laughed at that. "I don't know what that means."

"It might mean I don't think he needs saving. The police haven't got much on him. He's screwy, he was in town the day Julia was killed, and she had been gypping him. That's not enough to arrest him on."

She laughed again. "But with my contribution?"

"I don't know. What is it?" I asked, and went on without waiting for the answer I did not expect. "Whatever it is, you're being a sap, Mimi. You've got Chris cold on bigamy. Sock that to him. There's no—"

She smiled sweetly and said: "But I am holding that in reserve to use after this if he—"

"If he gets past the murder charge, huh? Well, it won't work out that way, lady. You can get him about three days in jail. By that time the District Attorney will have questioned him and checked up on him enough to know that he didn't kill Julia and that you've been making a chump of the D. A., and when you spring your little bigamy charge the D. A. will tell you to go jump in the lake, and he'll refuse to prosecute."

"But he can't do that, Nick."

"Can and will," I assured her, "and if he can dig up proof that you're holding out something he'll make it as tough for you as he can."

She chewed her lower lip, asked: "You're being honest with me?"

"I'm telling you exactly what'll happen, unless district attorneys have changed a lot since my day."

She chewed her lip some more. "I don't want him to get off," she said presently, "and I don't want to get into any trouble myself." She looked up at me. "If you're lying to me, Nick . . ."

"There's nothing you can do about it except believe me or disbelieve me."

She smiled and put a hand on my cheek and kissed me on the mouth and stood up. "You're such a bastard. Well, I'm going to believe you." She walked down to the other end of the room and back again. Her eyes were shiny, her face pleasantly excited.

"I'll call Guild," I said.

"No, wait. I'd rather—I'd rather see what you think of it first."

"All right, but no clowning."

"You're certainly afraid of your shadow," she said, "but don't worry, I'm not going to play any tricks on you."

I said that would be swell and how about showing me whatever she had to show me. "The others will be getting restless."

She went around the bed to a closet, opened the door, pushed some clothes aside, and put a hand among other clothes behind them. "That's funny," she said.

"Funny?" I stood up. "It's a panic. It'll have Guild rolling on the floor." I started towards the door.

"Don't be so bad-tempered," she said. "I've got it." She turned to me holding a wadded handkerchief in her hand. As I approached, she opened the handkerchief to show me a three-inch length of watch-chain, broken at one end, attached at the other to a small gold knife. The handkerchief was a woman's and there were brown stains on it.

"Well?" I asked.

"It was in her hand and I saw it when they left me with her and I knew it was Clyde's, so I took it."

"You're sure it's his?"

"Yes," she said impatiently. "See, they're gold, silver, and copper links. He had it made out of the first batches of metal that came through that smelting process he invented. Anybody who knows him at all well can identify it—there can't be another like it." She turned the knife over to let me see the CMW engraved in it. "They're his initials. I never saw the knife before, but I'd know the chain anywhere. Clyde's worn it for years."

"Did you remember it well enough that you could've described it without seeing it again?"

"Of course."

"Is that your handkerchief?"

"Yes."

"And the stain on it's blood?"

"Yes. The chain was in her hand—I told you—and there was some blood on them." She frowned at me. "Don't you— You act as if you don't believe me."

"Not exactly," I said, "but I think you ought to be sure you're telling your story straight this time."

She stamped her foot. "You're—" She laughed and anger went out of her face. "You can be the most annoying man. I'm telling the truth now, Nick. I've told you everything that happened exactly as it happened."

"I hope so. It's about time. You're sure Julia didn't come to enough to say anything while you were alone with her?"

"You're trying to make me mad again. Of course I'm sure."

"All right," I said. "Wait here. I'll get Guild, but if you tell him the chain was in Julia's hand and she wasn't dead yet he's going to wonder whether you didn't have to rough her up a little to get it away from her."

She opened her eyes wide. "What should I tell him?"

I went out and shut the door.

24

NORA, looking a little sleepy, was entertaining Guild and Andy in the living-room. The Wynant offspring were not in sight.

"Go ahead," I told Guild. "First door to the left. I think she's readied up for you."

"Crack her?" he asked.

I nodded.

"What'd you get?"

"See what you get and we'll put them together and see how they add up," I suggested.

"O.K. Come on, Andy." They went out.

"Where's Dorothy?" I asked.

Nora yawned. "I thought she was with you and her mother. Gilbert's around somewhere. He was here till a few minutes ago. Do we have to hang around long?"

"Not long." I went back down the passageway past Mimi's door to another bedroom door, which was open, and looked in. Nobody was there. A door facing it was shut. I knocked on it.

Dorothy's voice: "What is it?"

"Nick," I said and went in.

She was lying on her side on a bed, dressed except for her slippers. Gilbert was sitting on the bed beside her. Her mouth seemed a little puffy, but it may have been from crying: her eyes were red. She raised her head to stare sullenly at me.

"Still want to talk to me?" I asked.

Gilbert got up from the bed. "Where's Mamma?"

"Talking to the police."

He said something I did not catch and left the room.

Dorothy shuddered. "He gives me the creeps," she said, and then remembered to stare sullenly at me again.

"Still want to talk to me?"

"What made you turn against me like that?"

"You're being silly." I sat down where Gilbert had been sitting. "Do you know anything about this knife and chain your mother's supposed to have found?"

"No. Where?"

"What'd you want to tell me?"

"Nothing—now," she said disagreeably, "except you might at least wipe her lipstick off your mouth."

I wiped it off. She snatched the handkerchief from my hand and rolled over to pick up a package of matches from the table on that side of the bed. She struck a match.

"That's going to stink like hell," I said.

She said, "I don't care," but she blew out the match. I took the handkerchief, went to a window, opened it, dropped the handkerchief out, shut the window, and went back to my seat on the bed. "If that makes you feel any better."

"What did Mamma say—about me?"

"She said you're in love with me."

She sat up abruptly. "What did you say?"

"I said you just liked me from when you were a kid."

Her lower lip twitched. "Do—do you think that's what it is?"

"What else could it be?"

"I don't know." She began to cry. "Everybody's made so

much fun of me about it—Mamma and Gilbert and Harri-son— I—"

I put my arms around her. "To hell with them."

After a while she asked: "Is Mamma in love with you?"

"Good God, no! She hates men more than any woman I've ever known who wasn't a Lesbian."

"But she's always having some sort of—"

"That's the body. Don't let it fool you. Mimi hates men—all of us—bitterly."

She had stopped crying. She wrinkled her forehead and said: "I don't understand. Do you hate her?"

"Not as a rule."

"Now?"

"I don't think so. She's being stupid and she's sure she's being very clever, and that's a nuisance, but I don't think I hate her."

"I do," Dorothy said.

"So you told me last week. Something I meant to ask you: did you know or did you ever see the Arthur Nunheim we were talking about in the speakeasy tonight?"

She looked sharply at me. "You're just trying to change the subject."

"I want to know. Did you?"

"No."

"He was mentioned in the newspapers," I reminded her. "He was the one who told the police about Morelli knowing Julia Wolf."

"I didn't remember his name," she said. "I don't remember ever having heard it until tonight."

I described him. "Ever see him?"

"No."

"He may have been known as Albert Norman sometimes. Does that sound familiar?"

"No."

"Know any of the people we saw at Studsy's tonight? Or anything about them?"

"No. Honestly, Nick, I'd tell you if I knew anything at all that might help you."

"No matter who it hurt?"

"Yes," she said immediately, then, "What do you mean?"

"You know damned well what I mean."

She put her hands over her face, and her words were barely audible: "I'm afraid, Nick. I—" She jerked her hands down as someone knocked on the door.

"All right," I called.

Andy opened the door far enough to stick his head in. He tried to keep curiosity from showing in his face while saying: "The Lieutenant wants to see you."

"Be right out," I promised.

He opened the door wider. "He's waiting." He gave me what was probably meant to be a significant wink, but a corner of his mouth moved more than his eye did and the result was a fairly startling face.

"I'll be back," I told Dorothy, and followed him out.

He shut the door behind me and put his mouth close to my ear. "The kid was at the keyhole," he muttered.

"Gilbert?"

"Yep. He had time to get away from it when he heard me coming, but he was there, right enough."

"That's mild for him," I said. "How'd you all make out with Mrs. J.?"

He puckered his thick lips up in an *o* and blew breath out noisily. "What a dame!"

25

WE WENT into Mimi's bedroom. She was sitting in a deep chair by a window looking very pleased with herself. She smiled gayly at me and said: "My soul is spotless now. I've confessed everything."

Guild stood by a table wiping his face with a handkerchief. There were still some drops of sweat on his temples, and his face seemed old and tired. The knife and chain, and the handkerchief they had been wrapped in, were on the table.

"Finished?" I asked.

"I don't know, and that's a fact," he said. He turned his head to address Mimi: "Would you say we were finished?"

Mimi laughed. "I can't imagine what more there would be."

"Well," Guild said slowly, somewhat reluctantly, "in that case I guess I'd like to talk to Mr. Charles, if you'll excuse us for a couple of minutes." He folded his handkerchief carefully and put it in his pocket.

"You can talk here." She got up from the chair. "I'll go out and talk to Mrs. Charles till you're through." She tapped my cheek playfully with the tip of a forefinger as she passed me. "Don't let them say too horrid things about me, Nick."

Andy opened the door for her, shut it behind her, and made the *o* and the blowing noise again.

I lay down on the bed. "Well," I asked, "what's what?"

Guild cleared his throat. "She told us about finding this here chain and knife on the floor where the Wolf dame had most likely broke it off fighting with Wynant, and she told us the reasons why she'd hid it till now. Between me and you, that don't make any too much sense, looking at it reasonably, but maybe that ain't the way to look at it in this case. To tell you the plain truth, I don't know what to make of her in a lot of ways, I don't for a fact."

"The chief thing," I advised them, "is not to let her tire you out. When you catch her in a lie, she admits it and gives you another lie to take its place and, when you catch her in that one, admits it and gives you still another, and so on. Most people—even women—get discouraged after you've caught them in the third or fourth straight lie and fall back on either the truth or silence, but not Mimi. She keeps trying and you've got to be careful or you'll find yourself believing her, not because she seems to be telling the truth, but simply because you're tired of disbelieving her."

Guild said: "Hm-m-m. Maybe." He put a finger inside his collar. He seemed very uncomfortable. "Look here, do you think she killed that dame?"

I discovered that Andy was staring at me so intently that his eyes bulged. I sat up and put my feet on the floor. "I wish I knew. That chain business looks like a plant, all right, but . . . We can find out whether he had a chain like that, maybe whether he still has it. If she remembered the chain as well as she said she did, there's no reason why she couldn't have told a jeweler how to make one, and anybody can buy a knife and have any initials they want engraved on it. There's plenty to be said against the probability of her having gone that far. If she did plant it, it's more likely she had the original chain—maybe she's had it for years—but all that's something for you folks to check up."

"We're doing the best we can," Guild said patiently. "So you do think she did it?"

"The murder?" I shook my head. "I haven't got that far yet. How about Nunheim? Did the bullets match up?"

"They did—from the same gun as was used on the dame—all five of them."

"He was shot five times?"

"He was, and close enough to burn his clothes."

"I saw his girl, the big red-head, tonight in a speak," I told him. "She's saying you and I killed him because he knew too much."

He said: "Hm-m-m. What speak was that? I might want to talk to her."

"Studsy Burke's Pigiron Club," I said, and gave him the address. "Morelli hangs out there too. He tells me Julia Wolf's real name is Nancy Kane and she has a boy friend doing time in Ohio—Face Peppler."

From the tone of Guild's "Yes?" I imagined he had already found out about Peppler and about Julia's past. "And what else did you pick up in your travels?"

"A friend of mine—Larry Crowley, a press agent—saw Jorgensen coming out of a hock-shop on Sixth near Forty-sixth yesterday afternoon."

"Yes?"

"You don't seem to get excited about my news. I'm—"

Mimi opened the door and came in with glasses, whisky, and mineral water on a tray. "I thought you'd like a drink," she said cheerfully.

We thanked her.

She put the tray on the table, said, "I don't mean to interrupt," smiled at us with that air of amused tolerance which women like to affect towards male gatherings, and went out.

"You were saying something," Guild reminded me.

"Just that if you people think I'm not coming clean with

you, you ought to say so. We've been playing along together so far and I wouldn't want—"

"No, no," Guild said hastily, "it's nothing like that, Mr. Charles." His face had reddened a little. "I been— The fact is the Commissioner's been riding us for action and I guess I been kind of passing it on. This second murder's made things tough." He turned to the tray on the table. "How'll you have yours?"

"Straight, thanks. No leads on it?"

"Well, the same gun and a lot of bullets, same as with her, but that's about all. It was a rooming-house hallway in between a couple stores. Nobody there claims they know Nunheim or Wynant or anybody else we can connect. The door's left unlocked, anybody could walk in, but that don't make too much sense when you come to think of it."

"Nobody saw or heard anything?"

"Sure, they heard the shooting, but they didn't see anybody doing it." He gave me a glass of whisky.

"Find any empty shells?" I asked.

He shook his head. "Neither time. Probably a revolver."

"And he emptied it both times—counting the shot that hit her telephone—if, like a lot of people, he carried an empty chamber under the hammer."

Guild lowered the glass he was raising towards his mouth. "You're not trying to find a Chinese angle on it, are you?" he complained, "just because they shoot like that."

"No, but any kind of angle would help some. Find out where Nunheim was the afternoon the girl was killed?"

"Uh-huh. Hanging around the girl's building—part of the time anyhow. He was seen in front and he was seen in back, if you're going to believe people that didn't think much of it at the time and haven't got any reason for lying about it. And the day before the killing he had been up to her apartment, according to an elevator boy. The boy says he came down right away and he don't know whether he got in or not."

I said: "So. Maybe Miriam's right, maybe he did know too much. Find out anything about the four thousand difference between what Macaulay gave her and what Clyde Wynant says he got from her?"

"No."

"Morelli says she always had plenty of money. He says she once lent him five thousand in cash."

Guild raised his eyebrows. "Yes?"

"Yes. He also says Wynant knew about her record."

"Seems to me," Guild said slowly, "Morelli did a lot of talking to you."

"He likes to talk. Find out anything more about what Wynant was working on when he left, or what he was going away to work on?"

"No. You're kind of interested in that shop of his."

"Why not? He's an inventor, the shop's his place. I'd like to have a look at it some time."

"Help yourself. Tell me some more about Morelli, and how you go about getting him to open up."

"He likes to talk. Do you know a fellow called Sparrow? A big fat pale fellow with a pansy voice?"

Guild frowned. "No. Why?"

"He was there—with Miriam—and wanted to take a crack at me, but they wouldn't let him."

"And what'd he want to do that for?"

"I don't know. Maybe because she told him I helped knock Nunheim off—helped you."

Guild said: "Oh." He scratched his chin with a thumb-nail, looked at his watch. "It's getting kind of late. Suppose you drop in and see me some time tomorrow—today."

I said, "Sure," instead of the things I was thinking, nodded at him and Andy, and went out to the living-room.

Nora was sleeping on the sofa. Mimi put down the book she was reading and asked: "Is the secret session over?"

"Yes." I moved towards the sofa.

Mimi said: "Let her sleep awhile, Nick. You're going to stay till after your police friends have gone, aren't you?"

"All right. I want to see Dorothy again."

"But she's asleep."

"That's all right. I'll wake her up."

"But—"

Guild and Andy came in, said their good nights, Guild looked regretfully at the sleeping Nora, and they left.

Mimi sighed. "I'm tired of policemen," she said. "You remember that story?"

"Yes."

Gilbert came in. "Do they really think Chris did it?"

"No," I said.

"Who do they think?"

"I could've told you yesterday. I can't today."

"That's ridiculous," Mimi protested. "They know very well and you know very well that Clyde did it." When I said nothing she repeated, more sharply: "You know very well that Clyde did it."

"He didn't," I said.

An expression of triumph brightened Mimi's face. "You *are* working for him, now aren't you?"

My "No" bounced off her with no effect whatever.

Gilbert asked, not argumentatively, but as if he wanted to know: "Why couldn't he?"

"He could've, but he didn't. Would he have written those letters throwing suspicion on Mimi, the one person who's helping him by hiding the chief evidence against him?"

"But maybe he didn't know that. Maybe he thought the police were simply not telling all they knew. They often do that, don't they? Or maybe he thought he could discredit her, so they wouldn't believe her if—"

"That's it," Mimi said. "That's exactly what he did, Nick."

I said to Gilbert: "You don't think he killed her."

"No, I don't think he did, but I'd like to know why you don't think so—you know—your method."

"And I'd like to know yours."

His face flushed a little and there was some embarrassment in his smile. "Oh, but I—it's different."

"He *knows* who killed her," Dorothy said from the doorway. She was still dressed. She stared at me fixedly, as if afraid to look at anybody else. Her face was pale and she held her small body stiffly erect.

Nora opened her eyes, pushed herself up on an elbow, and asked, "What?" sleepily. Nobody answered her.

Mimi said: "Now, Dorry, don't let's have one of those idiotic dramatic performances."

Dorothy said: "You can beat me after they've gone. You will." She said it without taking her eyes off mine.

Mimi tried to look as if she did not know what her daughter was talking about.

"Who does he know killed her?" I asked.

Gilbert said: "You're making an ass of yourself, Dorry, you're—"

I interrupted him: "Let her. Let her say what she's got to say. Who killed her, Dorothy?"

She looked at her brother and lowered her eyes and no longer held herself erect. Looking at the floor, she said indistinctly: "I don't know. He knows." She raised her eyes to mine and began to tremble. "Can't you see I'm afraid?" she cried. "I'm afraid of them. Take me away and I'll tell you, but I'm afraid of them."

Mimi laughed at me. "You asked for it. It serves you right."

Gilbert was blushing. "It's so silly," he mumbled.

I said: "Sure, I'll take you away, but I'd like to have it out now while we're all together."

Dorothy shook her head. "I'm afraid."

Mimi said: "I wish you wouldn't baby her so, Nick. It only makes her worse. She—"

I asked Nora: "What do you say?"

She stood up and stretched without lifting her arms. Her face was pink and lovely as it always is when she has been sleeping. She smiled drowsily at me and said: "Let's go home. I don't like these people. Come on, get your hat and coat, Dorothy."

Mimi said to Dorothy: "Go to bed."

Dorothy put the tips of the fingers of her left hand to her mouth and whimpered through them: "Don't let her beat me, Nick."

I was watching Mimi, whose face wore a placid half-smile, but her nostrils moved with her breathing and I could hear her breathing.

Nora went around to Dorothy. "Come on, we'll wash your face and—"

Mimi made an animal noise in her throat, muscles thickened on the back of her neck, and she put her weight on the balls of her feet.

Nora stepped between Mimi and Dorothy. I caught Mimi by a shoulder as she started forward, put my other arm around her waist from behind, and lifted her off her feet. She screamed and hit back at me with her fists and her hard sharp high heels made dents in my shins.

Nora pushed Dorothy out of the room and stood in the doorway watching us. Her face was very live. I saw it clearly, sharply: everything else was blurred. When clumsy, ineffectual, blows on my back and shoulder brought me around to find Gilbert pommeling me, I could see him but dimly and I hardly felt the contact when I shoved him aside. "Cut it out. I don't want to hurt you, Gilbert." I carried Mimi over to the sofa and dumped her on her back on it, sat on her knees, got a wrist in each hand.

Gilbert was at me again. I tried to pop his knee-cap, but kicked him too low, kicked his leg from under him. He went down on the floor in a tangle. I kicked at him again, missed, and said: "We can fight afterwards. Get some water."

Mimi's face was becoming purple. Her eyes protruded, glassy, senseless, enormous. Saliva bubbled and hissed between clenched teeth with her breathing, and her red throat—her whole body—was a squirming mass of veins and muscles swollen until it seemed they must burst. Her wrists were hot in my hands and sweat made them hard to hold.

Nora beside me with a glass of water was a welcome sight. "Chuck it in her face," I said.

Nora chucked it. Mimi separated her teeth to gasp and she shut her eyes. She moved her head violently from side to side, but there was less violence in the squirming of her body.

"Do it again," I said.

The second glass of water brought a spluttering protest from Mimi and the fight went out of her body. She lay still, limp, panting.

I took my hands away from her wrists and stood up. Gilbert, standing on one foot, was leaning against a table nursing the leg I had kicked. Dorothy, big-eyed and pale, was in the doorway, undecided whether to come in or run off and hide. Nora, beside me, holding the empty glass in her hand, asked: "Think she's all right?"

"Sure."

Presently Mimi opened her eyes, tried to blink the water out of them. I put a handkerchief in her hand. She wiped her face, gave a long shivering sigh, and sat up on the sofa. She looked around the room, still blinking a little. When she saw me she smiled feebly. There was guilt in her smile, but nothing you could call remorse. She touched her hair with an unsteady hand and said: "I've certainly been drowned."

I said: "Some day you're going into one of those things and not come out of it."

She looked past me at her son. "Gil. What's happened to you?" she asked.

He hastily took his hand off his leg and put his foot down on the floor. "I—uh—nothing," he stammered. "I'm perfectly all right." He smoothed his hair, straightened his necktie.

She began to laugh. "Oh, Gil, did you really try to protect me? And from Nick?" Her laughter increased. "It was awfully sweet of you, but awfully silly. Why, he's a monster, Gil. Nobody could—" She put my handkerchief over her mouth and rocked back and forth.

I looked sidewise at Nora. Her mouth was set and her eyes were almost black with anger. I touched her arm. "Let's blow. Give your mother a drink, Gilbert. She'll be all right in a minute or two."

Dorothy, hat and coat in her hands, tiptoed to the outer door. Nora and I found our hats and coats and followed her out, leaving Mimi laughing into my handkerchief on the sofa.

None of the three of us had much to say in the taxicab that carried us over to the Normandie. Nora was brooding, Dorothy seemed still pretty frightened, and I was tired—it had been a full day.

It was nearly five o'clock when we got home. Asta greeted us boisterously. I lay down on the floor to play with her while Nora went into the pantry to make coffee. Dorothy wanted to tell me something that happened to her when she was a little child.

I said: "No. You tried that Monday. What is it? a gag? It's late. What was it you were afraid to tell me over there?"

"But you'd understand better if you'd let me—"

"You said *that* Monday. I'm not a psychoanalyst. I don't know anything about early influences. I don't give a damn about them. And I'm tired—I been ironing all day."

She pouted at me. "You seem to be trying to make it as hard for me as you can."

"Listen, Dorothy," I said, "you either know something you were afraid to say in front of Mimi and Gilbert or you don't. If you do, spit it out. I'll ask you about any of it I find myself not understanding."

She twisted a fold of her skirt and looked sulkily at it, but when she raised her eyes they became bright and excited. She spoke in a whisper loud enough for anybody in the room to hear: "Gil's been seeing my father and he saw him today and my father told him who killed Miss Wolf."

"Who?"

She shook her head. "He wouldn't tell me. He'd just tell me that."

"And that's what you were afraid to say in front of Gil and Mimi?"

"Yes. You'd understand that if you'd let me tell you—"

"Something that happened when you were a little child. Well, I won't. Stop it. What else did he tell you?"

"Nothing."

"Nothing about Nunheim?"

"No, nothing."

"Where is your father?"

"Gil didn't tell me."

"When did he meet him?"

"He didn't tell me. Please don't be mad, Nick. I've told you everything he told me."

"And a fat lot it is," I growled. "When'd he tell you this?"

"Tonight. He was telling me when you came in my room, and, honest, that's all he told me."

I said: "It'd be swell if just once one of you people would make a clear and complete statement about something—it wouldn't matter what."

Nora came in with the coffee. "What's worrying you now, son?" she asked.

"Things," I said, "riddles, lies, and I'm too old and too tired for them to be any fun. Let's go back to San Francisco."

"Before New Year's?"

"Tomorrow, today."

"I'm willing." She gave me a cup. "We can fly back, if you want, and be there for New Year's Eve."

Dorothy said tremulously: "I didn't lie to you, Nick. I told you everything I— Please, please don't be mad with me. I'm so—" She stopped talking to sob.

I rubbed Asta's head and groaned.

Nora said: "We're all worn out and jumpy. Let's send the pup downstairs for the night and turn in and do our talking after we've had some rest. Come on, Dorothy, I'll bring your coffee into the bedroom and give you some night-clothes."

Dorothy got up, said, "Good-night," to me, "I'm sorry I'm so silly," and followed Nora out.

When Nora returned she sat down on the floor beside me. "Our Dorry does her share of weeping and whining," she said. "Admitting life's not too pleasant for her just now, still . . ." She yawned. "What was her fearsome secret?"

I told her what Dorothy had told me. "It sounds like a lot of hooey."

"Why?"

"Why not? Everything else we've got from them has been hooey."

Nora yawned again. "That may be good enough for a detective, but it's not convincing enough for me. Listen, why don't we make a list of all the suspects and all the motives and clues, and check them off against—"

"You do it. I'm going to bed. What's a clue, Mamma?"

"It's like when Gilbert tiptoed over to the phone tonight when I was alone in the living-room, and he thought I was asleep, and told the operator not to put through any incoming calls until morning."

"Well, well."

"And," she said, "it's like Dorothy discovering that she had Aunt Alice's key all the time."

"Well, well."

"And it's like Studsy nudging Morelli under the table when he started to tell you about the drunken cousin of—what was it?—Dick O'Brien's that Julia Wolf knew."

I got up and put our cups on a table. "I don't see how any detective can hope to get along without being married to you, but, just the same, you're overdoing it. Studsy nudging

Morelli is my idea of something to spend a lot of time not worrying about. I'd rather worry about whether they pushed Sparrow around to keep me from being hurt or to keep me from being told something. I'm sleepy."

"So am I. Tell me something, Nick. Tell me the truth: when you were wrestling with Mimi, didn't you have an erection?"

"Oh, a little."

She laughed and got up from the floor. "If you aren't a disgusting old lecher," she said. "Look, it's daylight."

26

NORA shook me awake at quarter past ten. "The telephone," she said. "It's Herbert Macaulay and he says it's important."

I went into the bedroom—I had slept in the living-room—to the telephone. Dorothy was sleeping soundly. I mumbled, "Hello," into the telephone.

Macaulay said: "It's too early for that lunch, but I've got to see you right away. Can I come up now?"

"Sure. Come up for breakfast."

"I've had it. Get yours and I'll be up in fifteen minutes."

"Right."

Dorothy opened her eyes less than half-way, said, "It must be late," sleepily, turned over, and returned to unconsciousness.

I put cold water on my face and hands, brushed my teeth and hair, and went back to the living-room. "He's coming up," I told Nora. "He's had breakfast, but you'd better order some coffee for him. I want chicken livers."

"Am I invited to your party or do I—"

"Sure. You've never met Macaulay, have you? He's a pretty good guy. I was attached to his outfit for a few days once, up around Vaux, and we looked each other up after the war. He threw a couple of jobs my way, including the Wynant one. How about a drop of something to cut the phelgm?"

"Why don't you stay sober today?"

"We didn't come to New York to stay sober. Want to see a hockey game tonight?"

"I'd like to." She poured me a drink and went to order breakfast.

I looked through the morning papers. They had the news of Jorgensen's being picked up by the Boston police and of Nunheim's murder, but further developments of what the tabloids called "The Hell's Kitchen Gang War," the arrest of "Prince Mike" Gerguson, and an interview with the "Jafsie" of the Lindbergh kidnapping negotiations got more space.

Macaulay and the bellboy who brought Asta up arrived together. Asta liked Macaulay because when he patted her he gave her something to set her weight against: she was never very fond of gentleness.

He had lines around his mouth this morning and some of the rosiness was gone from his cheeks. "Where'd the police get this new line?" he asked. "Do they think—" He broke off as Nora came in. She had dressed.

"Nora, this is Herbert Macaulay," I said. "My wife."

They shook hands and Nora said: "Nick would only let me order some coffee for you. Can't I—"

"No, thanks, I've just finished breakfast."

I said: "Now what's this about the police?"

He hesitated.

"Nora knows practically everything I know," I assured him, "so unless it's something you'd rather not—"

"No, no, nothing like that," he said. "It's—well—for Mrs. Charles's sake. I don't want to cause her anxiety."

"Then out with it. She only worries about things she doesn't know. What's the new police line?"

"Lieutenant Guild came to see me this morning," he said. "First he showed me a piece of watch-chain with a knife attached to it and asked me if I'd ever seen them before. I had: they were Wynant's. I told him I thought I had: I thought they looked like Wynant's. Then he asked me if I knew of any way in which they could have come into anybody else's possession and, after some beating about the bush, I discovered that by anybody else he meant you or Mimi. I told him certainly—Wynant could have given them to either of you, you could have stolen them or found them on the street or have been given them by somebody who stole them or found them on the street, or you could have got them from somebody Wynant gave them to. There were other ways, too, for you to have got them, I told him, but he knew I was kidding him, so he wouldn't let me tell him about them."

There were spots of color in Nora's cheeks and her eyes were dark. "The idiot!"

"Now, now," I said. "Maybe I should have warned you—he was heading in that direction last night. I think it's likely my old pal Mimi gave him a prod or two. What else did he turn the searchlight on?"

"He wanted to know about—what he asked was: 'Do you figure Charles and the Wolf dame was still playing around together? Or was that all washed up?'"

"That's the Mimi touch, all right," I said. "What'd you tell him?"

"I told him I didn't know whether you were 'still' playing around together because I didn't know that you had ever played around together, and reminded him that you hadn't been living in New York for a long time anyway."

Nora asked me: "Did you?"

I said: "Don't try to make a liar out of Mac. What'd he say to that?"

"Nothing. He asked me if I thought Jorgensen knew about you and Mimi and, when I asked him what about you and Mimi, he accused me of acting the innocent—they were his words—so we didn't get very far. He was interested in the times I had seen you, also, where and when to the exact inch and second."

"That's nice," I said. "I've got lousy alibis."

A waiter came in with our breakfast. We talked about this and that until he had set the table and gone away.

Then Macaulay said: "You've nothing to be afraid of. I'm going to turn Wynant over to the police." His voice was unsteady and a little choked.

"Are you sure he did it?" I asked. "I'm not."

He said simply: "I know." He cleared his throat. "Even if there was a chance in a thousand of my being wrong—and there isn't—he's a madman, Charles. He shouldn't be loose."

"That's probably right enough," I began, "and if you know—"

"I know," he repeated. "I saw him the afternoon he killed her; it couldn't've been half an hour after he'd killed her, though I didn't know that, didn't even know she'd been killed. I—well—I know it now."

"You met him in Hermann's office?"

"What?"

"You were supposed to have been in the office of a man named Hermann, on Fifty-seventh Street, from around three o'clock till around four that afternoon. At least, that's what the police told me."

"That's right," he said. "I mean that's the story they got. What really happened: after I failed to find Wynant or any news of him at the Plaza and phoned my office and Julia with no better results, I gave him up and started walking down to Hermann's. He's a mining engineer, a client of mine; I had just finished drawing up some articles of incorporation for him, and there were some minor changes to be made in them. When I got to Fifty-seventh Street I suddenly got a feeling that I was being followed—you know the feeling. I couldn't think of any reason for anybody shadowing me, but, still, I'm a lawyer and there might be. Anyhow, I wanted to find out, so I turned east on Fifty-seventh and walked over to Madison and still wasn't sure. There was a small sallow man I thought I'd seen around the Plaza, but— The quickest way to find out seemed to be by taking a taxi, so I did that and told the driver to drive east. There was too much traffic there for me to see whether this small man or anybody else took a taxi after me, so I had my driver turn south at Third, east again on Fifty-sixth, and south again on Second Avenue, and by that time I was pretty sure a yellow taxi was following me. I couldn't see whether my small man was in it, of course; it wasn't close enough for that. And at the next corner, when a red light stopped us, I saw Wynant. He was in a taxicab going west on Fifty-fifth Street. Naturally, that didn't surprise me very much: we were only two blocks from Julia's and I took it for granted she hadn't wanted me to know he was there when I phoned and that he was now on his way over to meet me at the Plaza. He was never very punctual. So I told my driver to turn west, but at Lexington Avenue—we were half a block behind him—Wynant's taxicab turned south. That wasn't the way to the Plaza and wasn't even the way to my office, so I said to hell with him and turned my attention back to the taxi following me—and it wasn't there any more. I kept a look-out behind all the way over to Hermann's and saw no sign at all of anybody following me."

"What time was it when you saw Wynant?" I asked.

"It must've been fifteen or twenty minutes past three. It was twenty minutes to four when I got to Hermann's and I imagine that was twenty or twenty-five minutes later. Well, Hermann's secretary—Louise Jacobs, the girl I was with when I saw you last night—told me he had been locked up in a conference all afternoon, but would probably be through in a few minutes, and he was, and I got through with him in ten or fifteen minutes and went back to my office."

"I take it you weren't close enough to Wynant to see whether he looked excited, was wearing his watch-chain, smelled of gunpowder—things like that."

"That's right. All I saw was his profile going past, but don't think I'm not sure it was Wynant."

"I won't. Go ahead," I said.

"He didn't phone again. I'd been back about an hour when the police phoned—Julia was dead. Now you must understand that I didn't think Wynant had killed her—not for a minute. You can understand that—you still don't think he did. So when I went over there and the police began to ask me questions about him and I could see they suspected him, I did what ninety-nine out of a hundred lawyers would've done for their clients—I said nothing about having seen him in that neighborhood at about the time that the murder must have been committed. I told them what I told you—about having the date with him and him not showing up—and let them understand that I had gone over to Hermann's straight from the Plaza."

"That's understandable enough," I agreed. "There was no sense in your saying anything until you had heard his side of the story."

"Exactly and, well, the catch is I never heard his side of the story. I'd expected him to show up, phone me, something, but he didn't—until Tuesday, when I got that letter from him from Philadelphia, and there was not a word in it about his failure to meet me Friday, nothing about—but you saw the letter. What'd you think of it?"

"You mean did it sound guilty?"

"Yes."

"Not particularly," I said. "It's about what could be expected from him if he didn't kill her—no great alarm over the police suspecting him except as it might interfere with his work, a desire to have it all cleaned up with no inconvenience to him—not too bright a letter to have come from anybody else, but in line with his particular form of goofiness. I can see him sending it off without the faintest notion that the best thing he could do would be to account for his own actions on the day of the murder. How sure are you he was coming from Julia's when you saw him?"

"I'm sure now. I thought it likely at first. Then I thought he may have been to his shop. It's on First Avenue, just a few blocks from where I saw him, and, though it's been closed since he went away, we renewed the lease last month and everything's there waiting for him to come back to it, and he could have been there that afternoon. The police couldn't find anything there to show whether he had or hadn't."

"I meant to ask you: there was some talk about his having grown whiskers. Was he—"

"No—the same long bony face with the same ragged near-white mustache."

"Another thing: there was a fellow named Nunheim killed yesterday, a small—"

"I'm coming to that," he said.

"I was thinking about the little fellow you thought might be shadowing you."

Macaulay stared at me. "You mean that might've been Nunheim?"

"I don't know. I was wondering."

"And I don't know," he said. "I never saw Nunheim, far as I—"

"He was a little fellow, not more than five feet three, and would weigh maybe a hundred and twenty. I'd say he was thirty-five or -six. Sallow, dark hair and eyes, with the eyes set pretty close together, big mouth, long limp nose, bat-wing ears—shifty-looking."

"That could easily be him," he said, "though I didn't get too close a view of my man. I suppose the police would let me see him"—he shrugged—"not that it matters now. Where was I? Oh, yes, about not being able to get in touch with Wynant. That put me in an uncomfortable position, since the police clearly thought I was in touch with him and lying about it. So did you, didn't you?"

"Yes," I admitted.

"And you also, like the police, probably suspected that I *had* met him, either at the Plaza or later, on the day of the murder."

"It seemed possible."

"Yes. And of course you were partly right. I had at least seen him, and seen him at a place and time that would've spelled Guilty with a capital G to the police, so, having lied instinctively and by inference, I now lied directly and deliberately. Hermann had been tied up in a conference all that afternoon and didn't know how long I had been waiting to see him. Louise Jacobs is a good friend of mine. Without going into details, I told her she could help me help a client by saying I had arrived there at a minute or two after three o'clock and she agreed readily enough. To protect her in case of trouble, I told her that if anything went wrong she could always say that she hadn't remembered what time I arrived, but that I, the next day, had casually mentioned my arrival at that time and she had no reason for doubting me—throwing the whole thing on me." Macaulay took a deep breath. "None of that's important now. What's important is that I heard from Wynant this morning."

"Another one of those screwy letters?" I asked.

"No, he phoned. I made a date with him for tonight—for you and me. I told him you wouldn't do anything for him unless you could see him, so he promised to meet us tonight. I'm going to take the police, of course. I can't go on justifying my shielding him like this. I can get him an acquittal on grounds of insanity and have him put away. That's all I can do, all I want to do."

"Have you told the police yet?"

"No. He didn't phone till just after they'd left. Anyway, I wanted to see you first. I wanted to tell you I hadn't forgotten what I owed you and—"

"Nonsense," I said.

"It's not." He turned to Nora. "I don't suppose he ever told you he saved my life once in a shell-hole in—"

"He's nuts," I told her. "He fired at a fellow and missed and I fired at him and didn't and that's all there was to it." I addressed him again: "Why don't you let the police wait awhile? Suppose you and I keep this date tonight and hear what he's got to say. We can sit on him and blow whistles when the meeting's about to break up if we're convinced he's the murderer."

Macaulay smiled wearily. "You're still doubtful, aren't you? Well, I'm willing to do it that way if you want, though it seems like a— But perhaps you'll change your mind when I tell you about our telephone conversation."

Dorothy, wearing a nightgown and a robe of Nora's, both much too long for her, came in yawning. "Oh!" she exclaimed when she saw Macaulay, and then, when she had recognized him, "Oh, hello, Mr. Macaulay. I didn't know you were here. Is there any news of my father?"

He looked at me. I shook my head. He told her: "Not yet, but perhaps we'll have some today."

I said: "Dorothy's had some, indirectly. Tell Macaulay about Gilbert."

"You mean about—about my father?" she asked hesitantly, staring at the floor.

"Oh, dear me, no," I said.

Her face flushed and she glanced reproachfully at me; then, hastily, she told Macaulay: "Gil saw my father yesterday and he told Gil who killed Miss Wolf."

"What?"

She nodded four or five times, earnestly.

Macaulay looked at me with puzzled eyes.

"This doesn't have to've happened," I reminded him. "It's what Gil says happened."

"I see. Then you think he might be—?"

"You haven't done much talking to that family since hell broke loose, have you?" I asked.

"No."

"It's an experience. They're all sex-crazy, I think, and it backs up into their heads. They start off—"

Dorothy said angrily: "I think you're horrid. I've done my best to—"

"What are you kicking about?" I demanded. "I'm giving you the break this time: I'm willing to believe Gil did tell you that. Don't expect too much of me."

Macaulay asked: "And who killed her?"

"I don't know. Gil wouldn't tell me."

"Had your brother seen him often?"

"I don't know how often. He said he had been seeing him."

"And was anything said—well—about the man Nunheim?"

"No. Nick asked me that. He didn't tell me anything else at all."

I caught Nora's eye and made signals. She stood up saying: "Let's go in the other room, Dorothy, and give these lads a chance to do whatever it is they think they're doing."

Dorothy went reluctantly, but she went out with Nora.

Macaulay said: "She's grown up to be something to look at." He cleared his throat. "I hope your wife won't—"

"Forget it. Nora's all right. You started to tell me about your conversation with Wynant."

"He phoned right after the police left and said he'd seen the ad in the *Times* and wanted to know what I wanted. I told him you weren't anxious to get yourself mixed up in his troubles and had said you wouldn't touch it at all without talking it over with him first, and we made the date for tonight. Then he asked if I'd seen Mimi and I told him I'd seen her once or twice since her return from Europe and had also seen his daughter. And then he said this: 'If my wife should ask for money, give her any sum in reason.'"

"I'll be damned," I said.

Macaulay nodded. "That's the way I felt about it. I asked him why and he said what he'd read in the morning papers had convinced him that she was Rosewater's dupe, not his confederate, and he had reason to believe she was 'kindly disposed' towards him, Wynant. I began to see what he was up to, then, and I told him she had already turned the knife and chain over to the police. And try to guess what he said to that."

"I give up."

"He hemmed and hawed a bit—not much, mind you—and then as smooth as you like asked: 'You mean the chain and knife on the watch I left with Julia to be repaired?' "

I laughed. "What'd you say?"

"That stumped me. Before I could think up an answer he was saying: 'However, we can discuss that more fully when we meet tonight.' I asked him where and when we'd meet him and he said he'd have to phone me, he didn't know where he'd be. He's to phone me at my house at ten o'clock. He was in a hurry now, though he had seemed leisurely enough before, and hadn't time to answer any of the things I wanted to ask, so he hung up and I phoned you. What do you think of his innocence now?"

"Not as much as I did," I replied slowly. "How sure are you of hearing from him at ten tonight?"

Macaulay shrugged. "You know as much about that as I do."

"Then if I were you I wouldn't bother the police till we've grabbed our wild man and can turn him over to them. This story of yours isn't going to make them exactly love you and, even if they don't throw you in the can right away, they'll make things pretty disagreeable for you if Wynant gives us a run-around tonight."

"I know, but I'd like to get the load off my shoulders."

"A few hours more oughtn't to matter much," I said. "Did either of you say anything about his not keeping the date at the Plaza?"

"No. I didn't get a chance to ask him. Well, if you say wait, I'll wait, but—"

"Let's wait till tonight, anyhow, till he phones you—if he does—and then we can make up our minds whether to take the police along."

"You don't think he'll phone?"

"I'm not too sure," I said. "He didn't keep his last date with you, and he seems to have gone pretty vague on you as soon as he learned that Mimi had turned in the watch-chain and knife. I wouldn't be too optimistic about it. We'll see,

though. I'd better get out to your house at about nine
o'clock, hadn't I?"

"Come for dinner."

"I can't, but I'll make it as early as I can, in case he's ahead
of time. We'll want to move fast. Where do you live?"

Macaulay gave me his address, in Scarsdale, and stood up.
"Will you say good-by to Mrs. Charles for me and thank—
Oh, by the way, I hope you didn't misunderstand me about
Harrison Quinn last night. I meant only just what I said, that
I'd had bad luck taking his advice on the market. I didn't
mean to insinuate that there was anything—you know—or
that he might not've made money for his other customers."

"I understand," I said, and called Nora.

She and Macaulay shook hands and made polite speeches
to each other and he pushed Asta around a little and said,
"Make it as early as you can," to me and went away.

"There goes the hockey game," I said, "unless you find
somebody else to go with."

"Did I miss anything?" Nora asked.

"Not much." I told her what Macaulay had told me. "And
don't ask me what I think of it. I don't know. I know
Wynant's crazy, but he's not acting like a crazy man and he's
not acting like a murderer. He's acting like a man playing
some kind of game. God only knows what the game is."

"I think," she said, "that he's shielding somebody else."

"Why don't you think he did it?"

She looked surprised. "Because you don't."

I said that was a swell reason. "Who is the somebody else?"

"I don't know yet. Now don't make fun of me: I've
thought about it a lot. It wouldn't be Macaulay, because he's
using him to help shield whoever it is and—"

"And it wouldn't be me," I suggested, "because he wants
to use me."

"That's right," she said, "and you're going to feel very silly
if you make fun of me and then I guess who it is before you
do. And it wouldn't be either Mimi or Jorgensen, because he
tried to throw suspicion on them. And it wouldn't be
Nunheim, because he was most likely killed by the same person and, furthermore, wouldn't have to be shielded now. And
it wouldn't be Morelli, because Wynant was jealous of him

and they'd had a row." She frowned at me. "I wish you'd found out more about that big fat man they called Sparrow and that big red-haired woman."

"But how about Dorothy and Gilbert?"

"I wanted to ask you about them. Do you think he's got any very strong paternal feeling for them?"

"No."

"You're probably just trying to discourage me," she said. "Well, knowing them, it's hard to think either of them might've been guilty, but I tried to throw out my personal feelings and stick to logic. Before I went to sleep last night I made a list of all the—"

"There's nothing like a little logic-sticking to ward off insomnia. It's like—"

"Don't be so damned patronizing. Your performance so far has been a little less than dazzling."

"I didn't mean no harm," I said and kissed her. "That a new dress?"

"Ah! Changing the subject, you coward."

27

I WENT to see Guild early in the afternoon and went to work on him as soon as we had shaken hands. "I didn't bring my lawyer along. I thought it looked better if I came by myself."

He wrinkled his forehead and shook his head as if I had hurt him. "Now it was nothing like that," he said patiently.

"It was too much like that."

He sighed. "I wouldn't've thought you'd make the mistake that a lot of people make thinking just because we— You know we got to look at every angle, Mr. Charles."

"That sounds familiar. Well, what do you want to know?"

"All I want to know is who killed her—and him."

"Try asking Gilbert," I suggested.

Guild pursed his lips. "Why him exactly?"

"He told his sister he knew who did it, told her he got it from Wynant."

"You mean he's been seeing the old man?"

"So she says he said. I haven't had a chance to ask him about it."

He squinted his watery eyes at me. "Just what is that layout over there, Mr. Charles?"

"The Jorgensen family? You probably know as much about it as I do."

"I don't," he said, "and that's a fact. I just can't size them up at all. This Mrs. Jorgensen, now, what is she?"

"A blonde."

He nodded gloomily. "Uh-huh, and that's all I know. But look, you've known them a long time and from what she says you and her—"

"And me and her daughter," I said, "and me and Julia Wolf and me and Mrs. Astor. I'm hell with the women."

He held up a hand. "I'm not saying I believe everything she says, and there's nothing to get sore about. You're taking the wrong attitude, if you don't mind me saying it. You're acting like you thought we were out to get you, and that's all wrong, absolutely all wrong."

"Maybe, but you've been talking double to me ever since last—"

He looked at me with steady pale eyes and said calmly: "I'm a copper and I got my work to do."

"That's reasonable enough. You told me to come in today. What do you want?"

"I didn't tell you to come in, I asked you."

"All right. What do you want?"

"I don't want this," he said. "I don't want anything like this. We've been talking man to man up to this time and I'd kind of like to go on thataway."

"You made the change."

"I don't think that's a fact. Look here, Mr. Charles, would you take your oath, or even just tell me straight out, that you've been emptying your pockets to me right along?"

There was no use saying yes—he would not have believed me. I said: "Practically."

"Practically, yes," he grumbled. "Everybody's been telling me practically the whole truth. What I want's some impractical son of a gun that'll shoot the works."

I could sympathize with him: I knew how he felt. I said: "Maybe nobody you've found knows the whole truth."

He made an unpleasant face. "That's very likely, ain't it? Listen, Mr. Charles, I've talked to everybody I could find. If you can find any more for me, I'll talk to them too. You mean Wynant? Don't you suppose we got every facility the department's got working night and day trying to turn him up?"

"There's his son," I suggested.

"There's his son," he agreed. He called in Andy and a swarthy bow-legged man named Kline. "Get me that Wynant kid—the punk—I want to talk to him." They went out. He said: "See, I want people to talk to."

I said: "Your nerves are in pretty bad shape this afternoon, aren't they? Are you bringing Jorgensen down from Boston?"

He shrugged his big shoulders. "His story listens all right to me. I don't know. Want to tell me what you think of it?"

"Sure."

"I'm kind of jumpy this afternoon, for a fact," he said. "I didn't get a single solitary wink of sleep last night. It's a hell of a life. I don't know why I stick at it. A fellow can get a piece of land and some wire fencing and a few head of silver fox and— Well, anyways, when you people scared Jorgensen off back in '25, he says he lit out for Germany, leaving his wife in the lurch—though he don't say much about that—and changing his name to give you more trouble finding him, and on the same account he's afraid to work at his regular job— he calls himself some kind of a technician or something—so pickings are kind of slim. He says he worked at one thing and another, whatever he could get, but near as I can figure out he was mostly gigoloing, if you know what I mean, and not finding too many heavy-money dames. Well, along about '27 or '28 he's in Milan—that's a city in Italy—and he sees in the Paris *Herald* where this Mimi, recently divorced wife of Clyde Miller Wynant, has arrived in Paris. He don't know her personally and she don't know him, but he knows she's a dizzy blonde that likes men and fun and hasn't got much sense. He figures a bunch of Wynant's dough must've come to her with the divorce and, the way he looks at it, any of it he could take away from her wouldn't be any more than what Wynant had gypped him out of—he'd only be getting some of what belonged to him. So he scrapes up the fare to Paris and goes up there. All right so far?"

"Sounds all right."

"That's what I thought. Well, he don't have any trouble getting to know her in Paris—either picking her up or getting somebody to introduce him or whatever happened—and the rest of it's just as easy. She goes for him in a big way—bing, according to him—right off the bat, and the first thing you know she's one jump ahead of him, she's thinking about marrying him. Naturally he don't try to talk her out of that. She'd gotten a lump sum—two hundred thousand berries, by God!—out of Wynant instead of alimony, so her marrying again wasn't stopping any payments, and it'll put him right in the middle of the cash-drawer. So they do it. According to him, it was a trick marriage up in some mountains he says are between Spain and France and was done by a Spanish priest on what was really French soil, which don't make it legal, but I figure he's just trying to discourage a bigamy rap. Personally, I don't care one way or the other. The point is he got his hands on the dough and kept them on it till there wasn't any more dough. And all this time, understand, he says she didn't know he was anybody but Christian Jorgensen, a fellow she met in Paris, and still didn't know it up to the time we grabbed him in Boston. Still sound all right?"

"Still sounds all right," I said, "except, as you say, about the marriage, and even that could be all right."

"Uh-huh, and what difference does it make anyways? So comes the winter and the bank-roll's getting skinny and he's getting ready to take a run-out on her with the last of it, and then she says maybe they could come back to America and tap Wynant for some more. He thinks that's fair enough if it can be done, and she thinks it can be done, so they get on a boat and—"

"The story cracks a little there," I said.

"What makes you think so? He's not figuring on going to Boston, where he knows his first wife is, and he's figuring on keeping out of the way of the few people that know him, including especially Wynant, and somebody's told him there's a statute of limitation making everything just lovely after seven

years. He don't figure he's running much risk. They ain't going to stay here long."

"I still don't like that part of his story," I insisted, "but go
ahead."

"Well, the second day he's here—while they're still trying
to find Wynant—he gets a bad break. He runs into a friend
of his first wife's—this Olga Fenton—on the street and she
recognizes him. He tries to talk her out of tipping off the first
wife and does manage to stall her along a couple days with a
moving-picture story he makes up—what an imagination that
guy's got!—but he don't fool her long, and she goes to her
parson and tells him about it and asks him what she ought to
do and he says she ought to tell the first wife, and so she does,
and the next time she sees Jorgensen she tells him what she'd
done, and he lights out for Boston to try to keep his wife
from kicking up trouble and we pick him up there."

"How about his visit to the hock-shop?" I asked.

"That was part of it. He says there was a train for Boston
leaving in a few minutes and he didn't have any dough with
him and didn't have time to go home for some—besides not
being anxious to face the second wife till he had the first one
quieted down—and the banks were closed, so he soaked his
watch. It checks up."

"Did you see the watch?"

"I can. Why?"

"I was wondering. You don't think it was once on the
other end of that piece of chain Mimi turned over to you?"

He sat up straight. "By God!" Then he squinted at me suspiciously and asked: "Do you know anything about it or are
you—"

"No. I was just wondering. What does he say about the
murders now? Who does he think did them?"

"Wynant. He admits for a while he thought Mimi
might've, but he says she convinced him different. He claims
she wouldn't tell him what she had on Wynant. He might be
just trying to cover himself up on that. I don't guess there's
any doubt about them meaning to use it to shake him down
for that money they wanted."

"Then you don't think she planted the knife and chain?"

Guild pulled down the ends of his mouth. "She could've

planted them to shake him down with. What's wrong with that?"

"It's a little complicated for a fellow like me," I said. "Find out if Face Peppler's still in the Ohio pen?"

"Uh-huh. He gets out next week. That accounts for the diamond ring. He had a pal of his on the outside send it to her for him. Seems they were planning to get married and go straight together after he got out, or some such. Anyways, the warden says he saw letters passing between them reading like that. This Peppler won't tell the warden that he knows anything that'll help us, and the warden don't call to mind anything that was in their letters that's any good to us. Of course, even this much helps some, with the motive. Say Wynant's jealous and she's wearing this other guy's ring and getting ready to go away with him. That'll—" He broke off to answer his telephone. "Yes," he said into it. "Yes. . . . What?. . . . Sure. . . . Sure, but leave somebody there. . . . That's right." He pushed the telephone aside. "Another bum steer on that west Twenty-ninth Street killing yesterday."

"Oh," I said. "I thought I heard Wynant's name. You know how some telephone voices carry."

He blushed, cleared his throat. "Maybe something sounded like it—*why not*, I guess. Uh-huh, that could sound like it—*why not*. I almost forgot: we looked up that fellow Sparrow for you."

"What'd you find out?"

"It looks like there's nothing there for us. His name's Jim Brophy. It figures out that he was making a play for that girl of Nunheim's and she was sore at you and he was just drunk enough to think he could put himself in solid with her by taking a poke at you."

"A nice idea," I said. "I hope you didn't make any trouble for Studsy."

"A friend of yours? He's an ex-con, you know, with a record as long as your arm."

"Sure. I sent him over once." I started to gather up my hat and overcoat. "You're busy. I'll run along and—"

"No, no," he said. "Stick around if you got the time. I got a couple things coming in that'll maybe interest you, and you can give me a hand with that Wynant kid, too, maybe."

I sat down again.

"Maybe you'd like a drink," he suggested, opening a drawer of his desk, but I had never had much luck with policemen's liquor, so I said: "No, thanks."

His telephone rang again and he said into it: "Yes. . . . Yes. . . . That's all right. Come on in." This time no words leaked out to me.

He rocked back in his chair and put his feet on his desk. "Listen, I'm on the level about that silver fox farming and I want to ask you what you think of California for a place."

I was trying to decide whether to tell him about the lion and ostrich farms in the lower part of the state when the door opened and a fat red-haired man brought Gilbert Wynant in. One of Gilbert's eyes was completely shut by swollen flesh around it and his left knee showed through a tear in his pants-leg.

28

I SAID to Guild: "When you say bring 'em in, they bring 'em in, don't they?"

"Wait," he told me. "This is more'n you think." He addressed the fat red-haired man: "Go ahead, Flint, let's have it."

Flint wiped his mouth with the back of a hand. "He's a wildcat for fair, the young fellow. He don't look tough, but, man, he didn't want to come along, I can tell you that. And can he run!"

Guild growled: "You're a hero and I'll see the Commissioner about your medal right away, but never mind that now. Talk turkey."

"I wasn't saying I did anything great," Flint protested. "I was just—"

"I don't give a damn what you did," Guild said. "I want to know what he did."

"Yes, sir, I was getting to that. I relieved Morgan at eight o'clock this morning and everything went along smooth and quiet as per usual, with not a creature was stirring, as the fellow says, till along about ten minutes after two, and then what do I hear but a key in the lock." He sucked in his lips and gave us a chance to express our amazement.

"The Wolf dame's apartment," Guild explained to me. "I had a hunch."

"And what a hunch!" Flint exclaimed, practically top-heavy with admiration. "Man, what a hunch!" Guild glared at him and he went on hastily: "Yes, sir, a key, and then the door opens and this young fellow comes in." He grinned proudly, affectionately, at Gilbert. "Scared stiff, he looked, and when I went for him he was out and away like a streak and it wasn't till the first floor that I caught him, and then, by golly, he put up a tussle and I had to bat him in the eye to tone him down. He don't look tough, but—"

"What'd he do in the apartment?" Guild asked.

"He didn't have a chance to do nothing. I—"

"You mean you jumped him without waiting to see what he was up to?" Guild's neck bulged over the edge of his collar, and his face was as red as Flint's hair.

"I thought it was best not to take no chances."

Guild stared at me with angry incredulous eyes. I did my best to keep my face blank. He said in a choking voice: "That'll do, Flint. Wait outside."

The red-haired man seemed puzzled. He said, "Yes, sir," slowly. "Here's his key." He put the key on Guild's desk and went to the door. There he twisted his head over a shoulder to say: "He claims he's Clyde Wynant's son." He laughed merrily.

Guild, still having trouble with his voice, said: "Oh, he does, does he?"

"Yeah. I seen him somewhere before. I got an idea he used to belong to Big Shorty Dolan's mob. Seems to me I used to see him around—"

"Get out!" Guild snarled, and Flint got out. Guild groaned from deep down in his big body. "That mugg gets me. Big Shorty Dolan's mob. Christ." He shook his head hopelessly and addressed Gilbert: "Well, son?"

Gilbert said: "I know I shouldn't've done it."

"That's a fair start," Guild said genially. His face was becoming normal again. "We all make mistakes. Pull yourself up a chair and let's see what we can do about getting you out of the soup. Want anything for that eye?"

"No, thank you, it's quite all right." Gilbert moved a chair two or three inches towards Guild and sat down.

"Did that bum smack you just to be doing something?"

"No, no, it was my fault. I—I did resist."

"Oh, well," Guild said, "nobody likes to be arrested, I guess. Now what's the trouble?"

Gilbert looked at me with his one good eye.

"You're in as bad a hole as Lieutenant Guild wants to put you," I told him. "You'll make it easy for yourself by making it easy for him."

Guild nodded earnestly. "And that's a fact." He settled himself comfortably in his chair and asked, in a friendly tone: "Where'd you get the key?"

"My father sent it to me in his letter." He took a white envelope from his pocket and gave it to Guild.

I went around behind Guild and looked at the envelope over his shoulder. The address was typewritten, *Mr. Gilbert Wynant, The Courtland,* and there was no postage stamp stuck on it.

"When'd you get it?" I asked.

"It was at the desk when I got in last night, around ten o'clock. I didn't ask the clerk how long it had been there, but I don't suppose it was there when I went out with you, or they'd have given it to me."

Inside the envelope were two sheets of paper covered with the familiar unskillful typewriting. Guild and I read together:

Dear Gilbert:

If all these years have gone by without my having communicated with you, it is only because your mother wished it so and if now I break this silence with a request for your assistance it is because only great need could make me go against your mother's wishes. Also you are a man now and I feel that you yourself are the one to decide whether or not we should go on being strangers or whether we should act in accordance with our ties of blood. That I am in an embarrassing situation now in connection with Julia Wolf's so-called murder I think you know and I trust that you still have remaining enough affection for me to at least

hope that I am in all ways guiltless of any complicity therein,
which is indeed the case. I turn to you now for help in demon-
strating my innocence once and for all to the police and to the
world with every confidence that even could I not count on your
affection for me I nevertheless could count on your natural de-
sire to do anything within your power to keep unblemished the
name that is yours and your sister's as well as your Father's. I
turn to you also because while I have a lawyer who is able and
who believes in my innocence and who is leaving no stone un-
turned to prove it and have hopes of engaging Mr. Nick Charles
to assist him I cannot ask either of them to undertake what is
after all a patently illegal act nor do I know anybody else except
you that I dare confide in. What I wish you to do is this, tomor-
row go to Julia Wolf's apartment at 411 East 54th St. to which
the enclosed key will admit you and between the pages of a book
called The Grand Manner *you will find a certain paper or*
statement which you are to read and destroy immediately. You
are to be sure you destroy it completely leaving not so much as an
ash and when you have read it you will know why this must be
done and will understand why I have entrusted this task to you.
In the event that something should develop to make a change in
our plans advisable I will call you on the telephone late tonight.
If you do not hear from me I will telephone you tomorrow
evening to learn if you have carried out my instructions and to
make arrangements for a meeting. I have every confidence that
you will realize the tremendous responsibility I am placing on
your shoulders and that my confidence is not misplaced.

Affectionately,
Your Father

Wynant's sprawling signature was written in ink beneath
"Your Father."

Guild waited for me to say something. I waited for him.
After a little of that he asked Gilbert: "And did he phone?"

"No, sir."

"How do you know?" I asked. "Didn't you tell the operator not to put any calls through?"

"I—yes, I did. I was afraid you'd find out who it was if he
called up while you were there, but he'd've left some kind of
message with the operator, I think, and he didn't."

"Then you haven't been seeing him?"

"No."

"And he didn't tell you who killed Julia Wolf?"

"No."

"You were lying to Dorothy?"

He lowered his head and nodded at the floor. "I was—it was—I suppose it was jealousy really." He looked up at me now and his face was pink. "You see, Dorry used to look up to me and think I knew more than anybody else about almost everything and—you know—she'd come to me if there was anything she wanted to know and she always did what I told her, and then, when she got to seeing you, it was different. She looked up to you and respected you more— She naturally would, I mean, she'd've been silly if she hadn't, because there's no comparison, of course, but I—I suppose I was jealous and resented—well, not exactly resented it, because I looked up to you too—but I wanted to do something to impress her again—show off, I guess you'd call it—and when I got that letter I pretended I'd been seeing my father and he'd told me who committed those murders, so she'd think I knew things even you didn't." He stopped, out of breath, and wiped his face with a handkerchief.

I outwaited Guild again until presently he said: "Well, I guess there ain't been a great deal of harm done, sonny, if you're sure you ain't doing harm by holding back some other things we ought to know."

The boy shook his head. "No, sir, I'm not holding back anything."

"You don't know anything about that knife and chain your mother give us?"

"No, sir, and I didn't know a thing about it till after she had given it to you."

"How is she?" I asked.

"Oh, she's all right, I think, though she said she was going to stay in bed today."

Guild narrowed his eyes. "What's the matter with her?"

"Hysteria," I told him. "She and the daughter had a row last night and she blew up."

"A row about what?"

"God knows—one of those feminine brain-storms."

Guild said, "Hm-m-m," and scratched his chin.

"Was Flint right in saying you didn't get a chance to hunt for your paper?" I asked the boy.

"Yes. I hadn't even had time to shut the door when he ran at me."

"They're grand detectives I got working for me," Guild growled. "Didn't he yell, 'Boo!' when he jumped out at you? Never mind. Well, son, I can do one of two things, and the which depends on you. I can hold you for a while or I can let you go in exchange for a promise that you'll let me know as soon as your father gets in touch with you and let me know what he tells you and where he wants you to meet him, if any."

I spoke before Gilbert could speak: "You can't ask that of him, Guild. It's his own father."

"I can't, huh?" He scowled at me. "Ain't it for his father's good if he's innocent?"

I said nothing.

Guild's face cleared slowly. "All right, then, son, suppose I put you on a kind of parole. If your father or anybody else asks you to do anything, will you promise to tell them you can't because you give me your word of honor you wouldn't?"

The boy looked at me.

I said: "That sounds reasonable."

Gilbert said: "Yes, sir, I'll give you my word."

Guild made a large gesture with one hand. "Oke. Run along."

The boy stood up saying: "Thank you very much, sir." He turned to me. "Are you going to be—"

"Wait for me outside," I told him, "if you're not in a hurry."

"I will. Good-by, Lieutenant Guild, and thank you." He went out.

Guild grabbed his telephone and ordered *The Grand Manner* and its contents found and brought to him. That done, he clasped his hands behind his head and rocked back in his chair. "So what?"

"It's anybody's guess," I said.

"Look here, you don't still think Wynant didn't do it?"

"What difference does it make what I think? You've got plenty on him now with what Mimi gave you."

"It makes a lot of difference," he assured me. "I'd like a lot to know what you think and why."

"My wife thinks he's trying to cover up somebody else."

"Is that so? Hm-m-m. I was never one to belittle women's intuition and, if you don't mind me saying so, Mrs. Charles is a mighty smart woman. Who does she think it is?"

"She hadn't decided, the last I heard."

He sighed. "Well, maybe that paper he sent the kid for will tell us something."

But the paper told us nothing that afternoon: Guild's men could not find it, could not find a copy of *The Grand Manner* in the dead woman's rooms.

29

GUILD had red-haired Flint in again and put the thumb-screws on him. The red-haired man sweat away ten pounds, but he stuck to it that Gilbert had had no opportunity to disturb anything in the apartment and throughout Flint's guardianship nobody hadn't touched nothing. He did not remember having seen a book called *The Grand Manner*, but he was not a man you would expect to memorize book titles. He tried to be helpful and made idiotic suggestions until Guild chased him out.

"The kid's probably waiting for me outside," I said, "if you think talking to him again will do any good."

"Do you?"

"No."

"Well, then. But, by God, somebody took that book and I'm going to—"

"Why?" I asked.

"Why what?"

"Why'd it have to be there for somebody to take?"

Guild scratched his chin. "Just what do you mean by that?"

"He didn't meet Macaulay at the Plaza the day of the murder, he didn't commit suicide in Allentown, he says he only got a thousand from Julia Wolf when we thought he was getting five thousand, he says they were just friends when we think they were lovers, he disappoints us too much for me to have much confidence in what he says."

"It's a fact," Guild said, "that I'd understand it better if he'd either come in or run away. Him hanging around like this, just messing things up, don't fit in anywheres that I can see."

"Are you watching his shop?"

"We're kind of keeping an eye on it. Why?"

"I don't know," I said truthfully, "except that he's pointed his finger at a lot of things that got us nowhere. Maybe we ought to pay some attention to the things he hasn't pointed at, and the shop's one of them."

Guild said: "Hm-m-m."

I said, "I'll leave you with that bright thought," and put on my hat and coat. "Suppose I wanted to get hold of you late at night, how would I reach you?"

He gave me his telephone number, we shook hands, and I left.

Gilbert Wynant was waiting for me in the corridor. Neither of us said anything until we were in a taxicab. Then he asked: "He thinks I was telling the truth, doesn't he?"

"Sure. Weren't you?"

"Oh, yes, but people don't always believe you. You won't say anything to Mamma about this, will you?"

"Not if you don't want me to."

"Thank you," he said. "In your opinion, is there more opportunity for a young man out West than here in the East?"

I thought of him working on Guild's fox farm while I replied: "Not now. Thinking of going west?"

"I don't know. I want to do something." He fidgeted with his necktie. "You'll think it's a funny question: is there much incest?"

"There's some," I told him; "that's why they've got a name for it."

His face flushed.

I said: "I'm not making fun of you. It's one of the things nobody knows. There's no way of finding out."

We had a couple of blocks of silence after that. Then he

said: "There's another funny question I'd like to ask you: what do you think of me?" He was more self-conscious about it than Alice Quinn had been.

"You're all right," I told him, "and you're all wrong."

He looked away, out the window. "I'm so awfully young."

We had some more silence. Then he coughed and a little blood trickled from one corner of his mouth.

"That guy did hurt you," I said.

He nodded shamefacedly and put his handkerchief to his mouth. "I'm not very strong."

At the Courtland he would not let me help him out of the taxicab and he insisted he could manage alone, but I went upstairs with him, suspecting that otherwise he would say nothing to anybody about his condition.

I rang the apartment bell before he could get his key out, and Mimi opened the door. She goggled at his black eye.

I said: "He's hurt. Get him to bed and get him a doctor."

"What happened?"

"Wynant sent him into something."

"Into what?"

"Never mind that until we get him fixed up."

"But Clyde was here," she said. "That's why I phoned you."

"What?"

"He was." She nodded vigorously. "And he asked where Gil was. He was here for an hour or more. He hasn't been gone ten minutes."

"All right, let's get him to bed."

Gilbert stubbornly insisted that he needed no help, so I left him in the bedroom with his mother and went out to the telephone.

"Any calls?" I asked Nora when I had her on the line.

"Yes, sir. Messrs. Macaulay and Guild want you to phone them, and Mesdames Jorgensen and Quinn want you to phone them. No children so far."

"When did Guild call?"

"About five minutes ago. Mind eating alone? Larry asked me to go see the new Osgood Perkins show with him."

"Go ahead. See you later."

I called up Herbert Macaulay.

"The date's off," he told me. "I heard from our friend and he's up to God knows what. Listen, Charles, I'm going to the police. I've had enough of it."

"I guess there's nothing else to do now," I said. "I was thinking about telephoning some policemen myself. I'm at Mimi's. He was here a few minutes ago. I just missed him."

"What was he doing there?"

"I'm going to try to find out now."

"Were you serious about phoning the police?"

"Sure."

"Then suppose you do that and I'll come on over."

"Right. Be seeing you."

I called up Guild.

"A little news came in right after you left," he said. "Are you where I can give it to you?"

"I'm at Mrs. Jorgensen's. I had to bring the kid home. That red-head lad of yours has got him bleeding somewhere inside."

"I'll kill that mugg," he snarled. "Then I better not talk."

"I've got some news, too. Wynant was here for about an hour this afternoon, according to Mrs. Jorgensen, and left only a few minutes before I got here."

There was a moment of silence, then he said: "Hold everything. I'll be right up."

Mimi came into the living-room while I was looking up the Quinns' telephone number. "Do you think he's seriously hurt?" she asked.

"I don't know, but you ought to get your doctor right away." I pushed the telephone towards her. When she was through with it, I said: "I told the police Wynant had been here."

She nodded. "That's what I phoned you for, to ask if I ought to tell them."

"I phoned Macaulay, too. He's coming over."

"He can't do anything," she said indignantly. "Clyde gave them to me of his own free will—they're mine."

"What's yours?"

"Those bonds, the money."

"What bonds? what money?"

She went to the table and pulled the drawer out. "See?"

Inside were three packages of bonds held together by thick rubber bands. Across the top of them lay a pink check on the Park Avenue Trust Company to the order of Mimi Jorgensen for ten thousand dollars, signed Clyde Miller Wynant, and dated January 3, 1933.

"Dated five days ahead," I said. "What kind of nonsense is that?"

"He said he hadn't that much in his account and might not be able to make a deposit for a couple of days."

"There's going to be hell about this," I warned her. "I hope you're ready for it."

"I don't see why," she protested. "I don't see why my husband—my former husband—can't provide for me and his children if he wants to."

"Cut it out. What'd you sell him?"

"Sell him?"

"Uh-huh. What'd you promise to do in the next few days or he fixes it so the check's no good?"

She made an impatient face. "Really, Nick, I think you're a half-wit sometimes with your silly suspicions."

"I'm studying to be one. Three more lessons and I get my diploma. But remember I warned you yesterday that you'll probably wind up in—"

"Stop it," she cried. She put a hand over my mouth. "Do you have to keep saying that? You know it terrifies me and—" Her voice became soft and wheedling. "You must know what I'm going through these days, Nick. Can't you be a little kinder?"

"Don't worry about me," I said. "Worry about the police." I went back to the telephone and called up Alice Quinn. "This is Nick. Nora said you—"

"Yes. Have you seen Harrison?"

"Not since I left him with you."

"Well, if you do, you won't say anything about what I said last night, will you? I didn't mean it, really I didn't mean a word of it."

"I didn't think you did," I assured her, "and I wouldn't say anything about it anyway. How's he feeling today?"

"He's gone," she said.

"What?"

"He's gone. He's left me."

"He's done that before. He'll be back."

"I know, but I'm afraid this time. He didn't go to his office. I hope he's just drunk somewhere and—but this time I'm afraid. Nick, do you think he's really in love with that girl?"

"He seems to think he is."

"Did he tell you he was?"

"That wouldn't mean anything."

"Do you think it would do any good to have a talk with her?"

"No."

"Why don't you? Do you think she's in love with him?"

"No."

"What's the matter with you?" she asked irritably.

"No, I'm not home."

"What? Oh, you mean you're some place where you can't talk?"

"That's it."

"Are you—are you at her house?"

"Yes."

"Is she there?"

"No."

"Do you think she's with him?"

"I don't know. I don't think so."

"Will you call me when you can talk, or, better still, will you come up to see me?"

"Sure," I promised, and we hung up.

Mimi was looking at me with amusement in her blue eyes. "Somebody's taking my brat's affairs seriously?" When I did not answer her, she laughed and asked: "Is Dorry still being the maiden in distress?"

"I suppose so."

"She will be, too, as long as she can get anybody to believe in it. And you, of all people, to be fooled, you who are afraid to believe that—well—that I, for instance, am ever telling the truth."

"That's a thought," I said. The doorbell rang before I could go on.

Mimi let the doctor in—he was a roly-poly elderly man with a stoop and a waddle—and took him in to Gilbert.

I opened the table-drawer again and looked at the bonds, Postal Telegraph & Cable 5s, Sao Paulo City 6½s, American Type Founders 6s, Certain-teed Products 5½s, Upper Austria 6½s, United Drugs 5s, Philippine Railway 4s, Tokio Electric Lighting 6s, about sixty thousand dollars at face value, I judged, and—guessing—between a quarter and a third of that at the market.

When the doorbell rang I shut the drawer and let Macaulay in.

He looked tired. He sat down without taking off his overcoat and said: "Well, tell me the worst. What was he up to here?"

"I don't know yet, except that he gave Mimi some bonds and a check."

"I know that." He fumbled in his pocket and gave me a letter:

Dear Herbert:

I am today giving Mrs. Mimi Jorgensen the securities listed below and a ten thousand dollar check on the Park Ave. Trust dated Jan. 3. Please arrange to have sufficient money there on that date to cover it. I would suggest that you sell some more of the public utility bonds, but use your own judgment. I find that I cannot spend any more time in New York at present and probably will not be able to get back here for several months, but will communicate with you from time to time. I am sorry I will not be able to wait over to see you and Charles tonight.

> *Yours truly,*
> *Clyde Miller Wynant*

Under the sprawling signature was a list of the bonds.

"How'd it come to you?" I asked.

"By messenger. What do you suppose he was paying her for?"

I shook my head. "I tried to find out. She said he was 'providing for her and his children.' "

"That's likely, as likely as that she'd tell the truth."

"About these bonds?" I asked. "I thought you had all his property in your hands."

"I thought so too, but I didn't have these, didn't know

he had them." He put his elbows on his knees, his head in his hands. "If all the things I don't know were laid end to end. . . ."

30

MIMI came in with the doctor, said, "Oh, how do you do," a little stiffly to Macaulay, and shook hands with him. "This is Doctor Grant, Mr. Macaulay, Mr. Charles."

"How's the patient?" I asked.

Doctor Grant cleared his throat and said he didn't think there was anything seriously the matter with Gilbert, effects of a beating, slight hemorrhage of course, should rest, though. He cleared his throat again and said he was happy to have met us, and Mimi showed him out.

"What happened to the boy?" Macaulay asked me.

"Wynant sent him on a wild-goose chase over to Julia's apartment and he ran into a tough copper."

Mimi returned from the door. "Has Mr. Charles told you about the bonds and the check?" she asked.

"I had a note from Mr. Wynant saying he was giving them to you," Macaulay said.

"Then there will be no—"

"Difficulty? Not that I know of."

She relaxed a little and her eyes lost some of their coldness. "I didn't see why there should be, but he"—pointing at me—"likes to frighten me."

Macaulay smiled politely. "May I ask whether Mr. Wynant said anything about his plans?"

"He said something about going away, but I don't suppose I was listening very attentively. I don't remember whether he told me when he was going or where."

I grunted to show skepticism; Macaulay pretended he believed her. "Did he say anything that you could repeat to me about Julia Wolf, or about his difficulties, or about anything connected with the murder and all?" he asked.

She shook her head emphatically. "Not a word I could either repeat or couldn't, not a word at all. I asked him about it, but you know how unsatisfactory he can be when he wants. I couldn't get as much as a grunt out of him about it."

I asked the question Macaulay seemed too polite to ask: "What did he talk about?"

"Nothing, really, except ourselves and the children, particularly Gil. He was very anxious to see him and waited nearly an hour, hoping he'd come home. He asked about Dorry, but didn't seem very interested."

"Did he say anything about having written Gilbert?"

"Not a word. I can repeat our whole conversation, if you want me to. I didn't know he was coming, he didn't even phone from downstairs. The doorbell just rang and when I went to the door there he was, looking a lot older than when I'd seen him last and even thinner, and I said, 'Why Clyde!' or something like that, and he said: 'Are you alone?' I told him I was and he came in. Then he—"

The doorbell rang and she went to answer it.

"What do you think of it?" Macaulay asked in a low voice.

"When I start believing Mimi," I said, "I hope I have sense enough not to admit it."

She returned from the door with Guild and Andy. Guild nodded to me and shook hands with Macaulay, then turned to Mimi and said: "Well, ma'am, I'll have to ask you to tell—"

Macaulay interrupted him: "Suppose you let me tell what I have to tell first, Lieutenant. It belongs ahead of Mrs. Jorgensen's story and—"

Guild waved a big hand at the lawyer. "Go ahead." He sat down on an end of the sofa.

Macaulay told him what he had told me that morning. When he mentioned having told it to me that morning Guild glanced bitterly at me, once, and thereafter ignored me completely. Guild did not interrupt Macaulay, who told his story clearly and concisely. Twice Mimi started to say something, but each time broke off to listen. When Macaulay had finished, he handed Guild the note about the bonds and check. "That came by messenger this afternoon."

Guild read the note very carefully and addressed Mimi: "Now then, Mrs. Jorgensen."

She told him what she had told us about Wynant's visit, elaborating the details as he patiently questioned her, but sticking to her story that he had refused to say a word about anything connected with Julia Wolf or her murder, that in giving her the bonds and check he had simply said that he wished to provide for her and the children, and that though he had said he was going away she did not know where or when. She seemed not at all disturbed by everybody's obvious disbelief. She wound up smiling, saying: "He's a sweet man in a lot of ways, but quite mad."

"You mean he's really insane, do you?" Guild asked; "not just nutty?"

"Yes."

"What makes you think that?"

"Oh, you'd have to live with him to really know how mad he is," she replied airily.

Guild seemed dissatisfied. "What kind of clothes was he wearing?"

"A brown suit and brown overcoat and hat and I think brown shoes and a white shirt and a grayish necktie with either red or reddish brown figures in it."

Guild jerked his head at Andy. "Tell 'em."

Andy went out.

Guild scratched his jaw and frowned thoughtfully. The rest of us watched him. When he stopped scratching, he looked at Mimi and Macaulay, but not at me, and asked: "Any of you know anybody that's got the initials of D.W.Q.?"

Macaulay shook his head from side to side slowly.

Mimi said: "No. Why?"

Guild looked at me now. "Well?"

"I don't know them."

"Why?" Mimi repeated.

Guild said: "Try to remember back. He'd most likely've had dealings with Wynant."

"How far back?" Macaulay asked.

"That's hard to say right now. Maybe a few months, maybe a few years. He'd be a pretty large man, big bones, big belly, and maybe lame."

Macaulay shook his head again. "I don't remember anybody like that."

"Neither do I," Mimi said, "but I'm bursting with curiosity. I wish you'd tell us what it's all about."

"Sure, I'll tell you." Guild took a cigar from his vest pocket, looked at it, and returned it to the pocket. "A dead man like that's buried under the floor of Wynant's shop."

I said: "Ah."

Mimi put both hands to her mouth and said nothing. Her eyes were round and glassy.

Macaulay, frowning, asked: "Are you sure?"

Guild sighed. "Now you know that ain't something anybody would guess at," he said wearily.

Macaulay's face flushed and he smiled sheepishly. "That was a silly question. How did you happen to find him—it?"

"Well, Mr. Charles here kept hinting that we ought to pay more attention to that shop, so, figuring that Mr. Charles here is a man that's liable to know a lot more things than he tells anybody right out, I sent some men around this morning to see what they could find. We'd give it the once over before and hadn't turned up nothing, but this time I told 'em to take the dump apart, because Mr. Charles here had said we ought to pay more attention to it. And Mr. Charles here was right." He looked at me with cool unfriendliness. "By and by they found a corner of the cement floor looking a little newer maybe than the rest and they cracked it and there was the mortal remains of Mr. D.W.Q. What do you think of that?"

Macaulay said: "I think it was a damned good guess of Charles's." He turned to me. "How did you—"

Guild interrupted him. "I don't think you ought to say that. When you call it just a guess, you ain't giving Mr. Charles here the proper credit for being as smart as he is."

Macaulay was puzzled by Guild's tone. He looked questioningly at me.

"I'm being stood in the corner for not telling Lieutenant Guild about our conversation this morning," I explained.

"There's that," Guild agreed calmly, "among other things."

Mimi laughed, and smiled apologetically at Guild when he stared at her.

"How was Mr. D.W.Q. killed?" I asked.

Guild hesitated, as if making up his mind whether to reply, then moved his big shoulders slightly and said: "I don't know yet, or how long ago. I haven't seen the remains yet, what there is of them, and the Medical Examiner wasn't through the last I heard."

"What there is of them?" Macaulay repeated.

"Uh-huh. He'd been sawed up in pieces and buried in lime or something so there wasn't much flesh left on him, according to the report I got, but his clothes had been stuck in with him rolled up in a bundle, and enough was left of the inside ones to tell us something. There was part of a cane, too, with a rubber tip. That's why we thought he might be lame, and we—" He broke off as Andy came in. "Well?"

Andy shook his head gloomily. "Nobody sees him come, nobody sees him go. What was that joke about a guy being so thin he had to stand in the same place twice to throw a shadow?"

I laughed—not at the joke—and said: "Wynant's not that thin, but he's thin enough, say as thin as the paper in that check and in those letters people have been getting."

"What's that?" Guild demanded, his face reddening, his eyes angry and suspicious.

"He's dead. He's been dead a long time except on paper. I'll give you even money they're his bones in the grave with the fat lame man's clothes."

Macaulay leaned towards me. "Are you sure of that, Charles?"

Guild snarled at me: "What are you trying to pull?"

"There's the bet if you want it. Who'd go to all that trouble with a corpse and then leave the easiest thing of all to get rid of—the clothes—untouched unless they—"

"But they weren't untouched. They—"

"Of course not. That wouldn't look right. They'd have to be partly destroyed, only enough left to tell you what they were supposed to tell. I bet the initials were plenty conspicuous."

"I don't know," Guild said with less heat. "They were on a belt buckle."

I laughed.

Mimi said angrily: "That's ridiculous, Nick. How could that be Clyde? You know he was here this afternoon. You know he—"

"Sh-h-h. It's very silly of you to play along with him," I

told her. "Wynant's dead, your children are probably his heirs, that's more money than you've got over there in the drawer. What do you want to take part of the loot for when you can get it all?"

"I don't know what you mean," she said. She was very pale.

Macaulay said: "Charles thinks Wynant wasn't here this afternoon and that you were given those securities and the check by somebody else, or perhaps stole them yourself. Is that it?" he asked me.

"Practically."

"But that's ridiculous," she insisted.

"Be sensible, Mimi," I said. "Suppose Wynant was killed three months ago and his corpse disguised as somebody else. He's supposed to have gone away leaving powers of attorney with Macaulay. All right, then, the estate's completely in Macaulay's hands for ever and ever, or at least until he finishes plundering it, because you can't even—"

Macaulay stood up saying: "I don't know what you're getting at, Charles, but I'm—"

"Take it easy," Guild told him. "Let him have his say out."

"He killed Wynant and he killed Julia and he killed Nunheim," I assured Mimi. "What do you want to do? Be next on the list? You ought to know damned well that once you've come to his aid by saying you've seen Wynant alive—because that's his weak spot, being the only person up to now who claims to have seen Wynant since October—he's not going to take any chances on having you change your mind—not when it's only a matter of knocking you off with the same gun and putting the blame on Wynant. And what are you doing it for? For those few crummy bonds in the drawer, a fraction of what you get your hands on through your children if we prove Wynant's dead."

Mimi turned to Macaulay and said: "You son of a bitch."

Guild gaped at her, more surprised by that than by anything else that had been said.

Macaulay started to move. I did not wait to see what he meant to do, but slammed his chin with my left fist. The punch was all right, it landed solidly and dropped him, but I felt a burning sensation on my left side and knew I had torn the bullet-wound open.

"What do you want me to do?" I growled at Guild. "Put him in cellophane for you?"

31

IT WAS nearly three in the morning when I let myself into our apartment at the Normandie. Nora, Dorothy, and Larry Crowley were in the living-room, Nora and Larry playing backgammon, Dorothy reading a newspaper.

"Did Macaulay really kill them?" Nora asked immediately.

"Yes. Did the morning papers have anything about Wynant?"

Dorothy said: "No, just about Macaulay being arrested. Why?"

"Macaulay killed him too."

Nora said, "Really?" Larry said, "I'll be damned." Dorothy began to cry. Nora looked at Dorothy in surprise.

Dorothy sobbed: "I want to go home to Mamma."

Larry said not very eagerly: "I'll be glad to take you home if . . ."

Dorothy said she wanted to go. Nora fussed over her, but did not try to talk her out of going. Larry, trying not to look too unwilling, found his hat and coat. He and Dorothy left.

Nora shut the door behind them and leaned against it. "Explain that to me, Mr. Charalambides," she said.

I shook my head.

She sat on the sofa beside me. "Now out with it. If you skip a single word, I'll—"

"I'd have to have a drink before I could do any talking."

She cursed me and brought me a drink. "Has he confessed?"

"Why should he? You can't plead guilty of murder in the first degree. There were too many murders—and at least two of them were too obviously done in cold blood—for the District Attorney to let him plead guilty of second-degree murder. There's nothing for him to do but fight it out."

"But he did commit them?"

"Sure."

She pushed my glass down from my mouth. "Stop stalling and tell me about it."

"Well, it figures out that he and Julia had been gypping Wynant for some time. He'd dropped a lot of money in the market and he'd found out about her past—as Morelli hinted—and the pair of them teamed up on the old man. We're sicking accountants on Macaulay's books and Wynant's and shouldn't have much trouble tracing some of the loot from one to the other."

"Then you don't know positively that he was robbing Wynant?"

"Sure we know. It doesn't click any other way. The chances are Wynant was going away on a trip the 3rd of October, because he did draw five thousand dollars out of the bank in cash, but he didn't close up his shop and give up his apartment. That was done by Macaulay a few days later. Wynant was killed at Macaulay's in Scarsdale on the night of the 3rd. We know that because on the morning of the 4th, when Macaulay's cook, who slept at home, came to work, Macaulay met her at the door with some kind of trumped-up complaint and two weeks' wages and fired her on the spot, not letting her in the house to find any corpses or blood-stains."

"How did you find that out? Don't skip details."

"Ordinary routine. Naturally after we grabbed him we went to his office and house to see what we could find out— you know, where-were-you-on-the-night-of-June-6, 1894-stuff —and the present cook said she'd only been working for him since the 8th of October, and that led to that. We also found a table with a very faint trace of what we hope is human blood not quite scrubbed out. The scientific boys are making shavings of it now to see if they can soak out any results for us." (It turned out to be beef blood.)

"Then you're not sure he—"

"Stop saying that. Of course we're sure. That's the only way it clicks. Wynant had found out that Julia and Macaulay were gypping him and also thought, rightly or wrongly, that Julia and Macaulay were cheating on him—and we know he was jealous—so he went up there to confront him with whatever proof he had, and Macaulay, with prison looking him in the face, killed the old man. Now don't say we're not sure. It doesn't make any sense otherwise. Well, there he is with a corpse, one of the harder things to get rid of. Can I stop to take a swallow of whisky?"

"Just one," Nora said. "But this is just a theory, isn't it?"

"Call it any name you like. It's good enough for me."

"But I thought everybody was supposed to be considered innocent until they were proved guilty and if there was any reasonable doubt, they—"

"That's for juries, not detectives. You find the guy you think did the murder and you slam him in the can and let everybody know you think he's guilty and put his picture all over newspapers, and the District Attorney builds up the best theory he can on what information you've got and meanwhile you pick up additional details here and there, and people who recognize his picture in the paper—as well as people who'd think he was innocent if you hadn't arrested him—come in and tell you things about him and presently you've got him sitting on the electric chair." (Two days later a woman in Brooklyn identified Macaulay as a George Foley who for the past three months had been renting an apartment from her.)

"But that seems so loose."

"When murders are committed by mathematics," I said, "you can solve them by mathematics. Most of them aren't and this one wasn't. I don't want to go against your idea of what's right and wrong, but when I say he probably dissected the body so he could carry it into town in bags I'm only saying what seems most probable. That would be on the 6th of October or later, because it wasn't until then that he laid off the two mechanics Wynant had working in the shop— Prentice and McNaughton—and shut it up. So he buried Wynant under the floor, buried him with a fat man's clothes and a lame man's stick and a belt marked D.W.Q., all arranged so they wouldn't get too much of the lime—or whatever he used to eat off the dead man's features and flesh—on them, and he re-cemented the floor over the grave. Between police routine and publicity we've got more than a fair chance of finding out where he bought or otherwise got the clothes and stick and the cement." (We traced the cement to him later—he had bought it from a coal and wood dealer uptown—but had no luck with the other things.)

"I hope so," she said, not too hopefully.

"So now that's taken care of. By renewing the lease on the shop and keeping it vacant—supposedly waiting for Wynant to return—he can make sure—reasonably sure—that nobody will discover the grave, and if it is accidentally discovered, then fat Mr. D.W.Q.—by that time Wynant's bones would be pretty bare and you can't tell whether a man was thin or fat by his skeleton—was murdered by Wynant, which explains why Wynant has made himself scarce. That taken care of, Macaulay forges the power of attorney and, with Julia's help, settles down to the business of gradually transferring the late Clyde's money to themselves. Now I'm going theoretical again. Julia doesn't like murder, and she's frightened, and he's not too sure she won't weaken on him. That's why he makes her break with Morelli—giving Wynant's jealousy as an excuse. He's afraid she might confide to Morelli in a weak moment and, as the time draws near for her still closer friend, Face Peppler, to get out of prison, he gets more and more worried. He's been safe there as long as Face stayed in, because she's not likely to put anything dangerous in a letter that has to pass through the warden's hands, but now . . . Well, he starts to plan, and then all hell breaks loose. Mimi and her children arrive and start hunting for Wynant and I come to town and am in touch with them and he thinks I'm helping them. He decides to play safe on Julia by putting her out of the way. Like it so far?"

"Yes, but . . ."

"It gets worse as it goes along," I assured her. "On his way here for lunch that day he stops and phones his office, pretending he's Wynant, and making that appointment at the Plaza, the idea being to establish Wynant's presence in town. When he leaves here he goes to the Plaza and asks people if they've seen Wynant, to make that plausible, and for the same reason phones his office to ask if any further word has come in from Wynant, and phones Julia. She tells him she's expecting Mimi and she tells him Mimi thought she was lying when she said she didn't know where Wynant was, and Julia probably sounds pretty frightened. So he decides he's got to beat Mimi to the interview and he does. He beats it over there and kills her. He's a terrible shot. I saw him shoot during the war.

It's likely he missed her with the first shot, the one that hit the telephone, and didn't succeed in killing her right away with the other four, but he probably thought she was dead, and, anyhow, he had to get out before Mimi arrived, so he dropped the piece of Wynant's chain that he had brought along as a clincher—and his having saved that for three months makes it look as if he'd intended killing her from the beginning—and scoots over to the engineer Hermann's office, where he takes advantage of the breaks and fixes himself up with an alibi. The two things he doesn't expect—couldn't very well have foreseen—are that Nunheim, hanging around trying to get at the girl, had seen him leave her apartment—may even have heard the shots—and that Mimi, with black-mail in her heart, was going to conceal the chain for use in shaking down her ex-husband. That's why he had to go down to Philadelphia and send me that wire and the letter to him-self and one to Aunt Alice later—if Mimi thinks Wynant's throwing suspicion on her she'll get mad enough to give the police the evidence she's got against him. Her desire to hurt Jorgensen nearly gummed that up, though. Macaulay, by the way, knew Jorgensen was Rosewater. Right after he killed Wynant he had detectives look Mimi and her family up in Europe—their interest in the estate made them potentially dangerous—and the detectives found out who Jorgensen was. We found the reports in Macaulay's files. He pretended he was getting the information for Wynant, of course. Then he started worrying about me, about my not thinking Wynant guilty and—"

"And why didn't you?"

"Why should he write letters antagonizing Mimi, the one who was helping him by holding back incriminating evidence? That's why I thought the chain had been planted when she did turn it in, only I was a little bit too willing to believe she had done the planting. Morelli worried Macaulay, too, be-cause he didn't want suspicion thrown on anybody who might, in clearing themselves, throw it in the wrong direc-tion. Mimi was all right, because she'd throw it back on Wynant, but everybody else was out. Suspicion thrown on Wynant was the one thing that was guaranteed to keep any-body from suspecting that Wynant was dead, and if Macaulay hadn't killed Wynant, then there was no reason for his having killed either of the others. The most obvious thing in the whole lay-out and the key to the whole lay-out was that Wynant had to be dead."

"You mean you thought that from the beginning?" Nora demanded, fixing me with a stern eye.

"No, darling, though I ought to be ashamed of myself for not seeing it, but once I heard there was a corpse under the floor, I wouldn't have cared if doctors swore it was a woman's, I'd have insisted it was Wynant's. It had to be. It was the one right thing."

"I guess you're awfully tired. That must be what makes you talk like this."

"Then he had Nunheim to worry about too. After pointing the finger at Morelli, just to show the police he was being use- ful, he went to see Macaulay. I'm guessing again, sweetheart. I had a phone-call from a man who called himself Albert Norman, and the conversation ended with a noise on his end of the wire. My guess is that Nunheim went to see Macaulay and demanded some dough to keep quiet and, when Macaulay tried to bluff him, Nunheim said he'd show him and called me up to make a date with me to see if I'd buy his information— and Macaulay grabbed the phone and gave Nunheim some- thing, if only a promise, but when Guild and I had our little talk with Nunheim, and he ran out on us, then he phoned Macaulay and demanded real action, probably a lump sum, with a promise to beat it out of town, away from us meddling sleuths. We do know he called up that afternoon—Macaulay's telephone-operator remembers a Mr. Albert Norman calling up, and she remembers that Macaulay went out right after talking to him, so don't get snooty about this—uh—recon- struction of mine. Macaulay wasn't silly enough to think Nunheim was to be trusted even if he paid him, so he lured him down to this spot he had probably picked out ahead of time and let him have it—and that took care of that."

"Probably," Nora said.

"It's a word you've got to use a lot in this business. The letter to Gilbert was only for the purpose of showing that Wynant had a key to the girl's apartment, and sending Gilbert there was only a way of making sure that he'd fall into the hands of the police, who'd squeeze him and not let him keep the information about the letter and the key to himself. Then Mimi finally comes through with the watch-chain, but meanwhile another worry comes up. She's persuaded Guild to suspect me a little. I've an idea that when Macaulay came to me this morning with that hooey he intended to get me up to Scarsdale and knock me off, making me number three on the list of Wynant's victims. Maybe he just changed his mind, maybe he thought I was suspicious, too willing to go up there without policemen. Anyhow, Gilbert's lie about having seen Wynant gave him another idea. If he could get somebody to say they had seen Wynant and stick to it . . . Now this part we know definitely."

"Thank God."

"He went to see Mimi this afternoon—riding up two floors above hers and walking down so the elevator boys wouldn't remember having carried him to her floor—and made her a proposition. He told her there was no question about Wynant's guilt, but that it was doubtful if the police would ever catch him. Meanwhile he, Macaulay, had the whole estate in his hands. He couldn't take a chance on appropriating any of it, but he'd fix it so she could—if she would split with him. He'd give her these bonds he had in his pocket and this check, but she'd have to say that Wynant had given them to her and she'd have to send this note, which he also had, over to Macaulay as if from Wynant. He assured her that Wynant, a fugitive, could not show up to deny his gift, and, except for herself and her children, there was no one else who had any interest in the estate, any reason for questioning the deal. Mimi's not very sensible where she sees a chance to make a profit, so it was all O.K. with her, and he had what he wanted —somebody who'd seen Wynant alive. He warned her that everybody would think Wynant was paying her for some service, but if she simply denied it there would be nothing anybody could prove."

"Then what he told you this morning about Wynant instructing him to give her any amount she asked for was simply in preparation?"

"Maybe, maybe it was an earlier fumbling towards that idea. Now are you satisfied with what we've got on him?"

"Yes, in a way. There seems to be enough of it, but it's not very neat."

"It's neat enough to send him to the chair," I said, "and that's all that counts. It takes care of all the angles and I can't think of any other theory that would. Naturally it wouldn't hurt to find the pistol, and the typewriter he used for the Wynant letters, and they must be somewhere around where he can get at them when he needs them." (We found them in the Brooklyn apartment he had rented as George Foley.)

"Have it your own way," she said, "but I always thought detectives waited until they had every little detail fixed in—"

"And then wonder why the suspect's had time to get to the farthest country that has no extradition treaty."

She laughed. "All right, all right. Still want to leave for San Francisco tomorrow?"

"Not unless you're in a hurry. Let's stick around awhile. This excitement has put us behind in our drinking."

"It's all right by me. What do you think will happen to Mimi and Dorothy and Gilbert now?"

"Nothing new. They'll go on being Mimi and Dorothy and Gilbert just as you and I will go on being us and the Quinns will go on being the Quinns. Murder doesn't round out anybody's life except the murdered's and sometimes the murderer's."

"That may be," Nora said, "but it's all pretty unsatisfactory."

CHRONOLOGY

NOTE ON THE TEXTS

NOTES

Chronology

1894   Samuel Dashiell Hammett born May 27 on "Hopewell and Aim," tobacco farm of paternal grandfather Samuel Hammett in St. Mary's County, Maryland, second of three children of Richard Thomas Hammett and Annie Bond Dashiell. (Hammett family has been in America since the 17th century, Dashiell family since the 18th. Mother, who suffers from chronic tuberculosis, is of French Huguenot ancestry but converted to Catholicism on marrying Hammett. Father works on family tobacco farm and pursues career in local politics with little success.) Baptized a Catholic at St. Nicholas Church.

1895–97   Family, including older sister, Aronia, and younger brother, Richard, moves briefly to Philadelphia.

1898–1907 Family settles in Baltimore, where father works as clerk and later as salesman, bus conductor, factory foreman, and security guard. Hammett attends Public School 72.

1908–14   Attends Baltimore Polytechnic Institute in 1908. Leaves school after less than a year to work as newsboy, office boy and freight clerk for B&O Railroad, and clerk for Poe and Davies stockbrokerage. Family struggles financially. Paternal grandfather dies in 1911.

1915–17   Works as detective for Baltimore office of Pinkerton detective agency, located in the Continental Building. Learns job from older employee James Wright (later described by Hammett as model for his character the Continental Op).

1918   Leaves Pinkerton to enlist in army. Undergoes basic training at Camp Mead, Maryland; in July is assigned to a motor ambulance company. In October, complains of flu-like symptoms and is hospitalized with high fever; diagnosed with bronchopneumonia and released after 20 days.

1919   Hospitalized again in February; is diagnosed with tuberculosis and given discharge from army with small disability pension. Moves back with family. Despite frail condition, returns to work at Pinkerton; after six months is again hospitalized. Bureau of War Risk Insurance reviews his case and grants him a higher pension.

1920   Leaves home permanently in May; travels to Spokane, Washington, where he resumes work for Pinkerton. Serves as Pinkerton operative in Idaho and Montana, becoming involved as strikebreaker in Anaconda miners' strike. Health deteriorates; admitted in November to Cushman Hospital in Tacoma.

1921   Falls in love with nurse Josephine ("Jose") Dolan. After four months, is transferred to treatment center at Camp Kearny, near San Diego, California. Mother dies in April; Hammett does not return to Baltimore for funeral. Learns from Jose that she is pregnant; by letter, they agree to marry. Released from Camp Kearny in May, but physical condition remains fragile (will continue to suffer cyclical recurrence of lung problems). Moves to San Francisco in June. Marries Jose on July 7 at Saint Mary's Cathedral. Settles with Jose in apartment on Eddy Street and resumes work for Pinkerton. Daughter Mary Jane born October 15.

1922–23   Serious relapse makes it impossible for Hammett to work; reluctantly asks his family for financial help. With subsidy from Veterans Bureau, studies stenography and writing at Munson's Business College; decides to seek work in advertising. In October 1922 first published short story, "The Parthian Shot," appears in *The Smart Set*; publishes four more pieces in the magazine over the next year, including autobiographical "From the Memoirs of a Private Detective," based on his Pinkerton experience. Publishes "The Road Home," his first contribution to *Black Mask*, under pseudonym Peter Collinson in December 1922. In *Black Mask* story "Arson Plus" (October 1923) introduces anonymous operative later known as the Continental Op (the Op will be the protagonist of 28 stories and two novels).

1924–25   Wife and daughter go to live with her family in Montana for six months. Regularly publishes stories in *Black Mask*, including "The Tenth Clew," "The House on Turk Street," "The Whosis Kid," "The Scorched Face," and "Dead Yellow Women." Starts and then abandons a novel, "The Secret Emperor."

1926   Takes full-time job as advertising manager for jeweler Albert Samuels. Daughter Josephine Rebecca born May 24. Hammett, who has been drinking heavily for years, suffers lung hemorrhage and collapses at work in July. Diagnosed with hepatitis and is unable to continue working. Lives apart from family. Receives literary encouragement from Joseph T. Shaw, who assumes editorship of *Black Mask* in November.

1927   Begins reviewing crime fiction for *Saturday Review of Literature* in January (continues to publish there for next three years). After hiatus of a year, resumes writing fiction; continues series of Continental Op stories for *Black Mask* with "The Big Knock-Over" (February), "$106,000 Blood Money" (May), and "The Main Death" (June). Jose moves with children to San Anselmo in spring (family will live together only sporadically over next two years). Begins novel *Red Harvest* (originally titled "Poisonville"); first episode is serialized as "The Cleansing of Poisonville" in the November issue of *Black Mask*.

1928   Submits completed manuscript of novel to Alfred A. Knopf in February; Blanche Knopf offers publication but suggests revisions, including toning down of violence; Hammett agrees to some changes, and then makes extensive revisions in collaboration with Knopf editor Harry Block. Receives offer of scriptwriting work from William Fox Studios and goes to Hollywood in June, but no deal materializes. Completes second novel *The Dain Curse* in June (serialized in *Black Mask*, Nov. 1928–Feb. 1929). By end of year, completes his next novel, *The Maltese Falcon*.

1929   *Red Harvest* is published in February; Paramount buys movie rights. Knopf accepts *The Dain Curse* but requests extensive changes, which Hammett makes reluctantly. Hammett's health improves, and he moves into new, more expensive apartment with writer and actress Nell Martin, with whom he maintains longtime relationship. Manuscript of *The Maltese Falcon* is accepted by Knopf with requests for only minor revisions. *The Dain Curse* is published in July to favorable reviews and sells better than *Red Harvest*. *The Maltese Falcon* is serialized in *Black Mask* (Sept. 1929–Jan. 1930). Hammett and Martin travel to New York in the fall for extended stay; he works on new novel, *The Glass Key*.

1930   *The Maltese Falcon* is published in February; it receives excellent reviews from influential critics, including Will Cuppy and Franklin P. Adams, and is reprinted seven times in the course of the year. Paramount releases film *Roadhouse Nights*, loosely derived from *Red Harvest*. Hammett completes *The Glass Key* (serialized in *Black Mask*, March–June). Takes job as regular reviewer of crime fiction for the *New York Evening Post*. Warner Brothers acquires movie rights to *The Maltese Falcon* in June. At urging of David O. Selznick, Hammett is offered writing contract with Paramount, which he fulfills with hastily written seven-page story outline. Works on several other projects, and leaves Paramount at end of year. Meets Lillian Hellman, then married to writer Arthur Kober, at Hollywood party in November; they become lovers (relationship continues for the rest of their lives although they are frequently separated and often have other partners).

1931   Remains in Hollywood through the spring. Sees other writers socially, including Arthur Kober and Lillian Hellman, Dorothy Parker, and S. J. Perelman and his wife, Laura; drinks heavily and has many affairs. Writes treatment of an original Sam Spade story for Darryl Zanuck at Warner Brothers, but after receiving $10,000 for the story, it is rejected. *City Streets*, film based on Hammett's initial Paramount story, released in April. *The Glass Key* is published by Knopf in April, receiving strong reviews and selling well. Hammett moves to New York. Forms friendly relationship with William Faulkner. Completes first 65 pages of an early version of *The Thin Man*, then puts it aside. A film version of *The Maltese Falcon*, starring Ricardo Cortez and Bebe Daniels, is released by Warner Brothers in May.

1932   Found guilty in absentia on June 30 of battery and attempted rape in civil suit brought against him by actress Elise De Vianne, who is awarded $2,500 in damages.

Works on a second version of *The Thin Man*. Unable to pay his bill at Hotel Pierre, leaves surreptitiously and goes to live at Sutton Club Hotel on East 56th Street, which is managed by Nathanael West.

1933 Publishes novella "Woman in the Dark" as a three-part serial in *Liberty*. Finishes *The Thin Man* in May (condensed version appears in December *Redbook*). Travels with Hellman to Florida Keys for extended stay in fishing camp, where he helps her with her play *The Children's Hour*. Rents house in Huntington, Long Island, in summer.

1934 *The Thin Man* is published by Knopf in January. MGM movie version of the novel, starring William Powell and Myrna Loy, is released in June (five other movies featuring the novel's protagonists, Nick and Nora Charles, will be released between 1934 and 1947). *Secret Agent X-9*, King Features comic strip with script credited to Hammett and art by Alex Raymond, first appears in January (Hammett's byline is dropped after fifteen months). Publishes three stories in *Collier's*, January–March. Spends spring in Florida Keys with Hellman. Signs contract with MGM in October for a second movie in *Thin Man* series; stays at the Beverly Wilshire Hotel and socializes with friends, including Herbert Asbury, Nunnally Johnson, Joel Sayre, Arthur Kober, and Edward G. Robinson. Drinks heavily.

1935 Submits draft of story to MGM in January. Meets Gertrude Stein, who admires his work greatly, at dinner party in April. In June signs three-year contract with MGM, paying him minimum of $1,000 per week as writer and executive (Hammett frequently fails to meet terms of contract and is periodically taken off salary). Runs up heavy debts and is sued over the next several years by various creditors. Has brief affair with Laura Perelman during summer. In the fall divides time between Los Angeles and New York. Universal releases movie *Mister Dynamite*, starring Edmund Lowe, based on a Hammett story originally written in 1931; Paramount releases film version of *The Glass Key* starring George Raft and Edward Arnold.

1936 Meets Raymond Chandler at *Black Mask* dinner in January. Begins long-term affair with Pru Whitfield, wife of

Black Mask writer Raoul Whitfield. Becomes increasingly involved with Communist Party, which he joins as a secret member. Stays with Hellman on Tavern Island near Norwalk, Connecticut, during spring. Moves to Princeton, New Jersey, in October. *Satan Met a Lady*, a second film version of *The Maltese Falcon* starring Warren William and Bette Davis, released by Warner Brothers. *After the Thin Man*, based on Hammett's story, opens in December. Released from contract with Knopf after he fails to deliver promised novel.

1937   Returns to Hollywood in April to work on third *Thin Man* movie, under new agreement that pays him only for completed work. Publicly supports the Anti-Nazi League and the Western Writers Congress, and donates money to Abraham Lincoln Brigade fighting in Spain in support of Loyalist government. Becomes active in movement to gain recognition from studios for Screen Writers Guild. Begins 14-month period of abstinence from drinking. Jose Hammett files for mail-order divorce in Sonora, Mexico, court (after Hammett's death, divorce is ruled illegal and Jose is recognized as entitled to widow's benefits).

1938   Completes treatment for *Another Thin Man*. Along with other writers including Hellman, Langston Hughes, Dorothy Parker, and Malcolm Cowley, signs statement in defense of Moscow purge trials in April. Becomes ill after resuming drinking and is flown back to New York to enter Lenox Hill Hospital; moves into Plaza Hotel after his release in June. Signs contract with Bennett Cerf of Modern Library for new novel. Tells friends that he is at work on novel tentatively titled "My Brother Felix." Stays with Hellman on Tavern Island during summer and early fall, where he gives her detailed assistance on revisions of her play *The Little Foxes*. Speaks at anti-Nazi rallies sponsored by Communist Party in New York in November. MGM rejects his scenario for a *Thin Man* sequel.

1939   MGM cancels Hammett's contract in July. Modern Library announces new Hammett novel, "There Was a Young Man," for publication in the fall, but he does not deliver a manuscript. Hammett becomes member of editorial board of Equality Publishers, press sponsored by the Communist Party whose declared aim is "to defend democracy and combat anti-Semitism and Fascism" (press publishes monthly magazine *Equality* but ceases publication after signing of Nazi-Soviet pact in late August). Becomes a regular guest at Hardscrabble Farm, 130-acre property purchased by Hellman in Pleasantville, New York. *Another Thin Man* opens in November.

1940   Helps publisher Ralph Ingersoll in assembling staff for his newspaper *PM*; after public protests over Communist influence on the paper, Ingersoll repudiates Hammett in memo to stockholders. Serves as national chairman of Committee on Election Rights—1940, organization seeking to get Communist candidates on local ballots, and supports presidential campaign of Communist Party general secretary Earl Browder.

1941   In accordance with Communist policy shift following Nazi-Soviet pact, publicly opposes lend-lease policy of aid to Britain and American entry into war. (Becomes a supporter of the war effort following the shift in the Communist Party line after the German attack on the Soviet Union in June.) Elected president of League of American Writers. Receives $500 a week for nominal authorship of NBC radio serial *The Adventures of the Thin Man*, for which he does no writing. John Huston films highly successful adaptation of *The Maltese Falcon*, starring Humphrey Bogart and Mary Astor.

1942   Works on screen adaptation of Hellman's play *Watch on the Rhine*, with Hellman making extensive revisions (Hammett receives primary screen credit when film opens in September 1943). Returns advance on unwritten novel to Random House in March. Knopf issues all five novels as *The Complete Dashiell Hammett*. A second film version of *The Glass Key*, starring Brian Donlevy and Alan Ladd, opens. After previous rejections on health grounds, Hammett is accepted into the army as a private; he is inducted in September and undergoes Signal Corps Training at Fort Monmouth, New Jersey, where his tasks include composing lessons for trainees and giving orientation lectures.

1943   To avoid further dental problems, has all his teeth pulled at army hospital in March. Promoted to corporal in May.

Sent in June to Camp Shenango in Transfer, Pennsylvania, a facility used by the army to isolate soldiers with subversive political views. After he has been there a week, camp is dispersed following protest by Eleanor Roosevelt, and Hammett is sent to Fort Lawton near Tacoma, Washington, and then to Fort Randall, Alaska. Assigned to provide orientation for troops in the Aleutian Islands, arrives in September on small volcanic island of Adak. Starts a camp newspaper, *The Adakian*, under orders of Brigadier General Harry Thompson.

1944   First issue of *The Adakian* published in January (Hammett continues as editor for 15 months, contributing 13 signed articles). Establishes editorial staff that includes future journalists Bernard Kalb and Eliot Asinof and that is racially integrated, despite the overall segregation of the armed forces. Promoted to sergeant in August. *The Battle of the Aleutians*, pamphlet co-written by Hammett, published for distribution to troops. Sent on tour of the Aleutians to give educational lectures to servicemen.

1945   Joins training unit at Fort Richardson, near Anchorage. Promoted to master sergeant in June, and discharged in September. Moves to New York, living in apartment on East 66th Street. Lives on royalties from three radio serials based on his characters.

1946   Divides time between New York apartment and Hardscrabble Farm. Elected president of Communist-sponsored Civil Rights Congress of New York in June (position is nominal), and named a trustee of CRC bail fund. Begins teaching courses in mystery writing at Jefferson School of Social Sciences, devoted to "Marxism as the philosophy and social science of the working class" (continues teaching there until 1956).

1947   Moves to apartment in Greenwich Village. Hires full-time housekeeper, Rose Evans, who assumes close management of Hammett's affairs. Resumes contact with his brother Richard. Daughter Mary Jane stays with Hammett for an extended period; both drink heavily.

1948   Hammett's father, whom he had recently visited for the first time in nearly two decades, dies in Maryland in

March. Warner Brothers brings lawsuit against radio series *The Adventures of Sam Spade* on grounds that Warners owns all broadcast rights to *The Maltese Falcon*; Hammett files complaint seeking to affirm his right to use of the name Sam Spade. Health breaks after long period of heavy drinking and he is admitted to Lenox Hill Hospital; quits drinking permanently when warned that his life is in immediate danger if he continues.

1949   Lives mostly at Hardscrabble Farm. Loses suit against Warners regarding *Adventures of Sam Spade*; studio files plagiarism complaint against Hammett. Elected to board of trustees of Jefferson School of Social Sciences in August. Civil Rights Congress posts bail in November for eleven Communist leaders appealing convictions under the Smith Act of 1940 for conspiring to advocate the violent overthrow of the U.S. government.

1950   Goes to Hollywood to work on screenplay of William Wyler's *Detective Story*, but is unable to write. Lives with Jose during six-month stay, and enjoys company of daughter Josephine. Works with Hellman on her play *The Autumn Garden*.

1951   Visits Josephine and her daughter Ann in Los Angeles; returns with them for stay at Hardscrabble Farm. When four of the Communists convicted for Smith Act violations fail to surrender to authorities, subpoenas are issued for the trustees of the Civil Rights Congress bail fund. Hammett appears before U.S. District Court Judge Sylvester Ryan on July 9 and repeatedly invokes the Fifth Amendment when questioned about the CRC, the bail fund, and the whereabouts of the fugitives. At the conclusion of his testimony, Ryan finds him guilty of contempt of court and sentences him to six months in prison. Serves his sentence at the Federal House of Detention in New York until September, when he is moved to the federal prison in Ashland, Kentucky. Released on December 9 with time off for good behavior. Health is further damaged by imprisonment. Warner Brothers suit decided in Hammett's favor in December (studio's appeal is rejected in 1954).

1952   Finds himself impoverished due to cancellation of radio shows based on his work and liens on his income by

Internal Revenue Service for back taxes owed since 1943; all his books are out of print. Takes up residence at Katonah, New York, on estate of friend Dr. Samuel Rosen, living rent-free in gatekeeper's cottage. Writes 12,500 words of a novel which he abandons (it is published as "Tulip" in *The Big Knockover*, a collection of Hammett's stories published in 1966).

1953   Subpoenaed by Senator Joseph McCarthy to testify before his subcommittee of the Committee on Government Operations, where he is questioned about purchase of his books for libraries by U.S. State Department, and whether he ever donated royalties from such sales to the Communist Party. When asked by McCarthy whether he thinks it reasonable for the government to purchase and distribute books by Communists when it is fighting Communism, Hammett replies: "If I were fighting Communism, I don't think I would do it by giving people any books at all."

1955   Called to testify in February before New York State Joint Legislative Committee about his involvement with Civil Rights Congress; during questioning says, "Communism to me is not a dirty word. When you are working for the advance of mankind it never occurs to you whether a guy is a Communist." Suffers heart attack while visiting Lillian Hellman on Martha's Vineyard in August.

1956   Questioned by F.B.I. in March about his ability to pay tax judgment of over $140,000; Hammett asserts that he has no income or savings. In an interview given to the *Washington Daily News* the same month, states: "I stopped writing because I was repeating myself. It is the beginning of the end when you discover you have style." Fails to appear in court to answer federal suit for back taxes.

1957–61   Ordered to pay $104,795 in back taxes for the years 1950–54 in February 1957. Health continues to deteriorate severely; moves into Lillian Hellman's New York apartment in spring of 1958. Granted small pension by Veterans Administration in May 1959 on grounds of severe respiratory illness. Goes out in public for last time in February 1960 to see opening of Hellman's play *Toys in the Attic*.

Dies of lung cancer on January 10, 1961, at Lenox Hill Hospital. Funeral is held at Frank E. Campbell funeral home in New York. Buried at Arlington National Cemetery on January 13.

Note on the Texts

This volume contains the complete novels of Dashiell Hammett: *Red Harvest* (1929), *The Dain Curse* (1929), *The Maltese Falcon* (1930), *The Glass Key* (1931), and *The Thin Man* (1934). All of Hammett's novels first appeared in magazines—*The Thin Man* in *Redbook*, the others in the pulp magazine *Black Mask*—and were then published in book form by Alfred A. Knopf in New York. Hammett revised his novels, sometimes extensively, after their periodical publication, often in response to recommendations made by his editors at Knopf, but he did not revise his novels after their initial book publication; therefore, the texts of the novels printed here are those of the first American editions.

Red Harvest first appeared as four "novelettes" in *Black Mask*: "The Cleaning of Poisonville" (November 1927), "Crime Wanted—Male or Female" (December 1927), "Dynamite" (January 1928), and "The 19th Murder" (February 1928). On February 11, 1928, Hammett sent a typescript of the novel, then titled "Poisonville," to Alfred A. Knopf in New York. Blanche Knopf quickly expressed an interest in publishing the book, on the condition that Hammett make substantial revisions. Hammett agreed to most of her suggestions and rejected others, and he made smaller verbal changes in collaboration with Harry Block, a Knopf editor who would work with Hammett on all five of his novels. The text of the first Knopf printing, published on February 1, 1929, is presented here.

On June 25, 1928, Hammett sent Knopf a typescript of *The Dain Curse*, and on July 10 Harry Block suggested that a number of alterations would be needed before the novel could be published. In September Hammett wrote to Block that he had been revising the novel throughout the summer; on November 22, Block responded to a revised typescript with a request for still further changes. Hammett apparently complied, submitting his final revisions before April 1, 1929—a deadline Block specified in a letter of December 14. In the interim, the novel was serialized in *Black Mask* ("Black Lives," November 1928; "The Hollow Temple," December 1928; "Black Honeymoon," January 1929; "Black Riddle," February 1929). The text of the first Knopf printing, published on July 19, 1929, is presented in this volume.

Hammett sent Knopf his finished typescript of *The Maltese Falcon* in June 1929. In a letter of July 14, he responded to Block's requests for changes in what Hammett called the novel's "to-bed and homo-sexual parts": "I should like to leave them as they are, especially since you say they 'would be all right perhaps in an ordinary novel.' It seems to me that the only thing that can be said against their use in a detective novel is that nobody has tried it yet. I'd like to try it." Hammett was able to retain most of his original language, though he agreed to make some revisions. (Joseph Shaw, the editor of *Black Mask*, also made changes in *The Maltese Falcon*, which appeared in the magazine in five monthly installments, not separately titled, from September 1929 to January 1930.) This volume prints the text of the February 14, 1930, first Knopf printing.

The Glass Key was serialized in *Black Mask* in four parts—"The Glass Key," "The Cyclone Shot," "Dagger Point," "The Shattered Key"—from March through June of 1930. Hammett again made revisions for book publication; on December 20, 1930, he wrote to Knopf to complain about the number of changes that had been introduced into the novel. Hammett and Knopf had agreed earlier to postpone the American publication of the book, initially scheduled for the fall of 1930, until the following spring. In the interim, on January 20, 1931, the novel was published by Knopf in London; Hammett is not known to have been involved in the preparation of this edition, which alters his spelling, punctuation, and verbal usage to conform to British conventions. The text of the first American edition, published by Knopf in New York on April 24, 1931, is reprinted here.

Hammett began writing *The Thin Man* early in 1930 but set it aside until May 1933. In December 1933, an abridged version of the novel was serialized in *Redbook*; the first book edition followed on January 8, 1934. The text of the March 1934 sixth printing of the first Knopf edition of *The Thin Man*, which corrects "seep" to "sleep" (at 914.11 in this volume), is reprinted here.

This volume presents the texts of the original printings chosen for inclusion here, but it does not attempt to reproduce features of their typographic design, such as display capitalization of chapter openings. The texts are presented without change, except for the correction of typographical errors. Spelling, punctuation, and capitalization are often expressive features and are not altered, even when inconsistent or irregular. The following is a list of typographical errors corrected, cited by page and line number: 57.24, is'nt; 64.4, monacker; 77.25, After while; 129.15, started; 143.8, wooly; 143.9, bootle; 159.18, fragamentary; 173.28, terrior; 186.11, hear man's; 193.11, come; 207.26, happend; 224.7, musn't; 235.11, desirious; 236.32, have know; 242.25, asperin; 248.32, gratuitiously; 262.21, look up; 274.28, Manual; 274.33, her?; 277.1, Manual; 284.26, acting; 293.13, over him; 310.2, got most;

318.40, Collinson's; 327.8, had had; 334.37, g.m.; 337.25, things; 377.32, dopped in; 396.11, blustery,; 396.11, irritable,; 401.6, Let's; 408.19, store; 425.21, Mr Joel; 429.32, vised; 473.23, met in; 488.10, lost his; 509.24, ungents; 529.12, unbottoned; 545.3, it's; 582.4, get's; 713.20, get's; 836.21, Humphrey; 837.38, Moon; 866.7, Ill; 873.26, Ill; 918.6, get's. Error corrected second printing: 224.10, that. Errors corrected third printing: 375.27, learn; 385.20, it's; 612.7, its. Error corrected fifth printing: 461.3, turned.

Notes

In the notes below, the reference numbers denote page and line of this volume (the line count includes chapter headings). No note is made for material included in standard desk-reference books such as Webster's *Collegiate*, *Biographical*, and *Geographical* dictionaries. For further information and references to other studies, see Diane Johnson, *Dashiell Hammett: A Life* (New York: Random House, 1983); Richard Layman, *Dashiell Hammett: A Descriptive Bibliography* (Pittsburgh: University of Pittsburgh Press, 1979); Richard Layman, *Shadow Man: The Life of Dashiell Hammett* (New York: Harcourt Brace Jovanovich, 1981); Joan Mellen, *Hellman and Hammett: The Legendary Passion of Lillian Hellman and Dashiell Hammett* (New York: HarperCollins, 1996); and William F. Nolan, *Hammett: A Life at the Edge* (New York: Congdon & Weed, 1983).

RED HARVEST

47.25   *Rosy Cheeks*]   Song (1927) by Seymour Simons and Richard A. Whiting.

58.5   Fatimas]   Brand of cigarette blending Turkish and domestic tobacco.

83.32   iron men]   Dollars.

87.34   'cuter]   Prosecutor.

103.2   crush-out]   Jailbreak.

THE DAIN CURSE

216.24–25   rats and mice]   Dice; craps.

234.15–30   Iles du Salut . . . Aroa]   Approximately two thousand kilometers separate the Iles du Salut, off the coast of French Guiana near Devil's Island, from the Golfo Triste, west of Caracas, Venezuela. Aroa is inland from the Golfo Triste, in Yaracuy Province, Venezuela.

256.18   Tad]   Pseudonym of Thomas Aloysius Dorgan (1877–1929), Hearst newspaper cartoonist. His strips included "Indoor Sports" and "Silk Hat Harry's Divorce Suit."

278.36–37   Aimee, Buchman, Jeddu what's-his-name]   Aimee Semple McPherson (1890–1944), also known as "Sister Aimee," was a Los Angeles-based radio evangelist and founder, in 1927, of the International Church of the Foursquare Gospel; her books included *This Is That* (1919), *Divine Healing Sermons* (1920), and *In the Service of the King* (1927). The evangelist Frank Buchman (1878–1961) founded Moral Re-Armament, an organization promulgating absolute standards of morality and "the dictatorship of God." Jiddu Krishnamurti (1895–1986), an exponent of theosophy, was the author of *Who Brings the Truth* (1927), *Life in Freedom* (1928), and many other books.

279.5   Arthur Machen] Novelist, journalist, and short-story writer (1863–1947); his many books include *The Great God Pan* (1894), *The House of Souls* (1906), and *The Hill of Dreams* (1907).

288.12   orphan paper] Bad checks.

371.37–38   Charlie Ross] Four-year-old Charles Brewster Ross was kidnapped from his front yard in Germantown, Pennsylvania, on July 1, 1874, and held for $20,000 ransom. His abductors were mortally wounded during an attempted burglary on December 14; one, Joseph Douglas, confessed to the kidnapping but claimed that only the other, the already deceased Bill Mosher, knew the child's whereabouts. Ross was never found.

THE MALTESE FALCON

387.1   MALTESE FALCON] When *The Maltese Falcon* was included in the Modern Library series in 1934, Hammett added the following introduction:

If this book had been written with the help of an outline or notes or even a clearly defined plot-idea in my head I might now be able to say how it came to be written and why it took the shape it did, but all I can remember about its invention is that somewhere I had read of the peculiar rental agreement between Charles V and the Order of the Hospital of St. John of Jerusalem, that in a short story called THE WHOSIS KID I had failed to make the most of a situation I liked, that in another called THE GUTTING OF COUFFIGNAL I had been equally unfortunate with an equally promising dénouement, and that I thought I might have better luck with these two failures if I combined them with the Maltese lease in a longer story.

I can remember more clearly where I got most of my characters.

Wilmer, the boy gun-man, was picked up in Stockton, California, where I had gone hunting a window-smasher who had robbed a San Jose jewelry store. Wilmer's original was not my window-smasher, unfortunately, but he was a fair pick-up. He was a neat small smooth-faced quiet boy of perhaps twenty-one. He said he was only seventeen, but that was probably an attempt to draw a reform school instead of a penitentiary sentence. He also said his father was a lieutenant of police in New York, which may or may not have been true, and he was serenely proud of the name the local newspapers gave him—The Midget Bandit. He had robbed a Stockton filling station the previous week. In Los Angeles a day or two later, reading a Stockton newspaper—there must be criminals who subscribe to clipping services—he had been annoyed by the description the filling-station proprietor had given of him and by the proprietor's statement of what he would do to that little runt if he ever laid eyes on him again. So The Midget Bandit had stolen an automobile and returned to Stockton to, in his words, stick that guy up again and see what he wanted to do about it.

Brigid O'Shaughnessy had two originals, one an artist, the other a woman who came to Pinkerton's San Francisco office to hire an operative to discharge her housekeeper, but neither of these women was a criminal.

Dundy's prototype I worked with in a North Carolina railroad yard; Cairo's I picked up on a forgery charge in Pasco, Washington, in 1920; Polhaus's was a former captain of detectives; I used to buy books from Iva's in Spokane; Effie's once asked me to go into the narcotics smuggling business with her in San Diego; Gutman's was suspected—foolishly, as most people were—of being a German secret agent in Washington, D.C., in the early days of the war, and I never remember shadowing a man who bored me as much.

Spade had no original. He is a dream man in the sense that he is what most of the private detectives I worked with would like to have been and what quite a few of them in their cockier moments thought they approached. For your private detective does not—or did not ten years ago when he was my colleague—want to be an erudite solver of riddles in the Sherlock Holmes manner; he wants to be a hard and shifty fellow, able to take care of himself in any situation, able to get the best of anybody he comes in contact with, whether criminal, innocent by-stander, or client.

New York, January 24, 1934.
(Copyright 1934 by The Modern Library.)

398.18   *Celebrated Criminal Cases of America*]   By Thomas S. Duke; published in San Francisco in 1910.

425.31   *chypre*]   A heavy sandalwood perfume.

429.40   Geary Theatre]   Opened in 1910, on Geary Street in San Francisco.

435.2–3   George Arliss . . . Shylock]   Arliss (1868–1946) played Shylock, his last stage role, in New York and on tour in 1928. His many other stage vehicles included *The Devil* (1908), *Disraeli* (1911), and *The Green Goddess* (1921); he went on to star in such films as *East Meets West* (1934), *The Iron Duke* (1935), and *Dr. Syn* (1937).

471.26   Baumes rush]   In 1926, the New York State legislature passed the Baumes Law, which mandated life sentences for four-time criminal offenders.

472.2   Romeville]   New York City.

486.26   gunsel] Punk; young companion of a tramp; passive homo-sexual.

495.13   gooseberry lay] Stealing clothes from a clothesline.

515.13   stuss-games] Gambling games resembling faro.

515.14   twist] Woman; girlfriend.

515.16   Joliet] Illinois State Penitentiary at Joliet.

520.32   Arnold Rothstein] Gambler, bootlegger, drug dealer, and labor racketeer (b. 1882), Rothstein was fatally shot during a poker game in the Park Central Hotel in New York on November 4, 1928.

THE GLASS KEY

645.18–19   cyclone shot] The drilling of several holes in a safe for explosives.

645.20   come-along] Device for extracting a lock.

757.33   "That's keno,"] Exclamation given when a keno player has winning numbers, or more generally of approval or satisfaction.

THE THIN MAN

784.35   *Honeymoon*] A comedy by Samuel Chotzinoff and George Backer, starring Katherine Alexander, Ross Alexander, Rachel Hartzell, and Joseph Calleia; it opened on December 23, 1932, and ran for 73 performances.

785.5   Mayor-elect O'Brien] John Patrick O'Brien (1873–1951) won a special election in 1932 to complete the remainder of James J. Walker's term as mayor, after Walker's resignation following corruption charges.

788.9   *Rise and Shine*] Song by Nacio Herb Brown and Richard Whiting, first performed by Ethel Merman in the Broadway musical *Take a Chance* (1932).

789.33–34   Chaliapin's memoirs] Fyodor Ivanovich Chaliapin (1873–1938), opera singer; his memoirs were translated from the Russian as *Pages from My Life: An Autobiography* (1927) and *Man and Mask: Forty Years in the Life of a Singer* (1932).

804.24   Sullivan Act] 1911 New York State law restricting handgun ownership.

812.24–25   Haldeman-Julius Little Blue Book Number 1534] E. Haldeman-Julius (1889–1951) of Girard, Kansas, was publisher and editor, beginning in 1919, of a series of inexpensive "Little Blue Books" which ultimately included almost two thousand titles; number 1534 was written by B. C. Meyrowitz.

824.38   badger-game] The blackmailing of a man by a woman who places him in a compromising situation.

834.12   Stekel] Wilhelm Stekel (1868–1940), German psychoanalyst, author of many books including *Peculiarities of Behavior: Wandering Mania, Dipsomania, Cleptomania, Pyromania and Allied Impulsive Acts* (1922).

834.25   Jack Oakie] Actor (1903–1978) who starred in vaudeville and on Broadway, and appeared in *Close Harmony* (1929), *The Wild Party* (1929), *Let's Go Native* (1930), *Million Dollar Legs* (1932), *Dancers in the Dark* (1932), *Uptown New York* (1932), and many other films.

834.29   *Eadie Was a Lady*] Song by Nacio Herb Brown and Richard Whiting, first performed by Ethel Merman in the Broadway musical *Take a Chance* (1932).

835.19   *Celebrated Criminal Cases of America*] See note 398.18.

841.16–17   opening of the Radio City Music Hall] On December 27, 1932.

868.18   Levi Oscant] Play on Oscar Levant (1906–1972), pianist and friend of Hammett.

904.10   "Prince Mike" . . . "Jafsie"] "Prince Mike" was the nickname of Harry Gerguson, a Lithuanian immigrant and con man who attempted to pass himself off as Prince Michael Romanoff, cousin to the late Russian czar. "Jafsie" was the nickname of John F. Condon, a Bronx resident who in 1932 served as intermediary between the family of Charles Lindbergh and Bruno Hauptmann, kidnapper of the Lindbergh's infant son.

923.16   The Grand Manner] Published in 1929 by Louis Kronenberger (1904–80), the drama critic, essayist, and anthologist who was a friend of Hammett and Lillian Hellman.

928.38   new Osgood Perkins show] Osgood Perkins (1892–1937), stage and film actor, played an amorous novelist in *Goodbye Again*, written by Allan Scott and George Haight. The play opened at the Masque Theater on December 28, 1932, and ran for 212 performances.

Library of Congress Cataloging-in-Publication Data

Hammett, Dashiell, 1894–1961.
  [Novels]
  Complete novels / Dashiell Hammett.
      p. cm. — (The Library of America ; 110)
    Contents: Red harvest — The Dain curse — The Maltese
falcon — The glass key — The thin man.
  ISBN 1–883011–67–1 (alk. paper)
    1. Private investigators—United States—Fiction.
2. Detective and mystery stories, American.   I. Title.
II. Series.
PS3515.A4347A6 1999a
813'.52—dc21   98–53911
                                                          CIP

THE LIBRARY OF AMERICA SERIES

The Library of America fosters appreciation and pride in America's literary heritage by publishing, and keeping permanently in print, authoritative editions of America's best and most significant writing. An independent nonprofit organization, it was founded in 1979 with seed funding from the National Endowment for the Humanities and the Ford Foundation.

To subscribe to the series or to order individual copies, please visit www.loa.org or call (800) 964-5778.

This book is set in 10 point Linotron Galliard,
a face designed for photocomposition by Matthew Carter
and based on the sixteenth-century face Granjon. The paper
is acid-free lightweight opaque and meets the requirements
for permanence of the American National Standards Institute.
The binding material is Brillianta, a woven rayon cloth made
by Van Heek-Scholco Textielfabrieken, Holland. Composition
by The Clarinda Company. Printing and binding
by Edwards Brothers Malloy, Ann Arbor.
Designed by Bruce Campbell.